M. C. Beaton is the author of the hugely successful Agatha Raisin and Hamish Macbeth series, as well as a quartet of Edwardian murder mysteries featuring heroine Lady Rose Summer, the Travelling Matchmaker, Six Sisters, House for the Season and School for Manners Regency romance series, and a standalone murder mystery, *The Skeleton in the Closet* – all published by Constable & Robinson. She left a full-time career in journalism to turn to writing, and now divides her time between the Cotswolds and Paris. Visit www.agatharaisin.com for more, or follow M. C. Beaton on Twitter: @mc_beaton.

Back in Society

Being the sixth volume of The Poor Relation

M.C. Beaton

Canvas

Constable & Robinson Ltd.
55–56 Russell Square
London WC1B 4HP
www.constablerobinson.com

First published in the US by St Martin's Press, 1994

First published in the UK by Canvas,
an imprint of Constable & Robinson Ltd., 2013

A copy of the British Library Cataloguing in
Publication Data is available from the British Library

ISBN: 978-1-78033-322-9 (paperback)
ISBN: 978-1-47210-494-6 (ebook)

Typeset by TW Typesetting, Plymouth, Devon

Printed and bound by CPI Group (UK) Ltd, Croydon, CR0 4YY

1 3 5 7 9 10 8 6 4 2

*For Ann Robinson and her daughter,
Emma Wilson, with love.*

ONE

The poor always ye have with you.

THE BIBLE

The Poor Relation was no longer an apt name for what had become London's most fashionable hotel. The Prince of Wales's coat of arms gleamed over the entrance with that magic legend 'By Special Appointment.' In residence and taking up every guest room except one for his retinue of friends and servants was Prince Hugo Panič, from some Middle European country which everyone swore they had heard of but no one seemed to know anything about.

The owners of the hotel had been poor relations themselves when they founded it, that despised shabby genteel class eking out a difficult living. But Lady Fortescue, Sir Philip Sommerville, Colonel Sandhurst, and Miss Tonks, the owners, had made it prosper, at first by theft from their relations, and then by a combination of guile, hard business and luck. An actor, Mr Jason Davy, had recently bought his way into shared ownership, and yet, because of old Sir Philip's jealousy and dislike of him, had never felt he was one of them.

1

The open-handed prince paid hard cash as he went along and the hoteliers felt their days of penury were truly behind them. This gave them an added happiness and sparkle, and even Sir Philip had not been heard to utter anything loathsome for quite a number of days.

But their very happiness intensified the black misery of the occupant of the one apartment not taken up by the prince or his entourage. The occupant was Lady Jane Fremney, youngest daughter of the Earl of Durby. Through her refusal to marry the man her father had picked out for her, she had been cast out 'until she came to her senses.' That, her father considered, would not take very long as she had only one small trunk of clothes and none of her jewellery.

Lady Jane had used what was left of her pin money to travel from Durbyshire to London. She thought back on her miserable, lonely childhood, thought of her bullying governess, thought of the family servants who had treated her harshly because her father, the earl, encouraged them to do so. 'You have to break a woman's spirit to make her a good wife' was one of his favourite maxims, and Lady Jane often wondered whether that was why her mother had gone to such an early grave, when she herself was but two years old.

So she decided to put an end to her life. She had told the owner of the Poor Relation that her maid would be arriving shortly. Her empty jewel case was weighted down with stones.

She ate by herself at a corner table in the dining room, only half interested in the noisy, garrulous prince who sat at the centre table with his equally noisy mistress. She picked at the delicious food which the hotel always served, hardly tasting what she ate. She did not notice the owners much, and a London hotel being such an anonymous sort of place, she supposed that they barely noticed her.

In this she was wrong.

Four days after her arrival, the owners were gathered in their private sitting room at the top of the hotel. They looked very different from the threadbare people who had first banded together to share their lot. Lady Fortescue, in her seventies, tall and erect, wore a cap of fine lace on top of her snowy, impeccably coiffured hair, and a silk gown of expensive cut. Colonel Sandhurst, very grand in Weston's best tailoring, and occasionally glancing down at the shine on his flat pumps, fiddled with a diamond stickpin in his cravat and beamed around at everyone with his mild, childlike blue eyes. Also in his seventies, his one ambition now was to sell the hotel and marry Lady Fortescue.

Sir Philip Sommerville, equally old, was quite the dandy in a padded coat and enormous cravat. His tortoise-like face looked unusually benign, but then Sir Philip claimed that money could make a saint out of anyone.

Miss Tonks, fortyish, or, as Lord Byron put it, a lady of certain years, years uncertain, had a certain elegance, not entirely due to French taffeta and the clever hands of the royal hairdresser. She no longer blinked nervously or hung her head. She was as erect and confident a figure now as Lady Fortescue, and her gentle, sheeplike face turned from time to time towards the door, awaiting the arrival of the man of her dreams, Mr Jason Davy.

Just when she was beginning to think he would never arrive, Mr Davy entered. He was a middle-aged man, slim and nondescript, with bright eyes and thick brown hair streaked with grey. He, like Colonel Sandhurst, was impeccably dressed, and the only person who thought that he never could, never would look like a gentleman was Sir Philip Sommerville. Sir Philip had marked down Miss Tonks to take care of him in his declining years, but the 'silly' spinster did nothing but make sheep's eyes at the actor.

And Miss Tonks then proceeded to dent Sir Philip's new-found euphoria by saying eagerly, 'I am so glad you are come, Mr Davy. We have a problem.'

Mr Davy smiled and sat down next to her. 'What problem?' demanded Sir Philip with a scowl.

'Why, Lady Jane, to be sure,' said Miss Tonks.

'Oh, that one. I am sure she hasn't a feather to fly with, and what's more, doesn't mean to pay her bill.' Sir Philip tapped his nose. 'I can smell poverty. But does it matter? We're in funds. She's a beautiful lady, so we may as well be charitable for a change. She's in the poorest rooms. She can stay for a month and we'll give her a bill and if she don't pay it, we'll kick her out.'

'That is no answer to the problem,' said Lady Fortescue. 'I, too, have remarked on Lady Jane's downcast looks. She is the daughter of the Earl of

4

Durby and yet no one calls on her, nor does she call on anyone. The maid she spoke of has not arrived. She seems to walk and move in misery.'

'Do you mean she might commit suicide?' asked Mr Davy.

'Here now!' Sir Philip sat up straight, his pale eyes registering alarm. 'That would be a disaster. Get a suicide and the place is damned. Our prince would take himself off and it would be ages before anyone else would come. But what has she to commit suicide about? She may be poor and obviously in trouble with her family, but she is beautiful.'

'Perhaps she does not know it,' said Colonel Sandhurst. 'What lady so sunk in misery as she obviously is can think of her looks? How old is she, would you say?'

'Nineteen or twenty,' said Lady Fortescue. 'Her father is a brute, I believe, her mother dead, her four brothers in the military.'

'Let's get back to this suicide business.' Sir Philip was becoming increasingly worried. 'I mean, how do we stop her?'

'Perhaps,' volunteered Mr Davy, 'she might confide in one of us.'

'Meaning you?' jeered Sir Philip. 'Always the ladies' man, hey.'

'I was thinking of Miss Tonks here,' said Mr Davy, casting a forgiving smile on Sir Philip, which irritated that elderly gentleman every bit as much as Mr Davy had meant it to do.

'I have tried twice to engage her in conversation,'

5

said Miss Tonks, 'but she looks at me with such blank eyes that I cannot go on. But I will try to watch her as closely as I can.

'You can't be with her every minute of the day and night,' pointed out Colonel Sandhurst. 'Would not the best course of action be to write to her father? He cannot know she is alone and unchaperoned in London.'

'Let us see what Miss Tonks can find out,' said Lady Fortescue. 'We have had enough trouble in the past. It is time to enjoy comfort and to look after ourselves. Someone as young and as beautiful as Lady Jane may be distressed for the moment, but suicide! No, I think not.'

Miss Tonks slept late the following day. She had recently become accustomed to that luxury because the hotel had now a highly paid, efficient staff. It was well known among the servant class that the Poor Relation paid for the best and would sack anyone who was not willing, bright and efficient.

But her first uneasy thought was about Lady Jane. She washed and dressed hurriedly in her room in the apartment which the hoteliers rented. It was next door to the hotel.

When she entered the entrance hall, a heavily veiled figure walked past her and out into Bond Street. Sure that it was Lady Jane, Miss Tonks turned about and followed in pursuit.

Ragged clouds raced over the dingy sky above. Miss Tonks hoped it would not rain, for rain turned the streets of London into slippery, muddy hazards, and she was not wearing pattens, those wooden clogs with the high iron ring on the sole, so useful in wet weather. A strong wind was howling down the narrow streets and sending streams of smoke snaking down from the whirling cowls on the chimney-pots. Ahead of her, the slim figure of Lady Jane moved easily and quickly, heading always in the direction of the City. By the time Miss Tonks and her quarry reached the bottom of Ludgate Hill, Miss Tonks was feeling tired. Up the hill went Lady Jane and then turned off into one of the narrow lanes where the apothecaries had their shops. Miss Tonks saw her go into one of these shops and hesitated. outside, peering in over the display of leeches in jars and coloured bottles of liquid. She saw Lady Jane buy two flat green bottles of something. She drew back into a doorway as Lady Jane emerged, and then, as she watched her hurrying off, Miss Tonks wondered what to do. After a little hesitation, she pushed open the door of the apothecary's and went in.

'I wonder,' said Miss Tonks to the assistant, 'whether my lady's-maid has just been here. I sent her to buy something for me, but as I was in the City, I thought I would find out, you see, whether she had bought it. A heavily veiled woman.'

'I have just sold two bottles of laudanum to a veiled lady,' said the assistant.

'Oh, really? Yes, that is it. I have great difficulty sleeping at night.' And Miss Tonks chattered her way out of the door, discoursing all the while on her mythical sleeplessness.

On Ludgate Hill, she hailed a hack to take her back to Bond Street, where she called her partners together and told them of Lady Jane's purchase.

'A lot of ladies take laudanum,' said Mr Davy.

'Fool!' said Sir Philip. 'Not two whole bottles of the stuff. I have it. We'll get Jack, the footman, to collect her as soon as she has deposited the stuff in her room. I'll take her into the office and say that bills should be settled monthly, a new policy, and we will be presenting her with her account at the end of the month. I will hold her in conversation. Perhaps then Lady Fortescue and Miss Tonks can go to her room and change the mixture for something innocuous.'

'But why not confront her with the fact that we suspect she plans to do away with herself?' said the colonel.

'All she has to do is lie,' said Sir Philip. 'She'll leave a note for her father. Bound to. I know, leave enough laudanum in the bottles to knock her out. We'll keep checking on her and as soon as we find she's left a note, then we'll have her and out she goes.'

'Oh, no, we cannot do that,' exclaimed Miss Tonks. 'It would only add to her shame and wretchedness. Yes, we find her out and then we try to do something to help!'

Sir Philip groaned and clutched at his wig so that it slipped sideways. 'Look, we're happy and rich and we've got our generous prince to thank for it. Why bother ourselves with some mad girl?'

'Because it is our duty,' said Lady Fortescue awfully, and that silenced Sir Philip.

Lady Jane walked along Bond Street. Rain was beginning to fall, an appropriate day to end her life. She could feel the dragging weight of the two bottles of laudanum in her reticule. She had found her way to Ludgate Hill because one of the maids had drawn her a map. She would write a letter to her father and beg him to settle her account at the hotel. A smart carriage moved past. A pretty girl looked out of the window. Two soldiers on the pavement stared at her boldly. Three young matrons followed by their footmen and lady's-maids sailed into the hotel, no doubt to take coffee, because the Poor Relation was really the only place in London outside of Gunter's, the confectioner's, where ladies could meet.

In her rooms, Lady Jane unpinned her hat and veil and threw them on a chair. She put the two bottles on the toilet-table and then crossed to the writing-desk in her small sitting room. She was just sharpening a quill with a penknife when there came a scratching at the door and Jack, the footman, walked in.

'My lady,' he said, 'Sir Philip Sommerville requests the honour of your presence in the office.'

Lady Jane stood up. 'Where is this office?'

'At the back of the entrance hall, my lady.'

'Very well, I will follow you shortly.'

Jack hesitated on the threshold, remembering his instructions, which were not to leave her alone for a moment. 'I beg pardon, my lady, but Sir Philip said the matter was pressing.'

Lady Jane gave a little sigh. They had probably

guessed that she had no maid following on. They would have noticed that no one called on her. They would be anxious to find out whether she could meet her bill or not. Well, it didn't matter any more. All she had to do was tell more lies.

'I will come with you,' she said.

Colonel Sandhurst and Mr Davy were also in the small office. They stood up as Lady Jane entered.

She was wearing a plain grey gown of some shimmering stuff which seemed to highlight her extreme pallor. She was, despite the shadows under her eyes and the look of strain on her face, still very beautiful. Her skin was without blemish and her eyes, very large and grey, were fringed with thick lashes. Her mouth was perfect.

'Do sit down, my lady,' urged Sir Philip. 'May we offer you some tea, or wine? Perhaps a glass of negus or ratafia?'

'Nothing, I thank you.' She sat down with an unconscious grace. 'I believe you have business to discuss with me. What is it?'

'We have a new policy in this hotel,' said Sir Philip, speaking very slowly and hoping Lady Fortescue and Miss Tonks were fast about their work. 'We expect bills to be settled at the end of each month. I hope this does not disturb you.'

'Not at all,' said Lady Jane with the fleeting shadow of a smile. 'Is there anything else?' She began to rise.

'Yes, yes,' said the colonel hurriedly. 'We hope you will not consider this an impertinence, my lady, but because of your extreme youth and because you are unchaperoned, we are naturally concerned for you.'

Her voice was quiet and even.

'I do consider it an impertinence.'

Mr Davy spoke for the first time. His voice was kind. 'Do not be angry with us. We have noticed your sad looks. When one feels most alone, one should always remember that there is someone to help.'

Lady Jane's eyes were lit with a flash of anger. Why couldn't they leave her alone? She was angriest at Mr Davy for his kindness, for arousing that anger in her, for she preferred to stay wrapped in dull numb misery which would make what she had to do the easier.

She rose to her feet. Making an obvious effort, she said, 'I thank you for your concern, but it is not necessary, I assure you. Good day, gentlemen.'

'And that's that,' said Sir Philip gloomily. 'I hope she doesn't run into Lady Fortescue and Miss Tonks in her rooms.'

Lady Jane actually met both of them in the corridor outside. Lady Fortescue and Miss Tonks smiled and curtsied. She bowed her head and scurried past them and into her rooms. She locked the door behind her and then went to the writing-table. She sharpened the quill with swift, efficient strokes and drew sheets of writing-paper towards her. Should she blame her father for what she was about to do? No, she could not leave him with that misery. Perhaps he thought he had been doing only what was best for her. When she had turned out of her home, she had told him defiantly that she was going to stay with her old nurse in Yorkshire. The nurse, Nancy Thistlethwaite, had been the only person in her short life who had ever been kind to her and who had been fired as a result. Her father had laughed at her and had said that a poor existence in a cottage with that fool Nancy was just what was needed to bring her to her senses and agree to the marriage he had arranged for her.

So she wrote a letter saying simply that she had taken her own life and that she would like him to settle her hotel bill. Then she wrote another letter to Sir Philip Sommerville, apologizing for having committed suicide in the hotel and assuring him that her father would settle her bill. She sanded and sealed both letters and propped them up on the writing-table.

Then she brushed down her hair and took off her clothes and put on her nightgown. She poured the contents of both bottles into two glasses and, pinching her nose, swallowed down the contents, one glassful after the other.

She lay down carefully on top of the bed and sent a prayer up for forgiveness. She could feel herself becoming sleepy, and suddenly she began to fight against it. Out of nowhere came an intense desire to live. She dragged herself from the bed onto the floor. But a wave of misery hit her again and the desire to sleep was so very great. She would close her eyes just for a moment . . .

Jack, the footman, pressed his ear hard against the panel of the door. He thought he had heard a faint crash but Lady Jane's sitting room was on the other side of the door, not her bedchamber. He listened and listened but the following silence was absolute.

'Anything?' whispered Sir Philip behind him, making him jump.

'Nothing.'

'Then scratch the door and go in, man. Use your wits. Say it's a cold day and you wondered whether she would like the fires lit.'

Jack scratched at the panels and then turned the handle. 'It's locked!'

'Run and get the spare key our of the office, demme, and get the ladies up here.'

He fretted and chewed his knuckles in impatience. Jack returned, after what seemed to Sir Philip like an age, with not only the ladies but Colonel Sandhurst and Mr Davy as well. 'Now open the door,' whispered Sir Philip. 'You go in, Jack, and if all is well, ask her about the fires. If she's dead, call us.'

'She can't be dead,' said Lady Fortescue crossly. 'We emptied out most of the contents of the bottles and replaced them with plain water.'

Jack unlocked the door and went in, very nervously. He hoped she would be in the sitting room, for if she was not, that meant she would be in the bedroom and might have locked the door to her room for no more sinister reason than because she wanted to change her clothes.

But the sitting room was empty. With a dry mouth he approached the open bedroom door and peered around it. No one. He gave a little sigh of relief and was about to turn away when he noticed one small

13

bare foot sticking out from the floor on the far side of the bed. He walked round the bed and stared down at the still form of Lady Jane Fremney.

He rushed back through the sitting room, babbling, 'She's gone and done it. Oh, she's gone and done it.'

The others came in and crowded into the bedroom. Miss Tonks knelt down and bent over the girl. 'She is sleeping peacefully. God be thanked.'

Sir Philip retreated to the sitting room, where he found the two letters. He opened the one addressed to the hotel and let out a crow of triumph. 'We've got her!' he cried. He scuttled into the bedroom, waving the letter. 'And there's one addressed to her father.'

'Poor child,' murmured Lady Fortescue. 'Lift her onto the bed, Jack, and cover her with the quilt. Miss Tonks and I will be here when she awakes.'

Lady Jane slowly came awake. Her mind was immediately flooded with the realization of what she had done, of what she had tried to do. She was torn between misery that she was alive with her problems and relief that she *was* still alive. She struggled up against the pillows and her dazed eyes looked into those of Lady Fortescue and Miss Tonks, who were sitting beside the bed.

'What are you doing here?' she asked faintly.

Lady Fortescue ignored her. 'Tell Jack to bring the others here,' she ordered Miss Tonks.

'I must get up,' said Lady Jane feebly. She had just remembered the letters on the writing-desk.

Lady Fortescue held up one thin hand. 'In a moment. We know about the letters.'

Miss Tonks returned, followed by the colonel, Sir Philip and Mr Davy.

Lady Jane stared at them defiantly. She was beginning to remember falling on the floor. Someone had lifted her onto the bed and covered her.

'Now we are all here,' said Lady Fortescue, 'we would like to know how you came to take your own life.'

'A demned selfish action, too,' growled Sir Philip. 'Did you never think of us? A suicide could ruin us.'

'Do you mean the money for these rooms is all-important to you?' asked Lady Jane.

'Not the money – the scandal, the superstition. The next thing people would be seeing your ghost. Did it never dawn on you that your poor family would have to see you interred at the crossroads, with a stake through your heart?' complained Sir Philip, describing how suicides of the early-nineteenth century were buried.

'And did you not think of your immortal soul?' chided the colonel gently. 'What you planned on doing was a sin against God.'

'I know, I know,' said Lady Jane wretchedly. 'But what else could I do?'

'You could tell us how we may help you.' Miss Tonks pressed Lady Jane's hand. 'We are concerned for your plight.'

Lady Jane looked at the circle of faces around the bed.

15

'Very well, I will tell you. I had a most unhappy childhood. My problems really began when my father engaged a governess, a Miss Stamp, to educate me. Miss Stamp delighted in tormenting me and bullying me. When I appealed to my father, he told her about my complaint and suggested she beat me the harder because I was becoming wilful and spoilt. But I endured – how I endured! – for one day I knew her services would no longer be required and I would make my come-out and at least I would have a brief time when I could meet girls of my own age. But Miss Stamp was raised to the rank of companion and still had the schooling of me in etiquette and conversation. Still, there was hope of marriage to perhaps a kind man who would free me from bondage. I was allowed to attend balls at neighbouring houses, but always with Miss Stamp. I danced with some agreeable men, but when they came to call I was never allowed to entertain them.

'The final blow came when my father summoned me to his study and told me there would be no need to take me to London for a Season, for he had found a husband for me. This man he had chosen for me was Sir Guy Parrish, his friend, a man in his fifties, small and wizened, a five-bottle-a-day man. I said I would not marry him. I said I had lasted, had endured the tyranny of Miss Stamp, had endured his tyranny because one day, I thought, I would at least have a Season and a chance to find a man of my choice. He ordered me from the house, only allowing me to take one trunk. I took my jewel box, which had been emptied, and weighted it down with stones, for I knew what I meant to do. I would die in the London that had been forbidden to me. But I told him that I was going to stay with my old nurse in Yorkshire. He laughed and said a spell of poverty – for he knew Nancy, my old nurse, to be poor – was just what I needed to bring me to my senses. And so I came to you. I am so very sorry.' She turned her head away and tears rolled down her cheeks.

Sir Philip often admitted to himself that he was given to over-sentimentality. He surprised the others by saying in a rallying voice, 'Here, now. We are here to look after you. All you need, dear lady, is a little *fun*. I am the first to admit you have the dreariest apartment in the hotel and you should not be alone here. Not fitting. You can move in with Miss Tonks in our apartment next door.'

'Yes, do,' said Miss Tonks. 'We can have chats and look at the shops together.'

'Too kind,' said Lady Jane faintly, 'but I have no claim on you. You do not owe me anything. On the contrary . . .'

'It would amuse us,' said Lady Fortescue. 'I know that people of our rank are not allowed to talk about money, but we, being in trade, feel free to discuss our funds as much as we please. And we are in funds, thanks to the munificence of Prince Hugo. I think we should order some gowns for you. Gowns are very important in times of distress. We shall leave you to dress and pack. Miss Tonks will return in an hour to conduct you to your new quarters.'

17

The hoteliers left her and went down to the office for a council of war.

'She won't try it again, will she?' asked Sir Philip anxiously.

'I do not think so,' said Lady Fortescue. 'You are to be praised, Sir Philip, for the generosity of your nature.' She smiled at him, her black eyes almost flirtatious, and the colonel scowled. Sir Philip smiled back and then kissed her hand, remembering that not so long ago he had rather fancied Lady Fortescue.

'It is a pity that she cannot have a Season.' Miss Tonks looked wistful. 'She is so very beautiful, she could be all the rage.'

'She cannot.' Lady Fortescue looked around the small group. 'We are now pretty much socially acceptable again, although we are in trade. I am invited to several small functions, as is Colonel Sandhurst. But that is not the same. Besides, even if we could bring her out, her father would read her name in the social columns and post south to take her home. He may yet come looking for her. She is supposed to be with that nurse in Yorkshire, is she not? Then I suggest we give her some money to send to her old nurse and letters to post to her father, harsh letters which will keep him at bay for a little. If she learns how to enjoy herself – it will strengthen her character. Too much adversity, as we know, is very weakening.'

'She need not use her own name,' suggested Miss Tonks hopefully. 'No one knows she is in London.'

'We can't call her Lady Anything Else,' jeered Sir

18

Philip. 'The peerage would soon come alive to the fact they had an impostor in their midst.'

'She doesn't need to be titled. Something like Miss Jane North, heiress,' said Miss Tonks.

Lady Fortescue smiled at the middle-aged spinster indulgently. 'You are a matchmaker, Miss Tonks. You have dreams of finding her an eligible gentleman before her father finds *her*. But how could she be presented in society? Another ball here? We cannot while our prince is in residence.'

'What about Harriet?' asked Miss Tonks, looking eagerly around.

'The Duchess of Rowcester!' exclaimed Sir Philip. Harriet had been their cook when they first started the hotel. She had been a poor relation like the rest of them. Then the Duke of Rowcester had married her. She wrote to them all from time to time.

'Even if we should consider entertaining such a far-fetched idea,' said Lady Fortescue gently, 'you forget Harriet lost her child nearly a year ago.'

There was a sad little silence. Harriet's beloved baby daughter had been carried off in a typhoid epidemic.

'But don't you see,' said Miss Tonks stubbornly, 'helping Lady Jane would brighten her up. Give her an interest.'

'Her husband is her interest,' said Sir Philip, beginning to chew his knuckles, a sign he was worried. The others did not know that the necessary funds to start the hotel had been supplied by Sir Philip from a necklace he had stolen from the Duke of

Rowcester before he married Harriet. He had substituted a clever fake. He knew the real necklace had not been sold, for he had been paying the jeweller from time to time to keep it intact until such time as he might have enough to reclaim it. But of late he had forgotten to make the payments. He did not want to have anything to do with the formidable duke again.

'But the duke is abroad in Italy. Some elderly relative's funeral,' protested Miss Tonks. 'I read that in the newspapers. We could write to dear Harriet. She has only to refuse. I mean, we are not constraining her to come.'

'What ridiculous fustian,' snapped Sir Philip. 'What rubbish. The girl's lucky to be alive. Oh, amuse yourself for a little by taking her about and buying her gowns. But we have no need to become involved in plots and plans and schemes any more.'

'I would like to see Harriet again,' said the colonel. 'You could write, Miss Tonks, and send her our love and explain Lady Jane's situation.'

'I forbid it!' shouted Sir Philip, startling them all.

Had he not been so vehement in his protest, the others might, on sober reflection, have dropped the idea.

But Mr Davy said in a chiding voice, 'I really think what you want or do not want does not enter into the matter, Sir Philip. If Miss Tonks wishes to write to the Duchess of Rowcester, then that is her decision.'

This incensed Sir Philip the more. 'Miss Letitia Tonks used to be a quiet and respectable female before you came here with your nasty actor ways,' he said. 'You're always filling her mind with trash.'

'Please don't,' whispered Miss Tonks and began to cry.

'Now look what you've done,' raged the colonel.

'A pox on the lot of you,' howled Sir Philip and slammed out of the room.

'Do not cry,' said Mr Davy, putting an arm around Miss Tonks's shaking shoulders. 'You do what you think best.'

And the feel of that comforting arm sent Miss Tonks straight from the depths of misery to heaven.

TWO

I regard you with an indifference closely bordering on aversion.

ROBERT LOUIS STEVENSON

Harriet, Duchess of Rowcester, walked slowly along the terrace and thought of her husband. Things had been uneasy between them since the death of Emily, their beloved daughter. A peacock on the lawn in front of her let out a harsh scream and turned its moulting feathers to the sun.

She reflected that she had been glad to see him leave for Italy, for she could no longer feel affectionate towards him and shrank from his embrace. He had said that he would keep to his own bedchamber until she was fully recovered from the death of their child. Guilt and concern for him made her feel like a bad wife, and yet she could not bring herself to approach him, to heal the ever-widening breach she sensed between them.

She heard the post-boy's horn and wondered whether the duke had written to her from Dover, although he had said he would write when he reached Milan, his destination. But she hurried through the house, hoping all the same that he might have written, that he might have forgiven her. She stopped short in the middle of the Yellow Saloon as the awful thought struck her that he might never forgive her. She shook her head as if to dismiss it, but it obstinately would not go away. She had known for the past few months that his kindness and consideration towards her were slowly fading, to be replaced by resentment.

Sadly she walked on, through the chain of rooms, and so into the hall. The butler was arranging a small pile of letters on a silver tray.

'I will take them now,' said Harriet. She picked up the letters and retreated to the small morning room, which she had made her own. She put aside the ones addressed to her husband. There were three for herself. One was a bill from a London dressmaker, one a mercer's bill for a bolt of figured silk, and the third was from Letitia Tonks.

She opened Miss Tonks's letter, which was crossed and recrossed and difficult to read, Miss Tonks having written first across the paper and then diagonally one way and then the other. It started with news of how well they were doing since the prince had arrived, and then there was a long piece about how delightful a companion Mr Davy was and what an asset to the hotel. I wonder what happened there, thought Harriet, pausing in her reading and remembering an effusive letter a while ago in which a rapturous Miss Tonks had claimed that Sir Philip Sommerville was about to propose marriage to her. She tilted the page and started on the crossed writing. It took her some time to work out that it was a description of the attempted suicide of a certain Lady Jane Fremney, daughter of the Earl of Durby. Harriet read on through the long description of Lady Jane's running away from home, her penury, her desire for a Season, Miss Tonks's grand idea that if the young woman assumed another name and *if* someone like dear Harriet felt like opening up her town house and bringing Lady Jane out, then perhaps the dear girl might find herself a suitable husband instead of 'that monster' her father had chosen for her.

Harriet read the letter carefully to the end. She remembered her days at the Poor Relation with affection, the scares, the excitement, the warmth and the friendship, and gave a little sigh. To anyone else, Miss Tonks's suggestion would seem absolutely mad, but to Harriet, remembering her friends with affection, it was just the sort of idea they would dream up.

Why not? she thought suddenly. Why not find something unusual like this to occupy her mind instead of sitting and grieving for her lost child, and feeling guilty about her estranged husband?

She went to her writing-desk and penned a letter to Miss Tonks saying that she would be in London in two weeks' time and that they would discuss the matter then. Harriet did not want to give a definite yes until she had seen this Lady Jane. Anyone who did something so terrible, so drastic as trying to commit suicide might be mentally unbalanced.

* * *

Miss Jane North, as she was now called, submitted dutifully to the outings arranged for her by Miss Tonks and Mr Davy, who appeared to have been appointed her guardians. She tried hard to return their kindness by appearing cheerful, but she seemed to carry a greyness around with her, a remoteness. They promenaded around the shops, drove in the parks, took tea at Gunter's in Berkeley Square and went to the playhouse, where Mr Davy escorted them backstage and introduced them to the actors. Jane, who had never known any such freedom, could not yet appreciate any of it. She went everywhere heavily veiled, her eyes cast down, speaking in a low voice and only when spoken to.

Miss Tonks began to feel at her wits' end. Mr Davy said soothingly that it would take time. Someone who had so recently been in such despair as to want to commit suicide did not recover overnight. Jane had dutifully written to her old nurse, enclosing money and two letters for her father, one to be posted on immediately, the other in two weeks' time. But she did this on instruction, as she did everything else they told her to do.

And then the Duchess of Rowcester's letter arrived and Miss Tonks took it first to Lady Fortescue.

'Our cautious Harriet,' said Lady Fortescue, after she had read it carefully. 'And quite right to be cautious, too. She may decide against bringing out a young female who always looks as if she is about to attend her own funeral. The sad fact is that I find Lady Jane something of a bore.'

'Oh, no!' exclaimed Miss Tonks, clasping her thin hands together. 'She is always sad, but so *good* and so very beautiful.'

'You have always had a weakness for beauty,' said Lady Fortescue sympathetically. 'But there is nothing in her at the moment to attract any man. Even when she ate in the dining room, she failed to catch the eye of our most susceptible prince. Just in case Jane North, as we now must call her, has any hope left in her, we should not tell her about Harriet until Harriet has seen her and made up her mind what to do. Harriet may very well decide it is not worth the effort. The weather has been dreadful of late. If this incessant rain ever ceases, Jane might come about. Having to go abroad wearing calash and pattens is very lowering. Sensible dress does have a lowering effect on the spirits.

'Normally I would suggest putting her to work in the hotel, although we now do little work ourselves. Work might give her an interest. On the other hand, should Harriet decide to sponsor her, then having been seen about the hotel working would ruin her social chances. Then, of course, for it actually to work out, Jane has to be lucky enough to find a suitor able to stand up to her father, and one rich enough not to care if he decides not to give her a dowry. Where are you taking her on this awful day?'

'We are going to the Park in a closed carriage.'

'The day is depressing enough without being confined in a closed carriage and looking out at a lot of muddy trees. I think perhaps Sir Philip should take her in hand.'

Miss Tonks primmed her lips in disapproval. 'Sir Philip is enough to drive anyone to suicide.'

'He can be waspish and irritating. But perhaps the girl has been treated to *too* much kindness and understanding.'

Miss Tonks was about to protest, but then she thought that a day without Jane would mean she could go to the Park with Mr Davy alone. 'I do not know how Sir Philip will entertain her,' she said instead. 'He will probably take her to a cock-fight.'

Sir Philip received Lady Fortescue's suggestion without enthusiasm. 'I don't know where to take her,' he grumbled. 'Why should I waste time escorting a Friday-faced antidote? And she goes about so heavily veiled, it's like speaking to one of those horrors out of a Gothic romance. Oh, well, I can see from that militant look in your eye that there is no escape. And talking about Friday-faced antidotes, where is our Miss Tonks?'

'I think she is going out with Mr Davy.'

'Meaning you know she is going out with Mr Davy, as usual. She is wasting her time on that mountebank and becoming skittish and frivolous, which is disgusting in a lady of her years.'

'Then,' said Lady Fortescue drily, 'it follows that you are even more disgusting when you are skittish and frivolous because you are nearly twice her age. With any luck, at the end of the next Season, we will all be able to sell up and retire. You seem to harbour some odd notion of marriage to Miss Tonks. It would not serve.'

'Why?'

'I shall put it crudely and bluntly. Miss Tonks is a genteel virgin and you are an old rip with carnal lusts which seem to increase with age. One would have thought lust would have turned to rust by now.'

'We should all stay together,' said Sir Philip sulkily. 'Davy's an interloper.'

'Mr Davy is one of us. He has proved his worth by being a most efficient debt collector. We have not one outstanding debt now. And now that the prince is here and his secretary is paying everything at the end of each week, we have no worries on that score. Mr Davy has earned a holiday, as have we all.'

'He was not with us from the beginning,' protested Sir Philip. 'He has had an easy time of it.'

'I am not going to waste any more time talking to you.' Lady Fortescue rose to her feet. 'Do what you can for Jane. You are a kind man at heart, Sir Philip, so stop trying to pretend otherwise.'

Sir Philip found Jane in the room she shared with Miss Tonks. She was wearing a carriage dress and the inevitable depressing hat with a heavy veil.

'I'm taking you out, see?' said Sir Philip, 'So I'll wait for you in the hotel office next door while you change.'

'Change?' asked the voice softly from behind the veil.

'Yes, change. You're going out with a fashionable gentleman, so put on something pretty and leave off that demned veil!'

28

Sir Philip walked out before she could reply.

Jane rose stiffly – she always moved stiffly these days, as if the mental pain inside her head had affected her movements – a rheumatism of the very soul – and went to the large carved press next to the fireplace and opened it. There were four new gowns which had arrived from the dressmaker's, neatly folded. On the top shelf were new hat-boxes. Although she had stood patiently while she was fitted for her new clothes, she had not worn any of them.

She selected a morning gown of white lace and muslin and a pelisse of apricot silk lined with fur. On her head she put an apricot velvet hat with a low crown and wide brim. She studied herself in the long mirror, not really seeing herself, not noticing the fashion plate that looked back at her, searching only for bits of loose thread or hair that might be caught in her clothes.

Sir Philip, when he saw her entering the office, surveyed her with delight. 'Now you look more the thing,' he crowed. 'And bless us all, but the sun has begun to shine.'

'Has it?' asked Jane. 'I did not notice.'

He clicked his tongue in impatience. 'I have ordered an open carriage. I tried to persuade the others that it was time we had our own carriage instead of running up an enormous bill at the livery stables. But would they listen? Not them. Cheese-paring when they don't have to be, and profligate when times are hard. Come.' He held out his arm and she dutifully placed her gloved hand on it. Sir Philip

29

led her out into the hallway just as Prince Hugo was arriving. Prince Hugo was a large, ebullient man with bushy sidewhiskers and Slav eyes, intense blue eyes of an almost oriental cast. Those eyes fell on Jane and widened slightly. The prince's hand went up to his whiskers and gave them a twirl.

'Present me, Sommerville,' he said.

'Miss Jane North, Your Highness,' said Sir Philip.

The prince kissed Jane's gloved hand. She curtsied low. Sir Philip held out his arm again and they left the hotel while the prince stared after them.

'Made a conquest there,' said Sir Philip cheerfully as Jack helped them both into the carriage. 'Drive us around where we can be seen,' he instructed the coachman.

Jane sat rigidly beside him, missing the protection of her veil. So many people seemed to stop on the pavements to stare at her. She wondered if she had a smut on her nose.

She had never been told she was beautiful. It had been dinned into her mind from an early age that she was plain, and any hopes she had of attracting a man must be supplied by her rank and her dowry. At last the stares became too much.

'Sir Philip,' she said to that elderly gentleman, who was sitting with his arms folded, looking all about him with a complacent air. 'Why do people stare so? Do I have a mark on my face?'

'Pay them no heed and worry only when they stop staring. They like staring at beauties.'

He glanced at her astonished face and gave a cackle

of laughter. 'No wonder you didn't know you were beautiful, moping around behind a veil and wishing you were dead because of some nasty old tyrant of a father.'

A faint flush rose up in her pale face. Had either Miss Tonks or Mr Davy told her she was beautiful, she would not have believed them, would have thought they were being kind. But Sir Philip's blunt remarks had the ring of truth. She looked about her with a sort of wonder. A tall guardsman stopped short on the pavement and looked at her in open admiration and raised his hat. Jane gave a polite bow.

'Here now,' admonished Sir Philip. 'If you haven't been introduced to 'em, you don't notice 'em. Where will I take you to blow the cobwebs out of your brain? We'll go down to the river.'

He called to the coachman to take them to Westminster Bridge, and when they reached there ordered Jane to dismount and told the driver to wait.

They walked along the bridge and into one of the semi-circular bays which overlooked the river. London lay covered in a misty haze through which a warm sun shone, turning everything to gold. Upstream lay the terraces of trees and grey houses in front of Westminster Hall, the new Millbank Penitentiary, and low banks lined with willow trees. Downstream were the ramshackle taverns and the warehouses of Scotland Yard, the gardens of Northumberland House, the conical water-tower of York Buildings, Somerset House rising above the water, and St Paul's dome, dominating all the houses and spires. They stood in silence. The great stream flowed below them, green and grey, boats with white and brown sails scudding across it.

'It's beautiful,' said Jane.

'Nice enough on a good day,' said Sir Philip. 'I know, we'll go to the tea-gardens at Chelsea and enjoy the sunshine.'

The King's Road in Chelsea was a depressing sight with wounded soldiers standing outside the taverns, leaning on their crutches, their eyes wild with drink. But once Sir Philip and Jane were ensconced in the quiet of the tea-gardens, war seemed very far away, and Napoleon a forgotten ogre.

'Thank you. This is very pleasant,' said Jane. 'I am indebted to you, as I am to your friends.'

'Then you can repay us by stopping feeling so disgustingly sorry for yourself,' said Sir Philip.

She stared at him, shocked, and then said coldly, 'Perhaps we should be getting back.'

'Not till I've said my piece.' Sir Philip tapped his cup with his spoon. 'You have had a hard time of it, no doubt about that, but society is full of folk who were whipped by their parents, shut up in the cellar, and, yes, girls who were forced into marriage with men they don't like. It's the way of the world. But you lack bottom. If the rest of society were like you, there would be corpses from end to end of London. And what of those poor soldiers? Maimed and hobbled and on a pension of sixpence a day. The whole of life is compromise. You take what the Good Lord has handed you and make the most of it. Look at you!

You are beautiful and titled and well fed and well gowned. Come to think of it,' he went on cheerfully, 'you ought to be ashamed of yourself.'

Jane looked at him steadily, a high colour on her cheeks. 'I must think about what you have just said.' And she turned her gaze away from him and looked across the gardens.

It was just as well for her that Sir Philip's attention had been caught by the charms of a buxom waitress. He raised his quizzing-glass and for the moment forgot about his companion.

Jane struggled for words to explain why she had tried to commit suicide. How could she explain the cruel reality of being isolated in her father's mansion from any normal life? The only servant to ever show her any kindness, her nurse, had been dismissed. Her aunt, the earl's sister, was mostly in residence and ignored Jane as if she did not exist. Jane's young life had been ordered by the cruel tyranny of her governess. And having escaped from home burdened with guilt, lost in a strange world outside her 'prison,' she had felt without hope.

She felt a burning sensation of pure rage at this horrible old man opposite who was ogling the waitress. 'How dare you, sir!' she cried. 'How dare you mock me?'

Sir Philip reluctantly transferred his gaze from the waitress. 'I wasn't mocking you. I just got tired of seeing you mewing and whimpering.'

'Have you considered what my plight will be when my father finds me?'

Sir Philip sighed. 'He hasn't found you yet, and when he does, you've got all my soft-hearted friends to fight for you. Get it through your pretty head, you are not alone any more. Start living! Wake up! Drink your tea and let me feast my eyes on that shapely waitress.'

Jane glared at him but he appeared to have forgotten her again.

The sun continued to shine, and the river running at the foot of the gardens sparkled in the sun.

Still fuming and fretting over what Sir Philip had said to her, she turned her attention to the other people in the tea-garden.

And then a tall man entered the gardens with a stately lady on his arm. He was extremely handsome in a rakish and dissipated way. He had golden hair curling under a beaver hat. His clothes were beautifully tailored and his Hessian boots shone like the sun. He had broad shoulders and a trim waist and excellent legs. His eyes were very blue and heavy-lidded, which gave his mobile face a mocking look.

The lady was treating him with cold disdain, something which seemed to amuse him.

And then her voice, clear and carrying, reached Jane's ears. 'Is this your idea of entertainment, Monsieur le Comte? To take me to a common tea-garden and place me among common people?'

The comte's eyes ranged lazily about the garden and fell on Jane and widened slightly. Jane tried to look away, as she knew she ought, but felt trapped by that blue gaze. The lady with the comte followed his gaze and looked at Jane as well. Then she got to her feet. 'Take me home,' she ordered sharply. 'This place is a confounded bore.'

The comte dutifully rose to his feet. He bowed in Jane's direction and swept off his hat. The lady walked out of the tea-garden, her head held high. The comte flashed Jane a comical, rueful look and followed her.

Sir Philip's waitress disappeared indoors to the kitchen and he turned to Jane. He saw her face was flushed and her large eyes sparkling.

'You're still in a rage,' he said in a kind voice. 'I don't mind. Angry people don't try to top themselves. I'll take you back.'

The Comte de Mornay greeted his friend, Jamie Ferguson, in a coffee house in Pall Mall later that day.

'Sit down, mon ami,' he said, pulling out a chair with his foot. 'I am in love.'

'Again?' said Jamie with a grin. He was a tall, thin man with a clever, fox-like face, pale green eyes and sandy hair. 'What happened to the fair Clarissa?'

'I took her to a tea-garden in Chelsea.'

'What were you about? Only the best will do for Clarissa Vardey. What was wrong with Gunter's or the Poor Relation?'

'I knew she would not like it,' said the comte. 'I had begun to take her to unfashionable places. But although she did not like the tea-garden, I knew I could not move her from my side. So I used my most lethal weapon on her.'

'That being?'

35

'I told her I had lost all my money on 'Change.'

'She surely did not believe you!'

'Oh, but she did. I explained most carefully that the reason she had been recently subjected to the indignity of meeting me in such low places was because I could not afford anything higher. And just in case she might not believe me, I explained that she could help my life considerably by giving me back the diamond-and-sapphire necklace I gave her for her birthday. She took fright and went back to her husband like any good wife should.'

'So what is this about love?' asked Jamie, amused.

'While we were in the tea-gardens, I saw the most beautiful creature in the world. A face to dream about. She was with some old rip, her father or uncle, no doubt.'

'Or her protector,' said Jamie cynically.

'Never! She had an untouched air about her. I must find her again. She was exquisitely gowned, I mean gowned like a lady. And young. Not yet twenty.'

Jamie laughed. 'This I find hard to believe. You always court married matrons so that you never need to have any fear of marriage.'

'There was something very special about her. Tiens! When our eyes met, I could hardly drag mine away.'

'So when do you meet this paragon again?'

The comte spread his hands in a Gallic gesture of resignation. 'Who knows? Perhaps when the Season begins, I shall find her.'

'Are you so sure she will be there?'

'Her clothes were of the best.'

'She could be the daughter of a rich Cit.'

'The old gentleman with her was no Cit. In fact, I could almost swear I had seen him before.'

'You will amaze the hopeful mamas at the Season if you decide to put in an appearance. They've been after you for years.'

'I am thirty-two, old but not in my dotage.'

Jamie looked at him with affection. 'I always wonder why you never married.'

'Too busy having fun, too busy making the money. My feckless parents, God rest their souls, escaped the Terror with only their jewels. As soon as I came of age, I took what was left and gambled on the Stock Exchange, to great effect, as you know. It was my pleasure to take them out of that sordid lodging-house in North London and transfer them to a life of comfort in the West End.'

Jamie shook his head. 'I still don't know how you became so wealthy so quickly. You would occasionally disappear for months on end and then reappear, more plump in the pocket than before.'

'Business acumen,' drawled the comte. 'But you are not married yourself, hein? How do you account for that?'

Jamie sighed theatrically. 'A broken heart. But you know about that. When we first became friends five years ago, it was the very first thing I told you.'

'Ah, yes, Miss Fiona of the Highlands, who preferred a Scottish lord double her years and a life in a draughty castle. Mark this, my friend, she has probably got the chilblains all over, elbows like nutmeg graters and a red nose from drinking strong spirits to keep out the cold.'

'Oh, I forgot about her this age. She comes to London with her husband, Lord Dunwilde, for the Season.'

'And you will break her heart in revenge? That is what always happens in the romances.'

Jamie flushed guiltily because that was exactly what he dreamt of doing. 'Fiddle,' he said aloud. 'I shall join you at the Season and together we will hunt down your beauty.'

Harriet, Duchess of Rowcester, sat in the 'staff' sitting room and looked about her with pleasure. 'How good it is to be back,' she exclaimed.

'And how good to see you in looks,' said Lady Fortescue. 'We are so sorry about the death of your child. I lost all mine, one after another. But life goes on and you are still young and strong. You will have more.'

'Enough of my problems,' said Harriet hurriedly. 'When do I meet this Lady Jane?'

'We just call her Jane – Jane North. Jack has gone to fetch her. She is very beautiful, yes, but so downcast and sad that you may find the idea of sponsoring her a hopeless task. How was she today, Sir Philip?'

'Less dull than usual,' said Sir Philip. 'We went to the tea-gardens in Chelsea and you should see the waitress there. What shoulders!'

'Spare the ladies,' complained the colonel. 'If you

spent the time ogling some waitress, then I have no doubt Jane will be more in the megrims than usual – if that is possible.'

Jack opened the door and Jane made her entrance. She was wearing one of her new gowns of pale blue muslin cut low at the neck. Her glossy hair was elaborately dressed.

Head held high, she looked around the room and then her eyes fell on Sir Philip. 'I have thought about your strictures, sir,' she said, her eyes flashing, 'and I take leave to tell you you are an insensitive toad.'

She then stared around in surprise as Miss Tonks began to giggle helplessly. The colonel and Lady Fortescue were laughing openly, as was Mr Davy. Sir Philip had a malicious grin on his face.

The colonel clapped Sir Philip on the shoulder. 'You've done it, Philip. She's come to life.'

'Enough! Enough!' said Lady Fortescue. 'Jane, my dear, come here and make your curtsy to Her Grace, Harriet, Duchess of Rowcester.'

Bewildered by the response to her acid remark to Sir Philip, Jane nonetheless took in the beautiful and elegant figure of the duchess for the first time. She curtsied low. 'I beg your humble pardon, Your Grace, I did not know there was anyone else present.'

'You may call me Harriet and I shall call you Jane. We shall no doubt be a great deal in each other's company during the Season.'

'The Season, Your . . . Harriet?'

'Did Miss Tonks not tell you? I am to bring you out. We shall have such fun.'

'Fun,' echoed Jane, and then she sat down suddenly and began to cry. Harriet, suddenly overcome with longing for her dead child and absent husband, began to cry as well.

Sir Philip marched to the door. 'If this is your idea of fun, then I am going to Limmer's to get drunk!'

THREE

It is charming to totter into vogue.

HORACE WALPOLE

The next day Jane could hardly believe that she was going to have a Season after all. Not that her opinion had been asked. Harriet appeared to consider the matter settled and this beautiful duchess did not seem to think it at all odd that she would be chaperoning a fraud. Perhaps as she had previously worked at the Poor Relation and had probably been subjected to all sorts of adventures, the unusual to her had become everyday.

Jane stopped her packing, for Harriet's carriage was to arrive in an hour's time to take her to the duchess's town house in Park Lane.

She walked to the window and opened it and leaned out and looked down into Bond Street. It was early afternoon and the Bond Street loungers were just starting to go on the strut. A gentleman with a club-foot was heading in the direction of Gentleman Jackson's Boxing Saloon. Jane felt her interest quicken. Could this, then, be the famous Lord Byron? It was well known that Lord Byron, like other gentlemen of the *ton*, took boxing lessons. The art of boxing was considered a must for any gentleman of fashion. Thomas Assheton Smith, when Master of the Quorn, after a battle in Leicester Street with a six-foot coal-heaver, clamped raw steak on both black eyes and sent his defeated opponent a five-pound note for being the best man who had ever stood up to him. Some foreigners landing at Dover were amazed to see a Lord of the Treasury, also just arrived whose ministerial box had been taken away from him by customs-men, lashing out with his fists to regain it. Bottom, that quality in which Sir Philip had found Jane so notably lacking, was highly prized during the Regency.

After the man she believed might be Lord Byron had disappeared, her attention was caught by three dandies walking arm in arm along the pavement, indifferent to the passers-by whom their stately progress was crowding into the kennel. They were formidable figures with their wide-brimmed glossy hats, their spotless white starched cravats so tight and high that the wearers could scarcely look down or turn their heads, their exquisitely cut coats worn wide open to display waistcoats – from left to right – of buff, yellow and rose. Then there were the skin-tight pantaloons, or 'Inexpressibles,' gathered up into a wasp-waist; the fobs, jewels, chains and spotless gloves; the whitethorn cane to hint at the lands from which their incomes derived; and the wonderfully made boots whose surfaces shone like black glass.

Outside the perfumer's opposite, a carriage was

setting down a fashionable lady. Like a lot of her peers, the high-waisted fashions gave her a sort of hoisted-up look. She glanced up at the hotel and Jane, drawing back a little so as not to be noticed watching, saw that her face had an odd look, a cross between vacuity and insolence. She was soon to learn that this was the London look.

Her thoughts were in a jumble. She could not quite believe that, for the present time anyway, she was safe from tyranny. But she would need to be very brave and enjoy as much of each day as she could. For sooner or later her father would find her and bring with him the terrible Miss Stamp, and Jane shuddered at the thought of the dreadful punishments that woman would enjoy meting out.

She stayed so long buried in her thoughts that the chiming of the clock finally alerted her to the time, and she scrambled through the rest of her packing.

John, who, with his wife Betty, was personal servant to the hotel owners, came to carry down her trunks, her luggage having been augmented now by the clothes Lady Fortescue had ordered for her. Jane wished Miss Tonks had decided to come with her. She wondered what Harriet was really like.

'I have decided,' said Harriet, 'to start nursing the ground. To that effect, I think we should make calls. As Duchess of Rowcester, I am welcomed everywhere, a fact I still find strange, for when I was cook at the hotel, a Cit's family would not even have entertained me.'

Jane looked at the calm and beautiful face opposite, at the beauty of the duchess's jewels and the elegance of her gown and said, 'I cannot imagine you working in a kitchen.'

Harriet laughed. 'I was very good at it, but I must admit I was relieved when Sir Philip found a chef to replace me.'

'You are very good to do this for me,' said Jane. 'I . . . I do not deserve such kindness. I tried to take my own life.'

'Well, to be sure you must have been at your wits' end.'

'It must seem very odd to you who have so much courage that someone could be so cowardly as to contemplate suicide.'

Harriet's green eyes suddenly filled with tears and she turned her head away.

Jane rushed and knelt at her feet and took her hands in her own. 'What is it? You must not cry.'

Harriet took out a handkerchief and dried her eyes. 'I lost my daughter. She died of typhoid. I was distraught. I still grieve. Yes, I do know what it is like to want to take one's own life.'

'The duke, your husband?' said Jane. 'He is not with you?'

'He is gone to Italy to attend a funeral. We . . . we have become estranged over the death and it is all my fault. When my Emily died, I felt all love, all caring, all affection draining out of me. Dear me, Jane, and I am supposed to be entertaining you. I do not know what came over me.'

But Jane's sudden sharp concern for her hostess had made her temporarily forget her own troubles. 'If the idea of attending events at the Season is too much for you, Harriet,' she said, 'we could still contrive to have a pleasant but quiet time and we could talk often about your poor Emily. One must have someone to talk to.' She sighed. 'I never did, you see, and that is perhaps what magnified all my problems out of proportion.'

Harriet smiled. 'Rise. Or you will get a cramp kneeling at my feet. No, a few balls and parties will entertain me. We shall go on a call to a certain Mrs Haggard, a friend of my husband, who is *bon ton.* She has a daughter, Frances, to puff off, and so she will know all the eligibles. How are your water-colours? One must have a portfolio to show gentlemen callers.'

'I believe my painting is adequate. Painting, books and music were my only escape.'

'Pianoforte?'

'Again, quite good, I think.'

'And your singing voice?'

'Not good at all, I am afraid.'

'But you know how to receive and entertain gentlemen?'

'I have had experience of entertaining my father's friends, yes.'

'I understand from my friends that you are pretending to be staying with some old nurse and that you have forwarded money to her and letters for your father.'

'Yes, they are most kind. I must find some way to

repay them for their generosity. My new gowns were so expensive, they made me blink.'

'But you must have been aware of the high cost of dressmaking?'

Jane shook her head. 'A dressmaker came from the nearby town at home to fit me. The gowns were made and the bills sent to my father.'

'Never mind,' said Harriet. 'There is always some way to repay the poor relations!'

'The hotel owners? And yet they appear to be wealthy.'

'They lived through a series of adventures, I can assure you. Since my marriage I have been kept informed of everything that has happened by Miss Tonks and Lady Fortescue. Now you must change and look your best.'

Jane went thoughtfully off to her room. She found a lady's-maid waiting for her who introduced herself as Mary. 'You are Her Grace's lady's-maid?' said Jane. 'Perhaps you should attend to your mistress first.'

Mary curtsied. 'I am your lady's-maid, Miss North. I was elevated in station today from housemaid. If it please you, miss, I am perhaps not as practised as most lady's-maids, but I am willing to learn.'

Jane submitted to her ministrations, her brain in a turmoil. So much had happened to her emotions. She remembered her fury at Sir Philip and blushed. All he had spoken was the truth. How selfish she had been! And now here was Harriet, despite her great grief giving up time and money to bring out an impostor.

But it was not Sir Philip's criticisms which had brought Jane to life, but her deep concern for her hostess. Wrapped all her young life in her own misery, Jane had never been able to look out from her confined world and see any misery in others.

She resolved to do her very best to please this Mrs Haggard. She could only hope the lady would like her.

But from the moment she entered Mrs Haggard's saloon and made her curtsy, her heart sank. Mrs Haggard's cold, rather bulbous eyes raked her up and down. Then she delivered herself of a contemptuous sniff before turning away to introduce her daughter, Frances. Frances was a small girl with a great quantity of brown frizzy hair, a snub-nose, and a large mouth. There were four other matrons in the room. Harriet drew Jane forward and introduced her. Hard eyes stared at Jane's beautiful face. One of the matrons only gave her two fingers to shake.

'Come and look at my sketches,' said Frances.

Jane obediently followed her to the end of the long, dim room, leaving Harriet, the matrons and Mrs Haggard in a little island formed of chairs and a table next to the fireplace.

A desire to do her best for Harriet prompted Jane to say in a low voice, 'Did I do something wrong, Miss Haggard? I appear to be the subject of intense disapproval.'

'Of course you are,' said Frances. 'You do not have to look at these boring old drawings. I simply want to talk. It is because you are beautiful and that means

47

you are competition. The others there also have daughters to bring out. Any moment now, Mama will bring out the list of eligibles and the others will take notes and know to whom to send a card to a ball or rout. But you look quite clever as well. Are you?'

And Jane, reflecting on what she now saw as her gross lack of gratitude in that she had tried to commit suicide and then, having been saved from death, had not put herself out very much in any way to thank her benefactors, said, 'I think I am rather stupid.'

'Well, that shows you are clever. Only very clever people can afford to say they are stupid. I need your help.'

'In what way, Miss Haggard?'

'Call me Frances, for we are going to be such friends.'

'We are?' Jane was half amused, half taken aback.

'Oh, yes. We must combine forces. I have worked it out very carefully. The minute I saw you, I thought: If I make a friend of her and keep close to her at balls and parties, she will attract the gentlemen, and as she cannot dance with them all, they will be obliged, through politeness, don't you see, to turn to me and ask me.'

'Your remarks are very flattering, Frances, but I do not consider myself beautiful.'

'Oh, but you are. You could do with a little animation. I know it is fashionable to be poker-faced, but I notice that young ladies with animation are considered attractive. I note these things, don't you know, and write them all down. Then I study my notes as a student studies his professor's teachings.'

'Do the other ladies go to such efforts?' asked Jane.

'What are you talking about, Frances?' called Mrs Haggard.

Frances jerked open a portfolio. 'Miss North is advising me on how to better my technique with putting a wash on paper, Mama.'

'Very well.' Mrs Haggard turned back to her guests.

'No, I do not think so,' said Frances, turning back to Jane. 'I hope not, for then I will have the *edge*, don't you see? I have already selected my beau. I saw him driving in the Park and asked Mama who he was. She said he was a Mr Jamie Ferguson and not at all suitable.'

'In what way?'

'He is reported to be in love with a Scottish lady, Lady Dunwilde, and he is best friend of the rackety Comte de Mornay, who goes about breaking hearts and never getting married. I made a sketch of him. See, I have hidden it between the one of this boring cottage and this dreary tree.'

The rather foxy features of a gentleman looked up at Jane.

'You are awfully good,' said Jane.

'Yes, I am, aren't I? But Mama does not know that. Ladies should not be clever at anything to do with art. They are expected to confine themselves to pretty sketches. So this, then, is Mr Ferguson. So you must flirt with him and attract him to your side and then spurn him quite dreadfully so that he will turn to me for consolation. He is usually with the French comte. This is he.'

She slid out another sketch. Jane looked down at the man she had seen in the tea-gardens in Chelsea. 'You do not approve of him?' she asked Frances, for the comte's handsome face had a sinister cast.

'No, I do not. How can Mr Ferguson consider marriage with such a friend always near him?' She lowered her voice even more and leaned forward so that her frizzy hair tickled Jane's cheek. 'You will help me, will you not?'

Jane laughed and Harriet, at the other end of the room, turned and smiled. A small triumph to report to her friends at the Poor Relation.

'I think you are a romantic. You have written a play in which I shall attract this Mr Ferguson, make him fall in love with me, then jilt him so that he turns to you. I do have it correct?'

'Oh, yes, and a very sensible idea it is, too.'

'I fear you overestimate my looks. Perhaps we should just begin to be friends and then see what happens when the Season begins.'

Frances opened her brown eyes to their widest. 'Fiddle! We must seize the moment, Jane. We must hunt down Mr Ferguson *before* the Season begins. Mama is even beginning to mark down a Mr Thompson as a suitable beau, and he is only nineteen and has pimples.'

'And how can two young ladies hunt down a gentleman? We cannot go to a coffee house or yet to his club.'

'I've found out where he lives. He has lodgings in Curzon Street. We could drive out, so respectably,

50

don't you see, and alight to look at the shops. If we see him, I will faint, and you will call to him for assistance.'

'Frances, that is very bold. I should feel very embarrassed.'

'Would you? But will you drive out with me tomorrow at three just the same?'

'Yes, I would like that. Unless Her Grace has other plans for me, of course.'

'That was useful,' said Harriet as they drove home. 'You will be invited by Mrs Haggard to her daughter's come-out, and two of the other ladies will send cards to various functions.'

'I do not think Mrs Haggard likes me.'

'Of course not,' said Harriet. 'Nor did the others, not with daughters to bring out. How could they? You will put the other young misses in the shade. I told them roundly that to exclude a beauty who could be guaranteed to draw the gentlemen was sheer folly, and so they finally agreed with me.'

'How ruthless all this is,' said Jane wistfully. 'Not at all like books.'

'But you would not like life to be like books, or rather, romances. Were it so, you would spend your time being frightened by headless spectres and carried off to ruined Italian castles by foreign counts. You appear to have formed a friendship with Frances Haggard.'

'I like her.' Jane debated whether to tell Harriet about Frances's mad ideas of pursuit, but then said instead, 'Frances wishes me to go out with her tomorrow at three.'

'I have no plans for you. Do you wish the carriage?'

'No, I thank you; as we left, Frances said she would call on me.'

'Then you may send one of the footmen, when we get home, with a note to tell her that you may go. I myself will call on my friends at the Poor Relation. They are so tranquil now. No plots or plans or upsets. Such a relief!'

At the hotel Mr Davy, whose job apart from debt-collecting was to oversee the running of the coffee room, was rarely at his post these days. An excellent manager called Jobson, hired by Sir Philip, saw to everything. He had therefore decided to spend a pleasant afternoon taking Miss Tonks out on a drive. And so it was Sir Philip who was told the news that Jobson had requested the day off to go to his aunt's funeral.

'Send for Davy,' he told Jack, the footman, who had brought him the news.

'Mr Davy, sir, has gone on a drive with Miss Tonks.'

'Mountebank,' snarled Sir Philip. 'Oh, well, I may as well see to it myself.'

He went down to the coffee room in a bad temper. Now if there was one thing Sir Philip loathed, it was a Bond Street lounger, that breed of man who drawled at the top of his voice, insulted the waiters, stared at the ladies and complained about everything. Sir

52

Philip was not only angry, he was tired. He had been up half the night drinking at Limmer's, and his head throbbed and his old eyes burned.

He went into the coffee room. John, one of the waiters, took him aside. 'We have a gentleman, sir, who is ogling the ladies and behaving in an offensive manner. He is with, I believe, a foreign gentleman.'

'Walk outside with me a little,' said Sir Philip. 'I will deal with them presently.'

When they were outside in the hall under the great chandelier, which Sir Philip had blackmailed his nephew into giving him, he said testily, 'Has Davy shown his nose in the coffee room today at all?'

'No, Sir Philip,' said John. 'But Mr Jobson is usually always at his post. Today is the first time he has been absent.'

'That's no excuse,' said Sir Philip. 'It's Mr Davy's *duty* to see that all is well before he goes jauntering off around the Town like the gentleman he isn't. I suppose I had better go and get rid of the rats myself.'

'I must go down to the kitchens and bring up some more cakes,' said the waiter, and made his escape.

But in the brief time during which Sir Philip had been talking to the waiter, neither of them had noticed the gentlemen who had been creating the fuss in the coffee room leaving, and that Mr Jamie Ferguson and his friend, the Comte de Mornay, had taken their place.

'So this is the famous Poor Relation,' said the comte, looking around. 'It is kind of you to entertain me, Jamie. I do not know why I have not visited here before. They call it the marriage market and joke that any gentleman daring to enter its portals will shortly find himself engaged to be married to one of the servants.'

'There are no dazzlers here,' said Jamie, looking around. 'Only matrons. And there is a dreadful-looking old gentleman in an impossible wig and with his false teeth bared approaching us.'

Sir Philip stopped at their table.

'I must ask you to leave,' he said.

The comte leaned back in his chair and stared at Sir Philip.

'Why?'

'The ladies present find your manner offensive as do I.'

'Look here, madman,' said the comte in a gentle voice, 'get you back to Bedlam before I get someone responsible in this hotel to throw you out.'

'I,' said Sir Philip wrathfully, 'am Sir Philip Sommerville, owner of this hotel. Get out.'

The comte smiled lazily. 'Shan't.'

'Shall!' shouted Sir Philip. 'I am weary of clods like you, sir. We do not allow boorish manners here.'

'But you do. You do,' said the comte gleefully, 'because you've got plenty of them yourself.'

Beside himself with rage, Sir Philip spat at the table and his false teeth flew out and lay between the bemused comte and Jamie, winking in the light.

Sir Philip snatched them up and stuffed them in his mouth and ran out. 'Help! Help!' he shouted in the hall. The servants came running. John, the waiter, appeared up from the kitchens carrying a tray laden with cakes.

Lady Fortescue and the colonel emerged from the office. 'Sir Philip, what is the matter?'

He began an incoherent rant in which the perfidy of Mr Davy and the sheer evil of the pair in the coffee room were mixed up, ending with a shriek of 'Call the watch! Call the militia!'

But John, who had placed his tray of cakes on a side-table just inside the door of the coffee room, took a quick glance around and came back crying, 'They have gone!'

Sir Philip strode to the door of the coffee room and glared inside. 'They're still there!'

'Not *them*, sir. An uncouth lout of a gentleman and his German companion.'

Sir Philip clutched his wig and groaned.

'You had best go away,' said Lady Fortescue, 'and leave this to myself and the colonel. You have obviously made a stupid mistake. Just go away. Lie down. You look terrible.'

'Now what?' asked the comte, as he saw the stately figure of Lady Fortescue approaching on the arm of Colonel Sandhurst. 'It looks as if the old boy has summoned an equally geriatric couple to abuse us.'

Lady Fortescue curtsied and the colonel bowed. 'We apologize on behalf of our partner, Sir Philip Sommerville,' said Lady Fortescue. 'I am Lady Fortescue. This is Colonel Sandhurst.'

Both Jamie and the comte rose to their feet and bowed.

'Pray be seated, gentlemen,' said Lady Fortescue. The colonel drew out a chair for her and she sat down opposite them. The colonel joined her.

The comte introduced himself and Jamie, which involved everyone standing up again, the gentlemen bowing and Lady Fortescue curtsying.

'Now, Monsieur le Comte,' began Lady Fortescue, 'you and Mr Ferguson here have been victims of a sad misunderstanding. We are often plagued with un-couth Bond Street loungers. Sir Philip was told there was such a one in the coffee room, accompanied by a foreign gentleman. By the time Sir Philip entered to evict the nuisances, they had gone and you had arrived. We can only offer you our deepest apologies and assure you that such a mistake will not happen again.'

'Apology accepted,' said the comte. 'May I say, Lady Fortescue, that perhaps in future you should be sent to deal with any trouble, for the dignity of your presence and the stateliness of your mien would trounce even the most hardened lout.'

Lady Fortescue bowed and for a moment the ghost of the beautiful flirtatious girl she had once been showed behind the mask of paint and wrinkles on her face. Jamie noticed the way the colonel caught that look and the way he scowled.

Lady Fortescue turned and nodded to the waiter, who came hurrying up. 'Coffee and cakes for these gentlemen, John,' she said majestically. 'Do not present them with the bill. Their entertainment is our pleasure.'

John hurried off and Lady Fortescue smiled at the comte. 'Furthermore, you may have heard our cuisine is excellent. You may dine in our hotel any evening you want, as our guests, of course.'

'Too kind,' said Jamie. 'It is the talk of London, Lady Fortescue, of how you and your companions have made a success of business.'

'We have been fortunate,' said the colonel. He gave a little sigh. 'After this Season, we can sell and return to our rightful places in society.' He took Lady Fortescue's hand in his own. 'Lady Fortescue and I plan to settle down.'

'Congratulations, sir.' The comte was touched at this sight of elderly devotion, but it appeared that Lady Fortescue was not amused. She drew her hand away and said sharply, 'We have not yet made up our minds what we plan to do.'

The colonel looked like a sad old dog. The comte said quickly, 'You are very kind, and Mr Ferguson and I would be delighted to be your guests one evening.'

Lady Fortescue parted her thin rouged lips in a smile. 'Here is your coffee. We shall leave you. Again, our apologies.'

The comte and Jamie rose again and bowed. 'Think no more of it, dear lady,' said Jamie. 'All is forgiven.'

But Sir Philip Sommerville, watching sourly from the door of the coffee room, had no intention of ever forgiving this comte for his insolence.

The following day Frances and Jane drove out, accompanied by a footman. The day was fine and

Jane was enjoying Frances's company as they were set down at various shops in Pall Mall and then Oxford Street to examine the wares. Jane was just beginning to hope that Frances had given up any mad ideas of running this Mr Ferguson to earth when to her dismay she found their carriage turning into Curzon Street.

'There is a very good perfumer's here,' said Frances lightly. 'I have a mind to buy a bottle of scent.' She called to the coachman to set them down.

As they were about to enter the shop, everything seemed to happen at once. Frances looked along the street and spied Jamie and the comte walking along arm in arm. Sir Philip at that moment emerged from the perfumer's and stood watching.

'Here he comes,' he heard Frances whisper. Sir Philip immediately recognized Jane. He saw her companion put her hand to her brow and begin to sway. Sir Philip recognized the well-known signs of a lady about to pretend to faint so that the gentleman she had her eye on would run and catch her in his arms.

He would have let the comedy proceed had he not recognized the comte and Jamie.

He quickly stepped forward, just before both gentlemen came up to the ladies. Frances was swaying artistically. With a look of unholy glee on his face, Sir Philip darted forward and caught her in his arms.

'Sir Philip!' cried Jane, blushing with embarrassment.

'Can we be of assistance?' asked the comte.

Frances opened her eyes and looked up into the

tortoise-like features of Sir Philip Sommerville, gasped and tried to struggle free, but Sir Philip had her in a surprisingly strong grip.

'There is nothing you can do, gentlemen,' said Sir Philip. 'This poor young lady has the vapours and should be taken home immediately. Hey, sirrah!' – to the footman. 'Help me get your mistress to her carriage.'

Fuming inwardly, Frances submitted to being bundled into the carriage. Sir Philip leered up at her. 'You should stay at home if you're poorly. If I had not been on the scene, you might have found yourself in the arms of some mountebank or counter-jumper.'

'Dreadful old man,' said the comte. 'Come along, Jamie.'

Both men strolled off. Jane sharply ordered the coachman to drive on. Sir Philip swept off his hat and gave them a mocking bow.

'Who,' demanded Frances, fanning herself vigorously, 'was that old toad? He appeared to know you.'

'He is one of the owners of the Poor Relation and a friend of the Duchess of Rowcester.'

'Why did he have to be there at that moment?' demanded Frances.

'Well, Frances, my dear, perhaps it was just as well. I remember a lady at an assembly ball at home saying that London gentlemen were well used to ladies turning their ankles outside their houses or fainting in order to get attention.'

'Why didn't you tell me!'

'I just remembered,' said Jane ruefully. 'Frances, it

would be better to wait until the Season, when you will have a chance of meeting him properly.'

'By that time he will have eyes only for that Scotch lady he is reported to be so enamoured of. I am in need of a comforting ice at Gunter's. Coachman. Berkeley Square, if you please.'

'They're going into Gunter's,' remarked Jamie. 'Why did you suddenly decide to follow them?'

'I want to meet that beauty,' said the comte.

Because of the press of traffic, they had been able to stroll after the carriage.

'Take my advice,' said Jamie earnestly, 'and wait for the Season. Informal meetings do not work. Besides, that minx with your beauty staged that faint. Perhaps Sir Philip has charms for the young that we do not possess.'

'Perhaps the target was us,' pointed out the comte.

'Could hardly be us. They don't know us.'

'Still, I am suddenly determined to go to Gunter's,' said the comte. 'En avant!'

FOUR

It is under the trees, it is out of the sun,
In the corner where GUNTER *retails a plum bun.*
Her footman goes once, and her footman goes twice,
Ay, and each time returning he brings her an ice.

ANONYMOUS

Gunter's was set up in 1757 by the Italian pastry-cook Dominicus Negri, who later took Gunter into partnership 'making and selling all sorts of English, French and Italian wet and dry sweetmeats, Cedrati and Bergamet Chips, and Naples Divolini, at the sign of the Pot and Pineapple in Berkeley Square.' The shop was at number seven on the east side of the square, four doors away from Horace Walpole's house. Gunter's ices were famous, made from a secret recipe. In hot summer weather, it was the custom for ladies to recline in their carriages on the *opposite* side of Berkeley Square from Gunter's while waiters scurried back and forth across the square with trays of ices. It was also the only place in London before the advent of the Poor Relation's coffee room where a gentleman could be seen alone with a lady in the afternoon.

'So what do we do now?' asked Jamie. 'We cannot very well stroll in after them and sit at the same table.'

'It is she,' said the comte dreamily. 'The lady I saw in the Chelsea gardens.'

'Beautiful, I grant you, but somewhat masklike,' said Jamie. 'Very well. But let's hope Sir Philip does not appear again.'

Frances was just urging Jane to try a white-currant ice when she saw Jane staring beyond her and turned round, blushed and turned back.

'Do not be too forward, Frances,' counselled Jane, who was trying to save herself from embarrassment. The waiter arrived and they gave an order for two white-currant ices.

Then, to Jane's dismay, she found the comte at her side, making an excellent bow. 'Forgive me,' he said, 'but I feel we have met. I am the Comte de Mornay and this is my friend, Mr James Ferguson.'

'I am afraid that we have not met or ever been introduced,' said Jane.

'But I have heard of *you*, Mr Ferguson,' said Frances, sparkling up at him.

Jamie laughed. 'Nothing bad, I trust. Whom do I have the pleasure of meeting?'

'I am Miss Frances Haggard.' Frances held out her hand, which Jamie gallantly kissed. 'And this is my friend, Miss Jane North.'

Both gentlemen bowed. 'May we join you?' asked the comte. 'We are both much concerned about your health, Miss Haggard. We saw you faint in Curzon Street.'

'I am really quite delicate,' said Frances, looking the picture of robust health. 'But by all means, join us.'

Jane flashed her a worried look. Perhaps the ways of ladies in London were more free and easy than those of the provinces, but she felt that Frances was being too bold.

The gentlemen sat down. The waiter returned with the ices. The comte and Jamie ordered sorbets.

'I saw you in the Chelsea tea-gardens with Sir Philip Sommerville,' began the comte, turning to Jane. 'Is he some relative?'

'No, Monsieur le Comte,' said Jane. 'He and the owners of the Poor Relation Hotel are friends of my hostess, the Duchess of Rowcester. I am new to London and he was entertaining me.'

She addressed the table as she spoke, feeling uncomfortable, not wanting to meet his blue gaze.

'Let me tell you about Sir Philip,' said Jamie gaily. He began to tell the story about their experience in the hotel coffee room while Frances laughed – immoderately, Jane thought, picking at her ice and fretting about what on earth to do.

The comte studied her beautiful face and wondered why there was such an air of sadness about her. He had a desire to make her smile. He told several of his best anecdotes and Frances and Jamie laughed appreciatively, but still that beautiful face showed not the slightest trace of animation.

Jane found the comte terrifying. His mocking, glinting eyes that slanted mischievously at her, the splendour of his clothes and jewels, the light, intriguing scent he wore – it all made her feel confused and threatened. She had never dreamt of such a man.

The man of her dreams was solid and reliable, more like a father ought to be than a lover.

Harriet, passing in the square outside, recognized the Haggards's footman standing by the carriage and called on her coachman to stop. She learned that 'the ladies' were inside Gunter's. Followed by her maid, she entered the pastry-cook's and stopped short at the sight of Frances and Jane being entertained by two gentlemen.

Jane cast a mute appeal for help at Harriet and Harriet sailed forward. The gentlemen rose to their feet and then there was a great deal of bowing and scraping and curtsying before Harriet said, 'I was not aware that either Miss Haggard or Miss North was acquainted with either of you.'

'We have a mutual friend in Sir Philip Sommerville,' said Jamie.

'Indeed!' Harriet looked him up and down. 'And just exactly on what occasion did Sir Philip introduce you?'

Jamie looked awkward. 'We were not *exactly* introduced but . . .'

'I thought so,' said Harriet. 'Frances, Jane, come along. Gentlemen, good day.'

They both remained standing while Harriet ushered the girls out of the pastry-cook's. Frances hesitated, half turned and let her handkerchief drop to the ground, and then she hurried out after Harriet and Jane.

'Don't tell Mama,' cried Frances breathlessly. 'They were all that is correct, don't you know.'

'No, I don't know,' said Harriet crossly. She stopped by the Haggard carriage. 'Jane, you are coming home with me. But first, how did this come about? You will ruin your chances at the Season if it gets about that you are in the way of being entertained by the Comte de Mornay. I have heard of that gentleman, and he is a *rake*.'

'Frances felt faint in Curzon Street,' said Jane. 'Sir Philip was there to catch her just as the two gentlemen were passing. They must have seen us go to Gunter's and called to ask how Frances was.'

'Nonetheless, you must never do such a thing again.'

'Please don't tell Mama,' urged Frances again.

Harriet looked at the pleading face under that odd mop of frizzy hair and smiled. 'Not this time. Do not do such a thing again.'

'But Duchess, the comte may have the reputation of a rake, but surely there is nothing against his friend, Mr Ferguson.'

'Not that I know,' said Harriet. 'But if that gentleman wishes to make your acquaintance, then he must do it the usual way through formal channels.'

'So do I return this handkerchief?' asked Jamie with a grin.

'I think the minx is interested in you,' replied the comte. 'I shall come with you. In that way, I may get a chance to meet the beautiful Miss North again.'

'How do I find out where she lives?'

'Ask Josh, the porter, at the club. He knows the

direction of everyone. I would not tell her no-doubt-respectable mama that we sat down with her and I doubt if she will say anything, although that beautiful and stately duchess might. Simply say she dropped it as she was leaving.'

'And when should I call?'

'Leave a space of two days.'

'I hope the duchess isn't there.'

'Why? She is as beautiful as my Miss North.'

'I feel she does not approve of us one bit, my friend.'

But when they called after two days, it was to learn that Miss Frances and her mother, Mrs Haggard, were out on calls.

'That's that,' said Jamie.

'We could drive by the Duchess of Rowcester's,' pointed out the duke, 'and see if the Haggard carriage is there.'

'And what does the Haggard carriage look like? Will it have a crest?'

The comte smiled lazily. 'I neither know nor care. My tiger can quiz the coachmen outside the duchess's residence.'

The house in Park Lane was still protected from what had all too recently been Tyburn Way, where the condemned were taken to the gallows, followed by the mob, and so the entrance to the house was in Park Street. Both men waited while the comte's diminutive tiger questioned the coachmen of several carriages waiting outside. He came back to say that various ladies were calling on the duchess, among them Mrs Haggard and her daughter.

'So,' said the comte, 'in we go.'

Jamie hesitated. 'We do not really have an excuse.'

'Of course we do, mon ami. That handkerchief which Miss Frances so carefully let fall. Courage. I shall look on Miss North again.'

Harriet studied their visiting cards in dismay. She was about to tell the butler that she was 'not at home,' but a Mrs Bletchley, a friend of Mrs Haggard, said eagerly, 'You look dismayed. Who has called?'

'Monsieur le Comte de Mornay and his friend Mr Ferguson,' said Harriet.

'Oh, do have them up,' cried Mrs Bletchley. 'The comte is such a rattle.'

'You are surely not interested in a rattle for your Sarah,' said Harriet.

'Fiddle. This French comte is ridiculously wealthy and must settle down sometime. I beg you, dear Duchess, show them up.'

'Very well,' said Harriet but she was aware of Frances's shining eyes and the rigidity of Jane's face. Sarah Bletchley had run to the mirror to pat her curls. She was a dumpy little girl, and yet, to Frances's suddenly jealous eyes, she appeared to have hitherto unnoticed charms.

The ladies all sat in a half-circle round the fire. The two gentlemen entered. There were classes in Bond Street to instruct gentlemen of the *ton* in the correct way to 'break the circle,' as it was called. It was considered a superior grace to know how to enter a

67

drawing room, to penetrate the circle, to make a slight inclination as you walked around it, to make your way to your hostess unruffled, with your hat under your arm, with your stick, your gloves, and, possibly, since it was all the rage, an enormous muff. Gentlemen also took lessons in how to move. Gentlemen did not just walk, they glided. Fashion was all. There was even a whole chapter in a book on etiquette entitled, 'How to take off your hat and replace it.' The comte acquitted himself with elegance; Jamie, passably.

'To what do we owe the pleasure of this visit?' asked Harriet when all the introductions had been made and all the bowing and curtsying were over.

Jamie produced the handkerchief and presented it to Frances. 'You dropped this in Gunter's the other day.'

Frances flashed a guilty little look at her mother before she smiled and took it. 'How very kind of you, sir.'

But Mrs Haggard had been doing some quick arithmetic in her head. Mr Ferguson was not amazingly rich like this French comte, but tolerably well off. 'Show Mr Ferguson your portfolio, Frances,' she said.

Frances led James off to the end of the large saloon. With the grace of a dancing master, the comte took a chair, placed it next to Jane and sat down. Harriet watched this anxiously, but Mrs Haggard, on the comte's other side, said, 'Will you be honouring us with your presence this Season, my dear Comte?'

'Yes, I think I shall,' said the comte while he wondered what was wrong with this Miss Jane North. What was causing that aura of sadness?

Mrs Bletchley laughed. 'You will break hearts as usual and remain just as unwed at the end of this one as you have remained unwed at the end of all the others.'

'How ancient you do make me feel,' said the comte. 'But I may surprise you, madam. It is time I settled down.'

'You amaze us,' giggled Sarah. She hid her face behind her fan, then peeped over it at him. 'You sound as if you have met a lady of your choice.'

'I rather think I have.'

'Tell us,' urged Mrs Bletchley, thinking that Sarah had never looked so well.

'Ah, that is my secret. I fear the lady is not even aware of me.'

For a brief moment his eyes slid to Jane, who was sitting with her hands folded in her lap. Oh, no, thought Harriet. Very unsuitable. Jane needs a steady, reliable man, the kind of man I could take aside and explain her predicament to. Not this frivolous rake. He might even think the irregularity of her situation puts her in the mistress class!

Frances was showing her water-colours to Jamie, who was examining them with his quizzing-glass. Frances amused him. She was such a friendly little thing. 'Do you plan to find a bride at the Season, Mr Ferguson?' asked Frances.

'Alas. I fear I cannot. My heart is not yet mended and the lady who broke it will be at the Season ... with her husband.'

'Ah, Lady Dunwilde,' said Frances.

There is nothing more irritating than finding out that the secret of your heart is public property. Jamie's face darkened. He tucked away the quizzing-glass. 'I have stayed long enough,' he said abruptly.

'I am sorry,' said Frances impulsively. 'I should not have mentioned her name. But I could be of use to you, sir.'

He had begun to turn away from her, but at this he turned back and said in a voice in which irritation and amusement were equally mixed. 'How, my child?'

'I am not a child,' said Frances. 'I merely meant that I could make a confidante of this lady and find out what she thinks of you, don't you know, and if I found out that she cared for you just a little bit, you might feel better about things.'

'You would do that for me?'

'Oh, yes,' said Frances. 'You had best ask Mama if you can take me driving tomorrow and we will discuss strategy.'

He laughed. 'You are a minx and I should not encourage you. But yes, I would dearly like to know what the lady thinks of me.'

'Is she very old?'

'Old? Of course not. She is the same age as myself.'

'The prime of life for you, sir. You are in your early thirties, are you not? But middle-aged for a lady.'

'You are too harsh. I see my friend is ready to leave.'

He bowed before Frances, thinking again what a funny-looking little girl she was.

Meanwhile the comte had asked permission to take Jane driving, but Harriet had said firmly that as Jane's wardrobe was not complete, she had to be at home for fittings. The comte looked at Jane's still face for any sign that she might be either relieved or saddened by this decision but came to the conclusion that the mysterious Miss Jane North did not care one way or the other.

'How did you fare?' asked Jamie when the comte drove off.

'Very badly, my friend. I asked her to go driving with me, or rather, I asked the duchess, who refused permission, and the sad Miss North sat with her head bowed, caring neither one way nor t'other.'

'I am taking her little friend, Miss Haggard, on a drive tomorrow, so I will find out more about Miss North for you.'

'Miss Haggard is an engaging child,' said the comte. 'A much healthier pursuit than your mercenary Scotchwoman.'

'She is *not* mercenary.'

'My apologies. It was the title.'

'It was her parents, I am convinced of that. She had no choice in the matter. Miss Haggard has offered her help. She is to become a confidante of my Fiona during the Season and find out if she cares for me a little.'

'This being Miss Haggard's idea?'

'Yes, she is a good-hearted girl.'

And a devious one, thought the comte. But I am not going to put a spoke in her wheel.

Aloud he said, 'Do not quiz her about Miss North. I have lost interest.'

71

'So soon?'

'There is nothing there to be interested *in*. No sparkle, no wit, no humour.' The comte sounded almost angry.

'And no interest in you?' Jamie grinned. 'Your pride has taken a dent. Hitherto you have only been interested in eager matrons who wish to be unfaithful to their boring husbands. Still, it is not like you to give up so easily.'

'Then you do not know me very well. Who wants to make love to a statue?'

Although some of the following day was taken up with fittings, Jane found there were more calls to make. Harriet was taking her job of bringing Jane out seriously. 'I hope you did not mind me refusing the comte permission to take you driving. He is too old and frivolous for you. You need someone younger and of a serious turn of mind.'

'Yes, I am a trifle dreary, I confess,' said Jane. 'I feel the threatening shadow of my father always looming up behind me. I am so grateful to you, Harriet, for all your kindness, and yet I feel such expense and care are wasted on me. What serious and sober man is going to look on me favourably when he finds that I have been masquerading under another name? What if one of my neighbours who saw me at assemblies at home should turn up at the Season and recognize me?'

'Do you know, I don't think anyone would. No one surely is going to think that the beautiful Miss Jane

North, sponsored by the Duchess of Rowcester, is Lady Jane Fremney. They will merely think there is a striking likeness. I have a mind to go out this evening to the Poor Relation and visit my friends. They gather in their own sitting room after dinner and chat. It will remind me of the old days. Would you care to join me? It will not harm your reputation, for who will notice us? It is a very fashionable hotel and they will think we are going to pay court to the prince.'

Jane agreed that, yes, she would like to go, simply because she knew it would please Harriet.

Jamie and the comte made their way to the Poor Relation that evening, the comte saying he had every intention of taking up Lady Fortescue's invitation to a free meal. He also knew it would irritate Sir Philip. Jamie was in good form, having enjoyed his drive with Frances more than he had expected to. She was so easy to talk to, and because they were now conspirators in a way, he did not have to worry about making polite conversation. He had not told Frances anything about the comte's previous interest in Jane, for the comte had declared himself to have lost that interest.

Sir Philip was every bit as annoyed with their appearance as the comte had gleefully anticipated. But the food was excellent and it was amusing to see how Sir Philip, Lady Fortescue and Colonel Sandhurst appeared to serve the prince and his entourage while it was the waiters, in fact, who did all the work. The prince's mistress kept casting roguish looks in the comte's direction. Before, the comte would have enjoyed the game of flirting back, but for some reason he now thought it would be a rather childish thing to do. To his annoyance, he found his thoughts constantly straying to Jane North. He should not have given up that game so easily, not before he had managed to make her laugh.

He was facing the open door of the dining room and had just finished the pudding when he saw the Duchess of Rowcester and Miss Jane North arriving. They went past his vision in the direction of the stairs.

He saw that Lady Fortescue had noticed the arrivals. She said to the colonel, 'Harriet is here with Jane.' And then the colonel, Sir Philip, and Lady Fortescue left, leaving the waiters to collect the pudding plates and serve the nuts, fruit, wine, and butter at the end of the meal, some people preferring to eat butter with a spoon to finish off their dinner.

'How very curious,' said the comte. 'Miss Jane North and the duchess have just made their entrance and presumably gone upstairs. Lady Fortescue says to that colonel, "Harriet is here with Jane," and then the three owners take their leave. Ah, of course, the Duchess of Rowcester was once Harriet James, fallen on hard times, and rumour has it did the cooking in the kitchens here. So no doubt she has come to talk over old times. Where? They must have a private room somewhere, some parlour to which they retire.'

'You are never thinking of going after them!' exclaimed Jamie. 'Not the done thing. Not convenable, mon brave.'

'Your French accent is appalling. Why not? It is our

duty to thank the owners for this free meal and assure them all is forgiven. All very conventional.'

Jane, suddenly shy at finding herself back amongst the very people who had saved her life, sat next to Miss Tonks on the sofa. Sir Philip had just summoned Despard the cook, under the orders of Lady Fortescue. The prince, in raptures as usual over the excellence of Despard's cooking, had given ten guineas to Sir Philip to give to the chef. Sir Philip was all for pocketing it, grumbling that a Despard with too much money might be a Despard who would retire, but Lady Fortescue had insisted that the chef be paid.

Despard took the gold, his twisted face lighting in a smile. He would add it to the stack of gold which he had obtained as a bribe from a certain Lady Stanton who had wished him to flee the country and so leave the Poor Relation without their famous chef. Despard had betrayed her to Sir Philip and the rest and had kept the money. He turned and bowed to Harriet and then left.

'So,' said Mr Davy, 'what is the gossip of the day?'

'Our prince is still happy with us and everything goes smoothly,' said Lady Fortescue. 'No upsets or alarms. Does everything go well with you, Harriet?'

'I am assured of several useful invitations for Jane,' said Harriet. 'We had a visit yesterday from the Comte de Mornay and his friend, Mr Ferguson. I believe you experienced a certain difficulty with them here.'

'A misunderstanding,' said Lady Fortescue smoothly

as Sir Philip scowled. 'He is, I believe, rich and unmarried. Have you hopes there?'

'No, he is a rattle. Not at all suitable for Jane.'

'Perhaps Miss Jane needs a rattle,' said Mr Davy sympathetically. 'Opposites attract.'

'Like yourself and Miss Sheep Face there?' demanded Sir Philip waspishly.

'Your jealousy of the friendship between Mr Davy and Miss Tonks is becoming tiresome,' snapped Lady Fortescue, seeing poor Miss Tonks's nose turn red with embarrassment.

'I? Jealous . . . ?' Sir Philip was beginning wrathfully when the door opened and the comte and Jamie stood revealed on the threshold.

'My dear sirs,' protested the colonel, walking forward, 'you have strayed into our private quarters.'

'You must forgive us,' said the Comte ruefully. 'We have enjoyed your hospitality and are come to thank you.'

'You're welcome. Good night,' said Sir Philip, who had followed the colonel. He slammed the door in their faces.

'You impossible little toad,' raged Lady Fortescue. 'Now we shall have to invite them in before that comte decides to call you out for such an insult.' She opened the door. 'My apologies, gentlemen. Such a draught of wind. Pray do join us in a dish of tea.'

To Sir Philip's fury, both came in. Mr Davy had crossed to the piano. Miss Tonks followed him saying, 'If you intend to play, then I will turn the music for

76

you.' That left the place on the small sofa next to Jane empty, and so, with an expert flick of his long coat-tails, the comte sat down next to her. To Sir Philip's further fury, the comte handed his hat, cane and gloves to the poor relations' servant, John, a signal that he had every intention of staying longer than the usual ten minutes a formal call was supposed to take.

Lady Fortescue poured tea for the visitors and then turned to Mr Davy. 'Are you going to entertain us, Mr Davy?'

He smiled. 'Miss Tonks and I went to the Wells the other night to see Grimaldi. I was going to sing you one of his comic songs, but then I did not expect us to have such distinguished visitors.'

'Pray do not let us stop you,' said Jamie. 'Grimaldi is the greatest clown ever.'

'Alas, I will have to sing unaccompanied,' said Mr Davy.

'I'll accompany you,' said Sir Philip, startling everyone with his sudden change from bad temper to amiability. He gleefully thought that Davy had gone mad, and a rendition of a vulgar comic song was just the thing to give this comte a disgust of the company. He assumed Jamie was encouraging Mr Davy out of politeness. 'Hum the refrain,' said Sir Philip, rippling his small, well-manicured hands expertly over the keys.

Mr Davy hummed a jaunty refrain. Sir Philip went through it a couple of times and then Mr Davy began to sing.

The comte looked at him in surprise. The man was an actor, he thought, not knowing that until recently that had been Mr Davy's profession. The song was a simple one, about a man complaining about his bullying wife, but Mr Davy almost *became* Grimaldi as he sang, complete with funny expressions. There came an odd sound from next to the comte. He glanced in surprise at Jane. She had her handkerchief up to her mouth. He realized she was trying not to laugh. Ladies were supposed to emit tinkling chimes or show classical smiles. They were not supposed to laugh out loud. Society, he thought, has taken every natural expression away from us, from walking to laughing to how we eat. And then Jane gave way. She lowered the handkerchief and laughed out loud, and Lady Fortescue, usually rigid when it came to social behaviour, relaxed and laughed as well, half in amusement at Mr Davy's antics, half in delight at Jane's mirth.

By the time Mr Davy had finished, they were all, with the exception of a surprised and disgruntled Sir Philip, helpless with laughter. Mr Davy bowed before the applause and then said cheerfully, 'Now I will sing you a ballad. "The Minstrel Boy."'

'I don't know that,' said Sir Philip, scuttling away from the piano.

'You do, too,' complained Miss Tonks.

'I will sing unaccompanied,' said Mr Davy.

The words of Thomas More's lovely song sounded round the room in a clear tenor voice.

'The Minstrel Boy to the war is gone,
In the ranks of death you'll find him;
His father's sword he has girded on,
And his wild harp slung behind him.'

There was a little respectful silence when he had finished and then applause. Jamie, who was sitting opposite Jane, noticed with a sort of wonder that she had *thawed out*, as he described it to himself. Her large eyes were sparkling and there was a delicate pink bloom on her cheeks.

She heard the comte say, 'You ought to be on the stage, sir,' and then Mr Davy's reply, 'But I was until recently,' and that struck her as funny as well and she laughed helplessly while the comte looked down at her in sudden affection and wanted to take her in his arms.

He set himself to please, and entertained the company with various anecdotes about the follies of society while Sir Philip glowered and Harriet studied Jane's glowing face and worried about her. This comte was too frivolous, too unstable. All at once, Harriet longed for her husband, who would know exactly what to do. He would surely have reached Milan by now. But how long would it take for a letter to arrive? And what kind of letter? Why had she been so selfishly cold to him? But for the moment she must concentrate on Jane's safety. When the comte and Jamie at last took their leave, Harriet drew Sir Philip aside, waspish Sir Philip who nonetheless had proved so clever in the past at getting them out of scrapes.

'I am anxious about this comte,' she said in a low voice.

'And so you should be,' pointed out Sir Philip. 'His visit tonight was no accident. He is pursuing Lady Fremney.'

'Miss North,' corrected Harriet. 'It is better if we use her new name at all times. I think I need your help, Sir Philip. The comte is highly unsuitable. I am delighted to see Jane has recovered her spirits, but I am determined to find her a suitable beau and the comte is not my idea of a correct and stable gentleman.'

'I'll think o' something. In fact, I'll start now,' said Sir Philip, his pale eyes gleaming as he saw a way to get even with the comte. 'Leave her to me.'

He slid over and jerked his head at Miss Tonks, who was sitting beside Jane on the sofa. She rose after throwing him a suspicious look and went to talk to Mr Davy.

'Good to see you in high spirits,' said Sir Philip.

'Mr Davy is so very clever,' said Jane. 'I wish I had seen him on the stage.'

'Tol rol,' remarked Sir Philip dismissively. 'All these actors can do is perform. But nothing out of the common way. Sort of thing that amuses that French comte. We'll be the talk of London tomorrow.'

'How so?'

'Oh, he is such a gossip. He will rattle on about his unfashionable evening, listening to vulgar songs in an hotel sitting room and make a mock of all of us.'

Jane's eyes widened. 'He is not like that, surely.

There is a lightness of character about him, I admit. But he seems a gentleman.'

'Not where the ladies are concerned. That fellow has had more mistresses – you forgive me speaking so plain? – than I have had hot dinners. He is the despair of the Season. Rich and handsome, I will allow. He occasionally flirts with some gullible young miss, breaks her heart and then goes off to pay court to a flighty matron anxious for an amour.'

Jane thought of the little scene in the tea-gardens. Who had the lady been? A discarded mistress? What a wicked, dismal world it all was. She felt as depressed as she had recently been elated.

'Sir Philip!' Lady Fortescue's voice was sharp. 'What are you saying to Miss North?'

'Just tittle-tattle,' said Sir Philip quickly.

'I have been thinking,' said Harriet on the road home, 'that this comte's attentions cannot do you harm. Despite his reputation, he is accounted a great catch. Perhaps, should he ask again, I will give you permission to go driving with him.'

'I do not want to encourage the attentions of such a man,' said Jane in a low voice.

'As you will. But why?'

'Sir Philip told me of his mistresses, of his repu-tation.'

Harriet looked at her in dismay. 'I am afraid that was my fault. Seeing you so happy and animated, I thought . . . Well, in any case, I told Sir Philip to warn you off. I had forgot the sheer crudity of his methods. Oh, dear, I forgot, too, about his resentments. Because

81

he mistook the comte for a yahoo and got himself in disgrace with Lady Fortescue and the colonel, he will now want to get even with this comte. I am sorry, Jane.'

'In any case,' said Jane, striving for a lighter tone, 'I am sure there are safer, more charming gentlemen around. Have you heard from the duke?'

'Not yet,' said Harriet sadly. 'I wonder where he is.'

At that moment, the Duke of Rowcester and his servants were sheltering in a grimy tavern some miles from Milan. They had been forced to take shelter from a violent storm. The duke was seated in a dark corner, drinking a glass of the bitter local wine and thinking about his wife. He tried to remember how cold and distant to him she had been of late but could only remember the vibrant loveliness of her before the tragedy of their daughter's death. In and out of his thoughts came the sounds of rapid French from a couple of men, shielded from his view by the back of a high settle. The duke's French was excellent and he suddenly realized the two men were discussing possible ways to free Napoleon from his prison on Elba. He listened, half irritated, half amused, for Europe seemed to be full of Napoleonic plotters hoping to free their hero. What did another pair matter? And then he heard one say, 'You could go to Elba as a tourist after you have silenced that comte for us.'

'De Mornay has exposed plot after plot,' said the other voice. 'But never fear. He is in London and I shall make sure his death looks accidental.'

At that moment, the duke's valet arrived to say that a bedchamber had been prepared. The duke was conscious of two black figures disappearing out of the inn. He wondered who the plotters were but he was exhausted, and what did two more plotters matter? There had already been attempt after attempt to free the emperor, but all had failed.

It was only as he was falling asleep that he recalled the voices and with a little shock realized that the man speaking fluent French, the one who was going to London, had in fact probably been English. There had been something in the intonation and accent. And only an English tourist could go to Elba, and one of high rank. He decided to write to the authorities in Horse Guards in the morning about what he had overheard. But before that, he would write to his wife.

FIVE

It is impossible, in our condition of Society, not to be sometimes a Snob.

WILLIAM MAKEPEACE THACKERAY

A month had passed and the Season was about to begin. There was a hectic air about society, rather like that of actors before an opening night. Only Jane felt strangely unmoved. It still seemed to her an odd dream in which she was living, and yet the only road to freedom lay through marriage. Often she wished she had money of her own so that she might buy a partnership in the hotel. Her visits to the hotel had ceased, Lady Fortescue saying that although the hotel owners were *bon ton*, some slight taint of trade might stick to Jane were she to be seen socializing with them too often.

Frances, Jane knew, was disappointed because Mr Jamie Ferguson had not come to call. For her part, she was glad she had not seen the comte again. He made her feel . . . uncomfortable. Or rather that was the only way she could explain her feelings about him to herself.

Jane found Frances an agreeable companion because Harriet was often withdrawn and seemed to

84

live for the arrival of the post. And then, on the eve of the Season, Harriet received a letter from her husband. Jane did not know what it contained, only that Harriet looked transformed, radiant. The duke had not bothered to mention overhearing the conspirators. That news he had sent in a separate letter to Horse Guards.

Frances called that afternoon to discuss her coming out with Jane at a ball at Lady Farley's the following evening. Frances was unusually subdued. She had not told Jane that although she had gone to Curzon Street several times during the last month with her maid in the hopes of one glimpse of Mr Jamie Ferguson, she had been unlucky. She was plagued with dreams of this beautiful Scotchwoman, Lady Dunwilde. She had learned that she was in London but had not found anyone to describe her looks to her.

'Do you think Mr Ferguson will be at the ball?' she asked again.

'I do not know,' said Jane. 'Harriet has had a letter from her husband which has put her in alt. I could ask her to question Lady Farley as to whether Mr Ferguson has been invited.'

But Frances did not want that. For she suddenly knew if she found out before that ball that he was not going, then she would not look forward to the event at all. She had hoped that he would have called on her to discuss her plan of making Fiona a confidante, but only friends of her mother came to call, anxious matrons determined that their daughters should succeed in the marriage market.

'I think, dear Jane, that I should just wait and see. But you must remember to attract the gentlemen to your side and flirt with Mr Ferguson and then go off and dance with someone else so that he will be obliged to ask me.'

'You rate my looks too highly,' said Jane ruefully.

'Oh, no.' Frances shook her frizzy hair. 'Don't you dream of some gentleman walking towards you across the ballroom, Jane, and of you looking up and knowing this is your future?'

Jane gave a little sigh. She could not tell Frances that at the back of her mind was always the dread that she would see her father walking towards her, followed by Miss Stamp. Romance did not seem to play any part in this London of the early-nineteenth century. The heaths around London were decorated with corpses hanging from gibbets, the town was patrolled by window-smashing mobs, and gentlemen had to know how to defend themselves with stick or dress-sword. London was rich in brothels called bagnios, and in gin-shops where it was possible to get drunk for a penny and dead drunk for twopence. Unlike Frances, Jane read a great number of news-papers and magazines and was more aware of the violent life just outside the carefully protected world in which she lived. Because of her brutish father and his equally brutish friends, she saw the studied tenderness to the ladies of society by the gentlemen as a charade, as mannered as dancing. She thought of the Poor Relation Hotel and had a longing to visit the owners who knew her real name, to talk to them about her fears, the fears she did not want to burden Harriet with because Harriet was still in mourning for her dead child.

'You have gone all sad again,' said Frances. 'There is always a sadness about you, Jane, and you never talk of your family. Do they come to London?'

'No,' said Jane briefly. 'They are in the north. Let us change the subject. Is your gown very pretty, Frances?'

'I will sketch it for you,' said Frances, seizing her drawing-book. Her pencil moved rapidly over the paper. 'It is white muslin, of course, very suitable. Do you not wish we could wear scarlet or something like that? It has quite a low neckline, like so, and little puffed sleeves, but it has a gauze overdress with silver-and-sapphire clasps and *three* flounces at the hem. I am to wear a Juliet cap embroidered with pearls and sequins. My gloves are white kid but do not cover my elbows, which is a pity, for although I treat them nightly with lemon juice and goose grease, they are a trifle rough. And little slippers of white kid with rosettes of white silk.'

'Very fine,' said Jane.

'So what is yours like?'

'Come with me and I will show you.' Jane led the way to her bedroom where her gown was displayed on a dummy by the window. Like Frances's evening gown, it was of white muslin but decorated with a little green sprig and ornamented with a wide green silk sash. 'I have green gloves and green shoes to go with it,' said Jane, 'and green silk flowers for my hair. Do you not think the neckline a trifle low?'

Frances put her head on one side like an inquiring bird and studied the gown with interest. 'I do not think so. Low necklines are all the thing. I do wish these fashions which put the waist under the armpits would be exploded. My one claim to beauty is my tiny waist, but no one ever sees it.' She looked out of the window and down to the street below. 'Do you think it will rain? Oh, my heart. There is my Mr Ferguson walking below with that comte. Is he coming here?'

Jane joined her and looked down. The comte and Jamie were strolling arm in arm. As they came abreast of the duchess's house, Jamie said something to the comte as he looked up, and then both laughed.

About to turn away, because Jane felt that both men were probably joking about the bold misses who tried to accost gentlemen in Curzon Street, she suddenly stiffened and stared down. In a closed carriage on the other side of the street, she could make out the burning eyes of some man. His hat was pulled down over the top part of his face and a scarf up over the lower part. A ray of sunlight flashed on something metal and Jane realized with horror that he was holding a pistol and that that pistol was levelled at the two men walking below. She threw up the window and shrieked, 'Look out!'

The man in the carriage shouted something to his driver, who promptly whipped up his horses and the carriage bowled off.

The comte and Jamie looked up in surprise and then swept off their hats and made low bows. 'What is the matter, Jane?' cried Frances.

88

'I must tell them.' Jane was quite white. 'Some man was going to shoot them.'

'Capital!' cried Frances, clapping her hands. 'What a ruse!'

But Jane was already out of the room and running headlong down the stairs. A footman leaped to open the front door as she ran across the hall.

'Gentlemen!' cried Jane. 'Monsieur le Comte! You must listen.'

They had begun to move on, but at the sound of her voice they both turned about and hurried back to her.

'What is wrong, Miss North?' asked the comte.

Some fashionables passing by were turning to stare. Jane blushed, aware of how unconventional her behaviour must seem. 'Pray step inside,' she urged, 'and I will explain.'

'Delighted to oblige,' said the comte, his blue eyes sparkling.

Admiring what she considered Jane's unexpected boldness and improvisation, Frances came down the stairs as they entered the hall.

Jane led them into a rather gloomy saloon on the ground floor which was used for receiving the duke's business callers, such as his agent and his tailor. 'We should be chaperoned, Frances,' said Jane in dismay.

'Leave the door standing open,' said the comte, 'so that we will all be in full view of any servants. Or summon your maid, Miss North.'

'I will leave the door open,' said Jane, wondering whether she had imagined the whole thing. 'I was looking down from the window a moment before and

I saw a man with his face mostly covered in a closed carriage opposite. He . . . he was levelling a pistol at you.'

'Really?' said Jamie, thinking that Miss North was every bit as tricky as Frances.

But for a moment, the comte's usually lazy eyes were sharp and shrewd. 'Which one of us did he aim to kill?' he asked.

'I do not know,' said Jane wretchedly. 'I now think I must have imagined it all. And yet . . . and yet when I called to you, he shouted to his coachman and sped off.'

'Odd,' said Jamie, his eyes dancing. 'But London is full of footpads.'

But the comte, covertly studying Jane's pallor, was thinking of a meeting he had had earlier at Horse Guards where he had been told of a certain letter from the Duke of Rowcester in which the duke had explained some conspirator he believed to be an English gentleman was out to kill the Comte de Mornay. At Horse Guards, they knew that the comte's spying activities against Napoleon had in the past been a thorn in the side of the emperor's friends and supporters. They had urged him to use caution but at the same time to try to find out the name of this English traitor.

'Did you notice anything about the carriage, Miss North?' he asked. 'Any crest, any distinctive hammer-cloth? Surely the coachman was not masked?'

'It was just a plain carriage,' said Jane, 'and the coachman just looked like any other coachman.'

'No groom, footman or tiger on the backstrap? No livery?'

Jane shook her head.

Jamie gave a light laugh. 'We will watch very carefully how we go in future, Miss North. Our meetings seem destined to be dramatic. Firstly, poor Miss Haggard here faints nearly at our feet in Curzon Street and now you are on hand to prevent us being murdered.'

Jane looked at him haughtily. 'I did not make the whole thing up. Now, since your presence here is highly unconventional, gentlemen, I suggest you take your leave.'

But at that moment Harriet came in, followed by her maid, her eyes darting from one to the other. 'Explain,' she demanded curtly.

So Jane explained again, conscious all the time of the amusement in Mr Ferguson's eyes. Her story began to sound ridiculous in her own ears.

'How odd,' said Harriet coldly. 'Now, pray take your leave, gentlemen. You should not be here. We will no doubt see you at the Farleys' ball.'

'That will be our pleasure,' said the comte. With elaborate bows, both men made their farewells.

'Minx,' laughed Jamie as soon as they were clear of the house. 'How inventive! How cunning! And how flattering. Are you not flattered that such a beauty should tell such lies to catch your attention?'

'She had had a bad shock, my insensitive friend, or did her unusual pallor escape you?'

Jamie stopped short. 'You cannot mean she was telling the truth!'

'Trust me, mon ami. The beautiful Miss North really believed she saw a man with a gun.'

'Why would anyone want to kill one of us?'

But the comte had no intention of explaining anything. 'London is full of villains and footpads,' he said, tossing a coin to a diminutive crossing-sweeper.

Harriet had retired to write to her husband, and Jane and Frances were once more left alone. 'So you did not make it up?' asked Frances, her eyes round.

Jane shook her head in bewilderment. 'I really believe I saw a man with a gun. But in broad daylight and in Park Street! I feel so ashamed of myself. I must have imagined the whole thing. And your Mr Ferguson thought I had planned the whole thing to get their attention.'

'And so you did. No, I do not mean you lied. But you did get their attention, and now we know they are going to be at the ball.' Frances pirouetted about the room. Then she sank down next to Jane in a flurry of taffeta. 'But *she* will no doubt be there, Fiona Dunwilde, and I shall have to watch him making sheep's eyes at her. Tell me she will have changed, Jane. She is quite old now and the Scottish climate is reported to be harsh. The Scotch drink a great deal of claret and spirits, and so she may have a red nose and broken veins on her face.'

'We will know when we see her,' said Jane absent-mindedly, thinking all the time of that masked face at the window of the coach.

* * *

92

In their private sitting room that evening, the hoteliers gathered to discuss their future plans, the main one being that they were to organize and arrange the serving of the supper at Lady Farley's ball.

'I do not see why we should not tell Harriet we are going to be there,' complained Miss Tonks.

'She has much on her mind,' said Lady Fortescue. 'She is doing us a favour by bringing Jane out. We do not want her mind distracted by wondering in advance how to cope with her old friends acting the role of servants.'

'We ain't servants,' grumbled Sir Philip. 'We've engaged servants to do the work. It's Despard's famous cuisine Lady Farley is after.'

'But we ourselves have to appear to serve,' explained Lady Fortescue patiently. 'It is part of our cachet.'

'Cachet be damned,' growled Sir Philip. 'It's time we got back in society and took up our rightful places.'

'Which we could do,' said the colonel eagerly, 'if we were to sell this hotel.'

'Society isn't quite going to forget we were once in trade,' said Lady Fortescue.

'If you've got money,' said Sir Philip cynically, 'society will cheerfully forget everything.'

'Then why isn't Almack's full of Cits?' asked Mr Davy.

'Because Cits never were in our class to start with.' Sir Philip glared at him. 'They're all common . . . like you.'

'That will be enough of that.' Miss Tonks bridled.

'Let us change the subject. I gather our prince is not to be present at the ball.'

'He was asked but he don't want to go,' said Sir Philip. 'He uses this hotel like a small palace. He likes his own people about him. Lady Farley could have had him if she had invited his whole retinue. He never moves without 'em. How's Harriet?'

'The duchess sent a note by hand this morning,' said Lady Fortescue, 'to say that the duke had written her a wonderful letter. She says she will be so pleased to see him that she plans to wear some barbaric family necklace he is so proud of for the first time so that he will see her decorated with it on his return.'

Sir Philip felt quite cold with fear. He knew all at once that the necklace to which Harriet had referred was the one in the glass case in the muniments room at the duke's country home, the one he had thieved to raise money to start the hotel and replaced with a clever replica. Nestling as it was now in the dim light of the muniments room, the fake was safe from detection. But he had a sudden vivid little picture of a radiant Harriet wearing it and the duke smiling, taking out his quizzing-glass, and then beginning to shout he had been tricked.

'Think I'll stretch my legs,' he said, getting to his feet. Out in Bond Street, he hailed a hack and told the driver to take him to Holborn, upon which the driver promptly demanded payment in advance for venturing into an area which bordered on the Rookeries, those slums so full of crime and vice. Normally Sir Philip would have cursed and haggled but he was too worried to argue and settled for the fee of a shilling.

It seemed to take an age to get to Holborn but at last he was deposited outside the shop – or where the jeweller's shop used to be. He climbed stiffly down, calling sharply to the driver to wait. A sign above the door said 'Welsh Bakery.' Although the shutters were up, he could see chinks of light from inside the shop streaming through. He rapped furiously on the door with the silver knob of his stick and fretted and fumed as slow shuffling feet could be heard approaching from within. Bolts were drawn back, the door was opened a few inches, the end of a blunderbuss pointed at him, and a hoarse voice said, 'Who's there?'

'Where is the jeweller?' demanded Sir Philip, who had no intention of giving his name.

The door opened farther, revealing the baker himself, a small, squat, powerful man dusted with flour. 'Gone,' he said, 'two months since, and nothing but the constable and people like yourself a-hammering and trying to find him. The Runners have been round as well. Arsk at Bow Street.'

The door was slammed in Sir Philip's face. He stood irresolute on the greasy pavement, until the driver hailed him with 'I ain't going to wait about here all night.' Sir Philip climbed back into the smelly hack and asked to be taken back to Bond Street, his thoughts in a turmoil. The villainous jeweller had decamped and with him his stock and along with his stock that necklace which Sir Philip had been going to reclaim, and along with it all the money Sir Philip had been paying him in instalments to buy it back. Sir Philip decided to wait until daylight and then question his underworld contacts for news of the jeweller.

But although he searched and searched on the following day among the narrow streets and stews of London, no one had heard anything about the jeweller. Only the fact that he had to return to the hotel and change and go to Lady Farley's to take up his duties made him give up his frantic search.

Harriet was more like the débutante than Jane herself, reflected Jane as they set out for the ball. The duchess looked radiant, her green eyes sparkling like the emeralds about her neck. Beside her, Jane felt diminished, sad, and underneath it all she had a niggling feeling of dread that someone at the ball would recognize her. The only thing that gave her courage as they approached the large mansion in Grosvenor Square was a determination to do her best to shine to please her generous hostess and to try to help Frances with her romance. Frances, Jane knew, envied her, Jane's, looks. And yet Jane envied Frances her happy nature, her confidence, even her mad plans to secure the man of her dreams.

Lady Farley's town house was imposing, with a line of liveried footmen on either side of the red Turkey carpet leading up to the front door, but Jane's home was imposing as well, the earl liking to entertain with great ceremony, and so she did not feel intimidated.

They left their wraps with their maids in the

ante-room off the front hall and together they mounted the staircase to the 'ballroom' on the first floor, which was in fact made out of a chain of large saloons, with most of the furniture removed for the occasion. Lady Farley, a widow, stood at the top of the stairs with her son, the Honourable Clarence Farley, to receive the guests. She murmured a few gracious words and then Harriet and Jane walked into the main saloon, which was draped in gold silk and set about with banks of hothouse flowers. Frances came up with her mother to greet them and introduced Jane to her father. Jane had not until that moment met Mr Haggard. He was an older, masculine version of his daughter, his frizzy hair pomaded and powdered, and he had the same twinkling eyes and childlike air of geniality.

Frances drew Jane aside. 'She is here!' she whispered.

'Lady Dunwilde?'

'The same.'

'Which is she?'

'There. Dancing with that colonel.'

Jane looked covertly over her fan. Lady Dunwilde was a striking matron with auburn hair and eyes so dark grey, they looked black. She had a voluptuous figure shown to advantage in damped muslin. Beyond her, Jane noticed Mr Jamie Ferguson leaning against a pillar and staring intensely at the love of his life.

'Only see how he looks at her,' hissed Frances. 'We have our work cut out. This dance is over. Oh, pray someone asks me. I do not think I could bear to sit against the wall all evening, an object of pity. But if no one asks me, that is what I shall have to do. Be still, my heart, and fan me ye winds! Here comes your comte with my beloved. Smile!'

But Jane looked at the approaching comte with the same pleasure with which she would have observed an approaching snake. He was formidably handsome at the best of times, but in all the glory of evening dress and jewels, he seemed to eclipse every other man in the room. He bowed before Jane and said, 'Miss North, will you do me the very great honour of allowing me to lead you in a set of the quadrille?'

Jane curtsied low and said she would be delighted, although, the comte reflected wryly, she looked anything but happy.

They were joined in their set by Frances and Jamie. Jane noticed that Jamie was saying something in a low voice to Frances, and then how Frances's eyes flew to Lady Dunwilde and how she nodded. So they are going on with their plan, thought Jane. Frances is to make a confidante of Lady Dunwilde.

The comte, who had addressed her twice, asking if this were her first London ball, looked down at her, amused at his own sharp feeling of pique. He was used to ladies hanging on his every word. 'And only remark how Lady Farley has just slit her throat,' he said.

'Yes, indeed,' replied the preoccupied Jane politely, having become aware at the last moment that she was being addressed.

The music began and the couples twisted and turned in the intricate measure of the dance, which did not allow for any opportunity for conversation. Frances danced with great expertise and elegance, Jamie noticed, thinking indulgently that she was indeed full of surprises. When the dance was over, they promenaded in the round, as was the custom. Jamie contrived to come alongside Lady Dunwilde and her partner. He bowed low. 'Lady Dunwilde, may I present Miss Haggard; Miss Haggard, Lady Dunwilde.' Frances curtsied and then said, 'I am delighted to meet you, Lady Dunwilde. You are even more beautiful than I had been led to believe.'

Oh, silly little Miss Haggard, thought Jamie. No one could be pleased with such a blatantly insincere compliment. But to his surprise Lady Dunwilde smiled graciously and patted Frances's cheek. 'Dear child,' she murmured. 'Come and chat with me.'

With every evidence of gratified delight, Frances trotted off at Lady Dunwilde's side. They sat down against a bank of flowers on those uncomfortable seats called rout-chairs. 'Tell me,' said Lady Dunwilde, fanning herself languidly, 'have you been long acquainted with Mr Ferguson?'

'For about perhaps a little over a month,' said Frances, omitting the fact that apart from the day before, she had seen nothing of Mr Ferguson, despite her efforts, during that month.

Lady Dunwilde turned those very dark eyes of hers on Frances. 'You must not have hopes in that direction, my child.'

'Why not, my lady?'

She sighed. 'He was much in love with me before I

99

married Lord Dunwilde . . . and he still is. Alas, an undying passion, I fear.'

'It seems a pity that such devotion cannot be rewarded,' said Frances.

Lady Dunwilde's lips curved in a thin smile. The fan slowly moved. 'Oh, perhaps he may yet get his reward.'

Frances quickly raised her own fan to hide the sudden flash of dislike in her eyes. 'Where is Lord Dunwilde?'

'At home at present, although he will join me later. He is a martyr to the gout. But you must go and join the young ladies, and do tell Mr Ferguson that there is always hope.'

Frances rose and curtsied and gave Lady Dunwilde her best smile. 'Of course, my lady. Always at your service.'

'Do you know, I have taken quite a fancy to you, dear child. I shall call on you.'

'I am honoured and flattered, my lady.'

The fan flicked in a dismissive manner.

As Frances skirted the floor, she met Mr Ferguson just as that gentleman was bearing down on Lady Dunwilde. 'What did she say?' he asked eagerly. 'Did she speak of me?'

'Yes.' Frances stared down at her little kid shoes.

'What did she say?'

'You had better ask me to dance and I will tell you.'

'But it is the waltz and . . . and I wanted to ask Lady Dunwilde.'

'Oh, no, I would not do that, sir. I think you should hear what I have to say first.'

'Very well.'

He swept her onto the floor. Frances followed his steps, as lightly as a feather. He bent his head over hers. 'Now tell me.'

'Mmmm?' murmured Frances dreamily.

'Tell me what she said.'

Frances rallied. 'Lady Dunwilde asked me how long I had known you and I said over a month, which is quite true, don't you know. She said you had been madly in love with her.'

'Oh, my heart! And what did she say then?'

Frances looked up and met his eyes steadily. 'Lady Dunwilde said she had made the right decision in marrying Lord Dunwilde. She said that she believed you to be still spoony about her and that was a sign of great weakness in a man, in her opinion.'

'The devil she did!'

'But Lady Dunwilde is quite a kind matron, I think,' Frances said earnestly, 'and it is gracious in one of her years to befriend me.'

'You are to see her?'

'She is to call on me.'

They danced on in silence after that. When the dance was over, supper was announced. Jamie gloomily took Frances into supper. His friend, the comte, he noticed, was escorting Miss North.

The comte sat down next to Jane at one of the long tables, waited until she had been served with food and wine, and then said lightly, 'And you should be careful of that collection of spiders your duchess keeps in the attics. Some of them are, I believe, quite poisonous.'

Jane only heard the bit 'be careful' and assumed it was some caution about the dangers of the streets of London, for her worried mind slid away from what he was saying. There was a lady present who looked like one of her father's friends, a lady who kept sending curious little darting glances in her direction.

'And I am madly in love with you,' went on the comte. 'Will you marry me? I think we should deal very well together. Do you not think so?'

Worried and abstracted, Jane only heard his voice asking the latter question and said politely, 'Yes, I do agree.'

Those blue eyes of his flashed with humour. 'Good. That is settled. Will you tell the duchess I shall call on her tomorrow to ask permission to pay my respects? And, of course, I must call on your father and mother.'

'Mother? Father?' said Jane, coming out of her abstraction. 'What are you saying? My mother is dead.'

'Your father, then.'

'Why? Why are you talking about my father?'

'It is usual under the circumstances. Since we are to be married, I should seek his permission.'

Jane upset her glass of wine. A waiter darted forward to mop up the mess and pour her another.

Now he had her full attention. Her eyes were magnificent, he thought appreciatively. 'Marriage? What marriage? What are you talking about?'

'I asked you to marry me and you accepted, very sweetly, too,' he said, all mock patience.

She coloured to the roots of her hair. 'I know you

are funning, Monsieur le Comte. I was abstracted. Worried. Thinking of other things. I thought I was replying innocuously to polite questions.'

'So you are not going to marry me?'

'No. I mean, definitely no. I would not sound so harsh if I did not know you were bamming me.'

'Perhaps. But what do you have against my suit? I am rich, unmarried, good *ton*.'

'I am not used to London ways or London gentlemen, Monsieur le Comte. Some other lady, most other ladies, would probably be considerably flattered by your attentions.'

'Where is your home?'

'Durbyshire.'

'Do you know the earl?'

'No!' Sharply.

'Why so vehement, Miss North?'

'I . . . I have heard of this earl and do not like what I have heard. May we talk of other things?'

'Gladly. Do eat something. You will offend your friends from the Poor Relation if you do not.'

Jane looked across with surprise. She had been too abstracted to notice the presence of Sir Philip, Lady Fortescue, Colonel Sandhurst, Miss Tonks, and Mr Davy, but there they all were in various parts of the room, supervising the waiters, occasionally and graciously inclining to remove a plate or dirty glass with bejewelled hands.

'I hope nothing has gone wrong,' Jane heard the comte remark. 'That horrible old Sir Philip looks as if he is about to have an apoplexy.'

And Sir Philip felt so himself. For round the neck of Lady Farley lay a barbaric necklace he knew only too well. Somehow that perfidious jeweller must have sold it. What if Harriet knew that there could only be one like that? His heart was hammering with fear. Somehow he had to get that necklace from Lady Farley and replace it with the fake and put the real necklace back in the duke's muniments room.

When the supper was over he approached Harriet, who was being squired by an elderly military gentleman. 'A word with you, Your Grace,' he said and then glared at Harriet's escort, who was staring down his nose at him as if wondering at the sheer impertinence of these hoteliers.

Harriet murmured her excuses to her escort and walked off with Sir Philip. 'I just wanted to be sure you were enjoying yourself,' began Sir Philip.

'Yes, I thank you. I heard nothing but praise for Despard's cooking.'

'Know Lady Farley well, do you?'

'As much as one knows anyone in society.'

'Funny old necklace she's got on.'

'I remarked it,' said Harriet, 'because my husband has one like it at home. He wants me to wear it, although I do not like it much. I think he will be surprised to learn it is not unique.'

'I don't think anything is these days,' said Sir Philip. 'But it wouldn't surprise me to learn that Lady Farley's necklace is paste.'

Harriet laughed. 'You are the expert on such things. It looks very real to me. Jane appears to have some little animation this evening. Everyone is remarking on her beauty.'

'But you'll need to stop that comte from hanging about her,' said Sir Philip.

Harriet looked over his shoulder to the ballroom. 'Jane is dancing with Clarence Farley and getting on splendidly, by the looks of it. I shall endeavour to keep her away from the comte.'

Jane was enjoying the company of Clarence Farley. He was a serious man with a calm, courteous air. She felt safe with him in a way she did not feel at all safe with the handsome comte with his glinting blue eyes. When Clarence suggested she sit out the next dance with him she readily agreed. They talked of innocuous things such as the weather and balls and parties to come. Clarence had thick brown hair and a not very memorable face, small brown eyes and a rather large mouth, but he was well dressed and seemed very much at ease in her company.

'How long have you known de Mornay?' he suddenly asked.

'Not very long,' said Jane. 'And not very well.'

'You are new to London, Miss North. I feel I should warn you that de Mornay has the reputation of being an adventurer.'

For some obscure reason Jane could not fathom, she felt slightly annoyed at hearing the comte criticized. 'He is accounted well-to-go,' she said defensively.

'I did not mean adventurer in the sense that he pursues heiresses,' said Clarence. 'Only that he is flighty and breaks hearts.'

'My heart is quite safe, sir,' said Jane in a cold voice.

'Ah, now, Miss North, I would not offend you for the world. I feel we might be friends. May I ask Her Grace's permission to take you driving?'

'By all means.' Jane suddenly liked him again. 'When?'

'You will be receiving callers tomorrow, myself included. Shall we say the day after that?'

'Delighted.'

'The next dance is about to begin and here come your courtiers. Until then, Miss North.'

Jane, performing the cotillion with her next partner, was pleased to see Frances was on the floor. In fact, Frances had not been left sitting out once since her conversation with Lady Dunwilde. It was, thought Jane, because of her ebullience and friendliness. Little Frances would be engaged to be married before any of the belles.

Frances smiled and talked to her partners, prattling away as if she did not have a care in the world, when all the time she was aware of Jamie. He had not approached Lady Dunwilde. And then, just as the dance was finishing, she became aware of him edging around the ballroom floor in the direction of Lady Dunwilde. She suddenly could not bear it. What if he found out so soon that she, Frances, had lied to him about what Lady Dunwilde had said?

Just as Jamie had nearly reached his quarry, Frances pretended to turn her ankle and let out a piercing shriek and swayed dizzily. Her partner, a shy young man, stared at her helplessly. Jamie, with a mutter of annoyance, ran to Frances's side and caught her in his arms.

'My stupid ankle,' whispered Frances, tears starting to her eyes, because all the feelings she had for him welled up in her and overset her senses. She could feel his arms around her, smell the light scent he wore, feel the heat from his body.

'There now,' he said. 'Lean on me. Where is your mother? I fear your dancing is finished for the evening.'

He had quite forgotten Lady Dunwilde for the moment. Frances was a silly child and needed someone to look after her. Jane came up, full of concern. She had thought Frances was pretending to twist her ankle but became alarmed at the strain on her face. 'I will find your mother, Frances,' said Jane, 'and then I think your parents should take you home.'

'I would like to sit quietly and perhaps drink a glass of lemonade,' said Frances.

'I'll fetch it for you,' said Jamie. When he returned with the lemonade, he noticed that Lady Dunwilde had been joined by her elderly husband. She cast a languishing look in Jamie's direction, but he was still smarting from what he believed to be her cruel remark to Frances, and so he turned away and bent solicitously over Frances with the lemonade and then sat down beside her, so that when Mrs Haggard came hurrying up, it was to find a radiant daughter who said that she was quite recovered and would sit quietly with Mr Ferguson. Mrs Haggard was so pleased with her daughter's unexpected success at the ball, for she

107

had expected her to be totally extinguished by such dazzling beauties as Jane North, that she smiled indulgently on her and said they would take her home when she wished to go.

'I am so sorry,' said Frances to Jamie when they were alone. 'You must join your beloved.'

'I have no intention, Miss Minx, of joining my – as you call her – beloved. Her husband has arrived.'

'Do you mean to say she settled for that old man when she might have had *you*?' Frances's eyes over her fan were large and melting.

He laughed. 'You restore my amour propre, which has been sadly damaged. Why do you tap your little foot to the music? I thought that was the injured one.'

'It is,' said Frances quickly. 'It is when I stand on it that it hurts. Do you want me to convey any message to Lady Dunwilde for you when she calls?'

'I should hate her,' he said gloomily. 'But, in truth, you may tell her that I still love her with all my heart.' The light went out of Frances's face and she said sadly, 'My foot hurts rather a lot after all. I would like to go home.'

She looked around to say her goodbyes to Jane, but Jane was waltzing with the Comte de Mornay. Despite her misery, Frances could not help noticing that Jane was smiling at something the comte was saying to her while Clarence Farley leaned against a pillar and watched them both closely. There was something in Clarence's look that Frances did not like, but she put it to the back of her mind. When Lady Dunwilde called on her, she should tell her the truth, that Mr

108

Jamie Ferguson was still in love with her. Frances's lips set in a firm line. She had no intention of doing what she ought to do and she was suddenly determined to lie and lie until all hope was gone.

SIX

The comte, being barbered by his valet the following
day, roused himself from thought. 'You know I trust
you, Gerrard?'

'As you have every reason to do, Monsieur le
Comte.'

'I wish to send you on a mission of some delicacy.'

'Do you mean we return to France, milor?'

'No, I shall not be going. I wish you to travel to
Durbyshire and find out what you can about a certain
Miss Jane North who is being sponsored here by the
Duchess of Rowcester. She is unforthcoming about
her background and is quite vehement about the fact
that she does *not* know the Earl of Durbyshire. I
suggest you start with the earl's household. If he has a
secretary, seek the man out. It will be he who knows
all the ladies of the county who are invited to balls and
parties. Do we know an artist?'

'There is a certain gentleman of some little talent
known to my brother Lucas.'

'Find him today. Miss North is of outstanding beauty. She has black glossy hair and large grey eyes fringed with heavy lashes. He is to position himself outside the Duchess of Rowcester's town house in Park Street, wait until the lady emerges, and do a lightning sketch. She will probably go out this evening, and it is light quite late. He must give the sketch to you and then you may take my travelling carriage and go north.'

'Yes, milor. An affair of the heart?'

'An affair of the curiosity, mon vieux!'

Jane awoke as Frances bounced into her bedchamber. 'What brings you here so early, Frances?' she asked, struggling up against the pillows.

Frances perched on the end of the bed. 'I have done a wicked thing and it is on my conscience.'

'Then you had better tell me.'

Jane listened wide-eyed as Frances told of her lies of the evening before.

'But Frances,' she exclaimed, 'sooner or later they will meet and will find out you have lied and both will despise you!'

'I don't care about *her* despising me,' said Frances, taking off her straw bonnet and swinging it by its satin ribbons. 'She is determined to be my friend because she wants my Mr Ferguson as her lover. So immoral! Such women should be hung, drawn, and quartered, and whipped at the cart's tail.'

'All at once, Frances? Now, be sensible. The next time she gives you a message for Mr Ferguson, or he for her, tell the truth and then forget about Mr Ferguson. You were in demand last night. You should be at home preparing for your gentlemen callers.'

It was the custom for gentlemen to call on the ladies they had danced with the night before, although some merely sent a card with a servant.

'I am sure Mr Ferguson will call on me.' Frances pouted. 'And all to give me further messages for his lady-love. But what of you and Mr Clarence Farley? Solid, dependable, although I do think, dear Jane, your rakish comte puts all others quite in the shade.'

'Even Mr Ferguson?'

'With the exception of Mr Ferguson. You are so sad and serious, Jane, perhaps a rattle is just what you need. Still, I suppose everyone has warned you about him.'

'Nearly everyone, I think, including Mr Farley, who is, by the way, to take me driving tomorrow.'

'Do be careful. There is something about Mr Farley I cannot like.'

'He seems a kind and sensible man,' said Jane wistfully. 'Just the type of man I always imagined would make a good husband.'

'My nerves were overwrought last night,' said Frances, 'so I am probably mistaken about him. Now I am so tired, for I did not sleep well because of an uneasy conscience, don't you know.'

'So you will not lie again?'

Frances got off the bed and tied on her bonnet. 'I probably shall, dear Jane, but perhaps I should not feel guilty about it. I am protecting Lady Dunwilde from committing adultery, after all!'

That same morning, Lady Fortescue summoned Mr Davy to her bedchamber. 'I am sorry to disturb you so early,' she said as he entered wearing a dressing gown and nightcap. 'I need your help. Jack, the footman, came to me to say he had a message from Limmer's that Sir Philip is there and imbibing freely. It is bad for a man of his years to start the day drinking so early. Pray go and see if you can make him desist and get him to bed.'

Mr Davy held Lady Fortescue in high esteem, which is why he did not protest, for he would dearly have liked to refuse. He went gloomily back to his room and shaved and dressed and then made his way to Limmer's Hotel.

Sir Philip was in the coffee room glaring morosely at a half-empty bottle of wine.

His pale eyes focused on Mr Davy and he remarked, 'Why are you inflicting your presence of me, son of a whore, you bag of shite, you scum from the kennels?'

'I would gladly leave you to rot,' said Mr Davy amiably, 'were not Lady Fortescue concerned for your welfare. As a matter of interest, what drives you to the bottle at this early hour?'

Sober, Sir Philip would not have dreamt of telling him, but worry, drink, and a sleepless night had loosened his tongue. He had studied the doors and windows of Lady Farley's mansion before he had left and knew there was no way an elderly gentleman could play burglar and get through the many bolts and locks on the doors and windows. He felt everything was lost, and shame and exposure would result.

He made to pour another glass of wine but Mr Davy reached forward and caught hold of his hand. 'Drink coffee,' he urged. 'I might be able to help you.'

'You!' declared Sir Philip in accents of loathing. But he allowed Mr Davy to order a pot of coffee. All at once he had an urge to tell this actor his troubles, motivated by the knowledge that Mr Davy was not a gentleman and therefore would have no right to express shock or moral outrage had he belonged to that exclusive breed.

Mr Davy maintained a sympathetic silence until Sir Philip had drunk two cups of coffee. Then he said, 'Go on. What's it all about?'

So Sir Philip, in a flat, slightly slurred voice, told him all about the theft of the necklace to found the hotel, and its subsequent appearance on Lady Farley's neck, ending up with a moan of 'And how can an old man like me expect to broach the locks and bars of Lady Farley's house?'

'As to that,' said Mr Davy, 'I could help you.'

'You?' said Sir Philip contemptuously. 'How?'

'I still have many friends among the acting profession. Society is much given to amateur theatricals and like to employ people versed in the craft to show them how to go on. Were it to be suggested to Lady Farley that a little theatrical soiree would be just the thing,

114

and you know the man to arrange it, then I can fix things so that you will be there. Once indoors, when all are watching the play, you should have an opportunity to slide away. I have noticed at these events that the servants are allowed to watch as well. You should be able to get to my lady's bedchamber unobserved. But in order to arrange this for you, I expect something in return.'

'How much?' sneered Sir Philip.

'No money. I simply want your promise that you will not interfere in my friendship with Miss Tonks.'

Sobering rapidly, Sir Philip studied him, his brain beginning to work quickly. Say yes, promise anything, he thought. He could propose to Miss Tonks himself after it was all over, and claim that was hardly interfering in their friendship; he hoped they would still be friends, yes, all that. And call on Harriet and try to steal one of her seals and copy her handwriting, for he would need a letter, supposedly to have come from her, giving permission to take that fake necklace to London, ostensibly for cleaning. The duke's servants had met him when he had called on a visit before.

'Very well,' said Sir Philip. 'You have my promise. I must go to the country and get that necklace. Do you think you can have all arranged for the play by the time I return?'

'Yes,' said Mr Davy, rising to his feet. 'You must accompany me back to the hotel to put Lady Fortescue's mind at rest.'

'Do not tell the others any of this,' said Sir Philip.

'You have my word.' Mr Davy looked at him curiously. 'But I do not understand why you never did tell them. They must have known it was something of extreme value to raise the necessary sum to get the hotel started.'

'They would have been too afraid,' said Sir Philip as they walked together out of Limmer's. 'It all seemed like a joke then. Harriet was not yet married to Rowcester, and he seemed then like such a pompous idiot . . . well, I thought he deserved it. Then I let time slip by and slip by, and the longer time went by, the harder it seemed to tell any of them of what I had done.' He raised his cane and hailed a hack. 'Tell Lady Fortescue I am well. I must call on Harriet.'

Harriet was in her private sitting room when Sir Philip was announced. She looked at him half-annoyed, half-amused. 'It is an odd time to call, Sir Philip,' said Harriet. 'I am preparing to receive our callers, the gentlemen who danced with Jane and myself at the ball.'

Sir Philip's pale eyes turned thoughtfully in the direction of the little escritoire in the corner of the room. He must distract Harriet's attention. He could not pretend to suddenly feel faint, for she would simply ring the bell and summon her servants to help. He walked over to the window and looked down into the street. 'I am concerned about Jane,' he said. 'I do not think she should be encouraging the attentions of that comte.'

'Jane is not at all interested in the Comte de Mornay,' replied Harriet. 'Why! What is the matter?'

For Sir Philip had let out a stifled exclamation and was peering down into the street.

'Nothing,' he said hurriedly.

'There must be something.' Harriet went to the window. Sir Philip backed away. Harriet looked down but could only see a footman walking a dog. Sir Philip darted to that escritoire and pocketed a seal, a half-finished letter and a blank sheet of crested paper and thrust them both into his pocket just as Harriet turned round.

'I thought I saw an old friend,' said Sir Philip airily. Harriet looked at the old man suspiciously. 'Sir Philip, now I have assured you that Jane is well and not in danger of being seduced by the comte, is there anything else you wish to know?'

'Nothing, nothing,' said Sir Philip, backing to the door.

After he had gone, Harriet rang for her maid. 'Open the window,' she commanded. 'The room is airless.' The maid opened the window and a brisk breeze blew in and scattered the papers on Harriet's desk. The maid picked them up and put them under a paperweight. And later, Harriet, unable to find the letter she had started to write to her husband, assumed it must have blown away.

Jane, although she had had a rigid social training from Miss Stamp, found herself hard put to remember the names of the gentlemen who called that afternoon, with the exceptions of Mr Farley and the comte. The comte only stayed for ten minutes and was polite, courteous, and rather distant. She felt she should be relieved. Instead she found herself irritated with him and decided that his was the behaviour of a mounte-bank, proposing marriage to her one minute and ignoring her the next. And yet, despite that irritation, she often thought in wonder about her attempt at suicide. Day after day, there seemed to be so much to live for – Frances's friendship, the kindness of Harriet, the odd feeling of stability given by the knowledge that those hotel proprietors who had saved her life were still interested in her well-being, for Harriet told her that they always asked how she was getting along.

Pique at the comte's behaviour made her be very charming to Mr Farley, a fact that Harriet noticed with approval, although she would not have liked the reason for it.

When Jane left that evening for the opera with Harriet, Harriet said with some amusement, 'You really are London's latest beauty. A man across the road was sketching you!'

Jane flushed slightly. 'I never thought myself anything out of the common way.'

Harriet laughed. 'That is part of your charm. You are a sensible girl. I was glad to see you treat the comte with a certain amount of coolness.'

Jane, who had thought until then that she had behaved in no particularly remarkable manner to-wards him, began to wish she had not been so cold. Rake he might be, but the comte, apart from teasing her with that mock proposal, had been courteous.

'Although,' Harriet was going on, 'it will do your

consequence no harm if he is seen to be paying attention to you. Since I am now sure your heart is in no danger from that direction, I think I may allow him to take you driving. Mr Farley, of course, is an excellent suitor. So sensible!'

So dull, said a little voice in Jane's head. So very dull.

Frances was at the opera in an adjoining box to Harriet's. Lady Dunwilde paid her a visit at the first interval and drew her aside. 'Did you give Mr Ferguson my message?'

'Yes, my lady.'

'And what was his reply?'

'It was most odd,' said Frances. 'He just laughed.'

'Ah, he laughed with pleasure.'

'Well, no, it was a sort of mocking laugh, and then he said, "Too late."'

Lady Dunwilde bridled. 'Then you may tell him from me that I have no feelings for him whatsoever.'

'Would it not be better just to ignore him, my lady? Someone as beautiful and charming as yourself does not need to waste time on a heartless young man.'

'He is the same age as I!'

'For sure, for sure. As you wish. I shall tell him.'

'Do that, and I shall call on you tomorrow to hear his answer.'

'But I may not see him.'

'He is just arrived in the box opposite, with the Comte de Mornay.'

Frances looked across the lighted theatre and saw Mr Jamie Ferguson watching them avidly. He did not look at all like a man who had been put off the love of his life with lies. She felt very young and silly. Here she was being used by this harpy to set up an adulterous affair. And if Mr Ferguson was the type of man to want an adulterous affair, then she did not want to have anything to do with him. Lady Dunwilde left. Other young men crowded into the box and Frances forced herself to sparkle and flirt and did it to such good effect that the comte, levelling his quizzing-glass across the theatre, said to Jamie, 'Miss Haggard is in looks tonight. She is a fetching little creature.'

But Jamie only saw Frances as a conduit for his hopes and desires. The performance was beginning again. He would need to content himself until the next interval to find out what it was that Lady Dunwilde had said.

But at the next interval, he could not get near Frances. Her box was full of callers and she made no effort to speak to him alone. He would need to wait until the ball after the opera.

The comte was finding a similar difficulty in getting near Jane when he visited Harriet's box. Mr Farley was there and the comte heard that tiresome man remind Jane of their engagement to go driving on the following day. He was surprised to find himself experiencing a bitter, sour feeling which, after some quick thought, he identified, to his surprise, as jealousy. He slipped out of the box and summoned one of the opera footmen and told him to go into the Duchess of Rowcester's box and tell Mr Farley his mother wished his company immediately. He waited

120

until he saw Mr Farley leave, then re-entered the box and sat down quickly next to Jane.

'Alone at last,' he said.

'That is because the performance is about to begin,' said Jane.

'It is?' He settled himself more comfortably in his chair. 'Too fatiguing to return to my own box. I shall stay here.' Jane looked to Harriet for help, but Harriet's eyes were fixed on the stage. Jane was barely aware of the last act, only of the handsome figure next to her, aware that his eyes were often fixed on her face. Her breathing began to become rapid and shallow and she was relieved when at last the performance was over. But it seemed the comte was going to accompany them through to the ball, offering an arm to each and smiling all around in a sort of proprietorial way.

Harriet, noticing all the little envious glances cast in their direction, decided to indulge the comte. In Jane's averted glance, Harriet only read that Jane did not particularly care for the comte and decided it would be safe to use his escort to bolster Jane's standing in society. It did a lady no harm to be seen to be courted by a rich rake, provided that lady was well-chaperoned.

For her part, Frances knew the moment had come when she had to put an end to the lies. So when Jamie immediately approached her and asked permission to take her to the floor for a waltz, she sadly agreed. 'I have a confession to make,' she murmured. He bent his head and smiled indulgently, 'What have you been up to?'

'Telling lies,' said Frances.

'Bad lies?'

'Very bad.'

'Do you want to tell me?'

'I must. Lady Dunwilde did not say any of those cruel things. She wishes to have an affair with you.'

His face darkened. 'What? What is it you say?'

'I was to tell you there was still hope.'

'Why did you lie to me? Why?'

'I do not approve of adultery. I do not like Lady Dunwilde.'

She raised her eyes to his but he was looking across the room to where Lady Dunwilde was dancing and his face was suddenly radiant. 'I am sorry,' whispered Frances.

'Eh? Oh, all forgiven, I assure you.'

At the end of the dance, after the promenade, he escaped after surrendering Frances up to her next partner. As she was led off, Frances watched him cross the floor to claim Lady Dunwilde's hand for the dance, saw the quick exchange, saw the baleful look Lady Dunwilde cast in her direction, and tried to persuade herself she had done the right thing. Despite her distress, she noticed that Jane appeared to be enjoying the comte's company. They were sitting out, drinking lemonade, and Jane did not seem to be aware that Clarence Farley was glowering at them from behind a pillar.

'So although you tease me about my rakish disposition, Miss North,' the comte was saying, 'I am glad you can tease me about something. Do you think rakes can ever reform?'

'I am not well enough up in the ways of the world,' said Jane, 'but no, I do not think so. You are a sad flirt.'

'On the contrary, at the moment I am a very happy flirt. Tell me why you have honoured Farley with your company.'

'He is . . .'

'Safe?'

She gave a reluctant laugh and he was pleased to hear that laugh.

'Yes, safe. Talk about something else.'

'Let us observe Miss Frances. Smitten as I am by your charms, I remarked that Miss Frances talked very seriously to my friend Mr Ferguson during the waltz. Mr Ferguson looks startled, angry, then elated. Your little friend looks cast down, although she is putting a brave face on it. Off goes Mr Ferguson to Lady Dunwilde's side.'

'I do not know,' said Jane loyally, although she was sure that Frances must have told Mr Ferguson the truth.

'You even lie prettily. Another forbidden subject. So let us return to you. Do you have brothers and sisters?'

'Four brothers in the military,' said Jane.

'And are you fond of them?'

'I barely know them. I was born when they were grown men. My mother did not live for very long after I was born.'

'So you were raised by your father. Who is your father?'

'Mr North,' said Jane, opening and shutting her fan nervously.

'And Mr North is a landowner?'

'Yes, Monsieur le Comte.'

'How large is his property?'

'I do not know. How large is your property, sir?'

'I do not own land . . . yet. I was brought to this country by my parents after the Terror. They brought a quantity of jewels with them but settled down in an undistinguished suburb to eke out their remaining days by selling one jewel after another. I became interested in stocks and shares, a genteel form of gambling. I took the remaining jewels and was able to make a fortune for myself and them, so that their final days were passed in comfort. I keep thinking of the family lands in Burgundy. Perhaps they will be restored to me. Perhaps I may go back there one day. But I have a mind to buy myself a property in England. Perhaps in Durbyshire? What do you think, Miss North?'

'I have no views on the matter.'

He smiled at her, his blue eyes glinting in that mocking way which disturbed her so much. 'I can see it now – a pleasant mansion, some rolling acres, and children tumbling about the place. In my mind's eye, it is always sunny. I shall return from inspecting my property and she will be there to meet me with the children gathered about her skirts.'

'Monsieur le Comte,' said Jane with a slight edge to

her voice, 'you are a romantic. I am persuaded that your wife will be entertaining her friends while the children are abovestairs in the schoolroom being bullied by some ferocious governess.'

'Which is what happened to you, Miss North?'

'We were not discussing me.'

'True. But think again of my picture, Miss North. Do you yourself not have dreams? Do you not imagine having your own establishment with a loving husband? Close your eyes. Cannot you hear the laughter of the children and the sound of the wind in the trees?'

Jane thought of her grim childhood, and to her dismay a tear rolled down her cheek.

'Now what have I done?' asked the comte. 'I would not distress you for the world. Pray tell me what ails you, Miss North. Your servant, your devoted slave, ma'am.' The laughter had left his eyes. There was only kindness and concern.

Jane pulled herself together with a great effort, for that kindness in his eyes evoked in her a strong temptation to lean on him, to tell him everything, to ask for his help. But perhaps that was all part of the comte's lethal charm.

Clarence Farley bowed before her. 'Our dance, Miss North.'

She rose to her feet and curtsied. The comte rose at the same time and bowed and then went off in search of Harriet.

Harriet was talking to Mrs Haggard. 'Duchess, may I have your permission to take Miss North driving?'

Harriet looked up at him, thinking again how handsome he was. She thought quickly. It was only a drive in the Park. Jane could not come to any harm. She appeared to be getting on so well with Clarence Farley. That interest would keep her safe. And it would do no harm to give Mr Farley a little competition. 'Miss North is engaged to go driving tomorrow,' she said. 'Perhaps the day after? At five?'

'Delighted,' said the comte.

Mrs Haggard watched him go. 'Are you sure that was wise?'

'Oh, I think so,' replied Harriet. 'I have made extensive inquiries about this comte. He does not have a reputation for seducing virgins. He is amusing himself with London's latest beauty. To change the subject, Frances is quite a success.'

'Yes,' agreed Mrs Haggard complacently. 'We had many callers today. I am no longer worried about her prospects.' But she looked up in surprise as Frances came up to her at the end of the dance and said hesitantly, 'Would you mind very much, Mama, if I were to return with Jane after the ball?'

'I do not see why,' said Mrs Haggard rather crossly. 'It is Her Grace to whom you should be addressing your request.'

Harriet, seeing the pain at the back of Frances's eyes, said quickly, 'You know what it is like. They want to discuss beaux. Of course you are welcome, Frances. And there is no need for a footman to bring your night-rail, for I can supply you with anything that

126

is necessary, and one of Jane's gowns will serve you for the morning.'

Mrs Haggard opened her mouth to protest and then closed it. A duchess was a duchess, and it would do Frances's consequence no harm to be seen on such free and easy terms with the Duchess of Rowcester and her protegée.

So, at the end of the ball, an uncharacteristically silent Frances travelled home with Harriet and Jane. Jane was not surprised when Frances appeared in her bedchamber after she had courteously said goodnight to Harriet, crying, 'I must tell you all. It is all too dreadful.'

Jane listened sympathetically while Frances told her about revealing the truth to Mr Ferguson, ending up with a wail of 'And he was too happy to reprimand me!'

'I think you really must forget about him, Frances,' said Jane. 'You cannot still have any feelings for a man who is even contemplating an affair with a married woman.'

'It is the fault of that friend of his, that comte,' said Frances mulishly. 'Just because that frivolous Frenchman finds it amusing to court married ladies, there is no reason for Mr Ferguson to do the same. Do you think he can be reformed by the love of a good woman?'

'Meaning yourself?' Jane looked at her sadly. 'I do not think so. From my observation, the ladies of society marry for convenience and then fall in love afterwards, and not with their husbands.'

'But the Duchess of Rowcester is so in love with her husband, and he with her. Everyone talks of it.'

'There are exceptions, Frances, but it is not usual, or so I believe.'

'What of love? What of romance? Would you settle for someone like Clarence Farley?'

'Yes, I can see that I might. It would mean freedom of a kind, an establishment of my own, children.' A little smile curved Jane's lips and she said dreamily, 'Rolling acres and a tidy mansion and the children at my skirts when he rode home.' For a moment she saw herself on a summer's evening standing outside such a house, but the man on horseback coming down the drive was the comte, not Mr Farley. She blinked the bright dream away.

The comte, after having said goodnight to Mr Ferguson, waited in vain for his carriage to be brought round, finding after quite half an hour that someone had told his coachman to go home, that he intended to walk.

He set off through the dark streets in his evening finery, wondering what his valet would find out about Jane, marvelling the whole time that his mind hardly ever strayed away from her.

So absorbed was he in his thoughts that he almost did not hear the pounding of feet after him until it was too late. As it was, he swung around, drawing his dress-sword, and swerved to the side at the same time, just missing a murderous blow from a cudgel. With his back to the wall of a building, he faced his assailants, for there were three of them. They tried to rush him but his sword flickered like lightning, piercing the man with the cudgel in the arm and then sweeping round to dart at the other two, who fell back, turned round and took to their heels. The man with the wounded arm was stumbling off. The comte caught him, swung him round and held the point of his sword to his throat.

'What were you after, mon brave?' he asked.

'Your jewels, money, that's all. I swear.'

The point of the comte's sword pressed a little harder into the man's neck. 'Try again. Who sent you?'

'No one, yer honour,' gasped the man.

The comte thrust him away in disgust. 'Faugh, you smell abominably.' But his assailant, finding himself released, suddenly took to his heels and ran away with surprising speed, down a dark alley to his left. The comte debated whether to follow him but thought the man's friends might be waiting. He could not believe the attack was an accident. Someone had sent his coach away. Someone had wanted him to walk home.

Someone had wanted him dead.

SEVEN

I feel the pangs of disappointed love.
NICHOLAS ROWE

Two weeks had passed since Lady Farley's ball and Sir Philip and Mr Davy were closeted in the hotel office.

'You have the necklace?' asked Mr Davy.

'Yes, they handed it over with no trouble at all,' said Sir Philip. 'Now what about this play? I put the idea in Lady Farley's head before I left.

'It is Act Two of *The Beaux Stratagem*. We have a few professional actors, including myself, but Lady Bountiful is played by Lady Farley. You play the part of one of the stage-coach passengers at Boniface's inn. But as soon as Scene Two has been underway for a couple of minutes, you rise and exit. They will think you are playing the part of a departing passenger.' Mr Davy took out a roll of paper and spread it out on the desk between them. 'Here is a plan of the house which I have sketched for you. Here is my lady's bedchamber. If she plans to wear the necklace in the play, I will dissuade her and say it is not suitable for a Restoration comedy. You must make your way to her bedchamber by the back stairs. The servants are to be present at the play, standing behind the guests. Lady Farley wants as big an audience as possible for her talents.'

'Can she act?'

'Not in the slightest. She seemed surprised that she actually had to learn lines and could not command a servant to do it for her. But that is not your affair. I have had to endure such performances before.'

'What do you play?'

'Gibbet, the highwayman.'

'What if her jewel box is locked?'

'Sir Philip, unless I am not mistaken, you are perfectly capable of springing the simple lock usually found on jewel boxes.'

'Maybe. And when is this to take place?'

'This evening.'

'This evening!' echoed Sir Philip in alarm. 'Good God, man, what if I had not yet returned!'

'You sent an express to Lady Fortescue saying exactly when you were to return. It all worked out beautifully. You will not forget your promise?'

'No, no,' said Sir Philip testily. 'I shall not interfere with your friendship with Miss Tonks. Thinking of marrying her, hey?'

'I did not say that.'

Good, thought Sir Philip, then I shall propose, and I can say in all innocence that you talked only of friendship.

'What if it does not work?' he asked aloud, biting his knuckles nervously.

'Provided you are quick and deft, it should work.'

'That son of hers, Clarence; I don't want him snooping around.'

'He plays Aimwell. He fancies himself as another Kean.'

'Then it should work,' said Sir Philip. 'You have not told any of the others?'

'Of course not. You have my word.'

For what that's worth, thought Sir Philip nastily.

'I am becoming increasingly concerned about Sir Philip,' said Lady Fortescue to Colonel Sandhurst and Miss Tonks later that day. 'He is nervous and jumpy. He disappeared to the country and refused to tell us where he was going. I hope he isn't putting our money on horses.'

'He can't,' said the colonel. 'I keep tight control of the money, and Miss Tonks here does the accounting.'

'We are become so wealthy,' said Miss Tonks wistfully. 'Do we sell when our prince leaves, or not?'

The colonel held his breath.

'I think we might,' said Lady Fortescue.

A look of sheer gladness lit up the elderly colonel's face.

But Lady Fortescue's next words wiped it away. 'I thought,' she said in a considering way, 'that as we have all dealt so extremely well together, that we could all share a house in Town and begin to entertain.'

Colonel Sandhurst's happy picture of a trim manor in the country, shared with his bride, Lady Fortescue, whirled about his head and vanished.

Miss Tonks did not know what to think. Before the advent of Mr Davy she would have been delighted at the prospect of company for her declining years, but now she felt afraid. The magic title of 'Mrs' seemed as far away as ever. What if Mr Davy used his share of the money to launch some theatrical venture? The colonel, Lady Fortescue, and Sir Philip were all so very old that they might soon die and she would be left alone again. Mr Davy was pleasant and courteous to her at all times; in fact, he went out of his way to seek her company. But how could a man who had spent his life surrounded by beautiful actresses contemplate marriage to a faded spinster in her forties?

Also, Mr Davy had joined Sir Philip immediately on his return, and they had been closeted in the office. There was something conspiratorial about them. Besides, Mr Davy had organized a theatrical event at Lady Farley's, but when Miss Tonks had hinted shyly that she would like to go with him and be of help, he had not seemed to hear her.

She saw the pain on the colonel's face. She knew the colonel wanted to marry Lady Fortescue and so decided to leave him alone with Lady Fortescue while she herself tried to find out what Mr Davy was up to with Sir Philip.

When Miss Tonks had left the room, the colonel cleared his throat. He was about to remind Lady Fortescue of her promise to consider his offer of marriage and that they should retire together to the country, but all at once he found he could not. He dreaded an outright rejection. Lady Fortescue was talking about menus and the possibility of getting new curtains for all the rooms and the colonel took that to be a sign that she did not mean to sell up at all, for what was the point in refurbishing a place they were about to leave?

That evening Sir Philip, in the costume of a stage-coach passenger, which meant wearing his own clothes and having his elderly face smeared with nasty greasepaint, stayed on the stage for a whole two minutes before looking at his watch with a well-feigned start and taking his leave. He made his way to the back stairs with ease, having studied the map Mr Davy had drawn for him. As Mr Davy had predicted, most of the servants appeared to be at the back of the audience. He climbed to the upper floors, and consulting his map again by the light of an oil lamp in one of the passages, located Lady Farley's apartment. With a sigh of relief he looked around. He walked through her sitting room to her bedroom. The jewel box lay on the toilet-table, a large brass-bound affair. He took out his penknife and examined the lock.

Downstairs, Mr Davy saw trouble. Lady Farley, who had been like the worst prima donna during rehearsals, had considered the applause for her performance in the first scene of the Second Act not sufficient. To his horror, he saw her get up and stalk off in a sulk, followed by her maid. There was no way he could rush and warn Sir Philip.

Upstairs, Sir Philip had sprung the lock on the jewel box. With a smile of triumph, he took out the real necklace and substituted the fake. To his even greater relief, the lock proved undamaged and he was able to close the box again. There would be no signs of burglary. He was just making for the door when he heard Lady Farley's voice, high and petulant. 'I gave a fine performance, Clorinda, did I not?' and the maid's answering, 'Yes, indeed, my lady. You rivalled Siddons.'

'Then why did not they give me the applause I deserved?'

Sir Philip dived under the bed. He lay there sweating with fear while Lady Farley complained that her nerves were overset and she would retire early and that no one appreciated her, all punctuated by the sycophantic compliments of the maid.

Let her go to sleep, please let her go to sleep, prayed Sir Philip. He heard the maid retire. He heard the body on the bed above him turn and twist, searching for a comfortable position. And then his nose tickled. He grabbed it to stifle the sneeze he felt rising. In the treacherous way of sneezes, it appeared to subside, but the minute he released hold of his nose, the sneeze erupted.

He heard Lady Farley's cry of alarm. There was only one thing to be done. He shot out from under the bed, whipped back the bedcurtain, and cried, 'Do not betray me. I did all for love.'

In the light of a candle on the bedtable, Lady Farley shrank back against the pillows and stared up at Sir Philip's face, where the greasepaint had melted as he sweated with fear and was running in streaks.

'Do not cry out, beloved,' he panted. 'I love you!' Had he left it at that, then Lady Farley, whose hand was already reaching for the bell-rope, would have screamed for help, but fear had inspired Sir Philip. 'It was your performance, my lady,' he gabbled. 'Magnificent. I have never seen anything like it. You stole my poor old heart away.'

The fear and outrage vanished from Lady Farley's face and she actually simpered. 'Why, Sir Philip. You old rogue!'

'I cannot help it,' said Sir Philip, striking his bosom. 'I am ever susceptible to beauty. I had to see you alone, to tell you how I adore you. Now, having told you of my love, pray let me retire and leave you to your slumbers.'

What an awful woman she looked, he thought, with her skin ruined by too many years of application of white lead and her hair thinned by dyeing.

She gave him a flirtatious smile. 'Do you know, Sir Philip,' she said, 'I think such love should receive its reward, do not you?'

'I could not dare to hope for any favour,' cried Sir Philip in genuine anguish.

'Silly man. Come here.'

And just before he did what he had to do, Sir Philip thought of his colleagues with real hatred. The things he did for them!

The following day, Mr Jamie Ferguson prepared to meet his love. Lord Dunwilde was to be in the House of Lords that afternoon to make an important speech.

Lady Dunwilde had told him that she had given the servants the afternoon off. The road to adultery lay straight before him. He was just adjusting his cravat when the comte was ushered in.

'Good day,' said the comte, subsiding gracefully into a chair. ' I came to suggest you accompany me. I am to take Miss North driving. I have been deliberately cold in that direction so as not to alarm her or her protectoress. But Farley sees more and more of her at ball and party, the safe, so dull Farley. If you came with me, perhaps we could take up little Miss Frances. Then Miss North would relax more in my company.'

'Alas, my friend, I am bound for Lady Dunwilde's.'

'Oho, and his lordship is known to be giving an important speech in the House – or rather, important only to the old bore himself. So you are about to have your heart's desire? Eh, bien, I shall nonetheless call on Miss Frances first and see if she is free and allowed to come with such an old rake as myself, although come to think of it, she is so extremely popular that I shall probably find she is engaged.'

'Miss Haggard popular!'

'My dear Jamie, because she lied to you about what your soon-to-be mistress told her and you have been so studiously avoiding her, you must not yet have noticed that she never sits out a dance. She is a prime favourite.'

'To be sure, she has a certain charm.'

'She will make some man a good wife. All that liveliness and warmth and honesty. I shall leave you to your fate. Or rather, I can set you down at Lady Dunwilde's on my way there.'

Jamie glanced at the clock and gave a reluctant laugh. 'If I go now, I shall be too early and may meet his lordship on the doorstep. I tell you what, I shall call on Miss Frances with you. It is silly to bear a grudge against one so young and heedless.'

'Splendid. Let us go.'

To Jamie's surprise, Mrs Haggard's drawing room appeared to be full of gentlemen callers. To the comte's request to take Frances with him while he drove Jane, Mrs Haggard said, 'I am afraid, as you can see, Frances has too many people to entertain this afternoon. Perhaps another time.'

A footman carried around a tray with wine and cakes. Jamie helped himself to a glass of wine. He had come to talk to Frances and so he felt he may as well stay until he did. He still had plenty of time. Besides, Fiona Dunwilde had been cruel to him, damned cruel, and so she deserved to be made to wait a little. And now she is being damned cruel to her husband, said a voice in his head. He did not take her away from you by trickery or guile. She went gladly.

He joined the little court of men around Frances who were looking at her sketches. Somehow, by dint of inserting himself in front of her admirers, he managed to isolate her from them until they were left briefly alone.

'Forgiven me yet?' asked Frances in her usual direct way.

He smiled. 'Of course.'

Her face brightened. 'Why, then we can be comfortable again.'

He laughed. 'I could forgive the world this day. I am on my way to see Lady Dunwilde.'

Her expressive face became a mask of distaste and she said primly, 'Do not let me detain you. Ah, Mr Samson, you are lurking in the background and you will quite break my heart and you do not admire my sketches.'

A young man bounded eagerly forward. He was, Jamie guessed, only about a year or two older than Frances. He had an engaging smile and a mop of carefully coiffed blond curls. Jamie moved away. He heard Frances say something and heard this Mr Samson laugh.

All at once he felt rather grubby, and what had appeared to him earlier like a rapturous adventure seemed now in his eyes just to be another sordid society intrigue. The comte would not be troubled by conscience, he thought, looking across at his hand-some friend. But the comte, he realized with a little shock, despite his reputation, had never really hurt anyone. The ladies were either widows or racy matrons with philandering husbands who did not give a rap what their wives got up to, provided it did not appear in the windows of the print-shops or the daily newspapers. His feet felt like lead as he walked to the door. He looked back. Little Frances was once more surrounded by her admirers. She appeared to have forgotten his very existence. She looked young and happy and innocent.

'Are you coming?' asked the comte at his elbow. 'We have stayed our regulation ten minutes.'

'Yes, yes, I suppose so,' said Jamie fretfully. They made their goodbyes and walked together out to the comte's carriage.

The comte climbed in and took the reins. His tiger jumped on the back. 'Come along, mon ami,' said the comte lightly. 'I will leave you at your lady-love.'

'I will walk, thank you,' said Jamie abruptly. The comte gave a Gallic shrug and drove off As he turned the corner of the street, he twisted his head and looked back. Jamie was still standing there, his hat in his hand, looking up at the house.

Harriet walked into Jane's bedroom just as the maid was putting the finishing touches to Jane's hair. 'You have such a busy calendar these days that I cannot keep pace with your engagements,' said Harriet. 'Mr Farley again?'

'You forget, Harriet,' said Jane. 'The Comte de Mornay is to take me driving.'

'I suppose I must trust him to behave,' said Harriet doubtfully. 'I have been glad to see that he regards you with a certain indifference, Jane.'

And Jane should have been glad of that as well, instead of remembering all the times she had danced with Mr Farley conscious the whole time of the tall, handsome Frenchman moving about the ballroom.

'I am going to settle down and read a letter from my husband,' Harriet went on. 'I have been saving it for a quiet moment.'

They walked down to the drawing room together just as the comte was announced. Harriet was struck again by his looks and thought that he and Jane made a handsome couple. It was a pity their characters were so unsuited.

'I called to see if Miss Haggard would care to join us but found her surrounded by admiring gentlemen,' said the comte as he handed Jane up into his carriage. 'I am lucky to find you not similarly besieged.'

'The duchess sometimes refuses callers when she wishes a quiet day,' said Jane. 'She has received a letter from her husband which she has been treasuring so that she may read it when she is alone.'

They drove off in the direction of the Park in the comte's phaeton, his horses stepping out proudly. The day was fine and warm. Jane was wearing a broad-brimmed straw hat with lilac silk ribbons, a lilac silk gown embroidered with lilac flowers, and around her shoulders she wore a handsome Norfolk shawl. She looked around at the Fashionables strolling on the pavements and once more wondered how long this holiday, this respite from the agonies of home, would last. She had received a letter from her old nurse confirming that her letters had been sent on to her father and that he had not replied to any of them. But the day would soon come when his pride would not suffer a stubborn daughter and then he would go in search of her. When that day occurred, she had told her old nurse to tell her father the truth, that she was in London, or her father might take out his anger on the nurse.

The comte, glancing sideways at her, thought that the light and shade of different emotions chased across her face like cloud shadows over the countryside.

'So how are you enjoying the Season?' he asked, as he turned his carriage in at the gates of the Park.

'Very well, I thank you,' said Jane politely.

'Rumour has it you are to marry Mr Farley.'

'Indeed? Society is full of rumours.'

'He is not for you. He has a bad temper and would beat you.'

'Mr Farley? You are funning. He is all that is amiable.'

'I have warned you, Miss North. I do not think you know him very well. I have made certain inquiries and do not like what I have heard.'

'Would you like me to believe the rumours that I hear of you?' asked Jane, tilting her lilac silk parasol so that she could see his face. 'That you are a heartless philanderer?'

'I *was* a trifle flighty,' he said easily. 'But how I have changed! I am sedate and boring and highly respectable. Have you noticed me paying any particular attention to any female this Season?'

'I do not know, sir. I have not remarked your behaviour particularly.'

'Alas, all my good motives gone for nothing! You are heartless, Miss North.'

'Not I,' retorted Jane with a reluctant laugh.

'When you laugh like that with that beautiful mouth of yours, I feel like kissing you.'

'Monsieur le Comte!'

'Why not? Do you not think of me even a little, Miss Jane North? Do you never wonder what it would be like to feel my lips against your own?'

'If you are determined to continue in this strain; then I suggest you take me home.'

'Home being?'

'Why, Harriet's – the duchess. Where else?'

'I mean your home. You never said where it was.'

'Durbyshire.'

'Exactly where?'

The parasol tilted to hide her face. 'Oh, look,' said Jane, 'there is Mrs Barber.' The comte bowed in Mrs Barber's direction and Jane nodded. Mrs Barber, who barely knew either of them and whom Jane had only recognized as one of Mrs Haggard's friends who had been pointed out to her at a party, looked gratified.

Now they were among the throng of Fashionables and so were too busy nodding and bowing to make conversation. Jane began to relax. They would make the round a couple of times and then the comte would take her home and she could settle down again to contemplate the idea of marriage to Mr Farley. He was on the point of proposing, of that she was sure. All she had to do on the road home was to parry the comte's questions. Nothing out of the way would happen.

Harriet had been enjoying her husband's letter. He was on his way home and would shortly be in Paris. Paris! Her eyes glowed. He said that by the time his letter reached her, he might even be at the coast, finding a ship to Dover. The servants would meet him at Dover and he planned to drive to London as fast as possible. She relished every affectionate phrase. There was still pain over the loss of her child, but now sheer gladness as well that the estrangement between herself and her husband was over. And then she got to the end of the letter.

'*I did not tell you of an intriguing adventure on the road to Milan,*' the duke had written.

I was at an inn and overheard conspirators plotting the release of Napoleon. This, my dear, is nothing out of the common way, as many who gained power and influence under that monster's reign of terror wish their positions back. But one of them was English, I will swear, and they were planning to kill a certain Comte de Mornay who has, it appears, been instrumental in foiling other plots. A friend in Milan before I left told me that Mornay was in London. I wrote to Horse Guards telling them to warn him. And now, my beloved wife . . .

Harriet put down the letter. Jane was driving with the comte and someone was trying to kill the comte and that put Jane in danger. She called for her maid and changed into a carriage dress and sent a footman with an urgent note to the Poor Relation calling for help, never for a moment in her distress thinking that it would have been more sensible to call out the Runners than to send to such elderly people as the colonel, Sir Philip, and Lady Fortescue for help. Then, with her coachman driving, she set out for the Park herself.

The hoteliers felt they could not wait to order a carriage from the livery stables, and with Sir Philip, exhausted and shaky after his adventure of the night before, complaining loudly that this is what came of being too mean to own a carriage of their own, they hailed a smelly hack and howled to the driver to take them to the Park.

But when they got to the Park, they were stopped by a ranger who was not going to let a battered hack anywhere near the fashionable throng and so they had to get out and walk, with Sir Philip stumbling after them over the grass, clutching his side and moaning he was not long for this world.

The comte, unaware of all these people rushing to his rescue, reached the end of the second round and regretfully decided he must obey the dictates of fashion and take Jane home.

And then a shot rang out, a loud report, and he felt the wind of a ball as it whined past his face. His horses reared and plunged in fright and then took off across the grass, with Jane screaming and clinging to the rail. To Jane the Park passed her in a blur of frightened staring faces from carriages and trees and bushes. Shouting and swearing in French, the comte eventually controlled his maddened horses, hanging on to the reins, letting out a slow breath of relief when they finally slowed. He had left his tiger behind that day, so first he jumped down and ran to their heads, patting and soothing them, until the quietened horses began to crop the grass.

Then he returned to Jane. He lifted her gently in his arms down from the carriage and set her on the grass. He looked solemnly down into her white face and said gently, 'We are safe now.'

'That was a shot,' cried Jane. 'Someone was trying to kill us!'

'Me, I think. How white you are. You need colour. Even your beautiful lips are white.' He bent his head and kissed her on the mouth, and Jane, too overset, as she told herself later, to push him away, clung to his shoulders and let his mouth caress hers in a long, lingering kiss.

The comte at last freed her mouth and smiled down at her dreamily. 'Would that an assassination attempt happen to me every day so that I might claim such a reward.' He turned his head and looked across the Park. 'Good heavens, here comes your patroness, looking like thunder, and with those hoteliers.'

Harriet had taken up the hoteliers who, unlike Harriet, had not stopped to change into appropriate dress. Miss Tonks was wearing a morning gown and lace cap, the colonel certainly was as correct as usual, as was Lady Fortescue, but Sir Philip was in his dressing gown and nightcap and Mr Davy in his shirt-sleeves.

'We are safe,' said the comte, hoping Harriet had not witnessed that kiss.

'What happened?' demanded Harriet. 'People were shouting about a shot.'

'Someone shot at me,' said the comte pleasantly, as if, thought Jane, someone trying to kill you were an everyday occurrence. 'Why are you all here?'

'The Park rangers are coming,' said Harriet. 'I received a letter from my husband in which he said he had overheard a plot in an inn near Milan to kill you. I will take Jane home with me and perhaps when you have dealt with affairs here you may join us, Monsieur le Comte, and tell us about it. Jane, come with me.'

Jane, overset with conflicting emotions, felt that she should tell Harriet about that kiss, but at the same time she hoped Harriet had not seen anything, or she would forbid Jane to see the comte again. Not that it was important that she see the comte again, for she was surely going to marry the bad-tempered Mr Farley, was she not? Jane felt quite dizzy with all these thoughts. She was squeezed into Harriet's carriage beside the hoteliers.

As she was driven out of the Park, she saw Mr Farley standing up in his carriage and staring at her. Oh, heavens, he would call to see how she was. But if she was even considering marrying the man, she should not be, oh, dear, dismayed at the thought of his breaking into what, now the shock was receding, seemed like an exciting adventure.

She replied to the others' eager questions. All she knew, said Jane, was that there had been the sound of a shot which had narrowly missed the comte; his horses had bolted, but fortunately neither of them had come to any harm.

And then Harriet said, 'It would be as well, dear Jane, to keep clear of this comte in future if he is going to be the target for some assassin.'

'That seems too hard,' protested Jane. 'He needs our help, surely.'

'We will see what he has to say,' said Harriet. 'I think we could all do with a refreshing dish of tea.'

'Brandy, more like,' muttered Sir Philip. He was feeling old and tired and he knew he must set out for the duke's country home on the following day to return the real necklace to its case.

They had been seated a few minutes in Harriet's pleasant drawing room when Clarence Farley was announced. It was a day of surprises. Jane said hurriedly, 'I am too overset to see him. Pray say we are not at home.'

And so Clarence, looking every bit as angry as the comte had claimed he was, stomped off. But he waited outside in his carriage and had the doubtful pleasure of seeing the Comte de Mornay arrive and be admitted. He waited all the same, expecting the comte to reappear shortly, having been given the same message as himself, but as the minutes dragged on he realized to his increased fury that the comte was a welcome guest where he himself was not.

The news of the attempt on the comte's life spread through the West End like lightning. Frances and her mother received the news very quickly, for Mrs Barber had just been about to leave the Park when the

148

assassination attempt happened. She had driven straight to her friend, Mrs Haggard, to tell her the news.

'Poor Jane!' exclaimed Frances. 'Mama, I must have the carriage. I must call.'

'But Mrs Barber is just arrived.'

'I do not need you to come, Mama,' said Frances, already halfway out of the room, and without waiting to hear any protest from her mother she shouted down the stairs to the butler to have the carriage brought round and then called up the stairs to her maid to make ready to accompany her.

As she tripped out onto the pavement, she stopped in surprise. Jamie was standing there. He saw her and a rather sheepish smile crossed his face. Frances thought quickly. The other callers had left an hour ago. Either he had already visited Lady Dunwilde and returned, or he had been there all along.

He bowed low and said, 'It is late to go driving.'

'I am on my way to see Jane,' said Frances. 'Someone tried to kill your friend, the Comte de Mornay.'

'Good heavens! May I come with you?'

'I should be glad of your escort,' said Frances, wishing her maid were not with her, not to mention the coachman in front and the footman on the backstrap. She wanted to ask him about Lady Dunwilde, but could hardly ask him outright in front of the servants.

'What happened?' he demanded as the carriage moved off. She told him the little she knew and then said in a low voice, 'And how was your friend? Your *female* friend?'

'I am afraid I do not know,' he said. 'The air was so pleasant outside your house that I felt rooted to the pavement and could not move.'

Her eyes were shining under the little brim of her saucy hat. 'You did not go?'

'No, Miss Frances, I did not.'

'Why?'

'Later,' he said. He did not quite know himself. Only that as he stood outside her house, he had felt that as long as he stood there he was safe from taking an action which might leave him feeling nothing but shame. He felt he had managed to hang on to his immortal soul, and then almost laughed out loud at that dramatic thought.

When they were both ushered into Harriet's drawing room, they stared in surprise at the hoteliers. Sir Philip, in his dressing gown and nightcap, was curled up in an armchair by the fireplace, fast asleep.

They listened to the comte's account of his adventure. 'But why should anyone want to kill you?' asked Frances.

'I may as well tell you now that I am retired, so to speak, from business,' said the comte. 'I proved myself useful to the British government as a spy. In the earlier years, before I knew my City ventures would become profitable, it gave me adventure and provided me with an adequate income.'

'So you are not just a dilettante! You are a brave

man!' said Frances ingenuously. 'But what danger you are in! How can you protect yourself?'

'Things are not so black. I have a surprise for you. Just before you arrived, the authorities called here, for I told the Park rangers where I could be found. The culprit was seen.

'Who is he? Some ruffian?' asked Harriet.

'No, it was young Freemantle.'

Jamie gasped. 'Not Jerry Freemantle?'

'The same.'

'But he is of good family!'

'Let us think about Mr Freemantle,' said the comte. 'Deep in debt and duns at the door, as everyone knows. Cut off by his family. Wild, heedless, and usually drunk. Suppose someone approached him with an offer of money to shoot me? It would look like a very easy way of making money. I do not think for a moment that young Freemantle is a supporter of Napoleon. I think what is interesting is who paid him to try to kill me. The militia have gone to try to find him, and weakling that he is, I have no doubt he will talk, and then, dear Duchess, we will find the name of this Englishman your husband overheard. An Englishman who speaks fluent French is a rarity.'

'But we in society speak French the whole time,' exclaimed Jamie, who prided himself on his knowledge of that language.

'At the risk of hurting your feelings, mon ami, society appears, during the long wars with the French, to have developed a French language of its own which bears little resemblance to the original. I heard a

151

young lady say the other day, "Donnez-moi ça dos," by which she meant, "Give me that back."'

'And what was up with that?' asked Jamie, puzzled.

The comte raised his eyes to heaven. Harriet's butler interrupted by saying that there were 'some persons' below who wished to speak to the comte.

'I shall return soon,' said the comte, 'and hopefully with the news that young Freemantle has been found and has revealed the name of the arch-conspirator.'

They waited anxiously while he went belowstairs. 'I do hope it will soon be over,' said Harriet, finally breaking the silence. She looked up as her butler came back into the room. 'A message from Mr Farley, my lady,' he said, handing her a note folded in the shape of a cocked hat. She read it carefully and then looked at Jane with a little wry smile on her lips. 'Mr Farley is to call on me tomorrow afternoon to discuss a matter of some importance. You are, if I am not mistaken, to receive your first proposal, Jane.'

'A most suitable choice, if I may say so,' said Lady Fortescue. 'Quiet, stable, and worthy.'

'Eh, what?' demanded Sir Philip, who had woken up.

'I was commenting on the glad news that it appears Mr Clarence Farley is to apply for her hand in marriage of our Jane.'

'What's glad about it?' grumbled Sir Philip.

'He is surely a most suitable catch,' said Miss Tonks.

'Don't like him.' Sir Philip blinked sleepily about him. 'When we were catering at the ball, a little maid

152

dropped a glass. It did not even break, but Farley snarled at her, reduced her to tears and then told her to leave his mother's employ.'

'Perhaps we are all forgetting that the decision to marry Mr Farley or not is Jane's,' said Mr Davy.

All eyes turned on Jane. She pleated the fringe of her shawl nervously between her fingers. 'I do not know Mr Farley very well,' she said at last.

'Then I would counsel you to ask for time rather than throw away a good prospect out of hand,' said Lady Fortescue. 'Yes, I think that would be best. Plead for a little time to get to know each other better. He cannot take offence at that.'

All eyes turned to the door as the comte re-entered, his face grim. 'Young Freemantle hanged himself before they could get to him. This is a bad business.'

'Had he left no clues? No papers?' asked Jamie.

'Whatever he had, he had burned.'

'Then he must have had some loyalty to Napoleon after all,' exclaimed Jamie. 'Else why should he try to protect his fellow conspirators?'

The comte shrugged. 'Who knows? Perhaps he wanted only to protect other poor dupes like himself.'

'I do not want to appear too hard, Monsieur le Comte,' said Harriet. 'But as your life is in danger, it follows that anyone in your company is also putting their life in jeopardy. I must therefore suggest that Miss North should avoid your company for the present.'

'As you wish,' said the comte with seeming indifference. Jane found she was bitterly hurt. After that kiss, he should have at least shown some regret. He was a heartless flirt. She found herself becoming extremely angry indeed. She would see Mr Farley tomorrow, and although she would not accept his proposal, she would follow Lady Fortescue's advice and not turn him down flat.

EIGHT

Talk'st thou to me of 'ifs'? Thou art a traitor: Off with his head!

SHAKESPEARE

Jane could see no sign of the angry man that the comte had warned her about as Clarence Farley, seriously and intensely, got down on one knee and asked her to marry him.

'Please rise, Mr Farley,' she said, 'and sit by me.' Many of her doubts about him had receded. He looked so solid and dependable, a rock in a shifting world.

'I am very flattered by your proposal. You do me great honour. I have decided to be honest with you. Firstly, I would like a little time to get to know you better. Secondly, I am not Miss Jane North.'

His eyes were sharp. 'Who are you?' he asked bluntly.

'I am Lady Jane Fremney, daughter of the Earl of Durbyshire'

'But this is bewildering! Why the secrecy?'

In a low voice, Jane told him about how and why she had run away from home. She did not tell him of

155

her attempted suicide, something of which she was now bitterly ashamed. 'I must make it plain to you, sir,' she said earnestly, 'that even if we decide we do suit, then my father might not let me marry you and I will not have freedom to do so until my twenty-first birthday. I may have no dowry.'

His mind worked rapidly. His desire for her was waning fast. Because of the duchess's patronage, because of Jane's expensive clothes, he had expected a handsome dowry. He was all at once relieved that she had not accepted his proposal. On the other hand, he had a desire to spite the comte. It would also amuse him, he reflected, to send an express to the Earl of Durbyshire, telling him what his daughter was up to. In fact, he would do it as soon as he got home. Meanwhile he would pretend to want her despite her lack of dowry, and after hearing her story he was perfectly sure her father would not give her any.

He put his hand on his heart. 'Money means nothing to me. You are all I want. Pray say you will take tea with myself and my mother tomorrow. To get better acquainted, you should know my mother better.' And that would also keep his mother off his back, he thought sourly. She was always plaguing him to marry.

'I am honoured by your invitation and I accept,' said Jane. They both rose and he kissed her hands and bowed his way out.

Harriet entered almost as soon as he had gone. 'Did you accept him or tell him to wait?' she asked.

'I told him to wait,' said Jane. 'I also told him my true identity.'

'Oh, my dear, was that wise?'

'I warned him that I might not be able to marry him until I was twenty-one and that Papa might not give me a dowry and he said it did not matter. I am going to take tea with his mother tomorrow. I am . . . I am pleased with him, Harriet.'

Harriet looked at her shrewdly. 'But not in love with him?'

'I do not know what love is,' said Jane. 'But I trust him and respect him and that is surely a better basis for marriage than any easy, fleeting feelings.' And I cannot forget the comte's lips against mine in the Park, she thought with silent anguish, or how easily he accepted the fact that he should not see me while his life was in danger.

Frances was announced. Her eyes were sparkling and Harriet, guessing she had secrets to tell Jane, tactfully left the room.

'Mr Ferguson did not go to Lady Dunwilde yesterday,' said Frances breathlessly. 'He came here with me instead and he is to see me at the opera tonight. I am so happy I could cry.'

'I am happy for you.'

'And I have already received *two* proposals of marriage. Mama is in alt. I did not accept either, but it is very flattering to be in demand.'

'I, too, received a proposal of marriage today,' said Jane. 'Mr Farley.'

'Oh, dear.'

'Frances, you are incorrigible. He is all that is kind and good.'

'So you accepted him,' said Frances dismally.

'I told him to wait, that we should get to know each other better. And something else.' Jane told Frances of her real identity and Frances listened with avid interest to Jane's flight from home. To Frances it all seemed like some glorious Gothic romance. 'And you told Mr Farley all this? And he did not mind?'

'No, not in the slightest.'

'Well, to be sure, that was very noble of him. I must readjust my mind, for I had quite decided that it was to be the brave comte after all.'

'The Comte de Mornay has no interest in me.'

'He always watches you, even when he is putting up an appearance of ignoring you. I noticed that,' said Frances. 'I think he has been playing a game, playing a game of being cool towards you to animate your interest and not frighten you away.'

'*I* think he is a hardened flirt,' retorted Jane sharply.

'He has that reputation. Has he flirted with you?'

The desire to confide was too much for Jane. 'When the horses bolted with us after someone tried to shoot him, after they had quietened, he lifted me down and he kissed me . . . on the mouth.'

Frances heaved a sigh. 'Oh, that my Mr Ferguson would be so bold! Did you faint or slap his face?'

'Neither. I was too overcome. The shock, you see. But it meant nothing to him, for when Harriet told him that he should not see me so long as he was a target for an assassin, he accepted without a murmur.'

158

Frances looked at her doubtfully. 'A gentleman could hardly say anything else. And do you remember what Sir Philip said yesterday ... about Mr Farley's temper?'

'Sir Philip is always inclined to be waspish. I would guess that he would have encouraged me to go in any direction other than towards the comte.'

'I shall pray for you,' said Frances simply. 'I can see you are about to warn me not to tell anyone your secret and I shall not.'

The comte was reading a letter from his valet, Gerrard.

The Earl of Durbyshire employs a cook rather than a chef, and so I was able to ingratiate myself into her good graces, although she is like her kind, fat and bad-tempered and given to gin. I showed her the sketch and she cried out that it was a picture of Lady Jane Fremney, the earl's daughter. This Lady Jane is believed to be residing with her old nurse after having refused to marry one of the earl's elderly friends. Having learned what you wished, I changed the subject, claiming I was a London artist and that the sketch had been given to me by a fellow artist who must have taken the likeness when he was last in Durbyshire. The servants in general seem to hold this Lady Jane in great contempt for some reason, and I gather that her former governess, now elevated to companion, a Miss Stamp, is encouraged to treat her harshly.

The rest of the letter concerned the date of the valet's return to London.

So that explained the sadness at the back of her eyes, thought the comte, and then, with French pragmatism, he came to the conclusion that it was as well he was a wealthy man, for he doubted whether he could expect any dowry. The fact that he was determined to marry Lady Jane came first to him as a surprise, followed by tingling anticipation and then relief. Damn this assassin. He must find out who was at the back of the attempts on his life, or he would not only have to fight this earl for Jane's hand in marriage, but Harriet, Duchess of Rowcester, as well.

Frances called the next day just before Jane set out to the Farleys'. 'Such intrigue,' she cried. 'I met the comte with my beloved at the opera last night and could not but tell him of Mr Farley's proposal to you. He adopted an air of indifference, but I told him how you had said that you both must get to know each other better and that you were going to take tea with Lady Farley at four o'clock today. He stifled a yawn and drawled, "I hope she will be happy."'

'What else did you expect?' snapped Jane. 'That philanderer has no interest in me.'

'But I observed him when he thought I was not looking and his face was quite grim and set. I had not seen him look like that before. And he did not attend the ball but said goodnight and left at the second interval. Mr Ferguson, who knows him very well, said he looked very angry.'

'Pooh, it all means nothing to me,' said Jane, drawing on her gloves. 'I must go.'

Frances surveyed her anxiously. 'Do not be coerced into saying anything *definite*.'

'It is only tea, a brief visit.'

They walked down the stairs together. 'I mean,' persisted Frances, bobbing her head so that she could peer up under the brim of Jane's hat, 'do not let fear of your father drive you into an unsuitable marriage.'

'What my father planned for me was more unsuitable than you could possibly imagine, Frances. Do not worry about me. And I have something to tell you. I wager my best fan that Mr Ferguson will have asked for your hand in marriage by the end of the week.'

'If only that were true.' Frances looked rueful. 'He is so kind and friendly, but nothing of the lover there.'

'I am sure your efficient mama will have found a way to tell him of your two proposals of marriage. Harriet tells me that nothing spurs a man on like competition.'

'If that is true, your comte will be having quite a frightful time imagining you in the arms of Mr Farley.'

'What? Over the tea-tray?' Jane laughed and climbed into the carriage, which was waiting outside. 'Call on me tomorrow and I will tell you all about it.' She was driven off.

Frances climbed into her own open carriage. 'Home, miss?' asked the coachman.

'Yes, no, perhaps ... Let me think.' Frances sat scowling horribly, until she realized that she was being surveyed by the comte and Mr Ferguson from the pavement.

'Oh!' said Frances, blushing. 'I was just thinking of you.'

'Which one?' asked Jamie.

'You,' said Frances, pointing at the comte with her parasol.

'Pleasant thoughts, I hope?'

'No, not at all. I think you are being very stupid,' said Frances, looking intently into the comte's blue eyes. 'Jane has gone to take tea with Lady Farley and her son. She has not yet accepted his proposal, but I fear he may press her. You kissed her and then ignored her, Monsieur le Comte, and no lady will ever forgive anything like that.'

The comte's face became a well-bred blank. 'Yes, I know I am being impertinent,' said Frances, 'and you may stare down your nose at me as much as you like. But you should go to the Farleys' yourself and tell her you want her for your wife before she does anything stupid.'

To Jamie's amazement, the comte swept a low bow, said, 'Certainly,' and strode off down the street.

'I do believe he is going to do what you told him to do,' said Jamie.

Frances smiled at him shyly. 'May I take you up? Are you going anywhere in particular?'

He felt light-hearted. Sun was drying the morning's rain from the pavements. He sprang into the carriage. 'Let us just drive around.'

A little smile of triumph curving her lips, Frances

gave the orders to the coachman and settled back happily beside him.

Jane looked around the saloon of Lady Farley's home and said, 'Where is your mother, Mr Farley?'

'My mother had to rush off to see a sick friend. She sends her deepest apologies, but hopes to return in time to see you before you leave.'

Jane sat down on the very edge of a sofa, feeling nervous. Clarence had only spoken the truth. He had been annoyed at his mother's sudden departure, for all romantic feelings towards Jane had fled. The door of the saloon was wide open and servants came and went. Jane's maid was seated in the hall below. Despite his mother's absence, it was all very respectable.

The tea-tray was brought in with all the implements. Jane offered to make the tea, as it was the fashion for society ladies to make the precious brew rather than entrust the job to a servant. Clarence said he would prefer Indian tea, and so she opened up the lacquered teapoy and selected the correct canister. While she worked away, Clarence experienced a certain pang of disappointment that she was dowryless. He had sent an express the day before to the earl, so Jane would soon be removed from London and that would spite the comte. His eyes previously sharpened by jealousy, Clarence was well aware that the comte was fascinated by Jane. Now watching all that beauty bent over the tea-urn, he wondered whether it might not have been better perhaps to secure such a prize for himself, dowry or not. Although he had no longer any tender feelings for her, all men would admire and envy him. He knew that, in a day of dashing bucks and beaux, he was considered stodgy and dull.

The butler came in to say that there was a gentleman in the hall waiting to see him. Clarence studied the card, which had been proffered to him on a silver tray, and gave an exclamation of annoyance.

'Pray excuse me, Miss North,' he said. 'I shall only be a few minutes.'

Jane found that as soon as he had left the room, the very air seem to lighten. There was something threatening about Clarence Farley, almost oppressive.

She rose and walked to a low console table which held a few books: two bound volumes of the *Gentleman's Magazine*, one volume of the latest novel, no doubt Lady Farley's, and Foxe's *Book of Martyrs*. With a wry smile she picked up the *Book of Martyrs*. Miss Stamp delighted in reading aloud long passages of torture and death. Jane flicked back the cover and stared in surprise. The book was hollow. Inside was nothing but a small leather-bound notebook. Normally she would not have dreamt of looking through anyone else's private belongings, but the strangeness of the hiding-place caused her to open the notebook. There was a short list of names, with payments made to each in a neat column. She turned the pages. Always the same names, with regular payments. On the last page, one name had been scored through with a thin line, but she could still read that name – Gerald

Freemantle. Gerald . . . Jerry, the young man who had hanged himself!

She heard Clarence returning and slipped the notebook into her reticule and shut the fake *Book of Martyrs* but had not time to replace it exactly at the bottom of the pile of books, so she left it on the top and hoped he would not notice.

'A trifling matter of business,' he said. Jane sat down and began to dispense tea, proud in an odd way that her hands did not shake, for the import of those names was hitting her more and more. It could be innocent. They could be gambling debts and Jerry Freemantle's name was simply scored out because, being dead, he no longer needed to be paid. And yet she had taken that notebook and hidden it in her reticule and did not have the courage to question him about it. Her frightened thoughts turned to the comte. He would know what to do.

Her inner fear gave her an air of fragility which heightened her beauty. Clarence felt his senses quicken again. 'Have you considered my proposal?' he asked.

Jane forced herself to smile. 'It was only yesterday, Mr Farley. We are just starting to get to know each other.'

Mr Farley smiled back. 'Well, we shall see . . .' he began and then his wandering eyes came to rest on the console table, sharpened and remained fixed on it.

Then he turned his eyes back to Jane and studied her face and to her own horror she felt a guilty blush rising to her cheeks.

The butler entered. 'The Comte de Mornay,' he announced.

'We are not at home,' said Clarence, rising and going to the table. He picked up the *Book of Martyrs*.

'I would like to see the comte,' said Jane. She suddenly shouted, 'Monsieur le Comte. Here!'

There was the sound of a short altercation and then quick footsteps on the stairs and the comte entered just as Mr Farley opened the fake *Book of Martyrs* and saw that it was now empty.

'Shut the door, my lord,' he said. He crossed to a desk against the wall, opened it and took out a pistol. He swung round and pointed it at Jane. 'You have an item which belongs to me. I assume it is in your reticule. No, do not move, Monsieur le Comte, or I will shoot her dead. Throw the notebook on the floor, Lady Jane.'

'So you know who she is,' said the comte.

'And now her father will know where she is because I sent him an express yesterday,' said Clarence.

The comte was leaning against the wall, inside the door, looking cool and amused.

Jane took out the notebook and tossed it down in front of him.

'What was in it, my sweeting?' asked the comte lazily.

'A list of names and payments,' whispered Jane, 'and one of them was Gerald Freemantle. His name had been scored out.'

'So you are a traitor, mon brave,' said the comte. 'But you have not been out of the country recently.

But no doubt the gentleman who was plotting my death in an inn outside Milan has his name in your book. Why? Why work for a monster like Napoleon Bonaparte?'

'Because,' Clarence spat out, 'if he is restored he will not fail next time to invade England and then the scum of society with their drinking and whoring will be hanging from the lamps in the street.'

'Dear me, all the young bloods who dub you Dreary Clarence? And to get revenge on them you would betray your country! Just what do you plan to do now? You can hardly shoot us both dead in a houseful of servants in the middle of fashionable London.'

The pistol levelled at Jane's heart never wavered. 'I will take her with me. So long as she keeps quiet, her life will be safe.'

'Tut, tut,' said the comte reprovingly. 'What makes you think that I would assist you in betraying my adopted country for the life of one poor wench?'

'Because you are in love with her,' sneered Clarence.

'Alas, you have the right of it.'

And I love you, too, thought Jane miserably. I have loved you all along, and now it is too late. This monster will never let me live.

'Move towards the door, Lady Jane,' said Farley, 'and do not make any sudden moves. Stand aside, Comte.'

Jane was moving slowly towards the door when it suddenly opened and Lady Farley swept into the

167

room and walked directly between Jane and her son. She stared at the wicked-looking pistol in her son's hand. 'What are you doing, Clarence?' she screamed. In that moment, the comte moved forward, Jane darted behind him, and the comte clipped Lady Farley round the waist. 'Now what are you going to do, Farley?' he asked. 'Shoot your own mother?'

Lady Farley screamed hysterically and struggled in the comte's arms. Servants came running into the room. Clarence looked solemnly at all of them, put the pistol in his mouth and blew his brains out. The comte released Lady Farley, turned round and grabbed Jane and pressed her face into his breast, saying, 'Don't look, my love, my dear. It is all over.'

Harriet, fretting because Jane had not returned, decided to call on Mrs Haggard. Jane perhaps had gone straight from the Farleys' to call on Frances instead of coming home and getting ready to go out to the opera.

When she mounted the stairs to Mrs Haggard's drawing room it was to see Mr and Mrs Haggard outside the closed door with their ears pressed to the panels.

'What is the matter? Is Jane here?' asked Harriet.

'Shhh!' admonished Mrs Haggard. 'Mr Ferguson is proposing to Frances.'

'So you have not seen Miss North?'

'No! Shhh!'

Harriet, puzzled, turned away.

Inside the drawing room, Frances was being

ruthlessly kissed by Jamie and feeling she would faint from sheer ecstasy. 'And do you really want to marry me?' she asked when she finally could.

'Of course, you silly little thing.' And Frances gave a sigh of sheer relief and leaned her frizzy head against his chest.

Harriet, returning home, blinked at the scene in her own hall. Jane was crying quietly and being held closely by the comte while her little maid had hysterics in a corner, and then her bemused eyes focused on her husband and she hurled herself into his arms.

'What have I come home to?' he said, gathering her in his arms. 'Here is the Comte de Mornay with tales of murder, treachery and mayhem, and Miss North, who says she is not Miss North but Lady Jane Fremney and that her father has found out her whereabouts.'

Still holding Jane close, the comte said over her head, 'Lady Jane will tell you everything, Duke, but I have some business with the authorities which is pressing. Take care of her for me.' He bent his head and kissed Jane on the cheek.

Harriet, despite the fact that she did not want to leave her beloved husband's arms for one moment, moved to Jane's side and said quietly, 'Come with us. What happened? Do not cry. Is your father returned?'

As they moved up the stairs to the drawing room, Jane dried her eyes and tried to compose herself. In a flat voice she told them all that had happened to her at the Farleys'.

169

When they were seated in the drawing room, the duke said, 'He was probably nothing more than the paymaster for some inefficient organization of treacherous malcontents. De Mornay sounds like an efficient fellow. He will soon sort things out. All you have to do is try to recover from your shock.'

'Clarence Farley sent an express to my father telling him where I am,' said Jane, beginning to cry again. 'He will come and take me away.'

Harriet rapidly explained Jane's situation to her husband. 'Do not worry,' said the duke. 'We will give your father a hard time of it.'

'But I do not see what you can do,' wailed Jane. 'I am not of age and he has every legal right to take me away.' The duke and duchess exchanged rueful looks over her bent head. 'Perhaps the comte will think of something,' said Harriet in a comforting voice.

But Jane would only shake her head. He had said he loved her, he had held her and comforted her, but she could not believe he would propose marriage. And how could anyone stand up to the tyrant who was her father?

For Jane the following week was a dismal affair. Still suffering from shock and expecting her father to arrive any moment, she stayed mostly in her rooms at Harriet's. The comte had called twice, each time to report to her how the traitors had been rounded up and the ringleader had proved to be a rich and eccentric City businessman who had bribed weak young men to join his cause. He had been arrested and taken to the Tower. There would be no need for Jane to give evidence, the comte would handle all that with his lawyers. They would take a statement from her to be read out.

And Jane's misery seemed to be intensified by the happiness about her. Frances, newly engaged, was floating on air, and Harriet and her husband walked about in a glow of rediscovered love.

One afternoon, as Jane was trying to listen to Frances's happy confidences, the butler entered and the words she had been dreading to hear fell on her ears.

'The Earl of Durbyshire.'

Frances gave a squeak of dismay and darted from the room, almost colliding on the stairs with a burly middle-aged man and a thin angular lady.

When the earl entered, Jane was standing by the fireplace. She felt all her luck had run out. If only Harriet and her husband had been at home to lend her a little support.

Behind the earl came the dreaded Miss Stamp.

'So you lied and cheated and tricked me,' roared the earl. 'It's bread and water for you when we get you back home.'

Jane tried to summon up some courage. 'I do not want to go with you,' she said. 'I am a guest here.'

'You are my daughter,' howled the earl, 'and you will do what you are told.' He seized her by the shoulders and shook her and shook her until the bone pins rattled out of her elaborate coiffure onto the floor and her hair cascaded about her shoulders.

'You are a wicked and evil child,' said Miss Stamp, who appeared to be enjoying herself immensely.

'Please leave my fiancée alone,' came a measured voice from the doorway.

The earl stopped shaking his daughter and swung round and stared wrathfully at the elegant figure of the comte. 'What are you talking about, you jackanapes!'

'Your daughter is to marry me,' said the comte, 'whether you wish it or not. Stand away from her.'

'I can do what I like with her. She's my daughter. What are you going to do about that, hey?'

The comte drew his dress-sword and looked thoughtfully at the naked blade. 'Kill you?' he suggested amiably.

There came the sound of feet thudding up the stairs and Frances tumbled into the room, followed by the hoteliers, Harriet, and the duke. She had been lucky in finding Harriet and her husband as they were returning home, and even more fortunate on her road to alert the hoteliers, finding them all approaching in an open carriage after making a call on one of their clients.

The Duke of Rowcester glared awfully through his quizzing-glass at the enraged earl. 'What are you doing in my home, and who are you?'

'I am Durbyshire,' said the earl. 'I am taking my daughter home and none of you is going to stop me.'

'I had just been explaining that Lady Jane is engaged to be married to me,' said the comte.

'Over my dead body,' shouted the earl.

'Exactly.' The comte looked him up and down with contempt.

'You do not have my permission to marry her and there's nothing you can do about it,' said the earl. 'Take her away, Miss Stamp, and get her to do her packing now.'

'I'm tired of all this,' said Sir Philip suddenly. 'It is all very easy, though why I should help a churl like you, de Mornay, is beyond me.' He scuttled up to Jane and took her hand and led her to the comte. 'Take her, de Mornay, and get out of here. Haven't you heard of Gretna? Take her away, man, and put that sword away. You don't want to murder this nasty man and hang for it. He ain't worth it.'

The comte looked down at Jane, at her hair tumbled about her shoulders, at her tear-stained face, and he sheathed his sword and swept her up in his arms. The hoteliers crowded around the fuming earl, defying him.

'And if you do anything or make a scene, I'll have all this in the newspapers,' said Sir Philip. 'You'll be exposed to London society as the bullying old fool you are. I suggest you thank your stars your daughter is marrying well and get out of here and take that long drip of acid with you.'

'I have never been . . . !' began Miss Stamp furiously.

'I can see that,' said Sir Philip, maliciously misunderstanding her. 'What man would want to get his leg over the likes of you?'

'Where is your room, my darling?' asked the comte outside the door.

'Upstairs, but . . .'

173

'We are not going anywhere, my love. I cannot take you off just like that. You need your clothes and belongings.' He began to carry her up the stairs.

Jane looked up at him dizzily.

'Are you really going to marry me?'

'Oh, my love.' He kissed her passionately and then said softly, 'As soon as possible. Which way?'

'Put me down,' said Jane, 'and I will show you.'

She pushed open the door leading to her bedroom. 'Now we will stay here,' said the comte, 'until everything is quiet, and then perhaps next week we shall make a slow and comfortable journey north to Gretna.'

Jane looked at him shyly. 'I will have no dowry. And how did you ever find out my real identity?'

'I sent my efficient valet, Gerrard, into Durbyshire with a sketch of you to ferret out your secrets.'

'My father will never relent. I am penniless. I have nothing to give you.'

He wrapped his arms around her again and held her close. 'Oh, yes, you have,' he said softly. 'Kiss me!'

And Jane, brought up to be dutiful, did the very best she could.

NINE

To be in it [society] is merely a bore. But to be out of it simply a tragedy.

OSCAR WILDE

Three months had passed since the death of Clarence Farley, and the hoteliers sat in their private sitting room for the last time, each with their various thoughts.

Prince Hugo and his retinue had left, and below them the hotel was silent and empty of guests. Down in the kitchen Despard, once chef, now owner of the Poor Relation, which he had bought with all the money he had salted away, was entertaining Rossignole, his fellow chef, now partner, and a group of friends.

Sir Philip was moodily tapping out a tune with one hand on the piano. Lady Fortescue had had her way. They were all going to live together in a rented house in Manchester Square until such time when they found a suitable property, and only Lady Fortescue seemed happy with that arrangement.

Miss Tonks, who had wistfully dreamt of a home of her own and a husband of her own, thought drearily that they would all go on as usual until they died, even though they no longer had a hotel to run. Colonel Sandhurst had taken the arrangement to mean that Lady Fortescue did not want to marry him, and his life stretched out, dull and empty, to the grave. Mr Davy had been about to propose to Miss Tonks, but seeing with what seeming placidity she had accepted the new arrangement, he had come to the conclusion that she was happy for their friendship to continue, but nothing else. He was always conscious of the great difference between them in social status.

Sir Philip had not proposed to Miss Tonks either. There was no point. They would all be together just as before, and one of them would look after him in his rapidly declining years and he could not imagine why he felt so terribly old and depressed.

'I had a letter from Jane,' said Miss Tonks, breaking the moody silence. 'She says they were married at Gretna and are now staying with Scottish friends of Mr Ferguson outside Edinburgh. She thanks us all over and over again for saving her life. She is so much in love . . .' Miss Tonks fell mute again and silence came back, punctuated only by Sir Philip's playing the same phrase over and over again.

The door opened and Jack the footman and Lady Fortescue's old servants Betty and John came in, carrying bottles of champagne. 'A present from Despard,' said Jack, 'or Mr Despard, as I now must call him.' Jack looked very fine in a new coat of black superfine with black silk knee-breeches. He was to be the hotel manager, but Betty and John would follow their old mistress to Manchester Square.

'How kind,' said Lady Fortescue. 'Send Mr Despard our thanks and compliments, and do join us.'

'We are expected back at the party belowstairs,' said Jack. 'Do you wish us to stay and open the bottles for you?'

'I can do that,' said Mr Davy. 'Off you go.'

'Hark at him,' jeered Sir Philip, turning around on the piano stool. 'Gives the orders quite like the little gentleman that he ain't and never will be.'

Miss Tonks, correct to the last, waited until the servants had retired and said, 'Will you never have done with your nasty remarks, Sir Philip? The thought of putting up with your crotchiness from here to the grave depresses me beyond reason.'

'And the thought of looking at your stupid sheep face every day of the week is not much to look forward to either,' rejoined Sir Philip.

'Enough,' barked the colonel. 'Open a couple of bottles, Mr Davy, and pour us all a glass.'

Soon they were all sitting in a half-circle before the small fireplace, drinking champagne.

'A toast!' said Lady Fortescue, raising her glass. 'To our future together.'

'Future,' echoed several voices dismally.

She looked about her, her black eyes snapping. 'This is not a wake. We are rich, we are successful, and we are about to be back in society.'

Sir Philip, more affected by the champagne than the others, for he had been drinking earlier that day, said waspishly, 'You haven't got a heart.'

'I?' Lady Fortescue stared at him in amazement. 'I

am all heart. I may say what I have done in keeping us together was out of thought for you all.'

'So here we are,' said Sir Philip, 'with the old colonel pining away there. Ah, yes, Colonel, I know your dream. You hoped for a place in the country with Lady Fortescue as your bride, a fine place with your horses and hounds, and she never even gave you a thought.'

'But I did,' protested Lady Fortescue. 'Did you not think that I would not rather be alone with my husband? But I could not leave Miss Tonks, or you, Sir Philip, to fend for yourselves.'

'Do you mean,' said the colonel, 'that you are going to marry me after all?'

'I did think that was the arrangement,' said Lady Fortescue.

'But Amelia, my heart, you said nothing to me of this.'

'I am saying it now. You and I will be married and . . .'

'You cannot want the rest of us around,' said Miss Tonks. 'I would not, were I married.'

'Well, nobody's going to marry you,' said Sir Philip spitefully.

'I know,' said Miss Tonks, and began to cry.

Sir Philip felt a pang of remorse. He was just about to propose to her when Mr Davy suddenly got down on one knee in front of Miss Tonks and drew her hands away from her face.

'Letitia,' he said in a low voice, 'I would like to marry you, but I did not think I had hope because of the difference in our social situations, and because you seemed happy to live forever with the others.'

Amazement dried Miss Tonks's tears. 'But I want to marry you,' she shouted. 'I don't want to live with them.'

There was a stunned silence.

'More champagne, Colonel.' came Lady Fortescue's amused voice. The colonel refilled the glasses. 'It looks as if I have caused a lot of unnecessary suffering. And now we have this house, but only rented. So I shall marry my dear colonel and Miss Tonks her Mr Davy, and we will all go our separate ways. But what of Sir Philip?'

'Oh, don't mind me,' said Sir Philip. 'I'm as happy as a lark. I'll leave you love-birds together and find more congenial company.' He stomped out, but, sad to say, the two couples left behind were too happy that evening to worry about him.

After chatting for ten minutes, Miss Tonks and Mr Davy rose and left the sitting room and made their way down to the hall and stood together under the light of the great chandelier. The doors, usually open to the fashionable crowd on Bond Street, were that night closed and barred. From downstairs, in the kitchen, came the faint sound of someone singing a song in French.

Mr Davy reached out and took Miss Tonks's hand in his own. 'Dear lady,' he said, 'it was a clumsy way to propose.'

Miss Tonks's thin face was radiant. 'Where shall we live?'

'I think I am a town creature. Would it trouble you to live in town?'

'Not at all,' said Miss Tonks dreamily, 'anywhere will do.'

'This place will always hold some exciting memories for you.'

Miss Tonks looked around, remembering how she had come here nearly destitute, frightened and lonely, to find companionship, warmth, adventure, and now marriage. 'It will always be dear to me,' she said. 'People who came here seemed to be always lucky in love. Jane was our last success, in a way, although we did nothing really to bring her and her comte together.'

Mr Davy kissed her gently on the lips. And then he said, 'I think, Letitia, you can count yourself as the Poor Relation's last romantic success.'

Lady Fortescue and the colonel, and Miss Tonks and Mr Davy were to have a double wedding, a *quiet* double wedding. But the end of Lady Fortescue's brave venture into trade amused the Prince Regent so much that he declared he wished to be present. Slowly the quiet wedding grew and grew, to become a fashionable affair. The Duke and Duchess of Rochester were to be there; the Marquess and Marchioness of Peterhouse, the marchioness being none other than their former colleague Miss Budley; then Lord Eston and Cassandra, who had worked for them at the hotel when she ran away from home; and Arabella and her husband, the Earl of Denby; and

Captain Peter Manners and his little wife Frederica; and even Lord Bewley and his wife Mary. All the romantic successes of the Poor Relation were to be there. And then, just before the great day arrived, Jane and her comte turned up, declaring they would not miss the event for worlds. Society clamoured for invitations. It was decided to hold the wedding breakfast in the Poor Relation, now renamed The Grand, with Despard offering to supply the catering as his wedding present.

The Duke of Rowcester was the colonel's best man, and the Marquess of Peterhouse did the honours for Mr Davy, while his wife was bridesmaid to Miss Tonks, Miss Tonks's embittered sister having refused to even attend. Harriet was bridesmaid for Lady Fortescue. Miss Tonks was in white, as was Lady Fortescue – magnificent gowns of Brussels lace embroidered with gold thread and pearls, which had cost a fortune. Harriet was wearing that necklace, and Sir Philip could hardly bear to look at it. He had been through so much over that necklace and no one knew except perhaps that churl Davy, whose opinion did not count. The couples were married in the rented house in Manchester Square, which had been decorated with flowers for the occasion.

Lady Fortescue and her colonel were correct and dignified, as was to be expected, but the Marchioness of Peterhouse, the former Mrs Budley, declared that it was really Miss Tonks's day. Happiness had lent her a sort of beauty.

After the ceremony they all travelled to Bond Street

and to the Poor Relation for the breakfast. The Prince Regent, who had failed to put in an appearance at the ceremony, arrived with his friends for the breakfast and kissed both brides, and the new Mrs Davy thought she might faint from an excess of exaltation.

'How wonderful it all is,' said Jane to her comte. 'Everyone is so happy. I never thought when I first came here that such happiness would be the result.'

He laughed. 'Our happiness, you mean. I think the others have managed very well on their own. All I want to do is to take you away as soon as possible and kiss you senseless.'

Jane blushed, but her hand stole under the table and found his own.

Along the table from her sat Frances, drinking champagne and sparkling with happiness beside Mr Ferguson. 'It all ended well, don't you know,' said the irrepressible Frances. 'We will soon be married, and if I catch you even looking at middle-aged Scottish ladies, Jamie, I will scream!'

At the end of the breakfast, the Duke of Rowcester rose to toast the happy couples. 'The only sad thing about this day,' he said, 'is that it is the end of the Poor Relation as we all have known it, and there are many of us here who owe our happiness to the hoteliers.'

Sir Philip joined in the toasts. He was feeling increasingly miserable. They were all splitting up. The colonel and Lady Fortescue had found a pleasant house in Kent and would remove there on the following day, while Miss Tonks, now Mrs Davy, and her husband would take up residence in a handsome

182

apartment in South Audley Street. He himself would stay on in the rented house in Manchester Square until the lease ran out in four months' time. The fact that his clothes were now of the best and that his jewels winked and glittered could not comfort his lonely old soul. He wished with all his heart that he himself had proposed to Miss Tonks. She had, as he now knew, lost hope that Mr Davy would ever propose to her, and so she would have accepted him, and he, Sir Philip, would not be facing a lonely old age.

When the first guests began to leave, he slipped away and walked outside into Bond Street. The sun was shining, intensifying his loneliness. He looked up at the hotel, at the sign 'The Grand,' and thought it a silly sort of unoriginal name. No more guests to worry about, no more frights, no more adventures, no more poverty. He felt like crying. He would go to Limmer's and get drunk. Tears filled his eyes and he turned away blindly and collided with a lady who was walking along with her maid. He whipped off his hat and stammered out his apologies.

'Sir Philip!' exclaimed the lady, a statuesque matron with large teeth and improbable blonde curls peeping from under her rakish bonnet. 'Do you not remember me? Susan Darkwood?'

He bowed low and then realized she was dressed from head to foot in black. 'Your husband . . . ?'

'Lord Darkwood died six months ago.'

'I am so sorry. You and your husband were among our first guests.'

Lady Darkwood giggled. 'Did we not have fun then? And poor little Harriet came up from the kitchens to marry her duke. And now you are all so fashionable and little me was not even asked to the wedding. Still, it must be a happy day for you.'

'Not for me. I am alone again.'

She heaved a sigh. 'As am I. Ah, here is my carriage. You will come home with me and we will take tea and talk of old times,' said Lady Darkwood, who would not have dreamt of entertaining such a lowly creature as Sir Philip in the old days.

He hesitated. 'I am not very good company.'

She smiled down into his eyes. 'Then we must think of something to cheer you.'

His elderly heart suddenly began to thump against his ribs. He smiled back. 'I should like that. I *need* that. The company of a beautiful lady would do me a power of good.'

'Wicked man.' She tapped his hand with her glove. 'Come along.'

As happy as he had so recently been sad. Sir Philip climbed into her carriage and took the seat next to her. He pressed her hand and she gave him a languishing look.

The carriage moved on and rolled down Bond Street, away from the hotel.

And Sir Philip Sommerville did not look back.

Not once.

Magnificent Obsession

Victoria, Albert and the Death that Changed the Monarchy

H ELEN R APPAPORT

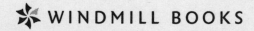
WINDMILL BOOKS

Published by Windmill Books 2012

2 4 6 8 10 9 7 5 3 1

First published in Great Britain in 2011 by Hutchinson

Windmill Books
The Random House Group Limited
20 Vauxhall Bridge Road, London SW1V 2SA

Addresses for companies within The Random House Group Limited
can be found at: www.randomhouse.co.uk/offices.htm

The Random House Group Limited Reg. No. 954009

www.randomhouse.co.uk

A CIP catalogue record for this book
is available from the British Library

ISBN 9780099537465

The Random House Group Limited supports The Forest Stewardship Council
(FSC®), the leading international forest certification organisation. Our books
carrying the FSC label are printed on FSC® certified paper. FSC is the only
forest certification scheme endorsed by the leading environmental
organisations, including Greenpeace. Our paper procurement policy
can be found at: www.randomhouse.co.uk/environment

MIX
Paper from
responsible sources
FSC
www.fsc.org   FSC® C016897

Typeset in Dante MT by Palimpsest Book Production Limited,
Falkirk, Stirlingshire

Printed and bound by CPI Group (UK) Ltd, Croydon, CR0 4YY

For Charlie Viney

Contents

Peel cut down my income, Wellington refused me rank, the Royal Family cried out against the foreign interloper, the Whigs in office were inclined to concede me just as much space as I could stand upon. The Constitution is silent as to the Consort of the Queen . . . and yet there he was, not to be done without.

Prince Albert, letter to Baron Stockmar, 24 January 1854[1]

He conquered my heart; so that I could not choose but to love him – there was an indescribable *something* about him – an elevation, an humility, a power and simplicity, a thorough *genuineness* of character, a style and tone in his whole manner, opinions . . . which made him to me my very ideal of a *Christian* Prince! What a Godfearing man he was! What a sense of duty he had.

Reverend Norman Macleod, 28 December 1861[2]

For me, life came to an end on 14 December. My life was dependent on his, I had no thoughts except of him; my whole striving was to please him, to be less unworthy of him!

Queen Victoria, letter to King of Prussia, 4 February 1862[3]

Preface & Acknowledgements

Queen Victoria is one of the most written-about women in British – if not world – history. Her consort Prince Albert has also been the subject of several biographies, as well as studies of his contribution to the arts and British culture. This book is neither a biography of the Queen nor of Prince Albert. Instead it focuses on what is, I argue, a crucial period in her life, one that completely changed the course her reign took for the next forty years and had a profound impact on Britain: the lost ten years from Albert's death at the end of 1861 to the beginning of her re-emergence from deep mourning in 1872.

Much has been written about Queen Victoria's later years as the gloomy, humourless, reclusive widow at Windsor, but virtually no attempt has been made to explore the nature of her grief or to describe the circumstances leading up to Prince Albert's death in December 1861 and its catastrophic impact on her. This book seeks to understand why the Queen reacted in the extreme way she did, by explaining her obsessive love for her husband and her total and utter reliance on him. The second half of the book considers Queen Victoria's untiring memorialisation of her dead husband – in biography, art and architecture – at a time when criticism of her withdrawal from public life was mounting.

Prince Albert's death, funeral and the public response to it have been paid surprisingly little attention to date; recent accounts tend to stop abruptly at his deathbed or fast-forward to the Queen's life thereafter. This book sets out to describe the effect that death had both on Prince Albert's contemporaries and on the nation at large. With this objective in mind, I have sought out unpublished, forgotten and neglected sources that comment on the Prince's declining health, his death and funeral and the Queen's reaction to it. In Britain we are blessed with a wealth of published letters, diaries and memoirs from the Victorian period, many of them by personalities who have long since been forgotten and consigned to obscurity, but which nevertheless contain valuable testimony on the impact of Prince Albert's death. It has been a pleasure to rediscover these now-neglected Victorian letter-writers and diarists, who have enlightened and enlivened my research and impressed me with their wonderfully perceptive comments about the Queen, Prince Albert and the true nature of their relationship.

A key resource in the writing of this book has been the Royal Archives in the Round Tower at Windsor Castle. I am indebted to their registrar, Pamela Clark, and her staff for making a range of fascinating material available to me during my research there, and for the permission of Her Majesty Queen Elizabeth II to quote from it, as well as use photographs and illustrations from the Royal Collection. My thanks also go to Sophie Gordon for her assistance in this latter respect.

From Germany, I was able to obtain copies of letters written at the time of Prince Albert's death by the Crown Prince of Prussia and Princess Alice of Great Britain. I am indebted to Christine Klössel at the Arkhiv der Hessischen Hausstiftung, Schloss Fasanerie, Eichenzell, for providing me with transcripts for those of the Crown Prince; and to Professor Eckhart G. Franz at the Staatsarchiv Darmstadt for making available digital images of the original letters by Princess Alice. Quotations from these letters are included with the gracious permission of Prince Donatus von Hessen. I am greatly indebted to Hannah Veale for translating both sets of letters from German, and in particular for her enormous patience in deciphering Princess Alice's difficult handwriting.

I would also like to thank a number of British archivists who provided valuable help and access to material: Alan Tadiello at Balliol College, Oxford, for the Queen's letters to General Peel in the Morier Family Papers; Nick Mays, at *The Times* Archive, News International Archive, for those of John Delane and Lord Torrington; Caroline Picco at Cheshire Archives, for providing a photocopy of the 'Descriptions of the Death of the Prince Consort, 1861' by Arthur Penrhyn Stanley, and for the permission of the present Lord Stanley to quote from it; the British Library, for permission to quote from the Duchess of Sutherland's letters in the Gladstone Papers and from Queen Victoria's 'Album Consolativum'; Colin Harris at the Bodleian Library Special Collection, for making available to me the diaries of Katharine Clarendon, John Rashdall and Charles Pugh and the Bodleian Library, University of Oxford for permission to quote from them; Briony Hudson at the Royal Pharmaceutical Society of Great Britain, for allowing me to access the account books of Peter Squire; Phil Tomaselli, for obtaining material for me from the Lord Chamberlain's papers at the National Archives, Kew; Helen Burton at Keele University Library, for information on Sarah Hildyard; and Ian Shapiro at Argyll Etkin, for allowing me access to the MS diaries of Sir John Cowell in his collection, as well as providing other materials for my research.

Many other people offered invaluable support, advice and information along the way: Denise Hesselroth alerted me to the underrated diaries of Lady Lucy Cavendish; Paul Frecker provided information on Victorian *cartes de visite* and images for this book; Kevin Brady shared his research on Princess Alice and her family; Marianne Kouwenhoven in The Hague investigated sources in the archives of Queen Sophie of the Netherlands; Geoffrey Munn at Wartskis kindly showed me items of jewellery relating to the Queen, Prince Albert and John Brown from their private collection; fellow historians David Waller, Matthew Dennison and Hugo Vickers answered my queries and suggested sources. Nicholas Janni and Juliet Grayson suggested sources on death and bereavement, and my dear friend Linda Blair gave me her invaluable views on the same, read sections of the manuscript relating to the Queen's grieving and offered insightful comments. Among royalty buffs, Sue Woolmans, Richard Thornton and members of the Royalty Weekend annual conference held at Ticehurst offered valuable support for, and interest in, this project. On a memorable research trip to Whitby to investigate the jet industry, Lynne and George provided a home-from-home at the No. 7 Guest House; Rachel Jones and Matt Hatch at Hamond's Jewellers on Church Street responded generously to my passion for Whitby jet; Peter Hughes, custodian of the wonderfully idiosyncratic Whitby Museum, which has an extraordinary collection of jet jewellery and artefacts, offered valuable background information.

The arguments contained in the Appendix to this book – 'What Killed Prince Albert' – are my own, based on extensive research and much deliberation. I arrived at my conclusions thanks to the assistance of doctors Simon Travis (Consultant Gastroenterologist) and Chris Conlon (Consultant in Infectious Diseases), who read my draft and offered their comments and observations. Professors Ronald Chaplain (Consultant Oncologist) and Neil Mortensen (Consultant Colorectal Surgeon) also offered valuable advice, as did Dr Anne Hardy on the incidence of typhoid fever in the Victorian period. But, in the end, the conclusions are mine. I would welcome comments and feedback on this book, to my website www.helenrappaport.com

Finally, my thanks as always go to my family for their support in all my work, in particular to my brothers Peter and Christopher, and also to my friend and fellow writer Christina Zaba, for her generous and unstinting encouragement in all my literary endeavours. My agent Charlie Viney, to whom this book is dedicated, has been a wonderful friend and guide over the last six years and will I hope support my efforts on many more books to come. I count myself enormously fortunate in having wonderfully supportive and sympathetic commissioning editors and friends, in Caroline Gascoigne at Hutchinson in the UK and Charlie Spicer at St Martin's Press in the USA.

Helen Rappaport
Oxford, August 2011

List of Illustrations

Colour section

Prince Albert by Robert Thorburn (The Royal Collection © 2011 Her
    Majesty Queen Elizabeth II)
Windsor Castle East Terrace (From the author's collection)
The Grand Corridor of Windsor (The Royal Collection © 2011 Her
    Majesty Queen Elizabeth II)
The Blue Room (The Royal Collection © 2011 Her Majesty Queen
    Elizabeth II)
V&A Christmas (Photo by Hulton Archive/Getty Images)
Marochetti statue (The Royal Collection © 2011 Her Majesty Queen
    Elizabeth II)
Design for the interior decorations of the Royal Mausoleum at
    Frogmore (From the author's collection)
Prince Albert on his deathbed (The Royal Collection © 2011
    Her Majesty Queen Elizabeth II)
Deathbed cut-out (From the author's collection)
Bertie (Photo by John Jabez Edwin Mayall/Hulton Archive/Getty
    Images)
Princess Louise (Photo by SSPL/Getty Images)
Princess Alice (Photo by Hulton Archive/Getty Images)
Commemorative pot lid (From the author's collection)
A Nation Mourns (Mary Evans Picture Library)
Framed mourning card (V&A Images/Victoria and Albert Museum)
Whitby Jet Factory © Frank Meadow Sutcliffe / Sutcliffe Gallery
The Royal Albert Hall (Monkey Business/Rex Features)
Wolverhampton Memorial © Spectrum Colour Library / Heritage-
    Images / Imagestate
Albert Memorial (Latitudestock/Getty Images)
Wedding (The Royal Collection © 2011 Her Majesty Queen Elizabeth II)
Thanksgiving (Mary Evans Picture Library)

PROLOGUE

Christmas 1860

It was the coldest Christmas for fifty years, so they said, a bitter winter having followed hard on the heels of a chilly and sunless summer. So cold was it that country people talked of the birds frozen on the trees and song thrushes dying in their thousands; so cold that the legs of waterfowl stuck hard to the ice on the surface of lakes and ponds. Londoners got the best of it – the ice on the Serpentine in Hyde Park was thirteen inches thick, providing welcome Christmastide recreation to the hundreds who skated there well into the night by torchlight. Indeed, such had been the unprecedented cold that year that there was talk of reviving the old seventeenth-century frost fair on the Thames.[1]

Out at Windsor, twenty-one miles west of London and south of the Great Western Railway junction at Slough, a heavy frost had descended across the bare chestnut trees of the park, above which Windsor Castle rose in all its magnificence. A great impregnable stone fortress of history and tradition, dating back to an original wooden structure built after the Norman Conquest, it was reached by climbing the hill from the King Henry VIII Gate down in the little town of Windsor below, and passing through the narrow archway of the Norman Gate that separates the Lower from the Upper Ward of the castle.

The week before Christmas the royal family had transferred from Buckingham Palace to their private apartments here in the Upper Ward for the festive season. In the 1840s the interior of the castle had been extensively remodelled to accommodate the rapidly growing royal family, and from their apartments on the first floor they could look out over the East Terrace, across the ornamental garden and fountain to the dry moat, and beyond it the open grassy swathes of Windsor Home Park. Outside, in the paved quadrangle, soldiers in bearskins perpetually on guard paced back and forth below their windows within sight of a bronze equestrian statue of Charles II.

A labyrinth of staircases and carpeted corridors greeted anyone venturing inside the apartments of the East Terrace, the interior shadowy on dark winter days until it was lit at four in the afternoon by huge lamps that were left to burn all night.[2] The royal family's rooms here – including the Oak Room, where they took informal meals, and a larger Dining Room and the White and Crimson Drawing Rooms for more formal events – were connected along a Grand Corridor, which stretched from Queen Victoria's rooms in the King's Tower at one end to the state rooms and the Prince of Wales's Tower at the far end. The Grand Corridor itself was a place of recreation and association for members of the royal household as they went about their duties, its walls hung with paintings and its length interspersed with white marble busts on pedestals, bronzes, fine inlaid cabinets and choice pieces of furniture. At regular intervals between them huge doors decorated with gilding opened into the royal apartments and guest rooms beyond.[3]

Despite the attractiveness of its interior, Queen Victoria had never found Windsor congenial, remarking that she hoped that 'this fine, old dull place' would never hold her bones. To return there from the more cosy, purpose-built family homes at Osborne and Balmoral that she and her husband so loved was always a wrench. 'I have no feeling for Windsor,' she once wrote, 'I admire it, I think it a grand, splendid place – but without a particle of anything which causes me to love it.'[4] Nevertheless, the royal couple had spent all their Christmases at Windsor since the birth of their first child, the Princess Royal, in November 1840 and, with Prince Albert's encouragement, the royal apartments each Christmas gave pride of place to a host of Christmas trees.

Windsor Castle came into its own at this festive time of year. The silence along its Grand Corridor, where noise was muffled by the red carpets and huge damask curtains that hung at the tall, arched windows looking directly into the quadrangle, was broken by the happy sound of laughter and children's voices. Games of hide-and-seek along the corridors and in the towers and staircases of the castle by the royal children ensured that it had a happy family atmosphere. Fires were kept blazing with beech logs in all the reception rooms – the Queen did not like the smell of coal, although her pathological intolerance of heat was such that she ordained that the rooms should be kept at a temperature of only sixty degrees and she had thermometers in ivory cases mounted on every chimneypiece in order to check that her directive was adhered to. Victoria liked the old way of things: she refused to concede to gas lighting, which had been introduced into the official state rooms at Windsor, insisting that her private apartments were lit only by candles. Such stubbornness might have been an inconvenience, but at Christmas time the softly flickering candlelight throughout the royal apartments lent a particularly romantic atmosphere to the surroundings.[5]

For the first half of December the rain had come down in torrents, but now in the final days before Christmas fine, cold weather and a sharp frost had arrived and would persist right through the holiday. From 5 p.m. on the afternoon of the 20th it had begun snowing and continued till midnight, the snow piling in drifts around the castle, as it rose up like a fairytale citadel in the dazzling white of the surrounding landscape. Prince Albert had always loved 'the dear Christmas Eve' and took great pleasure in his children's 'happy wonder at the German Christmas tree and its radiant candles'.[6] Christmas was a profoundly nostalgic time for him, reminding him of those he had spent with his brother as children. Separated from the home at Coburg that he so loved, he now had to 'seek in the children an echo of what Ernest and I were in the old time', as he mused to his stepmother.[7] By 1860 he and Queen Victoria had nine children, ranging from Vicky (aged twenty) to Beatrice the youngest, who was only three. Yet already, young though they were, the royal children had begun to fly the nest. Vicky, Albert's much-adored favourite, had been married at seventeen to the Crown Prince of Prussia, the first stage in a personal project nurtured by her parents to secure a united, democratic Germany under Prussian leadership. Already the mother of two children, Vicky was now resigned to having to spend Christmas isolated from her family at her palace in Berlin. Her sister Alice – Victoria and Albert's third child and second daughter – would be the next to marry. At the end of November she had become engaged to Prince Louis of Hesse; he was rather dull, but Alice had fortunately fallen in love with him, and Louis was visiting Windsor that Christmas in anticipation of their marriage in a year or so's time. Victoria and Albert had similar plans for their son and heir Albert Edward, better known as Bertie in the family, who had just returned from an official tour – his first on their behalf – to Canada and the USA. He had acquitted himself well, demonstrating his popular touch and natural social skills, although at a dance in his honour at Pike's Opera House in Cincinnati he had looked with rather too much pleasure on the 'vast array of beauties' lined up for him.[8] Such reports discomfited his parents; Bertie must be married off, and soon, in Albert's view.

It was an unusually large family gathering that year. The days before Christmas were full of laughter and activity as the family was reunited with Affie (Prince Alfred) who, having joined the navy at the age of only twelve, was home from sea, much to his mother's delight. Everyone busied themselves with present-wrapping in between frequent trips down the hill to skate on the frozen pond on the Slopes below the north-east side of the castle. On the 23rd Victoria was delighted to see that the severe frost persisted. Despite the freezing weather, everyone eagerly walked down to the pond again to skate, returning for an intimate family supper, after which, like any ordinary family, 'albums were looked at and Albert played at chess with Affie'.[9]

That particular Christmas, John Delane, editor of *The Times*, was fortunate to receive an insider's view of the royal family at their leisure, thanks to his friend at court, Lord Torrington – 'that arch gossip of gossips'.[10] Torrington had been a permanent lord-in-waiting to Queen Victoria since 1859 and, in a private joke with Delane, with whom he frequently corresponded, described himself as 'your Windsor special'.[11] In letters written that Christmas to Delane, Torrington vividly captured the happy and relaxed atmosphere at Windsor: how he played billiards with the two young princes, Arthur and Alfred, and had sat and chatted informally with the Queen and Prince Albert. On Christmas Eve he had ventured down to the castle's cavernous kitchens to see the great baron of beef – all 360 pounds in weight – that was being cooked on a huge spit with great iron chains, constantly attended by four men.[12] Elsewhere in the vast Windsor kitchen with its twelve ranges, other huge fires had roasts suspended in front of them – one alone had fifty turkeys. Yet everywhere the greatest calm and order prevailed among the kitchen's legion of white-jacketed and white-capped cooks.

Everyone was delighted to wake on the 24th to 'true Xmas weather, snow on the ground and sharp frost', as Victoria recorded. In the heart of his family and away from the limelight of public scrutiny and onerous official duty, Prince Albert took an almost childish delight in the pleasures of the Christmas season. In the morning he and the young princes went out for some invigorating shooting, while the others once more went down to the skating pond. The ice lured them all back in the afternoon to enjoy a game of ice-hockey, in which Victoria was delighted to see that the shy and nervous Louis 'joined with great spirit'. Back in their apartments after 4 p.m. as the dark of Christmas Eve drew in, the family set about arranging their many gifts to each other on the present tables.

It was, recalled Victoria, 'most bewildering' sorting them all out, but with her husband's 'great indefatigability' they succeeded.[13]

At 6 p.m. everyone in the royal household gathered in the Oak Room for the exchange of presents. Here they were greeted by the Queen and Prince Albert standing by a large table covered with a white damask cloth, in the middle of which stood a decorated fir tree surrounded by presents and handwritten cards for them. In addition, three artificial fir trees about eight feet in height had been specially put in place in each of the Queen's three private sitting rooms – one each for herself, the Prince and the Duchess of Kent – with another tree for the children in the nursery. Smaller fir trees imported specially from Prince Albert's childhood home at Coburg were on display elsewhere in the castle.[14] The chandeliers had to be taken down specially to accommodate the larger ornamental trees, which were securely suspended from the ceiling, their bases resting on the table. The ten rows of symmetrical branches of these trees were decorated with edible fancies: sweetmeats, little cakes, fancy French bonbons, gilt walnuts – and gingerbreads whose delicious aroma filled the air – the effect completed with coloured ribbons and wax tapers and a frosting of artificial snow and icicles. At each tree-top stood a Christmas angel of Nuremberg glass, its outstretched wings holding a wreath in each hand.

Lord Torrington watched as the family exchanged their presents. The largest drawing room was like an Aladdin's cave, 'fitted up with every-thing that was handsome, various, and in good taste', he wrote. 'Each member gave a present to one another, so that, including the Prince Louis of Hesse and the Duchess of Kent, [everyone] gave and received thirteen presents.' It was a most joyful sight, none more so than that of ten-year-old Prince Arthur – 'the flower of the flock' in Torrington's opinion – who 'speedily got into a volunteer uniform, which, with endless other things, including a little rifle, fell to his lot, took a pot-shot at his papa, and then presented arms'. Torrington could not help noticing how carefully chosen all the presents were, how 'beautiful in taste and suited to the receiver'. Those chosen by the children for their parents were selected with great care, so that 'even the Queen might find use for them'. Victoria was delighted with the gift of a bracelet containing small hand-coloured photographs of Louis and Alice. 'All the dear children worked me something,' she recorded with delight in her journal.[15]

After the family had exchanged their own presents, the Queen handed out gifts to the royal household. Torrington wondered whether the Prince

Consort had 'had a quiet joke in his mind' in the selection of somewhat
quirky presents for gentlemen members of the household – Charles
Phipps (Keeper of Prince Albert's Privy Purse), Thomas Biddulph (Master
of the Queen's Household), General Charles Grey (Prince Albert's Private
Secretary), and General Bruce (Governor to the Prince of Wales):

> Phipps had salt cellars resting on little fish with their mouths open,
> Biddulph a bread basket, Grey a sugar basin, and Bruce a claret jug; but
> at any rate, the four articles were somewhat true emblems of the loaves
> and fishes. The parties concerned have not observed the possible joke,
> nor have I suggested the idea.[16]

Torrington himself was delighted to receive 'a supply of studs, sleeve
buttons, and waistcoat ditto, handsome, plain gold; a pocket-book'. In
addition, everyone was presented with 'a large cake of Nuremburg
gingerbread'. That day at Windsor, he confided to Delane, he had never
seen 'more real happiness than the scene of the mother and all her
children'. Even Prince Albert, notorious for his reserve, had 'lost his
stiffness' and had allowed himself to rest and relax for once. All in all,
'your Windsor special had much cheerful and friendly conversation with
them both'. It was, he concluded, 'a sight I should have liked you to
have seen'. The Queen concurred in her journal that evening: 'As usual
such a merry happy night with all the Children, and not the least happy,
dear Alice and Louis.'[17]

On Christmas Day the family awoke to intense cold of minus two
degrees Centigrade and an icy fog hanging across Windsor Home Park.
'The windows were frozen, the trees all white with frost,' wrote the
Queen. After breakfast everyone gathered round to look at all the
unwrapped presents laid out round the Christmas trees on the tables.
Then once more they went down to the pond to skate. It was such a
wonderful fine day, the church bells echoing Christmas joy across the
crisp morning air, as the Queen recalled. The sound made 'such a beautiful effect' as they walked down the hill to St George's Chapel in the
Lower Ward for morning service.[18]

Christmas Dinner was a grand affair, once more enjoyed by the
entire royal household. 'How I live to tell the tale I don't know,'
Torrington told Delane, such was the vast banquet placed before them,
the centrepiece of which was the great baron of beef he had seen
cooking the previous day, surrounded by dozens of capons, turkeys,

pea-hens and Cochin China pullets. The two youngest children, Beatrice and Leopold, had been allowed down from the nursery to join the family for dessert, and after lunch Prince Albert played happily with his little daughter, who had brought some joy back into his life after the departure of Vicky – swinging her back and forth in a large table napkin to shrieks of delight.[19] Altogether it was a most 'jolly' day of relaxed informal conversation with the Queen and Prince Albert and family games of chess, pool and billiards.[20]

On Boxing Day, Prince Albert again took his sons out shooting while the Queen, Prince Louis and Princess Alice and the girls went down the hill to skate. Snow fell all that night and the following day, the 27th. As the candles on the Christmas tree were lit for the last time in the drawing room at 7 p.m. (all the trees in the royal apartments would be lit up again on New Year's Day and Twelfth Night), everyone gathered to dine 'en famille'. 'All were very gay,' the Queen recalled, 'and telling many stories.'[21] The happiness and informality of that memorable Christmas continued into the 28th, when everyone piled into sledges and took one last turn across the snowscape of Windsor Home Park before the time came to bid farewell to Prince Louis.

*   *   *

No one who was at Windsor that Christmas of 1860 could have failed to be impressed and moved by the conviviality of the British royal family at home. 'Even as in a public bazaar, where people jostle one another, so lords, grooms, Queen, and princes laughed and talked, forgot to bow, and freely turned their backs on one another,' Torrington told Delane. 'Little princesses, who on ordinary occasions dare hardly to look at a gentleman-in-waiting, in the happiest manner showed each person they could lay hands on the treasures they had received.'[22]

For Torrington, as for the vast majority of the British people, the royal family basked in a halo of sentimentality that reflected the affection that it was now increasingly enjoying as the model British family. No matter that the aristocracy had persisted in disliking Prince Albert and what they perceived as his disdainful and reserved German manner; he and Victoria – the virtuous and devoted couple with their nine pretty children – were idolised by the respectable classes as the epitome of the reassuringly bourgeois, Victorian domestic ideal. More importantly, their happy married life was confirmation of the stability and continuity of the British monarchy itself as a working monarchy, focused on the family and with pride in its material and social achievements. 'The more I see of the Royal domestic life, the more I am in admiration of it,' General Grey had written in 1849. He was convinced that 'so pure and exemplary a Court never before existed'.[23] Two years later the youthful Eleanor Stanley, who had been in waiting at Windsor that Christmas, had told her parents, 'you can't think how simple and happy all the Royalty looked, just like any other family, of the most united and domestic tastes'.[24] This reputation for informal happy domesticity was one that Prince Albert had worked hard to establish and was determined to maintain, as the archetypal paterfamilias. Torrington's admiration was much the same in 1860. There was no doubting the esteem in which Victoria and Albert were held, he told Delane. He had never seen 'a more agreeable sight' that Christmas: 'It was royalty putting aside its state and becoming in words, acts, and deeds one of ourselves, no forms and not a vestige of ceremony.'[25]

At the end of that year the royal family was at the height of its popularity, at a time of political stability and economic progress in Britain. After riding out much hostility in the early years of his marriage and a storm of controversy over his perceived meddling in foreign affairs during the Crimean War of 1854–6, Prince Albert was finally beginning to receive some grudging acknowledgement for his many contributions to the cultural, scientific and intellectual life of the country, for the efficient way in which he conducted official business and for the strict moral code he maintained in his family life.

Victoria herself had enjoyed twenty years of happy marriage, secure in her husband's love and fidelity. That in itself was a rarity, in an age when princesses had little choice in their life partners and were too often consigned to loveless marriages of dynastic necessity. For Britain's queen adored her husband with a fierce and unquestioning devotion that none dared criticise and nothing could dim. Quite simply, he was all in all to her: surrogate father, husband, best friend, wise counsel, amanuensis and teacher – King in all but name. And, thanks to his influence, the British monarchy had been reinvigorated under its queen as a democratic and moral example for a new age that had at last divorced itself from the lingering reputation of the unpopular Hanoverians.

As the Christmas holiday drew to a close and the members of the royal household dispersed and returned to their duties, the Queen and her husband settled down to watch the last hours of 1860 turn, Victoria as always confiding it all in meticulous detail to her journal:

Dearest Albert and I took leave of the old year and wished each other joy of the new, at 12, before going to bed. I felt much moved, so anxious for the future, that no War should come, and fear for the state of Europe. My precious Husband cheered me and held me in his dear arms saying we must have trust, and we must believe that God will protect us.[26]

God had indeed protected them; their children had all survived infancy, confirmation in itself, as Lady Lytton observed, of the 'numberless instances of *perfect awful*, spotless prosperity' that had blessed the royal family till now, in an age when around one in five children died in infancy.[27] Victoria and Albert had yet to endure the anguish, at first hand, of close family bereavements. Death was still a stranger to them; it had yet to cast its shadow over the grey stone battlements of Windsor.

PART ONE

Albert the Good

CHAPTER ONE

'The Treadmill of
Never-Ending Business'

At the age of only eleven, the precocious Francis Charles Augustus Albert
Emmanuel of Saxe-Coburg and Gotha had already planned his future.
'I intend,' he confided in his diary, 'to train myself to be a good and
useful man.'[1] It was a noble, if exacting aspiration for one so young, but
one that, as husband of Queen Victoria, he would more than fulfil in
his years of devoted service to the British throne and its people.

He had been born three months after his cousin Princess Victoria, on
26 August 1819, and was delivered by the same German midwife – Charlotte
Heidenreich von-Siebold – at the Schloss Rosenau, four miles from Coburg.
The second son of Ernst, Duke of Saxe-Coburg-Saalfeld and his wife Louise
(of the rather more wealthy and prestigious house of Saxe-Gotha-
Altenburg), Albert was very close to his older brother Ernst.[2] Theirs was
an idyllic and harmonious childhood, spent sharing a hedonistic love of
nature during their summers at the Schloss Rosenau on the edge of the
ancient Thuringian forest. Here they spent their time walking, hunting,
shooting and fencing, as well as indulging their fascination with science
and nature in a passion for collecting specimens. Both boys were trained
in musical skills by their father, Albert becoming an accomplished pianist
and organist as well as a fine singer and talented composer. He was always
at his most self-expressive when playing the organ; music, his greatest love,
providing a conduit for the reflective and melancholic side of his nature.
It was a refuge for the poetical streak in him, which rarely found an outlet
in his public life and which in adulthood was all too soon overwhelmed
by responsibility. Fearful of strangers and prone to outbursts of tears,
Albert had had his young life marred by the collapse of his parents' marriage
in 1824. His philandering father, who had never attempted to conceal his
extramarital affairs, had abandoned Albert's young and vulnerable mother

Louise to long periods of solitude while he went out shooting, hunting and womanising. When Louise later sought consolation elsewhere, he banished her from their home – and from their two sons. Albert was only five. Louise remarried, but died of cancer six years later in 1831, without ever seeing her boys again.

The loss of his mother affected Prince Albert deeply. His diffidence and insecurity manifested themselves in later life in a compulsion to be controlling over others; more significantly, his father's libidinous character and his mother's flirtations (which prompted later unproven rumours of Louise's promiscuity and Albert's illegitimacy) instilled in him a patho-logical horror of sexual licence and a fear of the seductive power of women.[3] The path of duty and usefulness was a far safer one and he expected life to be a 'hard school', where pleasure came second.[4] With this in mind, at the age of fourteen the young and idealistic prince estab-lished his own exacting curriculum of study: nine hours a day of ancient and modern history, theology, translation from Latin, geography, English, mathematics, logic, music and drawing – all overseen by one of the most formative influences in his early life, his tutor Herr Christoph Florschütz.

As the good Herr Florschütz proceeded with kind but Teutonic vigour to educate Albert, he was guided in his task by Baron Christian Stockmar. As Private Secretary and physician to Albert's uncle, Leopold King of the Belgians, Stockmar was the Machiavellian figure who would long lurk in the shadows of Albert's life – envisioning a future role for him leading the thrones of Britain and a united Germany in the cause of constitutional monarchy. The vehicle for this would be marriage to Leopold's niece Victoria, heir to the British throne, and Albert's future life was already being mapped out for him when he was in his early teens. The subordinate, if not redundant role of consort was not the future that the Prince would have wished for himself, but as the second son of the ruler of a minor duchy the size of Lancashire and with no throne coming his way, marriage to Princess Victoria was, as Stockmar told him, a responsible task 'upon the fulfillment of which his honour and happiness depend[ed]'. Such cold logic was the stock-in-trade of the punctilious Stockmar. It would shape the austere, intellectual Albert's mind for the ·roles to come, so much so that he would later tell the Queen, 'To me a long closely connected train of reasoning is like a beautiful strain of music.' Stockmar's rationale lent the indelible mark of dry, Germanic formulas to Albert's abstract attitude not just to the masses and the human condition, but also to his approach to history and politics – a fact that would later put him at odds with the instinctive, empirical way in which they were conducted in Britain.[5]

After a period of intense intellectual and cultural grooming in Brussels, the University of Bonn, the Swiss Alps and the art galleries of Italy, Albert was deemed ready to take up his burden of duty. The prospect made him fearful, for despite being the most handsome student prince in Europe, he had remained supremely indifferent to the charms of the opposite sex, preferring the man's world of the intellect and philosophical debate. He had heard tell that his putative bride was 'incredibly stubborn' and, worse, frivolous, delighting in 'court ceremonies, etiquette and trivial formalities'.[6] Albert was shocked that Princess Victoria took no apparent interest in the beauties of nature, but was prone to staying up late. She didn't like getting up early either, something he would have to change. For a young man of Albert's sober mentality, marriage to the English princess had, in his opinion, 'gloomy prospects'. When Leopold and Stockmar had stage-managed the couple's first meeting in England in 1836, Albert had come away thinking Victoria 'amiable', but little more. She, for her part, had found 'dearest Albert' handsome and kind, but rather pale and sickly. Although Victoria soon came to the conclusion that her putative husband was possessed of 'every quality that could be desired to make me perfectly happy', marriage to Albert after she became Queen in 1837 was not an immediate, foregone conclusion. For the first time in her life Victoria was independent of her mother's stifling control. She was determined to enjoy her freedom and have her own way in everything, as well as relishing her sovereign power, all of which was far more attractive than matrimony and the inevitability – and dangers – of childbirth. Besides, to her mind, Albert needed to gain wider experience and improve his English in order to be the consort of a queen. As princeling-in-waiting, Albert was therefore obliged to sit it out while the impressionable and impetuous Victoria was distracted by the claims of the other candidates jostling for her hand. Leopold and Stockmar, meanwhile, began to fear their long-held dream was slipping beyond their reach.

* * *

An absence of three and a half years and a string of unsuitable candidates changed everything. Just as Albert was losing patience with the long wait for Victoria's final approval, he was summoned to England in October 1839. The young queen was taken aback; the shy, podgy young man of 1836 had been transformed into a storybook-handsome prince who, with his large blue eyes and his 'exquisite nose', was both 'striking' and 'fascinating'.[7] She was swept off her feet by Albert's good looks, fine figure and youthful charm. What had begun as a stage-managed dynastic union now unexpectedly burst into the full bloom of ecstatic love, certainly on Victoria's part. Five days later, using her queenly prerogative, she proposed. Albert was far less certain of his feelings at this point, playing the role of acquiescent, if not bewildered mate, happy to bask in Victoria's passionate attachment to him: 'Victoria is so good and kind to me. I am often at a loss to believe that such affection should be shown to me,' he told Stockmar.[8] Mentally prepared though he may have been for the marriage to come, it was far harder for Albert to adapt in the four short months left to him to the idea of leaving his beloved Coburg for Buckingham Palace in the heart of sooty, polluted London. He contemplated his future life in England and the task of adapting to its language, the customs of its court, its chilly climate and its food with great apprehension. Marrying Victoria, and all the expectations that went with it, was a tremendous burden. He would have to leave behind everything that he loved, but he was characteristically single-minded about the sacrifice he was expected to make and the challenge that awaited him. 'With the exception of my relations towards [the Queen] my future position will have its dark sides, and the sky will not always be blue and unclouded,' he wrote resignedly to his stepmother. 'But life has its thorns in every position, and the consciousness of having used one's powers and endeavours for an object so great as that of having promoted the good of so many, will surely be sufficient to support me.'[9]

It was a terrible wrench for Albert to leave Coburg and especially the Rosenau, the 'paradise of our childhood', not to mention his brother Ernst, who had till then been his dearest and closest friend.[10] At the end of January 1840 Albert departed in floods of tears, accompanied by his faithful greyhound Eos and his Swiss valet Isaac Cart, vowing that he would 'never cease to be a true *German*, a true *Coburg & Gotha* man', and suffering violent seasickness all the way across the Channel.[11] Much as he loved Victoria, hers was the overwhelming passion. Young, introverted and inexperienced sexually, he did not know how to respond to her ardour and felt swamped by it. Never being one to express his feelings openly, he anticipated marriage more as a test of his purity of intent than as the fulfilment of any personal or emotional aspirations. Love, in his book, came second to the greater good; but for Victoria, it was absolutely everything. And even as Albert travelled, debate was raging in Britain on the thorny subject of his cost to the nation. Victoria's demand for an annual income for him of £50,000 had prompted much satirical comment on this German prince, who 'comes to take "for better or for worse" England's fat queen and England's fatter purse'.[12]

* * *

On a freezing cold 10 February 1840 Victoria and Albert were married in the Chapel Royal at St James's Palace, in a ceremony from which many of the leading members of Parliament were absent. Victoria allowed only five Tories to be invited, in retaliation for the open hostility of men in that political party to her choice of a German bridegroom: 'It is MY marriage,' she declared with her characteristic stubbornness, 'and I will only have those who can sympathise with me.'[13] Critics of her beloved Albert would henceforth be given short shrift. That day, as everyone agreed, Albert had never looked more handsome, nor she more radiant as she gazed up at his beautiful face. When asked by the Archbishop of Canterbury the previous day whether she wished to promise 'to obey', Victoria had replied that she wished 'to be married as a woman and not as a Queen'.[14] Her lifelong role as Albert's votaress was born on her wedding day. After only three days' honeymoon at Windsor, punctuated by walks on the terrace and duets at the piano, she was eager to get back to business, professing herself to be the 'happiest, happiest Being that ever existed'. Albert clearly had more than fulfilled his sexual expectations; but as for the rest – he was left to shift for himself, his only perceived role being that most marginal one of royal stud; 'we should erect a statue to Prince Albert for having provided us with this additional barrier against the King of Hanover', remarked one of the royal household when the Princess Royal was born that November.[15]

Prince Albert had been only too right to anticipate the sense of aliena-tion he would feel in England; it had been made far worse by the fact that he arrived in a country already disposed to dislike him as a German, as a 'pauper prince' and, even worse, that suspected him of being a secret Catholic. From the outset he was made fun of in the satirical press and among old-school Tories at court for his heavy German accent, his stiff and starchy manner and his outmoded style of dress. Soon after his arrival he was deeply affronted when Parliament voted to reduce his allowance to £30,000. But the worst of it was that, as a man driven by a sense of purpose, he found it very hard to deal with the idleness imposed on him by his role as husband to the monarch. He could not reconcile himself to being married to a wife who, whilst acknowledging at all times her husband's authority as head of domestic affairs, often treated him with brusque impatience and seemed intent on excluding him from any useful assistance in her official duties. In May 1840 he observed with some disgruntlement: 'In my whole life I am very happy and contented; but the difficulty in filling my place with the proper dignity is, that I am only the husband, and not the master of the house.'[16]

Albert's emasculation during these early months, as he struggled for a modicum of independence while Victoria demanded that he be at her constant beck and call on domestic matters, was frustrating and deeply humiliating. It took place against a backdrop of heated arguments between the Queen and the government over his precedence at court and his appointment as regent (should she die in childbirth). Having accepted naturalisation on his marriage to the Queen, Albert expected some official recognition of his position of pre-eminence – perhaps a peerage and, with it, a seat in the House of Lords. The Queen could not deny that she would have liked him to be accorded the status of King alongside her, but this was not to be. Albert's crippling shyness did not help matters. The artist Benjamin Haydon observed him at a ball in 1842, looking 'like a cowed and kept pet, frightened to sit, frightened to stand'.[17] Nevertheless Albert's patience paid off: he gained great influence over Victoria, subtly and by degrees, judiciously giving way in trivial things, so much so that he 'never finished a game of chess with her for the first three years'.[18] For the time being he established his influence in the only way open to him, by inculcating his own lofty ideals and interests in his impressionable wife. Victoria, whilst having natural gifts of intuition, was never his equal intellectually and accepted it. She was 'as full of love as Juliet', as Sir Robert Peel had observed, and, hungering as she did for Albert's praise and approval, submitted herself willingly, adoringly, to his greater wisdom.[19] Prince Albert became for her the much-longed-for father figure. Under his diligent tutelage, Victoria's mind was reformed: her slim grasp of the arts and science was enhanced. She eagerly accepted Albert's leadership as regards the books they read, the music they enjoyed, the paintings and sculpture they collected. She even modified her own 'bad' habits – as Albert perceived them – by ceasing to stay up late and giving over less and less of her time to dancing and idle gossip with her ladies-in-waiting.

But Albert, with his thirst for constant self-improvement, was discontented merely to sit by his wife's side, blotting her official letters as she wrote them; he sought to play an active role in the political life and culture of his adopted country. The first step came when in September 1840 a heavily pregnant Victoria made him a member of the Privy Council in order to stand in for her when she was confined; soon after she gave him a duplicate set of keys to her official boxes. From there Albert set about studying British laws and the constitution, educating Victoria, who by temperament was an autocrat, in the art of good administration and her sovereign duty. He worked hard to soften the obstinate and shamefully partisan attitude that she had displayed in the early years of her reign, weaning her away from her Whig bias towards an acceptance of the new Tory government and impressing upon her the all-essential political impartiality of the sovereign. Victoria was reluctant to relinquish any royal prerogatives, but understood the constitutional limitations placed on her, which her husband insisted she scrupulously observe. In so doing she ensured that her throne did not share the fate of those that later fell, like Louis Philippe of France's, in the revolutionary year of 1848.

In the battle to assert his supremacy over the Queen, in the autumn of 1842 Albert engineered the removal of her closest and most powerful confidante, her old governess, Baroness Lehzen. The first real opportunity to exercise his punctilious sense of order and frugality had come earlier that year when he had reorganised the royal household in a sweeping programme of cost-cutting and the rigid elimination of the 'canker' of waste, inefficiency and pilfering that had gone on for decades.[20] The money saved by this exercise would later be used to fund the building of Osborne House. By 1845, having endured the first years of his anticipated martyrdom uncomplainingly, Albert now held a position of moral and sexual power over his wife, as she slipped increasingly into the contented role of *Hausfrau*. Such was his concerted re-education of her as monarch that Victoria became convinced that her life before Albert had been worthless – entirely artificial and frivolous. The royal couple had become effectively a dual monarchy, receiving ministers together and talking of their role collectively, in terms of 'We think, or wish, to do so and so'. They even worked side by side at adjacent desks. Officially, the only title Albert was conceded was that of 'Husband of the Queen', but the marked elevation in his role by his wife prompted the court diarist, Charles Greville, to observe that 'He is become so identified with her that they are one person.' The Queen patently disliked official business, whereas Albert relished it; as a result, Victoria's dependency on him grew as her resistance to his control waned. It was obvious to Greville 'that while she has the title he is really discharging the functions of the Sovereign. He is King to all intents and purposes.'[21] And behind the scenes Albert worked hard to repel any encroachments on the power of the Crown that he now effectively controlled.

While he was set on a determined course of slowly winning the confidence of the British government as an unofficial, self-appointed minister, as the years passed much of Albert's time was necessarily consumed by domesticity. He was to provide patient and reassuring support to his wife through her successive pregnancies and bouts of post-natal depression. Victoria's histrionic outbursts were, however, extremely hard to deal with; as a natural introvert, Prince Albert hated emotional conflicts – and those with his wife were tempestuous, to say the least. He therefore developed a habit of avoiding confrontations and writing headmasterly notes to her about her behaviour, rather than dealing with it face-to-face, a practice that infuriated the headstrong and combative queen. Albert would not be diverted from his mission to remould his petulant wife; he doggedly and repeatedly urged her to curb her temper and learn self-restraint. Duly chastised, Victoria tried hard to rise to the challenge and aspire to the levels of perfection with which her adored husband was endowed. Little by little, Albert chipped away at his wife's impetuosity, and with it, one might also say, her instinctiveness and natural vivacity. Power and control were the aphrodisiacs that drove Albert; he might never be King, but all the time his wife was his creature, and so often physically sidelined by pregnancy that he could vicariously enjoy some of the power he knew he would never officially be given.

Without doubt, Albert's domestic life with Victoria brought many pleasures, as the children arrived in quick succession, from Vicky, their firstborn, in 1840 to their ninth child, Beatrice, in 1857. As a typical patriarch, he imposed his authoritarian attitudes on the royal nursery, putting his children in characteristic Victorian awe and fear of him. He oversaw their health, diet and welfare with Teutonic precision, recommending simple food and a rigorous curriculum. Much as he loved them and enjoyed their company, the Prince was a hard taskmaster. 'Upon the good education of Princes, and especially those who are destined to govern,' he remarked to his secretary George Anson, 'the welfare of the world in these days greatly depends.'[22] With this in mind, he closely supervised the schoolroom's day-to-day running with his children's governors and governesses. One of them, Madame Hocédé – French teacher to Prince Leopold and Princesses Helena and Louise – later recalled her regular consultations with the Prince about his children's education and how he never left her 'without my feeling that he had strengthened my

hands and raised the standard I was aiming at'.[23] Having a particular
interest in education, Albert personally devised his children's demanding
curriculum and administered corporal punishment (albeit reluctantly)
when they failed to toe the line. All of the children suffered, to varying
degrees, from the academic and personal pressures placed on them by
both parents, as well as the constant comparisons made with their sainted
father by the Queen. But whereas the intellectually gifted Vicky blossomed under Albert's favouritism and tutelage, his son and heir Bertie
wilted and rebelled under its rigour; the emotional scars Bertie suffered
in hopeless pursuit of academic achievements beyond his grasp set the
scene for future conflict between them.

*   *   *

Only a handful of people in the inner sanctum of the royal household
ever came to know Prince Albert intimately; even fewer won his friendship. The majority at court and in government – whom Albert always
held at arm's length – found it impossible to warm to his inhibited manner
and thought him cold and egotistical, like a 'German Professor', one of
several nicknames in circulation.[24] Even the Queen's jealous Hanoverian
relatives, such as her uncle the Duke of Cambridge, viewed him as a
'Coburg interloper'. She might promote her husband as a paragon of
virtue to anyone who would listen, but too often the Prince Consort
appeared inflexible, particularly over matters of royal etiquette and
protocol, and humourless too. He always seemed so decidedly superior
in his detachment from court circles, and in particular in his disdain for
the profligacy of the British aristocracy. They in turn could not understand
why the Prince had no mistresses, or, for that matter, any apparent interest
in women. It was only a matter of time, they assumed, before this would
change. 'Damn it, Madam,' Lord Melbourne had remarked to the Queen
when she was first married, 'you don't expect that he'll always be faithful
to you, do you?!'[25] But in fact Albert was. He refused to play the gallant
and was notorious for being offhand with ladies at court, so much so that
his secretary Anson noted that 'the Queen is proud of the Prince's utter
indifference to the attractions of all the ladies'.[26]

Albert's apparent incorruptibility was infuriating, for he did not seem to
be susceptible to the corrosive lifestyle of the typical courtier. He was
abstemious, ate frugally and stuck to the German habit of dining early,
never stopping to lounge around over the port and cigars; nor did he
frequent the London clubs or cultivate any English friends. Instead, he went

to bed early and walked every day with his wife and children, like any bourgeois paterfamilias. Even the way he rode to hounds was criticised: 'he did not fly his fences in true Leicestershire style,' carped the fox-hunting aristocracy who so despised him, and who hated him even more for regularly stealing the best prizes with his cattle at agricultural shows.[27] Everything about Albert was so proper; he was altogether 'too good'. The dullness and sanctimoniousness of the 'bourgeois court' over which he and Victoria ruled soon became legendary – both at home and abroad.

The prudish, antisocial streak in Albert's nature thus often made him appear more pedant than paragon, a man so formal and so circumspect that his real character was rarely divined by others. His reserve set up barriers to those who might otherwise have admired him, and people tended to respond to his personality as one of two extremes – as Queen Victoria's saintly 'Albert the Good', or as the much-disliked foreign interloper, 'Albert der King'. Steeling himself to this barrage of hostility, Albert meanwhile forged ahead with his wide-ranging interests in science, industry, education and the arts. He received a great fillip in October 1847 when – against considerable and undignified opposition – he was elected Chancellor of Cambridge University, in which capacity he would encourage a rapid and dramatic liberalising of its academic courses. In the visual arts he and Victoria collected paintings by Cranach, Dürer, Memling and Van Eyck, which would later greatly enhance the national collections; as patron of the Royal Photographic Society, Prince Albert was a passionate supporter of the genre and, with the Queen, amassed an unrivalled collection of early photographic work. In his reorganisation of the incomparable print collections at Windsor and his cataloguing of the royal collection of drawings by Raphael, Holbein and Leonardo da Vinci, the Prince left a lasting memorial to his own considerable scholarship as an art historian. In music, through his patronage of the Royal Philharmonic Society, Albert championed the work of his compatriots Wagner, Mendelssohn and Schumann.

Prince Albert's passionate interest in art and architecture had brought an invitation to join the Royal Commission of Arts, set up in 1841 to supervise the interior decorations of the new Houses of Parliament, inspiring him later to take a hand – in his spare time from all his many other pursuits – in supervising the design and construction of the royal family's new homes, at Osborne in the 1840s and Balmoral in the 1850s. As time went on he found himself increasingly in demand to give lectures on art, science, business and philanthropy, to attend exhibitions and play a high profile in the cultural life of the country. He sat on numerous humanitarian committees, such as the

Society for the Extinction of the Slave Trade and the Society for the Improvement of the Condition of the Labouring Classes. Duty and yet more duty was piled on him; as a connoisseur, humanitarian and polymath, Albert found it impossible to say no. But by 1848, during the year of revolutions in Europe – when it took him all day just to get through all the French, German and English newspapers – he was complaining to his stepmother in Coburg that he could not remember being 'kept in the stocks' of work as he was now.[28] His workload intensified at an alarming rate thereafter, culminating in the drain on his energies demanded by his visionary approach to the promotion of British excellence at the Great Exhibition, which he master-minded, as chair of the Royal Society of Arts, from 1849 until its opening in 1851. Similar, smaller exhibitions had taken place before in England, in northern cities such as Leeds, Liverpool and Sheffield during the 1830s and 1840s, but Albert's plan was far more ambitious. His objective had been nothing less than 'to give us a true test and a living picture of the point of development at which the whole of mankind has arrived . . . and a new starting-point from which all nations will be able to direct their further exertions'.[29]

The Exhibition proved to be the apogee of Prince Albert's civilising and cultural aspirations for his adopted country; it was also a triumphant celebration not just of British, but of international arts and industry. Throughout the planning Albert played the role, effectively, of a govern-ment minister and refused to be deterred by the many difficulties and disappointments he had to deal with along the way. Confirmation of his achievement – despite the continued sneering and sniping of the *beau monde* who still despised him – was only too visible when 34,000 people gathered at the Crystal Palace in Hyde Park on opening day, 1 May 1851. Victoria swelled with wifely pride: it was the happiest and proudest day of her life. The exhibition was entirely 'the triumph of my beloved Albert', she had no doubt of that. And for once the press grudgingly agreed; even the unbridled antagonism of *Punch* magazine at last abated.[30]

But it was a triumph achieved at the expense of Albert's always precarious physical well-being. Shortly before the Great Exhibition, in a written exchange with the Duke of Wellington over whether or not Albert should become Commander in Chief of the Army (which he wisely declined), the Prince defined the indispensable role that he felt he was now fulfilling at the right hand of the Queen. It was a role that had required him to 'entirely sink his *own individual* existence in that of his wife' so as to:

continuously and anxiously watch every part of the public business, in
order to be able to advise and assist her at any moment in any of the
multifarious and difficult questions or duties brought before her, sometimes international, sometimes political, or social, or personal.

Quite clearly, Albert believed that his wife, and more importantly the
monarchy, could not function smoothly without his own now-essential
input. With considerable self-satisfaction he enumerated his many roles,
as 'the natural head of her family, superintendent of her household,
manager of her private affairs, sole *confidential* adviser in politics, only
assistant in her communications with officers of Government', besides
which he was 'the husband of the Queen, the tutor of the royal children,
the private secretary of the sovereign, and her permanent minister'.[31] As
for Victoria, her emotional dependency on her husband was now total:
'You cannot think . . . how completely *déroulée* I am and *feel* when he is
away, or how I count the numerous children are *as nothing* to me when
he is away!' she told her uncle, King Leopold, in 1857.[32]

During the 1850s the prince's impressive job description was further
enhanced by his ambitions to break down British insularity with regard to
foreign affairs. 'His foreign correspondence alone, which the public here
knew nothing of,' remarked Albert's friend, the geologist Sir Charles Lyell,
'would have been thought sufficient occupation for one who had nothing
else to do.' In everything, the 'quantity of work he got through, in spite
of innumerable interruptions, was immense'.[33] It was during the Fifties
that Albert increasingly brought his years of political study into play, as
his insights deepened. He fired off endless memoranda to ministers, as
well as offering advice on every possible subject to his wife, so much so
that Victoria noted in her journal, 'He always lets me get the credit for
his excellent ideas, which pains me.'[34] Albert's grasp of foreign policy finally
found an outlet with the outbreak of war against Russia in 1854. But in
time of war Prince Albert was an all-too-obvious target for British xeno-
phobia. Government ministers and the press resented his perceived intrusion and during the war reverted to old habits, once more whipping up
hostility towards Albert as a foreigner and calling his political allegiances
into question. The gutter-press spread rumours that he might be a Russian
spy, and he was hissed at on his way to the state opening of Parliament
with the Queen in 1854. Rumours reached an absurd level when it was
suggested that the Prince was to be arrested for high treason and sent to

the Tower. But Albert endured the abuse and, as the war went on, boldly called into question its mismanagement, repeatedly urging the organisation of British militia forces to be sent as reinforcements to the exhausted and beleaguered British army in the Crimea. He wrote endless memoranda on every aspect of the military campaign – a body of work amounting to fifty folio volumes of documents – yet the only publicly acknowledged contribution that he was allowed to make during this time of national crisis was the design of the newly instituted Victoria Cross. However, by the end of the war he had gained one grudging admirer. Albert's old adversary, Lord Palmerston, who had been returned to power as Prime Minister during the war in January 1855, had by its end been forced to concede the Prince's value to the nation in promoting British prestige and interests in the royal courts of Europe, as well as his beneficial effect on the Queen and her conduct of royal business.

Through it all, his loyal wife remained Prince Albert's loudest and most vocal advocate, prompting one of her most spirited responses to criticism of his influence over her. 'A woman *must* have a support and an adviser,' she insisted to Lord Aberdeen, 'and who can this properly be but her husband, whose duty it is to watch over her interests, private and public?' Were it not for Albert, Victoria was adamant that her health and strength 'would long since have sunk under the multifarious duties of her position as Queen, and the mother of a large family'.[35] By the mid-Fifties she had firmly decided that 'we women are not meant for governing' and was increasingly happy to leave the job to Albert.[36] With this in mind, she had him elevated to the title of Prince Consort by royal decree in 1857 – the closest he would ever come to being named King.

*   *   *

Victoria might have become more and more content to play the role of wife rather than Queen, but by the end of the Crimean War in 1856 Prince Albert's untiring service to the monarchy and Britain had begun to take an alarming toll on his health. His constant sublimation of his own needs to his wife's far more volatile emotional ones had worn him down: always putting her first, advising, reassuring, consoling, shielding her from trouble and anxiety at every turn and being the crucial stabilising force that had enabled Victoria to fulfil her duties as Queen. Had she noticed it, her husband was already showing visible signs of chronic fatigue. He had, for most of his life, been plagued by ill health. A sickly child, he had suffered attacks of croup, anaemia and nosebleeds and had always tired easily, even to the extent of falling asleep at table. He had a slow metabolism and a low pulse rate, which made him prone to attacks of fainting and dizziness; since the age of fifteen he had suffered from rheumatic pain and, intermittently, from what was loosely referred to as a 'weak digestion' that brought on visitations by what Albert called 'his old enemy' – frequent, unspecified gastric attacks accompanied by spasms of intense pain, fever and shivering.[37] Stress clearly aggravated his condition; even Victoria noticed that whenever her husband was upset or anxious it would 'affect his poor dear stomach'.[38] Albert's own response to bouts of gastric illness was rigorous: he purged himself with hot water and applied his own 'fasting cure' – 'so as to rob my stomach of the shadow of a pretext for behaving ill', so he claimed.[39] What was clearly developing into a chronic condition appears never to have been subjected to any kind of rigorous examination or diagnosis by his doctors, medical science at that time defining a whole range of stomach complaints as 'gastric attacks' and having no means of differentiating between them.

As a compulsive obsessive and workaholic, the stress of the many speeches Albert had to give and the public functions he had to attend often brought on bouts of vomiting and migraines, which in turn affected his sleep. In the view of royal physician Sir James Clark, anxiety – 'the great waster of life' – was dulling his senses and wearing the Prince out.[40] In addition Albert hated the damp of the English climate and succumbed with alarming regularity in the autumn to feverish chills. His wife, however, who remained rudely robust for most of her life, never made any concessions to her frailer husband's need to ward off the cold. He was left to suffer in the underheated rooms in the royal palaces, permeated by gusts of cold air from the perpetually open windows that Victoria demanded, his only recourse being to enclose himself in thick long johns at night and wear a wig at breakfast to keep his balding head warm.

Yet still he laboured on, rising every morning at seven to do an hour's work in his study before breakfast; filling every day with a close reading of all the newspapers and the writing of endless letters – including a prodigious correspondence with his contemporaries on the Continent. In addition there were detailed memoranda to government ministers, as well as his extensive committee work; in every single thing he did he tried to 'do what was right by the Queen and the country'.[41] He walked fast and worked fast, often eating at speed as he did so, and rushed at 'double-quick pace' from one meeting to the next. He hated having to stop and his pace was remorseless: incessantly travelling up and down the country, making speeches, opening bridges and hospitals, laying foundation stones and appearing as patron or chair at the many scientific, cultural and academic organisations that he supported. The only respite from his self-imposed and onerous duties and so much nervous hurry came during family holidays at Balmoral and Osborne. Here Prince Albert would lose himself in his great love of the outdoors – hunting, shooting, fishing and overseeing the model farms he had created on the royal estates. But even recreation was given strict time limits and such holidays never restored his health and his spirits for very long. Work had become the all-consuming surrogate for a more normal, sociable life at court – a lifestyle he disdained and where he had never felt at ease. Prince Albert's unceasing pursuit of his many noble visions was sucking him dry. He had never got over his homesickness for Coburg, and his sense of isolation and disappointment had grown, as his mental and physical energies had dissolved. He had worked hard to make people admire him through his many services to the state, but getting them to like him in his own right (and not merely as an adjunct of the royal family) was a battle he had so far not won. He despaired at public indifference to his work and how little he was under-stood or appreciated in England: 'Man is a beast of burden,' he remarked gloomily in November 1856, 'and he is only happy if he has to drag his burden and if he has little free will. My experience teaches me every day to understand the truth of this, more and more.'[42]

Albert's growing sense of loneliness was exacerbated in 1849 by the sudden death of his secretary, George Anson, a loyal friend as well as servant, who had from the mid-1840s been extremely concerned at his master's punishing workload. By the late 1850s, with the departure of his adored daughter Vicky, who married the Crown Prince of Prussia in 1858, much of Albert's vital spark had irretrievably faded; he became increasingly stern and humourless, retreating into himself more and more. Without real friends or close intellectual peers, or his own entou-rage at court, or a supportive political faction in Parliament, his only consolation was his work. And much as he loved his wife, Albert's attach-ment to her was increasingly driven by the principles of reason and duty and doing the right thing. Victoria was fundamentally his '*gutes Weibchen*' – the good and loyal little wife – and mother of his children. She gave him her all, but for a man as restless as Albert it was never enough; she was not, and never could be, his soul's mistress. And for Victoria it was agony; there was nothing she could do to hold back the tide of melan-cholia and pessimism that was engulfing her husband. As Albert's chief acolyte, she could fulminate loud and often to their children about how their father was without equal – 'so great, so good, so faultless' – but his wife's admiration and praise were no palliative for 'the dragon of his dissatisfaction' that was now starting to consume him.[43] Nor could Victoria's obsessive love disguise the growing tension between them, brought on by Albert's impossible workload, which she increasingly resented for allowing them less and less time together.

In December 1858 came the first serious warning signs of the collapse of the Prince Consort's health, when yet another regular attack of gastric illness, supposedly the result of 'over-fatigue', laid him low in the weeks before Christmas. But although he confided to his diary his growing sense of utter weariness and despondency, those about him were not aware how deep his sense of exhaustion ran. For the truth was that Albert, Prince Consort was not only being progressively 'torn to pieces with business of every kind', he was physically broken and spiritually despairing.[44]

CHAPTER TWO

'The First Real Blow of Misfortune'

By the beginning of 1859 Albert, Prince Consort – the romantic Thuringian prince of 1840 – was sallow, balding and putting on weight. He was approaching forty, but already ageing fast as his reserves of strength evaporated and his virility waned. Fearful of confronting her husband's much deeper malaise, Queen Victoria put it down to overwork. Work always made Albert so irritable and 'very trying', in her view, but even she was becoming alarmed at how ill and 'fagged' he looked.[1] For now, quite apart from all his many public commitments, there were family problems preying on his mind. Ever a martyr to self-induced stress, Albert had a new and escalating anxiety, in his own and Victoria's worries about the future of the dynasty under their eldest son, Albert Edward, Prince of Wales.

'Poor Bertie', as his mother so frequently referred to him. He was a 'stupid boy' whose attention could not be fixed on anything useful, 'even at a novel'. He had grown up in the full glare of his mother's unending disappointment at his idleness and unprepossessing appearance, as well as his exacting father's constant pressure that he fulfil the impossibly high expectations they both placed on him.[2] As a child Bertie had craved parental affection and reassurance, but his naturally cheerful and ebullient nature had been cowed by the austere regime imposed by his father. Such repression had led to childish outbursts of understandable temper and frustration, a fact that caused the Queen to worry that Bertie's bad behaviour made him her 'caricature'.[3] She and Albert both dreaded that, in his laziness and egocentricity, their son and heir might grow up tainted by the blood of his disreputable Hanoverian ancestors. 'Remember, there is only my life between his and the lives of my Wicked Uncles,' Victoria retorted when later taken to task on this point.[4]

Albert's response to his son's weakness of character had been to impose a rigorous education that isolated him from his friends and would knock him into shape. A strict regime had worked for him, Albert, as a child and ought to do likewise for his dullard of a son. Bertie struggled to cope with his exacting timetable, but was endlessly chastised by his father for his poor academic performance. Albert's response to Bertie's tantrums at his workload was merely to make things even harder for him. Failure was not in Albert's lexicon. On the advice of Baron Stockmar, he demanded that Bertie study seven hours a day seven days a week, in a relentless quest for self-improvement. He personally checked his son's course-work and essays; any slight improvement in his performance was commended, but minor improvements never lasted for long. When Bertie reached seventeen he was therefore entrusted to the care of three equerries who took turns in ensuring that he behaved, as his father stipulated, like a gentleman. They were instructed to make sure he did not loll around in armchairs, or stand with his hands in his pockets. He was also to be kept from idle gossip and frivolous pursuits such as cards and billiards – and, the ultimate anathema, smoking cigars. He should be encouraged instead to be like his father and 'to devote some of his leisure time to music, to the fine arts . . . hearing poetry, amusing books or good plays read aloud, in short, to anything that whilst it amuses may gently exercise the mind'.[5] But it did no good; the more Bertie was controlled and chastised, the more he indulged, in secret, in all the things forbidden to him.

The Queen and Prince Albert dreaded Bertie's coming-of-age in 1859, a day on which he was greeted not with warm congratulations, but by a long, pedantic letter from his parents full of exhortations about his moral duties and that 'in due, punctual and cheerful performance of them the true Christian and the true Gentleman is recognised'. It was all too much for Bertie and he burst into floods of tears.[6] By the end of that year Prince Albert had reached a state of despairing resignation over Bertie's obtuseness, informing Vicky in Berlin that although he was 'lively, quick and sharp when his mind is set on anything, which is seldom', her brother's intellect was 'of no more use than a pistol packed at the bottom of a trunk if one were attacked in the robber-infested Apennines'.[7] By April of the following year the Queen had begun seriously to wonder to Vicky what on earth would happen should she die and Bertie become King. In their shared dissatisfaction with him, she and Albert concurred that the only thing that might save him from himself would be an early marriage. But how were they to keep Bertie on the straight and narrow until a suitable bride could be found? 'We can't hold him except by moral power,' the Queen concluded.[8] For now, a stretch at a Grenadier Guards camp at the Curragh in Ireland during the university vacation might help to make him knuckle under. It was only his father who had managed to keep Bertie out of trouble thus far. 'His only safety and the country's,' the Queen told Vicky, 'is in his implicit reliance in every thing on dearest Papa, that perfection of human beings!' But alarm bells were already sounding in Victoria's head: 'My greatest of all anxieties is that dearest Papa works too hard, wears himself quite out by all he does.' All this worry about Bertie, she was sure, was too much for her husband.[9]

With alarming predictability, in August 1859 Albert was laid low by yet another of his 'stomach attacks' and was unable to eat or drink anything but a little milk and water for days. Although he did his best to conceal from her how unwell he felt, even Victoria thought her husband looked 'fearfully ill'[10] Whenever sickness overwhelmed him, Albert felt the additional stress of being kept from his duties. There was always so much to do. In late October he was ill again, suffering one of the severest and most obstinate attacks the Queen had ever seen, 'the more annoying as it was accompanied by violent spasms of pain', which kept him in bed for two days. 'It has been such an unusual thing to see him in bed (never except for the measles),' she observed ruefully. Whenever Albert was ill, it 'cast such a gloom over us all', the Queen remarked, for when he was not able to be out and about as usual, it turned home life 'upside down'.[11]

Albert put his latest bout of sickness down to the 'sudden incredible change of temperature of the last fortnight', and resumed his duties without taking any real time off to convalesce.[12] The royal Physician-in-Ordinary, Sir James Clark, who had been with the Queen since her accession, but who was now in his seventies and approaching retirement, offered his own rather nebulous prognosis. It was, quite simply, all in the mind. Among the many causes of Albert's present condition, Clark reckoned that 'the worries both of body and mind to which you are daily exposed, the unusual heat of the year, and also the great strain on your strength [that] your position is constantly exposing you to' all increased the risk of him having his health 'deranged'. Clark, a physician of limited scientific understanding who had trained in an earlier, less sophisticated medical age, serving as a naval surgeon in the Napoleonic Wars, was noted for his faulty diagnoses and his timid 'watch-and-wait' policy. His presence at court, however, suited the Queen, who hated change and liked the reassurance of his familiar face. Clark, fearful always of demoralising her, kowtowed to Victoria and told her what she wanted to hear. To give him credit, Clark had at least emphasised the need for proper nursing and convalescent care, which Albert should have had whenever he was ill, but which he and his busy schedule never allowed.[13] But, for his own part, Albert placed little faith in the ageing Clark's diagnostic skills; the Prince had in the past been critical of his ineffectual management of the ailments of the royal children – most notably Clark's treatment of Vicky with asses' milk during a bout of illness in 1841.

Prince Albert was, however, only too well aware of the toll his never-ending catalogue of duties was taking on him physically and mentally. In his weekly letter to Vicky in Berlin, written on 23 May 1860, his sense of exhaustion was palpable. Spring in England was beautiful, he wrote: 'the most glorious air, the most fragrant odours, the merriest choirs of birds and the most luxuriant verdure', but he did not have time to enjoy any of it – not even the fresh primroses brought to his desk by his children, who knew how much Papa loved them. For Albert was totally and irrevocably chained to the 'treadmill of never-ending business'; so much so that he was 'tortured' at the prospect of his future commitments. Ahead lay two interminable public dinners at which he would be in the chair: 'the one gives me seven, the other ten toasts and speeches, appropriate to the occasion, and distracting to myself'. Later on he was to open the 'Statistical Congress of all nations' – yet more toasts and speeches – and in the interim he was faced with the prospect of:

> laying the foundation stone of the Dramatic College, etc. etc.; and this, with the sittings of my different Commissions, and Ascot races . . . and the Balls and Concerts of the season all crowded into the month of June, over and above the customary business, which a distracted state of affairs in Europe, and a stormy Parliament . . . make still more burdensome and disagreeable than usual.[14]

Later that year, during a visit to Coburg, Albert narrowly escaped serious injury in a carriage accident when the horses he had been driving took fright and bolted straight towards a railway crossing. Unable to prevent a collision with a stationary wagon, he had leapt from the carriage, anticipating oblivion. He escaped with cuts and bruises and made light of it, but the accident was yet another reminder, at a time when his spirits were already low, of his own mortality. Both Baron Stockmar and

Albert's brother Ernst, who saw him before he returned to England, were dismayed by the change in him. It was not just the despondency in his eyes, it was a sense they both felt that he had no fight left in him. Something was very wrong. 'God have mercy on us!' Stockmar confided to his diary. 'If anything should ever happen to him, he will die.'[15]

Not long after his return to England, Albert once again succumbed to stomach problems, suffering 'violent sickness and shiverings' in the night, and was confined to his room. The attack was severe, but as usual he concealed from his family how ill he felt. He remained weak for several days, referring to his illness as 'the real English cholera' – he also called it 'cholerina' – a term then in use for mild, choleraic-type attacks of diarrhoea. But as usual he returned to his work before recovering sufficiently, as he hated falling behind with his correspondence. Sensing his malaise, Victoria was loath to bother him on official business, as she 'knew it would distress or irritate him, and affect his delicate stomach'.[16] But Albert's depressed state of mind received a further blow in January 1861, when his much-valued and talented new physician, Dr William Baly, was killed in a railway accident. The forty-seven-year-old Baly, a doctor at St Bartholomew's Hospital in London and a specialist in enteric disease, had been appointed Extraordinary Physician to the Queen in 1859 on the recommendation of Dr Clark, in anticipation of Clark's imminent retirement. Prince Albert had taken to him from the first; Baly's death was 'a great, great loss' for them, he told Stockmar, 'as he had gained our entire confidence, and was an excellent man'.[17] Had Baly not died, it is possible that with his greater air of authority and experience in up-to-date medical practice than the ageing Clark – who on Baly's death was called back into royal service from retirement – he would have immediately insisted on complete bed-rest for the Prince.[18]

The year 1861 started badly for Prince Albert; even the popular *Zalkiel's Almanac* for 1861 warned that 'The stationary position of Saturn in the third degree of Virgo in May, following upon this lunation, will be very evil for all persons born on or near the 26th August.' Among the sufferers, it regretted to see 'the worthy Prince Consort of these realms'. 'Let such persons pay scrupulous attention to health,' it had prophetically intoned.[19] A replacement was soon found for Baly, Dr Clark this time suggesting another rising practitioner and colleague of Baly's, Dr William Jenner, who had gained considerable attention for his work at the London Fever Hospital in identifying the differences between typhoid fever and typhus.[20] The Queen was delighted with Clark's choice, pronouncing Jenner 'extremely clever' and with a pleasing manner.²¹ But the presence of another new doctor – albeit one who was the closest the royal family would have to a medical specialist – did nothing to change old habits: within days of his latest attack Albert was back at his desk struggling to keep up with his workload. In the light of his continuing poor health, on 10 February he and Victoria celebrated a rather low-key twenty-first wedding anniversary marked only by the playing of some sacred music by the Queen's Band that evening. Victoria was, as ever, grateful for her beloved husband's 'tender love'; Albert was less preoccupied by the particularities of shared affection, dwelling instead on the bigger picture of a working partnership – of things achieved and yet to be done. 'How many a storm has swept over it,' he told Baron Stockmar of his marriage, 'and still it continues green and fresh, and throws out vigorous roots, from which I can, with gratitude to God, acknowledge that much good will yet be engendered for the world!'²² But within days his grand designs were once more sublimated to physical pain, this time terrible toothache and a gumboil, which over the following two days led to inflammation of the nerves of his upper cheek.

'My sufferings are frightful and the swelling will not come to a proper head,' he wrote in his diary on 17 February. Enforced rest and restorative tonics brought some relief, but nine days of pain and two incisions of the gum by the royal dentist, Mr Saunders, in an attempt to provide some relief, 'pulled me down very much'.²³ Victoria remained entrenched in a stubborn denial of the seriousness of his condition. She grumbled to Vicky in Prussia about Albert's lack of physical stamina and hypochondria: 'dear Papa never allows he is any better or will try to get over it, but makes such a miserable face that people always think he's very ill'. In her view, it was the fault of his nervous system, which was 'easily excited and irritated'; Albert was 'so completely overpowered by everything'.²⁴ Nevertheless, in mid-February he resumed some of his duties, including, on the same day, a committee of the Fine Arts Commission and a visit to Trinity House (headquarters of the Lighthouse Service, of which he had been elected Master). But it was all too much and he returned exhausted. Within days his face and glands were swollen and painful.

On 21 February, once again confiding to Vicky her impatience at seeing Albert so weak and miserable, the Queen found it all 'most trying' and wearing; to her mind, it was part and parcel of the male inability to endure pain. Women, of course, were made differently. The trials of childbirth ensured that they learned to bear suffering with greater fortitude – 'our nerves don't seem so racked, tortured as men's are!'[25] A day later she complained that Albert had gone against doctors' orders to keep quiet and not go out, instead 'staying up talking too long and to too many people'.[26] He was his own worst enemy. The only recourse was to drag him away from business: to Osborne on the Isle of Wight, where he went at the end of February to recuperate.

But far worse trials and tribulations awaited Prince Albert on his return to Windsor in March. The Queen's seventy-five-year-old mother, the Duchess of Kent, who had been ailing for some time, was now seriously ill. She had been suffering from a severe case of the skin infection erysipelas for the last couple of years and, more recently, a swollen right arm, which caused her such pain that it had become useless. When it was operated on, the cause, as Dr Clark had privately predicted to Prince Albert some time previously, had proved to be a malignant tumour.

On the night of 15–16 March Victoria kept vigil at her dying mother's bedside at Frogmore. There, in the clutter of the Duchess's lilac-painted bedroom with its many visible mementos of her childhood, Victoria sat listening to the hours strike as the Duchess's face in its mob cap grew ever paler, the features 'longer and sharper'. From 8 a.m., as life ebbed away, Victoria knelt by her mother's bedside, holding her hand. 'It was a solemn, sacred, never-to-be-forgotten scene,' she later recalled, as her mother's breathing flickered and finally stopped at nine-thirty in the morning. It was also – in both her own and Albert's lives – their first experience, close to, of the grim ritual of the deathbed. Albert, much moved and in tears, gathered his distraught wife up in his arms and carried her into the next room – a paragon of tenderness and solicitude as Victoria dissolved into agonies of tears. The truth of her mother's condition had been kept from her and the shock was therefore intensified. How was she to endure the coming days and the thought of the 'daily, hourly blank' of life without her mother, she asked? It was all too dreadful.[27]

She felt abandoned, a helpless orphan; the whole of her miserable, repressed childhood flooded back to her, the days when she had fought her mother's control and then, on her accession, had ruthlessly replaced her, first with her governess, Baroness Lehzen, and then with Albert. It was thanks to him – for the Duchess was, after all, his aunt – that the two women had later been reconciled and had grown to love and appreciate each other. Victoria spent much time at Frogmore over the next few days sitting in her mother's room: feeling the 'awful stillness' of the house, struggling to recapture the shade of the mother she had in the past so shamefully maligned and had now lost. When she and Albert went through the painful process of sorting out the Duchess's effects – the accumulation of letters, the diaries, Victoria's own childish scribblings, and scrapbooks containing locks of her baby hair – she was shocked to find so much evidence of her mother's love and devotion. It opened the flood-gates to a torrent of unresolved guilt, remorse and grief, which brought with it total nervous collapse, so much so that some feared the Queen might go mad. Only her eighteen-year-old daughter Alice (the natural care-giver of the family) seemed equipped to offer consolation. 'Go and comfort Mama,' Albert exhorted her.[28] Alice did so willingly, just as she had spent much time nursing the Duchess and playing the piano to her during her final illness. Meanwhile, withdrawing into total seclusion, as the protocols of mourning demanded – and which she followed to the letter – Queen Victoria donned her crape. Her ladies did likewise. She specified no time for the termination of mourning for her mother, setting the burghers of the Chamber of Commerce aghast at how yet another period of protracted court mourning would affect trade in the British garment industry. For mourning had become a regular feature at Court.

* * *

Back in 1844 when news had come from Coburg of the death of his father, Ernst I, Albert and Victoria had both descended into paroxysms of grief, the distraught Queen begging her Uncle Leopold to now 'be the father to us poor bereaved, heart-broken children'. The couple's self-indulgent display at the time had alarmed their three-year-old daughter Vicky. She could not understand why 'poor dear Papa and dear Mama cry so', nor why all the blinds were pulled down on the windows and the rooms so gloomy.[29] Overnight, death had erased the pain from Albert's memory of his father's dissolute life, his cruelty to Albert's mother and his endless sponging for money. Albert and Victoria had now viewed the deceased old reprobate as a paragon of virtue, as one, so Victoria insisted, 'who was so deservedly loved' – this of a man she hardly knew. Indeed, Albert was disappointed in the British public's lack of grief. 'Here we sit together, poor mama [the Duchess], Victoria and myself, and weep, with a great cold public around us, insensible as stone.' But what significance did this obscure German royal have for the British public? Only Albert's devoted Victoria had been able to gauge the depths of his grief and offer solace; she was, he assured Stockmar, 'the treasure on which my whole existence rests'.[30]

Ever in tune with her emotions, Victoria had taken to the performance of bereavement with aplomb. This first experience in 1844 of 'real
grief', as she put it, made a 'lasting impression' on her, she told Uncle
Leopold, so much so that she admitted, 'one loves to cling to one's
grief'.[31] Years later, in a conversation with Vicky about ensuring that even
young children wore mourning, she had insisted: 'you must promise me
that if I should die your child or children and those around you should
mourn; this really must be, for I have such strong feelings on this subject'.[32]
By 1861, therefore, Victoria was already a master of the long and flamboyant mourning protocols that were in vogue, enthroning her own
particular maudlin celebration of grief as a virtue to be emulated by all.
She had by now been in and out of black for the best part of the last
ten years, marked in particular by the grand, theatrical state ceremonials
for the Duke of Wellington when he died in 1852 (the massive and ornate
funeral car designed in consultation with the ever-resourceful Albert).[33]
The Queen's intermittent wearing of black had continued through the
deaths of various members of her extended family: her Aunt Louise,
Queen of the Belgians, in 1850; her uncle, the King of Hanover, in 1851;
her half-brother, Prince Charles of Leiningen, in 1856 – for whom she
had indulged in an excessively elaborate six-month period of mourning.
Charles's death was closely followed by that of Victoria's cousin, the
Duchess of Nemours, in 1857, to which she responded by holding a
gloomy and 'interminable' black Drawing Room (as royal receptions
were called), with only the soon-to-be-married Vicky allowed to wear
white.[35] Then Victoria's brother-in-law, the Prince of Hohenlohe-
Langenburg, had died in April 1860, inaugurating yet another slavish
retreat into crape for three months – during which she had told Vicky
how 'lovely' her darling Beatrice (just three years old) had looked 'in
her black silk and crepe dress' – further fuelled by the death of Prince
Albert's stepmother, Marie of Saxe-Coburg.[34] Victoria had gushed
sympathy for both at a distance. Even when Tsar Nicholas I died on 2
March 1855 during the Crimean War she had insisted that the correct
protocols of mourning be observed at the British court – no matter that
this was for the monarch of a hostile nation. Royal blood was always
thicker than water. Most recently, the death of Friedrich Wilhelm IV, the
mad old King of Prussia, in January 1861 had propelled the disgruntled
ladies at the British court back into crape yet again.

Friedrich Wilhelm's death had provided twenty-year-old Vicky, as wife
of the Prussian Crown Prince, with her own first-hand initiation into

the solemn rituals of the royal way of death – something her mother had yet to experience. Informed in the middle of the night that the end was nigh, she and Fritz had hastily dressed, to hurry on foot across the frozen streets and stand vigil at the dying king's bedside at the Sanssouci palace at Potsdam. Soon the Queen was thrilling to Vicky's 'painfully interesting details' of the scene, with nothing but the great clock ticking the hours of the night away to the accompaniment of the 'crackling of the fire and the death rattle' and then the sight of the stiffened corpse the following morning. Etiquette had required Vicky to pay her respects to the laid-out body of the King on several subsequent days and she did not spare her mother the minutiae of the fearful altera-tion that she observed in it before the coffin was sealed, or the 'great shudder' she had experienced when forced to kiss its face on the pillow. This time, the corpse had 'looked like death and no longer like sleep'.[36]

Mourning protocols then current in Britain demanded twelve months of black for a parent or child (with only a retreat to half-mourning in the final three months); six months for a sibling, three months for an aunt or uncle; and six weeks for a first cousin. The strictest observance of such protocols was de rigueur at the British court, though it did reduce down to a few days for very distant royal connections. But 1861 began – and ended – in black; altogether that year the Queen would issue seven declar-ations of official court mourning. Nothing but black silk, bombazine and crape; black gloves, black collars, black flowers, feathers, lappets and fans and festoons of jet mourning jewellery were the order of the day – except for the younger, unmarried ladies-in-waiting, who were allowed to freeze in lily-white muslin well into the winter. The Queen herself remained in mourning for much longer than the statutory time. Her withdrawal into mourning for her mother was total, obliging members of the royal household to creep around on tiptoe, conducting conversa-tions in whispers in quiet huddles in corners, in order not to break the spell of silence that descended on Windsor. The social life of the British court was at an end. For months to come all royal family celebrations were cancelled: there were no birthday parties or outings to the theatre, and not even any music. By June everyone was complaining at the unremitting atmosphere of gloom in London. 'The Queen carries her sorrow at her mother's death to an absurd extent,' complained assistant secretary Benjamin Moran of the United States legation. 'There are no balls this season and in lieu thereof but one concert, and to this the Ministers, and their Ladies and Chief Secretaries only are to be invited.'[37]

The Duchess's funeral had been held in the strictest privacy at St George's Chapel, Windsor on 25 March. Unusually the pall-bearers had been six of her ladies, including her favourite, Lady Augusta Bruce. But neither the Queen nor her daughters had attended the ceremony, remaining, in Victoria's words, 'to pray at home together, and to dwell on the happiness and peace of her who was gone'. In Victoria's absence Albert had acted as chief mourner, assisted by Bertie and ten-year-old Arthur, in a chapel festooned in black and with the great bell tolling. After the service the Duchess's crimson coffin was lowered into the gloom of the vault beneath, to be temporarily housed there until the mausoleum being constructed for it was ready. Prince Albert was visibly moved during the ceremony, his eyes filling with tears when Mr Tolley, the soloist in the chapel choir, came to the words in Martin Luther's hymn 'The trumpet sounds, the graves restore/The dead that they contained before'.[38] That evening, he took a strange pleasure in sharing in his wife's grief, reading aloud to her the letters the Duchess had written to a German friend forty-one years previously, describing the illness and death of her husband and Victoria's father, the Duke of Kent.[39] For the first three weeks after her mother's death, until 9 April, Victoria wallowed in her grief, seeing only her closest attendants and taking no comfort in her children. She did not even come down to family meals. The relentlessly sombre mood in the household at Windsor was broken only by the pert little Princess Beatrice, entertaining everyone round the dinner table with her renditions of 'Twinkle Twinkle' and 'Humpty Dumpty' and other nursery rhymes.[40] Victoria's continuing orgy of grief disturbed many at court, particularly in the levels of bathos with which she now eulogised her once-hated mother. It undoubtedly was a form of atonement for her own past sins, but the Queen's instability alarmed people such as her friend the Earl of Clarendon, who worried about her state of 'great dejection' and her endless weeping. Her stubborn refusal to be consoled heralded what he felt was a return of the 'morbid melancholy to which her mind has often tended'. Clarendon knew it was a constant cause of anxiety to Prince Albert, who firmly begged his wife not to give way so completely and to be reconciled, remembering that 'the Blow was dealt by the Hand of the All Wise'.[41]

Not to receive this, the 'first real blow of misfortune' – a death in her immediate family – until the age of forty-one, and in an age when most couples lost more than one child in infancy, had meant that the Queen had taken her mother's death particularly hard. When Vicky arrived from

Berlin, no doubt glad to see her family again, she was chastised for being in high spirits. As for Bertie, he had failed his mother's litmus test of grief too, giving 'great offence' by not bursting into tears the moment he arrived at Windsor from Cambridge University for the funeral.[42] He was also reprimanded for not using writing paper with a broad enough black border. For the royal household the Queen's hysterical grieving was an annoyance; for the egocentric Victoria, it was cathartic: 'the general sympathy for *me*, and approval of the manner in which I have shown my grief . . . is *quite wonderful and most touching*,' she told Uncle Leopold. Weeping – 'which day after day is my welcome friend' – was her 'greatest relief'.[43] The more extravagant her mourning, the more she felt it demonstrated her devotion; and, as Queen, there were no limits placed on her right to indulge it. Her eldest daughter, however, was profoundly disturbed by what she saw during her visit: it was as though her mother *enjoyed* her sorrow, whilst turning a blind eye to how sick and exhausted her husband was. On her return to Berlin, Vicky discovered rumours had been circulating in the German court that her mother had lost her mind and that the mad doctors had been brought in to see her.

Absorbed in her own grief, Victoria entirely overlooked the fact that her mother's deathbed had also been Albert's first experience at close hand. Cast adrift in his own very private grief for a mother-in-law he had come to love dearly, he had little time to dwell on his own feelings; the comptroller of the Duchess's household, Sir George Couper, had also recently died suddenly, and Albert was charged – as her now sole executor – with taking on the onerous task of sorting out the Duchess's estate. He did so uncomplainingly, responding to the many letters of condolence from around the world and, more importantly, easing the mounting burden of his distraught wife's neglected dispatch boxes. Meanwhile Victoria took her mother's devoted lady-in-waiting and confidante, Lady Augusta Bruce, who had served the Duchess since 1846, to her bosom as her newly created, resident Lady of the Bedchamber. As a mournful cabal of two, they could wallow undisturbed in their shared remembrance of 'The Beloved'. Albert found himself of little use, but marshalled what remained of his emotional resources to sit with his wife reading consolatory prayers. Lady Bruce was much impressed by his tenderness and tact: 'Oh! He is one in millions,' she observed, 'well might she love him as she did!'[44]

Morning and evening Victoria persisted in feeding her grief by sitting in the Duchess's rooms at Frogmore, ensuring that all was kept exactly as it had been, even down to the little canary singing in its cage. Mama 'lives much in the past and future, perhaps more than in the present,' Albert explained to Vicky, which was why it was for her 'a spiritual necessity to cling to moments that are flown and to recollections, and to form plans for the future'. He continued to listen patiently and console when the couple went to Osborne the following month, but was increasingly worried by the state of his wife's mental health. Victoria's half-sister Feodora (from the Duchess of Kent's first marriage to the Prince of Leiningen) also sent endless exhortations from her home in Baden, urging Victoria to 'look round you and feel how rich you are; how much God has given you to be thankful for'. 'I do not wish to feel better,' the Queen insisted. She was determined to hold on to her grief: 'the more distant the dreadful event becomes, and the more others recover their spirits – the more trying it becomes to me'.[45] As for the children, they were 'a disturbance' to her and she could hardly bear to be around them, or show any real concern for the increasingly fragile health of her haemophiliac youngest son Leopold.

Thus, inevitably, the burden of official duty fell entirely on Albert. He was, he admitted to Stockmar, 'well nigh overwhelmed by business', but as always he soldiered on, with Victoria steadfastly refusing to leave off her mourning.[46] Her birthday on 24 May came and went in disconsolate, sombre retreat without even any music ('That would kill me,' she told Vicky).[47] It was not until 19 June that she made her first public appearance at a Drawing Room at St James's, in deep crape mourning – 'the deepest of deeps' – and with a headdress of black feathers.[48] It was crowded, hot and muggy and, after going through the barest of formalities, Victoria quickly retired. When King Leopold visited from Belgium at the end of the month he urged an end to full court mourning: he could see that Victoria's morbid state of mind was undermining Albert's health. Albert, however, would have none of it; the gloom at court was in tune with his own melancholic mood; besides, he knew that his wife would be unwilling to contemplate a transition – even to half-mourning – until six months of full mourning had passed, with her late mother's birthday on 17 August.[49]

CHAPTER THREE

'Fearfully in Want of a True Friend'

Queen Victoria's fitful waves of weeping for her mother continued throughout the summer of 1861, her grief reignited on 1 August with the removal of the Duchess's coffin to a polished blue granite sarcophagus at the mausoleum at Frogmore specially constructed for it. She herself did not attend the ceremony, but visited on her mother's birthday to lay a wreath of dried flowers, consoling herself that the Duchess's 'pure, tender, loving spirit' was hovering there above them.[1] For his own part, Albert was by now more preoccupied with the very real aches and pains that plagued him, particularly continuing bouts of high temperature and agonising toothache.

His tolerance of Victoria's retreat from view was heroic; he did his duty, continuing to defer to her grief – priding himself that court mourning had not 'deviated' from her wishes in this respect by 'one hair's breadth' – and standing in for her at various levees and Drawing Rooms that year, which she would not contemplate attending.[2] Much to her annoyance, however, he insisted on returning early from their holiday at Osborne to fulfil a commitment to open the Royal Horticultural Show (the forerunner of the Chelsea Flower Show) at the beginning of June. He went there without Victoria, taking Bertie, Alice, Helena, Louise and Arthur. But the brightness of the floral displays could not dispel the dark and showery weather as the royal party trudged up the wet and muddy gravel walks to the glasshouse, where 'an endlessly long address was read and responded to' and – in the mind of Victoria's cousin, Princess Mary Adelaide – 'an ill-timed prayer offered up'. Albert gritted his teeth, planted a Wellingtonia redwood tree and allowed the children to enjoy an ice cream. But the Queen's absence was noted, and many thought how pale and worn the Prince looked.[3]

Unseasonably hot weather later in the month and a stream of royal visitors further sapped Albert's energies: the bouts of feverishness and pain in his limbs persisted. It left him feeling 'very miserable', but he had to pull himself together to deal with their guests: King Leopold and his son from Brussels, Vicky and Fritz and their two small children from Berlin, Archduke Maximilian and his wife from Austria and other relatives from Hesse, Baden and Sweden, who all arrived in quick succession.[4] A trip to Ireland followed in August, primarily to see how Bertie was shaping up on his ten-week training course with the Grenadier Guards at the Curragh outside Dublin. Here he was enduring a strictly regulated regime laid down by his father, which, though it allowed for occasional dinner parties and meals in the regimental mess, endeavoured to keep him away from the corrupting influence of his more worldly fellow officers. Sadly, Bertie, while looking quite good in a uniform according to the Queen, proved to have absolutely no natural leadership skills; his disappointed parents were informed that he would not make the rapid rise through the ranks they expected of him. Indeed, his commanding officer had advised that the Prince of Wales would not even be capable of commanding a battalion by the end of his training, as he was 'too imperfect' in his drill.[5]

Whilst they were in Ireland the couple celebrated the Prince Consort's forty-second birthday on 26 August. But it was a subdued affair; Albert was in low spirits, sinking ever more into a mood of fatalism. Victoria refused to be downcast. 'God bless and ever preserve my precious Albert, my adored Husband!' she wrote in her journal. But, alas! 'So much is so different this year, nothing festive, we on a journey and separated from many of our children and my spirits bad' (only Alice, Helena and Alfred were with them). She wished her husband joy, but somewhere deep inside a germ of worry was growing: 'May God mercifully grant that we may long, very long, be spared to live together and that I may *never* survive him!'[6]

After a short stop in Killarney, where the Prince soaked up the scenery, finding the lakes 'sublime', the royal yacht took the family across the Irish Sea to Wales for the onward journey to their annual holiday at Balmoral, where they would be joined by Alice's fiancé Louis and Victoria's half-sister Feodora. When they docked at Holyhead, Albert sought some private pleasure in a day's railway excursion to nearby Snowdonia, as a prelude to the restorative peace and beauty of six weeks at Balmoral, which the family reached by special train to Aboyne station in Deeside, and thence by carriage to the castle.

* * *

Victoria and Albert's love affair with Scotland was a passionate, visceral one. When they were first married they had enjoyed Sir Walter Scott's romantic reinvention of a heroic, feudal Scotland in his popular novels such as *Ivanhoe*, and they made their first visit together in 1842. The dry air of Balmoral, redolent with the balsamic smell of heather and pine and birch, reminded Albert of the mountains and forests of Thuringia near the Rosenau. At Balmoral he felt he had come home and it always worked its therapeutic magic on him. Even now, with his energy levels at an all-time low, it did so once again. The brief respite from his workload gave precious time in which to shake off the black dog of melancholy, as he enjoyed some excellent deer-stalking – bringing down six stags in the space of three days – and grouse-shooting and excursions taking in the grandeur of the glens and lochs of the area. He shook off the worst of his fatigue (though the staff noticed how pale and tired he seemed) and planned another 'Great Expedition' by carriage and pony like the one they had enjoyed the previous year. On 20 September he, Victoria, Alice and Louis, plus a small retinue, travelled incognito forty miles south-east of Balmoral, up through the hazy hills of Lochnagar, down the wild glens of Tanar and Mark, wading on horseback across racing burns of crystal-clear, icy-cold water, to Invermark and its romantic old ruined castle half-covered in ivy. That evening, when they arrived at Fettercairn, they stayed at a local hostelry, the Ramsay Arms, under the guise of a 'wedding party from Aberdeen', taking great delight in not being recognised and enjoying a moonlit walk through the silent village before bedtime.[7]

Victoria was glad to see Albert relax, at last relinquishing his 'over-love of business' and she greedily consumed every precious moment in his company.[8] Another two-day round trip of 129 miles followed in October, in driving wind and rain for much of the time (Albert not helping his rheumatism by getting soaked through, while Victoria, who relished the invigorating cold of Scotland, had stayed cosy, wrapped in waterproofs and a plaid). With the light fading fast, they finally arrived at an inn in the village of Dalwhinnie, where the cold, wet and hungry travellers were disappointed at the sight of 'two miserable starved Highland chickens, without any potatoes' for supper, and nothing but strong tea to drink. And, worse, there was 'No pudding, and no fun', recorded a disgruntled Victoria.[9]

Despite the privations, she noted that this had been 'the pleasantest and most enjoyable expedition I *ever* made'. She had 'enjoyed nothing as much, or indeed felt so much cheered by anything, since my great sorrow'.[10] With her grief temporarily receding and Albert's spirits revived, the couple made one more expedition on 16 October – a beautiful autumnal day during which they picnicked out in the open on a steep and rocky hillside overlooking the narrow valley of Cairn Lochan, where Albert left behind a note in an empty bottle of seltzer water as a memento of their visit. They returned at seven that evening as the moon was rising, 'much pleased and interested with this delightful expedition. Alas!, I fear our *last* great one!' Victoria wrote, in anticipation of their imminent departure. Six years later she would add a plaintive note in the margin: 'It was our last one!'[11]

As always, Victoria and Albert were loath to leave Balmoral. On 22 October the Queen wrote to Vicky 'My heart sinks within me at the prospect of going back to Windsor', for she knew her return would rekindle painful memories of her mother, but she did at least depart with one positive thought in mind. During this latest visit she had taken great delight in the unstinting attention shown to her by their 'invaluable Highland servant' John Brown, who combined 'the offices of groom, footman, page, and *maid*'. Victoria was impressed: Brown was '*so* handy about cloaks and shawls' and all the paraphernalia required for their expeditions.[12] She would be certain to remember him as she took one last look at the sunshine on her beloved Highlands, blue with autumn heather, and one final lungful of pure mountain air. Sure enough, the day of their departure, as Albert told Stockmar, 'the Queen's wounds were opened afresh'; 'the void' of her mother's absence once more 'struck home to her heart'.[13] Albert knew how hard it was for his wife to get a grip on the whirlwind of her feelings; it had been one of the tasks he had set her in her self-improvement plan when they were first married. Now, as Victoria once more bewailed their enforced return to a place that held terrible reminders of the loss of her mother, he felt the time had come for some firm, but straight talking. He sat down and wrote her a letter. The best advice he could offer was that she try 'to be less occupied with yourself and your own feelings', for pain was 'chiefly felt by dwelling on it and can thereby be heightened to an *unbearable extent*'. 'This is not hard philosophy,' he went on, 'but common sense supported by common and general experience. If you will take increased interest in things unconnected with personal feelings, you will find the task much lightened of governing those feelings in general which you state to be your great difficulty in life.'[14]

*   *   *

On Sunday 6 October, whilst still at Balmoral, Victoria and Albert had as usual attended service at the modest little Church of Scotland kirk at nearby Crathie. The sermon that day was given by the Reverend Stewart, vicar of St Andrew's, Edinburgh, his text being 'Prepare to meet thy God, Oh Israel' from Amos 4:12. Now that she had had first-hand experience of death and had entered the inner sanctum of the initiated, Victoria felt the words of the sermon and its message so much more acutely. 'I feel now to be so acquainted with death – and to be so much nearer that unseen world,' she wrote to Vicky the following day, echoing a phrase of the Catholic cleric Cardinal Manning, whom she admired, that has long since been attributed to her.[15] The sermon had a profound impact on Albert, clearly feeding into the intimations of his own mortality that had preoccupied him since the Duchess of Kent's death, and the Queen requested that a manuscript copy of it be sent to him. She would later recall how often Albert had remarked on her own indomitable lust for life: 'I do not cling to life,' he had told her not long before his death, 'You do; but I set no store by it. If I knew that those I love were well cared for, I should be quite ready to die tomorrow.' More prophetically he had added that he was sure that 'if I had a severe illness, I should give up at once, I should not struggle for life.' It was an awful admission to make to a wife whose physical robustness was so visible, but he had, he told her, 'no tenacity in life.'[16] And yet he said these words cheerfully. They were, for him, a simple statement of belief – not a death-wish, as they have so often been interpreted. As a devout Christian, Albert was, as he had been throughout his life, ever ready to submit to God's will. 'I know of no public man in England,' remarked Sir Charles Lyell, 'who was so serious on religious matters, and so unfettered by that formalism and political churchism and conventionalism which rules in our upper classes.'[17] Such simplicity of faith had created in Albert an acceptance of what he was sure would be his own early death. His narrow escape from the carriage accident in Coburg the previous year, and his obvious distress on that visit at seeing his homeland for what he was convinced would be the last time, all fed into his increasing world weariness and spiritual detachment from the family.

The Queen remembered how strange it was in retrospect that her husband had 'dwelt so much on death and the future state' in the six months before his death, as though he had had a presentiment of its imminence. Had she given it closer thought perhaps, it might have occurred to her that her husband's lack of 'pluck', as she would later

call it, was in fact a reflection of his profound unhappiness.[18] Their shared
reading at the time – chosen of course by Albert – was dominated by
religious texts, including a collection by William Branks of the letters
of a religious evangelical, Sarah Craven, entitled *Heaven our Home*. Indeed,
the subject of the afterlife was something the couple often talked of,
Albert observing that although he had no idea 'in what state we shall
meet again on the other side', he was sure that he and Victoria would
recognise each other 'and be together in eternity'.[19] Of that he was
'perfectly certain'. And so, most determinedly, was she; for Albert was
hers for this life – and the next. Sarah Craven's letters, with their ecstatic
striving for perfection on the path to eternal glory and arrival at 'those
blissful shores' of heaven, endorsed the Queen and Prince Albert's own
belief that heaven was a familiar and comforting home, 'with a great
and happy and loving family in it' – a place indeed 'worth dying for'.[20]

The tenuousness of health and happy family life were brought home
again to Victoria and Albert in early November, when new worries
consumed them concerning their youngest son Leopold. Now aged eight,
he had always been a thin and sickly child, prone to knocks and bangs
that set up severe bouts of bleeding that laid him up for weeks. He had
finally been diagnosed with haemophilia a couple of years previously, a
fact that the royal family took care not to advertise at a time when the
disease was little understood. By 1861 Leopold had become so frail – a
'child of anxiety', as the Queen described him – that, after yet another
serious bleeding attack, the doctors had advised sending him to the
French Riviera for the winter, in the care of his rather aged governor,
the seventy-four-year-old General Bowater and a German physician, Dr
Günther. But Bowater himself was not in the best of health and Albert
worried for his son's well-being; he also grieved to see another child
removed from the family nest: Vicky in Berlin, Affie away at sea, Bertie
at Cambridge and now dear little Leopold gone from them on 2
November. Bertie, for all his failings, at least was not far away and came
back to Windsor on 9 November for his twentieth birthday. Bells rang
out across the town and – breaking her slavish observation of mourning
still for her mother – Victoria allowed a military band to celebrate the
occasion. She prayed to God 'to assist our efforts to make him turn out
well', but found it hard not to be reminded of past, happier days. Bertie's
birthday was the first family celebration spent at Windsor without the
Duchess of Kent. 'I nearly broke down at dinner,' she wrote in her
journal. '*The* contrast of former times – *all* in deep black . . . all was so

painfully forcibly felt!' And Albert had not been well either, suffering 'a very bad headache before dinner'.[21]

Gloom and yet more gloom piled up that month; the Queen was also fretting about Vicky, newly pregnant and sick with influenza in Berlin. She talked of sending Dr Jenner out to treat her, but then news arrived by telegraph on the 10th that the twenty-four-year-old Pedro, King of Portugal (to whom both Albert and Victoria were related through the Coburg line) was seriously ill with typhoid fever. His younger brother, Ferdinand, had died of the disease four days previously. Two days later Pedro too was dead. Victoria was stunned; in the habit of never taking any illnesses seriously other than her own, she had thought Pedro's complaint 'nothing but one of those frequent little feverish attacks which foreigners so continually have from not attending to their stomach and bowels'. She and Albert attended to their own digestive systems most rigorously. The royal pharmacist – Mr Peter Squire of Oxford Street – supplied them with monthly consignments of laxatives and purgatives such as tincture of rhubarb, syrup of ipecac, calomel, Rochelle salt, senna and bicarbonate of soda. But since their holiday at Balmoral, belladonna, sulphuric acid and tincture of paregoric had been added to the list to deal with Albert's continuing stomach cramps and diarrhoea.[22] Pedro's shocking and sudden death was a terrible loss for them both, but especially Albert, who had loved him as a son; more importantly, he had looked on the conscientious and hard-working Pedro as a young man in his own image, a 'model' king, whom he hoped to see uphold the integrity of the monarchy and democratise the throne of Portugal. Pedro was everything Albert had hoped to see in Bertie. These two deaths further fed into his morbid and religiose state of mind and his pathological dread of 'fever', which, in its various forms, carried so many off. The deaths of Ferdinand and Pedro were 'another proof', he told Vicky, that death might at any time come knocking on the door and that 'we are never safe to refuse Nature her rights'.[23]

The Portuguese deaths had once more plunged the court into black not long after the period of mourning for the Duchess of Kent had finally ended. Victoria's spirit was greatly knocked back by these two additional deaths in the wider royal family of Europe: 'We did not need this fresh loss in this sad year, this sad winter,' she wrote in her journal, for it had already been a year 'so different to what we have ever known'.[24] Pedro's death prompted her to recall the parting words of John Brown, the day they had left Balmoral, that the family should all remain well through the winter and 'return all safe'. Above all, he had added, he hoped 'that you may have no deaths in the family'. The concurrence of the two deaths in Portugal kept returning to her mind, 'as if they had been a sort of strange presentiment'.[25] Victoria and Albert remained 'much crushed' and kept to their rooms for meals for the next few days. Sensing how 'dejected' Albert was, as she told Vicky, the Queen did her best to bear up, but there was no disguising the atmosphere of increasing gloom that the deaths provoked in him.[26] 'The sad calamity in Portugal' haunted his already-restless nights. He seemed increasingly silent and listless; in later years Princess Beatrice remarked that after the death of King Pedro she did not see her father smile again. 'It was almost as if he had had a stroke,' observed others. Prince Albert seemed to be 'half in another world'.[27]

Nothing could cheer the ailing Prince Consort – not even the hopes of a marriage soon for Bertie. For the Prince of Wales had now been dispatched in obligatory pursuit of the most eligible bride that his energetic sister Vicky, enlisted by her parents, had been able to find for him: Princess Alexandra of Schleswig-Holstein-Sonderburg-Glücksburg, the sixteen-year-old daughter of Prince Christian, heir to the King of Denmark. Alexandra was pretty but poor, her father being descended from a marginal branch of the Danish royal family, and she came at the bottom of a list of other, more strategically desirable candidates who had been rejected for various reasons. Bertie travelled to Europe for a secret meeting with Alexandra in the Chapel of St Bernard at Speyer Cathedral near Baden-Baden, orchestrated by his sister. It brought no coup de foudre, though Bertie at least came away pleased with Alexandra's sweetness, her grace and charm. She would do well enough. Vicky was dismayed at her brother's indifference to an alluring young woman who, in her estimation, 'would make most men fire and flames'. The Princess's charms had, sadly, not produced enough of an impression on him even 'to last from Baden to England' and he remained hesitant.[28] Love was out of the question, agreed Victoria, for in her estimation Bertie was incapable of enthusiasm 'about anything in the world'.[29] She did not yet know it, but in fact his initiation into the pleasures of the flesh was well under way – and he was loath to cast them aside so soon for monogamy.

★   ★   ★

Just before he had left his training camp at the Curragh, after a lacklustre performance, Bertie had attended a rowdy party at the Mansion House

in Dublin. After it was over a group of his fellow officers arranged a
farewell present for Bertie, smuggling a young 'woman of the town',
Nellie Clifden, into his quarters. She was a regular favourite among the
Guards and knew her way around camp in the dark, so well indeed that
when Bertie staggered back to his bed that night, he found the vivacious
and willing young Nellie waiting for him. Having enjoyed Nellie's
welcome, he ensured her surreptitious exit via the window of his hut
and arranged further assignations with her back in England – right under
his parents' noses at Windsor. The gossips were quick to dub Nellie 'The
Princess of Wales', for she was unable to resist the temptation to brag
about her conquest around the dives and casinos of London.[30] The scandal
soon hit the London clubs and appeared in the papers on the Continent.
Bertie's parents remained blissfully ignorant of the fact until a letter
arrived in early November from Baron Stockmar in Germany informing
them of the rumours. The couple were deeply shocked, but before taking
any action, Albert checked with Lord Torrington, a regular of the clubs.
Confirmation that the rumours were true, Victoria later wrote, 'broke
my Angel's heart'; Bertie's behaviour was painfully reminiscent of that
of Albert's brother Ernst with a servant-girl in Dresden and of their
father's affair with a courtesan, Pauline Panam – better known as 'La
Belle Grèque' – who had later caused much royal embarrassment with
a kiss-and-tell memoir.[31] But in Bertie's case there was an empire, rather
than a duchy, at stake. A traditional rite of passage such as sexual initiation was par for the course in army life; but to Bertie's puritanical father,
this transgression – which was almost to be expected in the mind of
most Victorian fathers – was nothing short of a catastrophe. Albert's
stress levels went haywire: Bertie's transgression would, he told his son,
suck him irrevocably down into the vortex of sin and self-destruction.

Victoria would ever after lay at her son's door the devastating effect
of Bertie's indiscretions on Albert's precarious health. For they had
awakened Albert's innermost fears of the dangers of unbridled sexuality
and, with it, a return by his son to the old, profligate habits of the British
royalty. In his paranoia, Albert saw the spectre of vice opening the door
to blackmail, scandal, pregnancy and even disease; vice had always
'depressed him, grieved him, horrified him' – and the worry of the
dishonour that Bertie's encounter with a woman who was little more
than a prostitute might bring on him (and the monarchy) drained his
last reserves of energy.[32] A martyr now to his son's bad behaviour, he
paid the price with crippling insomnia and neuralgia.

On 16 November, 'with a heavy heart', Albert sat down and wrote a long and melodramatic letter to Bertie. His behaviour had caused him 'the deepest pain, I have yet felt in this life'. His son had 'wilfully plunged into the lowest vice', and Albert berated him for his thoughtlessness, weakness and ignorance.[33] The level of Bertie's depravity, as Albert perceived it, would be sufficient, should the woman fall pregnant and drag him before the courts, to provide her with an opportunity 'to give before a greedy multitude disgusting details of your profligacy'. But, far worse, the escapade might wreck the delicate marriage negotiations with Alexandra of Denmark. Four days later Albert wrote again in response to a letter from a contrite Bertie begging his forgiveness. He softened his tone; he was 'ever still your affectionate father' and entreated Bertie to make up for his behaviour by his future actions. Having eaten of the forbidden fruit of the tree, he must now hide himself from the sight of God, for nothing could restore him to the state of innocence and purity that he had lost. 'You *must* not, you *dare* not be lost,' Albert went on. 'The consequences for this country, and for the world at large, would be too dreadful.' The past was over and done with. Bertie 'had to deal now with the future' and the only thing that could save him was his marriage to Alexandra.[34]

While Bertie threatened to break his heart, the enduring consolation for Albert was his good and clever daughter Vicky in Berlin, to whom he wrote on her birthday a few days later. 'May your life, which has begun beautifully, expand still further to the good of others and the contentment of your own mind!' He had little hope of such worthy objectives from Bertie, who seemed utterly insensitive to the quest for 'true inward happiness', which in Albert's book was 'to be sought only in the internal consciousness of effort systematically directed to good and useful ends'.[35] The pursuit of such ends had sent him, ill though he was, on frequent journeys back and forth to London since their return from the Highlands. On 22 November Albert had visited Sandhurst in Surrey to inspect new buildings constructed there for the Staff College and Royal Military Academy. It was a gloomy day of incessant rain, but he stayed for three hours splashing about in puddles, looking over plans and performing his official duties in his usual businesslike manner. He returned to Windsor cold and soaked through, unable to eat and telling the Queen he felt tired, and complaining that he was 'much of the weather'.[36] Yet the following day, despite the rain, he went out shooting with Victoria's nephew, Ernst, Prince of Leiningen, who was over on a visit with his wife. Once again he got soaked through and afterwards sat around in his wet clothes. He confided to his diary that he was full of rheumatic pains and had 'scarcely closed' his eyes at night for the last fortnight. Victoria too was worried at how 'weak and tired' her husband was from sleeplessness, which had come on 'ever since that great worry and annoyance'. It was all too 'horrid'; and it was all Bertie's fault.[37]

While Victoria might find a pat explanation for it all, Albert's physical and mental malaise now went far deeper than mere worries about his errant eldest son. The years of self-imposed overwork and exhaustion had brought an overwhelming sense of isolation. Loneliness gnawed away at him and – though he never admitted as much – this loneliness extended even to his marriage. Victoria was always there ready to adore him, to hang on his every word, his every kiss, to praise unstintingly and monopolise his time, but Albert was tiring of her relentless, cloying admiration and her never-ending emotional hunger. Her love was too inverted; she enjoyed the satisfaction it gave her, without thinking of the good it should do him. He meanwhile longed for space, for spiritual companionship and the wisdom and cool detachment of his old friend and guardian angel, Baron Stockmar. He missed their close 'interchange of thought', particularly now that his few other male allies were dead. He had wept uncontrollably at the death of Anson in 1849 and at the time had begged Stockmar to come to England to console him. The loss of former Prime Minister Sir Robert Peel in 1850 had been a real blow too, for Peel had been Albert's true friend and political amanuensis and, in the opinion of Florence Nightingale, had taught him the political skills needed to be an unofficial minister.[38] Worse still, in 1858, had been the death of Albert's loyal Swiss valet Isaac Cart, who was his last link with Coburg and had been with him since the age of seven. 'I am fearfully in want of a true friend and counsellor,' he confessed in what would be his last letter to Stockmar on 14 November; but the ageing Stockmar, an unfailing stalwart through Albert's difficult years in England, was far away in Coburg, his own life now drawing to a close.[39]

At ten-thirty on the morning of 25 November Albert somehow found the strength to take a special train to Cambridge for a man-to-man talk with Bertie, feeling 'still greatly out of sorts'.[40] They met at Madingley Hall, where Bertie had been living with his governor, General Bruce, and his wife since going up to Cambridge in January; the location four miles out of town had been chosen by Albert, who had been unwilling to trust his son to the vicissitudes of college life. Bertie was mortified by his father's distress and was duly and lengthily chastised during a long walk with him down the wet Cambridgeshire lanes. But the strain of this excursion proved too much for Albert – Bertie had seemed oblivious to his father's ill health, and his poor sense of direction had got them lost, taking them on a longer route than planned. Albert paid the price when he returned to Windsor the following day and was racked with pains in his back and legs.

Victoria found her husband's continuing irritability most trying after his return from Madingley, remarking in a classic understatement to King Leopold that 'Albert is a little rheumatic . . . which is a plague'.[41] She could not, and would not, think the unthinkable: that her husband was seriously ill. And so she convinced herself that there was nothing ominous in his symptoms. After all, it was 'very difficult not to have something or other of this kind in this season, with these rapid changes of temperature', and, touch wood, he actually was 'much better this winter than he was the preceding year'. Albert, knowing his wife's propensity for hysteria, had determinedly kept the truth of his declining health over the last three years from her. And he would not disabuse her of the fact now, though he confided otherwise to his diary. 'Am very wretched,' he wrote, and for once he did not join the Queen on the terrace for their usual constitutional that day.[42] In contrast, the Prince's valet, Rudolf Löhlein, had by now become greatly concerned at his master's uncharacteristic listlessness and the way his mind had strangely wandered at times over the last couple of days. He was convinced that the badly drained town of Windsor (which had seen a typhoid epidemic in 1858 that had killed thirty-nine people) was a danger to him: 'Living here will kill your Royal Highness,' he had frequently repeated to him. 'You must leave Windsor and go to Germany for a time to rest and recover strength.'[43]

Talk of the notorious Windsor fever might have alarmed Albert, but he did nothing about it. He was no better on the 27th, when, after yet another sleepless night, he had a 'great feeling of weariness and weakness'. But still he refused to take to his bed. Victoria now admitted in a letter to Vicky, 'I never saw him so low'.[44] Dr Jenner visited and stayed for the night and advised Albert not to leave the castle. Rest indoors was one thing, but all hopes of unbroken sleep for Albert were removed when news broke in the British press on 28 November of a major diplomatic incident with America, now eight months into a bitter civil war. After the eleven southern states had seceded from the Union in March, forming a Confederacy, Britain – with strong economic links to the cotton-producing South, the mainstay of the Lancashire cotton industry – had given the South its tacit support. On 8 November a British West Indies mail packet, the *Trent*, which had been conveying envoys of the Confederate forces on a diplomatic mission to Europe, was stopped by a warship of the Federal Union (the Northern states) in the Bahama Channel off the northern coast of Cuba. The ship was boarded and four Southern officials were taken off under arrest: James Murray Mason, envoy to the Court of St James in London; John Slidell, envoy to the Court of the Tuileries in Paris; and their respective secretaries. The jingoistic Lord Palmerston's government saw this as a flagrant violation of international law and of British neutrality in the war. As the diplomatic crisis deepened, the press whipped up war fever, demanding reparations. Only five years after the end of the Crimean War, the British people found themselves contemplating the unthinkable: taking up arms against the American North. The primary concern of Foreign Minister Lord John Russell was to protect British cotton interests in the South, but taking on the North, at a distance of 2,500 miles, was a tall order. Nevertheless, British warships were ordered to deploy off the American coast, munitions factories went into overtime and 8,000 troops were shipped to Canada in case of war.

News of the 'astounding outrage of the Americans' greatly alarmed the Queen, as well as Prince Albert – who was still suffering what appeared to be the continuing aches and pains of a severe chill caught at Madingley.[45] Worry over the gathering political crisis further disrupted his already fractured sleep. Nevertheless, after dragging himself from bed and taking a hot bath on the morning of 29 November, he turned out to watch a review of the 200 boys of the Rifle Corps of the Eton Volunteers who paraded for the royal family beneath the East Terrace in Windsor Home Park. He knew that his absence would be remarked upon if he did not go; 'Unhappily I must be present,' he noted in his diary, before donning his fur-lined overcoat for the twenty-minute parade.[46] The weather was mild and muggy for November, but Albert was full of aches and feeling the cold. He looked decidedly unwell and could only walk slowly, because of the pains in his legs. He seemed to be shivering all the time and later told Victoria that he had felt 'as if cold water were being poured down his back'.[47] It was the last day that he was seen in public.

Later that day Dr Jenner visited and pronounced Albert much better; 'he would be quite well in two or three days,' he reassured him, and there was no need for a doctor to stay over in the castle. 'No, I shall not recover,' Albert told him, 'but I am not taken by surprise.' He was not afraid, he assured Jenner: 'I trust I am prepared.'[48] After eating a little supper, he revived that evening, or so the Queen thought. Privately, in a letter to Vicky, Albert confided – as he often did to her about the kind of things he would never tell the Queen – that 'Much worry and great sorrow (about which I beg you not to ask questions) have robbed me of sleep during the past fortnight.' The Bertie affair was haunting him and he confessed himself to be in a 'shattered state', made worse by heavy catarrh and headache and pains in his limbs for the last four days.[49]

He awoke on 30 November after another restless night that had left him wakeful from 3 a.m. Feeling weak and chilly, he ate a little breakfast, but he was suffering stomach cramps and was too ill to go out on the terrace to take the air. Besides, he was far too preoccupied with the *Trent* crisis. The prospect of war with the North was a very stark one, of which Albert was only too well aware. It would be a disaster for British trade, and worse, with the loss of American grain imports, it could bring with it bread shortages. Letters to *The Times* were already urging moderation – an apology should be demanded for what was now seen as an 'illegal and irregular proceeding' rather than an act of aggression. An editorial in *The Times* led the way, appealing to reason and self-restraint in the hope that 'our people will not meet this provocation with an outburst of passion'.[50] Counter to his wife and Palmerston's considerably more belligerent attitude, Albert sided with *The Times* and thought the incident was not something worth going to war over. The boarding of the *Trent* must, he suggested, have taken place without the assent of President Lincoln – an assumption that, whether true or not, might provide a way out of the impasse. He was still very depressed and eating very little, as Victoria told Vicky that day, but she persisted in her own logical explanation: it was a result of all the sleepless nights, which had lowered his spirits. She refused to take any of it seriously. 'Dear Papa is in reality much better', if he would only admit it, the fault being that he was 'as usual desponding as men really only are – when unwell'.[51] She was already looking forward to their departure from Windsor for Osborne on 13 December, for a cosy family Christmas. She was 'truly thankful' that they would soon have other scenery to look at, other than 'this most tiresome – and this year to me – most distasteful place'.

That evening a draft despatch from Palmerston's government to the Americans had arrived for the Queen's approval. Its tone was aggressive and strident; Albert was greatly alarmed: 'This means war!' he told Victoria, unless the uncompromising stance of the document could be modified.[52] That night he slept in a separate room, so as not to disturb her. He rose early the following morning, Sunday 1 December, lit his favourite green desk lamp (the one he had brought with him from Coburg) and sat down, still in his scarlet padded dressing gown, to draft a more conciliatory response. This allowed for the possibility of a misunderstanding and gave the Americans room for a dignified climbdown. Later, when the Queen got up, he wearily handed the draft to her, admitting that he had been feeling so ill when composing it that 'I could hardly hold my pen.'[53]

'He could eat no breakfast and looked very wretched' that morning, Victoria later recalled, but Albert managed a walk with her for half an hour on the lower terrace, though 'well wrapped up'. He also accompanied her to Sunday service in St George's Chapel, where he 'insisted on going through all the kneeling'.[54] He tried hard to make the most of a family Sunday, joining everyone for luncheon, 'but could take nothing', a fact that dismayed doctors Clark and Jenner when they visited. They were, the Queen wrote, 'much disappointed at finding Albert so very uncomfortable'. He came down to dinner that evening, but again was unable to eat, but he did his best not to show how ill he felt by chatting and telling stories and then sitting for a while listening to his eighteen-year-old daughter Alice and Marie, Princess of Leiningen, playing the piano. He went to bed at 10.30 'in hopes to sleep it off', but when the Queen joined him at half-past eleven, he was lying there, wide awake, shivering with cold and unable to sleep.[55]

Aware of the need for a prompt response to the Americans, to be sent that night by steamship, Victoria had reviewed Albert's draft memorandum on the *Trent*, made a few emendations – to what would be her husband's last act of public business – and sent it back to Whitehall in the hope that sufficient redress would be offered, along with a speedy apology.[56] It would take up to twelve days for the dispatch to reach America by sea. The British nation, with no real appetite for another war, went to church and prayed to God that a conflict could be averted. But Queen Victoria now had other far more immediate preoccupations – with her 'beloved invalid'.[57] The following morning, 2 December, after yet another night of shivering and sleeplessness, unable to eat and without even the inclination to get dressed, Prince Albert got up, sank onto a sofa and sent for Dr Jenner.

CHAPTER FOUR

'Our Most Precious Invalid'

With 'The American Difficulty' still preoccupying the British public and taking the lion's share of the newspaper columns, there was no inkling in the press on Monday 2 December 1861 that a very real crisis was brewing closer to home. As usual the Queen's every move over the weekend was reported in meticulous detail: on Saturday she had ridden out in the morning with Princess Alice and taken the air by carriage that afternoon, before holding a Privy Council meeting at five; the Prince Consort had accompanied her to Divine Service the following morning; the family was preparing to depart for Osborne for Christmas by the middle of December; and at the Birmingham Cattle and Poultry Show the Prince Consort's cattle had won first and second prizes in the Devon Steers class.

To the outside world all seemed well at Windsor. But for the Prince and his anxious wife it had been another 'sad night of shivering and sleeplessness', with Albert 'being awake at every hour almost'. When Dr Jenner arrived, he found him 'extremely uncomfortable and so depressed'. But he told the Queen that 'there was no reason to be alarmed', although he did fear that the Prince's condition was 'turning into a kind of long feverish indisposition'.[1] Albert lay listlessly on the sofa in his dressing gown and from time to time sat up in an armchair as Victoria or Alice read to him, but he was still very restless and uncomfortable when Jenner visited later that day. 'He kept saying, it was very well he had no fever, as he should not recover!', Victoria lamented in her journal, but she and the doctors persisted in making light of the Prince's neuroses. Such a thing, they all told him, 'was too foolish and he must never speak of it'. He tried to eat, but even some soup with bread tasted awful, 'making him feel nauseous and his stomach uncomfortable'.[2] Albert's mood was not lifted when his emissaries, Lord Methuen and Colonel Francis Seymour, returned from Portugal – where

they had been dispatched with letters of condolence – bringing accounts
of the death of King Pedro. The doctors had advised that Albert should
not speak to them, for fear of becoming demoralised, but he had insisted
on hearing all the details of the King's illness and death, at the end of
which he had asserted to Lord Methuen that his own illness also would
be fatal.[3]

That night, rather than disturb Victoria, Albert got up and went to
his own room, but sleep again evaded him as he lay there feeling cold.[4]
The following morning he could not eat breakfast or even take any broth
without being overcome by nausea. Seymour thought the Prince looked
'as if he was on the brink of a jaundice of no trifling kind', with 'severe
cold, bile and rheumatic aches in his back, legs, etc.' 'There is an end to
his shooting for a long time,' he remarked ruefully, seeing nothing else
to be concerned about.[5]

Although the British public was still oblivious to the Prince Consort's
rapidly declining health, the Prime Minister's concern was rising. At
seventy-seven years of age, Lord Palmerston was far from well himself,
suffering from agonising gout that caused such crippling pains in his
hands and feet that he could hardly get about or even open a letter.
Nevertheless he had come to Windsor for the Privy Council meeting on
30 November and had returned to the castle for a private dinner on the
2 December, when he had been concerned to hear of Albert's continuing
illness. He had had major problems in the past dealing with the Queen's
bouts of hysteria when under pressure, and dreaded any sidelining of
the Prince's role in affairs of state. Having long been sanguine about the
efficiency of the royal doctors, Palmerston was extremely uneasy and
requested that another medical man be called in to examine the Prince,
suggesting Dr Robert Ferguson, who had attended the Queen at the
births of all her children.

Queen Victoria was much put out by this. Despite her 'agony of
despair' at how listless and distracted Albert was, she was 'dreadfully
annoyed' by Palmerston's interference, and more so by what appeared
to be his covert calling into question of the medical skills of Clark and
Jenner.[6] She instructed Sir Charles Phipps, who during Albert's illness
was temporarily performing the role of her Private Secretary, to respond
very firmly, thanking Palmerston for his 'kind interest'. The Prince had
a feverish cold of the kind that he often succumbed to in winter and she
hoped it would pass off in a few days. She would therefore be 'unwilling
to cause unnecessary alarm where no cause exists for it, by calling in a

medical man who does not upon ordinary occasions attend at the Palace'.[7] The message was clear: Victoria and the royal doctors did not want to provoke an adverse response in the highly sensitive Albert by suggesting that his condition was in any way serious; nor, privately, did the doctors want any overattention to the Prince's worsening condition to cause the kind of hysterical outbursts that Victoria had shown over her mother.

And so a stubborn policy of cheerful optimism and illusory hope was adopted, in the face of all indications to the contrary. Victoria was already settled on a course of denial, confident there was nothing to worry about; after all, 'Good kind old Sir James' had reassured her, and that was enough in her book. 'There was no cause whatever for alarm,' Clark had told her and he felt sure that Prince Albert 'would soon be better'.[8] To reassure the Prince, Dr Jenner stayed at Windsor that night, but although Albert got some sleep between 8 p.m. and midnight, he was awake and restless for much of the remainder – wandering aimlessly from room to room, with a disconsolate Victoria trailing after him.

Was the royal doctors' decision not to take the Prince's illness with deadly seriousness at this early stage a fatal mistake? It certainly ensured that the patient was not firmly told to get into bed and stay there, in order to allow himself to be properly nursed. But the fact was that there was as yet no system of efficient nursing established in Britain to supplant the slatternly, untrained hospital nurses of Mrs Gamp fame, immortalised by Dickens in *Martin Chuzzlewit*. After her return from the Crimean War in 1856, Florence Nightingale had been given official approval to establish nurses' training at St Thomas's Hospital as a respectable profession for women, but the first Nightingale Training School had only opened in July the previous year. For now, the nursing of the sick poor was still largely carried out by nuns and similar lay orders. For the better-off, the best and often most hygienic care was that provided in their own homes by their nearest and dearest – in many cases the eldest unmarried daughter of the family.

The situation was no different at Windsor. With the Queen too emotionally unstable to cope with the stresses and strains of an increasingly irascible patient, the role of sick-nurse fell to the eighteen-year-old Princess Alice, who was assisted by the Prince's closest, but medically untrained personal attendants: his fellow Coburger, Rudolf Löhlein; his eighteen-year-old Scottish garderobier, Archie Macdonald; and his Swiss valet, Gustav Mayet.[9] For all her youth and inexperience, Princess Alice had from a young age shown a compassionate interest in the sick, visiting poor cottagers on the estate at Balmoral and, at the age of only eleven, going with her parents to see the wounded – many of them severely mutilated – of the Crimean War. Alice could see the grim reality where her mother could not, having long had an intuitive understanding of her father's state of growing weariness. From the start of this latest bout of illness Alice had had grave apprehensions. Writing to Louis in Hesse on 3 December, she openly admitted that 'poor mama' had no idea how to nurse someone, 'although she wants to help as much as she can'. (Augusta Bruce thought likewise: 'The Queen's little knowledge of nursing made her rather not the best nurse in the world.')[10] Alice was steeling herself to the role expected of her – that of the sentimental archetype, the 'Angel in the House' – on whom the family relied. But it was so hard with her father not eating, not sleeping and experiencing bouts of chronic pain, and refusing to allow that he would get better. 'I have to listen to the mutual complaints of my dear parents if I am to be really helpful to them,' she wrote, 'or even carry their burden, if that were possible,' she told Louis.[11] From now on she would be an almost constant presence, hovering devotedly over her father and sleeping in the room next to him so as to be always on call.

*　*　*

The first public inkling that something was amiss came in the morning papers of 4 December, which carried a small notice in the daily Court Bulletin that 'The Prince Consort has been suffering for the last three days from a feverish cold, which has confined His Royal Highness to his room.'[12] Over at Windsor the Queen had awoken after 'a very sad night' during which she had wept a great deal at seeing her husband in so much distress. After tossing and turning till 6 a.m., Albert had got up and sent for Dr Jenner, but refused to take any breakfast. Later he was persuaded to take some orange jelly and 'a little raspberry vinegar in seltzer water'.[13] Victoria pulled herself together to write a letter to Leopold in Cannes, telling him that Papa was suffering from 'a regular influenza', but when she returned from her walk on the terrace later that day she was dismayed to see Albert's looks and manner 'very sad and disheartening' and, worse, how little he smiled.[14] 'It was, from the first,' she later recalled, 'as if he could not smile his own expression.'[15]

Sir James Clark arrived, and was 'grieved to see no more improvement'. But he was still not discouraged, he told the Queen. Albert rested in the bedroom for most of the day and asked to be read to. But his irritable and restless state prevailed and 'no books suited him, neither

Silas Marner nor *The Warden'*. The Queen tried to raise his spirits with Charles Lever's *The Dodd Family Abroad* – a humorous novel about gauche British travellers on the Continent – but Albert did not like that either, so it was decided that the following day they would revert to an old favourite, a book by Sir Walter Scott.[16]

That night Albert's restlessness became even more marked; after tossing and turning in bed, he got up and once more walked distractedly from room to room in his quilted dressing gown. Dr Jenner arrived and administered a sedative, but it brought the Prince only a few hours' respite. After breakfast on the 4th the Queen found him looking 'dreadfully wretched and woe-begone', able only to take some tea, but no food.[17] Princess Alice did her best to soothe her father by reading Scott's *The Talisman* – a tale of Richard the Lionheart and the Crusades. After taking a short walk with her daughters that afternoon, the Queen found Albert no better. He was lying on the bed, but 'seemed in a very uncomfortable panting state, and saying "I am so silly" which frightened us'. Albert's persistence in taking no food roused even the usually conciliatory Dr Jenner, who told the Queen that the Prince *must* eat, 'and that he was going to tell him so'. Yes, it was tedious to have to eat when he felt so unwell, but 'completely starving himself, as he had done, would *not* do'.[18] For once Albert's self-administered starvation cure for his 'old enemy' was not working.

Albert was once more unsmiling and distant when Victoria went in to see him the following morning. It was deeply disturbing, for he seemed 'so unlike himself and he had sometimes such a strange, wild look' in his eyes, which she could not comprehend. After being persuaded to take some broth he slept for a while, and in the evening an ever-hopeful Victoria was encouraged that he seemed 'so dear and affectionate and so quite himself'. Earlier that day she had taken her youngest daughter Beatrice in to see him. 'He quite laughed at some of her new French verses which I made her repeat.' Then Albert lay there and 'held her little hand in his for some time' while a bewildered Beatrice stood gazing at him. But he refused to undress and get into bed when Dr Jenner again suggested it, eventually settling down to sleep in his dressing room, only to change rooms restlessly two or three times in the night.[19]

Victoria was awoken at one in the morning on 6 December, 'hearing coughing and moaning'. But Albert had at least taken some tea and broth during the night from Jenner, who had sat up with him by candlelight and once more reassured the Queen that 'there was nothing alarming'.[20] Thankfully, after Victoria had been out for a drive with one of her Ladies of the Bedchamber – the Duchess of Athole – Albert's mood lifted. Clark and Jenner were pleased, for the Prince had taken some broth and eaten two rusks, though he had 'vehemently remonstrated against taking any arrowroot in his broth, saying: "it is so offensive, that thick stuff"'.[21]

There were as usual urgent letters for the Queen to write, keeping her family up to date on Albert's condition. Despite her worst anxieties she confidently assured Uncle Leopold in Belgium that 'this nasty, feverish sort of influenza and deranged stomach is *on* the mend, but it will be slow and tedious'. But she had to admit how greatly alarmed she had been by 'such restlessness, such sleeplessness, and such (till to-day) *total* refusal of all food that it made one *very, very* anxious'. For four nights in succession she had got 'only two or three hours' sleep'.[22] She told a similar story to Vicky in Berlin, complaining of how irritable Albert was; she and the doctors would not of course be taking this all so seriously, were it not for the fact that 'the dear invalid' was 'the most precious and perfect of human beings'. Thankfully 'Good Alice' had been a 'very great comfort' to her; day after day, the Princess had sat reading to Albert, without ever betraying her own fears or allowing her voice to falter.[23]

That day Sir Charles Phipps wrote to the Prime Minister, having taken it upon himself to keep Lord Palmerston abreast of developments. The Prince's illness 'required much management', he warned, in order to fend off both Albert's natural depression at being ill and the Queen's extreme nervousness about it. In effect, the royal physicians were having to deal with two patients: the sick prince and his overwrought wife. As it was, a third practitioner was now also paying regular visits – Dr Henry Brown, the Windsor apothecary who, Phipps assured Palmerston, 'knows the Prince's constitution better than anybody'. But to call in any more doctors at this stage would do more harm than good, for 'the mere suggestion the other night upset the Queen and agitated her dreadfully'.[24]

On the morning of Saturday 7 December Victoria discovered that although Albert had had 'a good deal of sleep', he had again changed rooms several times during the night before returning to his original bed. Early that morning, as he had lain awake listening to the dawn chorus, he told her he had fancied himself back again in his beloved woods at the Rosenau; such thoughts were increasingly recurring as he sat in an armchair in his sitting room, 'looking weak and exhausted, and not better, complaining of there being no improvement, and he did not know what it could come from'. Victoria once more insisted that it was all the fault of overwork. For once Albert agreed with her. 'It is too

much. You must speak to the Ministers,' he told her.[25] Later Dr Jenner
came to see the Queen and told her that the doctors had 'all along been
watching their patient's state' and that, from their physical examination,
they now feared the Prince had a 'gastric or low fever'.[26]

The suggestion that Albert was suffering from some form of 'fever'
was an ominous one, for in Victorian times fever and its various
synonyms – 'low fever', 'slow fever', 'gastric fever' and 'bowel fever' – were
catch-alls for a whole range of complaints, of which typhoid fever was
the most common and the most dreaded. The word typhoid – if that is
what the doctors truly believed it to be at this stage, and it had puzzlingly
taken the supposed specialist Jenner a long time to reach this conclusion
– was never uttered in front of the Queen. The case was *quite* clear',
Jenner told her. 'He knew exactly how to treat him,' he went on, 'that it
was tedious and that the fever *must* have its course – viz – a month from
the beginning, which he considers to have been from the day Albert
went to Sandhurst – 22nd – or possibly sooner'.[27] This nebulous statement was the closest the Queen ever came to being given a diagnosis;
it would also give rise to 150 years of subsequent speculation that Albert
had somehow picked up a typhoid germ that day at the military academy,
or possibly back home at Windsor. Thus reassured by Jenner, all the
Queen had to do was wait patiently for the fever to run its course (just
like scarlet fever or measles) and all would be well. It was, however, not
advisable for the younger children – Louise, Beatrice and Arthur – to go
in to see their father, for fear of infection, though Alice was by now
indispensable and showed no fear of any perceived risk. The Prince, of
course, was not to know any of this because of his 'horror of fever'; it
would only bring him down in his present state.[28]

Another memorandum was sent by Phipps to Palmerston, confirming
that the Prince's illness 'is to-day declared to be a gastric fever'. But he
insisted there were no symptoms that gave cause for anxiety. Confidentially,
however, although the Queen was presently 'perfectly composed', Phipps
again reiterated to Palmerston that it required 'no little management to
prevent her from breaking down altogether. The least thing would alarm
her to a degree that would unfit her for the discharge of any duties.'
For this reason 'as cheerful a view as possible should be taken to her of
the state of the Prince'.[29] But it was already proving a struggle for Victoria;
she was by now exhausted, not just with her constant attendance in and
out of Albert's room, but with the task of having to deal alone with all
the unfinished official business in the dispatch boxes that were piling up.

Prince Albert spent the whole of the 7th in his dressing room lying on the sofa dozing, as his wife sat by him struggling to contain her emotions. 'What trials have we not had this year?' she wrote despairingly in her journal that day. 'What an *awful* trial this is – to be deprived for so long of my guide and my support and my all!' She felt as though she was living in a 'dreadful dream', and wept at the thought of what lay in store, of 'the utter shipwreck of our plans and the dreadful *loss* this long illness would be publicly as well as privately'.[30] Needing a close friend with whom to commiserate, she sent for Lady Augusta Bruce to come and stay, as Dr Jenner and Rudolf Löhlein settled in for another disrupted night watching over Albert.

The morning of 8 December gave rise to false hopes of the Prince's recovery. He seemed very weak, but was still walking about, and although extremely irritable and impatient, the doctors thought him 'going on well'. The Prince ate a little chicken and took some tea and wine during the day. Such minor improvements were sufficient to raise Victoria's hopes. When she returned from breakfast she found Albert lying on the bed in the King's Room, a small room used mainly by the royal family at Christmas time. It provided more air and light than the couple's bedroom and Albert specifically asked to be moved there. He seemed happy – 'the sun shining brightly and the room fine, large and gay; 'It is so fine,' he told her; he liked this room with its eastward view, out over the garden and the orangery, and, above, the blue sky and morning sunshine. For the first time since the onset of his illness Albert asked for some music: 'I should like to hear a fine chorale played at a distance,' he said. And so a piano was brought into the next room, where Alice played several of Albert's favourite pieces: Martin Luther's hymn 'Ein Feste Burg ist Unser Gott' and the Lutheran chorales 'Wachtet Auf' and 'Nun Danket Alle Gott'. The Luther hymn, a paraphrase of Psalm 46, which reassures the faithful that 'God is our refuge and strength/A very present help in trouble', seemed to offer great comfort to the sick man: 'he listened, looking upward with such a sweet expression,' the Queen noted, but then, soon wearied, he said in German, 'That is enough.'[31]

As it was Sunday, the royal family all headed off to service at St George's Chapel, leaving the Prince in the care of Princess Alice. The Reverend Charles Kingsley preached a 'beautiful' sermon, in the view of Lady Bruce, but the Queen professed she 'heard nothing', preoccupied as she was.[32] Alone with Alice, the Prince asked to have the sofa on which he was lying pulled closer to the oriel window 'that he might see the sky, and watch the clouds sailing past'. He once more asked her to play to him and lay there reflectively as Alice 'went thro' several of his favourite hymns and chorales', including another favourite, 'To Thee, O Lord, I yield my spirit', and 'Rock of ages, cleft for me'. When she turned from the piano to look, Albert seemed very still and serene with his eyes closed, his hands 'folded, as if in prayer'; her once-strong father was now as weak and helpless as a child. She thought he was asleep, but suddenly Albert looked up and smiled at her, and told her he had been having 'such sweet happy thoughts'.[33] Perhaps they were of the home in heaven that he had already contemplated at length in his reading of William Branks's book.

The fact that her father had chosen now to settle in the King's Room – the room in which both William IV and George IV before him had died – could not have escaped Alice (though the great state bed in which the kings had died had been moved out and replaced with two smaller ones). In such precious moments together during these final days, Albert often confided thoughts and feelings to his daughter that he would never dare share with his wife, for 'she could not bear to listen, and would not see the danger he felt, and only tried to argue him out of the idea'.[34] But, as Alice recognised that Sunday, her father was already resigned to dying and was preparing himself for it. It took all her strength of character and fortitude not to betray this knowledge to her mother, whilst drawing on her own emotional reserves for what now seemed inevitable. It was only when 'she felt she could bear it no longer' that she would 'walk quite calmly to the door', and then rush into her own room to weep. Shortly afterwards she would return, 'with her deadly white face, as fixed and calm as ever, with no trace whatever of what she had gone through'.[35] But in a long letter she wrote to Louis that day, Alice admitted how 'terribly difficult' the last week had been and how unbearable it was to see 'a strong, hard man like Papa . . . lying weak and helpless like a child' and listen to his pathetic groaning.[36]

After lunch on the 8th the Queen thought the Prince looked 'less ill than we expected' and took the Prince of Leiningen in to see him. Albert was by now drifting in and out of an almost constant doze. The doctors and his valets continued to fuss round him, especially the admirable Löhlein, but Albert's weakening state was occasionally broken by moments of irritability. At one point, much to Victoria's dismay, he became so impatient 'because I tried to help in explaining something to Dr Jenner and quite slapped my hand, poor dear darling'.[37] At other more lucid times his old affection resurfaced. 'When I went to him after dinner,'

Victoria recalled, 'he was so pleased to see me, stroked my face and smiled, and called me "dear little wife"'. She had spent the afternoon reading Scott's *Peveril of the Peak* and the *Memoirs* of the Prussian diplomat Varnhagen von Ense to the Prince. His tenderness later that evening, 'when he held my hand and stroked my face, touched me so much, and made me so grateful,' she recorded in her journal.[38] But Albert's occasional gentle and familiar commendations in German of Victoria as his *gutes Weibchen* and his *liebes Frauchen* were the only comfort now remaining to her.

The following morning – Monday 9 December – the British public was informed in the Court Circular of *The Times* that the Prince Consort had been confined to his apartments for the last week, 'suffering from a feverish cold, with pains in the limbs'. 'Within the last two days the feverish symptoms have rather increased, and are likely to continue for some time longer.' 'But,' the bulletin added by way of reassurance, 'there are no unfavourable symptoms.'[39] Such was not the prevailing view inside Windsor Castle. In light of the Prince's continuing poor condition, Phipps and the royal doctors were grappling with the problem of how to call in additional medical advice without undermining the Prince's morale. The men they had in mind were the socialite doctor Sir Henry Holland, who had been one of the Prince's Physicians-in-Ordinary since 1840 (and because of his status could not be 'passed over'), and Dr Thomas Watson, Physician Extraordinary to the Queen since 1859. Victoria had immediately started fretting about how this might affect her dear Albert, 'and fear I distressed both Sir James and Dr Jenner'.[40] But she was persuaded to agree, on the grounds that it was 'necessary to satisfy the public to have another eminent doctor to come and see him'.[41] When Holland arrived he was confronted with a desperate Queen: 'Oh, you will save him for me, Dr Holland? You will save him for me, will you not?'; while Watson's visit was rather more subdued. It 'went off quite well', Victoria later reported. Albert had found him a 'quiet, sensible man', but had thought it 'quite absurd' that Clark had wanted to send for Holland too.[42]

Watson, who was in the first rank of his profession after a long and distinguished medical career from 1825 and a period as chair of the Principles and Practice of Medicine at King's College, University of London, took a much more serious line than Clark and Jenner. Phipps was soon writing to Palmerston to say that Dr Watson considered Prince Albert to be '*very ill*'. 'The malady is very grave and serious in itself,' he had told Phipps, without enlightening him as to what exactly it was. The doctors were clearly still in the dark and hedging their bets: 'the symptoms exhibited were such as might precede the more distinct characterisation of gastric or bowel fever,' Phipps went on. 'The Prince's present weakness is very great,' Watson had told him, and 'it is impossible not to be very anxious'.⁴³ One ominous difference had now been noted: Prince Albert had finally stopped wandering around in his dressing gown and had undressed and taken to his bed – although during the day he was transferred to a couch in the Red Room beyond.

Albert passed a reasonable night and on the morning of the 10th his pulse was good. Victoria was therefore annoyed to hear that Lord Palmerston, having been alarmed by the news from Phipps, was nevertheless insisting that Dr Watson should remain on call at the castle and was pressurising Clark to call in more specialists. The Prime Minister did not mince his words: the Prince's fate was a 'matter of the most momentous national importance, and all considerations of personal feeling and susceptibilities must absolutely give way to the public interest'.⁴⁴ Other ministers were doing likewise, writing to Phipps in deepest anxiety. Sir George Lewis recommended they consult 'Dr Tweedie, an old longbearded Scotchman', who was founder and consulting physician to the London Fever Hospital in Islington; others, like the Duke of Newcastle, worried that the Queen might have become infected from her close contact with the Prince.⁴⁵ Many now realised with escalating alarm, as did Lord Granville, leader of the Liberal Party, 'how invaluable' the Prince's life was.⁴⁶

The Queen was, of course, oblivious to the backstage political drama that was unfolding. Later that day she went in to see Albert and 'found him wandering with the oddest fancies and suspicions', but the doctors reassured her that this was 'nothing' and quite common in such cases. Doctors Watson and Jenner in fact announced that they were both impressed with the Prince's progress over the last twenty-four hours, considering it to be 'a positive gain'.⁴⁷ Comforting herself with these small signs of progress, the Queen wrote to Vicky:

Thank God! Beloved Papa had another excellent night and is going on quite satisfactorily. There is a decided gain since yesterday and several most satisfactory symptoms. He is now in bed – and only moves on the sofa made like a bed, for some hours. He takes a great deal of nourishment – and is really very patient.⁴⁸

Sir James Clark, meanwhile, had been called away to his own sick wife at their home at Bagshot Park, but returned as often as possible, sleeping at Windsor every other night. But there was always Alice, as well as Löhlein – 'most attentive and devoted and indefatigable' – and Albert's valet, Gustav Mayet, who 'also does his best'.[49]

Victoria was able to thank and bless God for 'another reasonably good night' when she awoke on the 11th. She found her husband sitting up in bed taking his beef tea, 'which he always laments most bitterly over'. But 'his beautiful face, more beautiful than ever' had 'grown *so* thin'. A brief moment of tenderness, during which Albert lay for a while with his head on her shoulder, made her very happy. 'It is very comfortable so, dear Child,' he whispered to her and her eyes filled with tears.[50] Later, when he was being wheeled along the passage to the King's Room, he had turned to 'the beautiful picture of the Madonna' that he had given Victoria as a present three years previously, 'and asked to stop and look at it, ever loving what is beautiful'. To look on such things, he told his wife, 'helps me through half the day'.[51]

A reassuring letter had arrived that morning from Uncle Leopold: Albert's illness was just another of those regular and long-familiar indispositions that he often suffered at this time of the year. Victoria should not interrupt her 'usual airings' and must be sure to take a turn outside, for to be deprived of this 'would do you harm'. In reply Victoria was happy to tell Leopold that Albert had had another good night with no worsening symptoms. It was as much as they dared hope for: '*not* losing ground is a *gain, now* of *every* day'.[52] The doctors, however, continued to be highly circumspect in what they told her, which was always hedged around with elaborately contrived positives. The symptoms were still not unfavourable, in their view, but Victoria was apprehensive. Albert now looked 'so totally unlike himself', she told Vicky; again that day he 'was very wandering at times'.[53] She sat with him that afternoon and evening, reading to him and holding his hand, and, at his request, sharing a prayer together. Albert's irritability had at last receded and he seemed anxious for Victoria to stay close by. She returned to her husband's bedside after dinner and he sent for her again later, her hungry heart filling with joy: 'I flew over, so happy that he wished to see me.' Reluctantly she left him to rest, on Dr Brown's advice, but it was hard: 'God knows how happy I was to stay!'[54]

That evening an ominous change in the Prince was noted by Sir James Clark, who 'listened anxiously to his breathing, at his back'. But once again the Queen was fobbed off; when she asked Clark what this signified he 'said it was nothing, only a slight wheezing; of no consequence whatever'. So once more she went to her bed reassured that there was nothing to worry about, 'tho' sad to be so far' from her beloved Albert.[55] Clark was right to be worried: the wheezing suggested the onset of that dreaded complication: congestion of the lungs, or pneumonia as it is more commonly known today. Albert himself, in a lucid moment earlier that day, had recognised the danger. Princess Alice had been sitting with him at the time, when he had asked if the Queen was in the room. When Alice said no, he had told her that he knew he was dying. He wanted her to write immediately and tell Vicky in Berlin. Alice did so and when she returned he asked her what she had said in her letter. "'I have told my sister," she answered, "that you are very ill." "You have done wrong," he said to her; "You should have told her I am dying, yes I am dying."'[56]

Although Princess Alice and Albert had no illusions about his condition, the other members of the royal household were still clearly caught between a compulsion to deny what their eyes told them and confusion about the official diagnosis. Lady Ely, for example, that day told the Earl of Malmesbury that the Prince's illness was 'gastric fever and inflammation, of the mucous membrane of the stomach'.[57] Lord Palmerston, however, was now insisting to Phipps that the nation should be prepared for worse news to come – otherwise it would be 'thunderstruck and indignant' at having been kept in the dark.[58] The royal doctors were obliged to agree; the Prince's illness now presaged a national crisis. But how to convince the Queen of the danger? It was Princess Alice who took it upon herself to try and make her mother face up to reality: 'I will tell her,' she had said, and during a carriage ride that morning she had done her best, as gently as she could, to convince her mother that Albert could not recover.[59] That evening, a carefully worded bulletin was prepared: 'His Royal Highness is suffering from fever, hitherto unattended by unfavourable symptoms, but likely from its nature to continue for some time.'[60] It was signed by the four physicians: Clark, Holland, Watson and Jenner. But when the Queen asked to see it prior to it being sent out, she struck out the crucial word 'hitherto', refusing to accept even the remotest possibility of danger.[61]

Prince Albert's quickness of breath alarmed Dr Jenner the following morning, but like Clark he told the Queen there was no consequence to it, provided it did not increase. When the Prince took some broth and wine, the Queen noticed his hands were shaking; again Jenner told her not to worry; it was 'merely fever'. The Prince remained compliant and did what the doctors told him, though from time to time he seemed confused: this was yet another symptom of the fever, the doctors told her. It would work its way through Albert's system over the usual four-week course predicted in such cases. Taking them literally, Victoria recorded her false hopes in her journal: 'We rejoiced so to think tomorrow would be the 22nd day, and that in another week please God! he would be getting over it.' In anticipation of this, she 'talked with Dr Jenner of the happy convalescence, tho' always with trembling'.[62] Then she sat down and wrote a reassuring letter to Uncle Leopold stating that her husband 'maintains his ground well . . . takes plenty of nourishment, and shows surprising strength'. She was fulsome in her praise of the 'skill, attention, and devotion of Dr Jenner'. He was, after all, 'the *first fever* Doctor in Europe' and must know what he was doing.[63]

Lord Palmerston, however, remained far from impressed with the royal doctors and their persistent underrepresentation of the true seriousness of Prince Albert's condition and sent three letters to Windsor that day asking for news. Palmerston had no illusions that the Prince's illness was of a 'formidable character'. Aware that it was 'liable to take a sudden and unfavourable turn from day to day', he hoped therefore that Dr Watson, a man whose reputation he clearly respected, would stay in constant attendance at Windsor to monitor the Prince's condition, and that he 'would be allowed to have his own way as to treatment'.[64] He had no faith in Dr Clark, who in his view 'had already incurred a heavy responsibility by delaying so long to call in additional advice'. Clark had a great deal to answer for, in Palmerston's book, for not at once informing him of the graveness of the Prince's condition, 'instead of leaving me to find out by my own conclusions that it was of a much more serious nature than was represented to me by him' at Windsor the previous week. When later that day Phipps revealed the now worrying development of the Prince's impaired breathing and increasing listlessness, Palmerston was shocked. 'Your telegram and letter have come upon me like a thunderbolt,' he responded. The implications were 'too awful to contemplate'. 'One can only hope that Providence may yet spare us so overwhelming a calamity.'[65]

Refusing to contemplate the worst, the Queen was still clutching at straws that evening. The doctors were doing all they could to control Albert's rapid rate of breathing; 'another 24 or still more 48 hours without further increase of it would make one feel quite safe'.[66] But things were no better the following morning, Friday 13th. The Queen went in to see Albert in her dressing gown at 8 a.m. and noted that even the stoical

Jenner 'was anxious and tired'. After a carriage drive with Augusta Bruce, she returned at midday and 'found the breathing *very quick* which made me dreadfully anxious and nervous'.[67] The Prince was lying listlessly on his couch in the sitting room, only this time he had not even looked at his favourite painting of the Madonna and child as he passed it. He seemed now able only to recognise Carl Ruland, his German librarian, who came and read to him. For the most part he lay there with his hands clasped and with blank eyes gazing towards the open window, taking no notice of his surroundings and slipping in and out of consciousness, though Victoria was gratified that he did at one point take hold of her hand, calling her his *gutes Frauchen* and kissing her with affection.

At about four-thirty that afternoon, while the Queen was taking a short walk on the terrace, Dr Jenner hurried in to Augusta Bruce, telling her that 'such sinking had come on that he had feared the Prince would die in his arms'.[68] She must hurry to find the Queen and prepare her for the worst. In accordance with standard Victorian medical practice, Albert was now being dosed with brandy every half-hour in an attempt to raise his pulse.[69] By the time Victoria returned she found her husband very still and quiet. When Dr Clark arrived from attending his wife, he too was 'much perturbed' by what he saw. There could be no more prevarication: the Queen must be prepared, otherwise the shock would be too terrible.[70] Augusta Bruce and one of the children's governesses, Miss Hildyard, did their best to offer comfort to an increasingly distraught Victoria, who was now weeping in fear and dread of the worst. 'The country; oh, the country,' she kept repeating. 'I could perhaps bear my own misery, but the poor country.'[71] 'I prayed and cried as if I should go mad,' Victoria later wrote of that day. 'Oh! That I was not then and there crazed!' Desperation was now setting in: 'My Husband won't die.' No, he could not die, he must not die, she would not accept it: 'for that would kill me'.[72]

That evening the Prince's pulse improved and he appeared to have rallied; Victoria sat in a chair at the foot of his bed with Alice at her side, sitting on the floor; Augusta Bruce and Marie of Leiningen were close at hand in the next room. Albert 'was nice and warm and the skin soft', the Queen recalled. Dr Watson was gently reassuring: he had seen many infinitely worse cases recover. 'I never despair with fever,' he added – after all, as Augusta Bruce observed, hundreds of people had survived 'under far more aggravated forms'.[73] But clearly the crisis had come: it was 'a struggle of strength', the doctors told the Queen. Clark was again superficially hopeful, but the time had come, in the most roundabout way possible, to persuade the Queen that 'they must give a rather unfavourable Bulletin, which could be improved of course if our Treasure went on well'.[74] Phipps too was preparing Lord Palmerston: 'the Prince's disease has taken a very unfavourable turn,' he informed him, 'the Doctors are in the *greatest anxiety* – they have even fears for the night.' Shortly afterwards an urgent telegram followed: 'I grieve to say the Prince is much worse.'[75]

* * *

Over at his home at Ascot, where he was dining alone that evening, John Delane, editor of *The Times*, received a note from Lady Palmerston requesting him to come immediately to see the Prime Minister at his London home, Cambridge House on Piccadilly. 'I was both tired and sleepy but thought it right to go,' he recalled, 'and it was well I did.' Palmerston was in deep distress at the latest news from Windsor; the royal doctors were warning that Prince Albert was not expected to survive the night. Soon afterwards the Duke of Cambridge arrived with a 'despairing letter from the Queen'. 'I never saw such a party of ghosts as the few who had remained looked at the news,' Delane later told John Walter, the newspaper's proprietor. The truth, as Palmerston saw it with brutal honesty, was that at this present moment of political crisis over the *Trent* affair, 'the Queen would be a less national loss' than the Prince.[76]

Only the previous night, Thursday 12 December, 3,000 people had attended a Great Prayer Meeting of all Christian denominations at Exeter Hall in London, called by the Evangelical Alliance. But the prayers they had so fervently recited had not been for the Prince Consort, but for 'Almighty God to avert from us the calamity of war with the United States'.[77] With the political crisis still unresolved, and a wait of at least a fortnight expected before a response to Lord John Russell's dispatch would arrive from America, two great iron-clad steamships, the *Persia* and the *Australasia* were preparing to sail from Liverpool loaded with field batteries and more than 2,000 troops for Canada. In the face of the very real and present danger of war, there seemed little, in comparison, to worry about with regard to the Prince Consort. The papers had made little of his illness so far. Although the Prince's name had been omitted from the Court Circular for several days, his pack of harriers had gone out hunting as usual on the Friday, with no one at the meet suspecting the worst, though his absence had been lamented at the Smithfield Club Cattle Show (where as usual his steers were picking up prizes). A few papers had, however, noted the cancellation of a shooting party planned for Windsor, and that 'in consequence of the prince's indisposition' the removal of the court to Osborne for Christmas planned for the following Friday, the 20th, had been 'deferred for the present'.[78]

If there was one other person in the country who perhaps understood the Prince's national significance at that moment it was Florence Nightingale. Commenting on his illness in a letter that she wrote on the 13th to her friend Mary Clarke Mohl from her home on South Street in Mayfair, she recalled that the Prince had 'neither liked nor was liked. But what he has done for our country no one knows.' As for the Queen, Nightingale went on, she had 'really behaved like a hero. Has buckled to business at once. After all, it is a great thing to be a Queen. She is the only woman in these realms, except perhaps myself, who has a *must* in her life – who must set aside private griefs and attend to the res publica.'[79] Events were soon, however, to prove Nightingale entirely wrong in this regard.

At 5 p.m. on the evening of the 13th a subtle but significant change had come in the wording of the bulletin issued by the royal doctors for publication the following morning. 'His Royal Highness the Prince Consort passed a restless night', the public were to be told; 'the symptoms have assumed an unfavourable character during the day'.[80] It was only now that many members of the royal household, such as Prince Arthur's governor, Howard Elphinstone, began to realise how desperate the situation had become. Elphinstone first heard the grave news from one of the Prince's equerries, Charles Du Plat, and received further confirmation from Carl Ruland.[81]

It was at this point that Princess Alice made an important decision. All her gentle hints to her mother that she should prepare herself for the worst had gone unheeded. Nor had Victoria – in her total absorption in her own anxiety – given any thought to Bertie away at university in Cambridge, who had no inkling of how gravely ill his father was. The Prince of Wales should be recalled, the Queen was urged. But she refused; her husband's anguish at Bertie's recent bad behaviour was, she remained convinced, still at the root of his present illness. Without her mother's knowledge, therefore, Princess Alice sent a brief telegram to Bertie that night informing him that Papa was 'not so well. Better come at once'. The telegram arrived while the Prince of Wales was hosting a farewell dinner party for Cambridge dignitaries prior to leaving for the Christmas vacation. Two hours later he boarded a special train out of Cambridge. It was 3 a.m. when he finally arrived at a silent and watchful Windsor.[82]

CHAPTER FIVE

'Day Turned into Night'

With Christmas only a fortnight away, George Augustus Sala, an ambitious young leader-writer on the *Daily Telegraph* who had already shown a talent for florid obituary-writing, was looking forward to the festive season at his lodgings at Upton Court in Slough, a few miles from Windsor. 'A yule log had been ordered; there was to be snap-dragon in the Hall, the "mummers" . . . were to come over from Slough and sing carols on Christmas Eve; and the cook had made at least a dozen plum puddings and a whole army of mince pies,' he remembered with relish. At the time Sala had been turning in two 1,500-word leaders a day for the *Telegraph* with Saturdays off, but this weekend, with friends visiting, he arranged not to go into his London office on Sunday and Monday, in order to enjoy it at home – 'providing always,' he added, 'that something which the whole English nation was dreading, did not happen.'[1] For by the morning of 14 December 1861 the press knew that 'the wise and good Prince Consort' was lying desperately ill at Windsor Castle.

That day, according to the *North Wales Chronicle*, there were but three principal topics of conversation in London: 'the probability of war with America, the health of the Prince Consort, and the Smithfield Cattle Club Show'. An air of anxiety was clearly gathering with regard to how 'even the temporary loss' of the Prince Consort's services was 'a misfortune for the country'.[2] The *Birmingham Daily Post* spoke of 'much uneasiness' as to his health and the *Glasgow Herald* noted that his condition 'has not improved, and the symptoms of fever are not diminished'. What is more, 'owing to the number of inquiries at Buckingham Palace on Friday, including the French Ambassador, a bulletin will be issued there on Saturday, and a visitors' book opened'.[3] In an attempt to defuse public alarm, *The Times* hoped that 'it will be in our power shortly to announce an improvement in the state of the Royal patient'. It went on to observe that for more than twenty years now the Prince had 'been the guide and protector of the Queen, to a degree that is rarely found even in ordinary life, when the husband is both in law and in reality the guardian of the wife'; it was clear from these words that editor John Delane was preparing for the worst. Nor could public alarm be tempered by the assurances that followed that the disease would no doubt yield to the skill of the Prince's eminent physicians, or the erroneous assumption that he had on his side 'youth and strength and an unimpaired constitution'.[4] There was no denying the shock the country would sustain when the news of the Prince Consort's rapid decline became widely known. Having driven to Windsor that morning and spoken to several members of the royal household, Delane was back at his offices in Printing House Square, Blackfriars, already fine-tuning the obituary for Prince Albert that he had prepared when he had first heard of his illness.[5]

Much to the surprise of the royal doctors, the Prince had in fact been able to get a better night's rest on the 13th; the Queen was brought encouraging bulletins on his progress at regular intervals during the night and, when she awoke at 5.30 a.m. that Saturday, she was greeted by Dr Brown with further good news: the Prince appeared to have rallied. 'I think he is better than he has been yet; I think there is ground to hope the crisis is over,' he told her.[6] Such was Albert's all-too-brief rally that he even 'got up & walked across the room for a purpose of nature'. Phipps dared to send word to Palmerston by telegraph: 'We are allowed again *a hope*.'[7]

At 7 a.m. the Queen went in to see her husband. 'It was a bright morning, the sun just rising and shining brightly,' she recalled. But despite what Brown had told her, there was an ominous atmosphere about the room. It had 'the sad look of night watching, the candles burnt down to their sockets – the doctors looking anxious'. That morning Albert had about him a strangely calm and beatific air: 'Never can I forget how beautiful my Darling looked lying there with his face lit up by the rising sun, his eyes unusually bright, gazing as it were on unseen objects, and not taking notice of me.'[8] It was the calm of resignation to imminent death that lit up Albert's face, but Victoria would not – could not – see it. For her, Albert's tranquillity indicated hope of recovery and, much to the consternation of the royal household, she began talking as though the danger was over, hastening to telegraph the 'good' news to Vicky in Berlin. Others in the family, confused by the Queen's false optimism, 'began writing to everyone as if it were a trifling illness'.[9]

Bertie was now at his father's bedside and lucky to be one of the few he briefly recognised. At around midday the Queen asked the doctors if she might go outside for a short while to take the air. 'Yes, just close by, for half an hour,' was their response. Accompanied by Alice, she took a turn on the East Terrace, but leaving her sick husband even for a short while was more than she could bear: 'The military band was playing at a distance, and I burst out crying and came home again – my anxiety and distress were so great.'¹⁰ Hurrying back to Albert's bedside, Victoria asked if the Prince was any better. 'We are very much frightened,' Dr Watson said to her as gently as he could, 'but don't and won't give up hope.'¹¹

Princess Alice, however, knew that despite the fleeting and hopeful indications to the contrary, the turning point had come. Bertie wrote a note to Louis on her behalf: their father was 'fighting for his life. In 24 hours we will know for sure – almighty God hear our prayers.'¹² As the afternoon went on, hopes once more began to fade: the Prince's pulse dropped and his breathing became raspy and rapid as the congestion overwhelmed his lungs. By five-thirty he was perspiring heavily. The only recourse the doctors had was dosing him yet again with spoonfuls of brandy at regular intervals. 'The pulse keeps up,' they told the Queen. The Prince was not getting worse; Sir James was 'very hopeful, he had seen much worse cases'. But even Victoria could not ignore Albert's laboured breathing: 'the alarming thing – so rapid, I think 60 respirations in a minute, tho the brandy always made it slower when taken'. His hands felt cold and there was 'what they call a dusky hue about his dear face and hands which I knew was not good'. It was the onset of cyanosis – a loss of oxygen levels in the blood – indicating that the Prince's lungs were failing rapidly. Dr Jenner had noticed it too and could not explain it away to the Queen. Prince Albert was slipping in and out of delirium, his ramblings largely incoherent, except for the often-repeated name – of his son Bertie. He began fretfully folding his arms and then 'arranging his hair just as he used to do when well and he was dressing'. 'These were said to be bad signs,' Victoria later recalled. Anxious and bewildered, she dared not admit to herself what all this meant, but with hindsight, it was as though her husband was 'preparing for another and a greater journey'.¹³

Princess Alice was in unflagging attendance at her father's sick-bed – despite the doctors wishing to spare her the distress of it – assisted by Marie of Leiningen and Augusta Bruce, who were constantly in and out of the room. Miss Hildyard also hovered solicitously, offering support to the Queen.[14] And Phipps was there too, promising to help in every way that he could though his hands shook, for he found it hard to control his own deep anxiety. Victoria would not give up, constantly soliciting Jenner for signs of improvement. Was there any hope, she kept asking him? 'Humanly speaking, it is not impossible,' he told her. There was nothing to prevent the Prince 'getting over it', and yet it seemed to Victoria now 'as though that precious Life, *the most* precious there was, was ebbing away!'[15]

* * *

As Saturday 14 December unravelled, it was for many an agonising time – 'a horrible day of suspense waiting for further intelligences which still never came', with everyone in the royal entourage 'now hoping for the best, now again despondently fearing the worst'.[16] That morning, writing one of his regular letters to his friend and confidante the Duchess of Manchester, the Earl of Clarendon had no doubt that 'a national calamity may be close at hand'. It was not just a matter of the unique and extraordinary role that the Prince performed in ensuring the Queen's fulfilment of her public duties; it was the untold impact that his absence would have on her. 'The habit or rather necessity, together with her intense love for him, which has increased rather than become weaker with years, has so engrafted her on him that to lose him,' Clarendon warned prophetically, 'will be like parting with her heart and soul.'[17]

Phipps, meanwhile, was sending regular updates to Palmerston, lamenting that 'Alas! The hopes of the morning are fading away.' The third edition of that day's *Times* had unfortunately come out announcing the news issued by the royal doctors at 9 a.m. that there had been 'some mitigation' of the severity of the symptoms overnight.[18] It was therefore deemed necessary to send a further bulletin, admitting that since morning the Prince had lapsed into a 'very critical state'. Not surprisingly, with the time delay in updates on the Prince's condition being published, there was a considerable degree of public confusion as to how serious things really were. The editor of the *Medical Times and Gazette*, for one, had decided that it was time for an end to prevarication. The nature of the Prince's illness, he wrote that morning, was 'pretty clear to the medical profession'. But euphemism still prevailed in the journal's commendation of Dr Jenner's integrity. It was an advantage, it said, that the Prince was in Jenner's care:

for there is no living physician who has enjoyed a larger experience of fever in general, or to whom the profession are so much indebted for their present knowledge of its various forms, and especially of the characters which distinguish the precise form of fever under which the prince is now suffering from the dreaded typhus.[19]

But the fact was that Jenner had throughout seemed uncertain of his diagnosis and had been reluctant to admit to it.

Over in Berlin, Vicky, who was only just recovering from a bout of flu, had been extremely alarmed by the contradictory telegrams received from Windsor over the previous couple of days. Privately, Phipps had telegraphed her husband Fritz on the 13th advising him to prepare his wife for the worst, and then early the following morning they had received news of an improvement. Writing to her mother, Vicky expressed her bewilderment: 'The news I had been receiving every day were so reassuring and cheerful that I thought all was now going on perfectly well.' She wished she could be with her mother to 'try to comfort you and be of use', but because she was now in the early stages of her third pregnancy her doctors had refused to allow her to travel.[20]

In Windsor at least word was out: on Saturday afternoon a special service was held at St John's parish church to offer prayers for the Prince's recovery, and its congregation was large despite the short notice. The royal doctors could no longer prevaricate: at 4.30 p.m. a bulletin was issued informing the nation that the Prince was in a 'most critical state'.[21] Lady Biddulph (wife of the Master of the Queen's Household), who had been in attendance in Prince Albert's sick-room, slipped out to send the 'VERY, VERY bad news' to Earl Spencer – senior Lord of the Bedchamber and titular head of the royal household. The Prince was sinking fast, and 'the doctors say there is no hope not the slightest of His Royal Highness's life being spared,' she wrote, though 'None may say how long it may go on.'[22]

With the inner sanctum of the royal household gathering anxiously, at around 5.30 p.m. Prince Albert's bed was wheeled away from the window into the centre of the King's Room, as though to accommodate the watchers for the royal deathbed to come. The Queen, who had been resting in another room, came in and took up her place by Albert's bed:

> Gutes Frauchen, he said, and kissed me, and then gave a sort of piteous moan, or rather sigh, not of pain, but as if he felt that he was leaving

me, and laid his head on my shoulder and I put my arm under his. But the feeling passed away again, and he seemed to wander and to doze, and yet to know all.[23]

She could not catch what Albert said in his delirium; occasionally words came in French, but more often it was the words of Christian comfort that meant so much to him – 'Rock of ages, cleft for me'.[24] And yet, extraordinarily, when at around half-past seven that evening the doctors found it necessary to move the Prince to the other, cleanly made-up bed, in a moment of uncanny clarity, Albert insisted on rising from his bed unassisted, though he had to be helped back into it again by Löhlein and one of the pages.[25]

Ever since the previous evening, when he had heard of the Prince of Wales's recall to Windsor, Prince Arthur's governor, Howard Elphinstone, had 'felt some presentiment' of what was to come, but had done his best all day to keep the ten-year-old boy away from the gloomy atmosphere in the castle. But at about 8 p.m. that evening word was sent to Elphinstone to bring Prince Arthur down to the King's Room, where all the younger children were now gathering to say farewell to their father.[26] First Alice came, knelt and kissed her father, and he took her hand. The Queen asked if he wanted to see Bertie, who next approached the bedside, followed by the fifteen-year-old Helena, Louise aged thirteen, and then Arthur. 'One after the other the children came and took their father's hand but he did not really see or know them' – nor did he realise that three of them were absent: Affie away on naval manoeuvres in Mexico, Leopold recuperating in Cannes, and his beloved firstborn, Vicky, trapped in her gloomy palace in Berlin. Four year old Beatrice had been kept from her father for many days for fear of infection, Arthur had not seen him for some time either and was visibly shaken by the terrible change that had come upon him. Sobbing inconsolably, he 'lifted his father's hand to his lips and kissed it', but Albert did not seem to know him.[27] As Arthur was led away, Albert momentarily 'opened his dear eyes and asked for Sir Ch[arles] Phipps, who came in and kissed his hand, but then again his dear eyes were closed'. And he did not recognise Grey and Biddulph when they followed, or see how overcome they were. This leave-taking was, the Queen later recalled, 'a *terrible* moment, but, thank God! I was able to command myself and to be *perfectly* calm, and remained sitting by his side'. 'So it went on, *not* really worse but not better', she recalled of that terrible evening as she sat listening to her dying husband struggle for his breath, although she was not able to recall any of it in any coherent detail until more than ten years later. Dr Jenner now admitted to her that 'with such breathing it was of no avail'.[28]

After seeing Prince Arthur back to his room and to bed, Howard Elphinstone joined the other members of the royal household who were gathering in disconsolate groups in the guttering candlelight of the Grand Corridor. It was a place that was usually the scene of animated conversation among them, either before or after dinner, but which now 'presented a very dim aspect'. 'A few gloomy faces, fearing the worst, were patiently sitting, and anxiously waiting each doctor's face as they came from the Prince's room,' he recalled. But each report was different; 'hope and despair were alternately dealt out, that no one could form an idea of the truth'.[29]

Princess Alice spent the evening kneeling at Albert's bedside 'with his burning hand in mine', she later told Louis. 'I said to myself as I listened to that painful, difficult breathing, "Perhaps God will take him, and then we shall be parted from the dearest thing we have on earth – it cannot be." I expected that he would leave us, but I could not take it in.'[30] Lady Augusta Bruce had been deeply moved by Alice's conduct throughout these difficult days, dealing not just with her sick father and her anxious mother, but also with the stream of relatives who arrived at Windsor asking for news. She was, thought Bruce, quite 'wonderful'. The desperate situation had compelled the Princess, still so young herself, to 'suddenly put away childish things and to be a different creature'.[31]

As another telegram was sent to the city at 9 p.m., announcing that the Prince Consort's condition was desperate, the British public at large prepared for their beds, reassured by the third edition of the day's papers and unaware that the Prince lay dying at Windsor. 'I made up my mind that a favourable turn had been taken,' wrote Charles Pugh, a clerk in the Court of Chancery, in his diary. Like many others he was convinced 'that a sound constitution, temperate habits, and strength of manhood of the Prince would bring him through' and, with the rest of the nation, he went to bed in hopes of better news in the morning.[32]

In the King's Room at Windsor the Queen longed desperately for some sign of recognition from her husband. She leant forward and tenderly whispered in Albert's ear: '*Es ist kleines Frauchen*' – It is your little wife – and asked for *ein Kuss*, but he could barely raise his head from the pillow to do so. 'He seemed half dozing, quite calm and only wishing to be left quiet and undisturbed.'[33] And so she retired to the

(*Right*) One of the last official photographs taken of Prince Albert during a sitting conducted by the French photographer Camille Silvy on 3 July 1861.

(*Left*) This engraving, probably based on one of the photographs taken by Silvy, emphasises how exhausted and puffy-faced Albert looked in the last months of his life.

(*Right*) Queen Victoria made a major concession for Bertie's Thanksgiving Service at St Paul's Cathedral on 27 February 1872 by adding a deep border of ermine to the unrelenting black of her costume.

(*Below*) The Queen's youngest daughter, four-year old Beatrice, prettily decked out in baby black mourning, much to her mother's considerable pride.

(*Above*) Lady Augusta Bruce (later Stanley) the Queen's most trusted lady-in-waiting who with Princess Alice was her major carer in the first months after Albert's death.

(*Above*) A grief-stricken Bertie, Prince of Wales and his eleven-year-old brother Arthur, in Highland costume, were the only two of Albert's nine children to attend his funeral.

(*Top and above*)
Popular engravings such as these from the *Illustrated London News*, show the solemnity of the funeral held at St George's Chapel Windsor on 23 December 1861.

(*Left*) The Royal Mausoleum at Frogmore under construction, December 1863. It was not until 38 years later, 2 February 1901, that Victoria's coffin joined Albert's there.

(*Above*) William Jenner, the Queen's physician-extraordinary; (*Above right*) Henry Ponsonby, her long-suffering private secretary; (*Below*) the Queen's favourite physician, Sir James Clark; (*Below right*) Alfred Tennyson, her adored Poet Laureate.

(*Left*) John Brown, Queen Victoria's Highland Servant, filled much of the void left by Albert, after he was transferred from Balmoral to Windsor in December 1864. He loyally served the Queen until his death in 1883.

(*Right*) This popular cartoon, 'John Brown Exercising the Queen', highlighted the growing indispensability of Brown, a fact which disturbed many at court and laid the Queen open to ridicule.

(*Above*) This cartoon from the satirical journal *The Tomahawk* of 16 November 1867 entitled 'God Save the Queen – The Past and the Future' encapsulated popular disquiet about the Queen's continuing absence from public duties.

J A Y'S
LONDON GENERAL MOURNING WAREHOUSE,
247, 249, 251, REGENT STREET.

(*Left*) Jay's London General Mourning Warehouse at the corner of Regent's Street and Oxford Circus was one of several funeral outfitters that did a roaring trade after Prince Albert's death.

Nº 4 ANNA   Nº 5 KILLARNEY   Nº 6 EDGAR

(*Above*) This fashion plate from Jay's catalogue of 1862 typifies the stylish mourning dresses that were available.

(*Above*) Anxious crowds gather outside the Mansion House in the City of London to read the latest bulletins on the Prince of Wales's serious illness, December 1871.

Stamped Edition, 6ᵈ

THE ILLUSTRATED LONDON NEWS

No. 1566. — Vol. LV.   SATURDAY, NOVEMBER 13, 1869.   With a Supplement, Fivepence.

(*Left*) In November 1869 Queen Victoria was coaxed into a rare public appearance, to open London's newly constructed Blackfriars Bridge.

(*Above*) Members of the royal family and household gather on a mournful rainy
15 October 1867 for the unveiling of the statue to Prince Albert at Balmoral.

(*Left*) Benjamin Disraeli and (*right*) William
Gladstone, the prime ministers who made
concerted efforts during the 1870s to coax
Queen Victoria out of retirement.

anteroom for a while, where she sank to the floor exhausted, her hair awry and her face buried in her hands. The Dean of Windsor, who was standing close by, spoke to her gently: 'she had a great trial to undergo and [I] prayed her to nerve herself for it'; she had governed the country once without him and she would do so again. But 'Why?' she asked him plaintively, 'Why must I suffer this? My mother? What was *that*? I thought that was grief. But that was *nothing* to this.' She and Albert were one, she sobbed; 'it is like tearing the flesh from my bones'.[34]

Within half an hour a rapid change had set in; Prince Albert was now bathed in sweat as the fever of pneumonia took hold. The only sound in the King's Room was the dying Prince's increasing struggle for breath. Alice recognised it immediately: 'That is the death rattle,' she whispered to Augusta Bruce and went to get her mother. Victoria had herself heard Albert's heavy breathing from the adjacent room. 'I'm afraid this takes away all our hope,' Alice told her.[35] Upon which, Victoria 'started up like a Lioness rushed by every one, and bounded on the bed imploring him to speak and to give one kiss to his little wife'.[36] Prince Albert opened his eyes; he seemed to know her, but was too weak to raise his head from the pillow. Even now the doctors were still, fruitlessly, trying to dose him with stimulants, this time on a sponge: but 'he had cried out and resisted the brandy so much that they did not give it any more'. Utterly distraught, Victoria kissed Albert passionately and clung to him. His breathing became 'quite gentle'. 'Oh, this is death,' she cried out in a final agony of recognition, taking his left hand, which already felt quite cold. 'I know it. I have seen this before,' she sobbed as she knelt by his side.[37]

Outside in the Grand Corridor Elphinstone and the others, who had all been too fearful to go to bed, were still huddled anxiously when they saw a pale and drawn Dean of Windsor hurrying toward the King's Room. They knew what this signified: he had been summoned to read the prayers for the dying. Inside, Alice was kneeling on one side of the bed, with General Bruce beside her opposite her mother, and Bertie and Helena kneeling at its foot, and the Prince of Leiningen and Löhlein standing not far behind them. Beyond stood the four royal doctors – Clarke, Jenner, Holland and Watson – Sir Charles Phipps, and the Prince's closest equerries: General Bentinck, Lord Alfred Paget, Major Du Plat, Colonel Seymour and General Grey.[38] Lady Augusta Bruce and Miss Hildyard looked on from the doorway of the adjoining anteroom.

A terrible stillness had descended, broken only by the great clock in the Curfew Tower at the western end of Windsor Castle striking the third quarter after ten. It was hardly possible to say exactly when the moment came, but a few minutes later, as the Queen recalled, 'Two or three long but perfectly gentle breaths were drawn, the hand clasping mine, and . . . *all, all* was over – the heavenly Spirit fled to the World it was fit for, and free from the sorrows and trials of this World!' Victoria threw her arms around Albert's body, covering it with fervent kisses and calling out 'in a bitter and agonizing cry "Oh! My dear Darling!"', and 'he can't be gone, he can't be gone', before dropping to her knees 'in mute, distracted despair, unable to utter a word or shed a tear!'[39] Some would later recall a far more chilling, visceral sound – one, unforgettable 'piercing shriek', that had echoed out into the Grand Corridor and beyond.[40]

For some minutes the Queen would not be torn away from Albert's corpse, until Dr Jenner said firmly to her: 'Queen, this is but the casket, you must look beyond', after which the Prince of Leiningen and Charles Phipps raised her from her knees and led her, sobbing and with such a look of despair on her face, to the anteroom, where she lay down on the sofa, with Alice cradling her head.[41] One by one the gentlemen of the royal household came in and knelt down and kissed her hand, Lord Alfred Paget weeping out loud. Alice, with her uncanny composure, managed to hold herself together as Bertie came and threw himself in his mother's arms, vowing, 'I will be all I can to you.' 'I'm sure my dear boy you will,' Victoria replied with composure, as she held him and kissed him.[42] But when Howard Elphinstone approached hesitantly to offer his condolences, she reached out and clutched at his hand 'with a violent effort', beseeching him with a frantic look: 'You will not desert me? You will all help me?'[43]

Upstairs the Duchess of Athole, one of Victoria's three ladies-in-waiting on duty that day, had been sitting with Horatia Stopford and Victoria Stuart-Wortley. None of them had seen the Queen since the previous morning and they were all deeply anxious. Finally, at around 11 p.m., the Duchess had decided to venture downstairs to enquire how the Prince was, before retiring for bed, when she was met by a footman in red livery sent in search of her. As she arrived at the door of the King's Room, the Queen came out – white with shock – to meet her: 'Oh Duchess,' she cried, 'he is dead! He is dead!' She took the Duchess inside, throwing herself with open arms on the corpse in paroxysms of weeping.

Then she calmed a little and told the Duchess some of the details of Albert's final moments. They were joined by Miss Hildyard, who kissed the Prince's now-cold hands. Then Victoria dismissed her ladies, wishing to remain with Albert's body. It took some persuasion to get her to leave the room and try to rest; upon which she rushed straight up to the nursery, followed by the children, calling out as she went, 'Oh! Albert, Albert! Are you gone!'[44] One of the Queen's dressers, Annie Macdonald, recalled the awful sight: 'the Queen ran through the ante-room where I was waiting. She seemed wild. She went straight up to the nursery and took Baby Beatrice out of bed' and, 'clasping her tightly without waking her, lay her down in her own bed'. Midnight struck as the Queen, deranged by grief, still sat there 'gazing wildly and as hard as a stone' at her chambermaids Sophie Weiss, Emilie Dittweiler and Mary Andrews. Eventually she allowed them to help her undress, 'and oh, what a sight it was to gaze upon her hopeless, helpless face, and see those most appealing eyes lifted up,' wrote Augusta Bruce, as the Queen lay down next to the sleeping Beatrice, clasping Albert's nightclothes, and with his red dressing gown laid out beside her.[45] Alice settled down in the small bed at the foot of the Queen's to try and rest too, but her mother could not sleep, nor could she weep, and sent for Dr Jenner, who came and sat with her for a while, and then gave her some opiates. But Victoria slept only for a short while, 'then woke and had a dreadful burst of crying, which relieved me'.[46] For the rest of the night she slept intermittently, talking and weeping with Alice between times. As soon as she awoke, little Beatrice tried to soothe her mother with her caresses. 'Don't cry,' said she, 'Papa is gone on a visit to Grandmamma.'[47]

Late that night, before he went to bed, Howard Elphinstone went in to see Prince Albert's body. His face was calm and peaceful. Elphinstone had known all along that the Prince 'had a fixed idea, that he would die of the 1st fever he got', but nevertheless he was distressed that the Prince had not tried to fight his illness. 'He had gone without a struggle, but likewise without saying a word', to the end a stranger in a foreign land, and longing still for his beloved Coburg. Returning to his room, Elphinstone found a telegram awaiting him from Cannes: Prince Leopold's ailing governor, General Edward Bowater, had just died. A long way from home, the queen's eight-year-old youngest son was having to deal alone with two deaths on the same day.[48]

★   ★   ★

At his home at Upton Court that evening George Augustus Sala and his friends had enjoyed a convivial meal, although he would later admit that 'my mind was from time to time perturbed', and that it had 'wandered to Windsor and the illustrious invalid there'. Nevertheless he went to bed. It was left to another newspaperman to scoop the momentous news when it came. Thomas Catling, sub-editor on a popular new penny newspaper, *Lloyds' Weekly*, had earlier that evening been instructed to head for Windsor to await developments. He had arrived at 11 p.m. on the last train and made straight for the castle, only to find the bearded soldier on sentry duty there in tears. He allowed Catling to pass on up the hill to the castle itself, where the news of the Prince's death was confirmed. Catling asked the officials on duty to telegraph the news through to his paper, but was told that the wire at the castle was 'for Court uses only'. So he headed off in the dark to hunt out the home of the local clerk of the Electric and International Telegraph Company. The clerk was reluctant to get up in the middle of the night – he had 'taken nitre in gruel and put his feet in hot water to ward off a cold', he complained – but Catling persuaded him to send a telegraph to his newspaper office, after which a friendly policeman helped him find lodgings for the night.[49] His paper would be the first with the news.

That evening the Tory politician Henry Greville, a close friend of the Queen, had been dining at the home of the French ambassador, the Comte de Flahaut, with Count Lavradio of the Portuguese legation, during which they had concurred on the extent to which the recent deaths in Portugal had played on Prince Albert's anxieties and how he had been 'constantly harping upon it' during his illness. Greville had moved on to his club when a telegram arrived late, informing him of the Prince's death. 'Every one present (and the room was full), both young and old, seemed consterned by this event, so unlooked for, and possibly pregnant with such disastrous consequences.'[50] 'I tremble for the Queen,' he wrote, as too now did Sir Charles Phipps over in his room at Windsor. He had important things to do. First, a short message was sent by electric telegraph from Windsor to the Lord Mayor of London at the Mansion House informing him of the Prince's death, and then some urgent letters: one to the Duke of Cambridge, in which he attempted to find the words to describe how he had witnessed 'the last moments of the best man that I ever met in my life'. The Queen's strength was extraordinary, Phipps told the Duke, 'Overwhelmed, beaten to the ground with grief, her self-control and good sense have been quite wonderful.' As for himself, 'my heart is broken'.[51] He also wrote a message to Lord Palmerston, hoping that he had prepared him sufficiently for the 'dreadful event' and assuring him that the Queen was 'perfectly collected', and showing a self-control that was 'quite extraordinary'. When the Duke of Cambridge brought the letter to the ageing Prime Minister at his home in Piccadilly late that night, Palmerston was so knocked back by the shock that he 'fainted away several times' in front of the Duke, who feared he would 'have a fit of apoplexy'.[52]

Palmerston's response echoed the great distress of the entire royal household that night; the Queen's eerie state of composure, they knew, was a sign of her profound state of shock. 'She has not realised her loss,' Phipps observed, and he dreaded the moment when the 'full consciousness' of it would come upon her. Like Greville, he trembled at the prospect of the 'depth of her grief'. 'What will happen,' he asked, 'where can she look for that support and assistance upon which she has leaned in the greatest and the least questions of her life?'[53] It was a question that filled everyone with dread. It would not just be a matter of coping with their own private grief at the loss of the Prince, but of dealing with its catastrophic effect on the Queen – not to mention the everyday duties of the monarchy.

Over at Slough, George Augustus Sala had been unable to sleep and had got up at daybreak. 'I hastened into the garden and gazed across Datchet Mead towards Windsor,' he later recalled. He could just dimly see the Round Tower in the distance as the early-morning mist rose from the surrounding fields. And then he saw the irrefutable proof of the disaster that had befallen the nation. The royal standard was at half-mast, floating disconsolately in a chilly dawn, greeted only by the rooks cawing in the bare trees of Windsor Great Park. Grabbing his coat, Sala hurried down to a deserted station, boarded the first train to London and headed straight to his office to write the most important leader article of his career.[54]

CHAPTER SIX

'Our Great National Calamity'

That morning, 15 December 1861, there was a terrible tolling of bells across England. It had begun just after midnight when the great bell of St Paul's Cathedral in the city of London had begun sounding a long, slow lament across the wintry streets, rousing those within earshot from their sleep. Everyone knew what it signified, for the bell was only ever tolled in times of national disaster or on the death of monarchs. It went on echoing across the streets for the next two hours as hundreds of anxious citizens rose from their beds, dressed and began assembling in the churchyard outside St Paul's, their voices hushed, their faces drawn with shock as the news was passed from one person to the next that the Prince Consort was dead.[1]

A bulletin issued at 8 a.m. by the Mansion House confirmed the dreadful event, and thence an 'electric chain' rapidly united the whole nation in grief as the telegraphic wires hummed across England, and beyond – to Scotland, Wales and Ireland.[2] All the newspapers had gone to press by the time Prince Albert had died, so there was nothing in the first edition of the Sunday papers, although a few smaller news-sheets had managed to get the story out and were being sold at a premium. 'In almost every street crowds of persons were seen surrounding the possessors of these sheets,' one eyewitness recalled, 'anxiously listening while the statements contained therein were being read aloud.'[3] Soon the news was being chalked up on walls in the back-street tenements of London. By lunchtime that Sunday special editions of papers such as the *London Gazette Extraordinary* enclosed in heavy black borders were being sold by newsboys brandishing placards and shouting, 'Death of His Royal Highness the Prince Consort'.

But the first intimation that most of the general public had – particularly those in rural areas – came with the slow tolling of bells, many of them muffled, at intervals of half a minute, which echoed across the countryside as people made their way to Sunday morning service. Others did not hear the news until they were sitting in their pews and it was whispered as the collecting box was passed round; for some, the shocking realisation came when the prayers for the royal family read out by the priest omitted the Prince's name.

The diarist Arthur Munby vividly recalled that day:

> This morning came the astounding news of Prince Albert's death: so unexpected and sad and ominous, that people are struck dumb with amaze [sic] and sorrow. The news-offices in the Strand were open and besieged by anxious folk; a strange gloom was upon the town; in church, the preacher spoke of it, and an awful silence there was, with something too very like sobbing, when his name was left out from the prayers.

Attending service in Whitley, Surrey, that morning, the artist James Clarke Hook remembered that the rector had heard rumours that the Prince had died, but had decided nevertheless that it 'would be all right to pray for him'. Seeking confirmation, Hook later went down to the local railway station to ask if any bad news had been received by telegraph there. 'No, sir,' the stationmaster replied, 'but I'll ring the bell to Godalming, sir, and inquire.' Shortly afterwards, letter by letter, a reply came clicking back across the wire: 'P-r-i-n-c-e-C-o-n-s-o-r-t-d-e-a-d'.[4]

Everywhere, the response to the news was the same: up at Fylingdales on the remote North Yorkshire moors, the wife of a clergyman was preparing her usual class of farmers' daughters 'to read the Bible and settle the week's charities'. The fatal news came, she recalled, 'just as we assembled. We could not read; but we all knelt down and prayed for the Queen and wept bitterly.' News spread rapidly, even there, and 'In many parts of the wild moorland . . . the poor people have not gone to their days works without wearing some mark of mourning.'[5]

Few country vicars had time to record their reaction in their church sermons that day, but at St Paul's Cathedral a huge congregation heard Canon Champneys allude to the national bereavement and offer prayers for the Queen and the royal family in their great sorrow, before being played out at the end of the service to Handel's sonorous 'Dead March in Saul'. In Leeds, the vicar of St John's startled his congregation by reading the stark words from Samuel 3:38, 'Know ye not that there is a prince and a great man fallen this day in Israel?', without explaining its context to his bewildered flock until his sermon later on.[6] Other preachers improvised hastily revised sermons: from Bow Church in Cheapside, and the Poultry Chapel in the City, to the Lambeth Orphan Asylum and the Greek Orthodox church at London Wall, to the Roman Catholic church in Chelsea and the Scotch Church, in which the minister, Dr Cumming, deemed the Prince's best epitaph to be the text 'He doth rest from his labours and his works do follow him'. In Oxford, at St Mary's Parish Church, the Bishop of Oxford spoke 'in heart-stirring language' of 'the cloud which had that day spread over the land'. Throughout the day people everywhere instinctively turned to the Church for comfort; when Exeter Cathedral opened its great doors for afternoon service, it did so to a flood of people who filled it so quickly that many were turned away.[7]

By the time of the evening service the pulpits and lecterns of many churches were already draped in black crape. Across London the blinds of private houses had been drawn down, the brass plates on doors were surrounded with black, and mirrors and lamps indoors also covered. Omnibus drivers tied scraps of crape to their whips; in the countryside even beehives were draped in crape, as part of the age-old superstition of telling the bees of a death in the family. Many tradesmen either entirely or partially closed their businesses; steamers on the river stood idle, their flags at half-mast, as too did those of foreign vessels moored in London's docks. The royal standard was flying at half-mast everywhere across the capital, from the Victoria Tower of the Houses of Parliament to the Tower of London in the City.

But everywhere, in a spontaneous, haunting unison, it was the bells that spoke volumes for Britain's loss. Across the water meadows at Cambridge, where Prince Albert had been Chancellor of the university, the news had arrived at ten-forty that morning and spread with great rapidity, prompting the immediate announcement of the curtailment of all 'festivities incidental to the season'. The muffled peals of bells rang out all day – from Edinburgh in the north to Portsmouth in the south and across the major industrial cities of Manchester, Birmingham, Nottingham, Leeds, Huddersfield and Darlington. A similar response was recorded in Bristol, where the news had 'a most depressing effect upon all classes of citizens' as they pondered the flag at half-mast on the top of the cathedral. The burghers of Liverpool likewise spoke of a feeling of universal sorrow and regret in a town where 'his Royal Highness on several occasions endeared himself to all classes of the community by his affability and eloquence'; here, even American ships in port had lowered their flags. In Portsmouth in particular there was much grief among the army, navy and general public. On board Nelson's old flag-ship, the *Victory*, the royal ensign of England and that of the late Prince were hoisted at half-mast, as too 'above the town gates, the dock gate, the gun wharf, Southsea Castle . . . the fort, the ramparts, and all Government departments, as well as above the Sailors' Home'. In Southampton the 'whole of the mail packets and shipping plus various consulates and public institutions' all did likewise.[8]

Many people sat down in their homes that day confiding their thoughts to their diaries and writing letters to family and friends remarking on the mournful events at Windsor. The Prince's death would inevitably 'involve great changes', wrote the scholar Friedrich Max Müller to his mother, 'the queen can hardly bear the whole burden alone', and now she had no one who could help her in the unique way that the Prince had.[9] At Windsor, librarian Carl Ruland wrote to his family that Albert's death was 'a disaster for the entire family, for England, for the whole of Europe'. Working so closely with him, he had come to appreciate the depths of the Prince's character, for had Prince Albert not treated him 'as his own son'? Sir Moses Montefiore, a prominent leader of the Jewish community, had no doubts of its effect on them: 'we have lost a great and good prince', and also a friend, for the Prince had been 'most liberal as regards religious freedom to all'. In many cases, much as they mourned the loss of the Prince, the primary concern was its effect on the Queen; Charles Dickens predicted to his friend W. H. Wills, 'I have a misgiving that they hardly understand what the public general sympathy with the Queen will be.'[10]

The atmosphere of grief in Windsor town that grey Sunday morning was particularly acute – everywhere, even the poorest cottage, had its curtains drawn. Up at the castle 'an awful state of consternation and despair' reigned.[11] Within the royal apartments the Queen had now been joined, at her request, by her former Mistress of the Robes, the Duchess of Sutherland, who had herself been widowed earlier that year and who had driven over from her home at Cliveden to share in the Queen's grief. As the Duchess had entered the Queen's sitting room, Victoria had stretched out her arms to her. 'You know how I loved him!' she said, so plaintively, and took her in to see the Prince's body.[12] 'I feared the shock for her,' the Duchess later told her close friend, William Gladstone, for it was the first time Victoria had been back into the King's Room since the previous night when Albert had died. But she seemed extraordinarily composed, walked up to the bedside and reached out to Albert's body, which was laid out on the bed (though the doctors had forbidden her to touch it, for fear of infection). She raised her eyes, as though in a strange kind of trance, the Duchess recalled, 'and spoke every word of endearment as if he had lived'. Was he not beautiful, she said to the Duchess, who herself was greatly moved by the fine, spiritual look on Albert's face. 'Never could I have believed Death's finger could be so light,' she told Gladstone. The features were as delicately wrought as marble; it was only the paleness that betrayed the mark of death.

As Victoria described the events of the previous days to the Duchess, she confided that her sole comfort was the Prince's repeated reassurance that he had had no dread of death; she fondly recalled the words of 'infinite affection' that had passed between them during those last days, but as she did so, the Duchess also noted a creeping air of desperation in the Queen's voice. 'How could it be, what was it – what was she to do?' – she who had 'spoken every thought' to her husband and had always been reassured by him so that she 'had neither anxiety or worry'.[13] He was everything to her. How was she to manage without him? The level of the Queen's grief seemed 'so *intense*, so *all-absorbing*' to the Queen's cousin, Princess Mary Adelaide, Duchess of Teck, when she visited that afternoon. She recalled walking up the hundred stone steps to the castle, which, 'with all its blinds drawn looked dreary and dismal indeed'. In the Grand Corridor she had come upon the forlorn figures of Alice, Helena, Louise and Arthur, who 'all broke down in sight of me, though they strove to regain composure, and to remain as calm as possible for their widowed mother's sake'.[14]

The Queen's life would, she told Princess Mary Adelaide, 'henceforth be but a blank', though the Princess hoped that 'perhaps as months roll by the Children may in a *measure* fill it up'. But the brutal truth, as she saw it, was that the Queen's children were no substitute for their father and never would be: 'at the heart's core there must and will ever be an *aching void*'.[15] With Victoria clearly incapable of receiving consolation, yet alone giving it to her distraught children, how were they to cope with their own bereavement? 'Why did God not take me?' Louise had sobbed at her father's deathbed, sentiments echoed in a letter from her sister Vicky asking, 'Why has earth not swallowed me up?' Lord Clarendon had no doubt of the impact of his death on Albert's favourite child: 'I am afraid it will be the misery of her life not to have seen her father before he died,' he told the Duchess of Manchester.[16] As for Princess Alice, everyone marvelled at her dignity and composure: 'Could you but see that darling's face!' wrote one lady-in-waiting. 'Her great tearless eyes with their expression of resolutely subdued misery! No one knew what she was before, though I *marvelled* that they did not.'[17] Far away in Cannes, the most plaintive cry of all came from young Prince Leopold, who alone in his desolation, when told of his father's death, wept that he must go to his mother: 'My mother will bring him back again. Oh! I want my mother!' he had cried.[18]

For the moment, pending an onrush in the press the next morning, the only official words of condolence tentatively offered to the Queen were those of Lord Palmerston. Still laid up in agony with gout, and taking the Prince's death as a profound personal loss, he was unable to go to Windsor in person, but wrote that the Queen had 'sustained one of the greatest of human misfortunes'. But there was 'not one among the many millions who have the Happiness of being your Majesty's subjects, whose heart will not bleed in sympathy with Your Majesty's sorrow'. Nevertheless, as Prime Minister, there was one thing uppermost in his mind – distraught though he was – and this was the hope that the Queen's 'strength of mind and a sense of Duties' would help see her through.[19] In the meantime, from early on Sunday, members of the diplomatic corps as well as nobility and gentry had begun flocking to Buckingham Palace to enquire after Victoria's health and sign the book of condolences in a darkened and candlelit audience chamber. Emperor Napoleon III of France and his wife Eugénie, having already dispatched a senior emissary to London with letters of condolence, ordered three weeks of court mourning and sent frequent telegraphs from Paris, as also did the Emperor of Austria, the Duke of Saxe-Coburg and the King and Crown Prince of Prussia, where the court had immediately gone into mourning for a month. The event was announced across the Parisian newspapers 'in terms of unaffected regret' and nothing else was talked of; the flag at the Tuileries was at half-mast and British inhabitants of the city had immediately donned their black.[20] Meanwhile, in London, Charles Frances Adams, the new American ambassador, sent his condolences, recording in his diary sentiments similar to those already privately expressed by Florence Nightingale: 'The English will value him better now he is gone.'[21]

*   *   *

Traumatised though Victoria was by Albert's death, one thing was of immediate and overriding importance to her: to preserve the look and memory of him as he had been before he was taken from her for ever, down to the glass from which he had taken his last dose of medicine, which was left by his bedside.[22] Overnight, the body had been moved to the other bed in the King's Room and devotedly laid out by Albert's valet Löhlein, assisted by Macdonald. When Bertie took Princess Mary Adelaide in to take one last look 'at those handsome features', she had been touched by the wreath of white flowers at Albert's head, and single blooms placed on his breast and scattered across the coverlet; some of them sent as a gift by Prince Leopold from Cannes before he had known his father had died.[23] The room was full of people, the Princess recalled, including the artist Edward Henry Corbauld, who had come, at the Queen's request, to make a sketch of Albert on his deathbed. This would later be kept locked in a special case and circulated only within the family. The sculptor William Theed the Younger was also summoned to Windsor to take a cast of the prince's hands and a death-mask, reporting later that the Prince's face had been peaceful, bar the 'lines of suffering about the mouth'.[24] Although the Queen could not bear later to look at the mask, it was a sacred relic to be treasured. But she kept the marble hands near her bedside and would often clasp at them in the lonely moments of desperation that came during the night. The royal photographer, William Bambridge, was also called in that day to photograph Albert's private apartments as well as the King's Room, so that they could be cleaned, preserved and every object in them replaced exactly as they had been at the moment when he died – and remain so in perpetuity 'as a beautiful living Monument'.

To the Queen's mind, Albert was still very much with her in spirit, and their separation was only a physical, outward one. This emphasis on a *living* commemoration of her dead husband was fundamental to her future view of things. She resolved to fill the room with beautiful things: a bust of Albert, exquisite china, allegorical pictures – and fresh flowers. She wanted no morbid *Sterbezimmer*: the gloomy death-chamber preserved as a dusty sepulchre, so favoured by some of her German relatives, which was allowed to slowly decay and fade into dust untouched. Instead she wanted to preserve the King's Room as though her husband had just left it and would come in again at any time – his clothes and fresh linen laid out for him, hot water, towels and soap provided for his morning shave. Other, more mundane reminders were all left in their precise position too: in Albert's morning room, the reference books and directories, army lists, navy lists, clergy lists that he had regularly consulted; a small French book by the Abbé Ségur on the 'difficulties of religion'; and beyond, in his dressing room, Erskine May's book on parliamentary practice and Professor Max Müller's presentation copy to the Prince of his *Lectures on the Science of Language*.[25] But perhaps the most heartbreaking and intimate reminder of all was to be the hand-coloured copy of Bambridge's deathbed photograph of Albert, the chiselled features so fine in profile, with a small wreath of immortelles above it, which the Queen would hang above his side of their bed, in their homes at Windsor, Balmoral and Osborne.[26]

* * *

On Monday morning, 16 December, many public bodies and metropolitan vestries across the country gathered to pass resolutions expressing their profound sorrow at the Prince's death. In the City of London a Court of Common Council met at the Guildhall under the Lord Mayor to compose a loyal address of condolence, as other similar messages began to arrive at Windsor from the dignitaries of major provincial cities and towns. Along the great commercial thoroughfares of London – Cheapside, and Fleet Street in the city, the Strand, the Haymarket, Pall Mall, Piccadilly, Oxford Street in the West End, the majority of the shops 'had two or three shutters up'.[27] Theatres, concert halls and music halls all announced the cancellation of performances. The law courts, museums and art galleries were also closed, and even those places of public amusement not under the control of the Lord Chamberlain voluntarily shut their doors. Many cultural events were postponed, even those of the much-revered Charles Dickens, who was obliged, much to his annoyance, to cancel a lucrative series of six public readings in Liverpool and Chester for which thousands of tickets had been sold. Albert's death had also immediately thrown a veil of gloom over the forthcoming London Season: 'Farewell to drawing-rooms, balls, concerts, splendid soirées,' rued the exiled French politician Louis Blanc.[28] Within a day or so the stock market noted a considerable slump in trade and drops in the value of consols and railways stocks.

With so many public places closed, a distraught stream of people hungry for news flocked to the news-stands and public reading rooms. They were not disappointed in what they found. The tone set by all of the press on Monday 16 December was uniform in its portentousness:

a great calamity of biblical proportions had befallen the nation. John Delane of *The Times* gave saturation coverage in that day's edition ensuring that its circulation broke all previous records, rising to 89,000 copies. His words were stark and uncompromising: death had snatched from the nation 'the very centre of our social system, the pillar of our State' and it would be some time before the loss of the man and his services to the country could be estimated. The British people were unified in their grief, the classic adage that death was a great leveller being repeated by many papers, such as the *Morning Chronicle*, which observed that 'a bereavement such as this melts away the distinction of class'. With the country faced with such an 'incalculable affliction', the Prince Consort's death invited some of the best of contemporary obituary-writing, as well as some of the worst hyperbole: 'The eclipse of death is this day upon every home in England. More than that: a shadow has been cast over the world,' intoned the leader in the *Morning Post*. Most of the papers drew attention in particular to the destruction of the royal family as an idyllic domestic unit: 'Death has entered the highest, and what might but a few hours ago have been called the happiest, household in the land,' declared the *Scotsman*. The Prince had been 'the very stay and prop of the House which is identified with our dearest affections . . . The Home which all England recognised as the sweetest and holiest in the land is bereaved and desolate,' agreed the *Morning Post*; 'the serene unbroken happiness of a long reign had now been clouded by the deepest sorrow,' echoed the *Daily News*.[29]

Outstripping them all with his characteristic purple prose came George Augustus Sala of the *Daily Telegraph*:

It has pleased Almighty God to take unto himself the Consort of our beloved Queen. No pompous announcements in gazettes extraordinary – no sounding proclamations of his style and titles . . . no laborious enumeration of dignities telling us that he who now lies a cold corse [sic] in Windsor Tower was a Duke of Saxony and a Prince of Saxe Coburg and Gotha . . . none of the sonorous symbols of earthly state and grandeur, can abate one jot from the awful impressiveness, the ghastly puissance of those few naked words which tell us that Prince Albert is dead . . . Death has taken from us the most important man in the country.[30]

With such universality of grief and so many people automatically donning some form of mourning for the Prince, there would seem to be no need for official directives. Nevertheless, on 16 December the 'Orders for Court and General Mourning' were published in the *London Gazette Extraordinary*: 'The ladies attending Court to wear black woollen stuffs, trimmed with crape, plain linen, black shoes and gloves, and crape fans. The gentlemen attending Court to wear black cloth, plain linen, crape hatbands, and black swords and buckles.' More specific instructions followed for the Army, Royal Navy and Royal Marines. All army officers when in uniform should wear black crape 'over the ornamental part of the cap or hat, over the sword knot, and over the left arm, with black gloves, and a black crape scarf over the sash'. Military drums were to be covered with black, and black crape was 'to be hung from the head of the colour-staff of the infantry, and from the standard-staff of cavalry'. Beyond that, among the population at large, 'it is expected that all persons do forthwith put themselves into decent mourning'.[31] The middle classes needed no prompting and were already besieging the drapers and milliners' shops in order to order mourning outfits for themselves and their children; at the popular silk mercer's Lewis & Allonby on Regent Street 'people could not give their orders for crying'. But to do so was not without financial strain for many: the Chancery clerk Charles Pugh, with a wife and five daughters to support on a modest income, worried at the cost to low wage earners such as himself of putting their large families into mourning.[32]

In North Yorkshire, as in other rural areas, many of the churches and schools were 'put in regular mourning at the cost of the Inhabitants' – and everywhere the poorest of the poor found some way of demonstrating their grief, even if only by wearing black armbands.[33] But while advertisements carrying the patronage of Prince Albert were quickly amended as a sign of respect, elsewhere the world of commerce was quick to recognise the money to be made from this unexpected run on black. At the heart of the clothing industry in Leeds, the first advertisements appeared within two days, on 17 December:

> General Mourning – Death of the Prince Consort. C. Pegler & Co., 58 Briggate, Leeds, beg to call the attention of Ladies to their present large stock of black mourning silk and black glaces [silks] from Turin, which are of a very superior make, the whole of which are now offered at greatly reduced prices.

Rising to the competition, Messrs Hyam & Co. a few doors down Briggate announced that they were 'prepared to supply mourning to any extent at five minutes' notice, or made to measure in five hours'. The Leeds Mourning Warehouse joined in, offering 'an immense stock of black alpacas, so much in demand by the French, of the best make', whilst Mrs Hartley offered her stock of mourning millinery and any other accoutrements needed, down to black ribbons, gloves, veils, handkerchiefs, collars, cuffs and artificial flowers.[34] For men, black cravats and hatbands and even black shirt studs were now in huge demand. On Monday, at the opening of trade in the City of London, crowds of buyers had besieged wholesale dealers such as Morison's, Leaf's, Boyd's and Ellis's to buy in stock.[35] But a royal death, whilst filling the coffers of the trade in funeral goods and mourning, would have a significant impact on the general textile industry. It was therefore with some concern that William Synes, President of the Chamber of Commerce, had written on 16 December to the Lord Chamberlain expressing his concern that the period of public mourning for the Prince should, unlike that previously for the Duchess of Kent, be clearly stipulated in order to 'avoid excessive injury to the trades of the country'. 'Will you excuse me by suggesting,' Synes added, 'that on the present lamentable occasion not only the commencement but the *termination* of the mourning should be stated when the order is issued.'[36]

The deepest of mourning of course prevailed at Windsor; at midday on Sunday the public had been informed that, although overwhelmed with grief, the Queen was calm – her calmness having a strange kind of childlike simplicity about it that many remarked on. Some put it down simply to her 'Christian fortitude', but other ladies thought her 'unnaturally quiet' and feared for her sanity, as she sat in dumb despair, staring vacantly around her. In response to a consolatory remark offered to her she said, 'I suppose I must not fret too much, for many poor women have to go through the same trials.'[37] But it was clear she was numb with shock and exhausted. Nevertheless, on the 17th she composed herself enough to mechanically sign some important papers brought for signature. She seemed to remember, thought Lord Clarendon, how much Prince Albert had 'disapproved and warned her against such extravagant grief as she manifested at her mother's death' and appeared to be trying hard to remain calm. 'If she can support herself in this frame of mind, it is all one can hope for,' he added. Lady Normanby echoed this: the Prince's last words to the Queen, so she had been told by Lady Ely, were that 'she must not give way to her grief, she owed it to the nation, remember that!'[38]

On Monday, Victoria had struggled to write a few anguished lines to Vicky: she was, she told her, 'crushed, bowed down'. But since that morning 'a wonderful Heavenly Peace' had come over her. 'I feel I am living with him – as much as before – that He will yet guide and lead me – tho' He can't speak to me, while I can speak to Him.' She was resigned that henceforth her life would be one of sorrow, of duty, of self-abnegation and self-sacrifice. Two days later she had written again, telling Vicky that she had often prayed that she and Albert might die together or that he would survive her. All the joy had gone from her life now, all those happy times with Albert at Osborne, in the Highlands, those joyous family Christmases, their wedding anniversary – all belonged now to 'a precious past which will for ever and ever be engraven on my dreary heart'. Oh how she missed him, how she longed so 'to cling to and clasp a loving being'.[39] Close family members now began to rally round, but they were no substitute for her husband's arms. Arriving by train at Windsor from Kew, the Queen's aunt, the Duchess of Cambridge, was seen weeping bitterly on the concourse, the 'signs of her distress having a visible effect on bystanders' as she passed through. Up at the castle the strain of so much collective grief on the members of the royal household was terrible. 'We have indeed to bring all our faith and trust to bear,' wrote maid-of-honour Victoria Stuart-Wortley, for now 'this sad silent House is full of wailing and misery . . . I don't know when I shall get over it. The very fact of being *no use* is so dreadful.'[40]

*　　*　　*

In the nine days from Prince Albert's death to his funeral on 23 December, a profusion of eulogies filled the newspapers, for it took time for the nation to come to terms with the extent of its loss. The calamity of the Prince's death was like the 'sudden extinction of a light', wrote Delane in *The Times*, and 'an interval must elapse before we can penetrate the darkness'. This was no ordinary death, evoking 'conventional regret', but one that had brought 'real pain' to the entire nation. 'Wars and rumours of wars,' wrote the *London Review*, 'pass almost unheeded in the presence of this engrossing bereavement', for many felt as though they had lost a member of their own family. Albert's death was a personal blow that had touched everyone, and many ordinary people had been made 'dangerously ill by the shock'.[41] In the words of the *Illustrated London News*: 'Death stands within the walls of Windsor Palace – a Queen is widowed – Princes are orphans – and the Empire shrouded in mourning! Every family in the land is smitten with the awe and the sorrow which Death excites when he breaks into the domestic circle and snatches from it its chief pride and joy.'[42]

The eulogies for Prince Albert were in stark contrast to the many damning ones that had appeared on the deaths of George IV in 1830 and William IV in 1837. Previous kings, let alone prince consorts, had been nothing in comparison with him, according to the leader-writer of the *Glasgow Herald*, who described how the 'gloomy Philip of Spain', husband of Queen Mary, had been disliked, as too 'the 'reckless and unprincipled debauché' Lord Darnley, husband of Mary, Queen of Scots. In comparison with the 'dull-brained, wine-bibing' Prince George of Denmark, consort of Queen Anne, Albert had been a paragon.[43] The last time the nation had gone into mourning for a prince consort had been on the death of Prince George in 1708, but he had been a social and political cipher in comparison. The floodgates were now opened to a torrent of praise of Albert: as a man of genius, a wise and benevolent patron of art, science and industry with the welfare of the nation at heart, who was noted for his sagacity and eloquence, his nobility of character, his modesty, lack of ostentation and – most importantly – his domestic virtue. 'To the husband and father now lying dead at Windsor we owe the proof, new in our annals, that domestic life may be as pure, as free, as full of attachment, as pleasantly and rationally ordered, in a palace as in a country parsonage.' And yet none had really known the Prince; and many had underappreciated him and even thought ill of him; as *The Times* accentuated, Albert had been admired, certainly, but it was admiration at a distance. A distinct air of retrospective guilt about the extent to which the Prince had been underrated permeated the press. The *Guardian* emphasised how he had had to overcome the stigma of 'coming a foreigner, with foreign feelings and foreign sympathies', yet despite this 'so much good done, a most difficult part so wisely and honestly played, so many snares and stumbling-blocks escaped', adding that 'No one can say he has been an unimportant person in England.'

George Augustus Sala's uncritical hyperbole in the *Telegraph* continued to have considerable popular appeal, with its talk of 'the havoc of happiness, the blasting of prospects, the dislocation of love', and of Albert's phantom now hovering over the glistening domes of his great project, the Crystal Palace of 1851. When it came to bathos no one could touch the *Telegraph*'s leader-writer: England's queen was enduring her grief 'undaunted and indomitable, like some proud oak in Windsor Forest, from which the clinging ivy has been ruthlessly torn away, but which still stands unscathed, and defies the storm . . . She is not less the Woman, but she is more than ever the Queen!'[44]

There was, however, one other important issue already preoccupying the press – and that was Bertie. *The Times* had already given him dressing-down in its editorial on the 18th. It devolved to the Prince of Wales, Delane declared, to rise to 'all the solemnity of his position, and fit himself for the part to which he is destined'. For Bertie, the days of callow youth were over and he 'ought now to show the faculties which will make a good king'. He must 'make up his mind, if he wishes to gain the affection and esteem of the country' and choose between two paths: those of 'duty and pleasure'. But, even on his best behaviour, it was doubted that the Prince of Wales was capable of rising to the occasion. Lord Stanley thought him 'good-tempered, and apparently likely to be popular', but it was well known that he was 'not gifted with much ability', and his rebellious streak – a reaction to his repressed childhood – had left him prone to 'undignified' and immature outbreaks, 'which may be precursors of worse excesses'. He could not begin to fill the void left by his father; the writer Matthew Arnold had no doubts: there was no one with 'the Continental width of openness of mind of Prince Albert'. The worst fear was that, without Albert to guide her, the Queen would 'fall into a state of mind in which it will be difficult to do business with her, and impossible to anticipate what she will approve or disapprove'. The worst was yet to come, in the opinion of Lady Lyttleton: all the 'numberless, incessant wishes to "Ask the Prince", to "Send for the Prince", the never-failing joy, fresh every time, when he answered her call'. There was nevertheless 'such a feeling of unselfish goodwill towards Her Majesty,' wrote *The Times*, that the question of the Queen resuming public business immediately was out of the question. A degree of public forbearance would be required in the days to come, in the hope that her 'courage and independence of character' would equip her for resuming her duties. *The Times* was confident: 'we have on the throne a Sovereign whose nerves have been braced rather than paralysed by the chill of adversity'. But the newspapermen did not know the Queen as Lady Lyttleton did. Albert's death was, she had no doubt, a 'heart wound' that had torn her world apart.[45]

* * *

It was thus in considerable distress that Victoria prepared to leave Windsor for Osborne. Much to general consternation, she was not to remain there for the Prince Consort's funeral. In fact there had never been any question of her presence at the actual ceremony, for funerals were still very much a male preserve, with women being considered far too weak to conceal their grief in public. In her traumatised state the Queen would have been incapable of enduring it; indeed, she wanted nothing said to her at all about the arrangements, leaving it all to Bertie and the Duke of Cambridge. She had, however, been extremely reluctant to leave Windsor itself until everything was over. It was the royal doctors who prevailed on her to leave, fearful that she and the children might be infected by the supposed typhoid germ that had killed Albert. Victoria had protested: 'You are asking me to do what you would not expect from the humblest of my subjects.'[46] Alice too had remonstrated with them, but in the end Victoria had relented, having received a barrage of 'telegraphic entreaties' from her uncle, King Leopold of the Belgians, who insisted that she remove to Osborne.[47] The Queen's ladies thought this cruel in the extreme, as too did Lord Clarendon. In his opinion the Queen would have been better off staying at the White House – a small, comfortable mansion on the Beaumont estate nearby – or at Cliveden with the Duchess of Sutherland. Osborne was the worst possible place for her to retreat to, for, as Clarendon pointed out, it was a place 'where every object is so entirely associated with him'. Lady Geraldine Somerset (lady-in-waiting to the Duchess of Cambridge) agreed – going there would be agony for the Queen, but then 'every place she goes to must be a fresh *dagger*, each so *identified* with him'. Far worse, though, was the prospect of what the Queen would still have to endure: after twenty-two years of 'unparalleled happiness,' observed Lady Geraldine, 'she may live 30, 40 of as unequalled sorrow.'[48]

It had been intended that the Queen should leave for Osborne on the Wednesday, 18 December, and much of her luggage had been sent on ahead, together with the servants, but at the last minute she had not been able to tear herself away from the comforting darkness inside the castle, dreading as she did 'the sight of the glaring daylight'.[49] She told General Grey that all the time 'she felt that He was still in the room near her. She could not feel that she had lost His support.'[50]

Earlier that day she made the first gesture in what would become forty years of dedicated memorialisation of her husband by choosing a site for his final resting place. She and Albert had long since agreed that they did not want to be interred in the traditional royal burial place: the dark and gloomy crypt of St George's Chapel. And so in the morning Victoria drove down to Frogmore with Alice and found a spot, close to her mother's mausoleum in the south-western end of the gardens there, where she intended to erect a much grander sepulchre for herself and her beloved Albert.

Before she left for Osborne there were other, much more personal and final farewells that she wished to make. She gave instructions that Alice, Helena, Louise and Beatrice should each cut off a lock of their hair for placing in Albert's coffin before it was sealed, probably with some of her own, along with other tokens of special significance such as photographs of the children. (Locks of Albert's hair were also taken for preservation in a variety of ways, mainly in mourning jewellery.) Most significantly, Victoria arranged for a particular photograph to be placed in her husband's hands.[51] It was a reproduction of Albert's favourite portrait of her, by Franz Winterhalter, that she had given him on his twenty-fourth birthday in 1843 and which hung in Albert's morning room – a painting so intimate and so unlike all the official ones of herself as Queen, in which she was depicted with bare shoulders, her long, partially loose hair curving over her shoulder and down across her breast. It was an emphatic, parting reminder of herself as a sensual young woman: an evocation of the physical love that the Queen would now so miss about her husband, of the times 'when in those blessed arms' she had been clasped and held tight 'in the sacred hours at night'.[52] She had gone into the King's Room to see Albert twice on Sunday, but did not go again; she could not bear to, she told Vicky; she would rather keep in her mind 'the impression given of life and health' than that final vision of her husband's face so marble, and grown so very thin. Words of great affection and consolation flowed back from Vicky: 'None of us thought we could have survived this,' she comforted 'and yet we live, we love, we trust – and we hope still.'[53]

The following morning Victoria was still unable to steel herself to leave, and so at 10 a.m. Arthur and Beatrice were sent on ahead with the Leiningens.[54] Just before midday – the Duchess of Wellington would never forget the Queen's terrible sobbing – Victoria was led out to the great staircase, where she burst into 'a loud wailing cry and almost screamed "I *can't* go"'. With the greatest of effort she was assisted down the stairs and out to her carriage by Bertie and Alice on either side, whispering words of encouragement as they supported her.[55] 'It was a terrible moment,' recalled Augusta Bruce, who followed close behind. 'She felt on leaving that all that could be taken from her of him, had been.'[56] In the strictest privacy and with no servants in attendance, Victoria left a deserted South-Western Railway terminus at Windsor by royal train, in the company of Alice, Helena, Louise and Prince Louis and some of her ladies, including Augusta Bruce and the Duchess of Athole. At Gosport on the Hampshire coast she boarded the royal yacht, the *Fairy*, for the Isle of Wight and a cold and sadly inhospitable Osborne. For the house, with its warm Italianate architecture, had always been the family's summer home. Howard Elphinstone thought it 'so unsuited at this time of year'; all the colour was leached out of its usually vibrant gardens, which the Prince had so lovingly overseen, leaving the bare trees and flowerbeds and the empty ornamental urns on the terrace open to the bleak, cold wind from the Solent. The 'desolate look' of the frail, childlike Queen in her widow's cap was terrible: 'I felt – *what* was there that I would not do for her!' the Duchess of Athole recalled.[57] At midnight, Victoria was joined by Albert's brother, Duke Ernst, who had been brought over from Antwerp on the royal yacht and had stopped off to commiserate before proceeding to Windsor for the funeral. He came in cold, drenched and seasick, to find his unhappy sister-in-law 'bowed down with sorrow and utterly prostrate in the stillness of the night'. Soon that silence was broken by 'the loud grief which deprived us both of words'.[58]

After so many days of an icy composure that had made her entourage fearful for her sanity, arrival at Osborne finally brought home to Victoria the full force of her utter desolation, and she at last gave terrible vent to her grief. 'She cried for days,' remembered Annie Macdonald. 'It was heart-breaking to hear her.'[59] Osborne, that happy family home, had now for ever become a bitter place of mourning. All Victoria had left to cling to were the precious reminders of Albert that she kept constantly about her: his watch and chain, a golden cord with his keys and his quirky red pocket handkerchief, 'at which they had so often laughed in good old days'.[60]

Anticipating his imminent arrival, the first thing Victoria did at Osborne was to sit down and pour out her heart to Uncle Leopold, on writing paper with inch-thick black borders:

> The poor fatherless baby of nine months is now the utterly broken-hearted and crushed widow of forty-two! My *life* as a *happy* one is *ended*! The world is gone for *me*! If I *must live* on . . . it is henceforth for our poor

fatherless children – for my unhappy country, which has lost *all* in losing him – and in *only* doing what I know and *feel* he would wish, for he *is* near me – his spirit will guide and inspire me.

At last anger burned through the numbness of grief, arousing Victoria's indignation. How dare God take her precious Albert from her?

> But oh! To be cut off in the prime of life – to see our pure, happy, quiet, domestic life, which *alone* enabled me to bear my *much* disliked position, CUT OFF at forty-two – when I *had* hoped with such instinctive certainty that God never *would* part us, and would let us grow old together . . . is *too awful*, too cruel.[61]

*　*　*

On 22 December, after a week of prayer meetings up and down the country, another cold, grey Sunday dawned and the churches of Britain were packed with worshippers. The solemnity of the occasion was heightened by the surfeit of black everywhere: British churches that day were festooned with a 'crapery of woe'. Worshippers sat in muted grief listening to long sermons on the death of the Prince Consort by parish priests, many of whom grasped the opportunity for issuing exhortations to their flocks to prepare for their own ends by ensuring that they live untainted, Christian lives as the Prince had done.[62]

United in a 'bond of common sorrow,' the nation now gathered its strength for the heartbreak of the funeral to come, which promised a 'grand Gothic fane . . . completely draped and carpeted with black', with dirges and anthems and dead marches, and catafalques and a hearse 'drawn by plumed and mantled steeds and hung with escutcheons of the illustrious deceased', according to Sala of the *Telegraph*, once more rising to the occasion with a lugubrious flourish.[63] Overall the tone of the Prince's obituaries that week had reflected the public wish, as Lord Clarendon saw it, 'to make a serious *amende* for the injustice too often done to him in his lifetime'.[64] It was, however, the leader-writer of the *Observer* who best summed up, in a simple sentence quoting the words of Shakespeare's Hamlet, what other obituarists had taken columns to express:

> Peace to his ashes! A good husband, a good father, a wise Prince, and a safe counsellor, England will not soon 'look upon his like again'.[65]

In these final dark, sullen days of December yet more bad news arrived: ships from America had brought discouraging dispatches. The American cabinet in Washington, whilst deliberating its course of action, still appeared to be taking a belligerent stance over the *Trent* affair. At the US legation in London, Benjamin Moran continued to fend off anxious enquiries as to the outcome of the crisis, whilst observing the protocol of ensuring that all notes to the British government were now sent on black-edged paper in black-bordered envelopes sealed with black wax. Privately he expected a speedy reconciliation, but the British public at large, as the time approached for a receipt of America's answer, seemed convinced that war was inevitable. But, if a trade-off could have been possible, to the mind of Lord Palmerston it was 'Better for England to have had a ten-years' war with America than to have lost Prince Albert'.[66]

CHAPTER SEVEN

'Will They Do Him Justice Now?'

It had been forty-four years since the British nation had experienced a royal tragedy to match that of the death of Prince Albert. Back in 1817 the popular and vivacious Princess Charlotte of Wales, daughter of the Prince Regent, and – failing the birth of any other legitimate ones – heir to the British throne, had at the age of only twenty-one died of complications following the stillbirth of a son. For many people this sudden loss took on the dimensions of an everyday tragedy, for death in childbirth (of mother and child) was then such a common occurrence. Nevertheless, as a robust and healthy young woman, Charlotte should not have died, had she not been so unmercifully bled and starved by her misguided doctors during her pregnancy. With the Princess already fatally weakened, the failure of the royal doctors to intervene with forceps to progress her agonising two-day labour had resulted in her death from haemorrhage and shock on 6 November.[1]

Princess Charlotte's death, much like that of the Prince Consort later, was viewed as a great national disaster: 'The Catastrophe at Claremont'. It was commemorated in a torrent of sermons, discourses, dirges, elegies and epitaphs across the land, many of which were collected as 'A Cypress Wreath for the Tomb of Her Late Royal Highness the Princess of Wales'. Bonfires stacked to celebrate the impending birth were dismantled, shops closed and businesses suspended as many went into mourning. The unexpected deaths of two prospective heirs to the throne provoked much talk in the Continental press of a monarchical crisis and the looming fear – in the continuing absence of a legitimate heir of a foreign monarch yet again taking the British throne.

With perhaps the exception of the death in 1852 of the Napoleonic War hero the Duke of Wellington, the nation had 'never been afflicted by a loss at once so sudden and so overwhelming' and of such a prominent member of the royal family.[2] A great state occasion was made of the eighty-three-year-old Duke's death; an elaborate twenty-seven-foot-long funeral car, embellished with black and gold ornamentation and drawn by twelve black-plumed horses, had processed across London in front of around a million people, to St Paul's Cathedral, where the Duke was buried in the crypt alongside Admiral Lord Nelson. Prince Albert had taken a prominent role in national mourning for the Duke, and the funeral had been very much a mark of respect for a long life, well lived, that had come to its natural end. But the Duke's was the last of the great heraldic state funerals. By 1861 tastes had changed, particularly with regard to the outmoded convention of royal burial at night. This had been the norm for members of the royal family earlier in the century, including Princess Charlotte, the main reason being that the darkness reduced the need for the precise observation of the elaborate heraldic trappings traditionally required. The natural Gothic drama of such a funeral conducted in darkness was heightened by the flickering torchlight and ghostlike black weeds of the mourners. But when in 1837 the Duke of Sussex had had to endure the irreverent, overblown shambles of the funeral of William IV, he left instructions for a simple daylight funeral for himself without excessive pomp, which was observed when he died in 1843. When William IV's widow, Queen Adelaide, died in 1849, she left a similar request that her funeral be simple and conducted during the day. By then, even the royal lying-in-state had been abandoned – last seen at the funeral of Princess Sophia of Gloucester in 1844.

In his will, Prince Albert reflected the general and growing distaste among the aristocracy for pompous and protracted obsequies, stating: 'Everything I possess belongs to the Queen, my dear wife. I wish to be buried privately.'[3] The details of the will were never published, nor were any medical reports by Albert's doctors on the circumstances of his death, beyond the superficial content of the official bulletins. When King George IV had died in 1830 the royal doctors had published the gruesome details of his post-mortem in *The Times*; there had been post-mortems too for Princess Charlotte and her dead baby before they had both been embalmed, but Victoria flatly refused to allow any posthumous examination of her husband's sacred corpse, a fact that aroused considerable disapproval in medical circles.[4]

It fell to the Lord Chamberlain – Viscount Sydney – as chief officer of the royal household to make the arrangements for the funeral, in consultation with Bertie and the Duke of Cambridge. With the Queen wanting no involvement in its planning, it was assumed that a repetition of the private funeral overseen earlier that year by Prince Albert for the

Duchess of Kent would be the best option. The most urgent decision to be made was the actual date, which was decided on for Monday 23 December. The Lord Chamberlain and his staff were placed under considerable pressure to complete the arrangements in time, but it was seen as essential that the funeral be held before Christmas, in order to allow the nation some release from mourning over the coming festive season, even though, inevitably, it would be a very subdued one that year.

One thing at least could be relied on, and that was the discretion and efficiency of Messrs T. & W. Banting, who had conducted all royal funerals since 1811, as well as those of Nelson and the Duke of Wellington. From their fashionable premises in the West End, Banting's (like many other similar businesses of the day) combined a prosperous upholstery and cabinet-making enterprise with undertaking, contracting out the embalming and other aspects of the business. After his death Albert's corpse had been placed in the loving care of his valet Löhlein, who had laid out the Prince with the rings still on his fingers, dressed in the long dark-blue frockcoat of a field marshal, with gold cord aiguillette across one shoulder and a gold and crimson waist sash with tassels.

In accordance with royal tradition, Albert's body was placed within two coffins, similar in style and size to those used for the Duchess of Kent: the inner wooden shell lined with white satin had an outer casing of lead with massive silver-gilt ornaments and bore a Latin inscription:

Depositum
Illustrissimi et Celsissimi Alberti,
Principis Consortis,
Ducis Saxoniae,
de Saxe-coburg et Gotha Principis,
Noblissimi Ordinia Perisceldis Equitis,
Augustissimae et Potentissimae Victoriae Reginae
Conjugis percarissimi,
Obiit die decimo quarto Decembris, MDCCCLXI,
*Anno aetatis suae XLIII.**

---

* 'Here lies the most illustrious and exalted Albert, Prince Consort, Duke of Saxony, Prince of Saxe-Coburg and Gotha, Knight of the most noble Order of the Garter, the most beloved husband of the most august and potent Queen Victoria, who died 14 December 1861 in his 43rd year.'

On the evening of the 16th, officers of the Board of Works came and soldered the lead coffin down – Messrs Holland & Sons, undertakers of Mount Street, having placed charcoal around the corpse, again as per royal mortuary practice (in order to absorb any odours as it began to decompose).[5] Colonel Biddulph had arranged with Banting's that the entire ante-throne room be 'put in mourning to receive the body' with 'black druggett to cover floor, black cloth draperies over doors and windows'. In addition, a double-width of druggett was to be used to form an elaborate black pathway over the carpets, through two rooms, down the staircase and all the way to the entrance door of the castle, 'so as to form a mourning route for the remains', to be trod by those following the coffin.[6] When the coffin was moved down to the ante-throne room on the 22nd, it was placed inside a third, massive state coffin of mahogany covered with crimson velvet, over which a heavily embroidered black velvet pall lined with white satin was arranged, with Albert's coronet and his field marshal's baton, sword and hat placed on top.

On Saturday 21 December – for one day only – and in order to satiate intense public curiosity, Banting's had put the third, ceremonial coffin made in their workshops on public display at their premises at 27 St James's Street.[7] But this is as much as the public would get to see; the ceremony itself at Windsor would be strictly private and the British people were denied any opportunity of paying their final respects at a formal lying-in-state. Even when Princess Charlotte had died, only a limited number had been allowed into a cramped room at Lower Lodge, Windsor, for a few hours to take a brief glance at the coffin. This was a matter of some concern to the Mayor of Windsor, who was dismayed that no local people would be allowed to see anything of the funeral cortège. He requested a change in the route when the coffin was brought from the private apartments in the Upper Ward, suggesting that it might proceed down Castle Hill and out of the precincts briefly, before turning back to St George's Chapel. The palace and the Lord Chamberlain resisted this vigorously, insisting on absolute privacy.[8] As for the members of the press – as well as the necessary artists to illustrate the day's events – they would be allowed access, but hidden away in the organ loft above the main body of the chapel. The Mayor meanwhile persisted; there would, he argued, be 'intense disappointment' if the public were totally excluded. In the end he and a handful of people were allowed into the castle precincts, but the Comptroller would later complain that despite the tight security arrangements, a lapse by the Mayor had allowed

some 'strangers' to get in; worse, the policeman on duty at the door to
the organ loft had allowed the sister of the organist, Dr George Elvey,
to sneak in and watch the ceremony, 'an unpardonable piece of
impertinence . . . as he was perfectly well aware that no lady was to be
admitted excepting by the Queen's direct order'.[9]

Preparations for the funeral in St George's Chapel went on apace.
The stone flagging covering the entrance to the royal vault was removed,
and a raised dais constructed over it in the centre of the chapel to take
the state coffin and its huge velvet catafalque. The whole of the chapel
from its west door to the entrance of the choir was carpeted in black
and the doors draped with heavy black curtains. The empty oak choir
stalls and canopies of the Knights of the Garter were also festooned
with black, as were the steps up to the communion table. The only
colour breaking the pervading gloom was that of the glittering medieval
escutcheons and fringed banners high in the roof of the chapel and its
stained-glass window. Otherwise there was an 'utter absence of prismatic
colour'.[10]

As the days passed, one thing was all too clear, as the Duke of Argyll
observed: 'The whole nation is mourning as it never mourned before.'
'During the past week,' wrote Lord Hardman, 'every shop in London
has kept up mourning shutters, and nothing is seen in all drapers', milliners', tailors', and haberdashers' shops but black. Everybody is in
mourning.' For Albert's death had brought 'painful reminders of the
death of the Princess Charlotte and her baby' all those years before.[11]
The 200 shop assistants at Jay's vast London General Mourning Warehouse
on Regent Street were under siege, for, from the moment of the Prince's
death, there had been an 'incalculable demand for mourning'. Sales of
engravings and *cartes de visite* of the Prince Consort and the Queen had
also been unprecedented, the most popular being one by John Mayall
of the Prince seated, pen in hand, at his desk, which had been taken in
May 1860. The *carte de visite* was a recent innovation from France that
had immediately found favour with the public, with *cartes* of Mayall's
photographs of the royal family selling by the 100,000. Photograph dealers
were quick to capitalise on the windfall of the Prince's death and the
astonishing demand for images of him. Inside a week, 'no less than
70,000 *cartes de visite* had been ordered from . . . Marion & Co.', the
largest photographic wholesaler in England, located in Soho Square; in
Paris, a print-seller claimed to have sold 30,000 *cartes* in one day.[12] On the
afternoon of 21 December, Arthur Munby had fought his way through

the shoppers on Regent Street and found huge crowds outside the photograph shops, 'looking at the few portraits of the Prince which are still unsold'. He went into Meclin's to buy one: 'every one in the shop was doing the same. They had none left: would put my name down, but could not promise even then. Afterwards I succeeded in getting one – the last the seller had – of the Queen and Prince: giving four shillings for what would have cost but eighteen pence a week ago.' Munby concluded that the escalation in price was an indicator of the 'great conviction of his worth and value which the loss of him has suddenly brought to us all'.[13]

⋆   ⋆   ⋆

The morning of Monday 23 December 1861 dawned cold, grey and cheerless. 'The very air felt heavy with the general gloom,' recalled Princess Mary Adelaide when she got up at eight. She could already hear the tolling of the bells and later the minute guns in St James's Park, informing London that the 'last sad ceremony' was about to take place in St George's Chapel, Windsor. Nature itself seemed to sympathise with the national feeling of despondency, for the dull, damp, leaden sky showed no sign of clearing as people ventured forth to mark the day – a day when no respectable person was seen out of doors except in the deepest of mourning.[14]

The most profound gloom of all reigned in the town of Windsor, as the correspondent of *The Times* reported: 'every shop closed, every blind drawn down; streets silent and almost deserted'. The castle's great bell chimed out its doleful sound at intervals from an early hour, joined later by the minute bells tolling from nearby St John's parish church. Early that morning Bertie, Arthur, Duke Ernst, Prince Louis, the Crown Prince of Prussia and other male mourners in the royal entourage for Albert's funeral had left Osborne and travelled by special train from Southampton to Windsor, the shutters firmly drawn down as it passed through stations en route, observed by mute and grief-stricken crowds. The entourage brought with them wreaths of moss and violets made by Alice, Helena and Louise for their father's coffin, as well as a simple, touching bouquet of violets with a white camellia in its centre from their mother.[15] These would be the only flowers in evidence, fresh flowers as such not yet being part of British funeral culture.

At eleven o'clock the principal mourners gathered in the Oak Room, wearing, as instructed by the Lord Chamberlain, plain black evening coats and white cravats. Mourning scarves and armbands, as per funeral convention, were to be provided by Banting's at the chapel. Only those with a personal connection to the Queen and Prince Albert, plus the essential Cabinet ministers and the Archbishop of Canterbury, had been invited. Much to their dismay, the Duke of Cambridge and Lord Palmerston were both too unwell to attend; the Prince of Leiningen was also absent, having elected to remain at Osborne with the Queen. No foreign ambassadors were there either, bar the Portuguese envoy Count Lavradio, Count Brandenburg from Prussia and, on behalf of King Leopold who was yet to arrive in England, the Belgian ambassador, Sylvain Van De Weyer. Foreign royals present included the Duc de Nemours (married to Albert's cousin) and Albert and Victoria's cousins from Belgium: the Duke of Brabant and the Count of Flanders. 'Youth seemed out of place here,' remarked George Augustus Sala; the congregation for the funeral was 'a congress of old men, of patriarchs'. The only youthful exception, aside from Bertie and Arthur – and the only representative of Britain's many colonies (where the news of Albert's death was yet to arrive) – was the twenty-three-year-old former Maharaja of the Sikh Raj, Duleep Singh, now domiciled in England and a favourite of the Queen's. No women were present in the main body of the chapel, although, at Victoria's particular request, two of her closest friends – the Duchesses of Sutherland and Wellington (her former and current Mistresses of the Robes) – along with five other ladies, observed the proceedings out of sight in the Queen's Closet on the north side of the choir, specially fitted up with mourning on the Lord Chamberlain's orders. At Bertie's thoughtful request, Prince Arthur's nurse, Mrs Hull, was also at hand, in the organ loft.

As the journalists and congregation gathered in the chapel to a low sound of whispering and rustling, the faint sound of machinery could be heard as the mechanism for lowering the bier down into the vault was tested one final time. Elsewhere, workmen hurried to finish sweeping away the remaining mess from where the temporary black carpeting had been laid. Sala – whose account was published the following day across six columns of the *Daily Telegraph* surrounded in a heavy black border – had an excellent vantage point in the organ loft, from where he could see both east and west ends of the chapel. He was fascinated to note that one of the minor chapels had been converted into a temporary workshop by Banting's, where 'the busy bees of Death, the undertaker's myrmidons – plump men in raven black, rosy girls in brand new sables – [sat] stitching and tacking and folding scarves, and tying bands and sewing on rosettes, until the very last moment', these to be handed to the mourners as they arrived.

At midday the procession of fifteen mourning coaches slowly wended its way behind the hearse, under the Norman Tower and down the hill from the royal apartments in the Upper Ward. Its progress was witnessed by only a small group of spectators who were allowed to stand in front of the almshouses of the Poor Knights, immediately opposite the entrance to the south side of the chapel. As the procession drew to a halt, the minute guns were fired by members of the Horse Artillery beyond the castle walls in Long Walk, a couple of miles away. Outside the chapel Grenadier Guards, of whom the Prince had been Colonel-in-Chief, stood to attention and presented arms as the heavy black drapes at the chapel doors were pulled back to admit the coffin. From there, slowly, inexorably, it was edged forward into the chapel on a bier underneath its velvet pall (the assistants moving it, being unable to see, were guided by a narrow strip of white along the floor at their feet). Following the coffin came Lord Henry Lennox, bearing the Prince's baton, sword and hat on a black velvet cushion with gold tassels, followed by Earl Spencer with the Prince's coronet, which were all then placed on the coffin.

The mourners were led by Bertie and a grief-stricken Prince Arthur, his eyes red and swollen from weeping, who made the most poignant of figures in his black Highland dress. All around 'there was a dumb, cadaverous air about the chapel, swathed in its ghastly trappings'. Dukes, marquesses, earls, politicians and members of the royal household – from Albert's valets, to his farm bailiffs, his solicitor, librarian, apothecaries, doctors, and equerries – sat as one in their uniformly black and white garb, the scene relieved only by the occasional glitter of a bejewelled badge or order. As the muffled bell continued its melancholy chime a deep silence fell across those gathered. Gerald Wellesley, the Dean of Windsor, took his place to conduct the burial service, with music composed by the eighteenth-century organist and composer William Croft, which had been used at previous state funerals. A shudder of emotion went round the congregation as the choir burst into the chant 'I am the Resurrection and the Life', followed by 'I know that my Redeemer liveth' – the latter 'so touching, so inexpressibly mournful in its long, soft cadences,' as the organist Dr Elvey recalled.[16]

Of Albert's nine children, only two were present at the service: Bertie, who as eldest bore up as best he could, and little Prince Arthur, the Prince's eleven year-old younger son, who was consumed by grief throughout. When it came to the words 'So fall asleep in slumber deep,/ Slumber that knows no waking' – part of a favourite chant of their father's – the two brothers hid their faces and wept. Even Dean Wellesley's voice faltered many times and was sometimes inaudible, so overcome was he. For once some of the traditional conventions of royal funerals were broken, certainly with regard to the choice of music, which was strongly oriented to Albert's own musical tastes. The service included two of his favourite German chorales: the sixteenth-century 'I shall not in the grave remain/Since Thou death's bonds hast sever'd', by the Bavarian cantor and preacher Nicolaus Decius, which was 'chanted by the choir in whispered tones that seemed to moan through the building with a plaintive solemnity'; the other a favourite hymn by Martin Luther, 'Great God, what do I see and hear?', sung by the tenor soloist Mr Tolley. These had been requested by Victoria, having been privately printed in a pamphlet – *In Memoriam* – on the death of her mother, 'which the late Prince was constantly in the habit of using'.[17] Then the Garter King of Arms stepped forward to read the proclamation in which reference was made to Queen Victoria, 'Whom God bless and preserve with long life, health, and happiness'. There was, however, one significant change; having carefully studied the details of the funeral service before leaving for Osborne, Victoria had specifically ordered that the word 'happiness' be struck out and replaced with 'honour'. For her, all worldly happiness was now, and for ever, at an end.[18]

As the ceremony drew to a close, many in the all-male congregation openly wept as the pall was removed and the gold and crimson-covered coffin suddenly flashed into view, all too briefly, in all its magnificence. In the pause that followed as the congregation gazed in awe at Albert's coffin, the wind outside gathered and 'mourned hoarsely against the casements', accompanied by the quick, sharp rattle of the troops outside as they reversed arms, to the sound of the melancholy knell from the castle spire. Then the coffin was gradually lowered quietly down through the aperture in the stone floor to the royal vault below. As it finally disappeared from view a handful of earth was thrown down 'with a sharp rattle that was heard throughout the building'. The mourners then slowly advanced to take one last look down at the coffin before departing – to the sound of Dr Elvey playing the 'Dead March from Saul'. During the hour-long service everyone had perished with the bitter cold inside the chapel and now headed into the castle to be fortified with a champagne funeral luncheon, which Lord Torrington noticed that an exhausted Sir Charles Phipps devoured with relish, no doubt relieved it was all over.[19]

In his account the following day George Augustus Sala commented on the 'splendid but ghastly toilet of the grave' that Albert's magnificent funeral ceremony had embodied, contrasting it with the last rites for ordinary people, quietly laid to rest in 'green country churchyards, where the moon shines with a soft and tender kindness on the stones above them'. In contrast, Albert's great coffin had passed 'but a few paces from the Chamber of Death to the House of Silence' and now, as the mourners dispersed, the funeral attendants prepared it for its final resting place. At the end of a stone passage, six feet wide and nine feet high – past rows of tall, black, two-armed wooden candelabra in which torches were placed to light their way – the coffin arrived at two plain, rusty, barred iron gates, which marked the entrance to the royal vault. Inside this cold and silent stone vault with its groined roof stood four tiers of marble shelves on either side, with marble slabs in the centre (the preserve of monarchs only), on which were visible the deep-purple velvet-covered coffins of George III, George IV, William IV and their wives, and to the side the crimson coffin of Princess Charlotte. Queen Victoria had had a horror of Albert's coffin being placed there, alongside 'that huge, dingy coffin' of the venal old George IV.[20] And so here, at the gates to the vault, it would rest until his mausoleum was completed a year later.

Describing that day to his friend Delane at *The Times*, Lord Torrington said he was 'inclined to think that more real sorrow was evinced at this funeral than at any that has taken place *there* for a vast number of years'. 'Brave men sobbed like children,' agreed gentleman usher Lyon Playfair, and 'even the choristers broke down when they had to sing the requiem'. All around one saw 'old, dry, political eyes, which seemed as if they had long forgotten how to weep, gradually melting and running down in large drops of sympathy,' recalled Samuel Wilberforce, the Bishop of Oxford. Arthur Stanley, one of the chaplains to Prince Albert, would himself later recall that, 'considering the magnitude of the event and of the persons present, all agitated by the same emotion, I do not think that I have ever seen, or shall see, anything so affecting'.[21]

★   ★   ★

London itself that day had been 'like a city struck by the Plague'. An unusual stillness had prevailed everywhere; it was as though normal daily life was in a state of suspended animation. Private houses were dark and 'as much closed as though each household had lost a close relative'. Shops were shuttered up, labour was suspended, money exchanges were closed, as the country 'voluntarily imposed upon itself a fine which probably cannot be estimated at less than a million sterling, in order to mark its regret for the dead and its sympathy for its survivors'.[22] At Lockinge House in Berkshire, Lord Overstone, responding to the prevailing mood, had, first thing that morning, 'invited the whole house-hold (out of door as well as indoor servants)' to attend prayers inside the main house. 'They all attended readily I believe without a single exception,' he wrote. 'I read to them the Burial Service, with a few remarks of my own on the character of the Prince and the solemnity of the event whilst the Church Bell was tolling, almost as if it were in the very room.' All present, he recalled, were 'deeply affected; sincerely so I fully believe'.[23] No doubt many families began the day in similar manner, before heading for one of the many commemorative services held in Britain's churches, where the congregations were huge – with 3,000 crowding into St Paul's Cathedral alone. Many major towns staged large, solemn processionals ahead of the service: in Leeds not only was the parish church full to capacity, but mourners of all denominations and social classes lined the processional route all the way from the town hall. At Exeter there was again not enough room in the cathedral to take all those wishing to attend, prompting disgruntled local dignitaries to complain that hoi polloi had been allowed precedence.[24]

* * *

At a more modest level, among the working classes in the overcrowded East End, people were no less grief-stricken. At Bethnal Green there was 'hardly any noise in those usually noisy thoroughfares'; people gathered on street corners in subdued groups around street ballad-singers, 'whose utterances visibly moved their audiences' as they lamented the death of the Prince in song:

> Britannia, alas! is lamenting,
> And grief now is everywhere seen
> Oh think, you kind daughters of Britain,
> The Feelings of England's Queen
> What trouble and care does oppress her,
> Her loss causes her to deplore,

> The spirit of him is departed,
> And Prince Albert, alas! is no more.[25]

Philanthropists of the London City Mission noted considerable grief among the 'very poorest' of those families whom they visited at the time; one hospital visitor talked of how, when he did his round at St George's Hospital, 'not one patient spoke to him of his own wounds or ailments, while every one to whom he went up, was full of expressions of sorrow for the loss which the Country had sustained, and of tender enquiries about the Queen, in her cruel bereavement'. In rural areas Richard Monckton Milnes observed that 'The peasants in their cottages talk as if the Queen was one of themselves. It is the realest public sorrow I have ever seen – quite different from anything else.'[26]

But it was not just the Christian community that paid homage in their churches that day. Among the Jewish community, especially of London, Prince Albert was mourned in an atmosphere of profound melancholy. The Jews, who had much to thank the Prince for his impartiality on religious matters, marked the occasion with special services in synagogues, several of them draped in black. Sermons on the dead Prince were delivered at London's historic Sephardi synagogue (the Bevis Marks in the City) and the two Ashkenazi congregations (the Great and the Hambro synagogues). At the West London synagogue every seat was filled long before the service and the roads leading up to it were jammed with vehicles. Here the congregation heard a sermon by Dr Marks taking as its text the words of Jeremiah IX:19: 'A voice of lamentation is heard from Zion. How are we bereaved!' And at his own privately built synagogue on his estate in Ramsgate, the philanthropist Sir Moses Montefiore and his wife attended a special service where the reading desk was covered with black cloth, 'the only symbol of mourning we ever had in our synagogue'. All in all, as one British Jew later reported to a friend in South Africa, there had been 'not a dry eye in the synagogues'; prayers for Prince Albert had continued all day. 'The people mourned for him as much as for Hezekiah; and, indeed, he deserved it a great deal better' was his somewhat unorthodox conclusion.[27]

In all, seventy sermons preached on the Sunday and Monday would later be published in pamphlet form, their titles echoing the impact of Albert's death on the national consciousness – 'Britain's Loss and Britain's Duty', 'God's Voice from Windsor Castle', 'Death is Entered into Our Palaces', 'The Smitten Nation', 'A Nation's Lamentation over Fallen

Greatness', 'A Prince's Death, A Nation's Grief' – not to mention a plethora of poetry, good, bad and awful. Even the unremittingly satirical *Punch* magazine for once took a serious tone, rising to the occasion with its own moving offering 'How Do Princes Die', in which it reflected the universal feeling:

> It was too soon to die.
> Yet, might we count his years by triumphs won,
> By wise, and bold, and Christian duties done,
> It were no brief, eventless history . . .[28]

On the day after Albert died, when she had taken the Duchess of Sutherland into the King's Room to see his body, the Queen had turned as they both looked down at Albert's dead face and asked plaintively, 'Will they do him justice now?' By day's end, 23 December 1861, there was no one in the country who could have doubted the extent to which the nation had indeed done justice to its late Prince. The day had been a great celebration, not just of the Prince, but of sober British moral values. Benjamin Disraeli had no hesitation in his own paean to the late Consort: 'With Prince Albert we have buried our sovereign,' he confided unequivocally to Count Vitzthum, Saxon envoy to the Court of St James's. 'This German prince has governed England for twenty-one years with a wisdom and energy such as none of our kings have ever shown.' But as for the future: 'What to-morrow will bring forth no man can tell. To-day we are sailing in the deepest gloom, with night and darkness all around us.'[29]

Alone in Coburg, too sick and frail to travel, Albert's oldest and truest friend, Baron Christian Stockmar, was left to nurse his broken heart and the end of his life's work. 'An edifice, which for a great and noble purpose, has been reared with a devout sense of duty, by twenty years of laborious toil' had, with his protégé's death, 'been shattered to its very foundations'. He had an 'indisputable right', he wrote to Bertie, to say that 'in Him I have *lost the very best of* Sons'.[30] Stockmar would never recover from it; eighteen months later he too was dead, and the dream of a golden age of constitutional monarchy in Britain – and a united Germany – under Albert's enlightened guidance, died with him.

CHAPTER EIGHT

'How Will the Queen Bear It?'

In deep retreat on a bleak and cheerless Isle of Wight, Queen Victoria had sat watching the minutes tick by on the day of her husband's funeral, and then, as the clock struck, she had picked up her pen and written to Vicky. 'It is one o'clock and all, all is over!' Alone in Berlin, Vicky had spent the day sitting with her beloved father's photographs spread out on her knees, 'devouring them with my eyes, kissing them and feeling as if my heart would break'. She would have given anything to be there, with her family. Over at Osborne her mother had not wished to have any reminders of that day's solemnities. She made certain that she would not have to suffer within her earshot the agonising and very audible sound of the minute guns being fired by ships and batteries across the Solent. She therefore instructed Sir Charles Phipps to ask the Duke of Cambridge, as C-in-C of the Army, to see to it; 'nor should any guns for practice or other duties be fired at Portsmouth, or within reach of being heard at Osborne'. She had, she said, already found the constant practice-firing from Portsmouth on the morning of 20 December greatly distressing and shuddered at the thought of being further reminded.[1]

Sir Charles Phipps, who had remained with the Queen at Osborne until leaving for the funeral early on the Monday morning, had dreaded how she would react that day, but, he told Lord Sydney, was convinced that 'the coming here has been a *very good* measure'. Informing the Duke of Cambridge of the Queen's instructions, he hoped her deep grief would 'resume the same quiet, unexcited character' once the funeral was over.[2] Thin she might be, and still suffering from disrupted sleep, but the initial fears they had had when the Queen's pulse had dropped alarmingly had been unfounded and she was otherwise in good health. Her continuing state of calm, despite bouts of weeping, impressed everyone, as did her acceptance – Victoria claiming that she did not feel the same bitterness as she had when her mother had died. 'I was so rebellious then,' she admitted, 'but now I see the mercy and love that are mixed with my misery.'[3]

When he arrived by royal yacht from Prussia en route to the funeral, her son-in-law Fritz remarked on Victoria's composure and her 'greatness of spirit in such terrible times of grief'. They spent much time in quiet conversation, during which she told him how she had already plucked up the courage to go into Albert's rooms at Osborne. Fritz thought this highly therapeutic, urging her to 'seek out all the places they shared in times of happiness at the first sign of pain' in order to get herself 'used to the loneliness'.[4] On her arrival at Osborne, Victoria had sent for the gardener who had worked so closely with Prince Albert and had asked him to walk round the garden every morning with her, as Albert had done, and never to be afraid of speaking to her of his late master, 'as it was a solace to her to hear him spoken of.' She took a turn in the gardens too with Fritz, and went over to the Swiss chalet that Albert had commissioned in 1854 as a playhouse for the children. Victoria longed so much to have Vicky there, for she, of all her children, 'had her father's mind' and so would be able to 'help me in all my great plans for a mausoleum . . . for statues, monuments, etc.'[5]

But at least from 18 December Victoria's devoted relatives had begun arriving to offer moral support, ferried over from the Continent by a succession of royal yachts, most importantly her widowed half-sister Feodora from Baden. One person, though, was still absent and much missed – Victoria's uncle, King Leopold of the Belgians. Back in 1817 Prince Leopold of Saxe-Coburg, as he then was, had witnessed the dying agonies of his first wife, Princess Charlotte, and had taken centre stage during the days of public grief and mourning that had followed her tragic death. But now, faced with a horrifying repetition of events of forty-four years ago, as well as having lost a second wife (to tuberculosis) in 1850, he proved unequal to the task of supporting his widowed niece and did not arrive at Osborne until 27 December. (Others would claim that Leopold's motives were entirely selfish and that he had not wanted to go to Windsor for fear of infection.)

With her mother clearly unable to resume official business, Princess Alice had found the strength to take on the necessary day-to-day management of the household and deal with ministers and urgent letter-writing – all of it conducted on inch-thick black-bordered paper, with the help of Victoria's private secretaries, Phipps and Grey. But her heart, she told Louis, was 'quite broken' and her grief 'almost more than I can bear'.

With so much attention directed towards the Queen, some had failed to notice how shockingly frail Alice had become. When he arrived in England for the funeral, Louis had been disturbed to see her so changed – thin, pale, exhausted and overwrought. Fritz thought likewise: Alice was hardly sleeping, he wrote to Vicky on the 20th, she spent most nights in her mother's room. 'We're working to make sure that she doesn't do this too often, otherwise she will annihilate herself by her love of self-sacrifice.' Nevertheless Alice was consumed by a sense of duty to her mother and that she should remain with her to fill the gap left by Albert. She could not be persuaded even to take a break outside in the fresh air, noted Fritz, 'so much so that she, with strict admonishment, needs to be reminded not to overdo it'. Burdened by all her additional responsibilities, Alice admitted the great change in herself to Bertie: 'I feel years older since that dreadful time.'[6] Her wedding to Louis would, of course, have to be postponed.

One of Alice's most important tasks as the year drew to a close had been to send a message via Phipps to the Poet Laureate, Alfred Tennyson, requesting that he write something in memory of her father. Tennyson, who had met Prince Albert in May 1856, hated being asked to write to order, but the royal couple were among his most dedicated admirers and he could not refuse. Being unwell at the time, he protested that he did not at present feel able to do Albert justice and hoped, in due course, to be 'enabled to speak of him as he himself would have wished to be spoken of'. He therefore suggested that, rather than come up with something completely new, he should write a prefatory dedication to the Prince Consort, to be added to the new edition of his epic Arthurian romance in verse *The Idylls of the King*, which was due out the following year.[7] It was a work that Victoria and Albert had both been 'in raptures about' when they had first read it. For the time being, the Queen would continue to take comfort in his *In Memoriam*, which she and Albert had also greatly loved, a copy of which Tennyson had signed for Albert in May 1860. She felt 'much soothed' by it: 'only those who have suffered as I do, can understand these beautiful poems'.[8]

In the midst of her crippling grief the Queen was, meanwhile, very clear about one thing: she was determined to retain absolute control of matters of state. ('She has the *habit* of power and once taken it is hardly possible to live without it,' as Queen Sophie of the Netherlands shrewdly remarked to one of the ladies at court.)[9] With this in mind, Victoria told Fritz that she had made it known that all enquiries should be directed to her 'which would normally have gone to papa', and that nothing should be addressed to Bertie. 'Oh that boy,' she complained to Vicky, 'much as I pity I never can or shall look at him without a shudder'.[10] Others, in private, agreed that Bertie was a lost cause. There was, for writer and journalist Harriet Martineau, 'no hope in that wretched boy!' His 'natural goodness and docility' had given way to 'impenetrable levity'; Bertie had been fatally corrupted at the Curragh and at Cambridge, and 'there is nothing more to hope'. Even Lord Stanley gossiped that among Bertie's own entourage he was thought immature and childish and that they seldom addressed him 'when serious subjects were discussed'.[11]

The failings of her errant oldest son were uppermost in Victoria's mind when she wrote to Uncle Leopold on Christmas Eve, her sharp, angular hand scratching at and underlining the paper in an intensity of feeling that made plain her intentions for the future – intentions that would brook no interference, even from benevolent uncles:

> I am also anxious to repeat one thing, and *that one* is *my firm* resolve, my *irrevocable decision*, viz. that *his* wishes – *his* plans – about everything, *his* views about *every* thing are to be *my* law! And *no human power* will make me swerve from what he decided and wished . . . I live *on* with him, for him; in fact, *I* am only *outwardly* separated from him, and *only* for a *time*.[12]

Albert died in the belief, above all others, that he had trained his wife to do her duty. And in the dazed and disjointed days of grief that followed, Victoria kept repeating it like a mantra: yes, 'they need not be afraid, I will do my duty'. But she had yet to prove that she could, or would, do so, and meanwhile life for the royal household was in a state of stasis: 'the utter consternation of everyone – the standstill everything has come to – the spring and centre of each being gone, is more apparent every moment,' maid-of-honour Mary Bulteel admitted in a letter to her mother. 'I cannot *conceive* what she will do, for if her will were ever so strong, she cannot have the power or capacity to do his work.'[13]

* * *

As Christmas Eve 1861 drew in, everyone at Osborne, as well as in the royal family at large, was in a depressed state. 'We have not the heart to keep Christmas in the usual manner,' wrote Princess Mary Adelaide. 'The tree is at all events for the present to be dispensed with.'[14] For

Victoria the festive season that had once been such a joy was irrevocably
changed: 'Think of Christmas Eve and all!!!' she wrote to Vicky. 'It shall
never be spent at Windsor again – for he left us in those rooms.' That
same day, Vicky in Berlin also turned her thoughts to happier times:

> This is Xmas Eve! I should not know it sitting *all alone* – with none but
> my own sad thoughts for companions, but the noise in the streets, the
> merry bustle, forces the dismal contrast upon me . . . the bells are ringing
> – to me they seem tolling for the dear departed one! All the world is sad
> and dark and empty – mourning is the only thing that gives me
> satisfaction.

Christmas, Vicky concluded, *'never will* be *happy* again'.[15]

Osborne that year was, inevitably, a 'house of mourning'. Everyone
was looking thin and wan and exhausted, and even Christmas presents
took on a very different character: the household all received tokens of
remembrance of Albert – black-bordered photographs for the men, and
for the ladies lockets with Albert's portrait. Fritz had already been sent
back to Berlin with locks of Albert's hair and other mementoes for Vicky.
Casting his mind back to the happy Christmas he had witnessed at
Windsor the previous year, Lord Torrington could not help but make
comparisons in a letter to Delane. 'I need hardly say we are very dull
here,' he began, though personally he was not downhearted. 'All things
considered it is not so bad as I expected. People must eat & drink & in
spite of grief, we sometimes laugh.' But for the exhausted Phipps,
Christmas dawned no brighter. 'What a Christmas Day we have to pass
here!' he told the diplomat Lord Cowley. 'You can hardly form an idea
of the desolation of this house.'[16]

Back on the mainland, the British nation at large was doing its best
to overcome its still-profound grief at the Prince Consort's death, but
the prevalence of people in mourning on all the streets and in all the
shops continued to cast its gloom. In Manchester 'No one wishes each
other "a *merry* Xmas" this year,' observed the writer Elizabeth Gaskell,
whilst at the American legation in London, Benjamin Moran was resigned
that 'Xmas bids fair to be as funereal as the grave'.[17] A despondent press
reiterated what was in everyone's minds. 'What a sad and solemn
Christmas falls so unexpectedly upon us! What a dismal close of the
year!' ran the editorial in the *Morning Post*. 'These few sad days of
Christmas must be consecrated to grief,' lamented the *Daily Telegraph*.

Everywhere families were gathering around their hearths, where they would normally have raised a Christmas glass to the Queen, 'with an affectionate thought of her Consort, her children, our Princess in Prussia, our Prince coming of age, the young sailor, the sisters to be married, and the rest of the cherished family'. But now, 'The home which all England recognised as the sweetest and holiest in the land is bereaved and desolate,' observed the press, prompting many to remember 'those who are absent from the family gathering, and to forecast the further severing of family ties, which fate may have in store for us'. Recalling past Christmases at the close of this difficult year, George Augustus Sala in the *Telegraph* thought that 1861 would 'always to be associated with its numerals. When the hale among us are gray, and the gray are in their peaceful graves, it will be said: "At that Christmas the people buried the noble Consort of the Queen, and waited over their festal cheer to know if America would be at war with them or peace!"'[18]

Yet despite the continuing political crisis, war, mercifully, had not come. The American Civil War raged on – and with it the blockade of the southern ports, which was bringing short-time to the Lancashire cotton mills and an impending economic crisis at home. But life had to go on. And so, after the necessary respectful pause for the obsequies for Prince Albert, newspapers published the lists of theatrical entertainments on offer, as once again the pantomime season came around. Families could forget the mournful atmosphere at large with a trip to 'Little Miss Muffet and Little Boy Blue' or 'Whittington and his Cat', or take the train to the Crystal Palace at Sydenham and thrill to the heart-in-mouth spectacle of the French tightrope-walker Monsieur Blondin. Churches that had been festooned in mourning for Albert's funeral removed it – for Christmas at least – and brought in the holly and the ivy to try and cheer things up. In parishes everywhere, church dignitaries and charities handed out coal, food, warm clothing and other comforts to deserving families. Continuing a tradition started by the late Duchess of Kent, the poor in Kensington were given gifts of bread, meat, coals and blankets, and 'a good Christmas dinner' was provided by the Duke and Duchess of Cambridge to poor families in Kew. Appeals to Christian charity were also made to ensure that in Britain's 490 workhouses more than 14,000 inmates enjoyed a decent Christmas dinner of roast beef, potatoes, plum pudding and a pint of porter.[19]

★   ★   ★

Across the Atlantic, news of the Prince Consort's death had arrived in New York and Washington on Christmas Eve. *The Times* correspondent William Howard Russell, who had pioneered war reporting during the Crimean War and was now covering the American Civil War, remembered how the telegram when it came had 'cast the deepest gloom over all our little English circle. Prince Albert dead! At first no one believed it.' Their Christmas too would be a subdued one: 'the preparations which we had made for a little festivity to welcome in Christmas morning were chilled by the news, and the eve was not of the joyous character which Englishmen delight to give it, for the sorrow which fell on all hearts in England had spanned the Atlantic, and bade us mourn in common with the country at home.'[20]

In New York harbour the premier vessel of the Cunard line, the *Persia*, as well as other English steamers had lowered their flags to half-mast. The British Vice-Consul, Sir Edward Archibald, immediately convened a meeting of British residents in order to arrange a commemorative event, as too did residents in Nova Scotia and elsewhere in Canada. The *New York Times*, whilst of the opinion that the death of Prince Albert was 'without political significance', published the apprehensions of its London correspondent about its effect on Britain's 'nation of shopkeepers'. 'Christmas is just at hand, and the shops were hoping to make a little money for the first time this year. But now the death of the Prince, coming as it does, in the midst of the American difficulty, has reduced them to despair,' it reported, adding that 'The proprietors of the mourning establishments may be happy behind their bales of crape, but everyone else will lament.' Yet even here, in America, in the midst of a political crisis, the protocols of mourning were observed, with one Union lady complaining that at an official dinner in Washington the 'affectation of court mourning' for the Queen's loss was utterly absurd. 'It is too sad to see such extravagance and folly in the White House,' she wrote, 'with the country bankrupt and a civil war raging!'[21]

The state of agonising suspense over the 'American Difficulty' lasted to the very end of the year, as ships, guns and troops continued to sail for Canada from British docks. In Washington, Russell noted a rampantly bellicose attitude all around; 'press people, soldiers, sailors, ministers, senators, Congress-men, people in the street' were all agreed about the two arrested Southern commissioners: '"Give them up? Never! We'll die first."' The following day, therefore, he was greatly surprised to hear that Secretary of State William Seward – Abraham Lincoln's adviser on foreign policy – had capitulated to compromise. He had agreed to release the two men, after the President had argued during a heated cabinet meeting on Christmas Day that the North must at all costs pursue a policy of 'one war at a time'.[22] A climbdown by Seward in response to the British note drafted by Prince Albert was contrived that would not alienate American public opinion and was presented to the British minister to the United States, Lord Lyons, that day. News was telegraphed to Palmerston in England that Mason and Slidell were to be released, but the Prime Minister decided to suppress its announcement until after he knew for certain that this had indeed happened. The two men eventually sailed for Southampton on 14 January 1862. There would therefore be no crumb of comfort for the British nation that Christmas.[23]

But as one international crisis came to an end, another and very different domestic one loomed. With the Queen determined that her life was at an end 'in a worldly point of view', Sir Charles Phipps by now had very clear intimations of a catastrophe to come. The royal household was cast adrift, affairs of state abandoned, the Queen beyond consolation. He initiated a flurry of memos to government ministers about the ongoing and now even more crucial role of Private Secretary to the Queen – a role that Albert had long unofficially fulfilled. 'It must be evident to the world that there are many things which the Queen may, & indeed *must*, do through others,' Grey told Lord Glanville, as a clear rivalry developed between himself – as Albert's Private Secretary of twelve years – and Sir Charles Phipps.[24] It was essential that the Queen had someone confidential to take custody of her papers. Gossiping away to Delane, as was his wont, Torrington confided that Phipps and Grey 'although they keep up appearances *are at war*'. There was no unanimity of advice being offered the Queen and he expected that 'there will be trouble before long'. Everywhere people were whispering in corners, giving their own personal view of how and by whom the Prince's former roles should be taken over; 'but there is *no head* in the palace,' continued Torrington and he heard a different story from everyone.[25]

The true extent of the Queen's voracious, unquenchable mourning, as everyone now could see, was only just beginning to unravel. 'They cannot tell what I have lost,' she kept insisting, levelling the barrage of her grief at her devoted and uncomplaining half-sister Feodora, Princess Alice and Augusta Bruce – four women in black, who sat silently over meals together, day in, day out, all words of consolation long since exhausted. It was clear to Phipps that the Queen was incapable of thinking straight about anything: 'Her grief *gnaws* to the *very* core of her heart into the *very depth* of *her soul*!' True, Victoria did what she was asked by her doctors in order to sustain her health, but she was obsessed with one thought: to die, to 'join what was the *sun shine* of her *existence*, the light of *her life*'.[26] At the end of the year she gave instructions to the Lord Chamberlain that the public mourning for the Prince Consort should be 'for the longest term in modern times'; members of the royal household would not be allowed to appear in public out of mourning for a year.[27] Royal watchers in the press were becoming apprehensive, with the London correspondent of the *New York Times* already predicting that the Queen's seclusion would be 'as absolute as is possible'. 'My own belief,' he added, 'is that the glory of her reign is departed.' 'I have no hope that *she* will keep up her reputation now,' echoed Harriet Martineau – a regular, anonymous correspondent of the *Daily News* – 'Her temper is *not* cured; & of course we all fear for her brain . . . those who know what *his* trials were must have more depressing fears.'[28]

On New Year's Eve, looking out over the River Thames as the clocks struck midnight, the diarist Arthur Munby recalled events of the past two weeks. The whole nation had seemed 'sublimed by a noble sorrow and a noble anxiety, into a purity and oneness that I never remember to have seen before . . . England, knit together as one man by grief and indignation, has poured out its heart . . . in a passion of sympathy and love and veneration for the Queen, for which mere loyalty is a cold name indeed.' But for how long would that loyalty last, with a queen now in the deepest retreat from her public?

For Victoria, the days of her life at Osborne passed as one, in utter darkness and stark despair. And it was only now, as people gathered to lament the year that mercifully was over and raise a hopeful glass to a better one to come, that the full horror of the Queen's solitude began to sink in. For, despite being surrounded by loyal family and retainers, Queen Victoria had in reality 'none to cast herself upon and weep out her Soul'. Recalling a story he had once heard about the islanders of Honolulu, the country parson Robert Hawker noted in his diary that in the Pacific they called a king 'by a word which signified The Lonely One'. This was because 'their lofty place is shared by none and they are therefore solitary above their people'. Sympathy, he added, 'can only be complete among those who are equal', and who was the Queen's equal now that Albert had gone?[29] 'Oh! Who is so lonely as she,' echoed the *Daily News*, as one thought gained currency over and above all the many expressions of shock and grief and apprehension that had filled the press for the sixteen days since Albert's death. It lingered in every heart and on everyone's lips. In the days to come, they all asked, 'How will the Queen bear it?'[30]

PART TWO

The Broken-Hearted Widow

CHAPTER NINE

'All Alone!'

'What a sad new Year, what a cloud more impenetrable than ever has settled upon it,' wrote Lady Augusta Bruce to her family on 8 January 1862 as she contemplated the cheerless landscape at Osborne with the winter sea roaring in the distance. 'I can not tell you what it is to be here, to watch day by day the progress of this agony, and to see rising up one by one all the trials and difficulties that such a terrible visitation brings with it.' Osborne was still full of relatives who had arrived for Albert's funeral, yet for all of them New Year's Day had been, according to Lady Bruce, an intensely bleak one: 'The whole house seems like Pompeii, the life suddenly extinguished.'

For Queen Victoria, the New Year – like Christmas – brought only aching memories of what had gone before. 'This day last year found us so perfectly happy and now!!! Last year music woke us, little gifts, new year's wishes, brought in by [my] maid, and then given to dearest Albert. The children waiting with their gifts in the next room.'[1] All was so terribly, irrevocably changed; the clock of Victoria's happy life had stopped on 14 December 1861. Like Dickens's Miss Havisham, she had no desire to move forward but only to remain in stasis, locked into that terrible moment of loss, in perpetuity. She confidently expected to die soon, and made her will and arranged guardians for her children. Meanwhile, in anticipation of that longed-for day, she sank into a state of lethargy and gloom, enshrouding herself in the veil of widowhood as the sunshine of her marriage faded into the interminable monochrome of her new 'sad and solitary life'.[2] Day after day the great, inconsolable bouts of Victoria's weeping could be heard along the corridors of Osborne.

She had, at first, resolved differently: she would not give way to despair. Shortly after Albert had died, she had gathered her children round her and told them, 'Your father never blamed me but once and that was for my grief about my mother – that it was selfish . . . I will not do so now,' she promised them, 'I will have affliction, but not gloom.'[3] She had tried hard to remember those words of advice that Albert had given her after they left Balmoral the previous October – to be less occupied with herself and her own feelings. She had copied his letter carefully into the 'Album Consolativum' that she now kept as a compendium of personal consolation. Here Albert's wise counsel was joined by copious extracts from Tennyson's *In Memoriam* – its content so closely mirroring her own feelings on loss:

> Far off thou art, but ever nigh;
> I have thee still, and I rejoice;
> I prosper, circled with thy voice;
> I shall not lose thee tho' I die.
> (Canto CXXX)[4]

There were verses too by Goethe and Schiller, extracts from letters, and sermons and hymns – even by notable Roman Catholics such as John Henry Newman and Cardinal Manning. All were carefully copied mainly by her daughters or ladies-in-waiting in the neatest of handwriting, interspersed with a few in Victoria's own inimitable scrawl with significant words heavily underlined. The small gold-tooled, morocco-leather album with its gilt clasp went everywhere with her; by June it had already been filled.[5]

The courage needed to face up to her lonely task as monarch had, meanwhile, totally deserted her; her relationship with Albert had been crucial to her own sense of self and the way she lived her life, and without him she was rudderless. Indeed, her whole life had been one long pattern of reliance on others: during her childhood she had become used to incessant surveillance, imposed by her mother. She had never had to stand and act alone until the first months of her reign, after which she had quickly let go of her early promise as an active queen, to accept the guidance of a powerful man – her Prime Minister, Lord Melbourne. Then Albert had come along and, as she was sidelined by pregnancy after pregnancy, he had assumed many of the onerous responsibilities of state on her behalf. However, it went against the grain for Victoria not to fulfil her role conscientiously, as he had so assiduously trained her, but alone as she now was, she was so mistrustful of her own judgement that it was much easier simply to give way to grief and do nothing. Every act, every decision seemed so daunting without Albert. All she could do was filter things through the prism of what he would have said, or done, or wanted. Carl Ruland noted the dramatic change in the once-wilful queen: 'she used to say "I never will do it," and now it is "How shall I be able to do it?"'[6] Having lived her life in a unique position of power as a woman – enacting, initiating, granting permission and, when she chose, withholding it – Victoria was presented by Albert's death for the first time with something totally outside her control. She felt angry, worthless, inadequate and guilty too: that perhaps in her own self-obsession she had omitted to take her husband's failing health seriously enough and might even, somehow, have done something to prevent it. Unending grief was therefore not just an escape from responsibilities she did not wish to shoulder alone, but also a necessary form of harsh self-punishment.

'There is no one to call me Victoria now,' she had wept, though this is the popularly quoted version of a far more wrenching form of the loss of intimacy, as she expressed it to her German-speaking relatives: 'I have no one now in the world to call me "du",' she had told Princess Mary Adelaide.[7] The terrifying loneliness of her position was brought home to her even more at night when she missed Albert's presence the most. She was still young (only forty-three), still a sexual being full of longing: 'What a dreadful going to bed! *What* a contrast to that tender lover's love. *All alone!*'[8] The great waves of debilitating grief were relentless; how she envied her daughter Vicky, who had a husband 'on whose bosom you can pillow your head when all seems dark'.[9]

For the rest, Victoria remained calm and quiet and largely uncomplaining. No exhortations to find comfort in her children moved her. 'The children of lovers are orphans,' observed the writer Robert Louis Stevenson, and in Victoria's case it was only too apparent that her love for Albert had transcended her love for all her children, who remained the 'poor half' of her life.[10] Albert had thought it 'a pity', he told her in 1856, that she found no consolation in their company, and Victoria did not deny it. She was quite candid when Lord Hertford arrived for a private visit: 'she had never taken pleasure in the society of her children as most mothers did,' she admitted to him, 'but always preferred being alone with him [Albert].' It was Albert who 'gave all the gaiety and life to the house'. It made her so angry to hear people talk of '*her* management of the children, of *her* attention to business, and *her* doing this and doing that when they ought to have known it was all *him*, that he was the life and soul of the family and indeed of all her counsels'.[11]

Feeling as she did, Victoria made it much harder for her children to come to terms, in their own way, with the loss of their father. Rather than comforting them in their grief, she punished them, expecting them to share in the levels of her own conspicuous, unrelenting mourning. In so doing she cast a blight over their lives for many years to come. No one – in the family or entourage – was to be allowed any respite: she sent out an 'injunction' making clear the impossibility of her ever again joining in the 'frivolities of court'.[12] Personal pleasure, light-heartedness and laughter in her presence were absolutely frowned on, as too was all but the most necessary social contact. Anything more frayed her nerves. She who had so loved dancing as a young woman would never again attend a ball or give one. The private theatricals and fancy-dress parties that the children had so enjoyed during their father's lifetime were forbidden, and none of the family would be allowed to appear at the opening ceremony of the 1862 Great London Exhibition, despite their father's close involvement in its planning. The only exception made was for four-year-old Beatrice, whose disarming candour and innocent good humour were impossible to repress. 'Cousin Mary, am I too merry,' the little girl whispered guiltily to Princess Mary Adelaide when she visited in January. Poor Beatrice, 'prattling' amidst all 'the sad grave faces' as Mary noted, had heard her siblings wishing they could die and go to be with Papa. 'I don't wish to die,' Beatrice told her, 'I want to live, and want Mama to take care of me.'[13] 'I always hope her little innocent cheerfulness may be one of the first things to rouse the poor Queen,' wrote the Duchess of Wellington, but far from it: with time, even the irrepressible Beatrice succumbed to the overwhelming atmosphere of gloom at home, becoming strangely solemn and introverted.[14]

Weak and exhausted she may have been, but in a perverse way Victoria's thin, pale appearance made her look younger, more vulnerable, as though recovering from a severe illness. Indeed, she rather liked it when people told her how thin she had grown – it was comforting confirmation of the visible depths of her grief and her feminine frailty. Her sister Feodora and Princess Alice tried repeatedly to persuade her to engage in the gentlest of occupational therapy, some light reading or perhaps browsing the newspapers; she might even like to dictate her reminiscences. But nothing could rouse Victoria from her lethargy. She was suffering what no doubt today would be diagnosed as clinical depression. It left her incapable of doing anything more than reading the odd letter, taking short walks in the garden and talking – endlessly, obsessively – of Albert, as though by constant mention of his name she was keeping him alive, maintaining a seamless continuity between his death and her life, the only difference being that he was now invisible and she had yet to reach the end of her own mortal journey.[15] Soon there would be no avoiding a return to Windsor and to affairs of state and she dreaded the pressures already being put on her: 'The things of this life are of no interest to the Queen,' she told Lord John Russell wanly, but the excuse – for all the ready sympathy offered her – would not wash with ministers anxious for her to resume her official duties.[16]

For most of those first weeks of grinding melancholy at Osborne the Queen kept almost totally to the company of Alice, Feodora, her most trusted lady-in-waiting Augusta Bruce and her head-dresser, Marianne Skerrett. Augusta Bruce's growing power as right-hand woman did not go unnoticed, and was not without occasional jealous comment. When Vicky arrived in February she noted that Augusta Bruce had more influence over her mother than anyone else, 'simply because she said "Yes, Ma'am" to everything and that if she said "No, Ma'am" a few times the Queen would cease to think her the paragon of cleverness she now did'.[17] Augusta Bruce had been a lady-in-waiting for fifteen years; after Albert died she was offered a highly privileged, permanent place with the Queen (as opposed to the normal three-month periods on and off duty). Many of the Queen's other (unmarried) ladies during that first year never saw her from one day to the next and found their imposed idleness enervating. For, aside from Bruce and Skerrett, Victoria now demonstrated a decided preference for the company of widows such as the Duchess of Sutherland, Lady Ely and Lady Barrington, and, when she visited from Germany, her devoted friend Countess Blücher.[18]

But it was not just the well-born ladies-in-waiting and of the bedchamber who became the Queen's confidantes, for her dresser Marianne Skerrett played a key role. She was a tiny, thin creature, shorter even than the Queen (under five feet) and 'comically plain', but a good linguist and fiercely intelligent. Appointed in 1837 when Victoria came to the throne, Skerrett, a woman 'of the greatest discretion and straight-forwardness', became one of Victoria's most intimate and protective friends and played an increasingly important role, performing various personal and administrative tasks for her, as well as reading to her.[19] When Skerrett retired, Annie Macdonald (the widow of a footman), who had been Prince Albert's general cleaner, was promoted to wardrobe-maid and largely took over Skerrett's role. All of these women would increasingly be called upon – often unreasonably so – to fill the void of the Queen's loneliness, kowtowing to her often bullying demands during the first difficult ten years of her retreat. They formed a human barrier, used by Victoria to protect herself from what she saw as the unkind onslaughts of demanding ministers, and carried messages back and forth to male members of her entourage when she did not feel up to dealing with them.[20] Lady Ely rather enjoyed showing off her trusted position of important go-between – often on highly sensitive political matters – and delighted in whispering confidences in the Queen's ear in front of the other ladies. In general, though, self-effacement was an unwritten prerequisite of the job, as too was all thought of personal aspirations such as marriage. None of the ladies-in-waiting were supposed to keep diaries when on duty, but of course several did; with life at court so deadening and restricted, it was one of the few pursuits left to them.[21] The Duchess of Athole, with her vigorous common sense, was perhaps the most resilient and least awestruck of the Queen's ladies, under-standing the utter folly of trying to contradict Victoria's wishes and learning how to cleverly manage her intractability. The Queen *would* have her way and they had all better spare themselves the pain of trying to contradict it. Victoria in return recognised the Duchess's unique value and refused to allow her to retire.[22]

While the well-rehearsed commiserations of her ladies were all too readily available, Victoria found greater comfort in the honest words of ordinary people, who had sent endless 'expressions of universal admira-tion and appreciation of beloved Albert' since the day he died. 'Even the poor people in small villages, who don't know me, are shedding tears for me, as if it were their own private sorrow,' she noted in her journal.[23] When, in mid-January, there was a terrible disaster at the Hartley Colliery in Northumberland, in which 205 men and boys trapped below ground had suffocated and died, a distraught Victoria was quick to share in the sorrow of their wives and mothers, sending £200 to the disaster fund with her 'tenderest sympathies' and telling them that 'her own misery only makes her feel the more for them'.[24] On 11 January the Home Secretary, Sir George Grey, presented her with some of the many hundreds of addresses of condolence received from municipalities and other bodies across the country. There were in addition dozens of letters received at Windsor from heads of state – from the Emperor of Mexico to the Sultan of Turkey – all with their stereotypical expressions of grief and consolation, inscribed in immaculate copperplate handwriting. But none of them had the directness and honesty of the letter from the American President, received from Washington in February. 'The offer of condolence in such cases is a customary ceremony, which has its good uses,' he wrote, 'though it is conventional and may sometimes be even insincere.' Despite the recent political crisis, the bond of friendship between Britain and the USA ran deep and the American people deplored the Prince's death, sympathising in the Queen's 'irreparable bereavement with an unaffected sorrow'. Certain that 'the Divine Hand that has wounded, is the only one that can heal', he therefore commended Victoria and her family to God's mercies, concluding, with utter sincerity, 'I remain Your Good Friend, Abraham Lincoln'.[25]

It was the end of January before news reached South Africa via the paddle steamer *Jin Kie*, en route to China from Plymouth. It 'created great consternation here', wrote Lady Duff Gordon. Flags in the harbour were immediately lowered to half-mast and forty-two minute guns at the British fortress at Cape Town were fired as a mark of respect that evening. General mourning for the Prince in the Cape was called for the 1 February, and Lady Gordon noted that deep mourning was 'more general than in an average village of the same size at home' in England.[26] She also noted in particular the response of many Malays in the Cape, who 'hope the people will take much care of her, now she is alone', their feelings being 'all about her' – the Queen – rather than the dead man. In Penang in the Straits Settlement, British official Orfeur Cavenagh remembered the Prince's death casting 'a great gloom across the station'; all the residents of standing met to prepare a joint message of condolence to the Queen, reiterating their 'loyal attachment and sincere affection' for her in her affliction. On the island of Madagascar, which had come under British influence, King Radama ordered his court to go into mourning for Prince Albert for twenty-one days, as well as the firing of twenty-one cannons at Antananarivo and Tamtave.[27]

With the electrical telegraph in its infancy, it took some weeks before responses started trickling in from the Antipodes. The *Star of India*, an emigrant ship from Liverpool, brought the news to Australia and from there it was passed to New Zealand. A poignant response from Maori chiefs eventually wended its way back to London via the Governor of New Zealand. 'O Victoria, our Mother!' it lamented:

We, your Maori children, are now sighing in sorrow together with you
. . . who hast nourished us, your ignorant children of this island, even to

this day! We have just heard the crash of the huge-headed forest tree, which has untimely fallen, ere it had attained its full growth of greatness . . . Yes, thou the pillar that didst support my palace has been borne to the skies. Oh, my beloved! You used to stand in the very prow of the war canoe, inciting all others to noble deeds. Where, oh physicians, was the power of your remedies? What, oh priests, availed your prayers? For I have lost my love, no more can he revisit this world.²⁸

But it was one of Albert's own children, Prince Alfred, who was the last in the royal family to be given the news of his father's death, which finally reached him at sea off the coast of Mexico in early January, relayed to his governor, Major John Cowell, by a Spanish steamship, the *Ceballor*. But Affie did not arrive back in England until 16 February 1862.

★   ★   ★

From the moment Prince Albert's death was announced, British manu-facturing went into mass production of every conceivable kind of commemorative item: plaques and busts, plates, handkerchiefs, pot lids, jugs, book marks, even special mourning teasets, all feeding into the middle-class fashion for extravagant mourning. But this was nothing compared with the ambitious plans nursed by Victoria for 'numberless' memorials to her dear departed.²⁹ The process had already begun with the preservation of Prince Albert's rooms at Windsor, Osborne and Balmoral, as well as the King's Room in which he had died. Nothing connected to Albert and his memory and their life together was to be overlooked, even down to the first bouquet he had ever given Victoria, and her bridal wreath, which – like Miss Havisham's – was now slowly, inexorably turning to dust.³⁰ The cost of maintaining this meticulous status quo, and Victoria's insistence on keeping on all of Albert's personal retinue (albeit in reassigned roles), was placing additional strain on her overstretched finances. But Augusta Bruce understood precisely the impetus behind it: 'It was idolatry, but I am sure that God allowed and pardons it.'³¹ And the idols to Albert were many: in the months that followed, the Queen commissioned numerous busts and statuettes of him – in marble and in bronze – to be placed in her various homes as well as presented as gifts to her family and members of the household. A marble bust of Albert by William Theed, and garlanded with wreaths of immor-telles, became the centrepiece of a series of photographs Victoria commis-sioned from William Bambridge of herself and her children taken

at Windsor; several even more poignant ones of his mother and Alice
were taken by the young Prince Alfred when he arrived home from sea.[32]
With what some considered undue haste – given Victoria's absolute
retirement from society – mourning photographs of the Queen and her
children were being marketed as *cartes de visite* for public consumption
as early as March, providing an almost voyeuristic glimpse into her private
grief. The *London Review* decried these perversely distasteful, intimate
images and the role of the camera in spying on such 'sacred feelings . . .
to commercial account'.[33] But in fact Victoria *wanted* people to know
how grief-stricken she was; she wanted them to understand the great
gaping chasm in her life. By allowing the nation to see her grief she was
keeping Albert alive in their memories too. Many of these photographs,
showing even little Beatrice decked out in baby black mourning, were
beautifully framed and distributed by Victoria to friends, family and
politicians alike. Other photographs were set as miniatures into pieces
of gold and enamelled jewellery, such as lockets, bracelets, rings and
stick pins, by Garrard's, the royal jewellers, for the Queen, her children
and other favoured recipients.[34] A locket with Albert's hair was sent to
Leopold in Cannes with the instructions to wear it 'attached to a string
or chain round your neck'; Victoria also enclosed one of Papa's pocket
handkerchiefs, which he was instructed to 'keep constantly with you'.[35]

As early as 4 January, Queen Victoria had a conversation with General
Grey about her plans for a statue for Balmoral, and soon afterwards
began looking at sketches by William Theed of Albert in highland dress.[36]
In so doing she was immediately contravening one of her husband's
most explicit wishes, expressed in the wake of the excessive memorialisation of the Duke of Wellington in 1852: 'If I should die before you, do
not, I beg, raise even a single marble image to my name.' He had resisted
all suggestion that a statue of himself be placed in Hyde Park to celebrate
the success of the Great Exhibition of 1851. 'I would rather not be made
the prominent feature of such a monument,' he told Lord Granville, 'as
it would both disturb my quiet rides in Rotten Row to see my own face
staring at me, and if (as is very likely) it became an artistic monstrosity,
like most of our monuments, it would upset my equanimity to be
permanently ridiculed and laughed at in effigy.'[37] Having professed that
she would fulfil her husband's wishes to the letter, Victoria nevertheless
immediately set about spearheading a concerted nationwide memorialisation that would have appalled him. Lord Palmerston gave his full
support for a statue of the Prince 'of heroic size' to be erected on a

suitable site in London, and persuaded Parliament to agree to £50,000 towards the fund; anything less seemed paltry in Victoria's eyes, for she herself envisioned a great obelisk. Vicky, whose own ideas closely mirrored those of her father, objected, finding the idea lacking in artistic taste. As too did Lord Clarendon; the Queen, he remarked wearily, 'has no more notion of what is right and pure in art than she has of the Chinese grammar'.[38] Nevertheless the Duke of Argyll offered a 120-foot-long red granite stone weighing 600 tons from his Ross of Mull quarries. But the Lord Mayor, William Cubitt, doubted 'whether the roads would not fall in under such a weight or whether wheels could be made strong enough' to transport it.

Another plan, according to Lord Torrington, who was put in charge of inviting subscriptions to the fund, was melting down old cannons and 'making a column 400 feet high'.[39] It was also suggested that Cleopatra's Needle (languishing in Alexandria since being presented to the British in 1819 by Mohammad Ali, in gratitude for Nelson's victory on the Nile) should be brought to England for this purpose. This idea too was rapidly abandoned, as a Prince Consort National Memorial Fund Committee was established under Cubitt and the triumvirate of Sir Charles Eastlake (President of the Royal Academy) and a reluctant Lord Clarendon and Lord Derby, both of whom felt ill equipped for the task to which they had been co-opted. The committee's role would be to choose a design and fund-raise, through a network of sub-committees across Britain, for a lasting memorial to Albert, 'commemorative of his many virtues, and expressive of the gratitude of the people'. The obvious location for such a monument was Hyde Park, somewhere near the site of the Great Exhibition and just up from the Victoria and Albert Museum in South Kensington. Henry Cole, with whom the Prince had worked closely on the development of the museum and the planning of the Great Exhibition, suggested a more ambitious project to be located in the area: a whole range of institutions covering science, art and literature – an Albert University, which would serve as 'a palace of all learning, over whose gate his name should be written'.[40]

The Albert Memorial project was dogged by controversy from the outset, with the *Morning Post* firing a broadside at the committee, accusing them of favouritism over and above the wishes of the government. Lord Clarendon buckled at the onerous task foisted on him:

> we shall be inundated with designs of the late Consort in the robes of The Garter upon some furious and non-descript animal that will be called

a horse, and Albert Baths and Washhouses, and the good Prince inaugurating some drinking pump with the Q[ueen] and the royal children round
him looking thirsty: etc. etc.[41]

With the same thought in mind, Charles Dickens had refused point-blank
when invited by Henry Cole to join the committee. Despite his loyalty
to the Queen, he professed himself 'much shocked by the rampant
toadyism that has been given to the four winds on that subject'. He had
no faith in such a memorial, he admitted: 'With this heresy in my heart,
how can I represent myself as one of the Orthodox?'[42]

Many local municipal bodies up and down the country also broke
rank and ignored the national appeal, determined to make their own
mark locally. Lord Torrington feared that the impact of the national
memorial would therefore be dissipated, resulting in every town in
England having 'some miserable work of art, the production of a relation of the then mayor – aided possibly by some of the Corporation
who are bricklayers, painters, and what not'. Such 'local acts of folly',
in his view, would ruin the objectives of a grand and unifying national
work, but nevertheless local authorities went ahead with their 'little town
jobs' and raised statues to the Prince, not to mention renaming a plethora
of streets, pubs, tenement buildings, bridges, parks and wharves in
Albert's memory.[43]

Meanwhile Victoria had already initiated her own personal architectural project: the royal mausoleum at Frogmore. In accordance with
Albert's wishes, she settled on a Romanesque design inspired by the
mausoleum erected in Coburg for his father, Ernst I. It was to be built
by the architect Albert Jenkins Humbert from a design by the German
Ludwig Grüner, the two men having worked together on the Duchess
of Kent's mausoleum. It featured an octagonal copper dome over a
cruciform base, and would be constructed in British granite and
Portland stone with an interior decorated in the style of Albert's
favourite Renaissance painter, Raphael. From Berlin, Vicky liaised
closely on the design and execution of the project, wishing 'to
contribute in some measure to beautifying it'.[44] A favourite sculptor
of the Queen and Prince Albert, Baron Carlo Marochetti, came to
Osborne in January to work on a model of Albert's head from the
Theed death-mask, which would form the basis of a marble effigy of
the Prince wearing his robes of the Order of the Garter, to be placed
in the mausoleum in due course (Victoria's effigy was made

simultaneously, so that she would not look older than the eternally beautiful Albert when her own time came).

Excavation of the site began on 27 January, and Victoria began pumping the first of £200,000 of her own money into the project, having seen off one of its more unlikely opponents in Gerald Wellesley, the Dean of Windsor. The Dean, along with other churchmen, had feared that the loss of Albert's coffin from St George's Chapel would undermine its traditional associations with royalty. There was more than enough room: he wanted the side-chapel (now the Albert Memorial Chapel) to serve not just as Albert's memorial, but also as his mausoleum, and even sounded out the architect Gilbert Scott on ways of providing a private covered walkway to and from the chapel for the Queen. However, Victoria resisted, for nothing would deter her from erecting a purpose-built mausoleum for herself and Albert and, in order to spare her from criticism about its undesirability and 'foreignness', it was decided to release no details of the Frogmore project until it was completed.[45] Lord Clarendon was appalled that she had set upon such an insignificant location as 'that morass at Frogmore which is constantly flooded', and later heard that it would be necessary to heat the mausoleum all year round 'to keep off decay'; Bertie had already announced that he had no intention of being buried in such a place.[46]

*   *   *

From early January 1862 the Queen began receiving private visits at Osborne from individual politicians such as Lord Clarendon, who despite being out of office was her most trusted friend in Parliament, 'the *only* person who had quite understood her feelings and put himself in imagination exactly in her situation'.[47] Clarendon spent an exhausting day at the receiving end of her outpourings of grief, closely followed by those of Dr Clark, Princess Alice, King Leopold, Sir Charles Phipps and Bertie. For the time being, however, Victoria could only tolerate infrequent meetings with selected members of the Privy Council.[48] On 6 January she was nursed through her first such meeting by Arthur Helps, clerk of the Privy Council, whom she had already enlisted to edit a collection of Albert's speeches. Sitting in a darkened room swathed in black, she conducted the meeting through an open connecting door. Her ministers in the next room were obliged to shout, for fear the Queen could not hear. The official business was quickly wrapped up in a couple of paragraphs, with Helps even reading out the word 'approved' on Victoria's behalf.

She had been greatly relieved to be informed by Palmerston on 9 January that the Trent Affair had finally been resolved and that her husband's eleventh-hour intervention had contributed to a peaceful settlement of the dispute. Her ministers were by now extremely anxious that she should take up her dispatch boxes once more and return to the long-standing protocol on which she and Albert had insisted – of reviewing and commenting on every official document before it was sent out. For the time being Phipps marked the important passages for her, and that was all she would read. But she felt utterly unequal to the task; her 'reason', she feared, would not hold up to it. Nor would it hold up to the prospect of a change of government that was in the air: 'that would be what she could not stand'; it could well induce her to 'throw everything up', she warned Clarendon. The quickest way of killing her – 'and most *thankful* to them she would be for that result' – would be for Lord Derby, leader of the Opposition, to push for a general election. Nevertheless, it was the end of January before Victoria saw her Prime Minister, Lord Palmerston, for the first time since Albert's death. The old man was quite overwhelmed when he arrived at Osborne and could hardly speak for his tears, a fact that Victoria found unnerving when she thought of how she and Albert had so despised him in the past. But she also took comfort in it, for she liked to see others as grief-stricken as she was. 'I would hardly have given Lord Palmerston credit for entering so entirely into my anxieties,' she remarked, which is probably why she forgave him for overlooking the correct protocols of full mourning – by turning up in a brown overcoat, light-grey trousers, green gloves and blue shirt-studs.[49] Palmerston's genuinely expressed concern, his solicitousness over her health and whether she was eating enough went some way to easing the inevitable meetings with her other ministers, as too did Benjamin Disraeli's panegyric to the Prince when Parliament reconvened on 6 February. It prompted a grateful response from Victoria, struggling to come to terms with 'the afflicting dispensation of Providence which bows me to the earth'.[50] By now she had been obliged to resume the minimum of official business, but felt totally overwhelmed: 'so much to do, so many boxes, letters'; never before had she had to deal with so many responsibilities on a regular, daily basis.[51]

On 14 February, Victoria was greatly cheered by the arrival of the pregnant Vicky from Prussia. Yet despite her eldest daughter's presence, she was reluctant, even then, to allow an exhausted Alice out of her sight. In the end she was prevailed on to agree that Alice should go and rest with close friends, the Belgian consul Sylvain Van De Weyer and his wife, at their home near Windsor for ten days. Confronted with her mother's deep desolation and the helplessness of her siblings, Vicky thought they all seemed 'like sheep without a shepherd'. Her mother was as much in love with Papa 'as though she had married him yesterday', she told Fritz in Berlin. Vicky struggled hard with her grief; her mother's alone was more than she could contend with: 'there is always the empty room, the empty bed, she always sleeps with Papa's coat over her and his dear red dressing-gown beside her and some of his clothes in the bed'. As for Osborne, a home of which Vicky had till now had happy memories: 'It is nothing but a great vault; everything is so different, the old life, the old customs have gone'.[52] Like everyone else, she was greatly alarmed at how difficult it was to manage her mother or contradict her in the slightest degree; but even more alarming was Victoria's continuing, undisguised dislike for Bertie.

During his stay at Osborne, Uncle Leopold had done his best to try and reconcile mother and son, to no avail. Indeed, Victoria had openly admitted to Lord Hertford when he visited that she could never forget that her eldest son 'had been the chief cause of his father's illness'; she never could see Bertie 'without a shudder', she told Vicky. As soon as Bertie entered the room, Victoria became visibly agitated; his presence irritated her and from now on he would effectively be banished except for brief holidays. Such intransigence was 'a positive monomania with her', in the view of Lord Clarendon.[53] Lord Hertford begged Victoria to take her son into her confidence and 'give him something to do besides shooting and hunting – something that would make him feel himself of use to her and would improve his character'.[54] But Victoria would have none of it; there was no question of Bertie taking the place of his sainted father as her adviser, or of her giving him any useful employment in preparation for his own role one day as monarch. Palmerston presciently confided to Clarendon that he saw her 'unconquerable aversion' to her son and heir as a major problem 'looming in the distance'.[55] She had already resolved to go ahead with Albert's plans – shelved on his death – to send Bertie on a tour of Egypt and the Holy Land. He sailed from Osborne on 6 February; in his absence his mother would continue planning her son's road to salvation: marriage to Alexandra of Denmark. She and Vicky vetted the Danish royal family, gossiping about the Princess's various undesirable relatives and the financial embarrassment of her parents, Prince and Princess Christian, who had only a paltry £800 a year to live on. Nevertheless, as far as Victoria was concerned, Bertie was lucky to have Alexandra, though the prospect of a necessary meeting with the in-laws later in the year at Laeken in Belgium filled her with dread. Worse, though, was the prospect that Bertie, who still seemed utterly indifferent to his future bride, might change his mind. In this event, Victoria had a contingency plan: 'Affie would be ready to take her at once', for she was already sizing up possible other candidates for her second son too.[56] The complexities of royal marriage-brokering were one diversion from which even grief did not keep her.

For the time being, however, Victoria found no joy even in the approach of spring. Referring to herself in the third person, as was her wont, she lamented to Lord Derby that: 'She sees the trees budding, the days lengthening, the primroses coming out, but she thinks herself *still* in the month of December.'[57] The Duchess of Sutherland, who had joined Victoria's household on her accession in 1837, could see the potentially detrimental impact on the monarchy of the Queen's retreat. Whilst being sensitive, as a fellow widow, to Victoria's grief, the Duchess took advantage of her position of trust in these early months to try and persuade Victoria to return to her public duties. The Duchess's friend William Gladstone had written to her in alarm, 'we cannot afford to create an intense degree of pity for the woman at the cost of her character as a Queen, in which above all things balance and measure are required'. Whilst agreeing with Gladstone, Sutherland perceptively pointed out a necessary shift in how the public viewed the Queen – from active monarch to a revered national symbol of grieving; 'It is *The* Widow speaking to Her children,' she argued.[58] Several of Victoria's ladies-in-waiting already shared the Duchess's apprehensions about the Queen's insatiable commemoration of Albert. It seemed an 'unhealthy state of mind'; and one of them, when coming off her three-month period of duty, informed Charles Dickens that the Queen insisted on 'striking out the word "late" from all formal mention of him in documents that come before her'. This state of denial extended to the visitors' book at royal residences, where Albert's book was still maintained alongside that of Victoria and visitors were required to sign their names in it just as before, like 'calling on a dead man', as Disraeli noted.[59]

In March, when the mournful processional of the black-garbed royal household arrived back at the 'living grave' of Windsor, Victoria kept a close watch on the careful positioning of every last possession of her husband's in its correct place: his hat and gloves laid out, the handkerchief he last used lying on the sofa, 'the blotting book open with a pen upon it, his watch going, fresh flowers in a glass'. Without fail she daily cast freshly cut white flowers and cypress over the bed in which he had died – an act of display more Catholic than Protestant, as Clarendon noted – as well as stooping down to kiss the pillow whenever she entered. The last thing she did at night before retiring to bed was to kneel and pray by Albert's bed in the Blue Room, her communion with his spirit constant and all-consuming.[60]

Work on the mausoleum, meanwhile, had progressed sufficiently by 15 March (the anniversary of the death of the Duchess of Kent) for the Queen to lay the foundation stone, containing coins and photographs of the Prince, herself and the royal children. The project had raised her spirits: 'She is better, stronger, calmer, more resigned, more courageous and determined to walk in the path of duty,' thought Augusta Bruce.[61] On the given day, in front of 100 members of the royal household and workmen involved in the construction, a dignified Victoria fulfilled her task, 'laying the mortar and knocking the stone three times with the mallet just as any man would' and without shedding a tear. She later recorded her 'trembling steps' as she performed the ceremony, but her subjective view of her 'weakness' was not shared by those who watched; Lord Torrington thought she looked 'like a *young girl* and showed great nerve'.[62]

In addition to the mausoleum, Victoria now had a precious literary commemoration of her husband to cling to. In early January, Tennyson had sent the draft of his promised Dedication to the *Idylls of the King* for approval. The Duchess of Sutherland commended his 'beautiful verses' as 'worthy of the great and tragic subject', recommending one or two minor amendments, after which it was sent to Princess Alice on 13 January. In his verses the Poet Laureate expressed his profound admiration for the Prince as his own 'ideal knight':

> Who reverenced his conscience as his king;
> Whose glory was, redressing human wrongs;
> Who spake no slander, no, nor listen'd to it;
> Who lov'd one only and who clave to her . . .

> Dear to thy land and ours, a Prince indeed,
> Beyond all titles, and a household name,
> Hereafter, through all times, Albert the Good.[63]

The seductive image of Albert as the perfect, gentle knight of old, a heroic figure who wore 'the white flower of a blameless life', put into words Victoria's own long-held romantic fantasies about her husband. The verses, she said, 'soothed her aching, bleeding heart'.[64] Tennyson's idealised vision of Albert would be captured by Edward Henry Corbould in the Queen's favourite posthumous painting of him – as medieval knight in armour sheathing his sword, with the German inscription 'I have fought a good fight; I have finished the struggle; therefore a crown of rectitude is awaiting me' written below. Based on an 1844 portrait of Albert in armour by Robert Thorburn, this watercolour was set into the door of the Blue Room in 1863.[65] Tennyson's Dedication was rapidly taken to their hearts by the British public, setting its stamp on a century's hagiography of the Prince and forming the cornerstone of the cult of the Prince Consort of which Victoria would be the chief votary.

In April 1862, ten years after appointing him Poet Laureate, Victoria finally met her hero Tennyson when he visited her from his home at Farringford, not far from Osborne. Tennyson admitted to the Duke of Argyll to being a 'shy beast' who liked to 'keep to [his] burrow' and he was extremely apprehensive about what seemed an ordeal to come. The Duke reassured him: the Queen liked nothing more than 'natural signs of devotion and sympathy'. He should be guided by his feelings: 'what is *natural* is right – with Her'. He should talk to the Queen 'as you would to a poor Woman in affliction – that is what she likes best.' When the moment finally came, the Queen completely disarmed Tennyson. 'I am like your Mariana now', she told him, in an allusion to one of his poems about a widow who longed to be reunited with her dead husband in a much-repeated lament: 'I am aweary, aweary, / I would that I were dead!'[66] Despite her obvious state of deep melancholy, Tennyson found her sweet and kind; there was an extraordinary stateliness about her that set her apart from other women. He was so overcome by the emotion of the occasion that he could recall little of it later on. For her own part, Victoria had found the poet strange but arresting – 'tall, dark, with a fine head, long black flowing hair and a beard'. He may have been 'oddly dressed', but she had found him totally lacking in pretension.[67] Aware of Tennyson's strong mystical streak, she had had no inhibitions about discussing their shared experience of sudden death: he of his closest friend Arthur Hallam in 1833 and she of Albert. She recognised the poet as a kindred spirit who knew only too well that terrible feeling: the breaking of each 'blank day'.[68] *In Memoriam* had provided her with an emotional literary capsule

that mirrored her own torrent of fluctuating feeling, ranging from resignation, to morbidity, to hope, to anger, to a final overwhelming desire
for reunion with the dead, until which time she – like Tennyson of
Hallam – sought Albert's spirit reflected in everything around her.
Tennyson's portrait of Hallam reminded her greatly of Albert, she told
him – even down to the same blue eyes. 'He would have made a great
King,' Tennyson told her, to which she replied, 'He always said it did
not signify whether he did the right thing or did not, so long as the right
thing was done.'[69] Tennyson came away profoundly impressed with
Victoria's strength of character. A year later he was invited back with
his wife and two sons, on which occasion Emily Tennyson found the
Queen 'small and childlike, full of intelligence and ineffably sweet and
of a sad sympathy'. She too was captivated; Victoria talked 'of all things
in heaven and earth . . . laughed heartily at many things that were said',
but 'shades of pain and sadness' often passed over her face. 'The Queen,'
she concluded, 'is a woman to live and die for.' [70]

CHAPTER TEN

'The Luxury of Woe'

The year 1862 was a very good one for Messrs W. C. Jay's London General Mourning Warehouse. At its prime site on the south-east corner of Oxford Circus it was enjoying a boom in trade as never before in its twenty years of business. Although general public mourning had officially ended on 10 February, there was no let-up in what had become an 'almost incalculable demand' for mourning goods. Victoria herself had already sent out a memorandum explicitly stating that 'The Queen intends to wear her weeds (if she lives) at least till the beginning of 1864.'[1] Her intention to remain in full mourning – of the deepest, dullest crape – for the maximum two years was in itself not exceptional, but merely emphasised an already existing code of mourning observed by many pious widows. But such was the level of public sympathy for her at this time that many of the middle classes decided to follow suit and remain in mourning for longer – not just for the Prince, but, following Victoria's example, for their own deceased relatives.

Victoria soon changed her mind about leaving off mourning after two years, determining that although she might make the transition from the gloomy crape that was favoured in the first stage of mourning, she would remain in black for the rest of her life. She also demanded that her closest ladies-in-waiting remained in black with her when on duty. After the statutory two years, the rest of her female entourage and daughters would be allowed to wear half-mourning of grey, white or the newer shades of lilac, violet and mauve, which had become popular with the introduction of aniline dyes in the mid-1850s. The lugubrious drapes of crape – a matt gauze of silk and cotton tightly crimped like the crêpe paper named after it – were left off by most widows after the first, traditional stage of retreat of a year and a day, and replaced by lighter, shinier black fabrics such as satin and silk thereafter. But for now and throughout 1862 Victoria's children and the entire royal household, down to the footmen, remained in full mourning, and none of them was allowed to appear in public or receive anyone at home unless so dressed. Extra money was made available to less well-off members of her household, such as Marianne Skerrett and the Queen's two dressers and her wardrobe-maids, to buy additional clothes for this extended period of mourning.[2]

Mourning for Prince Albert predictably cast its pall over the London season of 1862, which was, as the theatrical newspaper the *Era* observed, 'at one blow strangled in its birth'. In anticipation, many of the aristocracy stayed put on their country estates that year or went abroad – to the detriment of the London trades that serviced their needs, as well as the theatres and concert halls. That year the mourning houses were the only businesses making money. The Victorian textile trade was in overdrive, offering a vast range of fabrics for mourning: 'black silks, crapes, paramattas, French merinos, Reps, Queen's Cords, Lustres, Barathea, Coburgs, French de Laines', and there was a huge demand too for the dye to make them black.[3]

Thanks to the unprecedented demand for its 'Noir Impériale' black silks and its best patent crape, Jay's had had to substantially enlarge both its 1862 catalogue and its premises on Regent Street.[4] The company's substantial intake of cheap imports, rushed in from the recession-hit trade in France 'under peculiarly advantageous circumstances', meant they could offer them at knock-down prices. French black silk was flying off the shelves at 2s. and 6d. (12.5p) per yard, and Jay's boasted that its stock of family mourning was now the largest in Europe.[5] By importing cheaply from France, Jay's and other mourning warehouses challenged the monopoly of the powerful Courtaulds, an Essex firm established by Huguenot refugees, which had since the early nineteenth century dominated crape manufacture and was even now developing a cheap substitute – the opportunistically named 'Albert Crape' – to cater to growing demand.[6]

Currently on offer at Jay's for the bottom end of the market was a 'complete suit of domestic mourning' at two and a half guineas, suitable for household servants. But for those seeking to indulge in the full 'luxury of woe', Jay's prided itself on ensuring that its morning and dinner dresses, capes and mantles, whilst scrupulously tailored to the distinct stages of bereavement, should follow the latest fashions. 'In the present day our ashes must be properly selected, our garments must be rent to pattern, our sack cloth must be of the finest quality,' observed social commentator Henry Mayhew sardonically after a visit to Jay's; grief, like everything else, counted for nothing if it was not fashionable.[7] With this in mind, Jay's brought out elegant outfits 'in accordance with the strictest Parisian taste and fashion' direct from top fashion houses such as Charles Worth of the rue de la Paix. The protocols were complex: the first year of deep mourning was followed by secondary mourning less dominated by crape; then three months of ordinary mourning (black of livelier fabrics, with ribbon and ornamentation); and finally six months of half-mourning, for which Jay's offered the best French silks in black, white, grey and suitable 'neutral tints'. The company's staff were the souls of discretion and calm within its harmonious, softly carpeted walls.

But Jay's was now facing stiff competition from Peter Robinson's Family Mourning Warehouse across the road in Regent Street, which kept a brougham ready to be dispatched, at a moment's notice, with two black-garbed fitters to the homes of distressed lady clients. Jay's too promised a similar rapid response on the fulfilment of orders, and delivery anywhere in the country. Its seamstresses were provided with hot dinners in Jay's own canteen, but such was the overload that for a time Jay's had to resort to laying on sandwiches and sherry in an adjoining room, so that the overworked seamstresses could 'run in and get a mouthful when they can'. But while Jay's employees enjoyed reasonably good working conditions, excessive workloads took their toll on the eyesight of the beleaguered armies of poor seamstresses working fourteen-hour days in ill-lit back rooms on black fabrics with black thread, which were particularly deleterious to the eyesight.[8]

In the rush to remain fashionable whilst in mourning for Prince Albert, publications such as the *Lady's Magazine* had been quick to feature do-it-yourself patterns for suitable black lace and beaded trimmings, for gowns, or handkerchiefs without their usual lace trimmings, but instead embroidered with mournful symbols such as black and white tears. Even Victoria had one of these, but otherwise she paid little attention to fashion in her own choice of mourning clothes; she was no longer dressing to please anyone. As a result, the Queen's spending on dress decreased noticeably, and with the years the corsets were increasingly left off as her waistline spread, and the same dreary gowns were made up in duplicate by her dressmakers Sarah Ann Unitt and Elizabeth Gieve with fabric from the local draper, Caley's opposite Windsor Castle.[9] The only additional trapping she wore was her widow's 'sad cap', as Beatrice called it, indented at the top in the style of Mary Stuart.[10] Framing her face in a heart shape of crisp white tulle, with a veil of black crape falling away behind, the cap enhanced Victoria's look of resigned, nunlike widowhood and accentuated the image of vulnerability that she sought to cultivate. Beneath her skirts, her white lingerie was threaded with black rather than coloured silk ribbon; black dyes were not yet stable enough to be used on fabrics worn next to the skin without discolouring it. As for jewellery, the Queen's strict rules on black applied equally here. Jet ornaments were de rigueur and dominated at court for the next thirty years or so, though diamonds, amethysts and pearls would be allowed during half-mourning. The Queen also favoured the morbid fashion for lockets and brooches made out of the deceased person's hair.[11] Her strict directives on appropriate jewellery would prompt Sir John Bennett, royal watchmaker and jeweller, who often attended court at Windsor with a selection of his wares, to complain that 'the Queen's deep mourning has utterly spoilt my market. If it were not for the honour of coming to Windsor, I should give it up.'[12]

As the trade in jet mourning jewellery expanded, so did the fortunes of a small fishing village, formerly a whaling port, on the north-east Yorkshire coast, which was the primary source of the best-quality jet. Layers of shale in the sea coast around Whitby had long been a rich source of fossils and petrified coniferous wood, of which jet – from a prehistoric tree similar to the monkey puzzle – had been the most prized, once cut and polished. Much of this jet was washed up on the Whitby coast, and was sought out by armies of beachcombers; as demand escalated, it was also mined inland at Bilsdale and Kildale and other locations on the North Yorkshire Moors. Jet from the area had been fashioned into jewellery for centuries (by ancient Britons and the Romans) and long prized as a kind of 'black amber'. With the coming of the railways and the influx of seaside visitors to Whitby, decorative household items made of jet – beaded lampshades, Bible and prayer-book covers, vases, seals, card trays, ink stands, paper knives, board games of all kinds, even doll's house furniture – had been produced as souvenirs and rapidly took their place in Victorian homes.

But it was the jewellery trade that catapulted local Whitby craftsmen and their wares unexpectedly into the limelight. It took considerable skill to work the brittle material without fracturing it, but jet jewellery manufacture rapidly extended to cover every aspect of Victorian mourning accessories, including beading for bodices, hair combs and headdresses, as well as jet birds, insects and clasps for hats and bonnets. In the 1830s the Whitby jet trade had employed around twenty-five people, but by the mid-1850s jet-working had become the principal occupation in the town, with 200 workshops accounting for an annual turnover of around £20,000. Jet ornaments became ever more popular and were shown at the Great Exhibition in 1851, and the trade received a further boost with the elaborate mourning for the Duke of Wellington a year later. In 1855, on a state visit to France, Victoria presented the French empress Eugénie with four bracelets of Whitby jet, setting a fashion soon followed by the French aristocracy.

But it was Prince Albert's death that sparked the meteoric rise of the industry, not just with jet jewellery, but also many commemorative mementoes of Albert: medallions, miniatures and even small busts. Lightweight jet was perfect for producing the kind of large and bulky jet jewellery needed to complement the full-skirted mourning dresses of the day, although during the first year widows did not wear the highly polished version of jet, and those with less money favoured the cheaper vulcanite, or bog oak – from semi-fossilized peat. Onyx and black enamel were also used, and cut-steel and Berlin ironwork were introduced later, but nothing had quite the cachet of the best-quality jet. The income of the Whitby trade rose rapidly to £50,000 in 1862 and reached its peak in the 1870s at £90,000, when it employed more than 1,000 local men and boys as jet-finders, carvers and polishers.[13] The highly paid workers even had their own pub, the Jet Men's Arms on Church Street, and the popularity of jet was further fostered at court by the Marchioness of Normanby on whose husband's estates much of the jet was found.[14]

* * *

The fact that the Queen had, inadvertently, set a fashion trend at the most unlikely and tragic time in her life was of little comfort at court. 'The dreary *painful* effect of all this *mass* of black all round one,' wrote Lady Geraldine Somerset, was 'altogether too inexpressibly sad and dreadful'.[15] They all now dreaded the Queen's return to Balmoral for the first time since Albert's death, which came on 30 April 1862, earlier in the year than her usual visits. Victoria wanted to be as far away as possible from London when the Great London Exposition of 1862 opened on 1 May, because of all its painful reminders of Albert; her son-in-law Fritz came over from Berlin to act as her surrogate. But the pain she felt on entering her Highland home for the first time since her beloved husband's death was acute. The 'agonising sobs' as she was assisted by Alice and Affie past the many everyday objects that reminded her of Albert: 'The stags heads – the rooms – blessed, darling Papa's room – then his coats – his caps – kilts – all, convulsed my poor shattered frame.'[16] Most of her time in Scotland was taken up with revisiting the places associated with her happy marriage and finding comfort in the homely sympathies of an old, recently widowed cottager on the estate. Victoria poured out pages of woe to Palmerston: her nerves were 'more shaken even than before,' she told him – he had only to look at her handwriting. No one knew or understood her bitter anguish and suffering. Her existence was pure 'torture'.[17] As the months of her intense, deranged state of grief wore on, with Victoria pausing to remember every significant date, object, memory connected with Albert, to the exclusion of everything else, those unaffected by such profound levels of grief found it harder and harder to sympathise.

But how could the vast majority of Victoria's staff and ministers begin to show sympathy for the turmoil, the sheer disorientation of her very personal sense of loss? She was after all the Queen and head of state; and in a court grounded in formality and protocol, they could hardly give her a hug or hold her hand, or offer the kind of intimate consoling gestures seen in normal families. Queen Victoria's regal authority, in all its terrifying loneliness, precluded that. It was therefore hard to commiserate, and all the Queen's entourage could do was carefully watch what they said, as the Duke of Argyll noted when he visited: 'one may easily say things which go against her, even when one least suspects it'. Holding a conversation with the Queen required considerable tact – and patience – for there was only ever one topic of conversation that interested her: Albert. The Duke tried hard to steer Victoria in conversation towards the 'hills, birds, and waterfalls' that he had seen at Balmoral. Such a change of tack would work for a few minutes, he later recalled, and even provoke a watery smile, but inevitably Victoria would turn the topic back to Albert: 'the birds *he* had liked, the roads he had made, his speeches, etc., but all as if he were still with her'.[18] Meanwhile, her forty-third birthday came and went in May in 'utter *loneliness* and *desolation*'. There was only one consolation – 'dear Baby' (Beatrice) – who was 'the bright spot in this dead home'.[19]

For all her stubborn insistence, others did not agree with Victoria's perception of her own physical frailty. When Lord Derby visited her on 16 June he thought she looked much better. Victoria was extremely put out to hear people say this; she had been 'much annoyed at a paragraph to that effect which appeared in *The Times*' and had, reported Derby, 'ordered it to be contradicted'.[20] She did not want to look or feel better and was convinced that she ate nothing and never slept; Lord Clarendon noted that she was even 'anxious that all her hair should be grey', as though by becoming so it would define her unending grief. Victoria had very good reason not to wish to recover, for when this happened she would be expected once more to take up her onerous ceremonial responsibilities as monarch – only this time alone, a thing she dreaded. This was not what she was used to: she wanted everyone else to shoulder her burden for her, to take care of *her*, as Albert had done. Her mind was set, as Phipps confided to Gladstone: 'I hope and believe that Her Majesty's health is not in that precarious state in which her Grief makes her almost wish it to be.'[21] For all her protestations and hypochondria, there were signs that Victoria's exceptionally resilient constitution – the 'vein of iron' that Lady Lyttleton back in 1844 had observed as the hallmark of her tenacious character[22] – was fighting back, but on 20 June she resolutely refused to acknowledge her Silver Jubilee. 'Beloved Albert had wished Fetes to take place in honour of it', but no, it had 'passed in complete silence'.[23] Her prolonged state of grief was making her unreasonable, irrational, impossible, in the view of those on the outside looking in. But Victoria was unable to help herself. She could not, however, ignore her daughter Alice's impending marriage at Osborne in July. It would be a wretched business and she wished it were 'years off', she told Vicky. She already expected it to be a 'dreadful, awful day' for her, with her broken heart and shattered nerves. Matters were made worse when Louis's aunt, Mathilde, Grand Duchess of Hesse, died shortly beforehand: 'The Angel of Death still follows us,' wrote Victoria, 'so now Alice's marriage will be even more gloomy.'[24]

* * *

Louis of Hesse was not the best, top-drawer royal bridegroom Victoria and Albert had hoped for; like Bertie's fiancée Alexandra, he was the product of a rather impoverished princely house that wasn't quite up to scratch – and, of course, not a patch on beloved Fritz, Crown Prince of Prussia. A couple of weeks before the wedding Victoria went to inspect Alice's trousseau. It was 'nothing but black gowns'.[25] In her present 'reduced state' she would not have allowed the marriage for another year, had not Albert already planned it, and had done so on the understanding that Alice would spend half the year with her, making over to her daughter and Louis the use of Clarence House for the purpose.

(Victoria was soon to be disappointed in her anticipation of having a married daughter to hand and a useful son-in-law around the house, for Louis's modest income would not stretch to the expense of living in London.)

As for Alice herself, just turned nineteen and still far from recovered from the stress of her father's death and the ceaseless demands made on her by her mother, she had been close to breaking point. Lord Clarendon admired her tenacity: 'there is not such another girl in a 1000,' he told the Duchess of Manchester. Despite being 'boxed up in a gilt cage all her life', Alice, for all her youth, had 'such sound principles, so great judgement and such knowledge of the world'; his only regret was that 'she is going with a dull boy to a dull family in a dull country'. He had a presentiment that she would not be happy.[26] But Alice could at least look forward to seeing her dear brother Bertie, back from his tour of the Holy Land in time for the ceremony. Bertie's return was not, however, a source of joy for Victoria. Before he arrived she sent a missive to Bertie's governor, General Bruce, telling him to warn the Prince that on his return he should be careful not to indulge in his mother's presence in 'worldly, frivolous, gossiping kind of conversation'. The Prince must be prepared to face 'in a proper spirit, the cureless melancholy of his poor home'.[27]

The morning of 1 July 1862 broke dull and windy; Alice had spent the previous night sharing her mother's room, listening to her toss and turn, not in anticipation of her daughter's happiness, but of her own ordeal to come. The modestly sized dining room at Osborne had been specially rearranged for the ceremony and filled with flowers, with a temporary altar covered in purple velvet and gold and surrounded by a gilt railing. This had been placed under one of Winterhalter's large canvases of the royal family in happier days, in which Albert took centre stage; there would be no avoiding his ghost at the wedding. Queen Victoria's ladies were hugely relieved to be allowed two days' respite from black – for 1 and 2 July – and wore half-mourning of grey or lilac for the ceremony; Alice too was allowed to get married in white. She looked delicate but lovely in her wedding dress, with its deep flounce of Honiton guipure lace and veil, both carrying a motif of rose, orange blossoms and myrtle, and the bottom of her skirt trimmed in artificial flowers of the same. On her head she wore an unostentatious wreath of orange blossom and wax flowers, much as her mother had worn at her own wedding in 1840. Eight bridesmaids had originally been planned for, but in the circumstances were reduced to four: Alice's sisters Helena, Louise and Beatrice and Louis's sister Anna. That morning Victoria had pressed her own special gift into Alice's hand – a prayer book similar to the one given to her by her mother on her wedding day.

Only a small gathering of hand-picked guests attended the wedding and were obliged to stand throughout: Louis's best man, Prince Henry of Hesse; the Cambridges; Louis's parents, Prince and Princess Charles of Hesse; Duke Ernst of Saxe-Coburg, who gave Alice away; Feodora; and a few other French and – in the eyes of Victoria's ladies – badly dressed Hessian relatives. The service was conducted by the Archbishop of York, standing in for an indisposed Archbishop of Canterbury. It was 'a *sad* moment, to see her come in leaning on her uncle's arm, instead of on *His!*' thought Lady Geraldine Somerset, as the service began just after 1 p.m. Alice's voice faltered during the ceremony, but she did not break down; it was the good Archbishop, himself recently widowed, who found it hard to hold back the tears. Victoria too retained the 'most wonderful command over herself' as she watched from the sidelines, seated in an armchair and protectively obscured from view by her four sons. The whole occasion had seemed to Lady Geraldine 'inexpressibly mournful'.[28] Despite being proud of Alice's 'wonderful bearing' throughout, the Queen had found it 'more like a funeral than a wedding'.[29]

Although a children's party was held in nearby Ryde to celebrate Alice's wedding that day, the local population saw no signs of the subdued celebrations going on at Osborne, and news reporters who headed there in search of a story came back empty-handed. The area had been as quiet as the grave; 'it certainly was a strange and solemn sight for the few of the public who flitted about the Osborne Road,' wrote the correspondent of the *Daily News*, for the surrounding park was deserted 'beyond a few servants, in the deepest mourning, passing almost stealthily up and down the avenue'.[30] Most of the papers covered this disappointing news story in brief; only the republican-minded *Reynolds's Newspaper* was bold enough to complain about the Queen's 'virtual abdication' and her continuing 'snug seclusion' at Osborne and Balmoral and its impact on trade, especially in the West End of London. For the milliners, tailors, dressmakers, perfumers and jewellers of the West End, who profited from catering to court dinners, balls and presentations, were now suffering a severe reduction in trade. Instead, the country had yet another royal to support, Louis of Hesse-Darmstadt, newly promoted by Victoria to His Royal Highness. Once more the nation was obliged to submit to 'those bleedings for the benefit of starveling Germans', while the Queen did nothing to revive severely depressed trade, with cotton famine – in the wake of the continuing war in America – now raging in Lancashire.[31]

Queen Victoria did not join her guests for the wedding breakfast held in a pavilion specially erected on the lawn at Osborne, but lunched in private with the newly weds in the Horn Room, surrounded by furniture made from stags' antlers purchased by Prince Albert. At 5 p.m. Alice left, complete with her black trousseau, for three days' honeymoon not far away at St Clair, the home of General Harcourt near Ryde. On 8 July she sailed on the royal yacht for Antwerp and her new home in Darmstadt, with a long memorandum provided by Dr Clark at her concerned mother's request, on how she should safeguard her frail health with lots of fresh air and cold baths. Victoria hoped her still-delicate daughter would not start a family too soon, but within the month Alice was pregnant.

At the end of July the Queen was only too anxious to escape once more to the quiet and stillness of Balmoral. A chink of respite for the younger children was allowed, when the artist William Leighton was asked to come and give them painting lessons, but he was shocked by the many great changes since his first visit:

> the joyous bustle in the morning when the Prince went out; the highland ponies and the dogs; the ghillies and the pipers. Then the coming home – the Queen and her ladies going out to meet them, and the merry time afterwards; the torch-light sword-dances on the green and the servants ball closing the day. Now all is gone with him who was the life and soul of it all.[32]

It was such a huge void to fill, and Victoria's every waking thought whilst in the Highlands was of Albert and his continuing memorialisation. At 11 a. m. on a bright, sunny 21 August, with the air soft with summer and the surrounding hills pink with heather, Victoria followed by her 'six orphans' was taken by pony carriage – led by her ghillie, John Brown – up the rugged hillside to the top of Craig Lowrigan, where a thirty-five-foot-high pyramid of granite dedicated to Albert was under construc-tion.[33] Here the family placed stones in the forty-foot-wide foundations, which would have their initials carved on them alongside a plaque: 'To the beloved memory of Albert the great and good Prince Consort. Raised by his broken-hearted Widow, Victoria R., 21 August, 1862.'[34] Four days later, on Albert's birthday, the whole family once more toiled up to the Craig for another mournful ceremony. Unable to join them, Alice wrote from her new home in Darmstadt, offering loving words of consolation and encouragement to her mother:

> Try and gather in the few bright things you have remaining, and cherish them: for though faint, yet they are types of that infinite joy still to come. I am sure, dear mamma, the more you try to appreciate and to find the good in that which God in His love has *left* you, the more worthy you will daily become of that which is in store. That earthly happiness you had is, indeed, gone for ever, but you must not think that every ray of it has left you.[35]

But it *had* left her. Could they not all see that it had? Like all the other words of comfort offered that year, Alice's did little to dent her mother's crippling, all-consuming grief. In September came yet another 'terribly trying ordeal' to be got through: the dreaded journey to Laeken, Uncle Leopold's palace near Brussels, where Victoria was to negotiate Bertie's formal engagement to Princess Alexandra with her parents. When she arrived, her nerves once again failed her and she declined to join the official luncheon, finally steeling herself to meet the party later that afternoon in an excruciatingly awkward and subdued exchange of pleasantries. Bertie, who was not present at the meeting, later formally proposed to Alexandra, though no public announcement was made till his twenty-first birthday on 9 November. Much to her surprise, Victoria was greatly taken by the gentle and unaffected Alexandra, to whom she touchingly presented a sprig of white heather sent from Balmoral by Bertie, but she made no bones about what lay in store for her: Alexandra would be welcomed, on her imminent visit to England (for initiation by Victoria into her duties as a member of the family), into a 'home of Sorrow'.[36] Back in London, Lord Clarendon sent the Queen his congratulations, though found it 'rather difficult to steer clear of the idea that the marriage could be any alleviation of her grief', for the Queen would countenance no such suggestions.[37] True to form, a few days later she was writing to Palmerston insisting that 'To the poor Queen this event can no longer cause pleasure, for pleasure is for ever gone from her heart!'[38] But at least she would, with this wedding, be acquiring a daughter-in-law, rather than losing a daughter; she only hoped that Bertie would be worthy of his lovely wife.

Whilst on the Continent, Victoria had travelled to Baden to see her half-sister, spending much of her time trying to persuade Feodora to live half the year with her in England as a glorified lady companion. But much as she loved her sister, Feodora politely declined, declaring that she did not wish to give up her independence at her advanced age. Privately she found Victoria's inexhaustible grief burdensome. They visited Albert's childhood home at Coburg together, where, amidst the expected anguish, Victoria also wallowed in recollections of happier times. Hearing Albert's native tongue and being in a place where the 'very air seems to breathe of her precious one' was a great comfort, she told Howard Elphinstone. Both were 'soothing and sweet in their very sadness to her bruised spirit and her aching, bleeding heart'.[39]

Back at Windsor she took almost daily walks to the mausoleum to inspect the building works. The dome was already in place and work on the interior had begun. She had already seen and approved Baron Marochetti's effigy of Albert, pronouncing it 'full . . . of peace, blessedness and beauty'.[40] Her thoughts increasingly dwelt on the anniversary to come, but meanwhile she had the diversion of Princess Alexandra's visit in November. 'This jewel!' she declared, was 'one of those sweet creatures who seem to come from the skies to help and bless poor mortals and lighten for a time their path!' Everyone could see how 'quite devotedly in love' Alix (as they all called her) was with Bertie, thought Augusta Bruce. She was being 'unutterably sweet' with the Queen, winning her over with her piety, gentleness and sympathy.[41] Her 'bright joyous presence has done much to rouse the poor dear Queen, who seems doatingly fond of her, and has her a great deal with her,' remarked a relieved Princess Mary Adelaide. The Queen was 'able to smile and even laugh cheerfully at times, and talks readily and with interest on every subject'. Well, for a little while at least; soon enough Victoria's conversation would revert to 'the sad, sad past'.[42] It was far too soon to hope for a fair-weather change to her deeply depressed state. As time moved remorselessly towards that first 'dreadful anniversary', Victoria went several times a day into the Blue Room (as the King's Room was now called, for the colour of its decoration) to pray, reiterating to Vicky that her misery was now a 'necessity'. She could not exist without it: 'yes, I long for my suffering almost – as it is blinded with him!' She would never adjust to 'that dreadful, weary, chilling, unnatural life of a widow'.[43] Fearful that the strain might provoke another mental and physical collapse, the pregnant Alice travelled over from Hesse to be with her, but once again Vicky could not join them.

At ten o'clock on 14 December 1862 the royal family gathered in the

Blue Room for a special service conducted by Dr Stanley, comprised of the Burial Service, hymns and prayers, and readings from Chapters 14 and 16 of St John on resurrection and reunion in the hereafter: 'A little while, and ye shall not see Me; and again, a little while, and ye shall see me, because I go to the Father.' Victoria knelt by Albert's bed, gazing at his white marble bust, with its fine profile and naked shoulders surrounded by flowers and palm leaves, which had been laid down there reverentially, replacing the living man a year since consigned to his coffin. But it was not a gloomy event. 'The room was full of flowers, and the sun shining in so brightly,' Victoria recalled. She told Dr Stanley that 'it seemed like a birthday', to which he answered reassuringly, 'It *is* a birthday in a new world.'[44] Two more services were conducted that day – at midday and 9.30 p.m. – inaugurating a sacred annual ritual that, like all others connected with Albert's life and death, would be followed to the letter till the day Victoria herself died.

Three days later the family made their way in the pouring rain down to Frogmore for the consecration of the mausoleum conducted by Samuel Wilberforce, Bishop of Oxford. The choir of St George's Chapel in their white surplices stood lining the steps as they entered. The sight, the Bishop recalled, was 'one of the most touching scenes I ever saw, to see our Queen and the file of fatherless children walk in and kneel down in those solemn prayers'.[45] Inside, a temporary wooden sarcophagus had been erected: it would be another six years before Marochetti's splendid double sarcophagus, to take both Albert's and eventually the Queen's coffins, was constructed from a single, enormous, flawless slab of Scottish granite. Meanwhile Albert's marble effigy had been placed in position and, one by one, the members of the royal family and household placed wreaths around it. During the service, verses from St John (19:41) were read: 'There was a garden, and in the garden a sepulchre', which everyone found most 'wonderfully appropriate' and moving. The process of investing Albert and his tomb with Christlike significance was completed the following morning at 7 a.m., when his coffin was quietly transferred from the crypt of St George's Chapel. Victoria did not attend, but was comforted that the sacred ritual of the 'translation' of Albert's remains was complete.[46] Henceforth he would always be near her, in their own private sepulchre in the garden. Later that day she was much comforted by the presentation of a sumptuously bound Lausanne Bible from 'loyal English Widows', the cost of which had been raised by a subscription set up by the Duchess of Sutherland. Eighty women who had lost their husbands in the Hartley

Colliery disaster in January generously donated to it. Victoria was deeply touched and, in a personal letter of thanks for the loyalty and devotion of her 'kind sister widows' and the nation in general, talked of how her one consolation was 'the constant sense of his unseen presence and the Blessed thought of that Eternal Union hereafter which will make the bitter anguish of the present appear as nought'.[47] Her heartfelt communion with other widows and her perception, by them, as a role model was an important saving grace during these dark years of retreat.

As December drew to a close, Victoria was relieved that 'One dreary, lonely year has been passed, which I had hoped never to live to the end of.' But now, 'with a weakened, shattered frame I have to begin the weary work again'.[48] The widows of England might grieve with her, but elsewhere in her kingdom sympathy for the Queen's unending grief was beginning to wane. 'Another year of royal mourning, another year of Queenly wo!' commented the leader in the *Era* for 28 December. 'A year and a week have come and gone, and we are sorry to learn that our prospects are not brightening, as we had trusted they would. We learn with sincere regret that her majesty will remain in mourning for another year.' Whilst the entire royal household and government might be tiptoeing around the Queen's extreme sensitivity on this point, the editor of the *Era* reminded his monarch that, for the good of the country, it was important she now resume her public life as sovereign and the 'mother of her people'. There were strong practical reasons for this: 'the manufacturers and artisans of England claim a public duty from her, as Sovereign, in return for the discharge of theirs, as taxpayers'. The Queen's retreat, and its effect on trade, was causing economic hardship to 'many, many thousands of struggling, hard working men'. The Prince of Wales was soon to be married, and Parliament would be asked to rubber-stamp an annual income of £100,000 a year to support himself, his wife and their household. Her Majesty therefore had 'an excellent opportunity to come into the sunshine again, brighten the gloom of the past, and inaugurate a brilliant series of London seasons!'

The *Era* – like *Reynolds's Newspaper* earlier in the year – was as yet a rare voice of dissent; speaking for the rest of a still largely sympathetic nation, the *Belfast News-letter*, without realising it, more accurately captured the Queen's present state of mind. Hers was 'a grief which cannot forget itself, and what is more, no longer desires to do so'.[49] All hopes of the Queen returning once more to the bosom of her people were still a very long way off.

CHAPTER ELEVEN

'A Married Daughter I Must Have
Living with Me'

In the spring of 1863 the British public resolutely shook off its gloom and enjoyed a few days of unprecedented national rejoicing. Its monarch might still be in self-imposed retirement, but a new and enchanting personality was about to shine a ray of light on the beleaguered royal family. On Thursday 7 March Princess Alexandra of Denmark arrived at Gravesend. Bertie was there to meet her and together they made their way across Kent by train, past cheering crowds and flags flying from every haystack and cowshed. Enormous numbers gathered in London for a glimpse of the Princess and something of the royal pageantry of old. The Corporation of London had spared no expense in anticipation of this precious respite from continuing royal despondency: £40,000 had been allotted for massed bands, decorated triumphal arches of evergreens and orange blossom, bunting and illuminations along the route. The windows and balconies of private houses too were festooned with flags, and some residents rented out their windows and balconies for large sums of money. The press took a vigorous interest in the story, whipping up public excitement at the prospect of seeing Bertie and his beautiful fiancée's royal progress. This ensured that their journey across London was witnessed by huge crowds, strung out across seven miles of streets, from the rather prosaic rail terminus on the Old Kent Road to Paddington, via London Bridge, Pall Mall, Piccadilly and Hyde Park. The crush was appalling, the journey interminably slow, the carriages laid on for the procession somewhat shoddy and, in the opinion of John Delane of *The Times*, 'unworthy of the occasion'.[1] But through it all Alexandra smiled warmly and bowed graciously 'as all those thousands of souls rose at her, as it were, in one blaze of triumphant irrepressible enthusiasm; surging round the carriage, waving hats and kerchiefs, leaping up here and there and again to catch sight of her; and crying Hurrah'.[2] Darkness had fallen by the time the couple arrived at Windsor station, where they were again enthusiastically greeted by patient crowds frozen from standing for long hours in the driving rain.

Victoria's greeting inside the castle had been warm and affectionate, but her self-absorption was such that she could not disguise how low and depressed she felt at what was to come, and she did not join the couple for dinner. Indeed, with undisguised bitterness she expressed her 'surprise' that the public had given such a warm ovation to the future wife of the Prince of Wales, 'when none was offered to the husband of the Queen' in his lifetime.[3] She had wanted the Prince of Wales's wedding to take place on her own wedding day of 10 February, but everyone had feared a repetition of Alice's funereal ceremony and she had been persuaded to postpone it to March. She overrode objections to it taking place in Lent, as she was determined to be rid of all her guests before Alice gave birth to her first baby – at Windsor, as she, Victoria, had ordained. Much to general disappointment, the Queen had resisted any suggestion of a grand state ceremony at Westminster Abbey, thus depriving the majority of her people of any glimpse of the proceedings. The wedding would take place under strict control at St George's Chapel, Windsor, where her privacy would be paramount and where she could not be made the object of unseemly curiosity.

In the fifteen months since Albert's death time had at least mellowed Victoria's attitude to her wayward son. She had to admit that there had been a distinct improvement in Bertie's looks and manner since his engagement to Alexandra, although he would always suffer by comparison with his absent married sisters Vicky and Alice. Bertie, for his part, was trying hard to be affectionate and 'do what is right', but Victoria still found his idleness and inattentiveness 'trying', as too his *joie de vivre*; his noisiness gave her bad headaches. She had been particularly anxious that he should be suitably 'Germanised' in time for his marriage, for she had been alarmed to discover that he wrote to his fiancée in English rather than his sainted father's native tongue: 'the German element is the one I wish to be cherished and kept up in our beloved home,' she told Vicky. To lose it would be a betrayal of Albert; it never occurred to her that to keep it would feed into already hostile feelings about the excessive favouritism of things German by the British monarchy.[4]

Before his death, and in anticipation of Bertie's marriage, Prince Albert had secured a 7,000-acre country estate for him at Sandringham in Norfolk for £220,000, paid for by the profits from the Duchy of Cornwall that Albert had so carefully managed during Bertie's minority. When in London, Bertie and Alexandra would reside at Marlborough House, but despite the couple's anticipated high profile, Victoria continued to veto any suggestions that Bertie take a greater role in public life, such as involvement in the learned and scientific societies that Albert had taken up, or attending the House of Lords. The problem, as Victoria well knew, was that Bertie was an incorrigible gossip and his indiscretion meant he could not be trusted with sensitive state papers. Ever mistrustful of him, she gave instructions for a close watch to be kept on the comings and goings at Marlborough House and on the calibre of people being invited there.

Having been instrumental in finding Bertie a wife, his sister Vicky was hugely excited at the wedding to come, which she would be attending with Fritz and their eldest son Wilhelm. Victoria was only too glad to delegate to her eldest daughter the task of receiving the many guests at the necessary official Drawing Rooms prior to the wedding, but nevertheless chided her: 'Dear child! Your ecstasy at the whole thing is to me sometimes very incomprehensible.' Neither Vicky nor anyone else would believe her when she insisted that she had to have quiet: 'I must constantly dine alone, and any merriment or discussion are quite unbearable.'[5] Besides, she already had enough to deal with, worrying about Alice's imminent confinement; and about Affie, who had committed a sexual transgression while away in Malta, prompting fears that he would turn out as much of a reprobate as his brother. It was all such a burden for her, not just as Queen, but as a lone woman with 'no near male relation of sufficient age and experience' to whom she could turn for advice. Who was there, Victoria asked General Peel, to 'help her with her sons' and 'keep them in the path of duty'?[6]

For the wedding on 10 March the Queen allowed one major concession: the guests could wear colours, although her own ladies, like her children, should be in the half-mourning colours of grey, lilac or mauve. She was choosy about who she invited – certainly not the immoral Frederick VII of Denmark or most of Alix's mother's questionable Danish relatives; nor too most of her own Hanoverian cousins. But even with such exclusions, the guest list was large, with 900 people in their best finery crammed into St George's Chapel. Many of the male VIPs were obliged to leave their wives at home, and others fought jealously for invitations to be there. It was a spectacular gathering: diplomats and distinguished Cabinet ministers, Knights of the Garter in their sumptuous robes, tiers of 'gorgeous Duchesses' in their bright colours and flashing tiaras, not to mention the glorious sight of 'beefeaters and gold-encrusted trumpeters and heralds in their tabards'. Ladies of fashion grasped this rare opportunity to vie with each other over the splendour of their jewels, Lady Westmorland's diamonds having the edge over Lady Abercorn's sapphires, in the view of Henry Greville, though he thought the beautiful young Lady Spencer, wearing Marie Antoinette's lace, was way and above the best dressed that day.[7]

Yet it was not the fashionable ladies, but their absent monarch, whom everyone really wanted to see. In her stiff, heavy crape and wearing Albert's badge and star of the Garter on its blue ribbon and a diamond brooch with his miniature, Victoria made her way to the chapel away from prying eyes via a covered walkway. She took her place in Catherine of Aragon's closet, specially draped with heavy purple velvet and gold, high up in the south-eastern corner near the organ loft, with Lady Churchill, Lady Lyttleton and the Duchess of Sutherland hovering in the background. All attempts to defuse morbid curiosity failed, as everyone craned their necks trying as discreetly as possible to catch a glimpse of this great figure of imperial grief. When Benjamin Disraeli raised his eyeglass to take a closer look, he was greeted with an icy stare.

Princess Alexandra, however, could not be eclipsed: her radiant beauty that day was breathtaking, as she entered pale and childlike in her dress of Spitalfields satin, covered with a skirt of Honiton lace garlanded with leaves and orange blossoms. Eight bridesmaids in lace and tulle decorated with rosebuds followed, carrying her long silver-moiré train. Bertie too looked the picture of nobility in his scarlet and gold of a general in the Guards, over which he wore the dark-blue robes of the Garter; Princess Mary Adelaide thought he demonstrated 'more depth of manner than ever before' that day, and his sisters Alice and Vicky wept with pride at the sight of him. The whole event had been a 'fine affair', in Disraeli's estimation: 'A perfect pageant with that sufficient foundation of senti-ment, which elevates a mere show.'[8]

But it was Victoria's haunted black figure watching the gathered guests from on high that everyone talked about afterwards. Whether by accident or design, the wedding had inevitably drawn attention to the widow as much as the bride, reigniting public sympathy for the bereaved Queen alone on her glorious pinnacle of solitude. Victoria had expected to find it all a 'fearful ordeal' and at times quivered with anxiety.[9] She had, however, borne up very well for most of the time, though certain key moments had brought back painful memories: the flourish of the trumpets reminded her of her own wedding day, and when she heard the glorious voice of the Swedish opera star Jenny Lind singing a chorale written by Albert she cast her eyes up to heaven. 'See, she is worshipping him in spirit!' remarked one of the deans of the Chapel Royal. Her face, to all those who caught sight of it that day, 'spoke all that was within'.[10]

Immediately after she had witnessed the signing of the register and embraced Bertie and Alix, Victoria fled, avoiding the assembled thirty-eight royals at the private wedding reception, or the crush of the general guests in St George's Hall, but dining alone with Beatrice.[11] There was only one place she wanted to be: at the mausoleum, communing with Albert. She kept the keys to it about her at all times, so that she could go down and let herself in to what had by now become an essential extension of home. The night before the wedding she had taken Bertie and Alix there to pray and receive Albert's blessing, and immediately after lunch on the 10th she returned once more. That evening she poured out her anguish in her journal. The wedding had been a day of pure 'suffering' for her without Albert, and she had only got through it 'by a violent effort'. She had consented to sit for her photograph with the happy couple, but resolutely refused to look to camera, instead gazing up in adoration at Albert's marble bust. After all was over, a despondency once more descended, made worse by an uncontrollable envy of her children's happiness: 'Here I sit lonely and desolate, who so need love and tenderness, while our two daughters have each their loving husbands and Bertie has taken his lovely, pure, sweet bride to Osborne.'[12]

As the overdressed members of the aristocracy engaged in an undignified scrum to find places on the special train back out of Windsor, a range of celebrations and parties took place that evening across London and elsewhere in Britain. At long last the nation was out enjoying itself: two and a half million people flooded the streets of London, 'dense enough to hide every stone of the streets from one who had seen it above'.[13] The night was cold and raw, and the crowds jamming central London to see the wedding illuminations at London Bridge, Nelson's Monument and the fountains in Trafalgar Square were 'frightful'; the monumental traffic jam of wagons, vans and omnibuses blocked the streets for hours. Privy Council member Frederick Pollock found himself trapped on Pall Mall, where he was jammed up against the lamp post in the middle of the road, unable to move. At Northumberland House near Charing Cross he witnessed 'a surging vortex of struggling humanity' unlike anything he had seen since the Queen's wedding day.[14] On Bedford Street the Archbishop of York's wife had her crinoline set on fire when their carriage became caught in the crush and some boys tossed a firework inside. All this mayhem, just to see 'a few gas stars and Prince's feathers', grumbled Henry Greville.[15] 'It wasn't worth the hours of jam and wedge,' agreed maid-of-honour Lady Lucy Cavendish. But it was proof, if ever it were needed, of how much the British people hungered for a renewal of the ceremonial of old. On the 11th sales of *The Times* containing an account of the wedding rocketed from its usual 65,000 to 112,000. Crowds turned out again in June for the public unveiling of the memorial to the Great Exhibition, featuring Albert's statue, at the Horticultural Society's Gardens. But it was the Princess of Wales who took centre stage. The monarch was nowhere to be seen.

★   ★   ★

On Easter Sunday, 5 April 1863, Alice's daughter Victoria was born 'at poor, sad, old Windsor' in the same bed in which Victoria herself had given birth to all her children and wearing the same shift her mother had worn. Victoria had sat up all night with Alice during her labour, even now approaching forty-three, wishing it could have been her giving one last child to Albert. The arrival of another grandchild and an improvement in her state of mind made her feel that she had at last made 'great progress' through all her burden of sorrow.[16] But the worm of jealousy kept gnawing at her – jealousy that her children one by one were entering into their own separate lives and she was no longer the centre of attention. With Alice now a mother, Victoria felt that only Baby (Beatrice) and Lenchen (Helena) still loved her 'the most of any thing'. She knew that this was the natural progression of things, but nevertheless it was a bitter pill to swallow: she who had been 'the dearest object of two beings [Albert and her mother] for so many years, is now daily learning to feel that she is only No. 3 or 4 in the real tender love of others'. She had to admit that she was sadly *de trop* in her married children's lives and that she did not belong to anyone any more. Soon Alice would be returning to Hesse and Victoria dreaded it. It was no good; her querulous self-centeredness once more rose to the surface. 'A married daughter I MUST have living with me, and must *not* be left constantly to look about for help,' she insisted to Uncle Leopold. The daughter designated to fill Alice's shoes and be sacrificed on the altar of her mother's neediness was the docile and dowdy Lenchen. A husband would have to be found for her who would agree to the couple spending the greater part of the year with Victoria in England; she could not give up another of her girls to a foreign country 'without *sinking* under the *weight* of my desolation'.[17] Nor was she willing for Helena to give her heart to one whom she, Victoria, deemed beneath her. After Albert's death Helena had developed a crush on his German librarian, Carl Ruland, and on discovering this Victoria had sent the loyal Ruland packing, even though she had begged him on Albert's deathbed: 'do not leave me and my children'.[18] Lucy Cavendish thought Helena already had that sad look – as had Alice before her – of 'one who has thought and done too much for her age and been a comforter'. She was 'cruelly overworked', the Queen having no notion of how her daughter's mind and body were strained by her onerous duties and her mother's endless dissatisfaction.[19]

Within months of their wedding, Bertie and Alix too fell under Victoria's critical eye: he for reverting to his old bad manners and hedonistic lifestyle, and she for looking thin and sallow and losing her '*fraîcheur*' – probably from too many late nights out socialising, in Victoria's view. Bertie should take better care of his wife, yet again he was no equal to his father, whose 'wise, motherly care' of her, when he was 'not yet 21', had 'exceeded everything'. Had Vicky noticed what a curiously small head Alix had? She had inherited her mother's deafness, too. Victoria dreaded the physiological outcome: combined with Bertie's 'small empty brain', their children, when they had them, might well prove 'unintellectual'.[20] Affie was a continuing worry as well; now home from sea, having survived a bad bout of typhoid fever, he was spending too much time at Marlborough House. Victoria feared that under his brother's influence he might once more 'fall into sin from weakness'. Time therefore to 'fix his affections securely' and see him married off as well. Once more a succession of German princesses – of Altenburg, Oldenburg and Wied – was put under the microscope, as Victoria discussed their relative merits with Vicky in Prussia.[21]

Although she continued to complain of feeling tired and overworked, the Queen had, throughout 1863, slowly begun to recover some of her equilibrium. But then, in July, a new death had knocked her back again – that of her 'dearest, wisest, best and oldest friend', Baron Stockmar.[22] That he was gone to 'brighter regions' where he would be in the company of Albert was at least a comfort and, like Albert, he must be commemorated. Did Vicky have 'plenty of the beloved Baron's photographs and also some of his precious hair?' she enquired. If not, she could send some.[23] Births, marriages, deaths and memorials were now increasingly the focus and pattern of Victoria's shrinking world and the morbid romanticism at the heart of her very existence. Even *The Times* noted that the Queen's unceasing grief had become 'a sort of religion' with her.[24] After her fleeting appearance at Bertie's wedding, the gentlemen of the press once more found their reporting on the Queen reduced to a daily catalogue of her brief walks and carriage drives. Her stay at Balmoral that autumn was particularly bleak in the face of the loss of Stockmar; as usual, the loyalty of the Scottish locals saved her from despair. 'There is nothing like the Highlanders – no, nothing,' she told Vicky.[25] But the loneliness of Balmoral was dreadful. She tried, and failed, to persuade a succession of relatives to come and keep her company, but they all made their excuses, leaving her with only Lady Augusta and Lady Jane Churchill for company, until the family gathered for the unveiling of a new memorial to Prince Albert.

On 13 October 1863 the Queen travelled from Balmoral to Aberdeen to unveil a statue of Albert by Baron Marochetti. It would be her first public appearance since her husband's death (the wedding in March having been by private invitation). But there were no bands or street decorations on this occasion and the public, who stood patiently waiting for two hours in the rain, were given strict instructions that there should be no cheering. Victoria was visibly agitated, but at least all her adult children had joined her – even Vicky was over from Prussia. But the day was filled with melancholy as she drove along the densely crowded, but respectfully silent streets, the dark, leaden sky unforgiving and the only bright point the profusion of flags on the ships docked along the quay, though even these hung limp and sodden in the drenching rain.[26] Victoria was anxious for it all to be over as quickly as possible and was clearly annoyed when – with the rain falling fast as she huddled under an umbrella held by Vicky – she had to endure a ten-minute-long prayer by the Principal of Aberdeen University prior to the unveiling. Even the spectators became restive, thinking the delay intolerable for their widowed Queen: 'Cut it short,' came a voice from the crowd. 'Ay man, gie us the rest on the neest Sabbath,' shouted another.[27]

As 1863 drew to a close, members of the royal household were on the constant lookout for hopeful signs of a return to normal. December would mark the end of the traditional two-year period of mourning and everyone hoped that her appearance at Aberdeen might mark the beginning of the Queen's return to public life. 'Two years it must be said, are a long period to be consumed in unavailing regrets and in dwelling upon days which cannot be healed,' observed *The Times*.[28] But for Victoria nothing had changed; her reaction to being on public display at Aberdeen had been no different from her other brief forays into the outside world: psychosomatic headaches, insomnia and stress preceded and followed every minor exertion and she continued to protest bitterly at being put upon. In response, Doctors Jenner and Clark stuck to the traditional line of petting her and pandering to her protestations, fearing her total mental collapse; thoughts of hereditary madness – she was, after all, the granddaughter of King George III – still lingered, in the absence of any real medical understanding of the Queen's psychological state. Victoria herself put it down to 'her *hard*, slavelike labour *for* the Country'. She felt persecuted, 'like a poor hunted hare, like a child that has lost its mother'.[29] Any disruption to her familiar daily routine was an extreme provocation for her, and she was beside herself with rage and disappointment in November when her most loyal lady committed an unforgivable act of betrayal: 'My dear Lady Augusta, at 41 . . . has most unnecessarily, decided to *marry*!!' she wrote to Uncle Leopold in high dudgeon. 'I thought she *never* would leave *me*!'[30] Victoria's own life might be in stasis, but the lives of others were not, and Lady Augusta, having long steeled herself, had finally plucked up the courage to grasp the happiness of marriage with Dr Arthur Stanley, Dean of Westminster. Victoria grudgingly gave her blessing, with the proviso that Lady Augusta would nevertheless be 'a great deal with me afterwards'; but for now Ladies Ely and Churchill would be the main butt of her increasingly volcanic personality.

The Queen's frequent explosions of temper and determined opinion prompted William Gladstone to think that he had detected signs of recovery and 'the old voice of business in the Queen' of late, and many of the newspapers were openly suggesting that she might even open Parliament the following year. 'There is strong pressure from without from almost the highest in the land down to the smallest boy in the streets of London to get the Queen once more to come to London,' Lord Torrington told General Grey:

> The public accept *no one* as a substitute and the danger is considerable if once that public cease to care or take an interest in seeing the Queen moving amongst them. It will not do for people to be accustomed to Her

Majesty's absence. Do away with the outward and visible sign and the
ignorant mass believe Royalty is of no value. There is not a tradesman in
London who does not believe he is damaged by the Queen not coming
to London.[31]

The suggestion that Victoria should open Parliament in 1864, however,
received a brisk refusal. Her health simply was not up to it; it was all
she could do just to keep up with the mountains of paperwork on her
desk. How could she perform any of these public duties, 'trembling and
alone at Courts, and Parties and State occasions, without her Sole
Guardian and *Protector*'?[32] Sir Charles Phipps and General Grey (with
whom Phipps shared the still-unofficial role of Private Secretary to the
Queen) were both beginning to detect worrying signs of avoidance in
their reluctant monarch, and one of their closest supporters in this view
was the Queen's own daughter, Princess Alice. She had seen her mother
that autumn on a private visit to Coburg, and had thought her very well.
Victoria had got through a formal luncheon with the Emperor of Austria
and eighteen other guests, talking animatedly and even running to the
window to see him off. In a private moment Victoria had even admitted
to Alice that she was 'afraid of getting too well – as if it was a crime
and that she *feared* to begin to like riding on her Scotch pony, etc.' Behind
the scenes, the royal entourage agreed that something must be done:
'after the next anniversary, we must all try, *gently*, to get her to resume
her old habits'.[33]

Ironically, it was one of the most complex political crises of the 1860s
that galvanised Victoria into a flurry of activity – be it only by letter and
memorandum – for although she continued adamantly to refuse to take
part in public ceremonial, she had by no means abandoned her vigorous
interest in foreign affairs. It was an interest she had shared with Albert;
this and her defence of her prerogatives as monarch had never dimmed.
Indeed, when she had travelled to Coburg in August she had specifically
instructed Gladstone that, in her absence, 'no step is taken in foreign
affairs without her previous sanction being obtained'.[34] For the Queen
was well aware that a political crisis of long standing was coming to a
head. It broke in November 1863 with the death of King Frederick VII
of Denmark and the accession of Alix's father, Christian IX. This had
prompted renewed calls for the independence of the Danish duchies of
Schleswig and Holstein, with the former being incorporated into
Denmark and the latter retaining separate status under Danish suzerainty.

Rival claims to the territories by the Duke of Augustenburg were disputed by the Prussian Prime Minister, Bismarck, who, supported by the Austrians, sought the ceding of both territories to Prussia.

The crisis forced a split in the deeply conflicted loyalties of Queen Victoria's European family and feelings became very heated, so much so that she forbade all political discussion at table. Like Albert, Vicky and Fritz, she was pro-Prussian; Bertie and his wife, naturally enough, supported the Danes; and Victoria's half-sister Feodora was firmly in the Augustenburg camp. Most of the British public sympathised with the underdog Denmark, abhorring Prussia, the aggressor. Ever the sabre-rattler Palmerston, now approaching eighty and fading fast, contemplated sending in British troops in defence of a beleaguered Denmark, but Britain had no stomach for war now, any more than it had in December 1861. Without the military support of France or Russia, it would have been madness to take on the Prussians.

Victoria was appalled at the prospect of conflict, but also wished to protect her own family interests. 'I have, since he left me, the courage of a lioness if I see danger,' she told Vicky, 'and I shall never mind giving my people my decided opinion and more than that!'[35] But she had to fight hard against her innermost prejudices: her 'heart and sympathies were all German', but she did not want to sanction 'the infliction upon her subjects of all the horrors of war'; or, on the other hand, see any help given by her government to the Danes. Publicly, she knew she had to do as Albert had so carefully taught her – be seen to be impartial, sticking to an insistence on British neutrality, as he had so honourably done over the American crisis. But oh, how she rued the inconvenient fact that her daughter-in-law Alix had not been 'a good German'.[36]

Such a shameful thought was soon forgotten when, as the crisis deepened, a pregnant Alix went into premature labour – giving birth two months early to a sickly son, Albert Victor, on 8 January 1864. In February Prussian and Austrian troops invaded Schleswig, prompting Victoria to seek comfort and courage from Albert's spirit by praying frequently in the Blue Room and at the mausoleum. She was pained by hostile comments in the press about her pro-German sympathies and was enraged when Lord Ellenborough criticised her in Parliament. Such accusations, she told Palmerston, 'ought to be put into the fire'.[37] She also had to ask Lord Clarendon to caution Bertie on his 'violent abuse of Prussia'; it was 'fearfully dangerous for the Heir to her throne to take up one side violently'. The British public, however, were on Bertie's side – anti-German feeling in Britain was 'quite ungovernable'. But it made no difference: in June the Danes were defeated, and in October Holstein and the German-speaking territories of Schleswig were ceded to joint Prussian and Austrian control.[38]

Victoria marked the end of the Schleswig-Holstein crisis by showing herself briefly to her public, taking a drive through Windsor Great Park in an open carriage, but only as far as the nearby railway station – a matter of a mile or so. Convinced that the newspaper criticism of her seclusion was unrepresentational of the view of the nation at large, she felt that this excursion and a couple of fleeting appearances at court that summer had 'pleased people more than anything'. 'If done occasionally in this way', she was sure such appearances would 'go farther to satisfy them than anything else'.[39] She was sadly deluded, for public sympathy was now clearly on the wane. The Queen's continuing absence from central London prompted some practical jokers to tie large placards to the palace gateposts, announcing: 'These commanding premises to be let or sold, in consequence of the late occupant's declining business.' The placards were immediately torn down and police duty outside the palace doubled, only for them to be posted again a few days later.[40] Some put it down to 'Republican propaganda', but gossip was further fuelled by an April Fool's joke published mischievously by Delane in The Times on 1 April, intended once more to draw Victoria out. 'Her Majesty's loyal subjects will be very well pleased to hear,' the paper announced, 'that their Sovereign is about to break her protracted seclusion by holding courts for the diplomatic corps at Buckingham Palace.' At long last the monarchy was about to 'recover from its suspended animation'. An aggrieved Victoria, who read her press cuttings avidly, immediately wrote her own anonymous rebuttal, which was published in The Times on 6 April:

An erroneous idea seems generally to prevail, and has latterly found frequent expression in the newspapers, that the Queen is about to resume the place in society which she occupied before her great affliction; that is, that she is about again to hold levees and drawing-rooms in person, and to appear as before at Court balls, concerts etc. This idea cannot be too explicitly contradicted.

She would, she said, do her very best to fulfil her duty in matters of national interest, and give the support to society and trade that was needed, but would not be put upon for the sake of expediency. At the core of Victoria's objections was her continuing and consuming sense of being overwhelmed – not just with work, but at the prospect of once more taking up those public duties 'of mere representation' and spectacle, which she had never enjoyed, even when Albert was alive. Her ceremonial functions, she insisted, could be 'equally well performed' by other members of the family. 'More the Queen cannot do; and more the kindness and good feeling of her people will surely not extract from her.' The British people had indeed been most forbearing for three years now, but it was precisely in the realm of theatre and ceremonial – as Bertie's wedding had all too clearly demonstrated – that the Queen was most missed and most needed. Her growing unpopularity was beginning to endanger the very fabric of constitutional monarchy, as Lord Cecil pointed out in the *Saturday Review*: 'Seclusion is one of the few luxuries in which Royal personages may not indulge. The power which is derived from affection or from loyalty needs a life of uninterrupted publicity to sustain it.'[41]

'The country knows nothing of the Queen's peculiar desolation,' sympathised Lucy Cavendish; it were better they prayed for her than goaded her. Within the safe four walls of her study Victoria felt she was as hard-working and conscientious as she had ever been, but the problem was that the public could not see this; her labours were 'as secret and invisible as those of the queen-bee in the central darkness of the hive'.[42] As a palliative, the Lord Chamberlain's office announced that three Drawing Rooms hosted by Princess Alexandra would be held during the London Season and three levees by the Prince of Wales. In addition, two state concerts and two state balls would be held at Buckingham Palace and, after a three-year lapse, Victoria ordered that her forty-fifth birthday – 24 May – be celebrated that year 'with trooping of the colours and general festivities, which had been suspended since the death of the Prince Consort'.[43]

But as spring turned to summer, discontent rumbled on and rumours continued to circulate: the Queen was ill, or mad; she would never live in London again, and – according to all the French papers – was about to abdicate, an event that had been anticipated on the Continent almost from the day of Victoria's widowing. Lord Howden agreed, confiding to Lord Clarendon that 'for her own interest, happiness and *reputation*', the Queen should have abdicated on Bertie's coming-of-age. 'She would then have left a great name and great regret.'[44] Instead, there was now much dissatisfaction among London tradesmen, as well as 'among that class to whom an invitation to a palace ball is a mark of their social position'.[45] Victoria was mortified by the gossip, but it did nothing to undermine her resolve or diminish her consuming self-absorption. Indeed, she appeared 'less inclined to appear than ever and more inclined to have her own way', according to Lord Torrington. The contradictions were boundless; claiming with one breath to have the business of the country at heart, time and time again Victoria forbade a topic of conversation which was 'precisely that on which it is most important that she should be informed'.[46] The problem, as Torrington explained to Delane, was that 'Every one appears more or less afraid to speak or advise the Queen', so much so that she now had a habit of sending word prior to any meeting with ministers on what she would and would not discuss, 'lest it should make her nervous'. If those about her had a little more courage, 'things might mend'.[47] But no one did.

The continuing failure of anyone to face up to the Queen's intractable personality was also creating diplomatic problems. She flatly refused to entertain visiting royalty or reciprocate hospitality given to her family abroad. The King of Sweden was obliged to stay at the Swedish legation on a recent visit to London, and during that of Prince Humbert of Italy in September 1864 the aged Lord Palmerston had had to traipse up from his home, Brockett Hall in Hertfordshire, 'to give him a dinner'. Later, when Prince Humbert visited Windsor, he had to be entertained with a modest lunch at the White Hart Inn rather than at the castle. Even when Alix's parents arrived for their daughter's wedding in March, they had been accommodated not at Windsor Castle, as would have been expected, but at the local Palace Hotel. Despite their conspicuous impoverishment they had, however, entertained Bertie and Alix lavishly when they visited Denmark later that year.

The Queen's neglect was verging on the rude as well as the mean, and was even more shameful when the Civil List could more than afford it.[48] Delane agreed, and published another pointed reminder in *The Times* of 2 November: the monarch's 'melancholy bereavement' might excuse her absence to visiting foreign dignitaries, 'but the presence of the Sovereign, although the highest ornament and the most attractive part of the nation's hospitality, is not absolutely indispensable to its exercise'. The Prince and Princess of Wales should, he argued, be given the task of entertaining foreign dignitaries in the Queen's continuing absence. They had already proved to be an enormous success at the heart of the

London Season and, with her grace and beauty, Alexandra was becoming a trendsetter in fashion, providing the best boost to trade in the absence of her mother-in-law. At a Drawing Room in May she had turned even the wearing of black into high fashion, appearing in full mourning for her maternal grandmother who had recently died, resplendent in a black silk train and skirt elaborately trimmed with jet beading, as well as a headdress and tiara of jet and black feathers. Going on this description, wrote the *Whitby Gazette*, 'the manufacturers of our town need not despair of the jet trade'.[49]

Before 1864 was out, as the country faced yet another year of the Queen's retreat, John Delane renewed his attack in *The Times*. 'In all bereavements there is a time when the days of mourning should be looked upon as past', he began:

It is impossible for a recluse to occupy the British Throne without a gradual weakening of that authority which the Sovereign has been accustomed to exert. The regulation of a household may be in the power of such a ruler, but the real sway of an Empire will be impossible.

For the sake of the Crown as well as of the public we would, therefore, beseech Her Majesty to return to the personal exercise of her exalted functions . . . and not postpone them longer to the indulgence of an unavailing grief.[50]

Inevitably Delane's editorial, measured though it was, provoked much controversy, with papers such as the monarchist *Morning Post* accusing *The Times* of disloyalty and rising to the monarch's defence: 'In seclusion or in society, Queen Victoria will reign in the hearts of her subjects.'[51] The *Observer* on the 18th agreed that the attack was unwarranted: only the sufferer could best judge when the time has come to give up mourning. Victoria thought *The Times* article 'vulgar and heartless'. Finding herself cornered, she resorted to her most effective and provocative weapon – emotional blackmail. Overwork had killed Albert; did they want it to kill her too? She was worn out with 'constant proposals as to what she is to do and not to do'. Privately, however, even her cousin the Duke of Cambridge had written to her begging her to come out of retirement and 'save her country'.[52]

The case for the Queen's continued seclusion was becoming increasingly difficult to argue, for her appearance now contradicted her repeated protestations of physical weakness. The logic shared by many was that she looked well and was therefore up to the job. Torrington 'never saw her in better health, spirits or looks' that summer. Yet such had been the rising levels of Victoria's perceived tetchiness that by the end of the year Jenner and Clark suggested a new form of therapy that might soothe the Queen's nerves and revive her interest in the outside world. If she were to go out for pony rides at Osborne, as she did at Balmoral, rather than just sitting in her carriage, it might do her a world of good. With the connivance of Phipps, and Princess Alice, who was eager to see her mother resume her public life, it was recommended that Victoria's Scottish ghillie, John Brown – so indefatigable in his attention and care of her, in Victoria's own view – should be brought down from Balmoral with her favourite pony, Lochnagar, for the winter. The monarchy in Britain was approaching crisis: 'Two years and a half have sufficed to destroy the popularity which Albert took twenty years to build up,' observed Lord Derby.[53] In that short space of time the Queen had disregarded every single lesson that her husband had taught her about her essential state duties in preserving the integrity of the throne.

CHAPTER TWELVE

'God Knows How I Want So Much to be Taken Care Of'

In January 1865, three years on from Prince Albert's death, the only visible evidence the nation had of its widowed queen's existence was vicariously, through the continuing memorialisation of her dead husband across the country – a process inherently more about Victoria's obsessive grief than her husband's increasingly elusive memory. For some, like Charles Dickens, the continuing cult of the Prince Consort was oppressive. 'If you should meet with an inaccessible cave anywhere to which a hermit could retire from the memory of Prince Albert and testimonials to the same,' he told his friend John Leech, 'pray let me know of it. We have nothing solitary and deep enough in this part of England.'[1]

The relentless dead march of Albert continued to echo across Britain throughout the 1860s, as the public, in deference to their grieving queen, loyally raised statue after statue on the urban landscape. After Victoria had unveiled the seated monument at Aberdeen, a succession of standing figures of the Prince, usually in his Garter robes or military dress, were unveiled in Perth, Dublin, Tenby, Birmingham, Edinburgh, Salford, Oxford (an uncharacteristic pose in informal dress for the Natural History Museum) and at Madingley – with Albert in his robes as Chancellor of Cambridge University. Although the consensus was to present the late prince as a man of learning, a few equestrian statues also appeared: at Liverpool, Glasgow and Holborn Circus in London.

Elsewhere in Britain, Prince Albert's name was being commemorated in the form of clock towers – at Hastings, Manchester and Belfast – while new buildings in his memory sprang up everywhere: the Albert Memorial College in Suffolk, the Royal Albert Memorial Museum at Exeter and the Albert Institute in Dundee. In central Manchester a large square named after the Prince was several years under construction on a derelict site that had been specially cleared for the purpose, its focus to be a seated statue under a medieval-style canopy similar to the one of Albert already commissioned in London, but finished long before it, in 1865. Plans in London were also under way, under the architect Captain Francis Fowke, to build a concert hall, an idea that the Prince had first mooted with Henry Cole at the time of the Great Exhibition, but which, after Albert's death, had been sidelined in favour of work on the national memorial in Hyde Park. The latter project was proving extremely protracted and costly. In 1864, after seven leading architects had been invited to submit designs, Gilbert Scott had been awarded the commission. His Gothic design was not favoured by the artistic establishment, who saw it as rather a safe and unchallenging variation on the traditional Eleanor Cross, and snobbery abounded in the professional press. 'Mr Scott's design is scarcely worthy of his reputation, and we should deem its adoption a discredit to the present state of knowledge of the principles of Gothic architecture,' sneered the *Civil Engineer and Architect's Journal*.[2] Queen Victoria, however, had executive power over the final decision; Albert had been a great supporter of Scott's work and the Gothic Revival, and what Albert liked the country got.

Work began on the Albert Memorial in the spring of 1864, when the site in Hyde Park was fenced off. But the money required was considerable – estimated at £110,000 – with £60,000 already raised by public subscription. In 1863 Disraeli and Palmerston persuaded a reluctant Parliament to come up with the balance. Grateful that in Disraeli she had found a soulmate who would endlessly gratify her adoration of Albert's 'spotless and unequalled character', Victoria sent her effusive thanks for his support together with a signed copy of Albert's collected speeches bound in white morocco.[3] Once the Queen had set her seal on Scott's design (though her critical powers stretched only so far as to deem it 'handsome') there was no toleration of further argument. By 1866 the *Art Journal* was agreeing with Disraeli that the memorial was 'worthy of its object' and that it resembled the character of the Prince Consort 'in the beauty and the harmony of its proportion'. It was, the editor concluded, 'the type of a sublime life, the testimony of a grateful people'. The satirical press disagreed, pointing out – presciently as it turned out – that such an ornate monument would soon succumb to the dirt and pollution of the London atmosphere and need 'periodical pumpings with a fire engine' to keep it clean.[4]

Scott's design was based on the style of ornate, canopied shrines found on the Continent in cities such as medieval Nuremberg and Renaissance Milan, taking inspiration too from the monument to Sir Walter Scott in Edinburgh and Scott's own design for the Martyrs' Memorial in Oxford's St Giles – both erected in the 1840s. The centrepiece was to be a gilded fifteen-foot seated figure of the Prince, wearing his robes of the Garter and holding the catalogue of the 1851 Great Exhibition, the objective being to promote the Prince as a patron of the arts, science and industry. Carlo Marochetti was commissioned to execute the statue in bronze, which would be placed under the canopy on a raised platform thirty feet above the ground. The canopy itself was to be decorated with mosaics and raised on granite marble columns, surrounded by carved angels. Below this central podium, and enclosing it on four sides, would be a frieze of sculptures in white Sicilian marble, with statues at each corner representing agriculture, manufactures, commerce and engineering. At ground level, at the foot of a series of marble steps, four further statuary groups would be placed at each outer corner, representing the continents of the British Empire: Europe, Asia, Africa and America. Marochetti's initial plaster model of the statue was, however, twice rejected by Scott, and when Marochetti died suddenly in Paris in December 1867 before completing his third version, the commission for the statue was passed to another favourite royal sculptor, John Foley. This, and other delays, as well as logistical problems and fierce arguments over escalating costs, meant that the whole project would take more than a decade to be completed.

In the meantime, in the summer of 1865, the entire royal family and more than a dozen near-relatives gathered in Coburg for the unveiling of a statue to Albert that was, of all of the many representations of him, perhaps the most personal, erected as it was so near to his birthplace and unveiled on Albert's birthday, 26 August. Victoria complained of having to endure the full glare of publicity during what was a particularly theatrical ceremony, and ensured that she arrived back in England unobserved, avoiding the public reception being prepared for her at Woolwich when she landed. Tickets had already been issued when she sent instructions that she wished for 'the greatest privacy' – a fact that rankled with the many dockyard workers and officials denied any sight of her. Her 'dismal debarkation' back home in England on 8 September was thus in marked contrast to all the pomp and ceremony indulged in at Coburg, where everyone agreed that she had, surprisingly, looked the picture of good health.[5]

To compensate her public for this disappointment, Victoria agreed to a rare public appearance the following year to unveil a statue of Albert on horseback at Wolverhampton, in the heart of the Black Country; 100,000 people turned out to see her, but the Queen's very name sounded 'strange and odd' to a mining community so far from the capital and whose denizens slaved for the most part in the darkness amidst its black slag-heaps. Victoria remained for the short time she was there a distant figure huddled in black, almost lost in the bleak industrial landscape.[6] As she drove back along a three-mile route through the poorest part of the town she was gratified to see flags and decorations celebrating her visit on even 'the most wretched-looking slums'. The people were half-starved and in tatters, she noted, but how comforting was the warmth with which they greeted 'their poor widowed Queen'. In reporting the visit, the normally uncontroversial *Ladies' Companion* could not contain its sense of cynicism: the good people of Wolverhampton had been 'mad with pleasure' at the all-too-rare sight of Her Majesty '*in propria persona*', but what was the point, it asked, of 'yet another statue to Albert the Good'? A better example had been set by the widow of the explorer Sir John Franklin – lost at sea while charting the North-West Passage in the Canadian Arctic. The bold and intrepid Lady Jane had 'not allowed her bereavement to drive her into retirement but rather to mix with human-kind to her own benefit and theirs'.[7] Far away on the Indian subcontinent the press was stirring, with the Calcutta-based newspaper the *Friend of India* remarking of the Queen's tedious inauguration of endless statues to Albert that her grief was 'overdone' and that, as sovereign, she had 'higher duties to perform': if Albert were alive, the paper had no doubt that 'he would have been among the foremost to discourage the redundancy of such displays'.[8]

In the meantime, all attempts at coaxing the Queen out of retirement other than to commemorate Albert (and no matter how subtle) were still being met with total obduracy. Nothing could supplant him as her first and greatest preoccupation: not her religious faith, not her children, not even her duty to her country. Duty had been the motivating force in Albert's life, but with Victoria it was different. She wanted more; she wanted love. Without it – without Albert – all she had to cling to was her great and enduring grief. But as her family and court watched in dismay, the damage of such pathological mourning to her normal func-tioning as monarch was becoming ever more apparent. Her recovery was not, as one might normally expect, contingent on the passage of time, as a simple matter of 'getting over it'. What was needed was a crucial and necessary shift in dependency, from her dead husband to a living substitute: a strong and protective male, who would look after her as Albert had done. This role now fell to the most unlikely of candidates – the blunt and down-to-earth John Brown, who after his arrival at Windsor at the end of 1864 had slowly begun to break down the incapacitating pattern of the Queen's grief at a time when every other option had failed.

* * *

The second of nine sons in a family of eleven children, the blond-haired, blue-eyed Brown had been an ostler at Balmoral when it was leased by Sir Robert Gordon prior to the estate being purchased by Victoria and Albert. It was Prince Albert who first spotted Brown's usefulness, and promoted him to the role of ghillie to the royal family in the autumn of 1849. In 1851 Brown found favour with the Queen when he began leading her out on her pony during her annual holiday at Balmoral. By 1858 Prince Albert had appointed him the Queen's 'particular ghillie' in Scotland, as one of several favoured Highland attendants, from which position he rapidly gained the ascendant by proving himself indispensable when accompanying Victoria and Albert on their incognito 'expeditions' in and around the Highlands during 1860 and 1861. Brown's roles were several: groom, ostler, footman, page, and even maid – for the terms of his employment included cleaning Victoria's boots and brushing her skirts and cloaks. He also performed the role of self-appointed bodyguard whenever the Queen drove out. In the autumn of 1863, returning as darkness fell from an excursion to Altnagiuthasach, Victoria, Helena and Alice had narrowly escaped serious injury when their carriage, thanks to the ineptitude of its aged and drunken coachman, had overturned on the road. Brown, who was thrown in the fall and clearly hurt, had immediately insisted on attending to them, wrapping them in blankets in the shelter of the overturned carriage and standing guard till help arrived. Such manly protectiveness went straight to Victoria's needy heart.

Within a couple of months of Brown's arrival at Windsor, the Queen's mood rapidly lifted, much of it down to the effect of his physical presence: she felt safe when he was around. Here was a strong arm on which she could depend, and whose every waking thought was concerned with her sole comfort, for, as she told Vicky, 'God knows how I want so much to be taken care of.' She poured out her admiration for Brown in a letter to Uncle Leopold, informing him that she had appointed the thirty-eight-year-old 'to attend me always'. She accorded him the title of 'The Queen's Highland Servant' on a generous salary of £120 per annum, making Brown second in rank only to Rudolf Löhlein, Albert's former valet, who on his master's death had been promoted by the Queen to Principal Personal Servant.[9] She was now riding daily, with Brown always at her side, and gave him sole responsibility for the organisation of her horses and carriages, as well as taking charge of her many dogs and even deciding which members of her household were allowed to ride which of her 'dear little Highland ponies' up at Balmoral.[10] Under Brown's influence, Victoria's adulation of all things Scottish – so far removed from the 'mere miserable frivolities and worldinesses of this wicked world' – swelled into panegyric. Highlanders, in her opinion, were 'high bred' and full of poetry, simplicity and truth, and 'might be trusted with all the secrets of the universe'.[11] She revered Brown's feral masculinity and brooked no criticism of him; he was 'superior in feeling, sense and judgment' to all her other servants, even her maids. She fretted when he got cold and wet out leading her pony in all weathers, bare-legged in his kilt and with no protective clothing. She was concerned that he never took proper care of himself and refused to take holidays, which is no doubt why she turned a blind eye to the essential whisky flask that accompanied him everywhere; in fact she issued a general order that all royal coaches should carry a bottle of whisky under the coachman's seat, in case of emergencies. Victoria herself had long enjoyed her favourite brands of Auld Kirk and Lochnagar whisky (the latter brewed on her own estates). She had been in the habit of taking whisky in a glass or two of burgundy at dinner and of adding it to her tea; in later years she increasingly enjoyed the medicinal benefits of whisky with Apollinaris mineral water, supposedly on her doctors' orders (whisky being considered beneficial in countering rheumatism). The comforts of whisky appear to have grown rather than diminished during her widowhood, no doubt easing the pain of her bereavement, but also conceivably triggering some of her more irascible and unreasonable behaviour.[12]

But Brown's meteoric rise to the position of favourite inevitably caused problems in the royal household. Her children remained stubbornly immune to his wholesome Scottish charms and were uneasy at his increasing influence over their mother. They were shocked to learn that she tolerated him – a mere servant – calling her 'wumman' with almost marital familiarity, and that she allowed him unprecedented access to her apartments. Soon Brown was gaining a say in everyday, domestic affairs, which alienated the other servants, who hated his gruff and autocratic manner. The Queen's entourage also bridled at his brusqueness and his crude political and religious views, in the main dismissing him out of hand as ill-mannered, coarse and dictatorial. In so doing they failed to understand the value of John Brown's essentially honest personality – which was so like the Queen's – and his absolute fidelity to her, as head of the clan. None seemed able to comprehend the power of his natural magnetism (as the epitome of the Noble Savage), any more than those at the Russian court would understand the similar influence Rasputin had over Victoria's granddaughter, the Tsaritsa Alexandra. The Queen's equerry Henry Ponsonby (who came to know the Queen very well later on as her Private Secretary) was perhaps the most tolerant and came closest to understanding Brown's charisma as a 'child of nature', but others, seeking to debunk him and his hold over the Queen, put it down to some kind of sinister mystic power – of supposed second sight – with Brown acting as the spirit medium through whom the Queen communicated with Albert on the other side.[13]

*   *   *

Persistent and unsubstantiated rumour that the Queen sought the help of spiritualists and mediums during her widowhood first reared its head in the 1860s and has never entirely gone away.[14] Much was made of Victoria and (prior to his death) Albert's passing interest in spiritism, mesmerism and magnetism, all of which had become fashionable when the cult of spirit-rapping and table-turning first arrived from the USA at the end of the 1840s. Since childhood Victoria had had a fascination for ghosts and hauntings, coupled with a tendency to be superstitious, and the enormous popularity of spiritualism fed into her natural curiosity. She and Albert had tried out table-turning, almost as a party game, when it had been all the rage, and they were said to have attended demonstrations by the sought-after medium David Dunglass Home, who was patronised by their friends Napoleon III and Empress Eugénie of France. But their interest in these and other such phenomena had been more as performance art – or, in Albert's case, as pseudo-science – rather than out of religious conviction. Many Victorian notables, from Gladstone to Harriet Martineau to Elizabeth Barrett Browning, Tennyson and Dante Gabriel Rossetti, had all, at one time or another, been drawn to psychic phenomena; as too were several ladies at court, such as the Queen's close friend Madame Van de Weyer, who was fanatically devoted to spiritualism.[15] But Prince Albert was too great an admirer of science and the rational, and Victoria too practical, too grounded in basic common sense, to be taken in by a spiritualist movement that was rapidly becoming tainted by fraudulence and deception.

The religious faith that Victoria and Albert had shared, and had openly discussed at length during their marriage, was based on a profound Christian belief in the spirit's survival after the death of the body. From the moment of his death Victoria had had a strong sense of Albert's continuing presence, both at home and especially in the mausoleum. In her widowhood she found her own very personal way of communing with him – often by sitting in front of his bust or holding some memento of him in her hand, such as the ivory miniature bust that she always carried in an oval case in her pocket. Before she signed any official documents Victoria was often seen to look up at Albert's marble bust and ask him whether he approved. Sometimes, when she was out driving in Scotland, she would open a small brooch that she wore with Albert's likeness in it and 'show' him an interesting view. She often talked out loud to him on a problem, or concentrated her thoughts on what he had said on a particular subject in a letter or memorandum in order to find inspiration.[16] With the reassuring presence of Brown close at hand (a man in whom Albert himself had invested great trust), she felt more connected to her dead husband and their former happy life together. Scotland – as represented by Brown – was the powerful, symbiotic link that bound her to Albert. She had no need, as the gossip alleged, of Brown's supposed psychic power (or anyone else's) to conjure Albert's spirit for her; her husband was there with her at all times, as a life presence.

John Brown's therapeutic effect on the Queen was in fact a quite simple one: like Albert before him, he took no nonsense from her and spoke his mind, treating her with the kind of male machismo that she admired. His presence gave her a new grip on life and, thanks to him, her depression had lifted and her terrible sense of yearning was, at last, abating, so much so that after visiting the mausoleum one day in June 1865 she confided to her journal: 'thank god! I feel more and more that my beloved one is *everywhere* not only there.'[17] Brown understood her loss; observing her at the mausoleum on Albert's anniversary that December, he told Victoria how sorry he felt that there was 'no more pleasure' for her, with her husband now in the tomb. 'I feel for ye but what can I do though for ye?' he had asked, adding, 'I could die for ye.' He promised her she would 'never have an honester servant', and she knew it, which is why any connivance at Brown's displacement failed dismally.[18]

John Brown was Queen Victoria's lifeline. Sensing the mounting resentment towards him in her household, she went to great pains to defend his position, even hiring a genealogist to trace his pedigree. An ancestral link with the Farquharsons of Inverey was discovered, which entitled Brown to carry a coat of arms and brought promotion and a role indoors, as well as out; soon afterwards Victoria further endorsed Brown's position of favour by commissioning a bust of him by the sculptor Joseph Edgar Boehm. Gradually a new, lighter tenor emerged in her journal and her letters to her family. Eulogies to Albert still played their part, as too did the constant insistence on her state of desolation without him, but there was room too for reiterations of her deepening romantic admiration for John Brown and his fine, upstanding qualities: his simplicity, kindness, disinterest, devotion, faithfulness, attention, care, intelligence, discretion and common sense. The Queen's comments were full of her usual, disarming truthfulness and innocence, yet there were already gossips on the lookout for something more sinister – if not sexually compromising.

* * *

On a rare outing in April 1866 to visit the army barracks at Aldershot, the press first noted the presence of the 'stalwart form and picturesque dress' of the Queen's ghillie John Brown 'seated in the rumble of her majesty's carriage'. 'Gillie Brown', it was noted, was to be seen in regular 'respectful attendance' on her; indeed, he seemed to already enjoy the unique position at court previously held by men such as 'Rustan, the Mameluke slave who had loyally served Napoleon the Great'.[19] Brown was now always at the Queen's side during her carriage drives or pony rides, morning and afternoon, whatever the weather. At Balmoral it was Brown, rather than her secretary, who brought Victoria each day's mail and remained alone in her study with her, ready to fold and seal her responses. He became extremely protective, defending her from anyone whom he felt to be a time-waster. Increasingly the royal household found themselves held at arm's length from the Queen, whilst Brown enjoyed unprecedented access to her behind closed doors. When she worked on official business in her sitting room at Windsor, Brown would stand outside, barring the way in and 'fending off even the highest in the land'.[20] He would often be the one chosen to pass on orders and even reprimands from the Queen to members of her household, a fact that particularly rankled with her secretary, General Grey. Such unconscionable familiarity with the Queen, combined with Brown's peremptory, tactless behaviour, provoked bitter complaints from the Queen's children, especially Bertie, who detested him. It also inspired jealousy in the household and sometimes led to outright quarrels in which Brown always got the upper hand. The gentlemen at court were greatly annoyed to discover that while the Queen disapproved of their drinking and smoking – notably that of her own sons – with characteristic inconsistency she indulged Brown's addiction to whisky and turned a blind eye to his regular bouts of inebriation and his stinking pipe, which she even allowed him to light in her presence.

As Victoria's friendship with Brown blossomed, the years 1865–6 were tempered by a succession of deaths. In October 1865 the loss of Lord Palmerston – who had doddered on in Parliament, dying in harness at the age of eighty-one – was a great sorrow, and another link with Victoria's safer 'happy past' gone for ever.[21] The death of her ailing Uncle Leopold was another blow when it followed on 10 December, with Victoria feeling even more the loneliness of her position as head now of the Saxe-Coburg family. In her widowhood she became accomplished at the art of heartfelt womanly condolence, writing with great kindness always to the widows of those who had served her, and in turn remembering those, when they died, who had commiserated with her own earlier distress. She was quick to pick up her pen and write to Mary Lincoln when the US President was assassinated in April 1865, offering her own 'deep and heartfelt sympathy', while taking advantage of yet another opportunity to reiterate how 'utterly broken hearted' she remained at the loss of her own husband.[22] She likewise consoled the widow of Sir Charles Phipps when he succumbed to bronchitis at the age of sixty-five in February 1865, prematurely worn out in loyal and unstinting service to her. Victoria insisted on paying her respects to his laid-out corpse. She did the same for John Turnbull, Clerk of the Works at Windsor, whom both she and Albert had regarded highly, when he died in April. 'I saw him lifeless in his coffin, looking like a fine old knight,' she told Vicky, adding rather proudly, 'It is the fifth lifeless form I have stood by within five months.'[23]

The rituals of death and mourning were so much part and parcel of her life now that she found their celebration consoling. She liked to be told the deathbed details of those she knew, went to see them laid out and, when she could not, requested photographs of them in their coffins to be sent to her. Even the tragic death of Vicky's two-year-old son Sigismund from meningitis that summer elicited requests for every last detail, which Vicky in her agony felt unable to write down. They discussed the power of sympathy and a comforting presence in their letters, but such was Victoria's solipsism that even this exercise in condolence was more about her own than her daughter's loss. 'There is one person whose sympathy has done me – and does me – more good than almost anyone's,' she told Vicky, 'and that is good, honest Brown.' His positive presence in her life was, however, also provoking a crisis of conscience: her grief, she had to admit to Vicky, was 'less poignant, less intensely violent' and was giving way to a 'settled mournful resignation', for now at last she had someone to fill the void of her 'dreadful loneliness'.[24]

*   *   *

In the autumn of 1865 Queen Victoria came to a decision about the future of her third daughter, Helena. After considering the limited choice of candidates, she had plumped for the rather unprepossessing Prince Christian of Schleswig-Holstein. He was about the best husband she could hope to find for her daughter, who at twenty-four was not blessed with good looks and was rapidly getting past a decent marriageable age. The Prince was already looking old for his thirty-five years; he had been rendered stateless as a result of the recent war, and was penniless to boot. With Christian having little to offer, as well as an unwholesome addiction to tobacco, Victoria was sure that he would not mind the fact that poor Lenchen had 'great difficulties with her figure'. She just wished he 'looked a little younger'; he needed to get out and exercise more, and stop coddling himself and eating so much.[25] The engagement was a relief, but brought with it an unavoidable duty that filled Victoria with terror. In order to obtain government approval for a £30,000 dowry for Helena – as well as a £15,000 annual income for Affie, who came of age that year – she would have to make a major concession and open Parliament in February 1866. It would be the first time since Albert's death that she would undertake a major state appearance. The cup of Victoria's anguish and resentment overflowed in a letter to the Prime Minister Lord John Russell, in which she compared the ordeal to come as an 'execution'. The public had a right to want to see her, she could not deny that, but it was unfeeling to insist on witnessing 'the spectacle of a poor, broken-hearted widow, nervous and shrinking, dragged in deep mourning, alone in State as a Show, where she used to go supported by her husband'. The thought of being 'gazed at, without delicacy of feeling' filled her with horror. [26]

In retaliation, Victoria made the occasion as difficult as she could for everyone involved; she changed the date of the ceremony because it did not fit in with her settled plans for travelling between Osborne and Windsor. She refused to travel in the usual, gilded state coach, but went in the dress-carriage instead, accompanied by Helena and Louise – though she did allow a brief glimpse of herself through its open windows en route to Westminster, despite the cold wind. She gave a small bow to the enthusiastic crowds when she got out of the coach on arrival. Arthur Munby thought his monarch looked 'very stout, very red in the face' and, although she was well received, her reception was not as warm at that for the Princess of Wales, who followed in the next carriage.[27] Victoria entered, dressed in her habitual crape with white lace cap and veil, though on this occasion there was a surprising addition – the cap was edged at the front with diamonds, and topped with a small diamond and sapphire coronet. Even thus subdued, she had an inescapable aura of queenliness, enhanced by the famous Koh-i-noor diamond, which she also wore, set as a brooch. But she refused to wear her ermine robe of state, which was instead draped across her chair; as she sat in it, Louise and Helena arranged it around her. Seeing Albert's robe lying on the vacant seat beside her, she paused and touched it, 'as a Catholic might a relic'.[28]

Victoria sat there motionless as she waited for the members of the Commons to be admitted; 'they came with a tremendous rush and noise and scrambling', in contrast to the members of the Lords in their robes already assembled.[29] Never, since Victoria opened Parliament in 1837, had 'so many peeresses applied for tickets for admission', wrote one commentator, all of them eager to see 'how the Royal widow would bear the sudden blaze of publicity'. To many, her presence that day seemed a long-awaited 'resurrection of royalty'.[30] Here was a scene of pageantry on a far grander scale than Bertie's wedding, of ladies in their finest jewels and court dress, the chamber 'billowy with necks and shoulders'; and there was the Queen, 'the only homely woman in the house', whose drab appearance was accentuated all the more by the presence of the superbly dressed Princess of Wales.[31]

Victoria's face remained stony and expressionless as her speech was read for her by the Lord Chancellor. She sat there stiff and erect, 'as though carved on the throne'.[32] 'Not a nerve in her face moved . . . but her nostrils quivered and widened . . . Tears gathered on the fringe of the drooping eyelids. A few rolled down the cheeks.'[33] After it was over, she made a slight bow, then bent and kissed a respectful and dignified Bertie, who escorted her out via the back door to her coach and thence, post-haste, to the privacy of Osborne. The following day she was, she claimed, in a state of physical collapse: 'shaken', 'exhausted' and still reeling from the 'violent nervous shock' of it all.[34] But like it or not, during 1866 she was coaxed out into public again: to London Zoo, the South Kensington Museum, the Union Workhouse at Windsor and even a visit to the women's wing at Parkhurst Prison on the Isle of Wight, where she was shocked to see the number of women incarcerated for murdering their illegitimate babies. During her stay at Balmoral she attended the Braemar Gathering for the first time in five years, and opened the sluice of the new waterworks at Aberdeen. But none of it – even her social appearances at a Drawing Room, two garden parties at Buckingham Palace and the weddings of Helena and Princess Mary Adelaide – changed her determination to 'lead a private life'.[35] She still felt hard done by, that she was being treated 'as an unfeeling *machine*' rather than the 'poor weak woman shattered by grief' that she really was.[36] The public had a rather different view of things: 'What do we pay her for if she will not work?' . . . 'She had better abdicate if she is incompetent to do her duty' were the kind of accusations now going round, according to Lady Amberley. Would it not be a good thing, pondered the *Pall Mall Gazette*, if the Queen could 'find in the capital itself her Balmoral? . . . If she needs comfort and consolation, let her know them among the denizens of her metropolitan city. The gratitude of a million hearts is worth a good many miles of Highland scenery.'[37]

The *Pall Mall Gazette* had good reason to carp: the Queen's clear preference for the company of John Brown and Scotland was beginning to cost her public image dear. Rumour and salacious gossip were circulating about the nature of their relationship and his seemingly insidious control over her. Some suspected it of harbouring a familiarity that went way beyond the bounds of decency, and the rumours in Britain and on the Continent prompted much satirical comment. *Punch,* in a parody of the dreary and uneventful Court Circular so typical of the Queen's sojourns at Balmoral, described a day in the life of Mr John Brown, who 'walked on the slopes . . . partook of a haggis' and in the evening 'was pleased to listen to a bag-pipe'. The local Scottish press took delight in spreading stories about 'The Great Court Favourite' and his fondness for whisky.[38] With the Queen now being widely referred to as 'Mrs Brown', it was insinuated that Brown was not only the power behind the throne, but that he had also found his way into the royal bed. Other papers, seeking to undermine his position, spread a story that Brown was about to leave to get married.[39]

Criticism of the Queen took a new turn in the summer of 1867 when a rival publication to Punch, the Tomahawk, launched a much more combative line on the Queen's favouritism of Brown and her continuing abdication of her duty. A major controversy had broken in May, when Sir Edwin Landseer had exhibited a painting at the Royal Academy's Spring Exhibition. Entitled 'Her Majesty at Osborne, 1866', this had depicted Queen Victoria sitting side-saddle in her widow's weeds on her pony Flora and reading a letter, with Brown standing at its head holding the reins. Such an informal painting of the Queen in close proximity with a servant provoked much sniggering by onlookers, as well as disapproval in the press for its 'imprudence'. 'A more lugubrious, disagreeable, and vulgar production we seldom remember to have seen,' remarked one reviewer.[40]

Rising to the occasion, the Tomahawk – which was subtitled A Saturday Journal of Satire and featured cartoons in the tradition of the Regency satirist Gillray – responded with a caricature of the Landseer painting, entitled 'All is black which is not Brown!'[41] The joke was picked up by Punch soon afterwards, but it was the Tomahawk that continued to lead the fray in ever bolder, more scurrilous challenges to the Queen, running a front-page leader entitled 'Where is Britannia' and a cartoon of the same title in its issue of 8 June; it followed on 10 August with a double-page pull-out cartoon, 'A Brown Study?', highlighting the Queen's symbolic abdication by showing a vacant throne with the discarded robes of state lying on it, the disused crown under a bell jar, and a nonchalant Brown, leaning against the throne, pipe in hand. The issue sent Tomahawk's sales rocketing to a massive 50,000 copies. Yet another Tomahawk cartoon followed soon after, entitled 'The Mystery of the Season', with Brown again leaning against an empty throne, accompanied by an article calling for a regency of the Prince of Wales: the Queen should retreat permanently 'to an honourable retirement' while she still had the affection of her people. She could then revel in the 'congenial solitudes of Osborne and Balmoral without any reproach'. With the *Tomahawk* putting the Queen's behaviour down to her 'deplorable mental health', the old rumours about madness once again surfaced, fanning the flames of gossip.[42] Some, like Harriet Martineau, rose to her defence: 'If the widowed grandmother of a dozen children is not safe from London tongues, the less we say about English morals and manners the better.'[43] But this was as nothing compared to the innuendo circulated on the Continent by the *Gazette de Lausanne*. The Swiss newspaper not only alleged a secret morganatic marriage between the Queen and Brown, but suggested that she was in an 'interesting condition'. This, in the view of the British consul in Berne, so seriously impugned the Queen's reputation that he lodged an informal complaint, but was forced to withdraw it by the Foreign Office because it had not been submitted through the proper channels. The British press respectfully declined to comment, though the republican-minded *Reynolds's Newspaper* could not resist the teasing remark, 'We do not care to reproduce in our columns the many extraordinary causes that are assigned for the Queen's seclusion in the pages of our foreign contemporaries.'[44]

Queen Victoria was kept in ignorance of this latest scandal on the Continent; as for the rest, she was adamant on the issue of Brown's incorruptibility. None of the gossip, or the publication of scurrilous penny pamphlets such as 'John Brown, or, The Fortunes of a Gillie', deterred her from her continuing preference for Brown's close attendance on her at all times. 'He is only a servant and nothing more', attested Henry Ponsonby. In his opinion, what had begun as a joke had been 'perverted into a libel'; the Queen understood only too well her unique position as monarch, and Brown's as her social inferior.[45] Nevertheless, yet another crisis involving Brown soon followed. In May 1867 he had been much talked about when he had appeared in the procession behind the Queen when she laid the foundation stone for the Royal Albert Hall of Arts and Sciences. Shortly afterwards Victoria announced that he would accompany her on the box of her open carriage to a Military Review in Hyde Park. Her Prime Minister, Lord Derby, and the Duke of Cambridge, as C-in-C of the Army, objected most forcefully, seeing such an appearance as seriously compromising to the integrity of the throne, in the light of so much unfavourable recent gossip. But all attempts to dissuade the Queen from taking her 'faithful Brown' with her that day failed – even warnings of anti-Brown demonstrations. Victoria professed herself 'astonished and shocked' at being 'plagued by the interference of others' and refused to go without him.[46] The monarchy was, however, spared a major public embarrassment when shortly afterwards Victoria's Hapsburg relative, Emperor Maximilian of Mexico, was executed by rebels during an uprising. An immediate – and in this case merciful – retreat into court mourning saved Victoria's face. But she made her feelings clear in no uncertain terms: 'The Queen will not be dictated to, or *made* to *alter* what she has found to answer for her comfort.' She put the whole affair down to 'ill-natured gossip in the higher classes, caused by the dissatisfaction at *not forcing* the Queen *out*'.[47] The more pressure was put upon her, and the more lies circulated about her 'poor good Brown', the more her hackles rose. Digging in her heels, she continued to punish them all for hounding her, and locked herself away at Balmoral.

The Queen's stubbornness about spending five months of the year at her Scottish home – 600 miles and a twenty-four-hour train journey away – involved her ministers in long and tedious journeys to Scotland in order to conduct essential business with her and was creating serious administrative problems. In the summer of 1866 political crisis in London had broken over the stormy passage of the 2nd Reform Bill to extend the voting franchise. Victoria had failed to remain in the capital to exercise her constitutional role as figurehead during the debates, instead decamping to Balmoral on 13 June in order to avoid the ugly experience of 'that stupid reform agitation'.[48] Lord John Russell's Liberal government fell on 20 June when they lost the vote by a narrow margin of eleven votes. Greatly inconvenienced by this turn of events and not wishing to leave Balmoral, Victoria insisted that, because the division had been so close, Lord John Russell should for the present remain in office. The Cabinet, however, pressed for him to do the right thing and resign. Constitutionally the Queen was obliged to return to accept her retiring ministers' seals of office, but she refused to budge until she was ready. Such a wilful reversion to the kind of old-style absolutism that she had first displayed as an inexperienced young queen in the late 1830s, and which Albert had worked so hard against, sent her household into despair. The Queen had been 'forgetting her duties in the pleasant breezes of Scotland', commented Henry Ponsonby. Lucy Cavendish, normally so loyal and defensive of her mistress, was shocked at 'the poor Queen's terrible fault in remaining (or indeed being) at Balmoral', for it had 'given rise to universal complaint, and much foul-mouthed gossip'.[49] This was not an action that would 'gratify the spirit' of her late husband, argued the *Tomahawk,* 'any more than it is consonant with the spirit of your people'. The Queen's behaviour was 'unbusinesslike' and 'childish', railed *The Economist.* The popular explanation was simpler: 'John Brown would not let her come.'[50]

At a public meeting in support of electoral reform held at St James's Hall in London, the Liberal MP Acton Smee Ayrton condemned the Queen's continuing retirement, only to be chastised by the Quaker John Bright, who like many in the middle classes was still prepared to defend her womanly grieving 'for the lost object of her life and affection'.[51] Bright's response rallied the crowd that night to loyal choruses of 'God Save the Queen', but dissent did not die down. Abandoned by its monarch, the capital seethed and buzzed with republican talk, as hopes of reform collapsed and the country was left in limbo until Victoria finally returned on 26 June. General Grey was no longer able to conceal from her the very strong feeling among the public that, in her retirement from view, the 'tone of society is much deteriorated'. The situation had been further exacerbated by the continuing absence of state ceremonial; already that year Victoria had adamantly refused to entertain Tsar Alexander II and the Khedive of Egypt when they were in London; and now she was doing her damnedest to avoid the Sultan of Turkey, who was due on a visit. Faced with this latest and most unwanted of duties, Victoria called on good Dr Jenner to produce a royal sick-note. He could always be relied upon to extricate her from duties that she did not wish to undertake, and obliged in the most lurid tones. The Queen's health simply was not up to it. 'Any excitement produces the most severe bilious derangement, which induces vomiting to an incredible extent,' Jenner told Grey. Just to be doubly certain, he waved the madness flag that always silenced Victoria's critics: any further undermining of the Queen's health might precipitate complete mental breakdown. At Victoria's request, Jenner also inserted an announcement about her indisposition in *The Lancet.*[52] In the end the Queen did not entirely wriggle out of entertaining the Sultan. The bulk of her duties were offloaded onto Bertie and Alix, but despite it being 'extremely inconvenient and disadvantageous' for her well-being, she grudgingly agreed to meet the Sultan on board the royal yacht at a naval review off Spithead, during which, despite all her protestations of ill health, her own sea legs proved a great deal stronger than his.[53]

* * *

By the end of 1867 it was clear that anti-monarchical, if not outright

republican sentiment was mounting in Britain. Victoria had been hissed
and booed en route to the state opening of Parliament, which she had
once more deigned to undertake that year. She saw at last the ugly faces
of anger in the crowd, and even admitted to Grey that she felt 'something
unpleasant' might happen 'with the existing agitation about Reform, and
the numbers of people out of employment'. Yet still she failed to connect
the pattern of overt public disapproval with her own stubborn behaviour;
still she clung to power and her royal prerogatives, while increasingly
lauding the homely Scots as being infinitely superior to the English
people who clamoured for her presence in London.[54] She remained
wilfully oblivious to the everyday realities of hunger and urban poverty
at a time when cholera was once more rife; of political unrest and
increasing class divisions. 'The Queen is teaching the people to think too
little of her office,' observed the *Daily News*. In the House of Commons,
Viscount Cranbourne went further, stating that in Britain 'the monarchy
was practically dead'.[55] By no means, responded *Reynolds's Newspaper*:
the monarchy 'lives, eats, drinks, and breeds as vigorously as ever'. In
all, the royal family plus 'the shoal of German and English parasites'
connected to it accounted for one million pounds of public spending per
annum.

General Grey had no doubt that unless something was done, the situation would get worse and 'very serious consequences may be the result'.
The Queen was the only person, he told her, who had the power to
stem the growing tide of her own public disfavour, 'by resuming the
place which none but Your Majesty can fill'. But he knew that putting
pressure on her would only undo what little power he had to do any
good.[56] Before Sir Charles Phipps's death, Grey had concurred with him
that 'The Queen is *perfectly* aware of what her subjects wish, nor can
she be ignorant of what her position requires.' But so far none in government had had any sway over the vagaries of her volatile temperament
and her stubborn self-interest. Only Prince Albert had known how to
handle what Dr Clark had called the Queen's propensity to 'mental
irritation'. Albert himself had said as much to Lord Clarendon. 'It is my
business,' he had told him, 'to watch that mind every hour and minute
– to watch as a cat watches at a mousehole.'[57] John Brown might be able
to boil potatoes and cups of tea by the roadside in Scotland, and bully
the Queen into wrapping up warm when out in her carriage, but only
Prince Albert had had the moral power to induce her to fulfil her much
more important constitutional duties when she least wished to.

Victoria meanwhile remained breathtakingly impervious to the criticism, confident as ever in the unassailability of her position. She thought the country 'never more loyal or sound'. 'I would throw myself amongst my English and dear Scotch subjects alone . . . and I should be as safe as in my room,' she told Vicky, shrugging off a recent Fenian plot to kidnap her that had been uncovered by the Home Office. 'There has been a great deal of nonsense and foolish panic, and numberless stories which had proved sheer inventions!' she continued, knowing full well that the hysteria generated by her household at the lack of security at her country residences was just another ploy, along with all the criticism of Brown, to get her to spend more time in London. With public disfavour mounting, she continued vigorously to fight off her critics, without the slightest inkling that help was about to come from the most unexpected of sources: the publication the following January of her 'poor little Highland book'.[58]

CHAPTER THIRTEEN

'The Queen Is Invisible'

From the moment Prince Albert died it had always been Queen Victoria's intention to commemorate his life, not just in visible monuments to him, but also in words. The process had begun soon afterwards, with her request to Alfred Tennyson to write a tribute in verse. This had been followed by a collection of *The Principal Speeches and Addresses of HRH The Prince Consort*, edited by Arthur Helps, which had been released for public consumption in 1863 after a private printing for the royal family the previous year. The speeches had rapidly sold thousands of copies, but Victoria was keen to establish a fuller written legacy of her beloved Albert and had herself embarked on a project to 'put down an exact account of our happy life' – again for family use.[1]

With this in mind, she started sorting through her mass of personal papers, but soon felt overwhelmed by the task and passed the commission over to General Grey, whose post as her Private Secretary had finally been officially ratified in 1866. Having already written a biography of his father, Grey was the obvious choice to write the first account of the Prince's life, although *The Early Years of the Prince Consort* would only cover the story up to the birth of Vicky in 1840. Grey's name might be on the title page, but in fact the book was written under Victoria's close instruction and supervision, using translations from the German of Albert's journals and letters provided by herself and Princess Helena. During the process Grey had had to tolerate the Queen's constant interference, to the extent that the bulk of the work – even down to the footnotes – was largely hers, with Grey fulfilling little more than the role of dutiful compiler, adding the Queen's personal interpolations in many places.[2] Having so much sensitive material put at his disposal, Grey worried that some of the book's candour, even for private circulation within the family, should be modified. As a former military man – bluff, stolid and formal, with a strong sense of his own independence – he found the experience of working on the book with the Queen a trial that had tested his patience to the limit.

Nevertheless *The Early Years of the Prince Consort* was an overnight success when Victoria agreed to its publication for general consumption; so much so that within two days of it going on sale in July 1867 not a copy of Smith & Elder's original print run of 5,000 was to be had in Printers' Row, home then to the British publishing industry. A second edition of 7,000 was immediately ordered, and a third shortly afterwards. An American edition and numerous translations followed, and soon it was announced that future volumes covering the rest of the Prince's life would be undertaken not by Grey, who was too overburdened by work, but by the Scottish scholar and German translator, Theodore Martin.

Predictably, the level of sycophantic review of *The Early Years* matched the hagiography of the original. Copious quotations from the book appeared across the press; *The Early Years*, it was asserted, provided the nation with a 'picture of purity, of self devotion to the claims of duty, of chivalric endurance of obloquy – in a word, of thorough high mindedness in every sense'.[3] The *Quarterly Review* went to extravagant excess in bolstering the inviolability of Albert's 'imperishable reputation'. Spanning twenty-three pages, its exhaustive and adulatory review commended Grey for his discretion as the Queen's amanuensis in 'thread[ing] together the pearls intrusted to him', adding that 'though the threading is his, the pearls are the gift to us of a higher hand'. In short, the book was an example of 'the Sovereign casting herself in her speechless grief upon the sympathy of her people'. Such emotive language of course drew the expected loyal response.[4] Elsewhere, the reviewer of the *Medical Times and Gazette*, while lauding 'the overwhelming affection of the wife' as demonstrated in the book, took this opportunity to suggest that it 'explains her Majesty's present position – a nervous system thoroughly out of gear' – the nearest any published observation on the Queen's state of mind had come to an overt assertion of mental depression. It also provided a typical Victorian circumlocution on her female frailties: 'If we have a queen, we must be content to bear the peculiarities of her sex, even though some of its distinctive virtues may be felt to have become, by excess, somewhat of defects.'[5]

Victoria's intention of producing edifying memorials to Albert for the benefit of her family did not stop with *The Early Years*. At the end of 1867, at a time when she was anxious to defend her favouritism for John Brown and all things Scottish, she was prevailed on by the Dean of

Windsor and others to actually publish something of her own: the journals of her life at Balmoral. The Dean had thought their 'simplicity' and
'kindly feelings' might do 'so much good' to Victoria's flagging reputation, but having allowed their private circulation in the family already,
she had had no intention of them being published.[6] The success of Grey's
biography, plus a desire to circumvent extracts from the Balmoral journals
appearing in garbled and pirated form, persuaded her to agree. At a time
of gathering crisis, they proved to be the perfect palliative. If the Queen
would not make herself visible to her public, then she could at least lift
something of the veil hiding her from view, vicariously, through her
Highland journals. It was an unprecedented royal act, the only previous
sovereign to have published his own opinions in any shape or form having
been King James I with his treatises on monarchy, and his famous and
idiosyncratic swipe at smoking, 'A Counterblaste to Tobacco' of 1604.

* * *

From the outset Queen Victoria was under no illusions about her creative gifts, modestly protesting that the journals were mere 'homely'
descriptions of her outings in and around Balmoral – which indeed they
were. That did not deter her, however, from sending a copy to Charles
Dickens, 'from the humblest of writers to one of the greatest'.[7] In
Victoria's case it was precisely the book's intrinsic qualities of simple
sentiment and mundanity that proved to be pure marketing gold. Arthur
Helps was once more recruited as editor and did his tactful best, as
unobtrusively as possible, to eradicate some of the Queen's lapses in
grammar, her repetition and use of colloquialisms and slang, as well as
expunging some of her more excessive underlining. The published edition
that appeared early in January 1868 was handsome to look at, bound in
moss-green leather with gold tooling; a large quarto edition that followed
a year later was illustrated, in addition to the original engravings, with
some of Victoria's own charming watercolours of Scotland. Entitled
Leaves from the Journal of Our Life in the Highlands, from 1848 to 1861, the
book was dedicated, of course, 'to the dear memory of him who made
the life of the writer bright and happy', its every page bearing the stamp
of the husband who had inspired it and of his wife's inexhaustible love
for him, in entries such as that for 13 October 1856:

> Every year my heart becomes more fixed in this dear paradise, and so
> much more so now, that all has become my dearest Albert's own creation,

own work, own building, own laying out, as at Osborne; and his great taste, and the impress of his dear hand, has been stamped everywhere.[8]

But while the book celebrated Albert as archetypal Highland laird, out shooting, fishing, riding and walking, it was the book's innate simplicity and warm-heartedness, and its projection of Victoria as an ordinary, private individual rather than as Queen, which immediately endeared it to the public and reviewers and restored something of her lost reputation. The British press in the main was disarmed by the lack of pretension of this 'woman's book'; to criticise its patently honest intentions would have been churlish, for here was something, in the estimation of *The Times*, that appealed 'directly to the common heart'.[9] Like *The Early Years*, it was heaped with excessive, if not outlandish praise, with the reviewer of the *Morning Post* commending it as being one of the best things ever written.

Victoria was delighted with her reviews, which came thick and fast. 'Newspapers shower in,' she told Vicky on 22 January.[10] She had even indulged in a little manipulation in the process; having liked the review of *The Early Years* by the Scottish writer and literary critic Margaret Oliphant, and expecting her to be likewise favourably disposed to her own modest offering, Victoria specifically requested that Oliphant review *Leaves*. Oliphant was extremely reluctant to be sycophantic to order; 'the queen's book,' she told a friend, 'looks mighty like a little girl's diary of travel and is innocent to the last degree. Would that it was consistent with loyalty to make fun of it.'[11] But she could not do so, for she was shrewd enough to know the value of the royal seal of approval and so she agreed, 'on condition that I am not asked to tackle the holy Albert again'. Privately Oliphant had scant regard for Victoria's amateurish literary endeavour and warned of the danger of her conceiving literary ambitions above her most limited ability. But she knew what the Queen could do for her, and so in her review in *Blackwood's Magazine* in February 1868 she admired the book's artlessness, spontaneity and simplicity, ensuring a generous fee of £100 and the award soon after of a Civil List pension, while keeping to herself her judgement on its literary merits.[12]

Other reviewers, however, could not restrain their excessive panegyrics to 'the queen's book'. 'She has claimed her place in that great freemasonry which is open to all ranks and races – the freemasonry of those who believe still in love, chivalry, romance,' proclaimed *Fraser's Magazine*. It was 'a homely book, made up of human nature's daily food,' extolled the *North British Review*.[13] The *Daily Telegraph* voiced the hope of many that in its very personal tone the book might in some way fill the void of the Queen's absence from view, by drawing her public 'nearer to the every-day life of a living QUEEN than any persons not courtiers ever came before'; and indeed, the archetype of virtuous family life celebrated within the book was set in stark contrast to the artificiality of court life. 'Thank GOD there are many thousand English homes like this,' it went on, for the Queen had 'no Royal monopoly of that pure light of household love which shines by so many English hearths'.[14] Only the *Tomahawk* dared to poke fun at the book's crippling ordinariness: 'the bubble about the queen walking about her royal parks in her coronation robes has long since been exploded,' it remarked. *Leaves* had little to tell Victoria's public, for 'we all know that Her Majesty wears a bonnet in private life'.[15]

Some papers, such as the *Chronicle*, derided the endless references to Victoria's humbler servants, particularly John Brown and the Queen's detailing of 'what he said of the Prince, how he got into the way of changing plates, how he brushed the queen's boots, and wore the royal plaid, how fast he walks and how loudly he cheers, and how much rather she would trust him than the Duke of Athole at an awkward ford'. Such mundanities did not fit the public profile of a sovereign, but, the *Chronicle* added, it 'would not have been made public if the public had not provoked it'.[16] *Reynolds's Newspaper* as usual pulled no punches:

> If this book were issued to the world as the work of Mrs Smith, instead of Victoria, Queen of England, it would not sell a dozen copies. People would wonder at how it came to pass that any sane individual could possibly be induced to publish so many pages of sheer and unmitigated twaddle. Readers would weary of the incessant laudation of her husband by the authoress, and, after throwing the book on one side, pronounce her an amiable monomaniac.[17]

But *Reynolds's* could not hold back the tide of enthusiasm for *Leaves from the Journal*. Respectable middle England fell upon it, attracted by the engaging spontaneity of the Queen's thought. With its warm depiction of the lower classes as embodied in her Scottish servants, *Leaves* was seen as an exemplary lesson in Christian goodness and social tolerance. Victoria knew that the book had no great literary pretensions, but felt that its popularity was a vindication of her own and Albert's deeply held values; 'the kind and proper feeling towards the poor and the servants will I hope do good, for it is very much needed in England among the higher classes'.[18] It was certainly a timely lesson in the virtues of the respectable lower middle classes, who admired the book and had been newly enfranchised with the passing of the 2nd Reform Bill. The aristocracy could not afford to be complacent about the voice of the common man, which was now demanding ever more to be heard, and Victoria was gratified that the public had appreciated how her book had got to the heart of 'what is simple and right'. A Mrs Everett Green, writing on behalf of English wives and mothers everywhere, agreed, telling Arthur Helps that the book provided 'a pattern for every home in the country'; after all, 'a royal example is more potent than a volume of sermons'.[19] In assessing its impact, the diarist Alfred Munby made the shrewd observation that *Leaves* 'may turn out to have been, by its very artlessness, a masterstroke of art', and he was right. Arthur Helps felt the same; the book provided a 'new bond of union' between the Queen and her people at a time when it was sorely needed.[20] Victoria was thrilled with the critical response, but determined not to let it go to her head. She was, she told Theodore Martin, 'much moved – deeply so – but not uplifted or "puffed up" by so much kindness, so much praise'.[21]

Not everyone, however, approved of the openness with which the Queen described her life at Balmoral; Lord Shaftesbury thought it entirely inappropriate that the monarch should reveal 'all that she thinks and does in the innermost recesses of her heart and home'.[22] The reaction in high society was one of horror; the Queen's otherwise devoted former ladies, Lady Augusta Stanley and Lady Lyttleton, had both been less than impressed with her uncritical admiration for all things Scottish, and Henry Ponsonby's bluestocking wife Mary sniggered at the Queen's rather amusing 'literary line'.[23] While Stanley admitted that the journal was 'nice' and 'very interesting', and that it evoked many happy memories of her own years in the Queen's service, she was also highly critical. Arthur Helps's 'apologetic introduction' had made her 'blood boil'; the frenzy of overpraise for this rather guileless book was excessive – as well as politically unfortunate. If the Queen had plumped for Ireland instead of Scotland as the object of her affections, Lady Augusta remarked, 'the ecstasies and interests that would have grown up would have been just as great – and fenianism would never have existed'.[24] Stanley's criticism like that of others in the royal household focused precisely on the element that had won it popular acclaim: the details of the lives of the lowliest of household servants at Balmoral, which gave the impression that the

Queen considered them on the same footing as the aristocracy. An entire entry for 16 September 1850, accompanied by an engraving of him, sang the praises of John Brown as having 'all the independence and elevated feelings peculiar to the Highland race'.[25] And the Queen's children, who thought their mother's book in poor taste, winced at her revelations of what, in their opinion, were far too many personal details. Ministers also worried that, with the decision having been made to exclude all comments relating to issues of public or political importance, it painted a false picture of the Queen's life. With its endless descriptions of picnics, drives, expeditions and pony treks, as well as Albert's voracious stag-hunting, it seemed to suggest that she and her consort had spent most of their time on holiday and at their leisure.

Nevertheless, the book was a huge critical and financial success and quickly became a best-seller, selling 80,000 during the first three months; by the end of the year it had sold 103,000 copies.[26] It was so in demand that 'the circulating libraries ordered it by the ton'.[27] On 14 March the Queen wrote excitedly to Vicky that her book 'had had such an extraordinary effect on the people' that a cheap, 2s. 6d. edition was coming out to deal with pre-orders of 20,000, and another 10,000 were to be printed.[28] In all, it is estimated that the royalties on *Leaves* totalled around £30,000 and most of the profits were given to charity, in the form of educational bursaries for pupils of parish schools, including the local one at Crathie near Balmoral. The book turned out to be an even greater publishing success in the USA; a German translation appeared within a couple of months, as too did one into Gaelic; and many others followed, including Hindustani, and – at the Shah's specific request – Persian.

The enormous success of *Leaves from the Journal of Our Life in the Highlands* was, as a bemused Dean of Windsor observed, 'a most curious turn of the wheel of fortune', for the Queen's book (in addition to General Grey's *Early Years*) had given the monarchy a much-needed boost when its popularity was hitting an all-time low.[29] Victoria felt vindicated by the popular success of her idyllic portrait of family life with Albert and was convinced of 'the good it will do the Throne'.[30] She was hugely relieved, for back in January she had had an anxious conversation with Theodore Martin in which she had urged him to find some way of letting the public know the truth about her withdrawal from public life. It was not her sorrow, great though it still was, she told him, that kept her secluded, but the 'overwhelming amount of work and responsibility':

From the hour she gets out of bed till she gets into it again there is work, work, work – letter-boxes, questions, etc., which are dreadfully exhausting – and if she had not comparative rest and quiet in the evening, she would most likely not be alive. Her brain is constantly overtaxed. Could this truth not be openly put before people?[31]

Martin himself had seen the piles of dispatch boxes requiring the Queen's attention, but had advised against making any public statement on her workload, telling Victoria that her people 'had entire trust in her doing what was best, and that she would appear in public whenever the necessity for doing so arose'.[32] Mercifully, the enthusiastic reception given to her book confirmed this. Scores of 'beautiful and touching' letters had poured in to the Queen, thanking her and 'saying how much more than ever I shall be loved, now that I am known and understood'. Having opened a window on to her private life with Albert, she hoped the book would act as a surrogate for her lack of personal appearances, and that that would be an end to criticism.[33] Slipping back into a dangerous complacency, Victoria felt her confidence further boosted by the attentions of a new and adoring Prime Minister – Benjamin Disraeli.

*   *   *

In February 1868 the seventy-five-year-old Lord Derby had been forced to retire, to be replaced by Disraeli, who had first entered government as Chancellor of the Exchequer under Derby in 1852. Victoria's first impression of him had been somewhat guarded; he seemed to her 'most singular', with his strongly Semitic looks and his shiny black ringlets. He 'had a very bland manner' and she thought his language 'very flowery', but after Albert died, Disraeli's gift for soothing flattery had worked its magic on Victoria with his eulogies to the late Prince as a sovereign manqué and his tributes to Albert's rich and cultivated mind.[34] In March 1863 Victoria, by now entirely won over, had deliberately passed over leading members of the aristocracy to grant seats to Disraeli and his wife at Bertie and Alix's wedding. 'The present man will do well,' she now told Vicky with confidence, for her new Prime Minister seemed 'particularly loyal and anxious to please me in every way'. But Vicky had heard differently; wasn't Mr Disraeli 'vain and ambitious', she asked? That might be so, but all that mattered to Victoria was that he had always treated *her* well and had 'all the right feelings for a Minister towards the Sovereign'; also to his credit was the fact that he had argued vigorously for additional government money for the Albert Memorial.[35] Disraeli's first fawning meetings with the Queen in the spring of 1868 demonstrated to her that he was 'full of poetry, romance and chivalry' – the emotional touchstones on which she thrived. His devotion, his penchant for kissing her hand and his saccharine praise of her authorial gifts, with remarks such as 'We authors ma'am' (he himself being the author of fifteen novels), clearly struck a chord.[36] After being sent a copy of *Leaves* hot off the press, he had lauded its 'essential charms'. 'There is a freshness and fragrance like the heather amidst which it was written,' he told Arthur Helps, words that no doubt found their way straight to the eager ears of the Queen.[37] In response she sent him primroses hand-picked by her at Osborne.

The narcissistic Disraeli had never easily won the admiration of other men, who had resolutely refused to take him seriously; there was just 'too much tinsel' about him, according to Lady Nevill, too much of the poser and dandy.[38] But he did have an extraordinary gift for winning the lifelong devotion of women, and soon proved to have a unique and winning way with his Queen, knowing full well that, in her case, the personal touch was all-important. Thanks to his charms and the warm public reception given to her book, Victoria's mood that year greatly improved. In March she attended her first Drawing Room in London since her widowhood, followed by another in April; she reviewed the troops at Aldershot and in Windsor Home Park, attended the Royal Academy exhibition and a 'breakfast' at Buckingham Palace. As an admirer of Florence Nightingale, she agreed to lay the foundation stone for the new St Thomas's Hospital, where Lucy Cavendish noted how she 'went thro' the ceremony with all her old grace and wonderful dignity, ending with several deep curtseys to the audience'. It was a 'sight to see', she wrote, confirming how well and cheerful the Queen now seemed: 'really our little Queen in her deep black was not outshone even by the lovely, radiant Princess of Wales'.[39]

However, Victoria continued to place very firm restrictions on more onerous public appearances, declining to open Parliament and continuing to resist being in London for more than a few days a year. She constantly complained of how exhausting and noisy she found it there – not to mention the terrible, dense yellow fog. But her spirits were clearly reviving: she started playing the piano again and sketching. She felt she was making a real effort, so she bridled at what she saw as the 'shameless' articles about her that continued to appear in some of the press, such as that in the *Globe* in May, which took her to task for preparing to disappear off to Balmoral while Parliament was in the midst of a crisis and Disraeli's government seemed about to fall.[40] For no sooner had she begun to bask in the warm glow of her new Prime Minister's flattery than in May the Conservative government lost the vote over Opposition leader William Gladstone's resolution to disestablish the Irish Protestant Church. Disraeli offered to resign; loath to lose him, Victoria sought to dissolve Parliament instead, hoping that by going to the country the Tories would be returned in a general election later in the year. Disraeli, after all, was already showing 'more consideration for my comfort than any of the preceding Prime Ministers since Sir Robert Peel and Lord Aberdeen'.[41] She fiercely resisted the pressures to shorten her visit to Balmoral, telling Disraeli that she would return to Windsor only if anything 'very serious should render it necessary', but that she was completely 'done up' by fatigue and worry.[42] Was not the whole week she had spent in London already that year enough to satisfy people?, she asked Theodore Martin, in a letter she sent enlisting his support and that of Arthur Helps in ensuring that no further swipes at her should follow in *The Times* and *Telegraph*.

It all seemed a case of the lady doth protest too much, for Victoria knew full well that later that summer she was planning to go on holiday yet again – this time abroad, to Switzerland – and that further criticism was bound to follow. But nothing for now would induce her to change her plans; on 18 May she departed for Balmoral. It was a highly provocative act: two days later Delane of *The Times* rightly objected to the fact that during this most difficult time 'the first person in the State, to whom recourse must be had in every momentous juncture, was hurrying at full speed from the neighbourhood of the capital to a remote Highland district, six hundred miles from her Ministry and Parliament'. The Queen, he pointed out, would be virtually incommunicado, and it was 'an act of culpable neglect' on the part of Mr Disraeli not to advise her against it.[43] The following day Denis Rearden, the MP for Athlone, submitted a question in the Commons for the Prime Minister as to whether, if the Queen's health 'appears to be so weak that she cannot live in England', she might not best be advised to abdicate or establish a regency under the Prince of Wales.[44] A month previously a seditious placard had been put up in Pall Mall to the same effect. Constitutionally, only the government could put pressure on the Queen, but Disraeli had little power over her at this stage. Victoria was enraged and responded from Balmoral two days later, making the ultimate threat in a letter to Disraeli. She had no doubt that she might look well, but people had no idea how much she really suffered: 'if the public will *not* take her – as she is – she must *give all up* – and give it up to the Prince of Wales'.⁴⁵ She felt totally justified in taking her two scheduled visits to Balmoral that year, which she did with Dr Jenner's full encouragement. Jenner himself saw the Home Secretary soon afterwards and assured him of the Queen's present state of agitation. Without rest he was convinced she would break down completely. Victoria was clearly most determined to have that holiday in Switzerland.

The idea of going there had sprung from accounts Albert had sent her of his travels in Switzerland in 1837 before they married. She had long planned it, in secret, but was determined to go somewhere completely secluded, where 'she can refuse *all* visitors and have *complete* quiet'. In the event, the compliant Disraeli made no objections and the Queen left England on 4 August 1868, 'entirely on the recommendation of her physicians', so the press were told.⁴⁶ She travelled under the rather transparent pseudonym of the Countess of Kent, with her three youngest children and a reduced entourage that included Dr Jenner and her favourite lady-in-waiting, Jane Churchill. Bringing up the rear came a disgruntled John Brown – who hated going abroad – following in a carriage full of all the Queen's picnicking equipment and a few bottles of best Scottish malt. For the next month Victoria made her home at the Pension Wallace overlooking Lake Lucerne. Never since Albert's death had she been so cheerful as during this holiday: talking animatedly and laughing at dinner and, despite the difficulty of her increasing weight and the terrible heat, taking sedate walks, drives and excursions to enjoy the view of mountains and glaciers. In Switzerland she was, for once, relieved of endless mournful reminders of Albert.

Back in England on 11 September, she barely made her presence felt at Windsor before, three days later, heading straight for Balmoral. She was dismayed at the prospect of the imminent general election and the possible loss of Disraeli, who paid her a ten-day visit there; after which she turned her attention resolutely away from politics to disappear off to a new holiday retreat that she had had built at Glassalt Shiel at the northern end of Loch Muick. She and Albert had in the past enjoyed the use of a small cottage three miles away at the other end of the loch, at Altnagiuthasach, but the memories were too painful for Victoria ever to return there. And so she had built this small hunting lodge, nestled in a wild spot at the base of the bare, snow-covered screes up at the northern end, as her 'first widow's house'. With its ten rooms, including her own with its single bed, it was modest by royal standards, but it was her own special refuge, 'not built by him or hallowed by his memory'. In October she held a house-warming there to which her servants were invited. Reels were danced and everyone drank 'whisky-toddy' toasts to the Queen's health and happiness.[47]

After almost two months at Balmoral, Queen Victoria finally arrived back at Windsor in time to regretfully say goodbye to the congenial Disraeli, whose government had been ousted by the Liberals in the general election. She was now obliged to welcome the dour Mr Gladstone as Prime Minister, a man who venerated her as Queen, but who, unlike Disraeli, had none of his gifts of flattery. Knowing this, the Dean of Windsor had advised Gladstone that he must treat his monarch with kid gloves: 'you cannot show too much regard, gentleness, I might even say tenderness towards her,' he had said, but when it came to it, Gladstone was a clodhopper in comparison with the swooning Disraeli.[48] Victoria was of course greatly inconvenienced by this changeover, but tried hard to like Gladstone at first. He seemed cordial and kind, but she soon came to dislike his heavy-handed manner and, worse, he talked too much. After thirty-one years on the throne she did not appreciate being lectured to by him. She missed Disraeli's gossipy informality and charm; nor was she protected any longer by an apologist for her entrenched behaviour. As another year turned, there was no doubt in the mind of Lord Clarendon that the Queen was perfectly up to the job. 'Eliza is roaring well and can do everything she likes and nothing she doesn't,' he told the Duchess of Manchester, using an irreverent nickname current in the royal household.[49] General Grey was in despair; his situation had become 'intolerable', he had told Disraeli; he had been on the brink of resigning and it was only Disraeli who had persuaded him to stay.[50] He shared his apprehensions with Gladstone; it was clear to them both that the Queen had got it into her head that she was far less capable of fulfilling her duties than she really was, that she was playing the feminine-frailty card far too often. What had become of the young queen who had been so anxious to fulfil her duties, when first married, that she allowed herself only three days of honeymoon, insisting to Albert that 'business can stop and wait for nothing'?[51] Seven years on from her husband's death, business had stopped and waited for far too long.

Grey had no doubts that they were dealing with a 'royal malingerer', but that 'nothing will have any effect but a strong – even a peremptory tone' with the Queen. Having convinced herself that she could not cope, she had become entrenched in a 'long unchecked habit of self-indulgence that now makes it impossible for her, without some degree of nervous agitation, to give up, even for ten minutes, the gratification of a single inclination, or even whim'.[52] Her children, particularly the twenty-year-old Princess Louise – who had assumed the role of resident daughter-on-duty after Helena's marriage in 1866 – were very worried about her continuing seclusion. In Louise's view, neither her mother's health nor her strength was 'wanting', as Victoria continued to insist. Grey found a new ally in Louise, who told him that she was 'very decided as to the ability of the Queen to meet any fatigue, and is most indignant with Jenner for encouraging the Queen's fancies about her health'.[53] As for her constant protestations about her volume of work, for all her claims to Theodore Martin, Grey of all people knew the true extent of the Queen's workload. It was as follows: 'In very short notes; in shorter interview, Her Majesty gives me her orders to "write fully" on this or that subject.' Beyond reading the letters or dispatches that Grey placed in front of her, the Queen, in his view, had little else to do, other than 'to approve of the draft which I submit to her'. The put-upon Grey felt that he was the unacknowledged one doing all the donkey work; the Queen only 'exercised her brain or her pen' on matters that affected 'her own comfort' and was happy to delegate the rest to him. 'Pray dismiss from your mind any idea of there being any "weight of work" upon the Queen,' he told Gladstone, adding, 'and this, Princess Louise, emphatically repeats'. Her sister, Princess Helena, had by now come to the conclusion that the only way to get their mother to cooperate was to 'put it plainly upon her duty as head of affairs, and above all, not use the "People say" argument', which 'exasperates Mama'.[54]

Grey anticipated a fight to come as Gladstone weighed in with attempts to persuade Victoria to leave Balmoral early in the autumn of 1869 in order to fulfil an important public engagement – a visit to the city for the first time in eighteen years, to open first the newly built Blackfriars Bridge and then the Holborn Viaduct constructed over the old Fleet Valley, connecting Holborn Hill with Newgate Street. Victoria agreed, on condition that the whole thing would be dependent on the state of her fragile health on the day in question. The Times feared that the many loyal Londoners eagerly looking forward to seeing her might be disappointed. A pavilion and stands to take 4,000 people were erected on the bridge, but what were 4,000 tickets compared to the half a million or so that *The Times* anticipated would assemble out of a 'natural yearning' to see their monarch?[55] High winds and heavy rain the night before spoiled the street decorations and dampened spirits, but Saturday 6 November dawned fine as special trains brought thousands of people into the city for the occasion. Many more flocked to Paddington Station to see the Queen arrive by train at 11.30 a.m. before processing by carriage with an escort of Life Guards (carrying loaded revolvers in case of trouble from Fenians) across London, past Buckingham Palace and over Westminster Bridge to the Surrey side of the river. After Victoria had speedily declared Blackfriars Bridge open, the royal carriage crossed over to the City and on up to the viaduct above Farringdon Street where even greater crowds awaited her. Here John Delane was waiting to see events for himself, having been apprehensive of demonstrations in the wake of a string of recent Fenian outrages and arrests. 'The cold intense, the show poor, but the loyalty great,' he recorded of the event in his diary.[56] Victoria thought the day had gone well, and the enthusiasm had been 'very great', though as usual it had been 'a hard trial' for her.[57] But not everyone that day came to admire, and hissing had been heard from the crowd when her carriage had passed along the Strand.

Victoria did not stay for the banquet given by the Lord Mayor at the Mansion House that evening, where her reply to the loyal address was read for her. Without being unduly overtaxed, she had left London on the royal train for Windsor by 1 p.m. Nevertheless, the *Morning Post* waxed lyrical on the magnanimous gesture she had that day bestowed on her adoring subjects. Her Majesty, it said, had 'broken through the habits of her ordinary life' to 'come up from that Highland Home in which she finds so much tranquil pleasure and consolation, to make evident to her subjects practically the interest which she takes in every occurrence that contributes to their welfare or adds to their enjoyment'.[58]

An hour and a half of the Queen's time in the capital had, however, been a paltry gesture and did nothing to prevent the spectre of unpopularity from rising once more. Victoria as usual remained oblivious to it. 'Nothing could be more successful than the progress and ceremony of Saturday,' she told Theodore Martin. 'The greatest enthusiasm prevailed, and the reception by countless thousands of all classes, especially in the City, was most loyal and gratifying – not a word, not a cry, that could offend any one.' There would therefore, in her estimation, be no need for any public statement on the reasons for her continuing seclusion; the story she would eventually tell in Martin's forthcoming life of Albert 'should fully open the eyes of her people to the truth'.[59]

Unfortunately, the first volume of *The Life of the Prince Consort* would not be published until 1874; meanwhile, early in 1870 the royal family was once more plunged into controversy, when Bertie, his reputation already plummeting thanks to his addiction to racing, gambling and clubbing, was called to give evidence in a scandalous divorce hearing. The petitioner, one of Bertie's acquaintances, Sir Charles Mordaunt, had threatened to cite him as co-respondent along with two others, but in the end had petitioned for a divorce on the grounds that his wife was insane. Nevertheless Bertie, who had written some innocent letters to Lady Mordaunt, was subpoenaed as a witness by her counsel. In the witness box he denied all accusations of misconduct. The whole scandal was, for Victoria, 'a painful, lowering thing'. She did not doubt Bertie's innocence, but she despaired at his imprudence in his choice of friends and his repeated social indiscretions. As his mother, she closed ranks to protect him, but not without lecturing him on abandoning his frivolous lifestyle. 'Thank goodness beloved Papa was not here to see it,' she told Vicky; he would have 'suffered dreadfully' with the worry of it all.[60] The case had come at a time when the press were once more on the attack, and a broadside entitled 'The coming K—', parodying Bertie's pleasure-seeking private life in the style of Tennyson's *Idylls of the King*, was doing the rounds. Echoes of the past dissolute behaviour of Bertie's Georgian ancestors reverberated across the accounts of the trial, with talk once more of the cost of the royal family to the nation when they did little in return to earn it.

*   *   *

Radical opinion in Britain, which had been on the rise since the agitation for the 2nd Reform Bill of 1866–7, had received a major boost in the summer of 1870 with the outbreak of the Franco-Prussian War, a conflict that had once again divided Victoria's loyalties – between her friend, the French emperor Napoleon III, and her Prussian relatives. The war had ended in the defeat of the French at Sedan in September and the flight of the Emperor into exile. The establishment of the Third Republic in France after the romantic heroics of the Paris Commune had prompted a surge in the political left in Britain, as middle-class radicals, trade union-ists and socialist-minded politicians gathered at a series of meetings at which calls were made for Queen Victoria to be deposed. Having let go of virtually all her ceremonial duties, she was accused of accruing large amounts from the Civil List for her own private use, while the Prince of Wales had been busy doing little but amass a pile of debts. The radical *National Reformer* argued that it 'seems proved by the experience of the last nine or ten years that the country can do quite well without a monarchy'.[61] *The Republican* – the organ of the Land and Labour League – equalled it, calling for social justice and an end to an oppressive government that cared nothing for the poor.[62] Republican clubs were springing up in major cities across the country: Aberdeen, Birmingham, Cambridge, Cardiff, London, Norwich and Plymouth, and with them came the increasing urgency, in Gladstone's mind, of addressing 'The Royalty Question' once and for all.[63] The fund of public goodwill for the monarchy was drying up and he did not see 'from whence it is to be replenished as matters go now'. 'To speak in rude and general terms,' he told Lord Granville in early December 1870, 'The Queen is invisible, and the Prince of Wales is not respected.'[64] If Victoria could not be coaxed out, then all he could do was campaign for better ways of showing the royal family 'in the visible discharge of public duty'. He therefore argued for a greater and more responsible role for the Prince of Wales, urging the Queen that Bertie be based in Ireland for half the year, as permanent Viceroy. Victoria was ruthlessly dismissive of the suggestion: the weather was awful, the damp climate would be bad for Bertie's health and the expenditure of money on royal public duties in Ireland would be a waste of time and money. As far as she was concerned, 'Scotland and England deserved it much more.'[65]

Ensconced at Windsor, Queen Victoria remained deaf to the warnings not far away in the heart of London. On 18 December a demonstration was called by the International Democratic Association in Trafalgar Square, at which up to 3,000 men and boys converged, carrying banners decorated with French republican mottoes and devices as well as the chillingly familiar red cap of liberty, 'to acknowledge the struggle of the people of France against despotism' and offer their full support for the new Republic, which the British government had yet to recognise. The aggression of Victoria's Prussian relatives in the recent war against France had further fuelled popular support for the republican spirit in France. *Reynolds's Newspaper* took advantage in its reporting to see the rally in Trafalgar Square as a sign of the stirring of allegiance among the working classes to 'the republican form of government'; it gave the lie to the supposedly monarchical loyalties of the British people that Victoria had for so long been cushioned by in her retreat from public view. 'Dynastic considerations are paralyzing the best energies of England, and rendering us the laughing stock of the whole world,' it warned. 'Englishmen are not the servile, grovelling idolaters of royalties and aristocracies our contemporaries delight in depicting them.'[66]

On a mild, calm afternoon in October 1870 diarist Arthur Munby had been out taking a stroll in Kensington Gardens. 'Close by was the gilded pinnacle of the Prince Consort's Monument, now all but finished,' he noted, but he was sanguine about its future, concluding that 'a hundred years hence' it would be looked upon as a 'tawdry yet interesting memento of an extinct monarchy'.[67] Earlier that summer, voicing the gathering anxieties of all his siblings, Bertie had tried to encourage his mother to show herself more to her people: 'If you sometimes came to London from Windsor and then drove for an hour in the Park (where there is no noise), the people would be overjoyed,' he had urged her, adding a sobering warning. 'We live in radical times, and the more *People see the Sovereign* the better it is for the *People* and the *Country*.'[68] In this view Bertie had the backing of Victoria's new Private Secretary, Henry Ponsonby, the exhausted and demoralised General Grey having collapsed and died on 26 March. The Prince of Wales would soon be thirty, but still had no useful ceremonial role; his mother, as she aged, was becoming increasingly intractable. With republicanism in Britain on the rise, a renewed and far more serious assault on the Queen's continuing seclusion was about to be launched.

CHAPTER FOURTEEN

'Heaven Has Sent Us This Dispensation to Save Us'

After less than a year in his new post as Private Secretary to the Queen, Henry Ponsonby was still very much feeling his way when, in 1871, the monarchy was confronted with its most serious crisis yet. The Queen's invisibility was not just a frustration to her public and her ministers; it extended to her staff and created many difficulties for Ponsonby in his job. Queen Victoria did not volunteer him much of her personal time, frequently sending scribbled notes rather than issuing verbal instructions, and not even calling for him when she dealt with her official dispatch boxes. The expectation of at least being solicited for advice had rapidly faded, and Ponsonby's role was often reduced to the farcical sending of the same papers back and forth, via footmen, to the Queen a few rooms away. He already had the distinct impression that his monarch did not work as hard as she claimed, despite the sycophantic protection of Dr Jenner. The perception of some, like Disraeli, that she worked tirelessly on Foreign and Colonial Office dispatches in the seclusion of her rooms was a fiction, in his view. And how could she do the work of government properly at Balmoral in isolation from her ministers? Ever more entrenched in going nowhere and seeing only the few people she liked, Victoria did not even enjoy having her children around her. If there was a choice between staying at Balmoral for one of the riotous ghillies' balls arranged by Brown or returning to London when the political situation demanded her presence, she always chose the former.[1]

The subtle and self-effacing Ponsonby had arrived at a time when the Queen most needed him. Unlike his predecessor – his uncle-in-law General Grey – Ponsonby was able to temper his exasperation at Victoria's most provocative bad qualities with a deeply felt affection and loyalty, where Grey had simply been worn down by them and, ultimately, alienated. Ponsonby demonstrated great skill in fielding Victoria's often irrational outbursts about the pressures placed on her with a discreet irreverence behind the scenes for their unreasonableness. But while his sardonic wit was his great saving grace, it required all his considerable resources of patience, tact and tolerance to carry out his duties in the face of the Queen's now-legendary intransigence. He was under no illusions as to the precariousness of the situation that year: 'If . . . she is neither the head of the Executive nor the fountain of honour, nor the centre of display, the royal dignity will sink to nothing at all,' he warned.[2] The Liberal minister Lord Halifax agreed: 'the mass of the people expect a King or a Queen to look and play the part. They want to see a Crown and a Sceptre and all that sort of thing. They want the gilding for their money.'[3]

Early in 1871, faced with the prospect of another daughter to marry – this time one of her least popular ones, Louise – Victoria for once showed no reluctance in doing her queenly duty by opening Parliament. It was a repetition of the situation she had faced in 1866 with Helena and Affie; she needed to secure a £30,000 dowry for Louise, followed shortly afterwards by an annuity of £15,000 for Prince Arthur when he came of age. But these further demands on the privy purse prompted renewed criticism of her failure visibly to earn her income, fuelled by publication of a pseudonymous pamphlet asking 'What Does She Do With It?', which accused her of secreting up to £200,000 a year of her Civil List monies, tax-free, for her own private purposes.[4] The immensely wealthy Argyll family into which Louise was marrying – and for once the groom was a British commoner rather than an impoverished foreign prince – hardly needed the money, and there was widespread public objection to the demand. Animosity was whipped up once more: it was time the Queen stepped down or the monarchy was done away with altogether. Charles Bradlaugh, President of the London Republican Club, argued that 'the experience of the last nine years proves that the country can do quite well without a monarch', urging not violent overthrow, but a peaceful transition. After so many years of only nominal monarchy, the Act of Settlement that had established the House of Hanover on the British throne in 1701 should be revoked on the Queen's decease.[5]

Gladstone loyally defended the Queen throughout the controversy and threw his full political weight behind her requests, but was not helped by gossip about Bertie's huge gambling losses in the casinos of Homburg; the Prince's popularity was plummeting in tandem with the

Queen's. Eventually Parliament agreed to both sums, though fifty-four members supported a call for Prince Arthur's annuity to be reduced to £10,000. Continuing demands for the Queen's greater visibility met with a tepid response from Victoria, who agreed to a couple of Drawing Rooms held consecutively at Buckingham Palace (so that she only had to tolerate one overnight stay there), a review of the troops in Bushey Park and a brief showing of herself in an open carriage on 21 March, when she drove with Princess Louise on her wedding day the short distance down the hill from the Upper Ward of Windsor Castle to St George's Chapel. But the ceremony itself, at which the Queen played a more prominent role giving Louise away, was witnessed only by the select few and the date, during Lent, was chosen entirely to suit the Queen's holiday schedule and not that of her churchgoing public, many of whom protested at its inappropriateness.

Eight days later Victoria re-emerged for the official opening of Prince Albert's brainchild, the Royal Albert Hall, which had been under construction for four years as a centre for the celebration of British culture. It was a key moment in the memorialisation of her dead husband, and the Queen faced this gathering of 8,000 – the biggest function she had attended since Albert was alive – with considerable trepidation. Her public were to be disappointed by her lack of visible engagement; during the brief ceremony, despite looking well and smiling and impressing everyone with her compelling regal dignity, Victoria could barely muster more than a brief sentence, in which she expressed her 'admiration of this beautiful hall' and her good wishes for its success.[6] Was she playing to the gallery, one wonders? When it came to the moment of declaring the hall open, she appeared totally overwhelmed and Bertie was obliged to say the words for her. Beyond this, she remained obdurate in her resistance to any other demands on her for the performance of ceremony. Gladstone, for all his loyalty to the throne, privately found her wayward-ness increasingly difficult – if not repellent in its self-servitude. But try as he might, his inducements to the Queen to increase her official duties brought only peremptory, if not hysterical lists of objections.

By the late summer of 1871, with the press warning that 'England might virtually be left without a Sovereign for half a century' if Victoria lived to a ripe old age, conspiracy was brewing even at Windsor.[7] The Queen's children were seriously alarmed that their mother was preju-dicing the future of the throne. Her conspicuous habit of grief had now become a habit of avoidance, made worse by Jenner's constant pandering to Victoria's neuroses, which they all felt had to be confronted once and for all. During a family gathering at Balmoral, and under the guidance of Vicky and a gloomily pessimistic Princess Alice, who were both visiting from Germany, they composed a letter to their mother in which they tried as respectfully and affectionately as they could to make her see the truth of her position. Signed by them all, the letter assured the Queen that they had '*each* of *us* individually wished to say this to you', and that they had done so from the conviction that had come upon them all 'that some danger is in the air, that something must be done . . . to avert a frightful calamity':

> No one has prompted us to write . . . No one knows except we ourselves . . . It is we your children, whose position in the world had been made so good by the wisdom and forethought, and the untiring care of yourself and dear Papa, who now feel how utterly changed things are, and who would humbly entreat you to enquire into the state of public feeling, which appears to us so very alarming.[8]

Just as the children were collectively gathering their resolve to hand the letter over to their mother, however, events overtook them. For Victoria fell ill – and seriously so – for once allaying any accusations of malingering. In early August what seemed like a bout of her usual insomnia and headaches was accompanied by a sore throat and complicated soon afterwards by the development of a painful swelling under her arm.[9] Her sufferings all the more justified Victoria's professed intention to decamp as swiftly as possible to the sanctuary of Balmoral. Gladstone objected, asking her to postpone her departure until after the Privy Council meeting to be held when Parliament had been prorogued – thus sparing her ministers the arduous journey north. Victoria was incensed by his 'interference with the Queen's personal acts and movements'; it was 'really abominable'.[10] She railed at the wicked persecution to which she was being subjected. Feeling ill as she now did, she had no intention of being further inconvenienced or made to stay in London to gratify what she saw as Gladstone's political ends, and once again she resorted to the bottom line: 'unless the Ministers *support* her . . . she *cannot* go on and must give her heavy burden up to younger hands'.[11]

With the Queen having protested endlessly for the last ten years about the precarious state of her health, no one believed her at first; but on 14 August her sore throat rapidly got worse, affecting her ability to eat and speak. Unaware of the true extent of her illness, Gladstone found her continuing protests 'sickening', confiding in Henry Ponsonby (who also felt she should stay until the prorogation) that 'Smaller and meaner cause for the decay of thrones cannot be conceived . . . it is like the worm which bores the bark of a noble oak tree and so breaks the channel of its life.'[12] Victoria was by now too ill to care; on 17 August she summoned all her strength to undertake the long train ride to Balmoral. Once there, she was soon bedridden. Although the agonising pain in her throat finally gave way on the 20th, she was in increasing discomfort from the swelling under her arm, which had developed into a large abscess; her appetite vanished and she rapidly lost weight.

With no sign of the abscess breaking, Dr Jenner was worried that it might lead to septicaemia. Although the public had had no inkling of it, nor too Victoria's ministers, Jenner even feared for her life. He dared not summon her children, knowing that their presence would only alarm Victoria and make matters worse; in any event, at such times she preferred the solicitous presence of Brown and her close personal servants Löhlein, Annie Macdonald and her dresser Emilie Dittweiler.[13] Unwilling to explain the true nature of her illness and uncertain as to what had provoked it, Jenner nevertheless felt compelled to defend the Queen against criticism from her ministers that she was once again crying wolf. From such a distance they could hardly be blamed, for they did not know the true facts. In an anonymous piece in *The Lancet* on 19 August he therefore catalogued her precarious physical state, her inability to tolerate crowded and overheated rooms and the continuing severe headaches, insomnia and loss of appetite that she was suffering. He also argued long and forcefully with Ponsonby about the necessity for her to spend any time in London. Ponsonby was dismayed by Jenner's action – he felt it played straight into the hands of those claiming the Queen was no longer fit to rule and should abdicate: 'Why should we wait any longer,' they would say, 'she promises not to do more, but positively to do less.'[14]

With complaints gathering in the English press, the Scottish papers loyally rebutted criticism of the Queen, praising her for not kowtowing to the trifling gestures of London life or suggestions that she allow Bertie to take over Buckingham Palace. Jenner weighed into the political arguments too: it wasn't the Queen's fault; all this criticism directed at her was symptomatic of the 'advancing democracy of the age'. 'It is absurd to think that it will be checked by her driving about London and giving balls for the frivolous classes of Society,' he told Ponsonby. Jenner felt beleaguered; in the end he could only warn, as he had done since the death of Albert, of the dark prospect of the Queen suffering a breakdown if pushed too hard: 'these nerves are a form of madness, and against them it is hopeless to contend'.[15]

Queen Victoria was little better by early September; she had not felt this ill, she said, since her bout of typhoid fever in 1835. It was therefore decided to call in a surgeon, Dr Joseph Lister, from Edinburgh. On the 4th he lanced the abscess, which had now reached six inches in diameter and was very deep-seated, first freezing it with ether. Lister was a pioneer of antisepsis and, in order to minimise the risk of infection, used his own carbolic-acid spraying machine – the 'donkey engine' as he called it – during the procedure. Jenner was enlisted to work the bellows of the spray, inadvertently choking the Queen in a cloud of pungent phenol.[16] When the wound still did not drain properly, Lister applied a rubber drainage tube, the first time this procedure had been used. It was, Victoria declared, 'a most disagreeable duty most pleasantly performed'.[17] Within a week she was showing clear signs of recovery. Thin and pale, she was wheeled around in a bath chair for days – everyone who saw her was shocked at her frailty. It was only now that news of the Queen's serious illness was released to the nation, prompting a mass stirring of public sympathy and anxiety, if not expressions of guilt for having accused her of malingering. The royal children, agreeing that any shock tactics with their mother might now backfire, quietly put their letter away, agreeing not to present it to her till early the following year – 'if at all'.[18] The illness had now played into Victoria's hands, and Princess Alice thought that nothing could be done to remedy her mother's infuriating compla-cency: 'She thinks the Monarchy will last her time and that it is no use thinking of what will come after . . . so she lets the torrent come on.'[19] Victoria was satisfyingly vindicated by the remorse of newspapers such as the *Daily News*, which on 15 September published a toadying apology. The people 'may have caught from a discontented Court a complaining spirit', it observed ingenuously:

> They may have been induced to feel that the Queen was hardly giving proper splendour to her Queenly position and was showing some slack-ness in her Queenly duties; but today all such complaints are hushed, the nation is ashamed of them and rebukes itself for uttering them, and feels nothing but an affectionate solicitude for her speedy recovery.

Three months on from the onset of her illness Victoria was still weak and in a lot of pain. Despite recovering from the abscess, she had been further disabled by a severe attack of rheumatic gout in many of her joints, and her hands and feet were badly swollen and bandaged; her nights were restless and she was dosing heavily on chloral. She felt utterly helpless, unable to feed herself or write her journal, which for weeks now she had been dictating to fourteen-year-old Beatrice. John Brown was constantly in attendance, carrying her to and from her bed, and her couch and up and down stairs. It was November before she could manage the stairs again. To be so incapacitated had been 'a bitter trial', and just as she was finally recovering her strength, a renewed attack on her was launched by the rising young Liberal MP for Chelsea, Sir Charles Dilke.[20] In a speech at Newcastle on 6 November 1871 he criticised the cost to the nation of the Civil List, particularly when the Queen rarely held court in London. He accused her of hoarding a private, untaxed fortune, as well as draining the royal coffers through the maintenance of an excessive number of obsolete sinecures – did Her Majesty really need a Hereditary Grand Falconer or a Master of the Buckhounds? Or, for that matter, did she require a collection of twenty-one assorted physicians, dentists, oculists and apothecaries to safeguard the health of the royal family? 'If you can show me a fair chance that a republic here will be free from the political corruption that hangs about the monarch, I say, for my part – and I believe the middle classes in general will say – let it come.'[21]

'Sir Charles Dilke has given the Queen notice to quit,' proclaimed the *Pall Mall Gazette*; and indeed his rhetoric was highly provocative.[22] But, when it came down to it, Dilke proved to be a man of words rather than action, prone to wild and unsubstantiated claims about Victoria's supposed squirelling-away of money from the privy purse. His stance was symptomatic of a groundswell of opinion that was inherently anti-monarchist rather than truly republican. But it lacked any real political – let alone genuinely socialist – backbone. *The Times* was quick to retaliate. On 9 November its editorial accused Dilke of 'recklessness bordering on criminality'. Victoria was incensed; press criticism of her had been cruel and heartless. Behind Gladstone's back, and oblivious to the extent to which her Prime Minister had doggedly defended her, she complained that he had not done enough to protect her against Dilke's treasonable onslaught, ungraciously telling Vicky that he was 'so wonderfully unsym-pathetic'. Yet at heart Gladstone held his Queen in awe. His instinct was to ignore Dilke (the loyalist reaction to the Queen's illness would take care of that) while voicing to his colleagues his continuing fears for the monarchy and his deep-seated distaste for the 'vehemence and tenacity' with which the Queen resisted the fulfilment of her sovereign duties.[23]

Dilke's attack was, in any event, rapidly laid aside when the Queen received a telegram at Balmoral on 21 November informing her that Bertie had fallen ill with typhoid fever at Sandringham. He had probably picked up the infection from contaminated drinking water during a recent pheasant-shoot at the estate of Lord Londesborough at Scarborough, where the lodge house in which he stayed was overcrowded and its drainage primitive.[24] The prognosis was enough to send shock waves of apprehension through the entire royal household. Victoria immediately dispatched Dr Jenner to Sandringham, and on the 24th the public were informed of the prince's illness, with the reassuring proviso that 'There are no unfavourable symptoms'. But they had all heard that line before – when Prince Albert had fallen ill exactly ten years previously.

Princess Alice was on a visit to Sandringham at the time Bertie fell ill and immediately did her best to take over the role of sick-nurse. Having nursed Louis through a mild attack of the disease in 1870, as well as organising field hospitals in Hesse during the Austro-Prussian War of 1866, she felt qualified to monopolise things, much to the annoyance of Alix, who had already proved herself more than competent at the task. Alice was ably assisted by two professional nurses, as well as Bertie's valet and a new and rising practitioner, Dr William Gull, who was Bertie's personal physician. Victoria arrived on 29 November to be met by Alix, 'looking thin and anxious with tears in her eyes'. When the Queen entered the sick-room the reminders of 1861 were many and vivid, and even more ominous when Jenner told her that 'it was a far more violent attack than my beloved Husband's'.[25] The following day Bertie's temperature was 105 degrees and his lungs were congested (bronchitis was setting in). But on the 1 December he rallied, enough for Victoria to feel it was safe to return to Windsor, after which she headed straight for Albert's mausoleum to pray. But hopes were not raised for long. On the 7th Bertie suffered a relapse and on the morning of the 8th Victoria received a telegram from Jenner: 'The Prince passed a very unquiet night. Not so well. Temperature risen to 104. Respirations more rapid. Dr Gull and I are both very anxious.' She hurried back to Sandringham with Louise, arriving late in the icy chill and snow, looking 'small and miserable' according to Augusta Stanley.[26] The press too were by now flocking to nearby Wolferton station, and from there to Sandringham on every gig and fly that could be hired, to camp out at the gates. Royal illness – particularly when knocking at death's door – was a great circulation-booster, as they all knew. Very soon word was out that the Prince had succumbed to the full force of the fever and had sunk into a terrifying, raging delirium.

No sooner had she arrived than Victoria took control of the household from under the nose of its mistress Alix and commandeered what little space remained for herself, her entourage and the rest of Bertie's siblings as they arrived. Alice and Alix's young children were all packed off to Windsor for their own safety. The atmosphere inside the newly built but overcrowded house, with its windows shut fast against the cold and snow outside, rapidly became noisy and quarrelsome as the various members of the family vied for space; others tiptoed round in sheer terror at being in such close proximity to the Queen, as 'dread and gloom' prevailed.[27] The Duke of Cambridge in particular was dubious about the sanitary arrangements, fearing the spread of typhoid germs among them, and went round the house inspecting it for bad smells.

Hour after hour Victoria watched over her son in the dark and claustrophobic room. 'It was too dreadful to see the poor Queen sitting in the bedroom behind a screen listening to his ravings,' recalled Prince Leopold later. 'I can't tell you what a deep impression it made on me.'[28] For once she was completely taken out of herself, mindful only of Bertie. The Queen's innate good qualities – her 'best self', as Lady Augusta Stanley called them – rose to the surface as, against the odds of her own recent debilitating illness, she drew on the great store of physical and emotional strength that she always had in reserve, when she chose to enlist it.[29] She was far from optimistic about the outcome, yet remained a paragon of calmness, patience and solicitude, listening to Bertie's stentorian breathing as he tossed and turned and raved. His outbursts of singing, whistling and talking – in several languages – were sometimes so embarrassing and compromising that his wife had to be kept out of the room.

Sunday 10 December was designated a day of national prayer, as the family and household gathered round, anticipating with dread the unthinkable: a repetition of the deathbed of Prince Albert ten years previously. Bulletins were being issued twice a day and posted at public places like the Mansion House and Charing Cross for all to see. Across Britain's places of worship the nation was once more united in a 'common

anxiety'. On Monday the 11th the doctors called Victoria from her
bed at 5.30 a.m. The patient had had a severe spasm, closely followed by
another. Jenner warned her that 'at any moment dear Bertie might go
off'.[30] She hurried to his bedside as the rest of the household congregated
outside the door in their dressing gowns. 'The awfulness of this morning,
I shall never, never forget as long as I live,' wrote the Duke of Cambridge
in his diary. Even outside the door everyone could hear Bertie's loud and
incessant delirious ramblings. 'All looked bewildered and overcome with
grief,' the Duke recalled, 'but the doctors behaved nobly, no flinching,
no loss of courage, only intense anxiety.'[31] All day an exhausted Victoria,
Alice and Alix kept vigil, as Bertie's life hung by a thread; by 7 p.m. that
evening the doctors were not expecting him to survive the night.

Letters and telegrams meanwhile poured into Sandringham, many
from the public with recommendations for homespun remedies for
typhoid, some 'of the most mad kind'.[32] Words of comfort and support
also came from ministers, including a heavy-hearted Gladstone, who
found it difficult to find words adequate enough that would not 'mock
the sorrow of this moment'. Even the chastened members of London's
republican clubs sent a joint message expressing their sorrow at the Prince's
illness and their hope that his life might be spared.[33] Reporter Henry James
Jennings of the *Birmingham Mail* remembered how he sat huddled in his
cold and draughty office for three or four days on end: 'we were there,
editor, compositors and machine men, from eight in the morning until
twelve or one at night, ready to bring out at short notice an edition
recording any important change'.[34] On the morning of the 12th, as he
went to his work at the Ecclesiastical Commissioners' Office, Arthur
Munby noticed how everyone felt as 'one family' at this time of crisis:

> Another day of public anxiety – shown more strongly in London than I
> ever remember. People asking for telegrams, listening for the passing bell;
> chance words heard in the street or elsewhere, showing that most men
> were thinking of the Prince. Home Office telegrams posted in our hall,
> as usual; at the Cheshire Cheese, the latest news written up in the dining
> parlour, in the Strand and Fleet Street, little details from the sickroom
> hastily brushed in with ink on large flysheets, which were stuck on shut-
> ters of newspaper offices; and crowds pressing to read them.[35]

Victoria was greatly comforted: 'The feeling shown by the whole nation
is quite marvellous and most touching and striking,' she noted in her

journal; it proved to her 'how really sound and truly loyal the people are'. For thirty-six hours the delirium consumed Bertie. On the 13th 'the worst day of all' as Victoria recalled, she was allowed to dispense with the screen and sit on the sofa within sight of her son as he battled for life. 'Alice and I said to one another in tears, "There can be no hope"'; all she could do as his temperature rose and he tossed and turned, clutching at the bedclothes and gasping between each incoherent word, was hold Bertie's hand and stroke his arm. In a brief moment of clarity he suddenly noticed her sitting there. 'It is so kind of you to come,' he whispered.[36]

Beyond the wintry flatlands of Sandringham the nation was gripped by 'an epidemic of typhoid loyalty' as *Reynolds's Newspaper* later described it, berating the fashionable journals for the 'mean, toadying, craven spirit of so-called loyalty' that covered their pages. Typhoid fever, as it rightly pointed out, was an endemic disease of the poor that brought grief and suffering wherever it struck: 'The Life of John Smith in Whitechapel, or of John Jones in the "Black Country", is exactly the same to a family as the life of the Prince of Wales.'[37] But nothing could dispel the collective sense of foreboding as the nation contemplated the significance of the date – 14 December – to come and the prospect of another funereal Christmas. The leader-writers were sharpening their pens and finalising their obituaries. George Augustus Sala at the *Daily Telegraph* geared himself up for a repeat performance of his 1861 panegyrics: 'All England may be said to have gathered at the little Norfolk cottage,' he gushed, 'in a thousand nameless households . . . hearts close together, and hands linked with hands . . . against the dreaded approach of death.'[38] Jay's were on standby for the stampede, having judiciously inserted an advertisement in *The Times* on the 13th announcing that its staff were at the ready to serve anyone, anywhere, 'in the event of immediate mourning being required'; over at St Paul's the bell-ringers were primed for action. With a longer run-in for its weekly deadline, *Punch* instructed illustrator John Tenniel to prepare two alternative cartoons: one entitled 'Suspense', depicting Britannia standing vigil outside Bertie's door; the other, 'In Memoriam', with her weeping in despair.[39]

Alone among newspapermen Wemyss Reid, editor of the *Leeds Mercury*, having received no telegram announcing the Prince's death by midnight, decided to go to press the following morning, the 14th, with an article assuming he would still be alive: 'in every other newspaper office the conviction that he was at the very point of death was so strong that no preparation had been made for his possible survival'.[40] His paper and *The Times* were the only ones to do so that day, most of the others having had to stall on printing the black-bordered obituaries they had prepared. As the 'dreadful anniversary' of Albert's death approached, a strange kind of fatalism gripped the royal family as they sat and watched through the evening, everyone filled with a superstitious dread that history might repeat itself. Mercifully, things improved late that evening. 'Instead of this date dawning upon another deathbed, which I had felt almost certain of, it brought cheering news,' recalled Victoria. Overnight Bertie's temperature began to drop; he slept quietly for several hours and his breathing eased. With all the royal family gathered at Sandringham, for once – and only once – there would be no commemoration that day of Albert's death in the Blue Room and the mausoleum at Windsor.[41]

Having issued six bulletins on the Prince's condition during the 13th, the doctors were very cautious about any immediate announcement of recovery. But with crowds huddled all day in the cold outside the newspaper offices and Marlborough House waiting for news, a bulletin was finally released at 1 a.m. on the 14th announcing that the prince was 'less restless'. Bertie's recovery from here on would be a slow and difficult one, with a worrying relapse on 27 December, but eventually he was on the mend. It was nothing short of a gift from providence to a beleaguered monarchy in a time of desperate need. 'What a sell for Dilke this illness has been!' wrote Lord Henry Lennox to Disraeli. 'The Republicans say their chances are up,' a relieved Duke of Cambridge told his mother. 'Heaven has sent us this dispensation to save us.'[42] Predictably the papers gushed with a tide of sentimental rhetoric honouring God's mercy in sparing Bertie and praising the fortitude of his mother and the devoted nursing of his virtuous sister Alice. Victoria, whose relationship with Alice was always difficult, was rather put out: 'beloved Alix I can never praise enough . . . so true, so discreet, so kind to all'; in Victoria's estimation, for all her frail constitution her daughter-in-law had more than equalled Alice in her sick-bed devotion.[43]

Despite Bertie's recovery, Christmas that year was a subdued one for the royal family. Victoria returned to Windsor on the 19th and spent the holiday there instead of at Osborne – for the first time since that last Christmas with Albert in 1860. But there was no tree and few festivities. 'It was, if not a sad, yet at any rate a very serious Christmas to us all,' she told the Duke of Cambridge, 'from the recent week of terrible anxiety and also for the consciousness that dear Bertie is still in an anxious state. His recovery is so slow, and there are such fluctuations from day to day, that I must own I do not feel easy about him.'[44] She professed herself humbled by the experience: 'It was a great lesson to us all – to see the highest surrounded by every luxury which human mortal can wish for – lying low and as helpless and miserable as the poorest peasant.'[45] On 26 December *The Times* published her letter of thanks to the nation:

> The universal feeling shown by her people during those painful, terrible days, and the sympathy evinced by them with herself and her beloved daughter, the Princess of Wales, as well as the general joy at the improvement of the Prince of Wales's state, have made a deep and lasting impression on her heart, which can never be effaced. It was indeed nothing new to her, for the Queen had met with the same sympathy, when just ten years ago, a similar illness removed from her side the mainstay of her life, the best, wisest and kindest of husbands.

Over in republican France, where the worst excesses of the Paris Commune had raised the ugly spectre of 1789 and soured the successful overturn of the monarchy, the response to the political turnaround in Britain was one of incredulity. England had supposedly been on the brink of becoming a republic, yet the last few days of the Prince's illness had been a lesson to all. As one Parisian journal observed, instead of mocking their royal family, the people had prayed, showing that they 'have the courage, the good sense not to disown either their history, their Government, or their God'. The British were still a free people and the French had much to learn from them about the 'powerful bonds of union' that a country relies upon in times of trouble. 'When shall *we* learn to pray altogether for anyone?' it asked.[46]

Gladstone had no doubt that Bertie's six-week near-fatal illness had provided the monarchy with a 'last opportunity' to capitalise on a renewal of public loyalty. 'We have arrived at a great crisis of Royalty,' he said, and he was determined to overcome it. The Queen had 'laid up in early years an immense fund of loyalty, but she is now living on her capital,' he told Ponsonby, who agreed that 'royal matters' had become stuck in a 'deep and nasty rut'.[47] Word meanwhile had come from Sandringham that some kind of service of thanksgiving might be in order, and Gladstone gave it his full support. Such a ceremony would set the seal on the important strengthening of the bonds between monarch and people that had occurred during the Prince's illness, as well as putting a

hopefully reformed Bertie back on track . . . For the Prince of Wales
had confided to his nurse when he first fell ill that 'if he got better he
should lead a very different life to what he had hitherto done'.[48]

* * *

Plans were put in place early in 1872 for a royal progress across London,
followed by a service at St Paul's Cathedral, with Gladstone providing
the Queen with supporting ammunition – a list of precedents, including
the celebrations there for the recovery from illness of George III in 1789.
Victoria immediately shrank at the prospect of being the centre of a
display of 'ostentatious pomp'.[49] She objected to St Paul's as a venue: 'a
most dreary, dingy, melancholy and undevotional church'; Westminster
Abbey was smaller and a lot nearer to Buckingham Palace.[50] Uppermost
in her mind was of course the physical strain on herself, not to mention
Bertie, of a long and fatiguing service, but in the end Alix persuaded
her. While the Princess of Wales agreed that her husband's illness had
been a very personal experience and that she, like the Queen, did not
want what was fundamentally a religious act being made a vehicle for
a grand public show, the nation – having taken such a *public* share in
our anxiety' – had shown such solidarity 'that it may perhaps feel that
it has a kind of *claim* to join with us now in a public and universal
thanksgiving'.[51]

Victoria had to concede, but her old, familiar obstructiveness ensured
that nothing went smoothly. Fraught discussions with Gladstone followed
over her various 'peculiar fancies', as he saw them: the length of the
service (which she wanted shortened to half an hour); the carriages to
be used (she vetoed a full state procession); the route (which was length-
ened to appease public demand); and the number of tickets to be issued
for the ceremony (under pressure from *The Times* this was increased
from 8,000 to just under 12,000). When it came to the question of who
was to pay for it all, Gladstone knew that the government must foot the
bill or Victoria would pounce on this as a reason to resist.[52] In the end
a series of compromises were made to ensure Victoria's participation,
with the Queen refusing to kowtow to the list of precedents presented
to her, but agreeing only out of personal recognition that some kind of
'show' was required as a thank-you to the nation.[53] 'I have no doubt that
he is "gauche",' thought Lady Augusta Stanley on hearing the news that
Gladstone had prevailed, 'but I must say I honor him for pressing her
duty on her – And Oh! That she should at this moment resent it!'[54] And

there were compensations for Victoria for this act of veiled capitulation: in return she was able to duck out of opening Parliament the same month.

The Service of National Thanksgiving held at St Paul's Cathedral on 27 February 1872 proved to be the long-wished-for public celebration of nationhood and monarchy. The whole of London was on the move from before dawn, on a day punctuated with bursts of chilly rain followed by sunshine.[55] Victoria and Bertie – he still very weak and haggard and walking with a limp (the result of a severe attack of gout) – traversed streets festooned with flags and bunting, floral wreaths and triumphal arches, with military bands playing 'God Save the Queen' and 'God Save the Prince of Wales'. Despite the cold, Victoria had specified an open landau so that the people could clearly see them in the convoy of nine carriages accompanied by a guard of honour. It took its route along Pall Mall, Trafalgar Square, the Strand and up Fleet Street, past tiers of specially constructed seating to Temple Bar, all to 'one mighty multitude and one continued acclamation'.[56] As on the occasion of Princess Alexandra's progress across London in 1863, the best vantage points were sold at a premium, from ten shillings, to forty guineas for a balcony view on Fleet Street. But this royal occasion saw crowds larger even than the 'Coronation, Exhibition, and Wellington mobs' of 1838, 1851 and 1852. A major lack of provision for viewing the procession led to chaos: many who climbed trees in St James's Park for a better view ended up in hospital with broken limbs, as did others who fell from windows and scaffolding; spectators were kicked by horses or knocked down by carriages; women and children fainted in the crush on Ludgate Hill and had to be hauled by ropes from the crowd.[57]

Victoria was still in deep mourning, though she had at least left off her crape in favour of black silk, her jacket and skirt trimmed with a deep border of ermine and her bonnet decorated with white flowers. She seemed happier than she had been in the last ten years, waving and at one point raising Bertie's hand and kissing it. He repeatedly lifted his hat in acknowledgement of the crowds; their deafening cheers as they passed were a 'wonderful demonstration of loyalty and affection, from the very highest to the lowest'.[58] The congregation at St Paul's had been awaiting them for several hours, but only fifty of these seats were set aside for 'working men', the rest having been fought over by the Upper Ten Thousand, as Reynolds's Newspaper noted. Why had there been no provision, it asked, for the 'people who labour', who instead were left outside, 'hustled, crushed and driven to and fro for the accommodation of "the quality"?'[59] French diplomat Charles Gavard and his entourage had gone to the cathedral wearing full ceremonial uniform – 'It would tickle the Republic to see us pass,' he quipped. 'What a human flood as we drew near the City, as foul too as the waters of the Thames,' he recalled. 'No mob is like an English mob; the signs of misery are so unmistakable. They are both violent and humble under the blows dealt by the police; and the ragbag reigns among them.' Gavard had taken up his place in the tiers of specially constructed benches at 11 a.m., 'in a draught of cold air that douched us till two o'clock'.[60] Arthur Munby had been in the cathedral even longer – since 8 a.m. to be sure of a good view.

At last the bells boomed out 'like a volley of artillery' as the Queen and Prince of Wales entered through the main doors, over which hung the inscription from Psalm 122: 'I was glad when they said unto me, I will go into the House of the Lord.' Victoria leaned heavily on Bertie's arm as they processed up the nave to the raised scarlet gangway lined with Beefeaters. There they took their special pew in the centre of the aisle, amidst a congregation of army and navy officers, peers, MPs and ministers, judges, Kings of Arms and royal heralds. The whole congregation, as they did so, was gripped by a 'royal silence that the sacredness of the place and the majesty of her office demanded – a real silence.' Gavard had not been particularly impressed with the sight of the Queen: 'fat and short . . . with a discontented-looking face'; but that silence – not the natural silence of the void, as he recalled, but 'the silence of thousands of people holding their breath at the presence of the monarch finally among them' – was quite extraordinary.[61] It was a 'thrilling moment', Munby recalled, when the organ sounded out, just as the sun broke through the clouds outside and 'sent beams of slanting light down through the misty vault of the dome, upon the gold and scarlet and purple crowds below'. As the 250-strong choir burst into the words of the *Te Deum*, Lucy Cavendish, like many others, felt a shudder of recognition: 'Never before had I realised what a Psalm of Thanksgiving it is, and most beautiful and moving were the words specially dwelt upon by the music: . . . "When Thou hadst overcome *the sharpness of death*".'[62]

After an hour-long service – 'cold and too long', as far as Victoria was concerned – the royal carriages returned to Buckingham Palace by a different route, taking an hour and a half to make their way the seven miles across the crowded streets.[63] Gratified by what had been 'a most affecting day', the Queen appeared shortly afterwards on the balcony to loud cheers, with Beatrice, Leopold, Arthur and Alfred.[64] As night fell the crowds were still out, as they had been in March 1863, linking arms, singing and dancing as they enjoyed the fireworks and gaslit illuminations across London. The dome of St Paul's was encircled with coloured lights, 'like St Peter's in Rome on Easter day', recalled Wemyss Reid; Fleet Street 'looked quite medieval again', thought Munby, 'its gabled houses bright as day with lights and colour – flags on the houses, flags festooned across the street, and legends, such as the Te Deum, stretching all down the way on either side, white letters on a scarlet ground nailed to the windows.'[65]

Inevitably criticisms were raised afterwards that the semi-state ceremony had not been sufficiently grand to match the significance of the occasion; *Reynolds's* took the opposite line. Under the banner 'Pinchbeck Loyalty: The Thanksgiving Tomfoolery', it damned the whole thing as 'a sickening display of hypocrisy, sycophancy, idolatry, idiocy and buffoonery'.[66] But such criticism was isolated; it had been, as Victoria herself noted, a 'day of triumph' during which both she and Bertie had been greatly moved and had found it hard to suppress their tears.[67] The common humanity displayed on the streets of London captured everyone's imagination; Thanksgiving Day had in the end been as much about the Queen reappearing to 'perform a function of Royalty in the Metropolis of her Empire' as it had been about Bertie's recovery.[68] In so doing she had prompted a resurgence of deep-rooted sentimentalism towards the monarchy that had not been witnessed since the early days of her reign. The real spectacle, though, as Gavard observed and the press echoed, was not that of monarchy on show, but of 'the people, the never exhausted masses which covered all the pavements, filled all the windows and balconies and stands from street to housetop and spread themselves even over the roofs'. All of them demonstrated 'the wisdom, the moderation, and the sound heart' that had merited their recent wider enfranchisement.[69] This great and potent human spectacle had not just been one for the monarchy to take note of; it had also underlined the collective power of the nation at large to ensure the throne's very survival.

Two days after the Thanksgiving Service a further and even more emphatic death-blow was dealt to the republican cause. In response to the enormous public affection shown to her at St Paul's, Victoria had driven out in Regent's Park late on the afternoon of 29 February in an open landau with Arthur and Leopold to show herself once more to her people. She had returned as usual via the Garden Gate, where a dense crowd awaited her as the carriage entered the palace grounds. Just as Brown dismounted to help Victoria's lady-in-waiting down from the carriage, a gaunt and shabby young man pushed forward, thrusting a pistol close to the Queen's face. As Victoria screamed out 'Save me!', Brown 'with a wonderful presence of mind' seized the man, even as Prince Arthur jumped out to do likewise.[70]

The author of this supposed 'assassination' attempt – the fifth that Victoria had faced since 1840 – was a seventeen-year-old Irishman named Arthur O'Connor, a great-nephew of the Chartist leader Feargus O'Connor. In the mêlée at the gates he had managed to climb unnoticed over the ten-foot-high railings into the courtyard beyond, in order to get close to the Queen. His flintlock pistol, bought for four shillings a few days previously in a pawn shop, was faulty and unloaded – filled with scraps of leather and blue paper. His intention had not been to kill, but rather to frighten the Queen into signing the petition he carried for the release of Fenian prisoners. He had wanted to press the petition on her during the service at St Paul's, but when he had been found lurking inside the cathedral the night before he had been ejected.[71] Soon after the attempt newsboys were, so Lucy Cavendish heard, running round the streets shouting, 'Assassination of the Queen'. 'If anything was wanted to send loyalty up to boiling-point, this attempt had done it!' she remarked. A couple of days later, when Victoria drove out in Hyde Park once again in an open carriage 'with no extra precautions', the crowds 'cheered famously'. Londoners once more returned to the gates of Buckingham Palace to stand and stare. When O'Connor's case was tried at the Old Bailey, Victoria was offended that he did not receive a stiff penalty, for she took the whole thing as a serious attempt on her life. *The Times* disagreed, viewing it as absurdly overhyped: 'Anything wilder or more irrational cannot well be conceived than this shop-boy's plan of over-awing the crown.'[72] Claims that O'Connor was deranged were dismissed and he was sentenced to twelve months' hard labour and twenty strokes of the birch. Victoria was relieved to hear later that he had accepted the option of a one-way ticket to Australia, but O'Connor returned a couple of years later and, after being caught loitering near the palace again, was locked up in a lunatic asylum.

Further outpourings of gratitude – this time for the Queen's safe deliverance from mortal harm – again boosted public sympathy for the monarchy in the wave of renewed loyalty that continued to spread across Britain. Back on the campaign trail in the provinces, Charles Dilke found that his republican speeches encountered an increasingly hostile response. At Bristol, Leeds and Birmingham his words were often drowned out by loud singing of the national anthem. His appearance at Bolton provoked a riot and numerous casualties. On 19 March, when he introduced a motion in Parliament calling for a full public inquiry into the Queen's personal expenditure, he was shouted down and defeated in the vote by 276 to two. Lady Lucy Cavendish had no doubts: these two recent, dramatic events had 'melt[ed] all hearts' and finally put paid to 'grumbling Republicanism'. 'What would seem like the one disloyal hand among three millions, and the fresh rush of loving feeling caused by it and by her courage', had finally brought an end to Dilke's cause. It had also raised the status and integrity of John Brown to new and unassailable heights. Certain that she owed her safety to him and him alone, Victoria rewarded her good Highland servant with a gold Devoted Service Medal, promoted him to the ancient title of Esquire and gave him an annuity of £25. The 'trusty, respectable yeoman' John Brown, so long despised by the royal household, was now a hero to the working classes.[73]

CHAPTER FIFTEEN

Albertopolis

The events of winter 1871–2 and the National Thanksgiving that followed proved to be a significant turning point for the British monarchy. By the end of 1872, with the return of economic prosperity and an easing of public disgruntlement, Charles Dilke and many of his supporters had retreated, realising that the future lay with increased representation of the people and the maintenance, however flawed, of the political status quo. When it came down to it, the Queen was a stabilising force, if only for her longevity, and they shifted their attention instead to the abuses of privilege among the aristocracy in the House of Lords. Working-class republicanism might stumble on for a year or two more, but it lacked political focus. The 'fearful storm of loyalty' that had marked the Prince of Wales's recovery had, declared the *National Reformer*, proved 'how little at present republicanism had permeated the general population', confirming that a deep-seated loyalty to the throne and a veneration of Victoria as monarch still largely prevailed.[1] The moral example of the throne, dormant for ten years since Albert's death, had found its renaissance in adversity.

Victoria's worries about her son and heir did not, however, abate for long; hopes that Bertie's near-death experience might reform his character faded as he slid back into old habits, confirming his mother's longstanding mistrust of him. By June 1872 she was once more bewailing the shortcomings of her thirty-one-year-old son: 'If only our dear Bertie was fit to replace me!'[2] Had Albert lived, she told Vicky, he would never have coped with the shame not just of Bertie, but also of his brother Affie's immoral behaviour: 'he would have suffered from many inevitable things which have taken place and which he never would have approved'. She was glad he had been spared this, for 'he could not have borne it'.[3] It was better to shoulder the burden alone. She would never relinquish any power to her son all the time there was breath in her body; nor did she feel the need for his advice on matters of state. Albert had set the template on that score, and to that she rigidly adhered. Since Bertie's illness she was more forgiving, learning to live with his inadequacies and appreciating better his innate kindness and affection. But for the rest of his mother's reign the Prince of Wales had to pay the price of a life of imposed idleness – frittering away his useful years in the shallow pursuit of women, horses and gambling in the watering holes of Europe and country houses of England.

As for a resumption of Victoria's public duties, the events of 1871–2, while doing much to turn the tide of her unpopularity, did little immediately to alter the deeply ingrained habits of the previous decade. The insularity and self-absorption of those lost years had seen a hardening of her least attractive image as the dour, prudish, humourless and repressive Widow at Windsor – an erroneous view that has come down through history, and which has marginalised the Queen's many good attributes. These worst excesses of stubborn self-interest had indeed seen her become at times 'maddening, cruel, hateful, pitiful, impossible'.[4] But out of so much darkness and negativity there finally emerged the monarch whose great virtues – lack of vanity, human sympathy, an absolute honesty and sound common sense – finally gained the ascendant in her later years. True, Victoria still stuck to her favoured routine of long periods out of sight at Balmoral and Windsor, and avoided Buckingham Palace at all costs. But her resistance softened after 1872, for she now better understood how crucial her public popularity was and that she could no longer remain totally invisible. Her increased appearances were never enough to silence her critics entirely; complaints about her seclusion persisted, with pamphlets such as 'Worthy a Crown?' and 'The Vacant Throne' raising the issue again in 1876 and 1877; but in general, by the end of the 1870s, public antipathy had waned and the level of complaint had died down. Much of Victoria's emergence from the cocoon of mourning at this time came thanks to the return to power of her adored Disraeli in 1874, when under his persuasive guidance she gradually became more visible at the head of the kind of informal, accessible monarchy initiated by Prince Albert before his death. Her elevation to Empress of India under the Royal Titles Act of 1876, at her own request, did much to swell national pride as well as Victoria's ego. The triumph of her Golden and Diamond Jubilees in 1887 and 1897 respectively incontrovertibly set the seal on the Queen as the figurehead of an ideology linking monarch and people with burgeoning colonial expansion, imperial greatness and national pride.[5]

While the Queen's grief for Prince Albert inevitably mellowed as the years passed, it was clear to all that the ageing monarch would never give up her widow's weeds. It suited her needs: Victoria might at last be reconciled to life without her husband, but to leave off her black, apart from being a betrayal of his sacred memory, would be to give notice of a return to normality – the one thing she wished to avoid. Her widow's weeds had become her shield and protector, and she clung steadfastly to them as she continued to battle with her irrational feelings of being overwhelmed and unable to cope. It was, to a certain extent, a very warped self-image; Victoria's perception of herself as the poor, weak, broken-hearted widow with shattered nerves had trapped her in a contradiction of what time and again she had demonstrated so clearly to others: her natural intelligence, the force of her indomitable personality and her great powers of endurance.[6]

Inevitably the ostentatious mourning rituals that she indulged in became outmoded, as social mores changed and the discussion of death increasingly became a taboo subject, but by now they had become the signifiers of Victoria's personal style as monarch, remaining very real, very visceral and absolutely central to who she was. Victoria's ladies-in-waiting, meanwhile, would continue to sigh about the cross they had to bear of wearing only lavender, white and grey for the remainder of her reign, for they were never allowed out of half-mourning when on duty; and time and again they were sent back into black as Victoria's friends and relatives died. If anything, the Queen's meticulous observation of the minutiae of bereavement deepened with the years, extending to her drawing-up of a detailed code of etiquette for the arrangement of all royal layings-out and funerals, which included specific instructions on the different types of shroud to be used for male and female, married and unmarried. With a series of deaths in the family and her entourage, she was kept indefinitely preoccupied, turning the performance of grief into her own very personal art form. There were many deaths for her to mourn, and in quick succession. In the 1870s she lost Lord Clarendon, Sir James Clark, General Grey, the former head of the royal nursery Lady Lyttleton, her favourite Scottish minister Reverend Macleod, her dear friend Countess Blücher, her old governess Baroness Lehzen, the devoted Lady Augusta Stanley, her literary hero Charles Dickens and her old friend Napoleon III – to name but a few. Dwelling on such losses was consoling for her; the constancy of the loyal mourner carrying the flame for the departed 'till all my widowed race be run' was a virtue

she had long cultivated.[7] None was more mourned than her dear
half-sister Feodora, when she died of cancer in September 1872. Victoria
saw it as a turning point, one of the last links with her past. 'God's will
be done,' she wrote in her journal, 'I stand so alone now, no near and
dear one near my own age, or older, to whom I could look up to, left.
All, all gone! She was my last near relative on an equality with me, the
last link with my childhood and youth.'[8]

For Victoria, the death of her half-sister was 'the third great sorrow
of her life' – along with the loss of Albert and her mother.[9] Reminders
of Feodora took their place amidst the busts, statues, mourning jewellery, photographs, memorial cards and all the other *memento mori* that
Queen Victoria gathered round her in one great mausoleum at Windsor
dedicated to her many dear and departed. The security offered by all the
paraphernalia of this 'obsolescent world' was infinitely preferable, always,
to the 'anxiety of reality'.[10] For her the celebration of death was a kind
of 'melancholy entertainment' – a piece of theatre that other pious
widows aspired to emulate – and the more mournful, the better. If a
ceremony was a tad cheerful the Queen 'always treated [it] with the
utmost indifference', recalled lady-in-waiting Marie Mallet.[11] Many felt,
as Mallet did, that Victoria's excessively lugubrious manner was perhaps
a reflection of 'the dim shade of inherited melancholy from George III'.[12]
She certainly made a great deal later in her reign of the funerary rites
for her devoted John Brown in 1883, her haemophiliac son Leopold when
he died in 1884, her grandson Eddy, Duke of Clarence in 1892, and
Beatrice's husband, Prince Henry of Battenberg, in 1896. But she took
a close interest too in the far more modest obsequies for lesser members
of her household. In 1891, when one of the servants who had accompanied her on her holiday to Grasse in the south of France died, she gave
instructions on the laying-out of the corpse, which were followed to the
letter. Marie Mallet found it very curious 'to see how the Queen takes
the keenest interest in death and all its horrors'. 'Our whole talk,' she
wrote home, 'has been of coffins and winding sheets.'[13] Nor did Victoria's
interest in the rituals of death stop at human beings; she went to equal
lengths when her favourite dogs died, ensuring they were buried with
great ceremony and that monuments were erected over their graves.[14]

Queen Victoria's long intimacy with death at least had one transforma-
tive effect: it opened up her naturally consoling heart and made of her,
in her old age, a great 'arbiter of grief'.[15] Always, and at every turn, she
drew strength and comfort from commiserating with others in their

bereavement, and many very personal and touching letters of condolence flowed from her pen. She of course continued to mourn the terrible void in her life left after Albert's death; forty years on from it she still missed his 'sheltering arm and wise help'.[16] Tennyson's great poem *In Memoriam* remained her touchstone, lines such as 'Ah dear, but come thou back to me' immortalising the longings of so many other widows and joining Victoria with them in 'one great rhythmic sigh of hopeless love'.[17]

With time and the deaths of so many she loved, public sympathy grew for the ageing queen. The British people respected her capacity for unending sorrow; there was something majestic, almost mystical about it. Victoria celebrated the mythic power of death like a pagan queen in tune with rituals beyond the understanding of ordinary mortals. And there were concessions in return: the remorseless black of her official image by degrees softened in its severity as the Queen took to relieving its monotony for official functions with white lace and diamonds, pearls and even her small diamond crown rather than her widow's bonnet. Eventually her long-familiar image in black had come to represent not just the monarchy and, by association, the age, but also Victoria's most-admired qualities of solidity, respectability and dignity as benevolent, matriarchal widow. By the end of her reign she had become an inspiration to middle-class women everywhere; women such as writer H. G. Wells's mother, who for forty years had followed 'her acts and utterances, her goings forth and her lyings in, her great sorrow and her other bereavements with a passionate loyalty'. For ordinary women such as her, Queen Victoria was their 'compensatory personality' – an 'imaginative consolation for all the restrictions and hardships that her sex, her diminutive size, her motherhood and all the endless difficulties of life, imposed upon her'.[18]

In a triumphant subversion of the traditional image of the monarch in splendid robes of state at the heart of great ceremonial set-pieces, by the century's end Queen Victoria dominated the national consciousness as its antithesis – in all her bourgeois ordinariness – as revered widow and 'Mother of the People', and (on an international scale) as Grandmama of Europe. It was an extraordinary alchemy, unique to Queen Victoria as monarch. For by the end of her reign there was no one to rival her in her wisdom, her years of experience and her grasp of statesmanship and international affairs. 'She was the grandmother of us all,' as one Eton schoolboy fondly remembered her:

She was our fond old lady, guiding the land, the nation, the world almost, with her venerable influence, but also sharing and living in our lives and fortunes, those of the simpler sort especially, and all without pomp or display, though with a dignity so massive, till the glitter of other courts, the brilliance of other times appeared meretricious and tawdry beside the homeliness that she loved . . . She belonged to us all, and none in the world beside ourselves had a queen and a grandmother to compare with her.[19]

The role of grandmother to her extended European family in Scandinavia, Germany and Russia had brought Queen Victoria many preoccupations as she spent her old age planning, negotiating and frequently meddling in her family's dynastic marriages, in the process maintaining a prodigious, opinionated and lively correspondence with them all. Although never particularly fond of children she was in the end greatly consoled by her grandchildren, particularly the children of Beatrice and her husband Prince Henry of Battenberg, who lived with her for much of the time. The proliferation of photographs, paintings and magazine articles about them all – with the comings and goings of their many christenings, weddings and funerals – satisfied public demand and kept the royal family in the public eye even when the monarch herself was still out of sight.

* * *

Queen Victoria had always viewed her bereavement as an inviolate 'sacred sorrow' and admitted to Vicky that 'those paroxysms of despair and yearning and longing and of daily, nightly longing to die . . . for the first three years never left me'.[20] But as she recovered from her debilitating grief – the grief 'that saps the mind', as Tennyson had called it – nothing would dim her determination to continue the public commemoration of Albert's memory and her own personal financial investment in it.[21] For the remainder of the century Albert's legacy proliferated in many more statues: some twenty-five in all, the one in Dublin narrowly missing destruction in a Fenian attempt to blow it up. Innumerable posthumous portraits, often based on *cartes de visite* of Albert, were commissioned for official bodies such as the Royal Society of Arts and municipal buildings across the United Kingdom, many of them paid for through public subscription. Stained-glass windows in churches were particularly popular, inspired by the one in St George's Chapel, Windsor, which had been constructed just in time for Bertie's wedding in 1863. Close by, the smaller Albert Memorial Chapel was remodelled by Gilbert Scott on the shell of the disused Wolsey Chapel and financed by Victoria, well in excess of the original estimate of £15,000. It opened to the public in December 1875, featuring yet another elaborate, Gothic cenotaph with a medieval-style recumbent effigy of Prince Albert in armour by the sculptor Henri de Triqueti.

By August 1871 the interior decorations of the Royal Mausoleum at Frogmore had been completed, using marble from Belgium and Portugal for the walls, altar and inlaid floor. But the beauty of the interior was only seen by the royal family and their entourage, and has been opened to general view only on a very occasional basis.[22] Its most frequent visitor for the forty years until her death was Victoria herself. Having her own set of keys, she would often go there to think and pray and contemplate Albert's effigy in times of trouble, national emergency and even moments of gratitude, such as Bertie's recovery from typhoid. In summer she often took picnics outside under the shade of a cedar tree. There was nothing morbid about it; it was her way of feeling close, of never forgetting. Above the entrance to the mausoleum she had had inscribed the words 'Farewell best beloved, here at last I shall rest with thee, with thee in Christ I shall rise again', but it was not until 4 February 1901 that she finally joined Albert there.

In the meantime, she had enough years and will left in her to oversee the expansion of the enduring national focus of Prince Albert's life and contribution to British art, architecture, science and culture. This was the complex of educational buildings popularly known as Albertopolis that sprang up in South Kensington in the last third of the century. The term had first been coined around the time of the Great Exhibition to refer to the land purchased with its profits – a site stretching from the northern to southern ends of what is now Exhibition Road. At one point Victoria had nursed ambitions to have all the great national collections of art and science collected here from across London, in one defining Albertian repository dominating the architectural landscape of late-Victorian London.[23] By 1866 the word 'Albertopolis' was in regular (though often irreverent) use; but it was many years before the entire complex was finished. The Victoria and Albert Museum was extended piecemeal until the mid-1880s, but the main frontage – for which Victoria laid the foundation stone in 1899 – was not completed till 1909. Albertopolis reached its full incarnation with the addition of the Natural History

Museum, the Science Museum, the Royal Albert Hall, the Royal College
of Art, the Royal College of Music and the Imperial College of Science,
Technology and Medicine. But the emotive focal point would always be
the Albert Memorial in Hyde Park, which gave a sense of unity and
identity to this ambitious Victorian exercise in Wagnerian grandeur.[24]
With her popularity still on a high after the assassination attempt of
February, on 1 July 1872 Victoria travelled to Hyde Park to inspect the
completed memorial prior to it being opened to the public, after years
of being surrounded by hoarding. However, only the outer shrine was
complete – the central statue of Albert by Foley had been delayed by
the sculptor's long illness and then death in 1874. It was not put in place
until November 1875 and finally unveiled, after it had been gilded, on 8
March 1876.

The architect – the newly knighted Sir Gilbert Scott – had designed
the Albert Memorial, he said, 'con amore', though the process had been
'long and painful'. He was proud of the 'exquisite phantasy' of its shrine-
like character, but knew that he would have to bear the brunt of criticism
of a work 'of a character peculiar, as I fancy, to this country'.[25] French
diplomat Charles Gavard thought that the late Prince (a man who was
very much 'comme il faut') would have been 'greatly embarrassed' by this
'temple, kiosque, pagoda' being erected to his memory. 'It is enough to
make Wellington jealous – he has only two statues,' he quipped.[26] On a
visit to London in 1872 the American writer Mark Twain took a drive
round Hyde Park and was struck by what he recalled as 'the brightest,
freshest, loveliest bit of gigantic jewelry in all this battered and blackened
old city'; Napoleon Bonaparte's tomb at Les Invalides in Paris paled in
comparison. Twain had nothing but praise for the memorial's attention
to detail and its artistry; but, having no idea at the time to whom the
monument was dedicated (the statue of Albert not yet being in place),
he assumed it was a memorial to Shakespeare. But no, it turned out to
be a tribute 'to a most excellent foreign gentleman who was a happy
type of the Good & the Kind, the Well-Meaning, the Mediochre, the
Commonplace'. But who was Prince Albert now to the nation? A man
who 'did no more for his country than five hundred tradesmen did in
his own time, whose works are forgotten'. The monument was magnificent, but Twain was discomforted by the fact that it did not celebrate
someone of the status of Shakespeare – but 'maybe he does not need it
as much as the other'.[27]

By the time the memorial was fully open, fifteen years after Albert's

death, its emotional impact had dissipated; for all its imposing magnificence, the Albert Memorial never won popular public approval. Viewed
as a 'hideous Germanised eyesore', it fell into such neglect in the late
twentieth century that there was talk of demolishing it. Several eccentric
schemes were mooted for protecting it from further decay, including
enclosing it in a massive glass box. Fortunately the Victorian Society
came to its rescue in 1987 and launched a concerted campaign that finally,
after numerous crises over funding, saw it restored to all its magnificence
(to the tune of £11 million) and reopened in time for the millennium in
October 2000, to a firework display spelling out 'Albert Saved'.[28]

The written legacy of Prince Albert's life and work also continued,
in tandem with the architectural one, at the Queen's behest and against
the odds of fading public interest. At the end of 1874 the first volume
of Theodore Martin's epic *Life of the Prince Consort* was published, but
it would not be completed till volume five in 1880, by which time it
already seemed passé in subject, sentiment and content. The dogged
Martin was knighted for his labours that year, but, despite its heroic
attention to detail, his *Life* was not a work of independent thought, but –
much like Grey's *Early Life* before it – set in stone the Queen's prescribed
view of her husband as plaster saint. It presented a portrait, wrote Lytton
Strachey, of an 'impeccable waxwork' rather than a more rounded one
of the real man. Nor did it go down well with some reviewers, due to
the extent to which it revealed Victoria and Albert's close involvement
in foreign affairs, to the point of interference. The real Prince Albert,
whom Martin's book and all the other written memorials to him in their
slavish hagiography had failed ever to capture – 'the real creature, so
full of energy and stress and torment, so mysterious and so unhappy,
and so fallible, and so very human' – had completely disappeared.[29] By
the 1880s public resistance was growing to any further representations
of a prince who had been dead for more than twenty years and whom
few had ever seen, let alone understood in his lifetime. People wanted
their living queen among them, not interminable marble and bronze
memorials to her dead, and increasingly remote, consort.

*   *   *

It took many difficult years of crucifying self-doubt for Queen Victoria
to overcome the sense of sexual inferiority that had become ingrained
during her marriage to Prince Albert. Her grief had been deeply disem-
powering for the best part of ten years, but the supreme irony is that

(*Above*) Prince Albert as Queen Victoria liked to remember him –
as a heroic medieval knight, in this painting by Robert Thorburn,
given to her by Albert for her 25th birthday on 24 May 1844.

(*Left*) The East Terrace, Windsor Castle, location of the royal apartments. Victoria never liked the castle very much and after Albert's death avoided spending much time here.

(*Right*) The Grand Corridor of Windsor Castle, a place of recreation where the royal children played and members of staff met and chatted, but which on the evening of 14 December 1861 was one of grim watching and waiting.

(*Left*) The Blue Room in which Prince Albert died, by John Simpson 1863. More fanciful popular representations of the size and layout of the room made it look far bigger than it was.

(*Left*) The one time Windsor Castle came into its own was for happy family Christmases during Albert's lifetime, such as this one c. 1850, promoting the public image of a happy, domestic royal family.

(*Right*) Carlo Marochetti's marble effigy of Prince Albert lying on a trolley waiting to be put into position inside the mausoleum *c*.December 1863.

(*Left*) Design for the interior decorations of the Royal Mausoleum at Frogmore, inspired by Albert's favourite painter, Raphael. His marble effigy was not placed in position on top of the granite sarcophagus there until November 1868; the interior was completed in August 1871.

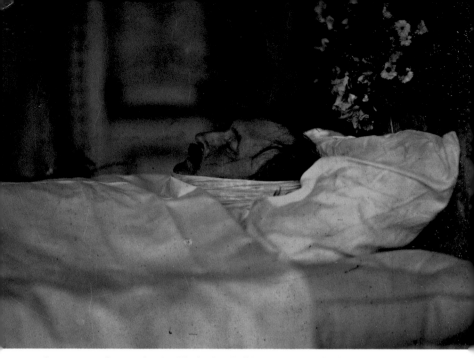

(*Above*) Prince Albert on his deathbed, a band of linen wound under his chin until rigor mortis had set in, in line with conventional Victorian practice. The photograph was taken in the Blue Room the day after his death by royal photographer William Bambridge.

(*Below*) A popular, but inaccurate Victorian scrap book cut-out of Prince Albert's deathbed, depicting Victoria, Alice, Bertie and Arthur. In fact, Arthur had not been present at the death, having said farewell to his father earlier that afternoon. Two of Albert's other sons were abroad at the time: Alfie at sea and Leopold in Cannes.

(*Left*) Bertie, Prince of Wales. Kind, sociable and well-meaning but academically underachieving, he failed to live up to the high expectations of both his parents.

(*Below*) Princess Alice, Victoria and Albert's second daughter, who took upon herself the devoted nursing of her father during his final illness and was the butt of her mother's agonising grief in the first six months after it.

(*Above*) Princess Louise, wearing jet, the only jewellery that the Queen would allow her daughters and her ladies to wear at court for more than twenty years after her husband's death.

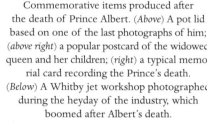

Commemorative items produced after the death of Prince Albert. (*Above*) A pot lid based on one of the last photographs of him; (*above right*) a popular postcard of the widowed queen and her children; (*right*) a typical memorial card recording the Prince's death. (*Below*) A Whitby jet workshop photographed during the heyday of the industry, which boomed after Albert's death.

(*Above*) Albert's brainchild, The Royal Albert Hall, constructed between 1867 and 1871 as an exhibition centre and concert hall for the promotion of British arts, industry and culture.

(*Left*) This equestrian statue of Prince Albert was the first public monument to be unveiled by Queen Victoria herself, in Wolverhampton in November 1866.

(*Right*) The gilded statue of Prince Albert at the newly restored Albert Memorial in Hyde Park. Completed with the statue in position in 1875, the memorial was never popular and came close to being demolished. It was saved and restored during the 1990s, thanks to a concerted campaign by the Victorian Society.

(*Above*) Bertie, Prince of Wales's marriage to Alexandra of Denmark, at St George's Chapel Windsor, 10 March 1863, with the widowed Queen watching the proceedings from Catherine of Aragon's closet, top right.

(*Below*) Bertie and Queen Victoria riding in an open landau to the Thanksgiving Service held at St Paul's Cathedral on 27 February 1872 for his recovery from typhoid fever. Note the presence on the box of the ubiquitous John Brown.

Albert's death was, perversely, the making of her as Queen, releasing her in the end from the perception of her own shortcomings as the dutiful 'little wife'. Despite all Albert's reassurances, Victoria had never been quite reconciled to what she considered the unseemliness of being a female monarch – consumed by official business at the expense of domestic and wifely duty. Albert, along with Melbourne and Peel, had taught her her trade as monarch and, had he lived, she would gladly, willingly, have given up her throne to him. Left without him, however, she had never for one moment – despite all her hysterical threats to abdicate – wanted to give up her sovereign power. That was the one thing she had always relished. Together, she and Albert had summoned an inglorious British monarchy from the dead during the years of their marriage, revolutionising the old Regency order and setting new moral standards. But had Albert lived, history would have been quite different; Victoria would have retreated further and further into the background, ceding much of the day-to-day control of affairs of state to her husband. It was Albert's voice that had rung out ever louder across the pages of her official memoranda during the 1850s as he increased his power base, seeking to aggrandise the prerogatives of the Crown over the position of the Cabinet.[30] Albert's burgeoning power had created apprehension even then among Victoria's ladies-in-waiting Lady Ely and Lady Churchill, both of whom felt that his virtual control of government business as uncrowned king would have led to political and constitutional difficulties resulting in 'direct conflict between the Throne and the People'.[31]

In the end, boosted by the assumption of her new title of Empress of India and her unrivalled supremacy over her royal relatives in Europe as 'the *doyenne* of sovereigns', Queen Victoria grew into the familiar, imposing image that has come down to us of '*Victoria Regina et Imperatrix*'.[32] The British monarchy retained its firm hold upon the affections of the middle classes, who could relate to Victoria and her 'comfortable' motherliness and, through her, 'felt related in some degree to something that [was] socially great' – their very own royal family. It is a sentiment that has survived into the reign of her great-great-granddaughter, Elizabeth II, a monarch whose unerring sense of duty bears all the hallmarks of the tradition set by Prince Albert. But whether it will survive beyond her is doubtful.[33]

In retrospect, the years 1840–61 of Queen Victoria's marriage to Prince Albert might be more accurately described as Albertian in tone, a fact of which, in deference to her late husband, Victoria wholly approved.[34]

For during the second half of the 1870s there came a sea change; people finally began referring to themselves as 'Victorians', endorsing what Victoria had herself said, after Albert's death in 1861, that it was 'the beginning of a new reign'.[35] By the 1880s Prince Albert's memory had so rapidly faded in rural areas, with no visible reminders of him, that villagers only knew that 'he had been the Queen's husband, though, oddly enough not the King, and that he had been so good that nobody had liked him in his lifetime, excepting the Queen, who "fairly doted"'.[36] The real man – so elusive to the British public in his lifetime, yet elevated by his grieving widow as a mythical, Arthurian figure – had by then been reduced to a cipher, languishing in the imposing shadow of his resurgent widow. Yes, hers had been a magnificent obsession and Victoria had stayed true to it, exhaustively commemorating her late husband in the way *she* saw fit. But the true Victorian age – of pageantry, pride and empire – was never his. It was entirely Victoria's. And it was yet to come.

EPILOGUE

Christmas 1878

For much of the 1870s Queen Victoria and her second daughter Princess Alice had been increasingly alienated from each other. Much of the breakdown in their relationship had to do with Alice's disapproval of her mother's retreat from duty and, by the same token, Victoria's dislike of her daughter's criticism and interference. Alice, in her view, could be tactless and unkind; she had become 'sharp and grand and wanting to have everything her own way'.[1] She was also rather too forward-thinking for Victoria's liking, affronted as she was by Alice's 'indelicate' interest in women's gynaecological matters and her passion for nursing. The truth of it was that so much enforced intimacy with her mother during Albert's last illness, and the six terrible months of grief she spent with Victoria until her marriage the following year, had left Princess Alice with a much deeper critical understanding of their mother than any of her other siblings, except perhaps Louise.

As a young girl Princess Alice had been shy, sweet-natured and compliant. She had shared many personality traits with her father, having the same thoughtful, studious nature. Prince Albert had always considered her to be the most beautiful of his children, although the severe features and sharp nose suggest a rather ethereal, mournful beauty and the last photographs of her convey a lingering sense of disappointment with life. She always seemed physically frail, particularly after an attack of scarlet fever in 1855, and her health (like her father's) began to deteriorate at an early age. Once married and removed from her mother's domineering presence, Alice rapidly proved to be less compliant than she had been of old, and more than capable of standing up to Victoria's endless demands that the members of her family should subordinate themselves to what suited *her*. On visits to England Alice began to question Victoria's dictatorial manner and, at times, resist it.

Her marriage to Louis had begun happily enough in 1862, but a perennial shortage of money had imposed considerable constraints on the
way Princess Alice ran her household and she was constantly having to
make economies (as well as regularly appealing to her mother for financial help). Darmstadt, situated in the hills of the Odenwald near the
River Rhine, was something of a social and cultural backwater. Alice
was a devoted wife and mother and unquestioningly loyal, but she was
not content to be consigned to a life that consisted solely of having
babies to populate the minor principalities of Europe. Like her father,
she wished to be of service to her adopted people and, also like him,
set herself high standards of duty. At times she would appear overwhelmed by her sense of *noblesse oblige*, of the onerous responsibilities
of her supposed position of privilege. 'Life was made for work and not
pleasure,' she once remarked, and stoicism – if not an unhealthy propensity to martyrdom – became her enduring quality.[2] As time passed there
was no disguising her increasing disappointment in her husband's
emotional and intellectual shortcomings, which heightened her sense of
loneliness and isolation. Louis, a born soldier, never shared Alice's
passionate interests in the arts, nor did he comprehend her wide-reaching
social concerns. She loved him as best she could, but she was disappointed. And so she found other channels for her personal frustrations,
between her seven pregnancies throwing herself into an enormous and
ever more consuming workload of philanthropic work, hospital visiting
and nursing, particularly during the wars of 1866 and 1870–1 into which
Hesse was drawn.

Princess Alice had always mourned her father with an intensity and
pain that were as private as her mother's were public, and spent much
of her time – like her sister Vicky in Berlin – writing long, consoling
letters focused on alleviating her mother's grief rather than her own.
On the anniversary of Albert's death in 1872 it was still hard for her to
find the right words: 'From year to year they can but express the same:
the grief at the loss of such a father, such a man, grows with me, and
leaves a gap and a want that nothing on earth can ever fill up.'[3] Alice's
personal sense of grief was made far worse by the tragic death of her
three-year-old haemophiliac second son, Frittie (Wilhelm Friedrich), in
1873, after he fell out of a window. Quite simply, it broke her heart and
also much of her spirit. She never recovered, succumbing more and more
to stress, headaches and insomnia. Her life in Darmstadt became stulti-
fying and her relationship with Louis ever more estranged. She was

weary and depressed. It was not Louis's fault, she told him, in a poignant and passionate letter written to him from Balmoral in October 1876:

> I am bitterly disappointed with myself when I look back, and see that in spite of great ambitions, good intentions, and real effort, my hopes have nevertheless been completely ship-wrecked . . . Rain – fine weather – things that have happened – that is all I ever have to tell you about – so utterly cut off is my *real self*, my innermost life, from yours . . . I have tried again and again to talk to you about more serious things, when I felt the need to do so – but we never meet each other – we have developed separately . . . and that is why I feel true companionship is an impossibility for us – because our thoughts will never meet.[4]

By the following year, when Louis succeeded his uncle as Grand Duke Ludwig IV of Hesse and by Rhine, Alice was dreading having to take up the even more onerous responsibilities of Grand Duchess. And then another tragedy struck. In November 1878 her fifteen-year-old daughter Victoria fell ill with diphtheria. Within eight days four of her other children, Alix, May, Irene and Ernie – as well as her husband – all contracted it; the remaining unaffected child, Ella, was sent to stay with relatives.

Alice nursed her family devotedly, day and night, but her five-year-old daughter May – her adored little May-flower 'with her precious dimples and loving ways' – died on 15 November.[5] She bravely kept the news from her other sick children for as long as she could, dreading that her only son Ernie might die; it would kill her, she said, 'to have to give him up too'.[6] Against all the doctors' warnings of the risk of infection, she could not however restrain herself from comforting Ernie with a kiss when he was told the terrible news of his sister's death. And it was not long after she had seen May's tiny little coffin covered with white flowers off to its funeral that Alice herself felt the first symptoms of the disease. The attack, coming on 7 December, was very severe.

As soon as she heard the news at Windsor, Victoria repaired to 'that sad blue room where darling Alice and I watched together 17 years ago, on this day' and prayed.[7] She sent Dr Jenner out to assist in Alice's care, but by the 13th Alice could no longer swallow. A telegram came from Louis: 'my prayers are exhausted,' he said. With the spectre of those two terrible Decembers of 1861 and 1871 hovering over her, Victoria headed down the hill to the mausoleum to pray. She was met en route by a footman with a telegram warning that things were desperate. The diphtheria membrane had spread across Alice's windpipe and she was having difficulty breathing. Later that day she rallied, but it was the same false hope as the hope they had had the day before Albert died. 'I sat in my room writing, watching anxiously for every footstep, every door opening,' Victoria recalled.[8]

In Darmstadt on the 13th Alice read the two letters from her mother brought by Dr Jenner. Then she lay down: 'Now I will go to sleep again,' she said, but overnight her condition deteriorated. At half-past eight the following morning – 14th December 1878, the seventeenth anniversary of her father's death – Princess Alice died, whispering the names of May and 'dear papa'.[9] She was thirty-five. It was John Brown who brought the telegram from Louis to Victoria as she sat down to breakfast that morning: 'Poor Mama, poor me, my happiness gone, dear, dear Alice. God's will be done.'[10] Victoria took the news with extraordinary calm; all the old animosity between herself and Alice forgotten in an instant. Her dead daughter – 'this dear, talented, distinguished, tender-hearted, noble minded, sweet child' – had now joined Albert in the pantheon of her personal saints. Victoria was convinced that it was an act of divine intervention, that God had called Alice away to be with her father, and she took great comfort in its terrifying logic. It was 'almost incredible and most mysterious'. Husband and daughter had both been 'for ever united on this day of their birth into another better world'.[11]

Queen Victoria ordered three weeks' public mourning for Princess Alice. She prayed often in the Blue Room over the days that followed and commissioned her favourite sculptor Boehm to make an effigy of Alice to join Albert's sarcophagus in the mausoleum.[12] Another Christmas in black loomed, as the public, who had long held the Princess in high regard for her dedicated nursing of her father and brother, responded with the same kind of grief-stricken loyalty as in 1861 and 1871. Princess Alice, Grand Duchess of Hesse – 'the model of family virtue, as a daughter, a sister, a wife and a mother' – was elevated to a state of beatitude that was never to be shared by any of her siblings.[13] Once again the letters and telegrams of condolence streamed in to Windsor; Victoria meanwhile waited anxiously for letters from Louis giving her 'every detail' of Alice's final hours and the funeral ceremony. 'You must treasure her in your hearts as a *Saint*,' she told Alice's children and siblings: they should do as she herself had done for Albert and 'mourn for their lost sister and mother, *more* and *more*, if not for a lifetime then for many years to come'.[14]

Princess Alice's funeral was held in Darmstadt on the afternoon of 18

December 1878; later that evening, in biting winter wind, her coffin was conveyed by torchlight to the Hesse family mausoleum at Rosenhöhe. Bertie and Leopold were there to watch as Alice's coffin was placed alongside those of Frittie and May, draped with the Union Jack, for Alice had always said that she wanted 'to go with the old English colours above me'.[15] In England the rest of the royal family attended a private service in her memory at Windsor. Once again the muffled bells pealed out the solemn threnody of royal death, British churches were draped in black, and shopkeepers put up their shutters as the nation mourned its lost princess. It was, as Christmas approached, 'a strange dreadful time', a time of mourning instead of celebration, now made doubly melancholy by the tragedy of yet another death in the royal family on the same day.[16] The presents the Queen gave to her servants that year were framed photographs of Alice. On 28 December her letter to the nation was published, thanking them for 'the most touching sympathy shown to her by all classes of her loyal and faithful subjects'. It was, she said, 'most soothing' to see 'how entirely her grief is shared by her people'.[17]

The loss of Alice was, for Victoria, a terrible landmark: 'the first break in my circle of children'.[18] As bereaved mother, widow and Queen, her position was now unassailable; her sacred monopoly on grief transcended all criticism. But it was a heavy burden. On New Year's Eve 1878 Victoria sat down, as she had so religiously done for forty-five years now, to write the daily entry in her journal. But how to describe 'The last day of this terrible year' as it sadly ebbed away? It had been punctuated by so much tragedy:

> the poor King of Italy, dying on Jan 8th, the Pope on the 23rd . . . the deaths of Ld Ailesbury and Ld Kinnaird . . . the awful loss of the 'Eurydice' . . . the first attempt on the Emperor William's life, the death of the poor Dss of Argyll of May 25th, the loss of the 'Grosse Kurfürst', the death of Lord Russell, the death of the King of Hanover on June 12th, and his funeral at Windsor on the 24th . . . the death of the poor young Queen of Spain, the illness and death of poor good Sir Thomas Biddulph, then the Affghan [sic] war, the awful illness at Darmstadt, dear little May's death on Nov 16th, the alarming account of dearest Alice, on the 8th, & the dreadful ending to her illness on the 14th![19]

Through the long years of her widowhood and the loss of so many she had loved, Queen Victoria had steadfastly held to the mantra she had chosen for herself, from the words written by Tennyson to commemorate Prince Albert in the Preface to *The Idylls of the King*: 'Break Not Oh Woman's Heart But Still Endure'. The dead would always be a necessary part of her, extending their lingering shadow over the unravelling of her own final mortal days. But she had found the courage to go on. And she had indeed endured. Yes, she had come through.

APPENDIX
What Killed Prince Albert?

Shortly after Prince Albert died, the registrar's office in Windsor town was notified by the Prince of Wales and a death certificate was issued, stating that the Prince had died from typhoid fever of a duration of twenty-one days.[1] Thus began 150 years of largely unchallenged thinking on the Prince Consort's final illness. One cannot know now what political or other pressures may have obliged the royal doctors to come up with this definitive diagnosis in the face of their undoubted and openly expressed uncertainty during the last month of the Prince's life. But the cause of death as given fell into line with their rather pat deduction that Albert's illness could be traced back to that day at Sandhurst on 22 November when he had got soaking wet and caught a chill.

The onset of the chill had, it was assumed, laid him open to infection by typhoid from contaminated drinking water or food – but not at Sandhurst for, feeling too unwell that day, the Prince ate and drank nothing while he was there. The logical conclusion to be reached was that he had contracted typhoid on his return to Windsor. By way of justification, in a front-page article on 28 December, the *Examiner* claimed that of late 'Her Majesty herself has been covering her nose on the way to the castle through the bad smells of the town', thanks to the supposed threat of 'Windsor Fever'. But this and similar reports in the press to the effect that there had recently been two or three cases of typhoid in the castle were later shown to be erroneous, and were rebutted by assertions elsewhere that 'the queen's household have been lately in the enjoyment of good health'.[2] Nevertheless the argument would not go away; some newspapers were quick to remind readers of an outbreak in 1858 in the town, which had carried off thirty-nine people, while others did the opposite and attempted to dampen claims that 'typhus fever or some similar disorder is raging at Windsor'. The town was 'in a very healthy condition', claimed the *Morning Star*, and in a long article on

21 December the *Medical Times and Gazette* presented a detailed discussion of the sanitation at Windsor, pointing out that the castle's drainage system was entirely independent of that in the town where the previous outbreak had occurred. Having conducted its own investigation, the paper asserted that it knew 'of no place where a more complete or more carefully worked system is to be found'. The only conclusion it could come to was that 'unless some dire and unsuspected source of danger should lurk in the royal apartments themselves – ample and well ventilated as they apparently are – the sewerage system of the castle must be acquitted of all share in the mischief, and the causes of the national calamity which we all deplore must be looked for elsewhere'.[3]

In 1860s Britain it was decidedly unfashionable for a prince consort to die of typhoid fever, and palace officials were clearly anxious to counter any public anxiety that the Queen and her family were at risk of infection. Typhoid fever was a disease that in the main decimated the poor – those who lived in squalid, urban areas where there was rudimentary sanitation and shared public water pumps. It is caused by the water-borne bacterium *Salmonella typhi* and is clinically and bacteriologically quite distinct from typhus, an illness that can only be spread from person to person by lice, through close contact in overcrowded slums or barracks. Although the bacterial cause of typhoid was not understood in the 1860s, its clinical distinction from typhus had been recognised by Albert's physician Dr Jenner a decade previously. In his 1850 study 'On the Identity or Non-Identity of Typhus and Typhoid Fevers', based on clinical and autopsy findings in sixty-six fatal cases, Jenner had applied the epithet 'typhoid', meaning 'typhus-like'. The association with poverty might explain the reluctance of the royal doctors to define the illness as such to the Queen and her entourage. Either way, they appear to have hedged their bets with regard to their diagnosis. If the Prince had indeed contracted typhoid fever at Windsor, then it would be expected (as a water-borne disease) that others in the castle sharing the same water supply would also have succumbed. But there is no record of anyone other than Prince Albert falling sick, and no evidence of him having come into contact with anyone suffering from the disease during the previous month.

The course of typhoid fever is a very emphatic one, with three clear stages: the first week (known as the invasive stage) is one of high temperature, agonising headache and extreme prostration. Also characteristic are muscular feebleness and tremor of the limbs with a low delirium, often accompanied by the involuntary passing of faeces and urine, as well as the accumulation of sordes (foul-smelling matter) around the lips and gums. In the first week of his illness Prince Albert, despite being clearly unwell and complaining of aches and pains and a furred tongue, was up and about and not displaying any of these extreme symptoms. The second week of the disease is marked by rising fever, tenderness, swelling and sometimes a gurgling sound in the abdomen, as well as diarrhoea and an enlarged spleen. Again, the intermittent symptoms Prince Albert was displaying of fever, occasional diarrhoea and wakefulness, accompanied by constant moving about, do not fit this scenario. In the third week and final stage – the point at which, on 8 December, the Prince finally took to his bed and became fitfully delirious and feverish – he should in fact, according to the classic typhoid pattern, have been moving into a slow and gradual recovery from temperature and other symptoms. With typhoid, however, relapses were often common and death from complications such as intestinal haemorrhage or perforation, or simply sheer physical exhaustion leading to pneumonia, often carried off patients who might otherwise have recovered.[4]

Medical knowledge in 1861 was in fact very limited in its ability to provide an accurate diagnosis of a whole range of gastroenteric fevers, irritation or inflammation, which have since been described and individually named. Prince Albert's typhoid-like symptoms may well have been a feature of acute deterioration of a chronic gastrointestinal inflammation (often referred to by Victorian doctors as 'catarrh of the stomach'), which had been developing over a long period of time. This would have been characterised by periods of remission during which he felt fairly well, followed by acute bouts or flare-ups, when the symptoms became very marked and at times intolerable. This might well account for Albert's frequent complaints about painful stomach cramps, vomiting and diarrhoea, as well as toothache or inflamed gums, which could well have been symptomatic of a chronic (meaning long-standing) condition. There seems little doubt that his poor health was aggravated by his excessive workload, his inability to sit still for long, eat properly without rushing his food or take adequate rest. Periods of stress in both his official life and his private one with the Queen – notably her bouts of post-natal depression and the excessive burden of her hysterical grieving when her mother died – would have made matters worse. Insomnia and worry, both of which Albert was plagued by, may have lowered not only his physical resistance, but also his mental state, leading to clear phases of apathy and depression. The only palliatives available for insomnia were ether-based proprietary drugs such as Hoffman's Drops – a popular, but highly addictive medication that was used for everything from coughs to croup and low fever.[5] They would have done nothing to relieve the Prince's symptoms, which collectively could be expected to exacerbate any underlying chronic condition. After the Prince caught a severe chill from his soaking on two consecutive days – inspecting the buildings at Sandhurst on 22 November 1861, followed by a day's shooting in the rain on the 23rd – the symptoms he complained of (chilliness, general aches and pains, waves of fever and sensations of cold running down the back alternating with bouts of heat) were all scrupulously noted by Queen Victoria. These are non-specific symptoms of infection, which could have been a predisposing factor to, or a feature of, a final and terminal deterioration in the insidious condition that had been present for at least the last four well-documented years of his failing health, and probably for much longer. Medical science knew even then that 'influenza opens the door to enteric fever so frequently that there would seem to be some relation between the two'.[6]

*   *   *

Two days after Prince Albert died, the first intimations of disquiet among medical practitioners were sounded, suggesting that perhaps officials at Windsor had not been entirely honest with the public over the circumstances of the Prince's illness, its diagnosis or treatment. In a letter to *The Times* on 16 December, headed 'The Medical Treatment of the Late Prince Consort', the pseudonymous correspondent 'Medicus' asked:

> When so valuable a life as the late Prince Consort's is taken by the particular disease stated, would it not be as well to publish for the satisfaction of the general body of the medical profession, as well as the public, an account of the treatment adopted by the acting responsible physicians who prescribed for and attended on his late Royal Highness from the commencement to the deplorable close of his illness?

It was a perfectly reasonable question and soon afterwards the *Morning Chronicle* reported that 'Information with respect to the fatal illness of the late Prince is being anxiously looked for, as well as the details of the medical treatment.' What is more, the medical profession, according to the paper, was divided in its opinion, although not for the first or last time. Doubt had been expressed 'in many quarters' that the Prince's treatment had been 'scarcely sufficiently vigorous, and that too much reliance was placed upon the previously sound constitution and temperate habits of the sufferer'. The paper was then bold enough – considering the Queen's deep sensitivity at the time – to express the one thought uppermost in every medical mind: 'The profession generally have been naturally anxious that a *post-mortem* examination should take place, but to such a proceeding Her Majesty expressed her decided unwillingness.'[7]

It is not surprising that the Queen resolutely refused to agree to such a thing, considering how traumatised she was by Albert's death, let alone the thought of his corpse being so horribly violated. This fact alone would have put pressure on the royal doctors to give a definitive diagnosis, for if any official doubts had been expressed about the cause of the Prince's death, a post-mortem might, legally, have been called for and would undoubtedly have sent the Queen into hysterics. It is possible of course that the doctors had indeed suspected something long-term or more deep-seated: if a post-mortem had proved this to be the case, they would also have been open to accusations of culpability through their perceived mismanagement or misdiagnosis of Albert's condition. In any event *The Lancet* called for an official account of the Prince's illness to be published, given that the unexpected rapidity with which he had sickened and died had run so counter to official bulletins that had played down the seriousness of his condition. *The Lancet* also raised the question of 'the discrepancies and manifold imperfections' in those bulletins. It was therefore with some disappointment, early in 1862, that the journal was obliged to announce, 'We are officially informed that the authentic and coherent account of the illness of the late Prince Consort, for which the profession and the public have manifested an anxious desire, will for the present be withheld.' Once again the palace had blocked freedom of information on the subject. The British medical profession remained far from satisfied, with *The Lancet* again echoing the view of many practitioners that such an omission 'leaves open to various conjectures a matter on which there should rest no shadow of doubt'.[8] The demands for clarification were, however, short-lived and rapidly receded in the light of the Queen's extreme grief. To persist on this point was deemed insensitive and intrusive.

On the medical fringe, however, accusations of mismanagement rumbled on. In January 1862 the *British Journal of Homoeopathy* criticised the attendance of four medical practitioners, feeling that this may have prompted a compromise in the treatment methods chosen: 'Under this heavy infliction of medical advice, the Royal patient had hardly a chance of recovery; for it is scarcely to be supposed that an intelligent or intelligible plan of treatment would be pursued under the direction of so many, and perhaps such opposite opinions.' In summary, the journal could not imagine the Prince's death occurring under 'the mild and efficacious medication' of homoeopathy. The Temperance movement too had its own uncompromising opinions. In an article entitled 'Alcoholic Medication' in the *Irish Temperance Journal*, John Pyper strongly criticised the constant dosing of the Prince with brandy during the last six days of his life. When a system was weakened by fever, Pyper argued, it needed rest – not alcoholic stimulation. 'Stimulation is not nutrition and the stimulant in fact becomes a depressant.' In the Prince Consort's case, 'keeping a person up' was 'a sure method of sinking him down'. The alcohol had merely provoked a 'still greater expenditure and waste of vital power'. In Pyper's view, any physician administering alcoholic stimulation was committing 'a grave, and also a grave-filling error'. A strong, hale man such as the Prince should not have died of 'gastric fever'. The opinion was of course misguided, though shared by many medical commentators at the time. Not being privy to the Prince's long-standing physical decline, they would have expected him – like similar men of his age 'of vigorous and athletic frame, a moderate liver, and with every thing conducive to health around him' – to have recovered from a bout of typhoid fever.[9] Pyper concluded that the 'gastric fever' had been complicated in the final stages by pulmonary congestion. This is reasonable enough, but pulmonary congestion is a pre-terminal event in any fatal condition as the heart fails or pneumonia develops.

Concerns about the Prince's treatment were not only posthumous. It is clear that Baron Stockmar, the person who knew Prince Albert best of all (from both a personal and medical point of view) had been greatly alarmed by Albert's failing health and his increasing malaise when he had seen him in 1860. By the end of that year Albert had endured a two-month attack of sickness, diarrhoea and pain; when he fell ill again in November 1861 Stockmar had sent regular messages to Windsor enquiring anxiously about the Prince's health. He had found the replies that he received evasive and unsatisfactory. Knowing that the royal family's medicines were supplied by the pharmacist Peter Squire of Oxford Street, he wrote directly to Squire, asking for details of the medication being prescribed. Correspondence between them on this matter has sadly not survived, though Squire's prescription book for the period reveals supplies of the antispasmodic and anticholinergic belladonna, a popular remedy for gastrointestinal disorders. No details of the amounts prescribed survive, nor is there (among all the other medications) any real sense of a concerted therapeutic regime for a specific condition in November to December 1861.[10]

Stockmar could of course do nothing from a distance, but whether or not accusations of gross mismanagement of the Prince's illness can be levelled at the royal doctors is still subject to debate. Lord Clarendon had, throughout, been scathing in his assessment. 'Nothing shall convince me that the Prince had all the assistance that medical skill might have afforded,' he wrote. Doctors Holland and Clark, in his opinion, were 'not even average old women; and nobody who is really ill would think of sending for either of them'. As for Jenner, he was a 'book physician' who 'had had little practice and experience'. William Gladstone certainly had no faith in Jenner and said that if he were his own doctor, he would 'get rid of him at once'. The vigour of the invective against the royal doctors by members of the government is in striking contrast to the pallid criticism of them elsewhere, but strong opinions are often founded on uncertainty. At least, however (and at Palmerston's stubborn insistence), another practitioner – Dr Watson – had been called in. 'But Watson (who is no specialist in fever cases),' Lord Clarendon observed, 'at once saw that he came too late to do any good, and that the case had got too much ahead to afford hope of recovery.' Jenner was very much the *parvenu* at court and still on trial. He would by necessity have been obliged to kowtow to Dr Clark's perceived superior wisdom and experience after twenty years in the job as the senior royal physician. Albert's fatal illness was his baptism by fire as a royal physician and, whether or not he was certain of the typhoid diagnosis – and the evidence suggests that he was extremely *uncertain* – typhoid fever can be difficult to diagnose even today, since it can be mimicked by several other illnesses marked by fever.

The biggest scorn, perhaps inevitably, has been heaped on Sir James Clark: he was incapable of treating 'a sick cat', in Clarendon's view, and had not just a past history of misdiagnosis, but also a habit of predicting recovery shortly before a patient died. He managed this unwelcome achievement not only in the case of Prince Albert, but also during the final illnesses of the former Prime Minister Robert Peel, Queen Louise of the Belgians, and Albert's secretary, George Anson. Queen Victoria's biographer, Elizabeth Longford, concluded that Clark 'erred on the side of optimism' out of an eagerness to please.[11] Yet when Victoria was sixteen he had nursed her through a severe attack of typhoid fever, so he was not unfamiliar with the disease. Clarendon put it all down to a matter of personalities and precedence: 'One cannot speak with certainty,' he added, 'but it is horrible to think that such a life *may* have been sacrificed to Sir J. Clark's selfish jealousy of every member of his profession.'[12] Whether he agreed with Clark's methods or not, Jenner was obliged to join in the misguided jollying along of Prince Albert by pandering to his restlessness, instead of sending him firmly to bed. Longford argues that by doing this Clark 'hoped to keep the sufferer going simply by refusing to let him lie down and die' – the continual dosing with brandy being a vain attempt to keep his pulse up (the alcohol's function being to dilate his blood vessels) and prevent him slipping into unconsciousness.[13] Whether or not the doctors concurred in the diagnosis of typhoid fever, it is clear that they remained highly reluctant to state its true nature, for fear of traumatising not only their patient, but also the Queen. Nebulous explanations therefore persisted: when Crown Prince Frederick arrived at Osborne on 19 December, the Queen told him that according to the doctors, Albert's disease in addition to its 'rheumatic character' had had 'a certain typhic element to it, without actually becoming typhus'. The confusion of typhus and typhoid here may well be the Queen's or Fritz's, or both – it was common enough at the time; but the following day, in a second letter, Fritz told Vicky that he had spoken at length to Dr Jenner, who had 'attributed dear Papa's suffering to "an abdominal typhus"' – a rather contrived euphemism at best.[14]

*   *   *

The claim that typhoid fever killed the Price Consort was not challenged in medical literature until 1993, but as early as 1977 historian Daphne Bennett offered alternative diagnoses in her biography of Prince Albert, *King without a Crown*.[15] In a brief discussion at the end of her book, Bennett suggested that perhaps the Prince had been suffering from a chronic wasting disease such as cancer, with the proviso that at that time doctors were unable to detect many of the deeper-seated or slow-growing cancers, relying largely on visual identification.[16] In his 1987 biography of Queen Victoria, the American historian Stanley Weintraub included a footnote regarding Albert's death in which he questioned the diagnosis of typhoid fever as the sole cause. He argued that Albert's frequent problems with sore and painful gums could have been caused by an oversecretion of hydrochloric acid in the stomach – caused perhaps by carcinoma of the stomach or a wasting disease such as a peptic ulcer, and arguing that perhaps he had been genetically predisposed to cancer (his mother died of cancer of the uterus at the age of thirty-one).[17] Another suggestion made to the author is that on the basis of known symptoms and their duration, stomach or bowel cancer is unlikely, but that Prince Albert might have been suffering from neuroendochrine tumours – or, more specifically, gastrinoma. This was accompanied by speculation that this rarer form of cancer could have been complicated by a secondary neuroendochrine tumour in the pituitary gland, which might have been responsible not just for Albert's increasing fatigue and weakness, but also for his distressed mental state – the irritability that Queen Victoria regularly commented on – and (though we have no way of knowing except by inference) a marked loss of libido. Gastrinoma is a type of malignant tumour that was first described in the 1950s; it usually arises in the pancreas or duodenum and grows slowly over many years, and is more common in men than women. Symptoms are often dramatic, since the tumour secretes gastrin, causing stomach ulcers, leading to intermittent stomach pain, vomiting and diarrhoea, all symptoms similar to those experienced by Prince Albert. In some cases gastrinomas metastasise in the later stages into the liver, causing it to become enlarged. Had this been the case with Prince Albert, it would not have escaped the notice of his Victorian physicians, who prided themselves on their clinical examination skills.

*   *   *

In December 1861 *The Lancet* came close to what is probably the most accurate contemporary assessment, when it pointed out soon after the Prince's death that 'there was enough of suddenness in the immediate termination of the disease to raise the question whether it might not have been due to ulcerative perforation of the bowel', adding 'that regrettably no facts had been provided to confirm this'. Quoting an article in the French medical press in January 1862, the *Medical Times and Gazette* supported this claim. The 'hints of "gastric fever" given by the first bulletin did not say much, and were anything but scientific'. But the account of the Prince's rapid decline and death suggested that 'a perforation of the intestines' had taken place.[18]

But what was the precise nature of the chronic, inflammatory

condition of the gut that had led to this perforation and from which the
Prince had suffered for so long? In 1993 J. W. Paulley was the first to
suggest that Prince Albert may have been suffering from ulcerative colitis,
or more probably a condition resulting from a fault in the immune system
with which it is often confused: Crohn's disease.[19] The possibility of
ulcerative colitis (first described in 1859, two years before Prince Albert's
death) can be dismissed, since the cardinal feature of this condition is
bloody diarrhoea and not recurrent abdominal pain, vomiting and fever.
The problem with a diagnosis of Crohn's, in the view of some commentators, is that it tends to be a genetic condition, particularly prevalent in
Jewish families. Such commentators misunderstand the condition, which
is today commonplace and affects any race or creed. The diagnosis,
however, inadvertently plays into arguments that Prince Albert was illegitimate and that his real father was a Jewish courtier, Baron von Meyer,
who had an affair with his mother, Louise. But so far absolutely no
substantive evidence in support of illegitimacy has come to light.[20] As it
happens, only about 5 per cent of sufferers of Crohn's disease have an
affected first-degree relative. Perhaps of more note is the predilection of
Crohn's disease to affect the upper socio-economic groups, and it remains
today much more common in the developed world than in developing
countries.

One other possibility remains: that the Prince had contracted abdominal tuberculosis, which can appear years after initial exposure to the TB
bacillus and cause symptoms clinically indistinguishable from Crohn's.
In 1861 it would have been impossible for the royal doctors to have diagnosed TB with any accuracy. The cause (the bacillus *Mycobacterium
tuberculosis*) and tissue diagnosis of it were only described by Robert
Koch in 1882 (work for which he was awarded the Nobel Prize in 1905).
Abdominal TB was at that time much more common than it is today;
it can affect the lining of the abdomen (the peritoneum) and, when it
does, fluid known as ascites accumulates in the abdominal cavity. It is
possible, therefore, that Prince Albert was suffering from ascites due to
abdominal TB, although the Victorian doctors should have been able to
detect this clinically by percussing his abdomen, which would have been
taut and uncomfortable.

The evidence, when carefully considered, would thus seem to favour
a diagnosis of Crohn's disease. But such a diagnosis is, of course, entirely
retrospective and anachronistic, for it was not described for the first time
until 1913 (by a Scotsman, T. Kennedy Dalziel) and then again in 1932 by

the Jewish-American gastroenterologist Burrill Crohn and colleagues. Nevertheless, Crohn's disease, which is gradually progressive and fluc-tuating in intensity, could explain the chronic, relapsing and remitting problems with his gut that Prince Albert had suffered from, undetected, over many years. It would have caused episodic partial obstruction in the bowel, which, if untreated, can be complicated by small perforations or abscess, leading to peritonitis, septicaemia and death. But only explora-tive abdominal surgery – at that time unavailable – would have revealed this. Crohn's disease is characterised in some patients by other, extra-intestinal problems that are quite independent of the activity of Crohn's itself, such as arthritis. It is conceivable that the Prince's frequent complaints of 'rheumatic' pain in his joints for much of his adult life, and which became so prominent in his final month, could also have been a manifestation of Crohn's disease. Such symptoms often persist even when the intestinal inflammation is inactive and are thus more compat-ible with this overall diagnosis. Like abdominal TB, Crohn's can be exacerbated by overwork and anxiety. A recent study by Charles Bernstein in Winnipeg has shown that the risk of relapse in Crohn's is almost doubled in those suffering high levels of perceived stress.[21] If this were true in Albert's case, then the ultimate irony is that Victoria's assertions that Bertie killed his father may in a way be true. Albert's extreme response to his son's escapade at the Curragh, and the excessive levels of anxiety and insomnia that followed, combined with a chill and over-work, may well have provoked a severe flare-up of his condition.[22]

In many respects, therefore, the natural history of Crohn's disease would fit the long-term pattern of Prince Albert's documented physical complaints: periodic diarrhoea due to inflammation of the gut, with abdominal pain and vomiting from intestinal obstruction, fluctuating between acute episodes marked by swinging fevers and periods of remis-sion. The bouts of depression and lassitude that he latterly suffered are also highly characteristic of an abscess or chronic sepsis. A pink rash of spots detected by the doctors on his abdomen in early December – which they seemed to fix on, almost with relief, as a sure sign of typhoid fever – could have been a consequence of cutaneous vasodilation brought on by septicaemia.[23] One must bear in mind how desperate the royal doctors must have been in those final days: their most important patient (apart from the Queen) dying at a young age; the eyes of Her Majesty, their (envious) colleagues and the world upon them; and there they were, uncertain of their diagnosis.

The final three-week cycle of illness would thus fit the time-frame for Crohn's, complicated by an abdominal abscess, developing into a terminal event with the opportunistic onset of pneumonia ('pulmonary congestion') in the last two or three days.[24] Although it was not widely reported at the time, this latter view concurs with that of other medical practitioners: what in fact carried the Prince off was that age-old nemesis of the sick and vulnerable – pneumonia.[25] In the absence of solid clinical evidence, or detailed autopsy notes, we can only ever make informed guesses. Whatever it was that killed Prince Albert – and we must now lay the ghost of typhoid fever to rest – no antibiotics, steroids or abdominal surgery were then available to help him. To Prince Albert himself must go the final word; if his condition had not killed him in 1861, it is likely, as he told his stepmother, that the 'weak stomach with which I came into the world . . . I shall take with me to my grave'.[26]

Notes

Epigraphs

1. Prince Albert, letter to Baron Stockmar, 24 January 1854, Martin II: 559–60.
2. Rev. Norman Macleod, RA VIC/MAIN/R/2/28.
3. Queen Victoria, letter to King of Prussia, in Gernsheim and Gernsheim, *Queen Victoria:* p. 140.

Prologue: Christmas 1860

1. For Christmas 1860, see Robert Chambers, *The Book of Days: A Miscellany,* vol. 2, 1878, pp. 760–1.
2. For descriptions and illustrations of the interior, see Girouard, *Windsor,* pp. 65–74; Hibbert, *The Court at Windsor,* pp. 207–8.
3. For descriptions of the Grand Corridor, see Stoney & Weltzien, *My Mistress the Queen,* pp. 40–1; Paget, *Embassies of Other Days,* vol. I, pp. 74–5.
4. Fulford, *Dearest Child,* p. 213; Hibbert, *Court at Windsor,* p. 107.
5. For the Queen's preferences for beech logs and gas lighting, see Girouard, *Windsor,* p. 72.
6. Martin, *Life of the Prince Consort* [hereafter Martin], I: 127.
7. Jagow, *Letters of the Prince Consort,* p. 134.
8. Moncure, Daniel Conway, *Memories and Experiences,* vol. I, New York: Houghton, Mifflin & Co., p. 256.
9. RA VIC/MAIN/QVJ/1860: 23 December.
10. In the words of Colonel Francis Seymour, Groom of the Bedchamber to Prince Albert; RA VIC/ADDC10/44.
11. Dasent, *Delane,* p. 13.
12. Ibid., p. 14; Stoney & Weltzien, *My Mistress the Queen,* p. 42 re kitchens at Windsor.
13. RA VIC/MAIN/QVJ/1860: 24 December.
14. See entry for 'Christmas', in Rappaport, *Queen Victoria,* pp. 90–3; 'How the Christmas Tree came to the English Court', *The Times,* 22 December 1958; Hibbert, *Court at Windsor,* pp. 207–8. For descriptions of Christmas at Windsor in 1847 and 1851 by lady-in-waiting Eleanor Stanley, see Stanley, *Twenty Years at Court,* pp. 155–7 and 201–3.
15. Dasent, *Delane,* p. 15; RA VIC/MAIN/QVJ/1860: 24 December.

16. Dasent, *Delane*, p. 16.
17. Ibid.; RA VIC/MAIN/QVJ/1860: 24 December.
18. Ibid., 25 December.
19. Dennison, *Last Princess*, p. 22.
20. Dasent, *Delane*, p. 17.
21. RA VIC/MAIN/QVJ/1860: 27 December.
22. Dasent, *Delane*, p. 15.
23. Wake, *Princess Louise*, p. 23.
24. Stanley, *Twenty Years at Court*, p. 202.
25. Dasent, *Delane*, p. 15.
26. RA VIC/MAIN/QVJ/1860: 30 December. The anxieties expressed about Europe refer to the ongoing struggle for Italian unification.
27. Wyndham, *Correspondence of Sarah Spencer*, p. 401.

Part One: Albert the Good

Chapter 1: 'The Treadmill of Never-Ending Business'

Title: Martin, V: 109–10.

1. Rhodes James, *Prince Albert*, p. 31.
2. In 1825 Duke Ernst succeeded his uncle, the Duke of Saxe-Gotha-Altenburg. The duchies shared with his estranged wife were reorganised and in 1826 Ernst assumed the new title of Duke of Saxe-Coburg & Gotha.
3. For a discussion of the unfounded rumours of illegitimacy, see James, *Prince Albert*, pp. 21–2; Hector Bolitho, who wrote extensively on Victoria and Albert, also scotched the rumours in a chapter, 'The Prince Consort's Mother', in his *A Biographer's Notebook*, pp. 102–22. For a recent argument in support of illegitimacy, see Richard Sotnick, *The Coburg Conspiracy*, London: Ephesus Publishing, 2008, esp. pp. 174–84.
4. Bolitho, *Prince Consort and His Brother*, p. 209.
5. Benson, *Queen Victoria*, p. 160; Ponsonby, *Mary Ponsonby*, p. 2.
6. Fulford, *Prince Consort*, p. 41.
7. Benson and Esher, *Letters of Queen Victoria 1837–1861*, II: 237 [hereafter Benson & Esher].
8. Jagow, *Letters of the Prince Consort*, p. 23.
9. Ibid., p. 24.
10. James, *Prince Albert*, p. 32.
11. Grey, *Early Years*, p. 200.
12. Duff, *Albert & Victoria*, p. 159.
13. Creston, *Youthful Queen Victoria*, p. 445.

14. Jerrold, *Heart of Queen Victoria*, p. 17.

15. Rosamund Brunel Gotch, *Maria Lady Callcott*, London: John Murray, 1937, p. 295. The remark was made by the Queen's dresser, Marianne Skerrett.

16. Jagow, *Letters of the Prince Consort*, pp. 347–8.

17. John Jolliffe, ed., *Neglected Genius: The Diaries of Benjamin Robert Haydon 1808–1846*, London: Hutchinson, 1990, p. 203.

18. Hewett, '. . . *and Mr Fortescue*', pp. 25–6.

19. Warwick, *Afterthoughts*, p. 4.

20. Martin, I: 160.

21. Fulford, *Greville Memoirs*, p. 223.

22. Emden, *Behind the Throne*, p. 68.

23. RAVIC/MAIN/R/1/193. This anonymous account of the last hours of the Prince Consort was written by one of the royal governesses, Madame Hocédé.

24. Tisdall, *Queen Victoria's Private Life*, p. 22. Other nicknames were 'The Pauper Prince' and 'Lovely Albert'. Lord Clarendon would privately refer to the Queen and Albert in correspondence as 'Joseph and Eliza' (ibid., p. 42); Victoria was also referred to as 'Queen Albertine'.

25. Hewett, '. . . *and Mr Fortescue*', p. 25.

26. Emden, *Behind the Throne*, p. 99.

27. Crawford, *Victoria, Queen and Ruler*, p. 52.

28. Pound, *Albert*, p. 182.

29. Martin, II: 248.

30. Benson & Esher, III: 317.

31. Martin, II: 60.

32. Benson & Esher, III: 240.

33. Clark, *Sir Charles Lyell*, p. 354.

34. Fulford, *Prince Consort*, p. 117.

35. Pound, *Albert*, p. 261.

36. Benson & Esher, II: 362.

37. Fulford, *Dearest Child*, p. 215.

38. Hibbert, *Queen Victoria in Her Letters and Journals* [hereafter *Letters and Journals*], p. 151; Bolitho, *Reign of Queen Victoria*, p. 147. For useful summaries of the Prince's health, see Duff, *Albert & Victoria*, pp. 24–5, and Bennett, *King Without a Crown*, pp. 239–44, 341–2, 352–4.

39. Jagow, *Letters of the Prince Consort*, p. 305.

40. James, *Prince Albert*, p. 211.

41. Stafford, *Henry Greville*, vol. 4, p. 227.

42. Bolitho, *Albert Prince Consort*, p. 166.

43. Magnus, *King Edward the Seventh*, p. 17; Strachey, *Queen Victoria*, p. 168.

44. Bennett, *King Without a Crown*, p. 360; Martin, V: 338–9; James, *Prince Albert*, p. 264.

Chapter 2: 'The First Real Blow of Misfortune'

1. Hibbert, *Letters and Journals*, p. 112.
2. Fulford, *Greville Memoirs*, p. 247. Downer, *Queen's Knight*, p. 104.
3. Corti, *English Empress*, p. 54.
4. Marie Louise, *My Memories of Six Reigns*, London: Evans Brothers, 1956, p. 113.
5. Fulford, *Prince Consort*, p. 25.
6. Phillipe Jullian, *Edward and the Edwardians*, London: Sidgwick & Jackson, 1967, p. 17.
7. Corti, *English Empress*, pp. 50–1; Pakula, *Uncommon Woman*, pp. 148–9.
8. Fulford, *Dearest Child*, p. 174.
9. Ibid, pp. 173–4.
10. Bennett, *King Without a Crown*, p. 341; Fulford, *Dearest Child*, p. 206.
11. Fulford, *Dearest Child*, p. 216.
12. Martin, IV: 500–1.
13. Ibid., 501–2.
14. Ibid., V: 109–10.
15. See Weintraub, *Uncrowned King*, pp. 393–4 ; Martin, V: 202–3; James, *Prince Albert*, p. 265; Jerrold, *Married Life of Queen Victoria*, p. 393.
16. Martin, V: 275; Bennett, *Uncrowned King*, p. 341.
17. Martin, V: 288.
18. See Robbins, 'The Missing Doctor', pp. 289–90.
19. *Zalkiel's Almanac* for 1861, London: George Berger, p. 19.
20. In 1850 Jenner published *On the Identity or Non-Identity of Typhoid and Typhus Fevers*, the result of two years' study of 'continued fever' at the London Fever Hospital. In it he defined the differences between the two fevers, typhoid being conveyed by contaminated food or water, typhus being carried by lice.
21. Fulford, *Dearest Child*, p. 309.
22. Martin, V: 292–4.
23. Ibid., 295–6.
24. Fulford, *Dearest Child*, p. 308.
25. Ibid., p. 310.
26. RA VIC/MAIN/QVJ/1861: 21 February.
27. Martin, V: 317–18. Martin's account of the Duchess's death is on pp. 316–19 and the quotations from the Queen's journal given in it differ from later published versions, in that these were used by Martin before the text was expurgated after the Queen's death.
28. Noel, *Princess Alice*, p. 70.
29. Wyndham, *Correspondence of Sarah Spencer*, pp. 338–9.
30. Martin, I: 202–3.
31. Benson & Esher, III: 6–7.

32. Fulford, *Dearest Child*, pp. 199–200, letter of 6 July 1859.

33. See K. D. Mathews and C. G. Reynolds, *Queen Victoria*, Oxford: Oxford University Press, pp. 50–1.

34. See Albert, *Queen Victoria's Sister*, chapter 9, and Fulford, *Dearest Child*, pp. 247, 249.

35. Strafford, *Henry Greville*, vol. 3, p. 33.

36. Fulford, *Dearest Child*, pp. 297–301.

37. Wallace, *Journal of Benjamin Moran*, p. 832.

38. For Victoria's response to seeing death for the first time, see her letter to Leopold of 26 March, in *Letters and Journals*, pp. 118–19. For the Duchess's funeral, see *The Times*, 26 March 1861.

39. Sarah Tytler, *Life of Her Gracious Majesty*, vol. 2, pp. 185–6.

40. For court mourning during these years, see Stanley, *Twenty Years at Court*, pp. 320–3, 376–7.

41. Kennedy, *My Dear Duchess*, p. 141; Wiebe, *Letters of Benjamin Disraeli*, vol. 8, p. 155, letter of Lord Henry Lennox, 18 December 1861.

42. See Lord Clarendon to the Duchess of Manchester, 3 April 1861, in Kennedy, *My Dear Duchess*, pp. 143–4.

43. See letters to King Leopold, 26 and 30 March, Benson & Esher, III: 436–7.

44. Windsor & Bolitho, *Letters of Lady Augusta Stanley*, p. 200. [Hereafter Windsor & Bolitho]

45. Albert, Queen Victoria's Sister, p. 189; Fulford, Dearest Child, p. 319.

46. Martin, V: 335.

47. Fulford, *Dearest Child*, p. 334.

48. RA LC/LCO/CER/MEMO, Drawing Room, St James's Palace, 19 June 1861.

49. Weintraub, *Uncrowned King*, p. 402.

Chapter 3: 'Fearfully in Want of a True Friend'

1. Martin, V: 374.

2. Ibid.: 369.

3. Cooke, *Memoir of HRH Princess Mary Adelaide*, vol. 1, p. 364.

4. Ibid.

5. Magnus, *King Edward the Seventh*, p. 47.

6. RA VIC/MAIN/QVJ/1861: 26 August.

7. Duff, *Queen Victoria's Highland Journals*, pp. 96–100.

8. Fulford, Dearest Child, p. 354.

9. Duff, *Queen Victoria's Highland Journals*, p. 106.

10. Ibid., p. 110.

11. Ibid., p. 114. Victoria added the postscript when preparing her Highland journals for publication in 1867.

12. Benson & Esher, III: 461–2.

13. Martin, V: 407.

14. Letter to Queen Victoria, 22 October 1861, quoted in Fulford, *Prince Consort*, p. 249.

15. Fulford, *Dearest Child*, p. 356. Victoria was in fact alluding to a favourite sermon by the Roman Catholic convert, Henry Edward Manning, 'The Commemoration of the Faithful Departed', in which he alluded to 'the habitual consciousness of an unseen world'. She had this quotation copied into her 'Album Consolativum' after Albert's death. See BL Add. 62089, fo. 95; *Sermons of Henry Edward Manning*, London: James Burns, 1846, p. 326.

16. Martin, V: 415; Fulford, *Dearest Mama*, p. 30.

17. Katharine M. Lyell, ed., *Life, Letters and Journals of Sir Charles Lyell*, vol. 2, London: John Murray, 1881, p. 352.

18. See Strafford, *Henry Greville*, vol. 4, p. 226; Longford, *Victoria*, p. 313.

19. RA VIC/MAIN/R/1/193.

20. Branks, *Heaven our Home*, pp. 8, 6, 70, 52. Branks was a minister at Torphichen, West Lothian; his book tapped into the vogue for consolatory literature and homilies on death that proliferated after Albert died; it was in its eighth reprint by 1876. *Meet for Heaven* followed in 1862 and *Life in Heaven* in 1863 – all three books selling in hundreds of thousands of copies in the UK and USA.

21. RA VIC/MAIN/Z/142: 9 November 1861. All comments by the Queen on Prince Albert's illness from this date to his death on 14 December are taken from her 'Account of My Beloved Albert's Last Fatal Illness from Nov. 9 to Dec. 14 1861'. Entries up to the 11 December were written at the time; those after were added in 1862 and 1872.

22. Royal Pharmaceutical Society: Queen Victoria's Account Book 1861–1869, which lists at the front the Queen's regular standing order for medical supplies, followed by monthly lists of additional supplies and their cost.

23. Martin, V: 411.

24. Longford, *Victoria RI*, pp. 292–3.

25. Fulford, *Dearest Child*, pp. 365–6.

26. Ibid., p. 367.

27. Wake, *Princess Louise*, p. 42; Jerrold, *Queen Victoria's John Brown*, p. 52.

28. Fulford, *Dearest Child*, p. 356.

29. Corti, *English Empress*, p. 72.

30. Hibbert, *Edward VII*, p. 40; St Aubyn, *Queen Victoria*, p. 279.

31. Bennett, *King Without a Crown*, p. 367; Scheele, *Prince Consort*, pp. 125–6.

32. Fulford, *Prince Consort*, p. 266.

33. RA VIC/MAIN/Z/141/94: 16 November 1861.

34. RA VIC/MAIN/Z/141/95: 20 November 1861.

35. Martin, V: 414.

36. RA VIC/MAIN/Z/142: 22 November.
37. Martin, V: 417; RA VIC/MAIN/Z/142: 23 and 25 November.
38. See Nightingale's letter to Mary Clarke Mohl, December 1861: 'Albert was really a Minister – this very few knew. Sir Robert Peel taught him'. Vicinus and Nergaard, *Ever Yours*, pp. 232–3
39. Martin, V: 412; James, *Prince Albert*, p. 270.
40. Martin, V: 417.
41. Benson & Esher, III: 468.
42. Martin, V: 417.
43. Wilson, *Life and Times of Queen Victoria*, vol. 2, p. 100. For an interesting medical article on the Windsor epidemic, see William Budd, 'On Intestinal Fever, *The Lancet*, vol. 1, 1860, pp. 390–1.
44. Martin, V: 417; Fulford, *Dearest Child*, pp. 369–70.
45. Ibid., 28 November.
46. Martin, V: 423.
47. Martin, V: 427.
48. Ball, *Queen Victoria: Scenes and Incidents*, p. 197.
49. Fulford, *Dearest Child*, p. 370; Corti, *English Empress*, p. 72.
50. *The Times*, 28 November 1861.
51. Fulford, *Dearest Child*, p. 370.
52. Bennett, *King Without a Crown*, p. 370.
53. Benson & Esher, III: 469.
54. Martin, V: 427.
55. RA VIC/MAIN/Z/142: 1 December.
56. For a detailed discussion of the Trent affair, see Weintraub, *Uncrowned King*, pp. 408–21.
57. Fulford, *Dearest Child*, p. 371.

Chapter 4: 'Our Most Precious Invalid'

Title: Queen Victoria to the King of the Belgians, 12 December 1861, in Benson & Esher III: 472.

1. RA VIC/MAIN/Z/142: 2 December 1861.
2. Ibid.
3. 'Descriptions of the death of the Prince Consort, 1861', Correspondence and Papers of Dean Stanley, Cheshire Archives, DSA 85.
4. RA VIC/MAIN/Z/142: 3 December.
5. RA VIC/Add MS/C/10/47: 2 December 1861.
6. RA VIC/MAIN/Z/142: 2 December 1861.
7. Connell, *Regina v. Palmerston*, p. 313.

8. RA VIC/MAIN/Z/142: 3 December.
9. Whittle, *Victoria and Albert*, pp. 106, 113.
10. Staatsarchiv Darmstadt: Briefe von Alice D24 Nr. 25/3–4 & 26/1: 3 December 1861; Windsor and Bolitho, p. 239.
11. Staatsarchiv Darmstadt: Briefe von Alice D24 Nr. 25/3–4 & 26/1: 3 December 1861.
12. See e.g. *Daily News* and *Morning Chronicle*, 4 December 1861.
13. RA VIC/MAIN/Z/142: 4 December.
14. Ibid; Benson & Esher, III: 470.
15. BL Add. MS 44325, Gladstone Papers vol. CCXL, letters from the Duchess of Sutherland; 19 December 1861.
16. RA VIC/MAIN/Z/142: 4 December.
17. Ibid.: 5 December.
18. Ibid.
19. Martin, V: 430. Excerpts from the Queen's account of Prince Albert's final days from 1 to 8 December as originally written by her can be found in Martin, V: 427–38. These original entries, published in 1880, differ slightly from their later edited transcription made after the Queen's death.
20. RA VIC/MAIN/Z/142: 6 December.
21. Ibid.
22. Benson & Esher, III: 470–1.
23. Fulford, *Dearest Child*, p. 372.
24. Connell, *Regina v. Palmerston*, pp. 313–14.
25. RA VIC/MAIN/Z/142: 7 December.
26. Martin, V: 431; Longford, *Victoria RI*, p. 296.
27. Ibid.
28. Ibid.
29. Connell, *Regina v. Palmerston*, p. 314.
30. RA VIC/MAIN/Z/142: 7 December.
31. Ibid.
32. Ibid.; Windsor & Bolitho, p. 240.
33. RA VIC/MAIN/R/1/193. Written on 23 December by Madame Hocédé to her family this letter was later, in all innocence, published by them in France, going against the Queen's demand for absolute discretion by members of the royal household. It appeared as a pamphlet, published by John Snow of Paternoster Row in 1864, and was syndicated in many journals as 'The Last Hours of Prince Albert' – see e.g. *Wesleyan-Methodist Magazine*, vol. 47, 1864, p. 906. Madame Hocédé had, by then, been quietly pensioned off for the additional indiscretion of encouraging the princesses to read 'unsuitable' books and went to Paris, where she set up a school for Protestant English girls. Kenyon, *Scenes in the Life*, p. 78.

34. Ibid.
35. Ibid.
36. Staatsarchiv Darmstadt: Briefe von Alice D24 Nr. 25/3–4 & 26/1: 9 December 1861.
37. RA VIC/MAIN/Z/142: 8 December.
38. Ibid.
39. *The Times*, 9 December 1861.
40. RA VIC/MAIN/Z/142: 9 December.
41. Fulford, *Dearest Child*, p. 374.
42. Holland, *Notebooks of a Spinster Lady*, p. 177; Fulford, *Dearest Child*, p. 177.
43. Connell, *Regina v. Palmerston*, p. 315.
44. RA VIC/MAIN/R 1/12: 10 December.
45. RA VIC/MAIN/M/R/1/58/9 and 18.
46. Martin, V: 435.
47. RA VIC/MAIN/Z/142: 10 December.
48. Fulford, *Dearest Child*, p. 373.
49. Ibid.
50. RA VIC/MAIN/Z/142: 11 December; part of this entry was written by the Queen that day, the continuation on 24 December.
51. Martin, V: 435.
52. Benson & Esher, III: 472.
53. Fulford, *Dearest Mama*, p. 374; RA VIC/MAIN/Z/142: 11 December.
54. RA VIC/MAIN/Z/142: 11 December.
55. Ibid.
56. Strafford, Henry Greville, vol. 3, p. 420.
57. Malmesbury, *Memoirs of an Ex-Minister*, p. 550.
58. RA VIC/MAIN/R/1/19, 22: 11–12 December.
59. Walsh, *Religious Life and Influence of Queen Victoria*, p. 114.
60. See e.g. *Morning Chronicle, Daily News, The Times* for 12 December 1861.
61. Walsh, *Religious Life and Influence of Queen Victoria*, p. 113.
62. RA VIC/MAIN/Z/142: 12 December.
63. Benson & Esher: III 472–3.
64. Connell, *Regina vs Palmerston*, p. 316; RA VIC/MAIN/M/R/1/58/19: 11 December.
65. Martin, V: 437.
66. RA VIC/MAIN/Z/142: 12 December.
67. Ibid.: 13 December, though the entry was actually written by the Queen on the 24th.
68. Windsor & Bolitho, p. 241.
69. Longford, *Victoria RI*, p. 299; Hibbert, *Letters and Journals*, p. 156.
70. RA VIC/MAIN/Z/142: 13 December.
71. Windsor & Bolitho, pp. 241–2.

72. RA VIC/MAIN/Z/142: 13 December.
73. Ibid., the remainder of this entry was written by the Queen on 27 March 1862; Windsor & Bolitho, pp. 241–2.
74. RA VIC/MAIN/Z/142: 13 December.
75. Connell, *Regina v. Palmerston*, pp. 316–17.
76. News International Archive, Delane Correspondence: TT/ED/JTD/10/131.
77. *Leeds Mercury*, 14 December.
78. *The Times*, 13 December; Walford, *Life of the Prince Consort*, p. 88; *Daily News*,9 December; *Newcastle Courant*, 13 December.
79. Vicinus and Nergaard, *Ever Yours*, p. 232.
80. *The Times*, 14 December.
81. Downer, *Queen's Knight*, pp. 121–2.
82. 'Descriptions of the death of the Prince Consort, 1861'.

Chapter 5: 'Day Turned into Night'

Title: written by Queen Victoria beneath a photograph of herself, Bertie, Helena and Vicky taken on 28 March 1862; Gernsheim & Gernsheim, *Queen Victoria*, p. 16.

1. Sala, *Life and Adventures*, vol. I, p. 373.
2. *North Wales Chronicle*, 14 December; *The Times*, 14 December.
3. *Glasgow Herald*, 14 December.
4. *The Times*, 14 December.
5. Dasent, *Delane*, vol. II, p. 38.
6. RA VIC/MAIN/Z/142: 14 December. This entry, not written by the Queen until February 1872, is preceded by this explanation: 'I have never had the courage to attempt to describe this dreadful day – but I will now at the distance of ten years . . . with the terrible facts imprinted on my mind as clearly as tho' they had occurred yesterday, and with the help of notes scrawled down at the time, try to describe it.'
7. Palmerston Papers, Broadlands Archive, quoted in Woodham-Smith, *Queen Victoria*, p. 428.
8. RA VIC/MAIN/Z/142: 14 December.
9. RA VIC/Add A/36/5: Henry Ponsonby to his mother, 14 December.
10. RA VIC/MAIN/Z/142: 14 December.
11. Ibid.
12. Staatsarchiv Darmstadt: Briefe von Alice D24 Nr. 25/3–4 & 26/1: 14 December, letter of Prince of Wales.
13. RA VIC/MAIN/Z/142: 14 December.
14. The children's governess, Sarah Hildyard, was another of the Queen's most

loyal servants, joining her in 1849. Known to Victoria as 'Tilla', she was forced to retire through ill health in 1867. Victoria found it a terrible wrench to lose her: 'I need not tell you how impossible it is to speak to you of your leaving us and indeed I will not call it by that name. It must be no real parting after 18 years . . . You have been a treasure to us.' Hildyard died in 1889. An album of photographs of the royal family collected by Sarah Hildyard can be found in the Raymond Richards Collection (M78), at Keele University Library, Special Collections. For extracts from Queen Victoria's letters written to Tilla, see *The Age* (Melbourne), 24 May 1956.

15. Ibid.
16. RA VIC/ADDC6, Lady Geraldine Somerset diaries: 14 December.
17. Villiers, *Vanished Victorian*, p. 309.
18. For the official bulletins issued from Windsor during 13 and 14 December, see Walford, *Life of the Prince Consort*, pp. 89–96.
19. *Medical Times and Gazette*, 14 December.
20. Pakula, *Uncommon Woman*, p. 159.
21. Walford, *Life of the Prince Consort*, p. 76.
22. Weintraub, *Uncrowned King*, p. 43.
23. Martin, V: 440.
24. RA VIC/MAIN/Z/142: 14 December; Walsh, *Religious Life*, p. 113.
25. Martin, V: 441.
26. Downer, *Queen's Knight*, pp. 122–3.
27. Aston, *Duke of Connaught*, p. 46; Downer, *Queen's Knight*, p. 123.
28. RA VIC/MAIN/Z/142: 14 December.
29. RA VIC/Add MS/4/25/819, diary of Howard Elphinstone: 14 December 1861.
30. Noel, *Princess Alice*, p. 78.
31. Windsor & Bolitho, p. 246.
32. Bodleian Library, Special Collections: MS.Eng.misc.d.472, Charles Pugh diary: 14 December 1861.
33. Martin, V: 441.
34. RA VIC/ADDU/416, account of Lady Winchester: 25 December 1861; RA VIC/ADDC6, Lady Geraldine Somerset diaries: 15 December 1861.
35. Windsor and Bolitho, p. 245; Noel, *Princess Alice*, p. 77.
36. RA VIC/ADDU/4, account of Lady Winchester: 25 December 1861.
37. Windsor & Bolitho, p. 245.
38. RA VIC/MAIN/Z/142: 14 December. A famous painting of the scene was later executed by William Walton, 'The Last Moments of HRH The Prince Consort', which slightly conflicts with some of the descriptions of where people were positioned in the room.
39. Battiscombe, 'Gerald Wellesley', p. 128; RA VIC/MAIN/Z/142; 'Descriptions of the death of the Prince Consort, 1861'.

40.   The earliest source for this much-repeated, and possibly apocryphal, story of the shriek is Augustus Hare, *The Story of My Life*, vol. 2, London: George Allen, 1900.

41.   RA VIC/ADDA8/377, letter from Miss Ella Taylor: 7 January 1872, p. 3.

42.   Kuhn, *Henry and Mary Ponsonby*, p. 82.

43.   RA VIC/ADDA25/819, diary of Howard Elphinstone: 14 December 1861.

44.   'Descriptions of the death of the Prince Consort, 1861'.

45.   Stanley, *Twenty Years at Court*, pp. 388–9; Windsor & Bolitho, p. 246; Tisdall, *Private Life*, p. 50; Duff, *Shy Princess*, p. 10; RA VIC/MAIN/Z/142: 14 December.

46.   RA VIC/MAIN/Z/142: 14 December. Martin's account, V: 438–41, of the deathbed from the Queen's journals has some slight variations, because it was taken from her journal before its later editing by Princess Beatrice. See n. 19 chapter 4 above.

47.   RA VIC/ADDA8/377, letter from Miss Ella Taylor: 7 January 1872, p. 3.

48.   RA VIC/ADDA25/819, diary of Howard Elphinstone: 14 December 1861; Downer, *The Queen's Knight*, p. 125.

49.   Thomas Catling, *My Life's Pilgrimage*, London: John Murray, 1911, pp. 75–6.

50.   Strafford, ed., *Leaves from the Diary of Henry Greville*, vol. 3, p. 417.

51.   Sheppard, *George Duke of Cambridge: A Memoir*, p. 222.

52.   Wilson, *Life and Times of Queen Victoria*, vol. 2, p. 98.

53.   Connell, *Regina v. Palmerston*, pp. 317–18.

54.   Sala, *Life and Adventures*, vol. I, p. 374.

Chapter 6: 'Our Great National Calamity'

Title: *British Mothers' Journal and Domestic Magazine*, 1 January 1862.

1.   Walford, *Life of the Prince Consort*, p. 125.

2.   Philip Hedgeland, 'National Grief and Some of its Uses' (sermon), Penzance, 1861, p. 3.

3.   *Morning Star*, 16 December.

4.   Hudson, *Munby*, p. 111; Pound, *Albert*, p. 350.

5.   RA VIC/R2/112, letter of Adam Sedwick to Sir Charles Phipps: 10 February 1862.

6.   *Leeds Intelligencer*, 21 December 1861.

7.   Walford, *Life of the Prince Consort*, pp. 142–7; Wolffe, *Great Deaths*, p. 83.

8.   Walford, *Life of the Prince Consort*, pp. 134–9; *The Times*, 16 December.

9.   Nirad C. Chaudhuri, *Scholar Extraordinary: The Life of Professor the Right Honourable Friedrich Max Müller*, London: Chatto & Windus, 1974, p. 255.

10. Chomet, *Helena*, p. 17; House and Storey, *Letters of Charles Dickens*, vol. 9, p. 540.

11. Sheppard, *George, Duke of Cambridge*, vol. 1, p. 223.

12. 'Descriptions of the death of the Prince Consort, 1861'.

13. BL Add. MS 44325, Gladstone Papers, vol. CCXL, letters from the Duchess of Sutherland: ff. 266–73, 19 December 1861.

14. Cooke, *Princess Mary Adelaide*, vol. I, pp. 377.

15. RA VIC/ADDA8/376 p. 4 and RA VIC/ADDU/396/2, letter of Princess Mary Adelaide of Teck: 16 and 19 December 1861.

16. Maxwell, *Life and Letters of the 4th Earl of Clarendon*, p. 253.

17. RA VIC/ADDU/396, undated letter, c. 17 December, from the Hon. Victoria Stuart Wortley.

18. Windsor & Bolitho, p. 246; Fulford, *Dearest Child*, p. 375; Smith, *Life of Her Majesty*, p. 356.

19. RA VIC/R 1/51: 15 December 1861.

20. Walford, *Life of the Prince Consort*, pp. 152, 155.

21. Martin Duberman, *Charles Francis Adams*, Stanford: Stanford University Press, 1968, p. 286.

22. Hibbert, *Court at Windsor*, p. 212.

23. Cooke, *Princess Mary Adelaide*, vol. I, p. 378.

24. C. E. Smith, *Journals and Correspondence of Lady Eastlake*, vol. 2, London: John Murray, 1895, p. 164.

25. 'Descriptions of the death of the Prince Consort, 1861'; Protheroe, *Dean Stanley*, p. 307.

26. Whittle, *Victoria and Albert*, p. 116; Dimond and Taylor, *Crown and Camera*, p. 23; Darby and Smith, *Cult of the Prince Consort*, pp. 4, 6; Fulford, *Dearest Mama*, pp. 27, 31.

27. Walford, *Life of the Prince Consort*, p. 130.

28. Louis Blanc, *Letters on England*, vol. 1, London: Sampson Low, 1866, p. 226.

29. *The Times, Morning Chronicle, Morning Post, Scotsman, Daily News*, 16 December 1861.

30. *Daily Telegraph*, 16 December 1861.

31. *London Gazette Extraordinary*, 16, 17 and 18 December 1861.

32. Chappell & Pollard, *Letters of Mrs Gaskell*, p. 671; diary of Charles Pugh, Bodleian Library, MS.Eng.misc.d 472.

33. RA VIC/R2/112, letter of Adam Sedgwick to Sir Charles Phipps: 10 February 1862.

34. *Leeds Mercury*, 17 December, 1861.

35. *Illustrated London News*, 28 December 1861.

36. PRO LC 1-90-005, 16 December 1861.

37. Wilson, *Life and Times of Queen Victoria*, p. 99; Walford, *Life of the Prince Consort*, p. 105.

38. Maxwell, *Life and Letters of the 4th Earl of Clarendon*, p. 253; Baroness Bloom-field, ed., *Extracts of Letters from Maria, Marchioness of Normanby*, London: Simson & Co., 1892, p. 424.

39. RA VIC/ADDU/32: 16 December 1861; Fulford, *Dearest Mama*, p. 23.

40. *Daily Telegraph*, 17 December; RA VIC/ADDU/396/1: undated letter, prob-ably 17 December 1861.

41. *The Times*, 17 and 18 December; *London Review*, 21 December; Journal of John Rashdall, 22 December, Bodleian Library MS.Eng.misc.e 359.

42. *Illustrated London News*, 21 December 1861, p. 616.

43. *Glasgow Herald*, 17 December.

44. *The Times, Guardian* and *Telegraph*, 17 and 18 December. For a résumé of major press coverage, see Walford, *Life of the Prince Consort*, pp. 157–83. An extensive body of newspaper cuttings can also be found in RA VIC/MAIN/M/64 and 66. Many press notices and magazine articles, as well as selected sermons and poetry, were collected by William Thomas Kime and pub-lished in a handsome large-format edition with embossed gold covers, as *Albert the Good: A Nation's Tribute of Affection to the Memory of a Truly Virtuous Prince*, London: J. F. Shaw & Co., 1862.

45. Vincent, *Disraeli, Derby and the Conservative Party*, p. 180. Cecil Y. Lang, ed., *Letters of Matthew Arnold*, vol. 2, Charlottesville: University Press of Vir-ginia, 1996, p. 111; Wyndham, *Correspondence of Sarah Spencer*, pp. 422, 423.

46. 'Descriptions of the death of the Prince Consort, 1861'.

47. Ibid.

48. Maxwell, *Life and Letters of the 4th Earl of Clarendon*, p. 255; RA VIC/ADDC6, Lady Geraldine Somerset diaries: 15 and 16 December 1861.

49. Weibe, *Benjamin Disraeli Letters*, vol. 8, p. 156, letter to Lady Londonderry, 19 December 1861.

50. Wake, *Princess Louise*, p. 45.

51. Dennison, *Princess Beatrice*, p. 26; Arkhiv der Hessischen Hausstiftung, Briefe 7.1/1-BA 3; letter of 19 December 1861.

52. Fulford, *Dearest Mama*, p. 23.

53. Ibid., pp. 24, 25.

54. Wake, *Princess Louise*, p. 45.

55. 'Descriptions of the death of the Prince Consort, 1861'.

56. Ibid; Longford, *Victoria RI*, p. 308.

57. Longford, *Victoria RI*, p. 308.

58. Jerrold, *The Widowhood of Queen Victoria*, p. 11.

59. Downer, *Queen's Knight*, p. 40; Tisdall, *Queen Victoria's Private Life*, p. 50.

60. Corti, *English Empress*, p. 77.

61. Benson & Esher, III: 473–4.

62. Smith & Howitt, *Cassells' Illustrated History of England*, p. 589.

63. *Daily Telegraph*, 19 December 1861.

64. Cowley, *Paris Embassy*, p. 228.
65. *Observer*, 16 December 1861.
66. Lyn MacDonald, ed., *Florence Nightingale's Theology*, Ontario: Wilfred Laurier University Press, 2002, p. 365.

Chapter 7: 'Will They Do Him Justice Now?'

1. See Kate Williams, *Becoming Queen*, London: Hutchinson, 2008, pp. 116–23, and Schor, *Bearing the Dead*, ch. 6, 'A Nation's Sorrows', for an account of the mourning for Princess Charlotte. For royal funeral conventions, see Curl, *Victorian Celebration of Death*, pp. 224–5.
2. *Lady's Newspaper*, 21 December 1861.
3. The will is as quoted in Corti, *English Empress*, p. 77. In it Albert nominated Victoria as executrix and provided for the distribution of the extensive property he had acquired in the UK, but it was never lodged at the wills registry at Somerset House and probate was therefore never formally granted. The full details of its contents were never revealed, for the Queen refused to allow it to be published, prompting later rumbling accusations of Albert's avariciousness in his acquisition of wealth as consort.
4. See the Appendix to this book, 'What Killed Prince Albert?'
5. The practice of embalming royal corpses had been discontinued by the time of Albert's death, hence the prompt sealing-down of the coffin on the evening of the 16th. See RA LC/LCO/CER/MEMO/Private Memoranda Ceremonials/93: Funeral of HRH the Prince Consort, Windsor, December 23rd 1861 – Lord Chamberlain's Account. For the coffins, see Walford, *Life of the Prince Consort*, pp. 112–13.
6. PRO LC 1-90-007, 17 December 1861. Drugget was a thick felted fabric of wool and/or cotton used as a floor covering.
7. *Morning Post*, 21 December 1861. Banting had also made the state coffin for the Duke of Wellington in 1852. The firm of Thomas and William Banting was one of the most prosperous London undertakers. William (1796–1878), who succeeded his father, died a very rich man with an estate valued at around £70,000 (equivalent to £3.3 million today), and is also notable as the originator of probably the first Atkins-type high-protein diet, which he devised to combat his own increasingly uncomfortable obesity. Published in 1863 as 'A Letter on Corpulence Addressed to the Public', it highlighted the dangers of excess sugar and fat in the diet and ran into four editions by 1869. Banting donated the profits to charity. The firm held the Royal Warrant for funerals until 1928; his sons organised Queen Victoria's funeral in 1901.
8. See Wolffe, *Great Deaths*, pp. 17–20, 194, 202–3.

9. RA LC/LCO/CER/MEMO/Private Memoranda Ceremonials/95: Funeral of HRH the Prince Consort, Windsor, December 23rd 1861 – Lord Chamberlain's Account.

10. The accounts of the Prince's funeral were extensive, with many papers running syndications of those in *The Times* and the *Daily Telegraph* of 24 December, which are the most detailed and graphic. Sala's highly colourful, Gothic account for the *Telegraph* can also be found as Appendix II to Duff, *Albert and Victoria*, pp. 270–84.

11. Argyll, *Autobiography and Memoirs*, vol. 2, p.184; Hardman, *Mid-Victorian Pepys*, p. 69.

12. Information from Paul Frecker. See also *Photographic News*, 28 February 1862, pp 104, 108.

13. Hudson, *Munby*, p. 111.

14. Cooke, *Memoir of Princess Mary Adelaide*, p. 379; Smith & Howitt, *Cassells' Illustrated History of England*, p. 589.

15. Downer, *Queen's Knight*, p. 127.

16. Elvey, *Sir George Elvey*, p. 183. Croft's settings of the burial service were composed for the funeral of Queen Anne in 1714; both these chants or 'sentences' formed part of the funeral service for Princess Diana at Westminster Abbey in 1997.

17. RA LC/LCO/CER/MEMO/Private Memoranda Ceremonials/93: Funeral of HRH the Prince Consort, Windsor, December 23rd 1861 – Lord Chamberlain's Account.

18. Jerrold, *Widowhood of Queen Victoria*, p.11; Elvey, *Sir George Elvey*, pp. 183–4; *The Times*, 24 December.

19. *The Times*, 24 December; Dasent, *Delane*, p. 40.

20. Duff, *Hessian Tapestry*, p. 73.

21. Dasent, *Delane*, p. 40; Playfair, *Memoirs*, p. 190; Ashwell, *Life of the Right Rev Samuel Wilberforce*, vol. 3, p. 44; Prothero, *Life and Correspondence of Arthur Penrhyn Stanley*, p. 61.

22. Darby, *Cult of the Prince Consort*, p. 1; Hardman, *Mid-Victorian Pepys*, p. 70; *Bell's Life in London*, 29 December 1861.

23. O'Brien, *Correspondence of Lord Overstone*, vol. II, p. 980.

24. Wolffe, *Great Deaths*, pp. 84, 97–8.

25. RA VIC/MAIN/R/2/22.

26. RA VIC/MAIN/R/2/15; Wolffe, *Great Deaths*, p. 195.

27. *Jewish Chronicle*, 27 December; Loewe, *Diaries of Sir Moses and Lady Montefiore*, p. 13; John Purves, ed., *Letters from the Cape*, London: Oxford University Press, 1921, p. 68.

28. *Punch*, 21 December 1861.

29. Lee, *Queen Victoria*, vol. 2, p. 320; Wiebe, *Benjamin Disraeli Letters*, p. 164.

30. Stockmar, *Memoirs of Baron Stockmar*, vol.1, p. xviii; RA VIC/

MAIN/M/64/28: letter of 9 January 1862. The existing German Confederation, created at the end of the Napoleonic Wars, consisted of thirty-eight states. They were finally unified under Bismarck, ten years after Albert's death, in 1871.

Chapter 8: 'How Will the Queen Bear It?'

1. Fulford, *Dearest Mama*, pp. 26, 28; Sheppard, *George Duke of Cambridge*, p. 223.
2. RA VIC/MAIN/R/1/181, Phipps to Lord Sydney: 22 December 1861; Sheppard, *George Duke of Cambridge*, vol. 1, p. 224.
3. RA VIC/MAIN/R/1/193: 23 December 1861 – letter written by Madame Hocédé.
4. Arkhiv der Hessischen Hausstiftung, Briefe 7.1/1-BA 3; letter of 19 December 1861.
5. RA VIC/ADDA8/377, letter from Miss Ella Taylor, 7 January 1862, p. 5; Fulford, *Dearest Mama*, p. 27.
6. Noel, *Princess Alice*, p. 77; Arkhiv der Hessischen Hausstiftung, Briefe 7.1/1-BA 3: 20 December; RA VIC/MAIN/M/64/6: 22 December 1861.
7. Land and Shannon, *Letters of Alfred Lord Tennyson*, vol. II, p. 291; RA VIC/MAIN/R2/6: 24 December; Dyson and Tennyson, *Dear and Honoured Lady*, p. 54.
8. Dyson, *Dear and Honoured Lady*, pp. 66–7.
9. Jackman and Haasse, eds, *Stranger in the House*, p. 227, Letter to Lady Malet, 30 December 1861. Queen Sophie exchanged numerous gossipy letters at the time with those privy to the events close to the Queen and the royal household, including Lady Malet, the Duchess of Westmorland, Lady Ely, Lord Clarendon, the Duchess of Cambridge and Lady Cowley, but sadly none of their letters to her survive in the Royal Dutch Archives at The Hague.
10. Fulford, *Dearest Mama*, p. 30.
11. Martineau, *Selected Letters*, pp. 196–7; Vincent, p. 181.
12. Benson & Esher, III: 476.
13. Ponsonby, *Mary Ponsonby*, p. 47.
14. RA VIC/ADDA8/376: letter of 19 December 1861, pp. 5–6.
15. Fulford, *Dearest Mama*, p. 27; RA VIC/MAIN/R/2/3: 24 December 1861.
16. Wake, *Princess Louise*, p. 4; News International Archive, TT/ED/JTD/A/022, Torrington Letters, c. 19 December; Wellesley, *The Paris Embassy*, p. 229.
17. Chapel & Pollard, *Letters of Mrs Gaskell*, p. 671, 26 December 1861; Moran, *Journal of Benjamin Moran*, vol. 2, p. 957, 24 December 1861.

18. *Morning Post*, 16 December; *Daily Telegraph*, 19 December; *Essex & West Suf-folk Gazette*, 20 December; *Daily Telegraph*, 25 December.

19. *Daily News*, 25 and 26 December.

20. Russell, *My Diary*, p. 218.

21. *New York Times*, 5 January 1862; Maria Lydig Daly, *Diary of a Union Lady* 1861–65, New York: Funk & Wagnalls, 1962, p. 106.

22. Charles Reynolds Brown, *Lincoln, The Greatest Man of the Nineteenth Century*, New York: Little & Ives, 1922, p. 58.

23. Russell, *My Diary*, pp. 218–19. News that Mason and Slidell and their secretaries had been released and put on a steamer for Southampton did not reach the British press till 8 January 1862.

24. RA VIC/MAIN/M/58/4: 19 December 1861.

25. News International Archive, TT/ED/JTD/A/022, Torrington letters: c. 19 December 1861.

26. RA VIC/MAIN/M/58/16: 26 December 1861.

27. Watson, *Queen at Home*, p. 156.

28. *New York Times*, 5 January 1861; Martineau, *Selected Letters*, letter to Henry Reeve, Christmas Day 1861.

29. C. E. Byles, *The Life and Letters of R. S. Hawker*, London: John Lane, 1905, p. 353.

30. *Daily News*, 20 December; *Morning Post*, 16 December.

Part Two: The Broken-Hearted Widow

Chapter 9: 'All Alone!'

1. Windsor & Bolitho, p. 251; RA VIC/MAIN/QVJ: 1 January 1862.

2. RA VIC/MAIN/QVJ/1862: 1 January 1862.

3. 'Descriptions of the death of the Prince Consort, 1861'.

4. Ricks, *Poems of Tennyson*, vol. 2, p. 451.

5. Queen Victoria's 'Album Consolativum' appears to have been passed on to her daughter Vicky in Berlin after the Queen's death in 1901 – perhaps to comfort the former Empress in her own terminal illness – she died of cancer seven months after her mother. The album is now in the British Library, BL Add. 62089; a second volume (62090) was started in 1872, but never completed.

6. Dasent, *Delane*, p. 48.

7. Bolitho, *Further Letters of Queen Victoria*, p. 118; RA VIC/ADDA8/390, Miss Ella Taylor's Reminiscences of HRH The Duchess of Cambridge, p. 51.

8. Longford, *Victoria RI*, p. 308.

9. Fulford, *Dearest Mama*, p. 47.

10. Jenni Calder, *Robert Louis Stevenson: A Life Study*, Oxford: Oxford University Press, 1980, p. 21; Wake, *Princess Louise*, p. 47.

11. RA VIC/ADDU/16, Lord Hertford's Account of Queen Victoria, Osborne, 1862, pp. 4–5.

12. Argyll, *Autobiography and Memoirs*, vol. 2, p. 188.

13. RA VIC/ADDA8/380: Miss Ella Taylor's Reminiscences of HRH The Duchess of Cambridge.

14. Erskine, *Twenty Years at Court*, p. 395.

15. Fulford, *Dearest Mama*, p. 47.

16. Buckle, *Letters of Queen Victoria* [hereafter Buckle], I: 9.

17. Kennedy, *My Dear Duchess*, p. 189; Dasent, *Delane*, p. 46.

18. Countess Blücher, née Madeline Dallas, was the daughter of the Lord Chief Justice. She married Count Gustavus Blücher von Wahlstadt in 1828. She was a close friend of Vicky in Berlin and attended the birth of her first child, Wilhelm, in 1859. The Countess died on 19 March 1870.

19. Sir Edwin Landseer said of Skerrett that 'If anything goes wrong in Buckingham Palace, Balmoral, or Windsor, whether a crowned head or a scullery maid is concerned, Miss Skerrett is always sent for to put it right.' Skerrett was the daughter of an officer who had served with distinction in the Peninsular War. See John Callcott Horsely, *Recollections of a Royal Academician*, London: John Murray, 1903, p. 128.

20. For an interesting discussion of Queen Victoria's ladies, see Reynolds, *Aristocratic Women*, pp. 212–17.

21. See Dulcie M. Ashdown, *Ladies-in-Waiting*, London: Arthur Barker, pp. 178–80.

22. The Duchess of Athole (1814–97) was widowed in 1864. Like Lady Jane Churchill (1826–1900), who remained with the Queen for forty-six years, Athole died still in service to Victoria. Lady Ely (1821–90) finally managed to retire in 1889 after thirty-eight years of devoted service.

23. Buckle, I: 12; RA VIC/MAIN/QVJ/1862: 21 January. Sadly, the spontaneous and more heartfelt expressions of popular support that must have been sent to the Queen from semi-literate, ordinary members of the public have not survived in the Royal Archives. The more formal tributes of monarchs and statesmen are, however, plentiful.

24. Kenyon, *Scenes in the Life of the Royal Family*, p. 224.

25. RA VIC/MAIN/Y/83/63: 1 February 1862.

26. Lily Wolpitz, ed., *The Diaries of John Rose of Cape Town 1848–1873*, Cape Town: Friends of South African Library, 1990, p. 97; Purves, *Letters from the Cape*, p. 47.

27. Purves, *Letters from the Cape*, p. 71; Orfeur Cavanagh, *Reminiscences of an Indian Official*, London: W. Allen, 1884, pp. 320–2; unpublished letter of Ra Haniraka, 3 March 1862, courtesy Ian Shapiro.

28. 'Address of the New Zealand Chiefs to Her Majesty, on the Death of the Prince Consort', forwarded by the governor of NZ, Sir George Grey, *Annual Register*, 1862, vol. 104, p. 503.

29. Buckle, I: 6.

30. Tooley, *Personal Life of Queen Victoria*, pp. 204–5.

31. Windsor & Bolitho, p. 257.

32. Another similar marble bust of Albert by Theed was completed in 1862 and two years later placed in the entrance hall at Osborne. See Darby & Smith, *Cult*, p. 7.

33. Plunkett, *Queen Victoria: First Media Monarch*, p. 181.

34. See *Crown and Camera*, pp. 23–5, and Gere and Rudoe, *Jewellery in the Age* of *Queen Victoria*, pp. 56–7.

35. Zeepvat, *Prince Leopold*, p. 32.

36. A plaster cast of the statue was placed at the foot of the staircase at Balmoral that August and replaced with the marble version in October 1863. A massive bronze version of the statue, on a bust of rough stone, was later erected in the castle grounds for all the Queen's staff to see. See Darby & Smith, *Cult*, p. 11.

37. Bennett, *King without a Crown*, p. 376; Martin, II: 537. A statue was eventually raised in 1863, though in front of the Royal Albert Hall, not far from the Albert Memorial, rather than in the park.

38. Kennedy, *My Dear Duchess*, p. 199.

39. News International Archive, TT/ED/JTD/A/022, Torrington Letters.

40. *The Times*, 15 January 1862; *Temple Bar*, vol. IV, 1862, p. 575.

41. *Morning Post*, 13 August 1862; Kennedy, *My Dear Duchess*, p. 199.

42. Storey, ed., *Letters of Charles Dickens*, vol. 10, pp. 28 and 69: 1 February 1862 and 10 April 1862.

43. Dasent, *Delane*, pp. 44–5.

44. Fulford, *Dearest Mama*, p. 36.

45. Battiscombe, 'Gerald Wellesley', pp. 134–5; Darby & Smith, *Cult*, p. 23.

46. Kennedy, *My Dear Duchess*, pp. 189, 207.

47. Villiers, *Vanished Victorian*, p. 317.

48. Ibid., pp. 317, 319.

49. Connell, *Regina v. Palmerston*, p. 323; Maxwell, *Life of Letters of . . . 4th Earl of Clarendon*, p. 257.

50. *Annual Register*, vol. 104, p. 10; Wiebe, *Letters of Benjamin Disraeli*, vol. 8, p. 170.

51. RA VIC/MAIN/QVJ/1862: 26 February; Hibbert, *Court at Windsor*, p. 212.

52. Epton, *Queen Victoria and her Daughters*, p. 102; Corti, *English Empress*, p. 81.

53. RA VIC/ADDU/16, Lord Hertford's Account of Queen Victoria; Fulford, *Dearest Mama*, p. 40; Kennedy, *My Dear Duchess*; Villiers, *Vanished Victorian*, p. 315.

54. RA VIC/ADDU/16, Lord Hertford's Account of Queen Victoria.

55. Villiers, *Vanished Victorian*, p. 313.

56. Fulford, *Dearest Mama*, p. 56.

57. Buckle, I: 20.

58. Gladstone to the Duchess of Sutherland, 24 February 1862, BL Add. MS 44, 326 fos 44–5, and Sutherland to Gladstone, 26 February, fos 46–51. See also Reynolds, *Aristocratic Women*, pp. 215–16.

59. Vincent, *Disraeli, Derby*, p. 198; Storey, *Letters of Charles Dickens*, vol. 10, p. 54.

60. Whittle, *Victoria and Albert*, p. 118; Kennedy, *My Dear Duchess*, pp. 186, 188–9, 191; Darby & Smith, *Cult*, p. 11; Downer, *Queen's Knight*, p. 129.

61. Windsor & Bolitho, p. 262.

62. Kennedy, *My Dear Duchess*, p. 189; RA VIC/MAIN/QVJ/1862: 15 March; Dasent, *Delane*, pp. 48–9.

63. Ricks, *Poems of Tennyson*, vol. 3, p. 263.

64. Dyson & Tennyson, *Dear and Honoured Lady*, p. 65.

65. Girouard, *Return to Camelot*, pp. 124–5.

66. Dyson & Tennyson, *Dear and Honoured Lady*, p. 124; Ricks, *Poems of Tennyson*, vol. 1, p. 207.

67. Dyson & Tennyson, *Dear and Honoured Lady*, p. 69.

68. 'On the bald street breaks the blank day', *In Memoriam*, canto VII, in Ricks, *Poems of Tennyson*, vol. 2, p. 326.

69. Dyson & Tennyson, *Dear and Honoured Lady*, pp. 69–70.

70. Ibid., p. 76.

Chapter 10: 'The Luxury of Woe'

1. RA VIC/ADDA22/77; Staniland, *In Royal Fashion*, p. 156; *Illustrated London News*, 28 December 1861.

2. Staniland, *In Royal Fashion*, p. 156.

3. *Leeds Mercury*, 17 December 1861.

4. *Illustrated London News*, 28 December 1861.

5. George Frederick Pardon, *Routledge's Popular Guide to London and Its Sub-urbs*, London, 1862, front advertising.

6. King, *The Dying Game*, pp. 106–7; Morley, *Death, Heaven and the Victorians*, pp. 63–4. Courtaulds soon developed large-scale production of its own cheaper, coarser fabric – 'Albert crape' – more durable and half the price, which during the 1870s was targeted at the burgeoning market among the lower middle and working classes.

7. Goldthorpe, *From Queen to Empress*, pp. 69–70. The expression the 'luxury of woe' or 'luxury of grief' was a commonly used one at the time in poetry,

philosophical writing; see e.g. *The Poetical Works of Thomas More*, 1826, Paris: Galignani, 1827, p. 246: 'Weep on, and as thy sorrows flow, I'll taste the luxury of woe'; Alison Adburgham, *Shops and Shopping*, London: Barrie & Jenkins, 1989, p. 66–7.

8. Christina Walkley, *Ghost in the Looking Glass*, London: Peter Owen, 1981, p. 29; Goldthorpe, *From Queen to Empress*, p. 76. A common complaint suffered by overworked seamstresses was temporary nystagmus, where the eye involuntarily flicks from side to side in rapid swinging motion and prevents the sufferer from fixing their gaze on an object. Kristine Hughes, *Everyday Life in Regency and Victorian Britain*, Cincinnatti: Writers Digest Books, 1998, pp. 217–18.

9. Staniland, *In Royal Fashion*, pp. 155–6.

10. RA VIC/MAIN/QVJ/1862: 1 July.

11. It was not until her Golden Jubilee of 1887 that the Queen was prevailed upon, thanks to the intervention of the Princess of Wales, to allow ladies at court to wear something other than jet. She agreed to silver and increasingly adopted it herself, thus sparking a new fashion and the further erosion of the jet trade.

12. Crawford, *Victoria, Queen and Ruler*, pp. 331–2.

13. The 1871 census listed 1,006 jet workers in the town. See Noreen Vickers, 'The Structure of the Whitby Jet Industry in 1871', http://www.localpopulationstudies.org.uk/PDF/LPS38/LPS38–1987 –8–17.pdf

14. McMillan, *Whitby Jet Through the Years*, pp. 74–6, 211, 226. The Whitby jet trade began to decline from the mid-1870s in the face of cheap foreign imports of imitation glass 'jet' from France, as well as vulcanite and poorer-quality jet from Spain. Thereafter trade in Whitby jet rapidly collapsed and the workforce shrank to 300.

15. RA VIC/ADDC6: 30 June 1862, diary of Lady Geraldine Somerset.

16. Fulford, *Dearest Mama*, p. 59.

17. Connell, *Regina v. Palmerston*, p. 327.

18. Argyll, *Autobiography and Memoirs*, vol. 2, p. 185, 187.

19. RA VIC/MAIN/QVJ/1862: 24 May; Fulford, *Dearest Mama*, p. 62.

20. Vincent, *Disraeli, Derby*, p. 187.

21. Bodleian Library Special Collections, Clarendon Papers, MS Eng.e.2122, Lady Katherine Clarendon diary for 3 February 1862; British Library, Add. MS 44289, Gladstone Papers, vol. CXCV: 16 March 1862.

22. Wyndham, *Correspondence of Lady Lyttleton*, p. 348.

23. RA VIC/MAIN/QVJ/1862: 20 June.

24. Noel, *Princess Alice*, p. 88.

25. Fulford, *Dearest Mama*, pp. 60, 83, 74.

26. Kennedy, *My Dear Duchess*, pp. 196–7.

27. Aston, *Duke of Connaught*, pp. 47–8.

28. RA VIC/ADDC6: 1 July 1862, Journal of Lady Geraldine Somerset.
29. Fulford, *Dearest Mama*, p. 85.
30. *Daily News*, 2 July 1862.
31. *Reynolds's Newspaper*, 6 July 1862.
32. A. MacGeorge, *Wm. Leighton Leitch Landscape Painter, A Memoir*, London: L. Blackie & Son, 1884, p. 63.
33. Fulford, *Dearest Mama*, p. 101.
34. Ibid., p. 102; the quotation is from Wisdom, chapter IV.
35. Anon, *Queen's Resolve*, p. 104.
36. Tisdall, *Queen Victoria's Private Life*, pp. 66–8.
37. Kennedy, *My Dear Duchess*, p. 201.
38. Connell, *Regina vs. Palmerston*, p. 331.
39. RA VIC/ADDA/25/85: 4 October 1862, letter to Howard Elphinstone; Connell, *Regina v. Palmerston*, p. 332.
40. RA VIC/MAIN/QVJ/1862: 22 July.
41. Fulford, *Dearest Mama*, p. 130; Windsor & Bolitho, pp. 272, 273.
42. RA VIC/ADDA/8/384: 'Miss Ella Taylor's Reminiscences of HRH The Duchess of Cambridge', p. 2.
43. Fulford, *Dearest Mama*, pp. 138, 139, 142.
44. RA VIC/MAIN/QVJ/1862: 14 December 1862.
45. Ashwell & Wilberforce, *Life of Bishop Wilberforce*, p. 72.
46. Fulford, *Dearest Mama*, p. 148.
47. Walsh, *Religious Life and Influence of Queen Victoria*, p. 116.
48. Fulford, *Dearest Mama*, p. 153.
49. *Belfast News-letter*, 1 December 1862.

Chapter 11: 'A Married Daughter I Must Have Living with Me'

1. Dasent, *Delane*, p. 64.
2. Hudson, *Munby*, p. 152.
3. Strafford, *Henry Greville*, p. 106.
4. Fulford, *Dearest Mama*, pp. 98, 126.
5. Ibid., pp. 172, 165.
6. Morier Family Papers, Balliol College, Oxford, K1/4/4, Queen Victoria, letter to General Peel, 25 January 1864.
7. Bailey, *Diary of Lady Frederick Cavendish*, p. 154; Greville, *Leaves*, vol, 4,. p. 109.
8. Cooke, *Princess Mary Adelaide*, vol. 1, p. 407; Wiebe, *Letters of Benjamin Disraeli*, vol. 8, p. 261.
9. Fulford, *Dearest Mama*, p. 180.
10. Hibbert, *Edward VII*, p. 62; Windsor & Bolitho, p. 308.

11. The wedding was extensively described in the newspapers and in journals such as *The Times, Telegraph, Daily News, Morning Chronicle,* etc. for 11 March. The Queen's own account can be found in Hibbert, *Letters and Journals,* pp. 172–4; the account of Disraeli is in Wiebe, *Letters of Benjamin Disraeli,* vol. 8, pp. 412–13; Windsor & Bolitho, pp. 281–8, 306–12; Lord Clarendon, in Kennedy, *My Dear Duchess,* pp. 210–15; Bailey, *Diary of Lady Frederick Cavendish,* pp. 154–7; Battiscombe, *Princess Alexandra,* pp. 43–50. Munby's vivid description of the crowds in London is in Hudson, *Munby,* pp. 149–53.

12. Hibbert, *Letters and Journals,* p. 172.

13. Hudson, *Munby,* p. 153.

14. Frederick Pollock, *Personal Reminiscences of Sir Frederick Pollock,* vol. 2, London: Macmillan, 1987, pp. 110–11.

15. Strafford, *Henry Greville,* vol. 4, p. 110.

16. Fulford, *Dearest Mama,* pp. 192, 193.

17. Hibbert, *Letters and Journals,* p. 177.

18. Chomet, *Helena,* p. 17.

19. Bailey, *Diary of Lady Frederick Cavendish,* vol. 1, pp. 199, 214.

20. Fulford, *Dearest Mama,* pp. 226, 209, 212.

21. Ibid., pp. 235, 213.

22. Hibbert, *Letters and Journals,* p. 178.

23. Elphinstone, *Queen Thanks Sir Howard,* p. 64; Fulford, *Dearest Mama,* p. 245.

24. *The Times,* 12 October 1863.

25. Fulford, *Dearest Mama,* p. 273.

26. *Morning Post,* 15 October 1863.

27. Ibid.

28. *The Times,* 12 October 1863.

29. Wake, *Princess Louise,* p. 75; Hibbert, *Letters and Journals,* p. 178.

30. Hibbert, *Letters and Journals,* p. 179; Windsor & Bolitho, p. 294.

31. Magnus, *Gladstone,* p. 160; Arengo Jones, *Queen Victoria and Switzerland,* p. 21.

32. Wake, *Princess Louise,* p. 74.

33. Arengo Jones, *Queen Victoria and Switzerland,* p. 18.

34. Hibbert, *Letters and Journals,* p. 178.

35. Fulford, *Dearest Mama,* pp. 205–6.

36. Hibbert, *Letters and Journals,* p. 181.

37. Connell, *Regina v. Palmerston,* p. 352.

38. Hibbert, *Letters and Journals,* pp. 184, 185.

39. Ibid., p. 185.

40. *Manchester Examiner,* 19 March 1864; Tisdall, *Queen Victoria's John Brown,* pp. 86–7.

41. *Saturday Review*, 26 March 1864.
42. Bailey, *Diary of Lady Frederick Cavendish*, p. 207; E. F. Benson, *As We Were*, London: Longman's, Green & Co., 1930, p. 38.
43. Watson, *Queen at Home*, p. 166; Tooley, *Personal Life*, p. 212.
44. Maxwell, *Life and Letters of 4th Earl Clarendon*, vol. II, p. 293.
45. Vincent, *Disraeli, Derby*, pp. 209, 210.
46. Ibid., p. 211.
47. Dasent, *Delane*, vol. II, pp. 108, 110.
48. Ibid., p. 130.
49. McMillan, *Whitby Jet Through the Years*, p. 212.
50. *The Times*, 15 December 1864.
51. *Morning Post*, 16 December 1864.
52. Balliol College Oxford, Morier Family Papers, K/Box 2/1, letter of 19 August 1864.
53. Vincent, *Disraeli, Derby*, p. 214.

Chapter 12: 'God Knows How I Want So Much to be Taken Care Of'

Title: Queen Victoria to Vicky, 5 April 1865, in Fulford, *Your Dear Letter*, p. 22.

1.   House and Storey, eds, *The Letters of Charles Dickens*, vol. 10, p. 425.
2.   *Civil Engineer and Architect's Journal*, vol. 37, January 1864, p. 27.
3.   Wiebe, *Letters of Benjamin Disraeli*, vol. 8, p. 270.
4.   *Art Journal*, 1866, vol. 5, p. 203; *Tomahawk*, vols 4–5, 3 April 1869, p. 148. This was indeed the case. By the time Foley's statue was finally positioned under the canopy in 1875 the monument was already blackened by ten years of London soot.
5.   *Pall Mall Gazette*, 11 September 1865.
6.   Hibbert, *Letters and Journals*, p. 196; Fulford, *Your Dear Letter*, p. 109; *Punch*, 15 December 1866, p. 238; *Morning Post*, 1 December 1866; *Illustrated London News*, 8 December 1866.
7.   *Ladies' Companion*, vol. 28, 1865, p. 324.
8.   *Friend of India*, 15 October 1865, no. 1605.
9.   Fulford, *Your Dear Letter*, p. 22; Hibbert, *Letters and Journals*, p. 187.
10. Lamont-Brown, *John Brown*, p. 79.
11. Hibbert, *Letters and Journals*, p. 189; Fulford, *Your Dear Letter,* p. 29.
12. In his travels through England in 1869 and published in 1870, Daniel Joseph Kirwan, a reporter for the *New York World*, painted a vivid and idiosyncratic portrait of the Queen, gleaned from his conversations with people at Windsor and elsewhere, as a result of which he felt compelled to 'lift the veil' on the true reason for the Queen's continuing seclusion. It was, Kirwan

claimed, due in part to her serious 'fondness for liquor', a fact that was 'continually hinted at obscurely in the more liberal organs'. What is more, Kirwan had it on good authority that the Queen 'was in the habit of drinking half a pint of raw liquor per day'. The fact that the Queen had found comfort in the bottle in her widowhood is no real surprise; it is an acknowledged fact that she enjoyed whisky, and entirely plausible that her need for its anaesthetising effect to counter the pain of grief may have grown in her widowhood. It would also explain the physical changes noted by many – of her increased weight (partly the result of a voracious appetite that she soon recovered) and her reddened and puffy face. But in the absence of further substantiating evidence, we only have Kirwan's word for it. See Daniel Joseph Kirwan, *Palace and Hovel or Phases of London Life*, reprinted by Abelard-Schuman in New York, 1963. See also Charles Morris & Murat Halstead, *Life and Reign of Queen Victoria*, International Publishing Society, 1901, p. 223.

13.   Longford, *Victoria RI*, p. 325. Rumours abounded during the Queen's reign and after her death that Brown had acted as a spiritualist medium in séances held in the Blue Room, during which the Queen had made contact with Albert on the other side. Despite exhaustive research, Victoria's biographer Elizabeth Longford found no evidence of either the Queen's indulgence in spiritualist practices or of Brown's role in them, nor did she of a sexual relationship between them. But unsubstantiated gossip and rumour – going so far as allegations of a morganatic marriage having taken place – persist to this day. No supporting evidence, however, survives in the Queen's journals – if it was ever there – though these were edited and bowdlerised by her daughter Beatrice after her death. Nor is there a mention of it in her thousands of uncensored letters to Vicky. All of the Queen's letters to Brown and his to her, as well as his diaries, which might have provided an answer one way or the other, were destroyed after the Queen's death, on the orders of Edward VII. See Rappaport, *Queen Victoria*, entries on John Brown, pp. 75–81, and the Paranormal, pp. 285–8; also Longford, *Victoria RI*, pp. 334–9; Cullen, *Empress Brown*, pp. 97–9; 'Victoria and John Brown' in Thompson, *Queen Victoria*, pp. 61–86; Lamont Brown, 'Queen Victoria's "Secret Marriage"', in *Contemporary Review*, December 2003, available online at http://findarticles.com/p/articles/mi m2242/is 1655 283/ai 112095011/ Perhaps the best summary of Victoria's relationship with John Brown, and one that clearly defines it in personal and social terms, comes in a letter she wrote to Viscount Cranbrook after Brown's death in 1883 and which recently came to light. In it she wrote, 'Perhaps never in history was there so strong an *attachment*, so warm and loving a *friendship* between the sovereign and *servant*' (my italics). Those three words – 'attachment', 'friendship' and 'servant' – define a close romantic friendship built on trust

and mutual respect, but one that was nevertheless contained within the parameters of Victoria's own very clear understanding of class difference. She was right to feel 'that life for the second time is become most trying and sad' after Brown's death. She had lost a friend, and true friends were a rare thing indeed to a lonely monarch, isolated by her position. Nevertheless some commentators appear to have totally misread this statement as alluding to Brown having taken the place, sexually and maritally, of Albert. Victoria in fact totally disapproved of the remarriage of widows. See Bendor Grosvenor, 'Dear John', *History Today*, January 2005, pp. 2–3.

14. For a discussion of Victoria's chronic grief, see Parkes, *Recovery from Bereavement*, pp. 129–31, 134–5; Jalland, *Death in the Victorian Family*, ch. 16, 'Chronic and Abnormal Grief', pp. 318–22.

15. Sylvain Van de Weyer died in 1874. Madame Van de Weyer (who died in 1878), was formerly Elizabeth Bates, daughter of a Barings banker, and had with her husband been a very particular friend of Victoria and Albert since 1840 and, with their close links to Uncle Leopold, were favourites at court. Victoria was godmother to their first child and after her widowhood frequently visited Madame Van de Weyer at her home, New Lodge, four miles from Windsor. Written evidence of their relationship is, however, extremely scant. See Paul Bishop, *Synchronicity and Intellectual Intuition in Kant, Swedenborg and Jung*, New York: Ewin Hellen Press, 2000, p. 314; *Spiritual Notes*, 1993, p. 52; Stanislaw Przybyszewski, *Erinnerungen an Berlin und Krakau*, 119, p. 123.

16. Crawford, *Queen Victoria*, pp. 327–8; Whittle, *Victoria and Albert at Home*, p. 142.

17. Longford, *Victoria RI*, p. 321.

18. Fulford, *Your Dear Letter*, p. 48; Thompson, *Queen Victoria*, p. 76.

19. *Morning Post*, 9 April 1866.

20. Lamont-Brown, *John Brown*, p. 69.

21. Hibbert, *Letters and Journals*, p. 191.

22. Justin G. Turner, ed., *Mary Todd Lincoln – Her Life and Letters*, New York: Knopf, 1972, p. 230.

23. Fulford, *Your Dear Letter*, p. 66.

24. Ibid., pp. 90–1.

25. Fulford, *Dearest Mama*, p. 211; Fulford, *Your Dear Letter*, pp. 56–7.

26. Hibbert, *Letters and Journals*, p. 193.

27. Hudson, *Munby*, p. 218.

28. Crawford, *Queen Victoria*, p. 328.

29. Russell, *Amberley Papers*, vol. 1, p. 466.

30. Crawford, *Queen Victoria*, p. 319.

31. Conway, David Moncure, *Autobiography, Memories and Experiences of Daniel Moncure Conway*, vol. 2, London: Cassell & Co., 1904, p. 65.

32. Ibid.

33. Crawford, *Queen Victoria*, p. 320.
34. Buckle, I: 299.
35. Longford, *Victoria RI*, pp. 348–9.
36. Arengo-Jones, *Queen Victoria in Switzerland*, p. 21.
37. Russell, *Amberley Papers*, vol. 1, p. 515; *Pall Mall Gazette*, 24 May 1865.
38. *Punch*, 7 July 1866; Tisdall, *Queen Victoria's John Brown*, pp. 105–6.
39. See, for example, *Examiner*, 7 September 1867.
40. *The Light Blue: A Cambridge University Magazine*, vol. 2, 1867, p. 330.
41. *Tomahawk*, 11 May 1867.
42. Ibid., 30 May 1868.
43. Martineau, *Selected Letters*, p. 212.
44. Cullen, *Empress Brown*, pp. 94–6.
45. Kuhn, *Henry and Mary Ponsonby*, p. 98.
46. Tisdall, *Queen Victoria's John Brown*, p. 109.
47. Ibid., p. 111.
48. Hibbert, *Letters and Journals*, p. 197; Fulford, *Your Dear Letter*, p. 120.
49. Kuhn, *Henry and Mary Ponsonby*, p. 97; Bailey, *Diary of Lady Frederick Cavendish*, vol. 2, p. 10.
50. *Tomahawk*, 8 June 1867; *Huddersfield Chronicle*, 30 June 1866; Russell, *Amberley Papers*, vol.1, p. 515; Cullen, *Empress Brown*, p. 94.
51. Longford, *Victoria RI*, p. 374; Tooley, *Personal Life of Queen Victoria*, pp. 217–18.
52. Cullen, *Empress Brown*, p. 113.
53. Hibbert, *Letters and Journals*, p. 198.
54. Cullen, *Empress Brown*, p. 104; Jerrold, *Widowhood of Queen Victoria*, p. 97.
55. *Daily News*, 13 June 1867; *Reynolds's Newspaper*, 21 July 1867.
56. Arengo-Jones, *Queen Victoria in Switzerland*, p. 24.
57. Downer, *Queen's Knight*, p. 170; Vincent, *Disraeli, Derby*, p. 242; Wake, *Princess Louise*, p. 75.
58. Fulford, *Your Dear Letter*, pp. 169, 51.

Chapter 13: 'The Queen Is Invisible'

1. Fulford, *Dearest Mama*, p. 219.
2. For a detailed discussion of the extent of the Queen's involvement in the compilation of *The Early Years*, see Homans, *Royal Representations*, pp. 115–31.
3. *Medical Times and Gazette*, 3 August 1867.
4. *Quarterly Review*, 1867–8, vol. 29, pp. 199, 304, 280.
5. *Medical Times and Gazette*, 3 August 1867.

6. Fulford, *Your Dear Letter*, p. 166.
7. Lee, *Queen Victoria*, p. 410.
8. Victoria, *Leaves from the Journal*, p. 106.
9. *The Times*, 10 January 1868.
10. Fulford, *Your Dear Letter*, p. 169.
11. Vineta and Robert Colby, *The Equivocal Virtue: Mrs Oliphant and the Victorian Literary Market Place*, Hamden: Archon Books, 1966, p. 117.
12. Gail Turley Huston, *Royalties: The Queen and Victorian Writers*, Charlottesville: University Press of Virginia, 1999, pp. 148, 142. In a study entitled 'Queen Victoria: A Personal Sketch', published in 1900 after her own death, Oliphant was less equivocal. In literary matters, the Queen was, she argued, 'no student of style, nor does she ever, we imagine, ponder and wait for the best word'. See also entry on Margaret Oliphant in Rappaport, *Queen Victoria*, pp. 271–3.
13. *Fraser's Magazine*, vol. LXXVII, February 1868, p. 154; *North British Review*, vols 5–6, 1868, p. 196.
14. *Daily Telegraph*, 10 January 1868.
15. *Tomahawk*, 18 January 1868.
16. *Chronicle* quoted in *York Herald*, 25 January 1868.
17. *Reynolds's Newspaper*, 19 January 1868.
18. Fulford, *Your Dear Letter*, p. 172.
19. Ibid., p. 171; Helps, *Correspondence of Sir Arthur Helps*, pp. 265–6.
20. Fulford, *Your Dear Letter*, p. 169; Hudson, *Munby*, p. 249.
21. Martin, *Queen Victoria As I Knew Her*, p. 28; Fulford, *Your Dear Letter*, p. 169.
22. Georgina Battiscombe, *Shaftesbury A Biography of the 7th Earl*, London: Constable, 1974, p. 298.
23. Cullen, *Empress Brown*, p. 128.
24. Windsor & Bolitho, p. 65.
25. Helps, *Leaves from the Journal*, p. 128.
26. Richard Altick, *The English Common Reader: A Social History of the Mass Reading Public 1800–1900*, Columbus: Ohio University Press, 1998, p. 388.
27. Tooley, *Personal Life of Queen Victoria*, p. 236.
28. Fulford, *Your Dear Letter*, p. 178.
29. Windsor & Bolitho, p. 73. For a detailed discussion of *Leaves from the Journal*, see Homans, *Royal Representations*, pp. 131–52.
30. Fulford, *Your Dear Letter*, p. 173.
31. Martin, *Queen Victoria as I Knew Her*, p. 29.
32. Ibid., pp. 38–9.
33. Fulford, *Your Dear Letter*, pp. 173, 171.
34. Hibbert, *Letters and Journals*, p. 90.
35. Fulford, *Your Dear Letter*, pp. 174, 175, 176.
36. Moneypenny & Buckle, *Life of Disraeli*, vol. II, p. 389; Fulford, *Your Dear Letter*, p. 174.

37. Helps, *Correspondence of Sir Arthur Helps*, pp. 264–5.
38. Nevill, *Under Five Reigns*, p. 177.
39. Bailey, *Diary of Lady Frederick Cavendish*, vol. 2, p. 49.
40. Hibbert, *Letters and Journals*, p. 205.
41. Ibid.
42. Arengo-Jones, *Queen Victoria in Switzerland*, pp. 29–30.
43. *The Times*, 20 May 1868.
44. Wake, *Princess Louise*, p. 81.
45. Arengo-Jones, *Queen Victoria in Switzerland*, p. 32.
46. Ibid., p. 43.
47. Duff, *Queen Victoria's Highland Journals*, p. 141.
48. Guedalla, *Queen and Mr Gladstone*, vol. I, p. 47.
49. Kennedy, *My Dear Duchess*, p. 248.
50. Arengo-Jones, *Queen Victoria in Switzerland*, p. 26.
51. Benson & Esher, I: 213.
52. Magnus, *Gladstone*, p. 200; Weintraub, *Queen Victoria*, pp. 351–2.
53. Magnus, *Gladstone*, p. 199.
54. Wake, *Princess Louise*, pp. 86–7; Bailey, *Diary of Lady Frederick Cavendish*, vol. 2 , p. 69.
55. *The Times*, 6 November 1870.
56. Dasent, *Delane*, p. 252.
57. Hibbert, *Letters and Journals*, p. 209.
58. *Morning Post*, 6 November 1869.
59. Martin, *Queen Victoria as I Knew Her*, pp. 39–40.
60. Fulford, *Your Dear Letter*, p. 263.
61. *National Reformer*, 18 September 1870.
62. Williams, *Contentious Crown*, p. 37.
63. Magnus, *Gladstone*, p. 111
64. Ramm, *Political Correspondence of Mr Gladstone*, p. 170.
65. Hibbert, *Letters and Journals*, p. 212.
66. *Reynolds's Newspaper*, 25 December 1870.
67. Hudson, *Munby*, p. 292.
68. Hibbert, *Queen Victoria*, p. 332.

Chapter 14: 'Heaven Has Sent Us This Dispensation to Save Us'

1. Tisdall, *Queen Victoria's Private Life*, pp. 106–7; Kuhn, 'Ceremony and Politics', pp. 160–1; Ponsonby, *Henry Ponsonby*, p. 71.
2. Ponsonby, *Henry Ponsonby*, p. 71.
3. Ibid., p. 72.
4. This accusation was entirely unfounded. Any monies saved from the

Queen's Civil List income were returned to the Exchequer and did not go into the royal privy purse. Ponsonby, *Henry Ponsonby*, p. 76. See also Kuhn, 'Ceremony and Politics', pp. 138–40.

5. Charles Bradlaugh, 'The Impeachment of the House of Brunswick', 1871, quoted in Thompson, *Queen Victoria*, p. 106.

6. For an exhaustive account of the ceremony, see for example *Daily News*, 30 March 1871.

7. Cullen, *Empress Brown*, p. 135.

8. Hibbert, *Queen Victoria*, p. 339, and Pakula, *Uncommon Woman*, p. 293.

9. It is possible that the abscess under Victoria's arm had been caused by germs spreading from her severely inflamed throat. No official diagnosis was ever announced, though it has since been suggested by Weintraub (*Queen Victoria*, p. 363) that she was suffering from quinsy.

10. Magnus, *Gladstone*, p. 209.

11. Longford, *Victoria RI*, p. 382; for Henry Ponsonby's memorandum on the Queen's seclusion in 1871, see Ponsonby, *Henry Ponsonby*, pp. 73–6.

12. Ponsonby, *Henry Ponsonby*, p. 75.

13. The loyal Emilie Dittweiler finally retired in 1892, after thirty-five years' service; Annie Macdonald remained with the Queen for an equal length of time, till her death in 1897. Both women were commended by the Queen in *More Leaves from the Journal of Our Life in the Highlands, from 1862 to 1882*, published in 1884.

14. Weintraub, *Queen Victoria*, p. 366; Longford, *Victoria RI*, pp. 384–5; Cullen, *Empress Brown*, p. 140.

15. Cullen, *Empress Brown*, p. 141; Jalland, *Death in the Victorian Family*, p. 320.

16. G. T. Wrench, *Lord Lister, His Life and Work*, pp. 227–8. See also Godlee, *Lord Lister*, pp. 305–6. Lister was honoured by the Queen with a baronetcy in 1893 and a peerage in 1897 for his pioneering medical work.

17. Godlee, *Lord Lister*, p. 306. The use of India-rubber drainage tubes for wounds had first been described in France in 1859, but Lister was the first to apply them in the UK. He finally described his procedure on the Queen in *The Lancet*, 1908, vol. I, p. 1815.

18. Longford, *Victoria RI*, p. 385.

19. Ponsonby Papers quoted in Cullen, *Empress Brown*, p. 143.

20. Hibbert, *Letters and Journals*, p. 226.

21. See *The Times*, 9 November, and *Newcastle Weekly Chronicle*, 11 November 1871; the speech was subsequently published as 'The Cost of the Crown'. For Dilke's accusations, see also Kuhn, 'Ceremony and Politics', pp. 140–3; Jerrold, *Widowhood*, p. 162–3.

22. *Pall Mall Gazette*, 9 November 1871.

23. Fulford, *Darling Child*, p. 29; Ramm, *Political Correspondence of Mr Gladstone*, vol. 2, p. 264.

24. One of the other guests, Lord Chesterfield, as well as Bertie's groom, Charles Blegg, contracted the disease. Both of them died.

25. Hibbert, *Letters and Journals*, p. 213. In addition to extensive newspaper coverage of the Prince's illness, the best first-hand accounts are to be found in the Queen's journals and in the letters of Alix's lady-in-waiting, Lady Macclesfield, written from Sandringham at the time, to be found at RA VIC/ADDMSS/C/18. See also Sheppard, *George Duke of Cambridge*, vol. 2, pp. 302–5.

26. Windsor & Bolitho, p. 148.

27. RA VIC/ADDC18, Lady Macclesfield letter: 8 December 1871.

28. Hibbert, *Queen Victoria*, p. 343.

29. Windsor & Bolitho, p. 149.

30. Hibbert, *Letters and Journals*, p. 213.

31. Sheppard, *George Duke of Cambridge*, vol. 2, p. 304.

32. Hibbert, *Letters and Journals*, p. 213.

33. Buckle, II: 177; Tisdall, *Unpredictable Queen*, p. 111.

34. Henry James Jennings, *Chestnuts and Small Beer*, London: Chapman & Hall, 1920, p. 81.

35. Hudson, *Munby*, p. 300.

36. Hibbert, *Letters and Journals*, p. 214.

37. See 'The Royal Fever and Our Feverish Constitution', *Reynolds's Newspaper*, 10 December 1871.

38. *Daily Telegraph* quoted in Cullen, *Empress Brown*, p. 156.

39. Morris, 'Illustrated Press', p. 118.

40. Reid, *Memoirs of Sir Wemyss Reid*, p. 157.

41. Hibbert, *Letters and Journals*, p. 214.

42. Cullen, *Empress Brown*, p. 157; Sheppard, *George Duke of Cambridge*, vol. 2, pp. 301–11.

43. Fulford, *Darling Child*, p. 20.

44. Sheppard, *George Duke of Cambridge*, vol. 2, p. 307.

45. Fulford, *Darling Child*, p. 20.

46. Tisdall, *Unpredictable Queen*, p. 113.

47. Kuhn, *Henry and Mary Ponsonby*, p. 155; Magnus, *Gladstone*, p. 211.

48. RA VIC/ADDC18, Lady Macclesfield letter: 29 November 1871.

49. Lant, *Insubstantial Pageant*, p. 29.

50. Weintraub, *Victoria*, p. 400.

51. Battiscombe, *Queen Alexandra*, p. 120.

52. For details of the fraught discussions with Gladstone over the arrangements, see Kuhn, *Democratic Royalism*, pp. 39–47.

53. Kuhn, 'Ceremony and Politics', pp. 153–4; Lant, *Insubstantial Pageant*, pp. 28–9.

54. Windsor & Bolitho, p. 151.

55. For discussion of the Thanksgiving Service, see e.g. *The Times*, *Daily News*, *Daily Telegraph*, 28 February 1872. It was also exhaustively reported in the popular weeklies, notably the *Illustrated London News*, which produced some thirty engravings depicting the celebrations over four issues between 24 February and 16 March. A useful summary of the press response is 'Epitome of Opinion in the Morning Journals', in *Pall Mall Gazette* for 28 February. See also, Lant, *Insubstantial Pageant*, pp. 26–33; Kuhn, 'Ceremony and Politics'.

56. Bailey, *Diary of Lady Frederick Cavendish*, vol. 2, p. 127.

57. Cullen, *Empress Brown*, pp. 159–61; Reid, *Memoirs of Sir Wemyss Reid*, p. 190; Morris, 'Illustrated Press', p. 120. The limited number of police on duty that day were totally unable to marshal the vast crowds surging forward to catch sight of the Queen, particularly at Ludgate Hill and Temple Bar – at which latter three people were suffocated to death in the crush. *Reynolds's* claimed that six people in all were killed that day and a hundred seriously hurt, with 227 being hospitalised. See issue for 3 March 1872: 'Tuesday's Tomfoolery' and 'Accidents at the Thanksgiving'.

58. Hibbert, *Letters and Journals*, p. 216.

59. *Reynolds's Newspaper*, 3 March 1872.

60. Gavard, *A Diplomat in London*, pp. 96–7.

61. Ibid., p. 97; Hudson, *Munby*, p. 305.

62. Hudson, *Munby*, p. 305; Bailey, *Diary of Lady Frederick Cavendish*, vol. 2, p. 127.

63. Buckle, II: 195.

64. Hibbert, *Letters and Journals*, p. 216.

65. Reid, *Memoirs of Sir Wemyss Reid*, p. 190; Hudson, *Munby*, p. 305.

66. *Reynolds's Newspaper*, 25 February 1872.

67. Fulford, *Darling Child*, p. 31.

68. *The Times*, 28 February 1872.

69. Ibid.; *Lloyd's Weekly* and *Reynolds's Newspaper*, 3 March 1872.

70. Hibbert, *Letters and Journals*, p. 227.

71. Ibid.; Bailey, *Diary of Lady Frederick Cavendish*, vol. 2, p. 128.

72. *The Times*, 20 March 1872.

73. Bailey, *Diary of Lady Frederick Cavendish*, vol. 2, p. 129; Cullen, *Empress Brown*, p. 156.

Chapter 15: Albertopolis

1. Williams, *Contentious Crown*, pp. 49–50: *National Reformer*, 21 January and 25 February 1872.

2. Hibbert, *Letters and Journals*, p. 228.

3. Ibid., pp. 228–9.

4. Tisdall, *Queen Victoria's Private Life*, p. 105.

5. See e.g. Williams, *Contentious Crown*, p. 209.

6. Parkes, *Recovery from Bereavement*, contains a fascinating case study of the Queen's grief. See especially pp. 129–31, 134–5, 138–42.

7. Tennyson, *In Memoriam*, Canto IX, in Ricks, *Poems of Tennyson*, vol. 2, p. 328.

8. Hibbert, *Letters and Journals*, p. 229.

9. Ibid.

10. Parkes, *Recovery from Bereavement*, p. 153.

11. Mallet, *Life With Queen Victoria*, p. 52.

12. Ibid., p. 122.

13. Ibid., p. 44.

14. See 'The Widow at Windsor', in Rappaport, *Queen Victoria*, pp. 407–11.

15. Craik, *Fifty Golden Years*, p. 45.

16. 'Letter from the Queen to Her People' on the occasion of her Jubilee, 24 June 1887, published in *Lloyd's Weekly News*, 26 June 1887.

17. Tennyson, *In Memoriam*, Canto XC, in Ricks, *Poems of Tennyson*, vol. 2, p. 408; A. S. Byatt, 'The Congugial Angel', in *Angels and Insects*, London: Vintage, 1995, p. 177.

18. H. G. Wells, *An Experiment in Autobiography: Discoveries and Conclusions of a Very Ordinary Brain (since 1866)*, vol. 1, London: Victor Gollancz, 1934, p. 46.

19. Percy Lubbock, *Shades of Eton*, London: Jonathan Cape, 1929, pp. 122–3.

20. Fulford, *Your Dear Letter*, p. 121

21. Tennyson, *In Memoriam*, Canto CVI, in Ricks, *Poems of Tennyson*, vol. 2, p. 427.

22. The Royal Mausoleum, open to the public once a year on the nearest Wednesday to Queen Victoria's birthday of 24 May, is now, sadly, closed indefinitely to the public, due to structural problems.

23. Weintraub, *Victoria*, p. 324.

24. For a detailed description of the many later memorials to Albert, see Darby & Smith, *Cult of the Prince Consort*. See also entries on Albert Memorial; Frogmore; Royal Albert Hall; Victoria and Albert Museum in Rappaport, *Queen Victoria: A Biographical Companion*

25. Stanford, *Recollections of Sir Gilbert Scott*, pp. 263, 264, 267.

26. Gavard, *Diplomat in London*, pp. 36–7.

27. 'Mark Twain's 1872 English Journal', in Lin Salamo and Harriet Elinor Smith, eds, *Mark Twain's Letters*, 1872–1873, Berkeley: University of California Press, 1997.

28. E. Beresford Chancellor, *Life in Regency and Early Victorian Times*, London: Batsford, 1926, p. 46. For a full account of the restoration project, see Chris Brooks, *The Albert Memorial: The Prince Consort National Memorial, Its History, Contexts and Conservation*, New Haven: Yale University Press, 2000.

29. Strachey, *Queen Victoria*, pp. 187–8.

30. See Williams, *Contentious Crown*, pp. 126–7. Criticism of the extent of Stock-mar's influence over Albert and the levels of the Prince's interference in government foreign policy during the Crimean War was prompted by revelations in the third volume of Martin's biography. See 'The Crown and the Cabinet: Five Letters on the Biography of the Prince Consort', published pseudonymously in *The Times* by Henry Dunckley as 'Verax' in 1878.

31. Warwick, *Afterthoughts*, pp. 3–4.

32. Aronson, *Grandmama of Europe*, p. 12. Victoria assumed the Latin title after 1876.

33. Henry James, *Portraits of Places*, Boston: James Osgood & Co., 1883, p. 310–11.

34. Williams, *Contentious Crown*, p. 210.

35. Grey, *Early Years of the Prince Consort*, p. 322.

36. Flora Thompson, *Lark Rise to Candleford*, Harmondsworth: Penguin, 1973, p. 295.

Epilogue: Christmas 1878

1. Noel, *Princess Alice*, p. 120.

2. Bennett, *Queen Victoria's Children*, p. 63.

3. *Alice, Princess of Great Britain*, p. 125.

4. Noel, *Princess Alice*, pp. 224–5.

5. *Alice, Princess of Great Britain*, p. 37. An account of the illness of Princess Alice and her children, written by her close friend Miss McBean, is on pp. 32–44.

6. Ibid., p, 41.

7. RA VIC/MAIN/QVJ/1878: 12 December.

8. Buckle, III: 653–4.

9. *Alice, Princess of Great Britain*, p. 44.

10. RA VIC/MAIN/QVJ/1878: 14 December.

11. Ibid.

12. The exquisite effigy of a recumbent Alice clasping her dead daughter May was executed in white marble by Boehm and was placed near her father's sarcophagus in the Royal Mausoleum at Frogmore, in time for the first anniversary of Alice's death in 1879.

13. *The Times*, 17 December 1878.

14. Richard Hough, *Advice to a Grand-Daughter: Letters from Queen Victoria to Princess Victoria of Hesse*, London: Heinemann, 1975, p. 10

15. Epton, *Victoria and Her Daughters*, p. 155.

16. RA VIC/MAIN/QVJ/1878: 19 December.

17. *The Times*, 28 December 1878.

18. Buckle, *Life of Disraeli*, vol. I, p. 341. Two more of Victoria's children died during her lifetime: Leopold in 1884 and Affie in 1900. Vicky outlived her mother only by seven months, dying of cancer in August 1901. A further tragic family death from diphtheria followed soon after Alice's, in April 1879, when Vicky's fourth son, Waldemar, died of the disease. The birth, in 1896, of Prince Albert, the future George VI, on the same day – 14 December – would add to the talismanic significance of the date for the royal family. Five months after Alice's death Queen Victoria took it into her head to try to marry Princess Beatrice off to Alice's widower, Louis, so that she could mother her dead sister's children, for the most part in England. She even persuaded Disraeli to try and get the law changed, permitting marriage with a sister-in-law, but it was thrown out by the House of Lords. See Mary Lutyens, ed., *Lady Lytton's Court Diary*, London: Rupert Hart-Davis, 1961, p. 47.

19. RA VIC/MAIN/QVJ/1878: 31 December. Victor Emmanuel II of Italy died on 9 January 1878; Pope Pius IX died on 7 February 1878. HMS *Eurydice*, a British training frigate, sank in a storm off the Isle of Wight on 24 March 1878; her crew of 376 drowned. In 1878 two assassination attempts were made in quick succession against Emperor Wilhelm of Prussia: on 11 May and 2 June. The German armoured frigate *Grosse Kurfürst* was damaged in a collision and sunk off Folkestone during manoeuvres on 31 May 1878; 284 of her crew drowned. George V of Hanover – the only son of the Queen's cousin, Ernest Augustus, Duke of Cumberland – died on 12 June 1878. María de las Mercedes d'Orléans, Queen Consort of Spain, died on 26 June 1878, of tuberculosis aged eighteen. The Second Anglo-Afghan War broke out in September 1878 and lasted till 1880.

Appendix: What Killed Prince Albert?

1. Fulford, *Prince Consort*, p. 270.
2. Walford, *Life of the Prince Consort*, p. 106
3. *Morning Chronicle*, 19 December; *Medical Times and Gazette*, 21 December, pp. 640–2.
4. For medical thinking on typhoid in the Victorian period, see: Alexander Duane, ed., *A Dictionary of Medicine and the Allied Sciences*, 3rd edn, New York: Leah Brothers, 1900, pp. 610–11; and Dr Montague Murray, ed., *Quain's Dictionary of Medicine*, rev. edn, London: Longman's, Green & Co., 1902, pp. 1764–7. Anne Hardy, *The Epidemic Streets: Infectious Disease and the Rise of Preventive Medicine*, 1856–1900, Oxford: Clarendon Press, 1993, has useful background on the incidence of typhoid fever in the 1860s.
5. Woodham-Smith, *Queen Victoria*, p. 424.
6. Murray, ed., *Quain's Dictionary of Medicine*, p. 1766.

7. *Morning Chronicle,* 20 December 1861.

8. *The Lancet,* 28 December 1861 and 11 January 1862.

9. *Irish Temperance Journal,* 1863, vol. 1, pp. 57–8; *British Journal of Homoeopathy,* 1862, vol. 20, pp. 174–5.

10. For Stockmar's communication with the royal pharmacist Peter Squire, see Dr G. C. Williamson, *Memoirs in Miniature: A Volume of Random Reminiscences,* London: Grayson & Grayson, 1933, pp. 253–4; Weintraub, *Uncrowned King,* pp. 426, 456. Thanks to the recommendation of Dr James Clark, Squire & Son had been appointed royal chemists on the Queen's accession in 1837. Squire's prescription and account book containing details of his supplies to the royal family for 1861–9 is in the archive of the Royal Pharmaceutical Society. It lists both regular monthly supplies and additional, variable orders, but unfortunately does not specify for whom particular medicines were intended. After Albert's death a large consignment of twenty bottles of smelling salts was sent by Squire's on 17 December, no doubt to deal with the flood of exhausted feelings among the ladies of the royal household at the Prince's death.

11. Longford, 'Queen Victoria's Doctors', p. 83.

12. Villiers, *Vanished Victorian,* p. 311; Cowley, *Paris Embassy* p. 229.

13. Longford, 'Queen Victoria's Doctors', pp. 85–6.

14. Arkhiv der Hessischen Hausstiftung: Briefe 7.1/1-BA 3: letters from Crown Prince Frederick, 19 and 20 December 1961.

15. In the medical press the following articles appeared concurring on the diagnosis of typhoid: Kevin Anderson, 'Death of a Prince Consort', *Medical Journal of Australia,* 9 November 1968, pp. 865–7. A. G. W. Whitfield, in his 'The Last Illness of the Prince Consort', *Journal of the Royal College of Physicians,* vol. 12, no. 1, 1977, pp. 96–102, offers a loose argument for typhoid, but with no compelling evidence. Michael Robbins in 'The Missing Doctor: An "If" of Victorian Medical History', *Journal of the Royal Society of Medicine,* vol. 90, March 1997, pp. 163–5, argues that had Albert's talented new physician Dr William Baly not been killed in an accident in January 1861, the course of the Prince's treatment – demanding complete bed rest and the removal of all stress, including the demands of the Trent affair – might have been different. For an interesting overview of Queen Victoria's relationship with Dr Clark, see Longford, 'Queen Victoria's Doctors'.

16. See Bennett, *King without a Crown,* pp. 371, 381–2.

17. Weintraub, *Victoria,* pp. 295–301, and Weintraub, *Uncrowned King,* pp. 435, 456.

18. *The Lancet,* 21 December 1861; *Medical Times and Gazette,* 11 January 1862. The French source for the latter article would appear to be *L'Union médicale,* 7 January 1862, vol. 13, no. 2, p 17.

19. J. W. Paulley, 'The Death of Albert Prince Consort: The case against typhoid fever', *Quarterly Journal of Medicine*, vol. 86, 1993, pp. 837–41.

20. See Sotnik, *The Coburg Conspiracy*, London: Ephesus Publishing, 2008, Ch. 18, 'Albert's Paternity'.

21. Charles N. Bernstein, Sunny Singh, Lesley A. Graff, John R. Walker, Mary S. Cheang. 'A prospective population-based study of triggers of flares of IBD', *Gastroenterology*, 2009; 136 suppl 1: A1106.

22. After Albert's death Victoria found a comment in his diary in which he said he had not slept for 14–16 days, as she later told Lord Clarendon – see Clarendon Papers, Bodleian Library Special Collections, Ms Eng. e. 2123, 5 February 1862.

23. Charlot, *Victoria, the Young Queen*, p. 421.

24. For further discussion of Crohn's, see: S. P. L. Travis and N. Mortensen, 'Anorectal and Colonic Crohn's Disease', in J.-C. Givel, N. C. Mortensen and B. Roche, eds, *Anorectal and Colonic Diseases: A Practical Guide to Their Management* (3rd edn), London: Springer, 2010, pp. 501–12.

25. Both the temperance and the homoeopathic medicine movements took a particular interest in the circumstances of the Prince's death, which provided them with an occasion for critiques of conventional allopathic methods. The *Water-Cure Journal* of 1865 (vols 39–40, p. 140) boldly stated that 'Alcoholic medication killed the Prince Consort'.

26. Letter to the Dowager Duchess of Coburg, 9 April 1857, in James, *Albert*, p. 254.

Bibliography

Archives

Arkhiv der Hessischen Hausstiftung, Schloss Fasanerie, Eichenzell:
Briefe Kronprinz Wilhelm von Preussen an Kronprinzessin Victoria, 1861, 7.1/1-BA 3

Balliol College, Oxford:
Morier Family Papers, K1/4/4, 1866–72, Queen Victoria's letters to General Peel

Bodleian Library Special Collections:
Diaries of Lady Katherine Clarendon, Clarendon Papers, MSS Eng. e. 2122–5
Diary of Charles Pugh, MS.Eng.misc.d472
Journal of John Rashdall, MS.Eng.misc.e 359

British Library:
Gladstone Papers, vol. CCXL, Add. MSS 44325 and 44326, letters from the Duchess of Sutherland; vol. CXCV Add. MS 44289
Queen Victoria's 'Album Consolativum', Add. MSS 62089, 62090

Cheshire Archives:
Correspondence and Papers of Dean Stanley, DSA 85

Public Record Office, Kew:
Lord Chamberlain's papers, PRO LC 1-90-005

Royal Archives, Windsor:
Letters and journals of Queen Victoria, Prince Albert and members of the royal household; memoranda from the Lord Chamberlain and Comptroller of the royal household [itemised in detail in the Notes]

Royal Pharmaceutical Society of Great Britain Collections:
Peter Squire, pharmacist: Queen Victoria's Account book, 1861–1869

Ian Shapiro collection:
Diaries of Sir John Cowell, 1861–2; letter of Ra Haniraka, 3 March 1862

Staatsarchiv Darmstadt:
Briefe von Prinzessin Alice, 1861, D24 Nr. 25/3–4 and 26/1

The Times Newspapers Limited Archive, News International Archive:
TT/ED/JTD/A/022, Lord Torrington letters to Delane
TT/ED/JTD/10–13, Delane Correspondence

Newspapers and Journals

British national and regional newspapers digitised in the online resource, 19th Century British Library Newspapers, available at the British Library, London, and other libraries and repositories. Major papers consulted:

Belfast News-letter
Daily News
Daily Telegraph
Leeds Mercury
Lloyds Weekly Newspaper
London Gazette
Morning Chronicle
Morning Post
Pall Mall Gazette
Reynolds's Newspaper

The Times Digital Archive 1785–1985

New York Times Article Archive 1851–1980

Magazines and journals digitised in 19th Century UK Periodicals, British Library, London (availability as per the newspaper archive):

Illustrated London News
The Lancet
Medical Times and Gazette
Punch
Tomahawk

Primary Published Sources

Alice, Princess of Great Britain, Grand Duchess of Hesse: Letters to Her Majesty the Queen, New and Popular Edition with a Memoir by HRH Princess Christian, London: John Murray, 1897.

Anon., 'The Last Hours of Prince Albert', in *Wesleyan-Methodist Magazine*, vol. 47, 1864, p. 906; published in pamphlet form as 'The Last Hours of HRH Prince Albert of Blessed Memory', London: John Snow, 1864.

Arengo-Jones, Peter, *Queen Victoria in Switzerland*, London: Hale, 1995.

Bailey, John, ed., *Diary of Lady Frederick Cavendish*, 2 vols, London: John Murray, 1927.

Bennett, Daphne, *King without a Crown*, London: Heinemann, 1977.

Benson, A. C. and Viscount Esher, eds, *The Letters of Queen Victoria, 1837–61*, 1st series, 3 vols, London: John Murray, 1911.

Bolitho, Hector, *Albert, the Good*, London: Cobden-Sanderson, 1932 [revised in 1970 as *Albert, Prince Consort*].

—— *The Prince Consort and his Brother: Two Hundred New Letters*, London: Cobden-Sanderson, 1933.

—— *Victoria and Albert*, London: Cobden-Sanderson, 1938.

—— *Further Letters of Queen Victoria from the Archives of the House of Brandenburg-Prussia*, London: Thornton Butterworth, 1938.

Buckle, George Earl, ed., *Letters of Queen Victoria 1862–85*, 2nd series, 3 vols, London: John Murray, 1926–8.

Connell, Brian, *Regina v. Palmerston: The Correspondence between Queen Victoria and her Foreign and Prime Minister*, London: Evans Brothers, 1962.

Corti, Egon, *The English Empress*, London: Cassell & Co., 1957.

Downer, Martin, *The Queen's Knight*, London: Bantam Press, 2007.

Erskine, Mrs Stewart, ed., *Twenty Years at Court: From the Correspondence of the Hon. Eleanor Stanley*, London: Nisbet & Co., 1916.

Fulford, Roger, *Dearest Child: Letters Between Queen Victoria and the Princess Royal, 1858–61*, London: Evans Brothers, 1964.

—— *Dearest Mama: Letters between Queen Victoria and the Crown Princes of Prussia, 1861–64*, London: Evans Brothers, 1968.

—— *Your Dear Letter: Private Correspondence of Queen Victoria and the Crown Princess of Prussia, 1863–71*, London: Evans Brothers, 1971.

—— *Darling Child: Private Correspondence of Queen Victoria and the German Crown Princess, 1871–78*, London: Evans Brothers, 1976.

—— *Beloved Mama: Private Correspondence of Queen Victoria and the German Crown Princess, 1878–85*, London: Evans Brothers, 1981.

Grey, Hon. Charles, *The Early Years of HRH The Prince Consort*, London: Smith, Elder & Co., 1867.

Helps, Arthur, ed., *The Principal Speeches and Addresses of HRH The Prince Consort*, London: John Murray, 1862.

Hibbert, Christopher, *Queen Victoria in Her Letters and Journals*, London: Viking, 1984.

Hobhouse, Hermione, *Prince Albert: His Life and Work*, London: Hamish Hamilton, 1983.

Hough, Richard, *Advice to a Grand-daughter: Letters from Queen Victoria to Princess Victoria of Hesse*, London: Heinemann, 1975.

Jagow, Kurt, *Letters of the Prince Consort, 1831–1861*, London: John Murray, 1938.

James, Robert Rhodes, *Albert Prince Consort: A Biography*, London: Hamish Hamilton, 1983.

Kime, William Thomas, ed., *Albert the Good: A Nation's Tribute of Affection to the Memory of a Truly Virtuous Prince*, London: J. F. Shaw & Co., 1862.

Longford, Elizabeth, *Victoria RI*, London: Weidenfeld & Nicolson, 1998 [1964].

—— ed., *Darling Loosy: Letters to Princess Louise, 1856–1939*, London: Weidenfeld & Nicolson, 1991.

Lorne, Marquis of, *VRI: Her Life and Empire*, London: Eyre and Spottiswood, 1901.

Martin, Sir Theodore, *The Life of HRH The Prince Consort*, 5 vols, London: Smith, Elder & Co., 1875–80.

—— *Queen Victoria as I Knew Her*, Edinburgh: William Blackwood & Son, 1908.

Pound, Reginald, *Albert: A Biography of the Prince Consort*, London: Michael Joseph, 1973.

Rappaport, Helen, *Queen Victoria: A Biographical Companion*, Santa Barbara: ABC-Clio, 2003.

Sell, Karl, ed., *Alice Grand Duchess of Hesse, Princess of Great Britain and Ireland, Biographical Sketch and Letters*, London: John Murray, 1884.

'Services Held in Windsor Castle on the Anniversary of the Lamented Death of the Prince Consort', London: privately printed, 1862.

Sheppard, Edgar, *HRH George, Duke of Cambridge, A Memoir*, vol. I 1819–1871, London: Longman's, Green & Co., 1906.

Victoria, Queen of Great Britain, *Leaves from the Journal of Our Life in the Highlands from 1848–1861*, ed. Arthur Helps, London: Smith, Elder, 1868.

Wake, Jehanne, *Princess Louise: Queen Victoria's Unconventional Daughter*, London: Collins, 1988.

Walford, Edward, *The Life of the Prince Consort*, London: Routledge, Warne & Routledge, 1862.

Weintraub, Stanley, *Victoria, Biography of a Queen*, London: Unwin Hyman, 1987.

—— *Albert, Uncrowned King*, London: John Murray, 1997.

Windsor, Dean of and Hector Bolitho, eds, *Letters of Lady Augusta Stanley: A Young Lady at Court 1849–1863*, London: Gerald Howe, 1927.

—— *Later Letters of Lady Augusta Stanley 1864–1876*, London: Jonathan Cape, 1929.

Woodham Smith, Cecil, *Queen Victoria: Her Life and Times*, vol. 1, 1819–1861, London: Hamish Hamilton, 1972.

Wyndham, Hon. Mrs Hugh, ed., *Correspondence of Sarah Spencer, Lady Lyttleton 1787–1870*, London: John Murray, 1912.

Secondary Published Sources

Airplay, F. (pseud.), 'Prince Albert, Why is He Unpopular?', London: Saunders & Otley, 1856.

Albert, Harold, *The Life and Letters of Princess Feodore: Queen Victoria's Sister*, London: Robert Hale, 1967.

Allan, Oswald, 'Worthy a Crown?', London: Head & Meek, 1876.

—— 'The Vacant Throne', London: E. Head, 1877.

Ames, Winslow, *Prince Albert and Victorian Taste*, London: Chapman & Hall, 1967.

Anon., *The Private Life of Queen Victoria: By One of Her Majesty's Servants*, London: C. Arthur Pearson, 1897.

Argyll, George Douglas Campbell, Duke of, *Autobiography and Memoirs*, vol. 2, London: John Murray, 1906.

Aronson, Theo, *Grandmama of Europe: The Crowned Descendants of Queen Victoria*, London: Cassell, 1973.

Ashwell, Arthur Rawton, ed., *Life of the Right Reverend Samuel Wilberforce*, 3 vols, London: John Murray, 1880–2.

—— and Reginald Garton, *The Life of Bishop Wilberforce*, London: John Murray, 1881.

Aston, Sir George, *HRH The Duke of Connaught and Strathearn*, 2 vols, London: George C. Harrap, 1929.

Auchinloss, Louis, *Persons of Consequence: Queen Victoria and her Circle*, London: Weidenfeld & Nicolson, 1979.

Ball, T. Frederick, *Queen Victoria: Scenes and Incidents of her Life and Reign*, London: S. W. Partridge, 1886.

Battiscombe, Georgina, 'Gerald Wellesley: A Victorian Dean and Domestic Chaplain', in 'St George's Chapel Annual Report to 31st December', 1963.

—— *Queen Alexandra*, London: Constable, 1969.

Bayley, Stephen, *The Albert Memorial*, London: Scholar Press, 1981.

Bell, George Kennedy, *Randall Davidson, Archbishop of Canterbury*, London: Oxford University Press, 1952.

Bellows, John, 'Remarks by J. Bellows on Certain Anonymous Articles Designed to Render Queen Victoria Unpopular', Gloucester, 1864.

Bennett, Daphne, *Queen Victoria's Children*, London: Gollancz, 1980.

Benson, E. F., *As We Were: A Victorian Peep-Show*, London: Longman's, Green & Co., 1930.

—— *Queen Victoria*, London: Longman's, Green & Co., 1935.

Bolitho, Hector, *Victoria the Widow and Her Son*, London: Cobden-Sanderson, 1934.

—— *Victoria and Albert*, London: Cobden-Sanderson, 1938.

—— *Romance of Windsor Castle*, London: Evans Brothers, 1948.

—— *The Reign of Queen Victoria*, London: Collins, 1949.

—— *A Biographer's Notebook*, London: Longman's, Green & Co., 1950.

Branks, William, *Heaven our home, or Memorials of Sarah Craven, gathered chiefly from her own letters*, London: Wertheim, Mackintosh & Hunt, 1859.

Brown, Raymond Lamont, *John Brown: Queen Victoria's Highland Servant*, Stroud: Sutton, 2000.

—— *Royal Poxes and Potions: The Lives of the Court Physicians, Surgeons and Apothecaries*, Stroud: Sutton, 2001.

Bullock, Rev. Charles, *The Home Life of the Prince Consort*, London: 'Home Words' Publishing Office, 1861.

—— *The Queen's Resolve 'I Will Be Good': with Royal Anecdotes and Incidents*, London: 'Home Words' Publishing Office, 1887.

Cannadine, David, The Context, Performance and Meaning of Ritual: The British Monarchy and the Invention of Tradition, c. 1820–1977 in Eric Hobsbawm and Terence Ranger, eds, *The Invention of Tradition*, Cambridge: Cambridge University Press, 1983.

Cartwright, Julia, ed., *The Journals of Lady Knightley of Fawsley (1856–1884)*, London: John Murray, 1915.

Chaple, J. A. V., and Pollard, Arthur, *Letters of Mrs Gaskell*, Manchester: Manchester University Press, 1966.

Charlot, Monica, *Victoria, the Young Queen*, Oxford: Blackwell, 1991.

Chomet, S., *Helena, A Princess Reclaimed*, New York: Begell House, 1999.

Clark, John Willis, ed., *Life, Letters and Journals of Sir Charles Lyell*, vol. 2, London: John Murray, 1881.

Cook, Edward, *Delane of the Times*, London: Constable, 1915.

Cooke, Clement K., *Memoir of HRH Princess Mary Adelaide, Duchess of Teck*, 2 vols, London: John Murray, 1900.

Cowley, H. R. C., Duke of Wellington, *The Paris Embassy During the Second Empire*, London: T. Butterworth, 1928.

Craik, D. M., *Fifty Golden Years: Incidents in the Queen's Reign*. London: n.p., 1887.

Crawford, Emily, *Victoria, Queen and Ruler*, London: Simpkin, Marshall, 1903.

Creaton, Heather, *Victorian Diaries, The Daily Lives of Victorian Men and Women* London: Mitchell Beazley, 2001.

—— *Unpublished London Diaries*, London: London Record Society, 2003.

Creston Dormer, *The Youthful Queen Victoria: A Discursive Account*, London: Macmillan, 1952.

Cullen, Tom, *The Empress Brown: The Story of a Royal Friendship*, London: Bodley Head, 1969.

Dafforne, James, *The Albert Memorial Hyde Park: Its History and Description*, London: Virtue & Co., 1877.

Darby, Elisabeth and Nicola Smith, *The Cult of the Prince Consort*, New Haven: Yale University Press, 1983.

Dasent, Arthur, *John Thadeus Delane, Editor of 'The Times': His Life and Correspondence*, vol. 2, London: John Murray, 1908.

De-La-Noy, Michael, *Windsor Castle: Past and Present*, London: Headline, 1990.

Dennison, Matthew, *The Last Princess: The Devoted Life of Queen Victoria's Youngest Daughter*, London: Weidenfeld & Nicolson, 2007.

Dimond, Frances, and Taylor, Roger, *Crown and Camera: The Royal Family and Photography*, Harmondsworth: Penguin, 1987.

Duff, David, *The Life Story of HRH Princess Louise, Duchess of Argyll*, Bath: Cedric Chivers, 1940.

—— *The Shy Princess: The Life of HRH Princess Beatrice*, London: Evans Brothers, 1958.

—— *Hessian Tapestry*, London: Macmillan, 1967.

—— *Victoria Travels: Journeys of Queen Victoria between 1830 and 1900*, London: Frederick Muller, 1970.

—— *Albert & Victoria*, London: Tandem, 1972.

—— , ed., *Queen Victoria's Highland Journals*, London: Webb and Bower, 1980.

Dyson, Hope and Tennyson, Charles, eds, *Dear and Honoured Lady: The Correspondence between Queen Victoria and Alfred, Lord Tennyson*, London: Macmillan, 1969.

Ellis, S. M., *A Mid Victorian Pepys: The Letters and Memoirs of Sir William Hardman*, London: Cecil Palmer, 1923.

Elvey, Lady Mary Savory, *Life and Reminiscences of Sir George Elvey*, London: Sampson, Low, Marston, 1894.

Emden, Paul, *Behind the Throne*, London: Hodder & Stoughton, 1934.

Epton, Nina, *Victoria and Her Daughters*, London: Weidenfeld & Nicolson, 1971.

Eyck, Frank, *The Prince Consort: A Political Biography*, Bath: Cedric Chivers, 1975.

Frankland, Noble, *Witness of a Century: the Life and Times of Prince Arthur Duke of Connaught 1850–1942*, London: Shepheard-Walwyn, 1993.

Fulford, Roger, ed., *The Greville Memoirs*, London: B. T. Batsford, 1963.

—— *The Prince Consort*, London: Macmillan, 1966.

Gardiner, A. G., *The Life of Sir William Harcourt*, 2 vols, London: Constable & Co., 1923.

Gavard, Charles, *A Diplomat in London: Letters and Notes 1871–77*, New York: Henry Holt & Co., 1897.

Gernsheim, Helmut and Gernsheim, Alison, *Queen Victoria: A Biography in Word and Picture*, London: Longman's, Green & Co., 1959.

Girouard, Mark, *The Return to Camelot: Chivalry and the English Gentleman*, New Haven: Yale University Press, 1981.

—— *Windsor, the Most Romantic Castle*, London: Hodder & Stoughton, 1993.

Guedalla, Phillip, ed., *The Queen and Mr Gladstone, 1845–1898*, vol. 1, 1845–1879, London: Hodder & Stoughton, 1933.

Handley, C. S., *An Annotated Bibliography of Diaries Printed in English*, 4 vols, Aldeburgh: Hanover Press, 1997.

Hardie, Frank, *The Political Influence of Queen Victoria 1861–1901*, London: Oxford University Press, 1938.

Hedley, Owen, *Windsor Castle*, London: Robert Hale, 1967.

Helps, Edmund A., ed., *The Correspondence of Sir Arthur Helps*, London: John Lane, 1917.

Hewett, Osbert, ed., '. . . and Mr Fortescue': A selection of the diaries from 1851 to 1862 of Chichester Fortescue, Lord Carlingford*, London: John Murray, 1958.

Hibbert, Christopher, *The Court at Windsor: A Domestic History*, London: Longman's, Green & Co., 1964.

—— *Edward VII: A Portrait*, London: Allen Lane, 1976.

—— *Victoria: A Personal History*, London: HarperCollins, 2000.

Holland, Caroline, *Notebooks of a Spinster Lady*, London: Cassell & Co., 1919.

Homans, Margaret, *Royal Representations: Queen Victoria and British Culture 1837–1876*, Chicago: University of Chicago Press, 1998.

—— and Munich, Adrienne, *Remaking Queen Victoria*, Cambridge: Cambridge University Press, 1997.

Hough, Richard, *Victoria and Albert: Their Love and Their Tragedies*, London: Richard Cohen, 1996.

House, Madeline and Storey, Graham, eds, *The Letters of Charles Dickens*, vol. 9, 1859–1861, and vol. 10, 1862–1864, Oxford: Clarendon Press, 1998.

'How the Christmas Tree Came to England', *The Times*, 22 December 1958.

Hudson, Derek, *Munby: Man of Two Worlds*, London: Abacus, 1974.

Jackman, S. W. and Haasse, Hella, eds, *Stranger in the House: Letters of Queen Sophie of the Netherlands to Lady Malet, 1842–1877*, London: Duke University Press, 1989.

Jerrold, Clare, *The Heart of Queen Victoria: True Anecdotes of Her Majesty's Life*, London: Jarrold, 1897.

—— *The Married Life of Queen Victoria*, London: Eveleigh Nash, 1913.

—— *The Widowhood of Queen Victoria*, London, Eveleigh Nash, 1916.

Kennedy, A. L., *My Dear Duchess: Social and Political Letters to the Duchess of Manchester 1858–1869*, London: John Murray, 1956.

Kenyon, Edith C., *Scenes in the Life of the Princess Alice (Grand Duchess of Hesse)*, London: W. Nicholson & Sons, 1887.

—— *Scenes in the Life of the Royal Family*, London: W. Nicholson & Sons, 1887.

Kharibian, Leah, *Passionate Patrons: Victoria & Albert and the Arts*, London: Royal Collection Publications, 2010.

Kiste, John van Der, *Sons, Servants and Statesmen: The Men in Queen Victoria's Life*, Stroud: Sutton, 2006.

Kuhn, William M., 'Ceremony and Politics: The British Monarchy 1871–2', *Journal of British Studies*, vol. 26, 1987, pp. 133–62.

—— *Democratic Royalism: The Transformation of the British Monarchy, 1861–1914*, Basingstoke: Macmillan, 1996.

—— *Henry and Mary Ponsonby*, London: Duckworth, 2002.

Lant, J. L., *Insubstantial Pageant: Ceremony and Confusion at Queen Victoria's Court*, London: Hamish Hamilton, 1979.

Lee, Sydney, *Queen Victoria, A Biography*, London: Smith, Elder & Co., 1904.

'Letter to the Queen on Her Retirement from Public Life', by one of Her Majesty's most loyal subjects, London: Samuel Tinsely, 1875.

Lindsay, W. A., *The Royal Household*, London: K. Paul, Trench, Trübner & Co., 1898.

Loewe, Louis, ed., *Diaries of Sir Moses and Lady Montefiore*, vol. 2, London: Griffith Farran Okeden & Welsh, 1890.

Longford, Elizabeth, 'Queen Victoria's Doctors', in Martin Gilbert, ed., *A Century of Conflict 1850–1950*, London: Hamish Hamilton, 1966.

—— *The Pebbled Shore: The Memoirs of Elizabeth Longford*, Stroud: Sutton, 2004.

McClintock, Mary Howard, *The Queen Thanks Sir Howard*, London: John Murray, 1945.

Macleod, Donald, *Memoir of Dr Norman Macleod*, vol. 2, London: Belford Brothers, 1876.

Magnus, Philip, *Gladstone: A Biography*, London: John Murray, 1963.

—— *King Edward the Seventh*, London: John Murray, 1964.

Mallet, Victor, ed., *Life with Queen Victoria: Marie Mallet's Letters from Court, 1887–1901*, London: John Murray, 1968.

Malmesbury, Lord, *Memoirs of an Ex-Minister*, 2 vols, London: Longman's, Green & Co., 1884.

Marie Louise, Princess, *My Memories of Six Reigns*, Harmondsworth: Penguin, 1961.

Maxwell, Sir Herbert, ed., *Life and Letters of the 4th Earl of Clarendon*, 2 vols, London: Arnold, 1913.

Millar, Delia, *Queen Victoria's Life in the Scottish Highlands*, London: Philip Wilson Publishers, 1985.

Moneypenny, William F. and Buckle, G. E., eds, *The Life of Benjamin Disraeli, Earl of Beaconsfield*, London: Smith, Elder & Co, 1910–20.

Morris, Frankie, 'The Illustrated Press and the Republican Crisis of 1871–1872', *Victorian Periodicals Review*, vol. 25, Fall 1992, pp. 114–26.

Munich, Adrienne, *Queen Victoria's Secrets*, New York: Columbia University Press, 1996.

Nevill, Barry St John, *Life at the Court of Queen Victoria: Selections from the Journals of Queen Victoria*, Stroud: Sutton, 1997.

Nevill, Lady Dorothy, *Under Five Reigns*, London: Methuen, 1910.

Nicholls, David, *The Lost Prime Minister: A Life of Sir Charles Dilke*, London: Hambledon Press, 1995.

Noel, Gerald, *Princess Alice: Queen Victoria's Forgotten Daughter*, London: Constable, 1974.

O'Brien, D. P., ed., *Correspondence of Lord Overstone*, vol. 2, Cambridge: Cambridge University Press, 1971.

Packard, Jerrold, *Victoria's Daughters*, New York: St Martin's Press, 1998.

Paget, Lady Walburga, *Embassies of Other Days*, vol. I, London: Hutchinson, 1923.

Pakula, Hannah, *An Uncommon Woman: The Empress Frederick, daughter of Queen Victoria*, London: Weidenfeld & Nicolson, 1996.

Ponsonby, Arthur, *Henry Ponsonby, Queen Victoria's Private Secretary: His Life from his Letters*, London: Macmillan, 1942.

Ponsonby, Frederick, *Side Lights on Queen Victoria*, London: Macmillan, 1930.

—— *Recollections of Three Reigns*, London: Eyre & Spottiswoode, 1951.

Ponsonby, Magdalen, ed., *Mary Ponsonby: A Memoir, Some Letters and a Journal*, London: John Murray, 1927.

Protheroe, Rowland E., *Life and Letters of Dean Stanley*, London: Thomas Nelson, 1893.

Purves, John, ed., *Letters from the Cape – Lady Duff Gordon*, London: H. Milford, 1921.

Ramm, Agatha, *The Gladstone–Granville Correspondence*, Cambridge: Cambridge University Press, 1998.

Rappaport, Helen, *Queen Victoria: A Biographical Companion*, 2 vols, Santa Barbara: ABC-Clio, 2003.

Reid, Stuart J., ed., *Memoirs of Sir Wemyss Reid 1842–1885*, London: Cassell & Co., 1885.

Reid, T. Wemyss, ed., *Memoirs and Correspondence of Lyon Playfair*, London: Cassell, 1899.

Reynolds, K. D., *Aristocratic Women and Political Society in Victorian Britain*, Oxford: Clarendon Press, 1998.

Richardson, Joanna, *Victoria and Albert: A Study of a Marriage*, London: Dent, 1977.

Rickman, John Godlee, *Lord Lister*, Oxford: Clarendon Press, 1924.

Ricks, Christopher, ed., *The Poems of Tennyson*, vols 2 and 3, London: Longman's, 1987.

Robbins, Michael, 'The Missing Doctor: An "if" of Victorian history', *Journal of the Royal Society of Medicine*, vol. 90, March 1997, pp. 163–5.

Russell, Bertrand and Russell, Patricia, eds, *The Amberley Papers: Diaries and Letters of Lord and Lady Amberley*, 2 vols, London: Hogarth Press, 1937.

Russell, William Howard, *My Diary: North and South*, vol. 1, London: Bradbury & Evans, 1863.

St Aubyn, Giles, *Queen Victoria: A Portrait*, London: Sinclair Stevenson, 1991.

Sala, George Augustus, *Life and Adventures*, vol. 1, London: Cassell & Co., 1895.

Sanders, Valerie, ed., *Harriet Martineau: Selected Letters*, Oxford: Clarendon Press, 1990.

Scott, Gilbert, *Personal and Professional Recollections*, Stamford: Paul Watkins, 1995.

Smith, G. Barnett, *The Life of Her Majesty Queen Victoria: Compiled from All Available Sources*, London: G. Routledge, 1887.

Smith, J. F. and Howitt, W., eds, *John Cassell's Illustrated History of England*, vol. 8, London: W. Kent & Co., 1864.

Stockmar, Ernest et al., *Memoirs of Baron Stockmar*, vol. 1, London: Longman's, Green & Co., 1873.

Stoney, Benita and Weltzien Heinrich C., eds, *My Mistress the Queen: The Letters of Frieda Arnold, Dresser to Queen Victoria 1854–9*, London: Weidenfeld & Nicolson, 1994.

Strachey, Lytton, *Queen Victoria*, Harmondsworth: Penguin, 1971 [1921].

Strafford, Alice, Countess of, ed., *Leaves from the Diary of Henry Greville*, London: Smith Elder & Co., 3rd series [1857–61] 1904 and 4th series [1862–72] 1905.

Thompson, Dorothy, *Queen Victoria: Gender and Power*, London: Virago Press, 2001.

Tinling, James Forbes, *Lessons from the Life and Death of the Princess Alice*, London: S. Bagster & Sons, 1879.

Tisdall, E. E. P., *Queen Victoria's John Brown*, London: Stanley Paul, 1938.

—— *Restless Consort: The Invasion of Albert the Conqueror*, London: Stanley Paul, 1952.
   Unpredictable Queen: The Intimate Life of Queen Alexandra, London: Stanley Paul, 1953.

—— *Queen Victoria's Private Life*, London: Jarrolds, 1961.

Tooley, Sarah, *Personal Life of Queen Victoria*, London: Hodder & Stoughton, 1896.

Tyack, Geoffrey, 'The Albert Memorial', in *Victorian Studies*, vol. 44, no. 2, Winter 2002, pp. 293–5.

Underwood, Peter, *Queen Victoria's Other World*, London: Harrap, 1982.

Van Der Kiste, John, *Queen Victoria's Children*, Stroud: Sutton, 2003.

Villiers, George, *A Vanished Victorian, Being the Life of George Villiers, 4th Earl of Clarendon 1800–1870*, London: Eyre & Spottiswoode, 1938.

Vincent, John, ed., *Disraeli, Derby and the Conservative Party: The Journals and Memoirs of Edward Henry, Lord Stanley*, Hassocks: Harvester Press, 1978.

Wallace, Sarah Agnes, ed., *The Journal of Benjamin Moran 1857–1865*, vol. 2, Chicago: University of Chicago Press, 1949.

Walsh, Walter, *The Religious Life and Influence of Queen Victoria*, London: Swann Sonnenschein, 1902.

Warwick, Frances, Countess of, *Afterthoughts*, London: Cassell, 1931.

Watson, Vera, *A Queen at Home: An Intimate Account of the Social and Domestic Life at Queen Victoria's, Court*, London: W. H. Allen, 1952.

Weibe, Mel et al., eds, *Benjamin Disraeli Letters*, vol. 8, 1860–1864, Toronto: University of Toronto Press, 2009.

Weintraub, Stanley, *Victoria*, London: John Murray, 1996.

Wheatcroft, Andrew, *The Tennyson Album: A Biography in Original Photographs*, London: Routledge & Kegan Paul, 1980.

'Where the Prince Consort Died', *The Times*, 13 December 1961.

Whittle, Tyler, *Victoria and Albert at Home*, London: Routledge & Kegan Paul, 1980.

Williams, Richard, *Contentious Crown: Public Discussions of the British Monarchy in the Reign of Queen Victoria*, Aldershot: Ashgate, 1997.

Wilson, Robert, *The Life and Times of Queen Victoria*, 2 vols, London: Cassell & Co., 1891–3.

Wrench, G. T., *Lord Lister, His Life and Work*, London: Unwin, 1913.

Zeepvat, Charlotte, *Prince Leopold: The Untold Story of Queen Victoria's Youngest Son*, Stroud: Sutton, 1998.

Sources for grief and bereavement, mourning dress and jewellery

Adburgham, Alison, *Shops and Shopping 1800–1914*, London: Barrie & Jenkins, 1989.

Arnold, Catharine, *Necropolis: London and Its Dead*, London: Simon & Schuster, 2006.

Behrendt, Stephen C., *Royal Mourning and Regency Culture: Elegies and Memorials of Princess Charlotte*, Basingstoke: Macmillan, 1997.

Bland, Olivia, *The Royal Way of Death*, London: Constable, 1986.

Bower, J. A., 'Whitby Jet and its Manufacture', *Journal of the Society of Arts*, vol. 22, 19 December 1873, pp. 80–7.

Bowlby, Richard, *Attachment and Loss*, Harmondsworth: Penguin, 1991.

Cooper, Diana and Battershill, Norman, *Victorian Sentimental Jewellery*, Newton Abbott: David & Charles, 1972.

Curl, James, *The Victorian Celebration of Death*, Stroud: Sutton, 2000.

Dawes, Ginny Redington, *Victorian Jewelry*, Ann Arbor: University of Michigan Press, 1991.

'Fashions for January', *Illustrated London News*, 28 December 1861.

Freud, Sigmund, 'Mourning and Melancholia', in *The Future of an Illusion*, London: Penguin, 2008.

Garlick, Harry, *The Final Curtain: State Funerals and the Theatre of Power*, Amsterdam: Editions Rodopi B.V., 1999.

Gere, Charlotte and Rudoe, Judy, *Jewellery in the Age of Queen Victoria*, London: British Museum Press, 2010.

Goldthorp, Caroline, *From Queen to Empress: Victorian Dress 1837–1877*, New York: Metropolitan Museum of Art, 1989.

Hayden, Ilse, *Symbol and Privilege: The Ritual Context of British Royalty*, Tucson: University of Arizona Press, 1987.

Jalland, Pat, *Death in the Victorian Family*, Oxford: Oxford University Press, 1996.

Kendall, Hugh P., *The Story of Whitby Jet: Its Workers from Earliest Times*, Whitby: Whitby Literary & Philosophical Society, 1988.

King, Melanie, *The Dying Game*, Oxford: Oneworld, 2008.

Kontou, Tatiana, *Spiritualism and Women's Writing from Fin de Siecle to the Neo-Victorians*, Basingstoke: Palgrave, 2009.

Kübler-Ross, Elizabeth, *On Death and Dying*, London: Tavistock Publications, 1970.

Luthi, Ann Louise, *Sentimental Jewellery*, Princes Risborough: Shire, 1998.

McMillan, Mabel, *Whitby Jet through the Years*, Whitby: privately published, 1992.

Morley, John, *Death, Heaven and the Victorians*, London: Studio Vista, 1971.

Muller, Helen, *Jet Jewellery and Ornaments*, Aylesbury: Shire Publications, 1980.

—— and Muller, Katy, *Whitby Jet*, Oxford: Shire Publications, 2009.

Parkes, Colin Murray, *Bereavement: Studies in Grief in Adult Life*, London: Penguin, 1996.

—— *Love and Loss: The Roots of Grief and Its Complications*, London: Routledge, 2006.

—— and Hinde, Joan Stevenson, *The Place of Attachment in Human Behaviour*, London: Tavistock Publications, 1982.

—— and Weiss, Robert S., *Recovery from Bereavement*, New York: Basic Books, 1983.

Powles, William E. and Alexander, Mary G., 'Was Queen Victoria Depressed?', *Canadian Journal of Psychiatry*, vol. 32, February 1987, pp. 14–19.

Puckle, Bertram S., *Funeral Customs: Their Origin and Development*, London: T. Werner Laurie Ltd, 1926.

Ramchandani, Dilip, 'Pathological Grief: Two Victorian Case Studies', *Psychiatric Quarterly*, vol. 67, no. 1, Spring 1996, pp. 75–84.

Schor, Esther, *Bearing the Dead: The British Culture of Mourning from the Enlightenment to Victoria*, Princeton: Princeton University Press, 1994.

Staniland, Kay, *In Royal Fashion: The Clothes of Princess Charlotte of Wales and Queen Victoria, 1796–1901*, London: Museum of London, 1997.

Taylor, Lou, *Mourning Dress – A Costume and Social History*, London: Allen & Unwin, 1983.

Walter, Tony, 'Royalty and Public Grief in England', in Tony Walter, *The Mourning for Diana*, Oxford: Berg, 1999.

Whaley, Joachim, ed., *Mirrors of Mortality: Studies in the Social History of Death*, London: Europa Publications, 1981.

Wheeler, Michael, *Heaven, Hell and the Victorians*, Cambridge: Cambridge University Press, 1994.

Wolffe, John, *Great Deaths: Grieving, Religion and Nationhood in Victorian and Edwardian Britain*, Oxford: Oxford University Press, 2000.

Index

gradually emerges into her public
role, 233

becomes Empress of India, 233

celebrates Golden and Diamond
Jubilees, 233

continues to wear widow's weeds,
234

and deaths and mourning, 234–6,
247–8

public view of, 236–7

and her extended family, 237

frequent visits to mausoleum, 238

and Martin's *Life of the Prince Consort*, 240

and the role of the monarch, 240–2

difficulties in relationship with
Alice, 243

and Alice's illness, 245–6

and Alice's death, 246, 247

journal entry for New Year's Eve
1878, 247

Victoria, Princess Royal *see* Vicky
(Victoria), Princess Royal, Crown
Princess of Prussia

Victoria, Princess of Hesse, 166, 245

Victoria and Albert Museum (South
Kensington Museum), 138, 139, 238

Victoria Cross, 25

Victorian Society, 240

Victory, 89

Vitzthum, Count, 117

Wagner, Richard, 22

Wales, 43

Walter, John, 72

Washington, 104, 124

Watson, Dr Thomas, 66–7, 69, 70, 71,
76, 81, 255

Weintraub, Stanley, 256–7

Weiss, Sophie, 83

Wellesley, Gerald, Dean of Windsor,
81, 112, 113, 140, 197–8, 202, 207

Wellington, Elizabeth Duchess of,
101, 111, 132

Wellington, Arthur Wellesley, 1st
Duke of, 23, 37, 105–6, 107, 137, 151

Wells, Mrs Sarah (mother of H.G.
Wells), 236

West End, 155

West London synagogue, 116

Westminster Abbey, 162, 226

Westmorland, Lady, 164

Weyer, Madame Elizabeth Van De, 184

Weyer, Sylvain Van De, 111, 142

Whigs, 19

Whitby Gazette, 175

Whitby jet trade, 150–1

White House (on Beaumont Estate),
100

White House (America), 124

Whitley, 87

Wied, Princess of, 167

Wilberforce, Samuel, Bishop of Oxford, 88, 114, 159

Wilhelm, Prince of Prussia, (son of
Vicky), 163

Wilhelm Friedrich (Frittie), Prince of
Hesse, 244, 247

William I, Emperor of Germany, 247

William IV, King, 65, 98, 106, 114

Wills, W.H., 89

Windsor (town), 1, 53, 55, 78, 89, 102,
110, 162, 174, 189, 249–50

Windsor, Dean of *see* Wellesley, Gerald, Dean of Windsor

Windsor, Mayor of, 108–9

Windsor Castle

honeymoon of V and Albert at, 17

royal collection of art at, 22

Christmas 1860 at, 1–9

mourning for Duchess of Kent at,
38

funeral of Duchess of Kent, 39

V reluctantly returns from Balmoral to, 45

Bertie's birthday celebration at, 47

Albert returns from Sandhurst to,
51

ROSANNA LEY

Return to Mandalay

Quercus

First published in Great Britain in 2014 by
Quercus Editions Ltd
55 Baker Street
7th Floor, South Block
London W1U 8EW

A CIP catalogue record for this book is available
from the British Library

PB ISBN 978 1 78206 762 7
EBOOK ISBN 978 1 78206 763 4

10 9 8 7 6 5 4 3 2 1

Printed and bound in Great Britain by Clays Ltd, St Ives plc

Typeset by Ellipsis Digital Limited, Glasgow

For Grey, with love.

And in memory of Peter Innes, John Sams
and all the men who fought in Burma.
Never forgotten.

CHAPTER I

'Could you come through to the office, Eva?' Jacqui Dryden's voice was, as always, cool and slightly irritated.

Eva was stooping over a Victorian dressing-table repairing the spring mechanism of a tiny drawer in the panelling. She straightened up. Ouch. Rubbed her back with the heel of her hand. It was a delicate job and she hadn't realised quite how long she'd been stuck in that position.

'Just coming,' she called back. Briefly, she touched the top of the walnut dressing-table with her fingertips as if promising her swift return.

Jacqui Dryden was standing staring out of the large bay window into the street below. It was a Thursday afternoon in late October and Bristol city centre was as busy as ever. The Bristol Antiques Emporium was well placed in a side street where rents were lower but there were still enough individual-looking shops to pull in passers-by. Vintage was in, business was brisk and Eva's boss should have been happy. She looked anything but. Her make-up was as flawless as ever, but there was something despairing in her blue eyes that Eva hadn't seen there before. Could it be anything to do with the raised voices she'd heard coming from the office this morning?

'Come in.' Jacqui turned towards her, the despairing expression vanished and Eva felt her scrutiny. Her boss had this way. She was a little over five feet tall, blonde and perfectly formed, and when she was around her, Eva invariably felt awkward, clumsy, too tall. She wasn't used to feeling like that. She brushed some sawdust from her jeans. Her hands were dusty too and she realised she had a splinter in her thumb. She kept her nails clipped short because of the nature of the job and at work wore jeans, a T-shirt and a pair of old Converse, tying her unruly dark hair back in a ponytail so that it wouldn't get in the way. She could imagine how she looked to Jackie, could see what she was thinking. She wasn't at her most glamorous. But this was work and Eva relished immersing herself in it.

Jacqui didn't invite her to sit down, didn't so much as smile. Several times over the past few months, Eva had been tempted to tap on her boss's shell, try and make it crack a little and take a peek inside. But she hadn't risked it – at least, not yet.

'I need you to go away on an assignment,' Jacqui said without preamble.

'Away?' Eva echoed. That was a first. 'What kind of assignment?'

She had worked at the Emporium for six months now. The job had attracted her because the company dealt mainly in Asian antiques. Thanks to her grandfather, as a child she had fallen in love with wood and with history; they were in her blood. At nineteen, she had left home in Dorset – a home that had splintered to pieces after her father's death when Eva was only six – and gone to university in Bristol to study antique furniture restoration with decorative arts. Specialist subject: Asian artefacts. And that was thanks to her grandfather, too. That was sixteen years ago now. But there was still so much, Eva reminded herself, to thank him for.

Jacqui didn't answer the question. Her partner, Leon – in business and life – hadn't answered her questions in the office this morning either. 'Why should you care? Tell me what's going on,' Jacqui had demanded. 'Or I walk out of here this minute.' But Leon hadn't and so Jacqui had. She had stalked out of her office in her pencil skirt and stilettos right past where Eva was busy repairing the scabbard of an old Japanese sword and pretending she hadn't heard what was being said.

'As you know,' Jacqui said to Eva now, 'our Asian stock is selling very well at the moment.'

'Yes.' Of course, she had noticed. The company were expanding that side of the business and soon perhaps Victorian walnut dressing-tables would be a thing of the past, so to speak. Many countries were opening up more than ever before and those in the Far East were in a position to take advantage of growing international interest in their colonial furniture, a legacy of days gone by, and in their cultural and religious artefacts too. Like their old stone Buddhas, for example – and they'd seen a few of those in the Emporium – often so badly eroded that they'd no doubt had new ones made by some local stonemason. The Bristol Antiques Emporium hadn't wasted any time in forging lucrative partnerships with Far East traders who wanted to sell.

3

'But there are problems.' Jacqui tucked back a strand of fine blonde hair that had dared escape the fifties' chignon she favoured. 'Too much stock is arriving badly damaged, for a start.'

'Which could certainly be avoided,' Eva agreed. She was the person who generally had to repair it. She had joined the Emporium hoping to make use of the expertise she'd gained doing her degree. At last, she'd thought. It had been thirteen years since she'd graduated, but none of her jobs had quite fulfilled her expectations. She'd worked in a second-hand furniture shop for a man who specialised in cold-calling with the express purpose of parting old ladies from family heirlooms with as little money changing hands as possible, until Eva could almost feel his smug smile destroying her soul. She'd worked in a museum shop, where she'd met her friend Leanne. And she'd spent over a year as a seamstress in vintage wedding hire. This was the time – she'd hoped – for her career to take off in the direction she wanted it to.

But the reality of the Emporium had proved another disappointment. Most of her time was spent doing run-of-the-mill repairs, cleaning, unpacking and often dealing with customers too. They might have formed a lucrative partnership, but the Bristol Antiques Emporium was under-staffed. Apart from Jacqui and Leon, there was only Lydia, who worked part-time in the antiques showroom above. And Eva who did just about everything else.

'If we can find a way of avoiding it, yes.' Jacqui frowned.

'Can't our contacts check the packaging before shipping?' Eva asked mildly. Many of the countries they dealt with packaged the goods poorly – often only with shredded newspaper. They didn't seem to appreciate the vulnerability of some of the more fragile pieces.

'And . . .' Jacqui dismissed this suggestion with a wave of her manicured hand. 'Our contact has come across some unusual items we may be interested in.'

'Unusual items?' Eva's interest flared.

'Statuettes, wooden furniture, eighteenth and nineteenth century – even earlier, some of it. Unique, primitive, just the sort of thing we're looking for.' For a second her eyes brightened with enthusiasm. 'But . . .' She hesitated. 'I don't fully trust our contact there.' She glanced at Eva as if to gauge her reaction.

Eva shrugged. She didn't need to ask why not. Firstly, six months working for Jacqui Dryden had shown her that her boss rarely trusted anyone, probably not even Leon, come to think of it. And secondly, she was aware that many of their contacts in the Far East had their own agenda. Why should they feel loyalty to their overseas dealers? Why shouldn't they look out first for their own families, their own countries, when so many of them had lived in poverty for so long?

'The provenance sounds more than plausible,' Jacqui told her. 'But they need to be authenticated.'

'Oh, I see.' Eva felt the fizz of anticipation. This was why she'd joined the company. Authentication, restoration, re-living history almost. And travelling too. That was an unexpected bonus. After the month she'd had, it sounded exactly what she needed.

'You could do that, couldn't you?'

'Of course.' It was what she'd been trained for. And this trip would give her the chance to prove her skills.

Once again, Jacqui frowned. 'You wouldn't object to going on your own?'

'Not at all.' Eva preferred to work independently. And it would be an adventure. 'I presume that you also want me to talk to our contact?'

'Yes.' Jacqui shot her an unfathomable glance. 'You'll need to reinforce our relationship with him.' She seemed to be choosing her words carefully. 'But it will need sensitive handling.'

'I understand.'

'And while you're there, you might also get the chance to look around.' Jacqui was still speaking cautiously, as if she wasn't sure how much to say.

'Look around?' Eva wanted to be clear. She twisted the ring she wore on her little finger. It was a cluster of diamonds shaped like a daisy and set in gold, a present from her grandfather on her twenty-first birthday and she wore it every day, work or no work.

'Explore other avenues. Go to some antique markets, chat to the dealers, make new contacts perhaps. Find some more items we may be interested in.'

Goodness. The thrill returned. Eva tried to hide her surprise. With so much at stake, why wasn't Jacqui going herself?

She couldn't be trying to get rid of her, surely? She'd only overheard an argument – although the embarrassment of that might be enough for someone like her boss. She was rather touchy, perhaps more so than usual.

'I'll be busy here.' Jacqui moved from the window to the large leather-topped mahogany desk that dominated the room, and pushed a pile of papers to one side as if to demonstrate just how busy she would be. 'There are some important shipments due to arrive.' Once again, she seemed to almost lose her drift. And then snapped out of it. 'I couldn't possibly get away at the moment.'

Leon, Eva thought. That was the real reason.

'These people won't wait forever. There'll be others interested, you can be sure. So there's nothing for it.' Jacqui sighed. 'You'll have to go. You're the only one there is.'

Praise indeed. Eva raised an eyebrow. 'And where exactly am I going?'

'Oh.' Jacqui plucked a piece of paper from her desk. 'Didn't I say? You're to leave next week if we can get you a visa sorted out by then. I'll book your flight and let you know the exact times. You'll have to bring your passport in tomorrow morning. I'll arrange for an agent to meet you at the airport and make the hotel reservations. Um . . .' With the tip of her forefinger – nail varnished deep plum – she traced a path along the paper. 'Yangon, Bagan and Mandalay,' she said. 'That's where you'll be going. Ten days should be long enough. You'll have to take internal flights. I'll give you all the details in advance, of course.'

7

Eva stared at her. She hadn't even dared hope . . . 'Burma?' she whispered. Her heart was hammering out an old tune, a familiar tune, the rhythm one that she had grown up with, that had become a part of her. She was going to Burma. She had heard so much about it. And now she was going to taste and experience it for herself. She wanted to fling open the window and shout it to the people down in the street below. There was a grin of pure delight bubbling inside and she wanted to let it out.

'Yes. But it's called Myanmar now, you know.'

'I know.' The grin emerged and Eva sent it Jacqui's way. What did it matter that Jacqui sometimes didn't seem to like her or felt threatened by her or whatever else it might be? What did it matter, when her boss clearly trusted her enough to give her this opportunity? What did it matter when Eva was going to Burma? She closed her eyes and felt the colours of the country flicker behind her eyelids. Blue and gold . . .

There wasn't much, she thought, that she didn't know about Burma. Her grandfather had spent some of his most formative years there. He had worked in the timber industry and he had fought against the Japanese. His life in Burma had touched them all in different ways. And the stories he had told Eva when she was a child had wound their way into her heart.

'You'll go, then?' Jacqui asked her. Though she didn't look as if she'd take no for an answer. 'I've printed out images of some of the things you'll be looking at because it's easier to have hard copy to hand. It's all here.'

'Oh, yes, I'll go,' Eva replied. She'd always known she'd visit Burma one day. How could she not? In her twenties and early thirties, holidays had been short, usually city breaks in Europe, since they gave her the best opportunity to explore antique markets and historic buildings. And during her now rather distant gap year she'd made it to Thailand, along with Jess, her friend from college. Burma was an expensive trip to fund herself but more than that, for a long time, the country had been a no-go area politically. Eva had read about the unrest among the hill tribes, the repressive government, and the house arrest of Aung San Suu Kyi, the woman they all adored, who had sacrificed her personal life in order to fight for democracy for her people. Eva knew about the sanctions and that although tourists had become welcome in Myanmar, money from tourism tended to go straight into the pockets of the military government. And she understood that to visit the country was to support them.

But things were different now. Aung San Suu Kyi had been freed, the political climate was changing and . . . Eva's child-hood dream was about to come true.

Should she pinch herself to make sure she wasn't dreaming again? She moved closer to the desk. The image of a seated and clear-eyed Buddha, probably gilded teak, gazed serenely back at her. Nineteenth century, she'd estimate from the picture, which wasn't terribly clear. She peered closer, looking for tell-tale patches of wear on the gilding but she'd have to assess the condition more thoroughly when she was actually there. There were other figures she recognised from her studies too, some carved and painted, some gilded and inlaid, some possibly as old as seventeenth century. A delicately carved angel, a monk sitting on a lotus flower, spiritual guardians and nats. There was what looked like a carved teak scripture chest, an ancient wooden crib and a pair of highly decorative doors – most likely ancient temple doors, she realised with a jolt of excitement.

Eva glanced across at Jacqui and met her gaze head on. Jacqui would no doubt have more information about these artefacts and she'd be giving it all to Eva to study before she left. But her boss was right. From the pictures alone, she could see that there were some remarkable pieces here. And she was being given the chance to see them, examine them at close hand, authenticate them and bring them back to the UK.

'Thanks, Jacqui,' she said.

Her boss gave her a quizzical look.

'For having faith in me. I won't let you down.'

And she left the office and drifted back to the Victorian dressing-table, her mind already halfway to Burma. She could still hardly believe it. Would it live up to her expectations? Would it fill the gaps in her grandfather's story? And what on earth would he say when she told him? Going to Burma had changed his life. Eva couldn't help wondering if it would do the same to hers.

Eva let herself into her flat and closed the door behind her. It had been quite a day. What she needed, she decided, was a large glass of wine and a hot bath – and then she'd phone him. He was the person she most wanted to tell. But first things first. She opened her laptop, located her music file and selected an album. *Japancakes*. The soft lilting melody of the first track 'Double Jointed' began to float through the room, rippling like water lilies on a lake.

The flat – the first floor of an Edwardian building on the outskirts of the city, hence the high ceilings, decorative coving and large bay windows – was relatively tidy, although she'd left in a rush that morning. As always, it had a rather transitory look about it, as if Eva might be about to gather up all her belongings and move out. Which was probably, she decided, down to her state of mind. She had stayed in Bristol because this was where the jobs were, as far as the West Country was concerned. But it was more than that. Since she was six years old, she'd lived in a world where something you loved could be snatched away from you and nothing in your life would be the same again. She didn't exactly love her flat, but it was practical, reasonable to rent and it suited her, for the moment.

There was only one bedroom, which housed her Chinese 'opium' bed, bought on a whim from eBay and a purchase she'd never regretted; every time she laid her head on the pillow, she imagined its possibly lurid history. It never gave her nightmares though, instead it seemed to be seeped in relaxation. But the living-room-cum-kitchen was a space easily large enough for one. Or even two, Eva thought ruefully, as she hung her autumn tweedy jacket on a peg and chucked her bag on the sofa. The music was building, the melody becoming more layered. Max's minimalist flat had been smarter but had less floor space and character. A bit, she thought, like Max himself. Or so it had turned out.

Eva owned only a few pieces of special furniture, acquired over the past thirteen years. Apart from the bed and a sprawling sofa, there was a hand-carved and sturdy Chinese camphor-wood trunk in the bay window, with cushions it made a perfect window seat; a hand-painted mango-wood cabinet from Rajasthan on the far side of the room, bought at auction a few years ago to house her novels and reference books from uni and beside that, her favourite piece, a Meiji-period Japanese red lacquered priest's chair that had turned up out of the blue in the Emporium only a month ago. She owned nothing from Burma yet. It was still early days for the country, which made it all the more exciting from Eva's point of view. What might she come back with for her own collection?

There was a Japanese print on the wall, and the kitchen cupboards held a motley selection of china, some Oriental, some English bone, so thin that when you held it up to the light you could almost see right through. Max would never have moved in here, Eva reminded herself. Their styles didn't match. They didn't match. She'd been fooling herself for two years, that was all.

Max. She poured that glass of wine, took a sip and went to run her bath. The sounds of *Japancakes* followed her through the flat, rising and falling, the perfect chill out music. She'd met him in a cinema queue. Someone in front of her had trodden on her toe, she'd taken a little jump back and managed to throw toffee popcorn all over Max, who was standing right behind her. It had proved to be quite an ice breaker. He had suggested they sit together, it had seemed natural to go for a drink afterwards to discuss the film, and the rest, she thought grimly, was history.

And now they were history too. Eva turned the hot tap and swirled in a generous dollop of her favourite bath oil. She wanted to lie back, relax, sip her wine and think about going to Burma. What did it matter that she hadn't yet met a man she wanted to spend her life with? What did it matter that she had spent two years with Max before she discovered his other agenda? If she were honest . . . Max had turned her head from the start. He was older, charming, sophisticated. He had not only taken her out to shows, events and to all the latest restaurants for dinner, but he'd often surprised her with gifts of jewellery and even weekends in Paris and Rome. Which was all very nice. Eva fetched her wine and began to peel off her dusty work clothes, piece by piece. The steam from the bath was already filling the room. She turned the tap and added some cold. But it wasn't really love, was it? Part of her had always known that.

And in two years their relationship had barely moved on. She began to hum as the track changed to 'Heaven or Las Vegas' – a good question, if it was one. Max had met her grandfather and she had met his formidable mother on one of the rare occasions when she'd swept through Bristol. But other than that . . . It was as if, she realised, they were still dating. They had often woken up together, but never discussed the future. They had given each other keys to their flats, but more as a matter of convenience, she suspected, than a wish to share their lives. Because they hadn't become close, at least not in the way that Eva imagined you became close with someone who was special. Apart from Lucas at uni – and that, she knew, had been more of a friendship than a love affair – Max was the nearest she had ever got to a full-time relationship with a man.

The water reached a perfect temperature and was as deep as Eva liked it. She lowered herself in, felt the liquid heat against her skin and smelled the neroli orange blossom rising from the essential oil. What would have happened, she wondered, if she hadn't gone round to his flat that afternoon one month ago? Would they still be together? Would she be thinking, even now, about where he would be taking her tonight, rather than contemplating a relaxing evening in alone?

It had been an unusual situation. Eva had stayed the night at Max's and the following day at work realised she didn't have her mobile and that she'd left it at his flat. She'd remembered a text that had come through; she must have left the phone on the coffee table after she'd answered it. She tried to call him, but his mobile was switched off; Max was a criminal lawyer so he was probably with a client. She'd nip round and get it at lunch-time, she decided. It wasn't far, he wouldn't mind . . .

Eva dipped her head back to soak her hair; she'd wash it under the shower later. She sank into the restful curve of the bath and had another sip of wine. From the moment she'd walked into the hall, she knew something was wrong. And she didn't have far to look. They were in the living room on the sofa, still adjusting their clothing, Max and some girl she'd never seen before, her make-up smudged over his pink shirt, her skirt still half way up her thighs. What a cliché. Eva hadn't hung around to witness their embarrassment or hear any pathetic excuses. She'd picked up her phone – still on the coffee table as she'd suspected, interesting that they hadn't even noticed it – and walked out, leaving his key on the hook by the door. Only afterwards did she remember the odd phone call which Max had left the room to take, once or twice when he'd cancelled their dates. The signs had been there, she supposed. She just hadn't let herself see.

More fool her. Eva began to soap her body, starting with her arms, generous with the lather. She'd been upset about Max, of course. But now . . . She was over him. She dipped under again. She'd reclaimed her life. And she was going to Burma.

When the water began to cool, she washed her hair and rinsed off under the shower and then climbed out, wrapping herself in a big white fluffy towel. He'd have finished his dinner by now. She paused the music. It was time to tell her grandfather.

He listened to the news without saying very much at first. Then, 'Well, Eva,' he said. 'My goodness. I can scarcely believe it. Burma. That's wonderful.' He drew in a shaky breath, perhaps remembering his own life there, she thought. 'Really wonderful.' He paused. 'Are you looking forward to it, my dear?'

Was she looking forward to it? 'I can't wait.'

'And when are you going?'

'Next week.' As soon as it could be arranged, she guessed. Jacqui didn't want any of those enticing antiques going anywhere other than to the Emporium. But there was a good deal of money at stake. Burmese traders, like any others, understood international markets: those artefacts wouldn't be going cheap.

'Next week!' He seemed quite shocked at this. 'So soon?'

'I think so.'

There was another long pause. What was he thinking? She imagined she could hear the cogs whirring. 'I wonder,' he said. 'I wonder.'

Eva smiled to herself. 'What do you wonder, Grandpa?'

She heard him take another breath. 'If you could possibly come here first, Eva?' he asked, his voice quavering just a little, the words coming out in a rush. 'Can you come to see me before you go?'

'Well . . .' She hadn't planned to. She adored her grandfather, of course, but this weekend would be quite a rush. Although it was tempting. Eva loved West Dorset and she still thought of it as home. Her mother no longer lived there . . . And Eva pushed that thought swiftly away. But her grandfather *was* her home – hadn't he always been?

'It's important, my dear,' he said. 'I wouldn't ask otherwise. I wouldn't expect it of you. Only . . .' His voice tailed off.

'Important?' Not just that he wanted to see her before she made the trip then? Eva hesitated.

'There's something that should have been done a long, long time ago,' he murmured. 'It's too late for me to do it now, of course. Perhaps I made a terrible mistake. I just don't know for sure. But if you . . .'

What was he talking about? Eva waited. She could hear his breath, thin and wheezy on the other end of the line. She didn't like the way he sounded. What should have been done a long time ago? What terrible mistake?

'It's such an opportunity, my darling,' he said, a sense of wonder in his old voice. 'For you and for me. Almost heaven-sent. But I'm wondering if it's too much to ask. And after all these years . . .'

'If what's too much to ask, Grandpa?' Eva was intrigued. 'What is it? Can you tell me?'

'Yes. I should tell you, Eva.' And just for a moment he didn't sound like her frail grandfather. Instead, Eva had a mental picture of him as a young man, before he went to Burma perhaps, when he was only seventeen.

'I'll come over tomorrow evening,' she said, making an instant decision. 'I'll stay the night.'

'Thank you, my darling.' He let out a breath as if he'd been holding it, waiting.

Eva was thoughtful as she ended the call and clicked on to her gmail. She re-started the music. It was a mystery, but she'd find out soon enough. At least her grandfather was pleased that she was going. It wouldn't be nearly so easy, she knew, to tell her mother.

CHAPTER 3

Eva parked her ancient but much-loved red-and-black Citroen 2CV in the drive and got out. She pulled on her jacket, grabbed her overnight bag from the passenger seat, slammed the door sufficiently hard for it to shut properly and walked up the path to the front door. The yellow stone was pock-marked by sea winds and the green paint on the door was a little cracked and faded, but otherwise the house of her childhood looked much the same as always, the orange rose climbing from its pot by the bay window up to the black roof slates and beyond, still in full bloom. Eva bent to sniff the nearest blossom. The scent of tea-rose immediately whirled her back to childhood days, making rosewater perfume and picnics on the lawn in summer. Those were the good bits. It was different – everything was different – after her world fell apart. But she wouldn't dwell on that now, not when she had Burma to look forward to. Not to mention her grandfather's mystery.

She lifted the brass door-knocker and let it fall. Pulled her hair out from under her collar. Waited.

Her grandfather opened the door, beaming. 'Hello, darling. Come in, come in.' He helped her with her bag, took her

19

tweedy jacket and hung it on a hook by the door. 'How was your journey? I suppose the roads were busy? They always are these days.'

'The journey was fine,' Eva reassured him.

He turned to her. 'Let me look at you.'

Eva pulled down the sleeves of her lacy blouse and slipped the silk scarf she was wearing from her neck, tucking it next to her jacket. 'Let me look at *you*,' she said. Her grandfather had always been tall and lean. But was he a little more bent than the last time she'd seen him? Was his kind and familiar face more lined?

'You look as lovely as ever.' He smiled. 'How about a hug from my favourite girl?'

Eva stepped into his open arms and closed her eyes, just for a moment. His hair was fine wisps of snow-white. His fawn woollen cardigan smelt of eucalyptus and wood, a fragrance she seemed to have lived with all her life.

'Do you mind if we eat in the kitchen tonight, darling?' he asked, holding her at arm's length for a moment, his hands on her shoulders. 'It's so much more cosy now that the nights are drawing in.'

'Of course not.' Eva followed his slow passage along the L-shaped hall past the shelf of memorabilia that her grandfather had brought back to the UK after his Burmese days. She knew it all so well, but now she lingered, taking it all in as if for the first time: the wooden elephant bells, a souvenir of his work in forestry; the set of opium weights made in the image of Buddha; the Burmese flowered paper parasol and finally the Japanese flag in a bamboo case, the silk burned by shrapnel during the war. And soon, she reminded herself, she would be experiencing her own Burmese days.

In the farmhouse kitchen at the back of the house, the Aga's reassuring warmth filled the room and one of Mrs Briggs's stews bubbled on the hob, a rich fragrance emanating from the pan. Two places had been set at either end of the old pine table and a bottle of red wine had been uncorked but not poured. Thank goodness for Mrs Briggs. Now that he was on his own, Eva's grandfather needed her help with cooking and housework more than ever. Eva knew how much he valued his independence. And she couldn't see him anywhere else but here, in his own house, big, rambling and impractical as it was. It was part of him. It always had been.

Eva pulled off her laced leather ankle boots and left them in the corner next to her grandfather's green wellies. That was better. The ridges of the flagstone tiles felt reassuringly familiar, and warm from the heat of the Aga on her stockinged feet.

Her grandfather was watching her appraisingly. 'How about a drink?' he suggested. 'I've opened a particularly pleasant Burgundy I'd like you to try.' His faded blue eyes held a definite twinkle.

Eva smiled. Her grandfather was quite a wine buff these days. And since Eva's grandmother's death, he had allowed himself to pursue his hobby even more keenly. 'That sounds lovely, Grandpa.'

With a shaky hand, he poured them both half a glass. 'Lovely to see you, my dear.'

'And you, Grandpa.' Eva took a sip. The wine was as mellow and rich as antique velvet. 'That is very good.' She put the glass down and lifted the lid of the stewpot. 'Mmm. And this smells wonderful. What would we do without Mrs Briggs?' She wouldn't rush him. Let him tell her what he wanted her to do in his own good time.

'What, indeed?' He chuckled. 'It's ready when you are.' He steadied himself for a moment on the antique dresser.

'Let me.' Eva put down her glass and fetched the plates from the warming oven. She began to ladle out the beef stew.

'I expect you've been wondering why I asked you to come here this weekend, hmm?' Her grandfather eased himself down on the chair. 'Selfish old fool that I am.'

'Nonsense.' Eva brought the plates over to the table. 'You could never be selfish.'

'Ah, well.' He shook his head. 'You wait till you hear what I've got to say before you decide.'

Eva smiled. 'Eat up.'

He smiled back at her and picked up his fork. Took a mouthful and chewed slowly, watching her all the while. 'I don't want to take advantage of your situation, my darling. But when you said you were going to Burma . . . I saw immediately. It is what you might say, fortuitous.'

'Fortuitous?' Eva picked up her glass and took another sip of her wine. It was a strange choice of words. But she trusted him. Her grandfather might be old and frail, but his mind was razor-sharp, it always had been.

He dabbed at his lips with his paper napkin. 'When you grow old, you have plenty of time to think,' he said.

'About Burma?' Eva guessed. She speared a potato and dipped it in the rich, fragrant gravy.

He nodded. 'And other things.'

'Such as?'

'Decisions that have been made, pathways that have been taken, wrongs that should have been made right.'

Eva reached across the table, which still bore the indentations of pens and pencils pressed a bit too hard during childhood crayoning sessions, and squeezed his hand. 'Everyone has regrets,' she said. It wasn't something reserved for the old.

'Even you, my dear?' He watched her sadly.

'Even me.' Eva thought of her mother. Too many regrets. Even at sixteen, you could make a decision that could snatch a person away from you. Was that what she had done? She wasn't sure though that she could have done it any differently.

He leaned forwards, those blue eyes as intelligent as ever and put his other hand over hers. 'But you're not talking about Max, I hope?'

'Oh, no.' He released her hand and Eva took another forkful of Mrs Briggs' beef stew. 'I'm not talking about Max.'

Her grandfather chuckled as he carefully topped up both their glasses. 'I'm glad to hear it. That man wasn't anywhere near good enough for my favourite girl.'

Eva smiled back at him. He'd never liked Max, and yet again, he'd been proved right. But she noticed that he'd pushed his plate away leaving most of the stew uneaten. 'Had enough?' she asked him. She didn't want to fuss, she knew that Mrs Briggs did enough fussing as it was. But she couldn't help worrying. He meant so much to her. He wasn't so much a grandparent as the life-force behind her childhood.

He nodded. 'My appetite isn't what it was, my dear.'

Head on one side, Eva regarded him. 'What is it that you regret, Grandpa?' she asked. She couldn't believe he'd done anything so very bad. Maybe things had happened in the war that had scared him or that he hated to think of, but he would never have willingly hurt anyone, not if he didn't have to.

He sighed. 'I kept something that didn't belong to me,' he said. 'I didn't find out the full truth when I should have done. And I never went back.' He heaved himself up, took the plates over to the kitchen sink and then slowly lowered himself down again into the old rocking chair.

Eva went over to him and took his hand. It was trembling. His skin felt paper-thin and it was threaded with blue veins and massed with liver spots from all those years of living in the tropics. 'You never went back to Burma?' she guessed. Did he mean after her grandmother had died? Why should he have gone back after all that time?

He nodded.

'And the truth?'

'That's what I would like you to find out, Eva, my dear,' he said.

She stared at him.

'I have an address.' There was a blue manila folder on the table next to the rocking chair, and from this he extracted two slips of paper. 'Two addresses,' he said, handing them to Eva.

She looked at the scraps of paper. He must have had them a long time. They were written in a younger man's handwriting and the paper was yellowing with age. *Daw Moe Mya*, she read. The same name, but a different address on each. Who was Daw Moe Mya?

'It's a long story, my dear,' he said.

Eva put the pieces of paper down on the table and moved over to the stove. 'I'll make us some tea.' She needed to keep a clear head. She filled her grandmother's ancient black kettle, her thoughts buzzing. A long story? Hadn't she heard all the stories about Burma?

She went back to sit by him. 'You'd better start at the beginning,' she said. 'And tell me exactly what it is that you want me to do.'

'I'm old, my dear,' he said. He leaned forwards and adjusted the red-tasselled cushion behind him. 'I've made mistakes. But perhaps it's not fair to ask you to help me. That's what your mother would say.' He shot her a look from under his bushy white eyebrows.

'I'm all grown up now, Grandpa.' Eva twisted her daisy ring. Thought of the email she'd sent to her mother last night. It was sad that these days they mostly communicated that way. More than sad, it was heart-breaking. But sometimes the fissures in a relationship only grew wider and deeper with time. And that's what seemed to have happened to theirs.

The kettle boiled and Eva got up to make the tea, using her grandmother's old floral patterned teapot. She assembled the porcelain cups and saucers and brought the tray over to the table by the rocking chair where he sat, went back to stack the dishwasher and put the pan in to soak, before returning to pour. She had the feeling that her grandfather needed a bit of thinking time. And so did she.

'What did you keep, Grandpa?' she asked gently as she placed a cup on the table next to him. 'What did you keep that didn't belong to you?'

'Get the chinthe,' he whispered.

'The chinthe?' Perhaps his mind was wandering after all? But Eva knew what he was referring to. The dark and shiny decorative teak chinthe – a sort of mythical lion-like creature, which always stood on her grandfather's bedside table – had been a feature of Eva's childhood, a feature of all those stories of Burma.

Eva had grown up sandwiched between her mother's flat and this yellow-stone, rambling house, between the gentleness of her grandfather's care and the brittle grief of Rosemary, her mother. Eva's grandmother Helen had been delicate, often tired, disliking noise and disruption. But her grandfather . . . He had picked her up from school and taken her on outings down to Chesil Beach and the Dorset sandstone cliffs, or off for muddy walks in the Vale. In the evenings they'd sat here in this kitchen and he'd made them mugs of hot chocolate and told her such stories . . . Tales of dark wood and darker mysteries. Of a land of scorching heat and drenching monsoons, of green paddy fields and golden temples, of wide lakes and steamy jungles. Those stories had become almost a part of her.

Eva went to fetch her grandfather's beloved chinthe from the bedroom. More than anything else, this symbolised his time in Burma, she supposed. She picked it up, looked for a moment into its iridescent, red glass eyes. It was a lovely piece, small and delicately carved in an eighteenth-century style, it looked a bit like a wild lion with a jagged tasselled mane and a fierce snarling face. It had a sturdy body and was made, she knew, of the rich burnished teak that her grandfather used to work with back in the days before the war, when he lived in the teak camps with elephants, sending the great logs that had been felled tumbling into the Irrawaddy River.

'Here he is.' She put the chinthe on the table next to the tea tray. Ran her finger across the carved mane. He was a proud animal and she'd always liked him despite his apparent ferocity. 'What is it that you want me to do, Grandpa?' she asked again.

Her grandfather stared at the little chinthe for a few moments and then looked back at Eva. 'It's a personal quest, my darling.' And to her horror his eyes filled with tears.

'Grandpa?'

'Those addresses I gave you,' he said. 'That's where she used to live, before the war, you know.'

'She?'

'The person I want you to look for,' he said. 'I need you to find out the truth of what happened.' He picked up the chinthe and held it gently in his hand. 'There's a promise I made many years ago, my darling Eva, that now I need you to keep.'

CHAPTER 4

Rosemary Newman read her daughter's email with a growing sense of dread. Burma. Would that country never loosen the claw-like hold it seemed to have on her life? She shuddered. First her father, and now Eva. What was it about the place?

She slumped slightly in her seat, then straightened, clicked back to her inbox. She wouldn't delete it, couldn't delete it, and of course she'd answer it, later. Or maybe she'd phone Eva, which was much harder. Face to face had become harder still. Not that she'd ever intended it to be that way . . .

Her daughter had explained that her company were sending her over there, but Rosemary knew she was delighted to go. Her excitement was written between the lines as clearly as the words themselves. *It'll be so interesting to see the place after all Grandpa's stories* . . . Grandpa's stories indeed. And a lot he hadn't told her too.

Rosemary got to her feet and walked over to the window. She and Alec lived in Copenhagen, in a penthouse apartment in a residential borough just outside the old ramparts of the medieval city and the sweeping view of the city which was theirs to admire every day included the spires of Christiansborg Palace and City Hall. The people who lived here were justifiably proud of Copenhagen. It was a thriving and cultural city and it was kept immaculately clean. Heavens, thought Rosemary, the harbour was so unpolluted you could apparently swim in it, not that she had tried. The city boasted plenty of parks and green spaces, wide promenades and waterfronts, and the infrastructure of cycle lanes, metro and other social services helped maintain a pleasant lifestyle. Alec earned a good wage working as a project manager for a large financial institution, and although taxes were high, the rewards were good. Rosemary couldn't complain. And it was hardly Alec's fault that sometimes she wanted to scream . . .

The apartment was smartly furnished, modern, all clean lines and up-market furnishings. Stylish and tasteful. And, she thought, a million miles away from the house in which she'd grown up, in West Dorset. Her parents' house, rambling both inside and out with its cubby holes, inglenook fireplace, winding stairs and bay windows looking out into the untameable garden. Her mother, Helen, had tried to keep it in check; they had even employed a gardener for a while. Helen and wild gardens were not a match made in heaven. But that garden, with its climbing roses, meandering paths, blowsy hydrangea bushes and pond with water lilies and frog spawn, would always go its own way.

Like Eva. Rosemary put a hand to her hair and tucked a few strands behind one ear. She kept it in a short, shaped bob these days, smarter, easier to control. Her daughter had always been headstrong. But Burma . . . It was almost more than she could bear. How much did Eva know?

When Nick had been alive, they'd laughed about their wild daughter, teased one another about who she took after, as she climbed trees or galloped across the beach playing what she called 'horsacs', her thick dark hair streaming behind her in the wind. She was a proper tomboy, unable to sit still for a minute. More than anything she had loved to spend time with her grandfather up at the house, and he'd been a wild one too in his time. For a moment Rosemary felt the bitterness creeping up on her. But their closeness had been a blessing, she reminded herself, after it had happened.

Oh, Nick. When Nick was alive, Rosemary had been happy, blissfully happy. She used to laugh. Rosemary looked around the swish apartment, all chrome and beige, cream and leather. Original art from local exhibitions on the walls, cool wooden parquet flooring. She used to get up in the morning and sing while she was in the shower. If she sang in the shower now, Alec would probably think she'd lost her mind.

She went into the kitchen and plucked her navy blue apron from the drawer. It was such a nice kitchen and everything was where it should be. And she wasn't *unhappy*. How could she be unhappy when Alec was such a good man who tried so hard? And really, she had everything she could ever need. *Apart from your daughter,* a small voice whispered back to her. *Apart from your father. Apart from Nick.*

She slipped the apron over her head and tied it behind her and round. This was a new apricot silk blouse and she didn't want to get any stains on it.

It was just that back then it was a different sort of happiness. The sort that made you feel truly alive. The sort that had nothing to do with a comfortable home or money. And everything to do with love.

Rosemary reached up to get the Kilner jars down from the top cupboard, everything she didn't use too often was kept there.

Back then, she'd had a job she enjoyed, working as a legal secretary to a friendly bunch at their local solicitors. And she had a daughter she loved – they had wanted to have more children but it just hadn't happened for them. She lived close to the parents who had brought her into the world, with whom she got on well and who were always there for her. And she had a husband she adored.

On the drainer was a basket of sloes, small and plump from the rain. Rosemary had picked them this morning from the patch of wasteland behind their apartment building. It wasn't a garden and it certainly wasn't countryside. Even so, the white flowers were pretty in springtime and in autumn the berries clustered like bunches of tiny black grapes. More importantly, they reminded her of England. Of hedgerows and country lanes in Dorset. And inevitably of her life in Dorset, of Nick.

Rosemary sighed. The problem had been, of course, that Nick was her life. You couldn't love like that more than once in a lifetime. And so when she lost that . . . Her house of cards had simply come crashing down. Which was what life was like, of course. Just when everything was going well, just when you thought you could relax and enjoy what it had to offer, that's when life would hit you for six. *Ouf*. Rosemary could feel the pain right in her belly – just as she'd felt it that day.

'Nick?' She'd come home for lunch. Cheese on toast, she decided, as she was walking up the path. Then she'd clear up – she hadn't had time that morning – before heading down to the supermarket to get a few bits and pieces before she picked Eva up from school. She only worked mornings, which was ideal, and in the holidays her parents were more than happy to step in, especially Dad. He adored his granddaughter, he seemed to have bucket-loads of patience and time for her. And Rosemary tried not to feel resentful. It was different when you were a grandparent, she reminded herself. You weren't working, you welcomed the chance to give your grand-children the time you hadn't given your own kids. Perhaps she'd be the same . . .

'Nick?' He always came back for lunch unless he was seeing a client who lived some distance away. Nick's workshop was only a few minutes round the corner. He designed and made stained glass for doors, windows, churches even. Beautiful stained glass that could recreate a bygone era, that could send an echo of the twenties or thirties in Art Nouveau or Deco geometrics and curves, that could send a warm amber glow into a hallway when the sun shone, a shaft of blue like a sum-mer's day, or even a spark of fire.

She went into the kitchen. 'Nick?' Dropped her bag.

He was lying, crumpled on the floor. He'd fallen. He was unconscious. 'Christ, Nick.'

She could still see it, see him; the image was branded on her memory. Rosemary picked one of the berries up and rolled it between her forefinger and thumb. She still had a few spines lodged in her fingers – blackthorns were not kind to predators and she supposed she was a predator in a way. And they weren't pleasant to eat raw, the taste was bitter and dry. But in gin . . . Sloe Gin at Christmas was Alec's favourite. The longer you steeped the berries, the richer the drink; Rosemary still had some left from three years ago. By now, it would taste of almonds on the tongue.

She closed her eyes. Nick had died from a blood clot which stopped the flow of oxygen to his brain. He'd had a massive stroke. He wasn't even forty. And Rosemary was left alone.

She realised that she was gripping the basket of sloes, white-knuckled. *Breathe, Rosemary.* The horror of it had never gone away. She had moved, unknowing, into some sort of dark place where she could survive, and she didn't even know, now, where that place was, how she had got there or what had happened to the people around her.

Rosemary took her large colander from the low cupboard left of the sink and shook in the sloes, ensuring that all the fruit was good, that she removed anything that was beginning to rot. She turned on the tap to wash them.

She came out of that dark place when her father grabbed her by the arm one day when she'd come to pick up Eva. Rosemary worked full time now. They needed the money and, besides, work was a distraction. When she was typing up a legal document or speaking to clients on the phone, she didn't have to think about what had happened. That she was now Rosemary Gatsby, widow. That her husband was dead. That, really, life should not have gone on.

'What?' Rosemary waited. Eva was still playing outside.

'She's just a child,' her father said.

'What do you mean? I know she's a child.' She frowned.

'I mean that you've got to pull yourself together, Rosie.' He put a hand on her arm. He was pleading with her.

She tried to tug her arm away, but he held fast. How could he possibly understand? How could anyone? Her world had no foundations anymore, no anchor. 'All very well for you to say,' she snapped. 'Do you ever think what it's like for me?'

He sighed, let her go. 'All the time,' he said. 'All the time. But you're her mother. It's your job to think what it's like for her.'

'I don't think I can do that job,' she had told him. 'Not anymore.' At least not in the way he expected her to. Since the cards had fallen, there seemed to be little reason to do anything. Why bother to get up in the morning when there was no one beside you to turn to? Why bother to clean the house? Make dinner? Pay the bills? Eva was the only reason Rosemary dragged herself out of bed at seven-thirty. The reason she shopped and cooked. The reason she forced herself to function.

'You've got to move on, Rosie,' he told her, his blue eyes burning with the need to get it through to her. 'It's not easy.

I know it's not easy. But you've got to do it,— for her sake, if not for your own.'

Rosemary tried. But Eva was not a comfort. She was a responsibility, a worry, one that was no longer shared and enjoyed with the man she loved. How could Rosemary hope to give her a balanced and positive upbringing after this? How could she do it alone? The task, even with her parents to help her, seemed insurmountable, a mountain with only a goat-track to follow. And at the top? All she could see was a very long drop down to rock bottom.

The berries had drained and now Rosemary prepared the Kilner jars; they must be sterilised with boiling water. She filled the kettle and switched it on. Pressed her weight against the counter.

Eva was tearful and needy and this had stretched her jangled nerves to the absolute limit. Of course the child had lost her father. *Yes, Rosemary,* she told herself sternly, *she's lost something too.* And at a vulnerable age when no one should have to experience such a loss, such a heart break, one she might never recover from, too. *And she needs you.* That was the thing, the certainty that hit her like an axe in the guts when she awoke from a fitful sleep every morning at dawn. She had to be two parents for Eva now. And the more her father reminded her of this fact, the more she cringed away from it. It was weak of her, she knew, but she simply couldn't think where to begin.

The kettle boiled and Rosemary poured the water into the tall jars quickly, feeling the hot steam licking like flames at her hands, her wrists, dampening the cuffs of her silk blouse. When Eva hurt herself and ran to her . . . Rosemary felt herself pulling back, her arms half-lifting and then falling impotent to her sides. She shrank from holding her own daughter. Why? Was she scared of loving her too much? When Eva woke up at night and her tears pulled Rosemary away from her dreams and her memories – the only things that seemed to keep her sane – she bitterly resented the intrusion. She wanted to shout at her: *Go to sleep. Let me be.* Did these things make her a bad mother? She loved her daughter and yet she couldn't love her, didn't dare to love her, couldn't risk being hurt that badly again.

Rosemary held everything back. She kept her distance. If she needed to, she walked away. And all that had become a part of her. She was now that woman. She couldn't hold her own daughter and she couldn't tell her she was safe. Because she wasn't safe. Neither of them were safe. The cards had fallen. Their anchor was gone. Where was there for them to run? Not to each other, it seemed. Eva turned more and more to her grandfather for her hugs and kisses. And Rosemary? She simply battled on alone.

She pricked the ripe sloes with a fork to release the flavour and weighed them out equally, tipping them into the jars. She weighed out the sugar too and added that. Measured the gin. Sealed the jars. And so . . . Eva was going to Burma – of all places.

Rosemary shook the jars, one by one. She shook them to dissolve the sugar but she felt as if she were shaking something out from deep inside of her. She shook them and shook them and then finally, she put them on a tray and carried them to the cupboard under the stairs. Placed them on the shelf in the dark. All she had to do now was wait.

She sat down on the cream leather sofa. It gave gently under her, cushioning and comforting. But cold, Rosemary thought. As she had been cold.

The fact was, that when Nick died, something had died in Rosemary too. After his death, she was only half living. And since then, she had never been able to get it back. Perhaps she never would. But so much, she realised, was lost when you only lived half a life. And the other people she had tried to love: her father, Alec, Eva. Would they ever find it possible to forgive?

CHAPTER 5

Eva woke up from a restless doze, the kind you have on a long-haul flight, still conscious of those around you, sensitive to your neighbour needing to squeeze past or the stewardess nudging you awake with a *sorry to disturb you, madam, but did you want breakfast/lunch/a snack/coffee,* whatever, each long hour was punctuated by something.

She'd been dreaming about her mother. She was five years old and her mother was reading her a bedtime story about Mister Fox; she could see that fox with his red waistcoat and bushy tail so clearly in her mind's eye. And hear her mother's voice, low, sing-song, her laughter that seemed to bubble up inside and tip from her like fizzy lemonade. She could feel her too, her warmth and her kisses better, she could even smell her scent, of springtime. Eva focused in hard. There were other sounds, her parents' banter and the rhythm of their voices, her father's booming: *What d'you reckon then, love? Don't give me that!* And then she was being swung between them. *One, two, three, up she goes.* The security of a hand being held.

Was she still dreaming? Somewhere inside, Eva knew she was in that strange state between sleeping and waking. She heard his voice again. Her father. Her memories were sketchy at times and at others clear as glass. He had taught her to swim in the sea, which she loved to do, even now. *Don't tense up, love. Let yourself go* . . . The water cool on her skin, the wave rising. *Ride with the swell. That's the way. You can't fight it.*

Eva couldn't fight it when she lost him. One day he was there, the next gone. No chance to say goodbye.

She blinked as her memory skittered back. She remembered that first day, that dark day. Grandpa picking her up from school. A hop, a skip and a jump. 'Where's Mummy?'

'She's busy. You'll see her soon.'

Eva didn't mind. She loved the secret games she always played in her grandparents' garden. But it was different today. Her grandparents were talking in hushed voices, watching her. Her grandmother turned to her in that too bright, bird-like way she had. 'How about a special treat for tea, Eva, dear?' Something was wrong.

When her mother arrived, she walked down the path very slowly. Her eyes were blank and red and when Eva shrieked, 'Mummy!' and ran towards her, she hardly seemed to hear or see. 'Mummy!'

It was as if her mother weren't there. She glanced at Eva and she seemed to look right through. Were neither of them there? Eva was scared.

'Hello, darling.' Absently, her mother touched her hair. She didn't lift her up and spin her around, she didn't hold her tight, she didn't kneel down and look her in the eyes, pulling a funny-mummy face. She just touched her hair. Eva knew that something was very, very wrong.

Every hour they were nearer to reaching their destination. Eva shifted in her seat. It had been a long journey, broken up in Doha for just an hour and a half before they were re-boarding. Fourteen hours in all, and the little sleep she'd had was fitful and crammed with these scenes from her past. How reliable were these memories? What she knew for sure was that life without her father had been as different as life could be. There was so much missing: his voice, his laughter, the presence of him. Even the house became silent and brooding, a house that had lost somebody. But at least there was still her mother. She had that to cling to.

Eva waited for her mother to come back to her. She waited for the stories, for the warmth of her arms, for the bubble of her laughter. But they never came. Her mother might still be there. But as the months went by, Eva finally learned the truth. There was something missing. Her mother had lost the heart of her. And so Eva had lost her mother too.

She stared out of the window at the blanket of cloud below and thought of what her grandfather had told her in the kitchen a week ago. Everything was a lot clearer now. She'd always known how much Burma meant to him, but this new story was different from any of the others. It was about the decorative teak chinthe that even now was tucked safely away in her cabin bag, protected by her bottle-green silk wrap. And it was about the woman whose address was written on the slips of paper in her purse.

'Take him back to Burma for me, Eva,' he'd said to her,

handing her the little wooden animal. 'Take him back to her family. Where he belongs.'

Her family . . . The family of the woman called Daw Moe Mya, or Maya, as he called her. This story was about what her grandfather had lost, and what he wanted to return to its rightful place.

'There is another chinthe,' he'd said, his faded gaze drifting off beyond Eva and the farmhouse kitchen in Dorset, back to the past and a far off place. 'This is one of a pair.'

'Yes.' She supposed it must be. They always came in pairs. They were guardians of temples and pagodas and were a feature of many Asian cultures, sometimes with animal, sometimes human faces and made of stone, wood and even bronze. Eva sipped the mineral water that the stewardess had just given her. She was so looking forward to seeing them in situ, particularly the famous fourteenth-century bronze Angkor Chinthe in Mandalay. She'd only seen a picture but open-mouthed and snarling, he looked satisfyingly ferocious.

'They need to be together, my darling,' her grandfather had said. 'To restore harmony.' But that was only the half of it. 'I should never have brought it back to England,' he murmured. 'It wasn't the right thing to do.'

Eva scrutinised the progression of the flight path of the Boeing on the screen in front of her. They were only forty minutes from touching down in Yangon. Her heart seemed to skip a beat. She peered through the window, anxious to catch her first glimpse of the place, longing to see what her grandfather had seen, feel what he had felt. She could make out the land mass already. The cloud was breaking, but with uncertainty, as if at any second it might fold into a blanket of leaden grey and unleash its contents on to the ground below. She felt the rush of adrenalin. It wouldn't be long . . .

'I loved her, you see.' Her grandfather spoke softly, tenderly, the memories lights in his eyes.

Eva wasn't even surprised. It was a moment when things from her childhood suddenly made sense, a jigsaw slotting into place. The way her grandparents always were with each other: his patience, her sadness, the polite distance between them. Eva had taken his hand in hers and squeezed it gently. A warm shiver spread through her. Her grandfather had come back to Dorset, and he had married her grandmother Helen. But . . . And she thought she was beginning to understand. No wonder her mother and grandmother had never been interested in his life in Burma.

'I have always loved her,' he said.

It was there in his face. All the answers were there. He had always loved her. She had forever usurped Eva's grandmother Helen in his affections, no matter how hard he must have tried for it to be otherwise.

'Then, why did you leave her?'

'It's a good question, my darling Eva,' he said. But he didn't give her the answer.

'And what makes you think she's still alive?' How old would she be? In her early nineties, Eva guessed.

Her grandfather nodded. He seemed very sure. 'If she were no longer alive,' he said, 'I think that I would know it.'

Now, as she watched, the dark sky lightened into streaks of pink and blue and began to give way to a misty dawn. The morning sun illuminated the crenellated tips of turrets of cloud. And there it was. Burma. What was it Kipling was supposed to have said? *It is quite unlike any place you know about.* Eva didn't doubt it. It was spread out there below her, kite-shaped, surprisingly green – but why not? The rains had barely finished. And the string of the kite was that winding river. She could see its many branches and the delta below. She checked the map in front of her, pushed her seat to an upright position, so she'd feel more ready for it all. The Irrawaddy, muddy brown in the milky morning light. It was another world.

Since her grandmother Helen had died . . . Eva frowned at this sobering thought, the rift between her grandfather and Eva's mother had grown. And she had to face it - the rift between Eva and her mother had done the same, as if moving in a perfect parallel. Did Rosemary blame her father for not making her mother happy? And if so, was it true? Eva gazed out of the window at the place that had perhaps been part of it, at the place that might give her the answers. But her grandfather was a good man. Whether it was true or not, Eva believed that he had done his best.

The stewardess brought round hot flannels and Eva held her hair up with one hand and let the scented towel rest on the back of her neck for a moment. She closed her eyes. Her mother's reply to her email had been brief and non-committal, like most of her communications, Eva thought. *Don't give anything away, Mother . . .*

Take care, Eva, she'd written. *Have a good time.* A few lines of news about Alec's company and what long hours he was working; in the world of computer technology everything moved so fast, there was a lot of pressure not to get left behind. And that was it. Nothing about Rosemary herself or when she might be coming over to visit. The word 'love', easy to write. A single kiss. But what did Eva expect? Especially now.

This was a work trip, yes, and she was looking forward to seeing lots of interesting antiques and artefacts, to have the chance to obtain some for the Emporium, to examine and authenticate. But that wasn't all. When she'd heard what her grandfather had to say, Eva had realised she couldn't do this in ten days. She couldn't do justice to Myanmar, to her work commitments, to her grandfather's request in such a short time.

'I've some holiday owing that I have to take before the end of the year,' she had said to Jacqui on the Monday morning after she'd visited her grandfather in Dorset. 'And so I was wondering . . .' Her grandfather had offered to help fund the trip, Eva had some savings. Financially it wouldn't be a problem, if Jacqui was prepared to be flexible. Eva was aware that her trip would take a huge chunk out of the Emporium's profits, though presumably the riches to be found in Myanmar must make it potentially worthwhile.

'How long do you want to stay?' Jacqui asked her when

45

Eva had explained a little of her family's connection to the place.

'Three weeks?'

Jacqui came to a quick decision. 'Why not?' she said. 'It could be useful. As long as you maintain email contact with me throughout, Eva.'

'Of course.'

Eva exhaled and let her shoulders release the tensions of the flight, of her tiredness, of her apprehensions. She was going to look for her grandfather's other life, the life that had excluded his wife and his daughter. She didn't know what she would find, but her mother wouldn't like it. She was going to a country that would be strange and unfamiliar in every way possible and she was doing it alone, apart from the slightly dubious contacts that Jacqui had arranged for her.

Eva opened her eyes and peered down at the great river looping its way over the marshland, dividing as if about to take some new path and then winding back again to join forces. Stronger together than alone. It had never been like that for Eva and her mother after Eva's father had died. Neither of them had been strong. Eva had been too young then to understand, but she'd had a long, long time to think about it ever since.

Eva had turned to her grandfather. But what she had always understood was that her mother had preferred to be alone.

'Not long to go now.' The man in the seat beside her spoke. He was a journalist and had been a pleasant enough companion. They'd had one or two brief conversations during the flight, which was all Eva had wanted with so much to think about.

Eva smiled. 'Can't wait,' she said.

The seat belt signs had been on for a few minutes. Now, the pilot put the air brakes on, the flaps went down on the wing. The land was becoming more cultivated, there were paddy fields, and in the half-light of the dawn Eva could see how much rain there had been. She could see rectangular shacks now too, randomly built on the river bank. Some kind of small settlement maybe; she was only too aware of Burmese poverty, although she knew about the riches to be found in this country too. There were clumps of palm trees and a very long straight road.

The plane banked as it turned into the wind, ready to make its final descent and Eva's head lurched with dizziness. Just tiredness or disorientation probably. And yet there was a familiarity to the land too. It didn't look as alien as she had expected. What *had* she been expecting? She wasn't really sure. She could feel the excitement though, it was tingling through her fingers and her toes, making her heart beat faster.

'Cabin crew, take your seats for landing, please.' The voice came over the tannoy.

And then she saw a golden pagoda, glinting in the sunlight. Its tapering spire stretched up towards the heavens, the cone of its body shimmered in the morning sun. This was Burma. Her journey lay ahead of her like the path of the winding Irrawaddy itself. She had arrived.

CHAPTER 6

The first time ever he saw her face.

Lawrence glanced at his bedside table, just for a second before he put out the light. Or to be more accurate, he glanced at the space on the table that the chinthe no longer occupied, though Lawrence could see it still in his mind's eye. *Watching over you.* He'd always kept it there, perhaps he thought it lessened the betrayal if he had even a part of her closest to him while he slept. Yes, or perhaps he was a fanciful old man. The truth was just touching the wood could take him back there. And then he looked at the clock, frowned, tried to work out if Eva would have landed. He must get it right. He wanted to arrive there as she arrived there, at least in his head.

He couldn't read, not tonight. When Helen was alive, she had loathed him reading in bed. 'Aren't you tired?' she would sigh as if it were his fault for not doing enough during the day to make him ready for sleep. And so then he would read maybe a paragraph or two of his book and leave it at that. Why upset her? It wasn't her fault, none of it was her fault. But now that he was alone . . . Now that he had the opportunity to read entire books if he wanted to, with no one to say a word about it . . . Well, his eyes just weren't up to it. He was tired in a way he had never been tired before.

The first time ever he saw her face.

There was a song, wasn't there, but he hadn't heard it back then when he was first in Burma. It hadn't even been written in 1937, though she could have been the reason why such a song had ever been born. He felt afterwards that he hadn't heard anything till then. Hadn't lived.

Mandalay, 1937

They were walking through the market, he and Scottie. There were market traders selling fish, vegetables and beans; many of the men and some of the women smoking Burmese cheroots or chewing betel and there were food stalls where people sat to eat under the shelter of a bamboo-walled hut crammed on wooden benches like pilchards in a tin. Steaming tureens of noodles and soup bubbled on open fires tended by proprietors in stained *aingyis*. It was hot, and a heavy humidity hung in the air like a quilt of mist. People milled around: Burmese and Indian in the main, though also a few Europeans, the men mostly dressed in thin jackets and *longyis*, the long wrap-around skirt worn by both men and women; the women's *longyis* tucked into the waist band, rather than knotted like the men's, and worn with bright colourful blouses, or in saris, draped elegantly around head and shoulders, falling to the dusty ground. Rain, Lawrence thought to himself. That was what they all needed.

'Was it what you were expecting?' Scottie had asked him when he first arrived at the chummery. Was it?

For a long time, Lawrence had craved adventure. Not just danger or girls, but travelling too. He'd wanted to see the world, at least as much of it as possible.

'What's wrong with us?' his father had demanded when Lawrence had finally plucked up the courage to tell them his intention. He'd meant, of course, the family firm. The shadow of Fox and Forster had loomed over Lawrence's childhood, a security and yet a threat. 'Why do you need to go anywhere, eh? We need you here.'

'He'll be back,' his mother had said. She was a diplomat, every glamorous inch of her from the top of her fair coiffured head to her immaculate shoes and stockings. 'Let him go and he'll come back.' She knew how to keep them both happy. It wasn't even a tightrope for her. All her life she'd twisted her father round her elegant little finger; it had become second nature to do the same with her husband and son.

Lawrence's father had grumped and growled and reached for the whisky decanter. But his mother had understood and so his father had let him go. He could never refuse her anything, all she had to do was allow a tear to creep into her blue eyes and he'd bluster his way back to getting a smile out of her. *Very well, my dear, if it will make you happy* were words Lawrence had heard frequently during his childhood and beyond. If Mother was happy then so was Pa. Simple. It was an equation that worked. But for himself, in whatever life he carved out for himself with a woman, Lawrence knew he'd want more.

Elizabeth had rumpled her son's hair affectionately. 'He'll

come back to us when he's needed,' she reassured them all. 'When he's got it out of his system. And be all the better for it. He wants to live a little, that's all. It'll do him good.'

Had it? Lawrence wasn't so sure. It had made him dissatisfied, he knew that much. But that was when he came back. As for the rest, she was right. Life was about seeing new places, wasn't it? Experiencing new things. Not sticking to what you knew and who you knew and staying in London working as a stockbroker in the family firm. There were worlds out there that others had explored and conquered. The British Empire was vast and he wanted to experience some of it. How could working in the family firm satisfy him? How could Helen? But he wouldn't think of Helen.

'Plenty of time for that,' his mother had told him, a gleam of satisfaction in her diplomat's eye. 'Plenty of time, my darling, for you to spread your wings a little.'

And fly, he thought. And fly.

Some of it, some of Burma, this land of dark-skinned people, overwhelming heat and golden temples, had been exactly as he had expected. It was different, it was exotic, it had a colour and a heady fragrance that made him dizzy. And it had its hard side too. It could be rough and uncomfortable. The heat could be unbearable. So could the mosquitos. There was poverty and hardship. One couldn't – or shouldn't – take Western comforts for granted.

Work had been a revelation. When he signed up at the company, Lawrence had given hardly a thought for the conditions he'd work under in the teak camps, for the labour he would be commanding in all weathers under pressure, getting as many good logs as humanly possible into the river and on their way down the raging Irrawaddy to Rangoon. Although in the end, humans didn't have as much to do with it as elephants.

And the people . . .

'They look up to us,' Scottie had said, trying to explain how things worked, how the system of the British clubs with their unquestioned luxuries, whist drives, cocktail parties and dances operated in apparently comfortable harmony with the poverty often seen on the streets, women begging, men in ragged clothes desperate to do a deal, children stealing scraps from the market in order to survive.

He seemed so sure. And yes, the Europeans were the undisputed masters, no doubt of that; the last Burmese dynasty had burned itself out in the previous century. Burned itself out, or been burned out by the British Empire, which had no qualms in using its superior weapons, knowledge and experience to get what it wanted. Or so some said. Scottie had all the stories. His father had been a witness to it all. Scottie and the rest of his family were bound up in the colonial web of imperialism more securely than anyone Lawrence had ever met. And that was good, because it was Scottie who had shown him the ropes and Scottie knew all the rules.

Lawrence had seen his fair share since he'd been here. He'd got into the rhythm of the weather, the heat and the rains which ruled everything, and he'd grown accustomed to the food, which wasn't so bad if you liked curry and rice. From February to May was the worst time, the hottest, when your shirt would stick to your back five minutes after you'd put it on and the white glare of the heat could drive you half-mad if you let it. In July and August the rains came with hardly a break in the monsoon, and this was when the real work was done with the timber, when the race was on to get the logs down the rivers and safely to the company's timber yard at Rangoon. Then the rains would tail off, ending with a final squall in October. The fields would dry up and there would be, at last, a wonderful short winter, when the breeze was mild instead of burning, when wild flowers reminiscent of those in English meadows grew in the rural areas, when the paddy grew and ripened into yellow and the nights and mornings could even be cold in the upper reaches of the country, with a cooling mist that filled the valleys and hung over the hills.

The company was generous in giving leave, perhaps it knew that it had to be in order to keep its young blood healthy and content, relatively speaking, at least. Like the rest of them, Lawrence enjoyed visits to Rangoon, going to the English bookshop to stock up on reading material for those long evenings alone in camp, out to sample steak dinners with as many G and Ts and as much ice as you wanted (there was no running out of ice in Rangoon . . .). He enjoyed his regular bouts of R and R up at the hill-station too and the easy camaraderie of the chummery there at Pine Rise in Maymyo, the guesthouse owned by the company and used as bachelor quarters for the single male employees. But there was something about the British clubs that left him cold.

They know who are the masters, Scottie had said. But sometimes Lawrence wondered. *Us and them.* Was it that simple? He thought not. It was a careless racism that was little more than an assumption. Could it be right to make such an assumption? It seemed to Lawrence that there was something in their eyes . . .

There was something in her eyes. She was standing by a stall and he could see her in profile. Small, neat, self-assured. And when she looked up . . .

The stall holder, an Indian, was selling hand woven rugs and blankets. The girl was inspecting a piece of cloth. She held it lightly between her fingers. She wore a *longyi* of bright orange and yellow like the streak of a sunset and her hair hung down past her shoulders as dark and glossy as a bird's wing slicked in oil. Her nails were pale pink, almost white, her lips a kind of bruised plum. And there was the slightest pucker of a frown on her brow. She was perfection, in miniature.

Scottie followed his gaze. He leaned closer to Lawrence. 'I know what you're thinking, old man.'

Lawrence ignored his grin.

'She's a stunner.'

But it wasn't that. Lawrence moved towards the stall, couldn't help himself. She was attractive, yes, but lots of girls were attractive. Helen was attractive – she was a beauty – or so his parents kept reminding him, a fragile, very English kind of beauty. And more significantly, she was the only daughter of his father's business partner and closest friend. But the look of this woman wasn't just striking, she'd walloped him right in the pit of his chest.

'Yes, sir?' The stallholder was quick to notice his interest. 'You like a nice new rug, sir? What colour is it to be? Red, blue, yellow? What size, sir?'

'A blanket.' Lawrence addressed him but looked at the girl.

She glanced up as he spoke, but immediately glanced down again. The Burmese were like that. They weren't meek, but they were self-effacing, the opposite, he thought now, of women like his mother, like Helen. *They know their station*, Scottie would say. Lawrence suspected they knew rather more than that. And no doubt were careful not to show it.

'What kind of blanket, sir? Wool? Cotton? Silk? I have very good collection. What colour? Red? Yellow? Brown?' Deftly, he swept first one blanket, then another, then another down from the display, flourishing each in front of Lawrence for his approval. Pretty soon the stall was in complete disarray, swathed in fabrics of every material and hue.

Scottie stood to one side and languidly lit a cigarette.

The girl seemed about to move away.

'That one,' Lawrence said quickly, indicating the blanket she still held lightly between her fingers. 'Let me see that one.'

'Indeed, sir, a fine choice.' The stallholder whisked it away from her.

She blinked and took a graceful step backwards. Lawrence noticed her feet which were tiny and clad in red silk slippers.

55

'Excuse me.' Lawrence addressed her. 'You were here first.'

She shook her head, took another step backwards.

Would she speak English, he wondered. Many of them did, and Hindustani too. Scottie spoke fluent Burmese. If she didn't speak English, would he act as interpreter? Lawrence hadn't had time to get to grips with the language yet.

'Really. Please. So rude of me.' Lawrence grabbed the blanket, which was made of a soft and fine wool. He handed it to her. 'It is a good blanket, is it not?' His voice to his own ears sounded tender, and this was a surprise.

She looked up at him. Her dark eyes were calm, but he saw in them a curl of humour that gave him hope. He'd been right. This wasn't some poor and lowly Burmese servant girl. This was a young woman of class. She understood him, he could tell.

'It is very fine,' she conceded in perfect English. Her voice was soft and gentle, it seemed to stroke his senses. And as he continued to hold the blanket out to her, she reached out her hand and again held the fabric, smoothing it with her finger-tips.

'Lawrence Fox.' He gave a little bow. 'Please excuse my bad manners. Blame the heat, it must be affecting me.' A weak attempt at humour, he knew. But it was all he could strum up at the present time.

Scottie cleared his throat. 'Jimmy Scott,' he said.

'We are both at your service.' Lawrence smiled.

She nodded her head in acknowledgement but made no attempt to reciprocate their introductions.

What next? Lawrence had always considered himself pretty expert at chatting up the girls. Warming them up with a compliment and a joke, making them laugh, moving in for the thaw, that sort of thing. Not that he had a wealth of experience to draw on. But somehow, knowing he was destined for Helen Forster had freed him to playing fast and loose whenever he had the chance. Cross that bridge when he came to it. But this girl wasn't like any of the other girls. She wasn't British for a start. He had no idea what to bloody do.

'And may I enquire your name?' he said, quietly so as not to intimidate her. At least she hadn't walked away.

'Moe Mya,' she said.

'Moe Mya,' he repeated. The short syllables were small and neat like her. And yet, as he looked into those eyes, he'd like to bet she could let go. Not in the way Scottie and the others in the club might joke about it, but . . . Well, in the real meaning of letting go.

She nodded. 'Some call me Maya,' she said. Her lips pursed together slightly.

I want to kiss them, he thought. *Jesus*. He felt an ache, almost a pain, in his groin. What was the matter with him?

He offered what he hoped was a suave, confident but reassuring smile. 'And you live here in Mandalay?' he asked.

'I live with my father, yes,' she said. 'Most of the time.'

'And the rest of the time?' Was there a man in the picture? Lawrence desperately needed to know.

'Sometimes we stay in Maymyo. My father has a house there.'

Lawrence acknowledged this with a nod. The hill station of Maymyo was situated at a higher altitude than Mandalay and was cooler and restful. Some said it was like England with its grass and neat manicured gardens, its road names reminiscent of his homeland, such as Downing Street and Forest Road. And Lawrence knew that its Englishness was confusing to the Burmese – even the notion of a garden planted with flowers was confusing, since wild flowers were so abundant, why would one plant one's own? But it wasn't just the British who went there. Any Burmese family in Mandalay who had money would generally also have a place in Maymyo for holidays and weekends. Her admission had reinforced his previous impression. She was not a poor native girl. She was, for Burma, a class act.

'And I have an aunt who lives in Sinbo. It is a small village on the Irrawaddy near Myitkyina.' She looked down at her feet in the red silk slippers. 'She lives alone and sometimes needs me to help her.'

'Indeed.' That was even more interesting. Because Lawrence was working in the jungle up near Myitkyina and her aunt's village was only a few miles away.

She looked back up at him from under her eyelids. Was she flirting with him? It wasn't the kind of flirting he was used to, but there was something, some dark knowledge in her eyes that drew him forward. He saw Scottie grind his cigarette under the heel of his boot, noticed that he was getting restless.

'See you back at the club, old man?' he asked with a wink.

'Yes. Perhaps . . .' What was the etiquette? Would she be welcomed in the bar there? Should he invite her? Lawrence wasn't sure of the form. He wasn't sure of anything anymore. 'You could tell me more?' he asked her, instead of what he had been going to say.

'More?' Her eyes were innocent and yet knowing.

'About Mandalay. About your life here.' Not the club, he decided. She didn't belong there, he wouldn't insult her.

She gave a little shrug as if Europeans waylaid her regularly to ask her such questions.

'You must know the city well?'

'My family has always lived here,' she said. 'My grandmother was a servant girl to the Queen.' Her slim back was already straight, but as she spoke these words she seemed to stand straighter still.

'Really? I say . . .' Lawrence was brave enough to take her arm. Scottie had already strolled off. He only had one chance with this girl and he wasn't going to chuck it away.

'Yes,' said Moe Mya. 'It is true.'

'About the blanket, sir?' The stallholder complained. 'You like the blanket, yes?'

'Shall we walk for a while?' Lawrence asked her.

She looked doubtfully around. And it was true that there wasn't really anywhere to walk to.

'To the Palace moat? It isn't far.' He could hear the recklessness in his own voice. But there was something. Perhaps she felt it too.

'The blanket . . . ?'

'I'll take it.' Lawrence reached for his wallet.

She drew back, shocked. 'You have not even agreed a price,' she said.

Lawrence grinned. 'How much?' he asked the stallholder. 'Name your figure and don't be greedy or I might change my mind.'

He could see the cogs spinning. *How much would lose the sale? How unpredictable might a man like Lawrence be?* By this stage Lawrence didn't even know the answers himself.

The stallholder named his price.

Moe Mya replied in Burmese. Lawrence had no idea what she said – he really must make more of an effort – but something must have been agreed because the stallholder argued briefly, then shrugged, nodded and began to fold the blanket into a neat square.

Lawrence passed over some money, tried not to feel that the initiative had somehow smoothly been taken out of his hands.

She passed him the blanket. 'They will not respect you if you let them cheat you,' she said softly.

He could feel her warm breath on his neck as she leaned closer. She smelt of coconut oil. This was the first time she had somehow separated herself from her people. Had she aligned herself with him? *Us and them.* Lawrence didn't understand it, but for him he felt it was no bad thing.

'You must barter. It is part of the game.'

The game . . . 'Thank you,' he said. 'And now?'

'We will walk towards the moat of the Royal Palace,' she said, as if it had been her idea all along. 'And I will tell you about Mandalay.'

CHAPTER 7

'Do you mind if I join you?'

Eva looked up from her guidebook to see a tall blond stranger smiling down on her. For a moment she was almost blinded by the reflection of the sun on his hair. 'Oh. Well . . .'

'Only there are no empty tables.' He indicated the café terrace around them and it was true, it was lunchtime and the place was heaving.

'Of course I don't mind, that's fine.' Eva was sorry for her initial hesitation.

She looked over at the busy street on the other side of the terrace. The people of Yangon were going about their business in the sweltering heat. Men and women in *longyis*, often carrying their wares on top of their heads in wide baskets as they elegantly threaded their way through the crowded streets. Different races, Sikhs, Shan, Indian, Thai, doing business on street corners. Street sellers and food-stalls, motor bikes and scooters with girls in *longyis* riding side-saddle, open-air trucks and trishaws . . . It was a riot of noise and colour. Eva had almost had heart failure when her taxi from the airport had hit a traffic jam. The driver had given a cursory glance at the road ahead and simply continued, driving on the other side. No one had seemed to care.

There still weren't many Westerners around in Yangon. And so when you saw one you tended to gravitate towards them to discuss local sights and the best places to eat. In other words, this blond stranger wasn't coming on to her, he just wanted to have lunch.

'Thank you. I appreciate that,' he said, as he perused the menu.

She could tell from his accent that he wasn't British. German, she guessed. His English was excellent though. And, like her, he seemed to be travelling alone. This was unusual. Most of the Westerners she'd spotted clustered in small groups with their tour guides as if Myanmar might otherwise taint them, though with what, she wasn't sure.

'*Min-ga-laba*. Welcome.' A young Burmese waiter appeared. Like many of the Burmese he kept grinning and saying hello to tourists all the time. She'd had no reason so far to worry about travelling alone. The people in this city were the friendliest and most helpful she'd ever come across.

Earlier today, Eva had taken a taxi to the randomly placed gilded stupa of *Sule Playa*, at forty-eight metres high and positively glowing in the sunlight, it sat slap bang in the middle of the British-constructed grid system that made up downtown Yangon. And then, thinking of her grandfather, she'd got out, paid the driver and walked on to the grand colonial buildings on the waterfront. Already, the heat was all-consuming, the pavements baking and the Burmese were using umbrellas as sunshades as they walked down the street. Her grandfather had told her what it was like arriving at Yangon on the steamer and, standing there, Eva could imagine. Stepping on to the jetty, walking on to the wide waterfront, faced by the Victorian High Court building, which could have been plucked from London's Embankment, and the classic Strand Hotel. If *Sule Playa* reminded her that even in bustling downtown Yangon she was still in the land of golden temples, then these colonial architectural masterpieces were an equally resonant echo of the grandness of Imperial Britain.

Her grandfather had stayed in the Strand and so Eva stepped into its cool, air-conditioned interior, admired the luscious creaminess of the walls which set off to perfection the teak staircase, gallery and furnishings in the high-ceilinged foyer. It was pure, understated luxury. But her grandfather hadn't strolled through hallways of precious Burmese art and jewellery as Eva was now doing. He would have stayed in a mosquito-infested room cooled by an electric paddle fan in those days. Even so, even before all its renovations, from what he'd told her, the colonial life in the Strand Hotel and elsewhere had been lavish and comfortable. At least compared to what most of the native Burmese had to endure.

After a restorative G & T in the plush bar, Eva had retraced her steps to the Indian and Chinese quarters where the locals squatted on their haunches among sacks of rice, lentils, heaps of noodles and, yes, definitely fried locusts. She grimaced. They chatted and laughed, their children playing nearby, as bicycles and trishaws careered along the narrow pot-holed streets, and as they cooked Burmese curries in huge cauldrons on top of braziers, the scents of spices, dried fish and nut oil hanging ripe and heavy in the air.

She laughingly refused a trishaw ride, a rejection which inspired the driver to spit betel juice forcefully on to the road. A nasty habit, she thought, noting his gory, red-stained teeth. The trishaw looked ancient and possibly dangerous, its saddles supported by two rusty springs and the driver himself was bow-legged and certainly no spring chicken. He rattled his money pouch enticingly at her, but she decided not to dice with death on Yangon's busy highway. Instead, she bought a bag of oranges and a pancake for her lunch and stood in the shade for a moment to take it all in. It was as if she'd moved from one side of the world to the other. A G and T in the Strand Hotel at one end and a Burmese pancake cooked in peanut oil at the other – the price of said G and T enough to buy dinner for six at the local open-air eatery.

Before coming here for lunch, Eva had visited Bogyoke Aung San market, where she purchased two *longyis* made to measure, one in magenta silk and one in indigo batik; two embroidered white cotton blouses and a pair of black velvety Burmese slippers, flip flops really, but made of softer fabric and clearly *de rigeur* in Yangon. And she'd enjoyed the shopping trip; the Burmese liked to barter, but it seemed it was just for fun. 'I am happy; you are happy,' more than one of the stallholders had said to her when they'd agreed a price. And they were right. Eva was glad that she had come here with some room in her suitcase, as her grandfather had advised.

Her companion, probably in his early forties, she guessed, had taken his time before ordering Myanmar beer and a Burmese noodle soup. There was a cultured look about him, in the suave confidence of his voice and manner, in the clothes he wore, which were casual but expensive. Was he a tourist? He looked as though he knew his way around.

He glanced across at her, friendly enough. 'It is your first visit here?' he asked.

She must have it stamped on her forehead under her wide-brimmed straw hat. An innocent abroad. 'Yes,' she admitted. 'I only arrived yesterday.'

Yesterday, the agent from MyanTravel had met her at the airport and accompanied her in the taxi to the Agency Offices housed in a huge old colonial building where she had been given green tea and slices of juicy watermelon. She would have the morning to settle in, he'd told her and then she would be meeting with her company's contact in Yangon who would collect her from her hotel at 3 p.m.

At three on the dot he had appeared in the hotel foyer. 'I, Thein Thein,' he said. 'Now, I take you to the showroom.' They had driven miles, finally arriving at a building that looked more like a shack than a showroom. The man who let them in looked rather shady too and already Eva was having doubts about what she was here to do.

The friendly little waiter brought the *kauk-sweh* soup, a thin broth with vegetables and stringy noodles.

'How about you?' Eva asked her companion. 'It's not your first trip, is it?'

'No, it is not. I have been here many times,' he told her. 'The first in 1999.'

'The city must have changed a lot since then.' Eva poured herself more jasmine tea. The hotels seemed full and although all visitors must still bring only pristine US dollars to the country and there were few ATMs and internet cafés, she could see that other changes wouldn't be long coming.

'It has, yes. And you are travelling for pleasure, is that so?'

'Yes and no. I've wanted to come here most of my life,' she admitted. 'But I'm here on behalf of the company I work for. I'm hoping to authenticate some antique pieces and arrange for them to be shipped back to the UK.'

'Indeed?' He took another spoonful of his soup. 'You work for an antique dealer? You are an expert, perhaps?' His blue eyes were twinkling and he had an open smile that she liked.

She tried to look modest. 'It's what I do,' she said.

'And what have you seen so far?' He called over the waiter and ordered more beer for himself and tea for Eva. 'If you do not mind me asking? I might even . . .' He leaned forwards confidentially, '. . . be able to help you, if you are looking for contacts, that is.'

Eva remembered what Jacqui had said about looking around for more stock. 'It's possible that I might be,' she said. He seemed nice enough and it was good to have some company for a change. Why not tell him what had happened?

'It was a bit of a disappointment, I'm afraid,' she said.

'Oh?'

'I can't possibly examine them in this light,' she had told Thein Thein. 'It's far too dim.'

A lengthy discussion followed between Thein Thein and the man in the shack. Voices had grown more and more heated but no one was actually doing anything.

'Come on.' Eva picked up one end of what she hoped was a nineteenth century scripture chest. 'Give me a hand. Let's get it outside.'

Eventually, amidst much grumbling, Thein Thein helped her and they heaved it into the open air. It was weighty enough to be solid teak . . . But there was a lot of damage, as she could now see. She ran her finger over the wood carving. It almost looked like termite damage, but teak was generally very resistant because it was so rich in natural oils. She examined the piece all over for colour consistency and patination. It had been extensively repaired, although the top was sound. But there was a muddy look to the wood grain that made her suspect it had been treated with something. 'What are you asking for this one?' She checked her paperwork. It would need considerable restoration.

Thein Thein translated. The Burmese dealer looked her up and down briefly as if to assess her wealth. Eva sighed. Hadn't it been explained to him who she was and what she was doing? He named a figure.

It didn't correspond to what was on the paperwork and Eva pointed this out to Thein Thein. He shrugged. 'He want to barter,' he said.

'Well, he can forget it.' Eva put her hands on her hips. 'We're not interested.'

'You do not think it genuine?' Thein Thein took off his battered straw hat, he seemed so shocked.

How could she explain to him? Authenticity was a blurred subject. How much an old piece had been worked on – restored, repaired, whatever you wanted to call it – could affect whether it was considered genuine or not. How much reconstitution was permitted before an item ceased to be an authentic antique? And how it had been repaired would certainly affect the price that could be obtained for it. Everyone had to make a profit, after all, this was a business.

The dealer burst out in a spate of outraged Burmese.

'He say it came from a sacred temple.'

Eva nodded. It might well have done.

'He say it has been protected by a special guardian, a nat, and that it once held holy scriptures on parchment.'

'Is there any documentation?' Eva asked. Not that she would understand it, but Thein Thein would presumably be able to translate.

Both men looked blank.

'Come on then,' she said. 'Let's look at the rest.' Experience had shown her that in every scrap heap there could be a pearl, and if it were here, she would find it. Otherwise Jacqui Dryden would certainly have something to say.

Eva gave her companion a condensed version of the story. She didn't want to say too much to someone who was virtually a complete stranger, but on the other hand he might be a useful person to know.

'And what about the rest of the pieces?' he asked. 'Was there anything interesting?'

'Not really.' She pulled a face. On behalf of the Emporium, she had purchased an old circular lacquer table, a carved teak screen and a few bits of colonial furniture that she knew would be highly saleable. But nothing that had made her heart beat faster. Still, onwards and upwards as they say. There were still Bagan and Mandalay. And she had also been able to talk to Thein Thein about the packaging and shipping damage that Jacqui had complained about. In fact she'd arranged an inspection the following morning of a shipment that was due out this week. She'd caught it just in time.

Thein Thein was doubtful about her conclusions. 'I am surprised that your company not want these special goods I have found,' he said. 'Very surprised they not want to take advantage.'

He could raise his eyebrows and widen his eyes as much as he liked, Eva thought. It wouldn't affect her judgement.

'You are likely to find better items in Mandalay,' her companion now told her.

'That's good,' said Eva, 'I'm going there next.' She eyed him curiously. 'And what about you?' she asked. 'Are you over here on business?'

'I am.'

She raised a questioning eyebrow.

'I have various interests,' he admitted. He sipped his beer

and regarded her appraisingly. 'I help to run a German charity which supports an orphanage in Mandalay.'

'That's nice.'

He sipped his beer, still watching her. 'And I like to buy gemstones.'

'Ah.' Eva's gaze was drawn to the signet ring he wore. 'From here?' she asked.

He nodded. 'A small Burmese ruby.' He smiled warmly. 'I'm sure a connoisseur such as yourself, knows that Burma is very famous for her rubies.'

Eva twisted her own diamond daisy ring. It was the only jewellery she was wearing. In this heat she had decided to dress light, in a simple white sleeveless cotton blouse and a flowery wrap-around skirt; she wanted to fit into the culture as far as possible and it was the best thing to wear to preserve the required modesty and to keep relatively cool. 'Hardly a connoisseur,' she protested. 'Especially not of jewellery.'

'Ah.' He smiled. 'Every beautiful woman is a connoisseur of jewellery, is that not so?'

'Perhaps. But tell me . . .' She leaned a little closer. 'How do you know the stones are genuine?' Her guidebook had advised not to purchase unless you could truly identify the real thing. And Eva had seen the jade and the rubies in the jewellery shops and on market stalls, there were so many, you couldn't help but. If they weren't genuine, then they were very clever imitations.

He touched his nose. 'Contacts,' he said. 'For those who

are interested in buying good stones, they must make contacts who can be relied on. It is like furniture, I think.'

'So it's all about who you know?'

'In Myanmar, yes.' He frowned. 'The government here is very strict about the export of gemstones. There are disreputable dealers. You must find a dealer you can trust.'

Disreputable dealers . . . Eva thought of the pieces she'd seen so far and the reaction of their contact Thein Thein. How trustworthy was he? He had seemed disappointed about the amount she had purchased and yet he must have seen for himself that some of the pieces were of dubious quality.

She looked thoughtfully at her companion, who seemed pretty knowledgeable about such things. Eva had gone into this business because she loved old artefacts and the history they could tell. But in the end, how could you make people really care that a diamond was a real diamond and not a piece of glass, or that an intricately carved teak Buddha painstakingly made by hand hundreds of years ago was still in its original condition?

'It is the price, of course,' her companion said when she put this to him. 'Look at the buses.'

'The buses?'

He was pointing towards the busy wide road. Two buses were creaking and hurtling down the street as if they were on fire, people hanging tightly on to the handrails. 'Why do you think they drive so fast?'

She shrugged. 'Because they're running late?'

He laughed. 'Because they are paid by the number of

passengers on board. So they race and overtake each other to get to the next stop first.'

She laughed with him. 'Really?'

'For sure.' He nodded. 'Always, everything is about money.'

Eva pulled a face. That wasn't what she wanted to hear, or believe. 'Not always,' she said. 'It's about history too. It's about the original source. The value of a genuine artefact. Its story.'

She realised that he was giving her that appraising look again.

'Your passion does you credit,' he said. 'But you should take care in this country when you say what you think.'

'About politics?' She had read that one shouldn't engage the Burmese in conversations about politics or their government – a loose tongue could get them into trouble.

He spread both hands. 'About many things,' he said. 'We take free speech for granted in Europe. The Burmese do not.'

Eva sat back in her chair, chastened. It was true though. She plunged in, whether to conversation or to love, and then considered the wisdom of it later.

'My name, by the way, is Klaus Weber,' he said.

She smiled at the fact that they hadn't yet even exchanged names. 'Eva Gatsby.' And shook his outstretched hand.

'And tonight?' he said smoothly. 'What plans do you have?'

Eva checked her watch to give herself thinking time. Had she really been talking to this man for almost two hours? And more to the point, did she want to spend any more time with him? She certainly wasn't looking for romance. But on the other hand, he had been very easy to talk to.

He shrugged. 'We are both travelling alone,' he said. 'I am staying at The Traders Hotel just down the road here. If you like, we could meet there for a drink and share a taxi to see the Shwedagon Pagoda at sunset. You have not yet seen it, I think? And it is the best time of day to experience its splendour.'

'No, I haven't.' Though she had seen the pagoda from a distance, of course, gilded and graceful, rising above the city like a halo. And the temple was apparently a 'must see'. She'd have to go tonight; tomorrow afternoon she was flying to Mandalay.

Mandalay. The next leg of her journey. Where she would be examining more antiques but also looking for a woman who might not even be there, who might be long dead in fact, for all she knew. And if she was dead? She had to find this woman's family then, if they existed, so that she could return her grandfather's chinthe to its proper home with its twin, in order to restore harmony. Not only that, but she had to try and discover the truth. Would she find Maya? And if she did, how would Eva feel about her?

'We could have dinner afterwards,' said Klaus.

'Well . . .' He was friendly and interesting and would be a lot more amusing over dinner than her guide book had proved to be.

He held up his hands and shot her again that open grin. 'No pressure. No ulterior motive. You are quite safe.'

Eva laughed. His attempt at humour had convinced her. 'Why not?' she said. Max was long gone. And anyway, this was just companionship and just for one evening. What harm could it possibly do?

CHAPTER 8

'You're early.' Rosemary looked up at the sound of Alec's key in the door. This was unusual. She knew that he was heavily involved in a project and that usually meant a late one.

'Uh huh.' He came closer, bent and kissed the top of her head.

Rosemary half-smiled, distracted. She'd been thinking about Eva. Eva in Burma.

'I'm just going to have a quick shower.' He was heading for the bathroom already. 'And then I thought maybe we could go for a walk.'

'A walk?' Mentally Rosemary calculated how long it would take to cook supper. 'Is there something wrong?' she asked him. It had rained earlier and already the light was fading.

'No.' His voice was muffled and then she heard the water coming through. 'Nothing wrong,' he called. 'I just need some fresh air. Want to clear my head.'

'OK.' But she knew there was more to it than that.

They walked along the promenade at Nyhaven, the seventeenth-century waterfront, one of their favourite strolls, where you could admire the brightly painted townhouses and the historic wooden boats moored in the canal. There were plenty of bars and restaurants too, but Rosemary could tell that Alec wanted to walk – and talk.

'I've been thinking,' he said, as they strolled along the wide walkway. 'It's been a long time since you saw Eva and your father.'

She glanced at him. *Was that it?* 'I know.' Almost a year to be precise.

Alec stuffed his hands in his pockets. 'Any reason?' He sounded casual, but Rosemary wasn't fooled.

'Not really,' she said. Other than the fact that during her last visit her father had been defensive and Eva more distant than ever. The truth was, it hurt. She wanted to see them both, of course she did. It was just that it was so hard. And surprisingly easy to lose yourself in a different life and not remember. Or at least to try. Alec wouldn't push it, he never did. Alec's parents had died several years ago and since then there was little reason for him to go back to the UK, apart from with Rosemary. He had one brother who was living in Australia and he'd lost touch with most of his British friends. It had happened to Rosemary too. Easier to bury yourself, easier to let them go.

They walked in silence for a moment. There had been a slight drizzle in the air and the sky was November-grey and dimming into dusk. The colour of the canal was a dull olive. Like the winter sea back in Dorset, thought Rosemary.

'Eva's in Burma,' she said, after a while.

'Burma?' he repeated. He pushed up his glasses which had slipped down his nose. 'Isn't that where—?'

'Yes.' She wasn't prepared to make any more connections at the moment. Eva had gone on a work trip. Whatever else she was doing there, Rosemary wasn't sure she wanted to know. 'She needs to authenticate some antiques.'

'Right.' Alec made to reach for her hand, she noticed the gesture but didn't respond. 'Rosemary?'

She felt his gaze upon her, the question in his eyes. Always the same question. *What's going on with you? What's going on inside?*

And she shot him a quick smile. It was her usual smile, the smile she'd perfected over the years which meant everything was OK, when it wasn't. That there was nothing to worry about, when there was. Which meant, which begged him, to let it be.

They passed the oldest house, number 9, built in 1661 she'd heard, painted blue and a different shape from most of the others. On the other side of the canal were the more lavish mansions, including the Charlottenborg Palace on the corner.

Alec didn't say anything else. And that was why they were together, Rosemary thought. Because he let her be. He accepted the distance which had become a part of her. And so she'd been able to let him get closer, in a way she had been unable to let her father or her daughter, because, unlike them, she knew he'd never get too close. Self-preservation. It was the most necessary thing in life. That was what Nick's death had taught her.

Rosemary had met Alec almost ten years after Nick had

78

died. Some might say it was a long time not to be involved with a man, but Rosemary didn't see it that way. It was more incredible that she had ever managed to be involved with a man again.

There was a female solicitor at the practice in Dorset called Selina, who had become something of a friend; her husband was a keen golfer and so Selina found herself with free time at the weekends which she sometimes spent with Rosemary if she was at a loose end. It suited them both.

'Come to dinner on Saturday,' Selina had urged her one Monday morning. 'One of Jon's friends will be there, and Jon's sister and her pal. It's just a casual get-together.'

'You're not matchmaking?' Rosemary was hesitant.

'Course not.'

But as a matter of fact, Rosemary had liked Alec from the first. Tall, thin and be-spectacled, with an obvious distaste for small talk, he was about as poles apart from creative, outgoing Nick as any man could be. But he wasn't just a computer science geek, he liked walking and he was into music. Turned out he was a bit of a foodie too and their conversation ranged from his love of Led Zeppelin, to walks along the South West Coast Path, to the menu of a particularly good local restaurant that had opened up in town. When they had a quiet moment to themselves, just before Rosemary said goodnight, he invited her there the following evening. And to her surprise, she heard herself accept.

'I can't believe it,' Selina had said. 'The first man you look at since Nick and he lives in Copenhagen.' She looked appraisingly at Rosemary. 'I suppose that makes him safe.'

'Maybe it does,' Rosemary conceded. But it was a step, wasn't it? She was still only thirty-seven. But not ready to run the mile.

Alec did work in Copenhagen but he was back for a month to see his parents and to carry out some programming research, and so Rosemary saw quite a bit of him. And she liked what she saw. He didn't expect too much of her. In fact he seemed to expect nothing. They could walk and talk, or they could walk in silence, it didn't matter to him. He liked her when she dressed up for dinner and he liked her just as much after a morning's gardening when she was wearing wellies and jeans. He didn't try to get her to talk about Nick (she was more than a little fed up with the 'better out than in' brigade), but once, when she did want to talk about Nick and even had a bit of a weep, he hadn't minded a jot. He met Eva and was nice to her, but he didn't pretend he wanted to adopt her or become her best friend. Some people might have said he wasn't very emotional. But that was what Rosemary liked most about him.

Two days before Alec returned to Copenhagen, Rosemary's mother, Helen, was diagnosed with a virulent form of cancer. It was a shock and yet hardly a surprise. She'd been getting paler and weaker for some time and her debilitating migraines had become more and more frequent. Rosemary was devastated. All she could think was, *another loss*. She had always adored her mother even though she was the first to admit that Helen wasn't easy. The trouble with her mother was that she'd always wanted everything to be perfect. Sometimes she had crackled with the pure tension of it. And what was perfect? What could be perfect? Certainly not life, which was ragged and raw and full of snakes and ladders around every corner which would always take you by surprise.

It was Alec who comforted her when she cried, who held her in his arms and eventually made love to her. And briefly, wonderfully, Rosemary found herself wanting it again, this closeness, this intimacy with another human being. It had been missing from her life for so long. She'd thought that it was another part of her that she would never find again.

'Will you come and visit me?' he asked her on the day he left. 'Copenhagen's a beautiful city. And it's only a short flight away. You could stay as long as you like.'

Rosemary wasn't sure exactly what he was asking. Was he proposing a long-distance relationship? She couldn't see herself flying out to Denmark every other weekend. Or was he suggesting something more permanent? What about work? What about her family? 'I can't leave my parents,' she said. 'My mother . . .' And then, of course, there was Eva. What sort of a proposition was she with a teenage daughter like Eva? She wasn't easy, she never had been easy and Rosemary's relationship with her was fraught at best. She was working towards her GCSEs and eventually she'd go on to university, or so Rosemary hoped. But what did Eva feel? Rosemary hadn't a clue. And worse still, she wasn't sure how it had ever got that way.

'You'd like it over there,' Alec said. 'It could be a new start.'

Magical words. If there was anything Rosemary needed, it was a new start.

'About Burma,' Alec said now. He paused to look at one of the old boats moored in the canal, but Rosemary had the feeling he wasn't looking at it at all.

'Yes?' She re-wound her soft pashmina scarf and tucked it back into the collar of her jacket. But she was mildly surprised. It wasn't like him to delve.

'Couldn't you put it behind you now?'

Could she? Rosemary thought of the day she'd made her discovery.

Alec had returned to Copenhagen and within months her mother had died. Her father had grieved for her, but there was something else. Relief, perhaps? Her parents were very different, she reminded herself, maybe over the years they'd even grown apart. But they'd been happy, hadn't they, in their own way?

The letters were tucked in his bedside cabinet and Rosemary only found them because she was sorting out some of her mother's stuff and had discovered a couple of pairs of her father's socks in Helen's drawer. The letters were tied with a red ribbon and her first thought was: love letters. And she felt a streak of happiness. Because this meant they had loved one another after all. They had written love letters and her father had kept every one.

She soon realised her mistake. She flicked through them.

Each envelope was written in her father's hand, but they weren't addressed to her mother. They were addressed to someone called Daw Moe Mya who lived in Burma. And they hadn't been sent.

Rosemary held them in her hands for several minutes. What did it mean? Who was this Daw Moe Mya? Why hadn't he sent any of these letters to her? What had he wanted to say, but not said? She was intrigued. And her father was out of the house.

Curiously, she eased open the first envelope that he hadn't even sealed, just folded.

My dearest Maya,

she read.

Will I ever send this? Or will I simply read the words over and over again? That, if I cannot talk to you, I need to do. So I doubt I will post this letter, my love. You see, sometimes it is enough just to write the words I want to say to you. It somehow loosens the constriction I have around my heart . . .

Rosemary gasped. She put a hand to her mouth. She checked the date. It was written only two years ago.

Constriction around my heart . . . That phrase had an awfully familiar ring. Rosemary knew exactly how that felt.

She rummaged through the letters then, read every one, about thirty in total. Love letters, yes. But written to a woman in Burma. And when she'd finished reading. Well, then she understood.

Her father had never really loved her mother. Through no fault of her own, Helen had always been second best. He had met this woman in Burma, and he'd never stopped loving her since. The dishonesty . . . Rosemary could hardly credit it. It left her with a bitter feeling, a taste in her throat of bile. He had come back to England and married Rosemary's mother, allowing her to think she was his chosen one, his special girl, the woman he wanted to marry.

But she wasn't. She never had been. And she must surely have known. No wonder he had never given Rosemary his time when she was a child and then a woman, no wonder her mother had always longed for everything to be perfect and had often looked so sad. No wonder that he was relieved now that he could stop pretending. He had always been in love with Maya, this woman from Burma. And his marriage, his English life with Helen, with Rosemary and, yes, even with Eva. It had all been a sham.

'The thing is, Rosemary . . .'

It took her a moment to realise that Alec was still talking.

'It doesn't matter too much to me because I've got no one left.'

She stared at him. No one left?

'But for you. You've got your father and you've got Eva.'

Had she though? Rosemary put a hand to her brow. He was really confusing her now.

84

'At first, I wasn't sure I needed another new challenge at my age,' Alec went on. 'I'm still not completely convinced.' He let out a short laugh.

He was walking more quickly now and Rosemary had to pick up her pace to keep up with him. She almost took his arm to slow him down, but they weren't really like that, she and Alec. They didn't link arms and they didn't hold hands, not usually.

'Convinced about what, Alec?' she asked him.

He glanced at her, distracted. He brushed back his thinning sandy hair. 'I mean it's nice that they're interested, of course. Flattering, you know.'

'Convinced about what?' Rosemary stopped walking.

He stopped too, put his hands on her shoulders and she felt the pressure through her leather jacket. 'I've been asked to join a different company, Rosemary,' he said. 'It means a promotion, more money, a complete change in fact.'

'A complete change?' she echoed. What did he mean, a complete change? Had he been head-hunted then? Was that it?

'Yes.' He relaxed his grip. She searched his expression, still waiting.

'It's in Seattle,' he said.

CHAPTER 9

The Shwedagon was so much more than Eva had expected. The pagoda was bigger, grander and more golden. The mosaiced glass of the walls and pillars glittered and the ornate teak carving around shrines and pavilions simply took her breath away. Eva was in awe. 'Did they really use sixty tons of gold to build this place?' she asked Klaus. Not to mention the diamonds decorating the top of the spire.

'I believe so.' He smiled. He seemed to be enjoying her reaction to the most famous temple of Myanmar.

Eva decided to get that information later from her guide book. For now, it was more important to absorb the atmosphere, to stare up at the golden stupa rising over 300 feet above her head, to absorb the wafting fragrance of incense sticks lit for various Buddhas and nats, the spirits of the place who must be appeased, and to listen to the soft chanting of men and women praying and meditating, sitting cross-legged, bowing forwards reverentially on the worn matting of the temple. None of her studies, none of her grandfather's stories had prepared her for this, the reality.

'You must take off your shoes at the bottom of the steps,' Klaus had told her, indicating where she should leave them.

But no sooner had she set them down than they were seized upon by two doe-eyed, raggedy children and carried triumphantly back to their stall. It seemed that they stored captured shoes and gave them back to their owners in return for a small donation.

Klaus clicked his tongue at them. 'No, no,' he said. 'Bring the shoes back here.'

But Eva just smiled. 'It's alright, really,' she said.

'They take advantage,' he told her. 'You should not encourage or this will become another culture of beggars rather than people trying to be independent.' But from his tolerant expression, she guessed that he understood how she felt on this, her first trip.

Because the children were being enterprising, surely? Eva was keen to support the community. And she didn't care a bit if they were taking advantage. Five hundred kyatts might do something significant for them, but for her it was less than fifty pence.

'It is traditional to visit the planetary post dedicated to your birth day,' Klaus told her as they commenced their walk around the stupa. 'Which day is it?'

'Saturday.' As in Saturday's child has to work for a living, thought Eva.

'*Naga*. It is the dragon, I think.' Klaus raised an eyebrow and took her to the post where people were strewing the Buddha with offerings of flowers and pouring water over him from a gilded cup, as was the custom. 'Astrology is very important to Buddhists,' Klaus told her. 'The day of the week when you were born, the position of the planets. They are considered to have great significance.'

They continued to wander barefoot around the stupa in a clockwise direction, pausing to admire anything that took Eva's fancy, a pavilion containing four teak Buddhas, house martins darting and diving in and out of the castellations of a temple, a group of black-haired children striking a big, golden bell. Klaus seemed quite happy to go wherever she wanted and Eva couldn't stop taking photos. She knew she was behaving like any other tourist, but how could she help it? There was so much to see, so much to capture. The dusty ceramic tiles were smooth under her feet and the air was warm, soft and fragrant, filled with that rhythmic prayer and chanting.

But when she put her camera to one side . . . That was when she felt it. The real and gentle spirituality of the place and the people. The sense of stillness. The shimmer of the gold and the warmth of the teak, the smoky incense and the fading light as the sun dipped and began to slowly set behind the greenery on the far side of the temple. It cast a shaft of red light that mellowed the pagoda into burnished amber and made it seem richer than ever. Darkness softly fell around them like a blanket. And the golden stupa, now bejewelled with lights, was outlined against the indigo sky, pinpricked by stars and cradled by the crescent moon.

'I am glad that you like the Shwedagon,' Klaus said to her. 'It is the glory of Myanmar, I think.'

She nodded. 'And perhaps it has its spirit too.'

He bowed his head in acquiescence. 'But now, you are ready to go?'

Most people had left the temple, but Eva and Klaus lingered to watch a procession of pink-robed, shaven-headed novice monks holding strings of jasmine flowers and paper parasols. They were just children, not more than nine or ten years old, and they were accompanied by members of their family dressed in their best *longyis* and most colourful shawls.

'It is the most important moment in the life of a young Burmese boy,' Klaus told her. 'His initiation.' He seemed thoughtful. 'It is when he becomes a proper and dignified part of the human race.'

'But will these boys stay monks for the rest of their lives?' she asked.

'No. Some do, of course. There are many *phongyis* who dedicate their entire life to the scriptures. But most of them simply withdraw from the secular world for a period of time in order to seek enlightenment, just as the Buddha did.' He shrugged. 'Or so they believe.'

But what did he believe? Eva liked him, but she guessed that there was more to him than met the eye. She sneaked a look at him as they proceeded down the marble steps and into the long aisle lined with handicraft stalls. He seemed cool and perfectly in control but she sensed that he was as deeply affected by this place as she was.

As they approached a small group sitting on the steps, Eva saw one of the Burmese men glance towards them. He got to his feet, re-knotted his green and red checked *longyi* and came a few steps closer.

Klaus saw him too. His brow clouded. Swiftly, he bent towards Eva. 'Excuse me for a moment, please, Eva,' he said. 'Will you wait here?'

'Of course.' He had indicated the doorway of one of the shops, which sold thin sandalwood fans and beaded purses and, although Eva was tempted to take a closer look at the goods on offer, instead she watched Klaus as he approached the man in the *longyi*. Who was that man? And what was he up to? She was curious.

Klaus and the Burmese man were soon deep in conversation. They moved round the corner and out of sight.

Eva frowned. She edged towards a nearby pillar. At first, there was no sign of them on the other side. But then she spotted the two figures standing in the shadows. They were talking animatedly, gesticulating with their hands. She studied the body language. The Burmese man, smaller and shorter than Klaus, seemed to be asking for something, hands outstretched. Klaus shrugged, peeled off some notes from his wallet and passed them over.

What was that all about? As Klaus looked over in her direction, Eva dodged out of sight behind the pillar and, somewhat unsettled, drifted back to the place where he'd left her. A souvenir seller materialised ahead. Her little cards had pictures made from black and gold bamboo, and Eva bought some, choosing at random, silhouettes of stilt houses, boats and palm trees, a big gold moon in the centre. She put them in her bag.

A few minutes later, Klaus appeared and took her arm. 'Sorry, Eva, that was a contact of mine. He was giving me some information, but not as much as I would have liked.' He smiled ruefully.

Eva relaxed. She was seeing drama where there was none, she decided. Klaus had business in Myanmar with some of the people who lived here. Nothing more, nothing less. He had moved away to shield her from what might have held a hint of unpleasantness, that was all. It was nothing. He was a nice man, but she must remember, he was still almost a stranger.

They had dinner in a small but smartish local eatery nearby and Klaus proved to be an entertaining companion. She was tempted to ask him about the Burmese man at the Shwedagon, but something stopped her. After tonight she'd probably never see Klaus again. So, what did it matter?

But in the taxi on the way back to her hotel, he withdrew a leather diary from his jacket pocket. 'I am staying at The Mandalay Royal. Are you?' he asked her. 'Most foreigners stay there so perhaps we can meet up again? I will see if one of those contacts I mentioned has something you might be interested in.'

'I am, yes.' Eva nodded. It would certainly be useful from a professional point of view.

He made a note. 'Then I hope I will see you, Eva, in Mandalay.'

They had arrived at her hotel and he got out to open the car door for her.

'Goodbye, Klaus.'

He dropped a platonic kiss on her cheek. '*Auf Wiedersehen.*'

She gave him a wave and watched as his blond head ducked back into the car and then disappeared out of sight. She'd had a lovely evening. But how well could you possibly know someone you'd just met?

At the desk, the receptionist handed her the room key. 'There is a telephone message,' she said. 'From England.'

'From England?' Eva felt a dip of panic.

'It is from the Bristol Antiques Emporium.' The girl read slowly from a notebook. 'Please telephone. Urgent.'

Urgent? Eva checked her watch. It would be around 6.30 p.m. in the UK. She'd switched off her mobile phone. Global roaming didn't work here in Myanmar and it wasn't easy for a tourist to buy a local SIM card, or so she had heard. Internet connections were awfully slow too. Jacqui had told her to call from a hotel if she needed to, but at over five US dollars a minute she'd be mostly on her own.

'Here is the number.' The girl handed her a slip of paper. It wasn't the office number though, it was one she didn't recognise. 'I dial, yes?'

'Yes, please.' Eva waited. It was painstakingly slow.

At last the girl spoke and handed the receiver to Eva. 'Hello?'

'It's Leon.'

Eva was surprised. Leon had never had much to do with

her side of the business, she'd always dealt with Jacqui. 'Is Jacqui alright?'

'She's fine,' Leon said. 'She asked me to call because she's a bit tied up tonight. Anyway, it's about the shipment that's due to go out. The one you wanted to check over.'

'Oh, I see.' Leon dealt with that side of things, deliveries, shipping and so on. 'What's the problem?'

'No problem,' Leon said. 'Not really. I just wanted to let you know that you don't need to check it. We only intended you to have a word with the people over there. We don't want to upset them, make them feel they're not doing their job properly. Do you see what I mean?'

'I suppose so. I just thought that as I'm here and it's about to go out . . . That it would be a good opportunity to check that packaging.'

'Best not to.' Leon sounded breezy. Clearly, he'd got over whatever had upset him before Eva left Bristol. 'There's too much red tape, to be honest with you, Eva. The shipment's already packed and ready to go. We can't afford any delays at this stage.'

'Oh, alright then. If you're sure . . .' It wasn't up to her, was it?

'We're sure.' Leon hesitated. 'And, like I said, it's a delicate matter, dealing with these people. OK?'

'Alright.' Though Eva felt snubbed. Didn't Leon and Jacqui realise that she could be tactful and diplomatic? She was hardly likely to go in there all guns blazing.

'And you can call me on this number if you have any more queries.'

'Fine.'

'Happy hunting.' And he rang off.

Eva stared at the phone. No enquiries about how she was getting on alone here in Burma, if everything was alright, if she had any problems . . .

'Thank you, madam.' The girl took the receiver back and made a note. Counting up the dollars, no doubt.

Had she misunderstood her role here? Eva didn't think so. Leon had always been difficult and she didn't envy Jacqui one bit. But she was faintly relieved that her duties in Yangon appeared to be over. She was thoughtful as she went up to her room. She draped her silk wrap on the chair and slipped off her leather sandals. She padded over to the window and looked out at the lights and night life that were Yangon, the golden stupa of the Shwedagon still glimmering in the distance against the night sky. Why should she bother about Leon? Tomorrow she'd be in Mandalay and there'd be more artefacts to examine. And lots of other things to keep her occupied too. Such as her grandfather's story and her promise to return the chinthe still nestling in her cabin bag at the bottom of her wardrobe, safe from the prying eyes of any chambermaids. Such as her mother's disapproval. And such as the elusive Maya who could, her grandfather had promised, tell her much more and who she might or might not find in Mandalay.

Quite often, Lawrence found that he'd fallen asleep during the day. He'd be sitting quietly, watching the sparrows and blue tits on the bird feeder, a cup of tea on the side table. And then he'd let his mind drift. Next thing, he'd wake up with the sound of Mrs Briggs or the postman at the front door, the tea stone cold and his head full of the place. Couldn't think where the hell he was for a minute or two. Old age, he supposed. Not that he'd ever stopped thinking about Maya entirely. But his life had been full enough. For many years there had been his work and Helen, then later Rosemary and Eva . . . But now. Well, his darling granddaughter, Eva, was in Burma and it was as if Lawrence had gone back there too, at least in his mind.

Mandalay, 1937

Back at the club, Lawrence couldn't stop thinking about her.

After meeting in the market, they had walked one quarter of the way around the still and calm waters of the moat, which was one mile, she told him, along a cool and wide walkway shaded by trees. The city within its confines, where the club was also located, had once housed the famous Royal Palace and Lawrence felt a swamp of shame when he remembered what Scottie had told him – how the British had ousted the last of the Burmese dynasty at this very place. Why had they done this? Was it purely a matter of greed?

They walked side by side, Lawrence conscious of her small body gently swaying with the rhythm of her steps and as they walked Moe Mya told him what there was to see in the city, the stone carvers and furniture makers, the Shwenandaw Kyaung gilded teak monastery, the Mahamuni, a golden Buddha on which men laid gold leaf in homage to the Great One and the U Bein teak footbridge across the River Irrawaddy.

'I want to see it all,' he told her.

She smiled at his enthusiasm. 'Then perhaps you will,' she said.

After their walk, Lawrence didn't want to let her go, so he took her to a tearoom where green tea was served in tall pots painted with flowers and bamboo and she talked of her family. Of her father who had commercial interests as a broker in the rice business, of her aunt, her mother's sister, who lived near Myitkyina and of her grandmother, Suu Kyi, who had been a servant-girl to Queen Supayalat back in 1885 when the King and Queen had been ousted from their thrones in the Palace and taken into exile.

'Where were they taken?' he asked her, trying not to be distracted by the rich purple of the high-necked blouse she wore, elegantly draped over her *longyi*. It wasn't so much the blouse, it was the metallic sheen of the purple against her burnished skin.

'Madras in India,' she said. 'It was considered to be a place of safety.'

'So far away?' Lawrence was surprised. He knew little of Burmese history, he realised. He had come to this land knowing it was different, but all the differences he had experienced to date concerned the countryside, the people and the culture. Scottie had told him stories, but they were always told by the voice of imperialism rather than the voice of the people. He realised that now. 'Were the King and Queen in so much danger then, to need a place of safety?' He was confused.

'The safety the British were thinking of was their own,' Moe Mya pointed out dryly. 'More tea?'

'Please.' He pushed his cup closer and she lifted the tall and decorative teapot once again. 'What were the British so worried about?' Though he could guess. And he realised that at this moment there was nothing he wanted more than to separate himself from those whom he called the British. He had always been a patriot, but it had been unthinking. Now, he was beginning to wonder.

'An uprising,' she said. 'Even peaceful people like the Burmese have such moments.'

He frowned. 'But the King and Queen were not harmed?'

She shook her head. 'No, they were not,' she said. 'There was a British Protectorate, to ensure that they were well looked after.' She passed him back his cup, now filled with the hot green liquid.

'And to ensure that they stayed put and didn't try to get back to Burma,' he added. It wasn't hard to work this out. How much support had the royal couple had among the Burmese people? It might have been possible for them to regain power. But the British clearly weren't going to take that chance.

'Precisely.'

Out of sight, out of mind. And now Lawrence felt more than shame, he felt guilt, for being British, for being part of imperialism, for the rout which must have affected so many, including Moe Mya's family.

'And what happened to your mother?' he asked her gently, for so far she had only talked of the aunt in Myitkyina and of her father and the close bond between them.

She bowed her head, but not before he had seen the tears fill her dark eyes. 'She died when I was a child.'

Moved, Lawrence reached for her hand, which was still resting on the handle of the teapot. It seemed so small next to his own and he marvelled at the tiny fingernails. 'I'm sorry,' he said.

She acknowledged this. She looked at his hand too although she did not attempt to take hers away. 'My father is a good man,' she said. 'If you like, you can meet him.'

'Of course.' Lawrence spoke automatically, though he was a bit surprised. After all she and he had only just met themselves. But he must see it as an honour and naturally he could not object. Damn it, he didn't want to object. He wanted to know all there was to know about her. 'I'd be delighted,' he added.

She smiled then and extracted her hand from his. 'It will not be easy,' she warned. She lifted her cup to her lips and he followed suit, watching her over the rim.

'Because he's very protective of you?' Lawrence would be protective of her too if he had the chance.

'Because you are British.'

Ah. Another reminder of the unpleasant fact that not all the Burmese were friendly and hospitable to their imperial masters. That some indeed would rather be free. 'I see.' He nodded. But he would still meet him. There was a lot, he realised, that he would do, for a chance to spend more time with this woman.

'Tell me about your work,' she said to him.

'Well . . .' The teak camp had not prepared Lawrence for any such notion of Burmese freedom. Every man who worked for him seemed loyal and accepting of his place. They had to be, otherwise the logging could not run smoothly. 'We are a team,' he said simply. And it was tough, demanding work. 'We have to be resilient.' It meant living for long periods in the teak camps away from civilisation and spending a lot of time in the jungle, along with the leeches, mosquitoes and the rest. And in a heat and humidity that could sap every ounce of energy from a man. But she would know all that, he realised.

'Why did you choose such a job?' Her eyes were wide. To her, such a choice must seem very strange for an Englishman.

'I often wonder.' Especially when the rains didn't come to take the logs off down the river, or when they lost an elephant to disease or accident. It was such bloody hard work. 'I like to be close to the earth, to the soil, to nature,' he told her, and perhaps this was what had first attracted him. He relished the rasping sound of the saw as the timber was felled, the creak of the complaining tree and the explosion as it fell, crushing everything in the forest within reach. He loved the sweet scent of the wood that could fill the hot, heavy air, and he had nothing but admiration for the elephant handlers who guided the great beasts, tied chains and fastened harnesses, so that the logs could be dragged to the banks of the *chaungs*, the wild and rushing mountain streams.

'You have taught us how to use the power of the river,' said Moe Mya. 'And to harness the power of the elephants too.' Although even as she acknowledged this, her small smile seemed to suggest that it was, after all, an insignificant thing.

What was not insignificant, thought Lawrence, was the way that with a boom and a crash, the logs would tumble downstream. And those logs could move. They'd hurtle singly or in packs, colliding into each other and everything in their path with a reverberation that could be felt all along the river bank. Or a log could get caught in rapids or heavy debris and in the blink of an eye there'd be a massive dam of the things until the force and weight of them made the obstacle give and a tidal wave of water carrying logs like missiles would pour down the mountainside. If you got in the way, you'd be a dead man.

'It's not all hard work, though,' he acknowledged. There were terrific cold-weather days too in Upper Burma when you could go on a jungle-shoot for fowl, geese or even bison. And there were the Forest Headquarter hill-stations like Maymyo where you could take leave to play tennis and enjoy a whisky in the club and plain home-cooked food and British camaraderie in the chummery or simply rest and recuperate before returning to camp. Even in camp, there were compensations; there were men who specialised in ferrying supplies and luxuries out there. You could more or less order anything you wanted: cigars, whisky, cans of meat or sardines. You just didn't know when it would arrive. 'You never know what will happen next,' he told her. 'That's what's so exciting. You're at the mercy of the elements. And you're living – do you see? Really living.' It was about as far from a desk job in the UK, working in the family stock-broking firm, as you could get.

'You have great passion,' she said, 'for your work.'

And he supposed this was true. He'd come to Burma to escape duty and the desk and he'd discovered the world of nature, the world of wood and a landscape and people that had already crept into his heart. It was indeed a different life.

Forestry was an old trade. Teak had been shipped from Burma to India as far back as the early eighteenth century though Lawrence's company had only acquired the forest leases, the elephant herds and the logging staff at the turn of this century when others had looked to the railways for their living. And the legislation was strict. Every teak tree in Burma belonged to the government and the Forest Department supervised which trees were chosen for felling. They must be mature, they must be dried out for at least three years and seasoned so that they could float. There was a hell of a lot of forest in Burma, but the amount of trees in any given area that were allowed to be felled was inconsistent and the terrain was tough. This made Lawrence's job still harder.

He quickly learnt to recognise unsound trees, to take into account irregularities of shape. The trees were felled by saw at ground level and that's when Lawrence and his crew would visit each one, to measure and hammer-mark it to indicate the points at which it would later be made into logs. It was indeed a trade dependant on nature: on the earth, on the trees, on animals and on the seasons. They needed the rainy season to move the logs down the rivers and they needed the elephants to haul them there. It was quite a spectacle. And the terrain was far too hilly and broken by *chaungs*, the spread of the extractable trees far too random to use mechanical haulage means. He explained some of this to Moe Mya.

She seemed interested, watching his face as he spoke, occasionally nodding or pouring more tea. 'And you like our elephants?' she teased. 'They work well for you, yes?'

'Oh, yes. Without them we couldn't do what we do,' he said. He worked closely with the forest assistant to look after these sagacious beasts and he got to know them individually, you couldn't help but. They were quirky and they had their likes and dislikes – which side they were approached from, for example (if you got it wrong, you'd get swiped from the swishing tail and that was no joke, as Lawrence had found out to his cost) and the spot from which they liked to feed. They were sensitive too and had to be protected from sores and disease. Anthrax was the worst; you could lose an entire working herd of a hundred in a matter of days. And they needed lots of food, sleep and baths in order to perform at their best.

Their working day might be only six hours – by noon they'd had enough – but by God did they put the work in. Lawrence was in awe. Between May and October during the rains, unharnessed elephants would follow the logs downstream, breaking up the jams of wood that tended to occur in the feeder streams and tributaries until they reached the main swollen river and the point where villagers could retrieve the logs (not a job Lawrence would care to undertake himself) and make up the raft. It was a bloody long and hazardous journey.

'I have seen the rafts many times,' Moe Mya told him. 'They are so big, yes?'

'They are. They need to be. They even have grass huts to accommodate the raftsmen, their families and possessions.' The whole family were involved with the retrieval of the logs, they would move location according to where was the best position to be stationed, children would keep lookout for the timber, skilled retrievers would bring in the logs which must be anchored, moored and then bound to make a raft of the size decreed by the timber company. But it was dangerous work. Men could die.

'How strange it all seems,' she murmured.

'It can take a long time to get to Rangoon by river,' he explained to her. 'Weeks, sometimes months. One has to take everything one will need.' The rafts were powered by the current of the river and guided by oars.

'And when they get there? What will they do then?' She was teasing him now, that spark in her dark eyes that he had noticed at the market, that meant that she understood him, even that she was laughing at him perhaps. Not that he minded. As long as she was there.

'The company gives them rail tickets to return to their villages,' he told her, keeping his back straight and proud. They weren't so bad, were they? It wasn't such an unsatisfactory job. What else would they do? 'And they stay there until the next rains.'

'Perfect.' She laughed.

The cycle of the seasons, the cycle of life. It was something that perhaps Britain had lost somehow with its city ways and industry. But it was here, Lawrence thought now. It was here.

'And when will you go back to camp?' Moe Mya asked him, her face serene. Was she wondering when she would see him again? Did she want to see him again?

'Just before the rains,' he said. There was no sign as yet, but it couldn't be long. All the extractions had been completed, the logs were arranged instream and the *ounging* herds were patiently waiting . . . It was a frustrating time. There was a sense of achievement but they needed that rain. And the heat went on.

'They will come soon,' she said. 'And now, I must go.' She rose to her feet. 'Please excuse me.'

'Oh.' He almost stumbled as he too got up from the chair. They had been sitting there for so long and he had quite lost track of time.

She shivered as they stepped outside, though to Lawrence the heat still seemed to hang heavy in the darkness that had now fallen.

'May I?' He put the blanket he was still holding gently around her shoulders. 'It is yours,' he said.

'Thank you.' She looked suddenly vulnerable as she stood there on the street with the thin blanket around her.

On impulse, he bent down and very gently brushed her lips with his. She didn't flinch as he'd thought she might, but neither did she respond. 'I can see you again?' He tried not to make it sound too much like a question – that way, she could refuse.

She bowed her head. 'Of course.'

'Good.' He came to a sudden decision. 'And I too will call you Maya,' he said.

Eva walked out on to the wooden verandah at Pine Rise in Pyin Oo Lwin, previously known as Maymyo. The goods she had come to see in Mandalay weren't ready to be inspected. She had emailed Jacqui who didn't seem overly concerned and who had agreed that Eva could take a few days of her leave here. There would be plenty for her to see, Jacqui had confirmed, when she returned to the city.

After the stifling heat, the hustle and bustle and traffic spilling in all directions in downtown Mandalay: rundown cars, scooters, trishaws, bicycles weaving around one other, signalling their intent with sharp bursts of the hooter or rings of the bell, this was an oasis of calm. And so it must have seemed to her grandfather when he stayed here. Eva took a deep breath of the clean air. A taste of paradise. The wide and dusty teak verandah felt solid and reassuring under her feet and there was a freshness in the air and a lushness to the planting that felt like silk on her somewhat frazzled senses.

In Mandalay, Eva had braved the city madness and taken a hair-raising taxi ride on the back of a scooter to the first address her grandfather had given her. She'd plucked up the courage to knock on the door of the rather smart traditional

Burmese house and wondered. *Could this be where she would find her?* But the young girl with ebony hair and a big smile who said, 'Hello, hello,' to Eva as if she were a long lost friend had not been able to help her.

'Gone ten year,' she'd said, holding up both hands.

'Do you know where?' Eva had gesticulated to try and get her meaning across.

The girl shook her head sadly.

'OK. Thanks.' But now she knew. The family, or some of them, had survived the war. They had lived in this house until ten years ago. And Eva still had address number two.

The address written on the second slip of paper was here in Pyin Oo Lwin.

As soon as she received Jacqui's email, Eva had checked out of her hotel in Mandalay and booked herself back in again for two days' time. Then she'd made a reservation at Pine Rise. Her need to follow the trail was all-consuming. It was easy to get a driver and she'd enjoyed the journey this morning as they drove from the broad plain of the Irrawaddy towards the old hill-station of Maymyo. Already the landscape had changed. The earth was a rich red and the vegetation more abundant; oleander and tall bamboo, poinsettia and mimosa lining the way with red and yellow and bursts of shocking purple.

Pyin Oo Lwin itself was an elegant and leafy town with avenues of eucalyptus trees hiding mock-Tudor houses, grand red-bricked villas and white bungalows positively shimmering in the sun. The houses were set far apart and in extensive grounds, their background, pine woodland and, in the distance, rolling hills of oak. They passed the Purcell Tower which her grandfather had told her housed a clock that used to chime with the same sound as Big Ben – how English was that?! – and a vibrant flower market. And finally, there it was. Pine Rise. Airy and light. All polished teak, clotted cream walls and glass chandeliers. Eva loved it on sight.

Her grandfather had spent a lot of time here, in the colonial guesthouse once owned by the company he worked for, now a hotel. It had provided rest and recuperation after a session working up in the jungle. It was a place in which to unwind, relax, recharge the batteries along with other company colleagues, before plunging back into the fray. He'd also spent time here recuperating from a bout of malaria.

Eva looked out over the lawn, where a carpet of yellow celandine-like flowers was just opening into bloom and, in the centre, a hexagonal wooden bench with a pergola above. Maya's family had also owned a weekend- and holiday-retreat here, hence the address written in her grandfather's hand in Eva's purse. Apparently, many of the well-off Burmese still did. It was two hours' drive from Mandalay, but at a higher altitude and so refreshingly cooler.

Eva trailed her fingers along the handrail. Her grandfather had stood here, perhaps even touching the same piece of wood, staring out at the same tropical gardens, which must have seemed a million miles away from the busy cities and steamy jungles he'd been working in. He, too, had climbed the highly polished teak staircase, which rose elegantly from the foyer to open out at the top like a tulip, forming a gallery from which you could promenade all the way around and gaze down into the foyer, where there was a Victorian fireplace twice as tall as Eva. He had stayed in one of these high-ceilinged rooms with disused fireplaces, maybe her room? The thought made her spine tingle. She didn't think she had ever felt so close to him. And the little chinthe was still safely tucked in her bag. He was on quite a journey too, though it wasn't his first. She thought of her grandfather in the jungle. Had he carried the chinthe with him when he went to war?

It was 2 p.m. She returned to her room, picked up her wide-brimmed hat and her new colourful Shan bag and left the hotel, the slip of paper in her hand, along with a road map provided at reception. The house that had been Maya's family retreat was less than ten minutes' walk away, the receptionist had told her, and now she was so close, Eva wanted to take it slowly.

She found the house on a dusty road at the top of a slight incline, its entrance framed by bamboo fencing wound with frangipani. She paused just for a moment to drink in the scent, which was so rich she almost felt dizzy, and made her way up the wide driveway. It was another traditional house but grander than the one in Mandalay. Built of teak and intricately patterned bamboo, it was made up of two storeys, the upper having a wide verandah which swept right around the house. There was so much wood. Even the roof was constructed with wooden tiles and the panelled door was framed by bougainvillea, which the Burmese called the paper tree, as her driver had informed her this morning on the way here.

Deep breath. Eva lifted the brass door knocker and let it fall. The sound seemed to reverberate around the walls of the house, shattering the air of tranquillity. In more ways than one, she thought ruefully.

A man opened the door. He was in his mid-thirties, with the dark hair of the Burmese, but with the features and height – he must be six feet tall – of a Westerner. Anglo-Burmese perhaps; Myanmar was a country of mixed races and influences: Japan, China, Thailand, India and Britain, for starters. He was clean-shaven, his skin a shade of dark olive.

Eva licked her dry lips. 'Hello.' She smiled. 'Do you speak English?'

'Of course.' He smiled back at her and his rather sharp-boned features were transformed. His accent was European, his tone soft and low.

She straightened her shoulders. 'I'm looking for the family of Daw Moe Mya,' she said. 'Do they live here, by any chance?'

He eyed her curiously, with just a hint of suspicion now. 'Why are you looking for them?'

A question for a question. Fair enough, she supposed. 'I have a message,' she said. 'For Daw Moe Mya, if she is still alive.' It still seemed so unlikely, but somehow Eva couldn't help trusting her grandfather's intuition; he had rarely been proved wrong.

The man frowned, calmly scrutinising her from hat to toe.

He seemed relaxed, she found herself thinking, but ready to pounce if necessary.

Eva fidgeted uncomfortably under his gaze. 'Does she live here?' she repeated. 'May I speak with her?'

He bowed his head slightly. 'My grandmother is old,' he said.

So she was alive! Grandpa, bless him, had been right. Eva wished she could tell him this instant. See the expression on his face when he heard the news . . . 'That's wonderful!' She beamed at the man in the doorway.

He raised dark eyebrows at her, a threat of a smile now touching the corners of his full mouth. 'It is?'

'Yes, it is. Not that she's old, of course, but that she's still . . .' She trailed off under his stare. 'I've come a long way,' she explained. 'From England.'

'England?' He blinked at her as if he expected her to break into a song-and-dance routine. He was wearing a short-sleeved, dove-grey shirt, and the traditional male *longyi* in a sage green and black check knotted at the front. And it was funny, but, as she'd already observed since she'd arrived in Myanmar, the effect was surprisingly macho.

'Yes. And I've come especially to see her.' Eva stood her ground.

'And who . . .' he said, 'are you?'

Ah. Here we go, she thought. Another deep breath. 'I'm the granddaughter of Lawrence Fox,' she said.

His eyes flickered. She realised that he had heard the name. Unlike most of the Burmese whose eyes were dark brown, sometimes almost black, his eyes were green, and with his dark hair and skin the effect was quite dramatic. But if he was surprised at her disclosure, he hid it well. He hesitated but then seemed to come to a decision. 'You may come in,' he said, his tone more guarded. 'I will see if my grandmother wishes to speak with you. But you must not stay long. Please,' and his eyes met hers, 'she is very frail.'

Alleluia, she thought. She was in and, 'I won't tire her,' she promised. But she wondered, was he just being protective? Or did he know their grandparents' story and resent what had happened between them all those years ago? What was more important, and rather scary, was that she was about to meet her, at last. Maya, the woman her grandfather had always loved.

The white entrance hall was open and airy and according to the custom, Eva slipped off her black Burmese slippers before following him into the next room. In the centre was a magnificent polished teak table. Eva couldn't help but reach out to touch its smooth and glossy surface, though as she did so, she caught him casting a probing glance her way. Around the table were several ladder-backed chairs, also beautifully made. On the far side of the room was a platform with blue-tiled walls and a shrine, placed high on the far wall. On it, looking down on the room below, was a small intricately carved Buddha and a vase of fresh flowers, their scent drifting through the air.

'Wait here,' he said. 'Please sit.' He gave her another assessing glance and in one fluid movement, turned and was gone from the room.

Eva sat. On the side wall were some photographs and she strained to see. A couple – presumably a King and Queen – seated on royal thrones. They looked very grand.

A few moments later, she heard the lightest of footsteps. She looked up. An old Burmese lady stood framed in the doorway. She was very tiny and her hair was white, but still, she held herself erect.

Maya.

Eva jumped to her feet. How would she be received? She hesitated for a moment, but Maya was already moving towards her, arms outstretched, her brown milky eyes filled with an expression of excitement and disbelief.

'Lawrence's granddaughter?' she breathed. 'But, yes. Look at you. You must be.' She seemed quite overcome.

'Yes. My name is Eva.'

Her grandson materialised from behind his grandmother and offered his arm, but the old lady grasped Eva's arms instead and pulled her into a close embrace. 'Eva . . .' she murmured. 'Eva.'

She smelt of oil and coconut and her grip was intense for such an old lady. *My grandfather's lover*, Eva thought, closing her eyes for a second. His Burmese lover. She didn't know why, but she was surprised that Maya spoke such fluent English. She'd known that the family were well-educated, cultured and well-off by Burmese standards. Even so . . .

Maya drew away and looked into her face, deep into her eyes as if she could look much further. With dry fingertips she traced a pattern over Eva's cheekbones. 'The shape of your face,' she murmured. 'It makes me remember . . .'

My grandfather. Eva had never thought they looked alike, but the family resemblance must be there, reminding Maya of what she had lost. But had she lost him? Or had she chosen to give him up? That, among other things, was what Eva intended to discover.

At last, Maya released her. 'Bring tea.' She clapped her hands. 'We must sit.'

Her grandson called out to someone in the far reaches of the house and Maya indicated to Eva that she should sit down again. The old lady was still smiling. There was no doubt that she was pleased to see her. Eva felt the relief wash over her. She wouldn't think about her mother and her grandmother, Helen, and whatever loyalties she should feel towards them, not now. First, she wanted to understand.

'You have come from England to see us?' Maya asked, her old eyes incredulous in her creased face. 'After all these years?'

'Yes. My grandfather asked me to bring something here for you.' Eva fumbled in her bag.

'He is still alive?' Maya's face lit up and for a moment she looked as eager as a girl. 'Lawrence is still alive?' She was holding on tight to the sides of her chair, her tiny body tense as a coiled spring. Slowly, she relaxed. 'I thought so,' she murmured. 'But I could not be sure.'

Just like Grandpa, Eva thought. They were as intuitive as each other. 'He certainly is.' With a flourish, Eva produced the decorative teak chinthe from her bag. She had wrapped him in tissue paper but his head and mane had escaped its confines. 'And he thought it was about time this little one came home.' Gently, she unwrapped the rest of him. Placed him on the table in front of her.

Maya and her grandson gasped simultaneously as they stared at the chinthe. The sight of it seemed to have an extraordinary effect on them both.

'Ah!' Maya's eyes filled with tears and she murmured something in Burmese. 'Lawrence,' she said softly. 'I knew, I knew.'

Eva was moved. She wasn't sure precisely what it was that Maya knew, but it was blindingly obvious that this woman had felt the same about her grandfather as he had felt about her. But if so . . . It seemed so wrong that they hadn't stayed together. What could be the reason? Eva glanced at Maya's grandson but he continued to stare at the chinthe as if still in shock. Had he known of its existence? She assumed so. Was he simply surprised that she had brought it back?

Maya must have married after Eva's grandfather had left Burma, Eva realised. She'd had a child, the mother or father of this man, her grandson. And that child must have married a Westerner for him to look as he did. Tall, green-eyed . . . A wing of his dark hair kept flopping on to his forehead, and he swept it away in an irritated gesture with the back of his hand. Did he know how Lawrence and Maya had felt about one another? How could anyone not know when the emotions were written so clearly on his grandmother's face?

He reached forwards, scooped up the chinthe in one brown

hand and frowned, turning it from left to right to examine it. She noticed his long fingers and short square nails. 'It seems undamaged,' he said. 'I do not think it has been tampered with.' With a swift glance at his grandmother, he got to his feet and took the chinthe to the other side of the room, where he got something out of a drawer.

He had his back to her, so Eva couldn't see. But . . . Tampered with? She bridled. 'My grandfather has looked after it.' She addressed Maya. 'He cherished your gift,' she assured her.

'Of course.' Maya bowed her head. 'Thank you, my dear child. Ramon . . .' she remonstrated.

With a nod, he came back, replaced the chinthe on the table. But he didn't sit down.

'So now he can be reunited with his twin.' Eva looked around the room. Where did they keep the other one? She would have expected it to be guarding the shrine. 'To restore harmony.' That was what her grandfather had wanted. That was how he had said it must be.

Maya and her grandson exchanged a look.

'Isn't that the belief?' Eva asked.

'Yes, it is.' Maya laid a gentle hand on her arm. Her skin was thin and papery but her hand was warm. 'But you see, Eva, it is not so simple.'

Her grandson muttered what sounded like a curse in his native language. He paced over to the other side of the room and then turned back to her. 'You brought this in your luggage from England?' he demanded.

'Yes. In my cabin bag.'

He shook his head. 'Incredible,' he muttered. 'Impossible.'

Eva was confused. 'Why isn't it so simple?' she asked Maya.

Maya sighed. Tenderly, she took the chinthe from the table, gazed into its red glass eyes. She shook her head sadly, running her fingertips over the carving of the face and mane Eva had always admired so much. 'Because,' she said, 'I no longer have the other.'

'Oh.' Eva hadn't even considered that possibility, and she suspected her grandfather hadn't either. 'Where is it?' she asked. 'Do you know?' But it had been a long time. Perhaps it had been naive of them to imagine that the chinthe's twin would have survived the war and its turbulent aftermath.

'It was stolen,' Maya's grandson said. He shot her another look. He still seemed angry. Perhaps that was his default emotion, Eva found herself thinking.

'Really?' She looked again at the little chinthe. It was a beautiful piece of carving, but, although old, she didn't think it would mean much to anyone other than the family who owned it. Why would it be stolen? 'Who by?'

'It is a long story.' Maya nodded and laid her hand again on Eva's arm. 'Do you know anything about the origin of Burmese chinthes, Eva?'

'A bit.'

'It is linked to our Buddhist philosophy,' she said.

'In what way?' Eva was intrigued.

'It is said that once, many moons ago, a princess was married to a lion and had a son by him,' Maya said, her voice slow, almost hypnotic. 'But later she abandoned this lion. He was

enraged and set out on a pathway of terror through the lands.'
She paused. 'The son went out to slay the terrorising lion.
Three times he shot an arrow at him. But so great was the
lion's love for his son that three times the arrow rebounded
from his brow.' Maya sighed. 'But the fourth time the lion
grew angry and the arrow killed him. Thus the lion lost his
life because he had lost his self-possession and allowed wrath
to invade his heart.'

'And what happened to the son?' Eva asked.

'He returned home to his mother who told him that he had
killed his father. The son then constructed a statue of the lion
as a guardian of a temple to atone for his sin.'

And the lion was the chinthe. Eva reached out to touch it
as she had done so often in her childhood. This was like listening to her grandfather's stories all over again. Burma must
be a land full of them. Myths, perhaps, but myths that had a
way of resonating and revealing some inner truth.

A young girl appeared with a tray of tea things and laid
them on the table next to Maya. The old lady picked up the
teapot, lifting it high and accurately pouring the stream of
green-gold liquid into three tiny cups.

'So, can you tell me what happened to your chinthe?' Eva
asked. She had come all this way. She wanted to know the
whole story and so, of course, would her grandfather.

Maya's grandson spoke swiftly to his grandmother in Burmese. It didn't take much imagination to guess that he was
warning Maya not to tell.

Maya nodded. 'What you say is true, Ramon,' she told

him. 'But she is Lawrence's granddaughter and she deserves to know.'

'We have a tradition in our country to pass stories from generation to generation.' She turned to Eva. 'Drink your tea, my dear,' she said. 'And I will tell you what happened.'

CHAPTER 12

Mandalay, 1885.

For Suu Kyi, the Royal Palace in Mandalay in the centre of
the walled city, a spread-eagled complex of red-roofed pavilions, towers and lush Royal Gardens, had always been the
safest place in her world. She was an orphan, from the Shan
states, and had been rescued and brought here to serve the
Queen, purchased by the Queen's agents and brought up at
the Palace, as was Nanda Li, another young maidservant of
her own age. She could barely remember living anywhere
else. The Royal Palace itself had been transported here and
rebuilt thirty years ago, long before Suu Kyi was born. Four
walls surrounded the citadel, and a moat deep and still. Their
position seemed impenetrable.

Many were afraid of Queen Supayalat; she was small but
had a fierce temper and there were those who said she had only
become Queen because she had seen to it that all the rivals
to her husband, King Thibaw's throne, seventy-nine princes
all told, were wrapped in carpets to prevent the spillage of
royal blood, bludgeoned to death and thrown in the nearest
river. Perhaps this was true. But she loved the King, Suu Kyi
could see that, and this impressed her greatly. She herself was

slightly afraid of him; he looked very handsome in his royal sash and golden slippers, though she was aware that he was half-Shan which accounted for his high cheekbones and fine eyes. Mostly though, she kept her eyes downcast when he entered the room. Suu Kyi was humble and she was happy simply to serve. Most especially she loved to serve the two princesses aged one year and three. Suu Kyi was proud that no one else – and especially not Nanda Li – could deal with the Second Princess's paroxysms of rage as well as she could. And now the Queen was in her eighth month of pregnancy and there would be a third child. No one could be more delighted than she.

But even Suu Kyi was aware that something was changing. Although their palace was guarded at all four corners by sentries of the King's bodyguard, and uniformed soldiers were all around, the Queen was jittery. And besides, Suu Kyi could hear the guns, the distant boom and grumble of cannon.

They all knew the origin of the problem; it had been much talked-of. There had been a dispute with a British timber company about the amount of duty that was being paid (Queen Supayalat insisted they were trying to avoid paying duty altogether) and the company had complained to the British Governor in Rangoon. The Queen was in favour of levying a substantial fine on the company. They must not think that they could behave as they liked, that they were in charge of this country, she said to her maidservants, to the King, to the Court and to anyone else who would listen. But the King's ministers had advised otherwise. A line should be drawn under the entire affair and the matter of paying duty on the timber should be forgotten, to ensure that the British allowed the King and Queen to remain on the throne. *Allowed* them to remain on the throne? The Queen had ranted and railed. Who did they think they were? She refused to give in and the King had followed her lead as he always did. And now . . .

Suu Kyi knew that the British had crossed the border; they all knew. But every time the King or the Queen asked for news, they were told that all was going well for the Burmese soldiers, that, indeed, there had been another victory and that there was no reason to worry. Even so, they all were worrying, the Second Princess was being even more difficult than usual and did not want to play five stones with rubies with her sister. Because they had all heard what the Queen had said. 'Those are not our guns. And they are getting closer and closer.'

It wasn't long before they found out the truth. The Burmese army had, in fact, disintegrated and fled to the hills, the war had lasted only fourteen days, the Royal Family were now being kept here as prisoners by ministers thinking only of their own personal gain and the British would be arriving very soon, to take them into captivity. Suu Kyi was shocked. How could this be? Who were these British who seemed to have so much power that even the might of the Burmese Army could do nothing against them?

'They have superior weapons,' Nanda Li said. 'I overheard the King talking to one of his men. There are thousands of them, not just British but Indian too, many Indians. They have big guns and cannon. We can do nothing against such a force.'

Indians too, thought Suu Kyi. And yet there were so many Indians living here in Mandalay, she had seen them. How was it, she wondered, that they came to fight for another side?

Nanda Li rolled her eyes. 'India is part of the British Empire,' she snapped. 'Do you never hear anything? Do you know even less?'

Sure enough, only a day later, the British soldiers came to the fort and they began to loot it, leaving the gates of the citadel unguarded when they left. There was so much, they could not take everything. The Queen seemed to go into a trance, as if the looting of her palace and her possessions was not real, as if it could not be happening. And it was up to Suu Kyi to care for the princesses, to shield them from harm, to prevent them from seeing the worst of it.

But more was to come. When they saw the soldiers leave . . . When they saw the citadel unguarded for the very first time . . . Then the people came. Suu Kyi saw their faces. At first, they must have been surprised that it was possible, since entering the palace unbidden would normally be punished by execution. Then they became greedy. They arrived in a jumble and a frenzy. They ran bare-footed, clutching their longyis close to them, right into the women's quarters where the Queen, the princesses, Suu Kyi and the few other maidservants who had not run away remained, bewildered and confused.

The princesses were both crying. Suu Kyi was trying to comfort them. The Queen, who because of her condition was supposed to be resting, simply lay on her royal couch and Nanda Li stood staring out of the window as if contemplating her next move.

Occasionally she shot a look of derision in Suu Kyi's direction. 'Why do you bother?' she hissed, when she could see the Queen was not listening. 'They are finished. Do you not see?'

But it was second nature to Suu Kyi. She loved the princesses and she would protect them with her life. Indeed, she could not imagine life without them, nor without Queen Supayalat for that matter, tyrannical and selfish though she could be. And besides, she, like Nanda Li, had no other family to go to. What choice did they have?

The noise from the mob increased until they could ignore it no longer. A man, a Burmese man, one of their people, had grabbed a rock and was trying to knock out the jewels from the jade-studded panels of the doors, someone else was throwing an offering box on the marble floor in an attempt to dislodge the gems within. And it was not all Burmese. There were many other nationalities apart from Indian living in the city of Mandalay and Suu Kyi could see some of Chinese and Thai origin also here in the chamber. But nationality was immaterial. They were all out for themselves. A woman was trying to dig jewels from the floor with the heel of her shoe, a child was even attempting to bite the rubies from the lid of a large, golden betel box with a lacquered dragon stand. People were grabbing what small objects they could, from decorated candelabra to jewelled hand mirrors, from filigree caskets to golden pitchers, using makeshift tools of rock or wood to gouge out the jewels from others. They were squabbling and fighting in the stifling heat, tearing things from each other's grasp. The beautiful wooden furniture, intricately carved cabinets and chests studded with precious jewels whose drawer handles were delicately moulded in the shape of elephant trunks and dragon tails, was being hacked to pieces. The walls of the chamber were tiled with clear and green glass and an oil lamp flamed, illuminating the carnage.

At first, the Queen continued to do nothing. She and the rest of them stayed in their candle-lit antechamber, and they listened helplessly to the raucous frenzy going on outside. Suu Kyi saw the Queen come out of the trance and begin to grind her teeth and look frantically from left to right. She knew that the Queen was not afraid; her face was purple with rage under the ivory *thanaka* face powder she wore.

She arose from her royal couch, made of teak and gold and studded with diamonds. And she stood in the doorway, next to the glass mosaic jade screen, her silk robes billowing around her. She was like a great ship in full sail. 'Get out!' she shrieked. 'How dare you come here like this? Go away! Get out!' And she shook her fist.

But what could she do against such a mob? Suu Kyi tried to hide the terrible sight from the princesses. Some of the looters had noticed Supayalat, some were clearly shocked to recognise their queen, and were bending and bowing into the reverential *shiko* that must always be afforded to royalty, some so low it looked like they were walking backwards. But even as they did this, others were dragging up the mat of silver and continuing to loot and steal from the Queen's chamber. Their supposed homage and respect meant nothing.

Before she had really thought about what she was doing, Suu Kyi leapt past the Queen and into the chamber where the people were rampaging and looting. 'The soldiers are coming back!' she yelled to the mob. 'Quick! Run! Soldiers are coming!'

Terror flamed briefly on the people's faces. They looked over their shoulders and then they ran. Fast and furious, they tumbled out of the glass-walled chamber as quickly as they had arrived, pushing and shoving to get through the tiny doorway, even dropping some of their booty in their haste.

The Second Princess was bawling. Her tiny bejewelled body was rigid and her fists were closed tight.

'Hush now.' Suu Kyi ran to her. She picked her up and held her close. 'Hush little one, for we shall be safe.' She crooned to her, she sang softly as if everything was not disintegrating around them. And she tried not to look at Nanda Li and the nasty sneer that seemed fixed on her arrogant face.

When the child was sleeping once more, Suu Kyi looked up to see the Queen standing beside her.

'Thank you, Suu Kyi,' she said, her eyes still angry. 'You have been very brave. But we cannot stop them. If these riches do not go to the people, then they will go to the British who are taking us prisoner.'

Suu Kyi nodded. She understood. She knew too that their

country housed the richest gem mines in the whole world and that the King and Queen were in possession, or had been, of a huge fortune in gemstones alone. It was their Royal Right and had been so throughout the Burmese dynasty.

'But we can gather up some things of our own.' With some difficulty the Queen reached down to a bag she was filling with her own personal jewels, necklaces of rubies and jade, rings of diamonds and gold and her own gold jewellery box with a lock and key. 'And these are for you.' From the bag she pulled two decorative chinthes. They were of the finest teak carving and their eyes shone.

'For me?' Suu Kyi could hardly speak. The Queen had never given her a gift before.

'For looking after the Second Princess so valiantly,' the Queen said. 'And for what you have done for us here today.' She nodded and bent as low as she was able. 'See here.' She demonstrated how skilfully they had been constructed. 'Look after these beasts and be careful who you choose to give them to,' she said. 'They may prove to be your security and your fortune. Use them well.'

Suu Kyi bowed as deeply as she could whilst still holding the sleeping princess. And it was when she arose that she saw it. The look on Nanda Li's face. It was a look of pure hatred and it made her shudder inside.

CHAPTER 13

Seattle.

'Seattle?' she'd echoed. 'But that's . . .'

'A long way away, yes,' he said grimly.

The United States. America.

'What did you tell them?' she'd asked him later, after they'd finished dinner, cleared up and gone to bed. It was king size, the duvet, goose-down, the sheets Egyptian cotton. Both of them were staring up at the ceiling. They were lying at least a foot apart. What would happen, Rosemary wondered, if she were to reach out for him?

'That I need time to think about it.' He glanced across at her. Without his glasses on he seemed naked, despite the cotton pyjamas he was wearing. 'To discuss it with my wife.'

'I see,' she murmured. All she could think was it seemed so far away.

Alex hiked himself up on one elbow. 'Rosemary, you hardly see your family,' he said.

'I know.'

'It's a great opportunity. I didn't think I'd ever get it at this stage.'

At this stage in his career, he meant. He was still only in his early fifties. But it was a young man's game.

'I know.'

He sighed. 'What do you want to do?'

That was three days ago and Rosemary wasn't any closer to giving him an answer. She filled the percolator with water and reached for the coffee beans. Did he want to go to Seattle? Did he want to uproot them and move to the US? She supposed that he did. Alec had always been ambitious, and she knew he'd always hoped to further advance his career, to be given a higher role in the company, to be a solution architect and actually in charge of designing interactive software rather than a senior developer. But she also knew that Alec was giving her some sort of choice. She had gone with him before, left the UK, moved to Copenhagen, followed that promise of a new start.

Rosemary switched on the grinder. She felt something painful in her chest. Was it regret?

She had never intended to leave her daughter behind. She had assumed — of course she had assumed — that when she decided to marry Alec and move to Copenhagen, Eva would come too. She was still only sixteen. Her place was with her mother. She could take her GCSEs in England and then finish her schooling in Copenhagen. And why shouldn't Rosemary marry Alec? After Nick's and then her mother's death, she was finally seizing a chance of some sort of happiness. And she had longed to get away. She had always loved West

Dorset. But now it stood for her marriage to Nick, her husband's death, the loss of her mother. As for her father . . . She was finding it hard to forgive him for those letters, for what had happened in Burma all those years ago before she was even born. She didn't want to be living in Dorset. Not anymore.

Rosemary switched off the machine and transferred the freshly ground coffee to the percolator, breathing in the rich, mellow fragrance that would always remind her of her honeymoon with Nick in the Cinque Terre of Italy; of the narrow streets and tall, colourful houses in the five mountainside villages; the scent of roasted coffee beans spilling out on to shady walkways and café terraces.

But there was also Eva. Transplanting her sixteen-year-old into a different lifestyle, with new opportunities, could only do her good, could only go some way towards healing the rift between them. That, at least, was what she had thought.

Rosemary screwed on the lid of the percolator and switched on the hob. She would never forget the day she came home from work and found Eva hunched and crying in her room.

'I don't want to go,' she had wept. 'I don't want to go.' Her dark hair tumbled, unruly as ever, over her shoulders. Her eyes were red and her lips swollen from her tears.

'To Copenhagen? But Eva, you'll soon make new friends. You'll go to a fantastic sixth-form college, have a great life, a much better time—'

'I've been talking to Grandpa.' Eva sniffed and hiccoughed. 'He says if I want to, I can go and live with him instead.'

Rosemary stared at her. Her mind was a blank. Where had she gone wrong? 'You don't want to come with me to Copenhagen?' she whispered.

'No.' And Eva had looked up at her with sad, dark eyes that were such an echo of Nick's, it almost broke her heart.

'You're sixteen,' she heard herself saying in a cool voice she hated. 'It's your decision. It's up to you.'

Rosemary had never forgiven her father for giving Eva the option. It hadn't been his place to. First Burma and now this, she had thought. Of course he'd been thinking of himself, as he always did. He didn't want to be apart from his precious granddaughter, he couldn't bear the thought of her living in another country. So why not stop it from happening? Rosemary was shocked at how bitter she felt towards him.

She stood by the stove and waited for the coffee to brew. She could have still changed her mind, of course; she didn't have to go. But she didn't. She told herself Eva would change *her* mind, but she hadn't. Once Eva had taken her GCSEs and it became clear that she was staying in Dorset whatever her mother did, then Rosemary had married Alec and moved to Copenhagen.

'It's not so far,' Alec had reassured her. 'We can come back for weekends as often as you like.'

And they had, at first. Rosemary had even wondered if they had more chance of rediscovering some mother and daughter bond if she was away. But that hadn't happened either. Wishful thinking, she supposed.

The coffee began to percolate and Rosemary put some

milk on to heat. She had to face it. As every year went by, she and Eva had become more and more estranged. Until it seemed to be too late.

By the time Alec came in from work, Rosemary had made a decision.

When they'd first moved here, she'd looked for a job as a legal secretary; that was what she knew, but the system was very different in Denmark and instead, she'd surprised herself by taking a part-time job in a local bookshop. She often used to drift in there to pick up copies of paperbacks and she had got to know the owner. But after a while, he admitted that he couldn't afford to keep her on, and so she left, feeling slightly guilty.

Alec had suggested that she take a break from the workplace. He earned more than enough for the both of them, he reminded her. She'd had a hard life working full time as a single parent, losing her husband so young. 'I want to spoil you a little,' he'd said. 'I want you to relax and take a rest. Have some me-time.'

And so she had. Over the years she'd got involved with various voluntary organisations: Stroke Awareness, in memory of Nick; Copenhagen Youth Project Support for disadvantaged kids and the Library Foundation. It took time and energy, but gave Rosemary a sense of self-worth. She was doing something. But now . . .

'I'm going back home for a while,' she told Alec. She

poured him out a bourbon with ice so that she wouldn't have to look at him as she said it.

She felt him exhale. 'Home?' And she heard the desolation in his voice.

'I need to see them both,' she said. She handed him the drink. Eva was in Burma but she would be back in a couple of weeks.

He downed it in one, never taking his eyes from her face. 'And America?'

'I don't know, Alec.' How much time did her father have left? She needed to make her peace with him.

'You don't know about me?' he asked her. He took off his glasses and rubbed his tired eyes. It made him seem so vulnerable somehow. 'Or you don't know about America?'

Rosemary didn't reply. She closed her eyes. All she knew for sure, at this moment in time, was that she must go back to where she had begun.

CHAPTER 14

'But that is only part of the story.' Maya took a deep and shuddering breath that seemed to come from the core of her tiny body.

Immediately, her grandson Ramon laid a gentle hand on hers. He spoke softly in Burmese, all his anger seeming to have evaporated. Eva was surprised at his tenderness. This was a different side to the man, one she hadn't expected, and she was glad that Maya had him there to look after her.

But as he turned to Eva, his gaze hardened. 'My grand-mother, she is tired,' he said. 'She must rest.'

'Of course.' Though Eva was aching to know the rest of the story. She had hoped to discover the heart of the Burmese tales from her childhood, the force behind them that seemed to have been absorbed into her very being. And she hadn't been disappointed. This story of Maya's was of routs and British imperialism, of precious jewels and royal shenanigans going right back to the final Burmese dynasty. Did her grandfather know all this? If not, Eva couldn't wait to tell him. Though he would be devastated to hear that the other chinthe had been stolen. She looked again at the photographs on the wall. 'The King and Queen?' she asked.

Maya nodded. 'Thibaw and Supayalat,' she said. 'And that is the Lion Throne.'

Eva got up to take a closer look. Unless she was very much mistaken, the throne was made entirely of gold. She looked at the other photograph. It was of an elderly woman sitting very upright in her chair, her eyes fixed with a great sense of stillness on the camera taking the picture.

'My grandmother, Suu Kyi,' Maya murmured. 'Servant-girl to the Queen. She told me the story when she gave me the two chinthes.' She turned to speak to her grandson in Burmese.

'She says I should take you to the National Kandawgyi Gardens for sunset,' he said. 'It is two-hundred-and-forty acres of botanical gardens and forest reserves. It is very beautiful there. Meanwhile, she will rest.'

'There's really no need for you to do that,' Eva said stiffly, since he hardly seemed enamoured at the prospect. And that was an awful lot of acres. 'I don't expect you to organise my sightseeing for me.' This came out more harshly than she'd intended and she noted the flicker of surprise and what might have been amusement cross his features.

'It has been decided.' He bowed his head. 'Then we will return here for dinner.'

'I see.' They seemed to have all her movements planned. Her first instinct was to refuse, to make her own arrangements. For a moment she thought of her mother's remarriage and the decision she'd made to stay in Dorset. Was that the reason they had grown apart? It would have meant leaving all her friends and her beloved grandfather. She couldn't do it, hadn't wanted to do it. Not even for the mother she had lost so many years before.

But this was Burma. Eva must respect their hospitality. She would be gracious and hopefully she'd then hear the rest of the story. 'That sounds lovely,' she said. 'Thank you.'

Maya beamed and rose to her feet. 'Ramon will look after you,' she said.

Eva glanced across at him doubtfully. But as Maya clasped Eva's hands in hers, she felt again the intensity of the old lady's emotion. 'I will see you in a few hours,' she said. She looked deep into her eyes, and Eva felt the potency of her gaze, her spirituality, she supposed. And she could imagine her as a young woman, as her grandfather must first have seen her. She could perfectly understand how they had come to fall in love.

On the drive to Kandawgyi Gardens, Ramon provided her with water and fruit magicked up by one of the girls in the house. Eva longed to ask about them all, find out who was who, but Ramon kept up a polite, detailed and impersonal commentary on Pyin Oo Lwin and their surroundings as he drove smoothly and confidently along the leafy roads, and so she didn't get the chance. He was clearly just doing his duty. And to find out anything more personal, she'd have to wait till later.

'When did Burma become known as Myanmar?' she asked him as he turned the car into the sweeping entrance to the gardens. 'Was it part of the move forward, of independence?'

'1989,' he said. 'Though it is more of a return to our cultural roots. It was the name originally given to our country by Marco Polo. It dates from the thirteenth century. Before that . . .' He raised a dark eyebrow. 'It is more complicated.'

Eva could well imagine. She had read something of the Indian and Cambodian tribes, the influx of early Thai and Tibetan people on the country. And later there were Britain, China and Japan, all getting in on the act. Even now, the hill tribes were separate and independent and there was much infighting. Which all explained the eclectic mix of races and nationalities on the streets of Myanmar. And some of the troubles that the country had been through, she supposed.

Eva looked around her as they drove towards the parking area. On the one hand, the planting was very British: pansies, petunias and roses arranged in neat rectangular beds. But on the other hand, the vast, rolling landscape of the park had retained its oriental feel, with bamboo thickets, palm trees and red pagodas.

Ramon pulled up in a parking bay and they got out of the car. He was only an inch or two taller than her, Eva realised, as they stood side by side for a moment, his body lean with not an ounce of spare fat. And he had an air of self-possession about him that intrigued her. Was he as calm and collected as he seemed? Or was he just good at pretending? She sensed he didn't want to be here, sensed he resented her intrusion into their lives. And yet . . .

'The pagodas house many collections,' he informed her, as he strode towards the lake. 'We will see the orchids. There are three hundred different varieties. And all collected from Myanmar forests.'

Goodness. She followed more slowly, not wanting to be hurried.

The orchids were stunning, row upon row of every stock and colour imaginable, each one with a glorious scent of honey. Eva took lots of photos, even managing to snatch a shot of Ramon bending to examine a vivid purple flower with an appreciative look in his eyes. He clearly enjoyed the beauty of nature. He glanced up at her though with a glower of irritation.

'You don't like the British very much, do you?' she asked him at last. Unless it was just her. Elsewhere, any mention of being English had created huge excitement among the Burmese. They immediately asked a multitude of questions about London, blithely assuming that anyone British must live there, and, rather bizarrely, premiership football, over which they became as animated as they did at any mention of 'our lady', Aung San Suu Kyi.

Ramon shot her an unfathomable look from under his dark brows. 'That is not so,' he said. He squared his shoulders. 'My father was English, of course.'

'Of course.' She looked at his face, the fullness of his lips, the unexpected green of his eyes. She'd thought as much. And she noted the tense he had used. *Was*. Well, she knew how that felt. 'Your father . . . ?' She trod carefully.

'Is dead.' He swung down the next path and, again, Eva had to hurry to catch up with him. He was so . . . well, blunt.

'I'm sorry,' she said. 'What happened to him?'

He was ahead of her and so she couldn't see his expression. 'He was a strong man.' His voice was bitter. 'But he died very suddenly. A massive heart attack, they said.'

'I see.' He was clearly very upset and she felt the impulse to reach out to him, but he was walking much too fast and she didn't think he'd appreciate it somehow.

They had left the orchids and now were heading back towards the lake, passing flower beds of petunias and yellow phlox. The scent of blackcurrant and freshly mown grass seemed to waft on the air. Very British, Eva thought. And as for Ramon's father, a strong man he might have been, but, unlike her own father, he was living in a country only a few steps away from being regarded as third world, one which had not yet benefited from advances in medical technology. Not only did it lack good hospitals but there was extreme poverty and hardship. Thanks to Western sanctions. Thanks to the repressive government. But hopefully, things were now changing.

'My father died when I was young as well,' she told him as they walked under the thicket of stripy bamboo.

He paused and stared at her, a sudden compassion in his eyes. 'I am sorry,' he said.

So was Eva. She had always wondered what it would be like to have a father who took you out bicycling in summer or tobogganing in the snow. Who was always available with a listening ear or a hug, or a lift back home when you'd stayed out late. She was lucky though, she'd had her grandfather.

139

Without him . . . Well, she couldn't think about where she would be without him.

'What about your mother?' she asked Ramon. Maya's daughter. They had reached the wooden bridge and at last he slowed and stood looking down into the water. She followed his gaze. Brightly spotted koi carp were meandering through the gentle ripples, every so often coming to the surface, mouths gaping open for food. Eva looked back at him. He seemed miles away. And he still hadn't answered her question.

'She died two years ago,' he said at last. 'She had leukaemia. It was a great sadness to us all.'

This time Eva touched his arm in a gesture of condolence. So he had lost his mother too . . . She thought of her own mother, just as lost in her own way. And now, by coming here, had she damaged their relationship still further? Or could she somehow find a way to become close to her again?

'Was your mother Maya's eldest daughter?' Eva asked gently. Maya must have married after the war, sometime after Lawrence had left the country. Had she known that Lawrence wasn't coming back?

But Ramon was eying her rather strangely. 'My mother was the only child my grandparents had,' he said at last.

And she had married Ramon's father. Like her mother before her, she had fallen in love with an Englishman. As if, Eva thought, it were in the genes. It was ironic. So the British had stayed, as it were, in the family, despite the fact that Lawrence had left them.

In the distance, Eva saw a pair of black swans with red beaks make their graceful way from the other side of the lake, gliding effortlessly side by side. A thought came randomly into her head. Wasn't it swans who mated for life? It hadn't been like that for Lawrence and Maya though, had it?

'You want the truth?' Ramon suddenly swung around to face her.

She jumped. 'Well, yes.'

'The truth is that I envy you,' he said.

'Me?'

'I envy the British and all you Westerners.' He turned away to stare back at the lake. His slick, dark hair hung in a wing across his forehead and he flicked it roughly back with his fingers.

'For what?' Although she could guess.

'For your freedom,' he said. 'It is so easy for you to come and go. To Europe, to America, to Asia. To trade, to speak your mind, to follow your beliefs.'

'But things are changing here,' Eva said gently. She was aware how hard it had been. The restrictions, the endless bureaucracy, the lack of civil and human rights. And she could only imagine what it must have been like to grow up in Myanmar with constant fear, intimidation and poverty.

'It is a slow process.' He met her gaze. 'And sometimes much slower than our government would have people believe.' He led the way from the bridge and back to the main path, easing off the pace, walking now in a more leisurely rhythm.

'You'd like to travel then?' she asked him.

'It is what I have always dreamed of.' His words were simple. But they said so much.

'Then you will,' Eva assured him.

He shrugged. 'I am one of the more fortunate ones,' he said. 'I come from a privileged family. For others . . .' He let this thought trail.

'But we should not talk of such things,' Eva murmured. Klaus had warned her about talking politics to the Burmese. They could get into trouble if anyone were to find out; the government still did all they could to limit what they called unnecessary contact between foreigners and the Burmese people. And apparently everyone was watched at some time while they were in Myanmar. Could that be true? It was hard to believe, here in these lush and well-manicured gardens. But the journalist she'd met on the plane coming over had told her he'd called himself a teacher on his visa application. Writers, he had said with a wry smile, are considered rather dangerous. So maybe it was true after all.

Ramon said nothing, just looked away towards the distant trees. They walked on beside the lake.

'And my grandfather?' Eva asked him.

'What about him?' But she could see that she'd touched a raw nerve.

'You think that he just left your grandmother after the war, don't you? You think he just went back to England without a second thought. That he didn't care.'

Ramon seemed about to say something. But he stopped himself. 'It was a long time ago,' he said instead.

'But he did care.' It was important to Eva that he believed her. 'There were repercussions for both our families. But whatever happened between them, he did care.'

Ramon held her gaze for a long moment before finally he looked away. 'We must find a place to watch the sunset,' he said. 'Or my grandmother will never forgive me.'

As the sun dipped lower in the sky, he led the way to a stylish café made entirely from teak, where they sat on the open terrace with a view of the lake and gardens. To their left, a group of students lounged under a broad leafed horse-chestnut tree and one of them started strumming his guitar. A couple of the girls sang softly as he accompanied them. It was a Bob Dylan song, 'Most Likely You Go Your Way', Eva recognised it; her mother had often played it and, for a second, she was transported from this landscape and back to Dorset, England and her mother's grief. 'Most Likely You Go Your Way'. Despite the heat, Eva shivered.

Ramon ordered soft drinks, which turned out to be a delicious cocktail of pineapple, ginger and lime, and they sat, more amicably now, watching the sky deepen from pale blue into dark grey and orange as the sun dropped laconically behind the distant forest of silver oaks. In the distance, a peacock strutted proudly towards his mate and some golden pheasants flew up into the trees.

'Where is it that you want to go?' Eva asked him, thinking of the lyrics of the Dylan song and of what he'd already told her.

'Many places.' He sipped his drink. 'I intend to expand my

business and increase my exports. It is not just a question of survival. I want to be successful.' He looked at her suddenly, sharply. 'Many of my countrymen, they are not ambitious. But me, I want to travel and I want to experience my father's world.'

Eva thought of her own father, the man she had hardly known. She had inherited his dark hair and eyes. But not the shape of his face, according to Maya. Eva sipped her fruit cocktail. She had a photograph of him taken by her grandfather when she was a child. He was sitting on a wooden bench in the garden. It was late springtime, the yellow forsythia was in bloom behind him and the roses on the trellis were tight orange buds. But what Eva loved about the photo was his expression, he was clearly unaware the photo was being taken and he was staring towards the lawn with such a look of contentment. That told Eva a lot about him and his life. Their life. Because her grandfather had told her what he was looking at – his wife and daughter sitting on the lawn making a daisy chain, and Eva had that photograph too. They were a pair. Whatever else had happened in her world, those photographs said it all.

With some effort, Eva brought herself back to the present. 'And what is your business?' she asked Ramon. She could see why he had been a little hostile at first. He had been through a lot and he felt protective towards his grandmother; there was nothing wrong with that. She had seen another side of him at Maya's house and the lakeside and she felt a bond with him because they had both, in different ways, lost their parents. And she liked the fact that he wanted more.

'I make furniture.' He sat up straighter, with pride. 'Quality furniture. From teak wood. The business was begun by my father when he first came to Myanmar. Everything is handcrafted. We are very proud of that.'

'Teak?' Eva's senses tingled. Could that be just a coincidence? Although she supposed it wasn't so strange. Her grandfather had come here to Burma to work in the teak industry because teak was something the country was rich in. And Ramon's father had no doubt come here for the same reasons. Both men had met a Burmese woman and fallen in love. But Eva's grandfather had left and Ramon's father had stayed.

As they finished their drinks, they watched the sun reddening, strands of pink and amber threading the sky around. Sunset in Asia. What could be more stunning?

'There she goes.' Ramon turned to her as the sun finally dipped behind the trees. 'Shall we leave, too?'

She smiled and took the hand he offered to help her to her feet. A craftsman's hand, she thought. Well shaped, slightly calloused from working with wood. 'Thanks for bringing me here,' she said. 'I don't have long to look around. Tomorrow, I have to get back to Mandalay.'

'Tomorrow is another day,' he said. And again, he gave her such a straightforward and thoughtful look that she struggled to understand. 'Do you think you were right to come here, Eva?'

She stared back at him. Right? What did he mean, right? Of course, he knew nothing about her job here. He hadn't asked. He had assumed, no doubt that she was just another tourist. 'Are you worried about me upsetting your grandmother?' she asked. Though she had the feeling that despite appearances, Maya was mentally very strong.

'It is not just my grandmother to think of.'

'Then who?' she asked. Or what?

But he just shook his dark head. 'The past is long gone,' he said. 'And is it right to open the box? That is what you must ask yourself.'

'The box is already open, Ramon,' Eva said. 'It's too late.'

CHAPTER 15

Lawrence replaced the telephone receiver. He was rather confused, what with all this coming and going. He wasn't sure what was happening. But it would all come clear. It usually did.

Had Eva found her, his Maya? Was she still alive, as he hoped? He had just wanted her to know. It was all such a long time ago and of course there was no need to send any of those letters. There never had been any need, they were for Lawrence and his peace of mind. But he wanted her to know what he still felt for her, what he had never stopped feeling for her, and the chinthe would tell her that more than words. Maya and Burma. They were entwined in his heart, always had been. He'd never been able to separate the two.

Mandalay, 1937.
Lawrence tried to tell Maya something of what he felt for Burma when they met again the following afternoon. They were walking along the downtown streets of Mandalay to her father's house. She had invited him there for dinner and he appreciated that this was an honour. He didn't tell anyone at the club where he was going, though Scottie probably sus-

pected. He didn't want to hear any of the jokes about native tarts and all the rest of it. It was commonplace to have a Burmese mistress, whether a man was married or no; Burma still wasn't as comfortable for colonial wives as India, with its longstanding *Memsahib* tradition. But Lawrence didn't care about all that. All he knew was that he didn't have long. Tomorrow, he must return to camp.

'You think we are a very simple race,' she teased. 'Living so much of our time outside and close to nature. Lacking many material things.'

'Is that so bad?' He did think that. But he'd tried to express it in a positive way. Spiritual contentment, people with smiles on their faces, with warmth. And now, once again, she was laughing at him.

She gave him a look. 'Wait till you meet my father,' she said.

Lawrence had been expecting their house to be quite basic – nearly all the houses he'd seen here had been quite basic – but in fact it was not. It was simple in construction, yes, but made of wood and bamboo with a wide verandah and a charming carved wooden frieze dividing ground and first floor to the eye from the outside. It was beautifully furnished too with cushions, embroidered tapestries and silk hangings, cane furniture and vibrant rugs strewn on the floor. The windows and doors, shaded with bamboo blinds and wooden shutters, which led into the front living room had all been flung open and a man in his mid-forties, or thereabouts, was lounging on a bamboo reclining chair, his dark head resting on a red satin pillow. There was, surprisingly, a black piano by the far wall. And the scent of burning incense oil wafted through the room.

Maya addressed him in Burmese. Then she turned back towards Lawrence. 'This is my father,' she said. 'And this is Lawrence.' And then she disappeared to prepare the food.

Her father got to his feet and nodded. 'How are you?' he asked. 'I can offer you a drink, perhaps?' He was polite, but not warm.

Lawrence accepted a beer but then felt embarrassed when his host only drank the tea Maya brought out for him a few minutes later. Of course, Buddhists didn't drink and Lawrence had already noted the shrine, the image of the Buddha, the fresh flowers in the room. Somehow, drinking when they weren't similarly indulging, made him feel a bit of a fool. It was that sense, again, that the Burmese always knew more and felt more than they'd let on. What did they really think about it all? He had a feeling he was about to find out.

But it wasn't until after they had eaten a simple meal of river fish, rice and a thin but spicy consommé that Maya's father finally opened up.

'Why did you come to Burma?' he asked Lawrence. And then before he could reply, 'I am not talking about the business you are in, I know about that. What I want to know is: do you mean to make it your home?'

'I don't know, sir.' Lawrence decided honesty was the best policy with this man. 'I wanted to see something of the world, I suppose. And I love your country, you can be sure of that.'

'You love the country?' he asked. His black eyes shone. 'Or you love being a master in our country?'

Lawrence considered this. Once again, Maya had disappeared, leaving them to talk. He guessed that she'd known what would be said. Maybe it was even a test. She had said it wouldn't be easy and talking to her yesterday about the last King and Queen of Burma had at least given him a taste of what might be to come. 'I see your point,' he said. 'Though in every job there's at least one master and at least one worker, isn't that so?' Maya had told him that her father worked as a broker in the rice business, and that his business was successful. Lawrence knew too that he had dealings with the British from time to time.

Maya's father nodded. 'This is true,' he said. 'But do not underestimate us. We know who is really in charge. And there is an old Burmese proverb: wise man's anger never comes out.'

Lawrence shrugged. Of course there must be resentment. But the situation in this country was hardly his fault. 'The legacy of the British Empire is not my responsibility,' he said. It sounded more pompous than he'd intended. He wanted the man to like him, but he had to be honest.

'But you are part of it,' the other man shot in.

'I am.' And proud to be British, Lawrence thought, despite everything he'd seen here. He'd talked to Scottie last night about the imperialist rout and now he knew that although the row had to all intents and purposes been about teak, the facts were more complicated. For many years the Burmese dynasty had simply been unable to keep control over its warring factions. Some might say (and Scottie did, rather loudly after several whiskies) that the British had been compelled to step in. That it had been almost a favour for them to take control out of the hands of those who simply couldn't cut the mustard. 'And then, of course,' he'd said to Scottie, 'there was the wealth we were taking from Burma – the jewels, the teak . . .' 'Ah yes,' Scottie had replied. 'Well, no man will do something for nothing, old chap. Fair dos.'

'The work's hard,' Lawrence told Maya's father. He hadn't signed up for this job to get rich quick. It was not a job for an ambitious man, far from it. 'And believe me, I'm not afraid to get my hands dirty.'

Maya's father smiled for the first time. 'I believe that you are not,' he conceded. 'And you must excuse me for speaking my mind.'

He continued speaking his mind for the next hour and a half. He talked of what he wanted for Burma: independence and personal freedom for the people. Yes, he knew that there had been considerable unrest between the hill tribes for centuries; yes, he understood that the British Empire was not a tyrannical master. But it was still a master.

'The British have brought some progress to your country, surely?' Lawrence asked. He was thinking of the law and order, the schools, the roads, the hospitals. It wasn't all bad. Even Maya had admitted that before the British came, the Burmese had had no idea of how to manage the elephants and the logging industry.

Maya's father took a cigarette from a lacquered box on the table and offered the box to Lawrence. 'Perhaps they have,' he conceded. 'But did we ask for such modern progress? Did we want it? Or was the giver thinking more of the people from your country who now live here? They would insist, I am sure, on not living in a slum. They are, I believe, the ones who benefit most from the progress you mention.' His lip curled. 'When you give without being asked,' he added, 'should you always expect gratitude and thanks? Should you expect some sort of payment too? Change is not always a good thing.'

Lawrence couldn't answer this question. He had never looked at it that way before.

'So what *has* our country paid? What have we given in exchange for this progress?'

Lawrence considered, but he wasn't sure what to say. Did he mean the teak? Did he mean the rice paddy fields? Both were a rich source of income for British companies, such as the one which employed Lawrence. Was that what he meant by payment?

'We have given our culture.' Maya's father nodded. 'We have given our freedom. Our natural riches. And we have given away our right to rule our own country.'

Lawrence wasn't sure that he could deny this. He almost

wished Scottie were here to make it all plain. 'I understand what you are saying,' he said. 'But—'

'And there are many much younger and more energetic than me,' Maya's father went on, 'who are determined to see some change of their own.'

'How will they go about it?' Lawrence enquired mildly, wondering what he was getting into. And where the hell was Maya?

'I am sure that they will try the peaceful way first,' he said. He inhaled deeply, blowing out the smoke in a perfect ring. 'After that, who knows?'

When Maya eventually re-entered the room, the talk turned to other things and very soon her father said goodnight and left them. But when he did, Lawrence was heartened by the warmth with which he shook his hand. Although British and a foreigner, perhaps he had, after all, passed that test.

'Your father's house is very fine,' Lawrence said to her. He indicated the silk hangings and the vibrant tapestries.

'Thank you,' she said. 'I embroidered the tapestries myself.'

'Did you, by Jove?' Lawrence took a closer look at the silver, gold and red threaded silk on black velvet. There was a depiction of a dragon and another which was a landscape with a river, a sampan and a house built on stilts. But the one that really caught his eye was of a golden temple with two silver chinthes guarding the gate, their eyes glowing red like fire. The tapestries were the work of a skilled needlewoman, he realised. The touch was so delicate.

Maya came to stand very close to him. He could smell the scent of coconut oil, feel the warmth permeating from her skin. 'So, do you still wish to know the daughter,' she said softly, 'now that you have met the father?'

He smiled. 'I do.'

'Then would you like to stay the night?' she asked.

He blinked in surprise. 'Here?'

'Yes.'

'With you?'

'Of course.'

'Maya . . .' He wanted it more than he could say. But . . . 'I can't promise you anything,' he said. Though the words stuck in his throat. Because he wanted to promise her things. Things that he had promised no woman. Already, he wanted to promise her the earth.

'I am not asking for your promises,' she said.

'And your father?'

She smiled. 'He does not want them either.'

That wasn't quite what he had meant. 'But—'

'Ssh.' She put her finger to his lips. 'My father is not like other men. You will discover.'

'Then . . .'

She wound her arms around his neck. They felt warm and surprisingly strong. She lifted her face to his. Her sleek black hair fell back from her face, revealing tiny and perfect ear lobes. 'Sometimes, there is no need for words,' she whispered.

And as she led him to her bedroom, as she untied her *longyi* and allowed the scarlet fabric to fall around her feet, as she came to him and he held her in his arms, slender, supple and warmer than he could ever have dreamt . . . Lawrence realised that she was right.

By the time they returned from the Gardens, Maya was rested and dinner had been prepared by a few of the younger women, under Maya's direction. She wanted to give Eva something simple but traditional, so she had chosen her special fish curry, the chicken with peanuts and a refreshing and spicy salad. She would serve these with *hin-jo*, *balachaung* and other accompaniments.

'What happened to your grandmother after the rout?' Eva asked her as they ate. 'Did she stay with the King and Queen?'

Maya smiled at her enthusiasm for the story. This girl could not wait, could she, to find out everything? She served her some of the curry and salad and thought back to her grandmother's old, brown face, her liquid eyes, her gentle voice as she told Maya what had happened all those years ago. She thought of other things too, of her grandmother's dark coiled hair which smelled of the coconut oil she poured over it once a month to keep it glossy and supple, a tradition Maya had continued with her own. Her grandmother, Suu Kyi, had washed Maya's hair too, when her mother was sick, washed it with tree bark, lemon and tamarind rind to create a giant lather and hair that was squeaky clean and smelled of the garden of paradise. Her grandmother's hands massaging her scalp, the scent of the spices . . . Maya could close her eyes and still smell it to this day. She sighed. 'Yes, she stayed with them.'

'And were they kept prisoner by the British?' Eva seemed outraged. She was looking very pretty tonight, Maya thought, tall and elegant in her simple blouse and long skirt, her skin slightly flushed from the heat and fresh air. Her hair too was dark and thick and it hung loose over her slim shoulders.

Maya tasted a little of the chicken. She remembered the details of the story very clearly for it had had a profound effect on her. Her grandmother had told her that the King had tried to sell certain jewels and possessions and that the British guards had found out, insisted he was being cheated and promptly appropriated everything of value that the Royal Family owned. But perhaps she should not tell the girl all these things. 'They were taken to India,' she said. 'And it is true that they were not free to come and go.'

'And your grandmother, Suu Kyi? Did she go to India too?' Her eyes were dark, not like Lawrence's eyes of clear sky-blue. Nevertheless, she had the shape of his face, the slant of his cheekbones. Maya had seen it, felt it. She had a certain look about her. And an honesty. Maya liked that.

'Yes, she did. Later, she was told she could return here . . .' Maya laid down her fork. These days she did not eat so much; her appetite was small. She was often tired too, she lacked the energy for long conversations and she needed help to prepare meals such as this one which once she would have loved to cook alone. 'But she did not return, not then.' She was loyal to the Queen and to the princesses. They had lost so much already.

'It must have been so hard for the King and Queen,' Eva murmured. 'After what they had been used to.'

'It was.' The girl was imaginative too. And Maya remembered making exactly the same observation to her grandmother. 'The Queen expected the old Burmese ways to still be part of her life,' she said. 'The reverence, the *shiko-ing*, the respect. But everything changed and most people in the royal entourage left before very long.'

Ramon dished out more food to Eva and offered some to his grandmother. She shook her head. But she accepted the glass of water he poured for her.

'What about the other servant girl?' Eva asked as Maya had known she would. 'What about Nanda Li? Did she leave too?'

'Not at first.' Maya frowned so as to remember more clearly every detail of what she had been told. 'But Queen Supayalat continued to prefer Suu Kyi and Nanda Li grew very bitter. She was lazy too. Often, she refused to serve her Queen and one day, the Queen simply sent her away.'

'And that was the last Suu Kyi saw of her?' Eva asked. She had a healthy appetite. Lawrence too had always eaten well; his job had been physically demanding of course. Maya had often wondered how he had managed during the war. Some of the men she saw after it was over had lost much weight. They were so thin, you could see their protruding bones.

'If only,' growled Ramon.

Maya saw Eva look across at him, surprised. There was some tension between these two, she could feel it, though she did not know the cause. Ramon was stubborn of course, very loyal and sometimes prickly like a wild bush on the plain. And Lawrence's granddaughter did not know the whole truth. Should she tell her? Maya had not yet decided. To tell Eva was to tell Lawrence. She did not have so much time left. But she would have to give it more thought.

'No, it was not the last time,' she said. 'The Royal Family were moved to Ratnagiri, many miles south of Bombay. They remained in exile, stripped of all power. But the people who looked after their interests were not always unkind.' She remembered what her grandmother had told her of the official's wife who had befriended her grandmother and made it her business to try and find a husband for Suu Kyi. She hadn't succeeded, but she had eventually persuaded her to return to Burma. There were new servants now, the Queen had become cantankerous and difficult, the princesses had grown and no longer needed her. The official's wife was of Indian origin but she had family in Rangoon who would give Suu Kyi work. 'I am giving you a chance of freedom,' she had urged her. 'You must take it.'

Suu Kyi had gone to the Queen and asked for her blessing. 'Go,' the Queen had told her. 'Go while you can. I would go myself, if I could. And, please God, my daughters will return to Burma themselves one day.'

Maya told Eva this part of the story.

'So she returned here,' murmured Eva.

'Yes, she did. The family she worked for moved to Mandalay,' Maya told her. 'My grandmother met my grand-father there, and she also met again with Nanda Li.'

The two families had had little contact. Maya remembered as a girl seeing Nanda Li's son and his wife in the bazaar, her mother ushering her quickly away. And she remembered the man's dark scheming eyes too, eyes that he had passed on to his own children, Maya's contemporaries, and on even beyond this. The family had grown in power and wealth, but their reputation went before them.

'One day, when I was a girl of sixteen,' Maya said, 'my grandmother gave me the pair of chinthes. And she told me the story of the rout of the last King and Queen of Burma, just as I have told it to you, my child.' She nodded. 'She told me to treasure them, and she warned me to keep them together for the sake of spiritual harmony. She told me that they would keep me safe and that the gift was the most special gift, that I should remember that.'

'But you gave one of them to my grandfather.'

The girl, Eva, looked so innocent sitting there. Maya's heart went out to her. 'Yes, I gave one to your grandfather,' she said. 'When he was about to go to war.'

'Before you leave, I have something I must give you.' That is what she had told him. And she had withdrawn the teak chinthe from the faded red Shan bag she carried over her shoulder. She passed it, almost reverentially, to him. It meant so much.

'What's this, my love?'

But she could tell that he knew. Everyone who had lived in her country knew the role played by the chinthes. They protected, they guarded, they kept from harm. Traditionally, they guarded the temple. But they had been given to Maya's grandmother because she had guarded the princesses. And now their strength was needed again. 'It is all I can give you.'

'And yet I have brought you nothing.' He frowned.

With her eyes, she told him that no, he was mistaken, he had given her everything.

He held the chinthe up to the lamp and looked into its red eyes. 'And where is his partner?' he asked softly.

'I will keep that one with me.' She bowed her head. 'They belong together. I hope and pray that he will bring you back to me.' It was the first time she had said this. No promises. That was what she had always said before. Nothing about belonging. Nothing about forever.

He dropped the chinthe into his backpack. 'I will take him with me wherever I go.'

Maya smiled to herself. If only he knew. But better he did not know perhaps.

'Many people in Burma bury their treasures,' she said. 'It may be that when you go to war, you will have to bury him too. If you do . . .' she smiled. 'You must remember where and mark the spot, my love.'

Gently, he held her face between his two hands. 'But I will never bury our love, Maya,' he said.

'Nor I.' She looked into his blue eyes. 'I will remember it for all of my days.'

He stroked her hair. 'I will come back.'

She put a finger to his lips. 'Whatever you do, my love,' she said. 'I will understand.'

She watched him go with his precious cargo slung over one shoulder. 'Keep him safe for me,' she whispered to the chinthe.

Later that night, after dinner, her father had grasped hold of her arm. 'Mya?'

'Father?'

'Where is the other chinthe?' He pointed up at the shrine where one lonely animal guarded the image of the Buddha who was, as he should be, placed higher than anything else in the room on top of a sandalwood box.

'I have given it away,' she said.

'Given it away?' He let out a curse. 'How could you give it away? We may need that, when . . . when . . .'

She put her arms around him. She knew that her father, for all his bravado, was frightened too. The war was getting closer. They were all in danger. But she would far rather have the chinthe guarding Lawrence, than have the pair confiscated by the Chinese or Japanese.

'He needs it more,' she whispered.

'So.' He looked mournful. 'You have given it to your Englishman?'

'I have.'

'Then you are a fool.' He sighed, ran his fingers through his hair.

'It was mine to give,' Maya remonstrated softly. 'My grandmother gave me the pair.'

'I know. But still, it is a family legacy.'

'I have respected the manner in which it should be given,' she told him, love giving her a stubbornness she hadn't known she possessed. 'And I believe that it will come back to our family one day.'

He looked up at the shrine. Shook his head. 'Does he know what it is?'

'No. But he knows what it means.'

He patted her shoulder. 'You must really love this man, my daughter,' he said. 'He must be your life.'

'He is,' said Maya. And that was the truth.

The rest of them were quiet as they listened to the remainder of her story. Maya wiped a tear from her eye.

'And what happened after the war?' Eva asked softly.

Maya could see that the girl was deeply moved. 'After the war, I kept my chinthe safe in the shrine in the house in Mandalay,' she said. 'I always felt that the other would return.' She smiled at Eva. 'One way or another.' Though she had never dreamt that it would be like this. That Lawrence's granddaughter would come from England and bring it back to her. It meant so much to her that he had done this. And it told her a great deal. If only her dear father had known that giving the chinthe to Lawrence before he went away to war, had in fact guaranteed the safety of them both . . .

'But one day,' she continued with the story. This girl,

bless her, was curious and wanted to know it all. And perhaps she too had in some way been sent? Perhaps she too could help? 'I returned from our house here in Maymyo with Ramon's mother to find that someone had broken in. They had smashed the windows to gain entry. And yet only one thing was taken.' She sighed, recalling the dread she had felt in the pit of her stomach. And with it had been the sense of inevitability, that one day . . . 'We always knew who was responsible. She had never forgiven my grandmother, you see, and neither had her family.' If both chinthes had been there, of course they would have taken the pair. What use was one without the other?

'Bitterness breeds bitterness,' she said sadly. 'Greed multiplies. They feel it all as if it were yesterday.'

CHAPTER 17

Even in the darkness, the yellow-stoned house looked as familiar as ever, but tired. Rosemary knew the feeling. Once she'd decided to come here, she'd acted quickly. She'd booked the next possible flight from Copenhagen and cancelled arrangements she'd made for the next couple of weeks. She didn't book the return flight. She wasn't sure how long this would take.

Alec had said very little. She just hoped he'd understand why she had to do this, and why she had to do it alone. It wasn't just a question of coming back to West Dorset, of seeing her father and Eva. But he'd probably know that too.

She trundled her case up the flagstones to the front door. The house seemed to be in darkness, but the lights were probably just on in the back. He'd always been conscious of saving electricity; his generation were. He'd be in the kitchen, probably, reading a paper and staying close to the Aga. Her father lived in that kitchen in winter months. Rosemary smiled at the thought. She'd missed him. But it was hard to admit that, even to herself. Anyway, she'd phoned, so he'd be expecting her.

At the front door, she hesitated. It was her childhood home

and she still had a key. But how would she feel, if—? No, she wouldn't barge in. She lifted the brass knocker and let it fall. Heard the sound echo as if the house were full of empty rooms. Along with the darkness, it gave her an uncomfortable sensation.

She pulled off her leather gloves and rubbed her hands together. It was chillier than it had been in Denmark. An English November. She thought of Bonfire Night, her father lighting Roman candles in the back garden. Rosemary holding sparklers in her gloved hands, shouting with delight, waving them round and making glitzy patterns of fire in the night air. The Catherine wheels he nailed to the fence that never spun properly, stopping halfway; the rockets spurting from an old milk bottle.

Rosemary sniffed. The shrubs hadn't been pruned, but her father wouldn't have noticed. And the paintwork on the door was starting to peel. She'd take a good look around and discuss it all with him, she decided, make a list of maintenance jobs for the spring. They mustn't let the place go to rack and ruin.

The phone call between them had been brief. 'Dad?' she'd said. 'I'm coming back for a visit. Is that alright?'

'Rosemary?' He had sounded vague and confused. She hated it when he sounded confused. And she noticed he never called her Rosie any more. When had he stopped?

'Yes. Can I stay at the house?'

'Of course, of course.' He paused. 'Will you want picking up at the station? The airport?'

'I'll arrange it all this end,' she reassured him. She told him when she would be arriving. 'I'll see you then.'

Alec had taken her to the airport. 'Take care, Rosemary,' he said when she got out of the car. 'Say hello to your Dad for me. And to Eva, when she gets back.'

'I will.' It was the first time she'd gone back to the UK without Alec. It felt very strange.

She knocked again. Still no answer. What on earth was he up to? She supposed that he couldn't hear her. He probably had the radio or the TV on and his hearing wasn't what it was.

After waiting for a minute or two, Rosemary groped in her bag for the house key. It slotted into the lock but the door held fast. She opened it with a good shove of the shoulder. That door could do with a plane. Draft proofing was all very well but you had to be able to open and shut the thing. Another one for the list.

'Dad?' she called. 'Hello!' She left her suitcase in the hall and after a quick glance into the lounge, went straight down the end into the kitchen. She switched on the light. Everything was scrupulously clean and tidy, the Aga as warming and cosy as ever, her father's rocking chair with the red tasselled cushion neat but unoccupied.

Silence.

'Dad?' Rosemary felt the panic stir, low in her chest. Had he forgotten she was coming? Gone out? But where on earth would he go out to on a cold November evening? 'Dad?'

Nothing. She pushed down the panic, retraced her steps and stood at the bottom of the stairs. Had he gone to bed, perhaps? That would explain why the whole house was so dark and quiet. She started up the stairs, heading for her parents' old bedroom. And then she remembered Eva telling her that he'd moved downstairs a few months ago; he couldn't manage the stairs like he used to.

She should have thought. 'Dad?' Rosemary hurried back to the downstairs bedroom next to the lounge. It was an en suite. 'Dad, it's me.' She spoke more quietly now. If he were asleep, she didn't want to wake him.

But she could see immediately in the light coming from the hall. The bed was made up and there was a glass of water on the bedside table, a towel hanging on the chair. But he wasn't here.

Now she was scared.

And then she realised that the light was on in the bathroom adjoining.

She rushed in. He was lying on the floor face down in his checked pyjamas and tartan dressing gown. 'Dad!' Rosemary put her hand to her mouth. It was an awful replay of the moment she had discovered Nick dead on the kitchen floor all those years ago. 'No,' she whispered.

She knelt beside him and she eased his face from the floor, frantically feeling for warmth, for a pulse. No, she was thinking. Not her father. Not now. Not like this. Please God. She couldn't go through this again.

CHAPTER 18

'But I don't understand,' said Eva. 'Can't you just report them to the police? The chinthe belonged to you and your family after all.' And if the Li family thought they had the right to steal one of them . . . She looked over at the little animal standing sturdily at the front of the shrine. Would they not also think they had the right to steal the other?

It was just 9 p.m. The rest of the family must have eaten earlier; only Maya, Ramon and Eva were sitting around the circular wooden dining table. And finally Maya had finished telling her story. Or had she finished? From the significant glances now passing between her and Ramon it seemed there might be more to come.

It had been quite a feast. Rice was at the core of most Myanmar cuisine but what Eva loved most were the side dishes that accompanied the curries, the spicy salads, with lime juice, peanuts and tamarind; the tart leaf-based soup known as *hin-jo*, Ramon had informed her; and *balachaung*, a pungent combination of chillies, garlic and dried shrimp fried in oil.

'It is not so easy here in Myanmar.' With his fork, Ramon deftly plucked a slice of papaya from the dessert of fresh fruit which sat in a simple white dish at the centre of the table. 'That family have connections.' His dark expression was the only indication as to what sort of connections these might be.

'And we have no papers to say that the chinthe is ours,' Maya agreed.

'Do *they*?'

Ramon shrugged. 'Probably. Forged ones, of course.'

'Why do you think it took them so long to steal it?' Eva wondered aloud.

'We used to take it with us when we travelled,' Maya admitted. 'This was perhaps the first time we left it in the house.'

But how would they have known that? Eva was indignant. She hadn't come all this way to fulfil her grandfather's last wishes, to return his chinthe to the place where it belonged, with its twin in the house of this family, to give up quite so easily. Nothing she had heard so far had convinced her it couldn't be done, the opposite in fact. Now that she knew the true provenance of the little animal . . . It made it even more important to get the other one back. 'But it isn't right,' she said.

'Many things are not right,' Ramon replied. 'It may not be right that we still do not have a full freedom of speech, or that those who we elect to government never have enough power. It may not be right that workers are paid so little for doing so much. Or that there are those in our country who still suffer.' He took a deep breath. 'Because it is not right, does not mean it does not happen.'

It was quite a speech. 'I appreciate what you're saying.' And she agreed with him too. 'But the fact that so many other things aren't right, doesn't mean we should take this lying down.'

'Lying down?' Ramon frowned.

'Accept it.'

He held her gaze. She recognised the passion there, and something else she couldn't define. 'No one is accepting it,' he murmured.

Maya intervened, laying a gentle hand on Eva's arm. 'It is not good to worry over things we cannot change,' she advised. 'All will come to those who have a clean heart.' She nodded sagely.

Was it her Buddhist faith that made her feel like this? Or was it living under a repressive regime for most of her life that had created such a sense of acceptance? But Eva was surprised at Ramon. He'd said he hadn't accepted it, but what was he actually doing? How long was it since the chinthe had first been stolen? It made her blood boil that this Li family could steal someone else's property and be allowed to get away with it.

'Who are these people anyway?' she asked. 'Where do they live?'

'What difference does it make where they live?' Ramon smiled grimly.

'Because if you know they've stolen the chinthe and if you know where they live, why couldn't we just steal it back again?'

Ramon let out a snort of laughter. 'Brave words,' he said. 'But you have no idea how dangerous that would be.'

Only if they found out who had taken it, Eva thought.

But Maya shook her head. 'Two wrongs do not make a right,' she said. 'It is wrong to steal and it will lead to no merit in the end.'

Eva sat back in her chair. Karma. But they must be able to do something. She looked Ramon straight in the eyes. 'So what *will* you do?' she asked.

He raised an eyebrow. 'Softly, softly,' he said.

Maya gave him a beatific smile. She reached for the teapot and poured out more tea. 'You must take care,' she warned.

Eva took the tiny cup that was offered to her. What was 'softly, softly' supposed to mean? Did Ramon have his own plan of trying to get the chinthe back? She hoped so. 'But the other thing I don't quite see . . .' She frowned. 'Is why they want it so badly.'

Maya and Ramon exchanged a look. Maya smiled and gave a small nod. Ramon shrugged.

'What?'

Ramon helped himself to more papaya, offering the fruit first to his grandmother and then to Eva. Maya shook her head, but Eva took a slice of watermelon, red and juicy. 'It is an important piece of history,' he said.

'Yes, of course.' The chinthes were originally the property of the last Queen of Burma. Eva looked across at the little animal she had brought all the way from Dorset. He had pride of place just below the Buddha in the shrine. He stood on guard, but Eva couldn't help thinking he still looked a little lonely.

'The decorative teak chinthes were among the treasures of the Royal Palace,' Ramon went on. His eyes were gleaming as he casually helped himself to more fruit. He bit into the dripping flesh of the watermelon, never taking his eyes from her face. 'And the Royal Palace was full of precious things,' he said. 'Teak carvings, golden images of our sacred Buddha, lacquer-work studded with gems. Even the walls were made of glass or decorated with jade and topaz.' He raised a dark eyebrow.

'Yes, I know.' But Eva still didn't quite understand. Naturally, the provenance of the chinthe gave it significance and value. It was what she had always believed: the story of an artefact was the one vital element that made it unique and special.

Ramon and his grandmother exchanged more significant looks.

What had she missed?

Lazily, Ramon got to his feet, stretched up to retrieve the chinthe from the shrine. He placed it carefully on the table between them. Watched her.

Eva smiled. The little chinthe was special. She would miss him. She ran her fingertip over the carving. 'Designed and carved by a royal master-craftsman?' she guessed.

'Of course. And?'

'And?'

He turned the chinthe to face her.

Eva looked into its red glass eyes as she had done so many times before. 'You might expect his eyes to be rubies,' she said. 'When you know the provenance. The fact that they're cheap glass, makes you think that the little beast isn't worth . . .' And then the penny dropped. 'That's the idea?' she breathed.

'That is the idea,' Ramon confirmed. He gave a grim smile. 'When you turned up with it earlier I checked all was in place. I could hardly believe it. But it was so.'

'All was in . . . ?'

Ramon picked up the little chinthe and, very gently, between his thumb and forefinger, he twisted its tail. In response, the head of the animal moved backwards to reveal a secret cavity inside.

Eva's eyes widened as she leaned closer. Of course, in her work, she had come across many antique wooden pieces with hidden compartments and sliding panels. But this was so delicate, so unexpected.

And inside . . . Ramon removed first one, then another from a nest of cotton padding. Two jewels sat in the palm of his hand.

Eva gasped.

The large rubies seemed to blink up at the light after the long period of darkness. Ramon held them out for her to see. They were dark red, almost purple in this light. Intense and passionate with a deep lustre and a blade that shimmered down the centre of each like an iris.

Rubies . . . She was speechless.

'Burmese Mogok Rubies,' he said. 'We call them pigeon-blood rubies, because of their colour.'

Eva was transfixed. They were stunning in both colour and luminosity.

'Would you like to take a closer look?'

Eva met his gaze, realised that for the first time today, he trusted her. Maybe he resented her grandfather and Westerners in general for the freedoms they took for granted. Maybe he didn't want her to open up the box of the past. But he and Maya were trusting her with something very special. 'Yes, please,' she whispered.

She held out her hand and he dropped one of the stones into her palm. She held it up to the light. There was a reflection that was like the sheen from a spool of silk. Why hadn't she guessed? But then again, why on earth should she have guessed? Ramon was right, red glass eyes, too obviously bright and glittering, had de-valued the piece. No one would guess. Unless they knew.

'And the other chinthe?' she asked.

'The same.'

'So . . . ?'

'The four Burmese Mogok rubies are very rare,' Ramon said. 'Suu Kyi suspected their value from what the Queen had told her and she knew of the existence of the secret compartments and of the mechanism with which to open it. It was then a simple matter for our family to have a master craftsman remove the rubies and insert the glass instead. The rubies must be kept in place for good luck, of course. But in front of them, for all to see, would be . . .'

'The red glass eyes,' Eva said.

'Yes.'

'And Nanda Li?'

Maya bowed her head. 'Of course, she, too, knew of the Mogok rubies, perhaps even of the secret compartment. She was there on that day with the Queen and Suu Kyi. She would have told her family. They would have known.'

Ramon glanced at his grandmother and murmured something softly in Burmese. 'They are a national treasure. It was illegal to take them out of the country.'

Maya nodded and smiled, patted his hand. She turned to Eva. 'But your grandfather did not know that,' she said.

'Illegal?' Eva echoed. So, she'd blithely transported an artefact of national importance and worth a small fortune from Britain to Myanmar, whisked it through security and deposited it back where it belonged, with hardly a second thought. No wonder they had both been so shocked. Eva had assumed it was the emotional trauma for Maya of the chinthe she'd given Lawrence being returned to her after all these years. Maybe it was that too, but it was so much more.

'The chinthe has always been a very special gift.' Again, Ramon looked at his grandmother. Maya nodded.

'And so my family thanks you from the bottom of its heart.'

Eva appreciated these words. But her mind was still spinning. Maya had said that her grandfather had not known he was not allowed to take the chinthe out of the country. What else had he known – or not known? Of course there would have been few checks during the aftermath of war. She thought of how dearly he had treasured the little beast. Could he possibly have known its value? For a moment Eva felt a flare of doubt. But he couldn't have known. He treasured it because it was a gift from the woman he loved. Her grandfather would never knowingly have placed her in danger.

Maya rose to her feet, which seemed to be a signal that the evening was at an end. Ramon got up too and so did Eva.

'But shouldn't you keep it under lock and key,' Eva said. 'If it's so valuable. I mean . . .'

Maya shook her head. 'What will be,' she said. 'We must trust him to do his job, to protect. We must trust him to be seen. And perhaps one day our missing chinthe will be drawn to return. If the Lord Buddha wills it.'

Eva nodded. She hoped she was right. But some sort of human intervention might be necessary too.

'We do not value either of the chinthes because of their material wealth,' Maya said softly. 'Nor even for their traditional symbolism. The ruby represents leadership and self-esteem and will bring wealth, good health and wisdom to its owner.' She smiled. 'We hope that this is so. But we value them for their history. For what each one represents and the spirit in which it was given.' She bowed her head and when she raised it again, there were tears in her dark eyes. 'But for others it is not the same. Which is why it would be such a dangerous task to try to reunite the two.'

'I understand.' Eva took Maya's outstretched hand. She respected what she was saying. But didn't everything that the chinthes represented make it even more important to reunite them? 'I've brought some photographs with me,' she said. 'Can I bring them to show you, tomorrow, before I leave for Mandalay?'

'Oh, yes. Please do.'

They said their goodbyes.

'Ramon will accompany you back to Pine Rise,' Maya said. And held up her hand when Eva was about to demur. 'I insist.'

'Very well.'

He held the door open for her and she slipped on her sandals before stepping out into the night air. Did Ramon really have a plan to get back the other chinthe? And if so, what was it? Eva decided that before she left Pyin Oo Lwin, she would make it her business to find out.

CHAPTER 19

Eva's mind was still back in the time of the final Burmese dynasty as they walked towards Pine Rise. In contrast, though, the night was silent and still, even the cicadas had been quiet since nightfall, the only other movement the faintest trembling of the velvety flowers which looked almost ghostly in the darkness, their scent more magnified than in the stark light of day. Eva's English life felt so far away, almost as if it belonged to someone else.

But she'd been wondering. She glanced at Ramon walking beside her. 'What happened to the other treasures from the Royal Palace?' she asked him. He had been subdued since they left the house; perhaps he, too, had a lot to think about. And now she sensed rather than saw his frown.

'Some are in the National Museum in Yangon,' he said. 'But most were plundered at the time of the exile.'

Plundered . . . Eva shivered, although the night air was still so warm she didn't even need a wrap. What had the King and Queen of Burma felt when they knew they had lost everything? And what had all that reverential bowing from their subjects really meant? Very little, it seemed, when there were riches to be had, beyond their wildest dreams. 'But where is it now?' she murmured. The ground was dry and hard under her thin sandals, still dusty from the heat of the day. They had taken the same route back to Pine Rise that she had taken earlier to get to Maya's. The lane was narrow but they were walking along the pathway that ran beside it.

'Sold many years ago and long gone,' he said. 'By now it will be in China, India, Britain, who knows?' But she wasn't fooled by the casual tone of his voice. Ramon cared. It was his country, she knew that he cared.

Eva paused to stare up at the canopy of the night sky. The whole galaxy seemed laid out before them. The sky was clear, never before had she seen so many stars. 'It was a sad end to the dynasty,' she said softly.

He followed her gaze. 'It was.' And he seemed to soften slightly.

'And what happened to the Royal Palace itself?' She refocused on the path ahead, allowed her hand to trail over the foliage of a eucalyptus tree as they passed by, its leaves glimmering blue in the light of the crescent moon.

'It was taken over by the British.' Once again, she heard the note of bitterness and Ramon's pace seemed to quicken as if he wanted this walk to be over.

'What did they do with it?' Though Eva could guess.

'The West Wing was converted into a club. The Queen's Audience Hall became a billiard room. The gardens were dug up to build polo fields and tennis courts.' His voice rang out in the darkness. He had moved ahead of her, but now he stopped for a moment to allow her to catch up with him.

'I see.' That didn't seem very respectful. She almost felt she should apologise.

'The Burmese, they call this period in our history, "The English time", he added, as the path narrowed and they moved once more into single file. 'Look around you at this town.' He waved his arms in an expansive gesture. 'It is full of the British legacy. It was even named after one of your Colonels. A Colonel May.'

'Really?' Eva hadn't known that, but she wasn't surprised. It was certainly true that Pyin Oo Lwin still looked very British, at least in the suburbs. But if the Burmese people had resented the 'English time', then why did they seem to like the British so much, she wondered. They were all so friendly, so eager to talk to her.

'And in the Second World War, the Palace was destroyed by fire,' Ramon continued. He glanced back at her, clearly expecting a reaction.

Also caused by the British, no doubt. Sometimes Eva felt more than a little ashamed of her heritage. But Ramon had an English father too, she reminded herself. Was he also ashamed? It didn't appear so. Hadn't he said that he wanted to go to the UK, to travel, to experience his father's world?

'And now?' she asked as she drew level with him. She had seen the wide moat that surrounded the old citadel. 'What's happened to the Palace now?'

'It has been reconstructed,' he said crisply.

'Oh?' It was hard to see the path ahead and Eva almost stumbled over a tree root. He heard the sound and turned to make sure she was alright, but she'd just lost her footing for a moment and she was fine. Ramon didn't seem to find their night walk such a problem. He could obviously see in the dark, she thought, like a cat.

'Perhaps you will visit the Palace when you return to Mandalay,' he said.

That sounded rather as if he couldn't wait for her to be gone. And once again he had become distant, that moment of trust back at the house when he'd shown her the rubies had disappeared. 'I will,' she told him. After what she'd heard tonight, it would be high on her list of must-sees.

The scent of the frangipani, rich and intoxicating in the night air, seemed to pull them along the road towards Pine Rise. Sometimes, Eva thought, it was almost too much, too cloying, too heavy. Even so, part of her longed to linger a little, to take her time dawdling and absorbing the sweet warmth of the night, which seemed so gentle on the senses. But Ramon clearly had other ideas and again, she had to hurry to keep up with him.

'Your country has many riches,' Eva observed, slightly out of breath as she thought again of those rubies. But it wasn't just the rubies and other jewels. There was also teak and oil, as well as rice, of course; she'd seen lots of paddy fields since she'd been here. No wonder the British and the Japanese had wanted a slice of everything.

'This is true.' He glanced across at her again and slowed his pace for a moment. 'But not many of our people are rich.'

She knew that too. Hadn't she seen them? Living in what

were little more than makeshift shacks? Begging by the road-side?

But, 'You have restored something of our family's heritage to us, Eva,' he said. His voice was surprisingly tender and, for a moment, Eva was aware of the proximity of him, tall and lithe just ahead of her in the darkness. 'We are very happy for that. And there is someone else, who will also be happy.'

'Your grandmother?' She heard the shrill cry of a bird or a bat from high above them. But she'd be happier still if the family had both chinthes, and the rubies, restored to them, Eva thought. She had read the mixed emotions in Maya's dark eyes. Bitter-sweet. And although her grandmother, Helen, had died and Maya's husband too, Eva knew that Lawrence and Maya would never be reunited – it would never be possible. Her grandfather was too frail to come here to Myanmar and Maya would never leave her country. For them, it was too late.

Ramon did not answer her. He was looking beyond her into the night. For the moment, she realised, she had lost him. 'And will you tell me your plan to get back the other chinthe?' she whispered.

'It is not your concern.' In a millisecond, he was back in the present and on red alert. And his voice had changed again. It sliced through the darkness.

No room for further discussion then, she thought. For now. 'Do you remember Maya's husband, your grandfather?' she asked. She was curious about the man who had stepped into the breach left by her own grandfather.

'Yes, I do.' He paused, seemed to rein himself back. 'He was a good man, a kind man.'

'And you had a happy childhood?'

He laughed. Perhaps he was amused by her questions. 'We survived very well,' he said. 'We were fortunate, compared to many of our countrymen.' He glanced back at her as if knowing what she were thinking. 'And if my grandmother ever missed your grandfather, then I never knew about it.'

Touché, thought Eva. 'But you always resented him.'

In the darkness she couldn't read his expression this time. 'Some might say that many Burmese women were taken advantage of by British men living in our country,' he said. He spoke clearly and there was no mistaking his meaning. 'They were not given the respect or the position that they deserved.'

Was that what had happened with her grandfather? 'Is that what your grandmother says?' Eva asked him.

He straightened and walked on. 'My grandmother is the most loyal woman I know.'

Which was, she knew, his way of answering the question. Maya would never criticise Lawrence. But Eva was sure it hadn't been like that. Theirs was a love story in a million. Her grandfather would never have left her if . . . But Eva stopped there. She didn't know the end of their story, not yet.

'Are you married, Ramon?' she asked him. He hadn't mentioned a wife. She wondered if they could ever be friends. He seemed to blow hot and cold and she never really knew where she was with him. Even so . . .

'No, I am not married,' he said. As he walked, he flipped his dark hair back from his forehead with that flick of his fingers, the gesture she'd noticed before, unconscious and unstudied. 'It is wrong to marry when I have so many plans.'

'That's very practical of you.' Though not terribly romantic. Eva recalled what he'd said before. 'You mean your plans to leave Myanmar?' She ducked to avoid a low branch.

'Perhaps.' He shot her a quick glance. 'And you?'

She shook her head. 'A couple of near misses,' she said. Though in truth they hadn't even been that. She thought of Max. Felt for the first time a sense of relief. She wouldn't have to try so hard anymore to be what he wanted her to be. She could just be herself.

Once again, she drew level with him. 'You will know when the right man comes along,' he said, the hint of a smile in his voice.

'Maybe I will.'

Now, he seemed to move a little closer to her as they walked along the path. She felt a sudden strand of tension between them, seeming to pull them closer still. It took her by surprise. In another time, she thought. In another place. But not here. And not with a man like this.

He pushed aside another branch hanging low over the path, so that she could walk through, and as she did so, her arm brushed against his. The jolt she felt almost stopped her in her tracks. Where had that come from?

'Eva?' he said.

'Yes?' She glanced up at him. His dark hair had once again

fallen across his forehead and he was looking at her intently. He wasn't moving. He stood perfectly still, as if he were waiting.

For her? Eva felt herself hovering on the edge. She felt as though she could move just a few centimetres closer and her body would be touching his. What would happen then? Would he kiss her? Did she want him to? If he did, she had the odd feeling that there would be no going back.

Once again, the thick, cloying fragrance of the frangipani wafted towards her, filled her senses like a drug. What was she thinking of? He was attractive, yes. Was it just that? Or was it the seductive scent of the flowers, the smooth darkness of the night?

She moved on, deliberately stepping away from him and he let the branch fall behind them. The moment was gone. And gone so completely that she half thought she'd imagined it. But she knew she hadn't. And she knew why she hadn't taken that extra step. It might mean nothing to him, but for her, there would be far too many complications. Her experience with Max was still fresh in her mind. She wasn't interested in any kind of one-night stand, and that was all it could ever be.

Their footsteps crunched on the gravel as they turned into the sweeping driveway of Pine Rise.

'Why did you come here, Eva?'

Had he felt it too? She had no idea. If he had, nothing in his voice, manner or body language betrayed the fact. His emotions seemed to be fully under control.

'To find out the truth of my grandfather's story.' She

looked up at Pine Rise gleaming at her in the moonlight. 'To see this country for myself. And to do my job, of course.'

'Your job?' He folded his arms and looked at her.

'I'm an antique dealer,' she told him. 'My company buys from your country.'

His lip curled. 'So the plundering continues,' he said.

'Well, hardly . . .' But before she could say more, he had already begun to walk away.

'Goodnight, Eva,' he called. And in seconds he was gone, swallowed up by the night.

It isn't like that, she wanted to say. They didn't take items of cultural or religious significance from the country. They were careful to check provenance. It was all above board. But . . . Eva sighed. For the first time, she felt a needle-prick of doubt. About her job, about what she was doing here.

She needed a good night's sleep, she decided. And she needed to get *her* emotions under control. In the meantime . . . She was left alone with only the soft sound of his footsteps on the gravel fading into the distance, the heady intoxicating scent of the frangipani and a long, pale sliver of moonlight.

Back inside Pine Rise she collected her key from reception. 'Is it possible to make an international call?' she asked. 'To the UK?'

'Yes, madam.' The girl lifted the telephone receiver and spoke to the operator. She looked back at Eva. 'The number, please?'

Eva told her. She waited.

'There is no answer,' the girl said at last.

'Are you sure?' Eva made a quick calculation. It would be around 7 p.m. Her grandfather was always home at this time. He would have just had his dinner. 'Can you try again?'

'Of course, madam.' Again, she went through the motions. Nothing.

'Thank you.' Eva walked away. It was probably nothing to worry about. Maybe he just hadn't heard the phone ring. She'd try again tomorrow. And if not . . . But she pushed the 'if not' away. Tomorrow, as Ramon had told her earlier, was another day.

CHAPTER 20

Lawrence could smell something metallic and unfamiliar. The bed he was lying on was narrow and hard and the sheets seemed to be clamped tightly to his body as if he were in danger of falling out. It wasn't his bed, which must mean that he wasn't at home.

Earlier someone had given him water and he'd drunk it through a straw. Was he in hospital? He hoped not. Everyone knew the food was bloody awful and the nurses woke you up every five minutes to take your temperature or your blood pressure or ask you if you needed to empty your bladder. But he had the feeling that someone had mentioned something about hospital.

What had happened? His head hurt when he tried to think about it. Had he collapsed? Had a heart attack? Was he dying, was that it? He hoped someone would tell Mrs Briggs. She'd be worrying if she came in to clean and he wasn't even there.

This thought almost made him chuckle but the chuckle turned into a cough and suddenly he couldn't breathe. That was it then. He'd choke to death. In a bloody hospital.

But she was there. Someone was there and she lifted him

slightly, enough to clear his lungs. 'Do you want to sit up?' she whispered.

But he was too tired to sit up. Too tired even to answer her. So instead he thought of Helen.

There had never been that spark between them, though they had been together for so long, shared good times and bad times and had a child together. They had rubbed along, one might say, and for most of his life with her, Lawrence had been contented enough. Contentment though, was flat, like a plateau. It didn't flow like the mountain streams of Burma in which ran both force and passion.

Lawrence also knew that he had not tried hard enough to forget, that Helen knew his thoughts and his heart lived elsewhere, in a country very far away. Many times he had tried to get close to Helen, to make some recompense perhaps, or to discover with her something that was more precious, more intimate than what they already shared. But he could not. She protected herself against him with the armours of prudery and convention, with the conservatism which grew more and more brittle inside her, until he felt she might break rather than let herself go.

Of course it was his fault. If he had been strong, Helen would have attached herself to some other man who would have made her so much happier. But it was too late for such regrets. He had done what he had done, rightly or wrongly. And he respected Helen, as both a wife and a mother. He believed that she too had tried her best. And even that was a sadness to him.

When Rosemary was born, it was almost a relief to hand the reins for his daughter's emotional welfare to Helen. Rosemary could give Helen what Lawrence could not. Helen could have all of Rosemary; he wanted her to have it all. He took a back seat and focused on making a living to provide for them, to give them a good life. Lawrence loved his daughter and would have liked to give her more. But he would not. He watched from the wings.

Now, he tried to remember when he had first felt an obligation to Helen, which was hard, because he felt as if it had always been there. Was it when his mother began hinting and his father began to slap him on the back as if he were a friend and contemporary, rather than a son? Was it when Helen's parents fussed over him and treated him as if he were one of their own? Or was it even earlier?

Helen was twelve the first time he kissed her. Or, he should say, the first time she kissed him. Lawrence was just thirteen.

His family had gone to a weekend lunch party at her house and it had drifted into late afternoon. They had a small swimming pool and even a tennis court; the family had money then, both families had money. Unlike others, they had benefited from the financial recession of the thirties; they had made some canny investments at the right time and now they were reaping the benefits.

Lawrence and Helen had been swimming in the pool, length after short length, racing each other and laughing and splashing and when they'd got out, she had taken his hand and pulled him towards the summer house. 'Come on. I want to show you something.'

It was a perfect summer's day, cloudless and blue, the way summer days often were in England back then, no breeze, bees idly buzzing around the clumps of lavender bordering the path. They sat on the decking of the summer house, which was hot from the sun, and stretched out their bare legs already dried from the pool. Helen's blonde hair was dripping on the bleached boards of the decking, the water almost sizzling as it landed. She moved close to him as if she might whisper in his ear and then shook her hair like a dog.

He laughed. 'What do you want to show me, Helen?'

'This.' And she'd pulled him close, put her lips against his and kissed him. Not just on the mouth, but prising his lips apart with hers until he felt her tongue, warm and moist on his.

He felt the stirring in his groin. 'Give over, Helen.' He half pushed her away, his hands on her shoulders, her wet hair trailing over his fingers.

'Why?' Dreamily, she looked up at him, batting wet eyelashes. Kissed him again, lightly this time. Her lips tasted of chlorine.

'Because.' He lay down and stared up at the sky, through the corrugated leaves of the apple tree next to the summer house, into the blue. Truth was, he didn't know why.

'One day we'll be doing this all the time.' She licked her finger and traced a path across his forehead.

'Doing what?' He grabbed her hand, held it pinned down by his side.

How stupid was he? Not to realise they had his whole life mapped out for him. His parents. Her parents. Helen.

'You and me,' she said.

'You and me?' He let go of her hand, leant up on one elbow and watched her. She'd picked a blade of grass and was dissecting it with her fingernail. He understood how it felt. She was a pretty girl. But he'd grown up with Helen. He knew her, warts and all. She was more like a sister.

'Don't you know?' she said, tickling his face with the grass. 'Don't you feel it?'

'Feel what?' He was scared of what might happen if she kept kissing him that way. Which was precisely why he had to stop her kissing him that way. It didn't feel right.

'Me and you,' she said again. 'We'll be married one day. We'll live in a big house. Maybe this house.' She waved vaguely towards where all the grown-ups were sitting outside, out of sight: his parents, her parents – colleagues and best friends – eating and drinking and planning someone else's future.

'Oh, yes?' He laughed. She was just a girl. What did she know?

'We'll have lots of furniture,' she said. 'And children.'

He laughed again, wondering if she'd detected the note of panic.

'And we'll have parties just like this one.'

Her parents' life, he thought. That was what Helen wanted.

'What makes you so sure?' he teased. He was still more curious than worried. It was just Helen's fantasy, it wasn't real.

She tilted her head towards him. Screwed her eyes up against the sun. 'It's what they want,' she said. 'So it'll happen.'

And Helen had been right. It had happened.

CHAPTER 21

The next morning, Eva took the photographs she'd brought from home to show Maya. It was too early to phone her grandfather again, but she'd try later, before she headed back to Mandalay. Fascinating though this trip to Pyin Oo Lwin had been, she mustn't forget that her contact would be waiting and that she had a job to do, whatever Ramon might think of it.

Eva handed her the first photo. 'My grandfather.' As he must have been when Maya first knew him. Had she had a picture of her lover back then? Possibly not. Certainly, her eyes filled.

'Lawrence,' she whispered. She held it carefully, as if it were so brittle it might snap.

'It was taken just before the war,' Eva said. It had *1939* scrawled on the back in her grandfather's hand. And he had told her that at the time he'd been on leave from camp.

'Yes. It was here in Maymyo,' Maya said. 'I remember that day.' She traced a fingertip over the picture. 'At Pine Rise.'

'Oh, yes, of course.' Eva recognised the carvings around the front door behind where he was standing. Now, she had seen them with her own eyes, run her fingers over that same wood . . .

Her grandfather was standing, legs akimbo, staring straight at the camera. He was wearing khaki shorts and a short-sleeved shirt. His eyes were pale and unblinking in the faded black-and-white shot. A young man ready to go to war. Had he known that? Had he been at all prepared for what he was about to go through? Eva doubted it.

'And this is Grandpa in the early nineteen fifties.' She produced the next, an early colour shot. Her grandfather was sitting in the window-seat at home, looking towards the garden, which was long and backed on to the Nature Reserve and the cliffs. The garden had a small pond with a yellow water lily, irises and carp and an old-fashioned crazy-paving path that meandered from the bench up to the vegetable patch. To Eva, it had always been a secret garden, because of the narrow paths that wound behind the sprawling hydrangea bushes, and the many places to hide behind the trellises of sweet peas and raspberry canes. The photo must have been taken less than ten years after he had left Burma. He looked wistful and, yes, a little lonely.

Maya nodded. 'It is a beautiful garden,' she said. 'And Lawrence looks just as I imagined.'

How many times had she pictured him, Eva wondered, thinking of what Ramon had said last night. Maya smiled, but again Eva could see the sadness in her dark eyes. How had she felt when this man whom she loved had gone off to war? Had she known she would never see him again? And how had she felt when he never returned? She seemed to have known that he had gone back to the UK rather than been a casualty and she must have accepted it long ago. But Eva wondered, nevertheless, how much had she suffered at losing him? She had married and she'd had a daughter. But so had Eva's grandfather. And yet he'd never stopped loving this woman sitting beside her now.

'It was taken not long before my mother was born,' she told Maya. Maya, too, must have been married by then. She and Eva's grandfather had been desperately in love. But they had parted. They had both moved on.

'Ah.' Maya held the photograph to her breast. 'What was she like, your grandmother? Did she make him happy?'

'Well . . .' Eva wasn't sure how to answer this. She didn't want to betray anyone, but she felt she must be honest with this woman who had already lost so much. 'He was content, I think,' she said. 'My grandmother loved him.' Which kind of said it all.

'Good.' Maya nodded. 'I am glad.' And her eyes were wise. 'It is good to be content, I think. Ramon . . .'

'Yes?' Though Eva wasn't sure she wanted to discuss Ramon, not after last night.

'He is not content. He is troubled. I know it.' Maya let out a small sigh and Eva could see the tension in the stiffness of her narrow shoulders.

Eva thought about what he'd said yesterday in the Gardens. 'He cares very deeply about things,' she said cautiously.

'He is political.' Maya took her hand. 'Just like my father. In this country, it is impossible to be content if you are a political animal.' She sighed. 'Could you talk to him, Eva,

197

my child? He would listen to you. He is drawn to you, I can see.'

'I really don't think—' Eva began.

'He imagines he protects me. But I worry . . .' She tailed off. 'Soon, I will no longer be here to worry.'

'I'll try.' Eva felt she had to be honest. 'But I'm not sure he would listen to me.' She was probably the last person he'd listen to, in fact. 'And I'm so sorry, but I must leave this afternoon. I have to return to Mandalay.' She changed the subject by producing the next photograph.

'Here's Grandpa with my mother.' This photo was very different. Her grandfather was holding her mother's hand and her mother, five or six years old perhaps, her hair a mop of blonde curls, eyes as blue as her father's, looked up at him with trust and love. And he gazed down at her adoringly. The photograph never failed to make Eva sad. What had happened between these two? Because once – and the evidence was here – they had been so close. But now . . . The rift between them seemed an insurmountable one. Copenhagen wasn't far away, but it was a while since her mother's last visit. And any meaningful reconnection between father and daughter would take a lot more than an email or a phone call.

Again, Maya nodded and took her time examining the photo. If anything, she seemed even more moved by this one than she had by the previous two. She clicked her tongue and murmured in Burmese. She peered at the photo, moving it closer to the light. 'Yes,' she said. 'His daughter. Yes, I see.'

Eva showed her some more photographs, one from each

decade, some of him alone, some with Rosemary, some with Eva. And Maya gave them all equal time, attention and care. Fortunately, the subject of Ramon appeared to have been dropped.

The very last photo Eva had taken herself last week before she left, printing it out so that she had a complete set. Lawrence here looked old and more fragile, his hair snow-white but his eyes as intelligent as ever. 'And as he is now,' she told Maya.

Maya let out a choked sob when she saw it. 'Look at us both,' she whispered, touching the face on the photograph. 'We are old . . . We have taken our chosen paths.' And then in a lower voice, 'Each without the other.'

Eva waited a moment for her to collect her emotions. Had she been right to bring this catalogue of memories with her? Her mother wouldn't like it. She would say that this was their life, that it had nothing to do with Maya. But it had seemed so important to Eva to show Maya the pictures of their family. And she was glad now that she had. 'Would you like to keep them?' she asked her.

Maya stared at her. Her hands were trembling. 'Truly?'

Eva was moved. She took her hand. 'I brought them for you.'

Maya bowed her head. 'Thank you, Eva,' she said. 'If only . . .'

But Eva never found out her 'if only' because at that moment, the door opened and Ramon strode in.

'Eva,' he said. 'Good morning. Did you sleep well?' His

gaze was distant as it swept over her. He was dressed as usual in short-sleeved shirt and *longyi*, in navy blue today, and was barefoot.

'Very well, thank you,' she said smoothly. Though she hadn't. She had tossed and turned half the night until a pale pink dawn had crept through the crack in the curtains. She was worried about her grandfather. And she had decided to steer well clear. Of moonlight, the scent of frangipani and Ramon.

'And when are you returning to Mandalay?' he asked, again.

'I've booked a driver for this afternoon.'

'You do not need a driver,' Maya said. 'Ramon is also returning to Mandalay this afternoon.'

'Oh?'

'I am needed at work,' he said. 'The city of Mandalay is where my business is located, of course.'

'Of course,' she echoed. She hadn't considered that. Not that it mattered. She needn't see him when she was in Mandalay. He would be busy and so would she. She was sorry not to be able to help Maya, but Ramon would never listen to her. And anyway, what should she say?

'Ramon will take you back with him,' said Maya.

'That's very kind . . .' Of Maya; the suggestion hadn't come from Ramon after all. Perhaps she was hoping the long drive would inspire confidences. 'But, as I said, I've already booked my driver.'

Maya got to her feet. 'We will cancel the driver,' she said regally.

Eva couldn't help smiling. Serene, but with a core of steel, she thought. 'But—'

'He will understand. Ramon will take you back to Mandalay. It is decided.'

Eva took a deep breath. 'Very well,' she said. 'Thank you.' The journey might have been more relaxing with a different driver. But she was an independent woman who could find her way around the world. What threat could a man like Ramon possibly pose for her peace of mind?

'How soon can you be ready?' Ramon glanced at his watch.

'In an hour?' She just had to pack a few things and make that phone call. She was eager now to get back to Mandalay. Work would distract her, it always did.

'And in a few days I, too, will be there.' Maya held out her arms and embraced her.

'Will you? I'll look forward to that.' Eva kissed her gently on both papery cheeks. She didn't want to betray anyone, and she knew her mother wouldn't approve, but she liked Maya. She appreciated her sense of calm, her strength, her connection to the grandfather Eva adored.

Maya nodded. 'There is more that I must tell you.'

'Oh?' And more that I should ask you, thought Eva.

Maya put a finger to her lips. 'When the time is right,' she said softly. She turned to Ramon. 'And in the meantime,' she said, 'you need have no worries and no problems. You will be perfectly safe. Because in Mandalay, Ramon will take care of you.'

★

Eva hurried back to Pine Rise.

At reception, the girl put her call through. Again, it was painstakingly slow. Finally, she handed the receiver to Eva.

'Hello? Grandpa?' she said.

'Eva?'

The voice was one she recognised. But it wasn't her grandfather. 'Mother?'

'Yes, darling, it's me.'

She sounded breathless but familiar, and Eva was surprised how glad she felt to hear her voice. But, 'What are you doing in England, Mother? There's nothing wrong, is there?' She felt a sudden churning in her belly. Grandpa?

'Everything's fine.' She heard her mother take a deep breath. 'I came over for a visit on the spur of the moment . . .'

While *she* was in Burma, Eva couldn't help thinking.

'And I found your Grandpa . . .'

'Found him what? Where?'

'He'd collapsed.' Another deep breath. 'But you mustn't worry. He spent last night in hospital and he's feeling much better now.'

He was feeling better. The churning subsided. He was alright. And her mother was with him. 'What happened?' she whispered. 'Was it a heart attack?'

'No, no.' Her mother's voice came across clear and reassuring. 'We think he just fainted. The doctor said he'd recently adjusted the pills he takes for high blood pressure. We think that's all it was.'

'Should I come home?' Eva found that she was clutching

202

the receiver close to her. Thank God her mother had turned up when she had. Supposing he'd been alone?

'There's absolutely no need.' Her mother sounded so in control, it was a huge relief. 'I'll stay here and look after him.'

'Can I speak to him? He's OK to talk, is he?' Suddenly Eva knew she had to tell him as soon as she could.

'I'll take you through. He's in bed, just resting.'

Eva heard her footsteps. 'Are you alright, Mother?' she asked.

'I'm fine, darling. What about you? How is everything?'

Everything. So much had been happening, Eva could hardly believe she'd been in Myanmar for only a week. 'It's going very well,' she managed to say. 'So far, so good.'

'It's Eva.' She heard her mother's voice. 'Calling from Burma.'

'Eva.' And here was her grandfather, sounding even more frail than usual. Perhaps it was the distance that separated them. She hoped so. 'Is that really you, Eva, darling? How are you? How's Burma?'

She chuckled. 'It's wonderful. And I'm very well too. But how are you, Grandpa?'

'Oh, I'm not so bad. Plenty of life in the old dog yet.' He laughed. 'Where are you, exactly, my dear?'

'Maymyo.'

He paused. 'And have you found her?'

Eva heard the emotion, the shaky exhalation of breath. She imagined him clutching the receiver closer too, just as she was clutching this old-fashioned black Bakelite receiver to her ear. 'Yes,' she said. 'I have.'

'What?'

'Yes!' She almost shouted. 'I've found her. She's well. Living here in Maymyo. I just wanted to let you know.'

'Thank you, my dear. Oh, thank you.' She heard in his voice a sweet relief that moved her so deeply. 'Thank you, darling Eva.'

'I'll tell you the rest of the news when I get back,' she said.

'You take care, my darling,' he wheezed.

'And you. I just wanted you to know . . .' The line had gone dead. But it didn't matter. She'd told him and he was alright. Her mother was there looking after him. Well . . .

'Could you make up my bill?' she asked the girl on reception. 'I'm almost ready to check out.'

'Yes, madam, of course.'

Eva took her key and went up to her room to finish packing a few bits and pieces. She could only imagine how that news had made him feel.

CHAPTER 22

Rosemary was building the fire in the living room. The kitchen was fine for eating in but it wasn't comfortable enough. He needed to be lying down and he wouldn't be wanting to stay in bed all day. If she made up the fire he could lie on the sofa and be warm. And it gave her something to do.

She started with scrunched up newspaper and old egg boxes. It was a long time since she'd been down on her hands and knees in front of a grate getting her hands dirty. The thought made her chuckle. It was a long way from the sleek radiators of their apartment in Copenhagen. She paused and sank back on to her heels for a moment. And how was Alec? He hadn't phoned since she'd left. But then again, neither had she.

Her father was asleep but she had her ears open for the moment he woke up. She hadn't lied to Eva, but on the other hand neither had she been scrupulously honest. They were so close and she didn't want to worry her, not while she was away in Burma. He wasn't well. He seemed to be . . . as Mrs Briggs had put it when she tried to explain to Rosemary this morning, *not quite with it*. Which itself seemed a bit of a betrayal. Her father had always been such an intelligent man, she'd been proud of that. And not only that, but according to Mrs Briggs, this wasn't the first time he'd had a fall. 'He asked me not to say,' she confided. 'I'm sorry. I wasn't sure what to do for the best.'

Rosemary began to build a little pyramid of kindling around the newspaper. Like a bivouac. Somewhere to hide, to shelter. But it was true, he wasn't with it, it was as if he were somewhere else.

That wasn't the reason he'd collapsed though. Rosemary shivered and thought back to the moment she'd arrived at the house, the moment she'd found him there, passed out on the bathroom floor. She'd found a pulse straightaway. Thank God. And she'd turned him into the recovery position. Talked to him, gently, tried to bring him round. At the same time, she'd groped for her mobile in her bag and dialled 999. He needed to be taken to hospital, now. She wasn't taking any chances.

In the ambulance she'd held his hand and he'd come round.

'Eva?' he'd muttered. He struggled to sit up. 'Eva, is that you?'

'It's Rosemary.' She had repressed a sigh and squeezed his hand. Even now he could upset her so easily 'Don't worry about a thing, Dad. You had a fall. We're on our way to hospital.'

'Hospital?' He pulled a face and the paramedic had laughed.

'Don't reckon you're too delighted about that then, Lawrence,' he remarked.

Rosemary leaned closer. He was so thin, so pale. His skin

was as pouched and creased as old paper, criss-crossed with lines she didn't even remember. He smelt of shaving cream and something vaguely medicinal which she couldn't quite place. She had left this visit far too long, she realised. But she'd make up for it now. 'Don't worry, Dad,' she whispered. 'You'll be fine.'

At the hospital he had shifted in and out of his usual sharp awareness. They had done lots of tests and concluded that there was nothing seriously wrong and that they could go home. No doubt he was taking up a bed needed by someone more ill. They would contact his GP, they told Rosemary, and tell him what had happened and he would probably make a home visit. Doubtless, it was the change in his prescription that had done it. Blood pressure could be hard to balance, not too high to risk a stroke, not too low to get dizzy and faint. But in the meantime, she should stay with him.

As if I'm going anywhere, she had muttered under her breath. He was her father. She should never have left him. It wasn't fair for him to be alone.

Rosemary picked up the matches and lit one, the scent of sulphur hitting her nostrils like some far off memory. She held it to the newspaper, it caught and she carefully added more kindling, building it around. She didn't let herself think about what he'd said to Eva on the phone, she was pretending she hadn't even heard. But at least Eva was well and it was good that she'd phoned, that Rosemary had been able to talk to her and fill her in on what had happened.

By the time she heard him stir, the fire was lit and blazing with life. It reminded Rosemary, more than anything, of her childhood growing up in this rambling house, of Christmas Day and a log fire burning. The tree in the corner decorated so carefully by her mother. She always allowed Rosemary to help, but Rosemary soon noticed that the bits she did would more often than not be done again by her mother. Made perfect. She sighed. How do you mend a broken marriagethough? How do you mend a marriage that had never been perfect, not even in the beginning?

She put a couple of logs in position and placed the guard in front of the growing blaze.

'Hello, love.' He was already sitting up and reaching for his glass of water. He seemed a bit brighter.

'Let me.' She passed it to him. Then she fussed with his pillows for a bit, to make him more comfortable. 'I've lit a fire,' she said. 'We'll give it half an hour to warm up and then I'll take you in there if you like.'

He was watching her. 'It's grand to see you, love,' he murmured. 'I never said. But it's grand to see you.'

'You too. How are you feeling after your nap?' She smoothed his fine white hair from his brow. Soft as baby hair, she thought, and something stirred inside her. She felt her eyes fill with tears. What on earth was the matter with her? Whatever she did, she mustn't let him see her cry.

'Cock a hoop,' he whispered.

She took his hand and gently patted it.

'Why did you come, Rosie? Why the sudden visit, eh?'

She was relieved to see a spark of animation in his pale blue eyes. How much could he see? 'I came to see you, didn't I?' And lucky I did, she thought.

He frowned. 'I'm not about to kick the bucket, am I, love?'

'Stop it.' She squeezed gently. 'Of course you're not. I just wanted to see you.' And she realised that it was true. She'd been so angry with him, hadn't she, over the years. But seeing him now, like this . . .

'I wanted to see you too,' he said. 'So that's alright then, isn't it?'

'That's alright,' she agreed. She was the woman who kept things at a distance, who had found it easier to bury herself in a new life in Copenhagen and to let the old life go. But this was her father and for a moment there she had thought she'd lost him. And she realised she didn't want to let him go.

She got to her feet. 'Fancy a cuppa?'

'Thought you'd never ask.' He grinned.

CHAPTER 23

Rather to her surprise, Eva found herself confiding in Ramon on the journey to Mandalay. She told him about the phone call and that her grandfather was far from well.

'I know you feel that he behaved badly,' she added. 'But it meant everything to my grandfather that I brought the chinthe back here to your family, that I found Maya and that she's still alive.'

Ramon glanced across at her. 'Perhaps I misjudged him,' he admitted. He swung the car out to overtake a smoke-belching truck that must have been fifty years old, full of local villagers squatting on pink plastic crates of live chickens and huge watermelons.

Health and safety hadn't made much impact on Myanmar, Eva noted and not for the first time.

'Or perhaps you do not know the full story.'

'It's possible,' she conceded.

He drummed long brown fingers on the steering wheel. 'Why, for example, did he never come back here? It has been many years since the war ended.'

Eva considered. 'Because he was married to my grand-mother,' she said. 'And then maybe he felt it was too late.'

'Too late to again disrupt my grandmother's life?' he asked.

'I think so.' She would have been married by that time. 'And your country was very isolated then,' she reminded him. 'It wasn't easy to get here. Politically—'

'Yes, that is also true.' He frowned. 'And I am sorry he is not well.'

So was she. They had left behind the leafy suburbs of Pyin Oo Lwin and were now descending towards the plains. The road to Mandalay, Eva thought nostalgically, lined with yellow mimosa. There was no sign of any tension from the night before and slowly Eva allowed herself to unwind and enjoy the journey through the red-earthed hills and lush vegetation. She leaned back in the seat. She had worn her hair up to keep cool but of course the car had air-con so she was perfectly comfortable. She closed her eyes for a moment, enjoying the sensation of the chill air on her skin. She had come to Pyin Oo Lwin not knowing if she would find Maya. And she had not only found her, but she had heard yet another story, one that had got her thinking and planning. Because there must be a way, mustn't there, to get that little chinthe back?

She stretched out her legs. She was wearing green linen cropped trousers and a sleeveless embroidered top and had already slipped off her leather-thonged sandals. 'It's been so lovely to meet your family,' she said.

He laughed. 'And you'll meet even more of them in Mandalay.'

Eva had a vision of more cousins, second cousins and

assorted ebony-haired children who seemed to belong to everyone. And she realised that it was assumed she would continue to see the family in Mandalay. It was a pleasant thought.

'Tell me some more about your furniture company,' Eva prompted, sneaking a look at him as he drove. He was a confident driver. Both hands rested languidly on the steering wheel, he looked casual but in charge. She'd like to know him a bit better, she decided, find out what made him tick.

'My father began the business in Myanmar,' Ramon said, 'but his father's family, the English side . . .' And she heard the pride in his voice. 'Were master craftsmen and furniture makers in Britain for more than four generations before that.'

'Really?' She'd find out the name, she decided, and look them up. 'So why did your father move here in the first place?'

'He was an explorer.' He looked swiftly across at her and then back to the road ahead. They were passing one of the many scatterings of shacks and dwellings with fruit and vegetable carts, children playing on the roadside, chickens pecking in the dust. 'At that time he was not sure his father's business was for him. He came out here at twenty-five, met my mother and decided to settle in this country.'

Again, Eva was reminded of her grandfather. He too had left England because he was an explorer and because he didn't want to join the family firm. But in his case, the war had changed everything. He had returned to Dorset when it was over and tried to rescue Fox and Forsters, but although he'd had some degree of success and the company had recovered to fight another day, Eva knew for a fact that her grandfather's heart had never been in it. He had left his heart, she supposed, in Burma.

'But your father became a furniture maker anyway?' she asked Ramon.

'Yes.' He nodded and swung the steering wheel to the left to follow the bend in the road. 'He had trained in London and always loved to work with wood. Very soon, he formed a Burmese furniture company with the same ethics as his father's.'

'Which were?'

'We pride ourselves on being environmentally conscious,' he said. He paused and accelerated smoothly to overtake a small truck. The journey was taking no time, already they were descending towards Mandalay, the sun low in the sky, visible through the trees to the west. 'We use only the best teak wood sourced from conscientious dealers with legitimate concessions.'

Eva was impressed. His words struck a chord with her own thoughts and values. 'But what happened to the business when your father—'

'Died?' He glanced across at her. 'My father had a loyal manager who has only recently left us to retire. He trained me and taught me the skills necessary to take over. From when I was only a young boy, it was always expected that I would grow up and take charge of the company.'

'And you did,' murmured Eva.

'And I did.' He braked at the junction and took the turning to the city. 'Each generation has a responsibility,' he continued. 'To develop the business as he sees fit, but to also remain loyal to the original ethos of producing high quality and hand-crafted furniture. To move forwards, but gradually and faithfully.' Once again, he glanced across at her. 'It is our way.'

'And your method is through expansion?' She recalled what he'd told her before, his dream of exporting his furniture to the UK and elsewhere.

'Not just expansion.' He shook his head. 'That is important, yes. But I have my own ideas too. You will see if you visit the factory.'

'I'd like to.' Eva was intrigued. 'Did your father try to merge his company with your grandfather's in the UK?' Had that been a possibility back then?

Ramon shook his head. 'They never had the chance to try,' he said. 'My English grandfather died only a year after my father arrived here. His heart, too, was not strong. There was, what do you say?'

'A family history?'

'Exactly.' He nodded. 'The company in Britain was terminated. It was even more important then for my father to make our business a success. He must continue his father's work. Now he was doing it for him and for his new family too, for us. And I must do the same.'

'I see.' She was certainly beginning to understand where Ramon's ambition came from and why the furniture company was so important to him. It was a legacy, a family tradition.

'And you?' Ramon asked as they entered the suburbs of the

city. 'You have antiques to view in Mandalay?' His voice was a little cooler, but thankfully he was less antagonistic than before.

'I have.' She watched him negotiate the busy road. 'But we're not depriving your country of anything iconic or culturally significant, you know,' she said. She twisted her daisy ring around her little finger as she spoke.

'Is that so?' He flicked back the wing of dark hair from his forehead. 'But who is to say? You?' He swerved to avoid a cyclist and sounded the horn of the car. 'Forgive me, Eva, but you are not Burmese, even though you may be an expert.'

'We are taking what the Burmese wish to sell,' she insisted. 'And we only buy from the legal owners. What's wrong with that?' Eva tried to control her rising anger. He was questioning her integrity, which she prided herself on more than anything.

Ramon braked sharply as a pedestrian loaded with watermelons stepped into the road. He swore under his breath. 'But why do they want to sell? Have you asked yourself that? Have you thought that perhaps they need to sell because they are desperate? Why not leave things where they are sometimes?'

'You can't take away people's right to sell their own possessions.' Though Eva knew it wasn't quite as simple as that. 'And anyway, lots of the things we buy came originally from the British.'

'Ah, the British.' His lip curled. 'Well, that is your history, Eva.'

'Your father was British too,' she said.

'Yes, and my mother was Burmese.'

Eva sighed. He was quite impossible. 'We are at least bringing money into your country.'

Ramon conceded this with a small nod. 'And we are grateful,' he said with some sarcasm. 'Just as we are grateful that the US has been good enough to lift some of the harmful sanctions against us.'

'Ramon—'

The tyres squealed as they drew up outside her hotel.

Eva didn't wait for him to open her door. She got out and practically dragged her suitcase out behind her.

'I apologise.' Ramon was standing in front of her, blocking her pathway to the hotel's swing door, long-limbed and with a determined look in his green eyes. 'It is your business. I must not interfere.'

'It's alright.' Eva had to concede that he had a point. And she would do what she could to ensure that everything she accepted for the Emporium had been checked and deemed appropriate for export.

'Perhaps in a day or two, you will be free to do some sight-seeing,' he suggested.

'I hope so.' Eva watched as he picked up her case and took it into the foyer, went in after him and gave her name to reception.

'Ah, madam, you have two messages,' the receptionist told her, checking a pigeon-hole. She handed Eva two slips of paper.

One was written neatly and signed *Klaus*, she'd read that

later. The other was from her contact in Mandalay, giving a phone number and the words: *it is ready for the view*.

'It looks as if you will be busy tomorrow,' Ramon murmured.

'Yes.' She smiled up at him. 'But thanks for bringing me back to Mandalay. I'm very grateful.'

'It was nothing.' He handed her case over to the porter. 'And at the weekend?'

'The weekend?'

'I can take you to visit Sagaing and Inwa, if you wish,' he said. 'They are special places. You must see more of our country to fully understand.'

Eva hesitated. Had his grandmother dictated that this was how he should behave? Or did it come from the heart? 'I'm sure you're very busy,' she hedged.

'Not really.' He shrugged. 'I would like to take you, to show you,' he said. He certainly seemed sincere. And again, he fixed her with that long, considering look of his.

'Then, yes. Thank you. I should be free at the weekend.' It would give her the chance to find out more about the location of the missing chinthe, and what exactly Ramon was planning to do to get it back. It would fulfil her promise to Maya to try and discover what was troubling her grandson. And it would help her to get to know this country even better. Which, more than anything, was what Eva wanted to do.

CHAPTER 24

She had found her. Eva had found her.

Lawrence watched his daughter bustle around the bedroom, tidying up things that really didn't need tidying up. They had Mrs Briggs for that.

But, 'Take a few days off, Mrs B,' Rosemary had said to her yesterday. 'I'll look after everything here.'

Him, she meant. Look after him. It made Lawrence feel like standing on top of the bed and shouting. *I'm here, don't you know? I can look after myself. I always used to look after you.*

But that was then. How could he look after anyone now? How could he even stand on top of the bed, come to that? It was as much as he could do to get out of bed and get to the bathroom.

'Leave it, Dad,' Rosemary said when he tried to do anything. 'Let me.'

He'd only be tidying a book away or hanging up his dressing gown. Nothing really. But he realised that she wanted to do those things, it was important to her. She wanted to feel useful. So he let her.

She wouldn't stay, though. He knew she wouldn't stay because she didn't live here anymore. He was sure of that, but for a moment it had slipped his mind where she had gone to.

And then Eva had telephoned from Burma. She had found her and Maya was alive and well. Lawrence had sunk his head back into his pillows that night and he was back there. Simple. He was back there and he could smell once more the jasmine in the porch outside her father's house, the coconut oil in her hair.

Upper Burma, 1937
Lawrence had returned to the camp. It wasn't much more than a forest clearing, a few huts with bamboo screens and thatched roofs for the timbermen surrounding the teal of the *tai*, a wooden house erected on a wooden platform and built on stilts, where, as Forest Assistant in charge of the camp, Lawrence lived. But he couldn't get her out of his head. Maya. She was the lightest of shadows in his daytime and his compelling silhouette after dark. And he could have stayed longer in Mandalay, because still the rains didn't come.

It had only been one night but their love-making had been a revelation. She had kept a lamp burning low and she had made him wait while she massaged his neck and shoulders with oil and kissed a trail from his lips down to his belly.

At last, with a groan, he could stand it no more and he had held her tightly and entered her with a passion he could barely control. The connection between them was immediate, electric.

'Touch me with your lips,' she said. And Lawrence remembered something Scottie had said to him, *there's no Burmese word for 'kiss'.*

So he kissed her throat, her hair, her mouth. Deep liquid kisses such as he had never experienced before. Lawrence had shuddered as he held her and he had felt her shudder too.

Later, he watched her sleep and it seemed her whole body was bathed in peace. Already he wanted her again and she opened her eyes as if she knew. Lazily, she arched her back like a sleek cat, moved towards him, her gaze fixed on his face.

'Maya,' he whispered.

Before Lawrence had left Mandalay, he had tried again to tell Maya about his life in England and Helen, about what was expected of him. He didn't want to pretend with her, he didn't want to simply leave one day and for her father to say: *I told you so. He never meant to stay. He just wants to seize all our country's riches and then leave, like all the rest.*

She turned on him, almost fierce. 'You owe me nothing,' she said. 'Nor I, you.'

'But Maya—' That wasn't what he had been trying to say.

'We have lain together in my bed,' she said. 'And we have talked. That is all.'

He took her arm. 'That is not all.'

She acknowledged this with a small nod. 'We are from different lives,' she said. 'And we do not have to say that we will always be together. We are together now. That is all that matters.'

'Are we together now?' He felt eager like a child. Because

he could hardly bear to have her like this and then leave. 'Are we? Can we be together again?'

'I will come to my aunt's house in Sinbo,' she said. 'Do not fear.'

Do not fear. With her, he had no fear. Better than that. With her he had a hope, more than he had ever known.

Now, Lawrence paced the *tai* and he walked around the camp. He climbed up the ladder and stood on his verandah, which gave him a very good view of the surrounding area, shaded by the vines grown around the structure for that purpose. As the sun set across the distant valley, he poured himself a whisky, sat on his chair outside, lit a cigarette and tried to relax. But he could not.

Desperate for something to take his mind off his need for her and his need for rain, he decided to visit a small village upstream from the camp where the logging of next season's out-turn was going on. He would go tomorrow to check on progress. Why not? There was nothing he could do here for now. And he was on a knife-edge just waiting.

He arrived the following day to find that the logging there was going to schedule. It was soothing to discover this, despite the heaviness of the heat and the tension of anticipation.

'The rain comes,' one of his men told him.

What was so different about tonight, he wondered. It was hot, as usual. The insects were persistent, as ever. There was no cloud to be seen, just a haze of heat that lifted only at sunset. And what a sunset. Even Lawrence, with so much on his mind, had to admit that the view was glorious. The darkening sky seemed shot with gold and amber as the blush filled the entire heavens over the forest. He sat there with his whisky long after he should.

And then he felt something change. There was a weight-lessness in the air, a sharpening of the senses and he knew what this meant. His man had been right. Lawrence was impressed. He went inside as the sky grew black, the wind blew and he could hear the thunder beginning to rumble. At last. Lawrence went to bed, still with the ache that he'd felt since meeting Maya, but at least feeling optimistic. And the rains came.

Even as he was falling asleep, he heard it. Rain, welcome rain, pattering at first on the roofs, getting louder and louder, sending him off into a deep sleep which included dreams of great rivers rising, logs tumbling and crashing downstream. And Maya.

In the morning the coolness of the temperature was another welcome relief after the heavy oppression of the past weeks. But now Lawrence had to get back to camp urgently. The paddy fields were awash and the two men he had sent ahead rushed back to tell him the news. There was flash flooding. The road back to camp was already impassable. Bloody hell. The rains had remained ferocious all through the night and even now they hadn't eased. Talk about one extreme to the other. The men were saying that the rivers had risen quicker than they'd ever known before.

He waited another day, but the rains didn't even stop to

catch breath. The incessant croaking of the bullfrogs was unnerving him. Lawrence took stock. He only had stores for a few days, but he mustn't panic. Still, the bungalow was built on low-lying ground and reports were already reaching him that all streams were in full spate so that not even elephants could ford them and that houses were being washed away, so great were the sudden floods. It was looking serious. Was he going to be marooned here? Or was the very water that he'd longed for going to snatch everything away? Nothing else for it. They had to get back – and fast.

The usual way back to camp involved crossing two large streams and it was clear this would be impossible. They'd have to go the long way round. There were still *chaungs*, but they were small ones, at least for the moment.

Not so small, it turned out. The first one was almost waist deep as they waded across and the current was swift. But they did it. The second fazed even the elephants. They screeched and bellowed at the sight of the raging torrent which was already uprooting trees and crashing them into the banks. Jesus. Lawrence shouted the order to the *oozies*, the elephant handlers, and the others to move upstream, though it was hard to even make himself heard with all the racket going on, and eventually they found a safer place to cross.

It was still hairy and there was only one way to do it. Halfway across, clinging on to his elephant, hoping they could avoid the debris being flung by the wild waters of the river into their path and praying they'd make it across, the elephant stumbled and Lawrence slipped and almost fell from its back. The driving rain was in his face, in his eyes, in his ears. He could barely see and all he could hear was the thundering of the river, all he could feel was the ponderous movement of the great beast on whom his life depended, trudging through the mud and waters of the *chaung*. Lawrence clung on with wet, numb fingers, regained his position on the elephant's back, thought of Maya's father. He was going to get his hands dirty today, alright. And more.

But at last they were over. Luck had been on their side that day. They stopped for breakfast, completely done in. They scraped the leeches off their legs since the puttees hadn't stopped the buggers getting through. But they had no choice. They had to go on. And on they went. At times the path wasn't visible and there was a lot more wading to be done before they eventually arrived back at the camp, wet through and exhausted.

Only then could Lawrence relax. He thought of Maya. She would be coming up to Myitkyina to her aunt's house in Sinbo in a few days and he would see her again. She seemed to want that as much as he. And then perhaps, he told himself, the ache would go away.

CHAPTER 25

The Emporium's contact in Mandalay was the main agent for all their dealings in Myanmar; his other men in Yangon and Bagan were apparently answerable to him. This, Eva found out within five minutes of arriving at his 'office', a dusty shack in downtown Mandalay on Eighty-fourth Street near the stone carvers' workshops in Kyauksittan. His name was Myint Maw, he talked very fast and he was extremely full of his own importance. Jacqui had warned Eva in her latest email. *You can be firm with him . . . But don't push him too far. If he gets at all funny with you, just walk away.* Funny with her? It sounded to Eva as if Jacqui were expecting her to walk a tightrope as far as diplomacy and tact were concerned.

'Now, what I can show you? What I can show you?' He shuffled through the heap of papers on his desk. 'What we have? What is to view?'

He seemed very disorganised. 'This is what I am expecting to see,' Eva said resolutely, consulting her own paperwork. 'Figures and statues, carved and painted.' She showed him the pictures of the delicately carved angel, the nats, the monk sitting on a lotus flower and the Buddhas.

'Ah.' He pressed his skinny hands together. 'So special, yes?'

'I hope so.' Eva picked up her bag. 'Shall we go?' She was determined to be businesslike and, with this in mind, had worn loose linen trousers and a smart silk jacket for the encounter. But she was getting awfully hot already.

The goods turned out to be in a storeroom several doors along. Between them the stone-carvers, their workshops so small that they worked by the roadside, sculpted Buddhas and other iconic images up to three metres high, working in white stone, marble and even jade for the smaller pieces. Men in *longyis* scurried around fetching and carrying and the noise of angle grinders and drilling throbbed dull and monotonous in the hot and dusty air.

'Who are their customers?' Eva asked.

Myint Maw dismissed customers and stone-carvers with a wave of his hand. 'Local business people,' he said. 'And foreign buyers perhaps.' He leaned towards her, so that Eva had a too-close-for-comfort view of the hairy mole on his chin. 'But as you know, most money in the old, not the new.'

Last night Eva had been happy enough to chill out at her hotel and take a walk alongside the Palace moat before finding first the nearest internet café and then a restaurant in the evening for dinner. She had tried to call the number Klaus had left for her. *Dear Eva, Sorry to miss you. Give me a call when you return to Mandalay . . .* But it wasn't available and there had been no sign of him at the hotel. It didn't matter. When you travelled alone, you grew accustomed to eating on your own. And after everything that had happened over the last few days, it was actually quite a relief to be alone with her thoughts and have an early night.

She'd also made an appointment with Myint Maw for 11.30 a.m. and so before coming here she'd taken the opportunity of visiting the silk weavers, where she watched, fascinated, as the Burmese women worked the looms, deftly threading the different colours of silk from their spools into intricate patterns with nimble fingers whilst working the pedals with their feet. They were so fast. Eva had moved from the factory at the back to the front of the shop and it hadn't taken much persuasion for her to add a silk scarf in delicate lavender to her growing collection of Myanmar souvenirs. Her mother, she'd decided, would just have to love it.

Now, they arrived at their destination and Myint Maw showed her into the storeroom. There were wooden objects crammed on to every dusty shelf and they were not, she saw immediately, quality goods.

'What's all this?' she asked.

But he hurried her through. 'This not for you,' he said. 'No, no.'

'Is it yours?' He seemed a little edgy. Eva paused to take a closer look but he pulled at her arm and she was forced to follow.

'No, not mine,' he said. 'It is shared storeroom. Do not worry. Come with me now, please.'

And that was a relief because it looked like cheap tat, very far from the sort of pieces she and the Emporium were interested in.

'Here.' Myint Maw led the way into a smaller room. He got a large box down from a shelf. 'This what you are here to view.' He nodded energetically. 'Yes, yes. I remember. I know. This is what you must see. Please.'

Eva took the first figure from the box. It was about thirty centimetres high, a female nat statue carved from wood with painted headdress, red lips and porcelain eyes, her expression regal but sad. Eva examined it carefully, using her eyeglass. The patina on the face was extraordinary, the glaze so cracked that it made her look like a very old lady indeed.

'Nan Karaing Mei Daw,' Myint Maw told her. 'Yes, yes. Beautiful nat, yes?'

'Part human, part buffalo.' Eva had done her homework. She knew the history. This particular nat destroyed her enemies when given offerings of fried fish. Like most of the other Burmese nats — there were thirty-seven in total — she had suffered a violent death and had become the Burmese equivalent of a martyr.

'You like?' Myint Maw rubbed those skinny hands together.

'I like.' It was nineteenth century, in excellent condition and perfectly genuine in Eva's opinion. Jacqui would love it.

Slightly taller was the seated Bhumisparsha Buddha in lacquered teak. As Eva knew from her studies, the style of Buddha images, from Mon to Taungoo and beyond, differed according to date and dynasty. This Buddha was, she recognised, from the Mandalay period with his youthful and innocent face, the hair tightly curled, the robes decoratively folded, the hand making the *mudra* gesture of touching the earth.

There was the angel, the *deva*, carved intricately in teak, and the rather gorgeous monk sitting on a lotus flower, lacquered teak with a gilded and glass inlay. She wasn't disappointed, although she did wish Myint Maw didn't feel compelled to keep up such a high speed commentary on everything she looked at. His English wasn't the best and it was distracting to say the least. He seemed nervous too, constantly checking his watch and looking towards the doorway as if they were about to be disturbed. But this was important and Eva was determined to take her time.

An hour later, she surveyed the collection of antique nats, Buddhas and other artefacts. It was impressive and she'd been able to confidently authenticate every one. She was so excited, she couldn't wait to see them in the Emporium. 'Prices have been agreed?' she checked with Myint Maw. That was her understanding; she didn't want to get into haggling.

Maw shrugged. 'Prices? Now, what you say?'

Oh dear. Once again, Eva produced her paperwork. And then she remembered Ramon. 'And where did all these pieces come from?' she asked the contact. 'Can you tell me?'

'Come from?'

'Where did you buy?' She included the statues in a wide gesture. Spread her hands into a question.

'All over,' he said. 'Private houses, monasteries, temples . . .'

'Monasteries?' That didn't sound right. 'Why are they selling?'

'They not want old things,' he said. 'They need the money. They want new.'

'And temples?'

'You go to Bagan?' he asked.

'Not yet.' But she would be going. And she knew there were hundreds of temples there.

He made a flicking gesture with his hand. 'When you go, you will see,' he said. 'Too many temples, much destroyed. Too many statues. Nowhere for them to go. But they want money. You see.'

Oh, dear. How could you balance the need for money with the need to keep iconic pieces in their original environment? It was a tricky question. 'And do you have the paperwork?' she persevered. She tried not to look at the mole and the long dark hair that sprouted from it. 'For the sales?' She wanted to at least check they had been paid for.

Myint Maw clutched his chest. 'You not trust? You think these things are stolen?' He seemed nothing less than devastated.

'Yes,' said Eva. 'No. That is . . .' She shrugged. 'My employer wants me to check.' Which wasn't quite true, but was good enough for the moment.

Maw seemed incredulous now. 'You joke?'

'No.' She shook her head but she wasn't sure they were getting anywhere.

'I show you other stuff,' he said. 'I know.'

Eva frowned. What was he talking about now? 'What other stuff?'

'I know,' he said. 'Why you care?'

Eva thought of what had happened in Yangon. 'Do you mean another shipment? Are there more goods being sent out to us?' She was confused. Why did she keep getting the feeling that everyone else knew a lot more than she did? She was the one inspecting all the artefacts, but there seemed to be another agenda. She liked transparency in her business dealings, with a mutual respect. Here, in both Yangon and Mandalay, dealings seemed to be decidedly muddy.

'You have no need to worry,' he assured her. She could feel him swiftly back-tracking. 'It is all good. Price is right. There will be no questions asked.'

But *was* that a good thing? Eva thought of all the roughly made wooden objects she'd seen in the other room and she thought of what Ramon had said. *Plundering* . . . Burma might be opening up to trade and to tourism. But who was benefiting? And she was pretty sure the answer was not the ordinary Burmese people.

CHAPTER 26

The doctor came in the afternoon. Rosemary felt that she'd known him forever; she had, more or less, he had been their family doctor since she was about ten years old and had looked after her mother when she was ill.

'Dr Martyn.' Warmly, she shook his hand.

'Rosemary. It's been a long time. How are you?' He looked much the same. Worn leather briefcase, scuffed shoes, green tweed jacket, his hair a bit thinner on top. Rosemary supposed that he'd be retiring soon.

'I'm alright,' she said. 'But Dad . . .' She told the doctor how she'd found him. 'And he did say his prescription had changed.'

'Mmm.' He frowned, pulled some notes from the briefcase. 'His blood pressure was getting a little high. We were trying to bring it down.'

'And he seems different,' Rosemary added in a low voice that she hoped wouldn't carry to the downstairs bedroom.

'Different?'

'A bit vague. Muddled.' She'd tried to explain to Alec on the phone last night too, but it was hard to put it into words.

'Do you want me to come over, Rosemary?' he had asked her. 'Give you a hand?'

'No.' And they both knew she had said it too quickly. 'I'm fine,' she told him. 'Thank you. I need this time with him.'

'Of course.' But he had rung off soon afterwards, saying he had a lot of work to get through, and she knew she'd let him down. *Sorry, Alec*, she whispered, in her head.

'Muddled, yes.' Dr Martyn nodded in that avuncular way that she remembered. But somehow it wasn't as reassuring as it used to be. 'A touch of dementia,' he said. 'But he's managing quite well, given his age.'

'Is it dementia, though?' she asked. 'He seems so clear about some things.' She frowned. 'And will it get worse?'

He raised bushy eyebrows. 'It might do, my dear. Or it might not.'

'I see.' She supposed it was a bit like asking if he would get older.

He took her to one side and put a reassuring hand on her shoulder. 'It's all part of the ageing process,' he explained in a low voice. 'Confusion, dementia, call it what you will. It's not uncommon, you know. And sometimes the long-lost past is a whole lot clearer than what happened yesterday.'

Rosemary nodded. 'Yes, that makes sense.' She forced a smile.

'So, where's the patient?' He rubbed his hands together. 'I'll look him over. My goodness, I remember your father from when I was first qualified.' He shook his head as if wondering where all the years had gone.

'Come through then.' Rosemary took him to the bedroom where her father was resting after lunch. Not a very substantial lunch, but she supposed a few spoonfuls of chicken broth and half a slice of bread was better than nothing.

She opened the door wider. 'Dad, Dr Martyn's here.'

'Now then, young feller me lad,' the doctor said. 'What have you been up to?'

Rosemary left them to it.

He emerged ten minutes later. 'His heart's tickety boo,' he said. 'Blood pressure fine. But I've adjusted the prescription slightly given what's happened. Here.' He handed her the new one. 'He's pretty stable, I'd say. For now.'

'Good.' Rosemary moved towards the front door. 'And we should check his blood pressure again once the new pills kick in, shouldn't we?'

He nodded. 'Ring the surgery in a week or so,' he said. 'I'll pop in again, no problem.'

'Thanks, Doctor.'

She opened the front door. 'And I was wondering . . .' She lowered her voice. 'Is there anything else we should be doing? Do you have any advice?'

'Let him rest,' he said. 'Plenty of fluids. Keep an eye on him.'

'Is that all?'

'And think of the future.' He fixed her with a penetrating gaze. 'You do realise, don't you, my dear, that before long your father might need more full-time care?'

Rosemary nodded. He seemed better now since his fall.

But what about the next time? By the next time it might be too late.

'You know where to find me if you want to discuss things.' He lifted a hand. 'And any further problems, just phone the surgery.'

'Alright. Thank you. Goodbye.' Rosemary watched him climb into his old black Renault and drive away.

She let out a small sigh and went back into the bedroom. 'Everything OK, Dad?'

'Rosie.' He looked tired. 'What did he say to you, then?'

'Nothing much.' She smoothed the cover of the bed and flicked back the curtain 'He said your blood pressure was fine. I'll make some tea, shall I?'

'I couldn't get much out of him either,' he said. 'They forget you have a mind once you hit eighty.' He coughed. 'Doctors. Treat you like a bloody imbecile.'

Rosemary chuckled. 'Doctor Martyn's not like that,' she protested. 'He's really kind.' But he had a point.

'Because I can get up, you know. I'm not just lazing around.' His breath rasped in his chest.

'Course you can,' she soothed. 'And we'll get you up later. Nothing wrong with having a little nap.'

He patted the bed. 'Come and sit by me for a bit. And stop looking so worried.'

'I'm not worried.' Though she was. And seeing him like this had made her worry even more. *And think of the future . . .* That's what Dr Martyn had said.

What did that mean? Full time care? A nursing home? She

couldn't imagine her father letting someone in to his house to wash him, shave him, change his sheets, and heaven knows what else if he wasn't capable of doing it himself. Mrs Briggs was one thing – that woman was an institution and she'd been here for ages. He knew her. He trusted her. But Mrs B couldn't afford to give them any more time and she wasn't strong enough to do any lifting. Neither was she a nurse. But nor could Rosemary see her father in a nursing home or retirement place. She shivered . . . She knew that many of them were very nice these days, and he had the money to choose a decent one. But he'd hate it. He belonged here in his own home, in their home. And he wouldn't want it to be filled with strangers.

'Pah, doctors . . .' He shifted into a more comfortable position, licked his dry lips. 'You don't want to let them worry you. I'll be on my feet in no time, you'll see.'

And if he wasn't? 'I'll make that tea,' she said.

'It's true I haven't been quite myself lately,' he mused, when she returned five minutes or so later. 'I've been thinking a lot about old times.'

'Old times?' she said. For a moment the bitterness resurfaced. Perhaps it was never that far away. 'The good old days in Burma, do you mean?' She put the tray down on the bedside table.

His serious gaze reproached her for her flippancy. 'Not so good during the war, love,' he said. He took the tea she handed him, the cup rattling in the saucer.

'Oh, the war . . .' She stilled it with her hand. 'It might be hot. Careful.' She took the plate from the tray. 'Biscuit?'

He shook his head.

'There were good times for you too,' she remarked. *Where are you going with this, Rosemary?* 'Before the war, I mean.'

'There were.' He met her direct gaze. ''Course there were.' Then he looked away and took a slurp of his tea. 'Ah, that's grand, love.'

She took her tea from the tray and sipped it, watching him over the rim of the teacup. One minute he seemed to know exactly what was going on, the next, off he'd drift into never-never land.

'But *we* had good times and all.' A small smile played around his mouth. 'You and me and your mum, didn't we, eh?'

'Of course we did,' she said. She thought back. She remembered him as a rough-and-tumble father who was always getting told off by her mother, always getting into trouble. He would take her out into the garden without her wellington boots on, so that they dripped mushy leaves and trod dirt into the pale green living-room carpet. And he would fail to bring her back from the seaside in time for tea. 'I don't know what I'm going to do with you,' Rosemary's mother would scold. 'You're like a child yourself, you are.' *Not always joking either . . .*

But most of the time . . . It had been her mother who looked after Rosemary, who taught her how to behave, who had brought her up to be whatever she had become. Her father had been busy with Fox and Forsters and his appearances were reserved for high days and holidays, not the everyday life in between. And she could remember hardly any times when the three of them were together and having fun. What good times? She must have frowned.

'No one gives you a manual, love,' he said. 'In those days, we had to make it up as we went along.'

And for the first time, Rosemary wondered. Had he wanted to have more of a share in her upbringing? Had he been excluded because he was too untidy, too careless? How had he felt being told off all the time? Helen had made of fun of him too. Sometimes even put him down. Had she been punishing him?

'She was a good woman, your mother,' he said, almost as if he knew what she was thinking. 'Thank heavens we had her to keep us on the straight and narrow, eh?'

Rosemary nodded. She thought of how she had felt when she'd lost her. Desolate. And yet at times it had been such a strain living up to all her expectations. Had he felt that too? She patted her father's hand. He must have felt that too.

CHAPTER 27

On Saturday morning, as planned, Ramon picked Eva up in his car and they drove towards Sagaing, stopping briefly at the Mahamuni temple. Sagaing was a highly religious site built on a hill, he told her, and she could see now that the green slopes ahead of them were studded with wooden monasteries and golden pagodas.

'Did you have a good day yesterday?' he asked pleasantly, as he changed gear to negotiate the hill.

'Yes, thank you.' It had certainly been full of treasures. But Eva decided not to tell him that; he might think that they were treasures which should stay in Mandalay. After her meeting with Myint Maw, she had emailed Jacqui to fill her in on the details and had received a reply straightaway. *Sounds good,* Jacqui had written. *Looking forward to seeing them.* Eva was confident she wouldn't be disappointed. Her boss had asked about Myint Maw too but Eva wasn't sure exactly what she wanted to know. *He's a bit shady,* she wrote back. *And he's never clear about provenance. But . . .*

'And your grandfather?' Ramon asked her.

'He's much better, thank you.' Eva had phoned again last night after dinner and spoken to her mother. 'Don't worry,' she had said. 'Just concentrate on what you have to do in Burma.' *What you have to do in Burma* . . . She wondered how much her mother knew about why she was here.

'And you?' Eva asked him. 'How are things at the factory?' He seemed very polite this morning and so she decided to reciprocate. He was wearing a black-and-yellow checked *longyi* and a white short-sleeved shirt which looked crisp and cool, considering the heat outside.

He nodded. 'Everything is good,' the hint of a smile touching the corners of his mouth. But not, she noticed, his eyes.

They passed a small wooden monastery and he stopped the car so that she could take a photo.

Eva decided to take advantage of his good mood. 'I've been thinking,' she said, when she'd climbed back in.

'Oh?' He raised a dark eyebrow, glanced in the mirror and drove on.

'About the chinthe.' She risked a look across at him.

He was focusing on the road ahead, which was narrow and steep with sharp bends. But now he was frowning.

'Do you really have a plan to get it back?'

Ramon let out a deep sigh. 'You are still thinking about that?' he asked. He didn't wait for her reply and he didn't look at her. 'I must tell you, Eva, to forget about it. You have done enough for our family in returning the other.' He braked sharply as a car came from the opposite direction. 'You can do no more.'

'But I could help,' she said. 'They don't know me. I'm not involved. I could at least—'

'No.' The car had passed and he drove on.

She blinked across at him. She'd had some thinking time since they'd last met. Couldn't she use what she was doing here for the Emporium as a cover? If she pretended she wanted to *buy* the chinthe . . . Wouldn't they be interested? They sounded very greedy. She suspected they would, if the price were right. And if she could draw them into the open, wouldn't they at least have a chance of getting the chinthe back?

'I know what you are thinking. But you must not become further involved.' And, once again, she was surprised by what sounded almost like tenderness in his voice. Taking his eyes off the road for just for a second, he pressed his palm on to hers in a swift and unexpected gesture. His hand felt so warm. 'You must leave it to me. You must trust me, Eva.'

Eva watched as he moved his hand back to the steering wheel. She would like to trust him, but he hadn't tried to get the stolen chinthe back before. Why would he do anything now?

'What will you do then?' she asked again. 'What are you planning? Can't you at least tell me that?'

He shook his head as the car continued to crawl uphill. 'It is dangerous.'

Which was all very well. 'But my grandfather—'

'They are dangerous.' His voice hardened. 'Do you hear me, Eva?'

'Yes, but . . .'

'We have our own ways of doing things here in Burma. I told you. You must not pursue this matter.' The road was getting even narrower and he bent forwards over the wheel. 'Please leave it alone, Eva.'

Eva sat back in her seat. But it meant so much to her grandfather to reunite the chinthes. She couldn't let him down. She couldn't just let it go, at least, not without a fight.

'Many Burmese people come here to Sagaing.' Ramon spoke in a clear voice, obviously determined that the subject be dropped. 'They spend weeks, months or even years in quiet contemplation.' He didn't look at her. 'Daw Moe Mya's grandmother, Suu Kyi, came here too at the end of her life.' He swung the car around a tight corner. On either side of them were traditional Burmese houses, simple but smart, tucked away behind bamboo fences and palm trees.

Despite herself, Eva's interest was piqued. 'How long did she live here for?'

'For the five years before her death. She ended her life here in Sagaing.' The car continued to crawl uphill. And they passed a golden pagoda, blinking in the sunlight from behind a thicket of trees.

'What was she looking for?' Eva tried to imagine.

'Enlightenment,' he said. 'She had been through much suffering. We call it *samsara*, *karma* is the force that drives it, the cycle of birth and death and the suffering therein.' He shrugged as if to lessen the intensity of his words. 'Many people come here to meditate and to live the right way, the non-harmful way, to find wisdom.'

Eva nodded. She could see that after the turbulent life Suu Kyi had lived, she would have wanted to end her days in peace and tranquillity. And she realised why Ramon had wanted to show her this part of Myanmar.

At last they came to the top of the hill and Ramon stopped by a golden temple.

'This is the highest pagoda,' he said. 'Shall we go in?' He shot her a broad smile.

The man's moods could change in an instant. But nevertheless, Eva got out of the car, put on her wide-brimmed hat, slipped off her leather sandals and followed him up the smooth dusty steps to the pagoda. And when she saw the view in front of her, her own frustrations instantly evaporated. The hill was cloaked with green and gold. She could almost feel a sense of quiet spirituality settling over her. This was it, she realised. This was what Myanmar and its people was all about. And it was something that she also longed for, for herself. That sense of peace.

'Where did she live?' she asked Ramon. He was gazing down the hill, past the bright pagodas and lush valleys, towards the wide silver curve of the Irrawaddy River and its two bridges, and he seemed lost in thought, as affected by the landscape as Eva, though he must have seen it many times before.

'You see the temple which looks like a giant cup?' He pointed, moving closer so that they shared the same sight line. 'Now go to the left.' He bent his head next to hers. She could smell the scent of him, oil and wood with the faintest hint of cardamom, and feel the heat of his dark-olive skin.

'Yes.' She followed his gaze.

'There is a tiny red-roofed building.'

'Like a Chinese pagoda?'

'A bit.' He smiled. 'That is the monastery where she lived her few final years. We can drive down and see it from the outside if you wish. But we cannot go in.'

She nodded. 'I'd like to.' It was her history too, she thought. Her grandfather was inextricably linked with Ramon's grand-mother. They had moved apart for almost their whole lives, but it seemed that what they'd shared was somehow greater than that.

Beside the steps to the temple, a woman was selling *thanaka*, the traditional Burmese make-up. Eva paused and watched her pounding the bark it was made from.

'You try?' the woman asked.

Eva stepped forwards and the woman smeared some of the light brown muddy substance on to her cheeks. It felt cold and grainy. Unlike Western make-up, it wasn't rubbed in, it was more like a tribal marking. 'It will protect you,' the woman said.

Ramon smiled when she got back into the car. 'Very nice,' he said. He touched her cheek. 'It will make your skin soft.' For a moment their eyes met.

They drove down to the monastery and stood outside, absorbing the atmosphere of the place. Despite the exterior glitz, it was a simple building. In the yard, a line of saffron robes were drying on a rope strung between two coconut palms, and a mangy dog was sleeping in the shade. Someone was cooking a huge vat of food over an open fire and one of the young novices was sweeping the floor with an old-fashioned broom. Eva could see the long tables in the refectory where the shaven-headed young monks would go with their black rice bowls for their lunch.

'They fast after midday,' Ramon told her as if he'd followed her thoughts. 'That is when they study English language and Buddhist Scriptures.'

Eva remembered what Klaus had told her about the monks. 'Were you a novice?' she asked him. She couldn't imagine it somehow.

'Of course.' He nodded. 'For a short time. In our culture it is thought an important part of development to make your *shin pyu.*'

'Your . . . ?'

He smiled. '*Shin pyu*. It is the highest way to pay respect. To your mother, to Lord Buddha. That is what Buddhists believe.'

With some difficulty, Eva visualised Ramon with a shaved head and a saffron robe. But he wasn't the type, she suspected, to be content just being a scholar. He was a worker, a master-craftsman. And she guessed that he was a good businessman too.

'We have one of the highest rates of blindness here in Myanmar,' Ramon told her. 'Hundreds of thousands wait for cataract operations. There are charities. European eye surgeons come here to this monastery to operate and help us.'

'That's great.' They needed that sort of help, she realised. It would be a long time before the country would catch up on medical advances, before their people could expect their health to be looked after as a matter of course.

As Eva took a last look around the monastery buildings, she wondered about the woman who had lived here, the woman who had first received the special gift of the two chinthes from Queen Supayalat, the last queen of Burma. Suu Kyi, Ramon's great, great grandmother. She had wanted enlightenment. Would she also want Eva to try and get the chinthe back?

From Sagaing, they took a small ferry over the river to Inwa, where the roads were red dirt tracks and the people got around by horse and cart or bicycle. 'This was once the capital of Myanmar,' Ramon told her, 'from the fourteenth to the eighteenth century. For me, the place most represents the past and what we, the Burmese people, have come from.'

Eva sat in the back of the brightly painted cart, buffeted by cushions, as they rocked and rolled along the rutted track. And once again she thought she knew why they were here. It was indeed like going back in time. The fields unfolding beside her were still ploughed by bullocks pulling a wooden plough, the crops still picked by women wearing broad bamboo hats. And as they passed, the one and only tarmacked road was being re-laid by an old-fashioned steamroller and a posse of women, some of them looking far too old for this kind of work, Eva thought, watching them load gravelly rock into wide baskets which they carried on their heads before throwing it on to the wet sticky tar.

'Inwa is often completely flooded by the river,' Ramon told her, and she could see that much of the area was one big lake covered in floating white water lilies and backed by distant romantic pagodas, whose reflected shapes fluttered on the surface of the water like a landscape from a fairy tale.

Eva tried to take it all in. It seemed to sum up the feeling of being in the tropics. Paddy fields and banana plantations; bullocks on the road, tied to a tree; ruined temples and ancient wooden monasteries. The palm fronds and banana leaves were so green, the landscape so simple and uncluttered. On the far side of the lake, she saw a small group of women washing. They had unwound their *longyis*, pulled them above the collar bone, refastened them and were washing underneath, in perfect modesty.

This was what Burma must have been like when her grandfather lived here, Eva thought. Apart from the invasion of British clubs and accompanying paraphernalia, of course. Here, she was aware of what he must have loved about the land. The gentle wooded hills, the red earth and the paddy fields of rice. The golden temples, the warm air, that sense of peace.

The horse and cart stopped at an old teak monastery and Ramon jumped off the cart and held out his hand to help Eva down from the back.

'Look!' A little girl materialised at the bottom of the steps. She held up a necklace for Eva to admire. Like Klaus in Yangon, Ramon had told her she should ignore the souvenir sellers, but it was hard when she knew they had so little.

'It's very nice,' Eva told her. 'But my suitcase is full.' Which wasn't far from the truth.

'Very cheap.' The girl grinned.

Eva's heart melted. These children were so sweet but they shouldn't have to become street sellers at such a young age. 'How cheap?' She smiled back at her.

'Three million dollars?' The girl laughed. 'You are very beautiful and he is very handsome.' She pointed at Ramon, who shrugged and walked on. 'Three million dollars from the pretty lady for the necklace? It is made of watermelon seeds.'

Eva laughed too. 'That's too much for me,' she said. And she offered a thousand kyat, a little less than a British pound. Immediately she was besieged by children selling crayoned fans, beaded purses and jade bracelets and it took her several minutes to escape and wave them all away. Ordinary Burmese people, she thought. Would the political reforms in the country help them? Or would they become greedy as they tried to extract money from rich Westerners? She hoped that in Myanmar, things wouldn't move too fast.

Inside the cool dim interior of the monastery, the ancient teak carving almost took Eva's breath away.

'I thought you would appreciate this place,' murmured Ramon.

And she did. Every doorway, every piece of panelling was exquisite and everything from floor to ceiling was made of wood, so that its sweet and musty scent filled her nostrils, pervading all her senses. She could almost taste the wood on her tongue. A ray of sunlight poured through the open door like a laser, lighting up dancing dust motes and the shaven heads of the boy novices who were sitting in the corner, learning from one of their elders. But this only seemed to enhance the feeling of calm.

The interior was high and cavernous and on a raised platform sat a gilded Buddha. Eva was about to step up for a closer look, but Ramon touched her arm and pointed to a sign. Ladies apparently were not permitted on the platform. Eva shook her head at Ramon's meaningful look. Myanmar, she thought, had a long way to go. At the Mahamuni temple in Mandalay, only men were allowed to add gold leaf to the Buddha, Ramon had told her earlier today, with some relish, it had to be said. The knobbly Buddha not only looked impressive but his covering of gold was now apparently over six inches thick.

'And is that a rule decreed by Buddha?' Eva had asked sharply. Because if so, she hadn't heard of it. 'Or by man?'

'Who knows?'

Eva guessed that Ramon wasn't used to women questioning a tradition that had been in operation for centuries. Or perhaps he simply dismissed Eva as feisty, as if she were some circus pony, she thought grimly. But she had been brought up to question things. It was the only way that any of society's wrongs could ever be changed.

They moved into the bright sunlight outside the monastery, where the wood was faded and sun-bleached. Eva turned to Ramon. 'Will your grandmother bring the chinthe back with her when she returns to Mandalay?' she asked him. 'Or will she leave it in Pyin Oo Lwin?'

He frowned. 'Why?'

'I just wondered.' Together they strolled back along the weathered teak flooring. The truth was, that she was concerned.

'You wonder about things a lot,' Ramon observed. 'I do not think that she will let it out of her sight.'

They walked down the steps of the monastery and back towards the cart.

'Then she should be careful.' Eva took the hand he offered to help her back in.

He eyed her gravely as she settled herself once more against the red cushions. 'For what reason?'

Eva leaned forwards. 'Because she told me that the Li family live in Mandalay. They might hear that she now has the other of the pair. They might try to steal it just like they stole the other one.' Why couldn't he see that something must be done?

'They will not hear.' Abruptly, he turned, went round to the front of the cart and swung himself up next to the driver. The driver took the reins and the little horse with the pink flower in its harness trotted off.

Ramon sat stiffly in front, his back only inches from her. His mobile rang and he pulled it from his belt in an impatient gesture. He listened for a few moments, then hurled a torrent of fast and furious Burmese into the phone.

Eva glimpsed the expression on his face, it was thunderous. What was the problem? She thought of Maya. His grandmother was right, something was certainly troubling him.

Ramon let out a final curse and ended the call, shoving his mobile back into the belt of his *longyi*. It amused Eva that in this country which was in so many ways old-fashioned and behind the times, where it was hard to find an internet connection or an ATM machine, that even the saffron-robed monks and market traders could be seen with mobile phones.

'Trouble?' she asked tentatively.

He didn't look round. His back was straight and unyielding. 'It is the factory.'

'I thought everything was fine?'

'It is not.' He half turned and glanced back at her.

Eva was touched by the sadness in his eyes. She knew how important his father's company was to him. If he lost that . . . 'What is it?' she asked.

'The company is not doing well.' He shook his head in despair. 'How can we hope to succeed when our prices are undercut by so many unscrupulous companies?'

'Unscrupulous companies?' she echoed.

'How can we be appreciated? If we respect our workers and pay them a good living wage, if we respect the environment and buy only legitimately sourced timber . . . If we do these things, we must ask a fair price for our furniture, yes?'

Eva was surprised at the outburst. 'Yes, of course you must.'

Some children passed by on their bicycles, their books in a basket, woven Shan bags slung over their shoulders. They waved cheerily at her and she gave a quick wave back. But her attention was focused on Ramon. She was beginning to understand. 'Buying timber from sustainable forests is more expensive,' she murmured. The felling of trees must be regulated, just as it had been in her grandfather's day, and trees needed time to dry out before they were ready. 'If others don't do the same . . .'

'How can we compete?' Ramon's voice broke and he put his dark head in his hands. 'It is another order lost,' he muttered.

Eva's heart went out to him. She wanted to reach towards him, tell him it would all work out in the end. But something stopped her. He was so fierce, so proud. 'I'm so sorry,' she said. He couldn't compromise on his father's ethics and standards. There would be no other way for Ramon.

'It is not your concern.' He lifted his head.

This was what he had said to her before. Eva watched the children slowly disappear down the red dirt track by the lake. But this time she saw the dignity in the set of his shoulders and the tilt of his head and she knew she had caught him off-guard. But at least she had found out what was troubling him. 'How bad is it?' she asked.

'Bad enough.'

'And who are the people using the illegally felled timber and undercutting your prices?' she asked. 'Who's your main competition?'

He turned around until he was facing her. His eyes were hard, his mouth unsmiling. 'Those who produce poor quality goods and pay their workers a wage they can barely survive on,' he said. 'Those who make their money by damaging the credibility of other Burmese traders. Those who care this much . . .' He snapped his fingers. 'For our country and our forests.'

'Who?' Eva asked again. It couldn't be just one company, could it?

'The most unscrupulous company of them all,' he said, 'is Li's.'

Li's . . . Eva thought of what Ramon had shown her today: the Burma of her grandfather's time, the spirituality, the search for enlightenment. And she thought of the artefacts that Thein Thein and Myint Maw had shown her. The treasures of Burma. Soon to be shipped to the UK, to the Bristol Emporium and sold on. Was this her destiny, she wondered. To buy from someone else's culture, to follow someone else's lead? Or was there another path she should be taking?

CHAPTER 28

She stood by the bed, keeping watch over him. Blood pressure, heart rate, pills for this and pills for that . . . Lawrence was getting more than a little fed up with it. Life was more than that, surely? It always had been. Lying in this bed, struggling to think, struggling to breathe . . . That wasn't living.

But he remembered his life, his real life. All of it. Not just Burma, like she'd said. Not just the war and his life with Maya. But England too.

West Dorset, 1939
Lawrence had been in Burma almost two years when he got a long leave to go to England. *Home.* They all said it, at the club and the chummery. *You're going home, you lucky bugger.*

Lawrence had mixed feelings. Of course he wanted to see his parents and some of his friends, those who were still around. And he was tired, God, was he tired from the endless heat and rain and sun, from the logging, from the malaria that he'd shaken off only a few months before.

But . . . Burma was warm and vibrant and it had got under his skin. And there was Maya. Their relationship had grown into something that meant so much to Lawrence. When he was away from her, he longed, more than anything, to see her, to sleep with her, to feel the warmth of her silken body. But it wasn't just sex – he'd known that from the start. And it wasn't just passion, though the passion burnt and flared in him like nothing he'd ever known. It was also her quiet and her calm. It was the long conversations they had in the sweet dead of the night when they were alone, it was the touch of her cool hand on his brow, it was the serene expression in her dark eyes. It was love. That's what it was.

And in England . . . Yes, he missed that green and pleasant land. But England also meant Helen.

She'd written to him – he could hardly stop her from writing to him – and her little notes, affectionate and sweet, all held a subtext that Lawrence didn't want to acknowledge. He knew that she was waiting for him. And he knew that he should be honest with her. This would ultimately be to his advantage. If Helen knew that he was in love with another woman, a native woman at that, wouldn't she free him from this family obligation? Wouldn't she have too much dignity to want him when she knew that Lawrence could never think of her that way?

He'd tell her, he'd decided, face to face when he was on leave. It was the most honourable thing to do.

In the event, his leave had flown by.

'You've hardly seen Helen,' his mother pointed out, the night before he was due to return to Burma.

This was true. He'd flunked it.

'My fault, darling.' She'd hugged him and he'd smelt the familiar fragrance of her, the powder and the lipstick and the light, floral overtones of her cologne. 'I wanted you all to myself.'

He laughed. And he hadn't complained. It had been good to see her, and his father too, though he'd had more than one grilling about how long it would be before Lawrence returned to the family firm and stopped all this 'messing around in foreign parts' as he'd put it.

'But you must see her tonight,' his mother decreed.

'Of course.' Though he felt a dip of foreboding. He'd have to tell her tonight.

'There's a dance at the Assembly Rooms. You must take her.'

Lawrence had bowed his head. It was out of his hands once again. His mother was right. He must see Helen. But he hadn't intended to tell her at a dance.

He drank a large glass of whisky before he even left home. Dutch courage. *And God knows he'd need it.*

How had it happened? He hardly knew. They were outside, round the back of the dance hall, for Christ's sake. It was so bloody tacky. They'd danced and he'd drunk a lot. He'd felt sick and he'd needed some air. Next thing he knew . . .

It was the whisky. He should never have had all that whisky. 'Oh, God. Oh, God.' He put his head in his hands. His own breath stank. He wanted to die. He was sweating and he wanted to die.

Helen wrapped her slim white arms around him. 'I've always loved you, Lawrence,' she murmured into his shoulder.

'It shouldn't have happened. It was a mistake.' He remembered that day she'd kissed him at her parents' party when she was only twelve. He remembered other times too. Times when he should have stopped it, when he should have told her 'no'. They had never gone this far. And all those occasions had been before he went away to Burma. Before Maya. But now, it felt as if all those times had led inexorably to this moment.

Helen guiding his hands to her breasts, Helen lifting the hem of her dress, slipping the buckle of his belt. Helen's kisses. *Now, Lawrence . . . I want you now.*

'It wasn't a mistake,' she said. 'It'll be alright.' Already, she had adjusted her clothing. No one would know.

He thought of Maya. Oh, but it won't be alright, he thought.

'You're mine now,' Helen whispered.

Every sense and fibre in his body screamed 'no'.

'We should never have done it,' he said. He thought of what he'd intended to say to her. How could this have happened instead? How had everything gone so horribly wrong? How could he ever justify it? How could he explain? 'I should never have done it. Helen, I'm so sorry . . .'

'I don't want you to be *sorry* . . .' she fired back at him. Her lip curled. 'Why should you be sorry? And why should we wait?' Her eyes were like liquid in the darkness.

'Wait?'

'Till you come back from Burma. You know what I mean.'

Oh, God. She had got it all so wrong. 'Helen,' he said. How could he break it to her gently? 'I love you . . .'

'I know you do, darling.' She began once more to pull him towards her.

He resisted. 'But I love you like a sister.'

She laughed, a tinkle of a laugh that had always sounded forced to Lawrence and had always irritated him. 'Like a sister,' she echoed. 'I hope not, my darling. Not after what we've just done.'

He gripped her shoulders. 'Which was why we shouldn't have done it. Don't you see?'

'No.' Her blue eyes hardened. 'I don't see. I only know that we're promised to one another, you and me, Lawrence, and that we always have been. I know what I feel. And I know that you've just made love to me.'

'It was wrong, I tell you.' He was angry now and he pushed her away. They shouldn't even have gone dancing. He should have refused to take her. But it would have been impossible, his mother would have seen to that. So, he should have seen her, told her the truth, even gone dancing . . . But he should never have allowed her perfume and the music to seduce him in a weak moment. And he certainly shouldn't have drunk all that bloody whisky.

'How can it be wrong?' She was crying, hanging on to his arm and crying.

He felt like a total bastard. He was one. And he was a fool.

Acting like a sex-starved boy. Why couldn't he have been stronger? 'I'm sorry, Helen.'

'It doesn't matter,' she said. 'I wish you'd stop apologising. I'm glad we did it. And I don't care what you say, because I can see further than you can see.' And she wiped the tears from her face, suddenly composed. 'We've sealed our promise. You're mine now, Lawrence.'

The last day of his leave was a miserable one. Lawrence said goodbye to them all, Helen's parents (though he could hardly look her father in the eye), his parents and Helen herself.

'I'll write to you, Lawrence.' Helen was weeping. 'Come home soon. For good.'

And their parents, looking on fondly, clearly thought they'd come to some sort of understanding. Christ. How could he ever come back to Dorset now? Worse, how would he ever be able to get that night out of his head? Not only had he given Helen the very hope he had intended to stub out completely, but he had betrayed the woman he loved.

Lawrence had hugged his mother, waved farewell and boarded the steamer that would take him back to Burma, back to Maya's arms. But Helen's words still echoed in his head. And perhaps they always would. *'You're mine now, Lawrence. You're mine now.'*

CHAPTER 29

Eva dressed for dinner in a cream silk blouse and the embroidered indigo *longyi* she had bought in Yangon. She wore her velvety Burmese slippers, and around her neck, the antique pearls that her mother had given her on her eighteenth birthday. She took a thin silk wrap in case it turned chilly later. Not that there seemed much chance of that, she thought, as she stood at her bedroom window looking out into bustling Mandalay at night. She could see the illuminated golden dome of a nearby pagoda outlined against the black velvet of the sky, and the distant moat that encircled the Royal Palace. There was a crescent arc of moonshine and the stars were like sequins stitched on to the night.

Ramon smiled his approval when she appeared in the hotel foyer. He was dressed in linen trousers and a light shirt and jacket. It was the first time she had seen him in Western clothes and it took her rather by surprise. He seemed though to have recovered his composure since yesterday afternoon. She wondered how bad things really were and if he regretted telling her about the problems with his business. Surely the company weren't in danger of actually going under?

After they had left Inwa they had driven back to the city

and down to the port. Eva thought that she might perhaps take the boat when she travelled to Bagan. It was a long journey but it would be a good opportunity to see some more of the real Myanmar on the way. She'd collected the departure information from the office on the portside and walked down to where Ramon was standing rather disconsolately on the muddy sand looking out to the Irrawaddy. A barge was moving slowly along the river. She could make out the logo on the hull. A peacock in blue and gold.

'One of Li's boats,' he said.

She watched as it motored past. They had a lot to answer for.

'Shall we go?' Ramon asked now. He escorted her to the car, swung the passenger door open for her to get in and closed it behind her. He went round to the driver's side and climbed in. For a moment, he leaned in close. 'May I say that you look beautiful,' he murmured. 'I love that you wear our traditional *longyi*.'

'Thank you.' Eva smiled back at him. Yesterday, their outing together had been a bit fraught, this evening, perhaps they could both forget their troubles for a few hours, relax and enjoy.

In his Western clothes, Ramon seemed so different, almost not part of this Eastern landscape to which she had already become acclimatised. It unsettled her slightly and she looked away, out of the window, as they drove alongside the dark still waters of the moat.

'How do you feel about our country now that you are wearing our clothes?' Ramon teased. 'Are you getting used to it yet?'

'I think I am.' She was getting used to the white heat that lay so heavy on the city, to the constant thrum of the air-conditioning, to the heavy rain that was still falling once a day without warning, tumbling from the sky and turning the dust to mud. She was used to the hooting and bell-ringing of endless streams of motorbikes, trishaws, bicycles and cars and the street sellers squatting on broken paving slabs beside rickety stalls, frying noodles, rice and fish, sorting heaps of crimson chillies, lentils and tiny peanuts, and peeling giant *pomela* fruit, while the fragrances of dried fish, cloves and anise rose thick and pungent in the warm air. She was getting used to it and she was loving it. Myanmar, with its vivid colours of landscape and *longyi*, its raucousness and its calm, its intense flavours and fragrances, was a country of extremities. No wonder its people liked to smile. Many of them were poor, yes, but perhaps they were rich in the things that mattered more: in spirit, in their quality of life. After the grey November days she had left behind in the UK, Myanmar was like a hothouse bloom. 'It's everything I hoped for,' she told Ramon. 'And more.'

'Good.' Ramon nodded as they drew up outside the restaurant. He glanced across at her. 'There is just one thing missing,' he said.

'Oh?'

He got out of the car and came round to her side to open

the door. Eva took the hand he offered to help her out and felt the weight of the warm air settle over her once again.

Ramon turned to a boy selling flowers on the street corner, handed over a few notes and was given a string of tiny white blooms in return. Eva had seen similar street sellers at the temples; the Burmese bought garlands of flowers and fruit to lay at the feet of the resident *nats* of the pagodas and shrines. Nats, who must be charmed and appeased. In Myanmar almost everything had one.

'Jasmine.' Ramon held the blossoms out to her.

Eva sniffed. 'Wonderful.' She didn't care if he was trying to charm or appease her. Their scent was like honey, it sweetened the night air.

'May I?' And before she could even wonder what he was doing, he had moved behind her and she could feel his hands on her hair, which she'd worn loose tonight, deftly weaving the flowers through, as if she were a bride. 'There.' He stood back to survey the effect. 'Now you are a perfect Burmese lady.'

She laughed and put her hands to her hair. He had a gentle touch. She could feel the furry softness of the tiny white flowers and smell their scent, far superior to any bottled perfume.

'Shall we?' Ramon indicated the restaurant.

'Of course.'

A boy pulled the door open and Eva felt the light pressure of Ramon's hand on her back as he followed her inside.

She looked around. 'What a fabulous place.' It was colonial

in decor and style. The high ceiling had decorative cornicing and a teak staircase with a polished banister rail rose gracefully on the left side of the room. The walls were painted white, there were fat teak pillars from floor to ceiling and people sat in cane and wicker chairs at wooden tables laid with white linen cloths. The bar in front of them was a sheet of solid black granite.

Ramon spoke to a waiter who led them to their table.

'I wondered, would you like to visit my factory tomorrow morning?' he asked her when they were seated. 'Or do you have more antiques to inspect?'

Eva laughed somewhat warily. That was a tricky subject. She picked up the creamy linen napkin by her plate and spread it on her lap. 'I am seeing some more,' she said. 'But not till the afternoon. So of course I'll come. I'd be delighted.' Myint Maw had telephoned her earlier today at the hotel with the news that some more items had become available. 'They very good,' he had said. 'You come see tomorrow 3 p.m., yes?' But Eva couldn't help wondering where they had suddenly appeared from. She had put in a quick call to Jacqui before she'd come out tonight, but she'd had no idea either. *Go and see them,* her boss had advised, *take care and keep me informed.* Eva had spent the day wandering around the markets and antique shops of Mandalay, but had purchased very little. It seemed that to buy anything of quality, it was indeed a case of who you know. Jacqui was right then to stress the importance of their contacts.

They both studied the menu. A jug of iced water had been

put on the table by the immaculately dressed waiter and she poured them both a glass. 'I'm looking forward to seeing the furniture you design and produce,' she said.

He smiled warmly and she was reminded of that moment when he'd first opened the door to her at Pyin Oo Lwin. It transformed his face and she couldn't help noticing that he was attracting admiring looks from other female diners.

'We should order some wine,' he said.

'Wine?' Eva was a little surprised.

'But, yes. There is a reputable vineyard just outside Mandalay.'

'Really?'

'Really. It is run by a Frenchman.' His green eyes gleamed. 'They produce an excellent pinot noir which I recommend we try.'

The food was Chinese, and they ordered river prawns which arrived nestling in a ginger salad with sesame seeds, chicken with peanuts and fish steamed with lime along with various vegetable side dishes and rice. And Ramon was right. The wine proved to be delicious.

Conversation flowed easily between them, but although they talked about styles of furniture and wood, about English antiques and even about British colonialism, they hadn't yet touched on the subject that had come up at Inwa yesterday.

While they were waiting for dessert, Eva leaned closer towards him. 'I had no idea that the Li family also owned a furniture company,' she said. She tried to keep her voice nonchalant; this would certainly be another touchy subject.

Ramon ran a finger around the rim of his wineglass. He had allowed himself only one glass, she noted. After a moment, he looked up. 'Not just furniture,' he said. 'Statues, too. Wooden models, Buddhas, you name it. If they can make money out of it, they will produce it.'

'So they have a factory here in Mandalay? A showroom?' Eva wondered if she had already unknowingly visited it.

'Eva . . .'

Their dessert arrived, semolina cake with fresh coconut milk, a Burmese speciality, Ramon told her. Eva tasted it. It was very different from the unpalatable and bland substance she remembered from school.

'I'm not asking where it is,' she protested.

'Very well.' He dipped a spoon into the pudding. 'Then, yes. They do have a showroom – a shop – and there is a factory behind.' He narrowed his eyes. 'But you must promise me . . .'

'Yes?' She adopted her most innocent look.

'That you will stay away.'

Eva finished up her dessert. 'How can I go there, Ramon?' she asked. 'I don't even know where it is.'

They had coffee and Eva was surprised to see, when she looked at her watch, that it was almost midnight.

'I will take you back to your hotel,' Ramon said. He had paid the bill already and pretended to be offended when she offered a contribution.

Outside, the darkness enveloped them, but the air was balmy and still. Eva was aware of the scent from the jasmine in her hair. And of Ramon, as he opened the door of the car and she slid silently into the leather interior.

At the hotel, he walked her towards the foyer. But just before they reached the swing door, he drew her to one side. 'Thank you for coming to dinner with me tonight, Eva,' he said. His voice held a low intimacy. Gently, he touched her hair.

'You mustn't worry about the company, Ramon,' she said. She took a step closer, put a hand on his shoulder. 'I'm sure it will survive the competition and end up even stronger and more successful than before.'

'I have misjudged you, Eva.' He looked deep into her eyes. 'I thought you had come here to interfere, cause trouble and upset my grandmother all over again. But that is not true. You have only come here for the sake of your grandfather. I wanted to blame you for all sorts of colonial wrongs. I was mistaken.'

Eva waited. The tension was palpable between them she felt as if she were balancing on a knife edge.

'In a day or two, my grandmother will be coming here to Mandalay,' he murmured, drawing her closer, whispering into her hair. 'And when she does—'

'Eva!'

She spun around. Who would know her, here of all places?

A blond head and broad shoulders. An air of suave confidence. Klaus was halfway through the swing doors of the hotel. 'Hey, Eva! Hello!'

She felt Ramon stiffen beside her and take a step away.

'Klaus. Hello. I did try and phone you.' Eva forced a welcoming smile. She wasn't unhappy to see him, but his timing was atrocious. What had Ramon been about to tell her, she wondered. And what had he been about to do?

'I have only just checked back into the hotel. I was away for a few days, on business.' He came up to her and kissed her lightly on both cheeks. 'Sorry. I am interrupting, I think?'

Eva could imagine how it had seemed. 'Not at all,' she said politely. 'This is Ramon. Ramon, Klaus, we met in Yangon.'

The two men shook hands. Klaus's non-committal smile seemed friendly enough but Eva sensed Ramon's wariness. 'Yangon?' he echoed.

'We met in a café.' Klaus chuckled. 'And then I dragged Eva off to see the Shwedagon and to dinner.' He made it sound, she thought, like some sort of willing abduction. 'I wondered what had happened to you.' She saw him take in the *longyi*, the Burmese slippers, the jasmine in her hair. 'I see you have settled in, for sure.'

She smiled. 'That's true.'

'So what have you been doing since we last met?'

She wouldn't know where to start. 'I went to Pyin Oo Lwin,' she said, 'and met Ramon and his family.'

'And have you purchased many wonderful antiques?'

Eva wished he hadn't put it quite like that. 'I've seen some interesting artefacts, yes,' she said.

'Good. And I have the name of that contact I mentioned.'

'You will excuse me?' Ramon cut in. 'I will leave the two of you to talk.'

'Oh, but . . .' Eva realised she didn't want him to leave. Not now, not like this.

'No, no.' Klaus gave a playful little bow which seemed to irritate Ramon still further. 'It is I who interrupts your evening. We could meet tomorrow morning, Eva, if that is convenient? We can talk then.'

'Of course. Let's have coffee in the hotel bar. Will 10 a.m. suit you?'

'Perfect.' And Klaus gave a salute of farewell as he strolled away.

'I'm sorry.' But Eva realised as she looked at Ramon's face that the moment was gone. Could he possibly be jealous, she wondered.

Ramon frowned. 'I recognise that man,' he said.

'Klaus? Where from?'

'I am not sure.' Ramon strode to the swing door and opened it for her. 'And now, Eva, I must say goodnight.' He took a card from his jacket pocket. 'The address of our factory,' he said. 'For tomorrow.'

'Thank you.'

Eva wondered why she felt disappointed. Why did she feel she was on the brink of something, standing on a kind of dizzy edge and that the something kept being snatched away from her? From the hotel foyer, Eva watched him drive away with mixed feelings. She was drawn to him, yes, but she wouldn't allow herself to get emotionally involved. There was absolutely no point. And she was glad she was meeting

Klaus tomorrow. Another contact would be useful from the Emporium's point of view. And she'd had another idea about how to retrieve the stolen chinthe. This would give her an excellent chance to put her plan into action.

CHAPTER 30

Rosemary took a deep breath. 'Dad?' she said. 'I've been wondering.' Was he up to talking about it? Would he even remember? He was usually at his sharpest in the mornings, but . . .

'What, love?'

'Why did you tell Eva all those years ago that she could come and live with you?'

'When, Rosie?' There was the confusion again, the vulnerability that stopped her from being angry with him. But there were things she had to talk about, things she had to find out before it was too late.

'When I was planning to go to Copenhagen with Alec.' She willed him to understand. 'She was only sixteen. Why didn't you talk to me about it first?'

'Ah.' His gaze rested on her face for a moment as if he couldn't quite remember who she was. Then it drifted towards the window and the hydrangea bush outside – still flowering, though the blooms were faded and edged with brown.

Rosemary waited. She should be patient with him. Give him time. Nick used to make Christmas wreaths from the hydrangeas, the ivy and the holly in her parents' garden.

He was good at that kind of thing. Their Christmas tree at home had never been decorated with neat silvery trinkets like Rosemary's mother's tree. It had cones Nick had spray-painted with Eva, stained glass lanterns and angels from the workshop, Eva's own cotton-wool bearded Father Christmas with the lopsided grin. Soon it would be Christmas again, she thought. And what then?

'She seemed so sad,' her father said, just when Rosemary had thought he wasn't going to reply at all. 'She really didn't want to go.'

Of course she didn't. But that wasn't the point. Abruptly, Rosemary got to her feet, went to stand by the window. Her arms were tightly folded as if she could squeeze it all inside. Some hope, she thought. She tried to relax. It was raining, huge drops splashing on to the path and the bushes, smattering the window pane. 'Children never want to leave their friends,' she said. She unfolded her arms, ran her fingers around the gold bangle on her wrist that Alec had bought her. 'But they get used to it, that's the point.' She turned around. 'She would have got used to it.'

Her father blinked up at her.

Yes, and perhaps you should have said this to him at the time, thought Rosemary. How could she be saying it to him now? Look at him. He didn't deserve it, it wasn't fair.

'I felt sorry for her,' he said. He frowned. 'I should have spoken to you first, Rosie, but—'

'Sorry for yourself too, I should think.' There, that was it, out in the open. After all these years. And if he dared to say:

I'd just lost your mother, she'd . . . Well, she wasn't sure what she'd do.

But he didn't. 'Perhaps you're right, love,' he said. 'I hated the thought of you both going. My girls.'

His girls. Now that he'd admitted it, Rosemary wasn't sure what there was left to say. He'd hated the thought of them both going. That was a bit different.

'She was crying.' His eyes slipped into that faraway look that she had begun to recognise. 'She begged me. I said we'd have to talk to you first, but . . .'

'You didn't think I should have gone,' she said. Outside, the wind was blowing through the trees. She could hear its soft whistle.

'You had to do what you thought was right,' he murmured.

'But did you think it was right, Dad?' Even to herself she sounded like a dog with a bone. 'Did you think it was right?' She came back to the bed and sat down beside him. He was her father. She supposed she was looking for some sort of absolution.

'Aren't you happy, love?' he asked. He took her hand in his dry and papery grasp. Squeezed.

Rosemary looked down. She was as happy as she'd ever expected to be. But she wasn't sure that it was enough. She wondered if Alec thought it was enough. 'I wanted a new life,' she whispered.

'I know. I understand that. You went through so much, Rosie. You had to be strong.'

She stared at him. He seemed so . . . together, all of a sudden, so wise. 'I wasn't strong.'

'But you were.' And his voice held all the reassurance that her father's voice had ever held. 'You kept it together for Eva.' He sighed. 'No one could have asked for more.'

Except Alec, thought Rosemary. Except Alec and Eva and even Rosemary herself.

She patted his hand. She could see him tiring. And suddenly, everything that had happened back then, the fact that he'd offered to look after his granddaughter when she'd needed it, as if he hadn't already done so much, took on a different dimension. He had done it because Eva felt sad. He had done it to help them, because Eva had needed him to.

Rosemary slipped out of the room to let him sleep. She thought of how he had been there for them both after Nick's death, how he had pushed her into carrying on. She hadn't seen it that way, not back then. But of course, he had done it out of love.

She phoned Alec after work, brought him up to speed on what was happening with her father. And, all the time, another part of her was listening to what she said, as if watching from the living room ceiling. They were so careful with one another, so polite. Neither of them mentioned Seattle. It almost made the watching Rosemary laugh.

'Is what we have enough, Alec?' she suddenly asked.

'Sorry?'

'Is what we have enough? For you? For us?' That's what

she had been thinking. So why not break the habit of the last thirty years and say it?

'Not always,' he said. She heard his breathing, calm, considered. 'I thought it would be, but it's not.'

And Rosemary remembered what she'd said to him when he'd asked her to marry him: 'I don't know if I can . . .'

'Marry me?' he'd asked.

'No. I don't know if I can give you what you want.' *I don't know if I can give you a hundred per cent*, she had meant. *I don't know if I can ever stop grieving, stop thinking about the first man I married. I don't know if I can love you in the way you deserve to be loved.*

And Alec had said, 'You don't need to.'

'What about you?' Alec said now, as if they were having a conversation about the weather. 'Is it enough for you?'

'I don't know.' Seattle lurked like a shadow on the wall behind her.

'Then perhaps it's a good thing to have this time apart, Rosemary,' he said more gently.

'Yes.' Because she was trying, wasn't she, to let loose this constriction around her heart.

CHAPTER 31

This morning, through the hotel, Eva had booked her river boat tickets for Bagan. Her departure was scheduled for four days' time. It would be hard to leave, but she had more items to see for the Emporium and she was looking forward to visiting the famous temples of Bagan too. This would give her three full days there before she flew back to Yangon. She waited for Klaus in the hotel café. It was air-conditioned and slick, all black and chrome, a total contrast to the dusty streets of Mandalay.

Klaus arrived promptly at 10 a.m. He was dressed casually today in a blue short-sleeved cotton shirt and beige shorts and was carrying the same leather bag that she'd seen him with when they first met. His blond hairline was glistening with sweat. He must have been out already and Eva knew that, even this early, it was thirty degrees outside.

She greeted him with a kiss on both cheeks and waved at the seat opposite. 'Sit down. It's good to see you.'

'And you.'

They ordered coffee and chatted easily about the sights of Mandalay until it arrived, strong and sweetened with condensed milk, as was the custom. He caught her eye and they both chuckled.

'Here is the name of the contact I mentioned.' Klaus placed a business card on the table between them. 'I think he is a reputable trader. He may have some things that will interest you.'

'Thank you.' Eva glanced at the card and slipped it into her bag.

'And now.' He steepled his hands together and regarded her with a serious expression. 'May I ask you something a little personal, Eva?'

'Of course.'

'Are you involved with the man I saw you with last night?'

That surprised her. 'Romantically, do you mean? No, I'm not.' Although she wasn't sure she liked the question. She couldn't help noticing the sweat still on Klaus's brow from the heat outside, the damp blond hair pressing against his forehead. She felt like telling him it was none of his business, but perhaps he only had her best interests at heart. She took another sip of her coffee. 'Why do you ask?'

'And you met in Pyin Oo Lwin?' His blue gaze searched hers.

It seemed an honest gaze. Eva hesitated. But she wouldn't tell him the story of the chinthe. She remembered what had happened at the Shwedagon, her feeling that Klaus might be hiding something. She liked him, but she wasn't ready to confide in him. 'Yes,' she said. 'My grandfather knew his family when he was out here working in the timber industry before the war.'

'I see.' Klaus stroked his chin, which was clean-shaven and

smooth. He seemed to relax slightly. 'But you do not know him well,' he pressed.

'Not really.'

He nodded and stirred his coffee. He seemed pensive, not quite the Klaus she had met back in Yangon.

Eva looked at the hand holding the spoon. The back of it was covered with a blond down of hair. 'Is something wrong?' she asked.

'It was just that you looked . . . close,' he said. 'And I was a little concerned.'

Close? It was, she thought, rather more complicated than that. And why should he be concerned? 'Ramon's family have a teak furniture business,' she said, trying to lighten the atmosphere. 'He runs the company but he's still very hands-on from what I can gather.' A master craftsman was always a master craftsman; it was his life.

'Yes, I know his company.' Klaus frowned.

'You do?'

'Yes. Look, Eva.' He took a swig of his coffee. 'Please forgive me for interfering. And I realise that we have only recently met. But I think you should know . . .'

'Yes?' She waited.

'I do not fully trust him.' He sat back in his chair.

Eva felt a cold and prickly sensation on the back of her neck. 'For what reason?' she asked.

'He has dealings with a disreputable company,' he said. 'In what capacity I do not yet know. But I am certain that their business is not a legal one.'

'And I'm certain that you're mistaken.' Eva finished her coffee and put her napkin to her lips. 'Ramon's company is independent. And totally above board.'

Klaus raised an eyebrow. 'Maybe not as independent and above board as you believe.'

Eva shrugged. Perhaps Ramon had decided to join forces with someone in an effort to get the company out of trouble. How would she know? And, come to think of it, how on earth did Klaus know his business dealings? 'What does it have to do with you, Klaus? If you don't mind me asking?'

He raised both hands in mock defence. 'I have an interest in the company he is working with, that is all,' he said. 'Perhaps this Ramon is an innocent in—'

'What company?' Eva was getting a bad feeling about this.

'Li's Furniture and Antique Company,' he said. He leaned back once more. 'But you will keep that to yourself, I hope.'

Eva felt that hollow feeling of dread, right in the pit of her belly. 'That's impossible.' She shook her head. And yet somewhere inside she was also conscious of a fleeting sense of inevitability. It was almost as if she'd known what he was about to say. Li's seemed to be everywhere, lurking at the bottom of every ocean.

'Nevertheless, it is the case,' Klaus said. 'I am sorry if that is a disappointment to you.'

Again, Eva shook her head. She thought of the dark expression on Ramon's face when he had seen that boat at the port. It made no sense. No sense at all.

'Sometimes, Eva,' Klaus said, 'we see only what we wish to see.'

Was that true? Eva frowned. 'Where do Li's operate from?' she asked him. 'Where's this showroom of theirs?' She pushed away her coffee cup.

'You do not wish to know,' he said.

But there he was wrong. Eva most definitely wished to know. And she was more than a little fed up with being fobbed off by everyone. 'I'll ask at reception then,' she said. 'They must have whatever's the Burmese equivalent of Yellow Pages.'

Klaus leaned over the table towards her. 'Please be careful, Eva,' he said. 'That is all I ask.'

She nodded, waited.

'It's on Thirty-Sixth Street,' he said. 'Just before the junction with Eighty-Fourth. Ask any taxi driver.'

'Thank you, Klaus.' But Eva was confused. Could this be why Ramon was warning her away from them? Because he actually had dealings with the company? She couldn't believe it. But she would go there, she decided. At the very least she could see what the place was like, perhaps talk to someone or even start putting her plan into action. She didn't have much time left and she had to do something. She wasn't scared either. If you wanted anything doing you had to do it yourself. She owed it to her grandfather. And Eva was determined to find a way.

CHAPTER 32

Of course, Lawrence could understand that Rosemary blamed him, about Eva.

He closed his eyes. That bloody ceiling. He hated that bloody ceiling. Sometimes it was close. Sometimes it was far away. Sometimes it stopped him from thinking, from remembering. And he wanted to be clear. So much, he wanted to be clear.

He hadn't thought much about becoming a grandfather, not until after Rosie had met her Nick and he'd seen that love light in her eyes . . . 'It won't be long,' Lawrence had said to Helen. She wouldn't have it of course, told him he was a silly romantic fool. Perhaps he was. Perhaps that's why he could see it.

Nick had come to him, a decent young man – no money, but honest and hard-working – and told him what they planned to do, how they'd manage, how he intended to build up a business from scratch. And Lawrence had felt only respect for him. 'Good luck to you,' he'd said. 'Good luck to you both.' And he knew there'd been a tear in his eye. That was the way things should be. Lucky Rosie.

When their daughter was expecting Eva, Helen had fussed

around like women do. And he had thought it wouldn't make much difference to his life. A grandchild to spoil, that was all. He hadn't realised Eva would make him feel young again, that as she grew a bit older, she'd want to listen to his stories of the old days, and listen open-mouthed with such a look of wonder in her dark eyes that he almost felt he was back there. He hadn't imagined that he'd be asked to look after her in a way he'd never really ventured to look after his own girl, because now Helen tired so easily and wasn't good with disruption and noise. He'd never dreamt he would feel such love.

So when Rosie took it in her head to remarry and leave West Dorset, well, he'd thought his heart would snap like a dry twig. His two girls. Something had happened with Rosie, she blamed him for something, she was still wrung out after Nick's death. And when Eva, his lovely granddaughter, had come to him crying . . . What was he supposed to do? He could never say 'no' to her.

Lawrence shifted on to his side. God knows what time of day or night it was, because he didn't.

Most of all perhaps, he hadn't imagined that Eva would inherit from him his love of wood. The smell of it, sweet and deep in your nostrils, the darker rings of age and history, the feel of it, raw and sappy, smooth as satin on the inside, rough on the out. That there would be such a bond between them.

Upper Burma, January 1942
'You are very quiet,' Maya observed. She was wearing a cream silk *longyi* and it rippled as she rose to her feet and took

the empty bowl from his place. But Lawrence noticed she didn't ask what he was thinking. Was it this that intrigued him about her? That she didn't need to know what he was thinking? That in fact she might already know?

'I was listening to the radio earlier,' he said. 'Catching up on the news.' He stretched out his legs. They were seated on low bamboo chairs on the verandah of her aunt's home and had just eaten a simple supper of noodles and *Ah Sone Kyaw*, stir fried vegetables cooked in a tamarind sauce. It was dark and clear, the stars sharply visible in the night sky, a perfect half-moon. Maya's aunt's house was more basic than her father's. It was made of bamboo and, like many of the traditional houses, was built on stilts. The furniture was plain and unsophisticated and this, too, was made of bamboo. The floor consisted of rush matting, but you still took your shoes off when you came inside.

'News of the war,' she said. She took a cloth to wipe the table and moved towards the back door.

'I want to enlist.' He hadn't meant to come out with it just like that. He hadn't fully decided, or so he'd thought. Clearly, he had. He remembered only too well sitting around the radio set in the logging camp with some of the other men on 3rd September 1939, glass in hand, listening to Neville Chamberlain telling them that once again the British were at war with Germany. Some of the men had wanted to book a passage west there and then, but there had been an immediate government order to block it. The British Empire had wide boundaries. Who knew where their skills would be most needed? It was far too soon to tell. But now . . .

She returned to the table. Observed him head on. 'You need to fight for your country,' she said. It wasn't a question.

'I can't not fight.' He was young, wasn't he, and fit? He couldn't do the work he did without possessing stamina. He had not yet received a call-up for military training. But it seemed like sheer cowardice to be out here in Burma living in relative peace while poor old Blighty was suffering from air raids and rationing and who knew what else. How could his mother be coping with that? He simply couldn't imagine her making do. And he was here being waited on by this beautiful woman while other men were fighting the enemy. Fighting, as Maya had said, for his country. *Your country needs you.* Lawrence wasn't a coward. He was more than willing to do his bit. But up till now he'd been playing the waiting game along with the rest. How long before it played itself out? How long before more countries got involved? Was this just the beginning? He feared so. Men were being enlisted into the Indian Army, the Burma Rifles, the Navy. It was time.

'You will return to England?' Maya asked him.

He examined the serenity of her face framed by her hair, almost indigo in the darkness of the night, lit only by the flickering lamplight on the porch. There was not a frown on her brow, not a flicker of anxiety in her eyes – or so it seemed. Like many Burmese people, she was Buddhist. But did she mind? He had no idea. Did she understand? Clearly.

Sometimes he believed she understood him better than he did himself.

And perhaps it was this that most drew him to her. On the level of language their communication was fluent but simple. But on a deeper level, there was a connection that made them as one. It wasn't sexual, as he'd realised long ago, though sex between them seemed natural and real, unfettered by convention. And it wasn't because she was different, other and exotic, though she was and he relished that too. It was, he realised, something in their twin souls. It was deeper even than love. It had scared him at first. But he had given himself over to it. It was, he thought now, a kind of peace.

England, Maya had said. For a moment he pictured the look of the docks when he had left last time. Last time . . . He tried not to think of Helen, though he could still see her in his mind's eye and she still wrote to him. Occasionally, he even wrote back: short, polite notes that said nothing and yet everything. But she didn't seem to understand what he was telling her, or she didn't want to. War had not yet been declared when he'd left the country. And yet there had been an uneasiness about England as if she might be preparing for it. He recalled the shouts and the whistles, the people rushing here, there and everywhere, boarding ships, standing on the docks with backpacks or suitcases, milling over the gangplanks, saluting, waving, shouting their last goodbyes into the grey skies and the murky sea. And he pictured his mother's face, her nod of encouragement. *This is what is expected. This is what you must do.*

'No,' he said to Maya. He spoke Burmese pretty well now. He knew the jungle and he had some understanding of the people. These skills would be appreciated in wartime situations. He had no military training, but Lawrence knew where he would be needed.

She poured him some green tea and he lit a cigarette. He drew in deeply, considering, and exhaled, watching the smoke spiral and disappear into the night. 'War is not only happening in Europe, my love,' he told her gently.

She looked up, startled. 'It will come here? To Burma?'

'I believe so.' He drew on his cigarette once more. He had heard rumours, you couldn't help but hear rumours if you kept your ear to the ground. The Japanese were already at war with Britain and, after Pearl Harbor, the United States of America. In his opinion they were on their way. 'The Japs are taking advantage of all the argy-bargy, no doubt about that.'

They needed to extend their boundaries. Japan, unlike Malaya and Burma, wasn't rich in rubber, oil or wood. In point of fact, when you looked at the history, Japan had long been after extending its power. They'd had an aggressive foreign policy for twenty years, since their invasion of Manchuria, and this had only fuelled their war machine. They had forces at the ready in Asia. They'd been fighting China and since the pact they'd signed with Germany a year and a half ago . . . Who knew how much else was going on behind the scenes? He had heard the Japanese described as a nation of fanatics. Maybe they were, although Britain had the fanaticism of Hitler to deal with at this moment in time. But he'd also heard that Japanese forward-planning was second to none.

Maya sat down opposite him and took his hands in hers. This was unusual. She, like many Burmese women, was not given to displays of affection. Often, she seemed strangely detached and unemotional. But he never doubted her love or loyalty. And more. Maya had set him free. 'They are striking while the enemy is looking the other way,' she said. 'Collecting the water while it rains.'

He smiled. 'I'm very much afraid that you are right.' Her hands felt so soft as they held his, so smooth where his were rough and calloused these days. He enjoyed the work and just the muted wooden tinkle of elephant bells could make his heart leap as he approached camp. Most of this was down to Maya, he knew that. And he had also long known that being in charge of a teak camp was a tough job, far from the white-skinned civilisation of an office job back in the UK. So how long did he have here, realistically? For how many years could he work here and survive the ravages of dengue fever and malaria and the rest, before he grew old before his time? This was not the job for a middle-aged man, only a young one. The company who employed him knew that, and Lawrence knew it too.

'So you will fight in Malaya?' Her eyes were wide. 'Or Burma?'

He brought her hand to his lips and kissed it. 'I will enlist with the Indian Army,' he said. 'Try to obtain an emergency commission. And then we will see how things develop.'

Another woman might have wept and begged him not to go. Another woman might have made him feel bad, as if he were deserting her. But Máya, of course, was different. And she had shown him the different possibilities for his life too.

So. It didn't matter how much he regretted what had happened, how bad he felt about Helen, and Maya too. Now, there was a war.

'You may never come back,' she quietly said. Her eyes were like the soft satin of the night sky. He wanted all his senses to sink into them and be lost.

'Perhaps not.' He released Maya's hand and held her face in his. 'But if I am alive, I will come back, my love.' And he meant it. God, how he meant it.

'Hush.' She put a finger to his lips. She did not believe in wasting words. She had a secret strength that had always drawn him, a dark strength of knowing. 'You do not have to give me your promises. You are a free man.'

They made love that night with a tenderness such as Lawrence had never known. Her dark and sinuous body seemed to wind itself around him in a way it never had before. Her hair, long and lustrous, trailed over his chest and his thighs, and her skin was silky to his touch, scented with a musky fragrance that seemed to take him to greater heights of passion.

'I love you, Maya,' he gasped as he felt himself climax inside her.

Her eyes were closed now, her brow smooth as a child's,

her lips slightly parted. 'And I love you, Lawrence,' she said softly.

It was, he realised, as he drew the mosquito nets over their bed and took her again in his arms, the first time.

CHAPTER 33

The moment Eva had said goodbye to Klaus, she grabbed her bag, left the hotel and took a taxi to Thirty-Sixth Street. She hadn't been here yesterday, but she found the showroom easily, though showroom was perhaps too grand a description for the rickety shop situated halfway along. It seemed to go a long way back and she saw that it was divided into two halves. One side was crammed with contemporary furniture, the other with what looked like old wooden artefacts. Dusty enough to be antiques. But . . . She decided to take a closer look. It was quite safe. She didn't even have to speak to anyone. She would look around and then work out her next move.

Outside on the street was a random collection of Buddha images, some made of stone, some wood. At first glance they looked worn and pretty ancient, it was true. She wet her finger with her tongue and traced it over the head of one of the wooden statues. The wood was dull and didn't have the richness of teak. And . . . She bent closer to take a sniff. It didn't smell of sandalwood either. A paler wood, sandalwood had a sweet sappy fragrance, even when dried and quite old. Teak, on the other hand, was deeper, it had more layers, more complexity.

She brushed some more of the dust aside. She'd hazard a guess that this was inferior wood, either felled much too early when it was too young or before it had been properly dried out. It could even have been recycled from some old or damaged furniture because the patina was uneven and inconsistent. Other pieces, she could see, had been none too cleverly distressed, discoloured, filed down in places. She ran her fingers lightly across the rough, amateur carving. It all seemed vaguely familiar. And it didn't take an expert to see what it was, or more accurately, she thought, what it wasn't.

Her thoughts drifted to Ramon. There was absolutely no way that he would work with these people. For one thing they had stolen his family's precious chinthe. And for another they represented everything that he detested in furniture-making and working with wood. As did she. Even if it were the only way to rescue his company from financial difficulties, even if it were the only way to retain his father's legacy . . . He wouldn't do it.

Eva edged past the Buddhas and into the dark, dingy shop, down a narrow aisle with shelves and glass-fronted cabinets on either side housing seated and reclining Buddha statuettes, elephants, horses and water-buffalo of wood, stone and perhaps even marble, and chinthes. Eva let out the breath she'd been holding. Chinthes of all sizes and types, some fierce-looking with snarling mouths, some proud, some grim-faced and indifferent. None, though, as charming or intricately carved as the chinthe her grandfather had given her to bring to Myanmar. And these were different in another way, too.

All these chinthes stood in pairs. Ready to guard the shrine of a seated Buddha, she found herself thinking. Ready to maintain harmony. Ready to protect a household.

'Can I help you? English, yes?'

Oh. Eva had been so lost in thought she'd almost imagined herself alone in the shop. But now she looked up. A small, Burmese man was standing, arms folded, beside her. He wore a stained *longyi* and a faded red shirt.'Yes, I am.' She pointed to a chinthe in the cabinet. 'Can I see this one?' Though her stomach gave a little lurch of nerves. Ramon had said these people were dangerous. And he would be furious if he knew she had come here.

'Of course.' He produced a key from the ring on his belt, though whether the cupboards were locked to discourage theft or to imply that the contents were more valuable than they really were, she didn't know.

'I have a special interest in chinthes,' Eva told him.

His expression didn't change, not a flicker passed across it as he unlocked the door and swung it open. 'Which one?' he asked her. 'This? This?'

She pointed. 'What's it made of?'

'Teak.' He reached in, lifted up the chinthe in question and handed it to her.

That was very unlikely. It was too light in weight for a start.

'How old is it?'

He squinted. 'A hundred years maybe,' he said.

'How interesting.' If it was, Eva would eat her hat. It was

dusty, yes, but the carving was rough, the wood discoloured – possibly with chemicals – and there were some very suspect markings. It had probably been knocked up in their own factory less than a month ago. It wouldn't even fool an amateur.

So not only were the Li family common thieves, but they were also selling fake antiques. Eva's blood boiled. The distressing of furniture was commonplace. But passing it off as antique? That was illegal, crossing a boundary that was unacceptable – to Eva and to anyone honest who appreciated the value of true provenance. Old objects had a past, a history, which was part of their intrinsic value. So that you could sit on a Victorian dressmaker's rocking chair and imagine her taking pins from the little drawer under the seat, rocking and sewing in the lamplight. You could open an eighteenth century casket and guess what had been kept inside. You could wear a 1920s bead necklace and almost see a girl doing the Charleston. A genuine antique had generally been made by a craftsman with love and care. And it had a story. These people were fakers and forgers. They were dishonest. Criminals, even. She took a deep breath. Tried to hold back the adrenalin.

'You like?' the man asked. He didn't look as if he could care less.

'Not really,' she replied.

Once again, he shrugged. And it was that careless shrug that made something inside her snap.

'Because it's not really old, is it?' she asked him.

He blinked. 'It was bought in good faith, isn't it? As to age, I do not know exactly.'

And yet he'd been willing to let her believe it was a hundred years old a few minutes ago. 'So it wasn't made here?' She pointed to the back of the shop. She knew that she should stop, that it was extremely rash to stand here in the enemy camp making accusations. Klaus too had warned her to be careful. But she was so angry. Why should they get away with it?

'No, not made here.' The man almost snatched it back from her and replaced it in the cabinet next to its twin. 'It look old to me. Why not? I am no expert, isn't it?'

No expert? Didn't he work in an antique shop?

The man turned around and let out a stream of Burmese clearly addressed to someone who must be lurking in the darker recesses of the shop. Eva tried not to panic. 'Are you the owner of this shop?' she asked him. Though she knew he couldn't be. The owner of this place would have others to deal with customers who wandered in off the street.

'It is my family who own this business.' A different man spoke. He was walking towards them. His dark hair was slicked back from an unsmiling and unshaven face. His eyes were limpid, his shoulders drooped. He was also dressed in the traditional *longyi* but looked much smarter, his shirt clean and white. He glanced at her with a distinct lack of interest. 'What it is to you?'

Li. This was the moment when she should walk out of

the shop. But she had to make sure. 'Who are you?' she said instead.

'My name is Khan Li.' He gave a curt nod. 'And what make you think the chinthe not old? You are expert, is that it?'

'As a matter of fact, yes I am. I have a degree in antique restoration and the decorative arts.' Eva spoke before she had the chance to think about it. 'And I can certainly differentiate between genuine antiques.' She paused. 'And fakes.'

He didn't even flinch. They stood there staring at one another, but Eva refused to be intimidated. She would not back down. She knew that she was treading a dangerous pathway, but would a man like him really be that concerned about the shop's authenticity being challenged by an English-woman? She doubted it.

Sure enough, he looked her up and down with a sneer on his swarthy face. 'You make accusation, yes?' he said.

Even Eva wasn't foolhardy enough to rise to that one. 'No,' she said. 'But I'm surprised that you don't value your compa-ny's reputation more highly.'

'My company reputation?' He stared at her in amazement.

She supposed he couldn't believe it, some young European woman coming in here daring to lay down the law. But this, she felt, gave her an edge. She thought of Ramon when he'd confided in her the other afternoon, she thought of Maya and Suu Kyi and the stolen chinthe, she thought of her grandfa-ther. She just couldn't stop herself. 'Don't you care about the credibility of antique dealers in Myanmar?' she asked him. 'How they are viewed by the rest of the world?'

He stared at her as if she were quite mad. And very probably, she was.

'What you want?' he growled. 'What it is you look for?'

Why would he assume she was looking for something? But his words gave Eva the opportunity she needed. It was heaven-sent. If she was ever going to flush him out into the open, she had to take it. She might never get another chance. Eva took a deep breath. 'I was hoping to buy something special,' she said. 'Something that is really old. That's my business, you see. I'm over here buying genuine antique artefacts for my company in England.'

'Something special, isn't it?' His eyes gleamed. 'Why you not say?'

Once again, his gaze flickered over her, top to toe. Eva shifted uncomfortably. It wasn't a pleasant feeling. But she could easily extricate herself from this situation at any time, she told herself. She knew what she was doing; this was her business. She would see what he had to offer and then she would leave. Simple.

'Come.' He beckoned her towards the back of the shop.

Eva saw that there was a desk and two chairs, one on either side. It felt a bit like venturing into the dragon's den and she hesitated. But she had to do it. For Maya and her grandfather, she had to do it.

She sat down. On the table was some paperwork and she recognised the stamped blue-and-gold peacock logo on the letter heading – the same logo she'd seen on the boat two days earlier.

'What kind of thing you want to buy?' Khan Li sat down opposite her and stared at her with his limpid gaze. It was unsettling.

'What do you have?' she hedged.

He called out something in Burmese. Eva fervently hoped no one else was going to appear.

'Some teak statuettes,' he said. 'Very old. Very unusual.'

'What kind of statuettes?' Eva couldn't believe she was sitting here talking business with Khan Li.

He shrugged. 'Robed Brahmin Priest blowing conch shell. Poona. Very good.'

And very expensive, Eva would guess.

'Water carrier, nats, ox-cart guardian. All very rare. All teak wood.'

'Can I see them?' It sounded like quite a collection.

His eyes narrowed. 'I not have them here,' he said, as if she were foolish to imagine this might be so. 'They special. But I can get them. If you want them, I get them.'

'I see.' What did he do, steal to order? He probably knew her own contact in Mandalay. They probably all knew each other. Heaven knows where they got all these artefacts from. Eva wasn't sure she even wanted to think about it. She sighed.

He leaned closer. Eva noticed the gold signet ring he wore, the dark hair from his chest curling over the top button of his shirt. 'What it is you want?' he asked again.

He was reading her like a book. Eva made a snap decision. It was now or never. What did it matter that five minutes ago she had let loose a tirade on fakes and forgery? Now, they were talking business. This wasn't the UK. Here, people didn't seem to get offended in the same way. Here, if the price was right, they would talk to anyone. About anything. She had to do it.

'My British client has an eighteenth-century decorative teak chinthe,' she said quietly. 'Very old and intricately carved.' She lowered her voice still further. 'With large ruby eyes.' There she'd said it. That should flush him out.

His expression changed. He looked decidedly shifty. He raised a dark and scraggy eyebrow and one foot jerked as if in a nervous reaction. But instead of answering her, he yelled out in Burmese again and this time a young girl wearing a red *longyi* and embroidered blouse appeared. He must have called for her before. She was carrying a lacquer tray, her face almost invisible behind a curtain of dark hair. On the tray was a teapot decorated with weeping willows and sampans in a lake, two tiny white cups and a plate of thin sesame biscuits. She poured out the green tea, handed a cup to them both, gave a little bow and disappeared.

He was rattled. Eva could see that he was rattled.

Khan Li offered Eva the plate of biscuits. Perhaps he was giving himself time to weigh the situation up, she thought. In his line of business he'd have to be careful, always on the lookout, always prepared.

'Your client owns one Burmese chinthe only?' he asked when a few moments had elapsed.

'He does.' She nodded. 'I see you have immediately grasped the point.' Flattery, she hoped, might help her.

'How big it is?'

She showed him with her hands.

'Carved teak?'

'Intricately carved, yes. Late eighteenth century.'

'With rubies for eyes, you say?'

'Yes.' There must have been quite a few. Burma had long been rich in rubies; gems had been mined for centuries and anyway, she hadn't told him how large the rubies were, or how rare. She hadn't told him where the chinthe had come from either. Its elusive provenance.

'But he is Englishman, yes?' he asked.

'Yes.' She threw caution to the wind. 'He is old. He lived here many years ago, before the war. He was very close to someone . . .' She tailed off. That was enough. She didn't want to overegg the pudding. 'He would very much like to own the other,' she said.

'Of course, yes.' He leaned forwards. 'But you know, I think, the value of such a piece?'

'Naturally.' Eva crossed her legs. She wished she were wearing something a bit more business-like this morning than her flowery wrap-around skirt and pink cotton blouse, but she hadn't expected things to develop quite so fast. This morning she'd planned to meet with Klaus and then visit Ramon's factory . . .

'And may I ask . . . ?' Khan Li's voice was smooth and pleasant – for the moment, Eva thought. 'Why you come to us?'

A good question. Eva bit into a sesame biscuit. She needed

some thinking time now. 'I have contacts,' she said. 'I had reason to believe you might be able to help me.' But perhaps she shouldn't be too specific? After all, the Lis had stolen the chinthe in the first place. She thought fast. 'My contact said that if any man could locate such a piece, it would be you.'

He frowned. 'And the name of your contact?'

Eva shook her head. 'I cannot say.'

He seemed to consider, but only for a moment. 'I am sorry,' he said. 'You have been misinformed, isn't it? This is not our speciality. We run a modest business. I do not think we can help you and your client.'

Eva hid her disappointment. So he didn't want to sell the chinthe. He wasn't as greedy as she'd thought. 'My client will be very disappointed,' she said. She sipped her tea. 'He is a rich man. He has owned the chinthe for many years and done much research on the provenance. But . . .' She shrugged. 'We will continue to look for its elusive twin.' She pushed her cup to one side and got to her feet. 'Thank you anyway.'

To her amazement, he chuckled.

Eva didn't get the joke. 'Sorry?' she said. 'What—?' His laughter scared her. *Had* she said enough? Or had she said too much? She thought of Ramon, and suddenly wished she hadn't come here alone.

'You or your client read too many novels, I think.' His eyes were hard now and unsmiling. But despite his calm demeanour, Eva sensed he was still on the alert. 'The selling and export of gems in our country is strictly regulated and controlled. I cannot help you.'

And as she shook hands with him and looked into those limpid eyes, Eva wondered. Had she misread the situation? Had she failed to take something else into account? It seemed so. She had taken a huge chance and walked straight into the dragon's lair. She could hardly believe she had done it. But it seemed that in the end, it had all been for nothing.

CHAPTER 34

Maya prepared for the journey to Mandalay. It was a mental preparation as much as anything. Eva's sudden appearance had been a shock, she felt quite dazzled by it all. Lawrence was still alive. Lawrence still thought of her. Lawrence had given his granddaughter the precious chinthe to be returned to her family where it belonged. And so there was something very important that she must do. She had made her decision.

As she organised her things – she might be old, but she was still capable, she would not be treated like a child – Maya let her mind drift back to the war, her war.

One particular peaceful April morning was branded into her mind. It was the first time she had heard the noise and it shattered the peace like nothing else on earth. She didn't think she would ever forget the sudden shriek coming from the sky outside.

'*Ba le?* What is that?' Maya's aunt had been confused. She turned from one side to the other, made to move towards the door of the house.

'Stop, Aunt!' Maya grabbed her and pulled her down. The shriek, high and inhuman, was the whine and whistle of falling bombs, followed immediately by the crashing explosions. Wide-eyed and terrified, they clutched one another. The earth trembled. *Lawrence*, thought Maya, as she often did. Where was he? Was he safe?

Maya and her aunt held fast. Maya could see the terror etched on her aunt's face. And it was not surprising. No one had expected this. Maya knew about the attack on Pearl Harbor, which had brought the Americans into both the war against the Japanese and a few days later the war in Europe, and she knew what Lawrence had told her about the Japanese invasion of Malaya and Thailand. She even knew that Japanese bombers had attacked Rangoon and, of course, that many of her countrymen had fled the capital and were travelling north upcountry. But somehow she, and most others she knew, had still not believed that they would be involved. They thought all the reports must be hugely exaggerated, they had imagined they would be safe here so far north of Mandalay; they had not felt the breath of the war coming closer.

When the low-flying Japanese bomber planes had let go of their load, they must have flown off to prepare for the next onslaught. Because there was more. Maya crawled from their hiding place behind the wooden sideboard. She put a hand to her mouth. She could see bodies strewn, injured and bleeding on the dusty ground, and that ground was stained with their blood. She could see an arm and, dear Lord Buddha, other dismembered limbs. Bullocks injured by flying shrapnel were bellowing in pain. Windows had been shattered. Bamboo huts and houses, even the stronger ones made of timber, had collapsed like dominos and were even now erupting into flames.

And then the planes returned and Maya crawled back to their hiding place. 'It is not over,' she whispered. It went on, hour after hour of ceaseless bombardment, the almost total destruction of the defenceless little town.

'It is market day,' her aunt whispered.

Maya knew what she was saying. If she had been in any doubt as to who were the heroes of this war – and in truth, she knew as all women knew, that there were no heroes, that war was a necessary evil that brought out as much cruelty and corruption as it did bravery and courage in the soldiers involved in it – this attack should have convinced her. For the Japanese bombers were not fighting the British here, although there were a few British living in the town. They were not fighting rebels, or even Burmese men who might rise against them. No. And the little town could have no military or strategic importance, surely? It was market day, as her aunt had said, and so the town was crowded with tribespeople selling fruit, fish, vegetables, woven goods. And the tribespeople tended to bring their families along for the ride. Largely then, they were fighting defenceless women and children. Those were the kind of heroes they were.

Maya's aunt began to weep and still the bombs were falling. When would it end? Maya thought of her father in Maymyo. Was he safe? Was he still talking of Japanese liberation? And if so, what would he say when he knew what had happened here on this day? He should know that the people he was looking to for granting Burmese freedom were capable of such things.

After what seemed like an eternity, the planes finally flew off, leaving nothing but an eerie silence in their wake. And then they heard the moaning, coming from the street. The moaning, the wailing and the crying. Once again, Maya crawled out from behind the sideboard and held her hand out to her aunt, helping the poor woman to her feet. She was distraught, clearly suffering from shock. Gently, Maya led her to an up-ended chair, righted it and sat her down. Somehow, Maya's aunt's house had survived the blasts, though the windows had shattered and, as she stood in the doorway, Maya could see that most of the houses in the street had been destroyed. The air was full of the stench of blood, the acrid smell of the explosions and the scent of scorched flesh, the street was lined with the charred remains of burned-out houses.

Maya's aunt came to stand by her side. 'Now what?' she whispered.

'Now we help to pick up the pieces.'

They proceeded to do what they could for the injured nearby, fetching dressings and binding wounds, bringing water to those who were probably dying, in order to ease their final moments on earth. Buildings were still burning and smoking. There was next to nothing left of Main Street where the Indian food shops were situated, now, it was just a row of charred shells. The small cinema had been destroyed and the shop that her aunt had always called the bits-and-pieces shop, because it sold everything you could need, was no more. The peaceful little town had, in a matter of hours, become one of mayhem and panic, noise and confusion, pain and bloody slaughter.

So many dead. And Lawrence? Was he still alive? '*Kador, kador . . .*' she muttered. Please, please let it be so. Maya liked to believe that she would know, in her deepest soul, if he were not. Was he at this very moment involved in the act of killing a man – a Japanese? Or was he one of the wounded, one of the dying? It was this thought more than any other that persuaded her to take the path she next took. How could she not?

Maya and her aunt ignored the corpses lying in grotesque positions on the streets, and concentrated on the survivors, helping to take them by barrow or on foot to the local hospital, which, miraculously, was still standing. It was a simple one-storey building made of brick and stone with a sloping zinc roof and it had always served the village well. But how would the small building and the limited staff cope with this?

'I would like to help,' Maya told the Scottish matron, who was clearly rushed off her feet and desperate. And the streets were still full of people wandering around in a daze or moving from one place to another in blind panic, often injured themselves, desperately searching for their loved ones or for a glimpse of some previous sanity. How many more of them needed to be in this hospital?

'It is dangerous,' the Matron said. 'Many people are leaving, if they are able. You should go too. The planes will surely come back.' She busied herself with the next patient, making her comfortable, preparing to tend to her wounds.

'Yes, we will go upcountry,' said Maya's aunt. 'We will be safe there.'

Maya turned to her. 'You must go, Aunt,' she said.

'Your father . . .' Maya could see the pain in her eyes. They both knew what he thought of this war, and what he thought of imperialism too.

'Perhaps he will come here,' Maya said. 'Or perhaps things will calm down and I can go and fetch him from Maymyo. We should be able to join you soon.' She had no idea though, if this were true.

Her aunt nodded. 'Very well,' she said.

Maya turned back to the matron. 'I'd like to stay and help,' she said. 'If you'll have me.'

'Bless you,' she said. 'We need to boil lots of water. And to stop the spread of disease we must start burying the dead without delay.'

And so . . . Maya's wartime nursing career had begun.

It was several days before she even had time to return to her aunt's house. There was very little worth saving, but some things might be useful, and these she gathered up to take back with her to the hospital. And then there was the chinthe. It was, she knew, her legacy and her security too. She tore a long strip from one of her *longyis* in the clothes drawer, and wrapped it up carefully in the fabric. She found an old trowel of her aunt's, went out to the red flowering *sein pan* tree and dug a deep hole in the dusty earth. She gave the chinthe one last kiss and put him in the grave. 'For safe-keeping,' she whispered. 'I will be back.'

And now, all these years later, the other had returned . . . Maya shook her head. The wonders of this world. And that was why she must do what she must do. It was a fair return.

CHAPTER 35

It was a relief for Eva to escape the stuffy, threatening atmosphere of Li's. How had she found the nerve to do it? There were beads of perspiration on her brow as she stood on the corner taking stock. She glanced back at the showroom, the furniture and the 'older' artefacts and she took a swig from her bottle of mineral water, as if she might rinse the feeling of the place away. She walked a couple of blocks to get her breathing back to normal and to think, dodging the broken paving slabs and avoiding looking at the sewer that ran, visibly, just below. She had taken a major risk with a dangerous man. She just hoped that Khan Li had written her off as deluded.

She stopped at an open-air bar on the corner for a quick coffee. It was sweet and milky as usual, but she appreciated the caffeine hit as she watched the traffic weave by, the metal on the cars and scooters shimmering in the heat haze that was downtown Mandalay. Outside the dingy shack next door, a public telephone was stationed rather bizarrely on a rickety table and beside this, on the pavement, some street vendors had set up shop under the shade of a tree and were squatting in a circle, eating their lunch from a tin. Perhaps it was her state of mind, but the noise and humidity were overwhelming.

Eva flagged down a taxi, got in and gave them the address of Ramon's factory. She sat back, relieved to feel the air-conditioning cool on her skin. But what would she say to him? Should she tell him where she had been? Confront him with what Klaus had told her? Eva sank further back into the leather seat. She would wait and see how things panned out, she decided.

Ramon's company, 'Handmade in Mandalay', was situated on the edge of town and so, although it was a factory, it had escaped most of the city's noise and pollution. The building was single-storey and made of wood and bamboo, and it was clear from the outset that it was mostly un-mechanised. Eva leaned forwards in the taxi as they approached. They might be having financial problems, but the place still seemed busy. A truck parked outside the building on the other side of the compound was being loaded with crates, presumably destined for shipping. A couple of men in flip-flops wearing *longyis* and loose shirts and carrying clipboards were talking by the factory entrance, another was taking some tools inside and several men were squatting as they worked on furniture on a wide terrace at the front.

Ramon was just coming outside. When he saw the taxi, he waved and came straight over.

'Eva, you made it.'

'Of course.' He looked happy to see her and, despite everything, this thought gave her a bit of a glow. She took the hand he offered to help her out of the taxi. And fervently hoped that Klaus had got it wrong.

Ramon spoke to the taxi driver and handed him two thousand kyatts.

'It's OK, I've got it.' Eva was fumbling in her purse.

'It is done.' Ramon waved her money away much as he had done after dinner last night, took her arm and led her towards the factory. His enthusiasm was obvious from the spring in his step. He was back in a red-and-black checked *longyi* and grey shirt this afternoon and Eva had to admit that it suited him. 'And now,' he said, 'I must show you what we produce.'

They began at the back of the factory. It was badly lit, the raw wood stacked on shelves up to the ceiling, the floor covered in shavings. 'This is where the process begins,' Ramon told her. 'The decisions of design have been made, the planks have arrived from the saw mill, we can now select the timber for each item of furniture.'

After this, she learnt, each potential piece – chests, cabinets, chairs, tables, some simple in design, some ornate – went on a journey through the factory, moving from one pair of practised hands to the next. It was about as different to what she'd seen at Li's as it could be.

It was a long process and everything was in a different stage of construction. 'Each piece must be sawn and planed using only traditional methods,' Ramon told her. Which explained the lack of mechanisation. Eva remembered what Ramon had said about his business ethics, about the importance of retaining the hand-crafted element in quality furniture. This was what they stood for. And practically the only bit of modern technology she spotted was the electric router, though the man wielding it sat shirtless and cross-legged on a plank of wood. Others squatted or crouched at their work, their dark hair matted with wood-shavings, their arms and legs bare and dusty. The sound of tapping, sawing and the occasional drone of voices filled the air.

'Some of our workers have been here for many years,' Ramon said proudly as they watched a man wielding an ancient saw. He was barefoot and stood on a plank, using his toes like a vice to help support the wood as he worked it. There was a real connection, she realised, between the craftsman and his materials, between the human body and mind and what he was making. It was humbling. It was how things used to be in the rest of the world too, she thought. Before production speed became the driving force. Before time was money. But where something was gained, something was also lost . . .

They picked their way past the low stools, mats and items of half-made furniture, and moved on to the next stage of the process.

'Who's this?' Eva paused by an old photograph in a frame on the wall. It was a black-and-white shot. A tall young man stood by an open topped British vintage car, one hand resting on it in a proprietorial gesture. He had longish dark hair, light eyes and Ramon's smile.

'My father,' he said. He straightened the frame. 'He began

this company in 1965. It was unusual in those days. A very brave step to take.'

Eva nodded. 'How old was he?'

'Only twenty-five.'

And Eva could hear the pride in his voice.

Ramon showed her how they used paper templates of most of their designs, which were then carved out with a chisel and a wooden pestle, working carefully with the grain of the wood. She watched his demonstration. Ramon worked with an easy confidence, his brown arms flecked with sawdust, his fingers applying the pressure, swift and sure. She could see the narrow blue veins on the inside of his wrist as he guided the chisel, in his hands the most delicate of tools. And she watched his face as he worked, observing his instant absorption in the job in hand, his eyes still and yet alert. A master craftsman, totally at one with his subject. An artist. Eva breathed in the scent of the wood, sweet and smoky, rich and mellow, sultry.

'We still have some of the traditional British hand-tools my father insisted were shipped over,' Ramon said. He pointed to the chisel. 'There is one. Also hand planes and saws. He thought British construction methods were the best and he taught some of our workers his own father's way.' He laughed. 'So now we have what you might call a fusion.'

East meets West, thought Eva. There were the hinges and the gluing and the cutting out for locks and handles. Sometimes there was delicate gilding work to be done. And then the final stages of staining, sanding and polishing. The final polishing of each piece was usually done outside and in day-light.

Much of the furniture was highly glossed. Which meant that it was coated with several layers of lacquer, each one left to dry, sanded down and polished until the piece positively shone. 'This is what most of our clients prefer,' Ramon told her. 'We cater mainly for the Oriental market, of course.' He leaned closer. 'Although, as I explained, we are hoping for that to change.'

Eva was aware that he had already begun shipping else-where. She just hoped that the little business wouldn't lose sight of its original values.

'What are these?' She picked up a small packet of coloured powder wrapped in cellophane from a whole stack lined up on a shelf. They looked like spices; turmeric or paprika.

'Dye.' He indicated the finished products: a set of dining chairs with long narrow spindles and curved backs in rich burgundy with gilded carving on their arms; a glass cabinet with ornate handles in the shape of swans in a teak so dark it was almost chocolate and a lamp-stand of light yellow wood, a delicate carving of a woman wearing a crown and a necklace of flowers carved on its base. Some were made of mixtures that had been subtly blended, and although the stained wood was not to Eva's taste – she preferred the natural shade of teak that was also very much in evidence – she had to admire the craftsmanship.

The golden teak wood was her favourite, a natural shade that had been hand rubbed until it shone. But there were also contemporary finishes such as lime wash and teak oil. The range was considerable and the pieces that emerged were breath-taking in their quality, workmanship and lustre. And they were so solid. Eva ran her fingers over the shiny surface of a table that was smooth as a baby's skin. But there the resemblance ended; these pieces were heavy. They were built to last.

'And what's the new development you mentioned?' she asked him, thinking about what he'd said when they were on the way to Mandalay.

'Ah.' He led her over to a far corner of the factory. Here, a carpenter was working on a different looking wood. Old wood, she thought. 'Recycling,' he said proudly. 'This is my new project. There will come a day when Myanmar must not destroy any more of its natural forest. And yet there are many neglected structures such as old cattle houses, derelict homes and bridges in our country that can provide old wood, good wood for the making of a different sort of furniture.' He picked up some old, very wide planking. 'We ensure that the wood is salvaged responsibly,' he said. 'And look at what we find. Its long seasoning time has given it good stability. It has weathered to show a richer heart within. Is it not beautiful, Eva? Look at the closeness and evenness of the grain. Does this piece not have a history?'

She nodded. Again their views were in unison. Why not use old wood to create new, rustic looking furniture with a unique character of its own? It was practical, environmentally friendly and creative.

'I am only beginning this idea for my company now,' he said. 'But it is, I think, the way of the future.'

But what about their financial problems? And what about Li's? It was impossible, surely, that Ramon could be involved with them. She thought of Klaus. If he could hear what she was hearing, if he could see Ramon's factory, then he too would realise how completely off the mark his accusations were.

'So what do you think?' he asked her at the end of the tour.

'It's very impressive.' She had seen the complete process involved in making a piece of hand-crafted furniture. It had been fascinating.

There was one room however, which Ramon didn't show her.

'What's in there?' she asked, pointing.

'Ah.' He seemed embarrassed. 'It is another workroom. Sometimes I go in there to work on a special piece.' He shrugged. 'But there is nothing in there at the moment to interest you.'

His secretive tone made Eva want to go in. She frowned. He had been so open as he'd shown her round his factory and yet now he had closed up again, albeit briefly. Why?

They had tea in his office and when he found out she hadn't had lunch, Ramon had a word with one of his female office workers who proceeded to conjure up *Pe Thee Thoke*, a salad with herbs and long beans, which proved delicious.

'Did you enjoy your coffee with your friend?' Ramon asked her, as he sipped his tea.

'Mmm.' Eva was non-committal. 'But he's not a friend, not really. I only met him in Yangon.'

'And you did not know him before?' Ramon seemed surprised, almost disapproving. His expression darkened.

She knew what he was thinking. But, 'It's different for Europeans,' she said. 'You're drawn together in a strange country.'

'So you are drawn to him, yes?' His brow knitted. 'In this strange country?'

Eva didn't like the turn the subject had taken. 'It's not like that.' She tried to explain, but in truth, she was beginning to feel some doubt herself. There had been that rather odd meeting at the Shwedagon. And now Klaus had tried to make her distrust Ramon. 'It wouldn't have happened like that at home,' she admitted. 'Or in Germany. But in Myanmar . . .'

'Strangers in a strange land.' He put down his tea-cup. 'Foreigners stick together.'

Fortunately, his mobile rang and effectively closed the subject. It was Maya. Like Eva with her grandfather, Ramon had forged such a strong bond with her, she could tell, made more so, no doubt, by having lost his parents. She heard him mention her name and his face broke once again into a smile. He was, she thought, such a mixture of a man.

He moved the phone from his ear. 'My grandmother has arrived in Mandalay,' he said to Eva. 'She asks if we will both join her at a local restaurant for dinner tonight?'

'That would be lovely.'

'She has something to tell you.' Ramon's eyes twinkled. 'I think you will be surprised – and pleased.'

More story-telling, Eva wondered? She hoped so. She couldn't get enough of hearing about the old Burmese days.

As Eva was just finishing her lunch, Ramon was called away and she sat alone in the little office for a few moments. One of his assistants came in to check something in the accounts book. He smiled and nodded to her.

'Do you speak English?' she asked him.

'Yes, a little.' He smiled again and bowed his head.

'You are happy working here?' she asked.

'Oh, yes.' He beamed. 'Mister Ramon is a good man, isn't it? A kind man. Yes.'

'I'm sure he is.' Eva smiled back.

'My brother, he work here too,' he went on.

'Oh yes?'

'He have operation for eyes, isn't it?' The man pointed to his own eyes.

'Cataracts?' she guessed.

He nodded. 'They do operation at monastery in Sagaing, isn't it?'

Eva remembered Ramon mentioning this on their day out. 'That's good,' she said. 'And he is better now?'

'Yes.' The man nodded furiously. 'Mister Ramon, he take him, he help family.'

'He took him to the monastery?'

'Yes, yes. Very good. Very kind. He pay him while he off

sick. He look after workers, isn't it?' He exited the room, still bowing and smiling.

Eva was thoughtful.

When Ramon returned, she got to her feet. 'I should be getting back to the hotel,' she told him. She had to meet Myint Maw at three and time was getting on.

'I will take you.'

'No, really. You've got so much to do here. I can easily—'

'I insist.' Ramon took her arm. 'Afterwards, I will return here for a few hours,' he said, 'and then pick you up tonight at eight.'

They left the building by way of the small front office door to the right of the warehouse area.

'I was talking just now to the brother of the man who had the cataracts,' Eva said.

'Oh, yes? Moe Zaw?'

Eva paused in the doorway. 'He told me you had paid the man all the time he was off sick.'

He shrugged. 'The family had need of the money. Any employer would do the same.'

She shook her head. 'I don't think so.' She glanced out at the terrace where men were finishing and polishing the gleaming furniture. 'Can the business afford to take on employees' health care?' she murmured.

He gave her a quick look. 'I can put my hand in my own pocket, Eva,' he said. 'It is not too much to do.'

They stepped outside into the blistering heat. So he had paid for it himself. No wonder his workers were loyal to him and his company. 'And the financial problems?' she said. 'The loss of orders?'

'We will overcome it.' Ramon flicked back the wing of dark hair. 'Just as my father overcame his problems. Our materials are not cheap. We have lost a few orders. So be it. I have to believe that our way is the right way. That we will be winners in the end.'

'I hope so.'

'And before you go, I have one more thing to show you,' said Ramon. 'It is over in the warehouse on the other side of the compound. It will only take a minute.'

'Very well.' Eva followed him to a small truck and climbed in beside him.

'We can do some more sightseeing tomorrow, if you like,' he said as they drove across. 'I could take an hour or two off. You must see the Royal Palace. It may be a replica, but it will give you an idea of the original.'

'I'd like that.'

As they got to the warehouse, a man came rushing out.

'Ah, Wai Yan.' Ramon introduced them. 'This is my warehouse manager,' he said to Eva. 'This is a family friend, Eva Gatsby.' They shook hands. 'Do you have the key to the garage, please?'

'The key, yes, pleased to meet you.' The man seemed a little nervous but produced a key from the ring looped into the belt of his *longyi*.

'Come.' Ramon led the way. He unlocked a door and flung it open. There was a car inside. And then she realised it was *the* car, the one in the photo. A gorgeous vintage car, all cream curves and red leather interior.

'Your father's car,' she breathed.

'It is a Sunbeam Alpine.' Ramon stroked the cream body-work lovingly. 'It was his prized possession. He had it shipped over here when he knew he would stay.'

Their eyes met and once again she felt it, that frisson she had felt in Pyin Oo Lwin as they had walked together towards Pine Rise, the roadside lined with the sweet scented blossom of frangipani. And that sense, last night, of feeling close to him.

'Ramon!' Suddenly one of his workers was at the ware-house door, waving his arms and gesticulating. The warehouse manager was beside him, tearing his fingers through his hair.

They looked at one another and laughed. It seemed they were destined to be interrupted.

'I can get a taxi,' Eva said. 'It's no problem.'

Ramon frowned. 'I will call a car for you. Excuse me for a moment, Eva.' He touched her face with his fingers. So briefly. But in that moment she knew. She wasn't mistaken. He'd felt that frisson just as she had.

Ramon stood in a huddle with the man who had just appeared and the warehouse manager, their voices rising, all talking at once, it seemed. They all sounded a little on edge, she thought.

Unnoticed, she wandered outside the warehouse and towards the truck still parked outside. So there was a spark and it wasn't just from the moonlight or the scent of frangipani. It was there in broad hot spanking daylight outside a furniture factory in Mandalay. Did that mean it was real?

She turned to look back at the factory building. It had taught her a lot about the man. He was a perfectionist and he was talented, for he had told her he still liked to get hands-on and she had observed that much of the furniture was designed and crafted by him alone. He cared about his work . . . She thought of the way he had run his hands over both the highly polished, finished pieces and the timber, raw, from where those pieces had begun. She thought of his expression when he'd been carving that piece of wood.

He cared for his employees. He loved his family too, especially his grandmother, and he cared deeply about Burmese trade and ethics. Eva wondered. How well did Ramon know the Li family and the business they ran? Would he be shocked if he knew how they were trying to hoodwink tourists, passing off old tat they'd artificially distressed as genuine antiques? But she couldn't tell him about it, not without admitting that she'd been there.

The sun was hot on her head despite the protection from her hat. Eva glanced at the old truck loaded with crates, wondered vaguely where the containers might be going. Japan, maybe, or China? She knew Ramon's dream was to export further afield, to expand, even set up a partner business elsewhere. Dreams . . . They could, she thought, be dangerous things.

She took a step closer. The door hadn't been closed properly and the wooden crate nearest to the back of the truck was clearly visible. She peered at the address label. Did a double-take. It couldn't be . . . She looked again. But it was. Her company's name *The Bristol Antiques Emporium* and their address in Bristol was written there, clear as day.

How odd. Eva frowned. But the Emporium was an antique company. Why would Ramon be sending a container of his handmade furniture out to them? And why on earth hadn't he told her? She had told him the name of her company, told him what she was doing here . . .

Eva ran her fingers lightly over the wooden crate as if it could tell her what was inside. And then she noticed something else. Under the stamp of the sender, 'Handmade in Mandalay', she could make out a different kind of marking, something that was familiar, something that made her blood run cold.

'Hey!' Wai Yan the warehouse manager was racing towards her. He looked furious. 'What you doing? Come away from there!'

Eva took a step back. 'Sorry,' she murmured. 'I was just curious . . .'

'You stay away!' He seemed quite threatening now as he brandished his clipboard, his face like thunder.

'What is going on?' Suddenly, Ramon was beside them. 'What has happened?'

The man muttered something in Burmese. He pointed to Eva, gesticulated at the truck, his voice seemed to go on and on in an incomprehensible stream.

Why wouldn't he stop talking? Suddenly, there didn't

seem to be enough air. Eva felt a wave of dizziness, her head was pounding and she swayed on her feet.

'Eva, are you OK?' Ramon's face swam in front of hers. His green eyes were concerned. Thankfully, the other man had stopped talking, though he was still standing there looking decidedly twitchy.

'It's alright, really.' She forced a smile.

'Your taxi is here.' He put an arm around her. Eva's first instinct was to shrug it off but she couldn't find the energy. 'I shouldn't have left you out here alone in this heat,' he was murmuring into her hair. 'I am so sorry. Take no notice of Wai Yan. I do not know what possessed him. He imagined you were stealing something.' He laughed.

'It doesn't matter.' She had only been out there for a few minutes. But her throat was parched and her lips dry.

'Are you sure you are OK?' He bent closer. 'You look as if you have seen a ghost.'

'I'm fine.'

Ramon opened the car door and helped her in, giving the hotel name to the driver and handing him a couple of notes. And this time Eva couldn't be bothered to protest.

He leant in, his eyes searching hers. But she couldn't even look at him.

'Later?' he said.

She nodded. 'Later.'

But as the taxi drove off and Ramon raised his hand in a wave goodbye, her head was reeling. What she had seen under the sender's stamp . . . Had it been some sort of a mirage from the heat? That distinctive blue and gold? No, it was real enough. It was the faded image of a blue-and-gold peacock, the logo of Li's Antique and Furniture Company. There was no doubt. Li's were sending stock to the Emporium. And they were using Ramon's company to do it.

CHAPTER 36

Rosemary took him in his breakfast. He was awake, but still looked a bit bleary. And old, she thought. And old.

'Morning, Dad,' she said, trying to sound cheery, although in fact she hadn't had a good night, outside the morning sky was leaden grey and she couldn't stop thinking about Alec.

'Oh.' He blinked at her. 'Hello, darling.' He frowned. 'For a second there, I thought you were—'

'I was what?' And then she realised. 'I was who?' Who was important in her father's life? Eva, obviously. Even Mrs Briggs, she supposed. She wasn't family, but she'd been helping them with cleaning for years and with cooking too since Rosemary's mother's death.

'Someone else,' he said. He looked lost. *Who, Dad?* But she didn't say it.

She helped him sit up, wrapped the old tartan dressing gown around his thin shoulders. When he was comfortable, she put the tray in front of him.

'Mm, porridge,' he said. 'I've missed that.'

'I tried to make it like Mother used to,' Rosemary admitted. Let it bubble for a few minutes, a swirl of honey, a flash of milk.

'Your mother always made the best porridge.'

She did something right then.

Rosemary rearranged the things on the bedside table. 'What used to be on here, Dad?' She had the sense of something missing. Like that old memory game with a tray and a tea-towel. It was elusive though.

He ate his porridge from the more solid edge, moving inwards. Tiny spoonfuls. Hardly enough to keep a bird alive, she thought.

'It was the chinthe.'

Of course it was. It had always been there. Rosemary's mother had hated it. *Evil little creature*, she used to say, and refuse to dust it. It was a small rebellion, but somehow Rosemary had come to think of it as malevolent too. When she was little and went into her parents' bedroom, she even used to snarl at it sometimes.

'How on earth did you persuade Mother to let you keep it there?' she asked lightly. All the rest of his Burmese souvenirs were relegated to the downstairs hallway where the light was dim and visitors might pass by the shelf, hardly noticing them. But the chinthe was the most iconic Burmese souvenir of them all. And Rosemary's mother must have seen it every night when she was about to go to sleep. No wonder she'd loathed it.

Her father put down his spoon. He'd only eaten about a quarter of the small bowl. But he exhaled with pleasure and she knew he'd enjoyed it. 'I didn't insist on very much,' he said.

She nodded. She understood. 'And where is it now?' But even as she asked, she knew the answer to the question.

'Eva took it to Burma.'

'I see.' Rosemary recalled what Eva had said in her email. Something that she was doing for her grandfather, wasn't it? But she *didn't* see. And suddenly, she couldn't bear it; he had confided in Eva and yet told her nothing. All these years. That she knew nothing of his Burmese days, apart from what she'd found out in those letters, apart from what she had imagined . . .

Rosemary took the tray off his lap and replaced it carefully on the bedside table. She passed him his tea. What if things had been different, she wondered. What if her mother hadn't deeply resented Burma and passed her own resentment on to her daughter? What if it had been Rosemary who had listened, enthralled to all those tales of a far-off place and far-off people, an exotic life that most people could only dream of? Instead of Eva?

She watched her father as he carefully sipped his tea. But that could never have been. Because . . . Rosemary realised that he was watching her.

'There was a woman,' he said. 'In Burma.' He reached for her hand. 'I'm sorry, love.'

'Before you met Mother?'

'No, not before that. There was always your mother.' He chuckled. 'I miss her, you know.'

'Me too.'

'You grew up together, didn't you?' she asked. 'You and Mother?'

'As good as.'

Rosemary listened to him talk. His voice was dry and thin, but the words rang true and she could fill in most of the spaces. She could imagine exactly how her mother had been, as a child, as a young woman. Demanding what was hers by right, refusing to take no for an answer, blindly believing that she could control everything and make him change. Make him love her . . .

It was part of her own childhood. *Of course you'll come to the shops with me . . . Of course your bedroom will be painted yellow . . .* Some people controlled by physical strength, some by mental domination. Her mother had controlled by her expectations, by her assumptions that there was a wrong way and then there was *her* way.

'I knew there was someone,' she told him when at last his voice faltered. 'But I didn't realise.'

'I had choices.' He nodded. 'I don't blame your mother at all. She did what she had to do. I was weak.'

'We can all be weak.' Rosemary squeezed his hand. She hated him talking like that. She wanted him to be as strong as the father she remembered.

'And Eva . . .' He stared out of the window as if he could see her there.

Rosemary waited. What exactly was Eva doing for him in Burma?

'She's given her back the chinthe,' he said. His eyes were

329

bright. 'It belongs with her family. It had so much history bound up in it, you see, Rosie.'

Rosemary nodded as if she understood, though she didn't, not really. She only understood that she'd wasted a lot of years without her father, blaming him for something that she should never have blamed him for. What had he done that was so different from what she had done – with Alec? Her father had not been able to give her mother one hundred per cent of his love, his life. But at least he had tried his best. Had Rosemary?

'Will you tell me about Maya?' she whispered.

He didn't seem surprised that she knew her name.

'If you want me to,' he said.

'Have you told Eva?'

'Some of it, yes.' He sighed. 'Some of it I don't even know myself. Not yet.'

Rosemary patted his hand.

'I'm waiting for Eva to get back,' he said.

And for an awful moment, she thought he meant *before I die.*

CHAPTER 37

Eva's head was still spinning when the taxi arrived back at her hotel. And she had to meet Myint Maw in less than half an hour. 'Can you wait for me, please?' she asked the driver. She would go up to her room, quickly get changed, collect her paperwork and the eyeglass she used to examine close detail and come straight back. And try not to think about what had just happened, she told herself, as she collected her key and took the lift to the seventh floor. Of Ramon and what she had discovered. Would he guess that she had seen what was in the truck? Probably. He must have thought she'd acted a little strangely. No wonder that warehouse manager had yelled at her like that. And yet . . . What *was* in that crate? And why in heaven's name was it being sent to the Emporium?

By 3 p.m. she was once again sitting in Myint Maw's stuffy little office. Thankfully, he had provided green tea.

'Miss Gatsby,' he was saying. 'I see this, I think to myself. I must show her. She must see it. She will not believe.' He shook his dark head, his entire scrawny body joining in the movement.

'What is it exactly?' Eva sipped her tea and wished she could summon up some enthusiasm. But it seemed her enthusiasm waned in direct proportion to Maw's sense of melodrama. Unless the events of a very long day were getting to her at last.

Myint Maw made a big pretence of looking first to the left then to the right although the office door was shut and they were alone in the room. 'Doors,' he said.

'Doors?'

'Not just doors. No, no, no.' He waved a long finger in front of him. Leaned closer so that Eva could smell his slightly rancid breath and see the hairy mole once again at close quarters. 'Special doors,' he said. 'Intricate carving, yes, yes. Big doors. Old doors. Monastery doors.'

'Monastery doors?' She was sure they were very interesting, but . . . 'Where did they come from?' she asked. 'What happened to the monastery?'

Maw gave his usual expansive shrug. 'Restoration?' But he seemed to be guessing.

And here we go again, she thought. Temples that were no longer prayed in, monasteries with no monks or novices living inside. Didn't they care that the ancient treasures of Burma were being pillaged by the West? And then her shoulders sagged. What was happening to her? She was beginning to sound like Ramon. And yet now she knew that Ramon . . .

'You will see, yes, I will take you in my car.' Maw was nodding energetically.

And Eva knew that she had to be professional. She was here to do a job. She must at least see the doors.

They were in the back of another shop a few blocks away. And they were stunning.

'Solid teak, yes, yes,' said Myint Maw. 'Two hundred centimetre high.' His eyes widened and he nodded even more frantically. She couldn't imagine the cost of the shipping.

She took her time examining them. Burmese woodcarvers were so skilled even from an early period, and the carving was both intricate and flamboyant. The doors featured two guardians, *devas*, holding sprays of foliage, and had been created in the mid-nineteenth century, she estimated.

'Built by King Mindon, yes, yes,' Maw was telling her, circling the doors like a terrier, flinging nuggets of information at her over his shoulder. 'From Amarapura, yes, yes.'

Although not built by him personally, one would assume. Eva moved closer to examine the carving more carefully. The pilasters and pediments were rosettes, horn shaped projections known as *saing-baung* and the flames of *nat-saw*. These monastery doors were indeed, exquisite specimens.

'You interested, yes?' Maw nodded as though this could not be in doubt.

Which it couldn't, Eva thought. Because even if she didn't buy them, how long before some other Western dealer snapped them up? They didn't belong on a monastery any more. They were for sale, in a shop. It wasn't her responsibility where they had come from. *Damn Ramon.*

'How much?' And Eva began the difficult process of negotiating a price. It was hard to haggle about pieces such as these and impossible to even estimate how much they were worth to the Emporium. But that was part of Eva's job, and her responsibility. And Jacqui would, she knew, be so impressed.

An hour later, Eva was back at her hotel. She put a call through to the Emporium and when Jacqui answered, Eva told her about the monastery doors.

'They sound magnificent,' her boss said. 'Can you email me a photo?'

'Will do.'

'And the contact?' Jacqui's voice changed.

'Myint Maw?'

'How does he seem on second meeting? Reliable, would you say?'

Eva remembered how edgy he had been the other day when she had talked about provenance. How he had seemed surprised that she even cared. 'He never knows where anything's come from,' she admitted to Jacqui. 'Like these doors, for example.'

'But if they're for sale . . .' Jacqui's voice was crisp and confident. 'They can't be stolen goods, can they? And if they're genuine . . . ?'

'Oh, yes, they are genuine.' Eva wished she could express what was bothering her. It was that feeling that something else was happening that she knew nothing about. Only now, perhaps, she might be closer to finding out what it was. 'And, Jacqui, do we have dealings with a company called Handmade in Mandalay?'

'I don't think so. Why?'

'It's just that I saw a crate . . .' Eva wasn't sure how much to say. She wasn't sure how much she knew either. And she certainly wasn't sure about the Emporium.

'What sort of a crate? Is something going on, Eva? Look . . .' And her voice seemed to change. 'You will take care, won't you?'

'Yes, of course.' Eva was surprised.

'And email me – if there are any problems that is.'

She hadn't asked Jacqui about Li's. And Eva wasn't quite sure why not. She took her time over coffee in the hotel bar but there were still three hours before Ramon was picking her up for dinner and she didn't think she could stay here alone with her thoughts for all that time. She needed to go out somewhere, anywhere.

Seeing that crate in the truck had shaken her up and she needed to make sense of it all. What should she do? What could she do? The Emporium weren't doing business with Ramon's company. Why would they? They dealt in antiques. She thought of the blue-and-gold peacock insignia that had not been entirely obliterated by the stamp of Handmade in Mandalay. Which meant that the Emporium must be doing business with Li's.

Eva didn't want to think about that. She stepped outside the hotel lobby and was promptly accosted by a friendly trishaw driver.

'You want to go on a trip, lady?' he asked hopefully. 'I take

335

you to Mahamuni temple. A good place. I very strong.' And he pounded his chest to demonstrate.

Despite everything, Eva had to smile. He was slight in build, but these trishaw drivers were sinewy and physically powerful. She'd often seen quite small men carrying two hefty tourists on their trishaws, one facing forward, the other back, their pedal–power truly impressive. 'I've been to the Mahamuni Temple,' she said. 'So, no, thank you.' It had been the same day Ramon had taken her to Inwa and Sagaing. Something she didn't want to dwell on. And yet he had pretended it was all so important, hadn't he? That she experienced the spirituality and the history. That she allowed Myanmar to touch something deep inside of her. And she had. She really had.

'The Royal Palace?' he persevered. 'You go there? It is close by.'

Eva considered. She had said she'd go to the Royal Palace with Ramon, and it was so connected with his family, to his grandmother's story . . . But now, everything had changed. Sooner or later, she'd have to confront him with what she'd seen. No wonder he hadn't wanted her to approach the Li family. He must know, mustn't he, exactly what they were? No wonder there was a back room in his factory that he hadn't wanted her to go in. It was unlikely that she'd be going anywhere with him in the future.

Eva glanced at the busy road. She couldn't walk anywhere, and it might be fun. 'Alright,' she told the driver. 'You're on.'

He frowned and shook his head. What now?

'You must ask me how much,' he told her.

Eva shrugged. 'OK. How much?'

'Five thousand kyatts there and back,' he said. 'This is good price.'

'Fine.'

Another frown. 'OK, lady, you drive a hard bargain. Four thousand it is.' And he grinned, revealing gappy teeth stained blood red and black from betel.

It was a ghastly sight, but Eva was getting used to it. Many of the Burmese didn't drink because it was against their religion. But Buddha had never said anything about betel. She climbed on board. Thought of her grandfather as she so often did. *Royal Palace, here we come.*

As Ramon had told her, the building was a replica since the original had been razed to the ground, and when they got there, after a nerve-jangling trishaw ride through the busy streets of Mandalay, Eva was disappointed. It was so different from what she'd imagined. Inside the city walls, it was a bit like being in the country, very green, with dirt roads and fields, which seemed bizarre after the griminess of the built up city outside. It felt peaceful but bare, with only the odd barrack-type building and a café shack breaking up the landscape and army personnel wandering around where once there must have been vibrancy, splendour, royalty and hangers-on. The palace was surrounded by lots of other tiered, red-roofed buildings. It was a maze. But what really dismayed Eva was that everything about the red pagoda

337

palace looked so modern. It seemed to be such a cheap replica. And she'd seen more than enough of those at Li's.

Inside, however, there were old sepia photographs of Queen Supayalat and King Thibaw in their extravagant royal robes, jewels and crowns and Eva stared at these, letting her imagination run wild, thinking of how life had once been for them. Queen Supayalat looked as Suu Kyi had described, diminutive but strong-minded, her expression almost surly. King Thibaw looked meek and sweet as a lamb but terribly regal with his high cheekbones, arched eyebrows and drooping moustache. She supposed that it was impossible to reproduce that time of glory, though the copy of the throne, *Sihasana*, built on a high platform supported by sculptured lions was certainly golden and glorious enough.

Li's . . . As Eva began to look around the impressive Audience Hall where important visitors of a certain rank would have been received, she couldn't help thinking about them. They were sending a crate to the Emporium. But why? What was in it? And if it were anything like what she had seen in their showroom, then why on earth would the Emporium be interested?

She wandered through past the *Sihasana* and the array of golden caskets, lamps, even royal sandals and shoes made of solid gold, silver and decorated with rubies. Eva was getting a good idea of just how rich in gems Burma's Royal Family had been. Along with wood, gemstones had been Myanmar's chief source of wealth for centuries. And she supposed the

Royal Family would ensure that they kept the best for themselves.

Unless it wasn't Li's fake statuettes in the crate. It could be something else. The crate could be full of the kind of artefacts Khan Li had said he could obtain for Eva. But if so, wouldn't Jacqui have wanted her to authenticate those pieces while she was here?

There were few other tourists and Eva was grateful for the information boards written in English which gave her all the guidance she required. She had no need, she told herself, of Ramon. And where did he fit in? If the goods being sent by Li were above board – and, privately, Eva found this hard to believe – then why not send them direct from their own premises? She'd seen the cargo boat on the river. Why send them via another company? Why send them via Ramon? But there was only one answer to this that she could think of. They would send them that way to provide a front. And you only needed to provide a front when you wanted to hide something.

Pushing these thoughts away once more, Eva meandered through to the Hall of Victory, with the *Hamsa* Throne, complete with a model of King Mindon seated on it, and found herself replaying the scene of the British rout of 1885, the people of Mandalay plundering the riches of the palace while the British were stashing their first haul, and Queen Supayalat, Suu Kyi, Nanda Li and the two young princesses watched from their chamber with horror.

But she couldn't get Ramon out of her head. Did he know

what was going on? Did Jacqui? Was Ramon's business, with his father's good name and ethics, a front for something illegal? Something criminal? Could it be possible that this man who – *admit it, Eva* – she had begun to have feelings for, was, for all his fine talk about business ethics, working with the Lis and involved in something decidedly shady? Klaus had been right. Fakes and forgery. That was the impression she'd had when she visited Li's. But Ramon . . . Could she have read him so wrong? Had he simply pretended to be passionate about his family business, about the superior quality of the furniture they produced, about their use of the hand-crafted traditions so intrinsic to Myanmar? While all the time . . .

Eva was now in the Glass Palace. Its walls tiled entirely with mirrors, it was the shimmering hub of the Palace complex, situated exactly in the centre. The Glass Palace . . . How mind-spinning it must have been just to stand here . . .

Why would he do it? Was it for the money? Was it part of his scheme, his dream, to spend time in the Britain of his father? Or was all that a pretence, too? And what about her own company? Jacqui had seemed very keen to get her out of the country when all these shipments were supposed to be arriving and Myint Maw had been more than a little edgy. Eva remembered how surprised he'd been when she questioned his sources, and how he'd back-tracked about all the other stuff that he'd apparently sent them. How she'd been convinced that she was being told only part of the story. So what was going on?

At the end of the rabbit warren of adjoining rooms that

made up the Palace, Eva came to the Cultural Museum. Inside, were more photographs, of ambassadors who had visited the Burmese court and of the Royal Family. There was King Mindon who had apparently ordered the building of the monastery from which her latest acquisition for the Emporium had come, the King who had also founded the City of Mandalay and had it built at the foot of the sacred mound of Mandalay Hill, in accordance with the prophesies of Buddha. And there was another representation that Eva loved, a colour drawing of King Thibaw and Queen Supayalat sitting high on the Lion Throne in the Audience Hall, with hundreds of subjects bending and *shiko-ing* before them. No wonder the Queen had a superiority complex, thought Eva.

In the central aisle was a line of royal wooden carriages with old photographs so faded and indistinct, she could barely make out the royal figures in their glamorous jewelled carriage, harnessed to and pulled by bullocks. Some of the costumes were displayed in glass cabinets though: a sequinned and beaded tapestry robe studded with rubies worn by Queen Supayalat; the gold-threaded brocade of a Royal Maid-in-Waiting – maybe even Suu Kyi's, Eva realised with a jolt – embroidered silk and hemp, sashes and shawls. And there was the famous four-poster bed made entirely of glass. No replica, this was the real thing.

The real thing . . . Eva paused as she left the building and wandered back to the entrance on the outside of the Palace this time. In the distance, she could see the glint of a golden pagoda on Mandalay Hill. Visiting the Royal Palace had given her an insight into the story of the chinthes and Suu Kyi. But what about the Emporium and her own position there? And what about Ramon? She had trusted him and now it looked as if he was no better than all the rest.

And for the first time since she'd been in Myanmar, Eva felt very alone.

CHAPTER 38

When Lawrence woke up, he was sweating, really sweating, just like he had in those days and nights in that interminable heat, oppressive and heavy. For a moment he didn't know where he was. Could he be back in Burma? In that dark green uniform, those boots and puttees? No, he was old and he had never been back, though for so many years he had longed to. But perhaps part of him was still there, in the jungle in 1943, weary and footsore, marching up to twenty miles a day with a seventy-pound rucksack on his back, leading his mule over hilly and jungle terrain, down almost impenetrable muddy paths in monsoon, exhausted from the searing heat, sweating from the humidity, hot and wet enough to rot your boots, waking up every morning to a jungle growth of light green mould even on his own skin. Jungle warfare.

Lawrence shivered despite the warmth of his bed. How had they kept going? People talked of morale and courage. But really you just kept going because you had to. You were as dependent on your comrades in arms as they were on you. You couldn't let them down. He found out later they'd been called the forgotten army, thanks to some war correspondent, he'd heard. But at the time . . . Yes, there was a sense of iso-

343

lation, a sense of marching to God alone knew where in a bloody evil terrain where typhoid or malaria might finish you off if the Japs didn't. They hadn't been forgotten by those who mattered, of course they hadn't. But their war wasn't the war in everyone else's minds and voices. Their war was more like a sideshow to what was going on in Europe.

How his shoulders had ached from carrying that pack. The puttees kept out the worst of the leeches. But his feet had suffered as much as everyone else's, blistered from the boots, thick, un-feeling, white-soled from the wet. His pack had held three grenades, meagre bedding, a mess tin and spoon, steriliser, salt tablets, rubber shoes and the little chinthe Maya had given him. *It had so much history bound up in it, you see.* He had said that recently, to someone.

He never considered leaving it behind though they all thought he was crazy. Others had pictures of their loved ones, well, he didn't need those; he could close his eyes and see Maya every night, clear as anything. And the chinthe would protect him, she'd said. Didn't that make it the most important thing of all? He'd carried a jack knife too, along with his gun, a length of rope and a water bottle. You tried not to drink it though. Not because it tasted brackish and of chlorine, though it did, but because you were rationed. Best to wait until you were desperate, with a throat parched and rough as sandpaper.

Lawrence remembered the food too, not so bad when the mules were carrying stocks or when the drops came through. Cans of stewed beef and carrots, bully and hard crackers, tinned fruit and condensed milk, rice pudding. But most of all he remembered the chilling sounds, stealthy footsteps that might belong to Japs in the pitch-black of night-time watch in the jungle, the whirr of a grenade, the crack of gunfire.

Lawrence thought of Eva. How long had she been in Burma? He wasn't sure of the days and nights like he used to be. When she first left, he had started counting. But then he lost track. What did she think of the place? And what did she think of Maya, his Maya? He had wanted to ask her when she telephoned, but he had been bowled over, utterly bowled over by the fact that his granddaughter had found her.

He had sensed that she was still alive. But . . . *You should have found out for sure.* Lawrence had always known this. He'd often wanted to tell Eva the whole story – she was the only person he could tell. A man didn't have conversations like that with other men. And then there was Rosemary . . . Once, she would have thrown a blue fit if she'd known her father had harboured longings for a woman other than her mother. And he couldn't blame her. But now? Things seemed different now. Eva, though, had the imagination and emotional intelligence to see how it could have been. They had always been close. And she would love Burma just like she loved wood, the feel of it: the rough and the smooth; the sweet and enticing forest-fragrance of it; the way it told its own age, its own story.

He shifted in his bed, avoiding looking at that ceiling. Something was telling him he'd been in this bed too long. The truth was that he had wanted to find out what had happened to Maya before now, had wanted to relive the memories and perhaps even meet again the woman who had stolen his heart. But he couldn't. He had committed himself to Helen and then he had fulfilled that commitment by marrying her. He had done it for his mother, for his dead father and because it was the right thing to do. Especially given what he had done. It was his duty. And that commitment, no matter how much he regretted it, meant he couldn't even take one step backwards to the past. That way would lead to something much darker than Lawrence could deal with. If he stepped back towards the past . . . He'd be done for. He knew it.

He closed his eyes. He was tired. Already, he was tired. After Helen's death, perhaps he could still have gone to find her. But something told him that it would be too late, that it would be wrong to intrude in her life now, so long after he had walked away from it. And then there were the politics of the matter . . .

Lawrence had told Eva many stories about his time in Burma. About the life on the streets where people crouched over open fires to cook their food, the spices smoking, rising and perfuming the air, the colourful bustling markets, the teak camps high in the hills built on stilts overlooking the River Irrawaddy and the elephants he had grown so fond of during his time there. He had talked about the wood, about the work, about the teak Buddhas and the golden pagodas of Mandalay, exotic fragments, he supposed, of what he thought of as his other life. His real life.

But he had never told Eva about his war. The war, he

didn't wish to remember. He'd seen men die from malaria and dengue fever and he'd seen comrades fall – too many of them. He'd killed men before they had the chance to kill him; you didn't think about it, you just made sure it was the enemy and then you fired. You ducked and you ran like blazes and you were glad that you were living another day. Some didn't, that was war. He'd seen blood and dismembered limbs and he'd walked away from it if there was nothing that could be done. He'd seen dysentery and disease and heard men going quite mad. He'd met women who had been tortured and raped, prisoners who had lived with only a handful of rice pushed through the bars of their prison cell to keep them going all day. He'd seen fear like he'd never imagined and he'd stared death in the face. Why would he want to remember such things?

But sometimes . . . The mind was a curious power. The mind and the memories could pick you up and toss you back there. Sometimes it was disconnected fragments, images that fast-forwarded through your brain. Sometimes you remembered every last detail. Back you went to the thick, cloying heat and damp of the jungle, back to the trenches, back to the stench of war. And you wondered how you'd got through it, just like Lawrence was wondering now.

Lawrence's emergency commission had taken him, on a train with no windows, to an officer training school in Mhow, India. Like Burma, this was a land of poverty. In the daytime there was plenty of action, even in training school. And more men were being trained as officers as the Japanese drew closer.

As he'd known it would be, it was a valuable asset to speak the language, to know the country and its people, even if one lacked military experience.

They woke at 4.30 a.m. Some of the lads were shaved in their beds by a barber and brought tea and biscuits by their personal bearer. It was laughable really, when you considered that they were preparing themselves for war. Lawrence always got himself up and ready for the 5.30 a.m. drill and weapon training that began the day. Especially after Maya, he couldn't bring himself to think of the natives the way a lot of the men did. Was it their right to be served? What gave them that right? There were many things he hadn't questioned when he first came to Burma. But since then, he had listened to Maya's father and others railing against colonialism and British rule. The Burmese wanted to be independent. Who could blame them? And was it for the British to decide whether they could control the in-fighting that made independence so fraught with difficulties? Lawrence didn't know. But he had come to think about these issues more deeply, had seen the other side of the coin. And it had left him feeling strangely disturbed.

At night, he used the light from the pressure gas butties to read and study the training manuals, details of weapons, drills, and soon Lawrence became an expert. But later, when the mosquito nets had been drawn over the bed and all he could hear were the crickets and the occasional far-off cry from someone in the village beyond, Lawrence thought of Maya. He thought of the seriousness in her dark eyes, the poise with which she walked around her father's house and the streets of Mandalay, the sleek sheen of her hair. And, worst of all, he thought of those nights spent close to her, drinking in her musky perfume and the faint fragrance of coconut oil, incense and sensuality that hung in the darkness, her supple body lying curled around his, her slender fingers tracing and trailing their way over his arms, his legs, his chest until he wanted to scream with frustration. Maya. In the day, he thought of his mother and sometimes he even thought of Helen. But in the night, always, he thought of Maya.

How was she? Where was she now? He had heard that the Japanese had carried out a series of damaging air raids on Rangoon and that people were fleeing and travelling up-country towards Mandalay and beyond. Would she be safe? In the depth of the night, Lawrence found himself praying for her.

In June the following year, Lawrence was commissioned into the Gurkha Rifles, with men recruited in Nepal from dependable tribes such as the Magars and the Gurungs, who'd already experienced crushing hardship. They were loyal, trustworthy and energetic; it was an honour to serve with them. Meanwhile, the Japanese had moved on. Their army had come up through Burma and was pushing India. The men were growing more restless, they wanted to be off, they wanted to be part of the war. Wingate's Chindits had done some damage to Japanese communications, having taken them pretty much by surprise, and now a force must be built to penetrate the back of the enemy and compel its retreat. This meant harsh jungle training to harden up the troops, build self-reliance and develop a knowledge of vegetation so that they could live off the land if needs be. There were many tricks. Some they learnt beforehand, some were instinctive or someone's bright idea, like the Gurkha who had the clever notion of catching lizards by putting a drop of Carnation milk in an empty tin. They'd used that a few times on the march, some of the little buggers weighed as much as half a hundredweight and tasted surprisingly good too.

Lawrence opened his eyes once again. Was it another morning or the same one? There was a shaft of light filtering through the curtain, reminding him that this was West Dorset and he should get up. *Mustn't let things slide*. He often said this to himself. He supposed he knew only too well how easy it would be.

He sat up slowly and reached for his dressing gown for it was chilly and he hadn't yet switched on the central heating. Sometimes it seemed almost a crime to be too comfortable, after everything.

At first, he thought as he tied the cord around his waist, the British had been slow and ill-prepared and the Japanese had made them suffer their worst military defeat for centuries. But . . . He chuckled to himself as he slowly made his way out into the hall and along to the kitchen to make his tea. None of that sweet char now. Now, he liked it strong and bitter. He looked around him. It was odd, but his kitchen seemed different and he couldn't remember coming in here for a while. He was feeling a bit wobbly. With some difficulty he groped his way to the rocking chair and sat down.

But once they realised what it would take to get going, the British had done it in style.

Because, despite everything, Lawrence remained a staunch patriot. Like terriers, the British forces were. There had been those who were little more than stuffy colonials and there were those who took advantage of the system they'd been born to. And then there were the others. The fighters. He straightened his back, heard the heating come on. Had he switched on a timer? Had he drawn the curtains? He heaved himself out of the chair and put the kettle on to boil. Sat down in the rocking chair again, just for a moment, and adjusted the red-tasselled cushion at his back. Had he taken advantage of Maya? He hated to think so. And yet . . . She had said he was a free man and it hadn't been true. He had never been free of her and he never would be. That was the sadness of it all.

In the dream-memory of his war, tramping through the heat of the jungle, his regiment had finally come to the end of the day's march. They had cut down banana leaves and bamboo to feed the mules – sensibly the animals preferred the latter, as if knowing they contained more roughage and less water – and they had unpacked them of the heavy burdens they carried: ammunition, reserves of food and the precious wireless of course, without which they wouldn't know what the hell was happening. Then they let them loose to graze. They had to look after the mules, they were more important than the men in many ways, especially when the air drops weren't getting through. The mules were their means of survival and the men got bloody fond of them too.

351

After they'd seen to the animals, they dug the slit trenches to protect themselves from the enemy, built their own shelter and laid out their sparse bedding, using the one blanket and groundsheet that each man carried in his pack. And they stayed on the alert. Two men stood watch in two-hour stags. Those bastards were never far away.

Lawrence thought he would collapse, from the heat, from the march, from sheer exhaustion. But he had dug because he had to dig. And as darkness fell he heard it: the whinny from a mule, the restlessness that could mean only one thing. The enemy approaching.

Where had they sprung from? Lawrence and his men were used to being taken by surprise. The Japanese were bloody good. In daylight, snipers sometimes stayed up the trees for hours; they had a roll of cloth round their waist full of cooked rice with bits of dried fruit and coconut, so the bastards weren't even going to get hungry. They always came down in the dark, though, to move position and to get drinking water as they only had small bottles. And they kept so bloody still. But when you spotted one, you knew there'd be others, so you had to spray the surrounding trees with a burst of Bren gunfire. That would bring the buggers down.

Lawrence crawled to the trench along with the rest. And as he peered over the edge, he saw him. A man. A soldier. Christ. His stomach lurched. The enemy.

Like lightning, Lawrence loosened the pin of his grenade, counted *one two three*, the longest three seconds he'd ever known. He chucked it and threw himself face down into the trench. He tasted the dusty earth and he waited for the crump of the explosion. *Him or me.*

Now, Lawrence shuddered at the memory. The kettle was whistling and he got up to see to it, but his legs were so weak that he had to sit down again. *Oh my Lord . . .* He had no strength. He had no strength to remember.

In that moment he had thought of her too, of Maya. A man like this might have denied her food. He might have hurled abuse at her, hit her on the back of her head with the butt of his rifle, raped her, shot her. *Him or me.* In an ideal world, he should have been a man before he was the enemy, with a wife, a family perhaps. A man like this could even have been a friend. But there was no time to think of such things. And Lawrence had been close enough to see the whites of his eyes.

At 8 p.m., Eva was waiting in the hotel lobby when Ramon's car drew up outside. She was conscious of a feeling of dread in the pit of her stomach. She had even considered cancelling their date; she really didn't want to see him. But there was Maya to consider. The evening had been at her invitation. And besides, Maya had said that she had something important to show her. Eva thought of her grandfather. She simply couldn't not go.

The doorman swung the door open as she approached and Eva stepped out of the cool air-conditioning of the hotel into the humid early evening of the street outside. Immediately, she was conscious of the noise of the traffic, the dust, the smell of the food sizzling in oily cauldrons nearby.

'Eva.' Ramon had got out of the car and now he approached, bent to kiss her. 'You look lovely as always,' he murmured.

'Hello, Ramon. Thank you.' After some deliberation, she had chosen a simple long white linen skirt and loose shirt, which she was wearing with her velvet Burmese slippers and embroidered Shan bag. Her hair, she had swept and pinned up, and, once again, she was wearing her mother's pearls. Rather primly, she offered her cheek.

'Are you feeling better? Did you have a rest?' He was all solicitousness and concern. He opened the passenger door and Eva climbed in.

'A lot better thank you,' she said. 'My head's so much clearer.'

He gave her an odd look, but shut her door, walked round and got into the driving seat. 'And did you meet up with your contact?'

'I did, thank you.' His back was to her now. Hypocrite, she thought. He had given her such a hard time about buying antiques from Myanmar, when all the time he was involved in . . . What was he involved in exactly? And what was the Emporium involved in? She still didn't have a clue.

'And you?' she asked politely. 'How are things at the factory?' She could hear the barely concealed sarcasm in her own voice.

Ramon edged the car out into the heavy traffic. 'There is some good news,' he said.

'Really?' Crime obviously did pay.

'Yes. I have had talks with a man I know. He has agreed to become my new business partner.'

'New business partner?'

'I do some work with him already.'

Surely he wasn't talking about Khan Li? This seemed to confirm what Klaus had told her. She found herself clenching her fist and forced herself to relax. *Shoulders down. Look out of the window. Breathe.*

Ramon wove his customary expert passage between lanes

of traffic, hooting sharply to indicate his intention or where he felt someone ought to be alerted to his presence. 'But if I make him a partner,' he continued, 'then he will be more committed. I will have more spare time. And he will make a big contribution to my business.'

'Money?' she snapped.

He glanced across at her in surprise. 'Of course, money. This is business, Eva. I told you the position we are in.'

Yes, he had. But couldn't he see that money wasn't everything?

Ramon gripped the steering wheel more tightly. 'But not only money. Also his time, his professional input, his directional skills.'

Again, she heard in his voice that passion for his work. The difference now was that she couldn't believe in it any longer. And she certainly didn't see Khan Li possessing the qualities Ramon had mentioned.

'And what makes you so confident that this new business partner will retain the ethics that your father held so dear?' Eva asked him. The mention of his father might even make him think again, bring him to his senses.

Once more, he glanced across at her, though as Eva could see, the road was busy enough to claim most of his attention. 'Naturally, I chose with great care,' he said. Now it was Ramon who sounded cool. 'As you know, I share the ethos and beliefs of my father. I would not do anything that might compromise them.'

Eva had to refrain from snorting with incredulity at this

statement. Who on earth did he think he was fooling? Certainly not her, not anymore. 'And what will you do with all that free time?' she asked.

They were driving next to the Palace moat now and she fancied she could almost see the red pagodas in the distance, but perhaps not; they were so far away. All roads in the city still led to the Royal Palace, although the palace was not what it had once been. Neither was the noisy, dirty city that sprawled untidily around it. King Mindon, thought Eva, would turn in his grave.

'I think I told you I wish to develop the export side of the business,' Ramon said frostily. 'And that I wish to go to England and visit the place where my father was born.'

'Where was that?' Eva softened slightly.

'A place called Ilfracombe in the county of Devon,' he said. 'My father told us it was very beautiful there. He often spoke of the harbour.'

She remained silent.

'Do you know it?' Swiftly, he glanced across at her once more.

'I went there as a child.' She decided not to tell him that it wasn't far from where she had been brought up in West Dorset. What was the point? She had to remember what she'd found out about him. She mustn't let him get to her now.

They drew up outside a restaurant with lanterns strung around the trees outside. 'Is this it?' Eva made a move to get out of the car, but Ramon laid a hand on her arm.

'What?' She looked down at his hand, warm on her bare

skin, at the slender craftsman's fingers, calloused from working with wood. She couldn't look up at him, didn't trust herself.

'What is it, Eva? What is wrong?'

She looked out of the window, tried to maintain control. She might have known this would happen. She'd never been any good at pretending everything was fine when it wasn't. 'I went to the Royal Palace this afternoon after I left you,' she said.

'Oh?'

'I decided I'd rather go there alone.'

'That is OK.' He took his hand from her arm. 'I am not offended. But did something happen there?'

She shook her head. Now, damn it, she felt like she was going to cry. 'And before I came to see your factory,' she said, 'I went to Li's showroom on Thirty-Sixth Street.'

'You went to Li's? For the love of sweet Lord Buddha, Eva!' He sounded angry now, just as she'd expected. 'Why did you go there? Did I not tell you—?'

'That it was dangerous? Yes, you did.' But now she had discovered his ulterior motive. She turned to him. 'But, you see, I made a solemn promise to my grandfather to do my best to reunite those chinthes. It may not mean much to you, but for him . . .' She tailed off. How could she begin to explain how much it meant to her grandfather, how much Maya and his life here had meant to him? How the chinthe had become symbolic of that life and their love and their parting?

'Ah, the chinthes.' He slapped his palms on the steering wheel.

'Yes.' She took a deep breath. 'I had to do something. Don't you see? I'm not here for much longer, I don't have much time.'

'And do you imagine that I too do not yearn for my grand-mother to hold those chinthes once again in her hands?' Ramon spoke quietly but his eyes glittered. 'Did I not tell you that I had a plan?'

'But you refuse to tell me what it is!' The man was so infuriating. Not that she even believed him. He would hardly hatch a plan to steal the chinthe back from a man he was about to make his business partner. Unless . . . Eva thought about it. Was that why he was shipping out their crates, not to make money but to try and get closer to them?

'Eva.' Ramon turned to her. He lifted her chin so that she was looking straight at him, at his green eyes, at the dark hair that flopped over his forehead, at the curve of his mouth. 'Can you not simply trust me?' he said.

If only. For a moment they stared at one another, eyes locked. But she couldn't do it, couldn't say it. Not after what Klaus had told her, and not after what she'd seen this after-noon with her own eyes.

He took his hand away from her face at last. 'I see that you cannot,' he said coldly.

'Well, what do you expect?' Eva was still close to tears, but she rounded on him. 'Aren't you about to make Khan Li your business partner? For heaven's sake! Is that likely to make me trust you? How could you? They're one of the unscrupulous

359

companies who have got you into trouble in the first place. You know exactly what they are.'

'What?' He looked truly baffled. 'Khan Li? Are you mad? Why do you think such a thing?'

'Well, because . . .' But her words tailed off. She wasn't going to tell him what she'd seen in the blue truck, at least not yet.

He sighed. 'What happened there, Eva?'

'Nothing much.'

'So you will not tell me?'

She looked down. Twisted the daisy ring on her little finger. How could she tell him anything? How could she trust him with anything?

'Khan Li is the last person I would ask to be my business partner, Eva,' he said. 'The man who is to be my partner is a man I have worked with for many years. A man who has money, yes. But a man I respect.'

Before Eva could respond, Ramon's mobile rang and he answered it, speaking swiftly and softly in Burmese. 'We must go in,' he said to Eva. 'My grandmother is waiting.'

'Of course.' Could she believe him? He sounded convincing. But nevertheless, Eva reminded herself, there was no doubt that he was working with them in some capacity. Something else was going on.

She followed him as he strode through the door held open by a waiter, his tall figure giving off some of the tension that Eva too was feeling inside. He was wearing the traditional male *longyi* again tonight – she supposed his grandmother preferred it – with a crisp leaf-green shirt. But there was a hardness about him, a kind of suppressed strength that was scaring her. She shivered.

Ramon looked around, waved and then led the way towards the far corner of the restaurant where Maya was sitting. The place was traditional Burmese in layout and decor, with lots of bamboo and wood, the chairs and table a burnished chestnut laid with gleaming cutlery and linen napkins.

'Grandmother. Auntie.' He gave a polite little bow.

Maya and another woman were seated at a table set for four. Maya rose to her feet. She looked as serene and elegant as ever in a lilac silk *longyi* with a matching embroidered blouse. Her white hair was coiled on her head and she wore a necklace of jade. It was almost . . . Eva thought back to what she'd seen at the Royal Palace . . . a ceremonial costume. The woman beside her, now also standing, looked vaguely familiar. Had they met before? Eva wasn't sure, perhaps she had been at Maya's house in Pyin Oo Lwin? She'd slightly lost track of the relatives. Eva smiled at her and the woman smiled back.

Maya embraced Eva, looking into her face in that direct way she had. 'Eva, my child,' she said. 'Thank you for coming.' She turned to the woman beside her.

She was, Eva supposed, in her late sixties, her hair still dark but greying and smoothed away from her face. She possessed the same look of serenity as Maya and there was definitely a resemblance between them; she must be another relative.

'I told you I had something to show you,' Maya said,

almost impishly, her old face wreathed in smiles, her dark eyes bright.

'You did, yes.' Eva smiled back.

'But it is not a "something" to be exact,' said Maya. 'It is a "someone".' She indicated the woman beside her. 'This is Cho Suu Kyi.'

'Oh.' Eva looked from one to the other of them in confusion. 'You have almost the same name as . . .' Maya's grandmother. The loyal maid-servant to the Queen who had first been given the pair of chinthes by Supayalat.

Maya nodded. 'We do not always use family names here in Myanmar,' she said. 'But we often name our children after our ancestors, as well as according to the day on which they were born. It is auspicious.' Once again, she smiled.

Eva's mind was racing. 'I'm pleased to meet you,' she said to Cho Suu Kyi.

'Suu is my daughter,' Maya said proudly.

Another daughter? Ramon had called her 'Auntie'. So was this . . . ?

'Yes.' Maya took Eva's hand and then Suu's hand and joined them, one to the other, so that Eva's hand was clasped in Cho Suu Kyi's. 'Suu is my first daughter, Eva,' she said. 'Cho Suu Kyi was named after my grandmother who left me the legacy of the teak chinthes. I gave your grandfather one of those precious chinthes. And this is the child your grandfather gave me.'

CHAPTER 40

Maya said goodnight to Cho Suu Kyi and went to her room. The evening had, in the main, been a successful one. There was a problem between her grandson and Eva, she could see that, of course. Something, or someone, had come between them and they were not the friends she had hoped they would be. She was old. Perhaps she was growing fanciful. But somewhere inside had been a small spark of hope . . .

She had agonised long over whether to tell Eva about her first daughter, the daughter she shared with Lawrence, but had never shared with Lawrence. Telling Eva would be to tell him, and that would be hard. But the girl had come all this way to Myanmar. Not only that, but she had brought back the chinthe, which told Maya that Lawrence had never forgotten her. It gave her such joy – a joy she had thought she would never feel in her life again.

And then . . . Cho Suu Kyi had wanted to meet Eva too, and why not, for she was family? And so the decision had been made. She must give Lawrence the gift of knowledge of his daughter, a gift that might also bring some pain, she guessed. But so often in this world, happiness and pain combine.

Upper Burma, 1943

It was exhausting work and sometimes Maya felt almost too weak to stand. But the matron and her two other assistants worked tirelessly day and night and Maya did the same. Matron Annie taught her how to carry out simple medical procedures and she had always been practical and capable. She learned fast because she had to.

The Military Hospital nearby had lost almost all of its staff and so they took on most of the patients, transporting them by a couple of bullock carts, which had somehow been overlooked in the mass evacuation from the town. Refugees, the hospital saw more than its fair share. Thousands of them lined the roads to India, often dying by the roadside from malnutrition, malaria, dysentery or cholera, if not from their wounds. The hospital was full to overflowing. Mattresses were put out on the verandahs and makeshift beds in the storerooms.

Maya often attended to the soldiers who had been brought in. She would chat to them and ask them, if it were not too traumatic, to talk about their experiences. She always hoped she might, by some wonderful coincidence, hear something of Lawrence. And she wondered too, one day, would it be Lawrence who came here to the hospital? Or would he be cared for by another woman such as she? Silently, she thanked that imaginary woman from the bottom of her heart.

One morning, she had to rush to the sink when she was in the middle of dressing a soldier's particularly nasty wound. It had become infected. Matron Annie had already carried out one emergency amputation, though she was hardly qualified to do so. Perhaps she would have to do another.

When she returned, Matron Annie was standing by the bedside looking serious. 'I see how it is,' she said gravely.

'Matron?'

'Soon, you will not be helping any longer, is that not so?'

'I do not understand.' Though of course she did.

They completed the work on the soldier's injury and then moved away. The matron took Maya to one side. 'You are pregnant?' she asked.

'Yes, I am.' She held her head high. She had known it, a few weeks after he had first left. She had known it when the town was bombed. And she was glad. She was proud to be carrying Lawrence's child. She would always be proud.

'What do you want to do?'

Maya knew what she was asking. Did Maya want to get rid of it? Did she really want to bring a child into this world and at this time in this place? It was madness, was it not? 'I will have the child,' she said softly. 'But until that day and after that day I will work as much as I can, here at the hospital. I will not need much time off, Matron.'

Gently, the matron touched her arm. 'I should tell you that you are a fool,' she said. 'And you know all the reasons why.'

Maya bowed her head.

'But I cannot help but admire you for your courage.'

If she only knew, Maya thought. It was not courage. It was just that she might lose him and so desperately she wanted to keep a small part of him. And she could not kill what they had created together in love. It was not possible. She could not live with that.

'And it is good to think of the possibility of new life,' said the matron. 'When this . . .' And she gestured to the ward full of injured and dying men, 'is all around us.'

Maya's daughter was born in the middle of the night on a Tuesday. It was a warm night and a long labour and she was attended by Matron Annie herself, who held her hand and boiled the water, examined her, comforted her and encouraged her to push when it was the right time.

When Matron Annie finally handed her the baby girl wrapped in a thin cotton sheet, Maya touched the screwed-up wrinkly little face and she wanted to cry. After all this pain and all this bloodshed all around her, it was down to this. Death and new life, and she held that new life in her arms.

By the following day, Maya was on her feet again and working. Wards must be cleaned, medicine administered and wounds dressed. She had a baby girl strapped to her chest. Apart from that, nothing had changed.

One day, a colonel turned up at the hospital and spoke to Matron Annie and Maya. They were more or less running the hospital between them now; everyone else had left. He was in command of a special unit trained in bridge demolition and this unit had been detailed to carry out an extensive programme of bridge blowing which would, he said, affect everyone remaining in the town. The Japanese were close and the unit must delay their advance in order to buy time. The unit had also been ordered to take possession of funds from the nearby Government House to keep the Shan riches out of the hands of the enemy. Silver, rare jewels, bullion, the place was full of the wealth of the Shan princes, much of it deriving from the profitable opium trade, as Maya was only too aware.

She thought of her own Shan grandmother, Suu Kyi, and the pair of rare and decorative jewelled chinthes she had given her. Like so many families she knew, Maya had buried her treasure in that safe place where she knew she could retrieve it when the war was over. Her aunt had even sewn jewels into her clothes, hidden in the knot of her *longyi*. It wouldn't be the first time the Burmese had used their family jewels to barter and survive. And Lawrence's treasure . . . ? She could only hope that somehow the little chinthe brought him back to her safe and well when the war was over.

After the demolition, the unit would be pulling out and who knew what would happen to their town. 'You are British,' the colonel reminded Matron Annie. 'They may not spare you. And you . . .' He looked at Maya who was walking now with the baby tied to her back like a papoose. 'The child is very pale,' he said.

Maya felt a tremor of fear. She understood his meaning. The light skin of her daughter gave her parentage away. She would be an innocent victim, but her mother would be viewed as a traitor.

'You could both be raped or killed without further

thought,' the colonel told the two women. 'The Japs don't take any prisoners. Or at least they do, but they won't give you that dubious privilege.'

But would they be any safer upcountry or on the road to India? Maya and Annie exchanged a look. Maya had heard how many of the refugees were dying from disease and starvation. And there were so many bandit gangs on the loose. People were desperate. At least here there was kindness, there was shelter and there was food. Their hospital store was meagre, but they had condensed milk, which was vital for a mother with a young baby, there was vegetable soup, there were eggs, rice and flour and there were occasional hens and ducks donated by villagers and refugees. And here Maya could continue to work and nurse – she would feel she was doing something to help the war effort, to help her people and the injured soldiers too.

'I cannot leave my patients,' said Matron Annie.

'And I can make her skin darker,' said Maya. With mud if need be. Fortunately, the baby had inherited her mother's dark eyes and Burmese nose, she did not look like a European child, although Maya would swear already that she had Lawrence's smile. And Maya and Annie had become close; they had already been through so much. If anything happened to Maya, she was sure that Matron Annie would look after her baby.

'So?' said the colonel.

'I will stay here at the hospital,' said Maya.

'We both will,' said Annie.

★

Maya told Eva some of this story over dinner. Ramon and Suu had heard it before, of course. And the girl listened, clearly enthralled, looking from one to the other of them as if she could hardly believe it.

But there was one part of the story that Maya did not tell them. She didn't think that she would ever tell another living soul.

CHAPTER 41

In 1943, after their parting, Maya had given birth to a child. Eva's grandfather's child . . . Eva continued to roll the knowledge around in her head as Ramon drove her back to her hotel. What a bombshell. And her grandfather didn't know. Which meant that Eva would have to tell him.

The tension between Eva and Ramon, so palpable she'd almost felt she could cut it with her butter knife, had increased during the evening as Maya told her incredible story. It was a tale that held Eva riveted. Of her nursing, of how she had kept her and her daughter alive in an occupied and poverty-stricken country at war, while Eva's grandfather had been fighting in another part of the country, with absolutely no idea of his daughter's existence. Her grandfather had wanted to know about Maya's war experiences and it had turned out that Maya's war had been an awful lot more complicated that he could ever have guessed.

Her grandfather had left Burma and returned to Dorset, still not knowing. If he had known, Eva wondered, would he have stayed?

The streets of the city were much quieter than when they had left a few hours ago. The street sellers had cleared their stalls and gone home, leaving just the hint of oil and fried spices in the air, the shops were shuttered and the bars were closing up too. Very few people remained on the dark pavements, for there were no street lights and this, along with the rickety kerbs and loose, broken paving slabs, plus the fact that it was virtually impossible to cross the road, was why it was hard to walk anywhere in the city at night. 'It is a lot to think about, isn't it?' Ramon said, as they drew up outside the hotel. 'It was a shock for you, finding out about my aunt, Cho Suu Kyi.'

'Yes.' And it would be a shock for her grandfather too. How would he react? How would he feel when he found out he had a daughter he had never known about, never had the chance to acknowledge, living on the other side of the world in Myanmar? And as for Eva's mother . . . Eva shuddered at the thought of what she might say.

'Tell me about your mother,' Cho Suu Kyi had said over dinner, which had consisted of a selection of delicious curries and salads. She served a small portion of *Bae Tha Hin*, a type of Burmese duck curry, on to Eva's plate, along with some rice. 'My mother has told me much about my father, I almost feel I know him. But I would so like to know about my other half-sister.' She smiled at Ramon and then back at Eva. 'About Rosemary, your mother.'

So would Eva. She would very much like to know about her mother. But she couldn't say that to Cho Suu Kyi. Even so, she wasn't sure where to start. 'She lives in Copenhagen,' she said. 'My father died when I was seven.' Which was nothing compared to Suu's experience, she realised. She had never even known her father. 'She married again when I was seventeen.'

And I chose to stay in Dorset. She didn't say this though. It would only confuse this new family that she now seemed to be part of. It confused Eva too. She knew why she'd chosen to stay: her grandparents and Dorset were her security, their home her home. They had seemed like the only thing that was holding her family together. But she didn't know why her mother had left. Was it out of love for Alec? Or did Dorset represent everything that she'd held dear and everything that she'd lost?

'Do you think your mother would come over here to visit?' Cho Suu Kyi was so excited, her dark eyes shone. And Eva could see why she had immediately found her familiar. She had the dark eyes of Maya. But her cheekbones, her mouth, her smile . . . She had the look of Eva's mother, even of her grandfather too.

'I'm not sure.' Ramon had told her about *arnadeh*, a kind of over-politeness and extreme consideration for other people's feelings, which was part of Burmese etiquette. It was why they served food to their visitors rather than inviting them to help themselves and it was important to observe it so as not to cause offence. So how could Eva tell Cho Suu Kyi that her half-sister Rosemary had never wanted to know anything about her father's Burmese days? She simply hadn't been interested. To her, they represented her father's disloyalty. Or so Eva supposed. She didn't really know, since her mother wouldn't talk about it. But she'd have to talk about it now. And perhaps Eva could make her see that this lovely Burmese family weren't a threat, with the possible exception of Ramon, she reminded herself. They were part of her past, her story.

'Would you care for a nightcap?' Ramon wasn't even looking at her. His green eyes were fixed resolutely on a point in the darkness in front of him.

Nothing between them had been resolved, had it? They had reached a stalemate. And if Eva were going to take any action regarding the crate she'd seen on the truck, then she couldn't confide in him. He was, though it was hard to accept, looking at him now, the enemy.

But she'd been only too aware of that enemy as she'd sat at the round table in the restaurant, Cho Suu Kyi placed on her left and Ramon on her right. They were almost terrifyingly polite with each other. *Can I pass you more fish curry? Would you like some vegetable salad? May I refill your glass?* Which was almost worse than having a full-scale slanging match.

'Is everything satisfactory?' Maya had asked mildly at one point. 'Has something upset you, Eva? Ramon?'

'No,' they both replied. 'Absolutely not,' Eva added.

But Maya was a wise one and despite the celebratory nature of the evening, her expression remained a little concerned.

'He is a good man, my grandson,' she whispered to Eva when they said goodnight. 'But I hope you found out what was troubling him.'

Eva crossed her fingers. 'Not really, I'm afraid.' It wasn't up to her to blacken his name, no doubt Ramon could manage it entirely on his own.

And now he wanted to prolong the evening?

'I don't think that's a good idea,' she said. She was tired. And besides, what more was there to say? He had talked of trust. But had he trusted her, by confiding in her, by telling her his supposed plan? No. Perhaps, because there was no plan.

'Eva——'

'No.' She fumbled with the door catch. The last thing she needed was to be caught at her most vulnerable, especially after a night like tonight. And besides, there was so much to think about.

Ramon whipped out of the car, came round to open her door. He took her hand as she climbed out and pulled her into a close embrace so swiftly that she was there before she had the chance to wonder if she wanted to be there.

'I cannot pretend to understand,' he murmured into her hair. 'But I just want you to know——'

She pulled away, but not far enough. He was holding her quite firmly by the shoulders and he didn't seem about to let her go.

'Ramon . . .' The sense of him seemed to envelop her. She tried to remind herself of what he was, but when he bent his head and his lips met hers, she lost all that and just felt it. His lips, firm, demanding. His kiss. The scent of him – of wood shavings and polish and just a hint of cardamom. The heat of him.

It was the sort of kiss you could drown in. The sort of kiss you wanted to go on forever. But. She pulled away.

'Eva.'

But she was gone. Literally running. Through the door of the hotel, grabbing her room key from the desk, leaning on the button to call the lift, almost sinking into it when the door opened. Thank God it was empty. She closed her eyes. Ramon . . .

The lift stopped at the seventh floor and she got out with a sigh, wandered down the corridor, put her key in the lock and—

And the door was already ajar.

It swung further open. The next moment seemed frozen in time. Eva stood there, taking in the scene. A man – a stranger, small, dark, Burmese, was rummaging through the clothes in her chest of drawers, her things thrown around the room, on the bed, on the floor. In that split second, she must have gasped. Because the man twisted round to face her. They stared at one another. Eva felt her legs almost dissolve with fear. She hung on to the door handle. And then she opened her mouth to scream.

CHAPTER 42

Rosemary had gone out to get some shopping, but she hardly liked leaving him, especially after this morning's episode.

She shivered as she arrived at the supermarket car park and parked the hire car in a vacant space. And not just because it was such a cold day. It had stopped raining at least, but now there was a winter bite to the air that reminded her: time was getting on, she had to decide what to do. Seattle was still looming on her horizon. Hers and Alec's.

Her father had been in the kitchen slumped in the chair, the kettle whistling full pelt. That's what had woken her, of course. She'd heard the noise and thought for a minute it was a siren, ambulance or police perhaps. Then she'd realised it was coming from the house, to be precise, from the kitchen downstairs.

Rosemary had grabbed her bathrobe, pulled it on and run down there. The kitchen was steamy and she didn't see him for a moment. Just thought, *what the . . . ?* And snatching the oven glove from the Aga rail, took the kettle off the heat.

Now, Rosemary got out of the car, plucked her shopping bag from the back seat and went to get a trolley. They had to eat.

As soon as she'd turned around, she'd seen him. 'Dad? Dad . . . ?' And her heart had flipped over in much the same way as it had when she'd first arrived at the house and found him out for the count on the bathroom floor. But fortunately, this time he was just asleep, bless him, waking even as she raced into the room, muttering something about 'holding fire'. How he could have slept through that racket, she had no idea.

'What are you doing, Dad?' Fear made her voice sharp and she saw him flinch. 'Did you put the kettle on?' she asked in a gentler tone.

'It was a long, bloody night,' he said. 'You can get fed up of marching.'

Ah. So he was back in wartime, was he? 'So you thought you'd come and make a cup of tea, is that it?' She took his arm. 'Let's get you back to bed.'

He blinked in confusion. But he went with her, like a lamb.

Rosemary picked up a bag of salad and some fresh noodles. Perhaps she should ring the doctor again. Later this morning he'd been so much better though. After he'd freshened up in the bathroom, she'd taken in some coffee and read him out bits from today's paper. Sometimes they even tackled the crossword, but Rosemary had something else on her mind today. Then they'd chatted about this and that. Not what she wanted to hear about though. She wanted to hear about Burma.

'I read the letters, Dad,' she told him. She wanted to confess. And she wanted to know more. 'The letters you keep in the drawer.'

'Letters?' But she saw the understanding touch his eyes. She nodded.

'When?'

'I found them after Mum died.' She realised that something had shifted inside her, that she wanted to tell him now. 'I wasn't snooping. Just tidying up. And then I couldn't resist reading them. I'm sorry.'

'Ah.' He shook his head. 'I knew there was something.'

Yes, she thought. Something to pull you apart.

'Perhaps I should have told you about her,' he said. 'But it was all so long ago. And I couldn't, not without upsetting your mother. You are our daughter, love.'

Yes, she was. His coffee cup was rattling in the saucer and Rosemary steadied it for him. 'You didn't send any of those letters though,' she said.

'No.'

'Why not, Dad?'

He fixed her with his honest blue gaze. 'Because I was married to your mother.'

'But you needed to write them?' She wanted to understand. Nick was dead, so there was no point in writing to him. Or was there? She had always thought that if only she could communicate with him one last time . . . Then perhaps it would somehow clear the way for her future. She looked helplessly at her father. Would he realize what she was asking him?

'I did. It helped, Rosie.'

'Why did you ever come back here?' Rosemary whispered.

She didn't want to hound him or upset him when he was so frail. But it was a question she'd wanted to ask for such a long time. She understood how her mother had been and the pressure the families had put on him. But why did he succumb? The way she'd loved Nick she would never have let him go. 'Why did you come back and marry Mum? When you were still in love with someone else?'

'Ah, Rosie.' He looked at her full on. 'It was Maya's decision, not mine,' he said. 'At least . . .' And he seemed to be remembering something. 'I could have done more. I should have done more.'

'Maya knew how it was back here in England?' Rosemary guessed. She could picture them all, waiting for his homecoming. His mother, Helen's mother, anyone else who was left of the family when the war was over. Everybody wanting him to marry Helen.

He nodded. 'She knew most things.' And smiled.

'She thought it was your destiny,' Rosemary murmured.

He folded the newspaper she'd left on the bed, smoothing it with his gnarled old hands. 'She let me go.' He exhaled with some difficulty and she saw him wince with pain.

And you didn't want to let everyone down.

'But you never forgot her.' She patted his hand.

'No, I never forgot her.' His eyes seemed to glaze over, as if he'd slipped back to the past once again. 'It's like that with love sometimes. I think you know that, Rosie.'

Rosemary looked away, beyond him and out of the window. The days were getting so short now, she hated that, longed for the stretched out days of summer. 'I do, yes,' she said.

He came back to her then, just for a moment, and he held out his arms.

She curled into them, like a child, eyes closed, feeling her father's frail warmth, feeling his comfort. It still didn't take much to make her think of Nick. And Alec knew that too. Did he also know that she had never been able to give herself to him in the way she had so carelessly given herself to Nick? Of course he did. He had said as much, he had said that he would take what was left. *Just like her mother had . . .* But she knew that something had changed for Alec. It wasn't just her going away. It had been building, in her, in him. And sooner or later there would be an explosion, or as near as Alec would ever come to an explosion. And why not? It was hardly fair. Seattle, she realised, was that explosion.

'First love . . . It takes some beating,' her father said. Gently, he stroked her hair.

Rosemary nodded. She swallowed. He was right. First love took some beating. 'Hard on number two though,' she said.

'I reckon so.' But his voice was faint and she realised he was drifting off again. Back to sleep or back to the past. The two seemed entwined into each and every day.

'Hard on number two,' she murmured. She eased herself off the bed without disturbing him. Smoothed the quilt. Touched his hand. And left him to it.

At the supermarket, Rosemary paid for her purchases and

wheeled the trolley out to the car. She wound her cashmere scarf more closely around her neck. All these years she'd blamed him. And yet . . . How much better was she?

CHAPTER 43

'Ssh, lady!' The man swore, pushed past her and was gone, racing towards the stairs.

What the hell? 'Hey!' Eva yelled after his retreating back. 'Stop that man! He's a thief! He's—' But no one was listening; no one was around. And the man was already out of sight.

Eva ran over to the phone, quickly dialled reception. Her hands were shaking. The phone seemed to ring and ring.

At last someone answered. 'There was a man,' she said. 'He was in my room. I walked in and . . . He should be there any second. He'll be coming down the stairs or in the lift or—'

'Excuse me, madam,' The girl on reception spoke slowly and clearly as if Eva were either deaf or insane. 'Please repeat?'

Eva repeated. But she knew it was useless. By the time she got the message through, he'd be long gone.

'Was anything taken?' the girl asked her. 'Valuables? Jewellery? Money?' Her voice was friendly, but not overly concerned.

'I don't know.' Eva sat down on the bed. She felt . . . violated. She looked around at the disarray in the room. Fortunately, she carried all her money with her, and she'd been wearing her pearls and her diamond daisy ring. But . . . Who would have done this? Hadn't she been assured that there was very little crime in Myanmar, and especially against tourists? And how had he got into her room?

'Please check,' the girl said. 'I will send someone up. Please answer the door.'

The door, Eva saw, was still wide open. 'Yes. Thank you.' She got to her feet, hung up and strode over to the door. Slammed it shut and locked it. Leaned on the back of it, trying to control her breathing. When she saw him, she hadn't had time to be scared. But now, she couldn't stop shaking.

After a few minutes there was a frantic hammering on the door.

Eva flinched. She had made a cursory check of her stuff and even put most of it back in the chest of drawers. Nothing seemed to be missing. 'Who is it?' She could hear the tremor in her voice. Once more she felt the sensation of being alone.

'It's me, Ramon. Eva, are you OK?'

Ramon. Relief flooded through her at the sound of his voice. In that moment, he certainly didn't feel like the enemy. She unlocked the door and was immediately wrapped in his arms.

'What happened, Eva?' He sounded angry.

'There was a man.' Her voice was muffled into his shoulder. She took a deep breath. And a step away. She was unhurt. She had to regain control of her emotions.

'What man?'

'I don't know what man . . .'

Ramon spoke rapidly in Burmese to one of the hotel staff

383

now hovering behind him. 'You need some brandy,' he said. 'And water.'

'Thank you.'

'Come. Sit down.' He took her arm and led her over to the bed. 'Tell me what happened.'

She sat down and began to explain.

His expression grew darker and darker as he paced the room. A boy came back with a bottle of brandy and Ramon poured a generous measure into a glass. He handed it to her. 'But you are not hurt?' he asked. 'He did not touch you?' His hand rested on her arm.

'No, no.' In fact he had run away like a rat up a drainpipe. No one had been hurt, or even threatened. Someone had been ransacking her room, but that was all. Eva sipped the brandy. It slipped down her throat like a flame. She supposed she was just suffering from the shock of it.

Ramon turned on the bedside lamp and flicked the switch of the main light off so that the room was suffused with a warmer glow. Eva was grateful. Her eyes were hurting. 'Do you want me to call the police?' he asked.

'No.' She didn't want to involve the police. What was the point if nothing had been taken?

He swore softly. 'They will not get away with this.'

And how did he propose to find out who *they* were? A thought occurred to her. 'But what are you still doing here?' The brandy had revived her somewhat. Hadn't Ramon driven home after he'd dropped her off at the hotel? How had he even known there was anything wrong? Eva didn't like the direction in which her thoughts were heading. He wouldn't have had anything to do with this, would he?

He took the glass from her and refilled it. 'I was still outside in the car. Thinking.'

Eva nodded. She knew very well what he'd been thinking about. That kiss.

'And I was about to drive off when I saw a man running fast out of the hotel.' He handed the glass back to her.

She frowned. 'But why did you think he was anything to do with me?'

'I did not. Not at first.' He sighed. 'And then . . .'

'And then?' She swirled the rich amber liquid around in the bottom of the glass. The scent of the brandy was strong, but somehow reassuring.

'I thought I recognised him.' He looked across at her. His eyes seemed to gleam in the light of the bedside lamp.

Eva's throat went dry. 'Who was he?' But already, she thought she knew.

'I think it was one of Khan Li's men. One of those he asks to do his dirty work when he wants to keep his own hands clean.' Ramon went into the bathroom and emerged with a glass tumbler. 'May I?'

She nodded and he poured himself a brandy from the bottle the hotel had provided.

Eva recalled her conversation with Khan Li. So he had taken the bait, after all. She supposed it would have been simple to find out where she was staying. But what had he been trying to discover by having her room searched? The name of her rich client who owned a certain Burmese decorative and jewelled teak chinthe perhaps? Or something else? The chinthe itself?

'Eva . . .' Ramon came and sat down on the bed beside her. He seemed to be considering how to continue. 'I have told you these men are dangerous, yes?'

She nodded. 'Yes, I know.' And she knew that she should have been more careful. It had been too risky to go there alone, foolish to think that she could get the better of someone like Khan Li.

'And I am aware you do not fully trust me.'

She made no answer to this. There wasn't much she could say.

'But you must now tell me exactly what happened when you went to Li's showroom.'

Eva considered this. If he was as in league with Li's as she suspected, then it would be very easy for him to find out anyway. And even if she couldn't completely trust him . . . She couldn't believe he meant her harm.

So she told him, every so often taking a sip of the sweet mellow liquid that had done its job of calming her down and was now making her feel pleasantly woozy.

By the time she'd finished, Ramon was shaking his head in disbelief. 'I cannot believe that you said these things to Li, Eva,' he said. 'You were foolish. But also brave.'

She shrugged.

'And did you tell him the name of your hotel?'

'Of course not!' She wasn't entirely stupid.

'So tell me this,' Ramon said. 'Why did you stop trusting me?' He got up from the bed and now knelt beside her, his green eyes pleading. He had to be genuine, she thought. No one could be that good an actor.

'I saw a crate in the truck outside your warehouse,' she said. At least she should give him the right to reply. 'It was being sent to the Bristol Antiques Emporium.'

He frowned. 'But that is the company you work for, isn't it?'

She nodded.

'Impossible.' He got to his feet. 'I know the name of every company we deal with. You weren't well. You must have imagined it.'

She watched him as he stood at the window, saw him flick back his dark hair with that irritated gesture of his hand.

'I didn't imagine it,' she said.

'But why did you not mention this before?' He turned around to face her. 'I could have shown you your mistake.'

She shook her head. There was no mistake and nothing would convince her otherwise. 'Because of the logo I saw under your company's stamp,' she whispered. 'It wasn't your crate.'

He shook his head. 'Eva, it has been a long and difficult evening,' he said. 'There has been . . .' He spread his hands, 'a revelation. And now a man has entered and ransacked your room.' He smiled. 'You have drunk a lot of brandy . . .'

She got to her feet. 'It was a blue-and-gold peacock

insignia,' she said. 'I wasn't mistaken, I wasn't seeing things and I certainly wasn't drunk.'

He came closer, put his hands on her shoulders. 'A blue-and-gold peacock, you say?'

She nodded.

Abruptly, his hands dropped to his sides. He muttered something in his own language that she couldn't understand. 'It is late. You must be exhausted.' He turned from her, went over to the door. 'Get some sleep, Eva,' he said, more gently. He opened it. 'We will talk again in the morning.'

Eva felt a sliver of fear returning and he seemed to sense it. 'He will not come back,' he said. 'I will have a word with reception on the way out. For one thing, I want to know how he got into your room. After I go, make sure you lock the door from the inside. You will be quite safe for now.'

'And tomorrow?' She realised she wouldn't feel safe here anymore.

He put his finger to his lips. 'We will talk tomorrow,' he said. 'You must not worry. I will pick you up at midday.'

She nodded. 'Alright.' She was exhausted, it had been a long day and she could hardly think straight. She wanted to trust him, she wanted to rest her head on his shoulder and close her eyes. And when they talked tomorrow, she would, somehow, make him tell her everything.

CHAPTER 44

Maya lay in her bed that night but she did not sleep. It would come; it always came, she must be patient.

She had relived so much of the war sitting at the restaurant table tonight, and now she recalled that one experience which she had talked of to no one. It had happened in the hospital when Cho Suu Kyi was still a baby . . .

Upper Burma, 1943
Maya had jumped with surprise. She had been doing some sorting in the hospital storeroom and had not expected to be disturbed.

The man who strode into the room as if he owned it was immaculately dressed in the uniform of a Japanese officer. His boots were polished and rose to his thighs and he carried a large sword at his side, one hand resting on the hilt.

'Can I help you?' she asked. But her mind went into overdrive. She was thinking, as she always was, of Cho Suu Kyi.

'Show me what food you have,' he said stiffly. He had arrived with one other soldier this afternoon. She guessed that they were an advance party, sent ahead to reconnoitre the area. So far they had been civil to herself and Matron

Annie and even to the inmates of the hospital. But they had also been guarded. And she didn't trust them.

Maya bowed her head. In the corner of the room little Suu was sleeping and she didn't want her to wake and be noticed. If the officer looked closely, he might see and he might suspect. Maya could not risk it. However, neither did she want to give the Japanese their precious food.

She opened the cupboard. 'We have very little,' she murmured. Pray to Buddha that he did not find their emergency store of condensed milk, soup and rice. 'What we have is for the sick.'

The officer turned up his nose in distaste. 'Why do you stay here in this town?' His gaze roved around the room. 'A woman like you?'

Maya moved quickly, placing herself between him and the corner of the room in which the baby was sleeping. What did he mean, *a woman like you*? 'It is everyone's duty to do something,' she said. 'And I like to help the wounded.'

'British soldiers?' he sneered.

'Any soldiers.' She looked him straight in the eye. 'We have Indian soldiers here and Chinese. And civilians too. Refugees. We do not differentiate.'

'Then you are fools.' He spat. 'You should learn where you will be looked after. If you can nurse, we need you at our hospital, not here tending to traitors.'

Maya thought quickly. 'I am not a nurse,' she said. 'Just an ordinary woman doing what she can.'

His gaze raked her from head to toe. 'Not so ordinary.' He licked his lips.

Maya felt her throat go dry and her legs weak. She had been warned of this. They both had. When the colonel had left, he had given her a .38 pistol with which to protect herself and she had it even now, tucked into the belt of her *longyi* at the back, hidden under the loose blouse she wore. But would she have any idea how to use it?

'Come.' He beckoned her closer.

Maya took a small step towards him, though all she wanted to do was run. In the next room, the ward, she would be safe for a while. He would not try anything when there were other people around. But how could she run anywhere when her baby was in here? She could not leave her. And anyhow, she would not be safe for long. She understood the mentality of the Japanese soldiers by now and she knew how they felt about honour and respect. If she humiliated this man in any way, he would never forget it. He would seek her out and she and the baby would never be safe. But if she complied . . .

He reached out, tilted her chin, sharply, and Maya looked up and over his shoulder. *Do not wake, my child* . . . He ran his fingers over her blouse, lingering at the buttons on the neck and then down towards her waist and the belt of her *longyi*. What if he felt the gun? She thought her heart would stop beating. 'Not here,' she whispered.

He cocked his head, surprised. Maya guessed that many women would die rather than be raped, especially by the enemy. She wasn't sure she counted herself in that category. She felt differently about her own survival since she'd had her child; the survival of each was linked. But her first priority was to get him out of the storeroom.

But just as she thought she might have achieved her aim, just as she saw the desire flare in his eyes, and as he gripped hold of her arms, Suu whimpered in her sleep, half-waking, and he blinked, pushed Maya out of the way. He stared down at the baby. 'Your child?' he demanded roughly.

'Yes.' She nodded. Maybe now she'd have to please him. Maybe now she'd have no choice. *Lawrence*, she thought, *where are you now?*

She resumed her position in front of the baby and put a hand on his arm. 'What do you like?' She heard herself saying it and hated herself. But she had to stop him looking at the child.

Once again, his surprise showed in his eyes.

But she had made an error of judgment and she saw that straightaway.

'You are a tart?' He sounded quite dispassionate now. 'What do you do it for? Money? Food? Jewels?'

She should have been more subtle. She should have thought. 'I am not a tart,' she said, speaking more loudly than she'd intended.

'Just looking out for yourself, is that it?' He eyed her curiously in his detached manner, his lust seeming to have abruptly dissipated. Perhaps it was the sight of the little one. In Maya's limited experience, men didn't much appreciate being reminded that sex might be connected with child-bearing. 'Or are you looking out for the child?'

Dear Buddha, but he was sharp. Maya decided that honesty might be the best policy with this man. 'I need to protect her,' she said simply. 'She is innocent. She has done no wrong. And she is all I have.'

He pushed past her again and moved closer to the make-shift cradle. He frowned. 'This is your husband's baby?' he asked.

'Yes.' The Japanese, she reminded herself, were strong on honour.

'And your husband is of your race?'

'Yes.' Maya began to pray, silently. *Holy Buddha, keep us safe, let him not see . . .*

'And he is where?'

'He died in Mandalay.' She answered quickly, not giving herself precious time to think.

He pulled her roughly towards him. She could smell him. Rancid and sour. 'Shall I tell you what I think?' He leered.

'Yes. Of course.' With some difficulty, Maya maintained her dignity.

Once again he put his hand to the collar of her blouse. 'I think that you are a tart,' he said. He pulled sharply and tore open the thin fabric so that her breasts were exposed.

It was all that Maya could do to just stand there in front of him. She let out a small gasp, grabbed the remnants of her blouse and held them to her breast. But she could hardly hide herself from his greedy gaze.

His eyes narrowed. 'I think you have slept with a European.' He pulled the torn blouse away from her again. 'Which was a stupid thing to do. That child is half-white. There is no doubt.'

'It is not true,' Maya whispered. 'She is Burmese. It is not true.'

'Ah.' He leaned closer and tapped his nose. 'But I see that it is true. The child is half-caste.'

She watched his expression as he looked from her to the sleeping child. She watched it change from greed to distaste to anger. She knew that the Japanese had a reputation for thoughtless cruelty and indifference to the suffering of others. That was part of their philosophy and it was one of the characteristics that made them so dangerous, and such strong warriors, for they carried that philosophy through to their own rank and file. How could she save them both? It was a moment in time that seemed to freeze. She dared not speak, hardly even breathe. Annie would say that the entire Japanese nation should not be judged by the actions of some individuals. But all Maya could see was the man before her.

In an instant he moved two steps to the cradle and wrenched Cho Suu Kyi from her resting place. The child blinked, opened her mouth and wailed.

He held her at arm's length. 'You are a traitor.' His eyes had gone quite mad. 'You are a murderous traitor.' He was speaking to Maya but looking at the child with an expression of such pure hatred, it sent a cold sliver of fear through Maya's

394

heart and mind. He was holding her baby as if he might fling her to the floor.

Maya made a snap decision. Her first instinct was to fly at him. But he was holding Cho Suu Kyi high and out of reach, and if she tried to wrest the child from him, Suu could fall, or he could simply push Maya aside and do what he wished. She had no option. The gun was in her hand before she could think twice.

She had taken him by surprise yet again and for a second he simply stared at her in disbelief. But pointing a gun at the man wasn't enough. She knew what he would do. She took aim with the instinct of a mother who knows exactly where is true. And she fired.

The explosion was deafening and she reeled back from the kick. Then she dropped the pistol to the floor, leapt forwards and, as he fell, she grabbed her child from his arms.

'What is happening here? What in God's name is going on?' Matron Annie was standing in the doorway. She looked from the Japanese officer who was clutching his chest, blood seeping from a wound, to Maya, huddled in the corner cradling her sobbing child. She looked at the pistol lying on the ground between them. She took a step towards Maya. 'The little one . . . ?'

'She is fine.' Maya let out a long breath, in a shudder. 'I had to do it,' she said.

'Yes.' Matron Annie dropped to her knees and felt the pulse of his neck.

But Maya knew already that he was dead. She had killed a

man. And suddenly she was shaking uncontrollably. *She had killed a man . . .*

'We must get rid of the body without delay.' Matron Annie's organisational skills came swiftly to the fore. 'Put the little one down. You must help me get him into the trench.'

Of course she was right. There was only one other Japanese soldier here at the moment and, with a bit of luck, he wasn't within earshot, but many more of them would soon be approaching. She could almost hear the sound of their army boots tramping through the jungle. And how many of them would see her baby and doubt Suu's parentage? How could she possibly protect her from them all? Maya could hardly bear to let go of Suu, not even for a moment. *She had killed a man . . .*

'First things first,' Matron Annie said briskly, indicating the dead Japanese soldier.

They took a leg each and dragged him out of the back door, checking the coast was clear before heaving him towards the small slit trench, leaving a trail of blood on the dusty ground. 'One, two, three,' said Matron and they hefted him in, watched the body fall to the ground, literally a dead weight, limbs splaying awkwardly to each side as it landed.

Maya realised that once again she was sobbing, wild sounds that seemed to come from somewhere else outside of her body. What had she done? She had never wanted to hurt anybody, it was against all the teachings to take a life. How could she have done it? And yet she knew how. She had done it because she and her baby were in danger.

'You had no choice,' Matron Annie said gruffly and placed a comforting hand on her shoulder. 'Come on. We don't have time for tears.'

And that was what they had come to, thought Maya. Having no time for tears.

Together, they collected firewood and kerosene, all the time looking out for the soldier's companion. 'He's probably looting the houses,' Matron Annie said with a shrug.

No doubt she was right. The Chinese soldiers who had come here only days before had been the same. They spoke of loyalty and they were supposed to be Allies, but all they cared for was what wealth they could find.

They piled the firewood over the body, working swiftly until they were both drenched with sweat, and then doused the wood with the kerosene. Although the flames caught and burnt the wood, the body remained virtually untouched, so they repeated the process again and then again until the body was unrecognisable. They piled on leaves and other rubbish and eventually the corpse burned and turned into a blackened mess that made Maya sick to the core as she looked at it. It could have been anything but it had been a man. Hurriedly, they dug up the earth and filled in the trench, raking over the soil and even the earth of the compound which had been stained with his blood. Maya knew they had to remove all the evidence or they would be dead for sure and it would all have been for nothing.

The Japanese were interested in total conquest of the Far East. A woman and a child, or two women and a child would not be allowed to get in their way. Their lives would mean nothing.

Maya made her preparations for sleep. She must put that experience behind her, as she had done so many times. Nevertheless, it haunted her and perhaps it always would. She prayed to the Lord Buddha that she might have to relive it no more. But how many experiences had Lawrence put behind him, she wondered. How much blood had stained his hands? She supposed that she would never know.

As she fell asleep she thought once more of Eva, that lovely girl and her grandson Ramon. What had happened between them? They were both unhappy, she could see. But it was not her affair. She would not interfere as her father had interfered between her and Lawrence, no good could come of that. She would wait and the right pathway would be revealed. That was the way that things must be.

CHAPTER 45

The following morning was as hot and humid as ever. After a somewhat disturbed sleep following the dramas of the night before, Eva got up late and went to the internet café to check her emails and send some more information to Jacqui. What else could she do at this stage but continue her work as planned? She was being paid by the Emporium to be out here, at least for part of the time. She still had the contact Klaus had given her to follow up, but she couldn't face that this morning. And it was too early now, but later she must phone her grandfather to tell him about Cho Suu Kyi. She wanted him to know. But how would he react? Would it be too much for him? Perhaps she should tell her mother instead, let her decide if he was well enough to hear the news, although she guessed it would be traumatic for her too. She decided not to tell either of them about the break-in, no need for them to start worrying over nothing. And she wouldn't send them any pictures of the family, not yet. She wanted to be with them, she wanted to see her grandfather's face.

Ramon was waiting for her in the lobby when she returned. 'Come to our house for lunch,' he said. 'I have something I want to show you.'

Not another long lost relative or vintage British car, she hoped. But she nodded and followed him outside. Perhaps now she'd find out the truth.

The house Ramon shared with Cho Suu Kyi and Maya was large by Mandalay standards, painted blue, pink and white, with a latticed balcony, blue shutters and a large verandah. The garden was small but there was a banana tree, a red flowering *sein pan* and some oleander and purple hibiscus. It was exotic and vivid and didn't seem to belong to the city at all.

Ramon showed her first into his own apartment which was an annex attached to the main building. The room they entered was small and almost bare, apart from an embroidered tapestry on the white wall, the depiction of a golden dragon, which made Eva give a little shiver. There was a low red chaise longue with blankets folded beside it, and the floor, she noted, was a gorgeous teak parquet. It was strange to be standing in his house, in his room.

Eva couldn't relax. She turned to him. 'Now will you tell me?' she asked. 'About the crate?'

'Ah.' He nodded. 'I spoke to Wai Yan this morning.'

'And what did he say?'

Ramon regarded her gravely. 'That he knew nothing about it.'

'But—'

'Hush, Eva. Please.' He made a gesture of invitation and led the way through to a small adjoining dining room where a low wooden table was set for tea. Around the table was an assortment of embroidered and beaded cushions, each one more vibrant than its neighbour. He indicated that they should sit. 'I saw the fear in his eyes,' he said.

What did he mean exactly? Eva waited.

'He knew something. He was scared. He did not want me to look in the warehouse, to investigate further.'

'But you did,' she breathed. She let herself sink into the cushions. They were very comfortable. She had known that man was hiding something, even when Ramon had first introduced him. She guessed that the warehouse was very much his domain. Ramon probably rarely even went over there unannounced. She exhaled with relief. Which might mean that he knew nothing at all about that crate.

'I did.'

'And?'

'I found another crate not belonging to us. When I examined it, like you, I could identify the blue and gold of the peacock insignia.'

Eva's eyes widened. 'What was in it?' she whispered.

'I don't know yet. It was sealed. Eva . . .' He grabbed her hand. 'It was also addressed to your company.'

She stared at him. She was still finding it hard to believe. Ramon didn't seem to be involved. *Thank God* . . . But what about Jacqui? What about the Emporium? And what were the crates doing in Ramon's warehouse?

'Can I ask you? Do you trust them? If that crate has been sent by Li's . . . We know what sort of a company he runs.'

Did she trust the Emporium? Eva didn't want to be disloyal, and despite their differences she had never doubted Jacqui's integrity, but . . . 'I don't know.' Miserably, she shook her head. Thought back to her conversations with their two contacts here in Myanmar, her sense that she wasn't completely in the know about what was going on, their edginess, Leon's reaction when he knew she was about to check the packaging of the shipment in Yangon. Not so much a string of coincidences, more like a string of similarities. A knotted rope, each knot leading to another section of the whole, each section unravelling the truth.

Ramon poured tea into the delicate white cups and passed one to Eva. Unlike the first room which had been so spartan, this room was painted in creams and reds and seemed almost opulent by comparison. And there was a faint scent of smoky incense in the air.

'Did you challenge your warehouse manager about the crate you found?' Eva asked him. She sipped the green tea. She had begun to develop quite a taste for it and she needed its calming influence right now.

'Of course.' His eyes positively glittered.

'And what did he say?'

'He denied any knowledge of it at first.' Ramon shrugged. 'And then he crumpled. He begged me not to tell them that I had found out what he was doing, he pleaded with me not to open the crate and he said that he had no idea what was inside.'

Eva raised her eyebrows. 'How many crates had he shipped out for them under your name?' she asked. She knew that Ramon must have gone through the same thought process as she had yesterday when she found out. And no doubt he had come to a similar conclusion: that his company was being used as a front for something that must surely be dodgy and possibly even illegal. She pushed the thought of the Emporium away for now. Whatever was inside those crates, his company's stamp was on the outside. And yet looking at him now as he sipped his tea, he seemed remarkably calm.

'It has been going on for several months apparently,' he said. 'Wai Yan promised this would be the last one, if I let it go.'

'But you won't let it go?' She stared at him. How could he?

Slowly, Ramon shook his dark head. 'I cannot. But neither can I trust him. So I let him think that I would.'

'We need to find out what's in the crate,' Eva murmured.

'Yes.' He frowned. 'And I do not have much time in which to do it.'

Because the crate wouldn't be left in the warehouse for much longer. Eva put her cup back on the tray. 'But why did he do it?' she asked. 'Why did he go behind your back like that?' She'd got the impression that Ramon was highly respected by his workers. It seemed a very odd way to repay him.

Ramon's mouth was set in a hard line. 'It seems that he is being blackmailed,' he said. 'There has been . . .' He hesitated. 'An indiscretion. He mentioned his wife who he loves very much.' His gaze strayed to a point beyond her and then returned to settle on her face. 'This is the sort of nasty game these people play, Eva. Men like Khan Li prey on people's

403

weaknesses.' Abruptly, he got to his feet. 'And so we must, as you might say, play them at their own game.'

Eva watched him as he walked over to the other side of the room and picked up a canvas bag that was lying there.

'So what will you do?' she asked.

'I am still considering my next move.'

She repressed a sigh. She knew he wouldn't be rushed. 'And what was it you wanted to show me?'

With a flourish, Ramon produced a parcel from the bag. He unwrapped the green tissue paper. Held it up triumphantly.

'Maya's chinthe,' murmured Eva.

He brought it over, knelt and held it out to her.

She took it. With her forefinger she stroked its carved mane. 'Did she bring it back with her from Pyin Oo Lwin?'

'That,' Ramon said, 'is good.'

'What's good?' Eva looked deep into the ruby eyes which had now replaced the red glass. Maya must have had them put in straightaway. It was odd knowing that they were rare, ancient and extremely valuable Mogok rubies. And yet . . .

'That you think this is my grandmother's chinthe,' he said. He was looking very pleased with himself.

Eva stared at him. 'But it's not . . . ?'

'The other one? No, it is not.'

'So there's a third?' Eva was confused. It certainly looked just the same. Although perhaps . . . She examined the eyes more closely. They were different from the rubies she had seen at close hand, she realised. Not so deep, not so intense.

'It is a replica.' Ramon took it back from her. He scrutinised it critically, holding it this way and that. 'I made it.'

'You made it?' Eva couldn't conceal her surprise.

'Yes.' He was trying to look modest now, but failing miserably.

And he had good reason. The wood was beautifully polished and exquisitely carved in the old primitive style. It was the work of a skilled master craftsman. Eva frowned.

'So the rubies are not real rubies?' She peered at them again. They were very convincing.

'Clever fakes.' He held the chinthe up to the light. 'They would stand up to the rough scrutiny of most people, apart of course from the scrutiny of an expert.'

'And you have aged it well,' she added dryly.

He shrugged. 'Everyone who makes furniture knows how to make wood look old,' he said. 'It is as simple a process as staining or polishing.'

Eva conceded the point. 'It's very good,' she told him. She was beginning to see what his plan might be. And presumably, he'd been secretly working on the carving of this little chap in the room in the factory which he hadn't shown her on his grand tour.

'I did a lot of it from memory after our chinthe was stolen,' Ramon admitted. 'And then you came along, Eva.'

She smiled. 'And provided you with the real thing.'

'Just for the finishing touches,' he admitted. 'Your timing was impeccable.'

'And you plan to swap them?'

He nodded.

She considered this. 'But how could you hope to do that? You're the last person they'd trust to get within spitting distance of the chinthe, given the history.'

He sat down again beside her. 'I have no hope of carrying out the substitution myself,' he said. 'But I hope that one day I will find someone . . .' He tailed off.

They stared at one another. His green eyes were warm. His lips curved into a slow smile. And it came to Eva, slowly but surely. She had no argument with this man. She could trust him. Because they were on the same side.

'I always knew that we could not simply steal the chinthe back,' he said. He stretched out his long legs. 'They would know who was responsible, there might be dangerous repercussions for my family and the matter would not be resolved.'

'That's true, I suppose,' Eva agreed. 'But it took you an awfully long time to come up with another plan.'

'Not really. My grandmother did not tell me the story of Suu Kyi, Nanda Li and the chinthes. Not until after my mother died. She said she was trying to protect me.'

Eva was surprised. 'So you didn't even know who had stolen it?'

'I did not. I think she imagined me too headstrong. She was afraid of me getting hurt. She thought I would charge straight round there and accuse them.'

Eva chuckled. And he probably would have. 'So she didn't tell you until she thought you'd grown a bit more sensible, is that it?'

He bowed his head, but when he looked up his green eyes held a smile.

'And that's when you started hatching your plan to carry out a swap?' It made sense, up to a point.

'Exactly.' He held the little chinthe at arm's length away from them. 'First, I had to find someone very accomplished at producing copies of Mogok rubies.'

'Which you seem to have managed.'

He laughed. 'Through a contact of Khan Li's,' he told her.

'But isn't that taking a huge risk? Mightn't he have told Khan Li?'

'No chance of that. They had a big falling out a while ago.' He gave her a knowing look. 'Most people fall foul of the Lis sooner or later.'

Eva didn't doubt it. 'And besides that, won't Khan Li be experienced enough to recognise them as fakes?' she asked. 'He must have seen a few rubies in his time.'

'You may be right.' Ramon frowned. 'It depends where they keep it, of course, and on the light. How often he picks it up to admire his little treasure.'

Eva was silent as she imagined this. She could almost see the gloating expression on Khan Li's face and she guessed that Ramon could almost see it too.

'And by the time he does realise,' Ramon said, 'or has it pointed out to him. By then it will, I hope, be too late.'

Because, she assumed, the chinthes would be far away. Or the Lis would have no idea whom among their acquaintances had done the swap. Though naturally, they would guess. It could work, she supposed. She tapped him on the arm. 'But how will you carry out the substitution?'

'That I do not know – yet.' He seemed deep in thought, his brow furrowed. 'But I know Khan Li. He would want to show it off. He does not keep it hidden away. I have already discovered that the original ruby eyes have been replaced in position. And if it is not hidden away . . .' He let this hang in the air between them.

Then it is up for grabs, thought Eva.

Ramon glanced at his watch. He jumped to his feet. 'But now,' he said. 'It is time for lunch.' He held out his hand and Eva took it. He pulled her to her feet and for a moment he kept her hand clasped in his, looked at her, in that considering way he had. Was he thinking about what he should do next? For Eva it was simple. She must phone her grandfather. And then she must, somehow, find out what was in those crates.

CHAPTER 46

Lawrence came to with a start, her cool hand on his brow. *Maya? Helen?* But of course he had lost them both. He struggled to wake. It was hard to prise himself away from the hospital; it clung like the sharp smell of iodine to his senses. He was there on R and R after a bout of malaria in the jungle, had been picked up by one of their light aircraft – a Dakota – carrying out a drop, brought back to India by a cheerful American pilot working double shifts and still with a grin on his face, bless his socks.

'How are you feeling, Dad?'

Rosemary. 'Just tired,' Lawrence croaked. 'Bad night.'

Too much to think of on those deep dark nights, sleeping under the mosquito net, listening to the sounds of the nurses changing shifts, discussing their reports and who needed what treatment the following day. A far off whistle from a train. The snoring of men in the ward, their sleep heavy from drugs, their occasional moans of pain, their nightmares. They all had those. And the sweats. A fever that seemed to carry him off to god knows where. The delirium.

He heard the sweeper climb the stairs and walk past, drunk as usual, humming to himself, smelling of alcohol and *bidis*, those cheap Indian cigarettes. It seemed a lifetime since Lawrence had been in India, at the jungle training camp in Rawalpindi, nipping down to Cooper's for coffee and a cake.

'There now, it'll pass,' said the nurse with the kind smile.

And she was right. Lawrence had been one of the lucky ones.

He wrote to Helen while he was in hospital. He still had the birthday card she'd sent him, tucked in his pack. He reached for it now. It had a picture of a gate and a lantern on it. *Your gateway to happiness*, it said. It had seemed bloody ironic to Lawrence, even then. But she had tried her best. *Happy birthday, my darling,* she'd written in her neat sloping hand. She'd remembered. And the least he could do was write to her occasionally, she deserved that much.

'I hope this finds you well, Helen,' he wrote. And as he re-read the words he sent a silent thought to Maya. *My love, my love.* 'I'm recovering in hospital from malaria, and am better now. They say war is glorious . . .' He stopped. That, it could never be. What was glorious about men falling by the way-side with disease and fever? They called that queasy dip in your stomach the thrill of battle. Some thrill. 'But it isn't,' he wrote. Stark but true. 'How was your Christmas? I hope you got something good to eat.' The politeness of his own words to a woman he had grown up with, who was practically a sister, to whom he had once, so wrongly, made love, shocked him.

Christmas . . . In the jungle, Christmas Eve had been a rare rest day. They'd spent it hunting and one of the chaps had nabbed a forty-inch-long Burmese black squirrel. It was bloody good, and they'd disturbed a flock of pea fowl that almost tasted like turkey if you closed your eyes and crossed your fingers.

Lawrence hardly knew what else to say to her. He could tell of the men and the marching, the true conditions of war, but she would only worry. He could tell her of the politics. But he had never discussed politics with Helen and it seemed bloody pointless now. Leave the politics to them in charge, he thought grimly. *They'll do us.*

He was unable, however, to forget about what she called his promise. *You're mine now . . .* Would she hold him to it? Was it even a promise at all? This was war and all the normal rules of behaviour went out of the window. Or did they? Wasn't a commitment still a commitment, even if it were unspoken? His pen hovered over the paper. 'Give my love to Mother when you see her,' he wrote instead. His father was dead. Christ, so many were dead. He had received the news in a letter from home that had taken months to reach him. In truth, he felt that he had hardly known his father and perhaps this was why he found it hard to grieve; his mother had dominated his childhood and his life since, until Burma. 'I think of you both often.'

They wouldn't mind that it was short, if they ever got it. He could hardly imagine that they would get it. It seemed a miracle that a letter could travel so far in wartime when all around was in chaos and turmoil.

The nurse took his temperature. 'You'll be out of here soon,' she said cheerfully, shaking the thermometer.

'Can't wait,' he laughed. 'Back to the jungle, eh?' What a prospect.

He stretched out in the narrow bed. How often did they have to change the sheets here because of the malaria and the dengue fever? But . . . Ah. The feel of the sheets around him. The softness of the bed after the hard ground of the jungle terrain . . . Even in the midst of his delirium, it had felt like heaven. And soap. The sensation of clean skin, he'd almost forgotten how it felt. It might have been exciting to rough it in the early days; they were marching to war, to victory, it seemed. That camaraderie around a section brew up. There had been moments and friendships he'd cherished.

But now the marching seemed interminable and victory still a long way off. Forty-five minutes every hour tramping through the jungle, driving the mule, hoping he was sure-footed enough to help show you the way, fifteen minutes rest. Not that the mules got any rest, it wasn't worth unpacking them for such a short time, poor buggers.

Some of the lads got fed up and tried to slip bits and pieces of their own load on to the mules. But Lawrence wasn't having that. 'Shape up,' he'd said. 'There's a limit to what they'll carry.' And he wasn't going beyond it. Those animals worked hard for the men and they'd be treated right.

Two days before he'd gone down with the fever, he'd lost him, Gallop, his faithful and strongest mule who'd been with him all the way, the best leader they possessed.

Lawrence had named him. 'Hope he bloody doesn't,' one of the men had said, getting a laugh.

He hadn't galloped but he always knew where he was going. The mule needed to be shod, Lawrence knew this and he had some spare shoes ready in Gallop's pack. But they also needed to cross the river and soon. He didn't show he was worried: it didn't do to show you were worried, or they'd all be in a funk. Lack of confidence saps confidence: if you don't feel brave, just look brave, that was as good. Once they got to the other side they'd be safe – relatively – and there was a paddy dried out to grass where the animals could graze for an hour or two before being rubbed down and picketed for the night. He could see what looked like a mass of yellow flowers in the marshes too. But as they got closer, he saw that his eyes had been playing tricks again. And he saw them disappear, because they weren't flowers but frogs, noisy as hell, each one the size of a man's fist. If they could catch some they'd be good for tonight's meal, he reckoned.

Last time they'd crossed a river, Lawrence had swum across first, blown a whistle, which he'd blown at feeding time in training, and then the mules had crossed one by one in a wavering line, Gallop leading the way, each driver holding on to a mule's tail. But this was the Irrawaddy, swift, muddy and cold. This time the river was deeper and wider, and Lawrence knew it well. He thought of all the times he'd used its power to transport the timber from upcountry down to Rangoon and he thought of the time he'd been stuck away from camp when the monsoon and the freak floods had hit. They'd never make it across here and they couldn't risk blowing whistles either, the enemy was too close.

They had a brief confab and decided. They'd use an eight-mule ferry, built in situ. Swiftly, they got to work. Lawrence's raft building experience from the logging came in useful, but this was something they'd also practised in training.

Soon, it was ready, and they began to cross, the ferry going back and forth. But Gallop was slow because of his leg, so he was one of the last and the sniper appeared from nowhere. The bullet came with a crack and with a yelp, he was down. Christ.

Jap. They were bloody effective in the jungle. How many times had they left gaps for the British troops to go through before closing the box? It was their military calling card, you might say, bloody devious too. But rumour had it they were using up their ammo and food. Meantime, British and American pilots were flying double hours to provide supplies for their men. They'd caught Jap off balance, it was said. Used observation patrols to go out and discover his concentration points, to break up attacks before they were launched. They were getting him out into the open and they were winning. But when would it end?

Now, Lawrence felt the tears wet on his face. He'd cried then too, cried for that mule who'd worked so hard on the march, plodding on, never kicking, never complaining. That animal could see a trail where a man could see bugger all. He was intelligent too. Mules could be stubborn but they were bloody strong. Gallop had never liked elephants but apart from that nothing would faze him, he wasn't one of the skittish ones.

Yes, Lawrence had cried for Gallop. So bloody what? He'd done it in private though, emotion had no part in war. Men died, animals died and more would follow, that was the nature of war and there was nothing more to be said. You got yourself up, you ate, you marched, you went to sleep: you carried on. Some called it the British stiff upper lip, not so popular these days, of course. But without it . . . Lawrence didn't think they'd have got through.

Two days later, he got the fever. But the march would be going on without him and he knew he'd be back. Someone would take him.

'Don't cry, Dad,' she said. 'Please don't cry.'

He squeezed her hand. 'I'm sorry, love,' he said. He couldn't seem to stop himself returning to the place. Did she realise?

'Eva will tell you all about it when she comes back,' she soothed. 'I've made you some nice soup for lunch. If you eat it up, you'll be strong enough to listen.'

Strong enough to listen.

It was almost as if she knew.

'Will you tell me about it?' Rosemary asked him. She had brought him lunch on a tray and was sitting with him while he ate. Lawrence wasn't hungry, but he was having a few mouthfuls, just to keep her happy.

'About what, love?'

'Mandalay.' She leant to pull his dressing gown closer

round his shoulders. 'It sounds so romantic, doesn't it? Bet it wasn't like that during the war though?'

She was trying. He knew how hard she was trying. And it had certainly been a shock to Lawrence when his men finally reached Mandalay that day in April. 'It was in ruins when we got back there,' he said. Though for a moment he'd imagined the city was as it had always been. 'It was criminal really. We knew it would never recover its former glory.' It had broken his heart.

'The road to Mandalay,' Rosemary said. 'What happened when you got there?'

Over the past days, weeks, months, they had marched on their own particular road to Mandalay. The war in Europe was long over and yet still their war went on. 'The Japanese were fanatics,' he told her. 'They never knew when they were beaten, would never accept defeat.' Lawrence and the Gurkhas had passed so many of their dead bodies, the jungle and mangrove swamps were full of them. Men who would not be taken prisoner, who would rather die in the jaws of a marsh crocodile. Men who would not give up. Tough in training and brutal, even to their own.

'Was the war in Europe still going on?' Rosemary asked.

'No, love.' Lawrence pushed his bowl away. Not that a little thing like that mattered to the Japanese.

He remembered VE day.

'We were in the jungle when we heard,' he told her. 'I'm not sure exactly where, but I bet you I could still find the co-ordinates on a map.' It was about 5 a.m. 'There was a signaller up a tree with an aerial wire picking up the BBC News no less, being relayed through All India Radio, Delhi.'

Rosemary smiled. 'Incredible.'

It was. All of a sudden the man let out a whoop.

'Jesus, soldier!' Lawrence was about to tear him off a strip but he didn't have a chance.

'The bloody war's over,' the signalman yelled down to them. 'We've done it. It's only bloody over.'

And then they were all whooping, even Lawrence, and the men went wild, shooting off their rifles towards the direction of the enemy, at random really. Rifles, Brens, mortars, the air was thick with the sound and smoke of gunfire.

Lawrence let it go on for a minute before he realised. 'Hold up!' he yelled. 'Enough!' They might have won the war in Europe, but this war was still going and they needed the ammo for more important targets.

Even so. It gave them hope and they marched bloody hard that day. They were winning this war too. The welcome drone of the big Dakotas circling in was becoming more frequent, the sight of those planes glittering in the sun as they banked and unleashed their canvas bundles of rations and ammunition into the drop zone, to hit the ground with a resounding thud, bouncing and careering over the paddy field, a few more delicate items fluttering down with the aid of small white parachutes billowing in the breeze. Confidence was returning. They might be weary and mere shadows of their former selves. But the enemy was on the run.

'And then you reached Mandalay.' Rosemary took the tray

from the bed. She sat down again and held his hand. 'At last. You got back there.'

'The outskirts of the city were easy to occupy,' he said. 'But Mandalay Hill was built up with brick and concrete buildings and honeycombed by tunnels and passages like you wouldn't believe.' He took a thin and rasping breath. His lungs seemed so weak these days. 'The area outside was open with no cover and the town was surrounded by a moat.' How big was the enemy's force in the city? They had little idea.

'So what did you do?' She was a quiet listener. She didn't listen like Eva did, wide-eyed and wondering. She listened calmly; she was taking it all in, as if she wanted to absorb his history.

'I took a few men and climbed up the city walls by ladder at dusk.'

'Dad!'

'I was careful. We did a quick recce of the straight grid of the main streets. Then we saw what had happened.'

'What was it?'

'The Japanese had left.' He patted her hand. 'They'd deserted Mandalay. In secret.' But much of the fort was already in ruins; the palace was half-destroyed by artillery fire and the old pavilions had been razed to the ground. The railway station was no more than a charred shell, the lines trailed with the mangled remains of coaches and engines. The streets that had once been full of Burmese people going about their business, market traders, bullock carts, saffron-robed monks begging for food and alms were almost deserted and the shops were empty too. Or bombed.

But despite the devastation, Lawrence had felt something leap inside him. Was it possible? No. She wouldn't be here. She couldn't possibly be here, not after so long. She wouldn't have stayed through it all, she must have set out like so many others for India. She could be a pilgrim, she could be a refugee, she could be dead. Nevertheless, he looked for her everywhere he went.

Some Burmese had remained in the city. And where did their loyalties now lie? It was a complex situation, Lawrence was aware. Some of them had given allegiance when it was demanded, whether to British or Japanese, it hardly mattered; they simply wanted to survive. Others had remained loyal to their British *thakins* whom they had served for perhaps as long as three generations and whom, Lawrence liked to think, had been fair masters. The hill tribes especially and those living in remote villages near the jungle had helped the Chindits and others hide from the Japanese, given them food and even guided them so that they could accomplish their missions of attacking the enemy routes of communication. Some, indeed, had died for it.

Then again he knew what Maya's father had believed, that Burma had a right to be independent, that the Japanese effort could justifiably claim Burmese support if it were to rid them of the yoke of imperialism. Perhaps Maya now thought the same. Perhaps she had even nursed Lawrence's enemy at one of the hospitals the Japanese had set up. Perhaps she'd been forced to. He'd heard that some women had been shot rather than allowed to nurse a British soldier. But he wouldn't think of that now.

Of course, things hadn't gone quite the way the new Burmese Independent Army and their supporters had expected. Anybody could see that the Burmese government installed by the Japanese were mere puppets and that the country had exchanged one master for another. Worse, this was a more brutal master, so much so that many Burmese had reverted to their previous loyalties, taking the side of the British once again, helping them finally expel the Japanese from Burmese soil.

Some of those who had stayed had been employed by the Japanese, as stenographers in their civilian offices running trades such as *saki* and ice-cream making. Lawrence talked to a few people. They'd been treated fairly, they said. The pay was low but had been supplemented by luxuries such as soap. The worst thing by far had been the surprise police raids. Always they were looking for hidden documents and for spies. Had that happened to Maya, Lawrence wondered.

He asked after her. But even those who knew her didn't know where she had gone.

And they couldn't hang around. Once Mandalay was taken, it was a race to retake Rangoon before the monsoons started up again. They couldn't give the Japanese the chance to re-group, they needed to keep up the impetus with the full force of aircraft, trucks and infantry, not risk getting stuck in a swamp in the middle of nowhere with the mozzies and the leeches and no help to hand. So . . . 300 miles, one road and the Japanese on either side. Afterwards, they called it the mopping up of Southern Burma. They knew they were beaten, but the enemy didn't recognise the word surrender.

And we made it.

'Are you tired, Dad?' she asked him. 'How about a little nap?'

'Good idea, love.' He could hardly keep his eyes open. He'd get up later. No harm done. Because that was just about the end of it. The war, his war, was over.

Lawrence returned to Mandalay as soon as he was able, though the post-war demobbing took longer than he'd expected. He hadn't weighed much more than seven stone when the war ended, but he was getting stronger with every day. He was released from military service and now he could return to his previous employer. Or could he? What was he looking for? Maya? His future?

Two letters had arrived for him c/o the company. One was from Helen.

She couldn't wait to see him, she wrote. *When will you be back?* She would count the days, she promised. *Every day I think of you. Every night I relive the last time we were together . . .* Lawrence threw the letter to one side. She wanted to remember. He longed to forget. *Coward.* He had been through this war and never thought himself that, and yet that was what he was.

How had things changed so little? How come everything – after this war – was exactly the bloody same? He might not wish to remember, but he had made a commitment to her, and wasn't he supposed to be a man of honour?

Lawrence paced to the other side of the dusty wooden verandah. Had he put down roots here in Burma or had he not? Did he want to return to Dorset? Or could he see himself permanently living here? He looked out over the hot and dusty ground. He was staying with a family he had befriended when he first returned to Mandalay. They had not known Maya and her father, but they were sympathetic to his cause and he had confided in them in part about her. And as for returning to his previous employer . . . Things were different now, he learned. The company Lawrence had worked for were finished, at least as far as logging in Burma was concerned. There was talk about re-establishment in the forests of Tanganyika and British Guiana, but it wouldn't be for him. One thing he knew, his work with timber was over. But was his life here over too?

It was dusk and nothing more could be achieved today. He should eat, try to relax, leave his decision till the morning. But . . . *A man of honour.* Did a man of honour leave the woman he loved and let himself be seduced by another, a woman who trusted him, whom he thought of more like a sister, for God's sake? Did a man of honour then marry that woman, a woman he did not love?

'*When you are home,*' Helen had written. '*Then our life together will truly begin.*'

Truly. Truly, it filled him with dread. She had not said how she felt about her father dying, she did not really say what she felt about him. But she had waited for six long years. He owed her.

Even so, today, like every other day, Lawrence walked the streets and looked for Maya. Every day more refugees were returning. And what would he do if she came? He could not answer that question.

The second letter was from his mother.

'How I have survived this terrible war, I shall never know,' she wrote. And Lawrence had to smile, for he could hear her voice saying it. 'But I have and now you must come home.'

Lawrence sighed. Typical black and white. Typical Mother.

'We need you. The company needs you to rescue it.'

She seemed to have considerable expectations of his skills. How would he rescue the family firm? Lawrence knew nothing about stock broking. He had never cared to know.

And then came the emotional twist she'd always been so good at. 'You owe it to your father to do this. He and Helen's father spent their whole lives working for the company's success.'

Which was true. But did that mean the son had to follow the father? What about the son's pathway? The son's destiny? Could he not choose his own?

'I need you,' she wrote. 'I need to see my son again, to see with my own eyes that he is alive and well, before I can believe it.' On the other hand, how could Lawrence deny her that? It had been seven years.

'And Helen needs you too. You made a commitment to that girl, Lawrence. I know it. Her father is dead now and you must take his place and look after her. It's the right thing to do. If you do not return, her heart will be broken.'

Because of course, his mother knew. Lawrence had never been able to hide anything from her. She had known about Maya, or at least that there was someone, on his last leave before the war. She knew her son. She always had, and that was why she had first let him go.

Days went by and Maya did not come. He delayed his return. Weeks passed and still he stayed. He asked after her and her father; no one knew where they were or what had happened to them. So many had got to India and might never return. So many had died in the trying.

He went to the house in Maymyo. It was a depressing visit. The house was still there, but shut up. Perhaps it had been requisitioned during the war, perhaps others had lived there, Lawrence had no idea and no one seemed able or willing to help him. Or perhaps there was no information to pass on. Much of the town had disappeared though, destroyed by bombs, and only a skeleton community remained. How long would it take them to recover, Lawrence wondered. To restore even half of the town's lush beauty and architectural grandeur? Nature would recover in time, but most of those buildings were lost and now would be lost forever.

He stayed for three days at Pine Rise, his old place of refuge, which had also survived the bombings, bar some damage to one side of the house and shattered windows and doors. And he remembered that last time he'd been there in March 1942, just before he was called up for action. He remembered a perfect day with Maya when she had given him the gift of the little chinthe, he remembered the photograph that one of the lads had taken. He remembered that last evening in the club, it was crowded because you could still get whisky there, when you couldn't in the shops. It was rationed though, they filled a glass barrel early every evening to limit the supply. Otherwise you'd hardly know there was a war on: there was still dancing at the club and even strawberries and cream for tea. And he remembered saying goodbye to the woman he loved.

But now he could stay no longer. If Maya were still alive and still in Burma, she would have come to Maymyo if not to Mandalay as they had agreed. He had to face it. He had lost her. And perhaps it was for the best.

Lawrence booked his passage. Another three weeks passed and still she had not returned to Mandalay. He tucked the little chinthe in his travelling bag. He'd keep a part of her though. He'd always keep a part of her.

He wrote to his mother and he wrote to Helen. He had no choice.

'I'm coming home.'

CHAPTER 47

They had lunch with Cho Suu Kyi, a clear soup with herbs and leaves followed by *Pa Zun Thoke*, salad with prawns. Maya was resting, Suu told them.

Eva made the most of her time with her, encouraging Suu to talk about her childhood and her life in Myanmar. Maya was linked to her grandfather by their love. But Cho Suu Kyi was actually related to Eva. She was her Auntie, well, half-Auntie, if such a thing existed.

She was just a baby and so did not remember the war, she said, though her mother had told her some stories. 'But after the war, I was happy.' Her expression was serene. 'Before my mother's marriage, we lived with my grandfather.' And it was clear that this arrangement had suited everyone. The family were not as well off as they had been before the war, but Maya's father had resumed his business interests as a broker in the rice industry and Maya brought in some money by doing fine embroidery work, a skill she had developed before she even met Lawrence and which she was able to pick up again after the war. They managed well enough to keep both a modest house in Mandalay and retain the one in Maymyo, which Eva, and her grandfather before her, had visited.

'We have some pieces of my mother's work here in the house.' They had finished lunch and Cho Suu Kyi got up to show Eva a vibrant embroidered silk tapestry in silver, gold and red threaded silk on a background of black velvet, which had been framed and hung on the wall. It was of a golden temple with two silver chinthes guarding the gate, their eyes red as rubies. And it was the work of the same skilled needlewoman who had embroidered the dragon tapestry in Ramon's quarters, Eva realised.

'And there is the quilt. You must see the quilt.' Cho Suu Kyi went to fetch it. It was sewn from multi-coloured patchwork squares, each one having an image from Myanmar embroidered within: there was a ruby of course, a golden temple, an orchid and a chinthe, to name but a few.

Eva fingered the delicate material. 'It's very fine,' she said. And it must have taken a long time to finish. But she wasn't surprised. Maya's patience was etched on her face and Suu, her daughter, had the same look about her. Not for the first time, Eva wondered if it was their religion, their upbringing or their character that gave them such a sense of acceptance and peace. She thought of her own life back in the UK, of her grandfather, who was becoming so old and frail, and of the Emporium. Whatever was going on there, did she want to spend the rest of her working life following other people's rules? Or did she want to work for herself, find her own pathway? Eva thought of Sagaing and the enlightenment people sought by going there. She needed to recapture her dream, the dream that had inspired her to do her degree in the first place, the dream that was about the scent of teak wood and the history of past lives.

Suu nodded with enthusiasm. 'Even now, my mother works most days for an hour or two,' she said. 'She says that her work gives her purpose and pleasure. She would not like that to end.' She smiled. 'But she often asks one of the young ones to thread the needle.'

Eva smiled too. How different would Maya's life have been if she had remained with Eva's grandfather? She didn't know. She just couldn't imagine it. But the fact that Maya could still undertake such work was a testament to her health, as well as her ability. She was not the kind of woman who would ever give up. So why had she given up on Eva's grandfather? Or had he given up on her? Eva was determined to find out.

'And then my mother met Ramon's grandfather.' Cho Suu Kyi put a hand on Ramon's arm. 'And he made her happy, I know.'

Ramon's Burmese grandfather, Eva discovered, had a small but successful business managing a tobacco factory, and it was clear that he had been more than willing to take on Cho Suu Kyi as his own.

Eva couldn't help thinking that perhaps Maya had enjoyed a more fulfilled personal life than her grandfather had had in England. He had never said a word against her grandmother to Eva, but there had always seemed to be something missing. Maya might have married primarily for the security of herself and her daughter, but she had married a good man and it had clearly developed into a rewarding kind of love. Eva was glad. And she was sure that her grandfather would be glad too.

'And they had a daughter,' Suu continued. 'Ramon's mother.' One of the younger girls had brought tea and now she poured the stream of green-gold liquid into the tiny porcelain cups with no handles.

'Who met and fell in love with a furniture maker from Devon.' Eva smiled. 'Thank you, Suu.' She took the cup that was passed to her.

'Exactly.' Ramon smiled too as he took up the story. 'My father's business did well in Burma. My family were able to build this house.' He sipped his own tea and looked at Eva across the rim of the tea cup. It was a disconcerting look. Perhaps, Eva thought, it was easier to know what you wanted to do in life when you were following in the footsteps of your mother or your father.

She looked at the smiling face of the woman sitting across from her. 'But you never married, Suu?' She hoped it wasn't too personal a question.

'No.' She looked down. 'I became a teacher and I was content in my job until I retired. But I never met a man I wished to marry.'

Eva nodded as if she understood, but she wondered how difficult it might have been for an Anglo-Burmese woman back in the early sixties. The streets of Myanmar were full of mixed races – she'd noticed this from the first – but back in the fifties when Cho Suu Kyi was growing up, it might not have been so easy. And how had Suu felt about the man who had unknowingly abandoned her, Eva's grandfather?

'Will you tell him about me?' Cho Suu Kyi asked, as if she had read her mind. She offered more tea.

'Of course.' Eva nodded and pushed her cup a little closer. He had a right to know. She was planning to phone him this afternoon. She didn't add that he had been ill, nor that she was worried about how her mother would take the news. But both these things were never far from her mind.

Suu glanced at her. 'But like my mother, he is very old now, I think?'

'He is.' Eva sighed. 'He would not be able to travel . . .' She tailed off. She didn't even know if Cho Suu Kyi wanted to see him, if she had forgiven him.

'Perhaps one day I can make a visit to England.' Suu looked down. 'If it is meant to be,' she said quietly.

If it is meant to be . . .

Eva took her hand. 'He'll be so happy to know about you,' she said.

Suu looked up, her eyes bright with tears. 'And he will forgive my mother for not telling him?' she asked.

'Oh, yes.' Eva was sure of that much. 'He'll understand. I'm sure he would forgive her anything. If he had known about you . . .' She squeezed her hand. 'He would have loved you.'

Suu nodded. She seemed to be hanging on Eva's every word.

'And if he could possibly come and see you, he would.'

She just hoped that she was getting the message across to this woman, who must still feel so abandoned.

'Thank you, Eva,' she said serenely.

Eva leaned closer towards her. 'He is a good man,' she assured her in a whisper. 'He would never have wanted to leave you.'

'I have been thinking,' Ramon said, on the way back to Eva's hotel.

He had been rather quiet at lunch, clearly still mulling it over. And yet he hadn't seemed in a hurry to get back to work this afternoon. Could that be because he wanted to spend more time with her? Eva thought of the look he'd given her earlier. 'About those crates?'

'Yes.' His eyes were fixed on the road ahead, his brown hands loose on the steering wheel.

Eva watched him, stapling the image into her mind, so that she could conjure it up whenever she wanted to in the future. She wasn't sure quite how she felt about him, but she certainly wasn't ready to forget him.

'It makes me very angry,' he said. 'That they have dared to use my name, my father's company, in this underhand way.' He glanced across at her as if considering how much he should say.

And for the first time Eva wondered, was he doubting *her* integrity? She couldn't blame him. After all, the crates were being sent to her company. 'I know,' she said. 'It's unforgiveable.' She hesitated. 'But what do you think is inside? Fake antiques?' It seemed the most obvious thing, given what she had seen in Li's showroom.

Ramon frowned and braked at the road junction. She could almost see his mind moving up a gear. 'Perhaps. But what sort of fake antiques can they be?'

He was echoing her own thoughts. 'Forged antiques can fetch a lot of money in Europe,' Eva pointed out. 'An ancient Buddha that once stood in the temple of Pashmina, you know the sort of thing.'

He laughed and indicated right by hooting and swinging the steering wheel around sharply. 'Pashmina is a shawl, Eva. Even I know that. But . . .'

'But?' She looked across at him. It sounded like a big 'but'. His features were concentrated, still on the problem rather than on the road, she guessed, though Ramon continued to weave the car in and out of lanes as deftly as ever.

'You are right, of course.' Now, Ramon turned left on to the road Eva always called the moat road, lined with trees and a walkway, the wide waters of the moat glinting in the after-noon sun on the other side of the railings. 'Perhaps that is all it is. And perhaps Li tries to implicate us because his family continue to hate my own. But still . . .' He let out a sigh, 'I would like to see.'

So would Eva. She would very much like to see. She had wanted to see inside those crates for a long time.

'And so . . .' Ramon pulled in to the kerb outside her hotel. 'There is only one possible thing to do.'

'Yes,' she breathed. And she knew what that was.

A group of men were squatting outside a shop doorway, playing *mah jong*. Beside them, a woman had set up a stall selling some sugary confection fried in oil. Eva could sniff it in the air. She was always tempted by the street food, and a couple of times she'd tried it, restricting herself to things that looked relatively safe and identifiable.

'Thanks for the lift.' She undid her seat belt. Earlier, he had asked her if she wanted to change hotels, or even come and stay at the house. There was plenty of room, he'd said, and Maya would be delighted, even though it was officially against the rules for a tourist to stay in a Burmese home. But Eva had turned down the offer. If she changed hotels, they'd soon find out where she was – if they were still following her. And if she went to stay at the house . . . Well, Ramon would be rather too close for comfort. She didn't want to get anyone into trouble. And why should she be driven underground? She wouldn't give them the satisfaction.

'Come.' Ramon got out of the car and went round to the passenger side. He opened the door. 'I will escort you to your room.'

'There's really no need,' she said.

But he wasn't taking no for an answer, so she followed him into the hotel, got her key from the desk and called for the lift.

'And how do you plan to find out what's inside the crate?' she whispered to him as they stood side by side. 'If your warehouse manager is always there keeping a watch on it?'

The lift arrived and they got in. 'He must go home some-time,' he said.

'And if the crate is sealed?'

He turned to face her. 'Anything that is sealed can be unsealed, Eva. Anything that is closed can be opened.'

For a moment, Eva wondered if he was even talking about the crates at all. Conscious of his proximity, she moved away, towards the far corner of the lift. She closed her eyes for a moment, breathing him in, it felt like. Even when he hadn't been at the factory, he smelt vaguely of freshly sawn timber and oily wood polish. 'When will you do it?' It was very melodramatic. But there was no going back, not now.

The lift was pinging its way up the floors. Finally it reached the seventh and the doors hissed open. 'It will have to be soon.' He strode out of the lift and she followed him. 'Tonight.'

'Of course.' If they left it any longer, the crate would be taken away for shipping. But her heart leapt. At last, things were happening.

She waited meekly while he inserted the key in the lock and flung the door open. He strode in, glanced in the bathroom, looked around the room, which, thanks to the chamber-maid, was pristine and tidy, and seemed satisfied that it was empty. 'I will go back to the factory,' he said. 'And when it gets dark—'

'Why when it gets dark?' She looked up at him. 'It's your factory. Why can't you just open up the crate in broad day-light?'

'No.' He frowned. 'It is better under the cover of darkness. Who knows who might be watching? Who knows who cannot be trusted?' He walked over to the window and surveyed the vista of downtown Mandalay, his arms folded. Not for the first time, Eva wondered what he really felt for this city and how much he wanted to stay.

'Take me with you.' She joined him at the window. 'I want to be there when you open up the crate. I want to see what's inside.'

'Impossible.' He glanced towards her and then away. 'It is far too dangerous. This is not work for—'

'A woman?' she challenged.

He shrugged. 'I will not put you in any more danger. That is all.'

Eva sighed. 'How can it be dangerous? It's your warehouse. All we have to do is slip in, open up the crate and take a quick look inside.'

His expression was inscrutable. He shook his head. 'Not "we", Eva. "I".'

'But I'm already involved.'

'No.'

'And you need my expertise. I can tell you—'

'No.'

She sighed. He was really very stubborn. 'Well, I'm coming anyway,' she said. 'I'll get a taxi as soon as you've gone. I'll stay there, out of sight, until it's dark.' She glanced across at him but there was no response. 'I'm going to be part of this, Ramon.'

Finally, he looked at her and she thought she saw the ghost of a smile turning the corners of his mouth. 'OK.'

'What?' She stared at him.

'I said OK. In England, it is different for women. I know that already. My father warned me.'

'Warned you?'

He raised both hands as if asking for mercy. 'No more arguments, please,' he said.

'No more arguments,' she agreed. After all, she was the one who had got them into this predicament. If she had only trusted him instead of rushing over to Li's . . . But it was hard to trust someone who was so secretive and who seemed to be living in the Dark Ages as far as women's liberation was concerned. He had an awful lot to learn.

'You will leave the hotel at sunset and not before,' he said. 'Walk two blocks before you get a taxi by the moat. Come straight to the warehouse door and I will let you in. Knock three times. Tell the driver not to wait. Can you do that?'

'Of course I can do that.' Eva bridled at his tone. He'd given in, but she knew he didn't like it.

Ramon moved towards her, his dark hair flopping over his forehead. She reached out, brushed it back gently with her fingers. It was almost an unconscious gesture. She held his gaze. But they both knew what it meant.

'So I will see you later, Eva.' He put his fingers on her mouth, then tilted her chin and brushed her lips with his. He still did not look away.

'See you later,' she whispered.

And she stood at the window while he went down in the lift and left the building. She stood there until he had got in the car and driven away. Until he was out of sight.

CHAPTER 48

'Eva? Is that you?' The phone line connection was fragile. Ironic, thought Rosemary. Something she would work on. 'How are you, darling?'

'Fine. Absolutely fine.' Eva sounded tired, but there was something else. A suppressed excitement.

'What's happened?' Rosemary glanced towards the open living room door. But he was sleeping. Sleeping or drifting. She'd left him with Mrs Briggs this morning, while she went out for a walk. She had to get some air, escape, just for an hour, and despite the chill wind she'd chosen to go to the golden sandstone cliff above Burton. She loved it there, it had been one of hers and Nick's special places. She tramped along the grassy cliff-top. The sheep were out grazing in the shorn November fields and she could see the grey church tower of the village beyond, the broad olive sweep of the ocean on the other side. *I'll come again tomorrow*, Mrs B had said. She seemed to know that while Rosemary didn't need her to cook or clean, she needed something else.

'You'll never believe it,' said Eva. 'How's Grandpa?'

Fading away, thought Rosemary. *Fading away before my very*

eyes. 'Not strong,' she said. 'Looking forward to seeing you, of course.'

'I don't know whether or not to tell him.' She heard Eva catch her breath. 'I don't want to give him too much of a shock. If he's not feeling strong, I mean.'

Tell him what? Rosemary sighed. 'You'd better tell me then.' She was her mother. 'Is it about Maya?'

'Oh.'

'He's told me about her.' Rosemary sat down on the piano stool her father kept by the phone table. She remembered her mother having it re-covered in this chintzy rose pattern over the old green velour. Funny, the things you remembered, the things you could visualise as if you'd seen them yesterday.

'How did that make you feel, Mother?' Eva asked. 'Are you alright?'

'Of course.' Rosemary spoke quickly, before she had a chance to consider. She ran her finger along the bevelled edge of the stool. 'It was a long time ago, Eva. It was well before he married your grandmother.' Though they both knew. Time had very little to do with it.

'Good.' Eva sounded decisive. 'But you'd better brace yourself, Ma.'

Brace herself? The thought of a plane journey filtered into her mind. *Get ready. Prepare.*

'For what?'

'Grandpa and Maya . . . Well, he didn't know, of course. She kept it a secret all these years.' Eva's voice held a note of wonder. And respect, Rosemary noted.

'Kept what a secret?' *Out with it, girl.*

'After Grandpa enlisted, Maya found out she was pregnant. She gave birth to their daughter during the war.'

Eva paused and the silence seemed to echo down the phone line. All of a sudden the connection was clear, uncluttered by all the things that didn't really matter.

'A daughter,' Rosemary said.

'Yes.' There was another beat of silence between them. 'Are you OK, Ma?'

Something fluttered inside her. Trepidation? Excitement? Disbelief? 'Yes.' She took a deep breath. 'I'm OK. Tell me.'

'Her name is Cho Suu Kyi. I met her yesterday. Maya introduced us. I had no idea either.'

'But how old is she? What's she like?' Again, Rosemary looked towards the door.

'She must be in her late sixties, I suppose. She's quiet and serene. Really quite lovely.'

A daughter, thought Rosemary. Maya and her father. So her father had two daughters. 'What does she look like?' she whispered. Or did she mean who? She couldn't imagine.

'Brown eyes. Dark hair. Greying. She has Burmese features. But the shape of her eyes is different. And actually . . .' She paused. 'She looks a bit like you.'

'Oh my gosh.' Rosemary blinked. She was still trying to take it in. Burma. His other pathway. Their parallel world.

Eva let out a low laugh. 'She was desperate to find out about you,' she said.

'Really?' Rosemary felt quite weak. Lucky she was sitting

down, she thought. 'What did you tell her?' *That your mother had left you when you were sixteen?*

'That you lived in Copenhagen. About Dad. About Alec.'

Goodness.

'You have a half-sister, Ma,' Eva said. 'Don't you think that's rather wonderful?'

'Well . . .' She wasn't sure what to think. But the surprising thing was, that 'wonderful' was in there somewhere. She'd always wanted a sister, she thought. And all these years . . .

'And Grandpa . . .'

'Heavens, yes.'

'Grandpa has another daughter.' Eva lowered her voice. 'A daughter living on the other side of the world.'

'Yes.'

'How do you think he'll take it?'

Rosemary frowned. 'He'll be pleased,' she said. 'Thrilled.' After all, Maya had been the love of his life and, much as she hadn't wanted to accept that, it was a fact and there was nothing she could do about it. She thought of Nick. You couldn't help who you fell in love with. This Cho Suu, who-ever she was, was a child born from love. Which had to be special.

'But he's missed out on all those years. He won't blame Maya will he, for not telling him?' Eva asked.

Oh, Eva, Eva, it was so long ago. And she didn't think her father was capable of blame, not now, when he was so frail. 'I'm sure he won't, darling,' she said. And there was some-thing ironic, Rosemary thought, in the fact that no sooner

441

had she found that bond with him, no sooner had she discovered her own father . . . That he should gain another
daughter.

'Will you tell him?' Eva asked. Suddenly, she sounded like
a child again. Rosemary thought of this daughter of hers,
who had been so irrepressible, so independent and who had
somehow grown up estranged from her. How she wanted
to get to know the real Eva, the Eva who probably still was
strong and independent, but who was vulnerable too.

'He should be told,' Rosemary murmured. 'Of course I'll
do it.'

'And as soon as possible.' Eva's voice was urgent now.
'That's why I phoned. I didn't want to leave it until I got back.
Just in case.'

In case it was too late, thought Rosemary. *Oh, my
heavens . . .*

'I'll tell him.' She straightened her shoulders. 'Don't worry,
darling. First chance I get.' *When I think he might understand
what I'm saying*, she meant.

'Good.' Eva sounded a little surprised. 'Thank you.' Rosemary guessed she'd been expecting the phone call to be much
harder than it was. And that's what she had done all these
years, she thought. She had made her daughter's life harder,
not easier. Not intentionally. She'd only been after damage
limitation, she'd done what she had to do. But nevertheless.
That's what she had to live with now.

'And everything else?' Rosemary forced a normality into
her tone that she didn't really feel. 'Is everything else alright?'

Eva exhaled loudly. 'There's a lot going on, to tell you the truth,' she said.

'With your work?'

There was a pause. 'I've got a suspicion that by the time I get back I won't have any work.'

'Why on earth not?' Rosemary felt a jolt of concern.

'It's a long story.' She sounded a little despondent. 'And it isn't over yet. But . . .'

'I worry about you being there on your own,' Rosemary said. The country was still such an unknown. And an awfully long way away.

'I'm not completely on my own.' There was a different note to her voice now.

'Oh?' Rosemary was intrigued.

'Maya and her husband had a daughter too. She married an Englishman who came over here in the sixties.'

'Quite a coincidence,' murmured Rosemary. Like mother, like daughter. So often, that seemed to be the way.

'And they had a son, Ramon.'

'Oh, yes?'

'He's been showing me round a bit. He's been very helpful, supportive.'

'Mmm?'

'He's really nice, Mother.'

Rosemary didn't have a problem reading between the lines. Eva was telling her that she had become somehow attached to Maya's grandson. *Oh, my Lord.* She didn't know whether to laugh or cry. But so long as someone was keeping an eye on her.

'I have to go now, Ma.'

'Take care, darling.' Half of Rosemary's mind was on her father. Could she make him understand? But the rest was with her daughter in Burma. 'Please take care.'

CHAPTER 49

Eva felt as if she'd side-stepped into a James Bond film as she slipped out of the hotel at sunset, walked a couple of blocks and crossed over to the wide and glimmering moat. The sun had dipped low behind the buildings and the sky was suffused with a deepening blush of red and grey. Another stunning sunset in Myanmar.

But Eva had other things to think about tonight. She was wearing close-fitting cotton jeans, sandals and a long-sleeved T-shirt to discourage mosquitoes. And she wanted to be able to run. She'd followed Ramon's instructions and had taken a circuitous route to the moat, dodging in and out of shop doorways, past the street sellers and market traders, whose stalls were piled high with crimson chillies, peanuts and pungent, colourful spices, swathes of fabrics in cottons and silk, patterned, embroidered, beaded. But she hadn't been tempted to stop and linger. She was on a mission and the adrenalin was rising high. She was pretty confident she hadn't been followed, but she couldn't be sure.

She waved down a taxi and gave the address of Ramon's factory, forgetting, as usual, to barter. By the time they arrived at the familiar building, dusk was drawing in. Eva got the taxi to drop her off by the main entrance and then walked quickly up the dusty track that led to the factory, forcing herself not to break into a run. She looked from left to right. There was not a sound to be heard, not even the faintest brush of the breeze through the thick clumps of bamboo and palm trees lining the track, and not a soul to be seen. And the building, as she'd expected, was in darkness.

She crossed the compound to the warehouse and knocked softly three times, trying not to think about what she would do if Ramon weren't there. There was no sign of his car, but then he'd hardly leave it at the front for anyone to see. She'd let the taxi go as he'd told her to. Her mobile didn't work in Myanmar and, anyway, she didn't know the numbers of any taxi-cabs. She thought she saw something – a bat? – flapping around near the roof. She shivered.

No one answered the door. Eva tried not to panic. She was miles away from anywhere and, with no streetlamps, it wouldn't be easy to walk back to civilisation either. Still . . . She thought briefly of the conversation she'd had with her mother earlier. A good conversation. She'd sounded so different.

She leant against the door. 'Ramon,' she whispered. She knocked again, three times.

As if by magic, the door creaked open at last. Thank God. She slipped through the opening.

'I thought I heard someone out there earlier,' Ramon said. He peered into the gloom. 'I was watching when you arrived, but there was nothing suspicious.'

'Good.' He shut the door behind her and Eva's eyes began to adjust to the light. Ramon was also dressed in jeans and a T-shirt and he was holding a large crowbar.

She gasped. He looked very menacing.

'It is to open the crate,' he hissed. 'Come on. It is through here.'

Eva followed him, stepping carefully past all the obstacles. The warehouse was strangely eerie in the near darkness, crates and packed furniture stranded here and there, the beam from Ramon's torch flashing briefly over them as they passed through. The scent of wood, newspaper and cardboard filled the air.

'Can't you switch the lights on?' Eva whispered. It was all very cloak and dagger.

'That is not a good idea, Eva. The lights could be seen from outside.'

He stopped, handed her the torch and when she shone it down, she saw a crate that had been separated from the rest. She directed the beam to the stamp of Handmade in Mandalay. And closer still . . . She could just make out the blue-and-gold peacock insignia half-hidden underneath.

'The dancing peacock was on our country's flag,' Ramon said sadly. 'And before that it was on King Mindon's silver coins. It is a disgrace for that company to abuse our heritage in this way.'

Eva couldn't agree more. But perhaps now was not the time. 'Let's get on with it,' she suggested.

'OK. Here we go.' Ramon lifted the crow bar and began to

lever the crate open while Eva continued to direct the beam. Breaking the seal was a simple enough matter. But the top of the crate was firmly fixed with nails and what looked like bits of old tin cans for reinforcement. Even so, Ramon worked quickly and in less than two minutes, he had prised off one of the planks of wood. Eva caught her breath.

'What was that?' He stopped. 'Did you hear something?'

She shook her head. 'It was probably the wind. Or bats.'

'Now we have it.' He eased open the crate. It was full of shredded paper. He dug his hand in and pulled out a package wrapped in newspaper. He looked up at Eva who was still standing, the torch-light directed at the crate. 'Yes?'

'Yes,' she breathed.

'Stop what you are doing, please.' The voice came from the other side of the warehouse.

The broad beam of a searchlight swept over them. Eva felt completely exposed. *What the . . . ?* Khan Li, was her first thought. But no, Khan Li wouldn't be speaking English for a start.

Ramon jumped up from where he'd been squatting by the crate. 'Who is there?' he demanded. 'You are trespassing. This is my property. Come out where we can see you.'

She heard the sound of footsteps coming closer. One pair of footsteps. One man.

'This crate. It is yours?' the man asked.

She knew that voice. There was a dryness to it that she recognised.

'That is my business,' Ramon growled.

'And mine too, I think,' the man replied.

With a click, the lights came on.

Eva stared at the man with his hand still on the switch. 'Klaus,' she breathed. What on earth was he doing here?

'You . . .' Ramon muttered a curse in Burmese under his breath. 'How did you get in?'

Klaus switched off the spotlight. 'Hello, Eva,' he said. 'Ramon. It was a simple matter to get in through the door. You must improve your security, I think.' His voice seemed to echo around the half-empty warehouse. 'And the crate . . .'

'It's not our crate,' Eva said. 'Otherwise, why would we have come here in the dead of night to break into it?' She didn't feel so scared anymore. This was Klaus, for heaven's sake.

But Ramon was glaring at him. 'This is my warehouse,' he said. 'What are you doing here? Why are you asking us all these questions?'

Klaus looked from one to the other of them. 'You say this is not your crate . . .' he began. 'May I ask you then, why you are so interested in it?'

'What is it to you?' Ramon was still bristling with anger. He took a step forwards, but Eva put a restraining hand on his arm.

'It's a long story,' she said. She was still trying to work out where Klaus fitted into all this.

'I am listening.' He folded his arms.

'Are you working for Khan Li? Is that it?' It was all she could think of. Klaus had admitted that he knew him.

'Most certainly, no.' Klaus reached into his jacket and flashed an identity card at them. 'I am part of a German investigation team,' he said.

'Police?' snapped Ramon.

He shook his head. 'We are professional, yes. And we work for a private individual. But now, we work alongside the Burmese custom authorities.'

Eva and Ramon exchanged a glance.

'So you're investigating Khan Li,' said Eva. She felt a wave of relief wash over her.

He raised an eyebrow and nodded.

'Then switch off the lights,' Ramon said. 'There may still be someone watching.'

'There is no one watching,' said Klaus. 'They have all left.'

Once again, Ramon muttered something uncomplimentary under his breath and Eva couldn't blame him.

Klaus turned to him. 'And you?' he asked.

'Me?'

'You are working for Khan Li, yes?'

Ramon swore again. He tore his hand through his hair.

'No, of course he isn't.' Eva had begun to grasp the situation.

Klaus looked disbelieving. 'Then why does the shipment go out from your factory?'

'I was not aware it did,' Ramon said. 'Until yesterday. My warehouse manager . . .' But he tailed off. Eva guessed that even after what the man had done, Ramon would make every effort not to get him into more trouble.

Klaus was still regarding him appraisingly. And of course it looked suspicious. Hadn't she thought the same thing herself? 'Have you been keeping watch on the factory?' she asked Klaus.

'I have.'

'Were you watching when I arrived?'

'Of course.'

Again, Ramon made a move towards him, and again Eva put a hand on his arm. 'To see what happens to these crates?' she asked.

'Exactly.' Klaus came closer, looked down at the crate. 'We have been following their progress,' he said. 'We have gathered the material and evidence we need. There are people who are very interested in what is happening here. Not only German people.' He nodded. 'Burmese too. Not everyone is corrupt.'

'Of course not everyone is corrupt,' Ramon said.

'And the man at the Shwedagon?' Eva asked. Had he given information to Klaus? He had certainly been paid for something.

'The man . . . ? Ah.' He nodded. 'You are very observant, Eva. And yes, he is a man who has been of some help in our investigations.'

How many more of them were involved? Eva could see it was a bigger enterprise than she'd ever suspected. 'Perhaps,' she suggested, 'we should all see exactly what's inside.'

Klaus frowned. 'I confess that I was not expecting this development,' he said. 'We do not wish to alert people too soon. It is a delicate matter. But when I saw that you two . . .'

Clearly, he remained unconvinced. She waited. It was blatantly obvious that she and Ramon were not involved in anything other than finding out what was going on.

'You must be tempted,' Eva said. The crate was already open.

With that, Klaus seemed to make up his mind. 'Why not?' He gestured to Ramon.

Ramon shrugged, but picked up the package wrapped in newspaper still on top of the crate.

They both watched as he uncovered a small wooden image of Buddha. There was nothing remarkable about it. It looked much the same to Eva as hundreds of others she'd seen at Li's, badly distressed and made of inferior wood, roughly carved, looking nothing like the antique it was presumably pretending to be.

Eva glanced at Klaus. 'How did your client get involved with all this?' she asked. Though she could guess. The questions she was trying to ignore were rather closer to home. Why would the Emporium be interested in this stuff? To what extent were they involved? And where did that leave her?

'All this?'

'Fake antiques.' It was, she had to admit, a disappointment.

Klaus raised an eyebrow. 'They have been exporting to Germany,' he told her. 'Many questions have been asked.' But his eyes were on the wooden Buddha in Ramon's hands. 'May I?'

Ramon handed it to Klaus, who turned it this way and

that, weighed it in one hand, shook it, examined it as if he were looking for something specific. 'Perhaps we must dig deeper,' he suggested.

Soon, they were surrounded by wooden Buddhas, elephants and chinthes scattered on the warehouse floor, all made of the same inferior wood with tacky coloured glass eyes. 'Should we keep going?' she asked.

'Yes, of course,' said Klaus. 'We keep going simply because most people would stop.'

She saw what he was getting at. But what was he hoping to find?

They reached the next layer and Eva unwrapped a small wooden tiger. It didn't look much different from the others. Apart from . . .

'Please, Eva?' Klaus was looking over her shoulder.

Eva handed it to him. 'Now it begins to make sense,' he said. He removed a handkerchief from his pocket, spat on it and rubbed.

All at once, Eva knew exactly what was going on. It was so obvious. So simple. It wasn't about fake antiques at all. This . . . This was what it was all about. The wooden tiger was of the same quality as the other pieces so as not to arouse suspicion from any custom officers who might be checking. But one thing was different. They had stolen the idea from the historic little chinthes.

Ramon squeezed Eva's hand. The wooden tiger had large, striking and quite perfect crimson eyes. Even in the artificial light from the bulb above, they glowed.

'Rubies?' Eva whispered.

'Rubies,' agreed Klaus. He whipped an eyeglass out of his shirt pocket and examined the tiger's eyes more closely. 'Just as I was expecting,' he said.

'You have a daughter. Another daughter.'

These words kept running in and out of his brain and Lawrence tried to make sense of them. Like a mountain stream, they tripped down from his consciousness, sometimes clear, sometimes picking up assorted debris on the way, winding and flowing towards the source. Only what was the source?

He sighed and tried to get more comfortable in the bed. So much of his life seemed to consist of this now, attempting to make sense of things that were happening, things that were being said to him. Sometimes he took it in. He always tried to take it in. Then he'd hear a voice whispering: 'Did he hear me? Do you think he heard me?'

And he'd want to shout: 'Yes, I heard you! You can talk to me. I can hear you.' But he couldn't. He couldn't shout. And although he had heard — he really had — already, he'd lost the sense of whatever it was that had been said. He tried to catch it, pull it back. He tried to prise the meaning out of it as if it were nothing more than a tin of sardines and he'd simply lost the key. He tried to grasp it. But it wasn't always possible. Not anymore.

Sometimes it stayed with him, for seconds, minutes, hours,

a day . . . Sometimes it vanished. Gone to gossamer, lightly floating away like a forgotten dream, like fairy dust. And just as bloody elusive.

'What's elusive? Dad, what's elusive?'

He must have said it out loud.

'Did you hear me? I was telling you about your daughter.'

'Rosie,' he croaked. She wasn't making any sense. 'You're my daughter. I've always loved you.' Tears were pricking at his eyelids, though whether this was due to frustration or what had happened with Rosemary, he couldn't say.

'Oh, Dad . . .'

He couldn't say either precisely what had happened with Rosemary or where he'd gone wrong. Though he knew he had. But he was sure that, very recently, he had understood and tried to put it right. That was all he could do now, try to put it right. And he had the feeling that she'd been trying too. He could also say, for certain, that he'd always loved her. And it'd be true.

He felt her cool hand on his brow. So sweet, so calming. It'd be true.

The past, now, that was another thing. It revealed itself to him every day and every night with such clarity. Those pictures in his head, flickering behind his eyelids, sleeping or waking, there was less difference now. Technicolour. Pure cinema.

He was young then and bold. He was with Maya, watching her at night time when the moon was hanging low like a cradle in the sky and the night was so clear you could count the stars, every one. She let down her hair and unwound the jasmine flowers from its dark sleek coils, their perfume filling the air with the sweetness of honey, the intoxicating richness of opium. She slipped off her blouse and untied her *longyi*. She let it shimmer down to her ankles as she took his hand and stepped out of it, into his arms. His arms. He'd been a lucky man.

'You have a daughter.'

The day before his ship was due to sail, Lawrence ran into an old neighbour of Maya's father, an Indian businessman. He could hardly believe his luck. But was it too late?

'Did they get to India?' he asked him. 'Did they survive? Do you know?' He had always felt that she was alive. It was almost as if he could feel her there, by his shoulder, whispering sweet words of support and love.

The man gave him rather a shifty look. 'They never went to India,' he said.

'Oh?' Lawrence's heart sank. Was she dead then? 'Do you have news?' he whispered. His legs felt weak as if they could no longer support him.

'Last I saw of them, they were living just north of Maymyo,' the man said.

In the heat, Lawrence could feel himself losing focus. 'How long ago?' he asked.

The man frowned. 'Just before it all ended,' he said.

Before it all ended . . . Lawrence knew what he meant. Less than six months ago then, Maya had been well and living with her father just miles from Maymyo. His first feeling was

457

one of relief. She was alive. It swept over him like a cooling shower, sheer joy. But . . . Why? Why hadn't she returned to Mandalay?

'Thanks,' he said gruffly and turned away.

His second thought was to cancel his passage, to travel back to Maymyo, go to the village and find her, have it out with her: why in God's name hadn't she come to meet him as they'd always planned? Wouldn't she want to see that he was still alive, if nothing else? His next thought was rather different. Clearly, she didn't want to. She no longer cared. The war could change people. He knew that better than most. And Maya? She wanted him to return to Britain. She had lost her love.

A sense of rejection and a burning anger, frustration, really, at the amount of time he had wasted here in Mandalay trying to find her when she was living tucked away just out of sight, took Lawrence on to the steamer and out of Burma on the ticket he had bought.

It was only on the long journey back to England staring into the depths of the endless churning ocean, that he had more time to reflect. Not turning up in Mandalay, not seeking him out to see that he was well and had survived the war, was completely out of character for the woman he loved. Even if her circumstances had changed, or her love had died, she would still have come to tell him. He remembered the chinthe, still in his pack. No. There was only one reason why she hadn't come, and that was because she hadn't trusted herself to come. He knew he was right. She had been trying to make it easy for him, he realised, thinking of what she had once said to him about promises. She had decided to let him go.

'You have a daughter.' The voice spoke again. Rosie.

'You're my daughter,' he whispered. Why couldn't she understand?

'Another daughter.' Her voice was more urgent now. 'Maya had your child. Many years ago. Her name is Cho Suu Kyi.'

Another child? Another daughter? Maya?

And a vision came to him of that same time just after the war when he'd left Rangoon and returned to Dorset. It hadn't happened, had it? But it could have. It was a vision of Maya, his baby daughter in her arms. And Maya was waving goodbye.

You have a daughter. Another daughter. These were the words that stayed with him, imprinted on his mind. He thought that now, he might remember those words forever.

CHAPTER 51

The following morning Klaus had arranged a rendezvous in a small backstreet café whose proprietor he knew and trusted and where they would have complete privacy. There were things they must discuss, Klaus had told them. It seemed that he had decided they didn't pose a threat to his investigation and that he could trust them. He needed their help too. He had asked Ramon to keep the crate in the factory for now, as it seemed the safest place, and they had repackaged and resealed it so that no one would suspect it had been tampered with. Within the next few days, he promised, everything would be resolved. He also guaranteed that the watch on the factory premises would continue.

Ramon had reluctantly agreed. As he said to Eva on the way back to her hotel, what else could they do? They had uncovered no more rubies, but they had to allow Klaus and his investigative team to follow the crate to its destination. And Eva knew only too well where that was. The Bristol Antiques Emporium. Her own company. It didn't bear thinking about.

'But how come Khan Li isn't still having the factory watched?' Eva asked Klaus after they'd ordered coffee from the female proprietor. It seemed unlikely that Li would let two of his precious rubies just sit in Ramon's warehouse without standing some sort of guard over them.

'I think I can explain that one.' Ramon leaned forwards. They were sitting at a round table on rickety chairs. In fact, the whole place was rickety and looked as if it could be blown down by the nearest ogre. But the floor was swept and the place seemed clean. 'According to my warehouse manager, nearly all the crates went out the day before yesterday. But that one was left behind. There was a small drama.' He smiled across at Eva. 'When Eva spotted one of the crates on the truck, and this provided an unintentional distraction. My manager decided that rather than tell Khan Li what had happened, he would keep quiet and simply send the final crate on later.'

Wai Yan wouldn't want to risk upsetting Li, Eva surmised. He wouldn't want to risk him carrying out that threat to tell his wife what he'd been up to. An indiscretion, Ramon had said. Eva wouldn't put it past Khan Li to have set a honey trap for the unsuspecting warehouse manager. And more fool him for walking into it.

'Following that distraction, it must have been easy to lose count of the crates being loaded into the truck,' Ramon continued. 'To assume they were all safely out and on their way and to cease the observation of the factory.'

'That must be it.' Klaus nodded.

He and Ramon seemed to have reached what Eva could only suppose was an uneasy truce. At least, to have accepted that they were both on the same side.

They paused in their conversation for a moment as the proprietor brought out three cups of milky coffee.

'For how long have you been watching my factory?' Ramon's eyes glittered, but his voice did not betray any emotion. Eva knew how hard it was for him to hear that his good name had been used in this way.

'For some weeks,' Klaus admitted. 'Our team has been watching their every move.' He shook his head. 'But I confess I did not expect the next move to be made by you, Eva.' He turned to her.

Eva shivered. She had been quite vulnerable there. It was a good thing that Klaus had turned out to be a friend and not an enemy.

'And you have still not explained to me how it is that you are involved,' he added.

Eva shrugged. 'It's a family affair.'

Klaus murmured something softly in German.

'What was that?' Eva asked.

'I said, perhaps not so much a family affair, as an affair of the heart.' He glanced knowingly at Ramon.

Eva flushed. But perhaps it was best that he thought that, for now.

'And you have suspected the Lis for some time?' Ramon asked, tactfully changing the subject. He took a sip of his coffee.

'Yes, we have. I am sure you know that Burmese rubies have been smuggled out illegally from your country for many years.'

'Of course.' Ramon nodded.

'At one time, ninety per cent of the entire trade was carried out illegally without regulation, now only fifteen per cent, I believe.'

'I did not know the figures were so high,' Ramon murmured. He glanced across at Eva. She too was somewhat taken aback.

'And naturally, the most precious and rare examples are much sought after in the German market.' Klaus pulled his coffee cup closer and eyed its milky depths with some suspicion.

'Are the ones in the tiger's eyes precious rubies?' Eva asked. They had certainly looked like it. Their colour was rich and full, almost blue-red, and they had a heat and a depth about them that reminded her of the rubies in the chinthe.

'I think they are Mogok rubies, yes,' Klaus said.

'How much are they worth?'

Eva wasn't fooled by the casual way in which Ramon put this question. The stones, after all, were still on his premises.

Klaus considered. 'It is hard to say without examining them more closely. But they are less than three carat, I am sure. Maybe thirty thousand US dollars each on the open market.'

Eva was stunned. She'd known they were lovely, but . . . She looked across at Ramon. He too seemed surprised, though less so. 'How do you know so much about rubies?' she asked Klaus.

'I have always had an interest in gemstones,' he said modestly. 'But for this case I have done much research. And . . .' He spread his hands. 'The more research I do, the more my interest, it grows.'

Eva nodded. 'And you can tell they are from Mogok just from the colour?' Mogok, Ramon had told her on the way back to her hotel in the car yesterday, was the city where most of the mining for Burmese rubies took place. They called it the Valley of Rubies. It was two hundred kilometres north of Mandalay, foreigners were rarely allowed in and the first rubies had been discovered there in the Stone Age. They had become more or less a royal monopoly, he had explained. All the best stones went to the crown, hence the Burmese chin-thes with the famous Mogok ruby eyes that had been given to Suu Kyi back in 1885.

'From the colour, yes.' Klaus's expression grew dreamy. Not only did he know his subject, but he really loved his rubies, thought Eva. 'But also from the lustre and the tone. The best rubies even change colour according to the time of day, the weather, the location. They are very hybrid, very complex. And if the stone is natural there may be an inclusion, a blade of a crystal, a delicate shimmer of light. We call this the silk. It is, you might say, nature's own fingerprint.'

'But why would your client object to receiving such a magnificent stone?' Ramon asked. 'I'm surprised he wants to put a stop to it at all.'

Eva could see what he meant. And all the time there was a market, there would be illegal exportation.

'This way there is no regulation and also no export tax

to be paid by the seller.' Klaus took a sip of his coffee. 'We do not know the provenance of the stones, maybe they have been stolen and are worth much less, of course. More importantly for us, not all the rubies have proved to be of the same quality. My client has been, he thinks, taken for a ride, as the English might say.'

Ah. Khan Li must have got greedy and seriously underestimated his client, Eva thought. But of course there could be no come back if the stones had been illegally exported in the first place. She drank some of her own milky coffee, which she had grown used to during her trip. In fact she found it quite comforting with all this talk about jewels and thieves.

'But this is a crime against my country.' Ramon sat up straighter. He frowned. 'It is us who should be pursuing them. Not you.'

'Yes, of course.' Klaus picked up a teaspoon and stirred his coffee thoughtfully. 'And I told you we were working together. Though we must tread carefully in that regard.'

Ramon nodded. Eva guessed they were referring once again to corrupt officials. Myanmar had lived for so long under the yoke of a repressive military regime, the kind of regime where corruption and greed could flourish. The people wanted 'The Lady' Aung San Suu Chi and her democracy party to come into power and introduce changes and reform. But Eva suspected that true democracy would be a long time coming.

The proprietor of the little café brought over a small plate of shortbread biscuits and left them on the table with a nod and a smile. She had placed a curtain over the door to discourage customers; in effect it was a secret meeting.

'My team will be taking care of the men at the other end, in Germany.' Klaus helped himself to a biscuit. 'You may be sure of that. But we did not want them simply to be replaced by new contacts. We needed to track down the source.'

'And not only in Germany.' Eva sighed. She had been through this in her head over and over since she'd first seen the crate addressed to the Emporium. She thought back to that moment. At first she couldn't accept it, despite the overwhelming evidence. Then she'd concluded that her own company was involved in something she despised: the buying and marketing of fake antiques, of forgeries. But it hadn't made sense, even then. Here she was in Myanmar meeting their contacts, examining Asian artefacts, authenticating goods on their behalf. Why bother if those contacts were corrupt? If those artefacts were forgeries? And besides, she knew what the Emporium sold. Genuine antiques; anything that wasn't authentic was weeded out at an early stage and sold off to a second-hand furniture dealer. They had ethics, they had integrity. Or so she'd always assumed. So what was going on?

She'd known something wasn't right, if only from what had happened since she'd been out here. The edginess of her two contacts, the back-tracking from Myint Maw, his attitude when she had questioned the provenance. But this . . . Finding the rubies had changed the picture entirely. This was big, this was something completely beyond her experience. Because the Emporium was involved in illegally importing rubies from Myanmar. And they were about to be found out.

'At least two of the crates were being sent to my own company in the UK,' she told Klaus. 'I can still hardly believe it, but . . .' She didn't need to say more.

Klaus nodded. 'We have contacts in the UK too,' he said. 'I am sorry, Eva, but I must confess that when we first met . . .' He sighed. 'I had been informed that you were in Yangon. We knew that you worked for the British company that was under investigation. But we did not know in what capacity.'

She stared at him. 'You mean you engineered our meeting?'

He spread his hands. 'I had no choice. But I liked you immediately. I was sure you were not involved, you can be certain of that. I even tried to warn you, if you remember.'

About Khan Li and Ramon, that was certainly true. 'And when you saw me going into the warehouse last night?'

He nodded. 'I assumed I had been mistaken at that point. I assumed you were involved after all and that my judgement, it was unsound. You were looking very guilty.'

Eva remembered the surreptitious knocking on the warehouse door. How she had slipped inside. The fact that they hadn't even put on the lights . . .

'I thought you an excellent actress,' Klaus said. 'Until I saw what the two of you were doing. As you pointed out, why would you be breaking into your own property? I knew then that you two were innocent, that you had stumbled on the truth.'

'But what should I do now?' Eva asked. She could hardly

go back to Bristol and pretend that everything was fine when her boss was about to get arrested for gem smuggling. She didn't even want to contact Jacqui by email. But she was still working for her, she had promised to keep in contact and in two days' time she was going to Bagan to examine more pieces that were for sale. She would have to do something.

Klaus frowned. 'Do you know who is responsible?'

'Not really.' She shook her head. Then she remembered how resistant Leon had been to her examining the packaging of that shipment. Jacqui had never really confirmed that, had she? She remembered Jacqui's questions and how she'd repeatedly told her to take care. She remembered the row between Jacqui and Leon too, before she left for Myanmar. Was it possible that Leon hadn't wanted her to come here at all? That he realised she might find out what was going on? 'But I have an idea,' she said. She told him what she knew.

'I will take it from there,' said Klaus. 'Do not worry. By the time you return . . .'

He didn't have to finish the sentence. By the time she returned, she would be looking for another job. Whether Jacqui Dryden had known what was going on or not, the Bristol Antiques Emporium would be finished. 'I'll have to resign,' she said.

'But not until you return to the UK, please, Eva,' said Klaus. 'We do not want to risk alerting them, not at this stage.'

'Very well.'

Ramon put his hand on hers, sending a signal of silent

sympathy. 'And what happens next?' he asked. 'To Khan Li, I mean?'

'I do not want to frighten him off too soon,' Klaus said. 'I have been trying to get close to the man.'

Eva shuddered. 'Why?'

Klaus spread a napkin on the table and pulled a pen from his shirt pocket. He made a drawing.

'A spider's web?' said Eva.

'Indeed.' Klaus drew the spider right at the centre. 'The more you can find out about him, the more easily you can capture him and his entire world. So you tantalise him. With a fly perhaps.' He drew a fly on the outside of the web. 'And out he comes to investigate. Out of his safety zone, you see? And then . . .'

'You move in for the kill?' suggested Ramon.

'Exactly.' Klaus screwed up the napkin and tossed it to one side. 'I posed as a buyer. I had to prove I had the necessary finances, I had to give evidence of my credentials, they were very thorough.'

'Yes, they would be.' Eva recalled her own rather pathetic attempt to do a similar thing.

'And how close did you get?' Eva could see where Ramon's thoughts were heading.

'What do you mean?'

'For example . . .' Ramon was unable to keep the excitement from his voice. 'Did Khan Li ever invite you to his house?'

'Yes, of course.'

Eva and Ramon exchanged a swift, conspiratorial glance. A rich buyer. How could Khan Li not want to show it off to him? But Klaus wouldn't help them, would he?

Ramon leaned forwards. 'Have you seen the chinthe?' he whispered.

'The . . . ? Ah.' Klaus tapped his nose. 'Yes, I know the piece you mean. It is a beautiful item. Very old, very rare stones. Pigeon-blood rubies as they are known, not after the blood of the bird, but the colour of the whites of their eyes. That piece is a master, an absolute master. And of course . . .'

Eva could see his mind working out the link, the resemblance to what they had found in the crate.

'Yes, they showed it to me.' Klaus finished his coffee and pushed his cup aside. 'That kind of man will always want to display what he owns to the rest of the world, I think.'

'I agree.' Ramon fell silent.

'It is only a pity,' Klaus said, 'that it is not part of a pair.'

Eva and Ramon exchanged another complicit glance.

'But of course it is not for sale,' said Klaus. 'It is far too fine. The price . . . We are talking a great deal of money here. It is part of your national heritage that piece, I think?'

'Did you wonder where they had obtained it from?' Eva asked, shooting a glance at Ramon. He shrugged and nodded.

'Yes, I did,' Klaus admitted. He looked from one to the other of them. 'But I did not want him to become suspicious of my motives. And so I did not ask.'

'It's part of the long story I mentioned last night,' Eva told him. 'It's the reason I got involved in the first place.'

Klaus sat back in his chair. 'As I said before, I am listening . . .'

'When I knew I was coming to Myanmar,' Eva began, 'I told my grandfather. He used to live here, you know. And he asked me to do something for him.' And between them, taking up the story when the other left off, Eva and Ramon related what had happened since the chinthes had first been given to Suu Kyi by Queen Supayalat at the time of the rout of the Royal Palace.

Klaus listened gravely, nodding from time to time. When Eva got to the bit about flying to Myanmar with the chinthe in her travel bag, he gaped at her in astonishment and then laughed so much he almost choked.

'It is so very interesting,' he said when they had finished. 'And naturally the pair – they should be together, as you say. But why are you telling me all this? How do you imagine I can help you?'

'Anyone who gets close enough to Khan Li to be shown that chinthe,' Eva said, leaning forwards, fixing Klaus with a gaze of entreaty, 'would be close enough to take it and return it to its rightful owner.'

Klaus laughed. 'Even if I could take it, Eva, and I might do it just to please you, you know'. He patted her hand. 'All hell would break loose. You would be in considerable danger. They might even stop you from leaving the country. And as for you . . .' He glanced at Ramon. 'Your family would never be safe.'

He was right, of course. The copy Ramon had made was of excellent quality. But was it good enough?

'You should tell the police.' Klaus addressed this to Ramon. 'You should perhaps have told them when the chinthe was originally stolen.'

Why hadn't they? Maya had insisted it was because she had no evidence of ever owning it, but Eva wondered. Had Khan Li or one of his associates got to one of Maya's household just as he had got to Ramon's warehouse manager? He had certainly found out somehow, where the chinthe was kept and that the family were not taking it with them to Maymyo.

'You know as I do, that would not work,' Ramon said. 'Men like Khan Li have too many contacts. And besides, we have no proof of ownership. It is our word against theirs.'

'Plus the fact that you now own the other chinthe once again,' Klaus said. 'But you are right about the police. They are idiots and usually in someone else's pay. What you need is a professional.'

'Like you,' said Eva.

Klaus shook his head. 'Do you not think they would notice their precious chinthe is missing?' He laughed. 'Though I would love to deprive them of it, for the personal satisfaction alone.'

Ramon pulled his bag towards him and took something out. Eva knew what it was. 'Can I trust you?' he asked Klaus.

'Of course.'

Ramon looked at Eva. They had gone so far. This might be their last chance. 'I think we can,' she said.

He nodded as if satisfied. 'I have a plan, Klaus,' he said. 'If you can go round there one more time before the family are exposed as the criminals they are . . .'

'Yes?' Klaus watched with interest. 'I think I can do that. They are waiting for me to make a decision about a certain gemstone I might buy.'

'Perfect. And when you go . . .' Ramon unwrapped the replica chinthe and handed it to Klaus. 'I want you to take this.'

He stared at it. 'But . . . ?'

Ramon leaned closer. 'It is not what you think,' he said. 'Please allow me to explain.'

CHAPTER 52

On today's walk round the lake at Mangerton Mill, Rosemary was on her mobile talking to Alec. It was almost, she thought, as if their previous conversation hadn't taken place. They skirted carefully around their danger zones, reverting to the politeness that had always served them well.

She had told him already about Eva's revelation. About Maya and that fact that she had a half-sister she'd never known about.

'That's amazing,' he said. 'How does that make you feel?'

Which was, she had to confess, getting a little bit close to that danger zone. 'Confused,' she admitted.

When she'd returned to Dorset less than two weeks ago, she had come because she needed to think about things, because she wanted to see her father, take stock. Rosemary looked around her at the smooth lake, the water ever so gently buffeted by the breeze, at the trees now a burnished copper and gold, the grass already cloaked with crumpled leaves. She'd never really admitted to herself why it was so necessary to come back here in order to think about these things and consider her future, but it was. Sixteen years ago she'd wanted nothing more than to escape from this landscape that held her so firmly in the painful grip of the past. But now . . . She seemed to need it in order to make sense of who she was, what she needed, what she had to do. Was it her roots? Her childhood? Her marriage to Nick? She didn't know. But while she'd been here, the vice-like grip of the landscape in which she'd grown up had relaxed into something that was still holding, but was now comforting too. A place where she felt grounded and complete. A sanctuary. She realised with a dip of panic that she didn't want to leave.

'And your father?' Alec asked. 'How did he take it?'

Rosemary couldn't help smiling. 'He was confused too. Actually, I'm not sure that he took it in, not properly. A couple of weeks ago he must have felt that he didn't have any daughters. And now he's got two.'

'He's still not quite himself then?'

'Not really.' Or perhaps he was himself. He was living far more securely in the past than the present, telling her long, rambling stories about his days in Burma, about Maya and the war, about his family, Rosemary's family, and his obligations. Perhaps he was more himself than he'd been for a long time.

'His mind's still wandering,' she said. 'But every so often he comes back to me and the here and now and he grips my hand – he's so strong still, it's astonishing – and I look into his eyes, Alec and . . .' She felt the tears welling again. They were never far from the surface these days.

'And?'

'And I know that somehow everything's alright between us again.'

475

'I'm glad,' he said. 'Really glad for you.'

It was hard to believe, Rosemary thought, that so much had happened since she'd left Copenhagen. But what about Alec? She surveyed the leaves on the path in front of her. It hadn't rained in the last couple of days and as she stepped forwards they crunched under her suede ankle boots. The scent of autumn, crisp and fungal, was in the air, the spiders' webs, spun between blackberry bushes, glittered in the weak sunshine. 'And what's been happening with you?' she asked.

'You mean, have I said "yes" to Seattle.'

Rosemary left the path and ventured on to the grass, still damp from the morning dew. The moisture began to seep on to the suede of her boots, darkening the tan. 'I suppose that I do.' Seattle, she thought.

'If I said "yes" to Seattle . . .' He paused. 'Would you come with me?'

That was a big question. But was it the right question? On the other side of the lake was a man with a toddler. They had a plastic remote-controlled boat and the man was stepping down into the reeds to launch it. Rosemary thought of her own child, Eva, and she thought of her father. He might not be with them very long; she knew in her heart that he was fading fast. But Eva . . . Alec was her husband. But, 'I can't leave her again,' she said.

There was a heartbeat of silence between them.

'She's a grown woman, Rosemary. She's not a child anymore.'

'I know that.' The child on the other side of the lake clapped delightedly and, together, father and son followed the progress of the boat as it chugged determinedly out into the centre of the lake.

'And you have your own life to lead.' He hesitated. 'We have our life. Don't we?'

'Yes.'

She heard him sigh.

'But I can't leave her again.'

There was a pause. 'I understand.' Nevertheless, she heard the impasse in his voice. And that was the thing with Alec. He always had understood. He had understood her grief over Nick and so he had never challenged it, never made her feel that it was time to move on. If he had forced her to confront it, she sometimes thought. If he hadn't simply accepted her for what she was . . . So, what? Was she now criticising him for being too compliant, too kind, too understanding? That was hardly fair. And yet only when someone really challenged you, could you discover where you stood.

The little boat was on her side of the lake now, heading for a tangle of rushes. There was a brief flurry of rudder and leaves, and then it choked and came to a standstill. On the other side of the lake there was a commotion and she heard the little boy begin to wail.

Gingerly, Rosemary stepped down on to the little beachy bit of the lake which had a damp sandy bottom and a few tiny pebbles. If she went a little further and reached out . . .

Her leather-gloved hand came into contact with the stern of the boat, she gave it a little push. And it was freed. She stepped back. Looked down at her boots. Ah, well. Over on the other side the man waved a thank-you and the little boy gave a whoop of delight. And the boat chugged on back to home straits.

'Rosemary?' said Alec.

'I'm still here.' She had gone with him to Copenhagen. She had lived the life he wanted to live, she had taken the escape route he offered her. 'What do you want, Alec?' she asked him. 'Do you want to move to Seattle?' It sounded large and alien. But Copenhagen had seemed that way at first.

'It's the way forward,' he said. 'As far as the job's concerned. And they won't wait forever.'

But was it the way forward for them? 'The job isn't everything,' she murmured. There was family too. A family she was only just beginning to rediscover. Alec could stay where he was. Why did everything have to change?

'Things always change,' Alec said softly.

Rosemary realised she must have spoken aloud.

'The job isn't everything, no, but things always change. If you're strong, you can accept change, go with it, benefit from it.'

If you're strong, you can follow your heart, she thought.

'If we're strong,' he said.

Rosemary realised what he was saying. This was the time when he was going to push her, when he was no longer going to be kind, compliant, understanding. 'So you have to do it?' she asked. 'You'll go to Seattle?'

'It's such an opportunity,' he said. 'What reason do I have to say "no"?'

CHAPTER 53

It was Eva's last night in Mandalay. During the day, she had gone to view the archaeological finds in the Cultural Museum and had visited the famous Angkor Chinthe, which was as impressive as she'd hoped. She had also finally met up with Klaus's contact in Mandalay, though there seemed little point. If the Emporium were finished, it would no longer need any contacts in Myanmar, whether dubious or not. But the man was pleasant, seemed honest enough and she kept his contact details. *You never know,* she thought.

The night before, Ramon had taken her to Mandalay Hill at sunset and to one of the famous puppet shows. And now, she was leaving on the river-boat for Bagan tomorrow, to fulfil the terms of her contract for the Emporium and to see the famous temples on the plain of Bagan before she flew back to Yangon and the international airport from there. And so . . . This would be her last evening with Ramon.

She had been invited to have dinner with Ramon, Maya and Cho Suu Kyi, but before this, Ramon picked her up in the car and drove her to Amarapura, once the capital of Myanmar, but now almost part of Mandalay's urban sprawl.

'Look.' He stopped the car.

In front of them a procession of ponies was approaching, decorated with red and gold garlands, wild flowers wound in their manes. On top of every pony sat a young boy in a crown and silk robes, holding flowers and strings of golden bells. An adult attendant walked alongside each one, holding a parasol over each boy's head. 'What's happening?' But even as she asked, Eva knew what this was. She had seen versions in the temples of Mandalay and Yangon. It was *shin pyu*, the Buddhist equivalent of a first communion. After this ceremony the boys would live for a time as *phongyis* with shaven heads and saffron robes, begging for alms and studying the Buddhist scriptures.

'Shall we?' Ramon was getting out of the car and Eva followed suit.

Behind the ponies came a lorry crowded with people. In the centre of the open truck a young girl was dancing. Ramon held Eva's arm. 'This is a *Nat Pwe*,' he murmured, his voice soft in her ear. 'A Burmese dance-drama to celebrate the occasion of the *shin pyu*.'

Eva watched, intrigued. The girl was about ten years old and wore a *longyi* and an embroidered blouse of shimmering red and gold. And she moved fast as a flame; leaping, arching, flexing, twirling, her palms stretched back towards her wrists, her tiny feet in red satin slippers flicking up the hem of her *longyi*. Her ebony hair swung up and out and around like a curtain of silk and the red and gold fabric moved with her, flashing in the early evening sun, a streak of arcing movement, a tongue of fire. The girl's face glowed and her eyes

481

were dense, lost in the drama of the dance. Until at last she paused, placed her palms together, head bowed and came to rest. It was enthralling.

They watched the small procession until it disappeared up the road behind them. 'Beautiful,' murmured Eva. She was glad that she had seen it, but the road seemed so quiet and empty now that the procession had gone. And she wondered if she would feel like that when she finally left this country. It had touched her grandfather with its magic and now, sixty-five years later, it had done the same to Eva.

They got back into the car. 'I am taking you to the famous U Bein Bridge,' Ramon told her, glancing across at her with a smile. 'The longest teak bridge in the world.'

Eva sat back, relaxed for once in his company. After all the drama of the last few days, it was good to be almost a real tourist for a change. Even though the shimmer of those rubies in the wooden tiger's eyes was never far from her mind. And whatever else they had done – and she was yet to discover the full extent of it – she knew that she couldn't forgive Jacqui and Leon for letting her come here, for putting her in such a potentially dangerous position and for allowing her to become involved.

'Who was U Bein?' she asked.

'The mayor of the time,' he said, accelerating smoothly. She knew they were close to the river now; in her heart she just felt it. 'He had it built with teak planking left over when the Royal Palace was moved to Mandalay.'

Everything, Eva thought, seemed to come back to the

Royal Palace sooner or later. It may have been moved and taken over and destroyed. But it still lived on. A bit like her grandfather's feelings for Maya, she couldn't help thinking.

And suddenly, there it was before them, the bridge stretched high over the wide river, the tall teak upright stilts reflected and glimmering in the surface of the Irrawaddy. The planking was strung loosely between the teak posts like a xylophone. More people were beginning to arrive, but at the moment there were just a few stragglers weaving across the bridge, and a group of monks, their saffron robes billowing gently in the breeze. It was quite a spectacle.

Ramon parked the car. 'Come,' he said.

And once again, she got out of the car and followed him.

At the bridge, they began to walk along the planking. Eva's steps were tentative at first; there were cracks in the wood and planks missing so you had to watch your footing. And the old wood had of course been repaired in places; with so many visitors, the work must be ongoing. It wasn't very wide and there wasn't much in the way of a handrail, the sides were mostly open. Eva stayed in the middle, trying to ignore the way the bridge undulated gently with the movement of people walking over it. It was a long way down to the River Irrawaddy.

'What do you think?' Ramon offered her his arm and she took it gratefully. He was dressed in a black *longyi* and shirt tonight, and he cut quite a dashing figure, his body moving with the gentle rhythm of the bridge, balanced and sure-footed.

'It's very special.' They paused and looked down into the rippling Irrawaddy, at the sampans helmed by men in conical bamboo hats, at the huge expanse of river and sky beyond. The clouds had built and the sun was sinking lower in the sky. Tomorrow, she would be on this river, Eva thought. Sailing towards Bagan.

'Have you heard from Klaus?' Eva asked Ramon. She had hoped that the matter of Maya's chinthes would have been resolved by now. Ramon had already told her that he'd had another meeting with Klaus in the back street café and that more information had changed hands. It looked as though Khan Li and his accomplices would be incarcerated for a long time once charges were brought, but Klaus was waiting, still gathering his final evidence. And once Khan Li was brought to justice, Eva had the feeling it might be even harder to get back the little chinthe. The family would close ranks. It would disappear, perhaps never to be seen again.

'Yes, I have heard from him.'

'And?'

'And he is having dinner with them tonight.'

Eva glanced across at him, at the inscrutable face she had become strangely accustomed to. They both knew what this meant. Ramon had given Klaus the replica chinthe. He would try to make the swap tonight. Eva shivered. The last supper, she thought. And it would be the same for her. Tomorrow, she'd be gone.

'You are cold?' He put a protective arm around her.

'No.' It was a warm evening with just a slight breeze.

But Eva was happy for him to leave his arm where it was. She wouldn't be enjoying the proximity of him for much longer.

There had been no further intimacy between them, no kisses, nothing to make her think that she meant anything more to him than a friend. And perhaps that was as it should be, because tomorrow she would be gone. And yet . . . With each day that passed, she seemed to grow closer to him.

They walked on in silence as the sun dipped lower and the trees on the little river islands became skeletal silhouettes. The sun was hazy now, half-hidden behind the clouds, sending a warm and gauzy glow on to the teak bridge and the water. Eva had experienced the sunset from the Shwedagon Pagoda in Yangon, from the road to Maymyo and, most spectacularly, two nights ago from the top of Mandalay Hill. But this, Ramon had promised her, would be the best. Saving the best for last, she thought.

'Will he tell us how he got on?' Eva asked. It would be wonderful to have some good news before she left, something she could tell her grandfather.

'I am sure he will,' said Ramon. 'If all goes well, there will be no further need for secrecy.'

Eva nodded. 'Good.' She was fortunate, she realised, that since her abortive attempt to lay a trap for Khan Li and since the ransacking of her hotel room, she had been left alone. Whatever happened now, it was up to Klaus. He had many more contacts, information and manpower at his disposal. But she liked to think that she had at least played a part.

She turned to Ramon. 'Who do you think found the first ruby in Mogok?'

He raised an eyebrow. 'They say it was an eagle.'

'An eagle?'

He smiled, warm and lazy. 'Long before the Buddha walked the earth, the north of Burma was inhabited only by wild animals and birds of prey,' he said.

'Yes?' And Eva moved in a little closer, their heads together as they walked along the rickety planking. How did he know she loved these sorts of stories?

'One day a huge, old eagle flew over the valley. On the hillside he saw a big piece of fresh red meat, bright and shining in the sun. He tried to swoop down to pick it up, but the meat was hard and he could not dig his talons into it. At last he understood: it was not meat at all, but a sacred stone, made of the fire and blood of the earth itself. The stone was the first ruby on earth and the valley was Mogok.'

'Is that true?' she asked him.

He shrugged. 'We do not question such stories,' he told her. 'We simply listen and we interpret.'

Another lesson to learn, thought Eva. The British had first colonised Burma, imagining that they could teach them so much, that they could bring progress in education, medicine, transport and material wealth. But as they imposed their will, their changes, their ways and their Imperial Rule on to these people . . . Had they ever stopped to think about what they could learn from the Burmese nation? Had they valued Burmese ways and Burmese culture – and not just for material gain? She thought that her grandfather had, she hoped that he had. He had, after all, fallen in love.

And what had she learnt? Eva thought of what Ramon had told her about Burmese culture and artefacts, the bitterness on his face as he had railed against those who had plundered Burmese wealth in the past and present. And she made a decision. She would not be responsible for taking any more Burmese artefacts away from the country, no matter how reliable the provenance. It was too easy to say that there would always be other antique dealers who would do the same. She was only responsible for own actions. She would go and see the temples, but, contract or no contract, she would not be buying anything for the Bristol Antiques Emporium in Bagan.

They stopped again, three quarters of the way across the bridge. The Irrawaddy had darkened now, the sky was suffused with red and indigo, the sun a ball of liquid fire sending a red torchlight streaming on to the water below. Despite the other people still on the bridge, there was a tranquillity about the setting that made Eva want to just stand there and absorb. She wanted to be able to remember this moment, this location, this exact and pure feeling, when she was far away. Ramon had been right. This was the best place to experience the Myanmar sunset. On the old teak bridge on the Irrawaddy river with this man by her side.

Ramon stroked Eva's hair from her face. 'This is an extraordinary place,' he whispered. 'Somewhere you might bring a lover.'

They were so close. Their arms and hips were touching, their faces only inches apart.

'You can bring them to the bridge to look down into the river,' he said.

Eva looked down. In places the water seemed deep and she couldn't see the bottom. In other parts, it was shallow and brackish with the little marshy islands that seemed to be used for duck farming. She watched the ducks waddling in a long line to form a group almost under the bridge.

'Or you can take them out in a boat,' he murmured, his voice hypnotic. 'It is the best view of the bridge, from the river.'

And she could see that this would be so. The U Bein was stark, rough and uneven. And yet the wooden bridge in its simplicity had blended into the natural landscape and become part of it, as it had indeed once been.

'And what about you?' Eva asked, stealing a glance across at him. All this talk about lovers, what exactly was he trying to tell her?

'Me?'

'What will you do?' When all this is over, she meant. When she had gone home.

He looked past her into the depths of the Irrawaddy. 'I will work at turning things around for my business,' he said. 'And I will continue pursuing my dream.'

His dream. The orange globe dipped towards the water, slowly sank into the horizon, washing the sky and the River Irrawaddy with its golden red flare.

His dream was to expand his family business, while keeping all its values intact. His dream was to travel, especially to the land of his father, and maybe even set up a business there in the UK. But dreams, well, they were just dreams, weren't they? You couldn't pin them down.

'But surely you must stay here and look after your grandmother,' Eva said. 'Won't she need you?' She knew that she was fishing.

He just turned to her. 'Perhaps,' he said.

Eva stared into the reddening sky. In a few weeks everything she had seen – every golden temple and saffron robed monk, every teak monastery, the *nat pwe*, even Myanmar itself, this river, this bridge, this man . . . Would those too all feel like a distant dream?

CHAPTER 54

For Eva's last supper, a feast of traditional Burmese food was served up by Cho Suu Kyi and Maya.

Ramon was quiet. Perhaps he, like Eva, was imagining Klaus, at dinner with Khan Li and his associates, maybe even at this precise moment performing the swap. He hadn't told them precisely how he intended to carry out the plan, but he had seemed quite confident.

'Leave it to the professionals,' he'd said as he'd left their clandestine meeting at the backstreet café. 'I assure you that I will do my very best.'

Under the table, Eva crossed her fingers. It was possible that tonight the two chinthes would be reunited and back with Maya where they belonged. If all went well . . .

'When you visit Bagan,' Maya was saying, as she forked more rice and fish curry with tomatoes on to Eva's plate. 'You must visit the Ananda Temple. It is a masterpiece of Mon architecture. There are four teak Buddhas there, each one facing a different direction. Two are originals.' She smiled, but Eva thought she was looking tired. 'It is my favourite temple in Bagan,' she added wistfully.

'And you must do a tour of the temples by horse and cart,' Cho Suu Kyi added. 'It is the only way.'

Eva looked across at Ramon. His eyes were sad. Was he remembering their visit to Inwa when they had taken a horse and cart together and visited the wooden monastery and the ruined temples? Or was he thinking of their imminent parting?

After dessert of fresh melon, papaya and a kind of sweet rice pudding, tea was poured according to the custom and they sat around chatting.

The knock at the door made Eva jump. Ramon glanced across at her, swiftly got to his feet and went to answer it. He returned with a package in a small box. 'For you, Grandmother.' He handed it to her, exchanged a complicit glance with Eva.

She wondered, could it be?

Eva watched Maya's face as she eased open the box.

'What is this?' she breathed. Slowly and carefully, she took it out. It was the other chinthe, the lost chinthe, the chinthe that was an exact twin of the one Eva had brought to Myanmar.

Eva beamed across at Ramon. 'He did it,' she whispered.

'Who did it?' Maya looked from one to the other of them. 'How can this be?'

'Never mind, Grandmother.' Ramon bent closer and murmured something softly to her in Burmese. 'Let us celebrate. A glass of our very best wine.'

'I will get it.' Cho Suu Kyi got to her feet. Eva knew that

491

although the women of the family kept to the Buddhist rule of no alcohol, they still kept wine in their house for Ramon and for visitors.

'I truly do not know what to say.' Maya was still staring at the chinthe. Her face was old and lined, but her eyes, in that moment, looked like a girl's. 'Can this really be him?' With her finger she stroked the carved mane, smoothed a fingertip over each of the magnificent ruby eyes. Even from where she sat, Eva could see their unmistakeable lustre and shine.

'It certainly can.' Ramon went to fetch the other chinthe from the shrine where he stood, now that the family had returned to Mandalay. He placed them side by side on the table.

'They are restored.' Maya's eyes filled with tears.

Eva and Ramon accepted a glass of sparkling white wine from Cho Suu Kyi and all four of them spent some time admiring the two rather extraordinary and special chinthes who, against the odds, had been reunited at last. Her grandfather would be so happy, thought Eva. If only he could be here now. It hadn't been easy and she'd needed a lot of help from Klaus and Ramon to succeed in her task. But they'd done it. She admired the rubies. They were quite breathtaking.

'Each ruby is perhaps twenty carat,' Ramon said casually.

'And they're from Mogok?' Eva asked. 'Pigeon-blood rubies?'

'Of course,' he said. 'They are from the Royal Jewel Box after all.' And his eyes gleamed.

'My grandmother told me that Queen Supayalat had an unrivalled collection of gems,' Maya added. 'As did the King.'

'Oh, yes.' Ramon laughed. 'Have you heard of the Nga Mauk ruby, Eva? It was named after the man who discovered it.'

She shook her head. 'No. What happened to it?'

'The story goes that at eighty carats, it was King Thibaw's prized jewel,' Ramon said. 'But it disappeared soon after the King and Queen's exile.'

'Who took it?' And Eva found herself wondering, first the chinthes and now this. How many other precious jewels had been looted from the palace or even lost and never returned?

'Opinion differs,' Ramon shrugged. 'Some say it was one of the Queen's maid-servants.' He smiled at his grandmother. 'Some say it was looted by one of the guards. And some . . .' He looked at Eva. 'Some say that it was stolen by the British colonel in charge of the exile and that it later turned up in Britain, in Queen Victoria's royal crown, no less.'

'Really?' Nothing would surprise Eva. Everyone seemed to have wanted something from the last Burmese King and Queen.

'The Nga Mauk is worth a small fortune,' said Ramon. 'And even these two little chinthes are—'

'Far too valuable for me to keep,' Maya said.

They all looked at her in surprise.

She nodded. 'They have not brought happiness, only bitterness and jealousy and parting.'

'Perhaps because of the manner in which they were first given,' suggested Ramon. 'It was a time of greed and betrayal.'

'You are right, Ramon.' She smiled. 'Through no fault of their own, they have caused pain. As it was in the original story. And so I have decided to give them on permanent loan to the National Museum,' she said. 'All the treasures of the Royal Palace – at least those that have been restored – are there. They will be safe and protected in its custody. And people may go to see them. They are an important part of our Burmese culture and heritage. It is where they belong.'

Ramon nodded. 'That is a good idea, Grandmother,' he said. And to Eva: 'Would your grandfather approve?'

'I think he would.' Eva smiled. 'But I also think you should write down the story of Suu Kyi and Queen Supayalat and the Chinthes with the Ruby Eyes. And I'll do an English version as well, if you like, before I leave. And then,' she said, 'everyone who sees them will know what really happened.'

Maya bowed her head. 'An excellent idea, Eva,' she said.

When the time came for Eva to leave, Ramon slipped out of the room for a moment, while she said goodnight and goodbye to Maya. It was surprisingly hard to leave this serene looking woman who had meant so much to her grandfather and still did. But she knew that Maya was tired and must rest. There had been a lot of excitement for one evening.

'I understand now,' Maya said, 'what was troubling Ramon. And I also understand how you have helped him.'

Eva blushed. 'Not really,' she said.

'And if there is ever anything you wish for . . .' She let the words hang.

'There is one more thing I'd like to know,' Eva admitted.

'Yes, Eva?'

'Why didn't you tell my grandfather about Cho Suu Kyi?' she asked. 'Why didn't you tell him that you – and he – had a child?'

CHAPTER 55

Why didn't she tell him that she had their child . . . ? It was a good question. Maya knew that both Eva and Lawrence deserved to hear the truth.

Upper Burma, 1944

Somehow – she hardly knew how – Maya remained with Annie at the hospital and they continued to nurse the sick, through the Japanese occupation and then the rest of the war. Maya could only hope that her aunt was safe, though she heard nothing. But she grew more and more worried over the whereabouts and health of her father. She had heard that some refugees were living in ramshackle huts made of palm leaves and bamboo in a small village near Maymyo, surviving from what they could forage, snare and grow, and she prayed that he was one of them and that he was safe. There was little freedom of movement, she could not go to him with a child to look after and she did not want to leave Annie. Together, they had managed to guard and protect Cho Suu Kyi from further Japanese curiosity and, in truth, Annie had been right: not all the soldiers were callous and cruel, others held them in some respect and it was this that kept them safe.

But one day she was given the chance to try and find him. There was a Japanese journalist with whom she and Annie had formed a good relationship after Annie had nursed him through a bout of malaria. He spoke fluent English, having been educated at mission schools in Japan and Canada and, more importantly, he was not one of those who believed in the Japanese conquest of the Far East. He was sympathetic and he was kind, even procuring rations of food for them when they were short. As a journalist, he enjoyed considerable freedom of movement. And he was on his way back to the headquarters for war correspondents, which was not far from Maymyo.

Before she left, there was something that Maya had to do. She returned to her aunt's old house and she dug up the little chinthe that she had buried there for safe-keeping near the red flowering *sein pan* tree. It took a while, she kept thinking that perhaps she was in the wrong place, but eventually she found it, still wrapped in the piece of fabric torn from her own dress in which she had buried it. The fabric was rotting and the dirt had got in but with a little polish from a rag, the chinthe's eyes gleamed as bright as they ever had. She could not leave without it. Who knew how long it would be before she could return? For now, she would take her chance and the chinthe would travel with her.

It took some persuading for Annie to join her. But everyone said it was becoming increasingly dangerous for a white woman to remain here in the village and since most of her patients no longer needed her and a Japanese hospital had been set up nearby, she finally agreed. Their Japanese friend provided them with the white armbands worn by reporters and settled them and Cho Suu Kyi on cushions in the back of the truck.

It was a long and uncomfortable journey along cratered and bumpy roads, but worst of all was the sight of so many refugees, some of them barely able to drag one foot after another, often diseased, all emaciated. And what were they heading for? Almost certain death, sooner or later. It nearly broke her heart.

It was July and unbearably hot in the truck. Maya's head was pounding, she felt dizzy and her eyes kept losing their focus. But every time she felt that she must surely pass out from the heat and the discomfort, Annie squeezed her hand and seemed to give her the strength to stay alert. And she must stay alert. Who knew when they might be stopped by the Japanese military or attacked by one of the gangs roaming the area? And she had her daughter to care for. At least they had some water, though Annie rationed it with care, ensuring that they all had enough to ease their sore throats and cracked lips.

The sight of Mandalay, when it came, almost finished her. The beautiful city was in ruins, almost totally devastated by bombings and explosions. The Palace of the Kings was full of Japanese soldiers. First British and then Japanese, she found herself thinking. Not since the time of her daughter's namesake had the palace belonged to Burma. The streets which had once been filled with noise and laughter, thronged with her people, with bullock carts, street sellers, craftsmen and monks in saffron robes begging for food and alms, were almost empty. There was an air of bleak desolation hanging over the city she had loved.

Maya was tempted to ask if they could drive to her old home, but she didn't dare. She wasn't sure she wanted to see it, because she knew what she would find. And they must press on to their destination. 'One day,' she breathed as they drove out of the city. 'One day I will return.'

After fourteen hours, they arrived at the village near Maymyo where they had decided to start their search. The refugees were living in ramshackle conditions, crowded, several families to a house, each of which had obviously been built from anything they could lay their hands that could provide shelter. And they were clearly starving. There was a sense of hopelessness in their dark eyes. They didn't know what to do and they didn't know where to go.

'Have you seen or heard of my father? His name is Sai Htee Saing.' Maya lost count of how many times she said these words.

Finally, a woman nodded. 'He was here,' she said. 'He moved on, to the next village, I think.'

Maya's heart soared. He was alive then! And off they went to the next village where conditions were only slightly better. More of the houses here had survived, but they had been abandoned, looted and were now housing families of refugees. 'Have you seen or heard of my father? His name is Sai Htee Saing.' The search went on.

'Does he play the piano?' an old woman asked her.

'Well, yes, but . . .' Maya was at a loss.

The woman pointed. 'The white bungalow at the end,' she said.

It was perhaps incongruous, considering his anti-British sympathies, that her father should be living in a colonial bungalow left by a British family who had simply locked the doors one day and left. But there he was.

Maya ran to him and at last in his arms she let herself weep. For he was thin and gaunt, but he was alive and she had found him.

'But who is this?' He was looking curiously at Annie, who was holding Cho Suu Kyi in her arms.

'This is my friend, Matron Annie,' said Maya.

'And her child?' her father added. 'How sweet she is.'

Cho Suu Kyi looked up at him and she beamed. It was clearly love at first sight.

Maya took her from Annie. 'My child,' she said. 'This is your granddaughter, Cho Suu Kyi.'

Maya and her father, Annie and Suu remained in the village until after the war ended. Annie's nursing skills soon came into play when people discovered her profession, and in turn this helped the little family to survive. Maya and Annie even took to using some of the old native remedies, taught to Maya by an old woman in the village, which meant foraging roots and herbs from the nearby jungle, some proving more effective than others. It wasn't easy, though, to get enough food.

The black market flourished, Japanese currency was almost worthless and they were increasingly dependent on gifts of eggs, rice or scrawny chickens from patients who often had nothing else left to give.

At first, Maya's father was wary of Annie. After all, she was British, and, having expected the Japanese to liberate the Burmese from British imperialism, here he was living with what must have seemed like one of the enemy. Only now though, was he realising that the second master of his beloved Burmese people was more cruel and much less forgiving than the first.

'But will her presence not inflame any Japanese soldiers who come into the village?' he asked Maya. 'We must put our own survival first, especially now that there is the little one to think of.'

Maya tried to persuade him that this wasn't the case, that in fact the Japanese had tended to treat Annie and Maya in exactly the same manner. 'And you have no idea, Father,' she added, 'how often Annie has put Suu and me first.'

What eventually changed his mind was Annie's generosity in treating anyone and everyone who needed her nursing skills, regardless of nationality or situation, and the way she had with Cho Suu Kyi, his granddaughter. That was what really made the difference, Maya thought.

And then news reached them that General Aung San, who had been made Commander-in-Chief of the Burmese National Independence Army, had changed allegiance, that he was no longer fighting with the Japanese and that he was supporting the British in driving back Japanese forces. He was not happy, it was said, with the Japanese treatment of Burmese soldiers, he had first responded to the Japanese in 1942 for the sake of Burmese independence, not to help Japan take control of his country. And had he also begun to doubt that Japan would win? Whatever the truth behind his decision, the British were gaining ground and the Japanese were staring defeat in the face.

'So be it,' Maya's father said, bowing his head.

Maya was aware that this news was another blow. They had received no word and believed her aunt, like so many others, had died as a refugee. And now this. Politically, her father had always supported the Nationalist Minority Group and General Aung San had certainly inspired some of his anti-British sympathies. 'Never mind, Father,' she said. 'It is for the best.'

'We will wait for Burmese independence,' he told her. 'That is all that matters. And it will come.'

And the end of the war would come, too. Rumours were rife that the British were advancing and would arrive soon. Let it be very soon, Maya prayed. Everyone was getting nervous, Burmese, British, Japanese alike. Air raids intensified as the British got closer and Maya began to worry that they might actually be killed, albeit accidentally, by their new liberators. But the air raids were concentrated on the railway, and their little village was spared. Soon Maya could almost smell it, the air of change. It was just a matter of time and once again, she started breathing his name with a new hope, that soon they would be reunited once more. *Lawrence . . .*

And then it really was over. A convoy of British and Ghurkhas arrived, a column of bullock-drawn carts led by two British officers on horseback. Maymyo had been taken and another force was heading for Mandalay. This convoy had broken away from the main platoon, travelling over little-known mountain tracks used by opium smugglers, catching the Japanese garrison to the east of their village unawares.

The people in the village were delirious with delight. 'We are free! We are free!'

Maya held her daughter close in her arms. And she prayed.

'Will you go back to Mandalay?' Maya's father asked her some weeks later. 'Will you try to find him? See if he is still alive?' It was the first time he had mentioned Lawrence since she and Annie had arrived here.

'I believe that he is,' she said. 'I feel it.' It was against the odds, she knew. But she did feel it, in her heart, and she was certain that the bond between them ran so deep that if he had perished, she would know. She looked up at the little decorative teak chinthe with the ruby eyes. Once again, he was guarding their Buddha in the shrine, once again he was on show, where he belonged. But what of his twin? Had he guarded Lawrence as well as she had hoped?

'It is unlikely.' Her father's expression was grave. 'And if he is still alive . . .'

'What, Father?'

He avoided her gaze. 'If he is still alive, he will have changed, my daughter,' he said. 'That is what war does. It changes everyone.'

Maya thought about this. Yes, he was right. War did change everyone. A man, or woman, could not witness a friend or comrade's pain and suffering, could not kill or maim, could not live in the conditions which Lawrence, as so many, must have lived, and not change. 'But that does not mean . . .' She faltered.

'That he no longer wants you? No, it does not mean that.' Her father reached out and patted her hand. 'Of course it does not mean that. Any man would want you.'

'And so how can what there is between us be wrong?' she asked. Her father had not said it was wrong. Indeed, he had never suggested it was wrong, even back in Mandalay before the war. 'Everyone has the right to do what she or he must do' had always been his watchword, the philosophy he lived by. He believed in individual independence as strongly as he believed in Burmese liberation.

'It is not wrong,' he said sadly. 'But you are from two different cultures, my daughter. Two different countries. And those countries have a relationship that has never been . . .' He hesitated. 'Equal.'

Maya digested this. She was aware, of course, that many British men had taken native Burmese women for their mistresses before the war. She and Lawrence had often discussed it. And she knew that those mistresses never dreamed that their lovers would stay with them, let alone marry them.

They were there to provide pleasure and comfort for their British masters who happened to be far from home. It was an accepted situation, by Burmese and British alike.

'But it is not like that for us,' Lawrence had told her, holding her close. 'For us, it is different, it is real. You know that, Maya, don't you?' And she had known it, she had told him she had known it. It disturbed her that her father hadn't known it too.

'It was not like that for us, Father,' she said, trying not to sound reproving. 'You know he loved me.'

'Yes, he loved you.' Her father left her side and wandered past the piano which had apparently been here when he moved in and which he still sometimes played, but not so often these days. He lightly ran his fingers over the keys, then walked slowly towards the window of the bungalow in which they still lived. Who would claim it now? Would someone simply return one day and tell them to go?

'Then why shouldn't we be together?' Maya asked.

He sighed. 'Because life and love is not just about two people whose worlds collide, my daughter,' he said. He stared out of the window, almost as if she were no longer in the room. 'It is about their backgrounds, their experiences, their cultures, too.' He tightened the knot of his *longyi* and straightened his back, as if he had come to a difficult decision. He turned to face her. 'It could never work between the two of you. For a short time, yes, your lives did collide. But now . . .'

Maya flinched. Was it over? Was it possible that Lawrence

no longer felt the same way about her? She too stared out of the window and into the distance, past the bright yellow flowers of the *ngu wah* tree in the garden outside, to the shacks and makeshift homesteads that had been built on the red earth by refugees. Her father had been lucky to find this place. He was still thin and gaunt and had a racking cough that worried her. But he was alive and now they were all safe at last.

She sighed. But was he right? Would their different cultures and backgrounds make it impossible for her and Lawrence to share a future? She could hear Annie at the other end of the bungalow talking to the baby in that sing-song way she had, her Scottish accent always able to sooth the child somehow. Was that all it had been between her and Lawrence? A collision?

'If it was just a collision,' she murmured. 'It was a very powerful one, Father.' Powerful enough to make her believe that they belonged, one to the other. She had always believed it, from the first moment they met. That belief had kept her strong throughout the war. At her lowest points, when she was in pain, terrified, or half-starving, at the time when she had killed a man, against everything she held dear, that belief had helped her through. 'I love him, Father,' she said. 'And I think that he will still love me.'

Her father turned from his stance by the window. 'If you love him enough, Maya,' he said, 'you will let him go.'

Maya let out a cry. 'I could not,' she whispered. She couldn't even think of it.

'It would be a sacrifice, yes.' Her father took a couple of

paces towards her. His dark eyes were fierce. 'But think not just of yourself,' he warned. 'Think of Lawrence. And think of his family too.'

'We are his family.' Maya was sobbing now. How could he be so cruel? 'Me and Cho Suu Kyi. We are his family.'

Her father came back to her side, cradled her in his arms as if she were a young girl again. 'You are Burmese,' he said. 'I am your family. But Lawrence has family back in England. Think of them. They have not even seen him for so many years.'

Maya could feel her tears wet on his shirt. Despite herself, she thought of Lawrence's mother. And then she thought of Helen.

'You told me there was someone else,' her father said. 'You can pull back the leg, but not the committed word.'

An old Burmese proverb. 'Yes.' She whispered the word. She had hardly dared think of her. Helen, whom Lawrence had been promised to. Helen, who was a white British woman and everything Maya was not. Helen, the woman everyone expected him to marry. And why not? Wasn't she from his world?

'Perhaps now that the war is over, if you are right and he has survived . . .' Her father let the words hang. 'You should allow him to return to her.'

Maya was silent. She had always told Lawrence that she wanted nothing from him, especially his promises. She looked up at the little chinthe standing in front of the shrine. But she had given him the other, to protect him from harm and return him to her arms. And she had believed they would be together.

Her father followed the direction of her gaze. He nodded. 'It takes a great deal of strength to turn your back on your past,' he said. 'On your family and your promises. On your country and your upbringing. To begin again in a strange land after you have lived through a war.'

'He could do it,' Maya shot back. She sat back on her heels. If Lawrence had lived through this war, he could do anything. And she would be by his side. She would help him.

'Yes, he could do it,' her father agreed. 'But would he thank you for it?'

Maya did not answer this. She did not know what to say.

'Or one day would he turn and look at you and think. *If not for her . . .*'

If not for her. Maya couldn't bear it. If he ever looked at her that way . . .

'He might be prepared to give up a great deal for you, my child.' Her father reached out and stroked her hair. 'His English life, his chance of promotion, perhaps even his career. But do you want him to? Do you expect him to?'

No, she did not. She never had. But she could not believe that now, after this terrible war, it would still be criticised or frowned on. To marry a native woman. If it was acceptable to bed one, why not acceptable to make her your wife?

A sound came from the kitchen. Maya got to her feet and straightened her *longyi*. 'There is our daughter,' she murmured. 'What of Suu? Does she not have the right to know her father? To live with him? To love him?'

'Yes, there is your daughter.' Her father drew away from her, his expression thoughtful. 'She is lucky to have escaped detection.'

'Detection?' But Maya knew what he was saying.

He turned back to her. 'She is neither one thing nor the other,' he muttered.

'And yet her features are more Burmese.' Fortunately for them all. Maya had continued to darken Suu's pale skin with a paste she made from bark and this had been sufficient for no one else to comment on her parentage. But in recent weeks Maya had let this practice slide. Could Cho Suu Kyi not now be who she was? Would she have to hide forever?

'Yes, that is true.' Her father frowned. 'But if it is known that she has a British father . . .'

What was that supposed to mean? 'Other children are of mixed race,' Maya began. Where there had been mistresses, there would be children. Would it really be such a disadvantage to Suu, having an English father?

'The British will have to leave Burma,' her father said. Once again he went over to the window. 'Their time is gone. What we need now is the freedom to rule our own country.'

She knew what he was thinking. Anything the British might have done for them was nothing; he believed that they had only ever done it for themselves. And perhaps this was true. The British would not want to lose a land with riches such as theirs.

'But it will not be easy.' He turned back to her. 'And it will not be easy for Suu. Trust me, my daughter. I cannot say how difficult her life will be.'

Maya thought about this conversation all evening and deep into the night. What she wanted more than anything was to be reunited with Lawrence, presuming that he was, as she fervently believed, still alive. She wanted it almost more than life itself. And yet . . .

In the early hours of the morning, she got up to look at her sleeping daughter. Would Lawrence think that she had trapped him? She could not bear that. What was best for Suu? What was best for Lawrence, the man she loved? What should she do, so that the two people she loved most in the world could be happy?

'So you didn't go back to Mandalay?' Eva asked.

'Not for six months.'

Eva raised an eyebrow. 'Six months?'

Maya smiled sadly. 'No man will wait forever, my dear,' she said. Six months might not seem very long, but it was what she had agreed with her father.

'If it is meant to be, it will survive six months,' he had said, when they had next discussed the matter. 'Stay here for six months. Think it over.'

It was perhaps the longest six months of her life.

'I thought it was for the best,' Maya told Eva.

Their eyes met. Maya didn't say more. This young girl, the

granddaughter of the man she'd never stopped loving, understood. She could see it. It was, perhaps, a sacrifice she should never have made. Only six months. But life went on.

In 1947, the entire Burmese Cabinet under Aung San had been assassinated and this was a blow her father hardly recovered from. Aung San had eventually secured Burmese independence from the British, but for what? Her father became faded and diminished, from politics as much as from his experiences in the war. As for Maya, she had met San Thein, her husband, and her life had been good enough. Not earth-shattering perhaps, but he had been a kind man, a hard-working man who had done his best for them all under the harsh regime that followed. It had all been so far from her father's hopes and aspirations, she thought sadly, and she almost thanked the Lord Buddha that he had not lived long enough to witness the worst of it.

And if she had ever wondered about Lawrence and what she had given up . . . Which she did. Oh, how she did. She could satisfy herself that she had done what she thought to be the right thing – for Lawrence and for Cho Suu Kyi.

CHAPTER 56

'Shall we have a last drink together before I take you back to your hotel?' Ramon murmured, as he and Eva finally left the house.

She turned to him, surprised. 'In a bar?' She had already stayed longer than she'd intended. But it had been worth it, to find out the truth.

'I was thinking of somewhere more private.' He raised an eyebrow, gestured towards his own apartment.

'Yes, let's.' Eva didn't even want to resist. It would at least put off the moment of parting. And she didn't want this evening to end.

She followed him inside.

But he walked right through the reception room and out of a door the other side on to a sheltered verandah with a bamboo roof. He held the door open for Eva.

She stepped through. Let out a small gasp. 'It's beautiful.'

The verandah was lit with a warm amber glow from two lanterns, one placed by the door and the other on a wooden table next to two cane deck chairs. Soft oriental music was playing and, as she looked up, Eva spotted the discreet speaker up in the corner on the wall. On the table was a bottle of champagne in an ice bucket with two glass flutes set beside it on a black and gold lacquer tray. Beside this, was a shallow ceramic bowl filled with water and floating hibiscus and jasmine flowers.

She turned to him. 'When did you do all this?'

'I took a moment to come out here earlier.'

Eva smiled. He'd certainly set the scene. She sat down on the chair he indicated. 'What a lovely idea,' she said. It was so very special. Did that mean that the time they'd spent together had meant as much to him as it had meant to her? She hoped so.

He shrugged. 'I wanted some time alone with you, Eva.'

'And why would you want that?' She watched his slender fingers as he loosened the cork in the bottle.

'Eva?' He stopped what he was doing and looked at her. 'Are you flirting with me?'

The cork popped, they both laughed and Eva quickly held up the two glasses for him to pour. 'Should I be?' she asked.

'Probably.'

They clinked glasses and he sat down in the chair next to her. 'To you and your grandfather,' he said.

'And to the chinthes.'

'Long may they live in the National Museum.' He smiled.

'Hear, hear.' At first, Eva had been surprised by Maya's decision, but now she realised that it made perfect sense. The family would no longer have to worry about owning something so valuable that might be stolen. And the chinthes could remain with all the other treasures from the Royal Palace, as part of Myanmar's history and heritage.

'Eva, when I first met you,' Ramon said, 'I may have been a bit unfriendly.'

'Just a bit.' She smiled back at him.

'The truth is that from the first moment I saw you standing there outside our house looking all earnest and asking to see my grandmother . . . I thought you were quite lovely.'

Eva felt a warm glow and it wasn't just from the champagne. 'You disguised it well,' she murmured, and took another sip. On top of the wine she'd already drunk this evening, it was going straight to her head. But it didn't matter. She was quite sure of what she wanted.

'But I also distrusted you,' he said. 'To suddenly appear in the way you did. And with the chinthe . . . It all seemed so unbelievable.'

'Yes.' She could see that. She watched as a huge dark moth fluttered around the orange glow of the lantern. The night outside was as still and the darkness as dense as she'd ever known it here in Myanmar. They were tucked away at the back of the building, with no houses in sight, no lights and no signs of civilisation. The fragrance of the flowers gently floating in the bowl wafted up to her, mingling with the dry citrus sparkle of the champagne.

'It seemed at first that you were only here to take from our country, our culture.'

Eva bowed her head.

'And then . . .' His voice tailed off.

She looked across at him. He seemed thoughtful. 'And then?'

'And then, when I realised who you were and what you were . . .'

Eva considered this. That she was the granddaughter of the Englishman Maya had loved? She supposed that was what he meant. That she was there to bring them their family's chinthe, to meet them and to listen to their stories, rather than ask for anything in return perhaps? Or did he mean something quite different?

'But it turned out by then that you distrusted me,' he said.

She nodded. Very true.

'And so we travelled full circle.'

'I suppose that we did.' Eva wasn't sure that she had ever felt such a sense of peace. She leant back in the cane recliner and closed her eyes. The oriental music played gently on as if it were caressing her senses. This might be her last magical experience in Myanmar, she thought. And she would make the most of it.

'Even so.' His tone changed. 'I have tried to resist you, Eva.'

And I you, she thought.

'Especially now, seeing you lying there in that chair looking like some sweet-faced angel.'

'Really?' Eva opened her eyes. She'd never been called an angel before.

He was staring at her, leaning forwards and looking very serious. The dark wing of his hair had flopped again over his forehead and again she reached out to brush it back, just as she had once before.

He caught hold of her wrist. 'You are leaving my country very soon,' he said.

She nodded. 'Yes.'

'You live in the UK. You belong to a different world.'

She couldn't argue with that. Eva waited.

'And yet,' he said.

'And yet,' she whispered. She knew exactly what he was thinking. Hadn't she been thinking the same thing these past days?

'And yet I feel that I cannot let you leave without telling you.'

'Telling me what, Ramon?'

'That I have begun to care for you.' He brought her hand to his lips and kissed it, not taking his eyes from her face. 'And I cannot let you leave without knowing what it would feel like to touch you, to kiss you once more, to feel you so close to me that nothing remains between us. Nothing at all.'

'And I you,' she said simply.

Ramon got up from his chair and he held out his hand to help Eva to her feet. She stood there in front of him, very close, and she looked up at him, recognised the desire in his eyes.

'Eva.' He held her face cupped in his hands.

When he kissed her, it felt good and it felt right. It began as a gentle kiss but as she responded to him, she could feel his urgency and answered it wordlessly with her own. He smelt

516

of wood and wax polish with that faint scent of cardamom and he tasted of champagne. His skin was smooth under her fingertips, his hair silky to the touch. His kisses became more demanding and their bodies cleaved together. Yes, she thought, she knew exactly what she wanted.

He led her into the adjoining bedroom and slowly, one by one, taking his time, he began to remove her clothes and she, his. He unbuttoned her blouse, she, his shirt. Their eyes met. She slid his shirt from his shoulders. Under the cotton fabric his chest was brown, muscular and almost hairless, his shoulders lean but strong. He unzipped her cotton skirt and she felt for the knot of his *longyi*. His hips jutted out and she ran her fingers gently over them and felt him shiver. He clutched her buttocks closer to him and then his hand was inside her bra, gently caressing her, the other hand unclasping the hook and eye. She nuzzled her lips into the softness of his neck, tracing the shape of his collar bone and he bent to kiss her bare shoulder.

'Ramon . . .' And then they were on the bed, pulling at the remainder of one another's clothes, passion overtaking them at last.

Later, much later, for the light of dawn was creeping through the window and Eva knew she must have slept, Ramon hiked himself up on one elbow. He stared down at her.

She looked at him, ran her fingertip along his collar bone, smiled lazily.

'There's so much I want to say to you, Eva,' he breathed.

She put her finger on his lips. 'Don't say it. Don't say a word.'

'Why not?' His green eyes seemed dark in the half-light. His hair was unruly, his lean brown body flexed and smooth.

'Because we may never see each other again, Ramon,' Eva forced herself to say. It had been a magical evening, but the night was over now. Soon it would be morning, reality would set in, and she would be gone.

'Do not say that,' he muttered.

'But it's true.' Dreamily she smoothed his hair from his eyes. 'You live in Myanmar and I live in the UK. And we both know that long-distance relationships never work.'

'But if we were determined for it to work . . .' he said.

She shook her head. It was sweet of him to say, but she had stayed here last night fully knowing that she would probably never see him again. She had stayed here last night because, like him, she had needed to feel him, love him, even if it was only to happen once. Only once, but she would never forget it, never forget his touch.

'I would like to say that one day . . .'

'Please don't,' she murmured.

'Don't what?'

'Don't encourage me to hope,' she said.

He stroked her hair, bent down and kissed her lightly on the lips. Now he tasted of night time, she thought. Night time and dreams. 'You are right. I cannot make any promises,' he said.

'I know,' she whispered.

★

An hour later, after they had dressed and showered, Ramon took her back to her hotel.

'I have something for you,' he said, as they drew up outside. 'A souvenir, to remember us by.'

'Oh.' Eva felt bad. She had nothing for him. She hadn't thought, hadn't expected . . . And she didn't need anything to remember them by.

'I made it myself.' He handed her a small intricately carved teak Buddha. 'It is not old.' He shrugged. 'But perhaps you will like it.'

'I love it.' Eva ran her fingertip over the carving. 'Thank you so much, Ramon.'

'Just remember,' he said gravely. 'He must always be the highest in the room.'

'Of course.' She smiled.

'And so . . .'

'No more goodbyes,' Eva said. In front of them, weaving down the road were two men on a scooter, a mattress held vertically between them. Only in Myanmar, she thought. 'Just kiss me once and then I'll walk away.'

'You won't look back?' he asked.

'I won't look back.'

How could she look back? That would mean Ramon would see her tears.

CHAPTER 57

Rosemary was giving her father a shave. 'Mustn't let your-self go,' she told him as she gently massaged the shaving foam into a lather over the grey stubble.

'You're right, love.' He sat up in bed, good as gold. The doctor was coming this afternoon, just to take a look at him. But Rosemary knew there was nothing any of them could do. The light was fading. Her job now was to make every-thing as comfortable as possible for him.

As she carefully manipulated the razor, Rosemary was aware of his gaze, fixed on her face. 'Alright, Dad?' she asked. He wasn't talking so much about Burma now. He wasn't talking about anything very much.

'Where's Alec?' he asked.

Rosemary was so surprised that she stopped shaving for a minute. 'Alec?' She rinsed the razor in the bowl on the bed-side table.

'Your husband.' He gave her a look.

She smiled, resumed the gentle strokes. 'He's still in Copen-hagen,' she said.

'Waiting for you to go back to him.'

'Don't talk,' she warned him. 'No, he's not really waiting. He knows why I'm here. He's happy for me to be here.' For the moment, she thought.

Her father gripped her wrist. Rosemary stopped what she was doing. Waited.

'Don't make him wait too long, Rosie,' he said.

'I won't.' She made her voice light. Little did he know. Alec wasn't waiting for her to return to Copenhagen. He was waiting for her to say yes to Seattle, to say yes to them. Which was, apparently, one and the same thing. *But not for me*, she thought. As she'd already realised. It was the wrong question. And both questions might need a different answer.

He relaxed his grip and she finished off. Put the razor in the bowl beside the bed to rinse it, took his blue flannel and gently wiped his face. It was perhaps the most intimate thing you could do for a man, shaving him. She still remembered when she was a girl, watching her father standing in front of the bathroom mirror, his face covered in shaving foam, sweeping the razor in confident strokes from neck to chin while she watched goggle-eyed, amazed he didn't cut himself to shreds. She remembered the scent of that shaving foam too, it was here now in the bedroom, sweet and soapy, with a hint of lemon.

'You love him, don't you?' her father wheezed.

Really, she could hardly believe it. These moments of lucidity might be few and far between, but when they came he could cut himself, he was so sharp. 'Course I do,' she said.

'Not like it was with Nick though, eh?' His eyes were actually twinkling.

She nudged him, patted his face dry with the towel. 'No, not like it was with Nick.'

'You put that man on a pedestal,' he said.

'Hardly.' Rosemary took the bowl into the bathroom and rinsed it out. She returned for the towel. He was still looking at her in that way. She sighed and sat down on the bed. 'What are you trying to say, Dad?'

He nodded. 'That you idealised his memory.' He got the words out with some difficulty. 'I know that's what you did. I did it myself with Maya.'

Rosemary wasn't having that. 'Nonsense,' she said sharply.

He closed his eyes. 'Ah, Rosie,' he said.

While he was sleeping, Rosemary thought about it. He'd written to Maya, hadn't he, though he'd never sent any of the letters. It was a connection that had helped him somehow.

She sat down at the kitchen table with a sheet of notepaper she'd found in the bureau.

My darling Nick,

she wrote.

> *If you are watching me, if you have ever watched me, you will know how much I miss you. You'll know what a terrible mess I made of things with Eva and with my father, too. And of course you'll know about Alec.*

She paused. Shivered, despite the heat of the Aga.

I saw it – marrying him – as a way out of the life I had in Dorset without you. But it wasn't fair, was it? She sighed. *And neither was it a way out.*

My father told me earlier, in one of his more lucid moments, that I had romanticised your memory, idealised you. He did that too, with Maya, he said.

Rosemary thought about this for a moment. She had denied it instinctively; it had seemed like an attack. But it was true.

The truth is that our love was special, and so was his with Maya. She understood that now. *But it's over, Nick. It wasn't over when you died, but it's over now.*

Rosemary took a deep breath. This wasn't easy. But then it never was easy to let go. *I tried to pretend that it wasn't over, but I'm not going to pretend any longer. I loved you but now it's over and I want you to set me free.*

Rosemary read the letter through. It was what she wanted to say. But, 'I'm sorry, Nick.' She fetched a bowl and the box of matches, struck one and held the letter over the flame. It curled, caught alight and she dropped it into the bowl, watched it flare briefly and then turn to ashes.

When Mrs Briggs arrived, Rosemary went out, back to Burton Cliff. It was cold, but she parked at the end of the no-through road and sat on the bench at the top of the grassy cliff, looking down. She wrapped her warm cashmere scarf more closely around her neck. She was wearing her thick coat, cord jeans and walking boots. To one side, she could see the old hotel and the sandstone path leading down to Hive Bay, to the other, the cliff-top walkway that led through to Fresh-water. And the sea stretched calmly out towards the horizon, the tide gently rippling, gleaming grey-green in the limpid autumnal sun. She had come here twenty-six years ago to scatter Nick's ashes. And this was another sort of goodbye. There was a moment when you had to discharge the past. And move on.

It was time. Rosemary got up from the bench and walked closer to the cliff edge. A young couple were strolling along the path, hand in hand. He paused, pointed out to her the church tower in the distance, in the village, beyond the river. It was a walk Rosemary and Nick had done so often, strolling along the top of the high golden cliff, down to Freshwater where the river emerged from a bank of tiny pebbles that had formed an island before it flowed into the sea. Then over the stile and back along the river bank, past the bridge, along the lane with the allotments and what used to be the Dove Inn. Back through the field and up the hill to the cliff top. If Nick were anywhere watching over her, he was here.

'No one should be second best,' her father had said.

This had been their special place. She had never come here with Alec. She had excluded him, just as her father had unintentionally excluded her mother. She supposed it had been their way of trying to keep it special. But . . . She groped in her bag for the little tin with the elephants on. Elephants were for remembering. And she would never forget.

She opened the lid. 'Bye, Nick,' she murmured. 'See you.'

She tipped the tin. And the ashes of her letter fluttered in the breeze, on to the pathway, on to the sandstone cliff. Some, she hoped, would make it down to the ocean below. Rosemary stared out to sea, almost thought she could glimpse the shimmer of Nick's smile shifting gently with the tide.

She stood there for a moment, watching, then she groped in her bag for her mobile.

He answered on the third ring. 'Alec?'

'Rosemary? How are you?'

'Not so bad.' She held the phone closer. 'I just wanted to speak to you. I wanted to hear your voice.' Here, she thought. Here in this place.

'Where are you?' She thought she heard his voice catch. Had he been thinking of her? Had he been wondering what to do?

'On top of a cliff.' She smiled. 'Surrounded by fields and sheep and seagulls.'

'Lucky you.'

'Can you hear the gulls?' She held the phone up. 'And the sea?'

He laughed. 'Yes, I can.'

'I miss you, Alec,' she said.

'I miss you too.' She heard the emotion in his voice. And she realised how unusual it was for them both to say those kinds of words. Words of love.

'Are you alright, Rosemary? I mean, your father . . .'

'Still the same. And I'm fine.' At least, she thought, I will be.

'I have to decide by tomorrow,' he told her.

She remembered what he'd said. Had she given him any reason to say 'no'? 'I can't come back to Copenhagen, Alec,' she said. 'I know this will be hard for you to hear. But I need to stay in Dorset, at least for a while.'

'For Eva?' His voice sounded very bleak. Rosemary knew she was hurting him. Sometimes it seemed that was all she had ever done. And yet she'd never wanted to.

'For Eva and for my father,' she said. 'But also for me.' The words tumbled from her in a rush. 'When I married you, when I came to Copenhagen, I was running away, Alec. Away from what had happened here and what the place meant to me. But running away from my emotions too. I thought I had to escape. I thought the most important thing in my life was self-preservation.'

'But it wasn't?'

'No, it wasn't.' Rosemary took a deep breath. 'The most important thing in my life was love.'

For a moment he was silent. 'So you regret marrying me?' His voice was thin. He sounded an awfully long way away. Rosemary knew she had to be honest with him, but she also had to get it right.

'Never.'

'Never?'

'I still don't.'

'And love?' He sounded sad.

'I love this place.' Rosemary opened her arms as if she

could hug it close to her. The sandstone cliffs, the pebbles of Chesil Beach, the cold and grey English Channel. 'I love my daughter and I love my father. And I love you.'

'So you've decided not to come to Seattle then, Rosemary?' His words cut through her like a winter wind.

But . . . Honesty. 'I'm sorry, Alec,' she said. 'But I can't.'

When she ended the call, Rosemary realised she was crying. Big fat tears rolling down her cheeks. She didn't reach for a tissue or wipe them away. She just let them come. She didn't know if she was crying for Nick or for her father or for Alec. It didn't matter. She just needed the release. She had to let it go.

CHAPTER 58

Eva was surprised to see her mother waiting for her at Arrivals. She'd emailed and asked her to organise a taxi; she knew the last thing she'd feel like doing after a long flight was travelling by train all the way from Heathrow to Dorset. But there she was, smiling, looking . . . Different, she thought.

'Eva.'

'Hello, Mother.' They kissed a little awkwardly. Eva was wary. Her mother had been so warm when they'd spoken on the phone. But it had been a while since they'd been face to face.

'How was your flight?' Rosemary's smile was encouraging and seemed genuine enough.

'Fine. How's Grandpa?'

'Not good,' she said. Her expression changed. 'I'm afraid to say that he's deteriorated a lot since you left.'

Eva's shoulders sagged. Just as she'd thought.

Rosemary patted her arm. 'Come on then, darling.' She took Eva's case and headed towards the exit and the car park. 'You'll see him soon. He'll be so happy you're back. You will come to the house before you go back to Bristol?'

'Of course.' Bristol. Eva wasn't looking forward to Bristol. 'Is Grandpa . . . ?'

'You'll see for yourself.' She turned around. 'But I should warn you, darling. He keeps slipping in and out of consciousness. Sometimes he's quite lucid . . .' She paused, and put her arm on Eva's. 'But other times, to be honest, we're not sure how much he hears, how aware he really is.' Her eyes filled.

'Oh, Ma.' Eva thought of how he'd been not much more than a month ago when she'd told him she was going to Burma. Frail, yes, but definitely still with all his faculties intact. *Slipping in and out of consciousness?* Shouldn't he be in hospital then? Shouldn't someone be doing something more for him? She looked helplessly at her mother, who was paying their car parking ticket at the machine.

She tucked the ticket into her bag. 'The doctor says he's comfortable.' And Eva saw her swallow back her tears. 'He's doing all he can for him. And he's in the best place, at home.'

'Good.' Then her mother's arm was around her shoulders. She hadn't felt that for a long time.

'We must be strong,' she whispered. 'We mustn't let him see.'

'Yes.' Eva nodded. 'I'm sorry. You're right.'

'Come on, darling.' Her mother's voice became brisk as she took hold of the case and again led the way towards the lift of the car park. Eva noticed as she followed her that her blonde hair was longer and less neat. That was new too.

'You said "*we're* not sure" how much he hears?' she asked, hurrying to catch up with her. 'Is Alec over here too?'

529

Something flickered over her mother's blue eyes. Her expression changed. 'I meant Ida Briggs and the doctor. Both of them have been marvellous.' She shook her head. 'No, Alec's not here. Just me.' She pressed the button and they waited for the lift.

'And . . . Ma?' She had to know.

'Yes?'

'Did you tell Grandpa? About Cho Suu Kyi?' This revelation had become, in its way, the most important part of the journey she'd made. The lift arrived and they both got in.

'Yes, I told him.' There was a silence as the lift winged them up to the second level of the short stay car park. The door opened and their eyes met, briefly, before Eva's mother scanned the level for the car. 'There it is.' She hurried over and unlocked it. Presumably it was one she'd hired for her stay here, Eva thought, since her grandfather no longer owned a car.

She followed her over. 'And what did he say?'

'Not much,' Rosemary told her. 'But he seemed to take it in. Finally.'

Her mother had opened the boot and Eva helped her heave in the case. Telling him couldn't have been easy for her, Eva thought. But there had been no other way. And it looked as if her worst fears had been realised. Now might have been too late.

But if her mother was upset, then she hid it well as she bundled Eva's hand luggage in with the case and shut the boot with a decisive clunk.

Eva slipped into the passenger seat. She was glad her mother had come to pick her up. It felt good to sit back and let her take over. But it wasn't just that of course.

Her mother started up the engine and put the car into gear. She turned to her. 'You'd better prepare yourself, Eva, darling,' she said. 'We think he's slipping away.'

Slipping away . . . Her grandfather had always been her rock. She didn't want him to slip away. Couldn't bear the thought of losing him.

Rosemary drove out of the airport terminal. It was drab, grey and industrial but they were still on the perimeter of the airport and Eva could see another plane landing, more passengers returning on a long-haul flight back to the UK. Even after just a few weeks away, everything here looked alien and strange. There was no colour, no red earth or vibrant flowers, no market stalls or street sellers. And it was so cold. Her mother had turned up the heating in the car, but Eva still had the shivers. She thought of those last days in Bagan, exploring the temples on the grand plain with an ever increasing sense of loneliness. She didn't want to think of her last night with Ramon. And she didn't want to think about her grandfather slipping away.

'Thank you, Ma,' she said.

'For what?'

'For telling him. For picking me up from the airport. For being here.'

Rosemary turned to her and smiled and Eva noticed her crimson-painted fingernails, her jewellery: gold, expensive, under-stated. Her jacket was gorgeous too, the softest of brown leather and her sweater was cream cashmere, which she wore with chocolate coloured trousers. Smart, thought Eva. But almost jarring to the senses after the simple white cotton blouses and embroidered *longyis* of Myanmar. After the poverty. They'd led such a different life, hadn't they, these two half-sisters? If it weren't for the unmistakeable resemblance between them, it would be hard to believe they were related.

'That's OK,' her mother said. 'It was my pleasure.'

Eva sneaked another glance at her. 'It must have been a shock for you too,' she ventured. 'Hearing about Cho Suu Kyi, I mean.'

'It certainly was. All these years thinking I was an only child . . .' But her mother didn't seem to want to say more. She glanced at Eva and then away.

'So tell me about your trip,' she said encouragingly as she took the motorway. 'That's if you feel like talking. But there's plenty of time. Rest if you want to rest.' She smiled.

Softer, thought Eva. That's what she was. Easier. For once in her life, she felt she didn't have to be walking on eggshells around her. After her father's death for as far back as she could remember, her mother had been so tense that Eva was afraid if she hugged her, she might snap. So she hadn't hugged her. She supposed she had responded to the vibe, kept her distance, confided in her grandfather rather than her mother. But what about the times before that? When she and her mother had cuddled and were close, when her mother had read Eva those bedtime stories about lions in the meadow and foxes in the fields in her low, sing-song voice, her laughter bubbling like fizzy lemonade? When her father had been working late and they'd stayed up to watch TV together, when her mother let her help bake gingerbread men. She hadn't forgotten those times. She'd thought of them on the way to Burma, on the flight, images of her childhood had fluttered like story-flags through her mind.

Once she started talking, it was hard to stop. Eva told her mother about her Myanmar impressions, the people she'd met, and even about Maya, though she didn't dwell on how much time she had spent with her; there was no point in rubbing salt into the wound. And then she told her about the rubies, the stolen chinthe and how Klaus had eventually got it back.

'My God, Eva,' Rosemary muttered under her breath as they eventually came off the motorway and headed towards West Dorset. 'I can't believe all this happened in less than four weeks. Are you alright, darling? It all sounds very dangerous.' She turned to look at her, her blue eyes full of concern.

'You sound just like Ramon.' Eva swallowed. She missed him already. He had phoned her at her hotel in Yangon before she flew back, but it had been a difficult conversation. She was leaving Myanmar and he was staying. What more was there to say?

'Ah, yes.' Rosemary raised her perfectly plucked eyebrows. 'Ramon. He seems to have had quite an effect on you.'

'He did.' Eva thought of the little carved Buddha in her

cabin bag. And she had a sense of déjà vu. She stared out of the window. Although the roads were clear, there was still snow on the hills.

'And?'

'And nothing.' Eva wasn't sure she wanted to be having this conversation. 'I'm British. He's Burmese. Well, half-Burmese anyway. We live in different worlds. There is no "and".'

'But there might have been?'

Eva shrugged. 'Maybe.' He had said he'd keep in touch. But she didn't know whether they would. Sometimes to keep in touch was even harder.

Her mother reached out and patted her hand. It was clearly an unconscious gesture and yet to Eva it was so unusual that it took her a moment to register it. 'If it's meant to be . . .' Rosemary said.

Eva stared at her. Wasn't that exactly what Cho Suu Kyi had said about seeing her father? *If it is meant to be.* And since when had her mother become so philosophical?

On both sides of the road now, the Dorset countryside stretched out around them as if it might enfold Eva in its arms. Green hills and lush valleys, the triangle of the distant ocean. The sky was still grey, but, as Eva watched, a shaft of feeble wintry sunshine peered through the clouds. Eva smiled. Another creature entirely from the sapping sun of Myanmar. She turned to her mother. 'And how about you?' she asked.

'Me?' Rosemary kept her eyes on the road.

'Yes. You seem pretty laid-back about my visit to Myanmar, all of a sudden. But I know you've always hated the place.'

'That's true.'

And now that she'd been there, Eva thought she understood why. 'So what's changed?' she asked.

'Let's say that while I've been looking after your Grandpa, I've had an awful lot of time to think,' she said.

'Oh yes?' Eva waited for her to elaborate. What had she been thinking about? The past? The present? The knowledge that she had a half-sister?

Rosemary glanced across at her. 'You and I have got a lot of catching up to do, darling,' she said. 'But there's plenty of time for that, too.'

Which sounded as if she intended to stay for a while. Eva relaxed into the passenger seat. But not plenty of time for her grandfather, by the sound of it. And so she willed the remaining miles to disappear. She wouldn't be going back to Bristol, not yet. She was going back to Dorset. Because she needed to see him now. She needed to get home.

CHAPTER 59

It was evening. Rosemary had lit the fire and they'd moved her grandfather into the lounge on the settee so that he could lie and look into the flames as they talked.

The doctor had been in earlier, and although he hadn't been so good when Eva first arrived, her grandfather had seemed to rally this evening. At last he seemed able to talk to her, able to listen to what she had to say.

She knelt beside him on a cushion on the floor, her mother sitting opposite in the floral armchair with the antimacassars Eva's grandmother had always insisted on.

'Well now, Eva, my dear.' He spoke softly, his pale blue eyes fixed on her face. 'How was she?'

Eva glanced up at her mother but she just smiled in a way that told her it was alright. Whatever her own feelings, she must have decided to put them aside, for her father's sake. 'She's very well.' Given her age. But Eva decided not to tell him how tired Maya had looked that last night in Mandalay. Tired but still peaceful, she thought.

'Ah.' He nodded as if this was the news he'd been waiting for. 'And was she pleased when you gave her the chinthe?'

'Pleased, yes. And very surprised.' Again, Eva glanced at

her mother. Before they went into the house they'd agreed not to tell him all the details. It might be too much to know that his granddaughter had been breaking into shipment crates and trying to inveigle her way into the homes of criminals, not to mention getting involving with illegal antiques and stolen rubies.

'Good, good.' He stared into the flames as if mesmerised.

'And I showed her the photos I took with me,' Eva added. She could see now why Maya had seemed so interested in that photograph of Rosemary. She'd been comparing Lawrence's daughter with his other daughter, she'd noticed that family resemblance right away.

'Did you take many photos while you were out there?' her mother asked.

Eva sat back on her heels. She'd already put them on to her laptop. 'Would you like to see?'

'Of course,' said Rosemary.

Her grandfather blinked at her and nodded.

She went to get her laptop and located the file, setting it up so that all three of them had a clear view. The first pictures were of Yangon, then Maymyo and then the orchids and Kandawgyi gardens.

'And who's this?' asked Rosemary. The picture was of Ramon. It caught him half in reverie as he examined a particularly stunning purple orchid, half indignant that he was being photographed unawares.

'Ramon.' The picture brought the memory of that afternoon back sharply into her mind. 'Maya's grandson,' she told her grandfather. 'He showed me around Maymyo and Mandalay.'

Her grandfather frowned and nodded. 'Ramon,' he said, as if committing the name to memory.

When she got to the picture of Maya, looking sweet and serene and white-haired, standing outside the house in Maymyo – the house that her grandfather had visited all those years ago – he caught his breath. 'She's hardly changed,' he murmured. And his head sank back onto the cushions.

Eva and her mother exchanged a small smile.

'She says hello,' Eva told him. 'And she asked me to give you her love.'

He nodded, as if he already knew, as if he already had her love. 'Did she have a good life?' he asked. 'Was she happy?'

'Yes, she did. She was.' That had certainly been Eva's understanding. And she recalled that this was what Maya too had wanted to know, *had he been happy? Had he been loved?* Maya might have regretted her decision, but if so she showed no sign. She had shown only acceptance; she had made the best of it. 'She married a good man,' Eva told her grandfather. 'And they had a lovely daughter.'

'And my daughter?' His voice was faint. 'My other daughter?'

So he had understood. Over in the armchair, Eva was conscious of her mother's silent presence. 'I have a picture of her,' she said. She clicked on it and her face filled the screen. 'Cho Suu Kyi,' she said.

Her grandfather and her mother stared at the image in

silence for a few moments. At last her grandfather nodded. 'She looks very fine,' he said. 'She looks . . .'

'Serene,' Eva's mother supplied.

'She is.' Eva looked appraisingly at her mother. 'And don't you think she looks a little like you, Mother?' she asked.

'Oh, she does,' her grandfather said firmly.

'A little.' A small smile played around her mother's lips.

'Maya wanted to tell you about her, Grandpa.' Eva willed him to understand. 'And she never wanted to lose you. But . . .'

He nodded. 'She thought it best to let me go,' he said.

Exactly. He knew the woman. Perhaps he had never doubted her. Eva moved on to the next photograph of Maya and Cho Suu Kyi together. 'Maya's husband brought Suu up as his own,' she told them. 'He looked after them both very well.'

'I'm glad.' Her grandfather reached out and squeezed Eva's hand. 'I'm glad they had a good life. As I did,' he added. He gave Eva a look. *Be patient with your mother*, it seemed to say, *try to understand*.

She did understand. And her mother too, Eva thought, was doing her best to understand. She moved on to the next pictures of the Royal Palace and other sights of Mandalay. There was the gaudily painted horse and cart which had carried she and Ramon around Inwa, the golden pagodas of Sagaing Hill and the glorious Mahamuni, covered in knobbly gold leaf by all his followers; a visual reminder of her entire journey. 'And the chinthes,' she said. 'Reunited at last.'

'Ah.' Her grandfather leaned closer.

They stared back at the camera lens with dignity, heads proud, eyes glittering. 'And here they are in the National Museum in Yangon.' Because Eva had taken another photo of them when she visited the museum the day before she left Myanmar. They were already installed beside an information board which told the story, in Burmese and English, of how Queen Supayalat had given them to her loyal maid-servant Suu Kyi in thanks for looking after the princesses and how they had now been given on permanent loan as a precious relic of Burmese culture. Beside them, was an old photograph of the King and Queen, the pair of chinthes unmistakeable, each one on an arm of Supayalat's throne. You couldn't, Eva thought, get a more reliable authentication than that.

Lawrence peered at the photo more closely. 'They look very grand,' he commented. 'And in a museum too.' He chuckled. 'Who would have thought it, eh? When one of them's been in the jungle and even to Dorset and back.'

Eva caught her mother's eye. She shrugged.

Eva leaned closer. 'The eyes of the chinthes are rare Mogok rubies, Grandpa,' she whispered.

He stared at her, then back at the laptop screen, then into the flames of the fire. 'Rubies?' he breathed. 'She gave me rubies?' He laughed, his chest heaving in an effort to get breath, but the laughter turned to a wheeze and then a cough. 'Rubies,' he muttered. He glanced at Eva. 'You know I've always admired an adventurous spirit, my darling,' he said.

'But I do hope you were careful.' And, once again, his eyes seemed to glaze over.

Rosemary got to her feet. 'Time for bed, Dad, I think,' she said. 'All this excitement. It's exhausting.'

Eva helped her support him and they got him into the bathroom and then to bed.

When Eva leaned over to kiss him goodnight, he gripped her hand. 'Did you like it, my darling?' he asked her. 'Did you like the old country?'

Eva smiled. 'I loved it, Grandpa. It was just as you always told me.'

He nodded, as if satisfied. 'And have you thought?' he asked her. 'About what you'll do next?'

Eva was surprised. She hadn't said anything. But it was almost as if he knew. 'I think so.' She hadn't quite thought it through, not yet. But she had a good idea. First thing tomorrow she was going to write her letter of resignation. And, in the circumstances, she hoped they would allow her to leave with immediate effect. But she was going to talk to Jacqui too, she'd decided. She would phone her tomorrow.

'I'm pleased to hear that.' He patted her hand. 'And he seems like a nice enough boy,' he said. 'Maya's grandson and my granddaughter. Well, I never . . .'

Eva smiled. He'd only seen a few photos of Ramon, but he'd still picked up on it, the old rascal. Her mother needn't worry. Grandpa was as sharp as he'd ever been.

He nodded. 'You'll come into some money soon, my dear,'

he whispered, his voice drifting. 'Think carefully about what you want to do with it.'

'Oh, Grandpa.' She didn't want to think about that at all, because of what it would mean.

'And thank you.' His eyes fluttered open and then closed. 'Thank you for taking Maya's chinthe back to Burma for me.'

'That was about the longest period of lucidity he's had since I got here,' Eva's mother said as they sat back in the lounge together, Eva on the settee this time. 'As if he were saving it up for your return.'

'Maybe he was.' She wouldn't be surprised.

'And what else was in the National Museum, darling?' her mother asked. 'It sounds a remarkable collection.'

'Yes, it was.' Despite being incomplete. Eva stared into the fire. The logs, burning orange, sparks flaring with red flames reminded her of the treasures she'd seen there. 'Gilded furniture studded with jewels,' she said dreamily. 'The Queen's couch – gold filigree with jade; the King's day bed – gold filigree with diamonds; a carpet woven of strips of silver.' She took a deep breath, remembering. 'Jewelled caskets decorated with elephants' heads. Royal costumes and state attire.' Their wide sleeves were threaded with gold lace, the body petalled with tiny bells and stiff with sequined rubies, the lapels embroidered with images of the peacock and the hare. 'Golden goblets, pitchers and salvers and betel boxes on dragon stands.'

Rosemary laughed, in her voice a note of wonder.

But Eva wasn't finished yet. 'Lacquered incense jars. Silver spittoons, swords and scabbards. A jewel-encrusted saddle, a hand mirror bordered with gemstones. Rings and bracelets and necklaces of silver, gold and jade, of diamonds and deep red rubies.' She smiled. 'The riches of Mandalay.'

'All taken from the Royal Palace,' murmured her mother. 'By the British, the Japanese, the Chinese, and by the Burmese themselves by the sound of it.'

'Yes.' Incomparable riches, in terms of precious metals and gems. How could a country that was so rich, also be so poor? Some of those riches, at least, had now been returned. But those weren't the only kind of riches the country owned, thought Eva, despite the poverty of many of its people. It also owned something even more precious. It owned riches of the heart.

In the morning, Rosemary knocked lightly on Eva's door and came in with a cup of tea. She sat on the edge of the bed and Eva knew.

'He's worse?' she asked.

'You'd better come in,' her mother replied.

Eva got up, put on her dressing gown and went into her grandfather's room to say goodbye.

CHAPTER 60

After her father's funeral, there was a reception back at the house, but one by one his friends and neighbours went home and just Rosemary, Eva and Alec were left.

'Thanks for coming,' Rosemary said to Alec. They were carrying bowls, plates and glasses from the living room back to the kitchen where Eva was clearing up and stacking the dishwasher. He had only arrived last night and they hadn't really had a chance to talk. Rosemary didn't know what he was going to do. She only knew that she was grateful for the support today. Her father's death had hit her harder than she ever would have expected.

'I'm your husband,' Alec said. 'Of course I'd come.'

Rosemary put glasses on a tray and took them into the kitchen. But what about Seattle? What about his ambition and his job? She returned to the living room and began stacking tea plates.

'Thank goodness you came back here when you did,' Alec said. He came closer, gently rested his hand on her arm.

'Yes.' She had made her peace with him, she had said goodbye, she had even come to comprehend the difficulty of the decisions he'd had to make, the pressure he'd been under and the effort of making a go of his life here in the UK with her mother. And the fact that he'd always loved her.

Alec's hand moved to her shoulder. Rosemary looked up at him. 'Put those plates down a minute,' he said.

She did as he asked. Turned to face him. What next? What would he tell her? She knew that she could manage alone, if she had to. She had made the decision, and she wouldn't go back on it.

He held her face in his hands. Looked straight into her eyes. 'Did you mean what you said the other day on the phone? When you said that you missed me? When you said that you loved me?'

'Of course I did.' Rosemary tried to smile but she wasn't sure that the right muscles were working. No doubt it was a very lopsided affair.

'I hoped so,' said Alec. He seemed to be searching her face for a clue.

Rosemary tried to give it to him, as much and as honestly as she was able. And surprisingly, she seemed more able than she'd expected. *How could you mend a marriage that had never been perfect?* You could start again, that's how.

'So I did some asking around.'

'Asking around?'

'To see what was available over here in the South West.'

'A job?' She was trying to take it in.

'A job.' He pulled a face. 'I'm not quite ready to retire yet, you know.'

'Me neither,' said Rosemary. She had already started

looking. She didn't want to be dependent on Alec, she had to do something for herself. Some sort of secretarial work perhaps, even working in the right kind of shop. She craved the personal contact. In Copenhagen, she'd been lonely, she realised.

Then it struck her what he was telling her. 'You'd come and live back here?' she said. 'To be with me?'

'I would.' He seemed very sure all of a sudden. 'You're my wife, after all.' His brown eyes twinkled behind his glasses.

'But what about Seattle?'

'Do I really need another challenge at my age? That's what I've been asking myself. And besides . . .' He pulled her closer.

'Besides?'

'You gave me enough reason to say "no",' he said.

Later, Rosemary and Eva went out together to scatter Lawrence's ashes in the garden he loved. 'In the spring, I think we should plant him a magnolia tree,' Eva said. 'In his memory.' And she squeezed her mother's arm.

'Yes, let's do that.' Rosemary turned to her and they shared a complicit smile.

Winter had now arrived in earnest and the lawn was still crisp with frost. The pond had iced over too and their breath warmed the air in gasps of steam as they made their way to the bench. Two weeks had passed since the morning he'd died, after his burst of energy following Eva's return. And Rosemary could understand, now, how he'd summoned up those final reserves in order to find out what he'd been waiting for,

546

to listen to what Eva had to tell him: that the chinthe had been returned to where it belonged; that Maya was well and had been happy; that she had never stopped loving him and had given birth to their daughter. It was like that sometimes. And when he was ready to go . . . He had gone.

In those two weeks, Rosemary and Eva between them had dealt with the awful administrative aftermath of death, which was the last thing you felt able to cope with when you'd lost a loved one.

'Where do you think?' Eva asked. In her hand was the urn containing his ashes.

More ashes, thought Rosemary. Another goodbye.

They had decided on the garden because he had loved it and lived here most of his life. From here, by the bench, he could see the raspberry canes he'd planted when he and Helen were first married, the crazy paving path he'd laid for Rosemary to run along when she was a little girl, and the pond where he'd grown purple irises and a sunshine-yellow water-lily.

Rosemary had brought a spade. She stuck it into the ground but it was rock-hard and resistant. 'Maybe we should have waited till the spring,' she said ruefully, resting her arms on the handle.

'Let me have a go.' Eva passed her the urn and took over.

In less than two weeks it would be Christmas. 'Will you spend Christmas here, with me?' Rosemary asked Eva, watching her daughter as she pressed in the blade, dug in with her heel, levered up a few miserable grains of earth and frost.

Alec wanted to go straight back to Copenhagen and start making arrangements for their move.

'I'd like to spend Christmas here – with Eva,' she had told him. 'I'll come back to Copenhagen for New Year. Will you join us – just for a day or two?'

'I'll do my best,' he said. 'But we've got plenty more times ahead, you and I.' He tilted her chin and dropped a light kiss on her lips. 'You're right. It's more important that you stay and keep Eva company. She needs you. You need each other.'

And Rosemary didn't have to be told just how lucky she was. To have him. To have this second chance, with Alec and with Eva.

Eva stopped her digging and turned to her, surprised. 'Of course I will.'

'Good.'

They both looked down at the ground. 'We're not getting very far,' Rosemary said wistfully.

'Tell you what . . .' Eva picked up the urn and took the lid off. She looked at Rosemary. She nodded. Eva up-ended it and scattered the ashes randomly into the winter air. 'To freedom,' she said.

'To freedom.'

They stood for a few minutes in silent contemplation, both saying their farewells in their own way. It was a good end to a life, Rosemary thought. To be free.

'Are you going back to Bristol, darling?' she asked Eva as they made their way towards the house. She rubbed her gloved hands together to keep warm. She knew that Eva had left the Emporium. She'd only returned once to her flat to collect some things which she'd brought back in her old red-and-black Citroen, since then she'd stayed at the house. But Rosemary didn't know her daughter's long-term plans. She just knew that in these two short weeks, they'd grown an awful lot closer. It would take time. You couldn't undo years of growing more distant in a fortnight. But it was a start. A good start. She wondered if her father was watching, if he knew.

'Only to pack.'

Goodness. She and Alec both. Rosemary felt a jump of panic.

'I've given notice to the landlord,' Eva told her. 'I'm moving out.' She opened the shed door and replaced the spade on the hook just inside.

'But where will you go?' Rosemary heard the jaggedy gallop of her own breathing. Not to Burma? Was it all going to be for nothing? Was Eva leaving, just as Rosemary was coming home?

'I'm going to make my life back here in Dorset,' Eva said. She shut the shed door with a clunk and replaced the padlock. 'I love it here.' She turned around, waved her arms to encompass this little part of it. 'There's nowhere else I'd rather be. It's where I belong.'

Rosemary felt the rush of relief. 'So you'll stay here?' Her father had left Eva the house as well as a good deal of money.

Rosemary had her share too, but her father had known Eva needed it more.

'I'm not sure. For a while, yes.' Eva turned to look at her. 'What about you, Ma?' Her tone was non-committal, but Rosemary wasn't fooled.

'We'll look for a place not too far from here,' she said. She led the way back into the house. 'By the sea. And we might go away on a trip somewhere.'

'A trip?' Eva looked curious. She shut the back door behind them and began to pull off her boots.

'Mmm.' In her leather bag Rosemary had Cho Suu Kyi's email address, set up and sent on to Eva by Ramon so that she could keep in touch with her English family. Rosemary was planning to write to her half-sister.

'She's always felt as if she were abandoned,' Eva had told her.

Much more abandoned than Rosemary had ever been.

And so, yes, she would write to her. She would tell her that their father had tried his best and that he'd been a good man. She would tell her that although he'd been unable to meet his other daughter, she would like to. If that would be alright.

Rosemary had tried all her life, especially after finding those letters, to shake off the thought of Burma and her father's time there, a world she had felt excluded from. But through Cho Suu Kyi, she was no longer excluded. She was linked to it, as was Eva. It was a part of her, because it had been a part of her father and she no longer wanted to pretend otherwise.

'Thanks for coming back, Ma.' Eva squeezed her arm.

Rosemary squeezed back. She was determined not to lose her daughter again and this time it was for keeps.

CHAPTER 61

Eva was in the process of restoring an Art Deco dressing table to its former glory. She had bought it from a dealer in the local market. Usually she only bought privately or at auction, but this piece had tempted her. It was a warm June day and she had flung open the double doors of her workshop-cum-studio to welcome the spring sunshine.

The dressing table was colonial in style and it reminded her somehow of Myanmar and her journey there. Much had changed in the six months since her return. Eva knew that her decision to live here in Dorset, her conviction that this was where she belonged, was due in part to what she had learnt on that journey. As was her decision to set up her own antiques restoration business. She missed Leanne and a few other friends, but she had contacts here too, it was where she'd grown up after all. And it was a good place for her new venture; the local antiques and vintage market attracted customers from all over the country and abroad and the area was developing quite a reputation for quality antiques at fair prices. As for furniture restoration, it was what she had always wanted to do and what she'd been trained for, but it was her grandfather's legacy which had enabled her to put it into practice, by buying a large unit which would house her workspace, selling space and a small office and where she could be her own boss. She was lucky, she knew that. She had managed to recapture her dream – the dream that had inspired her to do her degree, the dream that had the scent of teak wood and the history of past lives as its beginning and its end. She was following in her grandfather's footsteps. And she was moving towards, she hoped, that elusive sense of peace.

She already had a small staff of two, a couple, Kim and Jon, who helped out with the buying and the transporting and looked after the place when Eva was away. But like Ramon, back in Mandalay, Eva enjoyed being hands-on. Imaginative restoration of a piece of history was what she enjoyed the best. She had learnt the skills at uni: hand-finishing furniture, veneering and marquetry restoration; the conservation of upholstery and textiles. And now she was putting them into practice. The business, Gatsby's, was still in its infancy, but, like a proud parent, Eva was nurturing it every step of the way.

Last night she had gone round to her mother's for supper. She and Alec had bought a small cottage in Burton, the place her mother had always loved. The conversation had turned to Burma. Much to Eva's surprise, her mother and Cho Suu Kyi were now emailing one another regularly, and her mother and Alec had a trip to Mandalay planned for November.

'Have you heard from Suu lately?' Eva asked as they sat relaxing in the small sitting room.

'About a week or so ago, darling.'

'And did she say anything? About anyone?'

'Only that they were all well.' Her mother shot her a look. 'Have you heard from Ramon?'

'He emails occasionally.' Eva shrugged. 'But I don't encourage it. And I think he's more or less given up.' The last message had been three weeks ago. Three weeks and one day, to be precise. She had finally answered it last week, but she hadn't told him very much. *I'm fine. Working hard. Busy life . . .* That sort of thing.

'Why don't you encourage it?' Rosemary frowned.

Eva would have thought it was obvious. Her mother was sipping red wine and looked more contented than she'd ever seen her. She had grown out her neat blonde bob and wore her hair loose and free. She still looked stylish and elegant but was more likely, these days, to be found in a waxed jacket than a tailored one and green waterproof boots rather than calf leather and heels. She worked part-time in a local solicitor's, but she also kept chickens and was growing organic veg in their rambling cottage garden.

It was late and Alec had already gone to bed, pleading an early works meeting the following morning, hence this conversation á deux. 'He'll never be able to retire,' Rosemary had said as he went, a note of laughter in her voice. 'There's always some new project. I'll have to drag him away kicking and screaming.' But Alec had only laughed back at her and rumpled her hair. Things between them, Eva could see, had changed.

'I don't see the point,' she said, elaborating, since her

mother had raised an eyebrow and was clearly waiting for her to continue. 'We should both be free to get on with our own lives.' And she was getting on with her own life. Work kept her busy; it wasn't easy to set up a new business and take the step of becoming self-employed.

Eva had emailed Ramon to tell him of her grandfather's death. He could decide, she thought, whether or not to tell Maya. And he had a written a note of sympathy back. A week or so later, he had emailed to tell her that Khan Li and his corrupt associates had been arrested and would be charged. *I thought you would like to know*, he wrote. *His business is to be wound up*, he added. *It has been exposed as a discredit to Myanmar.* The way would be clear for reputable companies, like Ramon's, to trade legitimately with the rest of the world and progress, Eva thought, without unfair competition. And she was glad for him. He dealt in new furniture, she in old, but their values had always been the same.

It had been a strangely formal email, cool and distant, so maybe he felt the same way as she did. Eva wasn't sure she could deal with that sort of formal communication with him, as if they had never been lovers at all. He had big plans for his business, he wrote. As always. Big plans, thought Eva, but plans that didn't include her. Hadn't he said that because of his father he had a yearning for all things British? So why not include a fling with an English girl? She still had the little Buddha he had made for her; she would keep it forever. But as she'd told him before, a long-distance, email relationship was never going to work.

She had heard from Klaus too, that things had been taken care of on the European side. They had intercepted the crates and by the time Eva had tendered her resignation, he had passed on all relevant information about the Bristol Antiques Emporium to the authorities. Eva's phone conversation with Jacqui soon after her grandfather's death had not been an easy one.

'You know what's happened, I suppose?' she had said. 'I presume that's why you're leaving.'

'I'd rather not say,' Eva told her. The last thing she wanted was to get drawn into this sort of discussion. 'But I wanted to let you know. If not face to face because of my grandfather's death . . .'

'I understand.' And there was an empathy in Jacqui's voice that she didn't think she'd heard there before. 'And I apologise, Eva,' she said. 'I had no idea of the extent of what was going on. I knew there was something. But by the time my suspicions grew . . .' She sighed. 'I would never have wanted to put you in danger.'

Eva believed her. Whether or not Leon had initiated a relationship with Jacqui Dryden because she owned the Emporium was not Eva's concern. But Jacqui had been an honest antique dealer, of that she was sure.

These things will go on, Klaus wrote. *All we can do is continue the fight, Eva.* Less than a month later her friend Leanne had sent her a newspaper cutting reporting that the Emporium had closed down. And Leanne had done a bit more digging. Apparently Leon had been charged with handling stolen goods and illegal importing. And Jacqui . . . Eva did not know what had happened to Jacqui. She only hoped that she'd been able to start again.

But Eva, too, was continuing the fight in her own small way, for the future. She'd already formed GADA, the Genuine Antique Dealers Association, to support ethical trading in antiques, to create professional standards and to encourage dealers to buy and sell only genuine and authenticated pieces. This way, if they bought through dealers who belonged to the association, consumers could be sure, or as sure as possible, what they were getting for their money, with some sort of guarantee of authenticity, and with all available information provided about source, age, provenance and collection history.

Genuine dealers had already begun to show interest in GADA and Leanne, who had a background in marketing, was helping her spread the word. Hopefully, this would discourage outfits like Khan Li's from trying to fob off their fake Buddhas and chinthes and from being able to sell them on as genuine artefacts of Burmese history. Whether it was misrepresentation or just plain forgery, such activities would be considered illegal, as was the theft of any object which could be considered part of a country's heritage and cultural history. As far as Eva was concerned, GADA would strongly condemn any such action and would support law enforcement to forbid and eradicate it from the antiques trade.

Ramon and his passion for ethical standards and practice had started her on this pathway, she realised. And it had been reinforced by her other experiences in Myanmar. Eva wanted to bring the integrity and sense of history back into antiques. She wanted it to be a creditable and respected profession once again. She couldn't do it single-handedly, but as time went on, the more people in the business who supported her ideals and joined her association, the more chance she would have of making it a reality. But this didn't mean she no longer dealt with Asian artefacts. In fact the contact she'd made through Klaus did sometimes purchase antiques for her and she could always be sure of the provenance.

She thought of the replica chinthe Ramon had made out of his recycled ancient teak. That was a forgery too, of course. But she didn't feel it was hypocritical. Sometimes, the end justified the means.

'It was a healing journey, the one you made to Myanmar,' her mother said thoughtfully.

'Yes, you're right.' Though Eva hadn't fully realised it at the time. It had been healing for her grandfather, who could now be at peace; for Eva, who had finally seen for herself the Burma of all those childhood stories; for Maya, who'd had her family legacy returned to her. And for Rosemary, who had found the strength to understand, forgive and let go.

Eva thought of the way her mother had held her the morning after her grandfather had died. Her mother. It had been a healing journey for the two of them too, because Eva was getting close to finding her again. And there was no one else, she thought, who could hold her quite that way.

★

In the workshop, Eva glanced up as a man entered, a cap pulled down over his head.

'Morning,' she called.

'Morning,' he replied.

She let him browse. Eva loved the fact that people wanted to look around the studio, watch the repairs in progress, run their hands over furniture lovingly restored and polished and hopefully sometimes wanted to buy. Her prices were competitive, the pieces were hand-picked and everything was restored after considerable research and with meticulous attention to detail.

'I have something to sell.' The voice cut into her reverie.

She looked up, but couldn't see him. 'Oh yes?' For a moment, she felt a jolt of fear, but that was ridiculous. This was a lovely June day, it was broad daylight and they were in a studio in the middle of town. She wasn't in Myanmar now.

'What is it?' Though Eva didn't generally make purchases from people who came into the shop. The best pieces, she had to say, were somewhat more elusive and hard to find.

'A pair of chinthes.'

She gasped.

He stepped out of the shadows, came towards her, almost unrecognisable because of the hat.

Eva got to her feet, her polishing cloth still in her hand.

As he drew closer, she saw that he looked much the same, though more anglicised in that hat, black jeans and a leather jacket. He leant on the desk which she used as a counter.

Raised a dark eyebrow. 'They have very nice carving,' he said. 'And ruby eyes.'

'Ramon,' she breathed.

'But why didn't you tell me you were coming over to the UK?' she asked him half an hour later when they were sitting in her office, a cafetière of coffee between them. She couldn't stop staring at him, she was still getting over the shock.

'I wanted to surprise you.' He smiled.

'You did that alright.' She poured the coffee. Her hands were shaking and she hoped he wouldn't notice. 'How on earth did you find out my address?'

'Easy.' He shrugged. 'You are Eva Gatsby and you come from this town in West Dorset, is that correct?'

'Of course. But—'

'I Googled "Gatsby" and a website came up. *Gatsby's Antique Restoration*. Is this someone else, I ask myself. Or is this Eva? What are the chances?'

She laughed. 'I suppose it was pretty obvious.' She passed him his coffee. 'But why are you here, Ramon?'

He took off the hat and laid it on the desk next to his coffee cup. 'I told you I had big plans.' He shot her a reproachful look.

'The plans being . . . ?'

'To set up a sister company in Europe,' he said. 'I will keep the business in Mandalay. But I want to expand. Maybe even trade worldwide.'

'As your father wanted to do,' she murmured.

'Exactly.' His green eyes shone. He picked up the photo of her father on the bench in the garden, which she kept on the desk, alongside the one of Eva and her mother making a daisy chain, taken at the same time by her grandfather. 'Your father?' he asked.

Eva nodded. Everyone said they looked alike, not just in colouring but in her features too.

'Same dimples.' Ramon ran his fingers over the picture.

Eva tried not to blush.

'And your mother?' He picked up the other photo.

'Yes. My father was watching us make a daisy chain.' She shrugged. The photographs might not mean a lot to anyone else, but to her they represented the family past that she had lost. And they were special, because they too were a pair.

Ramon stared at them for a long time.

'And will you come and go between the two business premises?' Eva tried to make her voice casual. 'Between Europe and Mandalay?' She was trying not to analyse it. But what did this visit mean exactly? He hadn't said a word to make her think that anything had changed. And did she even want to hope? Seeing him here in Dorset, in her own workshop, just as she had once been in his, she wasn't sure what she felt. Perhaps she was still in shock.

'I will have overall responsibility of the two, yes,' he said.

'And how is your grandmother, Maya?' Eva asked. But she knew the answer almost as soon as she spoke.

His expression changed. 'It was only a few days ago.'

'I'm sorry,' she murmured.

'She rests,' he said simply. He bowed his head. 'She rests in peace.'

'Like Grandpa.' Maybe they were even resting together.

They looked at one another and then away.

'More coffee?'

He nodded and she poured.

'So, where will you—?'

'I wanted to—'

They both spoke at the same moment, both laughed uncertainly.

'You first,' she said.

'I wanted to write to you, Eva.' He reached out and took her hand. 'But there was too much to say.'

She nodded. Was this his way of trying to tell her it had all been a mistake?

'I told you once that I could promise you nothing.'

She nodded again, trying to smile, but feeling miserable inside. 'And I told you I didn't want your promises,' she reminded him. Just like Maya hadn't wanted Lawrence's promises. But that didn't mean . . .

'What were you going to say?' he asked gently.

'I was going to ask you where in Europe you were planning to set up your business,' she said brightly. Though it was an effort.

'Here,' he said.

'In Britain, you mean?'

'Here in Dorset,' he said. 'As close to you as possible. If that is OK.'

She stared at him.

'It will need someone here to set things up,' he said. 'And of course that person should be me.'

'Of course.' She beamed back at him, she just couldn't help it.

'And now, I think, I can make you that promise,' he said. 'If you will let me.'

Eva got up to stand next to him and she gently brushed his dark hair from his brow as she had done before. 'I'll let you,' she said softly.

'Your emails . . . ?' He took hold of her hands and got to his feet.

'There was too much to say.'

He nodded. 'I hoped that was it.'

Eva looked up at him. Was he really here? She could hardly believe it. And was he going to stay?

'Those chinthes that brought you and me together must be as powerful as my grandmother always believed,' he whispered.

'I think you're right.' And then she was in his arms again and his lips were on hers. Tasting as warm and golden as Myanmar itself and of the stories of her childhood, that had so long ago wound their way into her heart.

ACKNOWLEDGEMENTS

Thanks to my tirelessly supportive agent, Teresa Chris, whose intuition and 'eye' I greatly respect and to my talented editor, Jo Dickinson, and all the team at Quercus, especially Kathryn Taussig and Margot Weale. Jo and Teresa have helped me to mould this once unwieldy novel into its present shape and condition, and I am very grateful.

Thanks to the Sams family: Dee for her support; Mervyn and Jean for kindly lending me the memoirs of the late John Sams, in which he wrote about his time in the Gurkhas, training and then fighting in Burma. For John – Gallop, the mule! Thanks to Bill Johnson, who has delighted our Alston Hall writing group with his memoirs of his war in Burma and who was kind enough to read and comment on a section of the novel for me. And most importantly to my husband's father, the late Peter Innes, who fought in Burma in the Chindits and also worked in the timber industry there. Some of his Burmese artefacts are now in my husband's possession – including, of course, two chinthes. Although I have used aspects of John and Peter's lives and experiences in the novel, I must stress that Lawrence's story is entirely fictional and that none of the characters relate to any of their acquaintances, friends or loved ones!

My late mother-in-law, Hazel Innes, also acquired many books about Burma, which I have used in my research, notably Sue Arnold's autobiographical *A Burmese Legacy*, Helen Rodriguez's autobiography *Helen of Burma*, H.E.W. Braund's account of Steel Brothers and Company Ltd in Burma, *Calling to Mind* and Alan Carter's *Last Out of Burma*. *Helen of Burma* was particularly invaluable to me in writing about Maya's war. Again, my characters are not related to any real people I have read about here, many details have no doubt been absorbed into this story, but it is fictional and my own.

Of other books I have read during my research, the ones that stood out were *The Glass Palace* by Amitav Ghosh, which allowed me to dip fictionally into the world of the final Burmese dynasty in 1885 – and thanks to Claire Zolkwer for recommending this book to me – and of course George Orwell's wonderful *Burmese Days*. The story of the Ngau Mauk ruby is apparently a true one and was derived from information on the internet, as was other material about Burmese rubies and chinthes.

Thanks to my husband's 'Burmese family' especially Suu Suu and Tin Mya and the others we met during our stay in Myanmar in November 2012 such as Ben, the driver who took us to Maymyo. And to other people we met and talked with there who may have made a contribution, thank you too.

rateful thanks as always to Alan Fish, who read and commented on an early draft of this novel. And to my husband, Grey, who listens to every scene I read to him and always finds something useful to add. As I have said before, he is the best travelling companion a writer can have and a good problem solver to boot. Thanks to my daughters, Alexa and Ana, for answering random queries about language, music and things technical and for their unflagging support of my books. And to my son, Luke, for information about Copenhagen and computer scientists. Thanks to June Tate for her 'riches of the heart'. Finally, thanks to friends who have supported me during the journey of this novel and to readers who take the trouble to contact me to tell me that they enjoy my books. And to anyone I have forgotten. Thank you all!

567

The Creative Landscape

Rosanna Ley lives in West Dorset. Here she writes about the relationship between landscape and creativity . . .

There are little hotspots all over the world to which groups of creative people are drawn. But why? Surely it's not simply a question of contacts and existing artistic infrastructure – though clearly this helps. Is it something to do with landscape? And if some landscapes provoke more creative responses than others, which kind does it for you?

In the west country of the UK we can do wild and bleak or cute and scenic. We get a lot of rain – but this is why the grass is always greener. There are more writers, musicians, potters, artists, weavers, sculptors and glass blowers here than anywhere else in the UK. And tourists of all nationalities brave our English weather and come in their thousands to visit our galleries, exhibitions, mills, shops and craft centres. But what is it about the landscape that inspires creativity?

Is it perhaps the sense of history? Age can certainly give a landscape a vibe – Lyme Regis, Charmouth and the Jurassic Coast of Dorset have a sense of history which literally clings to the fossilized rocks, the cliffs and the beaches. Roman roads and ancient forts abound. In the novels of Thomas Hardy, Dorchester provides an artistic legacy too – of the writerly kind.

Visitors are equally inspired by the golden sandstone cliffs of West Bay – as recently featured in ITV's crime drama Broadchurch. Following Broadchurch, visitors (known locally as 'Broadies'!) have flocked to West Bay to see for themselves those amazing, towering honey-bricked cliffs.

Or is it perhaps the tranquillity of a natural landscape – be it coastal, woodland, upland or riverside – which appeals to the creative mind and feeds our desire to get back to nature and away from the noise, turmoil and stress of busy city life?

Sometimes, walking along the vastness of Chesil Beach, you feel solitary, humble, affected by Nature. It's liberating.

Artists here in Dorset often talk about the quality of the light for painting. The rocks range from the orange sandstone of West Bay through to the Blue Lias of Lyme; where there is light there is always shadow.

As for Fuerteventura . . . There is a late-afternoon light that tints the landscape with a deep yellow and turns the sand (and blonde hair!) an unearthly golden green.

Whatever the personal response to landscape, it seems that this is a relationship and a dialogue between individual and place. Landscape brings out the creativity in us all. It encourages us to reflect, express ourselves and even to change our thinking.

Landscape might offer a glimpse of memory and the past – as it does for Ruby in my second novel when she first sees the turquoise lagoon in Fuerteventura, otherwise known as the 'Bay of Secrets', which became the book's title. It might even offer a glimpse of the future.

I always felt I belonged to West Dorset. It's my 'soul home'. And I'm always happiest writing where there is a sea view. It may be in my local cafe in West Bay with the high bank of ginger pebbles and the waves right beside me, the harbour and the sandstone cliffs beyond. Or in Fuerteventura on the Playa de Castillo watching the surfers ride the wild waves. It might be a tranquil summer day or bleak mid-winter. The sea lets me dream – it does it for me every time.

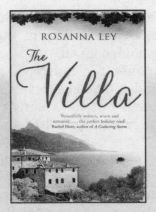
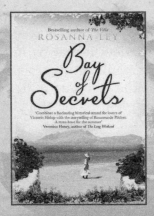

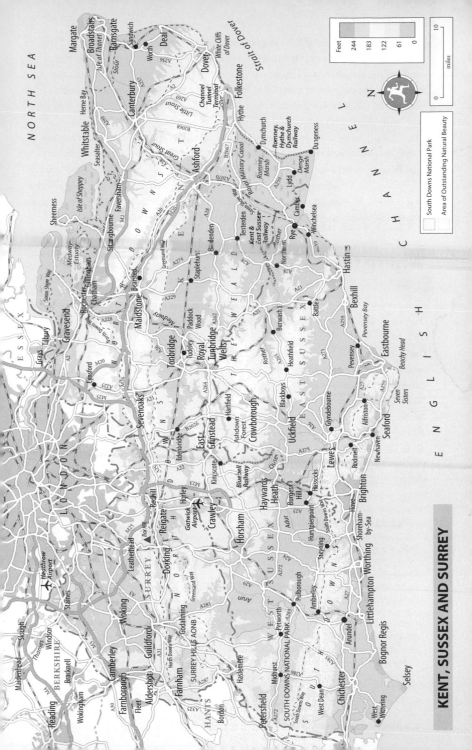

KENT, SUSSEX AND SURREY

invasion of England, in 1066, took place in Sussex, when the **Normans** overran King Harold's army at **Battle** near **Hastings** – and went on to leave their mark all over this corner of the kingdom, not least in a profusion of medieval **castles**. There are other important historic sights at every turn, from **Tudor** manor houses and sprawling Elizabethan and **Jacobean** estates to the old dockyards of **Chatham**, power base of the once invincible British navy.

You can also tackle some impressive long-distance **walks**, prime among them the glorious **South Downs Way** in Sussex and the gentler **North Downs Way** from Surrey to East Kent. Both Sussex and Kent – a county historically famed for its fruit and veg – are superb **foodie** destinations, with countless gastropubs, restaurants and farmers' markets providing delicious, local produce, from asparagus and wild cherries to fresh seafood and Romney Marsh lamb, as well as award-winning **vineyards** and **breweries** producing excellent wines and ales.

Where to go

On Kent's north coast the sweet little fishing town of **Whitstable**, famed for its oysters, is a favourite getaway for weekending Londoners. **Margate,** becoming cooler by the day, and the charmingly retro **Broadstairs** make good bases on the **Isle of Thanet**, with its clean sandy bays, while the east coast has the low-key Georgian seaside town of **Deal**, the mighty **Dover Castle**, **Folkestone** – home to the art Triennial – and the strangely compelling shingle headland of **Dungeness**. Inland is the university city of **Canterbury**, where the venerable cathedral dominates a compact old centre packed with medieval buildings, while Kent's Weald boasts a wealth of historic **houses**, among them the mighty **Knole** estate and **Hever Castle**, Anne Boleyn's childhood home, along with the glorious **gardens** at **Sissinghurst**, a stunning array planted by Vita Sackville-West. Exploring the many other historical attractions in the Weald – such as Winston Churchill's estate at **Chartwell** or Charles Darwin's family home at **Down House** – could fill a long and happy weekend; the Georgian town of **Royal Tunbridge Wells** makes an appealing base, as do countless peaceful villages.

ART ALONG THE COAST

One of the defining features of the Kent and Sussex coastline is its crop of exciting art galleries, which with their cutting-edge architecture and top-notch collections have brought fresh energy and glamour to the faded seaside towns of the Southeast. Regenerating ailing coastal communities with high-profile buildings is no new thing, of course – the **De La Warr Pavilion** (1935), Bexhill's Modernist icon, was built partly for that very reason, although it was originally an entertainment hall and not a gallery. Within a couple of decades it had fallen into decline, but a gorgeous restoration in 2005 saw it brought back to life. Nearby, in Hastings, the **Jerwood**, whose shimmering black-tiled exterior echoes the look of the local fishing huts, opened in 2012 to display a modern British collection, and has played an important part in the upwards trajectory of that town. Even Eastbourne, more associated with OAPs than YBAs, has the **Towner**, open since the 1920s but moved in 2009 to a sleek new location. In Kent, the **Turner Contemporary** was instrumental in returning a smile to the face of once-merry Margate; while Folkestone, if anything, has come even further, with the lively **Triennial** – a major public show that has featured artists from Tracey Emin to Cornelia Parker, first staged in 2008 – becoming a regular fixture.

CLOCKWISE FROM TOP LEFT *THE TIGER INN*, EAST DEAN (P.214); PUNCH AND JUDY SHOW, BROADSTAIRS (P.96); BODIAM CASTLE (P.189)

The jewel of **Sussex** is the **South Downs National Park**, a glorious sweep of rolling downland that stretches from Hampshire into Sussex, meeting the sea at the iconic chalk cliffs of **Beachy Head** and **Seven Sisters**. There's wonderful walking along the Downs, not least along the South Downs Way, but equally rewarding are the less-tramped pockets of countryside, from the gorse-peppered heathland of **Ashdown Forest** on the edge of the sleepy High Weald, to the sandstone cliffs of **Hastings County Park** on the coast.

In East Sussex, buzzy **Brighton**, a university town with a blowsy good-time atmosphere, makes an irresistible weekend destination, as does handsome **Lewes**, in the heart of the South Downs; **Hastings**, east along the coast, is an up-and-coming seaside town with lots to recommend it, including a pretty Old Town and the scruffy but hip St Leonards neighbourhood to explore. On the edge of lonely **Romney Marsh**, picturesque **Rye**, with its cobbled streets and medieval buildings, lies within minutes of the family-friendly beach of **Camber Sands**. In West Sussex, the attractive hilltop town of **Arundel**, surrounded by unspoilt countryside, boasts a magnificent castle; **Midhurst** – home to the national park visitor centre – is surrounded by gorgeous scenery and plenty of foodie pubs; while the lovely old cathedral town of **Chichester**, set between the sea and the South Downs, makes a perfect base for exploring the creeks and mudflats of **Chichester Harbour** and dune-backed **West Wittering** beach. Like Kent, Sussex abounds in great landscaped estates and gardens, among them seventeenth-century **Petworth House**, with its vast parkland roamed by deer, the Capability Brown-designed **Sheffield Park**, sprawling **Wakehurst Place** and the informal, imaginative garden at **Great Dixter**.

While **Surrey** boasts some attractive market towns, the chief appeal is in the **Surrey Hills**, in the North Downs, where ramblers and cyclists enjoy bluebell woods, mellow chalk grasslands and unspoiled hamlets such as **Shere** or Peaslake. The wild heathlands of the **Devil's Punchbowl** feel very different, but are equally good for walking. The county's main sights include the **Denbies** vineyard, where you can tour the winery and enjoy tastings; the stunning Arts and Crafts **Watts Gallery Artists' Village**; and the great gardens of **RHS Wisley**, dating back to Victorian times.

When to go

Kent, Sussex and Surrey often feel slightly warmer than the rest of the country, and the Sussex coast in particular sees a lot of sunshine – Eastbourne is regularly cited as the sunniest place on the UK mainland. Weather-wise, the **summer** is the best time to head for the coast, though it can get crowded – and more expensive – at this time, as well as at weekends and during the school holidays. Travel during the week, if you can, or book well in advance. **Spring** can be a lovely season, especially for ramblers and cyclists, with the wildflowers in bloom; given the profusion of woodlands, **autumn** is frequently glorious, with great banks of fiery foliage set off by bright skies and crisp air. **Winter** tends to be quiet, and is an ideal time to snuggle up with a pint of real ale in a country pub, or to enjoy the strange allure of an off-season English seaside town.

FROM TOP VINTAGE SHOP, BRIGHTON (P.259); ST THOMAS À BECKET, ROMNEY MARSH (P.132); WATTS CHAPEL, NEAR GUILDFORD (P.308) >

Author picks

Our authors have explored every corner of Kent, Sussex and Surrey, and here they share some of their favourite experiences.

Unique accommodation B&Bs are all very well, but for the utmost in unusual stays, try Margate's *Walpole Bay Hotel* (see p.94), the safari-style experience at Port Lympne (see p.129), the Belle Tout lighthouse at Beachy Head (see p.213) or the *Old Railway Station*, Petworth (see p.288).

Quirky churches There are some real gems in this region. Track down the Marc Chagall windows in Tudeley Church (see p.144), St Thomas à Becket, stranded in Romney Marsh (see p.132), and the beautiful Berwick Church with its Bloomsbury Group murals (see p.218).

Seaside fun Enjoy simple, old-fashioned pleasures at our favourite retro *gelaterias* – Morelli's in Broadstairs (see p.99) and *Fusciardi's* in Eastbourne (see p.210) – and while away a day crabbing at Whitstable (see p.80), East Head (see p.279) or Bosham (see p.277).

Vintage finds You can grab fabulous retro gladrags and funky vintage furnishings in Margate's Old Town (see p.92), along Harbour Street in Whitstable (see p.87) and in North Laine in Brighton (see p.241).

Festivals and events The Rochester Sweeps (see p.71), Jack-in-the-Green, Hastings (see p.182), Lewes Bonfire Night (see p.228) and the Bognor Birdman (see p.298): all fabulous fun and just a tiny bit bonkers.

Art off the beaten track The region has its fair share of big-hitting arty attractions (the Turner, Pallant Gallery and Charleston Farmhouse, to name but a few), but just as rewarding are the lesser-known gems of Ditching Museum of Art + Craft (see p.231), Farleys House and Gallery (see p.191), Derek Jarman's garden in Dungeness (see p.132) and the Watts Gallery Chapel in Surrey (see p.308).

Our author recommendations don't end here. We've flagged up our favourite places – a perfectly sited hotel, an atmospheric café, a special restaurant – throughout the guide, highlighted with the ★ symbol.

21

things not to miss

It's not possible to see everything that Kent, Sussex and Surrey have to offer in one trip – and we don't suggest you try. What follows, in no particular order, is a selective taste of the region's highlights, including gorgeous beaches, outstanding beauty spots, historic big-hitters and compelling cultural experiences. All highlights are colour-coded by chapter and have a page reference to take you straight into the Guide, where you can find out more.

1

1 THE SEVEN SISTERS AND BEACHY HEAD

The iconic, soaring Seven Sisters cliffs are the scenic highlight of the South Downs National Park.

2 CHARTWELL

Winston Churchill's country estate offers fascinating insights into the man, along with lovely grounds and local woodlands to explore.

3 THE TURNER CONTEMPORARY

The high-profile modern art gallery that kick-started Margate's rebirth hosts excellent temporary exhibitions, and all for free.

4 THE DEVIL'S PUNCH BOWL

Wild, raw and a little eerie – this Surrey heath is one of the county's more dramatic beauty spots.

7

8

9

14

19

20

21

Itineraries

Kent, Sussex and Surrey are wonderfully diverse, and these suggested itineraries offer a variety of different pleasures – from lively seaside fun in Brighton to a wealth of amazing historical sights and some of England's finest gardens. Mixing the big names with secret gems, they should help you discover some of the richness and diversity of this lovely region.

A WEEKEND IN BRIGHTON

FRIDAY NIGHT

Dinner Start off the weekend in style with champagne and oysters at *Riddle and Finns*. **See p.253**

Komedia Head to the hip *Komedia* theatre to catch some comedy or live music. **See p.259**

SATURDAY

Royal Pavilion Set aside a full morning to take in the splendours of George IV's pleasure palace by the sea. **See p.238**

The seafront Crunch along the pebbles, amble to the end of the tacky Palace Pier or swoop up the i360 tower, and grab a fresh mackerel sandwich from *Jack and Linda's Smokehouse* for lunch. **See p.241 & p.252**

Shopping Spend the afternoon exploring the independent shops of the Lanes and North Laine. **See p.259 & p.260**

Dinner Book a seat at the counter at *64 Degrees* to enjoy some memorably inventive cooking. **See p.252**

Nightlife Head out on the town – Brighton is positively bursting at the seams with über-cool bars and clubs, as well as a great collection of traditional boozers. A top spot to start the night is *The Plotting Parlour* cocktail bar. **See p.255**

SUNDAY

Brunch Try the *Flour Pot Bakery* or *Compass Point Eatery* for a lazy brunch. **See p.253 & p.254**

Yellowave beach sports venue Burn off the calories with a game of beach volleyball. **See p.249**

Duke of York's cinema If it's raining, hunker down at Brighton's independent cinema, or take in the exhibits at the Brighton Museum. **See p.258 & p.240**

Lewes If you fancy a complete change of scene, hop on a train to nearby Lewes (15min), where you can wander through the town's ancient twittens and visit a Norman castle. **See p.224**

THE HISTORY TOUR

There are enough historical attractions in Kent, Sussex and Surrey to fill a trip of three weeks or more. Here we cover the biggest hitters on a tour that could easily last a fortnight. None of the short hops between places on this itinerary will take more than an hour and a half by car.

❶ **Chatham Historic Dockyard** Explore historic ships, art and a working Victorian ropery in the colossal dockyard from England's Great Age of Sail. **See p.72**

❷ **Canterbury** With three sights – including the mighty cathedral and the ancient abbey – comprising a UNESCO World Heritage Site, this

ABOVE BEACH HUTS ON BRIGHTON SEAFRONT

venerable city is full of historic splendour. You'll need a couple of days to do it justice. See p.88

❸ **Dover Castle** The mighty cliffside fortress packs in millennia of history, from its Roman lighthouse to its claustrophobic World War II bunkers. See p.114

❹ **Battle Abbey** Site of the most famous battle ever fought on English soil, the 1066 Battle of Hastings, which saw the end of Anglo-Saxon England. See p.186

❺ **Royal Pavilion, Brighton** Opulent, quirky and marvellously OTT, George IV's Regency pavilion is quite unlike any other palace in the country. See p.238

❻ **Fishbourne Roman Palace** Head west to Chichester to visit the largest and best-preserved Roman dwelling north of the Alps. See p.274

❼ **Petworth House** Seventeenth-century Baroque mansion, with sweeping parkland landscaped by Capability Brown – and immortalized by J.M.W. Turner. See p.287

❽ **Polesden Lacey** Elegant and utterly Edwardian, with wonderful grounds just perfect for picnicking. See p.311

❾ **Knole** The fifteenth-century childhood home of Vita Sackville-West, eulogized in literature and film, is an immense treasure-trove with an irresistible, faded beauty. See p.152

THE GARDEN OF ENGLAND

All three counties are heaven for garden fans, with a wide variety, from formal to natural, to inspire even the most tentative of gardeners.

The following are the must-sees, visitable in a busy week; there are many more.

❶ **Sissinghurst** Abundant, romantic, nostalgic, witty – the bohemian cottage garden to end them all, designed by Vita Sackville-West and her husband. See p.148

❷ **Prospect Cottage, Dungeness** The late Derek Jarman's windswept shingle patch is a poignant, artistic memorial to an extraordinary filmmaker. See p.132

❸ **Great Dixter** The innovative, experimental garden of the late, great Christopher Lloyd features informal garden rooms set around a Wealden hall house, and is still very much living and evolving. See p.188

❹ **Sheffield Park** Beautiful at any time of year but especially famed for its autumn colours, when banks of flaming foliage are reflected in the mirror-like surfaces of the landscaped garden's lakes. See p.196

❺ **Wakehurst Place** A short hop from Sheffield Park, the country estate of Kew's Royal Botanic Gardens is a glorious 465-acre site taking in formal gardens, meadows, woodland, lakes and wetlands. See p.199

❻ **Hannah Peschar Sculpture Garden** A magical hideaway, with modern sculptures dotted around wild, lush woodland. See p.312

❼ **RHS Wisley** The Horticultural Society's flagship offers a huge amount, including a giant glasshouse and all manner of experimental gardens, plus an excellent shop. See p.313

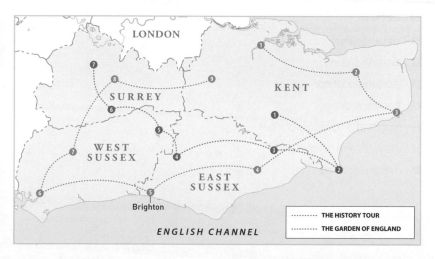

erries

30
ach

Katy Apples
from Bessborough
farm
£1.35/kg
.61p/lb

Blackberrys
£1.35
Each
from Bessborough
farm

Disco
Apple
£1.35
61p/l

Early
W
A

LOCAL FRUIT FOR SALE, THE GOODS SHED, CANTERBURY

Basics

Getting there

With London on their doorstep, the Eurotunnel at their eastern end, and Gatwick – Britain's second-largest international airport – to the west, Kent, Sussex and Surrey are easily accessible by air, road or rail, with excellent transport connections that include the country's first high-speed rail line in Kent.

By car

From the M25 London Orbital, several major **roads** strike off south: the A2/M2 to Canterbury and the North Kent coast; the M20 to Folkestone; and the M23/A23 to Brighton. The A27 runs west–east roughly parallel to the coast, giving access to coastal towns including Chichester, Brighton, Eastbourne and Hastings, though it can be slow going – the sixty-odd miles between Chichester and Hastings can take up to two hours to drive.

By train

Kent and the easternmost part of Sussex are served by **Southeastern** trains. By far the quickest way to travel into Kent is on Southeastern's regular **high-speed** services: one line (the HS1) zips from London St Pancras to Ashford International, taking under forty minutes; the other runs along the North Kent coast via Rochester, Faversham, Whitstable, Herne Bay, Margate, Broadstairs and Ramsgate, before heading inland to Canterbury and Ashford and across to Folkestone. There are also regular, slower services into Kent from London Bridge, Charing Cross, Waterloo and Victoria.

Sussex destinations served by Southeastern include Hastings (from Charing Cross or St Pancras via Ashford), Rye (St Pancras via Ashford) and Battle (Charing Cross). Hastings is also, along with the rest of Sussex, and parts of Surrey, served by **Southern Railways**, which in 2016 saw endless disruptions, delays and slashed services, with attendant industrial disputes. Southern's fast service to Brighton from London Victoria in theory takes just fifty minutes; the company also runs trains from Portsmouth along the coast to Brighton, and from London Victoria to Eastbourne, Lewes, Arundel, Littlehampton and Chichester. You can also reach Brighton from London Victoria

on the Gatwick Express, and from London Bridge and St Pancras International on Thameslink.

Southern also offers a service from London Victoria to Dorking in Surrey; elsewhere, the county is served by **South West Trains**, with regular services from London Waterloo to Farnham, Guildford and Dorking.

By bus

National Express (W nationalexpress.com) runs coaches from London's Victoria Coach Station to **Kent** (including Canterbury, Deal, Dover, Folkestone, Herne Bay, Hythe, Maidstone, Margate, Ramsgate, Sevenoaks and Tunbridge Wells), **Sussex** (Arundel, Ashford, Battle, Bexhill, Bognor, Brighton, Chichester, Eastbourne, Hastings, Littlehampton, Shoreham and Worthing) and Farnham in **Surrey**.

By plane

Gatwick Airport, just north of Crawley in Sussex, is Britain's second-largest international airport, and has good rail connections on to Brighton and other destinations within Sussex. In Kent, **Lydd airport** (W lyddair.com) in Romney Marsh sees services from Le Touquet (Feb–Oct only).

By ferry, Eurotunnel and Eurostar

Ferries run from France to Dover (W doverport .co.uk) and Newhaven (just east of Brighton; W newhavenferryport.co.uk). P&O Ferries (W poferries .com) and DFDS (W dfdsseaways.co.uk) operate the Calais-to-Dover route (hourly; 1hr 30min), and DFDS also runs services from Dunkirk to Dover (9–12 daily; 2hr) and Dieppe to Newhaven (2–3 daily; 4hr). Consult W directferries.com, W ferrybooker.com or W seaview.co.uk for up-to-date information, bookings and offers.

Often quicker and more convenient are the drive-on/drive-off shuttle trains operated by **Eurotunnel** (W eurotunnel.com) through the Channel Tunnel from Calais to Folkestone (35min). Book well ahead for the lowest prices, which start at less than €70 for a car with all passengers.

The **Eurostar** train service (W eurostar.co.uk) runs through the Channel Tunnel from Brussels, Amsterdam, Lille and Paris – plus, less frequently, from Lyon, Marseille and Avignon – to London St Pancras, with some trains stopping at Ashford International and Ebbsfleet International in Kent.

Getting around

Getting from A to B by public transport is generally pretty straightforward in Kent, Sussex and Surrey, at least when it comes to towns; the problem comes in getting to off-the-beaten-track attractions or villages deep in the countryside, which might only be served by one solitary bus, or involve a long hike from the nearest train station, making travel in anything but a car distinctly challenging.

Fortunately, some of the region's loveliest **countryside** – including Devil's Dyke, Beachy Head and the Seven Sisters in the South Downs National Park – has good public transport connections, and there is a huge range of wonderful long-distance walking and cycling routes too (see p.28).

Throughout the Guide we give public transport information for sights and attractions that are served by regular buses or trains.

By train

There are good connections around Kent, Sussex and Surrey with **Southeastern**, which covers Kent and the easternmost part of Sussex around Hastings, and runs the country's only high-speed rail services (see p.29); **Southern Railways**, which serves the rest of Sussex and some of Surrey; and **South West Trains**, which covers Surrey. The essential first call for information on routes, timetables, fares and special offers is **National Rail Enquiries**.

The key to getting the best **fares** is to book early and buy an "**advance**" ticket, which is only valid on the date and time specified; the most expensive tickets are "**anytime**" tickets bought on the day, which permit flexible travel on any train. You can buy tickets in person at train stations, or by phone or online from any train operator or simply by using a quick and easy online booking site like Ⓦthetrainline.com; the National Rail Enquiries website also offers direct links from its journey planner for purchasing specific fares. Bear in mind that some journeys (for example Hastings to London) are covered by more than one train operator, and an advance ticket bought from one operator will not be valid on the route run by the other. It's worth noting, too, that if you are travelling on one of the high-speed services operated by Southeastern you'll need a high-speed ticket, or else will be required to pay a supplement.

If you're spending time in Kent it's worth considering the **Kent Rover** travel pass, which gives you three consecutive days of unlimited train travel on Southeastern for £39.50 per adult (with up to four kids at £5 each).

Finally, it's worth bearing in mind that the region's **heritage railways** can be a useful means of getting to attractions otherwise not easily accessible, as well as being fun trips in their own right; the Romney, Hythe & Dymchurch Railway (see p.129) is a good way of getting to and from Dungeness; the Kent & East Sussex Railway (see p.151) connects Tenterden in Kent to the picture-perfect Bodiam Castle just over the border; and the Bluebell Railway (see p.196) links East Grinstead mainline station in Sussex with Sheffield Park.

By bus

The bus network in **Kent** is split into two: Stagecoach covers the east and south of the county, including Ashford, the Canterbury, Herne Bay and Whitstable triangle, Dover, Deal, Folkestone and Hythe; and Arriva covers the west and north, including Gravesend, the Isle of Sheppey, Maidstone, Sevenoaks, Tonbridge and the Medway towns.

In **Sussex** and **Surrey**, buses are run by a variety of operators including Arriva, Brighton & Hove Bus and Coach Company (which cover the surrounding area as well as the city itself), Compass Bus, Metrobus, Southdown PSV and Stagecoach, as well as smaller community operators. East Sussex County Council's website has links to bus timetables and a useful interactive bus map (Ⓦeastsussex.gov.uk; search for "bus timetables and maps"); West Sussex County Council (Ⓦwestsussex.gov.uk) lists local bus operators; and Surrey County Council's site (Ⓦsurreycc.org.uk) has a county-wide map of bus routes plus links to timetables.

In most cases, **timetables** and routes are well integrated. Buses between towns tend to be frequent and regular, but services can be sketchy once you get into the countryside, and on Sundays they sometimes dry up altogether.

Tickets are bought on board the bus, and it's generally cheaper to buy a return ticket than two single fares – check with the driver. Children under 5 travel free, and older children will generally pay half or two-thirds of the fare. For any but the shortest hops it's worth considering a **Discovery ticket**, which is accepted by all of the main bus operators in Kent, Sussex and Surrey; day tickets cost £8.50 per adult, £7 per child, or you can buy a family day ticket for £16.

The impartial official service **Traveline** has full details and timetable information for every bus route in Kent, Sussex and Surrey.

By car

Once you get away from the main towns and the coast, driving is, inevitably, the easiest way to get around the region – and in the case of many off-the-beaten-track attractions, it's the only practical means of transport.

If you are driving, keep plenty of change handy; some towns do still offer free parking but they're few and far between, and parking machines and meters never offer change. Pay-and-display car parks are generally cheaper than on-street meters. Both Brighton and Canterbury offer **park-and-ride** schemes, which can be a useful way to bypass the stress of parking, especially in Brighton where parking charges have risen through the roof in recent years.

The main **car rental** companies have branches all over the region; expect to pay around £30 per day, £55 for a weekend or from £120 per week. The price comparison website Ⓦ carrentals.co.uk is a good first port of call.

The AA (Ⓦ theaa.com), RAC (Ⓦ rac.co.uk) and Green Flag (Ⓦ greenflag.co.uk) all operate 24-hour **emergency breakdown services**, and offer useful online **route planners**. You can make use of these emergency services if you are not a member of the organization, but you will need to become a member at the roadside and will also incur a hefty surcharge.

PUBLIC TRANSPORT CONTACTS

Arriva ☎ 0344 800 4411, Ⓦ arrivabus.co.uk
Brighton & Hove Bus and Coach Company ☎ 01273 886200, Ⓦ buses.co.uk
Compass Travel ☎ 01903 690025, Ⓦ www.compasstravel.co.uk
Metrobus ☎ 01293 449191, Ⓦ metrobus.co.uk
National Express ☎ 0871 781 8181, Ⓦ nationalexpress.com
National Rail Enquiries ☎ 0845 748 4950, Ⓦ nationalrail.co.uk
South West Trains ☎ 0345 600 0650, Ⓦ southwesttrains.co.uk
Southdown PSV ☎ 01342 719619, Ⓦ southdownpsv.co.uk
Southeastern ☎ 0345 322 7021, Ⓦ southeasternrailway.co.uk
Southern Railway ☎ 0345 127 2920, Ⓦ southernrailway.co.uk
Stagecoach ☎ 0871 834 0010, Ⓦ stagecoachbus.com
Traveline ☎ 0871 200 2233, Ⓦ travelinesoutheast.org.uk

Accommodation

Kent, Sussex and Surrey offer a good range of attractive accommodation, from simple guesthouses to cosy village pubs, luxurious country retreats and cool boutique hotels. Camping is a good option, with glampers particularly well catered for in Sussex.

It is usually best to **book in advance**, especially in summer, and at certain times it's essential. Accommodation in Brighton, and all the seaside towns, is at a premium on summer weekends while festivals such as the Whitstable Oyster Festival, Broadstairs Folk Week and the Goodwood events near Chichester fill up their towns very fast. Some places impose a **minimum stay** of two nights at the weekend and/or in high season – this is practically universal in Brighton and the bigger seaside destinations, but can also be true of some of the more remote guesthouses or glampsites, too – though these conditions can often be waived at the last minute if an establishment has not filled its rooms. Most accommodation options offer **free wi-fi** as standard; we've stated in the Guide where this is not the case.

Hotels, inns and B&Bs

Hotels run the gamut from opulent country piles to (quite) cheap and (mostly) cheerful seaside guesthouses. The absolute minimum you can expect to pay is around £70 for a reasonable double room in a simple B&B, rising up to at least £200 for something more luxurious, be it a country manor set in its own grounds or a sleek sea-view affair in Brighton. For a good level of comfort, service and atmosphere you're looking at paying about £80–100, though of course there are exceptions.

Though we have quoted **prices** in our reviews (see box below), it is increasingly the case that rates are calculated according to demand, with online booking engines such as Ⓦ lastminute.com and Ⓦ booking.com often offering discounts on

---

ACCOMMODATION PRICES

For all accommodation reviewed in this guide we provide **high season** (July–Sept) weekend prices, quoting the lowest price for one night's stay in a double or twin room in a **hotel or B&B**, the price of a dorm bed (and a double room, where available) in a **hostel**, and, unless otherwise stated, the cost of a pitch in a **campsite**. For **self-catering**, we quote the lowest rate you might pay per night in high season for the whole property – and we've made it clear where there is a minimum stay. Rates in hotels and B&Bs may well drop between Sunday and Thursday, or if you stay more than one night.

last-minute reservations, and establishments raising or lowering their prices according to how busy they predict they might be.

Staying in a **B&B** will generally, but by no means always, be cheaper than a hotel, and will certainly be more personal. While often little more than a couple of rooms in someone's house, many B&Bs aim to offer something special, and the houses themselves may well be part of the appeal – a converted oast house in Kent, for example, or a Sussex lighthouse. In Surrey, certainly, staying in a rural B&B is by far the best accommodation option, allowing you to see the best of the county. Tea- and coffee-making facilities, en-suite or private bathrooms and a hearty breakfast are generally standard – certainly in the places featured in the Guide – and many will offer luxurious extras such as fluffy robes and posh bath products. Another good option, especially for foodies, is to stay in a **restaurant** (or gastropub) **with rooms**. Here the focus is mainly on the meal, which will invariably be good, with the added luxury of an extremely short and easy trip up to bed after dinner. Restaurants with rooms often offer meal-plus-bed deals, and a delicious breakfast to boot, which can prove good value.

Hostels

Even for those who can't face the idea of bunking up with snoring strangers, **hostel accommodation** is well worth considering. Most hostels nowadays, whether owned by the Youth Hostels Association (YHA) or independently run, have shaken off their institutional boy scouts/backpackers-only image, and offer a mix of dorms – with anything from four to twelve beds – as well as simple double, triple or family rooms.

There are nine **YHA** (W yha.org.uk) hostels in Kent, Sussex and Surrey: two in Kent – in Canterbury and out in the countryside near Gillingham; five in Sussex – Brighton, Eastbourne, Littlehampton, Southease (near Lewes) and Shoreham; and two in the Surrey Hills near Dorking. YHA hostels can offer very good value, especially for families. Many are in glorious rural locations, making great bases for walking or cycling holidays, and the costs (rates vary according to season and demand) are very competitive, with double rooms from as little as £40. Facilities, and atmosphere, vary; most have self-catering kitchens and some also have cafés, but all are reliable, clean and safe. Wi-fi provision, though free, also varies – where it does exist, it's generally only available in communal areas. The YHA is a member organization, part of the global HI (Hostelling International) group, but non-members are welcome to stay for an added fee of £3 per night. Annual membership costs £20 for an individual, which includes children travelling with you, £30 for two adults living at the same address, or £10 if you're under 26.

There are also a handful of **independent hostels** and **camping barns** (W independenthostels.co.uk) in the region. Of these, the *Kipps* hostels, in Brighton and Canterbury, are both highly recommended.

Camping

Camping is an excellent option in Kent and Sussex, whether you want a simple, wild camping experience, pitching your own tent in a car-free field, or a more luxurious all-in glamping holiday, snuggling up in a tipi, a compact shepherd's hut or a vintage Airstream caravan. Smaller, quieter sites dominate the scene, with a number of beautifully situated sites in bucolic countryside – in the North and South Downs, say, or on the clifftops along the east coast – though there are larger caravan sites clustered around the more popular seaside destinations such as Camber and the Thanet resorts. Sussex in particular has taken up the **glamping** trend with relish, with some of the best-equipped and most enjoyable sites in the country, though there are some excellent choices in Kent, too, including a safari-style option in a wild animal park (see p.129).

Most campsites close in the winter, though exact dates vary according to the weather during any one year; we've included the closing months in our reviews. **Prices** for pitches start at as little as £7 per person for the most basic site, but you could pay as much as £300 for a couple of nights in your own two-yurt hideaway, warmed by a wood-burner with kitchen and shower.

Several small outfits offer **retro VW campers**, or "glampervans", which cost from £60 per night; check out W theglampervanhirecompany.com (Kent), W plumcampers.co.uk (West Sussex) or W retrocampervan.com (Surrey). For an even more

---

TOP FIVE CAMPSITES

Blackberry Wood Sussex. See p.233
Palace Farm Kent. See p.78
The Warren Kent. See p.127
Welsummer Kent. See p.160
WOWO Sussex. See p.200

offbeat night, you could try "**champing**" in Kent or Surrey – setting up camp in an ancient church, with breakfast provided (May–Sept only; Ⓦchamping .co.uk) – or check Ⓦcampinmygarden.com, a directory of microsites in private gardens and fields.

Self-catering

Self-catering, whether in a rural cottage for two, a city-centre apartment or a family house by the sea, invariably proves cheaper than staying in a hotel and offers far more flexibility. Where once a week-long stay was standard, many places nowadays offer breaks of as little as one night, though there will usually be at least a two-night minimum stay at weekends and in the summer. Depending on the season, you can expect to pay around £350 a week for a small, out-of-the-way cottage or maybe three or four times that for a larger property in a popular spot. Note that properties owned by the National Trust and Landmark Trust, which are in historically significant and beautiful buildings, tend to be pricier than other options and are often booked up long in advance.

SELF-CATERING AGENCIES

Bramley & Teal Ⓦ bramleyandteal.co.uk. Stylish cottages in East Sussex and Kent, with good searches including "ecofriendly" and "dog-friendly".

Cottages.com Ⓦ cottages.com. Wide range of properties in the region, including some in Surrey.

Farm Stay UK Ⓦ farmstay.co.uk. Self catering – plus B&B, bunkhouses and camping – on working farms throughout the region.

Garden of England Cottages Ⓦ gardenofenglandcottages.co.uk. Classy self-catering in Kent and Sussex, with a good choice of traditional buildings in rural settings, and some large properties for big groups.

Kent & Sussex Holiday Cottages Ⓦ www.kentandsussexcottages .co.uk. More than three hundred pretty apartments, cottages and houses, on a user-friendly website with handy filters and searches for luxury, seaside and unique properties.

Landmark Trust Ⓦ landmarktrust.org.uk. A preservation charity that has converted historically important properties into characterful accommodation – from tiny Tudor cottages to Arts and Crafts mansions.

Mulberry Cottages Ⓦ mulberrycottages.com. Upmarket self-catering in Scotland and the south of England; including Sussex, Surrey and a particularly good selection in Kent.

National Trust Ⓦ nationaltrustcottages.co.uk. The NT owns many cottages, houses and farmhouses, most of which are set in the gardens or grounds of their own properties – the eight or so in Kent, Sussex and Surrey include a garden studio in Virginia Woolf's Monk's House, and a lighthouse keeper's cottage on Dover's White Cliffs.

Stilwell Cottages Direct Ⓦ cottagesdirect.co.uk. A good choice of properties in Kent and Sussex, with direct booking.

Food and drink

You're never far from somewhere really good to eat in Kent and Sussex, whether you want a simple Ploughman's lunch in a pub garden or exquisite Michelin-starred destination dining; Surrey, too, has its fair share of classy gastropubs and restaurants. Kent and Sussex, in particular, have embraced the local food movement with gusto, with countless gastropubs and restaurants sourcing food locally, naming their suppliers, and even growing their own.

Kent, which is traditionally famed for its fruit-growing, still produces delicious veg, soft fruits and juices, along with fish – Whitstable's oysters are famed – tasty lamb fed on the nutrient-rich Romney Marsh and lots of good cheeses. **Sussex**, too, offers fresh juices, artisan cheeses and Romney lamb, with fresh fish from the Hastings fleet and scallops from Rye Bay. **Surrey** has yet to attach itself to slow food principles with such vigour, but most of its best restaurants will list ingredients that have made the quick hop across the border from Kent and Sussex.

This part of the country is also excellent for **real ale** and **wine** – along with a couple of major historic breweries there are scores of local microbreweries and small-scale, award-winning vineyards producing delicious tipples, and no shortage of traditional country pubs or good restaurants where you can enjoy them. For more on local food see Ⓦ producedinkent.co.uk, Ⓦ www.sussexfoodawards .biz and Ⓦ southdownsfood.org.

Restaurants and gastropubs

One of the great pleasures of a trip to this region is to head out to a country **gastropub**, filling up on delicious, locally sourced food before or after a bracing walk. The distinction between restaurant and gastropub is becoming fuzzier every day, with the gastropubs tending to lead the way when it comes to innovation and high cuisine principles: the Michelin-starred *Sportsman* (see p.85), in Seasalter near Whitstable, for example, which is one of the best places to eat in the country, despite its humble pub exterior.

Beware, though – most places have caught on to the "gastro" buzzword, and not everywhere that calls itself a gastropub is going to be good. We've reviewed the very best places in the Guide, but as a rule of thumb it's worth checking to see if an establishment names its suppliers, has a regularly changing menu, and doesn't try to cover too many bases on the menu.

As for **restaurants**, most towns of any size that are geared up for tourists will have some very good options, from veggie cafés to classy bistros and seafood joints. The most popular seaside towns, including Whitstable, Broadstairs, Margate, Hastings and Brighton, as well as the countryside surrounding Chichester and Midhurst, and the area around Faversham in North Kent, are foodie hotspots, with creative restaurants and gastropubs garnering national attention.

Markets and farm shops

Kent, Sussex and Surrey offer rich pickings when it comes to **farmers' markets**, with an array of delicious seasonal produce and artisan bread, cheese, chutneys, fruit juices, beers and wines from local producers. These are lively, well-attended affairs, and always worth a visit, even if just to browse. We've reviewed the best of them in the Guide; you can find a comprehensive list of farmers' markets in Kent on ⓦkfma.org.uk; in Sussex on ⓦwestsussex.info/farmers-markets .shtml; and in Surrey on ⓦvisitsurrey.com /whats-on/markets. Farm shops are also good

TOP FIVE GASTROPUBS
The Compasses Inn Crundale. See p.63
George and Dragon Chipstead. See p.158
Griffin Inn Fletching. See p.201
Richmond Arms West Ashling, near Chichester. See p.272
The Sportsman Seasalter. See p.85

places to pick up picnic supplies or deli treats to take home – many have diversified to sell posh food and produce from other farms as well as from their own. We've picked out a few to review in the Guide, but it's always worth stopping off to nose around any you may come across on your travels.

Drink

Kent, Sussex and Surrey excel in traditional **country pubs**, often picture-postcard places with wonky oak beams, head-bumpingly low ceilings and roaring open fires. The vast majority have local ales on offer, and the best will also list wines from the local vineyards, and fruit juices and ciders from local suppliers. Most serve food, and though many have been gussied up to within an inch of their lives,

LOCAL SPECIALITIES
Cobnuts This tasty Kentish hazelnut, harvested between mid-August and October, can be bought at local farmers' markets and found as an ingredient on menus throughout the county.
Fruit Kent's mild climate and rich soil provide excellent conditions for growing fruit. Wild cherries have been eaten here since prehistoric times, and cherry and apple trees were planted by the Romans and the Normans, but it was Henry VIII who really developed a taste for fruit and veg varieties as we recognize them today. In 1533 he employed the first royal fruiterer to plant orchards in Teynham, a few miles west of Faversham, and the county, "the fruitbowl of England", never looked back.
Hops Though the industry has declined drastically in the last sixty-odd years, Kent in particular still has a strong emotional attachment to the hop, which was such a crucial part of the economy in the nineteenth century (see p.139). Local breweries, including the venerable Shepherd Neame in Kent and Harvey's in Sussex, still use local hops in their beers, and you can also buy live plants to grow, or dried garlands of bines for decoration – as seen in countless pubs and hotels in the Weald. Some artisan food producers also add hops to crackers or biscuits to add a unique, slightly bitter flavour.
Huffkins An old-fashioned Kentish speciality – a soft, flat, small oval loaf with a deep dimple in the centre, occasionally filled like a bap, and often served warm.
Lamb Though many of the famed Romney Marsh lambs are now farmed elsewhere (see p.130), the appearance on menus of their prized, tender meat is the sure sign of a good restaurant; the sweet, succulent meat of Sussex's Southdown lamb is equally prized.
Oysters The old fishing town of Whitstable, on the north coast of Kent, is the place to eat these briny treats (see p.84); there's even an annual festival to give thanks for them.
Rye Bay scallops The season for Rye Bay's prized bivalves –some of the best in the country – lasts from November to the end of April, and reaches its peak in February, when more than fifteen thousand are consumed during Rye's week-long Scallop Festival.

BEST FARMERS' MARKETS AND FARM SHOPS

Aylesford Farmers' Market Kent. See p.158
Cliftonville Farmers' Market Kent. See p.93
Cowdray Farm Shop Sussex. See p.285
The Goods Shed Kent. See p.54
Lewes Farmers' Market Sussex. See p.228
Macknade Fine Foods Kent. See p.78
Middle Farm Shop Sussex. See p.221
Penshurst Farmers' Market Kent. See p.143

Quex Barn Farm Shop Kent. See p.95
Rochester Farmers' Market Kent. See p.68
Sharnfold Farm Shop Sussex. See p.211
Shipbourne Farmers' Market Kent.
See p.155
Shoreham Farmers' Market Sussex.
See p.301
Tonbridge Farmers' Market Kent. See p.143

even the fanciest will have a room set aside for drinkers who simply want a quiet pint.

For cutting-edge **bars** and cool **cocktails** you'll do best in Brighton; even Kent's most popular tourist destinations, including Canterbury, Whitstable and the Thanet towns, have quite a low-key drinking scene, preferring quiet pubs over sleek see-and-be-seen joints. One trend that is making quite a stir in Kent in particular is the arrival of the **micropub** – minuscule, independently run and very simple places, often set up in old shops and open for limited hours, where a small crowd of real-ale fans can hunker down to enjoy beer, conversation and – well, nothing much else, really; that's the whole point.

Real ale

Both Kent, the heartland of the old hopping industry, and Sussex, which was also scattered with hop farms, are known for their **real ales**. The biggest local names are **Shepherd Neame** (Wshepherdneame.co.uk), the nation's oldest brewery, which operates from Faversham in Kent as it has for centuries, producing its characteristically earthy ales – Spitfire and Bishop's Finger among them – and running a huge number of local pubs; **Harvey's** in Lewes, Sussex (Wharveys.org.uk), which dates back to 1792 and is known for its traditional cask ales, including the flagship Sussex Best bitter; and the **Dark Star Brewing Co** (Wdarkstarbrewing .co.uk), which started out in 1994 in the basement of a Brighton pub and has grown to become Sussex's second largest brewery after Harvey's.

There is also an ever-growing number of **microbreweries**, some of them very small indeed, producing interesting, top-quality ales and porters. These outfits often apply traditional methods and creative innovations, selling their seasonally changing selections in local pubs, restaurants and farm shops, and occasionally online. In **Kent** look out for beers from Ripple Steam Brewery (Wripple steambrewery.co.uk), which uses no mechanization in its brewing process; the Tonbridge Brewery (Wtonbridgebrewery.co.uk), whose spicy Rustic

bitter is made with rare Kent-grown Epic hops; the Westerham Brewery (Wwesterhambrewery.co.uk), which uses nine varieties of Kentish hops in its Spirit of Kent pale ale; and Larkins Brewery (Wlarkins brewery.co.uk), whose peppery, chocolatey porter is particularly good. Great **Sussex** microbreweries include the Long Man Brewery in Litlington, which creates award-winning ales using barley grown on the farm (Wlongmanbrewery.com); Burning Sky in Firle, set up by ex-Dark Star brewer Mark Tranter and known for its pale ales (Wburningskybeer.com); FILO Brewery at the *First In, Last Out* pub in Hastings, which has been brewing since 1988 (Wthefilo .co.uk); the steam-powered Langham Brewery near Midhurst (Wlanghambrewery.co.uk); and a clutch of microbreweries in Brighton, among them Brighton Bier (Wbrightonbier.com) and the Hand Brew Co (Whandbrewpub.com). In **Surrey**, you can count on good ales from Hogs Back (Whogsback.co.uk) and Frensham (Wfrenshambrewery.co.uk) – both near Farnham – and the Surrey Hills Brewery (Wsurreyhills.co.uk) on the Denbies wine estate.

Wine

Kent, Sussex and Surrey, where the soil conditions and geology are almost identical to those in France's Champagne region – and where the climate is increasingly similar, due to global warming – are home to some of the country's most highly regarded vineyards. These chiefly produce white and sparkling wines, for which nearly all of them can claim a raft of prestigious awards, but there are some fine rosés and interesting reds out there, too.

Most good restaurants – and some pubs – in Kent and Sussex will make a point of listing local wines, and you'll be able to buy them in local farm shops and specialist stores such as the English Wine Centre near Lewes (see p.219) and the Exceptional English Wine Company near Midhurst (see p.285). You can also find bottles from the major producers in supermarket aisles: Marks and Spencer and Waitrose are the main sources. The best place to buy, of course, is from the **vineyards** themselves –

ENGLISH WINE: A SPARKLING SUCCESS STORY

English wine is fast shucking off its image as somehow inferior to its longer-established European counterparts, and the industry is booming. Nearly five hundred vineyards across the country produce about five million bottles a year (more than sixty percent of it sparkling), and the best of the harvest now more than rivals the more famous names over the Channel. **Sparkling wine** is the biggest success story, with several wines from the Southeast beating the best Champagnes in international blind-tasting competitions. New vineyards are springing up all the time: Rathfinny Estates, established in 2010 outside Alfriston, will eventually produce more than a million bottles of fizz a year, making it one of the biggest single vineyards in Europe. For more details of vineyards throughout Kent, Sussex and Surrey – including a downloadable wine routes map and an iPhone app giving full information on the region's growers and producers – check the website of the Southeastern Vineyard association, ⓦseva.uk.com.

Several vineyards offer tours and tastings. Among the best are:

Biddenden Kent. See p.150
Bolney Sussex. See p.197
Chapel Down Kent. See p.150
Denbies Surrey. See p.310

Hush Heath Kent. See p.146
Rathfinny Sussex. See p.217
Ridgeview Sussex. See p.231
Tinwood Estate Sussex. See p.275

most offer free guided tours and generous tutored tastings. As a very broad rule of thumb, in Kent **Chapel Down** does superb fizz and excellent whites, **Biddenden** has some fine off-dry sparkling wines and a distinctive, very delicious Ortega, and **Hush Heath** produces a superb pink fizz. In Sussex **Ridgeview** is renowned for its bubbly, while **Sedlescombe** (ⓦenglishorganicwine.co.uk) adopts innovative biodynamic principles for its wine making, with delicious results, and **Bolney**, unusually, is best known for its reds. Surrey's **Denbies** is another that specializes in excellent fizz.

While it's perfectly possible to visit the vineyards independently (see box above), a number of **tours** are taking advantage of increased interest in English wine. In Kent and Sussex, English Wine Tasting Tours (ⓦenglishwinetastingtours.co.uk) and Kent & Sussex Wine Tours (ⓦkentandsussexwinetours.co.uk) lead small-group tours of two to four vineyards a day, with tastings and lunch included; for a longer trip, Wine Rides (ⓦwinerides.co.uk) offers delightful three-day, two-night cycling/wine-tasting/camping breaks – tents, tastings, dinner and breakfast provided – in Carr Taylor and Sedlescombe vineyards in Sussex.

Sports and outdoor activities

Kent, Sussex and Surrey offer a good range of outdoor activities, chiefly walking and cycling, along with excellent sailing, watersports and birdwatching. There are also good opportunities for adrenaline junkies, including rock climbing and paragliding. As for spectator sports, Surrey boasts the Epsom Downs racecourse, home to the Derby for nearly 250 years, and Sussex is home to Goodwood, site of the UK's major horse and motor races. For something gentler, cricket is king in this part of England, still played on quiet village greens as well as on the bucolic county ground at Canterbury and at the lovely ground at Firle, near Lewes, home to one of the oldest cricket clubs in the world.

Walking

Perhaps unexpectedly, given how populated this corner of the country is, Kent, Sussex and Surrey are superb **walking** destinations, with plenty of trails, of all lengths and for all abilities, where you can get away from it all within minutes. From blustery seaside hikes atop towering chalk cliffs, to pretty rambles in ancient woodlands and undulating paths following ancient pilgrims' routes, the region offers a wide variety, whether you're after a country pub stroll or a long-distance trek.

The chalky hills of the **North Downs** and **Greensand Way** – both of which curve their way through Surrey to east Kent – along with the **High Weald** in Kent and Sussex, and the **South Downs** in Sussex, are all prime walking territory. **Long-distance paths** include the 150-mile-long **North Downs Way** (ⓦnationaltrail.co.uk/north-downs -way), which starts at Farnham in west Surrey and heads through the beautiful Surrey Hills, following old pilgrims' paths to Canterbury and Dover along the highest points of the Downs. Further south, and running roughly parallel, the 108-mile **Greensand Way** heads off from Haslemere in Surrey, traversing dramatic heathland, ancient woodlands and the pretty Kent Weald countryside before ending near the border with Romney Marsh.

In Sussex, the **Sussex Downs** – part of the **South Downs National Park** (Ⓦsouthdowns.gov.uk), which spreads into Hampshire and is crisscrossed by nearly two thousand miles of footpaths – provide fantastic walking opportunities, whatever you're after; the website details some good options that start and finish at a bus stop or train station. The jewel of the South Downs is the one hundred mile **South Downs Way** (Ⓦnationaltrail.co.uk/south-downs-way), which follows ancient paths and droveways along the chalk escarpment from Winchester all the way to the glorious Beachy Head cliffs. Running north to south through the South Downs, the 38-mile-long **New Lipchis Way** (Ⓦnewlipchisway.co.uk), from Liphook in Hampshire to West Wittering, affords you the special thrill of arriving in Chichester on foot. In the Weald, the largely rural and heavily wooded area that spreads through both Kent and Sussex, the 95-mile **High Weald Landscape Trail** (Ⓦhighweald.org), from Horsham to Rye via Groombridge and Cranbrook, takes you from bluebell woods to marsh-lands, via winding sunken lanes, past some of the area's prettiest villages. The North Downs Way and South Downs Way are linked by the eighty mile **Weald Way** (Ⓦexplorekent.org/activities/wealdway), a peaceful route that heads south from Gravesend to Eastbourne, spanning chalk downlands and valleys and taking you through Ashford Forest, and by the forty-odd-mile **Downs Link** (Ⓦwestsussex.gov.uk), which follows the traffic-free course of a disused railway line from near Guildford, winding through woods, heath and open country before linking up with the South Downs Way and following the River Adur down to Shoreham. The 150-mile **Sussex Border Path** (Ⓦsussexborderpath.co.uk), meanwhile, loosely follows that county's inland boundary with Hampshire, Surrey and Kent, starting in Thorney Island and ending in the lovely medieval town of Rye.

Long-distance **coastal paths** include the splendid 163-mile **Saxon Shore Way** (Ⓦexplore kent.org/activities/saxon-shore-way), which heads from Gravesend to Hastings, following the coastline as it would have looked 1500 years ago – which in some parts is now quite far inland encompassing the bays of Thanet and the White Cliffs of Dover, and taking in the appealing small towns of Faversham, Deal and Rye. Curving a twenty-mile course along the Thanet shore, from Minnis Bay in the west to Pegwell Bay near Sandwich, the **Thanet Coastal Path** (Ⓦthanet coast.org.uk) is an excellent way to experience the lovely beaches in this part of Kent.

We've flagged up especially nice walks throughout the Guide, and recommend some of the best walking books in our Books section (see p.327). There are countless more walks in Kent, Sussex and Surrey; check Ⓦvisitkent.co.uk, Ⓦeastsussex.gov.uk, Ⓦwestsussex.gov.uk and Ⓦvisitsurrey.com/things -to-do/activities/walking-and-hiking, as well as the

SEVEN SPLENDID WALKS

Ashdown Forest There are lots of good paths through the gorse-speckled heaths of Ashdown Forest, with the added fun for kids of tracking down Pooh Bear's favourite haunts. See p.194

The Crab and Winkle Way Follow the line of a disused steam railway from Canterbury to Whitstable, passing orchards and ancient woodland on your way. See p.60

The Cuckmere Valley and the Seven Sisters An eight-mile circular walk in one of the most beautiful parts of the South Downs National Park, offering magnificent views of soaring white cliffs and velvety green chalk grassland. See p.214

Herne Bay to Reculver A splendid stretch of the long-distance Saxon Shore Way, taking you from the old-fashioned seaside resort to the ruined clifftop church towers standing sentinel over wildlife-rich Reculver Country Park. See p.88

Kingley Vale Clamber up through dark, mysterious yew forest to rolling chalk grassland with panoramic views on this magical 3.5-mile circuit. See p.273

The Surrey Hills Using a country village like Shere or Peaslake as your base, the Surrey Hills offer countless rambles through Surrey's glorious old woodlands. See p.310

Whitstable to Seasalter Crunching along the shingle the two miles from the oyster-loving town of Whitstable to the superb *Sportsman* gastropub is a bracing way to experience this stretch of the North Kent coast. See p.82

South Downs National Park website (Ⓦ southdowns .gov.uk/enjoy/explore/walking), which has over two dozen downloadable walking trails. The **National Trust** (Ⓦ nationaltrust.org.uk/visit/activities/walking) is another good resource, with downloadable walks of varying lengths from most of their properties.

Cycling

Kent, Sussex and Surrey offer rich pickings for cyclists. From gentle traffic-free woodland trails suitable for family pottering to heart-thumping training routes, from invigorating coastal clifftop paths to sleepy country lanes, the routes are varied and well marked.

Of the **National Cycle Network** routes (Ⓦ sustrans.org.uk), Route 1, which runs from Dover all the way up to Scotland, takes in the East Kent coast between Dover and Sandwich before heading inland via Canterbury to meet the North Kent coast at Whitstable and Faversham, while Route 2 – also known as the **South Coast Cycle Route** – follows most of the south coast from Dover to Cornwall, dipping inland at various points, with an uninterrupted stretch between Dover and Worthing.

In Kent, the **Crab and Winkle Way** (Ⓦ craband winkle.org), also a walking path (see p.60), forms part of National Cycle Route 1 and provides a quick and scenic route between Canterbury and Whitstable on the coast. Just east of Whitstable, the seven-mile **Oyster Bay Trail** (Ⓦ explorekent.org/activities /oyster-bay-trail) is a family-friendly seaside path that leads to Herne Bay and the beachfront Reculver Country Park; from there you can join the start of the 32-mile **Viking Coastal Trail** (Ⓦ explore kent.org/activities/viking-coastal-trail), which follows the Thanet coast all the way round to Pegwell Bay, south of Ramsgate. You can also cycle from Hythe to Winchelsea in Sussex along the **Royal Military Canal** (Ⓦ royalmilitarycanal.com), a gratifyingly flat thirty-mile ride through quiet marshes. Shorter rides include the six-mile **Tudor Trail** (Ⓦ explorekent.org

/activities/tudor-cycle-trail), a largely traffic-free route between Tonbridge Castle and Penshurst Place; the flat, marshy lands of the Hoo Peninsula and the Isle of Sheppey are also very good for cycling. If you're after something more active, head to **Bedgebury Forest** (Ⓦ forestry.gov.uk/bedgebury), which is crossed by National Cycle Route 18 and features challenging off-road mountain bike trails.

In Sussex, the **South Downs Way** (see p.282) is as exhilarating for cyclists as it is for walkers, though bear in mind you'll be sharing the path with horses as well as pedestrians. The **South Downs National Park** website (Ⓦ southdowns.gov.uk) has a number of downloadable cycle rides that start and finish at a bus stop or train station. Two popular off-road cycle trails along disused railways are the fourteen-mile **Cuckoo Trail** (see p.192) and the nine-mile **Forest Way** (see p.196), while another great place to cycle is the flat **Manhood Peninsula**, with a good network of canalside towpaths and a couple of routes from Chichester, including the eleven-mile **Salterns Way** (Ⓦ conservancy.co.uk/page /cycling/346), which leads to East Head via country lanes, roads and designated paths. You can combine cycling with a spot of culture on the eighteen-mile **Coastal Culture Trail** (Ⓦ coastal culturetrail.com; see p.177), which links three art galleries along the Sussex coast; the section between Hastings and Bexhill is all off-road.

The pretty village of Peaslake in **Surrey** is a major centre for off-road cycling, with fabulous trails in the surrounding forest, while the steep zigzag road up **Box Hill**, long a popular route for training cyclists – and which formed part of the road race cycling event in the London 2012 Olympics – is particularly popular at weekends. A couple of National Cycle Network routes also run through Surrey – the quiet **Route 22** (Ⓦ sustrans.org.uk), which follows tranquil paths and bridleways between Guildford and Rowledge, south of Farnham, and the stretch between Guildford and Cranleigh on the **Downs Link** are particularly worthwhile.

ACTIVE FUN: A TOP FIVE

Paddle your own canoe along Kent's quiet waterways See p.61
Swoop above the South Downs on a paraglider See p.224
Outjump your opponents at Brighton beach volleyball See p.249
Pedal in the wake of Olympic champions at Box Hill See p.311
Catch some waves at the Joss Bay surf school See p.98

Watersports

With its long, varied coastline, its marshlands and its rivers, the Kent and Sussex region offers excellent watersports. Sailing, windsurfing and kiteboarding are especially good around **Whitstable** (see p.82), with good jet-skiing, sailing and kayaking in **Herne Bay** (see p.88), windsurfing and kiteboarding at **Margate** and superb surfing in Thanet's **Joss Bay** (see p.98), where there's a top-notch **surf school** (Ⓦ kentsurfschool.co.uk). The seaside town of Hythe, on Kent's east coast, is also something of a windsurfing centre (see p.128), while the nearby **Action Watersports** (Ⓦactionwatersports.co.uk), inland in Lydd, offers waterskiing, wakeboarding, jet-skiing and other activities on a purpose-built lake. Further down the coast, just across the border in Sussex, blustery **Camber** is another major centre for wind- and kitesurfing and paddleboarding (see p.173); the coast around **Worthing**, west of Brighton, is one of the best places in the country to learn how to kitesurf (see p.301); while at sandy **West Wittering beach** (see p.280) there's everything from kayaking to stand-up paddleboarding on offer.

Finally, if it's buff beach fun you're after, **Brighton** is the place, offering year-round beach volleyball and other sports at the brilliant **Yellowave Beach Sports Venue** (see p.249); local operators also offer scuba diving, kayaking, wakeboarding and sailing, with windsurfing, stand-up paddleboarding and cable wakeboarding on a beachfront lagoon.

There are some particularly nice spots for open-air **swimming** around Brighton, too: at the recently restored Grade II-listed Saltdean Lido (see p.245), accessible from the city along the Undercliff Walk; and in the nearby town of Lewes at Pells Pool (see p.227) – the country's oldest open-air freshwater pool. Arundel also has a fine lido (see p.291), which has the added bonus of a castle view.

Birdwatching

Birders are spoilt for choice in Kent and Sussex, with large swathes of lonely marshland, dense, ancient woods, and otherworldly shingle habitats all offering splendid twitching territory.

There are six major **RSPB reserves** (Ⓦrspb.org.uk) in **Kent**: the Blean Woods near Canterbury (see p.59); Cliffe Pools (see p.74) and Northward Hill (see p.74) on the Hoo Peninsula near Rochester; Capel Fleet on the Isle of Sheppey (see p.75); the headland of Dungeness down toward Sussex (see p.182), and Tudeley Woods in the Weald near Tunbridge Wells (see p.144). There are also good sightings to be had in the **nature reserves** at Stodmarsh near Canterbury (see p.60), around the Swale Estuary (see p.77) and at Pegwell Bay near Ramsgate and Sandwich (see p.108). Other good locations include **Reculver Country Park** between Herne Bay and Thanet (see p.88); **Romney Marsh** (see p.128); and the **White Cliffs of Dover** (see p.118) – though sadly you categorically won't see bluebirds over those. For more on birdwatching in Kent, check the website of the **Kent Ornithological Society** (Ⓦkentos.org.uk).

In **Sussex**, the **WWT Arundel Wetland Centre**, one of just ten Wildfowl and Wetland Trust (WWT) sites in the UK, is home to endangered waterfowl from around the world as well as a host of native birds (see p.291). You'll also spot birds in the shingle-saltmarsh **Rye Harbour Nature Reserve** (see p.170); in the heathland habitat of **Ashdown Forest** (see p.194); in the **Loder Valley Nature Reserve** (see p.199) at Wakehurst Place in the High Weald; at the **RSPB Pulborough Brooks** nature reserve (see p.295); and on the Manhood Peninsula around the beautiful **Chichester Harbour** (see p.277) and at the **RSPB Pagham Harbour** (see p.281) and **RSPB Medmerry** (see p.281) nature reserves. You can find out more about birding in Sussex on Ⓦsos.org.uk, the website of the **Sussex Ornithological Society**.

In the **Surrey Hills**, there's an RSPB reserve at Farnham Heath, an area of restored heathland and bluebell woods abounding in crossbills, nightjars, tree pipits, woodcocks and woodlarks.

Paragliding and rock-climbing

Would-be **paragliders** should make a beeline for the **South Downs**, where local companies (see p.224) offer lessons that mean you can be up there on your own within just one day.

Meanwhile, there's superb **climbing** around Eridge Green and Groombridge, on the Sussex–Kent border near Tunbridge Wells: **Harrison's Rocks** (Ⓦthebmc.co.uk) offers challenging routes for experienced climbers, and outfitters nearby offer lessons (see p.193).

Golf

Kent, Sussex and particularly Surrey are home to some of the finest **golf** courses in the country, including two at the Goodwood Estate in Sussex, and three near Sandwich (see p.106). For details of courses, see Ⓦsurreygolfguide.com, Ⓦsussexgolfguide.com and Ⓦgolfinkent.co.uk; the last of these sites also includes a downloadable map and links to Kentish golf breaks.

SPECIALIST OPERATORS

Canoe Wild Ⓦcanoewild.co.uk. Guided and self-guided canoe trips along the backwaters of Kent. See p.61.

The Carter Company Ⓦthe-carter-company.com. Cycling tours through Kent, with gourmet, arty, historic and family options.

Contours Ⓦcontours.co.uk. Walking holidays in Kent, Sussex and along the North Downs Way in Surrey.

Electric Bike Tours Ⓦukelectricbiketours.co.uk. Electric bike tours in

Kent. Itineraries include vineyards, hop and fruit farms, gardens and castles.

Experience Sussex ⓦ experiencesussex.co.uk. Activity and pottery holidays in Sussex, including guided walks and cycle rides.

Footpath Holidays ⓦ footpath-holidays.com. Self-guided and guided walking holidays in the South Downs.

Hatt Adventures ⓦ thehatt.co.uk. Climbing, abseiling and kayaking in Sussex.

The Kayak Coach ⓦ thekayakcoach.com. Kayak trips along the Ouse, Cuckmere and Arun rivers in Sussex, and along the River Medway in Kent.

Pear Tree Tours ⓦ footprintsofsussex.co.uk. Self-guided walking holidays and short breaks in the South Downs National Park.

South Downs Discovery ⓦ southdownsdiscovery.com. Self-guided walking holidays in the South Downs National Park, plus baggage transfers along the South Downs Way.

Walk Awhile ⓦ walkawhile.co.uk. Self-led and guided walking holidays in the Kent Downs, through the Weald and along the White Cliffs, with luggage transfers.

Festivals and events

Kent, Sussex and Surrey have a packed festivals calendar, which includes plenty of arts and music events and foodie festivals showcasing and celebrating the region's fantastic local produce. There's no shortage, too, of wonderful, quirky festivals and events that you won't find anywhere else in the country, from Sussex Bonfire Night to the Bognor Birdman.

JANUARY TO MARCH

Fat Tuesday Hastings, Feb. See p.182

Rye Bay Scallop Week Late Feb. Nine days of foodie events dedicated to the noble scallop: tastings, cookery demonstrations, live music and special menus, culminating in a scallop barrow race through the streets of Rye. ⓦ scallop.org.uk

Sussex Beer Festival Brighton, mid-March. Around two hundred real ales and forty ciders and perries on offer – many local to the Southeast – at this rollicking annual fest. ⓦ sussexbeerfestival.co.uk

APRIL & MAY

Brighton and Hove Food and Drink Festival Easter & May. The largest free foodie festival in the Southeast, running four times a year, celebrating local produce with workshops, tastings, markets and more. ⓦ brightonfoodfestival.com

Wise Words Festival Canterbury, late April. See p.59

Jack-in-the-Green Festival Hastings Old Town, end April/early May. See p.182

Rochester Sweeps Festival Early May. See p.71

Brighton Festival May. See p.248

Brighton Fringe May. See p.248

Elderflower Fields Festival Ashdown Forest, May. Family-friendly festival in Sussex woodlands, with music, local food and drink, a woodland spa and loads of kids' activities. ⓦ elderflowerfields.co.uk

Great Escape Brighton, mid-May. See p.248

Pantiles Food Festival Tunbridge Wells, mid-May. Stalls, celeb chefs and live music keep Tunbridge Wells' elegant Pantiles packed for this three-day foodie event.

Charleston Festival Late May. Ten days of author talks and events at Charleston Farmhouse, near Lewes, the former home of Sussex's Bloomsbury Set. ⓦ charleston.org.uk

Glyndebourne Festival Late May to Aug. See p.222.

JUNE

Whitstable Biennale Date varies, June. See p.86

Dickens Festival Rochester, early June. See p.71

Broadstairs Dickens Festival Third week June. See p.99

AEGON International Eastbourne, late June. International ladies' and men's tennis in the fortnight preceding Wimbledon, in the leafy surrounds of Devonshire Park. ⓦ lta.org.uk

Festival of Chichester Late June to late July. Month-long arts festival featuring music, theatre, film, spoken word, exhibitions, walks and tours. ⓦ festivalofchichester.co.uk

Festival of Speed Goodwood Estate, late June. See p.275

Brighton Kite Festival Date varies, but generally June/July. Long-running kite festival, with arena displays, team flying and kite fighting. ⓦ brightonkiteflyers.co.uk

JULY

Folkestone Triennial Date varies, but generally starts in July. See p.123

Deal Festival of Music and the Arts Early July. See p.114

Paddle Round the Pier Hove Lawns, Brighton, early July. See p.248

Beach Life Festival Eastbourne, mid-July. A free weekend of extreme sports action – from slalom to windsurfing, BMX to go-karting – with plenty of opportunities to get involved as well as watch. ⓦ visiteastbourne.com/events/beachlife

Hastings Pirate Day Mid-July. See p.182

Petworth Festival Mid-July. Two weeks of music (mainly classical and jazz), theatre, comedy and art. ⓦ petworthfestival.org.uk

Ramsgate Festival Third week in July. A multifaceted arts festival incorporating the Ramsgate Week sailing regatta, an old-style carnival with parades, floats and marching bands, and various exhibitions, concerts and events. ⓦ ramsgatefestival.org

Kent Beer Festival Near Canterbury, end July. Lively three-day real ale fest, featuring more than two hundred brews, held at Merton Farm (free shuttles from Canterbury). ⓦ kentbeerfestival.com

Leefest Near Tunbridge Wells, end July. Creative new music festival, born in teenager Lee Denny's back garden in 2009, which now has a larger (secret) base and attracts major international names from Young Fathers to Bastille. ⓦ leefest.org

Whitstable Oyster Festival End July. See p.86

Old Town Carnival Week Hastings, end July/early Aug. Nine days of festivities, which include concerts, walking tours, a procession and the ever-popular annual pram race. ⓦ oldtowncarnivalweek.co.uk

AUGUST

Bognor Birdman Aug. See p.296

Chichester International Film Festival Aug. Excellent festival with around three weeks of new movies from around the world, including open-air screenings and a drive in. ⓦ chichestercinema.org/festival

Airbourne Eastbourne, early Aug. Eastbourne's pride and joy and the biggest free seafront air show in the world – four days of historic aircraft and military displays. ⓦ eastbourneairshow.com

Chilli Fiesta Chichester, early Aug. A lively weekend devoted to the chilli, with cooking demos, talks and live music. ⓦ westdean.org.uk

Glorious Goodwood Early Aug. See p.275

Margate Soul Festival Early Aug. Big-name gigs – from Soul II Soul to CeCe Peniston – by the harbour, plus DJ stages, street performances and club nights. ⓦ margatesoulfestival.co.uk

Broadstairs Folk Week Early to mid-Aug. See p.99

Whitstable Regatta Early to mid-Aug. More than 220 years old, Whitstable's hugely popular weekend regatta offers boating fun for all the family, wacky water events and a yacht race, as well as fireworks and fairground amusements. ⓦ whitstableregatta.com

Herne Bay Festival Mid- to late Aug. Lively nine-day festival with lots of family events, a lantern parade, sandcastle competitions, fireworks, live music and workshops. ⓦ hernebayfestival.co.uk

Arundel Festival Second half Aug. This creative ten-day arts festival features everything from dragon-boat racing to treasure hunts, jousting to community samba, plus theatre, walks, workshops and tours. ⓦ arundelfestival.co.uk

Weyfest Near Farnham, third week Aug. Acclaimed grassroots music festival at the Rural Life Centre in Surrey – acts run the gamut from The Waterboys to The Wurzels, via The Orb, Wishbone Ash and The Boomtown Rats. ⓦ weyfest.co.uk

Medieval Festival Herstmonceux Castle, Aug bank holiday. The largest medieval bash in the UK, with costumed knights, men-at-arms, jesters, minstrels and traders descending on the moated castle for three days of jousting, tournaments, falconry and more, the highlights being the reconstructed siege and battle. ⓦ englandsmedievalfestival.com

Lewes Art Wave Late Aug to early Sept. The annual visual arts festival for Lewes and the surrounding area; a fortnight during which more than four hundred artists and makers open up their houses and studios to the public. ⓦ www.artwavefestival.org

Brighton Pride Date varies but generally Aug/Sept. See p.261

Brighton and Hove Food and Drink Festival Aug/Sept. The largest free foodie festival in the Southeast, running four times a year.

SEPTEMBER & OCTOBER

Coastal Currents Visual Arts Festival Hastings and St Leonards, throughout Sept. One of the biggest arts festivals on the south coast, featuring open studios, events, exhibitions and performances by local, regional and national artists. ⓦ coastalcurrents.org.uk

Rye Arts Festival Two weeks in Sept. Established festival taking in classical and contemporary music, opera and dance, exhibitions and literary sessions. ⓦ ryefestival.co.uk

Faversham Hop Festival Early Sept. Ebullient, family-friendly weekend celebrating the heyday of the hop with bands, food and lots of Shepherd Neame beer. ⓦ favershamhopfestival.org

In the Woods Kent, early Sept. New bands – Let's Eat Grandma, Kate Tempest and alt-J all played early gigs here – plus art installations, local food, a giant bonfire and twinkling trees in this intimate overnight festival, held in a different secret Kent woodland location each year. ⓦ inthewoodsfestival.co.uk

Goodwood Revival Mid-Sept. See p.275

Hastings Seafood and Wine Festival Mid-Sept. A weekend of live music, wine and local seafood down at The Stade. ⓦ hastingsfestivals.com/seafood

Art in Romney Marsh Mid-Sept to early Oct. Held across four weekends, this site-specific event has modern artists and musicians exhibiting work in five of Romney's most beautiful medieval churches. ⓦ artinromneymarsh.org.uk

OctoberFeast Lewes, mid-Sept to early Oct. Annual food and drink festival featuring markets, workshops, pop-up suppers, wine tasting, foraging excursions, brewery tours and more. ⓦ lewesoctoberfeast.com

Canterbury Food and Drink Festival Late Sept. This three-day weekend, with more local producers, suppliers, farms and restaurants set up in Dane John Gardens, along with arts and crafts stalls. It marks the start of Kent's Green Hop Beer Fortnight, which celebrates the distinctive ales made from fresh (rather than dried) green hops. ⓦ canterbury.co.uk and ⓦ kentgreenhopbeer.com

Small Wonder Charleston Farmhouse, end Sept. Annual short-story festival held at Charleston Farmhouse near Lewes, featuring workshops, discussions and performances. ⓦ charleston.org.uk/whats-on/festivals/small-wonder

Apple Affair West Dean Gardens, Chichester, end Sept/early Oct. Walks, talks and apples galore, plus cooking demos and live music in the beautiful setting of West Dean Gardens. ⓦ westdean.org.uk

Broadstairs Food Festival Early Oct. See p.99

Battle of Hastings re-enactment Mid-Oct. Annual re-enactment of the famous 1066 battle in Battle, featuring more than a thousand soldiers and living history encampments. ⓦ english-heritage.org.uk/visit/places/1066-battle-of-hastings-abbey-and-battlefield

Lewes Folk Festival Mid-Oct. A long weekend of folk gigs, workshops, singarounds and morris dancing all around town. ⓦ lewesfolkfest.org

National Apple Festival Brogdale, near Faversham, mid-Oct. A two-day celebration of Kent's finest fruit at the National Fruit Collection. More than a thousand apple varieties on display (with more than seventy varieties to buy), plus music, tours, food stalls, kids' entertainment and cooking demos. ⓦ www.applefestivalkent.co.uk

Canterbury Festival Mid-Oct to early Nov. See p.59

NOVEMBER & DECEMBER

Petworth Literary Festival Early Nov. Five days of talks and readings. ⓦ petworthfestival.org.uk

Folkestone Book Festival Nov. See p.127

London to Brighton Veteran Car Run First Sun in Nov. See p.248

Bonfire Night Lewes, Nov 5, or the day before if Nov 5 falls on a Sun. See p.230

Dickens Christmas Rochester, early Dec. See p.71

Brighton and Hove Food and Drink Festival Dec. The largest free foodie festival in the Southeast, running four times a year.

Burning the Clocks Brighton, late Dec. See p.248

Travel essentials

Costs

For the most part Kent, Sussex and Surrey, being generally well-heeled areas close to the capital, have prices on a par with London and the more **expensive** parts of England. There are some exceptions, but, especially when it comes to eating and drinking, you should be prepared to spend quite a bit. Your biggest expense will be **accommodation** (see p.23). If you camp, or stay in hostels, buy your own food from one of the region's excellent farm shops, and walk or cycle from place to place, you could get by on as little as £40 per person per day – more if you factor in sightseeing costs. Staying in a B&B and eating out once a day could easily double that, and above that the sky's the limit.

We have given full adult prices for **admission prices** in the Guide, and in the case of family attractions have quoted children's rates as well. Some places will have reduced prices for seniors, the unemployed and full-time students, but you will need to show ID.

Many of the region's major historic attractions are under the auspices of the private **National Trust** (Ⓦnationaltrust.org.uk) or the state-run **English Heritage** (Ⓦwww.english-heritage.org.uk), both of which are membership organizations. Prices can be steep for non-members, especially at the major attractions, but some NT properties offer discounts for people arriving on foot or by bike, and the generally excellent experiences offered by both organizations makes the cost worthwhile. If you're going to visit more than a handful of places run by either, it is well worth looking into membership, which will allow you free entry to – and free parking at – all their properties for a year. We've quoted the admission prices for non-members in the Guide, adding "NT" or "EH" as appropriate to indicate that members will not have to pay.

Prices for other attractions vary widely. Local town museums may well be free, while some of the major private attractions can charge as much as £20 per adult. Some of these pricier options, like Leeds Castle or Chatham Historic Dockyard, do allow you to return as many times as you wish in a year, however, which can work out as good value.

LGBT travellers

Brighton, of course, is the biggest draw for LGBT travellers in this region, with the lively Kemp Town area offering hotels, restaurants and shops all geared toward the pink pound, and an exceptionally lively and laidback LGBT nightlife scene packed into a compact area; **Brighton Pride** (Ⓦpridebrighton.org) is the big summer event. Countrywide listings, news and links can be found at Ⓦgaytimes.co.uk, Ⓦgaybritain.co.uk and Ⓦgaytravel.co.uk.

Maps

For an **overview** of the region on one map, the AA's *South East England Road Map* (1:200,000) is probably your best bet, and includes some town plans. There are also several good **road atlases** available: A–Z publishes a *South East England Regional Road Atlas* (1:158,400); *Kent Visitors' Map* (1:158,400); and *Surrey, East and West Sussex Visitors' Map* (1:158,400), as well as **street atlases** to East Sussex, West Sussex and Surrey (all 1:19,000) and Kent (1:20,267). OS *Explorer* maps (1:25,000) are best for **walking**.

Opening hours

We've given full **opening hours** for attractions, restaurants, cafés, pubs and shops in the Guide, though these do sometimes change from year to year – or even, in the case of the seaside resorts, depending on the season or the weather – so it's always worth calling ahead or checking the website before you set off.

Opening hours for most businesses, shops and offices are Monday to Saturday 9am to 5.30/6pm, with many shops also open on Sundays, generally 10.30/11am until 4.30/5pm. Big supermarkets have longer hours (except on Sun), sometimes round the clock. Banks are usually open Monday to Friday 9am to 4pm, and Saturday 9am to 12.30pm or so. You can usually get fuel any time of the day or night in larger towns and cities. Businesses and most shops close on bank holidays (see box opposite), though large supermarkets, small corner shops and many tourist attractions stay open.

Tourist information

The Southeast's regional tourist body, **Visit Southeast England** (Ⓦvisitsoutheastengland .com), has a comprehensive website, packed with useful tips and ideas. Within the region, **Visit Kent** (Ⓦvisitkent.co.uk), **Love Sussex** (Ⓦlovesussex.com) and **Visit Surrey** (Ⓦvisitsurrey.com) each have their own website; and further down the scale, individual cities, towns and groups of towns also have their

PUBLIC HOLIDAYS

New Year's Day (Jan 1)
Good Friday
Easter Monday
Early May Bank Holiday (1st Mon in May)
Spring Bank Holiday (Last Mon in May)
Summer Bank Holiday (Last Mon in Aug)
Christmas Day (Dec 25)
Boxing Day (Dec 26)
If Jan 1, Dec 25 or Dec 26 fall on a Saturday or Sunday, the next weekday becomes a public holiday.

own tourist information websites, which we list within the relevant destination in the Guide.

Local **tourist offices** are also listed in the Guide; at the best of these staff will nearly always be able to book accommodation, reserve space on guided tours, and sell guidebooks, maps and walk leaflets. The **South Downs National Park** has its own information centre in Midhurst (see p.284).

Travellers with disabilities

Kent, Sussex and Surrey have good facilities for travellers with disabilities. All new public buildings, including museums and cinemas, must provide wheelchair access, train stations are usually accessible, many buses have boarding ramps, and kerbs and signalled crossings have been dropped in many places. The number of accessible hotels and restaurants is growing, and reserved parking bays are available almost everywhere.

The **tourist bodies** for Kent, Sussex and Surrey, and for individual towns, have varying amounts of accessibility information on their websites; some allow you to search for accessible attractions and restaurants in the area. The **National Trust** gives general information about access at Ⓦ nationaltrust.org.uk/accessforall, where you can also download a PDF listing access information for their properties in the Southeast; **English Heritage** (Ⓦ english-heritage.org.uk) lists access information for each property on their website. Details of "Miles without Stiles" – accessible walks in the **South Downs National Park** – can be found at Ⓦ southdowns.gov.uk/enjoy/explore/walking.

A useful point of reference is **Tourism for All** (Ⓦ tourismforall.org.uk), which has general advice and listings. Also worth checking out is **The Rough Guide to Accessible Britain** (Ⓦ accessibleguide.co.uk), which has accounts of a few attractions in the region, reviewed by writers with disabilities.

Travelling with children

Kent, Sussex and Surrey have enough farm parks, castles, steam trains, off-road cycling trails, crabbing spots and beaches to keep even the most exacting of children happy. The best **beaches for families** are in Kent around the Isle of Thanet (see p.88), where there are fifteen sandy strands – seven of them have Blue Flag status, signifying a particularly good resort beach with safe water and lifeguard facilities – plus plenty of traditional family-friendly entertainment; in Sussex, the beaches are mainly pebbly, though there are two glorious exceptions at sand-dune-backed Camber Sands (see p.173) and West Wittering (see p.278).

Excellent **farm parks and zoos** in the region include the wildlife parks of Port Lympne (see p.129) and Howletts (see p.62) in Kent, and Drusillas (see p.219), Spring Barn (see p.230) and Fishers Farm Park (see p.289) in Sussex; there are **steam trains** on the Romney, Hythe & Dymchurch Railway (see p.129), the Bluebell Railway (see p.196), and the Kent & East Sussex Railway (see p.151) – the last of these an excellent way to get to Bodiam Castle (see p.189), one of many fine **castles** in this history-rich corner of the country. In North Kent, there is a knot of excellent family attractions around Rochester, where the huge ships of the Chatham Historic Dockyard (see p.72) are just a hop away from Diggerland (see p.72) and the Chatham Ski Centre (see p.72). For older children, there are a host of outdoor activities to keep them happy, from cycling and walking, to climbing near Tunbridge Wells (see p.193), canoeing in Kent (see p.61) or surfing at West Wittering beach or Joss Bay (see p.280 and p.98).

Child **admission prices** for all children's attractions are listed in the Guide. Attractions that are not geared specifically towards children generally admit under-5s for free, and have reduced prices for 5- to 16-year-olds. Under-5s travel free on **public transport**, and 5- to 16-year-olds generally at a fifty-percent discount.

Breastfeeding is legal in all public places, including restaurants, cafés and public transport, and **baby-changing** rooms are available widely in shopping centres and train stations, although less reliably in cafés and restaurants. Children aren't allowed in certain licensed (that is, alcohol-serving) premises – though this doesn't apply to restaurants, and many **pubs** have family rooms or beer gardens where children are welcome.

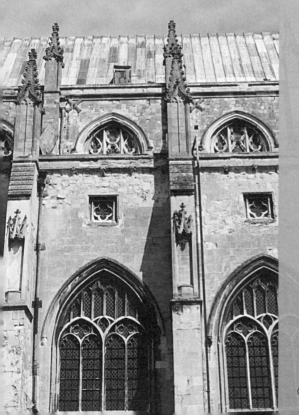

Canterbury
and around

CANTERBURY CATHEDRAL

1

Canterbury and around

Canterbury offers a rich slice through two thousand years of English history, with Roman and early Christian remains, a ruined Norman castle and a splendid cathedral that looms over a medieval warren of time-skewed Tudor buildings. It's a rewarding place to spend a couple of days, with important historic sights, peaceful riverside walks and a good number of hotels and excellent restaurants, and its small size makes it easy to get to know. Almost everything you will want to see is concentrated in or just outside the compact old centre, which, partly ringed by ancient walls, is virtually car-free. It's a delight to explore – though if you visit in high summer you should expect to share it with milling crowds. For a university town, things are surprisingly quiet after dark, which makes for a relaxing and restorative city break.

Canterbury is pretty laidback, but should you want to slow the pace even further, you can do so within minutes. Beyond the city a number of picturesque villages make good stop-offs for lunch or an overnight stay; indeed, it would be perfectly possible to base yourself outside Canterbury and make day-trips in, combining a city break with walking along the North Downs Way or even a canoe tour along the Stour. **South** of town, the Downs offer a couple of appealing family attractions as they begin their inexorable roll south, while to the north and west spreads the ancient, dappled woodland of the Blean and its nature trails and walking paths. From here you're a hop away from North Kent's foodie heartland, with both Faversham (see p.76) and Whitstable (see p.80) within easy reach. To the east, on the way to Thanet (see p.88) or the east coast, Stodmarsh Nature Reserve is an important birding spot and a lovely place for a stroll.

Canterbury

Most of the things you want to see in **CANTERBURY**, including the **cathedral**, are minutes away from each other within the bounds of the walled city. Just a short walk outside the walls are a handful of key historical sights – **St Augustine's Abbey**, **St Martin's Church** and **St Dunstan's Church** – while you may also want to head over to the campus of the University of Kent to catch a performance at the Gulbenkian Theatre (see p.58).

Brief history

The city that began as a Belgic settlement, spreading out on either side of the River Stour, was known as **Durovernum Cantiacorum** to the Romans, who established a garrison and supply base here soon after arriving in Britain. Life changed almost

Highlights

❶ Canterbury Cathedral Dominating this historic university town, the ancient cathedral – seat of the Primate of All England, the Archbishop of Canterbury – can't fail to inspire a sense of awe. **See p.41**

❷ Greyfriars Chapel This tiny Franciscan chapel, with its own pretty walled gardens, makes a tranquil hideaway just footsteps from the city centre. **See p.48**

❸ The River Stour Whether you stroll or cycle along its quiet banks, glide upon it in a punt, or leave the city behind on a kayaking adventure, the Stour provides charm in spades. **See p.52 & p.61**

❹ Crab and Winkle Way Cycling or walking along the old railway track between Canterbury and the seaside town of Whitstable, just seven miles away, is a lovely way to combine city, countryside and coast. **See p.60**

❺ Chilham An unfeasibly pretty village in the countryside surrounding Canterbury, this Tudor gem makes a great stop off, especially if you're walking or cycling the North Downs Way. **See p.62**

❻ Compasses Inn, Crundale This gorgeous country pub dishes up outstanding seasonal, rustic food, with lovely woodland and Downs walks all around. **See p.63**

HIGHLIGHTS ARE MARKED ON THE MAPS ON P.40 & P.42

1

immediately for the Cantii locals, who found themselves living in a thriving town with good roads, public buildings and a ring of protective city walls. After the Roman withdrawal from Britain the place fell into decline, before being settled again by the Anglo-Saxons, who renamed it Cantwaraburg. It was a Saxon king, **Ethelbert of Kent**, who in 597 AD welcomed the Italian monk Augustine, despatched by Pope Gregory the Great to reintroduce **Christianity** to the south of England. By the time of his death in 605, Augustine had founded an important monastery outside the city walls, and established Christ Church, raised on the site of the Roman basilica, which was to become the first cathedral in England.

After the Norman invasion, a complex power struggle developed between the archbishops, the abbots from the monastery – now St Augustine's Abbey – and King Henry II. This culminated in the assassination of Archbishop **Thomas Becket** in the cathedral in 1170 (see box, p.43), a martyrdom that created one of Christendom's greatest shrines, made Canterbury one of the country's richest cities – and effectively established the autonomy of the archbishops. Believers from all over Europe flocked to the cathedral on long pilgrimages, hoping to be cured, forgiven or saved; Geoffrey Chaucer's **Canterbury Tales** (see box, p.47), written towards the end of the fourteenth

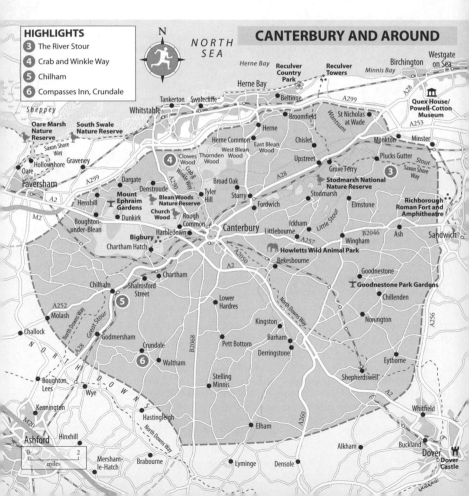

HIGHLIGHTS

3 The River Stour
4 Crab and Winkle Way
5 Chilham
6 Compasses Inn, Crundale

CANTERBURY AND AROUND

century, portrays the festive, ribald – and not always very pious – nature of these highly sociable events.

Becket's tomb, along with much of the cathedral's treasure, was later destroyed on the orders of Henry VIII, who also ordered the dissolution of St Augustine's Abbey. With its pilgrimage days effectively over, the next couple of centuries saw a downturn in the city's fortunes. However, following a period of calm and prosperity in the wake of the Restoration, in 1830 a pioneering steam passenger railway service was built, linking Canterbury to the seaside at Whitstable, and resulting in another bout of growth. Canterbury suffered extensive damage from German bombing on June 1, 1942, in one of the "**Baedeker Raids**" – a Nazi campaign to wipe out Britain's most treasured historic sites as described in the eponymous German travel guides. Nine hundred buildings were destroyed, and the city smouldered for weeks; the cathedral survived, however, and today, along with St Augustine's Abbey and St Martin's Church, has been designated as a **UNESCO World Heritage Site**.

Canterbury Cathedral

Buttermarket, CT1 2EH • **Cathedral** April–Oct Mon–Sat 9am–5.30pm, Sun 12.30–2.30pm; Nov–March Mon–Sat 9am–5pm, Sun 12.30–2.30pm; last entry 30min before closing • **Crypt** April–Oct Mon–Sat 10am–5.30pm, Sun 12.30–2.30pm; Nov–March Mon–Sat 10am–5pm, Sun 12.30–2.30pm • **Quire** Mon–Fri 9am–4.30pm, Sat 9am–2.30pm, Sun 12.30–2.30pm • £12, audio tours £4 • **Guided tours** Mon–Fri 10.30am, noon & 2pm (2.30pm in summer), Sat 10.30am (not in Jan), noon & 1pm; 1hr 20min; £5 • ☎ 01227 762862, ⓦ canterbury-cathedral.org

The Mother Church of the Church of England, **Canterbury Cathedral** may not be the country's most impressive architecturally, but it lords over the city with a befitting sense of authority. A cathedral has stood here since around 600 AD, established by Augustine; it was enlarged by the Saxons, but the building you see today owes most to a Norman archbishop, Lanfranc, who in 1070 rebuilt the place after a huge fire. Already on the medieval pilgrim route to Rome, the cathedral became an enormously important pilgrimage centre in its own right after the murder of Archbishop **Thomas Becket** here in 1170 (see box, p.43). In 1174 it was rebuilt again, and modified over successive centuries; today, with the puritanical lines of the late-medieval Perpendicular style dominating, its exterior derives much of its distinctiveness from the upward thrust of its 235ft-high Bell Harry Tower, dating from 1498.

Inside, it is the reminders of earlier days that have the most emotional impact – from the amazing carved columns in the crypt to the steep flights of stone steps worn away by millions of pilgrims – along with a couple of modern sculptures that recall the enormity of the events of 1170. It's well worth taking a guided **tour** to peel away the many layers of the building's fascinating history. There's quite a lot of walking, and climbing of stairs, if you want to see everything; if you're short of time, concentrate on the **crypt** and **Trinity Chapel**.

The precincts

The cathedral **precincts** are entered through the ornate, early sixteenth-century **Christ Church Gate**, where Burgate and St Margaret's Street meet. This junction, the city's medieval core, was originally called "Bullstake" – cattle were baited in the street here in order to tenderize their meat – but was renamed **Buttermarket** in the eighteenth century. Having paid your entrance fee, you pass through the gatehouse to be confronted by one of the finest aspects of the cathedral, foreshortened and crowned with soaring towers and pinnacles.

Note that you can exit the precincts via the large gift shop (see p.58) on Burgate; just next to it, within the grounds, is a little **refreshments hut** with outdoor tables; the close-up view of the cathedral, and the peace and quiet, make this one of the city's best-kept secrets.

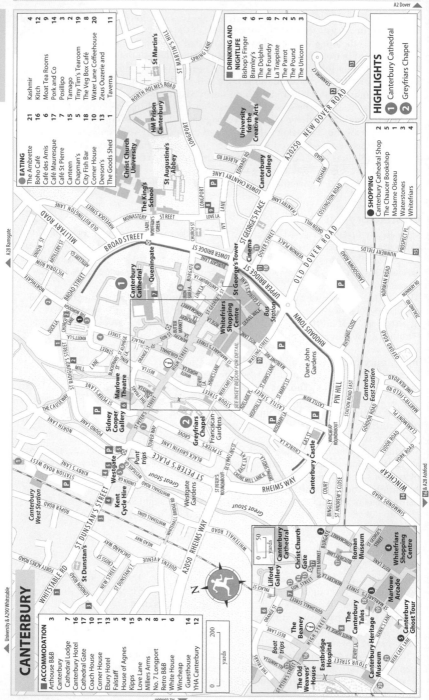

CANTERBURY

HIGHLIGHTS
1 Canterbury Cathedral
2 Greyfriars Chapel

The nave

The fourteenth-century **nave**, the largest space in the cathedral, would have been a bustling arrival point for weary pilgrims. With its soaring Perpendicular pillars and vaulted arches, its sweeping views and lofty gilt bosses, it was designed to inspire awe, but was more sociable, and less formal than the areas beyond. At the eastern end, an elaborate **stone screen** marks the entrance to the Quire. In the distance beyond, though barely visible from the nave, are the high altar and the Trinity Chapel; in medieval times, obscuring the view of the double ascent up to the holy relics would have added to the sense of expectation as the pilgrimage drew to a close, and even today the screen provides a dramatic pausing point on your journey through the cathedral.

The Martyrdom

The actual spot where Thomas Becket was murdered, known as the **Martyrdom**, is just off the nave in the northwest transept, marked by a modern-day flagstone etched simply with the name "Thomas". Next to it, the **Altar of the Sword's Point** – where, in medieval times, the shattered tip of the sword that hacked into Becket's scalp was displayed as a relic – is today marked by a modern sculpture of the assassins' weapons, suspended on the wall. Taking the form of two jagged swords attached to a similarly jagged cross, and casting sinister shadows, it is a striking image, at once violent and spiritual.

The crypt

From the Martyrdom you can descend to the low, Romanesque **crypt**, one of the few surviving parts of the Norman cathedral and considered to be the finest of its type in the country. Beneath the Quire and the elevated Trinity Chapel – but not actually underground – it is an unusually large space, dimly illuminated with natural light and with a number of chapels branching off from the main area. Becket's original shrine

---

THOMAS BECKET: THE TURBULENT PRIEST

The son of a wealthy merchant, Royal Chancellor **Thomas Becket** was appointed Archbishop of Canterbury in 1162 by his good friend and drinking partner Henry II. Becket had no particular experience in the Church, but Henry needed an ally against the bishops and monks who were, as the king saw it, getting far too above themselves and becoming a threat. The friends soon fell out, however, as Henry attempted to impose his jurisdiction over that of the Church and found that Becket seemed to have switched sides. After a six-year exile in France, Becket was reconciled with Henry and was allowed home in 1170 – only to find that his lands were being requisitioned by the king's officers. He incurred the king's wrath once more by refusing to absolve two bishops whom he had previously excommunicated, along with the family who had stripped him of his estates; Henry, in France, was told (untruthfully) that Becket was raising an army, provoking the king to utter the oft-quoted words, "Will no one rid me of this turbulent priest?" (Some sources claim he actually called him "low-born", or "meddlesome", but it is "turbulent" that has tended to stick.)

Hearing this, four knights took it upon themselves to seek out Becket and, on December 29, 1170, finding him in the cathedral, **murdered** him, hacking at him with their swords and slicing off the crown of his head. It was said he was praying when they found him, and was discovered to have been wearing a monk's habit under his robes, and a hair shirt underneath that – held to be proof of his great piety. The day after his murder, Becket's remains were taken to the crypt, for safety; within days miracles were said to be occurring at his simple stone tomb, and just three years later he was canonized. Hundreds of thousands of **pilgrims** from all over Europe, including kings and queens, flocked to the cathedral hoping to be healed or redeemed; one such pilgrim was Henry himself, who in 1174 walked barefoot and in sackcloth from St Dunstan's Church (see p.51) to the shrine, where he was theatrically beaten by eighty monks and a prior. Whether Henry was driven by a genuine sense of regret, or canny pragmatics – his pilgrimage was a statement to the world that he definitively did not order the murder of Becket, while also being an admission that his words may have inspired it – is open to debate.

1

stood down here, before being moved in 1220 to a more resplendent position in the Trinity Chapel.

Today, in the main body of the crypt, you can see amazingly well-preserved **carvings** on the capitals of the sturdy Romanesque columns, showing flowers, animals, scallops, sea monsters and winged beasts. There is a fine crop in **St Gabriel's Chapel**, which also boasts some intact, and colourful, twelfth-century wall paintings, uncovered in the 1860s. Among the usual stash of silver plate in the **treasury**, look out for the nineteenth-century brass high altar cross, studded with precious gems.

The Quire

In the main body of the cathedral, the **Quire** is one of the earliest examples of Gothic church architecture in Britain, built between 1175 and 1184 and replete with elegant pointed arches. As you enter from the nave, stop a while at the intricate **stone screen** and crane your neck upwards to gaze upon the interior of the **Bell Harry Tower**; a vertiginous pattern of arches, pillars and fan vaulting, this is a stunning sight, and all too easily missed. At the end of the Quire, at the top of the steps beyond the high altar, stands the thirteenth-century white marble **St Augustine's Chair**, on which all archbishops of Canterbury are enthroned.

Trinity Chapel

Beyond the Quire, climbing a flight of stone steps, polished and worn wonky by the knees of pilgrims, brings you to the **Trinity Chapel**, for centuries the cathedral's most venerated space. Becket's remains were moved up here from the crypt in 1220, with great pomp and ceremony; the new shrine, far more ornate than the earlier tomb, became a place of theatre and ritual. Each pilgrim would be shown the spot where Becket was murdered, taken to see the bust that contained the piece of skull dislodged by the fatal blow, and, as a grand finale, allowed to watch as a canopy was pulled up to reveal the ornate golden tomb, studded, according to the writer Erasmus in 1513, with jewels as big as goose eggs. The shrine shimmered in all its jewel-bedecked glory until being demolished during Henry VIII's Dissolution of the Monasteries in 1538, and all that remains today is a candle to mark where it once stood. You can get a sense of what it looked like, however, in the dazzling thirteenth-century stained-glass **Miracle Windows**, on the north side of the chapel, where along with Becket's life and miraculous works, you can see images both of the original tomb and the showier later version.

MURDER IN THE CATHEDRAL

A rain of blood has blinded my eyes. Where is England? Where is Kent? Where is Canterbury?
O far far far far in the past; and I wander in a land of barren boughs…

The Chorus, Part 2, *Murder in the Cathedral*

The American-born poet **T.S. Eliot** wrote his play **Murder in the Cathedral** for the 1935 Canterbury Festival, when it was performed in the cathedral itself. After converting to Anglicanism from Unitarianism in 1927 – the same year he took British citizenship – Eliot, a modernist, concerned himself increasingly with spiritual issues in his writing, and went on to become an important voice in the High Anglican Church, characterized by its emphasis on ritual and ceremonial. Written in a mixture of prose, blank verse and rhyme, and with its keening female chorus – who express their beautifully wrought, visceral anguish in lines like "O late late late, late is the time, late too late, and rotten the year" – *Murder in the Cathedral* recalls both Classical Greek drama and medieval morality plays. Though not quite as bleakly existential as Eliot's pre-conversion poems *The Waste Land* (1922) or *The Hollow Men* (1925), it is a profoundly personal work, written in his characteristically lean style. Even for non-believers, the genius he applies to both language and form in exploring vexed issues around faith, temptation, desolation and guilt render it a deeply moving piece of writing.

Also in the Trinity Chapel is the double tomb of **Henry IV** and his wife, **Joan of Navarre**, their heads resting on carved red cushions, and the (somewhat tarnished) gilt bronze effigy of Edward III's son, Edward Prince of Wales, or the **Black Prince**. The "achievements" hanging above him – his shield, gauntlets, sword and jerkin – are copies; the originals, which were carried in procession with his funeral in 1376, will return to the cathedral as part of a new display in 2017.

The Corona

At the far eastern tip of the cathedral, the **Corona** is where, until Henry VIII destroyed it, a silver bust of Becket held the piece of Becket's skull hacked off by his assassin's sword. Today the chapel is dedicated to saints and martyrs of our own time, among them Dr Martin Luther King, Jr and an Anglican archbishop, Janani Luwum of Uganda, murdered by Idi Amin's forces in 1977.

The Great Cloister

On the cathedral's north flank are the fan-vaulted colonnades of the **Great Cloister**, an atmospherically weathered and beautifully peaceful space. Look above you to see expressive little faces, bulbous flowers and heraldic symbols carved into the vaulting, and check out the carved graffiti and ancient, crumbling columns. The **Chapter House**, off the cloister, is relatively plain, though it does boast an intricate web of fourteenth-century tracery supporting the roof and two huge stained-glass windows.

The High Street and around

As it cuts a northwest–southeast swathe through the city between Westgate and St George's Gate, Canterbury's predominantly pedestrianized **High Street** changes its name three times: the stretch from Westgate to the river is St Peter's Street, followed by the High Street proper down to Longmarket, where it turns into St George's Street for the remainder of its length.

Each section of the High Street has its own character; **St Peter's Street** is relatively quiet, with low-key restaurants and shops occupying its hotchpotch of half-timbered, gabled and more modern buildings, while chain stores predominate along the **High Street** proper. Here, though, the side streets offer photogenic medieval vistas – the view up **Mercery Lane** towards Christ Church Gate, for example, a narrow alley of crooked, overhanging shops at the end of which stand the elaborate gatehouse and the cathedral's handsome towers. Much of **St George's Street**, meanwhile, is consumed by the Whitefriars shopping centre (see p.59), before ending up at the edge of the old city walls.

Westgate

St Peters St, CT1 2BQ • Daily 11am–4pm (closed 30min for lunch) • £4 • ☎ 01227 458629, ⓦ onepoundlane.co.uk

At the top of the High Street, the sturdy, 60ft-high **Westgate** is the largest and most important of Canterbury's seven city gates and the only one to have survived intact. With its massive crenellated towers, dating from 1380, it's a handsome structure, looming over the traffic below, and something of an icon for the city. A small museum inside includes intriguing historical snippets about the gate's days as a medieval and nineteenth-century gaol; best of all, you can climb up to the battlements for lovely **views** across to the cathedral and over the gardens below. Entry is in the lobby area of the neighbouring *The Pound* bar (see p.58).

Westgate Gardens

Westgate Grove, CT1 2BQ • Free • ⓦ westgateparks.co.uk

Across the road from the Westgate, and fringing the River Stour, the pretty, flower-filled **Westgate Gardens** make a splendid spot for a picnic or a riverside stroll. Like so many places in Canterbury, they're also historically significant, having been open to the

1

public since medieval times. You'll hardly be able to miss the two-centuries-old, unfeasibly chubby Oriental plane tree, with a girth of a whopping 29ft, give or take; more difficult to spot, however, is the underwater sculpture by the Westgate Bridge. Here, two female statues, one cast in cement and the other in grass resin, float eerily beneath the surface of the reed-tangled, shallow water like latter-day Ophelias. This is **Alluvia**, the work of Jason de Caires Taylor, an ex-graffiti artist from Canterbury who now creates such unsettling and sublimely beautiful underwater sculptures all over the world. It can be easiest to see the statues at night, when they are illuminated.

Sidney Cooper Gallery
22–23 St Peter's St, CT1 2BQ • Tues–Fri 10.30am–5pm, Sat 11.30am–5pm • Free • ☎ 01227 453267, ⓦ canterbury.ac.uk/sidney-cooper

An unobtrusive shopfront hides the **Sidney Cooper Gallery**, Canterbury Christ Church University's modern-art space. Hosting temporary shows from university staff, students and alumni, along with local and national artists of such calibre as Maggi Hambling, Louise Bourgeois and Anish Kapoor, it is always worth a look. Many, but not all, works have Kentish associations, and tend towards the cutting edge, featuring anything from sound art to animation to sculpture.

The Old Weavers' House
1–3 St Peter's St, CT1 2AT

The wonky, half-timbered **Old Weavers' House**, standing at the King's Bridge over a branch of the Stour, is one of the most photographed buildings in Canterbury. Built around 1500, the structure appears to be quintessentially medieval, but is actually a hotchpotch, constructed on twelfth-century foundations and with alterations made between the sixteenth and twentieth centuries. A couple of restaurants now inhabit the place, making much of their picturesque riverside location.

Eastbridge Hospital
25 High St, CT1 2BD • Mon–Sat 10am–5pm • £2 • ☎ 01227 471688, ⓦ eastbridgehospital.org.uk

Tiny **Eastbridge Hospital**, the ancient stone building standing just beyond the King's Bridge, was founded in the twelfth century to provide the poorest pilgrims with shelter (or "hospitality"). Following the Reformation it continued as an almshouse, offering permanent accommodation for people in need; today it is home to a small community of elderly people.

Beyond the handsome pointed arch doorway, a couple of steps lead down into the Gothic **undercroft**, the original pilgrims' sleeping quarters; you can see the cubicles they slept in, along with a few exhibition panels recounting the history of the building, and of pilgrimage in Canterbury. Upstairs is the medieval **refectory**, where a striking thirteenth-century wall painting shows Jesus surrounded by the four Evangelists (though only two of them remain), and the light-filled **pilgrims' chapel**, with its beautifully crafted, thirteenth-century oak-beamed roof.

The Beaney
18 High St, CT1 2RA • Mon–Wed, Fri & Sat 9am–5pm, Thurs 9am–7pm, Sun 10am–5pm • Free • ☎ 01227 862162, ⓦ canterburymuseums.co.uk/beaney

A sturdy terracotta, brick and mock-Tudor ensemble, built in 1898, the **Beaney** – officially the **Beaney House of Art and Knowledge** – started its days with the aim of improving the masses and retains a populist, welcoming feel. Today, despite its modern library and lofty, airy rooms, some of the exhibits have the – not unlikeable – feel of a Victorian collection, with cases of stuffed animals, pinned butterflies and **antiquities and archeological finds** creating a cabinet-of-curiosities thrill. Look out for the little mummified cat, baring its tiny sharp fangs, the terrifying angled temple sword from eighteenth-century Malabar, and the nineteenth-century face-slapper, used to hit female prisoners in Kashgar.

There is a lot to see here, but perhaps most interesting of all are the **paintings**, from the seventeenth century onwards. Among the images of Kentish notables, landscapes and historical moments, many of them painted by local artists, perennial favourites include a Van Dyck portrait of Kent MP Sir Basil Dixwell (1638), displaying his long, aristocratic fingers and showing off his expensive black silk robes; the tall, thin and enigmatic *The Little Girl at the Door* (1910), by local artist Harriet Halhed; a Reculver scene by Walter Sickert (1936), painted during his four-year stay in Thanet; and the vigorous images of 1930s hop-pickers by English Impressionist Dame Laura Knight. In addition, high-profile **temporary exhibitions** have featured artists such as Grayson Perry and Martin Parr.

Roman Museum

Butchery Lane, CT1 2JR • Daily 10am–5pm • £8; joint ticket with Canterbury Heritage Museum (see p.48) £12 • ☎ 01227 785575, ⓦ canterburymuseums.co.uk/romanmuseum

Following the devastating Canterbury bombings of 1942, excavations of the destroyed Longmarket area, between Burgate and the High Street, exposed the foundations of a Roman townhouse, complete with mosaic floors, now preserved in situ in the city's subterranean Roman Museum.

While historical panels give a good introduction to life in Durovernum Cantiacorum, it is the treasure-trove of **artefacts** excavated from the city and sites nearby that really brings it alive. This is a rich hoard: case after case filled with pottery, tiles and amulets (many of them phallus-shaped, a favourite among Roman soldiers), exquisite glass bottles, building tools, fashion accessories – the list goes on. Some are unexpectedly poignant – a commemorative stone for a 6-year-old girl, for example, marked with the words "May the earth lie lightly on thee"; the two crumbling military swords, found in a double grave; even the silver spoon marked with the words "I belong to a good man", which was buried for safety when the Romans withdrew in around 410, and which remained hidden underground for 1500 years.

The **remains** themselves come at the end of the display, protected behind glass in the dark. Here you can see the floor supports of an under-heated hypocaust, an undecorated stone corridor, and some stone floor mosaics decorated with geometric and floral patterns. If all this whets your appetite for Roman remains, plan a trip to Lullingstone Roman Villa, in the Weald (see p.153).

The Canterbury Tales

St Margaret's St, CT1 2TG • Daily: March–June, Sept & Oct 10am–5pm; July & Aug 9.30am–5pm; Nov–Feb 10am–4.30pm • £9.75, under-16s £7.50; discounts if booked online • ☎ 01227 479227, ⓦ canterburytales.org.uk

Housed in an old church a few yards off the High Street, **The Canterbury Tales**, based

THE CANTERBURY TALES

Geoffrey Chaucer's (unfinished) **Canterbury Tales**, written between 1387 and the author's death in 1400, are a collection of stories within a story in which a motley bunch of thirty pilgrims exchange a series of yarns to while away the time as they journey from a tavern in London to the cathedral. The group is a colourful cross-section of medieval society, including a knight, a monk, a miller, a squire and the oft-widowed, rather raunchy, Wife of Bath. At a time when French was very much the official language of literature, Chaucer chose to write their earthy and often ribald tales in English. That, and the fact that each story has a different narrator, with his or her own voice and personality – and that each character is linked by their common journey – is a structure that feels entirely natural to modern readers but at the time was entirely new.

The tales themselves are reworked stories, popular at the time, from around the world, ranging from oral folk tales to classic myths – the *Prologue*, however, is entirely Chaucer's work, introducing each character and giving a wonderfully vivid, and humanistic, portrayal of early medieval England. All this, combined with the lively language and universal themes, keep the *Canterbury Tales* as fresh and engaging today as they ever were.

1

on Geoffrey Chaucer's medieval stories (see box, p.47), is a quasi-educational, and fun, attraction. Equipped with audio guides, visitors set off on a 45-minute wander through atmospheric, odour-enhanced fourteenth-century tableaux, following the progress of a group of pilgrims (or rather, suitably scrofulous mannequins) from the *Tabard Inn* in London to Becket's atmospherically lit, and fabulously ornate, shrine. Each new space provides a setting for one of Chaucer's famous tales – edited-down versions of stories from the Knight, the Miller, the Wife of Bath, the Nun's Priest and the Pardoner. Each is told in a slightly different way, using animatronics, shadow play, video, or a combination of the three, with helpful interventions from costumed guides acting their hearts out in character – and though it's not slick it's all done rather well, with lively lighting, sound effects and tongue-in-cheek dialogue. The bare bum revealed in the scatological Miller's Tale is always a cheeky crowd-pleaser, and it's hard not to get caught up in the bawdy fun of it all.

Canterbury Heritage Museum

Stour St, CT1 2NR • 11am–5pm: April–Sept Wed–Sun; Oct, half terms and some hol weeks daily • £8; joint ticket with Roman Museum (see p.47) £12 • ☎ 01227 475202, ⓦ canterburymuseums.co.uk/heritagemuseum

The **Canterbury Heritage Museum** provides an illuminating trot through the city's history. Though there are a couple of Iron Age treasures – including a rare, early mirror made from bronze, found buried with the cremated remains of a young woman, and marked with swirling Celtic designs – the story sets off in earnest with the Roman city, displaying a selection of jewellery, pottery and house deities. The **Norman** room features grotesque eleventh-century stone carvings of mythical beasts, and a rather splendid 60ft-long, 1980s wall **frieze** from Canterbury-born Oliver Postgate (he who brought us *Bagpuss* and *The Clangers*). Deftly outlining the complex story of Thomas Becket and his relationship with the king, the colourful frieze portrays the adversaries as well-matched and largely self-serving, living in brutal times – although as you might expect of Postgate's work, everyone looks pretty affable. The **medieval** pilgrimage souvenirs – tin lead badges portraying Becket's reliquary bust (see p.45) – are intriguing, while in the **Tudor** room you can see sections of rose-pink marble capitals that were found on Canterbury's riverbank in 1983 and are believed, by some, to be from Becket's tomb, destroyed by Henry VIII. Highlights from the **Elizabethan** and **Stuart** eras include a beautiful wall painting, alive with roses, carnations, tulips, cherries and acorns, found in a Tudor house nearby. One section covers local-born playwright/poet and alleged spy **Christopher Marlowe**; another is dedicated to novelist **Joseph Conrad**, with a re-creation of his study.

A room at the end pays homage to the beloved **Oliver Postgate**, with nostalgic TV footage and cabinets of real-deal Clangers, while beyond that the tartan-trousered philanthropist **Rupert Bear**, created by local-born Mary Tourtel, practically has a museum all to himself. Here you can see all manner of bear memorabilia, including the very first Rupert book, dating from 1921.

Greyfriars Chapel and Franciscan Gardens

Behind 6 Stour St, CT1 2NR • **Chapel** Easter–Sept Mon–Sat 2–4pm; Anglican Eucharist Wed 12.30pm • **Gardens** Daily: summer 9am–5pm; rest of year till dusk • Free; donations welcome • ☎ 01227 471688, ⓦ eastbridgehospital.org.uk

A delightful surprise hidden off Stour Street, literally spanning the river and with pretty, peaceful gardens, the stone-built **Greyfriars Chapel** is the only surviving building from England's oldest Franciscan friary (1267). In the thirteenth century the friary was home to sixty or so friars; it was closed by Henry VIII in 1538 and sold on. This little building was, it is thought, the guesthouse of the friary, and home over the years to Huguenot and Belgian refugees; one room was also used as a prison in the nineteenth century, as its grim, studded iron door attests. In 2003 a group of Anglican Franciscan friars returned to Canterbury, and they now use Greyfriars as their chapel.

The interior, though unadorned, is fascinating, with its original beams and prisoners' graffiti carved into medieval wooden panelling. A small **exhibit** illuminates the history of Greyfriars and of the Franciscans; upstairs, the whitewashed, vaulted **chapel** still hosts a weekly Eucharist, open to all. Take time to stroll through the **Franciscan Gardens**, a haven of serenity with the river gurgling past a drift of scattered wildflowers.

Canterbury Castle

Castle St, CT1 2PR • Daily morning to dusk • Free • ☎ 01227 862162, ⓦ canterbury.co.uk

Walking down Castle Street, which grows quieter and increasingly residential as it approaches the city wall, brings you to the ruins of **Canterbury Castle**. Replacing a simple wooden structure built by William the Conqueror around 1070, this motte-and-bailey affair sitting hard by the Roman town walls was started in around 1086 and considerably altered in subsequent years; by the late twelfth century its importance had dwindled to nothing in the light of Henry II's mighty castle at Dover. For many years it existed as a rather neglected prison, until it fell into ruin in the sixteenth century and was pretty much pulled apart in the eighteenth and early nineteenth centuries.

Today, you can explore the substantial roofless **keep**, built by Henry I and made of locally quarried flint, Kentish ragstone and Roman bricks. It's an evocative spot, with its sturdy walls silhouetted against the sky and sprouting luxuriant vegetation; most days it is silent but for the wheeling birds tending to their nests, stuffed in the many huge arches and empty windows.

Dane John Gardens

Watling St, CT1 2QX • Free • ☎ 01227 862162

Dane John Gardens, an attractive and well-used park near the castle, was laid out in the eighteenth century with lawns, flower beds and a stately avenue of lime trees, along with a bandstand that still hosts concerts in summer. Bordering the southern edge of the gardens are the city walls and the Dane John Mound, a Romano-British burial mound that was incorporated into the city's original castle and now affords good views across the city. There's a refreshment kiosk, and in late September a **food and drink festival** (ⓦ canterbury.co.uk/canterburyfoodfestival.aspx), with more than one hundred food stalls, plus live music and children's entertainment.

The King's Mile

The **King's Mile** – the stretch from the cathedral up Sun Street and Palace Street, also including Guildhall and the Borough – is a quieter and more characterful place to shop than the High Street, its picturesque historic buildings housing a number of quirky independent shops, galleries and restaurants. Palace Street is the prettiest section; at the top, where it meets the Borough, a sturdy stone gate screens off the medieval buildings of the **King's School**. Commonly believed to be the oldest continually operating school in the world, King's has an impressive list of alumni, from Elizabethan dramatist Christopher Marlowe to author Patrick Leigh Fermor and movie director Michael Powell. Beyond the Borough, Northgate is home to a clutch of **Asian restaurants**, groceries and businesses – it might be stretching it to call this Canterbury's Little Asia, but you could perhaps get away with it at a push.

Outside the city walls

From Burgate, it's just a three-minute walk east of the city walls to the vestigial remains of the sixth-century **St Augustine's Abbey**, and then another five minutes on to **St Martin's Church**, possibly the oldest church still in use in the English-speaking world. The two, along with the cathedral, comprise UNESCO's **Canterbury World Heritage Site**; for any full account of the city's history, or indeed the history of Christianity in

1

England, they are a must-see. Northwest of town, **St Dunstan's Church** – where Henry II paused on his 1174 pilgrimage to shed his shoes and don his hair shirt, and where the remains of another martyr, Sir Thomas More, are interred – is also worth a look.

St Augustine's Abbey

Longport, CT1 1PF • April–Sept daily 10am–6pm; Oct daily 10am–5pm; Nov–March Sat & Sun 10am–4pm • £5.80; EH • ☎ 01227 767345, ⓦ english-heritage.org.uk/visit/places/st-augustines-abbey

While Canterbury Cathedral gets most of the attention, the ruined **St Augustine's Abbey**, founded in 598, is just as historically important. Founded as a monastery by the Italian monk Augustine, tasked with re-introducing Christianity to the English, it was vastly altered by the Normans, who replaced it with a much larger abbey; in turn, most of this was later destroyed in the Dissolution before falling into ruin. Today, it is an atmospheric site, with more to see than its ruinous state might at first suggest. Its 'various ground plans, clearly delineated in stone on soft carpets of grass, along with scattered semi-intact chapels, altar slabs and tombstones, evoke the original buildings almost as powerfully as if they were still standing. Standouts include the ancient **tombs** of the early archbishops and the remains of the seventh-century **St Pancras Church**, which survived the Norman expansions, and where you can see the Roman brick used in its construction.

Illustrated information panels admirably recount the changing fortunes of the abbey, but to get the most out of a visit, pick up an audio guide from the excellent interpretive

---

THE RISE AND FALL OF ST AUGUSTINE'S ABBEY

In 595 Pope Gregory the Great dispatched **Augustine**, a Benedictine monk from Rome, on an evangelical mission to restore Christianity to England after a couple of centuries of Anglo-Saxon paganism had all but wiped it out. The kingdom of Kent seemed like a good place to start: not only was it conveniently close to the continent, but also its king – **Ethelbert**, the most powerful Anglo-Saxon ruler of the time – had a Christian wife, Bertha, and was open to the idea of conversion.

Augustine, reluctantly, fearing he was not up to the task of converting the barbarian Angles, set off with between twenty and forty monks. At one point he turned back, begging the Pope to send someone else; his entreaties went unheard, however, and he finally arrived on the Kentish coast in late 596 or 597. He baptized Ethelbert in 601, an act that effectively rubber-stamped his mission, and immediately set about founding a church within the walled city (today's cathedral), and a **monastery** outside the walls to the east. Following a tradition that forbade burials within city walls', the monastery's first church, dedicated to saints Peter and Paul, became the final resting place of both Augustine (in 605) and Ethelbert (in 616), along with successive archbishops and kings of Kent right up until the middle of the eighth century.

Augustine's monastery continued to thrive after his death. Two more churches, St Mary and St Pancras, were added in the first half of the seventh century, with further extensions being made in the eighth and ninth centuries; by the 900s it was well established as a major seat of learning. The most dramatic changes came in the eleventh century, with the arrival of the **Normans**, who in 1072 established a Benedictine **abbey** here, replacing the relatively simple Anglo-Saxon structures – and moving the holy remains of St Augustine from their original tomb into a far more ornate, jewel-bedecked shrine – with a huge Romanesque church similar in size to today's cathedral. The abbey continued to grow, becoming an important centre of book production, until the **Dissolution**. After being disbanded in 1538, it was converted into a royal palace, with apartments for Anne of Cleves (who never actually stayed here), and following Henry VIII's death it was rented by a string of noble families. In the eighteenth and nineteenth centuries the abbey precinct fell into relative ruin, though it was used variously as a brewery, hospital, jail and pleasure gardens; shocked at such sacrilege, local MP Alexander James Beresford Hope bought the site in 1844 and opened a missionary college four years later. These Victorian buildings are now part of the King's School (see p.49); other buildings in the precinct are owned by Christ Church college, Canterbury prison and English Heritage.

centre. These describe not only the more dramatic incidents in the site's history, but also its domestic routines, and really bring the place to life.

St Martin's Church

Corner of North Holmes Rd and St Martin's Lane, CT1 1PW • Tues, Thurs & Sat 11am–3pm, Sun 9.50am–10.20am • Free • ☎ 01227 768072, ⓦ martinpaul.org

In a slightly incongruous location behind the city jail, the lovely **St Martin's Church**, one of England's oldest churches, was built on the site of a Roman villa or temple and used by the earliest Christians. Although medieval additions obscure much of the Saxon structure, this is perhaps the earliest Christian site in Canterbury – it was here that the Frankish Queen Bertha worshipped with her priest Liudhard, welcoming Augustine and his monks after their arrival in England in 597. After King Ethelbert was baptized in St Martin's, Augustine's mission was deemed to be a resounding success, and he was able to go on to build the church and the abbey that dominated Canterbury for centuries.

Entering the church through an ancient shady graveyard, where nearly a thousand gravestones pepper the grassy hills, you'll find a few intriguing vestiges of the building's long history. Beyond the nave – a very early Anglo-Saxon structure of mortared brick and stone, with a fourteenth-century beamed roof – you can see a wall of long, flat Roman bricks in the chancel, dating back to the fourth century, and opposite it a flat-topped Roman doorway. Other highlights include an angled "squint", through which medieval lepers would have watched Mass from a safe distance outside the church.

St Dunstan's Church

80 London Rd, CT2 8LS • Mon–Sat 9am–5pm, Sun during services only; weekday hours dependent on volunteers, so call ahead to check • Free • ☎ 01227 786109

Though many people pass it without a second thought, the tenth-century **St Dunstan's Church** was an important stopping-point for medieval pilgrims on their journey to the city via Westgate – it was from here that King Henry II proceeded barefoot to the cathedral when doing penance in 1174 (see box, p.43). The church is also remarkable for holding the eternal remains of **Sir Thomas More**, executed upon the orders of Henry VIII in 1535 for refusing to accept the king's desire to split from the Catholic Church. More's head, removed from a spike outside the Tower of London by his daughter, Margaret Roper, is enclosed in a lead casket in the Roper family vault, beneath a stained-glass window portraying scenes from his life. A marble slab marks the spot

ARRIVAL AND DEPARTURE
CANTERBURY

BY TRAIN
Canterbury East Canterbury East station (in the south) is a 15min walk from the cathedral.
Destinations Bekesbourne (hourly; 5min); Chatham (every 20–40min; 45min); Dover (every 30min–1hr; 15–30min); Faversham (every 20–40min; 15min); London Victoria (every 30–40min; 1hr 35min); Rochester (every 20–40min; 40min–1hr).
Canterbury West Canterbury West (in the north), a 15min walk from the cathedral, is used by the high-speed train from London St Pancras.
Destinations Ashford (every 10–30min; 15–25min); Broadstairs (hourly; 25min); Chartham (hourly; 5min); Chilham (hourly; 10min); London Charing Cross (Mon–Sat hourly; 1hr 45min); London St Pancras (hourly; 55min); Margate (hourly; 30min); Ramsgate (every 20–40min; 20min); Sevenoaks (hourly; 1hr 5min);

Sturry (hourly; 5min); Tonbridge (hourly; 1hr 5min); Wye (every 30min; 15min).

BY BUS
National Express services and local Stagecoach East Kent buses use the station just inside the city walls on St George's Lane beside the Whitefriars shopping centre. The travel office here sells tickets and has timetables (Mon–Sat 7.30am–6pm; ☎ 0345 600 2299).
Destinations Broadstairs (hourly; 1hr–1hr 30min); Chilham (Mon–Sat hourly; 30min); Deal (Mon–Sat every 30min–1hr; 45min–1hr 20min); Dover (every 15min–1hr; 45min); Faversham (every 10–20min; 30min); Folkestone (every 15min–1hr; 45min); Herne Bay (every 15min; 35min); Hythe (every 30min; 1hr); London Victoria (hourly; 2hr); Margate (every 30min; 1hr); Ramsgate (hourly; 45min); Sandwich (every 20min; 40min); Whitstable (every 15min; 30min).

1

INFORMATION AND GETTING AROUND

Tourist office In the Beaney, 18 High St (Mon–Wed, Fri & Sat 9am–5pm, Thurs 9am–7pm, Sun 10am–5pm; ☎01227 862162, ⓦcanterbury.co.uk).

By car Parking in town can be problematic. There are off-street pay car parks throughout the centre, including on Watling Street, Castle Row, Rosemary Lane, Northgate and Pound Lane.

By bike Kent Cycle Hire, based at the *House of Agnes*, 71 St Dunstan's St (see opposite), rents bikes for £20/day or £90/week; kids' bikes, tandems and tagalongs are all available (book in advance; ☎01227 388058, ⓦkentcyclehire.com). You can drop off your bike at their sister outfits in Whitstable (see p.83) or Herne Bay (see p.89), if you wish.

ACCOMMODATION

A crop of fine old **hotels and B&Bs** in the city centre offer all the creaking, authentic antiquity you could ask for, and there's a host of good-value B&Bs just outside the city walls. Prices are reasonable for such a popular city, though many places ask for a two-night minimum stay at the weekend and it can be difficult to secure a room in July and August, when rates tend to increase; book well in advance if possible. If you're driving, check if your accommodation has on-site **parking** – many places in the centre don't, and this will add to the cost.

HOTELS AND GUESTHOUSES

Arthouse B&B 24 London Rd, CT2 8LN ☎07976 725457, ⓦarthousebandb.com. Occupying an old fire station a 10min walk from Westgate, the *Arthouse* offers a variety of options, and delicious seclusion. The main Victorian house has two doubles (each with private bathroom) sharing a lounge and kitchen – you could rent both and have the place to yourself. There's also a modern Scandinavian-style timber property, *Cedar House* (sleeps six) in the back garden, and more self-catering in the

Fireman's Cottage next door (sleeps four). Breakfast costs £5 extra. Two-night minimum stay. **£75**

Canterbury Cathedral Lodge The Precincts, CT1 2EH ☎01227 865350, ⓦcanterburycathedrallodge.org. Modern hotel, owned by the cathedral and with an unbeatable location within the precinct grounds – you can eat breakfast outside in good weather. Rooms in the main building are unfussy and contemporary, with something of the feel of conference accommodation; cheaper annexe rooms lack the cathedral views. Rates vary depending on

CANTERBURY TOURS

Canterbury is small enough to find your own way around very easily, but various **tours** are available should you want a knowledgeable overview. A trip along the **River Stour**, in particular, either on a rowing boat or a chauffeured punt, is a relaxing and picturesque way to get to know the city.

RIVER TOURS

Canterbury Historic River Tours ☎07790 534744, ⓦcanterburyrivertours.co.uk. Informative rowing-boat trips, with lively narration, along the River Stour (March–Oct daily 10am–5pm; every 15–20min; 40min; £9.50). No reservations necessary; simply turn up at the bridge by the Old Weaver's House (see p.46).

Canterbury Punting Company ☎01227 464797, ⓦcanterburypunting.co.uk. Chauffeured river tours (March–Nov; around 45min) on wooden punts, with historic commentary; cushions, blankets and rain canopies are provided if necessary. Choose from shared tours (every 15min; £10), candlelit "ghost" tours (6–8pm; £12) or a private "romantic" tour for couples (10am–8pm; £50). Reservations can be made at their base – *Water Lane Coffeehouse* on Water Lane (see p.56) – at the tourist office, by phone or by email.

Westgate Punts ☎07816 760869, ⓦcanterburypunts.uk. Chauffeured punting trips (mid-March to Oct daily, weather permitting,

10am–6pm or later in summer) along the Stour through the city, and out into the countryside. These are private trips only, with a minimum of two adults/group (35min–1hr 5min; £10–17). Call to reserve, or find them at Westgate Bridge opposite *Café des Amis* restaurant (see p.56).

WALKING TOURS

The Canterbury Ghost Tour ☎0845 519 0267, ⓦcanterburyghosttour.com. A tongue-in-cheek mix of supernatural spookery and local folklore, leaving from *Alberry's Wine Bar*, 38 St Margaret's St (Fri & Sat 8pm; around 1hr; £10). You can book by phone or online, or simply turn up on the night.

Canterbury Guided Tours ☎01227 459779, ⓦcanterburyguidedtours.com. Informative walking tours of the city and the cathedral precincts, leaving from the Buttermarket (daily: April–Oct 11am & 2pm; Nov–March 11am; 1hr 30min; £7.50). Buy tickets at the tourist office or the Roman Museum (see p.47).

availability, but booking well in advance will bring costs down, as will special offers. Rates include one free admission/person to the cathedral. **£95**

Canterbury Hotel 140 Wincheap, CT1 3RY ☎01227 453227, ⓦthecanterburyhotel.co.uk. Solid hotel in a Georgian building, about a 10min walk from Canterbury East train station. The rooms are fine, but it's the suntrap garden and (small) heated indoor pool and spa that give this place the edge – and there's a guest bar specializing in whisky. **£100**

Cathedral Gate 36 Burgate, CT1 2HA ☎01227 464381, ⓦcathgate.co.uk. Built in 1438 and with a fantastic location next to the cathedral gate, this ancient pilgrims' hostelry is a warren of a place, all crooked, creaking floors, timber beams and narrow, steep staircases (no lift). It's in no way fancy, but it's comfortable and efficient, with cathedral views from many of the rooms. They also provide a simple continental breakfast, which you can eat in your room. The cheapest rooms share toilets and (tiny) showers but have basins, and all have tea- and coffee-making facilities. In summer you might get better value for doubles elsewhere, but for singles (who pay around £50, with shared facilities), this is a particular bargain. **£82**

Coach House 34 Watling St, CT1 2UD ☎01227 784324, ⓦcoachhouse-canterbury.co.uk. Six B&B rooms (including a good-value single and a family option) in a Georgian house, not luxurious but with creaky character. Some are en suite, others have private bathrooms; all are comfy, with original features, and there's a courtyard garden. On-site parking. Two-night minimum stay at weekends. **£85**

Corner House 1 Dover St, CT1 3HD ☎01227 780793, ⓦcornerhouserestaurants.co.uk. Set on a busy corner just outside the city wall, this superb Modern British restaurant (see p.57) offers three gorgeous B&B rooms that combine rustic charm and contemporary cool – the romantic attic features an in-room roll-top bathtub. **£130**

Ebury Hotel 65–67 New Dover Rd, CT1 3DX ☎01227 768433, ⓦebury-hotel.co.uk. Comfortable, reliable and rather old-fashioned Victorian hotel, with fifteen en-suite rooms. There's plenty of on-site parking, a large leafy garden and a heated indoor pool with jacuzzi, all of which make up for the slightly out-of-the-way location a 15min walk from the cathedral. **£130**

Falstaff 8–10 St Dunstan's St, CT2 8AF ☎01227 462138, ⓦthefalstaffincanterbury.com. A handsome fifteenth-century coaching inn, with a little bar, by the Westgate. Rooms vary, so it's an idea to call to discuss your preferences: those in the old building have lots of creaky historic atmosphere (some have four-poster beds), while the cheaper options in the annexe behind (£105) are less interesting. Singles and family rooms available. **£139**

★**House of Agnes** 71 St Dunstan's St, CT2 8BN ☎01227 472185, ⓦhouseofagnes.co.uk. You can't fail

to be charmed by the crooked exterior of this B&B near Westgate, and the experience inside is great, too. The main fifteenth-century house (mentioned in *David Copperfield*) has eight stylish rooms, each different, with eight more rooms in the old stable block in the large walled garden (£95). There's also a funky little library and guest lounge. There can be street noise from the front, so if that bothers you, or if you want a more spacious room, let them know when you book. Some on-site parking. **£115**

Love Lane 14 & 15 Love Lane, CT1 1TZ ☎01227 455367, ⓦ7longport.co.uk. Two three-bedroom early Victorian cottages, each sleeping five, backing onto and owned by the same people as *No. 7 Longport* (see below). Each has a kitchen, sitting room and dining area, along with sweet courtyard gardens with barbecue; you can get a B&B room, or rent a whole cottage on a self-catering (minimum three nights in high season; £193/night) or, if available, B&B basis (minimum two nights; £270/night). Breakfasts are delicious. **£100**

Millers Arms 2 Mill Lane, CT1 2AW ☎01227 456057, ⓦmillerscanterbury.co.uk. The USP at this nineteenth-century Shepherd Neame pub, a 5min walk from the cathedral, is its location opposite a weir on the Stour – you can be lulled to sleep by the sound of rushing water from the rooms at the front. The en-suite B&B rooms come in a variety of sizes (including singles), with tasteful, contemporary decor – comfortable, friendly and good value. **£110**

★**No. 7 Longport** 7 Longport, CT1 1PE ☎01227 455367, ⓦ7longport.co.uk. This fabulous little hideaway – a tiny, luxuriously decorated fifteenth-century cottage with a double bedroom, wet room and lounge – is tucked away in the courtyard garden of the friendly owners' home, just opposite St Augustine's Abbey. The breakfasts are wonderful, with lots of locally sourced ingredients, and can be eaten in the main house or the courtyard. It gets booked up fast. The same owners run *Love Lane* (see above). **£100**

Retro B&B 63 Whitstable Rd, CT2 8DG ☎01227 455727, ⓦtheretrobandb.com. A 10min walk from Canterbury West station, this late Victorian red-brick house offers six spacious, thoughtfully styled en-suite B&B rooms, each on a different theme, including a family suite with a London-bus bunkbed. Rooms at the back are quieter. It's newish, so everything is spick and span – the friendly hosts and attention to detail make it a winner. **£100**

White House 6 St Peter's Lane, CT1 2BP ☎01227 761836, ⓦwhitehousecanterbury.co.uk. If the medieval look doesn't float your boat, you could try this B&B in a Regency townhouse within the city walls. Each of the seven contemporary rooms is different, in both decor and size (there's one single; £80), but all are en suite. The location, just off the High Street and near the Marlowe, is handy, and the street, being residential, is relatively quiet. **£105**

1

Wincheap Guesthouse 94 Wincheap, CT1 3RS ☎01227 762309. A very welcoming Victorian B&B on busy Wincheap, a few minutes' walk from Canterbury East station. They have a range of en-suite double and family rooms; the nicest is Room 1, a double, which has French doors leading to a small private patio. The ample free parking is a plus. £75

HOSTELS

★**Kipps** 40 Nunnery Fields, CT1 3JT ☎01227 786121, ⓦkipps-hostel.com. This early twentieth-century house, a 10min walk from Canterbury East station, is home to an excellent self-catering hostel. It's spruce and clean, with homely touches and a large cottage garden, but above all it's the friendly staff who make *Kipps* special. Along with

mixed en-suite dorms, they have single, double and twin rooms. Nightly events mean you can be as sociable as you wish, but it's more a home from home than a party hostel, and quiet after 11pm. Breakfast £2.50. Dorms £18, doubles £63

YHA Canterbury 54 New Dover Rd, CT1 3DT ☎0845 371 9010, ⓦyha.org.uk/hostel/canterbury. Half a mile out of town, and 15min on foot from Canterbury East station, this YHA hostel occupies a substantial Victorian villa. In addition to the four- and six-bed single-sex dorms (some of which are en suite), and one twin (with shared facilities), they offer little wooden cabins, sleeping five, which are en suite with mini-kitchenette. Breakfast costs £5.25, with evening meals also available, and there are self-catering facilities. Dorms £19, twin £69, cabins £89

EATING

With its lively student population and year-round tourist trade, Canterbury is not short on places to eat. The old core is **tearoom** territory, of course, but the city is establishing itself as a credible foodie destination, too, with a good number of places focusing on **Modern British** cuisine and Kentish produce – the **Goods Shed** farmers' market blazes the trail – and plenty of restaurants offering food from around the world. Meanwhile, if you have a car and fancy getting out of town, you can choose from some excellent gastropubs in the villages around Canterbury (see p.61 & p.63).

CAFÉS, COFFEE SHOPS AND TEAROOMS

Boho Café 27 High St, CT1 2AZ ☎01227 458931, ⓦbohocafecanterbury.co.uk. This cheerful café-bar, with its quirky decor (paintbox colours, kitschy oilcloths, wonky lampshades, vintage clocks) is a popular spot with an informal neighbourhood feel. The menu (lunch dishes from £8) offers something for most people, from full English fry-ups via tapas and overstuffed ciabatta sandwiches to home-made veggie burgers, gluten-free options and meaty Mediterranean-influenced mains. You could also simply pop in for coffee and cake. There's seating on the street, and a pretty suntrap garden at the back. Mon–Thurs 9am–6pm, Fri & Sat 9am–9pm, Sun 10am–5pm.

Café St Pierre 41 St Peter's St, CT1 2BG ☎01227 456791. Bijou French patisserie and café with streetside tables and a small paved garden. The pastries are divine, from apricot *feuilleté* to buttery *palmier* biscuits, and you can make a light lunch of their *croques monsieur*, quiches and savoury croissants (£3.20–4.80). The baguettes

(£5.20; takeaway £3.80) include *du jour* specials (mushroom with melted raclette, say, or *andouillette* with Dijon mustard). Mon–Sat 8am–6pm, Sun 9am–5.30pm.

Canteen 17 Sun St, CT1 2HX ☎01227 470011, ⓦcanteenfresh.co.uk. *Canteen* is a no-fuss spot for fresh juices and coffee, along with light lunch dishes (from £4.50) – flatbread wrap with houmous and falafel, perhaps, or a roasted veg and feta toastie. Take away or eat in one of their little rooms, ranged across three floors. Mon–Fri & Sun 10am–5pm, Sat 9am–6pm.

City Fish Bar 30 St Margaret's St, CT1 2TG ☎01227 760873. Sometimes only fish and chips will hit the spot, and this cheery, central family-owned chippie is a reliable place to get your fried fish fix. A fish supper costs £7, but you can also get your chips with sausage, battered mushrooms or a pasty for around £4. There are a couple of tables squeezed into the shopfront, and a few more outside, but it's mostly takeaway. Mon–Sat 10am–7pm, Sun 10am–4pm.

THE GOODS SHED

The **Goods Shed farmers' market** (Tues–Sat 9am–7pm, or 6pm in winter, Sun 10am–4pm, some food counters keep their own hours; ⓦthegoodsshed.co.uk), housed in an old brick goods shed next to Canterbury West train station, is a highlight of any foodie visit to Canterbury. With traders selling local cheeses, breads, charcuterie, fresh produce, wine, beer and deli items, along with a couple of places for coffee, breakfast, posh sandwiches, tapas and sharing plates, it's a fantastic place to pick up picnic food, to stock up (or fill up) before catching a train, or to treat yourself to a special meal at the mezzanine **restaurant** (see p.57).

1

Kitch 4 St Peters St, CT1 2AT ☎01227 504983, ⓦwww
.kitchcafe.co.uk. This airily pretty, if slightly squeezed, café
– in a heavily trafficked spot next to the Old Weaver's House
– offers healthy breakfasts, superfood salads and grazing
plates using wholefoods and unprocessed ingredients. Try
one of the all-day breakfasts (£5–8.50), which range from
home-made date and coconut granola via free-range bacon
butties to kale scramble on sourdough. Mon–Fri
8.30am–4pm, Sat & Sun 9am–4pm.

Moat Tea Rooms 67 Burgate, CT1 2HJ ☎01227 784514,
ⓦmoattearooms.co.uk. Sweet, traditional little tearoom in
a beamed and mullioned old building with cake stands piled
high with scones, cupcakes and scrumptious home-made
sponges. The loose-leaf teas include black, green and
jasmine varieties – and although they serve decent
breakfasts, light lunches and sandwiches, it's the good-value
afternoon teas you should go for (cream teas from £6.95).
Mon–Fri 9am–5pm, Sat 8am–5pm, Sun 11am–5pm.

Pork and Co 18 Sun St, CT1 2HX ☎01227 450398,
ⓦporkandco.co.uk. Dude food comes to the pilgrim city
at this little takeout place, which announces its credentials
with the pig's head and piles of succulent pulled pork in the
window. Slow-cooked pulled pork in a brioche bun is the
mainstay (£3/£5.50), but you can also get those juicy
scraps in a pot, with trimmings, for just £4, or with mac and
cheese for £6 – they also offer scotch eggs, pork pies and
sausage rolls. Their sit-down restaurant, a few doors down
at no. 27, adds buttermilk-fried chicken, burgers and
toasties to the menu. Daily 11am–5pm.

★**Tiny Tim's Tearoom** 34 St Margaret's St, CT1 2TG
☎01227 450793, ⓦtinytimstearoom.com. There's
actually nothing very Dickensian about this upmarket
1930s-style tearoom, which offers some thirty blends of
loose-leaf tea, an indulgent choice of hot chocolates, and
filling afternoon teas (available all day, from £18.50) with
finger sandwiches, scones, pastries and cakes all made in
house. Smaller appetites might prefer the cream teas, all-
day breakfasts or lunches – the Kentish huffkins (£8.95),
large filled baps, are a tasty local choice, or you could
simply choose a fat, fruit-packed "Plump Pilgrim" scone
with butter and jam (£3.95). In good weather the cute back
garden makes a good retreat from the tourist crowds.
Tues–Sat 9.30am–5pm, Sun 10.30am–4pm.

The Veg Box Café 17b Burgate, CT1 2HG ☎01227
456654, ⓦthevegboxcafe.co.uk. This simple veggie café
does delicious things with alfalfa and tofu, using organic,
local ingredients, and with lots of vegan and gluten-free
options. The daily changing menu will feature a soup,
curry/stew, quiche, burger and bake, plus mixed salads
(mains from £6), while breakfast features home-made
granola and spicy "eggs in purgatory" for £4.50. The
location, with tables under the arcades near the cathedral,
is good, though as the food is served in cardboard boxes
with compostable cutlery, it's more of a quick lunch pit stop

than a place to linger. Cash only. Mon–Sat 8.30am–5pm,
Sun 9am–4pm.

Water Lane Coffeehouse Water Lane, CT1 2NQ
☎01227 464797, ⓦwaterlanecoffee.co.uk. Laidback
riverside hangout in a quiet corner, serving great coffee
(from Square Mile and Caravan roasters, among others),
with a few cakes (from £3.80) and interesting veggie salads
(£4). Relax on a sofa in the light-bathed room, dotted with
pot plants, and consider jumping on one of the punt trips
that sets off from outside (see box, p.52). Mon–Fri
9am–5.30pm, Sat 9am–6pm, Sun 10am–5pm.

RESTAURANTS

The Ambrette 14–15 Beer Cart Lane, CT1 2NY ☎01227
200777, ⓦtheambrette.co.uk. With a sister restaurant in
Margate (see p.94), *Ambrette*'s Canterbury branch brings
Dev Biswal's nouvelle Indian cuisine to a smart, good-
looking pub conversion on a quiet street. The focus on local
produce is strong, with delicious flavours infusing
everything from quinoa and mushroom biryani to shoulder
of Kentish venison with carpaccio of venison loin – for
dessert try the chocolate samosas with passionfruit and
guava parfait. Mains £17–30; two-/three-course lunch
menu £22.95/£28.95. Mon 11.30am–2.30pm &
6–9.30pm, Tues–Thurs 11.30am–2.30pm & 5.30–
9.30pm, Fri & Sat 11.30am–2.30pm & 5.30–10pm, Sun
noon–2.30pm & 5.30–10pm.

★**Café des Amis** 95 St Dunstan's St, CT2 8AD ☎01227
464390, ⓦcafedez.com. Don't be misled by the name (it's
short for *Café des Amis du Mexique*) – this is not a French
bistro, but a lively Mexican/Tex-Mex/South American place.
Funky decor, carnival colours and papier mâché artwork set
the scene for the vibrant food – from the hot goat's cheese
tostadas (£6.50) to the paella (£26.95 for two) or the crispy
duck confit fajitas (£28.95 for two), you can't go wrong. The
weekday set menu (noon–6pm) gets you two courses plus
nachos for £13.95. Mon–Thurs noon–10pm, Fri noon–
10.30pm, Sat 11am–10.30pm, Sun 11am–9.30pm.

Café Mauresque 8 Butchery Lane, CT1 2JR ☎01227
464300, ⓦcafemauresque.co.uk. Moroccan-style
restaurant with southern Spanish accents (all tiles,
lanterns, scatter cushions and brass candlesticks) a few
steps from the cathedral. You can go for tasty tapas –
anything from tabbouleh to squid and chorizo skewers
(£3.75–5.95, mixed platters for two from £13.95) – or
plump for tagines, couscous or paella. The weekday lunch
menu (actually served noon–5pm, during which time you
can also order baguettes and soup) gets you a main for
£8.95–11.95. Wash it all down with a jug of sangria or a
pot of fresh mint tea, and save room for the sticky date
cake. Mon–Fri & Sun noon–9pm, Sat noon–9.30pm.

Chapman's 89–90 St Dunstan's St, CT2 8AD ☎01227
780749, ⓦchapmanscanterbury.co.uk. An old-school
seafood restaurant offering simple, well-executed food. The

menu runs the gamut from crab pâté with toasted sourdough (£7) to an abundant *fruits de mer* platter (£32) via the likes of seared tuna, fish pie or fish and chips, plus daily specials. Regular themed evenings (all-you-can-eat mussels, perhaps, or half-price lobster) and a two-/three-course menu (Tues–Fri noon–2pm, Sat noon–5pm; £12/£15) are great value. Mon 6–9pm, Tues–Thurs noon–2pm & 6–9pm, Fri noon–2pm & 6–9.30pm, Sat noon–9.30pm.

Corner House 1 Dover St, CT1 3HD ☎01227 780793, ⓦcornerhouserestaurants.co.uk. The location on the noisy main road isn't idyllic, but indoors all is calm in this upmarket Modern British restaurant, soothingly kitted out in dove grey and rich wood, with bare beams and bare-brick walls creating a rustic feel. Locally sourced ingredients are used in seemingly simple dishes such as guinea fowl with haricot beans or garden pea pannacotta, with daily fish and veggie specials and tempting desserts – including home-made ice creams. Mains from £16, with hearty sharing plates (for two or more, from £17/head) that might feature stuffed Stour Valley rabbit loin with black pudding sausage rolls or Romney Marsh lamb with *Dauphinoise* potatoes. Tues–Fri noon–2.30pm & 5.30–9.30pm, Sat noon–9.30pm, Sun noon–3.30pm.

Deeson's 25–26 Sun St, CT1 2HX ☎01227 767854, ⓦdeesonsrestaurant.co.uk. With its funky feature wallpaper, linocuts and local art, its dark wood furniture and fresh flowers, *Deeson's* is a warm, comfortable setting in which to enjoy creative Modern British cuisine. The quality is not always *quite* as high as the prices (mains £15–21) might lead you to expect, but the tapas menu allows you to pick at tasty dishes such as haggis poached egg with parsnip chips or twice-baked Old Winchester cheese soufflé (£2.50–10.50). Based on Kentish produce, the menu changes regularly, but mains such as pork tenderloin with black pudding and candied walnuts, or cod fillet with celeriac *rösti*, are typical. Mon–Sat noon–3pm & 5–10pm, Sun noon–10pm; tapas Mon–Thurs noon–3pm & 5–7pm, Fri & Sat noon–3pm.

★**The Goods Shed** Station Rd West, CT2 8AN ☎01227 459153, ⓦthegoodsshed.co.uk. It doesn't get any more locally sourced than this – a buzzing, shabby-chic restaurant in the excellent Goods Shed farmers' market (see box, p.54), where most of the ingredients are provided by the stalls themselves. You can get anything from a build-your-own full breakfast to a formal supper: the regularly changing menu, Modern British with flashes of Mediterranean flair, might feature dishes such as turnip soup with wild garlic (£6.50), monkfish with parsley dumplings and *anchoïade* (£20) or guineafowl with lentils, spinach and black pudding (£17.50). Prices can mount, though at lunchtime they are happy for you to select a couple of starters. While the bustling ambience during the day is a delight, it can feel a little subdued at the end of the night, with the market stalls closed. Tues–Fri 8–10.30am, noon–2.30pm & 6–9.30pm, Sat 8–10.30am, noon–3pm & 6–9.30pm, Sun 9–10.30am & noon–3pm.

Kashmir 20 Palace St, CT1 2DZ ☎01227 462050, ⓦkashmirtandoori.co.uk. Though there's no reason to think it from the outside, this north Indian curry house is a winner: a large, friendly place with a long menu of tandooris, biryanis, baltis and the like (with some great Punjabi veg choices). House specials (tandoori butter chicken, for example) from £8, thalis from £11; set meals from £10.95. Daily noon–2pm & 5–11.30pm.

Posillipo 16 The Borough, CT1 2DR ☎01227 761471, ⓦposillipo.co.uk. A long-established trattoria, a real local favourite, serving robust Neapolitan dishes, crispy wood-fired pizzas (£5.95–13.95), fresh pasta (from £8.95) and rustic fish and seafood specials, including a lip-smacking cod dish with olives, capers, anchovies and oregano (£13.95). The prices are reasonable, for such a classy place, and there's a kids' menu, too (£6.50). Daily noon–late.

Tamago 64 Northgate, CT1 1BB ☎01227 634537, ⓦtamago.restaurant. This minimalist, casual Japanese café, just north of the King's Mile, brings an authentic slice of Tokyo to Canterbury, dishing up hearty *ramen*, *katsu* curries and *bento* boxes (from £9.90) – along with beer and sake cocktails – to a brisk, youngish crowd. Mains from £9. Mon–Fri 5–9.30pm, Sat noon–3pm & 5–9.30pm, Sun noon–4pm.

Zeus Ouzerie and Taverna 2–3 Orange St, CT1 2JA ☎01227 788072, ⓦzeuscanterbury.com. Authentic Greek cuisine gets an update in this smart and stylish contemporary taverna, which does all the standards very well, from the meze (£3–10) to the moussaka, the *sheftalia* to the *souvlaki*. It can get pricey, with mains from £12, but various lunch menus offer good value (Tues–Fri noon–4pm; £9.95–12.50). The delicious honey-drenched puds make a perfect finale. Tues–Thurs & Sun noon–10pm, Fri & Sat noon–11pm.

DRINKING AND NIGHTLIFE

Canterbury is a nice place for a drink, with more than its fair share of pubs serving **real ales** in cosy, historic buildings. The Shepherd Neame-owned places are in the majority, but look out, too, for beers from Canterbury's own Wantsum, Canterbury Brewers and Canterbury Ales breweries. Generally **nightlife** keeps a low profile – many people are happy to while away their evenings in the pubs.

Bishop's Finger 13 St Dunstan's St, CT2 8AF ☎01227 768915, ⓦbishopsfingercanterbury.co.uk. Unpretentious, popular old pub, just outside the Westgate, with Shepherd Neame ales, five large-screen TVs showing major sports events and a patio at the back. Mon–Thurs & Sun noon–midnight, Fri noon–1am, Sat 11am–1am.

1

★**Bramley's** 15 Orange St, CT1 2JA ☎01227 379933, ⓦbramleysbar.co.uk. One of the quirkier central venues, this cocktail bar offers bohemian-speakeasy ambience – all candles, sexy lighting and mismatched retro styling – and well-mixed drinks at not-bad prices (cocktails from £8). A mixed bag of live events includes vintage clothes sales, jazz jams and Charleston dance classes. Mon–Thurs 6–11pm, Fri & Sat 6pm–12.30am.

★**The Dolphin** 17 St Radigund's St, CT1 2AA ☎01227 455963, ⓦthedolphincanterbury.co.uk. A likeable old 1930s pub that's both quite cool, in a shabby way, and relaxed. With a good selection of local real ales (including Gadds and Hopdaemon), a real fire in winter and a big, grassy beer garden, the emphasis is on chatting, hanging out and playing board games, with no loud music or TVs to spoil the ambience. Tasty food, too, with few pretensions. Mon–Wed noon–11pm, Thurs–Sat noon–midnight, Sun noon–10pm.

The Foundry White Horse Lane, CT1 2RU ☎01227 455899, ⓦthefoundrycanterbury.co.uk. Tasty craft beers and lagers from the on-site Canterbury Brewers microbrewery in this big old foundry building; you can watch the whole brewing process as it happens, while you drink. They offer guest ales, ciders and bottled beers, too, and the food (burgers, ribs, pies and the like), isn't bad. Mon–Thurs noon–midnight, Fri & Sat noon–12.30am, Sun noon–11pm.

La Trappiste 1–2 Sun St, CT1 2HX ☎01227 479111, ⓦlatrappiste.com. The best thing about this capacious, European-style café-bar – apart from its location on the King's Mile near the cathedral – is its long list of Belgian beers, among them Lambic, Trappist and Abbey, and including wheat, fruit and white varieties. The roof terrace is a draw, too. Mon–Thurs & Sun 8am–11pm, Fri & Sat 8am–midnight.

The Parrot 1–9 Church Lane, CT1 2AG ☎01227 454170, ⓦtheparrotonline.com. Venerable hostelry – the oldest in Canterbury, in a fourteenth-century building groaning with dark-wood beams – in a quiet spot. The interior has loads of character, and they serve a choice of ales along with hefty portions of high-quality Modern British pub grub. Daily noon–11pm; kitchen Mon–Sat noon–10pm, Sun noon–9.30pm.

The Pound 1 Pound Lane, CT1 2BZ ☎01227 458629, ⓦonepoundlane.co.uk. Tucked away at the bottom of the medieval Westgate, this historic spot – which has housed both a Victorian jail and an Edwardian police station – has reinvented itself as a slick bar, its bare-brick vaults now filled with comfy armchairs, burnished bronze decor and vintage-style neon. There's some riverside seating, though it's on a busy road. Mon–Thurs 11am–2.30pm, Fri & Sat 11am–3.30am, Sun 11am–1am.

The Unicorn 61 St Dunstan's St, CT2 8BS ☎01227 463187, ⓦunicorninn.com. There's a neighbourhood feel at this seventeenth-century, family-run tavern, popular with the CAMRA set; settle down by the wood-burning stove with a Kentish brew, or enjoy a game at the bar billiards table. Quiz night on Sun. Mon–Thurs & Sun 11.30am–11pm, Fri & Sat 11.30am–midnight.

ENTERTAINMENT

Gulbenkian University of Kent, CT2 7NB ☎01227 769075, ⓦthegulbenkian.co.uk. The excellent arts centre on the university campus offers a consistently interesting programme of high-quality cultural events, including contemporary drama, dance, comedy, concerts and film.

Marlowe Theatre The Friars, CT1 2AS ☎01227 787787, ⓦmarlowetheatre.com. This modern theatre, cutting an audacious dash right in the centre of the city, is a popular venue for music, dance, stand-up, cabaret and plays. Shows range from the mainstream, with West End musicals and crowd-pleasing touring acts – Sarah Millican, Elkie Brooks, Toots and the Maytals and the like – to gigs from up-and-coming acts.

SHOPPING

Canterbury Cathedral Shop 25 Burgate, CT1 2HA ☎01227 865300, ⓦcathedral-enterprises.co.uk. You can enter the huge cathedral shop either from the precincts or from Burgate. It's worth a browse – though the wide range of products tends, naturally, towards the religious or spiritual (Thomas Becket tree decorations; stained-glass earrings; CDs of choral music), there is also a selection of books, foodie gifts, ceramics, magnets and the like. Mon–Sat 9.30am–5.30pm, Sun 10.30am–4.30pm.

★**The Chaucer Bookshop** 6–7 Beer Cart Lane, CT1 2NY ☎01227 453912, ⓦchaucer-bookshop.co.uk. A bibliophiles' delight: a friendly, sixty-year-old secondhand bookshop in a crooked old building with two storeys packed to the rafters. It's strong on rare and antiquarian titles – hardbacks predominate, with lots of history and local interest, plus vintage prints, maps and postcards – but you can hunt down anything from popular literary fiction to *Just William*, via art, travel, food and all sorts. Pretty cards and wrapping paper, too. Mon–Sat 10am–5pm, Sun 11am–4pm.

Madame Oiseau 8 The Borough, CT1 2DR ☎01227 452222, ⓦmadame-oiseau.com. A cupboard of a shop on the King's Mile, where they make and sell classy artisan chocolates. The emphasis is on the feminine – the heart-shaped bonbonnière, for example – but there are big chunky slabs, too, crammed with fruits and nuts, along with

CANTERBURY FESTIVALS

The year-long arts programme offered by Wise Words – chiefly focused on poetry, but with storytelling, arts workshops and music too – peaks during the **Wise Words literary festival** (ⓦ wisewordsfestival.co.uk), held over ten days in late April. Centred on the beautiful Franciscan Gardens (see p.48), the quirky performances and events spill out all around town – from busy street corners to River Stour punts – creating a feel-good buzz.

The **Canterbury Festival** (mid-Oct to early Nov; ⓦ canterburyfestival.co.uk), meanwhile, is the *grande dame* of the city's arts events, a high-culture affair offering an international mix of music, theatre and performance, with poetry, lectures, classes and live events thrown in. You'll catch anything from Americana to Gregorian chants, tango to *chanson*, in a variety of venues including the cathedral, the Marlowe and the Gulbenkian.

chocolate gingers, chocolate-covered chillies and cute chocolate cats for the kids. Mon–Sat 9.30am–5.30pm.

★**Waterstones** 20–21 St Margaret's St, CT1 2TH ☎ 01227 456343, ⓦ waterstonescanterbury.co.uk. An excellent branch of the bookshop chain, filling three storeys of a venerable building. The love for books is palpable, with regular big-name author events; a good few staff members (among them novelist David Mitchell) have gone on to be famous writers in their own right. There's a good, spacious independent café upstairs, too, with free wi-fi. Check out the (scanty) remains of a Roman

bathhouse in the basement. Mon–Sat 9am–6pm, Sun 10.30am–5pm.

Whitefriars Between St George's Lane and St George's, St Margaret's and Watling streets, CT1 2TF ☎ 01227 862760, ⓦ whitefriars-canterbury.co.uk. Gobbling up a substantial chunk of town between the bus station and the High Street, Canterbury's major mainstream shopping mall has the big high-street names – Fenwick to H&M, Specsavers to Boots – plus banks, supermarkets and places to eat (most of them fast-food, but there is a *Carluccio's* café in Fenwick). Daily; opening hours vary.

North of Canterbury

Covering around eleven square miles between Canterbury and Kent's north coast, the ancient broadleaf woodland of the **Blean** is a wonderful area for walking. Accessible from the North Downs Way – which passes the South Blean – the Saxon Shore Way in the north, the Pilgrims' Way from Winchester to Canterbury, and the Crab and Winkle Way between Canterbury and Whitstable (see box, p.60), these dappled and wildlife-rich **woodlands** feature around 120 miles of footpaths, taking in not only woods but villages, hop gardens, orchards and historical sites. Dominated by oak and sweet chestnut trees, but also featuring silver birch, hazel, beech and ash, among many others, it's an area rich in **birdlife**, with nightingales, nightjars, woodpeckers and tawny owls all making their homes here. The Blean is an easy place to head for a short day-hike from Canterbury, but there are also plenty of nice spots to stay and eat should you want to enjoy a more leisurely visit.

The area **northeast of Canterbury**, meanwhile, fanning out towards the coast, offers a number of water-based diversions. The **River Stour** courses through on its way to the sea at Pegwell Bay; bordering it to the east, the lonely **Stodmarsh Nature Reserve** is a fabulous birding spot.

Blean Woods Nature Reserve

Rough Common, CT2 9DD • Free • Access on foot at all times • ☎ 01227 464898, ⓦ rspb.org.uk/reserves/guide/b/bleanwoods • Buses #4/#4A (daily) and #27 (Mon–Sat) from Canterbury

Covering more than eleven square miles, **Blean Woods Nature Reserve**, near the hamlet of Rough Common a couple of miles northwest of Canterbury, offers some wonderful walking opportunities through the woods; five waymarked trails, the longest of which is eight miles, crisscross this peaceful site. In addition to the warblers, nightingales and woodpeckers, watch out for the flutter of the Heath

1

THE CRAB AND WINKLE WAY

A **cycling and walking route** that follows the line of the old steam railway from Canterbury to Whitstable (see p.80), and forms part of National Cycle Route 1, the **Crab and Winkle Way** is a delight. Some 7.5 miles long, and largely traffic-free, it starts at Canterbury West train station, heads up to the University of Kent campus (via two different routes), then passes through orchards, ancient woodland and gentle rolling pastures before ending in Whitstable; the midway point at Winding Pond is a nice spot to take a break, with a grassy area and picnic bench. Whitstable itself, a lovely little seaside town on the north coast, is well worth a stay of a night or two. For more, including a downloadable map, see ⓦ crabandwinkle.org.

Fritillary butterfly, seen in few other places in Britain. Note that dogs are only permitted on one of the trails.

Mount Ephraim Gardens

Staplestreet Rd, Hernhill, ME13 9TX • April–Sept Wed–Sun 11am–5pm • £6 • ☎ 01227 751496, ⓦ mountephraimgardens.co.uk

The elegant Edwardian gardens at **Mount Ephraim**, a private estate a couple of miles west of Bossenden Wood in the Blean, provide an appealing contrast with the woodlands around them. Here you can wander through ten acres of landscaped, terraced gardens – among them a fragrant rose garden, a Japanese rock-and-water garden, and an unusual medieval-style "mizmaze", with soft raised turf paths fringed with wildflowers and swaying grasses. Many people bring picnics, but there is also a tearoom.

Stodmarsh National Nature Reserve

Stodmarsh, CT3 4BP • Dawn–dusk • Free • ☎ 07767 321053, ⓦ gov.uk/government/publications/kents-national-nature-reserves/kents-national-nature-reserves#stodmarsh • Buses along the A28 between Sturry (3 miles southwest) and Upstreet stop nearby

The lonely **Stodmarsh National Nature Reserve**, a square mile of reed beds, fens and pools in the Stour Valley, is accessible from the village of Stodmarsh, six miles northeast of Canterbury, and Upstreet/Grove Ferry, three miles further north. This marshy wetland is especially good for **birdwatchers**, with bitterns, kingfishers and marsh harriers, among others, in residence – plus swallows and housemartins in summer, and starlings in winter – but it's a peaceful place for anyone to enjoy a bracing country walk. Footpaths (from 0.3 to 3 miles) include a couple of nature trails, with five designated hides.

ACCOMMODATION   NORTH OF CANTERBURY

The Grove Ferry Upstreet, CT3 4BP ☎ 01227 860302, ⓦ thegroveferry.co.uk. Location is key at this friendly, relaxed pub, in a handsome ivy-festooned building with an unbeatable setting on the River Stour near Stodmarsh. The willow-fringed riverside terrace and big beer garden are lovely places to enjoy a local cask ale, and the six quirky boutique B&B rooms, decked out in cool vintage and Pop Art style, are great value, with lots of space and nice details including real coffee and bottled water. A couple have their own balconies overlooking the river at the back. Full meals are available in the pub. **£89**

★**The Linen Shed** 104 The Street, Boughton-under-Blean, ME13 9AP ☎ 01227 752271, ⓦ thelinenshed .com. Shabby chic meets froufrou vintage glamour in this quirky weatherboard home, fronted by lavender gardens.

The guest rooms, two of which have private bathrooms and one of which shares a bathroom with the friendly owners, are gorgeous, ranging from faded French Provincial to Art Deco in style, with French linen sheets, fresh flowers and fluffy robes. Gourmet breakfasts are served in the lovely garden in good weather. Minimum two-night stay at weekends. **£85**

Nethergong Nurseries Upstreet, CT3 4DN ☎ 07901 368417, ⓦ nethergongcamping.co.uk. A simple, peaceful and spacious riverside campsite, 8 miles northeast of Canterbury, with room for forty tents in woodland or open meadows, and glamping in Romany wagons and bell tents; there's also a shallow paddling pond and a fishing lake. Campfires are allowed (£5) and they sell their own fresh veg. Minimum two nights. Closed Nov–Easter. Tents **£25**, bell tents **£80**, wagons **£80**

EATING AND DRINKING

1

★**Butcher's Arms** 29 Herne St, Herne, CT6 7HL ☎01227 371000, ⓦmicropub.co.uk. Fantastic micropub – open for more than a decade – in an old butcher's. Behind the unassuming shopfront is a fifteen-seater cubbyhole crammed with bric-a-brac, with a crowd of real-ale fans having a good old natter. There are always at least four ales on the weekly changing selection. Tues–Sat noon–1.30pm & 6–9pm or later, Sun noon–2pm.

The Dairy 40 The Street, Boughton-under-Blean, ME13 9AS ☎01227 750304, ⓦthedairyrestaurant .co.uk. In an old 1930s dairy building, this family-friendly restaurant goes for a retro vibe and stays on brand (milk churn seats, milk bottle light shades) with the decor. The informal menu – bar snacks, light bites (from £5), bistro standards (scotch eggs, burgers, fishcakes; from £11), coffee shakes and puds – focuses on Kentish produce. Wed–Fri 6 11pm, Sat & Sun 11am–11pm.

The Dove Plumpudding Lane, Dargate, ME13 9HB ☎01227 751360, ⓦthedovedargate.co.uk. This easygoing country pub welcomes drinkers and diners alike, serving simple British food done well – grilled sardines, steak pies, ham hock terrine, Eton Mess – in a relaxed space. Mains start at £13, with wood-fired pizza (from £9) in the evenings and all day Sat. The garden has its own bar and traditional bat-and-trap game. Mon & Sun noon–10pm, Wed–Sat noon–11pm; kitchen Mon & Wed–Sat noon–2.30pm & 6–9pm, Sun noon–5pm.

Fordwich Arms King St, Fordwich, CT2 0DB ☎01227 710444, ⓦfordwicharms.co.uk. Behind the handsome ivy-strewn red-brick exterior is an unpretentious real-ale pub. The daily-changing menu (starters from £5, mains from £10) offers dishes such as crispy pork belly or sea bass with garlic mussels – plus lunchtime sandwiches and ploughman's lunches. There's a riverside garden and terrace, and regular live jazz and folk music. Mon–Sat 11am–11pm, Sun noon–11pm; kitchen Mon–Sat noon–2.30pm & 6.30–9.30pm, Sun noon–3pm.

★**Gate Inn** Church Inn, Chislet, CT3 4EB ☎01227 860498, ⓦgateinnchislet.co.uk. Friendly Shepherd Neame pub, in a very pretty part of Kent, with a streamside garden shaded by willows and with its own resident ducks

and chickens. Inside it's cosy and unpretentious, with a big log fire, board games and an eclectic library. Good cask ales are offered, with a tempting menu of simple, home-made food including pies and chunky black-pudding sandwiches (mains from £6). Booking advised for meals. Mon–Fri noon–3pm & 6–11pm, Sat & Sun noon–11pm; kitchen Mon–Fri noon–2.30pm & 6–9pm, Sat & Sun noon–4pm & 6–9pm.

Kathton House 6 High St, Sturry, CT2 0BD ☎01227 719999, ⓦkathtonhouse.com. Just a 7min drive from Canterbury, this unassuming-looking restaurant offers special-occasion fine dining in an intimate setting. The food, on monthly changing menus, is classic, with an emphasis on meat and lots of rich sauces – duck breast in green peppercorn sauce, guinea fowl breast in creamed apple brandy, supreme of halibut in lime and butter sauce – and delectable puddings. It's just for two, and three course menus £22/£26.50 at lunch, £39/£46.50 at dinner. Reservations essential at weekends. Tues–Sat noon–2pm & 7–9pm.

Old Coach and Horses Church Hill, Harbledown, CT2 9AB ☎01227 766609, ⓦtheoldcoachandhorses.co.uk. This relaxed village pub, just a 20min walk from Canterbury, serves local ales and good, locally sourced food (starters from £7.50, mains from £12.50) from a regularly changing menu – typical choices might be leg of Kentish saltmarsh lamb or veggie burger with halloumi. The courtyard garden is a nice spot in summer, with great woodland views. Mon–Sat noon–11.30pm, Sun noon–7pm; kitchen Mon–Fri noon–3pm & 6.30–9pm, Sat noon–9pm, Sun noon–4pm.

Red Lion Crockham Lane, Hernhill, ME13 9JR ☎01227 751207, ⓦtheredlionhernhill.co.uk. On the village green, in a quaint fourteenth-century building, the *Red Lion* is a smartened-up old pub with a big grassy garden and a kids' play area. The contemporary menu tends toward the fancy, with Moroccan pork cheeks with harissa joining gastropub staples including pies and burgers. Starters from £6, mains from £11. Mon–Sat 11.30am–10.30pm, Sun 11.30am–7pm; kitchen Mon–Sat noon–2.30pm & 6–9.30pm, Sun noon–4pm.

MESSING ABOUT ON THE RIVER

Canoe Wild (☎01227 469219, ⓦcanoewild.co.uk), with bases in Fordwich (2.5 miles northeast of Canterbury) and Grove Ferry (some 5 miles further), offers canoe, kayak and paddleboard rental (March–Nov daily 9am–5pm, other times on request; £20/canoe/hr, or £45/£80 for a half/full day) and guided canoe/kayak paddles – from seal-watching at Pegwell Bay to sunset wildlife tours in Stodmarsh – for all abilities (May–Oct days and times vary; from £25/person for a 3hr tour). Booking is advised, but not essential. For something less active, try a river cruise on the electric launch **Mary Ellen**, moored at the *Grove Ferry* inn (see opposite) – no reservations required (March, April & Oct Sat & Sun; May–July & Sept Wed–Sun; Aug daily; hourly from noon; 50min; £9; ☎07985 273070, ⓦgroveferryrivertrips.co.uk).

1

South of Canterbury

The area **south of Canterbury**, though often overlooked in the dash from the city to the villages of the Weald or the iconic white cliffs of the coast, holds a couple of places of interest: the well-respected **Howletts Wild Animal Park** and gardens at **Goodnestone** are worthwhile paying attractions, while a number of sleepy little hamlets, including the village of **Chilham**, are appealing pit stops along the North Downs Way.

Howletts Wild Animal Park

Bekesbourne, CT4 5EL • Daily: April–Oct 9.30am–6pm; Nov–March 9.30am–5pm; last admission 1hr 30min before closing • £15.95, under-16s £12.95; Treetop Challenge £7/person; Animal Adventure £2.50/child • ☎ 01227 721268, ⓦ aspinallfoundation.org/howletts • Call ahead for free minibus from Bekesbourne train station, a mile to the southwest (Sat & Sun 10am–4pm)

Working alongside the Aspinall Foundation conservation charity, which also oversees Port Lympne near Folkestone (see p.129), **Howletts Wild Animal Park**, three miles south of Canterbury, is highly regarded for its conservation efforts, saving and breeding rare species from around the world, and, where possible, returning them to the wild. Spread across the ninety-acre site, the animal enclosures are, in the main, well designed and equipped, with scope for the creatures to retreat if necessary; this is not a zoo, as such, and you are not guaranteed to see all the animals if they are not in the mood to be seen. Though the park is home to black rhinos, snow leopards, Siberian tigers and the largest **African elephant** herd in the UK, along with many other species – check out the extraordinary red river hogs – the stars here tend to be the primates, including **gorillas**, lemurs and a large number of lively langurs. Other diversions include the **Treetop Challenge**, an elevated adventure course with zip-lines, nets and rope-bridges, and the **Animal Adventure Challenge**, a less daunting adventure play area for smaller kids. Reckon on a bare minimum of two hours for a visit.

Goodnestone Park Gardens

Goodnestone, off the A2 Canterbury to Dover, CT3 1PL • April & Sept Sun noon–4pm; May–Aug Wed–Fri 11am–5pm, Sun noon–5pm • £7 (no credit cards) • ☎ 01304 840107, ⓦ goodnestoneparkgardens.co.uk

Goodnestone Park Gardens, spread across eighteen acres around eight miles southeast of Canterbury, present a romantic ensemble. Part of an early eighteenth-century estate (which was home for a while to Jane Austen's brother and sister-in-law, and where the novelist was a frequent guest), the gardens were designed in the formal style so fashionable in the 1700s. The high point remains the seventeenth-century **walled garden**, its mellow, centuries-old walls tangled with clematis, wisteria and jasmine, and with deep borders spilling over in a profusion of English country flowers. There's also a **woodland** of old sweet chestnut and oak trees, carpeted with bluebells in spring and alive with vivid blue hydrangeas in autumn, and an **arboretum**, planted with ornamental trees that erupt into blossom in springtime.

Chilham

Country villages don't come much prettier than **CHILHAM**, a ten-minute drive southwest of Canterbury in the Stour Valley. This is chocolate-box stuff, a cluster of beamed and tiled fifteenth- and sixteenth-century dwellings, tangled with flowers and centring on a market square – no surprise, then, that it's been used in a number of movies, among them Michael Powell and Emeric Pressburger's delightfully odd *A Canterbury Tale*, and period TV adaptations from Jane Austen to Agatha Christie. It offers more in the way of dozy English charm than actual sights, though **St Mary's Church**, with its looming tower, and **Chilham Castle**, a Jacobean country house whose gardens are occasionally open to the public (ⓦ chilham-castle.co.uk), give you something to look at on opposite ends of the square. There's also a tearoom and a pub on the square for food.

ACCOMMODATION   SOUTH OF CANTERBURY

Duke William The Street, Ickham, CT3 1QP ☎01227 721308, ⓦthedukewilliamickham.com. Owned by local celebrity chef Mark Sergeant, this smart village gastropub offers four contemporary B&B rooms, each named for a famous cook, with recipe books and local guidebooks to browse. Some have lovely countryside views and a little roof terrace, and all have Nespresso machines and access to a pantry of essentials. Choose from a good full breakfast or a hamper in your room. **£100**

Waterlock House Canterbury Rd, Wingham, CT3 1BH ☎01227 721792, ⓦbranchingoutwingham.co.uk. This elegant Georgian townhouse, in a medieval village near Goodnestone, offers B&B for two in a two-storey loft apartment with its own private entrance. The lovely ambience, all shabby chic elegance and soothing bleached colours, has been beautifully created by the French/English antique-dealer owners, and there's a flower-filled cottage garden. Two-night minimum. **£120**

Woodland Farm Walderchain, Barham, CT4 6NS ☎01227 831892. Simple, secluded and sheltered camping spot, a mile or so from the village of Barham and around 20min drive from Canterbury, with great views of the North Downs and space for around fourteen tents in an open field and its surrounding woods. It's a friendly place, with basic (but clean) facilities, and allows fires in braziers. Closed Nov–Feb. Per person **£5**

Woolpack Inn The Street, Chilham, CT4 8DL ☎01227 730351, ⓦwoolpackinnchilham.co.uk. On the edge of Chilham, this Shepherd Neame pub, dating back to 1480, has fifteen en-suite guest rooms – including a single, three family rooms and an apartment – spread through the main pub, a rear building and a converted stable block. A couple have four-poster beds and some have access to a little garden; all are decorated in a simple, rustic style. The food, focusing on traditional British gastropub staples, is not bad at all (mains from £13); breakfast is not included in rates. **£85**

EATING AND DRINKING

Artichoke Chartham Hatch, CT4 7JQ ☎01227 738316, ⓦshepherdneame.co.uk. Quietly doing its thing, this fifteenth-century Shepherd Neame pub – with several good walks nearby – is pleasingly unreconstructed. The pub grub, from the simple (ham, egg and chips; pies) to slightly fancier (duck confit) is equally unpretentious, with starters from £5 and mains from £10. There's a cute beer garden, too. Mon–Thurs & Sun noon–11pm, Fri & Sat noon–midnight; kitchen Mon–Sat noon–3pm & 6–9pm, Sun noon–5pm.

★**Compasses Inn** Sole St, Crundale, CT4 7ES ☎01227 700300, ⓦthecompassescrundale.co.uk. Perhaps the perfect country inn, reached via winding hedgerow-lined lanes and with North Downs walks from the door – and offering outstanding eating in a quirky, hop-strewn space, all open fires, fresh flowers, vintage knick-knacks and horse brasses. Food is a bit English, a bit French, quite meat-focused and very local; everything – from hunks of warm sourdough bread with home-churned butter to triple-cooked dripping chips with truffle salt and Kentish cheese, from rabbit and cider pie to loin of cod with crispy ox cheek – tastes amazing. Mains from £13, two-/three- course lunch menu £14.95/£17.95. Book ahead. Tues–Sat noon–3pm & 6–11pm, Sun noon–6pm; kitchen Tues–Sat noon–2.30pm & 6–9.30pm, Sun noon–4pm.

The Duck Pett Bottom, CT4 5PB ☎01227 830354, ⓦtheduckpettbottom.com. The delightfully named hamlet of Pett Bottom is home to a great food pub – a favourite haunt for Ian Fleming, who supposedly wrote much of *You Only Live Twice* here. The food is a cut above the norm – mainly British but with Mediterranean accents, and full of

flavour. Menus change regularly, but you might start an evening meal with spiced lamb terrine and grilled flatbreads, following with pan-fried sea bass with *salsa verde* (mains from £12); two-/three-course lunch menus (£14.50/£16.50; £20/£23 on Sun) list such dishes as lobster bisque, sausage cassoulet or ricotta and parmesan gnocchi. There's a nice garden for sunny days. Tues–Sat noon–11pm, Sun noon–8pm; kitchen Tues–Thurs noon–2pm & 6.30–8.30pm, Fri & Sat noon–2pm & 6.30–9pm, Sun noon–4pm.

★**The George** The Street, Molash, CT4 8HE ☎01233 740323, ⓦthegeorgemolash.co.uk. The focus on local ingredients, including veg, fruit and salad from their own smallholding, has won this old North Downs coaching inn a firm following, with a daily changing menu listing traditional, well-executed dishes such as shoulder of lamb braised in ale or home-made suet steak-and-kidney pud. Mains start at £12, and there's a great-value two-/three-course set lunch menu (Mon–Sat) for £8/£10. The woodland walks on the doorstep, and the big beer garden, are bonuses. Mon–Fri noon–2.30pm & 6–9pm, Sat noon–9.30pm, Sun noon–7pm.

Mama Feelgoods Chalkpit Farm, School Lane, Bekesbourne, CT4 5EU ☎01227 830830, ⓦmamafeelgoods.com. Packed with local produce and posh artisan treats, this deli and café, just a 10min drive southeast of the city, is a go-to lunch spot for Canterbury locals. Food is simple and inexpensive (from £6) – quiche, sandwiches and soups – with breakfast (until 11.45am), good coffee and home-made cakes. Mon–Sat 9.30am–5pm, Sun 10.30am–4pm.

North Kent

BOTANY BAY

North Kent

With a coastline that takes in creek-laced marshlands, shingle and sand beaches and dramatic, sea-lashed chalk cliffs, North Kent offers a splendid variety of attractions. It's perhaps best known for its bucket-and-spade resorts, but anyone with time to spend will uncover medieval castles and lonely bird reserves, ancient festivals and weird museums, cutting-edge galleries and historic villages abounding in places to eat. This coast has traditionally been London's seaside playground, and today, easily accessible on the high-speed train from St Pancras, it still offers blasts of sunny fun within a hop of the capital.

Beyond the scruffy edges of London and Essex, the **Medway towns**, clustered around the estuary of the same name at the point where the North Downs fall down to the coast, have two big highlights in Rochester and Chatham, where a knot of important historic sights and family attractions – chief among them the mighty Chatham Historic Dockyard, founded by Henry VIII and for centuries the base of the Royal Navy – are less than an hour from London. From the estuary, the lowlying North Kent marshes creep along the coast to Whitstable, offering excellent birdwatching, particularly on the quiet Hoo Peninsula and Isle of Sheppey. Tucked just inland on the edge of the North Downs, alongside a winding creek, is medieval **Faversham**. Home to Shepherd Neame brewery and the national fruit collection, it's an underrated base for this part of Kent, with a good foodie scene. Most people are ploughing on to artsy **Whitstable**, a bolthole for weekending Londoners, famed for its oysters and its lively shops and restaurants. Neighbouring **Herne Bay** offers invigorating clifftop walks all the way to the **Isle of Thanet**, on Kent's northeastern tip – where you'll find an almost uninterrupted sequence of sandy beaches and bays fringed by tall chalk cliffs. The "isle", though not literally cut off from the mainland, has a distinct personality, its trio of appealing historic resorts – brash Margate, genteel Broadstairs and handsome Ramsgate – each offering something different. Since the opening of Turner Contemporary in Margate, linking it culturally both with Whitstable and Folkestone further down the east coast, Thanet has grasped with aplomb its mantle as queen of Kent's coastal art scene.

The Medway towns

The estuary towns of the **River Medway**, which stretches seventy miles from West Sussex to the sea, have historically been defined by their naval and shipbuilding industries – a heritage celebrated by the enormous **Chatham Historic Dockyard**, which records more than four hundred years of British maritime history. Of the towns themselves **Rochester** is by far the most appealing, with a clutch of interesting sights

WIIITSTARI F

Highlights

❶ Rochester With its Dickens connections, cathedral and castle, plus Chatham Historic Dockyard on its doorstep, this good-looking Medway town makes a rewarding day-trip. **See p.68**

❷ Faversham Sweet little creekside town with a good food scene, a historic brewery and an orchard to explore, and lonely marshland walks all around. **See p.76**

❸ Whitstable It's hard not to fall for laidback, oyster-loving Whitstable, where weekenders rub shoulders with seasalts and artists. **See p.80**

❹ The Sportsman, Seasalter This "grotty pub by the sea", as it calls itself, is in fact a Michelin-starred treat, one of the best restaurants in the UK. **See p.85**

❺ Margate's Old Town Pronounced "romantic, sexy and fucking weird" by local girl Tracey Emin, mad Margate is fast becoming one of south England's hippest destinations. **See p.92**

❻ Botany Bay Thanet has many superb beaches, but with its huge chalk pillars and its sweep of clean sand, Botany Bay is the most dramatic. **See p.93**

❼ Broadstairs Folk Week Quaint Broadstairs, the prettiest of the Thanet resorts, becomes a lively hotbed of music and street parades during this annual festival. **See p.99**

HIGHLIGHTS ARE MARKED ON THE MAP ON PP.68–69

2

and good places to eat. The surrounding mudflats and saltmarsh are a big draw for **birdwatchers**, with the depopulated **Hoo Peninsula** and **Isle of Sheppey** boasting a number of important **nature reserves**.

Rochester

The handsome town of **ROCHESTER** was first settled by the Romans, who built a fortress on the site of the present **castle**; some kind of fortification has remained here ever since. With a Norman **cathedral** and an attractive high street, the town is probably best known for its connections with **Charles Dickens**, who spent his youth and final years near here, and wrote about it often. Mischievously, perhaps, it appears as "Mudfog" in *The Mudfog Papers*, and "Dullborough" in *The Uncommercial Traveller*, as well as featuring in *The Pickwick Papers* and his last novel, the unfinished *The Mystery of Edwin Drood*. Many of the buildings he described can be seen today.

Everything you'll want to see is either on or just off the **High Street**, an unspoiled parade of wonky half-timbered, brick and weatherboard buildings that heads southeast from the River Medway. Lined with independent, old-fashioned shops and coffee houses, it's a great place to wander; there's an excellent **farmers' market** on the third Sunday of the month (9am–1pm), held in the Blue Boar Lane Car Park nearby.

Huguenot Museum

95 High St, ME1 1LX • Wed–Sat 10am–5pm; last admission 4.30pm • £4 • ☏ 01634 789347, ⓦ huguenotmuseum.org

Above the tourist office, the **Huguenot Museum** makes interesting connections between the fifty thousand French Protestants who fled France for Britain between 1685 and 1700 and modern-day refugees. The three-room display focuses on the dire religious persecution that drove them to flee their homes, the hostility they faced on arrival, and the huge contribution they made to British culture. Though many Huguenots settled in east London, there were significant populations in Kent – including an important silk-weaving

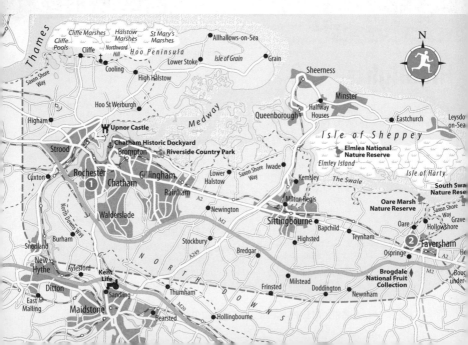

community in Canterbury – and in 1960 the Huguenot Hospital, established in 1718 in London, was moved to a new site on Rochester's high street. A couple of minutes' walk south of the museum, it still provides accommodation for Huguenot descendants fallen on hard times. The museum itself exhibits fine examples of Huguenot craftsmanship – in weaving, clockmaking, glassmaking, gold- and silversmithing – while temporary shows highlight specific strands of the Huguenot experience.

Guildhall Museum

17 High St, ME1 1PY • Tues–Sun 10am–5pm • Free • ☎ 01634 332900, ⓦ medway.gov.uk

At the riverside end of the high street, the **Guildhall Museum** – the old magistrates' court, where Pip was bound over as apprentice to Joe in *Great Expectations* – holds a chilling interactive exhibition on the grim prison ships, or decommissioned **hulks**, used to house convicts and prisoners of war in the late eighteenth century. The next-door building holds the **Dickens Discovery Rooms** – a wordy display on the author's life and a short film about locations that feature in his work, along with more general exhibits (on Victorian domestic interiors, toys and local theatres) that stretch the Dickens connections somewhat.

Rochester Castle

Northwest end of the High St, ME1 1SW • Daily: April–Sept 10am–6pm; Oct–March 10am–4pm; last entry 45min before closing • £6.40; EH • ☎ 01634 335882, ⓦ www.english-heritage.org.uk/visit/places/rochester-castle

Built around 1127 by William of Corbeil, Archbishop of Canterbury, the dramatic **Rochester Castle**, though now ruined, remains one of the best-preserved examples of a Norman fortress in the country. The stark 113ft-high Kentish ragstone tower-keep – England's tallest – glowers over the town, while the interior is all the better for having lost its floors, allowing clear views up and down the dank shell. The outer walls and two of the towers retain their corridors and spiral stairwells, allowing you to scramble up rough and uneven damp stone staircases to the uppermost battlements.

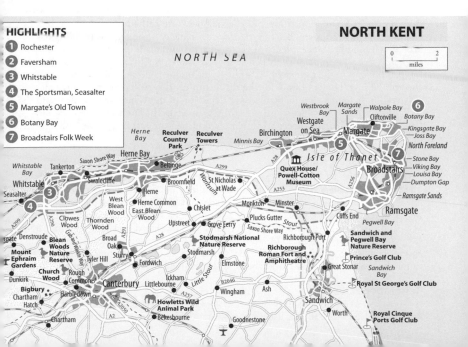

HIGHLIGHTS

1. Rochester
2. Faversham
3. Whitstable
4. The Sportsman, Seasalter
5. Margate's Old Town
6. Botany Bay
7. Broadstairs Folk Week

2

ON THE DICKENS TRAIL

Charles Dickens (1812–70) spent many of his formative years in Chatham, and returned to live near Rochester for the last thirteen years of his life with his long-time lover Ellen Ternan, a local actress. They met when she was 18 and he 45, and after his separation from his wife Catherine, lived together until his death.

In addition to the main **sights** the town also hosts two Dickens **festivals** (see box opposite); there's another, along with more Dickens-related sightseeing, in **Broadstairs**, along the coast in Thanet (see box, p.99).

ROCHESTER AND CHATHAM

Eastgate House High St. The Elizabethan Eastgate House features as the Nuns' House in *Edwin Drood*, and Westgate in *Pickwick Papers*. Inside, an exhibition covers the history of the building, while in the garden you can see Dickens' summer study, a Swiss chalet with gingerbread trimmings, which was moved here from Gad's Hill in the 1960s.
Royal Victoria and Bull Hotel 16 High St. This run-down hotel, opposite the Guildhall, stood in for the *Bull* in *Pickwick Papers* and the *Blue Boar* in *Great Expectations*.
Dickens Discovery Rooms, Guildhall Museum See p.69.
Restoration House See below.
Six Poor Travellers House See below.
Chatham Historic Dockyard In 1817 Dickens' family moved to a small house in Chatham, where his father was a clerk in the dockyards, and lived there for six years. See p.72.

BEYOND ROCHESTER

Gad's Hill Place Higham, ME3 7PA. Now a private school, three miles west of town, this is the Georgian house that Dickens dreamed of owning as a child and bought at the height of his fame in 1856, and where he died in 1870. The Dickens Fellowship runs occasional tours, which must be prebooked (April–Oct; £9.50; 🌐 dickensfellowship.org).
St James's Church Cooling. See p.74.

Rochester cathedral

Boley Hill, ME1 1SX • Mon–Fri & Sun 7.30am–6pm, Sat 7.30am–5pm• Free; audio tours £1 • ☎ 01634 843366, 🌐 rochestercathedral.org

Built on Anglo-Saxon foundations, Rochester's beautiful **cathedral**, at the northwest end of the high street, dates back to the eleventh century – though the building has been much modified since. Plenty of Norman features remain, however, particularly in the handsome west front, with its pencil-shaped towers, richly carved portal and tympanum, and in the nave, with its stout Romanesque columns, arches and jagged chevron carving. Look out, too, for the thirteenth-century wall painting (only half survives) in the quire – a remarkably vivid depiction of the Wheel of Fortune – and the zodiac image in the tiled floor in front of the high altar. The latter was the work of famed architect George Gilbert Scott, who remodelled the east end of the cathedral in the 1870s.

Six Poor Travellers House

97 High St, ME1 1LX • March–Oct Wed–Sun 11am–1pm & 2–4pm • Free • ☎ 01634 842194, 🌐 richardwatts.org.uk/poor-travellers

The **Six Poor Travellers House**, an almshouse founded in 1579 to house impecunious travellers for the night – anyone, from scholars to blacksmiths, on the condition they were neither "rogues nor proctors" – was also used for a while in the eighteenth century as a prison for drunkards and runaway servants, and described by Dickens in his 1854 story *The Seven Poor Travellers*. "A clean white house", as the author put it, "of a staid and venerable air". Today you can wander through a set of small rooms, including three simple bedrooms with their truckle beds, and a fragrant courtyard herb garden.

Restoration House

17–19 Crow Lane, ME1 1RF • June–Sept Thurs & Fri 10am–5pm • £8.50; gardens only £4 • ☎ 01634 848520, 🌐 restorationhouse.co.uk

Restoration House is not your usual house museum. An elegant Elizabethan mansion, given its current name after Charles II stayed here in May 1660 before his restoration, and the inspiration for Miss Havisham's Satis House in *Great Expectations*, it was, incongruously enough, owned for a while by Emu-toting entertainer Rod Hull. In fact, he saved it from being demolished – it was eventually taken from him by the taxmen, however, and left to dilapidation. The current owners have avoided the manicured restorations of so many old houses; its ragged, crumbling beauty reveals far more about the house's long life and many alterations than something more formal. This is a lived-in place, full of whimsical juxtapositions and evocative details: plaster is cracked and wood is buckled and chipped; mottled Georgian mirrors share space with Renaissance drawings and Gainsborough paintings, while Jacobean furniture sits upon undulating elm floorboards and fresh wildflowers tumble from vintage china. The walled garden is charming, too, with fountains, fruit trees and fairytale topiary.

2

ARRIVAL AND INFORMATION   ROCHESTER

By train Trains arrive in the heart of town just east of the High St, opposite the back entrance of the tourist office. Destinations Canterbury (every 20–45min; 40–50min); Chatham (every 5–25min; 3min); Faversham (every 10–20min; 30min); London Charing Cross (Mon–Fri every 30min; 1hr 20min); London St Pancras (every 30min; 35–40min); London Victoria (every 10–20min; 45min–1hr 20min); Ramsgate (every 5–40min; 1hr 10min).
By bus Regular Arriva buses to and from Chatham stop on Corporation St (the A2), which runs parallel to the train line

and the High St (every 7–20min; 5min).
Tourist office 95 High St (April–Sept Mon–Sat 10am–5pm, Sun 10.30am–5pm; Oct–March Mon–Sat 10am–5pm; 01634 338141, visitmedway.org). In a good central location, this is the hub for the Medway region, with lots of information, an art gallery and a café.
Tours The City of Rochester Society offers free guided walking tours, leaving from outside the tourist office (Sat, Sun & Wed 2.15pm; 1hr 30min; city-of-rochester.org.uk/guided-tours).

ACCOMMODATION

Golden Lion 147–149 High St, ME1 1EL 01634 405402, jdwetherspoon.com. Rochester's newest and most central option, with nine spick-and-span, well-equipped en-suite rooms above a Wetherspoons pub on the high street. Breakfast (available in the pub) is not included, but with a/c, double glazing and free tea and coffee this is very good value. __£60__
North Downs Barn Bush Rd, Cuxton, ME2 1HF 01634 296829, northdownsbarn.co.uk. Three luxurious B&B rooms (two en-suite doubles; one single, with private bath, £45) in a gorgeous barn conversion on the North Downs Way four miles south of Rochester. __£85__

Ship & Trades Maritime Way, Chatham, ME4 3ER 01634 895200, shipandtradeschatham.co.uk. This lively waterside brasserie-bar near the dockyard offers fifteen smart, contemporary B&B rooms, many with Chatham marina views and some with capacious terraces. __£90__
YHA Medway 351 Capstone Rd, Gillingham, ME7 3JE 0845 371 9649, yha.org.uk/hostel/medway. Rochester's nearest hostel is four miles southeast, in an old oast house opposite the lovely Capstone Farm Country Park. There's a small kitchen, and a café. March–Oct Sat, Sun & school hols only; Nov–Feb groups only. Dorms __£19__, doubles __£39__

EATING

The Deaf Cat 83 High St, ME1 1LX thedeafcat.com. A hop away from the cathedral, this independent coffee shop, dedicated to the memory of Dickens' deaf cat, is a laidback place serving espresso drinks, cookies, cakes and

sandwiches to a mixed crowd of tourists and locals. Try to bag a sofa seat. Mon–Sat 9am–5pm, Sun 10am–5pm.
The Seaplane Works 132 High St, ME1 1JT facebook.com/TheSeaplaneWorks. Something a little different in

ROCHESTER FESTIVALS

Rochester hosts not one but two annual **festivals** devoted to **Charles Dickens** (rochesterdickensfestival.org.uk). Early June sees a weekend of parades, readings and street entertainment, while the Dickens Christmas in early December is a festive flurry of falling snow and candlelit parades, with much emphasis, of course, on *A Christmas Carol* and Scrooge. Just as much fun is the **Rochester Sweeps Festival**, a three-day May bank holiday celebration that re-creates the Victorian sweeps' May Day holiday; a rumbustious street affair featuring a Jack in the Green ceremony, folk music, parades and morris dancing.

2

these parts: a vegan coffee house/restaurant in a bare-bones, boho space (scrubbed wood, school chairs) that's as simple and appealing as the food. Dishes are creative and colourful, using local produce – hearty stews, over-stuffed wraps, vegan pizzas, raw cheesecake and the like, with top-notch Square Mile coffee to boot. Mains from £6. Mon–Wed 8am–5pm, Thurs & Fri 8am–8pm, Sat 9am–5pm, Sun 10am–4pm.

Sun Pier House Sun Pier, Medway St, Chatham, ME4 4HF ☎01634 812805, Ⓦsunpierhouse.co.uk. Friendly, arty tearoom in a small gallery by the water. With its comfy sofas, board games and views across to Rochester – they provide binoculars for a better look – it's a relaxing spot for

a coffee and cake, a light lunch or a traditional afternoon tea (£12; book 48hr in advance), all freshly made. Tues–Sat 10am–4pm, Sun noon–4pm.

Topes 60 High St, ME1 1JY ☎01634 845270, Ⓦtopesrestaurant.com. Rochester's fanciest restaurant, very near the cathedral, serves inventive dishes – such as chargrilled herb bread pudding with wild mushroom broth, or duck breast with braised puy lentils and duck spring roll – in a wood-panelled dining room with sloping ceilings. It's prix fixe; the good-value set menus include two courses for a midweek lunch/dinner for £16/£19.50. Wed–Sat noon–2.30pm & 6.30–9pm, Sun noon–2.30pm.

SHOPPING

★ **Baggins Book Bazaar** 19 High St, ME1 1PY ☎01634 811651, Ⓦbagginsbooks.co.uk. England's largest secondhand bookstore is a neverending warren of a place, filled with specialist, antique and rare titles on anything from fungi to UFOs. Daily 10am–5.45pm.

The Hendersons 44 High St, ME1 1LD ☎01634 400781, Ⓦthehendersonsshop.co.uk. It's always worth

a rummage in this personally curated lifestyle store – selling a mix of quirky vintage and playful contemporary design – where the gifts and homeware range from 1920s jam jars to Midcentury Modern armchairs, with stocking fillers including patches, brooches and French school jotters. Mon–Fri 10am–5pm, Sat 10am–5.30pm, Sun 11am–4pm.

Chatham Historic Dockyard

About one mile north of Chatham along Dock Rd, ME4 4TE • Daily: mid-Feb to end March & Nov 10am–4pm; end March to Oct 10am–6pm; Victorian Ropery and *Ocelot* tours by timed ticket only • £24; under-15s £14; family ticket from £63; tickets are valid for a year • ☎01634 823800, Ⓦthedockyard.co.uk • Bus #190 runs to the docks from Rochester; there are also trains to Chatham station from Rochester (see p.71) and St Pancras International (every 30min; 40min) – from the station you can walk (30min), take a bus (#101; 15min) or hop in a taxi (£7)

Two miles east of Rochester, the colossal **Chatham Historic Dockyard**, founded by Henry VIII, was by the time of Charles II the major base of the Royal Navy. Britain led the world in ship design and shipbuilding for centuries, and many Royal Navy vessels were built, stationed and victualled here. The dockyards were closed in 1984, with the end of the shipbuilding era, but reopened soon afterwards as a tourist attraction.

With an array of fine historic ships, exhibitions and important buildings spread across the eighty-acre site it would take days to explore the whole place – if pushed for time, concentrate on the **Ocelot sub**, the **Victorian Ropery** and the **Command of the Oceans** displays. The main attractions are reviewed below, but there are more detailed on the website and on the map boards dotted throughout the docks.

FAMILY ATTRACTIONS AROUND ROCHESTER

Chatham Historic Dockyard (see above) makes a great family day out, and there are two more excellent family attractions, especially good for active types, nearby.

Chatham Ski Centre Capstone Rd, Gillingham, ME7 3JH ☎01634 827979, Ⓦjnlchatham.co.uk. Excellent skiing and snowboarding on the artificial ski slope, plus tobogganing and sno-tubing down the longest track in the UK. There are lessons for kids as young as 4. Prices vary. Mon–Fri 10am–10pm, Sat & Sun 9.30am–6pm.

Diggerland Roman Way, Medway Valley Leisure Park, Strood, ME2 2NU ☎0871 227 7007,

Ⓦdiggerland.com. Good mucky fun – especially on rainy days – on this small plot, crammed with diggers and dumpers of every shape and size, with plenty to drive, some to operate, and others mutated into fairground-type rides. Children can drive unaccompanied – but check the height restrictions before booking. £19.95; free for anyone under 90cm tall. Sat, Sun & school hols 10am–5pm; closed winter.

Command of the Oceans

The interactive **Command of the Oceans** exhibits offer some real highlights, vividly portraying the dockyard as a colossal, dynamic and ever-changing factory. The **Heart of Oak** walkthrough experience uses digital graphics to follow a grandfather and grandson as they explore the docks in 1806 – just after Nelson's flagship *Victory*, devastated in the Battle of Trafalgar, returned here for repair – illuminating the processes of building timber-hulled sail-powered ships, and how Nelson's new "cutting the line" strategy changed the face of sea battle, and warship design, forever. **People, Tools and Trades**, meanwhile, focuses on 1803, with touchscreens zooming in on the individual workers – more than 2500 of them – and dockyard trades of that year.

2

Perhaps best of all, however, is the **Ship Beneath the Floor** exhibit, which tells a fascinating tale. In 1995, archeologists discovered 168 frame timbers below the floorboards of Chatham's wheelwright's shop; these were identified as having come from *Namur*, a "second rate" ship launched in 1756. The *Namur* saw battle in the Seven Years War and the Battle of Lagos, among others; one member of its crew was slave boy Olaudah Equiano, who went on to become a famous abolitionist. The timbers were placed below the floor in 1834, but why there is quite so much of it is a mystery – saved as a mark of respect, perhaps, or, in a new age of iron and steam, as a memorial to a bygone era of timber and sails. Whatever the reason, they're a strangely moving sight in situ.

HMS Gannet

The Victorian sloop **HMS Gannet**, built at nearby Sheerness in 1878, is the most beautiful of Chatham's three historic ships, its elegant rigging and fine teak-planked hull evoking the glorious era of British naval supremacy. Unusually, *Gannet* also has a funnel – steam was not yet a tried and trusted form of naval power, so the ship was designed to be able to use both steam and sails. Nimble and fast, she was typical of the patrol ships deployed to impose the "gunboat diplomacy" that ensured Britannia ruled the waves.

HMS Cavalier

HMS Cavalier, built on the Isle of Wight in 1944, was known as the fastest destroyer in the fleet, equipped with all the latest technology and remaining active until 1972. You don't need to be a naval buff to get something from walking around this mighty "greyhound", the last of its kind in existence; the ship is kitted out as it would have been in the 1940s, and fascinating audio tours, which include testimony from men who served on destroyers, illuminate just how harsh conditions were on these mighty warships.

Ocelot submarine

Tours of the **Ocelot submarine** – the last Royal Navy warship to be built at Chatham, launched in 1962 – are not for the claustrophobic. You'll need to climb narrow, steep staircases, squeeze along low-ceilinged, one-person-wide passageways and shoot yourself from room to room through knee-high circular hatches. However, the opportunity to experience the astonishingly cramped quarters that housed a crew of 69 men for months at a time, and to peer through the periscope at the outside world, make it perennially popular; the fact that *Ocelot* was a Cold War spy ship, and that her movements are shrouded in a certain mystery, only lends it more intrigue.

The Victorian Ropery

The **Victorian Ropery** is one of the surprise hits of the dockyard, its lively tours, led by guides in Victorian costume, using the history of rope-making to illuminate the history of the docks themselves, and to reflect upon life at sea in the nineteenth century. Rope was made at Chatham from 1618 until the docks closed. During the "Age of Sail", warships would have needed some twenty miles of the stuff for the rigging alone; HMS *Victory* needed thirty miles at least, using it for everything from bucket handles to hammocks to cat-o'-nine-tails.

2

In 1790, the quarter-mile-long **Ropewalk**, the longest brick building in Europe, was built at Chatham; it is now the only one of its kind left in the world, and rope is still made here for commercial use. Here you get the opportunity to make rope yourself, and during the week can watch ropemakers at work, "walking the rope out" in the lengthy hall upstairs, using traditional machinery dating from 1811.

No. 1 Smithery

Chatham's smithy – built in 1808, at the point when wooden ships were being replaced by iron and steam – now houses the **No. 1 Smithery**, which, along with temporary art exhibitions, features a splendid **Maritime Treasures** gallery. The highlights are undoubtedly the **ship models**, peaks of artistry and engineering made for a variety of reasons – as part of the design process, as prototypes, or simply as a way for sailors or naval POWs to pass the time. Look out for the fully rigged model of the wrecked HMS *Victory* (1806), carved by prisoners of war from bones saved from their meat rations, and a model of HMS *Ormonde* (1918), a World War I ship "dazzle painted" with jarring angular designs that, while looking for all the world like eye-catching Jazz Age modernism, provided highly effective camouflage at sea.

The Big Space

The Big Space is indeed very big, and full of very big things – including a Midget submarine, hulking mine-clearance equipment, massive steam hammers, a D-Day locomotive and a grim-looking tank. The building, a covered slip built in 1838, is impressive, a colossal wide-span timber structure with a cantilevered frame and an apsidal end that resembles the bow of a ship. From the mezzanine you can take a closer look at the roof, with its dramatic exposed timber skeleton.

The Hoo Peninsula

The marshy **Hoo Peninsula**, jutting out into the Medway and the Thames estuaries north of Rochester, is a lonely area rich in birdlife, attracting migrating and nesting waterfowl. The **Heron Trail** cycling route covers a loop of around seventeen miles, linking the **Cliffe Pools**, **Buckland Lake** and **Northward Hill** reserves, while the **Saxon Shore Way** walking path, which passes through Rochester, is also handy for Cliffe Pools and Northward Hill.

RSPB Cliffe Pools

Cliffe • Daily dawn–dusk • Free • ☎ 01634 222480, ⓦ rspb.org.uk/cliffepools • Bus #133 from Chatham (1hr) and Rochester stops in Cliffe; by car, park in Cliffe and walk down Pond Lane into the reserve

One of the most important wildlife reserves in the country, the 550-acre **Cliffe Pools**, a watery landscape of brackish pools, grasslands and salty lagoons right by the Thames, attracts large flocks of wading birds and waterfowl. Stars include avocets, little egrets, nightingales, turtle doves and lapwings, and, in summer, godwits, sandpipers and stints. A number of trails, including the Saxon Shore Way, cross the reserve, offering brilliant views.

Cooling

The village of **COOLING** is an isolated spot, stranded in the Hoo marshes around seven miles north of Rochester. On the main road, the thirteenth-century **St James's Church** (ⓦ coolingchurch.org.uk) is where Pip meets Magwitch by his brothers' gravestones in *Great Expectations*; you can still see the thirteen sad little lozenge-shaped stone tombs that inspired the scene. Nearby, within a private estate owned by musician Jools Holland, the ruined **Cooling Castle** was built in the fourteenth century to guard the River Thames; due to land reclamation it now sits around two miles inland.

RSPB Northward Hill

One mile from High Halstow • Daily dawn–dusk • Free, donations welcome • ☎ 01634 222480, ⓦ rspb.org.uk/reserves/guide/n/northwardhill

In a remote location on a ridge overlooking the marshes, **Northward Hill**, its beautiful bluebell woods filled with nightingale song in spring, boasts the largest **heronry** in the UK. With nearly 150 pairs of grey herons and around fifty pairs of little egrets, the marshes are also a rich breeding ground for lapwings. Three trails, the longest at 2.3 miles, offer views of the marshes and the Thames Valley, and lead you to a heronry viewpoint.

Isle of Sheppey

The **ISLE OF SHEPPEY**, a flat clump of marshy land measuring just nine miles by four, separated from the mainland by the Medway and the Swale estuary, is often overlooked on a Kent itinerary. That's not to say it hasn't got a certain cut-off appeal: beyond its fifty-odd caravan parks, amusement arcades and industrial estates, beyond the ranks of enormous pylons and its trio of prisons, the island offers an odd, otherworldly sense of isolation and a few quiet attractions, from wide beaches crunching with London Clay fossils to empty, shimmering marshlands rich in **birdlife**. For an offbeat, nostalgic experience, the **Bluetown Heritage Centre** (see below) in Sheerness, Sheppey's main resort, can't be beat, but otherwise the south of the island is the most appealing – a serene, big-sky landscape where contented cows and fat sheep graze upon the salty marshlands of the isolated **Isle of Harty** and the wetland wilderness of **Elmley National Nature Reserve**.

Isle of Harty

The **Isle of Harty**, on Sheppey's southeastern tip, may not literally be an island, but separated from the rest of Sheppey by a number of channels it certainly feels cut off. With a few narrow country lanes winding through the watery landscape, this is good walking territory, and a favourite spot for birders; the **RSPB Capel Fleet viewpoint** is one of the best places in England to see birds of prey, including peregrines, while the coastal strip between **Shell Ness**, on the island's eastern tip, and Harty's *Ferry House Inn* (see p.76) is designated as the **Swale National Nature Reserve** (ⓦ naturalengland.org.uk), an excellent spot to see waders, waterfowl and birds of prey, along with rare plants and butterflies.

Elmley National Nature Reserve

Kingshill Farm, ME12 3RW • Mon & Wed–Sun 8am–8pm (or sunset if earlier) • £3 • ☎ 07706 333331, ⓦ elmleynaturereserve.co.uk

The trip out to the **Elmley National Nature Reserve**, a 3000-acre wilderness area of open grassland, mudflats and saltmarsh on the southwest of the island, is half the fun. The sign from the A249 heralds a two-mile drive through lonely wetlands, with big skies stretching out to either side, before you even reach the farm car park – from there some 3.5 miles of footpaths provide fabulous views. The privately owned reserve is famed among birders for its breeding waders and birds of prey; in spring and summer you'll see displaying waders, including redshanks and lapwings, along with rare breeding species including grey partridge and yellow wagtail, while in the cooler months you may spot short-eared owls and wigeon. Hares are also common, along with seals basking on the mudflats. Uniquely for a national nature reserve, Elmley also offers a handful of luxurious **shepherd's huts** – there could hardly be a more peaceful place to stay.

ARRIVAL AND INFORMATION	ISLE OF SHEPPEY

By car Sheppey is linked to the mainland by the A249 and the huge Sheppey Crossing bridge. You can also take the smaller road running alongside the A249, which has a small drawbridge and provides faster access to Elmley.

By train There are connections with Sittingbourne on the mainland from Sheerness (every 30min; 20min) and Queenborough (every 30min; 15min).

Tourist information The Bluetown Heritage Centre, 69 High St, Blue Town, Sheerness (Tues–Sat 10am–3pm, later for some movie/music hall shows; £2; ☎ 01795 662981,

2

ⓦthecriterionbluetown.co.uk), is a fascinating little volunteer-run information centre/museum – complete with a genuine old-time music hall and cinema (additional charge) – which concentrates on the history of Sheerness. The cosy tearoom serves home-made cakes and cream teas. **Website** ⓦvisitsheppey.com.

ACCOMMODATION AND EATING

Ferry House Inn Harty Ferry Rd, Harty, ME12 4BQ ⓣ01795 510214, ⓦtheferryhouseinn.co.uk. A friendly sixteenth-century pub, in a remote spot on Sheppey's southern coast. With its sweeping Swale views, the large, flower-bedecked garden is a peaceful place to eat good, fresh, Kentish food; they have a kitchen garden, and all beef and lamb comes from their own farm (mains from £11; two-course set lunch menu £11). It's a popular venue for weekend weddings, so it's best to call in advance if you want a meal. They also offer B&B rooms and self-catering cottages (from £560 for two nights). Mon–Fri 11am–10.30pm, Sat 11am–11pm, Sun 11am–5pm; kitchen Mon–Fri noon–2.30pm & 6.30–8.30pm, Sat 12.30–4pm & 6.30–8.30pm, Sun noon–4pm. **£80**

The Three Tuns Lower Halstow, ME9 7DY ⓣ01795 842840, ⓦthethreetunsrestaurant.co.uk. On the way to Sheppey, this fifteenth-century country inn, with a huge streamside beer garden, serves great local ales and ciders and good, seasonal gastropub grub. Tuck into a "Kentish pub board" (Scotch egg, apple and black pudding sausage roll, toasted huffkin, Kentish cheeses; £12.95), a mixed grill meze, a wild mushroom risotto or a steak; they also do great gourmet sandwiches (from fish fingers to grilled halloumi; from £6). Daily noon–11pm; kitchen noon–9pm.

Faversham and around

Site of an important medieval abbey (long since gone), the good-looking creekside town of **FAVERSHAM** was famed from Elizabethan times for its thriving boatyards, fitting and repairing the wooden barges that worked their way along the estuary to London. Once surrounded by hop gardens, it is still home to the **Shepherd Neame Brewery**, while the importance of fruit-growing hereabouts is celebrated by the **Brogdale National Fruit Collection**. For many years, too, Faversham was at the centre of the nation's explosives industry, with **gunpowder** produced in the nearby marshes for three centuries before fizzling out in the 1930s. On the edge of the North Downs Area of Outstanding Natural Beauty, and separated from the Swale by a web of **marshes** and winding creek inlets, it's a neat, pretty place, its core boasting a well-preserved mix of buildings from medieval via Elizabethan to Victorian. **Market Place** (markets Tues, Fri & Sat 8.30am–3/4pm; ⓦfavershammarket.org) is the hub, fringed with cafés, the independent **Royal Cinema** (ⓦroyalcinema.co.uk) and a handsome sixteenth-century Guildhall elevated on stout columns. From here, medieval **Abbey Street** runs down to the peaceful **creek**.

Fleur de Lis Heritage Centre Museum

10 Preston St, ME13 8NS • Mon–Sat 10am–4pm, Sun 10am–1pm • £5 • ⓣ01795 590726, ⓦfavershamsociety.org

The **Fleur de Lis Heritage Centre** should be your first stop; not only does it house the excellent information office and bookshop (see p.78) but also a fabulous local **museum** that punches way above its weight for a town of this size. Packed with lively exhibits on everything from brewing to boat building, agricultural riots to local pirates, the Tardis-like space also illuminates Faversham's social history with its reconstructed domestic interiors, while offbeat objects, from a mammoth's tooth to a magic lantern, greet you at every turn.

Faversham Creek

Faversham grew up alongside its **creek**, a tidal inlet of the Swale that was used from at least Roman times as a harbour. In the sixteenth century it was crowded with small merchant ships, many of them built locally, and it remained busy until Victorian times, swarming with deft Thames barges. **Standard Quay** (ⓦstandardquay.co.uk), downstream of the swing bridge at the end of Abbey Street, was until 2012 one of just two remaining wooden boat repair yards in Britain; though you will still see old barges, fishing boats and historic ships moored by the quayside, the cluster of workshops, lopsided timber-framed buildings and weatherboard grain warehouses today hold antique, vintage and craft stores, art and carpentry workshops and a garden centre (with coffee shop). You can walk along the creek to the nearby marshes and a couple of nature reserves (see below).

Shepherd Neame Brewery

11 Court St, ME13 7AX • Daily, though closed occasional days; tour schedule varies, but there is usually a 2pm tour and often another in the morning, and occasionally more at weekends • £12.75 • ☎ 01795 542016, ⓦ shepherdneame.co.uk/tours-functions/brewery-tours

It's rare to find a pub in these parts that isn't owned by the **Shepherd Neame Brewery**, the oldest in Britain, whose Spitfire, Bishops Finger and Master Brew ales are household names among beer fans. A brewery has stood on this site since at least 1573, drawing water from an artesian well; now this fifth-generation, family-owned business is best known for their quintessentially Kentish ales, made with hops from local fields. Lively **tours** take you through the process, from soaking the barley to conditioning the ales and adding special ingredients — oysters, rose petals — for their speciality brews. It's a working facility, thrumming, humid and pungent, and tours are enjoyably interactive: peer into the steaming, churning mash tuns, the oldest in England, and try all the key ingredients, from the burnt toast-tasting chocolate malt used in stout and porters, to wincingly bitter dried hop pellets and fresh spring water from the well. The grand finale is a tutored beer-tasting, after which you can choose a sample of your favourite to drink with free snacks.

Brogdale National Fruit Collection

Brogdale Rd, ME13 8XZ • Daily: April–Oct 10am–5pm; guided tours (1hr) daily 11am, 1pm & 2.30pm • £12, lasts a year • ☎ 01795 536250, ⓦ brogdalecollections.org

On the southern edge of town, **Brogdale Farm** is home to the largest collection of fruit trees in the world, with thousands of varieties of apple and hundreds of pears, plums, cherries and nuts. It's above all a research facility; you can wander around freely, but you'll get the most from your trip if you join a guided **tour** or come for one of their regular themed days or festivals. A little marketplace includes a café, a nursery stocked with heritage fruit trees, a fruit shop (summer only), the excellent **Butcher of Brogdale** (ⓦ thebutcherofbrogdale.co.uk) and Tiddly Pomme (ⓦ tiddlypommeshop.co.uk) for fresh local juices and ciders.

The Swale

From the sixteenth to the twentieth century gunpowder was manufactured in the marshes northwest of Faversham on the south bank of the Swale; today these tranquil, sheltered mudflats and saltmarshes, cut through with fresh and brackish creeks, are prime habitat for migratory, overwintering and breeding birds, among them black-tailed godwit, dunlin, curlew, avocet, redshank and snipe. The **Oare Gunpowder Works Country Park** (Mon–Fri 9am–5pm, Sat & Sun 10am–4pm; ⓦ gunpowderworks.co.uk), a mile west of town, just off the Western Link road to the village of Oare, is intriguing, its wildlife trails weaving through woodland, past abandoned works buildings and along ponds and canals. A couple of miles further north the **Oare Marsh Nature Reserve** (ⓦ wildlifetrusts.org/reserves/oare-marshes), at Harty Ferry, just north of Oare, has good birdwatching hides and views across the estuary to Sheppey. You can also walk along the creek east of Faversham, following the coast through the **South Swale Nature Reserve** (ⓦ wildlifetrusts.org/reserves/south-swale) – rich in wading birds and wildfowl, and flecked with glorious wildflowers – the six or so miles to Seasalter and its famous gastropub, *The Sportsman* (see p.85).

ARRIVAL AND INFORMATION

By train The station is on Station Rd; it's a 10min walk up Preston St to Market Place.

Destinations Broadstairs (every 10–40min; 35min); Canterbury (every 15–40min; 15min); Dover (every 30min–1hr; 30–40min); Herne Bay (every 10–40min; 15min); London St Pancras (every 30min–1hr; 1hr 10min); London Victoria (every 30min; 1hr 10min–1hr 35min); Margate (every 10–40min; 30min); Ramsgate (every 10min–1hr; 40min); Rochester (every 10–20min; 30min); Whitstable (every 10–45min; 10min).

By bus Buses to Boughton (frequent; 20min) and Canterbury (every 15min–2hr; 40min) stop in the centre of town, on Court St near Market Place.

By car Skirted by the A2, Faversham is just half a mile off the M2 and a 20min drive from the M20.

Fleur de Lis Heritage Centre 10 Preston St (Mon–Sat 10am–4pm, Sun 10am–1pm; ☎01795 534542, ⓦ faveshamsociety.org). Faversham's splendid visitor information centre has a fantastic local history bookshop (there's a second branch, selling used books, around the corner on Gatefield Lane) and a museum (see p.76); it also organizes 1hr 30min walking tours (Feb, March, Nov & Dec 1st & 3rd Sat 10.30am; April, May & Oct Sat 10.30am; June–Sept Sat 10.30am & 2.30pm; £5, including museum entry).

Website ⓦ visitfaversham.org.

ACCOMMODATION

Faversham Creek Hotel Conduit St, ME13 7DF ☎01795 533535, ⓦ favershamcreekhotel.co.uk. A mere splash away from the creek, this restaurant with rooms offers great food in the classy *Red Sails Restaurant* (see below) and six individually styled boutique B&B rooms, each named after a famous Kentish personality. **£85**

★ **Palace Farm** Down Court Rd, Doddington, ME9 0AU ☎01795 886200, ⓦ palacefarm.com. A peaceful family farm in a North Downs village six miles southwest of Faversham, with ten comfortable, hostel-style B&B rooms around a courtyard or in a converted granary. They're all en suite, with bunks and/or double beds, with a communal kitchen, lounge and dining room, plus outdoor eating areas. There's tent camping and a few tipis (May–Sept), in a quiet field; you can rent firepits and bikes. Campsite closed mid-Oct to March. Camping/person **£8**, tipis **£50**, doubles **£50**

Railway Hotel Preston St, ME13 8PE ☎01795 533173, ⓦ railwayhotelfaversham.co.uk. Opposite the station, this hotel has been hosting train travellers since Victorian times; today it's a Shepherd Neame inn, with en-suite rooms above the pub. Clean, comfortable and friendly, with some nice stylish flourishes and good bathrooms. The on-site *Carriage* restaurant is not bad, either, serving bistro favourites including steak and ale pot pie or pan-fried sea bass (mains from £10). Breakfast costs extra. **£75**

Sun Inn 10 West St, ME13 7JE ☎01795 535098, ⓦ sunfaversham.co.uk. Lovely old coaching inn, owned by Shepherd Neame, in a good central location near Market Place. There are twelve rather luxurious B&B rooms, many of them crisscrossed with oak beams, and a smart food menu in the pub. **£95**

EATING AND DRINKING

As the home of Shepherd Neame, Faversham has more than its fair share of real ale **pubs**, most of them in lovely historic buildings – you can't go very wrong with any of them. Many also serve terrific **food**: this is one of Kent's foodiest towns.

Jittermugs 18A Preston St, ME13 8NZ ☎01795 533121, ⓦ facebook.com/Jittermugs. Friendly little coffee shop, with distressed wooden floors, sofas and bookish bits and bobs scattered around the place. Come for an espresso or fresh Moroccan mint tea with a slab of cake, a light meal (£4–6) of antipasti, salads, toasties and the like, or evening tapas (from £3). Mon–Thurs 8.30am–10pm, Fri & Sat 8.30am–10.30pm, Sun 10am–5pm.

★ **Macknade Fine Foods** Selling Rd, ME13 8XF ☎01795 534497, ⓦ macknade.com. Just outside town, *Macknade*'s is more of a gourmet food hall than a farm shop. It's the foodies' go-to for the best local produce, from wines and fish to fruit and herbs, plus bread, cakes and posh deli stuff. The café serves excellent Italian espresso, cheese and artisan meat platters (£6–15), sandwiches,

salads and all-day brunch (from £2.50 for a slice of sourdough with butter and honey). Food hall Mon–Sat 9am–6pm, Sun 10am–4pm; café Mon–Sat 9am–5pm, Sun 10am–4pm.

Red Sails Restaurant Faversham Creek Hotel, Conduit St, ME13 7DF ☎01795 533535, ⓦ favershamcreekhotel .co.uk/menu. The menu at this Modern British restaurant is full of fresh flavours, running the gamut from local oysters (pre-order only) to "textures of cauliflower" or hazelnut-crusted sole, with Kentish wines available by the glass. Mains from £16, and a good range of set menus from £14.95. Wed–Sat noon–2.30pm & 7–9.30pm, Sun noon–4.30pm.

Shipwrights Arms Hollowshore, ME13 7TU ☎01795 590088, ⓦ theshipwrightsarmspub.co.uk. Time seems

2

to have stood still in this cluttered, seventeenth-century weatherboard pub – peacefully set in the marshes next to a boatyard – where the real ales are very local, as are the regulars. It's on the Saxon Shore Way, so you can walk here in around 40min through the marshes from Faversham, after which it's a treat to settle down to a quiet pint in the garden. Food is traditional pub grub. Hours can vary, so it's worth calling ahead. Usually May–Oct Mon–Fri 11am–3pm & 6–10pm, Sat 11am–11pm, Sun noon–10pm; Nov–April closed Mon; kitchen May–Oct Mon–Thurs noon–2.30pm, Fri & Sat noon–2.30pm & 6.30–8.30pm, Sun noon–2.30pm; Nov–April closed Mon.

★**Three Mariners** 2 Church Rd, Oare, ME13 0QA ☎ 01795 533633, ⓦ thethreemarinersoare.co.uk. Appealing eighteenth-century pub, in a creekside village 1.5 miles north of Faversham, with a garden and terrace for alfresco dining. Serving good local ales, it excels with its food: perfectly executed dishes such as linguine of sea urchin roe and bottarga, or herb-crusted rump of lamb. Mains start at £14, with set dinner menus at £17.95/£21.50 – you could cut costs with the three-course walkers' menu (Mon–Sat lunch; £13.95), but it's worth splashing out. Book ahead. Mon–Sat noon–11pm, Sun noon–9pm; kitchen Mon–Thurs noon–2.30pm & 6.30–9pm, Fri & Sat noon–2.30pm & 6.30–9.30pm, Sun noon–6.45pm.

★**The Yard** 10 Jacob Yard, Preston St, ME13 8NY ☎ 01795 538265, ⓦ facebook.com/TheYardFaversham. This laidback community café, tucked away in a mews near the railway station, scores high for its fresh, creative food, on a daily changing menu – veggies will love the vegan breakfasts and sunny meze platters, but the home-made scotch eggs and pork pies are delicious, too. Good coffee and cakes, and lots of community events, including yard sales and live music, make this a favourite local haunt; the little cobbled yard is a delight on sunny days. Dishes from £6.50. Mon–Sat 9am–5pm.

Whitstable and around

The most charming spot along the North Kent coast, and a popular weekend destination for capital-dwellers, **WHITSTABLE** is a lively, laidback place. Fishermen, artists, yachties and foodies rub along here, and the sense of community, and tradition, is strong. By the Middle Ages this fishing village was celebrated for its seafood, and though it's nowadays more dependent on its commercial harbour and seaside tourism, the **oysters** for which it has been famed since classical times still loom large – you can tuck in at dozens of restaurants, or celebrate them with gusto at the lively annual **Oyster Festival** (see box, p.86).

Formal sights are few, which is part of the appeal. It's a great place simply to hang out, with a busy little **harbour** and an attractive **High Street** lined with independent restaurants, delis and shops. The **beach**, an uncommercialized shingle stretch backed by flower-filled gardens, weatherboard cottages and colourful beach huts, offers broad empty vistas and blustery walks for miles in each direction, and with its shallow bays and clean, flat waters Whitstable also offers good **watersports**.

Whitstable Harbour

Whitstable's **harbour**, a mix of pretty and gritty that defines the town to a tee, bustles with a fish market, whelk stalls and a couple of seafood restaurants, and offers plenty of places to sit outside and watch the activity. Built in 1832 to serve the **Canterbury & Whitstable Railway**, which carried day-trippers to the beach and back, today it's a mixed-use port, backed by a hulking asphalt plant; the handsome 1892 Thames sailing barge moored on the South Quay, **Greta** (see p.83), offers boat trips around the estuary.

The high street

Whitstable's high street runs through town from the railway up to the harbour. Adopting three different names as it goes, it links to parallel streets, and to the sea, via a number of narrow alleys. Starting as **Oxford Street** in the south, it segues into the **High Street** proper beyond **Whitstable Museum**, then transforms itself again at

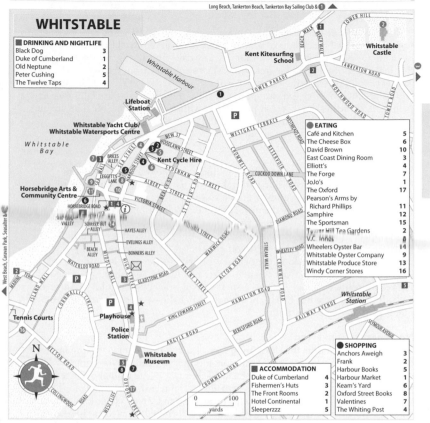

WHITSTABLE

■ DRINKING AND NIGHTLIFE

Black Dog	3
Duke of Cumberland	1
Old Neptune	2
Peter Cushing	5
The Twelve Taps	4

Long Beach, Tankerton Beach, Tankerton Bay Sailing Club & ❶ ▲

Kent Kitesurfing School

Whitstable Castle

Whitstable Harbour

Lifeboat Station

Whitstable Yacht Club/ Whitstable Watersports Centre

Whitstable Bay

Kent Cycle Hire

Horsebridge Arts & Community Centre

West Beach, Caravan Park, Seasalter

● EATING

Café and Kitchen	5
The Cheese Box	6
David Brown	10
East Coast Dining Room	3
Elliott's	4
The Forge	7
JoJo's	1
The Oxford	17
Pearson's Arms by Richard Phillips	11
Samphire	12
The Sportsman	15
Tower Hill Tea Gardens	2
V.C. Jones	8
Wheelers Oyster Bar	14
Whitstable Oyster Company	9
Whitstable Produce Store	13
Windy Corner Stores	16

Whitstable Station

Tennis Courts

Playhouse

Police Station

Whitstable Museum

■ ACCOMMODATION

Duke of Cumberland	4
Fishermen's Huts	3
The Front Rooms	2
Hotel Continental	1
Sleeperzzz	5

● SHOPPING

Anchors Aweigh	3
Frank	2
Harbour Books	5
Harbour Market	1
Keam's Yard	6
Oxford Street Books	8
Valentines	7
The Whiting Post	4

the **Horsebridge**, once home to the jetty where cargo was loaded and unloaded onto the Thames barges, and now a knot of activity where the town meets the beach. Here marks the start of **Harbour Street**, Whitstable's showpiece shopping stretch, lined with wonky and jauntily painted old buildings housing excellent restaurants and shops.

Whitstable Museum

5 Oxford St, CT5 1DB • 11am–4.30pm: Easter–Sept Thurs–Sun; Oct–Easter Sat; hours may change during school hols, so call to check • £3 • ☎ 01227 276998, ⓦ canterburymuseums.co.uk/coastal-museums

The friendly **Whitstable Museum** is full of curiosities. One corner is dedicated to ex-local **Peter Cushing** – the assertion that the man best remembered as Dr Frankenstein was an accomplished model-maker, who also designed scarves for Marks and Spencer, may come as a surprise. Evocative photos recall the days of the **Canterbury & Whitstable Railway**, the world's first scheduled steam passenger service, while local maritime history is covered with figureheads, ships' models, hulking old tools and the odd bit of oyster paraphernalia. The **fossils**, and an **Ice Age mammoth tooth** and tusk, both found nearby, are a hit with kids, while the local "pudding pan pots" are pretty extraordinary, too. Officially known as **Samian ware**, these pottery dishes date back to Roman times, conserved underwater in silt for thousands of years before being hauled up by fishermen and used in local homes.

2

The beaches

A swathe of shingle punctuated by weathered groynes, backed for most of its length by seaside houses and beach huts in varying states of repair, **Whitstable beach** is a glorious place for a stroll, a crabbing expedition or a lazy day's sunbathing, with a gentle slope that makes swimming possible in summer. Just steps away from the high street, it feels a world away, uninterrupted by commerce or cars and bathed in pearly light. Its elemental beauty, brightened by ragged clumps of tough beach plants, splashy wildflowers and peeling, upturned fishing boats, is picturesque without being twee; the skies are huge here, and the sunsets dramatic, with locals and tourists gathering most nights to watch the horizon bleed from orange to purple.

West to Seasalter

You mustn't leave Whitstable without taking a seaside walk **west from the Horsebridge**, where a beachside path takes you past abundant, unruly gardens, weatherbeaten beach huts and covetable seaside houses on one side with the huge open horizon expanding on the other. The *Old Neptune* pub (see p.86), standing alone on the shingle, marks the start of the town's **West Beach**, a good spot for crabbing and fine for swimming at high tide. Busy with families in summer, the beach gets quieter the further west you go – beyond the caravan park you can either continue by crunching along the pebbles, or keep to the path behind the beach huts. Around two miles from town you arrive at lonely **Seasalter**, marooned between birdlife-rich marshes and a shell-strewn beach with muddy offshore oyster beds. It's an unlikely but lovely spot for the Michelin-starred *Sportsman* (see p.85), one of Britain's best restaurants.

Northeast to Tankerton

Walking **northeast from the Horsebridge**, passing the thicket of clattering masts next to the yacht club, then the lifeboat station and the harbour, and trudging along the shingle beyond, you'll join a broad seaside walkway. On the road above, accessible by a short path, sits **Whitstable Castle** – actually an eighteenth-century manor house and beautiful flower-filled public park, with great sea views, an excellent kids' **playground** and a couple of cafés (see p.84). Well below and sheltered from the road, the path fringes Whitstable's broad, shingle **Long Beach** before emerging at the Blue Flag **Tankerton beach**, where there's good swimming and a **lifeguard service** (May–Sept Sat & Sun, daily during school summer hols). At low tide you can take a stroll along "**the Street**", a half-mile-long clay sandbank that juts out at a right angle to the beach and provides sandy bottomed, shallow swimming on either side. Ranks of brightly coloured beach huts sit staggered on the grassy **Tankerton Slopes** rising by the path – Tracey Emin's beach hut installation, *The Last Thing I Said To You Is Don't Leave Me*

WHITSTABLE WATERSPORTS

Whitstable is an excellent place for **watersports**, with a number of clubs based here and a laidback social scene. There are sailing races most summer weekends, and **windsurfing** and **kitesurfing**, concentrated around Long Beach and the Street, are popular.

Kent Kitesurfing School Boardworx Watersports Store, Beach Walk (☎07597 048858, ⊛kentkitesurfingschool.com). Kitesurfing coaching and beginners' lessons (from £100 for a 2hr 30min taster) at Tankerton and Pegwell Bay near Ramsgate.

Tankerton Bay Sailing Club Tankerton Slopes (⊛tbsc.co.uk). Small, friendly sailing club, below *JoJo's* restaurant (see p.85), offering beginners'

courses and three free "joyride" taster sessions a year (May–July).

Whitstable Watersports Centre Whitstable Yacht Club, 3–4 Sea Wall, next to the harbour (☎07936 031149, ⊛wyc.org.uk). Top-class lessons in sailing (from £60 for a 3hr taster), windsurfing (from £50 for a 2hr taster) and paddleboarding (£20/hr) in association with Whitstable's prestigious yacht club.

WHITSTABLE AND AROUND **NORTH KENT** 83

Here, which was bought by Charles Saatchi for £75,000 in 2000 and later destroyed in a warehouse fire, hailed from here. Scattered with rare hog's fennel, the slopes are classified as a Site of Special Scientific Interest and provide a lovely barrier from the road above. Climbing the steps next to the sailing club brings you up to **Marine Parade**, the road to Herne Bay, and an excellent restaurant, *JoJo's* (see p.85) – about thirty minutes' walk from Whitstable.

ARRIVAL AND DEPARTURE

By train From the station it's a 15min walk north to the harbour, or the same distance southwest along Cromwell Rd to West Beach.

Destinations Broadstairs (every 10–45min; 25min); Faversham (every 10–45min; 10min); Herne Bay (every 10–45min; 7min); London St Pancras (hourly; 1hr 15min); London Victoria (hourly; 1hr 30min); Margate (every 10–45min; 20min); Ramsgate (every 10–45min; 35min).

WHITSTABLE AND AROUND

By bus Buses stop on the high street, running to Blean (frequent; 20min), Canterbury (every 15min; 30min) and London (3 daily; 1hr 45min).

By car Whitstable lies around five miles north of Canterbury on the A290, easily accessible from the M20. Parking is tight: if you can't find a space on the street, try the pay car park behind the harbour or at Keam's Yard near the Horsebridge.

INFORMATION AND ACTIVITIES

Tourist information The Whitstable Shop, 34 Harbour St (Jan–March Mon–Sat 10am–4pm, Sun 11am–4pm; April–Dec Mon–Fri 10am–4pm, Sat 10am–5pm, Sun 11am–5pm; ☎01227 770060, ⓦseewhitstable.com). You can also check ⓦcanterbury.co.uk/whitstable in advance.

Sailing trips The *Greta* (☎07711 657919, ⓦgreta1892 .co.uk), a lovely old Thames barge moored in the harbour,

offers regular trips, including seal-spotting, around the Thames Estuary (May to mid-Oct; around 6hr; from £48).

Bike rental Kent Cycle Hire, 61 Harbour St (booking essential; ☎01227 388058, ⓦkentcyclehire.com), rents bikes for £20/day or £90/week; kids' bikes, tandems and tagalongs are all available. Conveniently, you can drop off your bike in their sister branches in Canterbury (see p.52) and Herne Bay (see p.89), if you wish.

ACCOMMODATION

Though there are some great places to stay in Whitstable, the choice of **hotels** and **B&Bs** is surprisingly limited, and prices aren't low, especially at the weekends (when there may be a two-night minimum). Many people choose **self-catering**: check ⓦwhitstableholidayhomes.co.uk, ⓦwhitstablecottagecompany.com and ⓦplacestostayinwhitstable .co.uk.

★ **Duke of Cumberland** High St, CT5 1AP ☎01227 280617, ⓦthedukeinwhitstable.co.uk. Eight comfortable and good-value en-suite B&B rooms above a friendly music pub (see p.86). It can be noisy on weekend nights, when they have live bands, but the music (which is generally excellent) tends to wind up around midnight. On sunny mornings breakfast in the garden is a treat. **£70**

★ **Fishermen's Huts** Near the harbour ☎01227 280280, ⓦwhitstablefishermanshuts.com. Run by the same people as the *Hotel Continental*, these thirteen two-storey weatherboard cockle-farmers' stores (sleeping two to six), offer cute, characterful accommodation by the sea wall near the harbour. Most have sea views, and some have self-catering facilities. Rates include breakfast, served at the *Continental*; rates drop considerably out of season. Two-night minimum stay on Fri and Sat. Mon–Thurs & Sun **£125**, Fri & Sat **£195**

The Front Rooms 9 Tower Parade, CT5 2BJ ☎07738 013768, ⓦthefrontrooms.co.uk. The three guest rooms in this B&B – a Victorian townhouse near Long Beach – are soothingly stylish, decorated in pale, heritage hues. One

en-suite room with balcony, and two with shared shower; you won't have to share with strangers. A continental breakfast is brought to your room. Two-night minimum stay on Fri and Sat. Mon–Thurs & Sun **£130**, Fri & Sat **£120**

Hotel Continental 29 Beach Walk, CT5 2BP ☎01227 280280, ⓦhotelcontinental.co.uk. The 1930s *Hotel Continental*, the only hotel in town, has a relaxed atmosphere and a peaceful location overlooking the sea at the start of the path to Tankerton. The rooms, all different, are being refurbished with a seasidey vibe, and you get great sunset views from the bar/bistro. Rooms with sea views are almost twice the price of those quoted here. Rates include a good buffet breakfast. **£85**

Sleeperzzz 30 Railway Ave, CT5 1LH ☎01227 636975, ⓦsleeperzzz.net. Though it doesn't look like much from the outside, and the location near the train station has more convenience than wow factor, *Sleeperzzz* B&B offers good value and a friendly welcome, with three large, comfortable, clean en-suite rooms decorated with a dash of seaside style. Continental breakfast included; full breakfast £5 extra. **£75**

2

WHITSTABLE NATIVES: THE WORLD'S YOUR OYSTER

Few molluscs have as much romantic allure as the **oyster**: unadorned, raw food redefined as a delicacy and attributed with aphrodisiac powers. For seafood fans, tucking into a half-dozen oysters is an essential part of any trip to Whitstable – ideally slurped down raw with a dash of Tabasco and a squeeze of lemon, accompanied by a crisp white wine or a hearty local stout – but their resurgence as a local icon is relatively recent. The shallow Swale estuary, fed by nutrient-rich brackish water from the marshy coast, has long been an ideal breeding ground for the bivalves, which are thought to have been eaten around here as far back as Neanderthal times. Certainly the Romans were so taken by their delicate flavour that they towed them by sea back to Italy, and the industry as we know it began in earnest in the Middle Ages. By the mid-nineteenth century Whitstable had close to one hundred oyster dredgers, with the heavy, rocky-shelled "Whitstable Native" oysters being shucked in their millions and sent up the river to Billingsgate fish market in London. Though for centuries oysters were largely seen as poor people's food, in 1894 the Whitstable Oyster Company received the royal warrant to supply Native oysters to the queen. The twentieth century saw a run of bad luck – disease and overfishing, bad winters and big freezes – and by the 1970s oysters had fallen out of fashion, until the opening of the *Whitstable Oyster Company* restaurant (see p.86) in the 1990s saw the tide turn once more. Note that **Whitstable Natives** are strictly in season from September to March only; outside these months you may find yourself eating the perennial **Pacific oyster** – a larger, prolific breed, some of which are cultivated on the seabed and some of which are dredged wild. Occasionally, when the crop has been particularly bad, oysters have even been imported in order to meet demand.

EATING

Whitstable is one of the best places to eat in Kent, with a scene that extends beyond oysters and seafood into a relaxed and very good neighbourhood bistro scene. Many restaurants close surprisingly early – for all its pockets of sophistication, this is a sleepy place at heart – and opening hours may change during the off-season or at quiet times, when it's an idea to call ahead. There's a **farmers' market**, with lots of organic produce, at St Mary's Hall, on Oxford Street, every second and fourth Saturday of the month (9.30am–2pm).

CAFÉS AND DELIS

Café and Kitchen 61 Harbour St, CT5 1AG ☎01227 276941. Cute and informal café serving tasty home-made breakfasts, brunches and lunches (rarebits, pies, quiches, salads – also available to take away) and hosting themed suppers and pop-ups. Wed–Sat 10am–3pm & 6–9pm, Sun 10am–4pm.

The Cheese Box 60 Harbour St, CT5 1AG ☎01227 273711, ⓦthecheesebox.co.uk. Heaven for turophiles, specializing in British farmhouse and artisan cheeses to take away. On Fri and Sat evenings you can eat in, dropping in for a cheese platter or a fondue with a glass of local wine, beer or cider. Wed & Thurs 10am–5pm, Fri & Sat 10am–9.30pm, Sun 11am–4.30pm.

David Brown 28a Harbour St, CT5 1AH ☎01227 274507, ⓦdavidbrowndeli.co.uk. Excellent little deli with Mediterranean flair, selling posh store-cupboard staples plus pastries, savoury tarts, sausage rolls, charcuterie, cheese and flavour-packed salads, along with superb coffee. You can eat in, in the tiny attached café – breakfast is popular, while lunch (from £6) might feature antipasti plates or fresh pasta. On sunny days the two outdoor tables are highly prized. Mon–Sat 8am–5pm, Sun 8am–4pm.

★ **Elliott's** 1 Harbour St, CT5 1AG ☎01227 276608, ⓦno1harbourstreet.co.uk. At a glance you'd have this pegged as a cheery neighbourhood café – which indeed it is – but the quality of the ingredients, and the tempting menu, elevates the food to something special. Breakfasts range from porridge with brown sugar to scrambled eggs and smoked pancetta on sourdough; at lunch you could try pan-fried crevettes with garlic; whole baked camembert; a burger; or the best crab sandwiches in town (£6.95). The evening menu changes regularly (mains from £12), but typical choices include lemon sole, rump of veal or cauliflower velouté with truffle oil. Mon–Wed 8am–4pm (later in summer), Thurs–Sat 8am–4pm & 7–11pm, Sun 9am–4pm (later in summer).

The Forge Chandlers Way, Sea Wall, CT5 1BX ☎01227 280280, ⓦwhitstablefishermanshuts.com/the-forge. This rickety little shack, an oyster-shell's throw from the beach, is a real crowd-pleaser, with day-trippers enjoying Whitstable oysters (from £1.50 each), lobster and chips (£13.50) and glasses of chilled white wine rubbing shoulders with families refuelling on mugs of tea and piping hot fresh doughnuts (five for £2.50). Local beers, too, plus ice cream. Sit at communal picnic tables, or bag a deckchair. Opening days and hours are weather dependent – they'll open in good weather for most of the day and sometimes into the night; if you're coming in winter, call ahead. Daily, depending on weather.

Whitstable Produce Store 33 Harbour St, CT5 1AJ ☎ 01227 277643, ⓦ whitstableproduce.co.uk. Friendly grocer-cum-deli specializing in Kent produce, with farm-fresh fruit and veg, juices and smoothies, home-made sausage rolls, quiches and tempting cakes. You can also eat in. Mon–Fri 9am–5pm, Sat 9am–6pm, Sun 10am–5pm.

Windy Corner Stores 110 Nelson Rd, CT5 1DZ ☎ 01227 771707, ⓦ facebook.com/windycornerstoresandcafe. Homely neighbourhood grocery shop/café, where locals gather to enjoy coffee and home-made cakes, read the papers and chat; there are a couple of outdoor tables on the quiet residential street, and it's all very informal. The menu, freshly prepared with local ingredients, is short but tempting. Breakfasts (£3–7) include a great full veggie option or a bacon sarnie, while lunch extends to creative salads, sandwiches and daily specials (from £7) – roast pepper and lentil gratin, say, or rump steak with coconut rice and Thai salad. Mon–Fri & Sun 8am–4.30pm, Sat 8am–5pm.

RESTAURANTS

East Coast Dining Room 101 Tankerton Rd, CT5 2AJ ☎ 01227 281180, ⓦ eastcoastdiningroom.co.uk. Fine dining without fuss at this pared-down restaurant in an unlovely spot on a busy road. The accomplished food is hearty, but not heavy – you might see leek and cider soup with crumbed quail egg; roast mallard breast; or salt cod and chorizo beignets, with perhaps a whisky-and-treacle tart for pud. Mains start at around £17, but there's a great-value two-/three-course set lunch menu for £12.95/£16.95. Wed noon–2.30pm, Thurs & Fri noon–2.30pm & 6.30–9.30pm, Sat noon–3pm & 6.30–9.30pm, Sun noon–4pm.

JoJo's 2 Herne Bay Rd, Tankerton, CT5 2LQ ☎ 01227 274591, ⓦ jojosrestaurant.co.uk. With a breezy sea-view terrace atop Tankerton slopes, *JoJo's* is a great option. The coffee shop offers cakes, juices, fresh salads and gourmet sandwiches (from £4.50), while the back-room restaurant buzzes with happy diners feasting on Mediterranean sharing plates (from £4; up to £35 for a mixed plate) and gazing out at the sea. Good choices might include grilled cod cheeks with white-wine butter, risotto balls with pea and mint, or chargrilled sardines with chorizo. Reservations recommended for dinner; cash only. Coffee shop Tues–Sun 9am–5pm; restaurant Wed (school hols only) 6.30–11pm, Thurs–Sat 12.30–3pm & 6.30–11pm, Sun 12.30–3pm.

The Oxford 27a Oxford St, CT5 1DB ☎ 01227 265717, ⓦ theoxfordwhitstable.co.uk. Appealing bistro serving

accomplished Modern British food in a lively, elbow-to-elbow dining room with a courtyard garden. Seasonal dishes run the gamut from risotto of slow-braised beef shin with Gouda to hake with brown shrimp, orange and spring onion, plus burgers at lunch and generous Sunday roasts. Mains from £11 at lunch, £15 at dinner; mid-week two-course lunch/dinner £13.95/£16.95, both including a drink. Wed & Thurs noon–2.30pm & 6–9pm, Fri noon–2.30pm & 6–9.30pm, Sat noon–3pm & 6–9.30pm, Sun noon–3pm.

Pearson's Arms by Richard Phillips Horsebridge Rd, CT5 1BT ☎ 01227 773133, ⓦ pearsonsarmsbyrichardphillips .co.uk. In a prime location right by the shingle, this is a restaurant in a pub rather than a gastropub per se; local celeb chef Phillips produces gutsy Modern European food, served here in a warmly weatherbeaten first-floor room with gorgeous sea views. The locally sourced, seasonal menu – Sussex goat's cheese parfait with roasted beets, maybe, or pan-fried bass with clam and cockle chowder – is wholesome and good (mains from £12.50; two-/three-course Mon–Sat lunch menu £13/£15). Mon noon–2.30pm, Tues–Sat noon–2.30pm & 6.30–9.30pm, Sun noon–7pm.

Samphire 4 High St, CT5 1BQ ☎ 01227 770075, ⓦ samphirewhitstable.co.uk. This welcoming bistro – all timeworn wood, bright cushions, fairy lights and fresh flowers – has been serving locally sourced Modern British food for nearly a decade. Mains, from £12, might include baked aubergine with rose harissa, fregola and pomegranate; roast duck breast with smoked fennel; or mussels with Biddenden cider. Mon–Thurs & Sun 10am–9.30pm, Fri & Sat 8.30am–10pm.

★ **The Sportsman** Faversham Rd, Seasalter, CT5 4BP ☎ 01227 273370, ⓦ thesportsmanseasalter.co.uk. The dull pub exterior belies the Michelin-starred experience within: *The Sportsman* gastropub, in a lonesome spot between marshes and beach four miles west of Whitstable, serves faultless, deceptively simple food. This is local sourcing to the extreme: fresh seafood, of course, plus lamb from the marshes, meat and veg from farms down the road, seaweed from the beach, bread and butter made right here – even the salt comes from the sea outside. Start, perhaps, with salt-baked celeriac, apple and fresh cheese (£9.95), and follow with thornback ray with brown butter, razor clams and sherry vinegar dressing (mains from £19) – or splash out on the £65 tasting menu (book in advance). Tues–Sat noon–2pm & 7–9pm, Sun 12.30–2.45pm.

Tower Hill Tea Gardens Tower Hill, CT5 2BW ☎ 01227 281726. A delightful spot towards Tankerton, across the road from but officially part of Whitstable Castle garden. The tearoom in the castle itself, the *Orangery*, may be smarter, but on a sunny day this simple thatched hut has the edge, offering mugs of tea, ice creams, sarnies and snacks, in a shady, flower-filled

2

WHITSTABLE FESTIVALS

Based on a medieval thanksgiving ritual, the annual **Whitstable Oyster Festival** (Ⓦ whitstableoysterfestival.co.uk), held for ten days or so at the end of July, is a high-spirited, very crowded, affair. There are food stalls, oyster eating competitions, parades, live music, exhibitions and loads of kids' activities, with a traditional "Landing of the Oysters" ceremony at Long Beach, blessing the first catch of the season. Quite different is the highly regarded **Whitstable Biennale**, a week or so of experimental art, film, theatre and performance, held in June, and next due in 2018 (Ⓦ whitstablebiennale.com).

garden with glorious sea views. April–Oct daily 10am–5pm, depending on weather.

V.C. Jones 25 Harbour St, CT5 1AH ☎ 01227 272703, Ⓦ vcjones.co.uk. Friendly chippie, run by the same family since 1962, with a reassuringly unreconstructed old-timers' dining room at the back and takeaway at the front. From £8.50 for a huge portion, more if you add mushy peas and all the trimmings, and around half that for takeaway. Cash only. Tues–Thurs 11.30am–8pm, Fri & Sat 11.30am–9pm, Sun noon–5pm.

★**Wheelers Oyster Bar** 8 High St, CT5 1BQ ☎ 01227 273311, Ⓦ wheelersoysterbar.com. A Whitstable institution, dating back to 1856 – and not related to Marco Pierre White's London oyster bar of the same name – this is a quiet contender for the best fish restaurant in Kent. It's an informal and friendly old place, with a tiny back parlour and a few stools at the (invariably sociable) fish counter at the front. The inventive, super-fresh seafood is stunning, whether you go for tapas (John Dory ceviche with white crab salad; devilled herring roe on hot buttered toast; steamed prawn dumplings; £7–9), half a dozen oysters

(£6–13) or more substantial mains like caramelized scallops with Parma ham, pickled cucumber, cauliflower purée and a pea and ham fritter. They offer takeaway, too, including delicious flans. BYO (no corkage); cash only; reservations recommended. Mon & Tues 10.30am–9pm, Thurs 10.15am–9pm, Fri 10.15am–9.30pm, Sat 10am–10pm, Sun 11.30am–9pm.

Whitstable Oyster Company Horsebridge Rd, CT5 1BU ☎ 01227 276856, Ⓦ whitstableoystercompany .com. With the best location in town, in the Victorian Oyster Stores building by the beach, the "oyster house" opened in 1989 and put Whitstable on the foodie map. Many former fans have moved on, put off by the high prices, but this remains a lovely spot for a treat, serving perfect, simply prepared fish – from roast gilthead bream with garlic and rosemary to smoked eel with creamed horseradish – in a sun-warmed (or candlelit) room with bare brick walls and checked tablecloths. Mains from £15; half a dozen local oysters £16. Mon–Thurs noon–3pm & 6.30–9pm, Fri noon–3pm & 6.30–9.30pm, Sat noon–9.45pm, Sun noon–8.30pm.

DRINKING AND NIGHTLIFE

Whitstable's nightlife revolves around its **pubs**, with a handful of places hosting excellent **live music**. Microbrews from the **Whitstable Brewery** (run by the people behind the *Oyster Company* restaurant, but based in a village some miles away; Ⓦ whitstablebrewery.co.uk) are well worth trying – the oyster stout in particular is good, with a dark, chocolatey taste that goes down very well with the town's most famous snack.

★**Black Dog** 66 High St, CT5 1BB Ⓦ facebook.com/ TheBlackDog13. Don't be daunted by the vaguely Goth exterior – this quirky, cluttered little micropub, with something of the feel of an old gin palace, is all heart, with the focus on the (mainly) Kentish ales, ciders and wines, the inexpensive local snacks, and the friendly regular crowd. No cards, no vaping and no children. Mon–Wed noon–11pm, Thurs–Sun noon–midnight.

★**Duke of Cumberland** High St, CT5 1AP ☎ 01227 280617, Ⓦ thedukeinwhitstable.co.uk. This roomy central pub, with cool music-themed decor and a pretty beer garden, has a name for its live music (Sat evening and Sun afternoon, with DJs on Fri) – an impeccable programme from jazz, folk and blues to soul, big bands and retro pop. They have rooms, too (see p.83). Mon–Thurs 11am–11pm, Fri & Sat 11am–midnight, Sun noon–7pm.

Old Neptune Marine Terrace, CT5 1EJ ☎ 01227 272262, Ⓦ thepubonthebeach.co.uk. A white weatherboard landmark standing alone on the beach, the "Neppy" is the perfect spot to enjoy a sundowner at a picnic table on the shingle, gazing out across the Swale to the Isle of Sheppey, or to hunker down with a pint in the compact tongue-and-groove interior after a bracing beach walk. Some real ales, plus live acoustic music at the weekend. Mon–Wed 11.30am–10.30pm, Thurs–Sat 11.30am–11.30pm, Sun noon–10.30pm.

Peter Cushing 16–18 Oxford St, CT5 1DD ☎ 01227 284100, Ⓦ jdwetherspoon.com. Quite extraordinary: a vast Wetherspoon's pub in a 1930s cinema, with a soaring, opulent Art Deco interior filled with retro movie memorabilia and Cushing paraphernalia. Join locals and old-timers for its inexpensive beer and grub and soak up the old-school glamour. Mon–Thurs & Sun 8am–11pm, Fri & Sat 8am–11.30pm.

★**The Twelve Taps** 102 High St, CT5 1AZ 📞01227 770777, 🌐thetwelvetaps.co.uk. This welcoming, café-bar-style craft beer place, with a little back garden,

offers a rotating selection of twelve keykeg beers, plus speciality gins, wine, cider and coffee, and sparkling wine on tap. Try the beer flight – three third-pints for £5. No children after 6pm. Tues–Sat noon–11pm, Sun noon–10pm.

ENTERTAINMENT

Horsebridge Arts Centre 11 Horsebridge Rd, CT5 1AF 📞01227 281174, 🌐horsebridge-centre.org.uk. With a gallery and café, and lots of community events, this splendid arts centre also hosts acoustic gigs, theatre, comedy and movie screenings. Mon–Sat 9am–6pm, Sun

10am–5pm; performances from 7pm.
Whitstable Playhouse 104 High St, CT5 1AZ 📞01227 272042, 🌐playhousewhitstable.co.uk. Variety, dance, movies, drama and music at this local theatre in a converted church.

2

SHOPPING

Whitstable is a great place for shopping, with **Harbour Street** in particular known for its shabby-seaside-chic boutiques and vintage stores. The rest of the high street, while slightly less hip, has far more character than most, with barely a chain to be seen.

★**Anchors Aweigh** 63 Harbour St, CT5 1AG 📞01227 263647, 🌐facebook.com/anchorsaweighvintage. This little closet of a vintage store is always worth a browse for saucy seaside postcards, textiles, homewares, furniture, frocks and men's jackets, mainly from the mid-twentieth century, and all at good prices. Mon 10am–3pm, Thurs 10am–4pm, Fri & Sat 10am–5pm, Sun 11am–4pm.
Frank 65 Harbour St, CT5 1AG 📞01227 262500, 🌐frankworks.eu. Colourful, creative and contemporary British graphic design and crafts, with handmade ceramics, prints, jewellery, cards and stationery, in a light, airy store. Mon, Tues, Thurs & Fri 10.30am–5pm, Sat 10.30am–5.30pm, Wed & Sun 11am–5pm.
Harbour Books 21 Harbour St, CT5 1AQ 📞01227 264011. Two floors of novels, local titles and books on art, politics, travel and photography, many discounted, along with cards and gifts. Mon–Sat 9.30am–5.30pm, Sun 10.30am–5.30pm.
Harbour Market South Quay, Whitstable Harbour, CT5 1AB 🌐harbourmarketwhitstable.co.uk. A colony of fishermen's huts on the harbour, populated by around thirty local retailers – mostly food and drink stalls, but with crafts and gifts too. March–Oct Mon, Thurs & Fri 11am–5pm, Sat & Sun 10am–5pm; Nov–Feb some stalls open on occasional days.

Keam's Yard On the shingle near the Horsebridge, CT5 1BU 📞07970 633112, 🌐facebook.com/KeamsYard. Artist Bruce Williams' freestanding little workshop, facing the sea, exhibits quirky and interesting work in all media, much of it seaside-related, at good prices. Usually daily 11am–5pm.
Oxford Street Books 20a Oxford St, CT5 1DD 📞01227 281727, 🌐oxfordstreetbooks.com. Sprawling place selling a great selection of secondhand and antiquarian books, with out-of-print and rare titles sharing shelves with 95p paperbacks. July & Aug Mon–Fri 9.30am–5pm, Sat 9am–5pm, Sun 11am–4pm; Sept–June Mon, Tues & Thurs–Sat 9.30am–5pm.
★**Valentines** 21 Oxford St, CT5 1DB 📞01227 281224, 🌐valentines-vintage.com. The perfect vintage furnishings store, selling good-looking, high quality, handpicked homewares, ceramics and glass, from the 1950s to the 1970s, at competitive prices. Mon–Sat 10am–5.30pm, Sun 11am–4pm.
★**The Whiting Post** 57 Harbour St, CT5 1HW 📞01227 275900, 🌐thewhitingpost.com. Colourful, feminine and whimsical womenswear store, with an irresistible selection of vintage-style frocks, accessories and shoes from brands including Saltwater, Seasalt, Lotta's and Noa Noa, plus homewares from the likes of Orla Kiely. A few men's clothes, too. Mon–Fri 9.30am–6pm, Sat 9.30am–6.30pm, Sun 10.30am–5.30pm.

CYCLING AROUND WHITSTABLE

The 7.5-mile **Crab and Winkle Way** (🌐crabandwinkle.org), following the old steam railway line to Canterbury (see box, p.60), is a popular cycling – and walking – route from Whitstable (though it's a little easier doing it in reverse), as is the enjoyable **Oyster Bay Trail**, a traffic-free seaside path that follows the coast round from Swalecliffe, just beyond Tankerton, to Herne Bay and Reculver Country Park (6.7 miles in total). From here you can hook up with Thanet's 32-mile-long **Viking Coastal Trail** (see p.30), which takes you along the shore to Birchington, Margate, Broadstairs and Ramsgate.

2

Herne Bay and around

The holiday destination of choice for Bertie Wooster's long-suffering butler Jeeves in the P.G. Wodehouse stories, **HERNE BAY** keeps a lower profile than the other seaside towns on Kent's north coast. Most of the appeal is on the seafront, where a two-mile prom fringes a typically British combination – caffs, ice-cream parlours, tourist shops and run-down amusements, alongside enormous bow-fronted houses, abundant flower gardens and a bandstand that recall the town's heyday as a Victorian resort. There's a stubby pier, with safe swimming nearby, and in summer the shingly beach is dotted with families. Look out to sea and you'll see the former end of the pier, marooned in the waves since a storm in 1978. Further out still are the menacing outlines of the **Maunsell Forts** – World War II anti-aircraft structures, long since abandoned to the elements. The waters around here are good for **jet-skiing**, and there are clubs in town devoted to dinghy sailing (wⓗhpyc.org.uk) and family-friendly sailing, canoeing and kayaking (wⓗhernebaysailingclub.co.uk). The main reason to come, however, is to take the invigorating walk to the **Reculver towers**.

Reculver Country Park

Reculver Lane, CT6 6SS • Visitor centre March, Sept & Oct Sat & Sun 11am–4pm; April–Aug Mon, Tues, Thurs & Fri 10am–4pm, Sat & Sun 11am–4pm • Free • ☎ 01227 740676, ⓦ kentwildlifetrust.org.uk/reserves/reculver-visitor-centre-and-country-park

From Herne Bay you can take a glorious coastal walk along the Saxon Shore Way, or a cycle along the Oyster Bay Trail, to the twelfth-century **Reculver towers**, three miles east in **Reculver Country Park**. The park – an area of flat, fossil-flecked beaches and dramatically eroding soft sandstone cliffs topped with velvety meadows – is remarkably peaceful, with only the sound of waves crashing beneath you and wide-open views across to Thanet stretching ahead. It attracts many migratory birds; you can check recent sightings at the visitor centre, which also fills you in on local history, in particular Reculver's fame as the testing ground for the bouncing bombs used by the World War II Dam Busters. From the towers it's another appealing walk or cycle of around four miles along the Viking Coastal Trail to **Minnis Bay**, where there's a sandy Blue Flag beach and good kitesurfing.

Reculver towers

Reculver, CT6 6SS • Daylight hours • Free; EH. Pay-and-display car park not owned by EH • ☎ 01227 740676, ⓦ www.english-heritage .org.uk/visit/places/reculver-towers-and-roman-fort

The flat-topped twin **Reculver towers** make a dramatic display on the clifftop, silhouetted against the sky. Built on the site of a Roman fort that protected the Wantsum Channel – which once separated Thanet from the mainland – the towers are pretty much all that remains of a twelfth-century remodelling of an earlier Anglo-Saxon monastery church. They were the only part of the structure to escape demolition in 1805 – by which time most of the local village had been abandoned due to drastic coastal erosion – and were kept here as navigational aids. Crouching low behind them are some rather more decrepit remains of the original church, bitten away by centuries of weather.

ARRIVAL AND DEPARTURE   HERNE BAY AND AROUND

By train The station is on Station Rd, on the south side of town; it's a 12min walk up Pier Ave or Station Rd to the sea.

Destinations Broadstairs (every 10–30min; 22min); Faversham (every 10–40min; 15min); London St Pancras (hourly; 1hr 25min); London Victoria (hourly; 1hr 30min); Margate (every 10–30min; 15min); Ramsgate (every 10–30min; 30min); Whitstable (every 10–45min; 7min).

By bus Buses from Canterbury (every 15min; 35min) and Margate (hourly; 50min) stop on the high street, a couple of blocks back from the seafront.

INFORMATION AND GETTING AROUND

Tourist information There's a small info centre in the clock tower at 81 Central Parade (Fri & Sun noon–2pm, plus occasional Sats; ⓦ clocktowerfriends.org), and some Herne Bay information on ⓦ canterbury.co.uk/herne-bay.

Bike rental *Le Petit Poisson* (see below) is the Herne Bay HQ for Kent Cycle Hire (see p.52); you can drop off your bike here or in Whitstable or Canterbury.

EATING AND DRINKING

★A Casa Mia 60 High St, CT6 5AJ ☎01227 372947, ⓦ acasamia.co.uk. This humble old-style pizzeria, the first in the UK to be approved by the rigorous Associazione Verace Pizza Napoletana, serves the best wood-fired pizza you'll get this side of Naples – authentically soft, charred and pliable, full of simple, good, Italian flavours, and a snip at £5–11. They also cook up a mean risotto and fresh pasta, but it's the pizza that steals the show. Takeaway available. Mon–Thurs & 11pm, Fri & Sat noon–3.30pm & 5–11.30pm, Sun noon–10pm.

Le Petit Poisson Pier Approach, Central Parade, CT6 5JN ☎01227 361199, ⓦ lepetitpoisson.co.uk. Don't be misled by the plain exterior – inside, the wooden-floored and brick-walled dining room, particularly appealing at sunset, is a relaxed setting for excellent seafood. The menu changes according to the seasons, but you might see sea bream with spicy crab cake, mussels in Kentish cider, or salt-cod fritters with hazelnuts; wash it all down with a cold dry white from Kent's own Chapel Down

vineyard. Mains from £14. Tues–Fri noon–2.30pm & 6.30–9pm, Sat noon–3pm & 6.30–9.30pm, Sun noon–3.30pm.

Oyster and Chop House 8 High St, CT6 5LH ☎01227 749933, ⓦ oysterandchophouse.co.uk. Small restaurant using local suppliers and mostly organic ingredients. The regularly changing menu is particularly strong on meat and fish – mallard with beetroot or Dover sole with red quinoa are typical. Lunch starters £5.95, mains £12.95; dinner £7.95/£16.95 Wed–Sat noon–2pm & 6.30–9pm, Sun noon–2pm.

Wallflower The Mall, 116 High St, CT6 5JY ☎01227 740392, ⓦ wallflowercatering.co.uk. The setting isn't inspiring, but the home-made veggie/vegan food in this casual boho bistro is great. Most ingredients are sourced locally, and it's all delicious, from the generous breakfasts to the colourful, superfood-packed salads to the raw lemon cheesecake; unusually, they offer lots of coeliac choices. Takeaway available. Mon–Sat 9am–5pm.

Isle of Thanet

Fringed by low chalk cliffs and sandy bays, the fist of land at Kent's northeastern corner, the **Isle of Thanet** (ⓦ visitthanet.co.uk), may now be attached to the mainland, but still has the feel of a place apart. That's not to say it's inaccessible – it's just ninety minutes from London by train, with regular transport connections to Canterbury and Dover – but taken together, the resorts of **Margate**, **Ramsgate** and **Broadstairs** have a distinct personality of their own. Having developed as seaside getaways in the eighteenth and nineteenth centuries, by the mid-twentieth century Thanet's sandy beaches had become the favoured bucket-and-spade destinations for Londoners seeking seaside fun. The arrival of cheap foreign holidays put paid to those glory days, but each town clings to its traditional attractions to varying degrees. There is a whiff of nostalgia about them all, from Broadstairs' quaint cobbled streets and old wooden pier to Margate's kiss-me-quick charms. J.M.W. Turner, who spent much of his time in Margate, said the Thanet skies were "the loveliest … in all Europe", and watching the sun set over the sea from one of its many glorious **beaches** – seven of which have Blue Flag status – it's hard to disagree.

THE THANET BEACHES

Thanet's chalk coastline, starting with Minnis Bay in the west and curving all the way round to Ramsgate Sands, features more than a dozen fine bays and clean, safe, sandy **beaches**. We've only covered the major beaches in this chapter, but each of them is worth visiting. All are accessible from the Thanet Coastal Path, or, by bike on the Viking Coastal Trail, and you could feasibly walk from Margate to Broadstairs, and then on to Ramsgate, at sea level – but you'd need to check the tides carefully. For more, see ⓦ thanetcoast.org.uk.

2

Margate and around

"There is something not exactly high class in the name of Margate. Sixpenny teas are suggested, and a vulgar flavour of shrimps floats unbidden in the air."

Marie Corelli, novelist, 1896

While the sixpenny teas and whiff of shrimps may have long gone, there is still something "not exactly high class" about **MARGATE**, a quirky resort that relishes eccentricity, nostalgia and brash seaside fun. As England's earliest seaside resort – in 1736 the country's first seawater baths were opened here, starting a craze for sea bathing and cures (among them a tasty concoction of seawater mixed with milk) – Margate grew in importance to score a number of firsts, including the first canopied bathing machines in 1750, seaside boarding house in 1770, donkey rides in 1790, and beach deck-chairs in 1898. At its peak, thousands of London workers were ferried down the Thames every summer to fill the beaches of "merry Margate", and on a fine weekend the place still throngs with day-trippers enjoying fish and chips, candyfloss and sandcastle-building. As elsewhere along the British coast, the arrival of cheap overseas holidays in the 1970s ushered in long decades of decline; today, though the poverty of those years has left its mark, the tide in Margate is turning. Following the opening of the spectacular **Turner Contemporary** in 2011, a stream of artists and creatives was drawn to Margate by the faded seaside charm, the glorious skies so beloved of Turner, and the low rents. Concentrated initially in the pretty **Old Town**, the artsy buzz – which fuels some cutting-edge indie galleries, scores of **vintage shops** and an increasingly good food scene – is slowly spreading. That irresistible energy – and not forgetting those huge, clean sandy **beaches** – has made Margate a must-see once more.

Turner Contemporary

Rendezvous, CT9 1HG • Tues–Sun 10am–6pm • Free • ☎ 01843 233000, ⓦ turnercontemporary.org

Rearing up on the east side of the harbour, the angular, opalescent **Turner Contemporary** gallery is a landmark on the seafront. Named for J.M.W. Turner (who went to school in

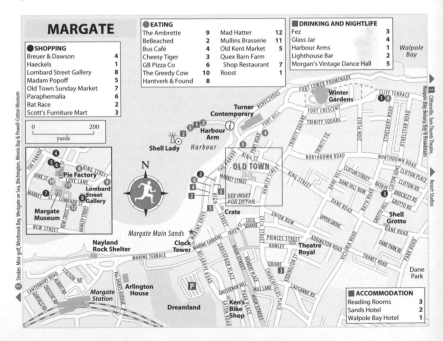

the Old Town in the 1780s, and who returned frequently as an adult to take advantage of the dazzling light), the modern gallery is built on the site of the lodging house where he painted some of his famous seascapes – and had a long love affair with his landlady, Mrs Sophia Booth. Inside, in addition to framing fantastic views of the seascape through its enormous windows, the gallery hosts regularly changing exhibitions of high-profile contemporary art, including shows devoted to Turner himself.

Harbour Arm

Margate's Georgian stone pier, or **Harbour Arm**, crooking out into the sea from next to the Turner gallery, is a funky little enclave, with a parade of old coal stores and fishermen's huts housing cafés, bars and artists' studios. It's de rigueur to walk over to the 85ft-high concrete **lighthouse** at the end, where the views across the little harbour and the broad sweep of Margate's beach are fantastic – especially at sunset. The oxidized bronze **"shell lady"** statue gazing out to sea is a homage both to kitsch seaside ornaments and to Mrs Booth, Turner's beloved landlady.

2

Marine Terrace

Fronting the beach, Margate's **Marine Terrace** has a rough-and-ready charm. You can sit in the Victorian **Nayland Rock shelter** where T.S. Eliot stared out to sea and drafted his poem *The Wasteland*. "On Margate Sands. / I can connect / Nothing with nothing", he wrote: who knows what existential angst he might have wrought from the seafront today, with its jangling amusement arcades – the flashy **Flamingo** sign has a dash of sub-Vegas pizzazz – and the towering **Arlington House**, a brutish concrete 1960s housing block that's regarded as a hideous eyesore or a modernist treasure, depending upon your bent. To be fair, a growing number of good restaurants and bars, and the revitalized **Dreamland** amusement park, are bringing new life to this seafront stretch, and, surveyed from the sea or the Harbour Arm, the view of low-slung buildings fringing the long beach is undoubtedly appealing, evoking something of the resort's nineteenth-century heyday.

Dreamland

Marine Terrace/Belgrave Rd, CT9 1XG • April opens for easter, days and hours vary; May & June Sat & Sun, hours vary; July & Aug Mon–Thurs 11am–6pm, Fri 11am–8pm, Sat 11am–9pm, Sun 11am–7pm; Sept to mid-Oct Sat & Sun 11am–5pm; occasional days and events in other months • Free; attractions individually priced – buy tokens for £1 each at the entrance • ⓦ dreamlandmargate.com

Margate's **Dreamland**, which grew from Victorian pleasure gardens to become a wildly popular theme park in the 1920s, the very epitome of brash seaside fun, stood derelict on the seafront for nearly ten miserable years following its closure in 2003. Once a poignant symbol of the town's decline, it has now become the flagbearer for the new, improved Margate – restored in 2015 under the guiding eye of designers Wayne and Geraldine Hemingway, it's a hit with hipsters and hen dos alike. There's more to Dreamland than knowing vintage cool, however. Certainly the look of the place

---

ARTY MARGATE: THE INDIE GALLERIES

While Turner Contemporary rules the roost, Margate has a lot of indie art galleries for a town of its size, most of them artist-led and all of them exhibiting accessible contemporary works in most media. New ones pop up all the time, making use of Margate's interesting abandoned spaces, from butchers' shops to electricity substations, but the following are good bets. Opening days and hours will vary according to what's on.

Crate 1 Bilton Square, High St, CT9 1EE (ⓦ cratespace .co.uk).
Lombard Street Gallery See p.96.
Pie Factory 5 Broad St, Old Town, CT9 1EW

(☎ 01843 294175, ⓦ piefactorymargate.co.uk).
Resort Studios Pettman Building, 50 Athelstan Rd, Cliftonville, CT9 2BH (☎ 01843 449454, ⓦ resortstudios .co.uk).

– old-school **roller disco** and retro **pinball machines**, jaunty **helter skelter** and 1920s wooden **rollercoaster** – plays on beloved memories of the traditional British seaside, but the place offers lots for today's kids, too. From the mermaid and pirate "schools" to the gravity-defeating Barrel of Laughs ride, there's something very sweet about Dreamland. The park also has a full calendar of cool **events**, from LGBT outreach projects and tea dances to music festivals and free gigs; some very big names appear here, from Grandmaster Flash to Slaves.

The beaches

It's not all about art and vintage shopping: even today most of Margate's visitors come to enjoy the sandy beaches. Though the mass community singsongs that were held here in the late nineteenth century are no more, the town beach, **Margate Main Sands**, a glorious golden swathe, is a family-friendly delight, with a tidal pool, kiddy rides and beach volleyball, tennis and football. Quieter **Westbrook Bay**, to the west, offers shallow water that's great for paddling and watersports, especially windsurfing, and an eighteen-hole mini-golf course (Ⓦ strokesadventuregolf.com) nearby.

The Old Town

Margate's hipster reputation was largely spawned in the **Old Town**, a compact area roughly bounded by Hawley Street/Trinity Hill to the east, the waterfront to the west, and the blocks north of New Street up to Northdown Road. This is where Margate began, as a seventeenth-century fishing village, and in its narrow lanes is an energetic concentration of **vintage shops**, galleries and studio spaces, centring on lively little **Market Place**, lined with outdoor cafés.

Margate Museum

Market Place, CT9 1ER • 11am–4pm: May–Sept Sat, Sun & Wed; Oct–April Sat & Sun • £1.50 • ☎ 01843 231213, Ⓦ margatemuseum
.wordpress.com
Secreted away in the old town hall/police station/magistrate's court (built in 1820), the volunteer-run **Margate Museum** is easy to miss but worth seeking out. Enjoyable, if old-fashioned, exhibits illuminate the town's social history, covering a broad range of subjects from early sea bathing to Margate's role in the Dunkirk evacuations.

Shell Grotto

Grotto Hill, CT9 2BU • Easter–Oct daily 10am–5pm; Nov–Easter Sat & Sun 11am–4pm • £4 • ☎ 01843 220008, Ⓦ shellgrotto.co.uk
Discovered, or so the story goes, in 1835, by the children of the Newlove family who were renting the land above it, Margate's mysterious **Shell Grotto** opened as a paying attraction soon after and has been captivating visitors ever since. Resembling a slightly shabby gift shop from the outside, and reached via a short, winding and damp subterranean passageway, the grotto is an extraordinary and rather unsettling sight, its hallways and chambers entirely covered with intricate mosaics made from shells – more than 4.5 million of them, from clams to mussels to oysters, tinted silvery grey and black by the fumes of Victorian gas lamps. The origins and purpose of the grotto, decorated with all manner of symbols and imagery, remain a mystery. Some believe it to be an ancient pagan temple, others a more recent Regency folly, and others still are convinced that the Newloves themselves built it, with a canny eye to the tourist trade. Whatever the truth, were it a hoax it was certainly an elaborate one – transporting and storing all the shells alone would have been a superhuman undertaking, not to mention the many years it would have taken to build such a place, and the impossibility of doing so in secret.

Cliftonville

A climb up from the main town, the clifftop neighbourhood of **Cliftonville** was, in Victorian times, Margate's snooty suburb, and until the 1930s its fashionable sea-facing hotels hosted such illustrious guests as T.S. Eliot, who recuperated from a nervous breakdown here in 1921. During Margate's dark years, Cliftonville declined and became one of the town's more impoverished neighbourhoods, its huge properties given over to bedsits and hostels. Today the creative types are moving in, and though gentrification would be too strong a word for it, it is definitely perking up. There's not a huge amount to see – a striking, deserted 1920s Lido, a clifftop adventure playground and the historic **Walpole Bay Hotel** (see p.94) – but there are a couple of good places to eat, and the sandy beach, **Walpole Bay**, has a Victorian tidal swimming pool. Cliftonville also hosts an excellent **farmers' market** on the last Sunday of the month (Jan–Nov; 10am–1pm).

Botany Bay

Around 2.5 miles east of town, beyond Cliftonville, the Blue Flag **Botany Bay** is the flagship Thanet beach and quite different from others in the Southeast. Its towering chalk stacks, sheared off from the cliffs by narrow, winding sand corridors, create dramatic silhouettes, while the caves, shallow rockpools and stepping stones of creamy white boulders, capped with seaweed moptops, make a veritable seaside play- and fossicking ground.

Powell-Cotton Museum

Quex Park, Birchington, CT7 0BH • Museum & gardens mid-Jan to mid-Dec Tues–Sun 10am–5pm • House April–Oct Tues–Sun 1–4pm • Museum, house & gardens £8.50, gardens only £4 • ☎ 01843 842168, ⊛ quexmuseum.org

As if Margate itself wasn't offbeat enough, the **Powell-Cotton Museum**, in the village of Birchington, five miles west, offers another dose of magnificent eccentricity. Opened in 1896 to house the hunting trophies of Major Percy Powell-Cotton – whose expeditions, made between 1895 and 1939, included such far-flung corners as Abyssinia and Kashmir – this old-fashioned museum is most astonishing for its enormous **wildlife dioramas**. Crammed with staggering numbers of well-preserved and disarmingly expressive creatures, from aardvarks, bongos and dog-faced baboons to snarling tigers and mighty African elephants, these vivid scenes are even more astounding today than when they were made, giving a shocking sense of the abundance of wildlife that humans once took for granted. Highlights in the adjoining world-class **ethnographic collection** include bronze casts from Benin, an Angolan initiation costume woven from tree bark, and fabulous sacred and early Christian Abyssinian paintings.

Several rooms of the Powell-Cotton family home, a Regency mansion, are open to visitors, as are the lovely Victorian **gardens**, with pathways tumbling with abundant plantings and strutting peacocks. It's a great spot for picnics; stock up (or eat a meal) at the estate's excellent **Quex Barn Farm Shop** (see p.95).

Minnis Bay

Five miles west of Margate, near **Birchington**, the big, gently shelving sandy beach at **Minnis Bay** often has space when others get full, despite its many obvious charms. It's popular with kitesurfers, windsurfers and sea canoeists, and has good facilities, including showers and a paddling pool, along with a restaurant-bar on the cliff above.

ARRIVAL AND DEPARTURE
MARGATE AND AROUND

By train Margate's station is near the seafront on Station Rd. Destinations Broadstairs (every 5–30min; 5min); Canterbury (hourly; 30min); Faversham (every 10–30min; 30min); Herne Bay (every 10–30min; 15min); London St Pancras (every 25min–1hr; 1hr 30min); London Victoria (Mon–Sat hourly; 1hr 50min); Ramsgate (every 5–30min; 15min); Whitstable (every 10–45min; 20min).

By bus Buses pull in at the Clock Tower on Marine Terrace. Destinations Broadstairs (every 10–30min; 30min); Canterbury (every 30min; 1hr); Herne Bay (hourly; 50min); London (7 daily; 2hr–2hr 30min); Ramsgate (every 10–15min; 45min).

INFORMATION AND GETTING AROUND

Tourist office The visitor information centre for all Thanet is in the Droit House, Stone Pier, next to the Turner Contemporary (10am–5pm: April–Oct daily; Nov–March Tues–Sat; ☎ 01843 577577, ⓦ visitthanet.co.uk).

By bike Ken's Bike Shop, 28 Eaton Rd, opposite Dreamland's side entrance (shop Mon–Sat 10am–4pm, rental daily 9am–7pm; ☎ 01843 221422, ⓦ kensbikes .co.uk) rents bikes from £15/day (£25 for two days, £30 for three) – with reductions if there are more than one of you – and offers a delivery and collection service. They also cover Broadstairs and Ramsgate.

ACCOMMODATION

★**Reading Rooms** 31 Hawley Square, CT9 1PH ☎ 01843 225166, ⓦ thereadingroomsmargate.co.uk. Stunning boutique B&B set in a handsome, peaceful Georgian townhouse. The three big guest rooms have artfully distressed walls, gorgeous furnishings and huge, luxurious bathrooms; a classy breakfast is served in your room. Two-night minimum at weekends. No children. £160

Sands Hotel 16 Marine Drive, CT9 1DH ☎ 01843 228228, ⓦ sandshotelmargate.co.uk. With an unbeatable location, this airy boutique refurb of an old seafront hotel is a popular choice. The twenty luxe rooms, some of which have balconies and sea views, are soothingly decorated in tasteful cream and black, while the swanky dining room has glorious sunset views – bag a table on the balcony if you can. £130

★**Walpole Bay Hotel** Fifth Ave, Cliftonville, CT9 2JJ ☎ 01843 221703, ⓦ walpolebayhotel.co.uk. This family-run hotel has changed little since Edwardian times, and exudes an air of faded gentility from its pot-plant-cluttered dining room to its vintage trellis-gated lift. Offering a chunk of classic Margate eccentricity – the "living museum" and collection of napery art, for example – it's an old favourite of Tracey Emin, who threw parties here. Rooms vary, but most have sea views, many have small balconies, and all are comfy, clean and well equipped. The occasional wear and tear just adds to the character. £85

EATING

OLD TOWN

The Ambrette 44 King St, CT9 1QE ☎ 01843 231504, ⓦ theambrette.co.uk. Margate's fanciest restaurant doesn't look like much from the outside, but head through the tatty old pub doors to discover superlative modern Indian food served in a serene dining room. Beautifully presented dishes are light and delicately spiced, featuring ingredients not often seen in Indian restaurants – rock samphire, wood pigeon, venison – most of them locally sourced. Starters from £7, mains from £17; pre/post-theatre and lunch menus £19.95 (two courses) and £24.95 (three courses). Mon–Thurs 10am–4pm & 6–9.30pm, Fri–Sun 10am–4.30pm & 5.30–10pm.

The Greedy Cow 3 Market Place, CT9 1ER ☎ 01843 447557, ⓦ thegreedycow.com. Everything in this charming deli, from the mismatched retro decor to the Middle Eastern-accented menu, welcomes you in. Food is healthy and creative – you don't often see home-made tahini on toasted sourdough with red apple, honey and cinnamon on a Kentish breakfast menu – with flatbread sandwiches (from £6.50), tempting salads (£7), pulled pork and gourmet burgers (both from £8). Tues–Fri & Sun (plus Mon in summer) 10am–4pm, Sat 10am–5pm.

★**Hantverk & Found** 18 King St, CT9 1DA ☎ 01843 280454, ⓦ hantverk-found.co.uk. This tiny gallery café is causing quite a stir with its fabulous fresh fish menu, poshed up with on-trend ingredients. From the deliciously simple (local lobster with chilli and garlic; dressed crab with charred sourdough) to the simply delicious (mussels with harissa; clams in dashi miso broth with wakame), you can't go wrong – or just order half a dozen oysters (£9.50) with a glass of Basque Txakoli. Starters from £7, mains £13–20. Thurs noon–4pm & 6.30–9.30pm, Fri & Sat noon–4pm & 6.30–11pm (last orders 10pm), Sun noon–4pm.

Mad Hatter 9 Lombard St, CT9 1EJ ☎ 01843 232626, ⓦ facebook.com/TheMadHatterMargate. One-of-a-kind tearoom, in a crooked seventeenth-century building packed with kitsch royal memorabilia, Margate paraphernalia, stodgy Victoriana and year-round tinsel; the lack of irony makes it all the more appealing. The menu features old-school treats – casseroles, toasties, apple pie with custard – but it's best to concentrate on the cakes and scones. Cash only. Sat 11.30am–5.30pm.

Mullins Brasserie 6 Market Place, CT9 1EN ☎ 01843 295603, ⓦ mullinsbrasserie.co.uk. Lunch at this upscale, comfortable contemporary Caribbean restaurant sees jerk chicken, rotis and Creole mains from £9; more elaborate evening dishes (parmesan- and herb-crusted mahi mahi, say, or curried goat), start at £12. The two-/three-course lunch menu is great value at £12.95/£14.95. Mon–Thurs noon–3pm & 6–9pm, Fri & Sat noon–3pm & 6–9.30pm.

OUTSIDE THE OLD TOWN

BeBeached Harbour Arm, CT9 1AP ☎ 01843 226008, ⓦ bebeached.co.uk. On a sunny day you can't do better than bag an outside table – or a deckchair – under a tropical parasol at this friendly Harbour Arm café. Food is locally sourced, home-made and often organic, with dishes ranging from meatloaf to beetroot tart, sausage cassoulet to halloumi kebabs, plus great brunches. Mains £7–10, slightly more in the evening. Feb–Dec Wed, Thurs & Sun 11am–4.30pm, Fri & Sat 11am–4.30pm & 7.30–9.30pm.

★**Bus Café** 16 Fort Rd, CT9 1HF ☎07936 076737, ⓦthebuscafe.co.uk. The wraps and boxes dished up from this red double-decker bus are really tasty – filled with barbecue chicken, halloumi or courgette steaks, and served with crunchy, fresh salads – and for £6 you can't go wrong. Posh hash browns are also an option for breakfast (£7.50), jumbling rösti and eggs with anything from chorizo to horseradish. Eat on board or, on sunny days, on pre-loved furniture in the quirky junkyard outside, full of dusty treasures. The bus might occasionally be out at a festival, so check their website first. Mon & Fri–Sun noon–4/5pm.

★**Cheesy Tiger** 7–8 Harbour Arm, CT9 1AP ☎01843 448550, ⓦfacebook.com/cheesytigermargate. A *petite tranche* of Europe in the heart of Thanet, this rickety little deli/café/wine bar offers classy tapas, wine and – above all – cheesy dishes, made with the finest ingredients. The menu changes regularly, but you might find tallegio and truffle on toast, rich French onion soup, burrata with pink peppercorn oil or a sinfully unctuous toastie – you could also sit with a simple cheese platter and glass of red gazing across at the sands. Dishes from £6. Thurs noon–10pm, Fri noon–11pm, Sat noon–5pm & 6–11pm, Sun noon–4pm.

★**GB Pizza Co** 14 Marine Drive, CT9 1DH ☎01843 297700, ⓦgreatbritishpizza.com. A Margate must – this buzzing contemporary pizza joint on the seafront, with smiley staff and a lively vibe, dishes up delicious gourmet crispy pizza (from £6) made with ingredients from small producers. Mon–Fri 11.30am–9.30pm, Sat & Sun 10am–9.30pm.

Old Kent Market 8 Fort Hill, CT9 1HD ☎01843 296808, ⓦtheoldkentmarket.com. A great stop if you're after food on the go, this indoor market, in an old cinema near the Turner Contemporary, has stalls selling sushi, Afro-Caribbean curries, pies and more – including a red bus serving Full Englishes, burgers and camembert fondue with organic bread. Daily 8am–8pm.

Roost 19 Cliff Terrace, Cliftonville, CT9 1RU ☎01843 229708, ⓦroostmargate.com. Casual dining with a creative twist in this funky restaurant, where the staple rotisserie chicken is joined by many delicious things – mac and cheese, seaweed salt-and-pepper squid, a "dogster" (lobster and chorizo in a hotdog bun, with sweet potato fries) – all locally sourced. Dishes £7.50–15. Thurs–Sat 10am–3pm & 5.30–9pm, Sun 10am–5pm.

AROUND MARGATE

Quex Barn Farm Shop Restaurant Quex Park, Birchington, CT7 0BB ☎01843 846103, ⓦquexbarn .com. A no-fuss café with small garden, linked to the excellent Quex Park farm shop, one of the best in Kent, selling fabulous produce and deli specialities. Food, much of it organic and sourced from the Quex estate, is wholesome and good, whether it's the fresh-baked bread, the farm's sausages, vegetarian stuffed peppers or slow-roast belly pork. Mains from £10. Mon–Thurs 9am–3pm, Fri 9am–3pm & 6–9pm, Sat 8.30am–4pm & 6–9pm, Sun 9–11.30am & noon–3pm.

DRINKING AND NIGHTLIFE

★**Fez** 40 High St, CT9 1DS. Join an interesting mix of locals in this relaxed and eccentric micropub, stuffed to within an inch of its life with recycled vintage memorabilia, where young mods and old soulboys alike perch on Waltzer ride carriages, barber chairs or cinema seats to enjoy a good chinwag and a pint of real ale or speciality cider. Mon–Sat noon–10.30pm, Sun noon–10pm.

Glass Jar 15 Marine Drive, CT9 1DH ☎ 01843 290448, ⓦtheglassjarmargate.co.uk. With its scrappy furniture, scuffed floorboards and skewiff piano on the wall, this little bar doesn't take itself too seriously, making it a popular local spot for cocktails and dude food. Mon–Wed & Sun noon–midnight, Thurs–Sat noon–1am.

Harbour Arms Harbour Arm, CT9 1JD ☎07776 183273, ⓦharbourarmsmargate.co.uk. Cosy, cluttered micropub, with a nautical, seasalty atmosphere, serving cask ales and ciders to a loyal local crowd. In warm weather the outside benches are at a premium – nursing a pint while watching the sun set over the sea is sheer delight. Mon–Thurs noon–10pm, Fri & Sat noon–11pm, Sun noon–9.30pm.

Lighthouse Bar Harbour Arm, CT9 1JD ☎01843 291153, ⓦlighthousebar.co.uk. This chilled-out bar has a prime spot at the end of the Harbour Arm, with windows overlooking the sea on two sides and more space than its neighbours. Sit outside to enjoy the fresh air, or on a comfy sofa inside; in winter the wood-burning stove keeps things toasty. Live music and DJ nights. Daily noon–midnight; kitchen Mon–Thurs noon–6.30pm, Fri & Sat noon–9.30pm, Sun noon–4pm; hours may change in winter.

Morgan's Vintage Dance Hall 46 High St, CT9 1DS ☎01843 229009, ⓦmorgansmargate.co.uk. Glamorous yet unintimidating old-style ballroom with lovely sea views and a fabulously eclectic programme of live music, club nights (rockabilly to ska via disco) and cabaret. The gorgeous seaview balcony is an unrivalled spot for a sundowner, and you can even enjoy a retro cream tea during the day. The drop-in dance classes, from hip hop to tango, are great fun. Tues–Sun from noon; closing hours vary.

ENTERTAINMENT

Theatre Royal Addington St, CT9 1PW ☎01843 292795, ⓦtheatreroyalmargate.com. This grand old theatre, built in 1787 (but converted in Victorian times) is the second oldest in England. Crowd-pleasers and stand-up comedians share the schedules with challenging, contemporary theatre, dance and opera.

★**Tom Thumb Theatre** 2 Eastern Esplanade, Cliftonville, CT9 2LB ☎01843 221791, ⓦtomthumbtheatre.co.uk. Nostalgic, witty and warm hearted, this is quintessential Margate: a tiny, family-owned rep theatre (just fifty or so seats) in a nineteenth-century coach house, offering cinema clubs, spoken word, live gigs (from bluegrass to electronica) and stand-up, along with straight theatre.

SHOPPING

Margate's shopping scene yields rich pickings, with creative indie shops and pop-ups, once the preserve of the Old Town, spreading into the High Street and Cliftonville. The town is **vintage** heaven, with prices for clothes and furniture far lower than in the big cities.

Breuer & Dawson 7 King St, CT9 1DD ☎01843 225299, ⓦbreuerdawson.com. Though they do have the odd item for women, the focus here is on men's vintage gear, including Hawaiian shirts, 1940s jackets and 501s, in a handsome Old Town shop run by Camden Market alumni. Pricey, but you can find some bargains. Usually Tues–Sun (plus sometimes Mon in summer) 11am–5pm.

Haeckels 18 Cliff Terrace CT9 1RU ☎01843 447234, ⓦhaeckels.co.uk. Margate reaches peak artisan in this exquisite lab/showroom where organic candles, fragrances, teas and beauty products are created by hand from natural ingredients – wild herbs, seaweed, chalk, saltwater – harvested from the Margate coast. Daily 10.30am–5pm.

Lombard Street Gallery 2 Lombard St, CT9 1EJ ☎01843 292779, ⓦlombardstreetgallery.co.uk. The shop at this sunny art gallery sells a very good, original range of postcards, posters, notebooks and crafts, much of it with a seaside, Margate-specific bent. Tues–Sat (plus sometimes Mon in summer) 11am–5pm, Sun noon–4pm.

Madam Popoff 4 King St, CT9 1DA ☎01843 446072, ⓦmadampopoff.com. Charming array of vintage clothes for women, some of them dating back to the 1930s, with an emphasis on glamour and feminine frocks. Tues–Fri & Sun (plus sometimes Mon in summer) 11am–5pm, Sat 11am–6pm.

Old Town Sunday Market Market Place, CT9 1ER ☎07976 051915, ⓦfacebook.com/MargateBazaar2011. Weekly outdoor community market, with stalls selling funky crafts, antique jewellery, upcycled treasures and collectible junk. Easter–Oct Sun 11am–4pm.

Paraphernalia 8 King St, CT9 1DA ☎07534 707105. Intriguing choice of stuff from around 1800 to 1980, including books, prints, furniture, stuffed stoats and saucy postcards – anything you might imagine – in this cut-above junk shop. Mon–Fri & Sun 11am–5pm, Sat 10am–6pm.

Rat Race 32–36 High St, CT9 1DS ☎01843 230397, ⓦratracemargate.co.uk. Mods, soulboys, rude boys and rockers kit themselves out here in classic British gear, new and vintage, including sharp suits, Harringtons and Brutus jeans for the men, and prom dresses, minis and pedal pushers for the women. Mon–Sat 10am–5.30pm, Sun 10am–5pm.

★**Scott's Furniture Mart** Bath Place, CT9 2BN ☎01843 220653, ⓦscottsmargate.co.uk. Whether you're after a shell-encrusted poodle ornament or an old-school board game, you'll find it in this cheery, family-owned flea market, occupying an old ice factory. Also on the premises – which covers three floors and 16,000ft – is Junk Deluxe (Thurs–Sat only; ⓦjunkdeluxe.co.uk), specialists in Midcentury Modern furniture. Mon, Tues & Thurs–Sat 9.30am–1pm & 2–5pm.

Broadstairs and around

The smallest, quietest and most traditional of the Thanet resort towns, unspoiled **BROADSTAIRS** stands on top of the cliff overlooking the golden arc of Viking Bay. At the northern end of the bay, a sixteenth-century timber **pier** curves out from the picturesque cluster of old flint and clapboard buildings that surround its venerable fishing **harbour**; the sandy **beach** alongside, which can only be reached by foot – or by elevator – feels deliciously sheltered from the town above. Up on the cliffs, the neat gardens, ice-cream parlours and seaview terraces of the large Victorian and Regency buildings give the place an almost Mediterranean flavour, while the large

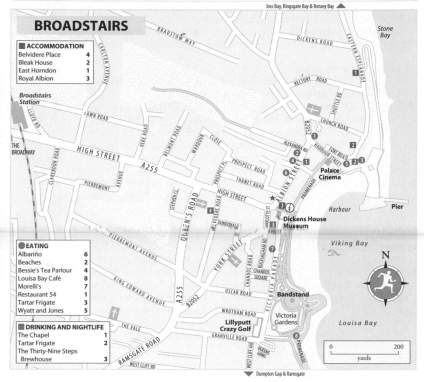

BROADSTAIRS

■ ACCOMMODATION	
Belvidere Place	4
Bleak House	2
East Horndon	1
Royal Albion	3

● EATING	
Albariño	6
Beaches	2
Bessie's Tea Parlour	4
Louisa Bay Café	8
Morelli's	7
Restaurant 54	1
Tartar Frigate	3
Wyatt and Jones	5

■ DRINKING AND NIGHTLIFE	
The Chapel	1
Tartar Frigate	2
The Thirty-Nine Steps Brewhouse	3

bandstand hosts concerts of all kinds, and the kitschy **Lillyputt crazy golf** course offers old-fashioned seaside fun and a nice tea garden (£4.50; ⓦ lillyputt.co.uk). Linked to the prom by tiny alleys, sloping **Albion Street** behind is lined with higgledy-piggledy Georgian buildings housing restaurants, bars and shops.

A fishing village turned popular Victorian resort, Broadstairs still benefits from its location within walking distance of several excellent sandy **bays**. Renowned for its excellent **folk festival**, it also has strong connections with **Charles Dickens**: from 1837 until 1851 the author stayed in various hotels here, and eventually rented an "airy nest" overlooking the sea, where he finished writing *David Copperfield*. A festival and a small **museum** play up the associations, and the house he rented is now open as a B&B.

The bays

Broadstairs' town beach, sandy **Viking Bay**, is a lovely golden crescent at the foot of the cliffs, and accessible, in summer, by lift. Fringed with beach huts, Viking Bay has a surf school (see p.98) and a few children's rides – and gets crowded on hot days. This is just one of seven sandy coves in the vicinity, however; on the northern edge of Broadstairs, walkable from Viking Bay, you'll find **Stone Bay**, where a staircase winds down the wildflower-tangled cliff-face to a curved Blue Flag beach, submerged at high tide. Quieter in summer than Viking Bay, it's great for rockpools and for sunny morning swims. Beyond is **Joss Bay**, another Blue Flag beach which, with its long sands and shallow waters, offers the best surfing in the Southeast – it's home to the **Joss Bay Surf School** (see p.98) – and a refreshments kiosk. Further north are quiet **Kingsgate Bay**, with its sea caves, and best of all, the stunning **Botany Bay** (see p.93).

In the other direction, **Louisa Bay**, easily reached on a sea-level prom from Viking Bay, is a quiet spot beneath cliffs shored up with concrete. Good for rockpooling, it does disappear entirely at high tide, but there's a superb beach caff (see opposite).

Dickens House Museum

2 Victoria Parade, CT10 1QS • Easter to mid-June & mid-Sept to mid-Oct daily 1–4.30pm; mid-June to mid-Sept daily 10am–4.30pm; Nov Sat & Sun 1–4.30pm • £3.75 • ☎ 01843 861232, ⊛ dickensmuseumbroadstairs.co.uk

2 One block back from the clifftop prom, the broad balconied cottage that now houses the **Dickens House Museum** was once the home of Miss Mary Pearson Strong, on whom Dickens based the character of Betsey Trotwood in *David Copperfield*. (In the book, this "house on the cliff", outside which the donkey fights that so angered Miss Trotwood took place, was moved to Dover.) Its small rooms are crammed with memorabilia, including Dickens' letters, illustrations from the original novels, a reconstruction of Betsey Trotwood's parlour, and the author's desk, which he modified to include a rack for six bottles of wine. In addition, Victorian posters, maps, photography and costumes do a splendid job of evoking old Broadstairs.

ARRIVAL AND INFORMATION

By train Broadstairs station is at the west end of the High St, a 10min walk to the seafront.
Destinations Canterbury (hourly; 25min); Faversham (every 10–40min; 35min); Herne Bay (every 10–30min; 22min); London St Pancras (every 25min–hourly; 1hr 20min–1hr 45min); London Victoria (Mon–Sat hourly; 1hr 50min); Margate (every 5–30min; 5min); Ramsgate (every 5–30min; 6min); Whitstable (every 10–45min; 25min).

BROADSTAIRS AND AROUND

By bus Buses stop along the High St.
Destinations Canterbury (hourly; 1hr–1hr 30min); London (7 daily; 2hr 45min–3hr 20min); Margate (every 10–30min; 30min); Ramsgate (every 5–20min; 15min).
Tourist information The nearest tourist office is in Margate (see p.94); there's also a small information kiosk on the Promenade by the *Royal Albion* hotel terrace (⊛ visitthanet.co.uk).

GETTING AROUND AND ACTIVITIES

Bike rental Ken's Bike Shop in Margate (see p.94) also covers Broadstairs and Ramsgate.
Watersports Joss Bay Surf School (lessons from £35; ⊛ jossbay.co.uk), based at the area's prime surfing beach, offers lessons for all levels. Kent Surf School

(⊛ kentsurfschool.co.uk), on Viking Bay, is great for beginners; it rents equipment and runs year-round surfing and stand-up paddleboarding lessons, with kids' three-day summer camps (lessons from £35) and kayaking tours (£45).

ACCOMMODATION

★**Belvidere Place** 43 Belvedere Rd, CT10 1PF ☎ 01843 579850, ⊛ belvidereplace.co.uk. This stylish, quirky boutique B&B, in a gorgeous Regency townhouse, is at once warmhearted and extremely hip, its five rooms featuring sleek bathrooms, cool art and one-off vintage finds. The gourmet breakfasts are superb. **£130**
Bleak House Fort Rd, CT10 1EY ☎ 01843 865338, ⊛ bleakhousebroadstairs.co.uk. An irresistible lure for Dickens fans, who can stay in the castellated house the writer rented for some twenty summers. The four guest rooms are decorated in slightly stuffy Victorian style – the Dickens room (£225) even features a bed in which Queen Victoria slept. **£195**

East Horndon 4 Eastern Esplanade, CT10 1DP ☎ 01843 868306, ⊛ easthorndonhotel.com. Friendly, comfortable, old-school B&B in a large Victorian house overlooking Stone Bay, just a 5min seaside stroll from the centre of Broadstairs. Rooms are large, spruce and well equipped, some with sea views, and there's easy access to the sandy beach opposite. **£86**
Royal Albion 6–12 Albion St, CT10 1AN ☎ 01843 868071, ⊛ albionbroadstairs.co.uk. Grand eighteenth-century sea-facing hotel, now owned by Shepherd Neame, in a central location and with a sociable terrace bar (it's probably best to eat elsewhere, though). Rooms are clean, contemporary and comfortable; the best have sea views and little balconies. **£100**

EATING

Albariño 29 Albion St, CT10 1LX ☎ 01843 600991, ⊛ albarinorestaurant.co.uk. Authentic tapas served in a small, simple room that can get rather full. Cheese or

meat platters start at £12, while the tasty tapas (£2.50–12.50) range from the familiar (tortilla; *gambas*; *padron* peppers) to the more unusual (crab on toast with

BROADSTAIRS FESTIVALS

The town bursts into life each August during **Broadstairs Folk Week** (ⓦbroadstairsfolkweek .org.uk), one of England's longest-standing folk and roots music events, which features big names and up-and-coming singers, bands and dancing, with workshops, kids' events and a spine-tingling torchlight parade. Just slightly less crowded, the **Dickens Festival** (ⓦbroadstairsdickensfestival. co.uk), spread across the third week in June, sees enthusiastic Dickens fans, many of them dressed in Victorian garb, flock through the town enjoying dog shows, Dickens dramatizations, afternoon teas and traditional music hall. In early October, **Broadstairs Food Festival** (ⓦbroadstairsfoodfestival.org.uk) is a three-day foodie event focused on locally sourced produce; there are more than one hundred exhibitors at the fair itself, with demos, tastings and events all around town. There's a smaller version, the **Broadstairs Spring Fair**, at the end of March.

2

pancetta; ox cheek with liquorice and sweet potato), all nicely washed down with a sherry or the eponymous Galician wine. Mon–Thurs 6–9.30pm, Fri 6–10pm, Sat noon–2.30pm & 5–10pm.

Beaches 49 Albion St, CT10 1NE ☎01843 600065, ⓦfacebook.com/beaches.broadstairs. With a surfy vibe and friendly crowd, *Beaches* is a colourful, laidback place with a varied menu. Choose from fresh fruit smoothies, all-day breakfasts, meze platters, veggie chilli, baked Camembert, burritos, big salads and more – all from £4.95. No cards. Easter–Oct Mon–Thurs & Sun 8.30am–6pm, Fri 8.30am–9pm.

Bessie's Tea Parlour 45 Albion St, CT10 1NE ☎01843 600189, ⓦbessiesteaparlour.co.uk. This dinky café, all vintage crockery, fresh flowers and bunting, is the perfect spot for traditional home-baked cakes, scones, pastries and finger sandwiches accompanied by a pot of loose leaf tea. Afternoon teas, of course, are a speciality (from £12.50), including savoury and champagne options. Daily 10am–6pm.

★**Louisa Bay Café** Louisa Bay, CT10 1QE. It doesn't look much, but this beach cabin is a local hit for its fabulous bacon butties (from £3.50), made with the best back bacon and thick fresh bread, and eaten alfresco by the sand; the local sausages and breakfast baguettes are good too, with prime steak burgers, panini and Greek salads for a casual lunch (around £5). Easter–Oct daily 9.30am–4.30pm, weather permitting.

Morelli's 14 Victoria Parade, CT10 1QS ☎01843 862500, ⓦmorellisgelato.com/stores/broadstairs. Deliciously retro, very pink, 1930s ice-cream parlour, whose formica, leatherette and wicker decor, including an Italian water fountain, is a vintage lover's dream – as is the jukebox. Scoops of home-made gelato cost from £2.50,

with all sorts of fancy sundaes for a splurge; order a frothy cappuccino, too, for the full experience. Daily 8am–10pm.

Restaurant 54 54 Albion St, CT10 1NF ☎01843 867150, ⓦrestaurant54.co.uk. Fine Modern British dining served in a soothing, candlelit room. Mains (£15–25) might include cod deep-fried in gin-and-lime batter with pea croquettes; seared Barbary duck breast with orange and mango salad; or roast leek, pine nut and blue cheese Wellington. Mon–Sat 6–9pm, Sun noon–3pm & 6–9pm.

Tartar Frigate Harbour St, CT10 1EU ☎01843 862013, ⓦtartarfrigate.co.uk. Reserve a window table if you can, and enjoy local seafood and sea views in this popular restaurant above a historic harbourside pub (see below). Classic mains, including skate with capers and black butter or lobster thermidor, cost from £17, with meat options for non-pescatarians. Sun lunch sees things go off-piste, with a traditional four-course roast (£19). Mon–Sat noon–1.45pm & 7–9.15pm, Sun seatings at 12.30pm & 3.30pm.

★**Wyatt and Jones** ☎01843 865126, ⓦwyattandjones.co.uk. This place looks great – fresh flowers, scrubbed-wood tables, soothing grey tongue-and-groove, Viking Bay views from the lower dining room – and the Modern British food, all locally sourced, is fantastic. Options run the gamut from anchovy toast or a superb warm crab tart starter to lobster in wild garlic butter; mains (from £18 at dinner, less at lunch, when small plates are also available from £6) might include harissa lamb with smoked aubergine or baked cod in brown butter with cep and marjoram pearl barley. Tasty breakfasts, too, whether you fancy toast and Marmite or eggs Benedict. Wed & Thurs 9–11am, noon–3pm & 6.30–9pm, Fri & Sat 9–11am, noon–3pm & 6–10pm, Sun 9–11am & noon–5pm; sometimes open daily in summer.

DRINKING AND NIGHTLIFE

★**The Chapel** 44 Albion St, CT10 1NE ☎07837 024259. Offbeat, ramshackle alehouse-cum-library in a dimly lit old chapel, with lots of nooks and crannies to curl up with an erudite or obscure used tome while you sip a local ale. Good local pub grub, too, and regular live folk/blues music. Daily 11am–2am (or earlier on quiet nights).

Tartar Frigate Harbour St, CT10 1EU ☎01843 862013, ⓦtartarfrigate.co.uk. By the harbour, with a seafood restaurant (see above) upstairs, this eighteenth-century flint-and-weatherboard pub is a terrific place to spend an evening, especially during one of their folk jam sessions. Regular live music. Mon–Sat 11am–11pm, Sun 11am–10.30pm.

★ **The Thirty-Nine Steps Brewhouse** 11–13 Charlotte St, CT10 1LR. Friendly – and dog-friendly – pub with craft ales on tap and its own on-site brewery. The changing selection of cask ales, fruit ciders and unusual perries is always interesting, and the food is great – excellent cheese platters and home-made pork pies from just £3, much of it sourced from their deli down the road at no. 5. Occasional live acoustic music. No cards. Daily noon–11pm.

ENTERTAINMENT

Palace Cinema Harbour St ☎01843 865726, ⓦthepalacecinema.co.uk. Hidden away at the bottom of Harbour St, in a Grade II-listed 1911 flint building, Broadstairs' tiny indie cinema is a gem, with a programme that ranges from world cinema to crowd-pleasers.

Ramsgate

RAMSGATE is the largest of the Thanet towns, its robust Victorian redbrick architecture and elegant Georgian squares set high on a cliff linked to the seafront by broad, sweeping ramps. Down by the bustling **harbour** (ⓦportoframsgate.co.uk) – Britain's only royal harbour, designated after George IV visited in 1821 – a collection of cafés and bars overlooks the bobbing yachts, endowing the place, in summer at least, with a cosmopolitan buzz. The small, busy **Ramsgate Sands**, a Blue Flag beach complete with children's rides and jet-ski area, lies just a short stroll away. Other sights include the **Maritime Museum**, in the old Clock House on the quayside, which chronicles local maritime history in great detail (Easter–Sept Tues–Sun 10.30am–5.30pm; £2.50; ⓦramsgatemaritimemuseum.org), and the excellent flea market **Petticoat Lane Emporium**, with hundreds of stalls selling arts and crafts, vintage and antiques, on Dumpton Park Drive (Mon–Sat 10am–5pm, Sun 10am–4pm; ☎01843 599005, ⓦpetticoatemporium.com).

Ramsgate Tunnels

Marina Esplanade, CT11 8NA • Tours Wed–Sun 10am, noon, 2pm & 4pm; 1hr • £6.50 • ☎01843 588123, ⓦramsgatetunnels.org

Many mocked when a team of engineers, championed by A.B.C. Kempe, Ramsgate's eccentric mayor, suggested in 1938 that a set of underground train tunnels could be refashioned into air-raid shelters. The scheme went ahead, however, and during a devastating air attack in August 1940 the **Ramsgate Tunnels** – equipped with bunk beds, electric lights and lavatories – saved thousands of lives. After World War II, the tunnels, which had provided safety, warmth and even a sense of makeshift, ragtag community to the many local families made homeless by the war, were closed. **Tours** today explore nearly a mile of largely empty, chilly tunnels, dotted with the odd piece of original memorabilia – though the atmosphere is palpable, it's the stories told by your guide that bring the place alive.

The Grange

St Augustine's Rd, CT11 9NY • Wed 2pm & 3pm, call (6–8pm) to reserve; also occasional open days • £4 • ☎01843 596401, ⓦlandmarktrust.org.uk

The Grange is the former family home of **Augustus Pugin**, best known for designing the interiors of the Houses of Parliament, who lived his last ten years in Ramsgate. Designed by Pugin and built in 1843–44, the house is Gothic Revival in style and filled with dark wood, rich wallpapers and decorative tiles – its emphasis on functional interior layouts over exterior symmetry marked a revolution in house design. Only some of the property is open to the tours, but you could stay here; it's rented out as self-catering accommodation by the Landmark Trust. Pugin and his family are buried at **St Augustine's church**, another of his works, and perhaps his favourite – "my own child", he called it – next door (ⓦwww.augustine-pugin.org.uk).

ARRIVAL AND DEPARTURE   RAMSGATE

By train Ramsgate's station lies about 1.5 miles northwest of the centre, at the end of Wilfred Rd, at the top of the High St.
Destinations Broadstairs (every 5–30min; 6min);

Canterbury (every 20–40min; 20min); Faversham (every 10min–1hr; 40min); Herne Bay (every 10–30min; 30min); London St Pancras (every 10min–1hr; 1hr 15min–1hr 45min); London Charing Cross (hourly; 2hr 10min); London Victoria (Mon–Sat hourly; 2hr); Margate (every 5–30min; 15min); Whitstable (every 10–45min; 35min).
By bus Buses pull in at the harbour.
Destinations Broadstairs (every 5–20min; 15min); Canterbury (hourly; 45min); London (7 daily; 2hr 30min–3hr); Margate (every 10–15min; 45min).

INFORMATION AND GETTING AROUND

Tourist information The nearest official tourist office is in Margate (see p.94) but there's an info point in Customs House, Harbour Parade (daily 10am–4pm; ☎01843 598750, ⓦvisitthanet.co.uk). Another useful resource is ⓦramsgatetown.org.
Bike rental Ken's Bike Shop in Margate (see p.94) also covers Ramsgate and Broadstairs.

ACCOMMODATION

★**Albion House** Albion Place, CT11 8HQ ☎01843 606630, ⓦalbionhouseramsgate.co.uk. This elegant clifftop Regency house is now a boutique hotel, oozing luxurious, quirky charm. The fourteen rooms are all different, but most offer harbour views, some have balconies and each is decorated in soothing contemporary style. The on-site brasserie/bar is good, too, serving anything from afternoon tea to Mediterranean sharing boards or rack of lamb. **£155**
The Corner House 42 Station Rd, Minster, CT12 4HD ☎01843 823000, ⓦcornerhouserestaurants.co.uk. In the pretty old village of Minster, six miles west of Ramsgate, this corner restaurant has quietly been making a name for itself for its superb locally sourced food – Romney Marsh lamb; Stour Valley rabbit; mushroom, spinach and Kentish blue cheese tart (mains from £16). The fact that they also offer two spacious, stylish en-suite rooms upstairs makes it a very credible rural bolthole for a tour of the coast. **£90**
Royal Harbour Hotel 10–12 Nelson Crescent, CT11 9JF ☎01843 591514, ⓦroyalharbourhotel.co.uk. Two interconnecting Georgian townhouses above the harbour house this welcoming hotel, a friendly place with nautically themed decor and lots of personal touches. Rooms range from tiny "cabins" to larger options with balconies, and many have sea views; the walled herb garden, cosy lounges (with open fires) and complimentary evening cheese board are all plusses. **£110**

EATING

Flavours by Kumar 2 Effingham St, CT11 9AT ☎01843 852631, ⓦflavoursbykumar.co.uk. The food on offer at this cheery restaurant is a cut above your standard curry house, with tasty, traditional dishes executed with great flair by a chef who used to work at the famed *Ambrette* in Margate (see p.94). The *amuse bouches* between courses are a nice touch. Mains from £10; the two-/three-course lunch menu, which offers lots of choice, is excellent value at £9.50/£11.50. Daily noon–2.30pm & 5.30–10pm.
Ship Shape Café 3 Military Rd, CT11 9LG ☎01843 597000. Cosy old-school caff tucked under the arches by the harbour, full of nautical bits and bobs and favoured by a seasalty crowd tucking into all-day fry-ups, mugs of strong tea and home-made puds. On a sunny day the outdoor tables make a fantastic vantage point. Daily 7am–5pm.
★**Vinyl Head Café** 2 The Broadway, Addington St, CT11 9JN ☎07901 334653, ⓦfacebook.com /vinylheadramsgate. Friendly, chilled-out little neighbourhood hangout offering coffee, juices and home-made cakes, crepes and veggie food, plus interesting events, from haircuts to art classes – and vinyl for sale, of course. The tiny courtyard is a great spot in summer. Daily 9am–5pm.

DRINKING AND NIGHTLIFE

Belgian Café 98 Royal Parade CT11 8LP ☎01843 587925, ⓦwww.belgiancafe.co.uk. Big, brash brasserie-style place near the seafront, its outside tables usually full with an eclectic crowd enjoying Belgian beers, real ales and marina views. Mon–Thurs & Sun 7am–2am, Fri & Sat 7am–3am.
Conqueror Ale House 4c Grange Rd, CT11 9LR ☎07890 203282, ⓦconqueror-alehouse.co.uk. Ramsgate's unassuming, award-winning micropub offers a quiet, friendly space to linger over excellent local ales and ciders. Tues–Sat 11.30am–2.30pm & 5.30–9.30pm, Sun noon–3pm.
Queen Charlotte 57 Addington St, CT11 9JJ ☎01843 570703. Cool and quirky little pub with an up-for-it, bohemian crowd, an eclectic playlist, exhibitions and events, pop-up restaurants and live music. Wed 5.30–10pm, Thurs 5.30–11pm, Fri & Sat 5.30pm–midnight, Sun noon–9pm.
Ramsgate Music Hall 13 Turner St, CT11 8NJ ☎01843 591815, ⓦramsgatemusichall.com. Outstanding live music venue – with room for just 125 people – with a fabulous roster of acts in all genres; though it's hard to pick, recent highlights have included Teleman, the Pop Group and Imaani.

East Kent

DUNGENESS

East Kent

As the closest part of Britain to the Continent, the east coast of Kent has long been a frontier. Historic evidence of its vulnerability to invasion is at every turn, from stout Tudor castles and Napoleonic fortifications to poignant memorials to World War II, when gunfire in France could be heard from across the sea and entire towns were evacuated. Proximity to the Channel has brought Kent good fortune, too – not least in medieval days, when its Cinque Ports were granted enormous privileges and wealth. In Victorian times tourism entered the fray, with Folkestone in particular attracting the great and the good to its grand seafront hotels. Things are far quieter today. Defined by its iconic White Cliffs and lacking the big tourist towns of Kent's north coast or the Sussex shore, the east coast abounds in quiet bays, rugged headlands and lonely marshes, its low-key seaside towns and villages offering plenty of laidback appeal.

Pretty, medieval **Sandwich**, once an important Cinque Port (see box, p.107) but now no longer even on the coast, makes a charming overnight spot, while further south the former smuggling haven of **Deal** has a certain raffish energy. Its two castles, built by Henry VIII, may be less famous than the mighty complex at Dover, but they're fascinating in their own right: Deal Castle reveals the most sophisticated military engineering of its day, while just a seafront walk away is Walmer Castle, once home to the Duke of Wellington, among other luminaries. **Dover** – Britain's principal cross-Channel port, a mere 21 miles from mainland Europe – is not immensely appealing in itself but it does provide a springboard for the magnificent **Dover Castle**, and for the stupendous chalk banks of the **White Cliffs**, which offer glorious walks. South of Dover lies **Folkestone**, a plucky resort valiantly re-energizing itself as an arts destination, and **Romney Marsh**, with the eerie, arty shingle headland of **Dungeness** at their southernmost tip.

The East Kent coast offers outstanding walking and cycling. The coastal stretch between Folkestone and Dover forms part of the North Downs Way, while the section of the Saxon Shore Way between Deal and Dover is one of the most picturesque on the entire path. **The Warren**, Folkestone's very own stretch of white cliff, offers dramatic vistas and a broad, fossil-studded beach, while **Samphire Hoe**, an incongruous knob of land created from spoil during construction of the Channel Tunnel, is an intriguing place for a stroll.

Sandwich and around

SANDWICH, on the River Stour six miles north of Deal, is one of the best-preserved medieval towns in England. Hard to believe today, but this small, pretty place was a major commercial port, chief among the Cinque Ports (see box, p.107), until the Stour started silting up in the 1500s; unlike at other former harbour inlets, however, the **river**

SANDWICH

Highlights

① Sandwich With its sleepy quayside and glorious Edwin Lutyens gardens, its nature reserves and its seal-spotting trips, this medieval gem is a delight. **See p.104**

② Deal The quiet seaside town of Deal boasts a proud maritime history, two Tudor castles, an atmospheric conservation area, great walking, and some superb places to stay and eat. **See p.109**

③ Dover Castle A visit to Dover's mighty castle, which dominates the skyline for miles around and spans Roman remains to World War II bunkers, could fill an entire day. **See p.114**

④ White Cliffs of Dover An exhilarating walk along these imposing white cliffs is an

unmissable East Kent experience. **See p.119**

⑤ The Warren Wildlife-rich and geologically fascinating, the cliffs and beach of the Warren have a rugged, handsome beauty. **See p.126**

⑥ Rocksalt, Folkestone This glamorous harbourside restaurant, right on the water, is just one of the many good reasons to visit the up-and-coming town of Folkestone. See p.127

⑦ Prospect Cottage, Dungeness Pay tribute to the artistic vision of late filmmaker Derek Jarman at his seaside garden, gazing out from the windswept shingle of Dungeness. **See p.132**

HIGHLIGHTS ARE MARKED ON THE MAP ON P.106

hasn't vanished completely and still flows through town, its grassy, willow-lined banks adding to the sleepy charm.

Though the **Secret Gardens** are the biggest formal attraction, it's a pleasure simply to wander around Sandwich, with its crooked half-timbered buildings, narrow lanes, peaceful quayside and riverside path. Shops are few, and very low-key, while historical markers relate fascinating snippets. Just outside town lie a handful of **nature reserves** and the remains of **Richborough Roman Fort**, which you can reach by boat. It's also a major destination for **golfers** – the **Royal St George's** course, which fringes the coast to the east, with the Prince's Golf Club to the north and the Royal Cinque Ports Club a mile or so south.

Secret Gardens of Sandwich

Knightrider St, CT13 9EW • Daily: April–Sept 10am–5pm; Oct–March 10am–4pm • Jan & Dec free; Feb–Nov £7 • ☏ 01304 619919, Ⓦ the-salutation.com/the-gardens

Designed by Sir Edwin Lutyens and heavily influenced by his famous gardening partner Gertrude Jekyll, the 3.5-acre **Secret Gardens of Sandwich** were restored in 2007 after being abandoned to the wilderness for 25 years. While they largely retain the design of the original gardens, a few new features, including a tropical border (we can

THE CINQUE PORTS

In 1278 Dover, Hythe, Sandwich, Romney and Hastings – already part of a long-established but unofficial confederation of defensive coastal settlements – were formalized under a charter by Edward I as the **Cinque Ports** (pronounced "sink", despite the name's French origin). In return for providing England with maritime support, chiefly in the transportation of troops and supplies during times of war, the five ports were granted trading privileges and other liberties – including self-government, exemption from taxes and tolls and "possession of goods thrown overboard" – that enabled them to prosper while neighbouring ports struggled. Some benefitted during peacetime, too, boosting their wealth by such nefarious activities as piracy and smuggling.

Rye, Winchelsea and seven other **"limb" ports** on the southeast coast were later added to the confederation. The ports' privileges were eventually revoked in 1685; their maritime services had become increasingly unnecessary after Henry VIII had founded a professional navy and, due to a shifting coastline, several of their harbours had silted up anyway, stranding some of them miles inland. Today, of all the Cinque Ports only Dover is still a major working port.

3

thank global warming for that), have been added, the lake, with its little island, dates back to the 1970s. It's a tranquil spot, with plenty of benches and secluded nooks, and a perfectly nice place simply to wander. The informal, country-garden style beautifully offsets the classical lines of the 1911 house (now a private residence and hotel, home to Steph and Dom of TV's *Gogglebox* fame), with bold, splashy plantings, unexpected combinations and discrete areas linked by winding brick paths.

The quayside

Sandwich's riverfront **quayside**, peaceful today, was once the heart of a great medieval port, when the wide river estuary known as Sandwich Haven lapped at its banks. While the Haven began silting up in the sixteenth century, and the sea is now miles away, the waterfront gives the place a breezily nautical atmosphere, with small boats moored by the toll bridge, open countryside stretching out across the river, and the cry of seagulls raking the air. **Boat trips** (see p.108) run from the toll bridge over the Stour – note the sixteenth-century **Barbican**, a stone gateway decorated with chequerwork, where tolls were once collected – up to Richborough Roman Fort (see p.108) and down to the estuary to spot seals and birds. You can also **walk to Sandwich Bay** from the quayside, following the river and heading across the Royal St George's Golf Course to the sea – it's just a couple of miles, depending on the path you take.

The Guildhall

Cattle Market, CT13 9AH • Museum April–Nov Tues, Wed, Fri & Sat 10.30am–12.30pm & 2–4pm, Thurs & Sun 2–4pm • Free • ☎ 01304 617197, ⓦ sandwichtowncouncil.gov.uk/guildhall

At the centre of Sandwich, the handsome sixteenth-century **Guildhall** houses the tourist office (see p.108), various venerable council chambers, and displays recounting the history of the town. For centuries, the open square around it hosted a busy cattle market; today there's a small market every Thursday morning.

Royal St George's Golf Course

1.5 miles east of Sandwich, CT13 9PB • Visitors (Mon–Fri only) need to be introduced by a member, or to email a letter of introduction from their club and to produce evidence of a handicap of 18 or better • ☎ 01304 613090, ⓦ royalstgeorges.com

Sandwich is separated from the sandy beaches of Sandwich Bay by the **Royal St George's Golf Course**, perhaps the finest links course in England. Set in the undulating dunes, and boasting the deepest bunker in championship golf (on its fourth hole), St George's was established in 1887 and has been a venue for the British Open fourteen

---

THE NOBLE SANDWICH

Perhaps surprisingly, Sandwich makes little of what might seem an obvious claim to fame. The town's eponymous snack was created, so the story goes, in 1762, by John Montagu, the fourth Earl of Sandwich. Absorbed in a game of cards and on a winning streak, the peckish earl ate his beef between two bits of bread so as to be able to focus on the game, thus inadvertently inventing what went on to become the nation's favourite lunchtime staple. However, as this fabled event didn't happen in Sandwich, and as the earl's connections with the place were largely limited to his name, it seems fair enough that the town resolutely ignores any possible punning potential.

---

times since 1894 – most recently in 2011. Laid out in sympathy with its natural surroundings, it's a stunning spot, with wonderful views of the sea.

3 Richborough Roman Fort and Amphitheatre

Richborough Rd, Pegwell Bay, CT13 9JW • April–Sept daily 10am–6pm; Oct daily 10am–5pm; Nov–March Sat & Sun 10am–4pm • £5.80; EH • Parking free • ☎ 01304 612013, ⓦ www.english-heritage.org.uk/visit/places/richborough-roman-fort-and-amphitheatre • The best way to get to the fort is on a river boat from Sandwich (see below); trips take about 1hr

Marooned in the marshy lands that fringe Pegwell Bay, two miles northwest of Sandwich, stand the remains of **Richborough Roman Fort and Amphitheatre**, one of the earliest coastal strongholds built by the Romans. Originally a military garrison, the fort developed into first a civilian town and then a major port. Though its sheer size, and its lonely setting, is evocative – the coast that it guarded is now a couple of miles distant – Richborough's historical significance outshines its appearance. All that can be seen within the huge and well-preserved Roman walls are the remains of an early Saxon church and a little museum; nearby, a large hollow marks the site of the third-century amphitheatre.

Sandwich and Pegwell Bay Nature Reserve

Three miles north of Sandwich, off the A256, CT12 5JB • Daily 8.30am–7pm (or dusk if sooner) • Free • ☎ 01622 662012, ⓦ kentwildlifetrust.org.uk/reserves/sandwich-and-pegwell-bay

The broad expanse of the **Sandwich and Pegwell Bay Nature Reserve**, on the River Stour estuary between Sandwich and Ramsgate, is a superb spot for birdwatchers, boasting a wide variety of seashore habitats including tidal mudflats, shingle beach, dunes, saltmarsh, chalk cliffs and coastal scrubland. The best time to view the wading birds is in winter, or during the spring and autumn migrations, but even in summer you'll spot redshank, shelduck and oystercatchers, along with ringed plovers and little tern. The reserve is on the Viking Coastal cycling trail and the Saxon Shore Way (see p.30).

ARRIVAL AND DEPARTURE   SANDWICH AND AROUND

By train Sandwich station is off St George's Rd, from where it's a 10min walk north to the town centre and the quay. Destinations Deal (every 30min–1hr; 6min); Dover (every 30min–1hr; 25min); Ramsgate (hourly; 15min).

By bus Buses pull in and depart from outside the Guildhall. Destinations Canterbury (every 20min–1hr; 45min); Deal (every 20min–1hr; 25–35min); Dover (every 45min–1hr; 45min–1hr); Ramsgate (hourly; 45min–1hr).

INFORMATION AND TOURS

Tourist office The Guildhall (April–Oct Mon–Sat 10am–4pm; ☎ 01304 613565, ⓦ sandwichtowncouncil .gov.uk or ⓦ whitecliffscountry.org.uk).

River tours Sandwich Riverbus boats, by the toll bridge, head out on seal-spotting jaunts in the estuary (30min–1hr) and on longer wildlife-spotting trips (2hr),

and provide a ferry service to Richborough Roman Fort (1hr); you'll need to call to reserve (roughly Easter to mid-Sept Thurs–Sun & school hols 11am–6pm; mid-Sept to Easter Sat, Sun & school hols 11am–dusk, dependent on weather; £7–35; ☎ 07958 376183, ⓦ sandwichriverbus.co.uk).

ACCOMMODATION

Bell Hotel The Quay, CT13 9EF ☎01304 613388, ⓦbellhotelsandwich.co.uk. Sandwich's largest hotel is a rambling hostelry that has stood on this site since Tudor times; the present building is largely Edwardian. Rooms are comfy, in an uncontroversial, upscale style; the best (£165–195) have balconies overlooking the quayside and the Stour. There's a bar, and an in-house restaurant serving Modern European food (mains from £13). Minimum two nights at weekends June–Sept. **£115**

Kings Arms Strand St, CT13 9HN ☎01304 617361, ⓦkingsarms-sandwich.co.uk. No surprises at this old pub, all carpets, dark wood and horse brasses, with a roaring fire in winter – it's geared up for eating (steaks, pies, curries, burgers), but there's a pretty garden in

summer for when you just fancy a pint. Upstairs is a selection of plain, comfortable en-suite rooms; not fancy but good value, with a tasty breakfast included. **£85**

Molland Manor House Molland Lane, Ash, CT3 2JB ☎01304 814210, ⓦmollandhouse.co.uk. The history is palpable in this thirteenth-century manor, full of original features, 3 miles west of Sandwich. It's family friendly, with kind hosts and a big garden with swings and a slide; you'll be welcomed with a delicious cream tea and lots of little luxuries. Six of the seven B&B rooms are en suite, and the other has a private bathroom. All are attractive, light and comfortable. Usually two nights minimum March–Oct, but it's worth checking if they have last-minute availability. **£115**

EATING

Elizavet 3–5 Bell Lane, CT13 9FN ☎01304 619899, ⓦgreekrestaurantsandwich.co.uk. This convivial restaurant, squeezed into a narrow cobbled lane off the quayside, serves good, old-school Greek food to an appreciative crowd. Mains (£9.50–19) include all the classics done well, and you can put together a tasty meze platter (£3.50–7) with dolmades, halloumi, smoked red peppers and the like. And yes, the occasional music nights do feature plate-smashing and dancing. Tues–Sat noon–2pm & 6–11pm, Sun noon–3pm.

★**George and Dragon** 24 Fisher St, CT13 9EJ ☎01304 613106, ⓦgeorgeanddragon-sandwich.co.uk. A fifteenth-century inn and popular, unpretentious gastropub, with great food, good cask ales, roaring real fires in winter and a courtyard garden for alfresco summer dining. The menu changes fortnightly, but dressed crab with new potato salad (£11) or duck breast with potato and beetroot croquette (£15) are typical; each dish can be matched with a real ale. Booking advised in the evening. Mon–Sat

11am–11pm, Sun 11am–4pm; kitchen Mon–Sat noon–2pm & 6–9.15pm, Sun noon–2pm.

Hop and Huffkin 10 New St, CT13 9AB ☎01304 448560, ⓦhopandhuffkin.co.uk. Locally sourced, home-made food, wines and ales served in a good-looking contemporary dining room or a courtyard. Mains (£9–18) focus on casual crowd-pleasers – burgers (in huffkins), sausage sandwiches, mussels, steaks – with good daily specials and a couple of veggie options. Occasional live music. Mon–Sat 10am–9.30pm, Sun 10am–8.30pm.

No Name 1 No Name St, CT13 9AJ ☎01304 612626, ⓦnonameshop.co.uk. For picnic supplies, including baguettes, delicious cheeses and artisan bread, look no further than this excellent French deli near the Guildhall. You can also eat in, choosing from a daily-changing blackboard menu of light dishes – tartines, soups, quiches – with heartier mains such as baked mussels, duck confit and thyme-roasted chicken in the bistro upstairs. Dishes around £7–14. There's another branch in Deal (see p.113). Mon–Sat 8am–5pm, Sun 9am–4pm.

Deal

The low-key seaside town of **DEAL**, six miles southeast of Sandwich, is an appealing place, with a broad, steeply shelving shingle **beach** backed by a jumble of faded Georgian townhouses, a picturesque **old town** redolent with maritime history, and a striking concrete **pier** lined with hopeful anglers casting their lines. Henry VIII's two seafront **castles**, linked by a seaside path on the Saxon Shore Way, are the main attractions, along with walks and cycle rides along the coast, but above all Deal is a place to simply potter around. Its relaxed vibe and strong community spirit give it a likeable air of confidence; this, along with a very good selection of **restaurants** and B&Bs, makes it an increasingly popular weekend destination.

Brief history

It was on this stretch of coast that, in 55 BC, **Julius Caesar**, daunted by the vision of Dover's colossal white cliffs further up the shore, first landed in Britain. **Henry VIII** built three castles in the area, compact coastal fortresses designed to scare off the Spanish and the French; having been named a **limb port** of the Cinque Ports in the thirteenth century (see box, p.107), by Elizabethan times Deal was one of the most important ports in the country. It was renowned for its skilled boatbuilders and courageous sailors – men able to navigate the perilous offshore Goodwin Sands, where countless ships had met their doom, to reach safe harbour in the "**Downs**" anchorage, the sheltered waters closer to land – and by the eighteenth century had become a notorious centre for smuggling. Privateering boosted the local economy until well into the Victorian era.

The seafront

At first glance, Deal's **seafront** promenade may not be the best advertisement for the town. Though handsome, many of its buildings have become a little shabby – on the outside at least – and lack the picture-postcard appeal of the sprucer old-town lanes just inland. That said, it has a likeable charm, with small, independent hotels and restaurants far outnumbering the few amusement arcades and tourist shops; **Beach Street**, the parade of pastel-painted Georgian and Victorian buildings north of the pier, is its prettiest stretch.

Deal beach

The **beach** itself is a long, uninterrupted shingle swathe, almost entirely uncommercialized and perfect for bracing walks. Steeply shelving, it's also a popular spot for sea fishing and even, for the very bold, a circulation-zapping swim. The wide coastal path alongside, suitable for walkers and cyclists, takes you past a picturesque ensemble of fishing boats, tatty lobster pots and chalky white fishing huts via **Walmer Castle**, the largest of Henry's local coastal defences, to the laidback little village of **Kingsdown**, at the edge of the White Cliffs.

Deal Pier

Built in 1957, **Deal Pier** is almost defiantly unprepossessing, a brutal concrete affair that replaced a more decorative Victorian iron pleasure pier destroyed by a run-in with a Dutch merchant ship in 1940. You can't leave town without walking its length – all 1026ft of it – however; lacking amusement arcades or end-of-the-pier entertainments, it has its own appeal, offering splendid views back over the town and a good family restaurant, *Jasin's*, at the end (see p.113). It's also a renowned spot for **fishing**, the water yielding bass, ray, smooth hound, dogfish and mackerel in summer, and codling, whiting and flatfish in winter. Channel Angling, at the pier entrance, sells bait and tackle (Mon–Thurs & Sun 7am–5pm, Fri 7am–6pm, Sat 7am–10pm; ☏01304 373104, ⓦdealpierfishing.co.uk).

Timeball Tower

Victoria Parade, CT14 7BP • 11.30am–4.30pm: May Sat & Sun; June–Sept Wed–Sun • £3 • ☏ 01304 362444, ⓦ dealtimeball.co.uk

Facing the sea, Deal's **Timeball Tower** was used, in the early nineteenth century, as a semaphore tower in an attempt to monitor local smuggling activity. Abandoned in 1842, the tower was transformed by the addition of a timeball in 1855; the ball dropped down a pole on the roof at exactly 1pm in summer, providing an accurate time check for ships at sea attempting to navigate the offshore Downs. Although the coming of radio put paid to that, the timeball still drops regularly in summer, and at midnight on New Year's Eve. Inside, you can see an array of exhibits relating to communications and signalling, including rare timepieces, telescopes and ingenious Victorian telegraph mechanisms.

The old town

Middle Street is the prettiest road in Deal's **old town**, its cute pastel cottages, elegant Georgian houses and narrow alleys making perfect photo opportunities. *Carry On* fans should stop by no. 117, a compact cottage with a blue plaque commemorating Charles Hawtrey, who by all accounts lived out his later years here in eccentric and alcoholic promiscuity. Middle Street's picturesque tranquillity belies the fact that this was the de facto high road for the town's smugglers and pirates – the northern end, marked by the small Alfred Square, was a particularly nefarious stretch, and it's said that a network of secret tunnels still lies beneath the street today.

Deal's lively **High Street** has more character than many of its kind; the best shops are to be found in its old town stretch, with a scattering of independent boutiques, delis, vintage stores and coffee shops north of Broad Street. Off the High Street, at 22 St George's Rd, the **Deal Museum** (April, May, Sept & Oct Tues–Fri 2–4.30pm, Sat 11am–4.30pm, Sun noon–4pm; June–Aug Tues–Sat 11am–4.30pm, Sun noon–4pm; £3; ⓦ dealmuseum.co.uk) illustrates the town's social and seafaring history.

Deal Castle

Marine Rd, CT14 7BA • April Sept daily 10am–6pm; Oct daily 10am–5pm; Nov–March Sat & Sun 10am–4pm • £5.80; EH • Parking free • ☎ 01304 372762, ⓦ www.english-heritage.org.uk/visit/places/deal-castle • Buses #12, #13 #13A, #14, #80A, #82, #82A and #93

3

Diminutive **Deal Castle**, at the south end of town, is one of the most striking of Henry VIII's forts. Hastily built in 1539–40, along with Sandown Castle (now destroyed) to the north and Walmer Castle (see below) to the south, as part of a chain of coastal defences against potential invaders – and in particular, Henry's French and Spanish Catholic enemies – this was a castle designed to face battle. Its distinctive **shape**, which viewed from the air looks like a Tudor rose, has less to do with aesthetics than sophisticated military engineering: squat rounded walls were effective at deflecting cannonballs and provided less surface area to be hit. Inside the six outer bastions, themselves mounted with heavy guns, a second set of six semicircular inner bastions protected the cylindrical central keep, its own 14ft-thick walls providing stout defence.

Perhaps disappointingly, after all this effort, the castle never did see serious fighting, though there was a brief skirmish during the Civil War. The castle was garrisoned one last time during the Napoleonic Wars, but again little fighting actually took place.

Self-guided **audio tours** outline every detail of the state-of-the-art military design. Bare rooms reveal how the castle changed over the years and give a good sense of how the soldiers lived; check out the claustrophobic privies with their deep, dark wells. Descending through gloomy cobbled passageways brings you to the basement and the Rounds, a subterranean warren equipped with yet more cannon, facing potential enemies across the dry moat.

Walmer Castle

Kingsdown Rd, 1 mile south of Deal, CT14 7LJ • Mid-Feb to March Wed–Sun 10am–4pm; April–Sept daily 10am–6pm; Oct daily 10am–5pm; Nov to mid-Feb Sat & Sun 10am–4pm • £10.10; EH • Parking free (weather dependent) • ☎ 01304 364288, ⓦ www .english-heritage.org.uk/visit/places/walmer-castle-and-gardens • Hourly buses (#82/#82A) from Deal; also accessible on foot along the seafront (30min) or from Walmer train station, a mile away; in addition to the on-site parking there's free public parking opposite the entrance

The southernmost of Henry VIII's trio of "Castles in the Downs", **Walmer Castle** is another rotund Tudor-rose-shaped affair, built to protect the coast from its enemies across the Channel. Like Sandown Castle (which no longer stands) and its neighbour at Deal, Walmer saw little fighting; unlike those, however, it changed use when it became the official residence of the Lords Warden of the Cinque Ports in 1708 (which it still remains, though the title itself is now strictly ceremonial).

Adapted over the years by its various residents, today the castle resembles a heavily fortified **stately home** more than a military stronghold. The rooms – many of them

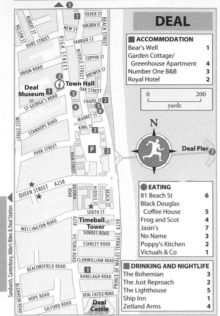

DEAL

ACCOMMODATION
Bear's Well	1
Garden Cottage/	
Greenhouse Apartment	4
Number One B&B	3
Royal Hotel	2

EATING
81 Beach St	6
Black Douglas	
Coffee House	5
Frog and Scot	4
Jasin's	7
No Name	3
Poppy's Kitchen	2
Victuals & Co	1

DRINKING AND NIGHTLIFE
The Bohemian	3
The Just Reproach	2
The Lighthouse	5
Ship Inn	1
Zetland Arms	4

4, 4, 5 Paddling Pool, Bandstand & Walmer Castle

fan-shaped, due to the unusual circular walls – are filled with the memorabilia of previous Lords Warden, including the late Queen Mother and Winston Churchill. Walmer is most associated, however, with the **Duke of Wellington**, who was given the post of Lord Warden in 1828. In his bedroom you can see his simple camp bed, with its original bedding, and the armchair in which he died in 1852. The Iron Duke lay in state in this room for two months before being buried at St Paul's Cathedral; in the two days before his body was taken to London, some nine thousand local mourners trooped past to pay their respects. Other Wellington memorabilia includes his sunken bronze death mask and a pair of original leather "Wellington" boots, designed by the Duke after the Battle of Waterloo to be cut lower than the usual boot and thus easier to wear.

The castle's eight acres of terraced **gardens** are a delight. Begun by Lord Warden William Pitt in 1792, with help from his famous and eccentric adventuress niece, **Lady Hester Stanhope**, they offer all manner of walks and picnic spots. Make a beeline for the Broadwalk, where colourful, cottage-garden-style borders are backed by a stunning yew "cloud" hedge, its surreal bulging undulations caused by a period of neglect during and after World War II.

ARRIVAL AND INFORMATION   DEAL

By train The station is on Queen St, a 10min walk from the sea.

Destinations Dover (every 15min–1hr; 15min); Ramsgate (every 30min–1hr; 20min); Sandwich (every 30min–1hr; 6min); Walmer (every 30min–1hr; 3min).

By bus Buses run from South St and Queen St near each other in the town centre.

Destinations Canterbury (hourly; 1hr 15min); Dover (every 30min–1hr; 45min); London Victoria (2 daily; 2hr 50min–3hr 45min); St Margaret's-at-Cliffe (hourly; 30min);

Sandwich (every 20min–1hr; 25–35min); Walmer (every 15min–1hr; 15–30min).

By bike There are lots of good cycling paths around Deal. For rental – including kids' bikes and tagalongs – try Mike's Bikes, just outside Deal train station (from £9/half day or £27 for two days; ☎07484 727755, ⓦmikesbikesdeal.com).

Tourist office Town Hall, High St (Mon–Fri 9.30am–1pm & 2–4.30pm, Sat 10am–2pm; ☎01304 361999, ⓦdeal .gov.uk or ⓦwhitecliffscountry.org.uk).

ACCOMMODATION

Bear's Well 10 St George's Rd, CT14 6BA ☎01304 694144, ⓦbearswell.co.uk. In a peaceful Old Town spot near the High St and the sea, this is an airy boutique B&B in a gorgeous Georgian home. The three en-suite rooms are comfortable and uncluttered, with views of the church or pretty back garden, and the breakfasts, made using local produce, are great. **£115**

Garden Cottage/Greenhouse Apartment Walmer Castle, Walmer, CT14 7LJ ☎0370 333 1187, ⓦwww.english-heritage.org.uk/visit/holiday -cottages/find-a-holiday-cottage/garden-cottage or

ⓦwww.english-heritage.org.uk/visit/holiday -cottages/find-a-holiday-cottage/greenhouse -apartment. Breaks of three, four or seven nights in these self-catering options, both of which sleep four, in the castle grounds. In a gorgeous spot overlooking the eighteenth-century kitchen garden, both are decorated in an inoffensive contemporary style. Minimum three-night stay; nightly rate lower for longer stays. **£284**

Number One B&B 1 Ranelagh Rd, CT14 7BG ☎01304 364459, ⓦnumberonebandb.co.uk. Occupying a handsome Victorian townhouse, this good-value B&B is near Deal Castle and just a minute from the beach. The four rooms each have a dash of quirky design flair, with luxurious extras including bathrobes and coffee makers. Two-night minimum stay June–Aug, and at weekends April, May, Sept and Oct. No under-16s. **£85**

Royal Hotel Beach St, CT14 6JD ☎01304 375555, ⊛theroyalhotel.com. Things have quietened down since

Admiral Nelson scandalized society by entertaining Lady Hamilton in his bedchamber here, but there's still a thrill to staying a pebble's throw from the shingle beach – especially if you get one of the sea-facing rooms with large balconies. Rates include a breakfast buffet, and there's a bar and bistro on site. **£130**

EATING

81 Beach St 81 Beach St, CT14 6JB ☎01304 368136, ⊛81beachstreet.co.uk. Upscale contemporary brasserie with a changing fusion menu. Dinner (small plates from £5, large plates £13–23) might include shredded pork and chorizo risotto or red onion and mozzarella tarte tatin; two-/three-course lunch menus (Mon–Sat) are £12.80/£15.90, or £15.95 on Sun (two courses). Mon–Sat noon–3pm & 6–10pm, Sun noon–4pm.

Black Douglas Coffee House 82 Beach St, CT14 6JB ☎01304 365486, ⊛blackdouglas.co.uk. Boho seafront place, with a cosy, cluttered interior and a focus on locally sourced home-made food. While you can pop in for coffee and cake, they also do breakfast (pancakes, Eggs Benedict and the like; £5–12), lunch (maybe a feta, houmous and roast beetroot salad), and a short supper menu on Fri and Sat. No cards. Mon–Thurs 9am–5pm, Fri & Sat 9am–5pm & 7–10pm, Sun 10am–4pm.

★**Frog and Scot** 86 High St, CT14 6EG ☎01304 379444, ⊛frogandscot.co.uk. The Scottish/French couple who own this bijou bistro have created a delightful neighbourhood haven where happy locals linger over genuinely delicious, authentic French dishes, from slow-braised ox cheek to lobster mayonnaise with frites, and a fabulous wine list featuring many biodynamic varieties. Mains from £15; two-/three-course lunch menus £13.95/£16.95. Wed–Fri noon–2.30pm & 6.15–9.15pm, Sat 10am–2.30pm & 6.15–9.15pm, Sun 10am–3pm.

Jasin's Deal Pier, CT14 6HZ ☎01304 366820, ⊛jasinsrestaurant.com. With its picture windows and pared-down timber decor, perched over the water like a ship's lookout, *Jasin's* is a pier caff with panache.

Family-friendly, serving honest grub – fish and chips, home-made lasagne, toasted wraps and the like – it's great for breakfast (till 4pm), when fishermen, laptop-toting freelancers and tourists alike tuck into Full Englishes (from £5), croissants or chunky bacon sandwiches. There's outdoor seating too, right above the water, and a few takeaway options. Mains £5–10. Mon–Thurs & Sun 8am–8.15pm, Fri & Sat 8am–9.15pm.

No Name 110 High St, CT14 6EE ☎01304 375100, ⊛nonameshop.co.uk. This excellent French deli (takeaway only) is a good place to stock up on baguettes, cheese, hams and olives for an upmarket beach picnic. There's another branch in Sandwich (see p.109). Mon–Thurs 8.30am–5pm, Fri & Sat 8.30am–4.30pm.

★**Poppy's Kitchen** 119 High St, CT14 6BB ☎01304 371719, ⊛poppyskitchen.co.uk. Simple, fresh and utterly delicious salads, quiches, soups and tarts, with a focus on healthy organic ingredients. The regularly changing lunch menu, though small, packs in a good choice, from chard and Cheddar tart to kohlrabi, beetroot, garlic and feta salad (dishes from £5.50), while breakfast ranges from home-made granola to a Full English. Mon–Sat 9am–5.30pm, Sun 10am–3pm.

Victuals & Co 2 St George's Passage, CT14 6TA ☎01304 374389, ⊛victualsandco.com. Tucked away in a lane off the High St, this upscale restaurant has made quite a splash with its global fusion food. Short menus (two-/three-course lunch £19/£21; dinner mains from £16) might include such dishes as pan-fried scallops with Asian salad, venison carpaccio or chicken Massaman curry. Wed–Fri 6.30–9pm, Sat noon–2.30pm & 5.30–9.30pm, Sun noon–2.30pm & 5.30–8.30pm.

DRINKING AND NIGHTLIFE

The Bohemian 47 Beach St, CT14 6HY ☎01304 361939, ⊛thebohemian.co.uk. The seafront "Boho" attracts a lively crowd with its mishmash decor – vintage mirrors, quirky art, retro bits and bobs – along with its suntrap garden, its late hours and its long list of spirits (from absinthe to bourbon), real ales and bottled beers. Chunky sandwiches, pub grub and pizza are on offer, too (£4–16). Mon–Wed 11am–midnight, Thurs 11am–1am, Fri 11am–2am, Sat 10am–2am, Sun 10am–11pm; kitchen Mon–Fri 11am–3pm & 6–9pm, Sat 10am–9pm, Sun 10am–4pm.

★**The Just Reproach** 14 King St, CT14 6HX. With no phone or website (and only a minimal Facebook page), this dinky, dog-friendly micropub offers British microbrews, local cider and wines in a snug, bare-bones room livened up with retro memorabilia, and with no TV, music or digital devices to interrupt the conversation. Good, simple food – pickled onions, pork pies and cheese platters – too. Mon–Thurs noon–2pm & 5–9pm, Fri noon–2pm & 5–11pm, Sat noon–11pm, Sun noon–4pm.

The Lighthouse 50 The Strand, Walmer, CT14 7DX ☎01304 366031, ⊛thelighthousedeal.co.uk.

Friendly, community-minded music pub with an eclectic range of live music (folk to Klezmer), DJ nights (Northern Soul to Disco), stand-up and quizzes – usually free. Book for the popular "reggae roast" – an English/Caribbean roast dinner – on Sun (£7.50). Thurs–Sun & occasionally Wed.

Ship Inn 141 Middle St, CT14 6JZ ☎01304 372222. Venerable old-town pub, popular with a local and laidback crowd enjoying a quiet pint, with a gorgeous early nineteenth-century interior and a walled garden. Lots of real ales on offer. No cards. Mon–Sat 11am–midnight, Sun noon–midnight.

Zetland Arms Wellington Parade, Kingsdown, CT14 8AF ☎01304 370114, ⊚zetlandarms.co.uk. Around a 45min walk from Deal along the beach, the *Zetland* is a favourite stop for walkers and cyclists, perched on the shingle and with great views of the White Cliffs. Ales come from Shepherd Neame, and there's pub grub (from £9), too. Mon–Sat 10am–11.30pm, Sun 10am–10.30pm.

ENTERTAINMENT

The well-regarded **Deal Festival of Music and the Arts** (usually first fortnight of July; ⊚dealfestival.co.uk) is at the highbrow end of the scale. A variety of venues – as far afield as Sandwich, Dover and Margate – host chamber music, opera, classical music, modern dance and jazz from around the world, with big names, young performers, and a programme of talks and events.

Astor Community Theatre 20 Stanhope Rd, CT14 6AB ☎01304 370220, ⊚theastor.org. A lively arts centre in a handsome old Edwardian theatre, hosting live music – local and low-key national bands – big-name literary events, rep theatre, comedy, and the best world movies and classic films.

Dover and around

Given its importance as a travel hub – it's the busiest ferry port in Europe – **DOVER** is surprisingly small. Badly bombed during World War II, the town centre is unprepossessing, with just a few low-key attractions; the seafront is equally unassuming. The main attractions are **Dover Castle**, looming proudly above town and clearly visible from the sea, and just a walk along the legendary **White Cliffs**.

Dover Castle

Castle Hill, CT16 1HU • Mid-Feb to March Wed–Sun 10am–4pm; April–July & Sept daily 10am–6pm; Aug daily 9.30am–6pm; Oct daily 10am–5pm; Nov to mid-Feb Sat & Sun 10am–4pm; last entry 1hr before closing • £18.30, under-16s £11; EH • Parking free • ☎0370 333 1181, ⊚www.english-heritage.org.uk/visit/places/dover-castle • Stagecoach buses from the centre of Dover #15, #15X, #80, #80A & #93 (hourly; 20min)

No historical stone is left unturned at **Dover Castle**, an astonishingly imposing defensive complex that has protected the English coast for more than two thousand years. A castle stood here as early as 1068, when **William the Conqueror**, following the Battle of Hastings, built over the earthworks of an Iron Age hillfort; a century later, the **Normans** constructed the handsome keep that now presides over the heart of the complex. The grounds also include a **Roman lighthouse**, a **Saxon church** and all manner of later additions, including tunnels built in the Napoleonic Wars and World War I signal stations. Indeed, the castle was in continuous use as some sort of military installation right up to the 1980s, and its network of **tunnels**, used during World War II, are huge attractions in their own right.

Ideally you should allow a **full day** for a thorough visit, including time for a battlement walk (which takes around 1hr in total); if time is short, head first to Operation Dynamo, where long queues build up as the day proceeds, before making your way to the Great Tower.

Operation Dynamo: Rescue from Dunkirk

Tours leave at regular intervals; 40min

One of Dover Castle's most popular attractions is its network of **secret wartime tunnels**, dug during the Napoleonic Wars and extended during World War II. It was from these claustrophobic bunkers in 1940 that Vice Admiral Ramsay set out the plans for **Operation Dynamo**, the evacuation of Dunkirk, which successfully brought back some 330,000 stranded British and Allied troops from the Continent, helped by a small flotilla of local fishing and pleasure boats – the "little ships" – sailed by civilians. Defined by J.B. Priestley as "so absurd yet so grand and gallant that you hardly know whether to laugh or cry", Dunkirk marked a turning point in the war. Though "wars are not won by evacuations", as Churchill put it – and it was clear that the need to evacuate marked a serious defeat – a new determination to win, the so-called "Dunkirk Spirit", was born.

Operation Dynamo tunnel **tours** are lively and affecting affairs. Guides lead groups through the dark warrens while dramatic vox pops, sound effects and film footage flickering across crumbling tunnel walls shed light on the build-up to the war and how the evacuation came about. The detail is impeccable, from the graffiti on the walls, scrawled over a period of two hundred years, to the reconstructed chart rooms and repeater stations, eerily alive with the sounds of ringing phones and crackling messages.

The Underground Hospital

Tours leave roughly every 30min; 20min

In 1941–42, a new network of tunnels was hurriedly built beneath the castle to create a medical dressing station where patients, most of them from the castle garrison, could be bandaged and stabilized before being transferred to hospitals with better facilities. Billed as a walkthrough experience, tours of the **Underground Hospital** are impressionistic affairs, with rather less hard information than the Operation Dynamo tours next door. Loosely following the journey of a fictitious injured pilot brought to the hospital in 1943, you stride (at quite a pace) through corridors and wards, mess rooms and dorms, all filled with surgical instruments and the accoutrements of hospital life, as a somewhat surreal soundtrack booms around you. Dark, stuffy and claustrophobic, the tunnels can feel nightmarish as lights flicker and bombs rumble, spectral patients groan and shadowy nurses gossip; eerily, in the operating theatre, as you hear (invisible) doctors talking around their (invisible) patient, the smell of surgical spirit is overpowering.

Dover Secret Wartime Tunnels Uncovered

Though somewhat overshadowed by the high-profile subterranean tours around the corner, the **Dover Secret Wartime Tunnels Uncovered** exhibition shouldn't be overlooked. Lively panels give information on the tunnels themselves, apposite quotes and historical snippets illuminate the Dunkirk expedition, and intriguing photos and memorabilia include bricks from Nagasaki and Hiroshima. Meanwhile, listening stations tune into personal D-Day accounts from the people who were there, from fishermen sailing the "little ships" to a member of the Women's Land Army waiting for the boats to return.

The Great Tower

At the heart of Dover Castle is the inner bailey and the amazingly well-preserved **Great Tower**. Built by Henry II as a palace and a residence to welcome important visitors – including those on pilgrimage to Canterbury – this was the last and finest of the enormous rectangular royal towers that had begun with the Tower of London a century earlier. Despite subsequent modernization, notably under Edward IV and in the seventeenth century, it remains one of the best-preserved medieval royal towers in existence.

Inside the tower itself, a series of rooms linked by steep and narrow stone staircases have been painstakingly re-created to look ready to receive Philip, Count of Flanders, in 1186. Everything from the pots and pans in the kitchen to the chess set and richly coloured furniture and wall hangings in the **King's Chamber** has been meticulously reproduced using, where possible, the materials and methods of the time. The chambers in particular reveal a surprising blaze of paint-box colours and jaunty designs – rich turquoises, reds and gloriously decorative golds designed to flaunt the king's colossal wealth and influence. Climbing to the **roof** of the tower, passing other visitors huffing and puffing as they descend, rewards you with fabulous views of the castle grounds, the sea, and Dover itself.

The medieval tunnels

Following a nearly disastrous siege by the French Prince Louis and rebel barons in 1216–17, Dover Castle saw a number of improvements in its defence system – not least a complex set of subterranean **tunnels**, entered from a spot near the Great Tower. These were altered and expanded during the Napoleonic Wars and in the 1850s, but their original plan remains largely intact. There is little to actually see, although a set of lever-controlled doors that could be closed remotely to trap invaders is undeniably impressive, but the dramatically sloping declines, damp, drippy darkness, mysterious nooks and steep staircases are irresistibly atmospheric.

The Roman lighthouse

The Romans put Dover on the map when they chose the harbour – Portus Dubris – as the base for their northern fleet, and, probably in the second century AD, erected a clifftop **lighthouse** (*pharos*) to guide the ships into the river mouth. The remains of the chunky octagonal tower, made from local flint and bricks and refaced in medieval times, still stand – only the four lower stages survive, but you can walk inside the hollow shell.

St Mary-in-Castro

Standing beside the remains of the Roman lighthouse, the **St Mary-in-Castro** church dates back to around 1000 AD. Though subsequently remodelled, it remains a very fine, late-Saxon church, with original cruciform layout and soaring internal stone arches. Under Henry III, St Mary's became a church for soldiers – Richard the Lionheart's knights took shelter here before setting out on a crusade, and you can see their graffiti scratched into the wall just above ground level in the original stone arches near the pulpit. Over the next few centuries the church fell into ruin, to be restored by famed Victorian architects Sir George Gilbert Scott and William Butterfield; the latter is responsible for the decorative mosaic tiling that covers the walls.

Roman Painted House

New St, CT17 9AJ • Early April & June–Sept Tues–Sat 10am–5pm, Sun 1–5pm; mid-April to May Tues & Sat 10am–5pm; last entry 30min before closing • £3 • ☎ 01304 203279, ⓦ theromanpaintedhouse.co.uk

Built around 200 AD, the **Roman Painted House**, once a rest house for official guests from across the Channel, was demolished around seventy years later. Today, in a purpose-built building near the Market Square, you can see the remains of five rooms, including evidence of the hypocaust (underground heating system) and various mosaics, along with – the chief attraction – vibrant Roman wall paintings relating to Bacchus, the god of wine. Roman objects found during the 1971 excavation are also on display.

Dover Museum

Market Square, CT16 1PH • April–Sept Mon–Sat 9.30am–5pm, Sun 10am–3pm; Oct–March Mon–Sat 9.30am–5pm • £4.50 • ☎ 01304 201066, ⓦ dovermuseum.co.uk

Dover Museum is an appealing, slightly old-fashioned place, packed with enthusiastic displays on the town's past. The star attraction, protected behind glass in its own

FROM TOP ST THOMAS À BECKET, ROMNEY MARSH (P.132); PROSPECT COTTAGE, DUNGENESS (P.132) >

gallery, is a **Bronze Age boat** that was discovered in Dover in 1992, immaculately preserved by river silt for more than three thousand years. The vessel – the oldest-known seafaring boat in the world – is an astonishing sight, long, dark and sinewy like tough black seaweed; it took ten carpenters one month to build it, using holly, plum, oak, ash, apple, elm and yew, plus dense wodges of moss for waterproofing.

The White Cliffs of Dover

Shingly Dover beach may today lack the romance invested in it by Matthew Arnold (see box opposite), but the iconic **cliffs** flanking the town on both sides retain their majesty. Stretching sixteen miles along the coast from Kingsdown to Folkestone, a towering 350ft high in places, these vast banks are composed of chalk – plus traces of quartz, shells and flint. Much of the cliffs lie within the Kent Downs Area of Outstanding Natural Beauty, and with their chalk grasslands home to an exceptional number of rare plants, butterflies and migrant birds, have been designated a Site of Special Scientific Interest.

The most dramatic **views** of the cliffs themselves, of course, come from miles out to sea, either from a ferry or on a short tourist cruise from Dover (see p.121). Best of all, though, is to take a **walk** along them, which affords you amazing views of the Straits of Dover – the world's busiest shipping lanes. On a clear day it's even possible to catch a glimpse of France.

Shakespeare Cliff

A couple of miles west of Dover • Bus #60, #61 or #61A from Pencester Rd towards Aycliffe

West of Dover, **Shakespeare Cliff**, named for its mention in *King Lear* (see box opposite), is almost ferociously daunting, a towering bastion of chalk leaning backwards as if straining to hold back the sea. The bracing clifftop walk here offers a sweeping panorama – and an excellent, unusual view of Dover and the surrounding cliffs – but anyone with vertigo will want to stay well clear of the edge.

Samphire Hoe

Below Shakespeare Cliff, off the A20 from Dover to Folkestone, CT17 9FL • Daily 7am–dusk • Free, but pay parking • ☎ 01304 225649, Ⓦ samphirehoe.co.uk

Created in 1997 from some 175 million cubic feet of chalk marl reclaimed during the building of the Channel Tunnel, **Samphire Hoe**, the nature reserve at the foot of Shakespeare Cliff, is an unsettling spot. Wild and exposed, its chalk meadows, dotted with rock samphire, orchids and wildflowers, have a raw beauty that evolves with each passing year. On the other hand, this is clearly a man-made landscape, blocked off from the sea by a sea wall and wire fence, and with brutish Channel Tunnel ventilation buildings welcoming you at the entrance. Walking around the Hoe (a total loop of around 45min) does, however, offer invigorating blasts of fresh air, along with splendid views of the sea and of the awe-inspiring Shakespeare Cliff looming above – this is a good **birdwatching** spot and you may see kestrels, guillemots and kittiwakes swirling overhead.

To reach Samphire Hoe, pedestrians, cyclists and cars alike enter through a dark single-lane **tunnel** that descends through the cliffs; this was built in the 1880s, an aborted early version of today's Channel Tunnel.

Langdon Cliffs

Langdon Cliffs, a couple of miles east of town, above the port of Dover, are home to the National Trust White Cliffs of Dover Visitor Centre (see p.121), and a popular starting point for clifftop **walks**. Following cliff-edge paths and ploughing through chalk downland meadows, you can walk in around fifty minutes to the Victorian **South Foreland Lighthouse** – via **Fan Bay**, with its World War II tunnel complex – but if time is short it's well worth taking a briefer stroll, enjoying unsurpassed

THE WHITE CLIFFS OF DOVER

There is a cliff whose high and bending head
Looks fearfully in the confinèd deep
Bring me but to the very brim of it,
And I'll repair the misery thou dost bear
With something rich about me. From that place
I shall no leading need.

Earl of Gloucester, *King Lear*, Act 4 Scene 1

The sea is calm tonight,
The tide is full, the moon lies fair
Upon the straits; on the French coast the light
Gleams and is gone; the cliffs of England stand,
Glimmering and vast, out in the tranquil bay,
Come to the window, sweet is the night air!

Dover Beach, Matthew Arnold, 1867

3

Ah, God! One sniff of England
To greet our flesh and blood
To hear the traffic slurring
Once more through London mud!
Our towns of wasted honour
Our streets of lost delight!
How stands the old Lord Warden?
Are Dover's cliffs still white?

The Broken Men, Rudyard Kipling, 1902

There'll be bluebirds over
The White Cliffs of Dover
Tomorrow, just you wait and see.

(There'll Be Bluebirds Over) The White Cliffs of Dover, sung by Vera Lynn, 1942

As the first and last sight of England for travellers throughout the centuries, the **White Cliffs of Dover** play a complex role in the English psyche. A symbol of national fortitude, independence and pride, they have long represented a barrier for potential invaders; like mighty natural fortresses, they inspire awe and fear. **Julius Caesar** mentions them in his *Commentaries, Book IV*, recounting the Roman invasion of Britain in 55 BC – "steep cliffs came down close to the sea in such a way that it is possible to hurl weapons from them right down to the shore. It seemed to me that the place was altogether unsuitable for landing." Daunted, the invaders sailed further north to Deal and landed there instead.

In Shakespeare's **King Lear** the cliffs represent certain death to the abject and blinded Gloucester, who plans to commit suicide by jumping from them; in a later scene, his son Edgar, lying, convinces his father they are at the cliff edge with the words "the murmuring surge/That on the unnumber'd idle pebbles chafes/Cannot be heard so high. I'll look no more/ Lest my brain turn, and the deficient sight /Topple down headlong". Poet Matthew Arnold, meanwhile, gives them a similarly melancholic resonance, invoking their massive grandeur in his famous elegy for lost belief, **Dover Beach**, while for Kipling's home-sick emigrants the cliffs, and the old Dover pub the *Lord Warden*, are among quintessential images of home.

Perhaps the most famous mention of the cliffs, however, comes in **Vera Lynn**'s wartime anthem, a rallying call for Britons to keep dreaming of a peaceful future in the wake of the Battle of Britain. It's ostensibly a hopeful song, but the plaintive tune, and the fact that no real bluebird ever flew over the cliffs, imbues the uplifting words with a poignant uncertainty.

views. Watch out for kittiwakes in the summer, along with pretty Adonis blue butterflies fluttering among the wildflowers, and perhaps even an Exmoor pony or two, grazing on the velvety grass.

Fan Bay Deep Shelter

Fan Bay • Tours April–Oct Mon & Fri–Sun every 30min 11am–3pm; 45min • Admission on prebooked, timed tours only, from the office next to the National Trust White Cliffs Visitor Centre (see opposite) • £10, no under-12s; NT • Parking (at the Visitor Centre) £3.50 • ☏ 01304 207326, Ⓦ nationaltrust.org.uk/white-cliffs-dover

In 1941, at the height of World War II, a **gun battery** was installed on the White Cliffs to monitor and attack enemy ships in the Channel. Below it, hidden behind the face of the cliffs and carved out in just one hundred days, lay an **underground labyrinth** that housed 185 troops. The battery and all visible traces on the surface were destroyed in the 1970s, but the tunnels themselves remained; they've since been cleared and restored by the National Trust as a historical attraction.

Visiting **Fan Bay Deep Shelter** is quite an undertaking. First you have to walk for around forty minutes along the clifftop trail from the White Cliffs Visitor Centre (see opposite); then you don a hard hat with head torch and set off on the tour, descending down into the cliff via 125 steep stairs. Guides lead you through the dark, damp warren that once held dorms, hospital beds and storage rooms. Though the tunnels are largely empty, the anecdotes, stray pieces of memorabilia, and wartime graffiti etched into the chalk bring the place eerily alive. Some way down, you emerge onto an open-air ledge that holds two concrete "sound mirrors" – early-warning devices, designed to amplify the sound of approaching aircraft, built during the previous war in 1914.

South Foreland Lighthouse

The clifftop, St Margaret's Bay, CT15 6HP • Tours Mid-March to Oct Mon & Fri–Sun 11am–5.30pm • £6; NT • Parking (at the National Trust White Cliffs Visitor Centre) £3.50 • ☏ 01304 852463, Ⓦ nationaltrust.org.uk/south-foreland-lighthouse

South Foreland Lighthouse, a fifty-minute walk from the White Cliffs Visitor Centre, marks the end of the National Trust-owned clifftop path. Built in 1843 to guide ships past the perilous Goodwin Sands, three miles offshore, the chunky, icing-white tower offers (on clear days) amazing cross-Channel views. This was the site of Marconi's first international radio transmission, and the first lighthouse to be powered by electricity; guided **tours** detail the history, while touchscreens allow you to monitor the comings and goings on the busy Dover Strait. The **tearoom** downstairs is a vintage-lover's dream, complete with vinyl playing on the record-deck and yellowing antique newspapers to flick through. You can **stay** in the lighthouse, too (see opposite).

St Margaret's-at-Cliffe and around

Tucked away off the A258 Dover–Deal road, four miles northeast of Dover and around two miles inland, **ST MARGARET'S-AT-CLIFFE** was a major smuggling centre in the eighteenth century. There's very little evidence of that today, however; it's a sleepy spot, set on a glorious stretch of the **Saxon Shore Way** (see p.29) and on National Cycle Route 1. The local beach, **St Margaret's Bay**, is charming.

St Margaret's Bay

St Margaret's Bay, a twenty-minute walk down from the village, is the closest point on the British mainland to France, just twenty miles away. A secluded cove of shingle-sand beach, sheltered by white cliffs and with rockpools to explore and the odd fossil to be found, it's a nice spot for a seaside sojourn, with kayaking, canoeing and occasional surfing from the wave-cut platform off Ness Point. In the years following World War II St Margaret's was quite the artistic colony, an exclusive summer getaway for wealthy Londoners; **Noël Coward** and friends bought up the four Art Deco houses at the end of the beach and hosted the great and the good for seaside sojourns. By 1951 Coward deemed the bay too "crowded with noisy hoi polloi", however, leased his house to his friend **Ian Fleming**, and returned to his home in Aldington, in Romney Marsh (see p.130).

If you fancy a break from the beach, pop into the organically managed **Pines Garden** (10am–5pm: Jan–March Wed–Sun; April–Dec daily; £4; Ⓦ pinesgarden.co.uk), with its lake, mature trees, kitchen gardens and lovely **tearoom**. If you're feeling more energetic, you could walk up to South Foreland Lighthouse (see opposite) – follow Lighthouse Road up for a mile or so, and note that the path is poor in places.

ARRIVAL AND DEPARTURE

By train Dover Priory station is off Folkestone Rd, a 10min walk west of the centre.

Destinations Canterbury (every 30min–1hr; 15–30min); Deal (every 15min–1hr; 15min); Faversham (every 30min–1hr; 30–40min); Folkestone (every 10–50min; 20min); London Victoria (every 30min–1hr; 2hr); Sandwich (every 30min–1hr; 25min).

By bus The town-centre bus station is on Pencester Rd.

DOVER AND AROUND

Destinations Alkham (5 daily; 20min); Canterbury (every 15min–1hr; 45min); Deal (every 30min–1hr; 45min); Folkestone (every 20–30min; 30min); Hythe (every 20–30min; 1hr); London Victoria (11 daily; 1hr 55min–3hr 20min); St Margaret's-at-Cliffe (hourly; 20min); Sandwich (every 45min–1hr; 45min–1hr).

By ferry P&O ferries run between Dover and Calais, while DFDS car ferries run to Calais and Dunkirk.

INFORMATION AND TOURS

Tourist office Dover Museum, Market Square (April–Sept Mon–Sat 9.30am–5pm, Sun 10am–3pm; Oct–March Mon–Sat 9.30am–5pm; ☎01304 201066, ⓦwhitecliffscountry .org.uk).

National Trust White Cliffs of Dover Visitor Centre Langdon Cliffs, Upper Rd (daily: March–June, Sept & Oct 10am–5pm; July & Aug 10am–5.30pm; Nov–Feb 11am–4pm; free, NT; parking £3.50; ⓦnationaltrust.org .uk/white-cliffs-dover). A few panels illuminate the ecology and history of the local coast and countryside, and

there's a secondhand bookshop, but most space is devoted to the coffee shop and its huge outdoor deck – the ideal vantage point from which to watch the port activity below.

Dover Sea Safari Based in the Dover Sea Sports Centre on the beach, Dover Sea Safari (ⓦdoverseasafari.co.uk) offers a selection of high-octane speedboat tours – including harbour and White Cliffs jaunts (1hr 30min; £35), seal-watching trips at Pegwell Bay (2hr; £40) and occasional low-tide trips out to Goodwin Sands, where you are left for an hour to roam free (3hr; £60).

ACCOMMODATION

DOVER

Maison Dieu Guest House 89 Maison Dieu Rd, CT16 1RU ☎01304 204033, ⓦmaisondieu.co.uk. Friendly guesthouse in a central location, with seven attractive and very comfy single, double, twin and family rooms, some with shared facilities. A few have good views over the garden to Dover Castle. An optional breakfast costs £6.50 extra. **£50**

Marquis at Alkham Alkham Valley Rd, Alkham, 5 miles west of Dover, CT15 7DF ☎01304 873410, ⓦthemarquisatalkham.co.uk. This swanky restaurant-with-rooms offers ultramodern boutique-style accommodation within a 200-year-old inn. The ten chic rooms have huge windows, many with picture-perfect views across the Downs. Alkham itself, while pretty, is a sleepy place; the hotel restaurant (see p.122) is the main draw. Rates drop during the week, and there are numerous dinner-and-accommodation packages. **£149**

Peverell's Tower Dover Castle, CT16 1HU ☎0370 333 1187, ⓦenglish-heritage.org.uk/visit/holiday-cottages /find-a-holiday-cottage/peverells-tower. Be king or queen of the castle at this lovely self-catering option (sleeps two), a thirteenth-century tower set within Dover Castle's walls. Well-equipped and contemporary – though keeping its twisty stairs and medieval quirks – it also has its own roof terrace with amazing views. A stay here includes access to the castle. Three-, five- or seven-night stays only; nightly rate lower for longer stays. **£238**

THE WHITE CLIFFS

East Cottage South Foreland Lighthouse, St Margaret's Bay, CT15 6HP ☎0344 800 2070, ⓦnationaltrustholidays.org.uk//holiday-cottage /east-cottage-st-margaret-kent. Comfortable National Trust accommodation (one twin and one double) in a nineteenth-century lighthouse-keeper's cottage. Near the cliff edge, it's a magnificent spot (see opposite) – though if you stay in high season, or during a public event at the lighthouse, you'll be in the thick of things – and the Channel views are fabulous. There's no mobile reception up here, but that's all part of the charm. Minimum three-night stay; nightly rate lower for longer stays. **£271**

ST MARGARET'S-AT-CLIFFE AND AROUND

White Cliffs Hotel High St, CT15 6AT ☎01304 852229, ⓦthewhitecliffs.com. Chilled-out, friendly place – a great hit with walkers and cyclists – with a sociable restaurant/bar and really nice accommodation. The rooms tucked away in the warren of corridors in the main building – a sixteenth-century weatherboard house – come in all shapes, sizes and styles, from rustic and cosy to huge and glamorous, some with four posters; the smaller, less expensive options in outbuildings around the grassy beer garden are not quite so special, but all are super-comfortable. A tasty full breakfast is included. **£120**

EATING AND DRINKING

DOVER

Allotment 9 High St, CT16 1DP ☎01304 214467, ⓦtheallotmentdover.co.uk. A light-filled oasis on Dover's run-down High St, this place serves tasty, unpretentious food in a soothing space with a pretty courtyard garden. They keep things simple at breakfast (Full English; smoked salmon and scrambled egg) and lunch (bangers and mash; baguettes), but the dinner menus branch out into such dishes as black and white pudding on spicy chickpeas, or Whitstable fish stew. Starters from £5; mains £7–16. Tues–Sat 8.30am–11pm.

Blakes of Dover 52 Castle St, CT16 1PJ ☎01304 202194, ⓦblakesofdover.com. Cosy, wood-panelled basement bar offering real ales and local ciders, with a small beer garden at the back. Food – steaks and traditional pub grub – is served upstairs. Live music on Sun afternoons. Mon–Sat 11am–11pm, Sun noon–10pm.

Hythe Bay Seafood Restaurant at Dover The Esplanade, CT17 9FS ☎01304 207740, ⓦhythebay.co.uk. Sister restaurant to the original in Hythe (see p.129), this seafood place has a great location on Dover's seafront, and a traditional menu of simply prepared fish and seafood – from scallops to Dover sole, sardines to lobster – in a bright dining room with broad sea views. There's an outdoor deck for sunny days. Starters from £6, mains from £14. Daily noon–9.30pm; coffee served from 10am.

Marquis at Alkham Alkham Valley Rd, Alkham, 5 miles west of Dover, CT15 7DF ☎01304 873410, ⓦthemarquisatalkham.co.uk. A restaurant with rooms just a 10min drive from Dover. The chef applies a nouvelle, fusion sensibility to local ingredients, creating dishes such as local cod with Jerusalem artichoke, shiitake mushrooms and samphire, or roast rack of lamb with pickled beetroot and smoked aubergine; daytimes also

see a casual terrace menu of sandwiches, and afternoon tea is served daily. Mains from £16; tasting menus (request in advance) £35/£65; two-/three-course weekday lunch menus £14.95/£19.95. Mon–Fri 7.30–10am, noon–5pm & 6.30–9.30pm, Sat 8–10am, noon–5pm & 6.30–9.30pm, Sun 8–10am, noon–5pm & 6–8.30pm.

ST MARGARET'S-AT-CLIFFE AND AROUND

Cliffe Kitchen White Cliffs Hotel, High St, CT15 6AT ☎01304 852229, ⓦthewhitecliffs.com. Cheery, informal dining in a seaside pub/restaurant, lined with splashy local art and with a big, walled beer garden. Kentish wine and keg ales are on offer, while monthly changing menus list such dishes as wood pigeon with black pudding or Deal plaice with brown shrimp (starters from £5, mains £12.50–18.50). Outside formal meal times, doorstep sandwiches and cream teas are available; weekends see a short menu of sourdough pizzas from £6. Daily 7am–11pm; full meals served Mon–Sat noon–2pm & 6–9pm, Sun noon–3pm & 6–9pm.

The Coastguard St Margaret's Bay, CT15 6DY ☎01304 853051, ⓦthecoastguard.co.uk. This smartish, nautically themed beachside pub/restaurant is a good spot for a summer drink; enjoy a Kentish cask ale on their large terrace (separated from the beach by a car park) or the small beer garden that stretches practically down to the shingle. A short menu lists traditional English dishes (fish and chips, quiche, burgers, pies) with interesting daily specials (razor clams with garlic and toasted nuts, say). Starters from £5.50; mains £10–20. Mon–Sat 10am–11pm, Sun 10am–10pm; kitchen Mon–Sat noon–2.45pm & 6–8.45pm, Sun 6–8pm.

Folkestone

In the early 2000s, depressed after the demise of its tourist industry and the loss of its ferry link to France, **FOLKESTONE** was a doleful place. Like all the settlements on the east coast, it had long been defined by its relationship to the sea: starting out as a fishing village, it thrived as a smuggling centre in the seventeenth century, then grew in Victorian times to become a busy cross-Channel ferry port and upmarket **resort**. The ravages of two World Wars, followed by a rash of rebuilding, did the place no aesthetic favours, however, and the rise of cheap foreign travel hit hard. With the **Channel Tunnel**, west of town, whisking passengers direct from the M20 to the Continent, and the curtailment of the ferry service to Boulogne in 2000, reasons to stop in Folkestone were diminishing.

Thus began a concerted effort to start again, with many hopes pinned on the arts and the creative industries. Cue Folkestone's **Triennial**, which premiered in 2008. Spearheaded by the multimillionaire Roger de Haan (owner of Saga holidays, which is based here) and his Creative Foundation charity, the acclaimed art show brings considerable attention in festival years, and, spawning other cultural events in its wake, is gradually bringing Folkestone out of its extended limbo. Some parts of town – the seafront alongside Marine

Parade, for example – remain bleak and shabby, but with the regenerating **Creative Quarter** and the salty little fishing **harbour** (both owned by de Haan), the glorious **Lower Leas Coastal Park**, a sandy town **beach**, and the wild **Warren** cliffs and beach nearby, Folkestone has plenty to offer. Less than an hour from the capital by train, and with some stylish places to eat and stay, it's making waves as a seaside weekender.

The Creative Quarter

Occupying a small corner of town down by the harbour, Folkestone's **Creative Quarter** (🌐creativequarterfolkestone.org.uk) is a redeveloping slum area now owned by the Creative Foundation, who rent out the workspaces, commercial units and flats to artists. The steep and cobbled **Old High Street**, lined with brightly painted higgledy-piggledy seventeenth- and eighteenth-century buildings, holds most of the independent shops, cafés and galleries; it snakes its narrow way up to **Rendezvous Street**, another appealing little enclave. In Triennial years the Creative Quarter is Folkestone's beating heart; things are quieter at other times, with many shabby buildings boarded up or

3

THE FOLKESTONE TRIENNIAL

The **Folkestone Triennial** (dates change, generally two months in summer/autumn; 🌐folkestonetriennial.org.uk), a public art project first held in 2008, has played a major part in changing the town's image. Attracting big British names from Tracey Emin to Cornelia Parker and Martin Creed, as well as artists from around the world, the Triennial's importance to Folkestone as a confidence boost is inestimable. While many works are linked explicitly to the town, and most are location-specific, with soundscapes, performance art and mobile installations encouraging visitors to roam around and discover Folkestone itself, this is by no means a parochial event. Each year has a different theme, which, from dislocation and transience to the art of "looking", are universal. Talks, tours, workshops and live events keep energy levels high, with eminent critics and curators rubbing shoulders with curious locals – above all the Triennial aims for accessibility over elitism.

SIX INSTALLATIONS

Following each Triennial a selection of the exhibits are made permanent, cumulatively transforming the town into a giant outdoor gallery. The following are particularly striking; there's a full list, a map and a downloadable audio guide on 🌐folkestoneartworks.co.uk.

18 Holes Richard Wilson (2008). Look twice and you'll see that the three concrete-and-green-felt beach huts on the coastal promenade, around 500m west of the Leas Lift, are actually made from a crazy-golf course, the last remaining part of Folkestone's last remaining amusement park, finally demolished in 2007 after promises to redevelop and regenerate went by the wayside.

Baby Things Tracey Emin (2008). Blink and you'd miss them; these seven small bronzes from Kent-born YBA Emin – baby mittens, tiny cardies, teddies and lone bootees discarded on benches, railings and pavements – comment on the high teenage pregnancy rate in Folkestone and towns like it. Ostensibly ephemeral scraps of jetsam, they pack a surprisingly poignant punch.

The Folkestone Mermaid Cornelia Parker (2011). Parker's naturalistic version of Copenhagen's idealized Little Mermaid, a bronze life-cast sculpture modelled on a Folkestone woman, sits on a boulder by the harbour, overlooking Sunny Sands beach.

Out of Tune A. K. Dolven (2011). Norwegian-born artist Dolven has strung a discarded sixteenth-century church bell from a steel cable 65ft high, suspended between two posts on a lonely spot near the Leas Lift, where Folkestone's last amusement park once stood.

The Luckiest Place on Earth Strange Cargo (2014). Folkestone Central's railway bridge is transformed into a site of great fortune – four 3D-printed sculptures, each representing a genuine Folkestone resident and clutching good luck talismans, join the interactive *Recycling Point for Luck and Wishes*.

Whithervanes: a Neurotic Early Worrying System Cézanne Charles and John Marshall (2014). Five headless chickens dotted across rooftops act as weathervanes for online anxiety, monitoring digital news sources for alarmist language; how brightly the vanes are lit, and the speed at which they're turning, indicates the amount of online panic they are picking up.

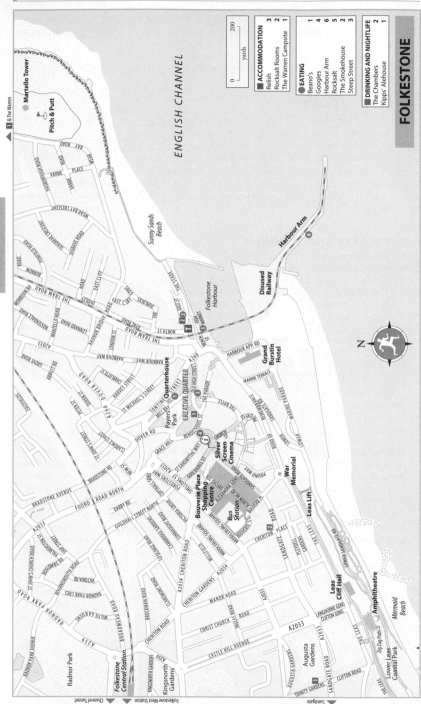

FOLKESTONE

ACCOMMODATION
Relish	3
Rocksalt Rooms	2
The Warren Campsite	1

EATING
Beano's	1
Googies	4
Harbour Arm	6
Rocksalt	5
The Smokehouse	2
Steep Street	3

DRINKING AND NIGHTLIFE
The Chambers	2
Kipps' Alehouse	1

ENGLISH CHANNEL

empty, but tantalizing pop-ups come and go and the community vibe is tangible, with flyers for local events and fundraisers plastered on windows everywhere.

Lower Leas Coastal Park and around

Folkestone exists on two levels – down by the sea and up on the cliffs, with steep hills and zigzag steps linking the two. Taking up a large, long swathe below the clifftop Leas promenade and above the beach, the **Lower Leas Coastal Park** is a glorious expanse of lush plantings, winding paths and pretty footbridges, all accompanied by sea views that on a sunny day have a distinctly Mediterranean flavour.

A man-made creation, made possible following a massive landslide in the eighteenth century, the park – which stretches west of the Leas Lift practically as far as the neighbouring village of Sandgate – was the talk of Victorian and Edwardian Folkestone, its landscaped promenades prime attractions of this genteel resort. Today it also features wildflower meadows and shady woodlands; behind the grassy outdoor amphitheatre, a dramatic zigzag path scales the rockface, complete with mysterious grottoes, up to the bandstand on the Leas. At the park's heart, thrillingly hidden in the woods, is an outstanding **children's playground** (free entry), with tube slides, zip-lines and all manner of adventure equipment for all ages. Beyond the point at which steps descend to the seafront *Mermaid Café* the park becomes wilder and less landscaped; it all culminates in a staircase leading up to the *Grand* and *Metropole* hotels on the Leas, relics of the resort's Edwardian heyday.

Leas Lift
Lower Sandgate Rd, CT20 1PR • Daily 9.30am–5.20pm; shorter hours in winter • £1.20

The last of Folkestone's four Victorian lifts, and one of only three water-powered funicular lifts remaining in England, the 1885 **Leas Lift** chugs up between the Leas seafront parade, with its lawns, formal flowerbeds and bandstand, down to the seafront at the end of Marine Parade, which is somewhat neglected at this spot.

Mermaid Beach

The shingle beaches below the coastal park are not bad for swimming, though you should watch out for rocks; the area around the *Mermaid Café*, unofficially called **Mermaid Beach**, is the best, a gently shelving slope with a rough sand bottom. The beach huts here – large concrete and hardboard boxes, painted in bright ice-cream colours – have a poignant, quintessentially Folkestone feel, being at once jaunty, pretty and a little rough.

THE MARTELLO TOWERS

Built during the Napoleonic Wars, and based on a Corsican design that had thwarted British troops in 1794, Kent's clumpy **Martello towers** formed part of a chain of more than one hundred such defences that ran along the coastline from Sussex to Suffolk. Resembling giant – and malevolent – upturned flowerpots, around 30ft or 40ft high, with walls some 8ft thick on the landward side and 13ft thick seaward, the towers were designed to house more than twenty men in cramped quarters above the ground-floor arsenal and below the rooftop gun platform. The predicted French invasion never came, but the towers were handy for keeping an eye on local **smuggling**, and some served as observation decks during **World War II** before being left, as a rule, to rack and ruin.

Some forty or so towers survive in England, many of them listed, and they're becoming desirable as property conversions. Folkestone boasts four of them; walk along the clifftop to the Warren and you will first encounter **Martello No. 3**, which acquired its ugly rooftop accretion in World War II. You can climb the rickety external staircase to the entrance (well above ground level, to confound attackers) for a bird's-eye view of the town and the Strait. There's another tower nearby, off Wear Bay Road, with more in Sandgate, Hythe and Dymchurch (in varying states of decay), and still more along the Sussex coast from Rye to Seaford.

The harbour and around

Split in two by the long-defunct railway viaduct, Folkestone's **harbour** was crowded in Victorian days with ships and pleasure vessels, and with fishermen hauling in their huge catches. Today, it's an atmospheric spot, fishing boats bobbing in the tidal waters and wildflowers sprouting from its rocky walls, the cobbled **Stade** (or "landing place") studded with black weatherboard fishermen's huts. Small-scale fishing still goes on here, with a couple of seafood stalls (the whelks are delicious), plus a brace of excellent restaurants (see opposite) joining the chip shop, caff and pubs. On the other side of the harbour, beyond the 1980s *Grand Burstin* hotel – an outrageous eyesore looming over the water like a half-built cruise liner – the regenerating **Harbour Arm** (daily 7am–7pm; ⓦ folkestoneharbourarm.co.uk) is one to watch. Terminus for Folkestone's old cross-channel boat trains, and fenced off for years, the arm now provides a good focus for seaside walks, and its food carts, restaurants and bars (see p.128) promise a welcome blast of energy in this corner of town.

Sunny Sands beach

It may not always be sunny at **Sunny Sands**, the little beach by the fishing harbour, but it's undeniably sandy, which is a rarity along this shingly shore. The golden stuff is celebrated every summer with a popular annual sandcastle competition, a cheery affair watched over by the *Folkestone Mermaid* (see box, p.123), and on fine weekends it can get packed. From here you can climb a zigzag staircase and walk along the East Cliff to the very different beach at the Warren, enjoying glorious sea views as you go.

The Warren

Accessible only on foot, fossil-bedecked **Warren Beach**, which fronts the **Warren**, a clifftop nature reserve and Site of Special Scientific Interest, feels wonderfully remote (though it's no secret in these parts, and when the tide is out you may well be joined by fossicking school groups and chilled-out families from the nearby campground). Getting there, a twenty-minute walk from Sunny Sands, is something of an adventure. Having ascended from Sunny Sands to the East Cliff clifftop, recent landslides mean you have to dip inland for a while, via a pitch-and-putt course, and passing a Martello tower on your way (see box, p.125), before rejoining the cliff-edge path. The gradual descent entails a bit of up and down along overgrown paths, and some minor scrambling over rocks – the official path takes the longer route round to the beach, but many people head down through the undergrowth to get to the sands sooner. Broad, flat and gleaming, punctuated by dilapidated groynes, seaweed-slick rocks, fossils and sea shells – and backed by a rather forbidding concrete sea defence – the Warren has a wild, raw magnificence, with huge, open views across to Samphire Hoe and the White Cliffs.

ARRIVAL AND INFORMATION   FOLKESTONE AND AROUND

By train Folkestone Central station is off Cheriton Rd, just under a mile northwest of the Cultural Quarter.
Destinations Dover (every 10–50min; 20min); London Charing Cross (every 30min–1hr; 1hr 40min); London St Pancras (every 30min–1hr; 55min); Sevenoaks (every 30min–1hr; 1hr 10min).
By bus The bus station is in the centre of town near Bouverie Place Shopping Centre.
Destinations Dover (every 20–30min; 30min); London Victoria (4 daily; 2hr 10min–3hr).
Tourist office Town Hall, 1–2 Guildhall St (Mon–Fri 9am–5pm; ❶ 01303 257946, ⓦ discoverfolkestone .co.uk); also includes information on Hythe and Romney Marsh.

ACCOMMODATION

Relish 4 Augusta Gardens, CT20 2RR ❶ 01303 850952, ⓦ therelish.co.uk. An attractive Regency building next to the green Augusta Gardens and not far from the Leas, with ten quiet, comfortable boutique-style rooms, a comfy lounge and an outdoor terrace where you can eat your cooked breakfast. Little extras include complimentary home-made cake, juices and a welcome glass of wine. No lift. __£98__
Rocksalt Rooms 1–3 Back St, CT19 6NN ❶ 01303 212070, ⓦ rocksaltfolkestone.co.uk. Four "boutique bolt

holes" (they're small) in an unbeatable harbourside location above the *Smokehouse* restaurant, and brought to you by the *Rocksalt* crew. Those at the front are by far the best, with French windows and water views – those at the back can get stuffy – but they're all chic and super-comfy, with scrubbed bare-brick walls, plump duvets, espresso-makers and tiny wet-rooms; a tasty continental breakfast is delivered to your room in a hamper. **£85**

The Warren Campsite The Warren, CT19 6NQ ✆01303 255093 (no calls after 8pm), ⓦ campingandcaravanning club.co.uk. Eighty pitches in a quiet cliffside location by the Warren nature reserve and beach, walkable (just about) from Folkestone. The views are glorious, but be prepared for the poor, pothole-scarred approach road. Non-members pay thirty percent more. Minimum stay two nights in summer and on Fri & Sat all season. Closed Nov–Easter. **£13.30**

EATING

Beano's 43 Tontine St, CT20 1JT ✆01303 211817. This simple little veggie/vegan restaurant is a reliable stalwart in the Creative Quarter. Come for Mediterranean-inspired breakfasts (till 11.30am), goat's cheese toasties or fancy sandwiches, or fill up on falafel, quinoa burgers or spinach and almond curry. Mains £6–8. Mon–Sat 8.30am–5.30pm, Sun 9am–5.30pm; occasionally open Fri eves.

Googies 15 Rendezvous St, CT20 1EY ✆01303 246188, ⓦ googies.co.uk. Exhibiting local art and hosting regular gigs in the basement, bohemian *Googies* offers a home-made menu using Kentish produce and suppliers. From big breakfasts and eggy brunches (from £5) via small plates – hot smoked salmon fritters; brisket and whipped bone marrow on sourdough (from £4) – to home-made burgers and Modern British mains (from £11), everything tastes great. Mon & Tues 9am–6pm, Wed & Thurs 9am–9pm, Fri & Sat 9am–11pm, Sun 10am–6pm.

Harbour Arm Folkestone Harbour, CT20 1QH ⓦ folkestoneharbourarm.co.uk. Long neglected and out of bounds, the restored Harbour Arm features a string of food carts serving global cuisine. There's waterside seating, with restaurants and bars in the restored buildings behind. It's early days, but the Harbour Arm is looking set to become a foodie focus in Folkestone. Note that individual businesses keep different hours, and that the opening days and hours of the Harbour Arm itself may extend in the future; check the website. Spring Fri & Sat 9am–10pm, Sun 9am–7pm; summer Mon–Sat 9am–10pm, Sun 9am–7pm; autumn Fri 5–10pm, Sat 9am–10pm, Sun 10am–7pm.

★**Rocksalt** 4–5 Fishmarket, CT19 6AA ✆01303 212070, ⓦ rocksaltfolkestone.co.uk. A beautiful cantilevered glass-and-wood restaurant with a deck on the harbour, a whelk's throw from the fishing boats, *Rocksalt* is a sophisticated setting for flawless Kentish food. The fresh local fish is a winner, of course, from plump mussels via roast mackerel to whole local lobster with garlic butter, but the meat and veggie choices, made with produce from their own farm, are delicious too – roast cauliflower with cheese fondue, wild garlic pesto and hazelnuts, say, or rump of spring lamb with tarragon broth. Starters from £7, mains from £13; two-/three-course set lunch (Mon–Fri) £21.50/£25. Mon–Sat noon–3pm & 7–10.30pm, Sun noon–3pm.

The Smokehouse 1–3 Back St, CT19 6NN ✆01303 884718, ⓦ thesmokehousefolkestone.co.uk. *Rocksalt*'s sister restaurant, a modern, brick-and-glass affair on the harbour, serves fantastic fish and chips (from £7) to eat in or take away. Though portions are unceremoniously heaped in cardboard boxes, this is no run-of-the-mill chippie – along with cod and haddock, and all the usual accompaniments, you could go for mackerel, ray or scallops, with starters including mussel bhaji or salt-and-pepper squid. The toughest choice is whether to have the fish healthily baked or in *Smokehouse*'s fabulous, crackly crisp batter. Mon–Sat noon–9pm, Sun noon–6pm.

★**Steep Street** 18–24 Old High St, CT10 1RL ✆01303 247819, ⓦ steepstreet.co.uk. This gorgeous coffee house, lined ceiling to floor with vintage books, buzzes with a Cultural Quarter crowd chatting, reading or tapping on laptops. The food, from sandwiches to salads, quiches to cakes, is simple but good, and inexpensive (cakes from £2). Arm yourself with a cappuccino, a home-made flapjack and a couple of books, head up to the mezzanine, settle down in a plump armchair and prepare to linger. Mon–Fri 8.30am–6pm, Sat 9am–6pm, Sun 9am–5pm.

3

FOLKESTONE FESTIVALS

Other than the Folkestone Triennial (see box, p.123), the town's main event is the ten-day **Folkestone Book Festival** (Nov; ⓦ folkestonebookfest.com). Largely based at the Quarterhouse (see p.128), the book festival brings in a host of big-name crowd-pleasers, from Jonathan Coe to Rose Tremain, along with TV and radio folk and local historians. Events include screenings, plays and workshops; many are free. **Open Quarter**, meanwhile, an open studio event in mid-June, is a lively time to be in the Creative Quarter, with special exhibitions, performances, workshops and "meet the artist" events (ⓦ creativequarterfolkestone.org.uk).

DRINKING AND NIGHTLIFE

The Chambers Radnor Chambers, Cheriton Place, CT20 2BB ☎01303 223333. The location, in the shopping streets some way from the seafront, isn't inspiring, but this laidback basement café-bar is a popular spot for local ales and ciders, with good pub food, DJ nights and live music. Mon–Thurs & Fri noon–11pm, Fri & Sat noon–1am; kitchen closes a little earlier.

Kipps' Alehouse 11 Old High St, CT20 1RL ☎01303 246766, ⓦfacebook.com/Kippsalehouse. Informal pub/live music venue with a relaxed, cosy feel, serving real ales, craft beers, traditional ciders and inexpensive global food to a friendly, lively crowd. Mon–Thurs & Sun noon–10pm, Fri & Sat noon–11pm; kitchen closes a little earlier.

ENTERTAINMENT

Quarterhouse Mill Bay, CT20 1BN ☎01303 760750, ⓦquarterhouse.co.uk. The anchor of the Creative Quarter, the Quarterhouse hosts a variety of live music, comedy and theatre, along with festival events and film screenings, in a striking modern building.

3 Hythe and around

Just five miles south of Folkestone, at the northeastern edge of Romney Marsh, the ancient town of **HYTHE** was a Cinque Port (see box, p.107), and an important entry point for pilgrims crossing the Channel to visit Becket's tomb in Canterbury. Today it's an attractive little seaside town, the northern terminus of the **Romney, Hythe & Dymchurch Railway** (see box opposite), with a broad pebbly beach. During Hythe's heyday and before the silting up of the harbour, the High Street was at the sea's edge; today it lies north of the A259 and the Royal Military Canal, which runs prettily through town on its thirty-mile journey to Sussex. The beach here is good for **watersports**, especially windsurfing; contact the Hythe and Saltwood Sailing Club (HSSC; ☎01303 265178, ⓦhssc.net) on the waterfront.

Royal Military Canal

ⓦroyalmilitarycanal.com

Fringed on both sides by tree-lined banks, the **Royal Military Canal** was built, like the Martello towers (see box, p.123) – of which Hythe has five – to defend the coast from potential attack by Napoleonic troops. Today it runs for nearly thirty miles from Seabrook, just east of town, through the marshes to a point south of Winchelsea in Sussex; you can walk or cycle its entire length. Cutting through town, the canal gives Hythe its distinctive character, its grassy banks dotted with sculptures and making a splendid place for a shady picnic. **Rowing boats** can be rented from next to Ladies' Walk Bridge (Easter–Sept; £12/hr; ☎07718 761236, ⓦelectricboathythe.co.uk), and every other year in August the canal hosts a **Venetian Fete** (ⓦhythe-venetianfete.com), with a floating costume parade. Further out of town, the canal becomes increasingly peaceful, with swans gliding on the water, herons and kingfishers in the trees, and bright-yellow water lilies and irises in the shallows.

St Leonard's Church

Oak Walk, CT21 5DN • Ossuary Mon–Sat 11am–1pm & 2–4pm, Sun 2–4pm • Church free; ossuary £1 • ☎01303 262370, ⓦstleonardschurchhythekent.org

The Norman church of **St Leonard's**, high on a hill on the north side of town, is a handsome building, with a soaring thirteenth-century chancel boasting some fine stone carving, but its main appeal is of a more eerie kind. Step into the ambulatory, where an **ossuary** confronts you with a startling pile of thousands of thigh bones and shelves of grinning jawbones and skulls, neatly packed as if on some ghoulish supermarket shelf. Dating back to medieval times and earlier, they're thought to be the remains of locals buried in the churchyard and moved when the church was expanded in the thirteenth century – some show signs of being descended from Roman settlers. Medieval church officials immediately saw the potential of such a gruesome tourist attraction, and charged pilgrims on their way to Becket's shrine in Canterbury for the privilege of a peep.

Port Lympne Reserve

Lympne, CT21 4LR • **Reserve** Daily: April–Oct 9.30am–6.30pm, last admission 3pm; Nov–March 9.30am–5pm, last admission 2.30pm • £25, under-16s £21 • ☎ 0844 842 4647, ⓦ aspinallfoundation.org/port-lympne • **Dusk safaris** May–Aug Wed & Thurs 6pm • £45 • ☎ 01303 234111 • Bus #10 from Folkestone to Ashtead stops near the reserve

Set in around six hundred acres five miles west of Hythe, **Port Lympne Reserve**, along with Howletts near Canterbury (see p.62), works with the charitable Aspinall Foundation on a conservation and breeding programme for wild and endangered species. The park is home to more than seven hundred animals, many of them rare – along with a pair of adorable spectacled bears and some Western Lowland gorillas, it has the largest herd of endangered black rhino in the UK. Port Lympne isn't a zoo, so you're not guaranteed a view of all the animals – visits start off safari-style, with bone-rattling trucks taking you around the hundred-acre "African Experience" (wildebeest, giraffes, zebras, black rhino), "Asian Experience" (bears, rhinos, cheetahs), "Carnivore Territory" (big and rare cats, including Barbary lions, now extinct in the wild), and the primate enclosure; some areas, including the new Dinosaur Forest (populated with life-sized models of historic crowd-pullers from T-Rex to pterodactyls) are also accessible on foot. The Serengeti it isn't, and the vision of exotic creatures, should you be lucky enough to see them, roaming through the gentle Kent countryside, with views over Romney Marsh to the Channel, is incongruous to say the least – but it's a commendable enterprise, and quite an adventure in this quiet corner of Kent if you manage to be here on a sunny day.

The best way to see the park can be outside opening hours: **dusk safaris** including drinks and dinner are available in summer, while a number of **accommodation** options range from romantic overnight glamping safaris (see below) to family glamping and camping pods, a couple of smart hotels and a luxurious cottage, sleeping eight, with its own private chef.

ACCOMMODATION AND EATING   HYTHE AND AROUND

Hythe Bay Seafood Restaurant Marine Parade, CT21 6AW ☎ 01303 233844, ⓦ hythebay.co.uk. With a nice setting on Hythe's seafront, this once-smart but now slightly tired dining room has a breezy front terrace. It's less upmarket than the newer branch, in Dover (see p.122), but the menu is mostly the same, and the simple, traditional fish dishes are largely good, especially if you choose the local catch. Starters from £6, mains from £14. Daily noon–9.30pm; coffee served from 10am.

Livingstone Lodge Port Lympne Reserve, Lympne, CT21 4LR ☎ 01303 802457, ⓦ aspinallfoundation .org/livingstone-lodge. A safari in Kent may not be the

---

ROMNEY, HYTHE & DYMCHURCH RAILWAY

The **Romney, Hythe & Dymchurch Railway** (RH&DR), a fifteen-inch-gauge line running the 13.5 miles between Hythe and Dungeness (1hr), offers an enjoyable way to travel through this quirky corner of Kent – stops include Dymchurch, St Mary's Bay, New Romney and Romney Sands, named for the neighbouring holiday camp, near Greatstone Beach (mid-March to Oct daily; Nov to mid-March Sat & Sun, plus special events and tours; £17 for a Hythe–Dungeness return or a rover ticket including the railway exhibition at New Romney station; shorter journeys are cheaper; ☎ 01797 362353, ⓦ rhdr.org.uk). Built in 1927 as a tourist attraction, its fleet of steam locomotives are mainly one-third-scale models made during the 1920s and 1930s, so taking a long ride can feel a little cramped, but if Laurel and Hardy – who reopened the line from New Romney to Dungeness after the war in 1947 – could do it, anyone can. Hythe station is a fifteen-minute walk west of the town centre, on the south bank of the canal by Station Bridge, while the end of the line, in Dungeness, is near the Old Lighthouse (see p.131). New Romney, the original station, is the railway headquarters, with play parks and a model railway exhibition (£2).

most obvious of holidays, but among the many accommodation options offered by this wildlife reserve (see p.129) these luxurious overnight adults-only glamping breaks (April–Oct Wed–Sun) offer a unique experience, including park entry, a game drive, African-inspired buffet dinner, full breakfast, and accommodation in opulent "tents" (some have four-poster beds and en suites; all have private terraces) overlooking a watering hole. **£340**

★ **Saltwood on the Green** The Green, Saltwood, CT21 4PS 01303 237800, saltwoodrestaurant .co.uk. Buzzy local bistro in a village a mile or so north of Hythe, dishing up exciting, beautifully presented food from an accomplished chef. The inventive menu, using local and foraged ingredients, lists dishes that you won't see for miles around – pumpkin cornbread with chorizo jam and goat's curd, for example, or steamed bun with bacon and onion ash – along with simple, flavour-packed options such as open ravioli of broad beans, spinach and cottage cheese or local plaice with charred spring onion and giant couscous. Desserts are pretty special, too. Small plates from £6; large plates from £12; two-/three-course lunch menus £15/£18. Wed–Sat 9am–3pm & 6–11pm, Sun 11.30am–5pm.

Romney Marsh

In Roman times, what is now the southernmost chunk of Kent was submerged beneath the English Channel. The lowering of sea levels in the Middle Ages, however, along with later reclamation, eventually created a hundred-square-mile area of shingle and marshland now known as **ROMNEY MARSH**. Once home to important Cinque and limb ports (see box, p.107), along with villages made wealthy from the wool trade, this now rather forlorn expanse stretches inland for around ten miles from Hythe and skims the eastern edges of the Weald before curving around to meet Rye in Sussex. The "marsh" is in fact made up of three marshes – Romney proper extends as far south as the road from Appledore to New Romney, Walland lies to the south and west, and Denge spreads east of Lydd. Together they present a melancholy aspect, much given over to agriculture and with few sights as such, unless you count the **sheep** (see box below), the birdlife and several curious medieval **churches** (see box, p.132). While this flat, depopulated area makes grand walking and cycling country, its salt-speckled, big-skied beauty can also be appreciated on the **Romney, Hythe & Dymchurch Railway** (see box, p.129). The little train is in particular an excellent way to reach lonely **Dungeness**, the shingle promontory presided over by two colossal nuclear power stations that is so beloved of artists.

ROMNEY SHEEP

The salty, mineral-packed Romney marshes are famed among foodies for their indigenous breed of **sheep**, a hardy, independent and low-maintenance creature with a stout body and stubby legs. In addition to producing excellent meat, Romney sheep have heavy, dense and long-woolled fleeces; the local woolmaking industry, which started in medieval times, was hugely profitable, spinning off a flourishing smuggling trade that lasted into the nineteenth century. In the 1800s nearly a quarter of a million Romneys roamed this waterlogged landscape, and in 1872 the first of them were exported to Australia. Itinerant shepherds, or "**lookers**", followed the flocks as they wandered, shacking up in small brick huts (just a few of these shed-like structures remain today, identifiable by their rusty iron roofs and squat chimneys). There are fewer genuine Romneys around the marsh nowadays – you'd see more in New Zealand – and, as improved drainage has seen much of the land turned over to agriculture, many are bred on farms elsewhere. You may spot a few as you explore, however, foraging in the lush grasses and samphire.

Much **Romney lamb**, which is juicy, tender and sweet (not, surprisingly enough, salty), is exported to France, but it's also a regular on the menus of good Kent and Sussex restaurants, and you can buy it at some of the better farm shops. Vegetarians can enjoy the bounty of the marshes at **Romney Marsh Wools**, a sheep farm near Ashford, which sells luxurious Romney wool products including throws, moccasins and wool-fat soaps (romneymarshwools.co.uk).

Dymchurch and around

Five miles from Hythe, **Dymchurch** is torn between defining itself as a cheery family resort and playing up its smuggling associations, particularly its location as a base for the marvellously named Dr Syn, the smuggling, swashbuckling vicar featured in the early twentieth-century novels of Russell Thorndike. The wide, three-mile-long **beach** is a good one: clean, sandy and family-friendly, with donkey rides. There's another nice beach at **St Mary's Bay**, the next stop down on the Romney, Hythe & Dymchurch Railway. Just a hop away is the hamlet of **St Mary in the Marsh**, a scrap of a place with a couple of literary associations – Noël Coward lived in a cottage next door to the *Star Inn* pub before moving to Aldington nearby, while his friend, Edith Nesbit, who also lived nearby, is buried in the twelfth-century churchyard (see box, p.132). Once a busy Cinque Port at the mouth of the River Rother, **New Romney** lost its importance after a series of dramatic storms in the thirteenth century silted up its harbour and changed the course of the river, sending it out to the sea at Rye; today it's the hub of the RH&DR (see box, p.129), with an interesting Norman church whose western door is sunk beneath ground level.

3

Dungeness

An end-of-the-earth feel pervades **DUNGENESS**, the windlashed headland at the southern extremities of Romney Marsh. The largest expanse of shingle in Europe, presided over by two hulking nuclear power stations (one of them decommissioned), "the Ness" is not conventionally pretty, but there's a strange beauty to this lost-in-time spot with its landmark **lighthouses** and its clanking miniature **railway** (see box, p.129). Many of the little cottages standing higgledy-piggledy on the golden shingle date back to when this entire area was owned by Southern Railway, and train workers converted old carriages into simple homes; today they're joined by high-concept architectural conversions, fishing boats both dilapidated and jaunty, forbidding watchtowers, rusting winches, long-obsolete "listening ears" (pre-radar early warning devices built in the 1920s and 30s) and decrepit concrete bunkers. Stubborn wildflowers, grasses and lichens cling to the pebbles like spillages of bright paint, adding a palette of splashy colour. Many artists – most famously the late filmmaker Derek Jarman, whose **Prospect Cottage** continues to draw garden lovers and movie fans alike – have been inspired by the area's extraordinary light, its colossal skies and its quiet weirdness, setting up home in the ramshackle cottages and fashioning gardens from beachcombed treasures.

With its steep beach and fierce current, Dungeness Point is no place for a swim, although you can do so further north towards Lydd, if you take great care with the tides, and it's possible to fish from Dungeness beach. The headland has been designated a **National Nature Reserve**, with no new development allowed. Its unique and fragile ecology supports a huge variety of vegetation, from wild red poppies and deep-pink sea peas to inky-blue sea kale, and animal life – including large populations of the endangered great crested newt – and it's renowned for superb **birdwatching**.

Old Lighthouse

Next to the RH&DR station, Dungeness, TN29 9NB • 10.30am–4.30pm: March–May & late Sept to Oct Sat & Sun; June Tues–Thurs, Sat & Sun; July to late Sept daily • £4 • ☎ 01797 321300, ⊕ dungenesslighthouse.com

Decommissioned since the erection in 1961 of its smaller successor nearby (the "New Lighthouse"), the 143ft-high **Old Lighthouse**, built in 1904 and painted the same velvety black as many of the beach cottages, displays navigational equipment and information panels on its four floors and affords sweeping views from the top. It's nearly two hundred steps up, with an extremely steep final stretch, and can be dramatically windy – vertigo sufferers should beware. The large, round structure next to the Old Lighthouse is the base of the oldest lighthouse of all, built in the eighteenth century and long since gone. It is now a private residence.

FIVE ROMNEY MARSH CHURCHES

The dozen or so **medieval churches** of the Romney marshes are atmospheric and often isolated places, whose largely unrestored interiors provide evocative reminders of the days when the area thrived on the lucrative wool trade and wealth from its ports. The following are the pick of the bunch; for a full list, see ⓦ rmhct.org.uk.

St Augustine's Brookland. Decidedly odd thirteenth-century church, with its conical wooden belfry standing beside it rather than on top of it. Inside, note the wall painting on the south wall, showing the murder of Thomas Becket, and the unusual lead font marked with signs of the zodiac.

St Clement's Old Romney. Filmmaker Derek Jarman has his simple gravestone in the churchyard of this lovely Norman church. The restful whitewashed interior, with its Georgian minstrel gallery and rose-pink box pews, can be seen in the 1962 Disney movie *Dr Syn, Alias the Scarecrow,* which starred Patrick McGoohan of *The Prisoner* fame.

St Dunstan's Snargate. The terracotta wall painting of a ship (c.1500) in the north aisle of this thirteenth-century church is locally believed to have been a secret signal to smugglers that this was a safe haven.

St Mary the Virgin St Mary in the Marsh. This peaceful ancient church, parts of which date back to 1133, is notable for being the burial place of author E. Nesbit; her grave is marked by a simple wooden sign.

St Thomas à Becket Fairfield. The iconic Romney church, standing like a lonely sentinel upon the Walland Marsh, is all that survives of the lost village of Fairfield. Its largely Georgian interior, with herringbone floor and exposed beams, is beautifully tranquil.

Prospect Cottage

Dungeness Rd, TN29 9NE • Roughly a 20min walk from the RH&DR station

The late **Derek Jarman** (1942–94), artist and avant-garde filmmaker, made his home at **Prospect Cottage**, a black weatherboard cottage with sunshine-yellow window frames, and the shingle garden he created in his final years from stones, rusty sea treasures and tough little plants remains a poignant memorial. The flowers may not always bloom quite as brightly today, without Jarman's guiding hand, but the poetry of his vision lingers, not least on the side of the house, where a long quote from John Donne's poem *The Sunne Rising* is carved black on black.

As everywhere in Dungeness, there is no fence, and the current resident, Jarman's friend Keith Collins, is used to people nosing around – but do bear in mind that both the garden and the house are private.

RSPB Dungeness Reserve

Off the Lydd road, three miles from Dungeness, TN29 9PN • **Reserve** Daily 9am–9pm or sunset • £4 • **Visitor centre** Daily: March–Oct 10am–5pm; Nov–Feb 10am–4pm • Free • ☎ 01797 320588, ⓦ rspb.org.uk/Dungeness

The marshy Dungeness promontory, poking out vigorously into the Channel, attracts huge colonies of gulls, as well as bitterns, little ringed plovers, Slavonian grebes, smews and wheatears. You can see them, and all manner of water birds, waders and wildfowl, from the huge picture windows at the excellent **RSPB visitor centre** and from half a dozen hides in the reserve itself, accessible on three easy trails.

ARRIVAL AND INFORMATION   ROMNEY MARSH

By train There's a mainline train station at Appledore, on the Ashford-to-Hastings line, while Dymchurch, St Mary's Bay, New Romney, Romney Sands and Dungeness are all on the miniature RH&DR (see box, p.129).

Romney Marsh Visitor Centre Dymchurch Rd, on the A259 between Dymchurch and New Romney (Easter–Sept

daily 10am–5pm; Oct–Easter Wed–Sun 10am–4pm; ☎ 01797 369487, ⓦ wildlifetrusts.org/reserves/romney -marsh-visitor-centre). This ecofriendly centre is packed with information on the wildlife of the marsh, with marked trails and organic gardens.

ACCOMMODATION

Beach Sun Retreat 21 Sycamore Gardens, Dymchurch, TN29 0LA ☎ 07830 182380, ⓦ beachsunretreat.com. This

self-catering house is perfect if you're sick of the British weather – its "sun room", complete with tropical mural, fake

ACTION WATERSPORTS

The coast around Camber in Sussex is renowned for its watersports (see box, p.173); just six miles away in Lydd, **Action Watersports** (📞01797 321885, 🌐actionwatersports.co.uk) is a top-notch facility offering sheltered waterskiing, wakeboarding, paddleboarding, flyboarding and jet-skiing on a purpose-built, 22-acre freshwater lake. Lessons and equipment rental are available, with packages from £27.50 for a fifteen-minute water-ski or wakeboard session to £275 for a jet-skiing package. There's a huge pro shop and showers on site, along with a relaxation area and kids' playground.

palms, DJ decks and gurgling waterfall, is bathed in replica natural sunlight. Though undeniably kitsch, it's more hip than tacky – on the ground floor of an old, timber-clad hotel, the property has a luxurious, airy feel with two double rooms and a single, a movie-screening room, and extensive grounds with access to Dymchurch's sandy beach. Minimum three-night stay; nightly rate lower for longer stays. **£260**

Romney Bay House Hotel Coast Rd, Littlestone, TN28 8QY 📞01797 364747, 🌐romneybayhousehotel.co.uk. Accessed down a potholed road near Dungeness and presiding alone over the lonesome shingle like a fading *grande dame*, this 1920s beauty was built by Sir Clough Williams-Ellis, who designed Portmeirion in Wales, for the Hollywood gossip columnist Hedda Hopper. Today it's a quirky hotel, with ten en-suite double/twins (some with sea views), a cosy drawing room, and a light-filled lounge overlooking the sea, which is just footsteps away. The restaurant (Tues, Wed, Fri & Sat) serves a four-course set dinner for £45. No children under 14. **£110**

Shingle House Dungeness Beach, TN29 9NE

🌐living-architecture.co.uk. A breathtaking modern self-catering house, offered by Alain de Botton's Living Architecture programme, blending in beautifully with its surroundings. Behind the tarry black timber exterior it's designed to the very last inch – all white tongue-and-groove, stained wood, warm concrete and vast glass walls opening out onto the shingle – and offers seriously luxurious accommodation for up to eight people. It books up very fast and very far in advance. Three-night or weekly stays only. Minimum three-night stay; nightly rate lower for longer stays. **£792**

★**The Watch Tower** Dungeness Rd, TN29 9NF 📞01797 321773, 🌐watchtowerdungeness.com. Originally a lookout post built in the Napoleonic Wars, this is a peaceful and very welcoming one-room B&B on the northern edge of the Ness. A private guest entrance leads through the arty back garden, via your own light, plant-filled conservatory – where a splendid breakfast is served – into the comfortable twin room (can sleep up to four) with its cheery Dungeness-themed bathroom. **£99**

EATING AND DRINKING

Britannia Inn Dungeness Rd, TN29 9ND 📞01797 321959, 🌐britanniadungeness.co.uk. At Dungeness Point, right by the RH&DR station and squatting beneath two fluttering Union and St George's flags, this unfussy place serves Shepherd Neame ales and pub grub. Mon & Tues 11am–3.30pm, Wed–Fri 11am–3.30pm & 6.30–9pm, Sat 11am–9pm, Sun noon–7pm; kitchen Mon & Tues noon–3pm, Wed–Fri noon–3pm & 6.30–8.30pm, Sat noon–8.30pm, Sun noon–6pm.

Dungeness Snack Shack Fish Hut, Dungeness Rd, TN29 9NB 📞07825 598921, 🌐dungenesssnackshack.net. It doesn't get much fresher, or more local, than this – the day's catch, brought ashore and sold straight off the boat, to take away from this little hut. Try a lobster or crab roll, a fisherman's roll (fresh grilled fish served in a bun), or a Mexican roll (served in a flatbread with lime, chilli and sour cream). They're open in winter, too, dishing up a warming chowder – and all as cheap as chips (baps from £3.50). Usually Fri–Sun 11am–3.30pm.

Pilot Inn Battery Rd, TN29 9NJ 📞01797 320314, 🌐thepilotdungeness.co.uk. The vaguely nautical *Pilot* pub, just north of Dungeness lifeboat station, is the local

favourite for fish and chips (from £11.25) – other options, from pies via burgers to a vegan stew with dumplings, are also on offer. Richardson's, opposite, sells superb smoked and fresh wet fish. Mon–Sat 11am–10pm, Sun 11am–9pm; kitchen until 1hr before close.

★**Red Lion** Snargate, TN29 9UQ 📞01797 344648. Take a trip back in time at this gem of a pub, which has been in the same family for more than a century and changed little since the 1940s. World War II memorabilia fills the place, Kentish cask ales and ciders are served at a cluttered marble bar, and they've even got a selection of vintage pub games. Daily; hours vary.

Woolpack Inn Beacon Lane, Brookland, TN29 9TJ 📞01797 344321, 🌐thewoolpackinn.org. Family-friendly country pub in a quiet village, retaining many of its fifteenth-century features, including a head-bangingly low ceiling and wattle-and-daub walls. You can drink in the large garden or the cosy, hop-strewn interior, and eat satisfying, home-cooked pub grub – steaks, fresh local fish, veggie dishes and burgers. Mains £7–20. Mon–Fri 11am–3pm & 6–10.30pm, Sat 11am–11pm, Sun noon–10pm; kitchen Mon–Fri noon–2.30pm & 6–9pm, Sat & Sun noon–9pm.

The Kent Weald

OAST HOUSES, SISSINGHURST

The Kent Weald

The Kentish Weald, wedged between the North Downs and the High Weald of Sussex, is defined by its gentle hills and country lanes, shallow valleys and tangled broadleaf woodlands. This landscape is at once quintessentially English, and, with its historic orchards and old brick oast houses – testament to the days when the Weald dominated England's hopping industry – has also come to symbolize Kent as a whole. The entire region, packed full of historic sites, royal estates, fairy-tale moated manor houses and some of England's loveliest gardens, makes splendid day-trip territory – the western Weald, in particular, is an easy journey from London.

It's perfectly feasible to plan a longer break, too, basing yourself in or around any one of numerous villages – Cranbrook, say – or in **Tunbridge Wells**, by far the nicest of the Weald's large towns. Both sit in the beautiful **High Weald**, scattered with gorgeous hamlets, with lots of country walking, peaceful places to stay and more gastropubs than you can shake a pint of real ale at. Some of England's finest **vineyards** are scattered around the east of the region, where the chalky soil yields dry whites and sparkling wines as good as any from France.

The commuter towns of **Sevenoaks** and **Maidstone**, on the fringes of the Weald, are surrounded by tourist attractions. Big hitters include Leeds Castle and **Hever Castle** – Anne Boleyn's family home – Winston Churchill's estate at **Chartwell**, and the jaw-dropping treasure house of **Knole**, the childhood home of Vita Sackville-West, who went on to create the sublime gardens at **Sissinghurst**. Less known, but with big appeal, are the Roman villa at Lullingstone; the fascinating Down House, where Charles Darwin lived and worked for forty years; and the delightful Elizabethan manor and gardens at Penshurst, along with a host of smaller historic houses and gardens. The Kentish Weald is renowned for its bluebells, which carpet the woodlands with a shimmer of mauve each spring – you'll find stunning woods around Chartwell and Sissinghurst, as well as near Ightham Mote, a charming Tudor manor house, and at the Edwardian Emmetts Garden.

Much of the Weald is commuter territory, so public transport to the main towns is good, but you'll need to drive – or even better, walk or cycle – to explore the countryside in depth. Long-distance walking routes include the Greensand Way from Surrey – which runs through the Weald before ending at Hamstreet, on the border with Romney Marsh – and many shorter loops and trails link the area's heritage sights. The North Downs offer excellent walking opportunities, with peaceful villages just a hop away from the busy Eurostar hub of **Ashford**.

Royal Tunbridge Wells

It seems unfair that **ROYAL TUNBRIDGE WELLS** is still associated, in many minds, with the fictional letter-writer known as "Disgusted of Tunbridge Wells", a whingeing Little Englander renowned for blustering and umbrage. Don't be misled – this handsome spa town, established after a bubbling spring was discovered here in 1606, and peaking

---

Hopping mad p.139
Cycling the Tudor Trail p.143

The Kent & East Sussex Railway p.151
Shipbourne Farmers' Market p.155

DEER AT KNOLE

Highlights

❶ Bedgebury This ancient broadleaf forest and world-renowned pinetum is a glorious spot to commune with nature, with countless options for all the family to get active. **See p.145**

❷ Vineyard tours Strolling through vineyards, learning about English viniculture, and tasting excellent, award-winning wines is a wonderful way to spend a sunny Kent afternoon.
See p.146 & p.150

❸ Sissinghurst Breathtaking gardens created by Vita Sackville-West – who defined her planting style as "cram, cram, cram, every chink and cranny" – and her husband. **See p.148**

❹ Smallhythe Place Picture-postcard Tudor cottage, once home to the glamorous Victorian actor Ellen Terry. **See p.150**

❺ Knole This magnificent old estate, with its glorious medieval deer park, is a classic English beauty with a fascinating history. **See p.152**

❻ Chartwell Along with lovely gardens and countryside walks, Winston Churchill's family home reveals a touchingly personal side of this gruff statesman. **See p.154**

❼ Hever Castle Gardens Laid out between 1904 and 1908 by Waldorf Astor, these showpiece gardens include gorgeous Italianate statuary, rose gardens and trees planted in the time of Anne Boleyn, who spent her childhood here. **See p.156**

HIGHLIGHTS ARE MARKED ON THE MAP ON P.138

THE KENT WEALD

HIGHLIGHTS

1 Bedgebury
2 Vineyard tours
3 Sissinghurst
4 Smallhythe Place
5 Knole
6 Chartwell
7 Hever Castle Gardens

HOPPING MAD

Unlike their neighbours on the Continent, medieval Brits preferred their ale syrupy sweet, made with malt and flavoured with spices. Tastes changed in the fifteenth century, however, after Flemish merchants introduced them to beer made with **hops** – which, quite apart from their distinctive flavour, have strong preservative qualities. In 1520 the first hop garden opened, near Canterbury – the Kentish soil provided perfect growing conditions, and the local woodlands supplied essential poles, for training the vines, and charcoal, for drying the hops. Just as significant, however, was the wealth of medieval Kentish farmers, which meant they could invest in new, labour-intensive and untried agricultural ventures. Almost immediately English beer was being exported to the Continent, much to the concern of the Dutch growers, and the industry boomed so dramatically that laws were passed preventing farmers rejecting all other forms of agriculture in favour of hop-growing. By the 1650s, hops were grown in fourteen English counties, with Kent producing one third of the total, and by the 1870s, around 72,000 acres – most of them in Kent – were devoted to the industry. The distinctve round **oast houses**, used for drying hops and topped with tiptilted white cowls, rapidly became as familiar a feature on the Wealden landscape as its woods and orchards.

The harvest required **casual labour** almost from the start. After the coming of the railway, thousands of **"hoppers"**, generations of families and entire neighbourhoods, mainly from London's East End, were migrating to the fields of Kent for six weeks every autumn. Taking special "hopper trains", or piling into trucks and buses, joined by gypsy families in their caravans and itinerant workers chancing their luck, the hoppers originally lived in rough tents, but by the early twentieth century these had been upgraded to tiny "huts" – tin shacks, or stables. Some would bring bedding and curtains from home, covering unglazed windows and lining walls with newspapers; others would simply shack up in the straw, wrapping themselves in sacks. Everyone cooked and ate outside on faggot fires, sharing rudimentary washing and toilet facilities.

Days were strictly regulated, with hoppers working in teams (or "drifts"), tearing down the climbing vines ("bines"), stripping them of their cones, and filling their baskets as fast as they could. Pay was calculated per bushel, and often settled at the end of the season (by which time the rate had often plummeted); more skilled jobs, paid by the day, included that of the stiltmen, balanced on high stilts, who cared for the wires at the top of the wooden hop poles. **George Orwell**, who went hopping near Maidstone in 1931, stated that "as far as wages go, no worse employment exists" – and it was tiring, often painful, work, with hands ripped by prickly stems and covered in rashes from hop resin. But the chance to escape the cramped, polluted East End, the health benefits of fresh air, and the opportunity to meet up with old friends seemed to override all that. Each farm effectively became its own community, with parties, dances and a Hop Queen crowned; temperance workers, the Salvation Army and the Red Cross would set up camp nearby to provide spiritual and medical care. In local villages, meanwhile, there was much mistrust of these rough Cockney incomers: shops battened down the hatches, and pubs, if they served them at all, consigned hoppers to special areas. Following mechanization in the 1950s the need for hoppers dwindled to almost nothing, and the majority of the oast houses that remain have been converted into private homes.

4

during the Regency period, is an appealing destination. There are a couple of low-key sights, but above all it's a nice place simply to stroll around, with a pretty Victorian **high street** leading down to the pedestrianized **Pantiles**, and some excellent restaurants and pubs. Surrounded by gorgeous High Weald countryside, the town also has lots of lovely green space: the **Grove** and, to the north, **Calverley Grounds** offer formal gardens, paths and splendid views, while the wilder, wooded **Common**, spreading out to the west behind the Pantiles, is laced with historic walking paths.

The Pantiles

Tucked off the southern end of the High Street, the colonnaded **Pantiles** – named for the clay tiles, shaped in wooden pans, that paved the street in the seventeenth century

– is a pedestrianized parade of independent shops, delis and coffee houses that exudes a faded, almost raffish elegance. In Georgian times the fashionable set would gather here to promenade and take the waters, and it remains a lively stretch, especially in sunny weather, when the alfresco restaurant tables are buzzing with people-watching crowds. Hub of the Pantiles is the original **Chalybeate Spring**, in the 1804 Bath House. For £1, a costumed "dipper" will serve you a cup of the ferrous waters (Easter–Sept Wed–Sun 10.30am–5.30pm), a tradition that dates back to the eighteenth century.

Tunbridge Wells Museum

Mount Pleasant Rd, TN1 1JN • Tues–Sat 9.30am–5pm, Sun 10am–4pm • Free • ☎ 01892 554171, ⓦ tunbridgewellsmuseum.org

A Tardis of a place above the library, **Tunbridge Wells Museum** offers an intriguing mishmash of local history, its old glass cabinets filled with everything from fossils to dandy Georgian glad rags, fading maps and scruffy stuffed animals. With an offbeat section on local cricket-ball manufacture and a spooky cabinet of Victorian dolls, it's particularly worth a look for its exquisite collection of **Tunbridge ware**, the finely crafted wooden marquetry, dating from the late eighteenth century and popular until the 1920s, that was applied to everything from boxes to book covers to furniture, and created a wealth of Tunbridge Wells souvenirs.

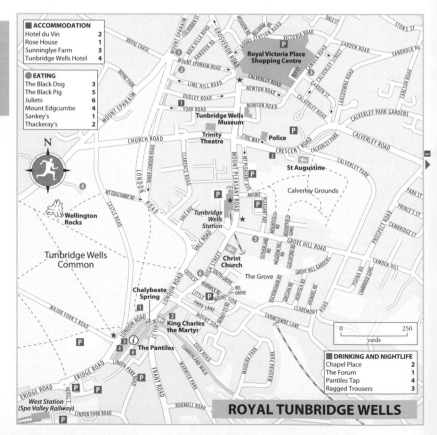

King Charles the Martyr

Chapel Place, TN1 1YX • Mon–Sat 11am–3pm • Free • Ⓦ kcmtw.org

The first permanent building in Tunbridge Wells, the Restoration church of **King Charles the Martyr** (1676) was the brainchild of Thomas Neale, the entrepreneur who, having built the Pantiles to exploit the tourist potential of the spring, went on to provide a place of worship and an assembly room for visitors. Behind the forbidding exterior lies a beautiful space. Its exquisite domed ceilings, their plasterwork emblazoned with flowers, grapes, cherubs and foliage, remain amazingly intact, while in the north gallery you can perch on the young Queen (then Princess) Victoria's very own pew. Other highlights include hand-written lists of early congregations, including Samuel Pepys, and, as you might expect from its name, a few pieces of memorabilia relating to Charles I.

ARRIVAL AND DEPARTURE

ROYAL TUNBRIDGE WELLS

By train The train station stands where the High St becomes Mount Pleasant Rd.

Destinations Hastings (every 30min–1hr; 40–50min); London Charing Cross (every 15–30min; 55min); Sevenoaks (every 20min; 20–25min); Tonbridge (every 15–20min; 10–15min).

By bus Buses set down and pick up along London Rd and

Mount Pleasant Rd.

Destinations Brighton (every 30min–1hr; 1hr 50min); Cranbrook (every 30min–1hr; 1hr 10min); Hever (Mon–Sat 2 daily; 40–50min); Lewes (every 30min–1hr; 1hr 20min); London Victoria (1 daily; 1hr 40min); Maidstone (every 30min; 1hr 20min); Sevenoaks (every 30min–2hr; 45min); Tonbridge (every 15–30min; 10min).

INFORMATION AND TOURS

Tourist office Corn Exchange, The Pantiles (April–Sept Mon–Sat 10am–3pm; Oct–March Tues–Sat 10am–3pm; ☎ 01892 515675, Ⓦ visittunbridgewells.com). Guided walking tours set off from here (Easter–Dec Thurs & Sat 11.30am; 1hr; £5).

Spa Valley Railway Based at West Station, a few minutes'

walk southwest of The Pantiles, this historic railroad, with steam and diesel locos, runs short trips via Groombridge to Eridge in Sussex, passing lovely Weald countryside (days vary, but generally Sat, Sun & hols April–Oct, with extra days in summer and special trips in winter; £11 return; total 1hr–1hr 30min trip; ☎ 01892 537715, Ⓦ spavalleyrailway.co.uk).

ACCOMMODATION

Hotel du Vin Crescent Rd, TN1 2LY ☎ 01892 320749, Ⓦ hotelduvin.com. Elegantly set in a Georgian mansion overlooking Calverley Grounds, this member of the *Hotel du Vin* chain is quietly classy with a cosy bar and romantic French restaurant, and an atmospherically sloping old staircase leading up to the contemporary rooms. The best are at the back, with views of the lavender-filled grounds, the hotel vineyard and the park beyond. **£145**

Rose House 42 York Rd, TN1 1JY ☎ 01892 537123, Ⓦ rosehousetw.weebly.com. This hospitable B&B scores for its central location, its pretty courtyard garden and its friendly hosts, but there's just one room, so book well in advance. **£85**

Sunninglye Farm Dundale Rd, TN3 9AG ☎ 01420 80804, Ⓦ featherdown.co.uk/location/sunninglye-farm. Four miles

southeast of town, across the border on a hilltop copse in Sussex, this glampsite – one of the boutique Feather Down Farms chain – offers seven opulent tents (sleeping six), with beds, wood-burning stoves and flushing loos, on a family farm. The surroundings are bucolic, with a little nature-spotting area and a pond with rowing boats and materials for raft making, and campfires are permitted – you collect firewood yourself from the local woods. Two-/three-night minimum. **£100**

Tunbridge Wells Hotel 58 The Pantiles, TN2 5TD ☎ 01892 530501, Ⓦ thetunbridgewellshotel.com. Location is key in this period hotel, which offers quirky charm in cosy B&B rooms above a smart Modern British restaurant on the Pantiles – there's no lift, so ask if you don't fancy a room on the higher floors. **£150**

EATING

The Black Dog 20 Camden Rd, TN1 2PY ☎ 01892 549543, Ⓦ blackdogcafetw.co.uk. This excellent little Aussie-run coffee house flies the flag for Camden Rd, the (slightly) boho face of Tunbridge Wells. It's not all flat whites and macchiatos; they're licensed, and offer tasty, on-trend food, from breakfast (new potato and spinach hash, say) via brunch (walnut and raisin French toast with ricotta and berries) to lunch (smoked haddock and dill

fishcakes on sweet potato and assiago rösti). Dishes from £4. Mon–Fri 8am–4pm, Sat 8am–5pm, Sun 9am–2pm.

The Black Pig 18 Grove Hill Rd, TN1 1RZ ☎ 01892 523030, Ⓦ theblackpig.net. Pig out without guilt at this gastropub, where locally sourced, free-range and organic dishes might include slow-roast pork belly, a wild game platter or roasted bream – or simply settle down with a charcuterie plate and a glass of wine in the sunny beer

4

garden. Mains from £12.50. Daily noon–1pm; kitchen Mon noon–2.30pm & 6.30–9pm, Tues–Sat noon–2.30pm & 6.30–10pm, Sun noon–9pm.

Juliets 54 High St, TN1 1XF ☎01892 522931, ⓦjulietsandmore.com. Don't be misled by the twee window display; this is a lovely independent café whose warm, exposed-brick interior, filled with splashy paintings and mismatched furniture, invites you to linger. The home-made food is a winner, from the fab breakfasts (till 11.30am) – hop sausage sandwiches, pancakes with syrup, avocado on toast – to the daily-changing salads, soups, smoothies and cakes. Mains from £6. Takeaway available. Daily 8am–5pm.

Mount Edgcumbe The Common, TN4 8BX ☎01892 618854, ⓦthemountedgcumbe.com. Hidden away on the Common, this friendly food pub makes a cosy, offbeat place for a meal – from superfood salad to fish and chips – or a pint of local ale. With a lovely garden, it has a deliciously rural feel; in bad weather, check out the real cave in the bar area, strewn with fairy lights. Small plates from £6, mains from £11. Mon–Wed 11am–11pm, Thurs–Sat 11am–11.30pm, Sun noon–10.30pm; kitchen Mon–Thurs noon–3pm & 6–9.30pm, Fri & Sat noon–9.30pm, Sun noon–8pm.

★**Sankey's** 39 Mount Ephraim, TN4 8AA ☎01892 511422, ⓦsankeys.co.uk. Cosy seafood brasserie – with a sunny patio – serving great fish and shellfish (from fish stew to fish cakes, oysters to paella) from £9, with a two-course menu for £10.95. You can get the same menu, plus simple grub – grazing boards, burgers, Sunday roasts –in the buzzy pub upstairs, decked out with enamel signs and brewery mirrors, with comfy sofas around a wood-burning stove and a large selection of specialist beers. Brasserie Tues–Fri noon–3pm & 6–7pm, Sat noon–3pm. Pub Mon–Wed & Sun noon–11pm, Thurs–Sat noon–1am; kitchen Mon–Thurs noon–3pm & 6–10pm, Fri & Sat noon–10pm, Sun noon–8pm.

Thackeray's 85 London Rd, TN1 1EA ☎01892 511921, ⓦthackerays-restaurant.co.uk. Named for the novelist William Makepeace Thackeray, who lived here for a time in 1860, this tile-hung seventeenth-century building offers top-notch French dining in a smart room or alfresco courtyard. Dishes such as roulade of marinated foie gras or sautéed chive and Parmesan gnocchi are conjured from fresh market produce, with fine wines to match. Set menus only, from two-course options (lunch only; Tues–Sat £18, Sun £29.95) up to the six-course tasting menu (£68). Tues–Sat noon–2pm & 6.30–10pm, Sun noon–2.30pm.

DRINKING AND NIGHTLIFE

Chapel Place 18 Chapel Place, TN1 1YQ ☎01892 522304, ⓦchapelplacetw.co.uk. Bijou cocktail bar that pulls a cool but relaxed crowd for its on-trend rustic/industrial decor and well-mixed drinks (from £5). They're big on the gin here, but also offer wine and craft beers, with local cheese and charcuterie platters to snack on, and coffee during the day. Tues–Sat noon–11pm, Sun noon–10pm.

The Forum Fonthill, The Common, TN4 8YU ☎08712 777101, ⓦtwforum.co.uk. Highly regarded 250-capacity music venue that pulls an enthusiastic, in-the-know crowd for its lively programme of indie and up-and-coming bands, club nights, poetry slams and burlesque.

★**Pantiles Tap** 39–41 The Pantiles, TN2 5TE ☎01892 530397, ⓦthepantilestap.co.uk. A brilliant destination for beer-lovers, this sweet spot is tucked away just behind the Pantiles with a tiny terrace and a frequently changing selection of keg and cask ales and ciders from microbreweries all around the UK. Local wines and an interesting range of bottled beers are on offer, too. Mon 4–11.30pm, Tues–Sat noon–11.30pm, Sun noon–10.30pm.

Ragged Trousers 44 The Pantiles, TN2 5TN ☎01892 542715, ⓦraggedtrousers.co.uk. This popular, relaxed bar, in the eighteenth-century Assembly Rooms, sees a high-spirited crowd enjoying real ales and lively chat, with decent pub grub during the day (£5–15). Daily noon–11pm; kitchen Mon–Fri noon–3pm, Sat & Sun noon–4pm.

ENTERTAINMENT

Thanks to **Leefest** (see p.32), Tunbridge Wells is a firm fixture on the summer festival circuit. Held in a secret location near town, this excellent music festival showcases everything from alt-cabaret to the coolest big names.

★**Trinity Theatre** Church Rd, TN1 1JP ☎01892 678678, ⓦtrinitytheatre.net. You'll catch art movies, world cinema and cult classics in the excellent Trinity, which also stages top-quality rep theatre, music and stand-up in an atmospherically converted church.

Around Royal Tunbridge Wells

Set in the High Weald, **Tunbridge Wells** is moments away from Sussex; the historic **Spa Valley Railway** (see p.141) chugs through lovely countryside from here to Eridge. This area is particularly good for **climbing**, with Nuts 4 Climbing in nearby Groombridge offering taster sessions and lessons (see box, p.193). To the north is the Elizabethan estate at **Penshurst**, with its glorious grounds, and **Tonbridge**, a quiet town long overshadowed by its neighbour, where you can tour the gatehouse of the once-mighty medieval castle. The tiny hamlet of **Tudeley** nearby offers a surprise in its local church – a set of ravishing windows designed by the artist **Marc Chagall**.

Penshurst Place

Penshurst, TN11 8DG • House April–Oct daily noon–4pm, mid-Feb to April Sat & Sun noon–4pm; gardens April–Oct daily 10.30am–6pm; mid-Feb to April Sat & Sun 10.30am–6pm; grounds all year • £10.80, grounds & gardens only £8.80; £1 discount if arriving by bike/bus • ☎ 01892 870307, ⓦ penshurstplace.com • Bus #231 or #233 from Tunbridge Wells (Mon–Sat)

Tudor timber-framed houses and shops line the pretty main street of **PENSHURST**, set in countryside five miles northwest of Tunbridge Wells. Presiding over it all is **Penshurst Place**, a magnificent fourteenth-century manor house that has been home to the Sidney family since 1552 and was birthplace of Sir Philip Sidney, the Elizabethan soldier, poet and all-round Renaissance Man. The jaw-dropping **Barons Hall**, dating from 1341, is the glory of the interior, with its 60ft-high chestnut-beamed roof still in place; it's all the more stunning for being largely unadorned, with amazingly well preserved life-sized carved wooden figures – satirical representations of local peasants and manor workers – still supporting its vast arched braces. Elsewhere, the formal staterooms are packed with furniture and art, featuring important Elizabethan portraits, some fabulous tapestries and a fine room of armour with some savage-looking halberds; curiosities in the small **toy museum** include a painting on a cobweb and a Noah's Ark made from straw.

The 48 acres of grounds offer good parkland walks, while the eleven-acre walled **garden** is a beautiful example of Elizabethan garden design, with formal, yew-edged "rooms" ablaze with tulips, peonies, roses and lavender. There's also an adventure playground, and an excellent **farmers' market** on the first Saturday of the month (9.30am–noon; ⓦ kfma.org.uk/penshurst).

Tonbridge and around

With its prime location and its good road and river connections, **TONBRIDGE** was for centuries far larger and more important than Tunbridge Wells. It's much quieter today – though Jane Austen's father was born here, and fans can pick up a self-guided walking-tour leaflet in the tourist office to follow in the family footsteps – and chiefly of interest for the mighty gatehouse of its medieval **castle**. If you're here on the second Sunday in the month, be sure to check out the **farmers' market** (9.30am–1.30pm; ⓦ tonbridgefarmersmarket.co.uk), which is the largest in Kent and one of the best.

Tonbridge Castle

Castle St, TN9 1BG • Mon–Sat 9am–5pm, Sun 10.30am–4.30pm; last tour 1hr before closing • Audio tours (1hr) £8.50, under-16s £5 • ☎ 01732 770929, ⓦ www.tonbridgecastle.org

A huge motte-and-bailey affair, later home to a large, self-sufficient feudal community, **Tonbridge Castle** was built in 1068 and heavily fortified over the following centuries.

CYCLING THE TUDOR TRAIL

The ten-mile, mostly traffic-free **Tudor Trail** (download maps at ⓦ explorekent.org), which runs along Regional Cycle Route 12, allows you to combine a cycle ride with some of the Weald's most popular sights. Starting from **Tonbridge**, which has a train station (see p.144), the six-mile route west to **Penshurst Place** (see above) takes you along the Medway, through broadleaf woodlands, and past wildflower meadows and lakes. From Penshurst continue to **Hever Castle** (see p.156) along country lanes and peaceful bridleways, perhaps stopping off at the pretty village of **Chiddingstone** (see p.156). It's just a mile to Hever train station, or three miles to Edenbridge station, from Hever Castle.

Controlling the bridge across the Medway, in a key position between London and the coastal ports, it remained effective as a fortress until the Civil War, using the most advanced design to repel attackers. Today, **audio tours** lead you around its impressively intact four-storey **gatehouse**, which in size and might is almost a castle in itself. Imparting lots of lively information on the castle's preparations for battle, it's all enjoyably interactive, with re-creations of thirteenth-century life including subterranean storerooms where disconcertingly life-like mannequins lurk in the half-light, and supper tables where rumbustious guards joke and banter. You might even come across the odd poor soldier taking a moment for himself in one of the gloomy privy chambers.

All Saints' Church

Tudeley Lane, Tudeley, TN11 0NZ • Summer daily 9.30am–6pm; rest of year daily 9.30am–4pm • £2.50 donation requested • ☎ 01892 836653, ⓦ tudeley.org/allsaintstudeley.htm

It would be easy to drive through **TUDELEY**, a scrap of a hamlet on the outskirts of Tonbridge, were it not for **All Saints' Church**. In this simple stone-and-brick structure, peacefully overlooking fields at the edge of the village, you'll find an unexpected surprise: twelve stained-glass windows designed between the 1960s and 1980s by the Russian artist **Marc Chagall** (1887–1985). Commissioned to create a memorial window by the parents of a local woman who died young, Chagall was so taken with the spot that he decided to design the rest of the windows too. They are an extraordinary sight, set low in the walls and easy to approach – the artist's marks are clear to see, while the dreamy golds, turquoises, rose pinks and inky violets wash over each other to create folkloric, almost abstract ensembles of birds, animals and deft floral motifs. It's undeniably moving to see the artist's humanistic and spiritual vision on such a grand, close-up scale, especially when the sunbeams stream through and flood the church with washes of jewel-like colour.

Tudeley Woods RSPB Reserve

Between Tunbridge Wells and Tonbridge on the A21 • Free • ☎ 01273 775333, ⓦ rspb.org.uk

An invigorating mix of woods and heathland, **Tudeley Woods RSPB Reserve** is a haven not only for birds – lesser spotted woodpeckers, nightjars, woodlarks and marsh tits among them – but also butterflies and woodland flowers, including bluebells and rare orchids. It's especially interesting during the autumn migration season, and a profusion of **fungi** – more than a thousand species at last count, including the endearingly named Puffballs, Deceivers and Chickens of the Woods – sprouts along the woodland floor. You can follow three nature trails, each between one and three miles in length.

ARRIVAL AND INFORMATION · AROUND ROYAL TUNBRIDGE WELLS

By train Tonbridge train station is a 10min walk from the castle along the High St.
Destinations Ashford (every 30min; 35min); Canterbury West (every 30min–hourly; 55min); Edenbridge (hourly; 15min); Hastings (every 30min–1hr; 50min–1hr); London Bridge (every 30min; 45min); London Charing Cross (every 10–30min; 50min); London Victoria (hourly; 50min); Penshurst (hourly; 8min); Tunbridge Wells (every 15–30min; 10min).
Tourist office Castle grounds, Castle St, Tonbridge (Mon–Sat 8am–5pm, Sun 10am–4pm; ☎ 01732 770929).

EATING AND DRINKING

Bottlehouse Inn Coldharbour Rd, Penshurst, TN11 8ET ☎ 01892 870306, ⓦ thebottlehouseinnpenshurst .co.uk. A smart food pub in an updated fifteenth-century tavern, serving accomplished contemporary food, from butter-roasted plaice to sweet potato, butternut and feta curry (mains £11–25), on a seasonally changing menu. Eat outside on the flower-filled terrace or in the tasteful interior with its beams and plaster walls. Mon–Sat 11am–11pm, Sun 11am–10.30pm; kitchen Mon–Sat noon–10pm, Sun noon–9pm.
The Dovecote Alders Rd, Capel, TN12 6SU ☎ 01892 835966, ⓦ dovecote-capel.co.uk. Two miles southeast of Tudeley, this is an unreconstructed, friendly country pub with excellent real ales and reliable, unpretentious pub grub (from £7.50). It's usually buzzing with a cheery, laidback local crowd. Mon 5.30–11pm, Tues–Sat

noon–3pm & 5.30–11pm, Sun noon–10.30pm; kitchen Tues–Sat noon–2pm & 7–9pm, Sun noon–3pm.

Fir House Tearoom Penshurst, TN11 8DB ☎ 01892 870382. Quaint Tudor tearoom, right outside Penshurst Place and once part of the estate, with a flower-filled cottage garden and a cosy open fire in winter, serving home-made cakes, afternoon teas and high teas, along with soups and light snacks. April–Oct Tues–Sun 2.30–6pm.

George and Dragon Speldhurst Hill, Speldhurst, TN3 0NN ☎ 01892 863125, ⓦ speldhurst.com. Smart gastropub in a medieval inn three miles southeast of Penshurst. Mains such as slow-roast Old Spot pork belly start at £12.50, but lunchtime sees cheaper options, like Applewood cheddar sandwiches, from £8.50. Make sure to pop into St Mary's Church across the road to see the Pre-Raphaelite Burne-Jones windows. Daily Mon–Sat noon–11.30pm, Sun noon–10.30pm; kitchen Mon–Fri noon–2.30pm & 6.30–9.30pm, Sat noon–3pm & 6.30–9.30pm, Sun noon–4pm.

The Hare Langton Rd, Langton Green, TN3 0JA ☎ 01892 862419, ⓦ brunningandprice.co.uk/hare. Next to the village green, this family-, walker- and dog-friendly Greene King pub offers a nice beer garden, a lovely, spacious interior and great food, with global dishes – Malaysian fish stew, say, or cauliflower, chickpea and almond tagine – plus gastropub staples like bangers and pies. Mains from £11. Mon–Thurs noon–11pm, Fri & Sat noon–midnight, Sun noon–10.30pm; kitchen Mon–Thurs noon–9.30pm, Fri & Sat noon–10pm, Sun noon–9pm.

Little Brown Jug Chiddingstone Causeway, Tonbridge, TN11 8JJ ☎ 01892 870318, ⓦ thelittlebrownjug.co.uk. Easy-going, good-looking pub with a huge beer garden (complete with BBQ hut) and spacious interior – there's lots to look at here, from the walls lined with pictures and old news cuttings to the bookshelves packed with vintage titles. Food runs the gamut from grilled mackerel with couscous or seared lambs' liver (mains from £10), and there's a great selection of beers. Cosy, friendly and charming. Mon–Thurs 10am–11pm, Fri & Sat 9am–midnight, Sun 9am–11pm; kitchen daily noon–9.30pm.

The Spotted Dog Smarts Hill, Penshurst, TN11 8EP ☎ 01892 870253, ⓦ spotteddogpub.com. With its charming, old spotty dog sign, flower-bedecked weatherboard exterior and wonky tiled roof, this looks like the perfect country pub. Inside is just as attractive, a sixteenth-century burrow of sloping floors, low beamed ceilings and inglenook fires, with a terraced garden at the back sheltered by tall trees. Reasonably priced local and guest ales are on offer, while the menu offers traditional English favourites such as gammon steak, roast chicken and home-made fishcakes (mains from £10). Mon–Sat 11.30am–11pm, Sun noon–10.30pm; kitchen Mon noon–2.30pm, Tues–Fri noon–2.30pm & 6–9pm, Sat noon–3pm & 6–9pm, Sun noon–4pm.

Kent's eastern High Weald

As you head further east into Kent's High Weald from Tunbridge Wells, things get sleepier. This is the domain of one-street villages and tidy market towns; the largest, like **Cranbrook** or **Tenterden** – their quaint, well-heeled high streets lined with antiques shops and upmarket restaurants – feel positively metropolitan compared with the rural hamlets hereabouts. Star attractions include the ravishing gardens at **Sissinghurst**, the award-winning vineyards at **Chapel Down** and **Hush Heath**, and **Bedgebury forest**, with its excellent cycling and walking opportunities, but you should seek out some quirkier destinations, too – Victorian actress Ellen Terry's Tudor cottage at **Smallhythe** and the idyllic **Scotney Castle** gardens among them.

Goudhurst and around

Surrounded by orchards, woods and hop fields, and offering uninterrupted views across the Weald, the hamlet of **GOUDHURST** has just one main street, its array of weatherboard, half-timbered and tile-hung buildings tumbling down from a sturdy ragstone church towards a duck pond. With some good places to eat and stay nearby, it's a handy base for a stay in this part of Kent.

Bedgebury National Pinetum and Forest

Bedgebury Rd, Goudhurst, TN17 2SJ • Daily: Jan & Dec 8am–4pm; Feb & Nov 8am–5pm; March & Oct 8am–6pm; April & Sept 8am–7pm; May–Aug 8am–8pm • Free; parking Mon–Fri £10, Sat & Sun £12 • ☎ 01580 879820, ⓦ forestry.gov.uk/bedgebury

Brilliantly set up for outdoor activities, the Forestry Commission-owned **Bedgebury National Pinetum and Forest** comprises not only a glorious 2500-acre spread of broadleaf

4

woodland, but also a world-renowned pinetum, established with Kew Gardens in the 1920s. The forest is a beauty, particularly stunning in spring when carpeted with drifts of bluebells, and a lovely place to spot wildlife, from goldcrests to wild boar; the pinetum, meanwhile, is home to more than twelve thousand **conifers** – 630 of the world's 810 species, from redwoods to Norway spruce, many of them rare and endangered.

Whether you fancy a gentle stroll and a lakeside picnic, a vigorous forest hike, a horseride, or a high-adrenalin zip-line adventure at the **Go Ape** treetop park (Ⓦgoape .co.uk), Bedgebury delivers. It's brilliant for kids, with tree-dappled adventure play areas, special orienteering trails and a junior Go Ape area. The forest is also very popular with **cyclists** (no bikes are allowed in the pinetum): National Cycle Route 18 runs through on its way between Goudhurst and Cranbrook, and there are off-road **mountain-bike trails** for all abilities, plus a freeride/dirt jump area, with **bike rental** (Ⓦquenchuk.co.uk) and showers on site.

Scotney Castle

Lamberhurst, TN3 8JN • March–Nov daily: house 11am–5pm; garden and estate 10am–5pm; last admission 1hr before closing • £13; NT; free (limited) parking • ☎ 01892 893820, Ⓦ nationaltrust.org.uk/scotney-castle

The ravishing ruin of **Scotney Castle**, a moated fourteenth-century manor house set in 750 gorgeous acres, presents a breathtakingly romantic vision, particularly in spring when tumbling white wisteria and tangles of old roses fight for space on the honey-coloured sandstone, and the **gardens** blaze with huge clouds of rhododendrons and azaleas. The gardens and castle – intentionally ruined by its owners in 1830, in order to create a picturesque folly in the grounds of their new home – are by far the main attractions, but you can also visit the mock-Elizabethan **"new house"**, a stolid Victorian pile. There's not a huge amount of interest inside, but the estate itself is a stunner, with three designated **trails** (30–45min) taking in bluebell woods, a working hop farm and wonderful views of rolling parkland.

Hush Heath vineyards

Five Oak Lane, Staplehurst, TN12 0HT • Daily 11am–5pm • Free self-guided tours; some free guided tours, most guided tours £15 – pre-booking essential • ☎ 01622 832794, Ⓦ hushheath.com

A family-owned estate of more than four hundred acres, centring on an early sixteenth-century manor house, **Hush Heath** devotes around twenty acres to Chardonnay, Pinot Noir and Pinot Meunier vineyards and thirty acres to apple orchards. While this is one of the newer Kentish wineries – its first wine was released in 2007 – Hush Heath soon became famed for its sparkling wines, made using traditional Champagne methods, and in particular the outstanding **Balfour Brut Rosé**, a delicate, very dry pink fizz that won the first gold medal for English wine at the prestigious International Wine Challenge. Other stars include a gorgeous ruby-red 1503 sparkling Pinot Noir, with its hint of cherry and berries, and a flinty Chardonnay reminiscent of a fine, crisp Chablis.

The self-guided **trail** through the estate is a stunner, a walk of an hour to ninety minutes, taking in not only ranks of vines, but also wildflower meadows, orchards and ancient woodlands, with generous Downs views sweeping off into the distance. Finishing up your walk with free **tastings** on the pretty terrace is a delight.

ACCOMMODATION

Chequers Inn The Broadway, Lamberhurst, TN3 8DB ☎ 01892 890260, Ⓦ chequerslamberhurst.co.uk. Nothing fancy at this fifteenth-century coaching house near Scotney Castle: just five good-value en-suite B&B rooms above a decent pub and restaurant with a riverside garden and an open fire for chilly nights. **£70**

GOUDHURST AND AROUND

Goudhurst Inn Cranbrook Rd, Goudhurst, TN17 1DX ☎ 01580 211451, Ⓦ thegoudhurstinn.com. Owned by the Hush Heath vineyard, a 10min drive away, this family-friendly pub/restaurant (see p.148) has four contemporary B&B rooms, with super-comfy beds and quirky design features. **£85**

CLOCKWISE FROM TOP LEFT LEEDS CASTLE (P.158); SISSINGHURST (P.148); HEVER CASTLE (P.156) >

EATING AND DRINKING

★**Frankie's** Staplehurst Nurseries, Clapper Lane, Staplehurst, TN12 0JT ☎01580 890713, ⓦfrankiesfarmshop.co.uk. Let yourself in on a local secret and head for this superb farm shop café. Linked to an excellent plant nursery, the shop is stocked with local goodies, with a busy open kitchen baking bread and serving simple farm-fresh breakfasts and lunches – Kentish rarebit, seafood platter or tortilla with a herb salad, for example – plus amazing home-made cakes. It can get crowded at lunchtime, but on sunny days it's a pleasure to eat alfresco under the beady eye of the local alpacas. Mains from £8. Mon–Sat 9am–5pm, Sun 10am–4pm.

Goudhurst Inn Cranbrook Rd, Goudhurst, TN17 1DX ☎01580 211451, ⓦthegoudhurstinn.com. You get good Downs views from the beer garden of this Hush Heath-owned hotel (see p.146) and restaurant, which also has a kids' play area and all-you-can-eat barbecues on summer weekends (£15). The menu (mains around £14) focuses on tried-and-trusted pub grub staples, with clay-oven pizzas and lighter dishes served in the bar and garden. Kitchen Mon–Thurs & Sun 7am–11pm, Fri & Sat 7am–midnight.

Green Cross Inn Station Rd, Goudhurst, TN17 1HA ☎01580 211200, ⓦgreencrossinn.co.uk. This ordinary-looking little redbrick pub is actually more of a restaurant, serving delicious fish and seafood – dressed crabs and fresh oysters, Rye Bay skate, lobster spaghetti, paella – prepared with love by the Italian chef-owner. Mains from £12. Kitchen Mon–Sat noon–3pm & 6–11pm, Sun noon–3pm.

★**Halfway House** Horsmonden Rd, Brenchley, TN12 7AX ☎01892 722526, ⓦhalfwayhousebrenchley .co.uk. Unpretentious old country pub about five miles northwest of Goudhurst, popular with walkers, families (there's a big garden and separate play area) and beer lovers – there are at least seven real ales available at any time, with local cider, too. Crammed with old farm implements and dried hops, the interior is rustic, if a little hokey, and they serve simple, filling pub grub from around £8. Daily noon–11pm; kitchen Mon–Fri noon–2.30pm & 6–9pm, Sat noon–3pm & 6–9pm, Sun noon–3pm.

4 Cranbrook and around

Kent's smallest town, **CRANBROOK** (ⓦcranbrook.org), was at the heart of the Weald's thriving medieval cloth industry, and home to a group of Victorian painters, the Cranbrook Colony, who enjoyed a brief spurt of popularity with wealthy London art collectors for their romanticized renditions of English country life. Today the place has the nostalgic and well-heeled air of a Sunday evening BBC TV drama: Stone Street, along with the busy little high street, offer a Wealden hotchpotch of medieval, Tudor and Georgian buildings, and lots of spruce, white weatherboard weavers' cottages, all watched over by the handsome 1814 **Union Windmill**, still grinding today (2.30–5pm: April–June & Sept Sat; July & Aug Wed, Sat & Sun; free; ⓦunionmill.org.uk). With excellent places to eat in town and nearby, it's an ideal base for the fabulous **Sissinghurst** gardens.

Sissinghurst

Biddenden Rd, off the A262, 2 miles northeast of Cranbrook, TN17 2AB • Gardens mid-March to Oct daily 11am–5.30pm; last admission 45min before closing; estate daily dawn–dusk • £12.05; NT • Parking £3 • ☎01580 710700, ⓦnationaltrust.org.uk/sissinghurst

When she and her husband, Sir Harold Nicolson, took it over in 1932, **Vita Sackville-West** described **Sissinghurst** as "a garden crying out for rescue". Over the following thirty years they transformed the neglected five-acre plot into one of England's greatest and most popular country gardens, a romantic and breathtaking display that continues to inspire gardeners today. Spread over the site of an Elizabethan estate, which generations of neglect had left in a dismal condition (only parts of the old house remain), the gardens were designed to evoke the history not only of the ruined site itself, but also of Vita and Harold's beloved Kent – a heartfelt endeavour that was to absorb them for the rest of their days, and the anchor at the heart of their unconventional and open marriage.

The garden is in fact a set of gardens, each occupying different "rooms" within Tudor brick walls; the classic lines of the design are beautifully offset by the luxuriance of the planting, the flowers and foliage allowed to spill over onto the narrow pathways and the crumbling red brick. Perhaps most famous is the **rose garden**, stunning in late June and early July, when it's at its lush, overblown richest, and the fragrance, described by Vita as reminiscent of "those dusky mysterious hours in an Oriental storehouse", is heavy in the air. The exquisite abundance of tumbling old roses is set off by Japanese anemones, peonies, alliums and irises, among others, and vines, figs and clematis creep over the crumbling brick walls. The **cottage garden**, meanwhile, blazes in shades of orange, yellow and red – a fiery "sunset" scheme that is stunning year round. Sissinghurst has two areas that feel particularly unique: the **nuttery**, a glade of gnarled old Kentish cobnuts that is especially lovely in spring, when its carpet of woodland flowers is in full bloom, and the magical **White Garden**, with its froth of pale blooms and silvery grey-green foliage.

Focal point of the estate is the tall, brick Tudor **tower** that Vita restored and used as her quarters. You can climb 78 steep wooden stairs to the top, from where you get a bird's-eye view of the gardens, the estate and the ancient surrounding woodlands; halfway up, peep through the iron grille into Vita's **writing room**, which feels intensely personal still, with faded rugs on the floor and a photo of her lover, Virginia Woolf, on her desk.

There are a number of **trails** in the woods around Sissinghurst – pick up a guide at reception or online – and, of course, a superb **plant shop** at the entrance. Meanwhile, regular talks, **workshops** and courses focus on all things garden related, from scything to garden writing.

ARRIVAL AND DEPARTURE

By bus Bus #29 offers services (Mon–Sat 7–10 daily) to Goudhurst (11min), Tenterden (30min) and Tunbridge Wells (50min), the stop is on the High St, west of Stone St.

CRANBROOK AND AROUND

ACCOMMODATION

★**Hallwood Farm** Hawkhurst Rd, Cranbrook, TN17 2SP ☎01580 712416, ⓦhallwoodfarm.co.uk. Two spacious and pretty en-suite B&B rooms – rustic beams and fresh flowers, plus fresh milk and soft drinks in your own fridge – in an oast house conversion on a working fruit farm, surrounded by 200 acres of farmland, bluebell woods, blackcurrant fields and apple orchards. You can sample their produce at the huge farmhouse breakfasts. No under-12s. Minimum stay two nights. **£100**

The Queen's Inn Rye Rd, Hawkhurst, 4 miles southwest of Cranbrook, TN18 4EY ☎01580 754233, ⓦthequeensinnhawkhurst.co.uk. This sixteenth-century inn offers smart boutique B&B rooms (including two family rooms; £140) and friendly service, plus good food in the gastropub downstairs (see p.150). **£100**

Sissinghurst Castle Farmhouse Sissinghurst, TN17 2AB ☎01580 720992, ⓦsissinghurstcastlefarmhouse .com. Stunningly located on the estate, less than 100m from the gardens, Sissinghurst's Victorian farmhouse building – a huge, spacious affair, rich in old wood – offers seven luxurious, comfortable and tasteful B&B rooms. You can wander around the farmhouse's own pretty gardens, or just curl up in the comfy living room. **£150**

EATING AND DRINKING

The Bull The Street, Benenden, 3.5 miles southeast of Cranbrook TN17 4DE ☎01580 240054, ⓦthebullatbenenden.co.uk. Though it can get crowded, especially during the Sunday carvery, this is a cosily classy, rustic pub in a charming hamlet. They serve excellent home-made pub grub – pies, fish and chips, suet puds and juicy burgers – from £11, plus a handful of Modern European mains (from £13.50), good sandwiches and Ploughman's lunches, and local ales, ciders and perries. Daily noon–midnight; kitchen Mon–Sat noon–2.15pm & 6.30–9.15pm, Sun noon–2.15pm.

The Great House Gill's Green, Hawkhurst, 4 miles southwest of Cranbrook, TN18 5EJ ☎01580 753119, ⓦelitepubs.com/the_greathouse. Modern European kitchen in a smart but cosy sixteenth-century weatherboard pub. The regularly changing menu lists such treats as goat's cheese and wild garlic salad, roasted poussin or lamb and feta burger, with mains from £12. The sunny terrace and pretty garden are great in summer. Daily 11.30am–11pm; kitchen Mon–Thurs noon–3pm & 5.30–9pm, Fri noon–3pm & 5.30–9.30pm, Sat noon–9.30pm, Sun noon–8.30pm.

★**The Milk House** The Street, Sissinghurst, TN17 2JG ☎01580 720200, ⓦthemilkhouse.co.uk. Lovely, light restoration of a sixteenth-century building, all whitewashed beams, pale wood, sisal flooring and plaster walls, with delicious, farm-fresh food – sourced from within twenty miles – and local ales and wines. The top-quality ingredients pack a massive punch in dishes that run the gamut from Old Spot ham, duck egg and chips to clam, cockle and corn chowder; from courgette, feta and *freekah* fritters to polenta and parmesan-crusted hake. Small plates from £5; mains (which are really quite big) from £14. Flatbread pizzas are served in the garden. The four gorgeous B&B rooms (from £120) continue the soothing tone – this is a delightful place to spend the night. Mon–Thurs & Sun 9am–11pm, Fri & Sat 9am–midnight; kitchen Mon–Sat noon–3pm & 6–9pm; grazing menus and pizzas all day Mon–Sat till 9pm Sun.

The Queen's Inn Rye Rd, Hawkhurst, TN18 4EY ☎ 01580 754233, ⓦ thequeensinnhawkhurst.co.uk. Handsome tavern serving on-trend gastropub food (mains from £11) – sweet potato and spinach tagine, pan-roasted pheasant, *moules frites* and the like – made using fresh Kentish produce. You can stay here, too (see p.149). Mon–Thurs 11am–11.30pm, Fri & Sat 11am–midnight, Sun 11am–11pm; kitchen Mon–Thurs noon–2.30pm & 6–9.30pm, Fri & Sat noon–2.30pm & 6–9.45pm, Sun noon–8pm.

Tenterden and around

Historically a major weaving centre and a limb port (see box, p.107) for Rye, **TENTERDEN** (ⓦ tenterdentown.co.uk) used to sit on the River Rother. Now lodged ten miles inland on the borders of the High Weald, it's a handsome, well-to-do little town, its broad, tree-shaded high street fringed with bow-windowed weatherboard and tile-hung buildings. From here you can hop on a **steam train** to Bodiam or take a trip out to lovely **Smallhythe Place**, once home to the great actor Ellen Terry, perhaps taking in one of the superb local **vineyards** on the way. The south-facing, chalky slopes nearby, very similar to those in the Champagne region of France, make perfect conditions for grape-growing – you can stock up on award-winning wines at **Biddenden** and **Chapel Down**.

Biddenden vineyards

Gribble Bridge Lane, Biddenden, TN27 8DF • Jan & Feb Mon–Sat 10am–5pm; March–Dec Mon–Sat 10am–5pm, Sun 11am–5pm• Free; occasional free guided tours (booking essential) • ☎ 01580 291726, ⓦ biddendenvineyards.com

Spread across 23 acres on a gentle, sheltered south-facing slope, five miles northwest of Tenterden and just outside the half-timbered village of Biddenden, the family-owned **Biddenden vineyards** have been established here since 1969. With a long scroll of awards, they set the bar high for England's wine-making, growing eleven varieties – mostly German, including Ortega, Schönburger, Huxelrebe and Bacchus – from which they produce single-variety white, red, rosé and sparkling wines, plus excellent ciders and juices. The medium-dry, fruity Ortega is particularly fine; it's worth trying the smoky, digestif-style, Special Reserve cider – aged in whisky casks – too, and the red apple juice made from red-fleshed and -skinned apples. The vineyards are free to visit, with a friendly, no-pressure atmosphere – either take a twenty-minute self-guided stroll, finishing with free **tastings** in the farm shop, or, to better understand what you're seeing, book one of the occasional free **tours** (roughly weekly, more in summer).

Chapel Down vineyards

Small Hythe, TN30 7NG • Daily 10am–5pm • Free • **Guided tours & tastings** April–Nov daily; 1hr 45min • £10 • ☎ 01580 763033, ⓦ chapeldown.com

Chapel Down, established in 1977, is a multi-award-winning winemaker, growing eight varieties – chiefly Bacchus, Chardonnay, Pinot Blanc, Pinot Noir and the complex Rondo, as well as the Siegerrebe, which goes to make Chapel Down Nectar, their delicious and non-syrupy dessert wine. The country's biggest producer of English wine, using grapes grown here and in Sussex and Surrey, they supply Jamie Oliver and Gordon Ramsay, among others, and have branched out into brewing lager, too, using the same Champagne yeast as in their sparkling wines to create the zingy, refreshing and award-winning Curious Brew. The enjoyable **tours** are brisk and informative, following the wine-making process from vine to bottle and outlining the traditional methods used to create sparkling wines. A tutored **tasting** at the end gives you generous glugs of around seven or eight wines – and with no compunction to spit them out. You can buy bottles (and taste more) at the **shop**, or order yourself a glass or two at the on-site **restaurant**, *The Swan*.

Smallhythe Place

Small Hythe, TN30 7NG • April–Oct Wed–Sun 11am–5pm • £7.70; NT; free car park nearby (not owned by NT) • 01580 762334, ⓦ nationaltrust.org.uk/smallhythe-place

An unfeasibly picturesque early sixteenth-century cottage, all beams, time-worn wood

THE KENT & EAST SUSSEX RAILWAY

From Tenterden you can take a nostalgic train excursion on the **Kent & East Sussex Railway** (April–Sept, with some special services at other times, up to five services daily in Aug, fewer in other months; unlimited all-day travel £17, under-16s £11.50 ☎01580 762943, ⓦ kesr.org.uk), a network of vintage steam and diesel trains that trundle their way 10.5 miles to the medieval Bodiam Castle in Sussex (see p.189). Following the contours of the land, the fifty-minute trip is a scenic, up-and-down affair, passing through the Rother Valley and the marshy, sheep-speckled Rother Levels; stops include Northiam (a mile from the village) near Great Dixter (see p.188).

and warped mullioned windows, the rambling-rose-tangled **Smallhythe Place** is particularly interesting for having been home to the unconventional, charismatic actor **Ellen Terry** (1847–1928). The house was opened to the public after Terry's death by her daughter, Edith Craig, and thus it remains, packed with her belongings and all manner of theatrical memorabilia. (Edith was herself a fascinating character: theatre director, actor, costume designer and suffragette, she lived in a lesbian ménage à trois – the "three trouts", near-neighbour Vita Sackville-West called them – in a house on the grounds for thirty years until her death in 1947. But that's another story.)

Wandering through this crooked little dwelling, with its wonky floors and creaking staircases, is like following a treasure trail. Display cases are crammed with mementos, relics, letters and **costumes**, the walls cluttered with theatrical posters and illustrations. It's a dynamic and intimate exhibit, shedding light on the woman who, born into a family of travelling players, became a child actor and model, married three times, had two illegitimate children, lit up the stage with her naturalistic performances and became the toast of the theatrical, literary and artistic world.

Don't leave without a stroll around the lovely cottage **garden**: plays are staged in the rustic, thatched seventeenth-century **barn**, opened to the public by Edith in 1929, and the vintage-style **tearoom**, with tables beside the reed-fringed pond, is a treat.

ACCOMMODATION   TENTERDEN AND AROUND

The Bakehouse 10 High St, Biddenden, TN27 8AH ☎01580 292270. Two quirky B&B rooms above a cosy, hop-strewn coffeehouse/bistro. The medieval building seeps history, with gnarled beams and creaky floorboards, crooked stairs and low ceilings, and the rooms, while not luxurious, are comfy and cheery with fairy lights, throw rugs and colourful bedding. **£80**

Bloomsburys Sissinghurst Rd, Biddenden, TN27 8DQ ☎01580 292992, ⓦ bloomsburysbiddenden.com. Friendly, not over-manicured glamping in tipis and yurts. Good home-made food is served in the pretty flower-filled café/restaurant, and there's a farm shop/deli on site, along with a wellness centre offering massage, yoga and various therapies. They even host occasional (low-key) acoustic live gigs. **£180**

Brook Farm Brook St, Woodchurch, TN26 3SR ☎01233 860444, ⓦ brookfarmbandb.co.uk. This

seventeenth-century farmhouse, set in five acres three miles east of Tenterden, offers spacious and friendly B&B in a smartly converted barn. The en-suite rooms are comfortable, un-chintzy and feature lots of warm oak – all have great views, and the largely organic breakfast, taken in the farmhouse, is something special. There's a heated outdoor swimming pool and pond. No under-12s. **£95**

Little Dane Court 1 Ashford Rd, Tenterden, TN30 6AB ☎01580 763389, ⓦ littledanecourt.co.uk. Though this fifteenth-century house near the centre of Tenterden offers comfortable, oak-beamed B&B rooms, it's the Japanese-themed cottage (sleeps four; £220) in the back garden, complete with futon and *shoji* window screens, that gives it the edge. The East-meets-medieval Kent combo can feel a little incongruous, but it's different, and nicely done – you could even order a Japanese-style breakfast, and eat it in the sunny courtyard. **£100**

EATING AND DRINKING

The Lemon Tree 29–33 High St, Tenterden, TN30 6BJ ☎01580 763381, ⓦ lemontreetenterden.co.uk. This traditional tearoom/restaurant, in a fourteenth-century timber-framed building, is great for afternoon tea (with home-made cakes, scones and rarebit), but also offers cooked

breakfasts and old-school comfort food, including pan-fried liver, pies and sausage and chips (mains £9–12), with lots of local ingredients. Mon–Sat 9am–5pm, Sun 10am–5pm.

Nutmeg Deli 3 Sayers Lane, Tenterden, TN30 6BW ☎01580 764125. You'll get the best espresso in town at this snug, buzzing little deli, tucked away on a pedestrianized lane off the north side of the High St. There are also cakes, healthy organic sandwiches, savoury tarts, salads and gluten-free options, along with local cheeses and deli goods. Dishes from £6. There are just a handful of tables, so you may have to wait. Mon–Sat 9am–5pm, Sun 10am–4pm.

★**Three Chimneys** Hareplain Rd, Biddenden, TN27 8LW ☎01580 291472, ⊛thethreechimneys.co.uk. Dating from 1420, this shabby-chic free house – blistered plaster and exposed bricks, dried hops tumbling over wonky beams – is a lovely place to stop for a pint of real ale. The locally sourced food is generally very good; mains on the seasonally changing menu can get pricey (£14–20), but the bar menu is good value (£6.50–9). Dishes might include duck and bacon hash, pan-roasted fish, or three-cheese croquettes, all of which you can eat in the pub (candlelit in the evening), in the restaurant (in a light-bathed conservatory), or on the terrace. They also offer B&B rooms (£120). Pub and kitchen Mon–Sat 11.30am–11.30pm, Sun noon–10.30pm;

The West House 28 High St, Biddenden, TN27 8AH ☎01580 291341, ⊛thewesthouserestaurant.co.uk. Michelin-starred Nouvelle British dining in a beamed sixteenth-century cottage. The ambience is laidback rather than stuffy, and – befitting the warm, rustic atmosphere – dishes, while small, are umami-packed and gutsy. Try Iberico pork *presa* with razor clams and wild garlic butter, perhaps, or ragout of white beans, artichoke, feta and olives. Three-course menus £25 (weekday lunch) and £45 (dinner); six-course tasting menus £50 (vegetarian) or £60. Tues–Fri noon–1.45pm & 7–9.30pm, Sat 7–9.30pm, Sun noon–2.30pm.

Sevenoaks and around

Set among the greensand ridges of west Kent, 28 miles from London, **SEVENOAKS** is a thriving, well-heeled commuter town. Dating back to Saxon times, and with several historic buildings, mostly from the seventeenth and eighteenth centuries, it is not an unattractive place; its real appeal for visitors, though, is as a jumping-off point for the immense baronial estate of **Knole**, which is entered just off the High Street. Other day-trip attractions nearby include the mosaics at **Lullingstone Roman Villa**, Winston Churchill's home at **Chartwell**, and the ravishing Elizabethan estate of **Ightham Mote**.

Knole

Entered from Sevenoaks High St, TN15 0RP • **House** March–Oct Tues–Sun noon–4pm • £8.15; NT • **Gatehouse tower, courtyards, Orangery/visitor centre & conservation studio** Daily: mid-March to Oct 10am–5pm; Nov–Feb 10am–4pm • Gatehouse tower £3.15; courtyards & conservation studio free; NT • **Garden** April–Sept Tues 11am–4pm • Included in house price; NT • **Parkland** Daily dawn–dusk • Free; NT • Parking £4 • ☎01732 462100, ⊛nationaltrust.org.uk/knole • The High St entrance to Knole estate is a mile south of Sevenoaks train station and half a mile south of the bus station; it's a 15min uphill walk from the entrance through the estate to the house

Covering a whopping four acres, **Knole** is an astonishingly handsome ensemble, with an endlessly fascinating history. Built in 1456 as a residence for the archbishops of Canterbury, it was appropriated in 1538 by Henry VIII, who lavished further expense on it and hunted in its thousand acres of **parkland**, still home to several hundred wild deer. Elizabeth I passed the estate on to her Lord Treasurer, Thomas Sackville, who remodelled the house in Renaissance style in 1605; it has remained in the family's hands ever since.

The house is given extra dash from being the childhood home of Bloomsbury Group writer and gardener **Vita Sackville-West**, whose bohemian tendencies, by all accounts, ran in the family; one of the great sadnesses of her life was the fact that as a girl, despite being an only child, she was not able to inherit the house she loved with an "atavistic passion". She wrote about it often, and in great detail in her loosely autobiographical novel, *The Edwardians* (see p.325); her one-time lover, Virginia Woolf, made it a fairy-tale castle in her novel *Orlando*, a flight-of-fancy love letter to West herself.

Knole is currently in a state of **flux**. Such was the state of deterioration in many of the rooms, and the poor condition of some of their most precious contents, that the estate is undergoing **major restoration work**, slated for completion in 2018; note that all admission prices will increase once the conservation work is complete. While some star pieces may not be on show when you visit, many others have been brought out on display for the first time. There is plenty still to see, including the new **conservation**

studio, where you can watch precious items being restored with the utmost skill, and the parkland offers splendid **walking**; pick up a map from the ticket office.

The house

Quite apart from the building itself, which, unusually for an English country estate, largely retains its Jacobean appearance, Knole is famed for its enormous collection of **Stuart furniture**. Much of this was acquired at the end of the seventeenth century, by Charles Sackville, Lord Chamberlain to William III, whose "perquisites" – or "perks" – of the job meant he could keep any unwanted royal furniture.

Beyond the **Great Hall**, it's in the showpiece **Great Staircase** that Knole's wow factor really kicks in: a Renaissance Revival delight with dashes of Rococo, it's alive with decoration and flamboyant murals. Upstairs, long galleries and apartments are packed with Jacobean portraits, eighteenth-century pictures of Tudor notables, Renaissance sculpture and fine old furniture. Highlights include the **Spangled Bedroom**, with its amazing bed, draped in a crimson silk canopy stitched with once-glittering sequins (due to return in 2018); the **King's Room**, gleaming with silver furniture and gold brocade; and, perhaps most evocative of all, the lustrous **Venetian Ambassador's Room**. This eighteenth-century beauty – described by Woolf in *Orlando* as shining "like a shell that has lain at the bottom of the sea for centuries" – boasts another staggering carved and gilded bed, once belonging to James II. The bed, and its hangings of sea-green, blue and gold velvet, were literally crumbling away due to a poor restoration job in the 1960s, and will be returned to their original splendour in 2018.

There's an altogether more domestic scene revealed in the **Gatehouse tower**, where two private rooms belonging to a more recent occupant, Eddy Sackville-West, a Bloomsbury Group stalwart who lived here from 1926 to 1940, are filled with his books, records and private possessions. Climbing the 77 steep steps to the top of the tower gives you amazing views over the estate.

Lullingstone Roman Villa

Lullingstone Lane, Eynsford, 8 miles north of Sevenoaks, DA4 0JA • April–Sept daily 10am–6pm; Oct daily 10am–5pm; Nov–March Sat & Sun 10am–4pm • £7; EH • Parking £2.50 • ☎ 01322 863467, ⓦ www.english-heritage.org.uk/visit/places/lullingstone-roman-villa • The villa is a 2-mile walk from Eynsford train station

The remains of **Lullingstone Roman Villa**, excavated in the 1950s and protected in a purpose-built building by a trickle of the River Darent, reveal much about how the Romans lived in Britain. Peacefully located in a rural spot, Lullingstone was typical of many houses in this area – indeed, the Darent Valley had the highest density of Roman villas in the country. Believed to have started as a farm around 100 AD, it grew to become a large estate, home to eminent Romans (including, it is thought, Pertinax, governor of Britain in 185–6 and, for just three months, emperor) and was occupied until the fifth century.

The site is known for its brilliantly preserved Roman **mosaics**, but excavations also unearthed rare evidence of early **Christian** practices – the so-called **Orantes paintings**, showing six large standing figures with their hands raised, and the Chi-Rho, an early Christian symbol. These unique finds are now held by the British Museum, but you can see reproductions here, along with replicas of fine marble **busts** found on the site.

The first-floor balcony is the best place from which to view the **mosaic floor**, which depicts Bellerophon riding Pegasus and slaying the Chimera, a fire-breathing she-beast. Displays throughout give lively glimpses into Roman domestic life – from decorated glass gaming counters to impossibly delicate bone needles and stunning bronze jewellery, with recipes for such dishes as mussels with lentils and peppered sweet cake revealing the Romans to have eaten very well indeed. Clay slabs marked with the imprints of paws, hooves or the maker's fingerprints have a poignant immediacy, as do a couple of **human skeletons** – one of a young man in a lead coffin decorated with scallops, the other of a tiny baby, one of four found at the villa.

Ightham Mote

Mote Rd, Ivy Hatch, TN15 0NT • **House** March–Oct daily 11am–5pm; Nov Sat & Sun 11am–3pm; Dec daily 11am–3pm • **Gardens** Daily: March–Oct 10am–5pm; Nov–Feb 10am–3.30pm • **Estate** Daily dawn–dusk • Jan & Feb £2.70; March–Oct £11; Nov & Dec £5.50; NT • Parking £2 • ☏ 01732 810378, ⊚ nationaltrust.org.uk/ightham-mote

Hidden in a pretty wooded valley around seven miles east of Sevenoaks, **Ightham Mote** – when you eventually find it – is a magical sight, a fourteenth-century, half-timbered beauty sitting on its own moated island, fringed with a soft stone wall spilling over with colourful wildflowers. There's plenty to see in its twenty-plus rooms, though as it has been much adapted over the centuries by its various owners, from Tudor courtiers to a wealthy American businessman, it is a bit of a mishmash. Every room is different, from the medieval Great Hall to the Victorian servants' quarters to the 1930s Oriel Room, where you can settle down on the sofa and listen to the old wireless; for anyone interested in architecture, or conservation, it's a treat. Highlights include the fifteenth-century **chapel**, with its stunning mid-sixteenth-century painted oak ceiling, and the **drawing room**, dominated by an elaborate Jacobean fireplace and lined with exquisite hand-painted eighteenth-century Chinese wallpaper. The **gardens**, encompassing an ancient orchard, woods and lakes, offer pretty walks, while the 550-acre estate, waymarked with trails, includes natural springs and bluebell woods to explore.

Emmetts Garden

Ide Hill, 4.5 miles west of Sevenoaks, TN14 6BA • Daily: March–Dec 10am–5pm (or dusk if sooner) • March & June–Dec £8.10; April & May £10; NT; parking free • ☏ 01732 868381, ⊚ nationaltrust.org.uk/emmetts • Bus #404 bus from Sevenoaks (Mon–Fri) to Ide Hill, 1.5 miles south

Kent's ancient woodlands hold a good share of England's **bluebell woods**, and some of the very best are to be seen at the Edwardian **Emmetts Garden**. Sitting at the top of the Weald, one of the highest points in Kent – and with wonderful views over the grasslands of the North Downs – the six-acre garden is fringed with woodland whose slopes are carpeted with a violet haze in springtime. The woods, which include a wild play area for kids, make for gorgeous walks at any time of year, and in the formal garden itself you can see some surprisingly exotic plantings, many from East Asia, along with a rose garden and rock garden. There's plenty of space to stroll on hillside paths or picnic in the meadows.

Chartwell

Mapleton Rd, Westerham, 6 miles west of Sevenoaks, TN16 1PS • **House** March–Nov Mon–Fri 11.30am–5pm, Sat & Sun 11am–5pm; Dec (some rooms only) Sat & Sun 11am–3pm • **Studio** March–Oct daily noon–4pm; Nov & Dec noon–3.30pm • **Garden** March–Oct daily 10am–5pm; Nov–Feb 10am–dusk • £13.50; garden, studio & exhibition only £6.75; NT • Parking £3 • ☏ 01732 868381, ⊚ nationaltrust.org.uk/chartwell

Packed with the wartime Prime Minister's possessions – including his rather contemplative paintings – there is something touchingly intimate about **Chartwell**, the country residence of **Winston Churchill** from 1924 until his death in 1965. Churchill bought the house in 1922, bowled over by the expansive Weald views; his wife Clementine always had her doubts, however, fearing it would be too expensive to maintain. Indeed, Chartwell had to be put on the market in 1946, when it was bought by a consortium of the Churchills' supporters; the family then had the right to live there until they died, after which it was left to the nation.

Built on the site of a sixteenth-century dwelling, the house was extended greatly in the eighteenth and nineteenth centuries; the imposing 1920s exterior dates from Churchill's era. Filled with fresh flowers and personal effects, Chartwell is set up to look largely as it would have in the 1920s and 1930s, revealing the personal side of this gruff statesman – and Clementine's superb eye for design. A Monet hangs in the light-filled **drawing room**, with its colour scheme of soft primrose, lavender and rose, while the **dining room** features fashionable custom-designed Heals furniture. Cabinets of **memorabilia** include a medal given to Lady Churchill by Josef Stalin for her charitable work during World

SHIPBOURNE FARMERS' MARKET

A couple of miles south of Ightham, **Shipbourne Farmers' Market** is consistently rated as one of the best in England, with excellent local produce, a very friendly, sociable vibe, and a real focus on the community. Held every Thursday from 9am to 11am, in and around St Giles' Church, on Stumble Hill, it has some twenty stalls piled high with the freshest local fruit, veg, meat, cheese and bread; profits go to agricultural charities in the UK and in Africa.

War II, Churchill's 1953 Nobel Prize for Literature, and a Wanted poster offering £25 for his capture, dead or alive, following his escape in 1899 from a Boer POW camp. His flamboyant side is not forgotten, not least in his jaunty velvet **"siren suit"** – a self-designed boiler suit to be pulled on over pyjamas in the event of an Air Raid. An **exhibition** at the end includes a sweet series of notes between him and Clementine, and an illuminating letter from his father written when he was a young man, expressing his fears that he was to become "a social wastrel" and a "public school failure".

Chartwell's rolling **grounds**, bobbing with flowers, dotted with lakes and ponds and studded by mature fruit trees, are perfect for a picnic. Take a stroll around the romantic English cottage garden, and look out for three small stones by a path – these are the **graves** of Churchill's beloved brown poodles, and his marmalade cat, Jock. The estate also makes a good starting point for a couple of appealing waymarked **walks**; pick up guide sheets from the visitor centre.

The studio

Churchill defined himself as a have-a-go artist, and openly acknowledged that he painted to combat the "black dog" – he coined the term – of his depression. His **studio**, lined ceiling to floor with more than one hundred canvases and including his easel, brushes and palette, reveals him to be an enthusiastic and not untalented painter; the works are of varying quality, however, and some of the best can be seen in the house itself. Of these, standouts include an effervescent black-and-white 1955 portrait of Clementine at the launch of HMS *Indomitable* in 1940, and a rather lovely, delicate *Magnolia* (1930).

Down House

Luxted Rd, Downe, 10 miles northwest of Sevenoaks, BR6 7JT • Mid-Feb to March Wed–Sun 10am–4pm; April–Sept daily 10am–6pm; Oct daily 10am–5pm; Nov to mid-Feb Sat & Sun 10am–4pm • £11.10; EH; parking free • ☎ 01689 859119, 🌐 www.english-heritage.org.uk/Darwin

Down House, where Charles Darwin lived and worked most of his life, is a treat, revealing a wealth of snippets about an extraordinary man and an extraordinary age. Darwin moved here from London in 1842 with his wife Emma and their first two children (they went on to have eight more), and remained until his death in 1882. This unremarkable family home – an "oldish, ugly" Georgian house, according to Darwin – provided sanctuary from the social demands of the capital, and was itself a living laboratory. All the family were involved in his work – his children would collect and label specimens from the garden, help look after his pigeons and map the flight paths of local bees – as were his butler, the governess and even the local vicar.

Exhibition rooms offer an overview of Darwin's life and times, including a replica of his tiny cabin on the HMS **Beagle**, the ship that housed him on the five-year voyage that he called "by far the most important event in my life". The scrawled **list** of his father's objections to his *Beagle* trip – including it being a "wild scheme" and "disreputable to my character" – is just one of many lists on display. Darwin was an inveterate list-maker; they make fascinating reading, exposing a thoughtful, meticulous and somewhat anxious individual. Domestic rooms reveal a comfortable, well-worn upper-class Victorian family home, filled with pictures, mementos and memorabilia, but above all dominated by Darwin's work. In the **drawing room**, for example, look beyond the bourgeois trappings and you'll see a terracotta jar on Emma's beloved piano. This would have been filled with

4

earthworms, as part of an experiment to see if they could hear or sense music. While you can see a reconstruction of Darwin's **bedroom**, the cluttered **study** perhaps reveals most. In the centre sits his battered old horsehair armchair and writing board; in the corner, a screened-off privy. Darwin suffered from regular vomiting, painful wind, dizzy spells and headaches, along with eczema and skin complaints. Some have attributed his symptoms to Chagas disease, caught after being bitten by a bloodsucking South American bug during his *Beagle* journey; others believe that his illness was aggravated by stress.

Don't miss the **garden** – Darwin's outdoor laboratory, where he could observe the natural world in situ, as well as cultivate plants for investigation. A gate opens onto the **Sandwalk**, the path through the meadows that he followed three times a day without fail on what he called his "thinking walks".

Chiddingstone

Some nine miles south of Sevenoaks, **CHIDDINGSTONE**, surrounded by soft rolling hills, ancient woodlands and hedge-tangled country lanes, is ridiculously picturesque. "Village" is too grand a name for this tiny place; the one street comprises just a handful of half-timbered Tudor gems and sixteenth- and seventeenth-century buildings, including **St Mary's Church** (ⓦ chiddingstonechurches.org), a general store (former residence of Thomas Bullen, Anne Boleyn's father), a tearoom and a school, all owned by the National Trust (the excellent pub, the *Castle Inn*, is currently closed while the Trust assesses how much conservation work it requires). Things were not always so quiet; by the early sixteenth century this was a prosperous place, at the centre of the local wool and iron industries. Unsurprisingly, it has often been used as a movie location and stood in for the fictional village of Summer Street in Merchant Ivory's *A Room With a View*.

Chiddingstone Castle

Hill Hoath Rd, TN8 7AD • Easter–Oct Mon–Wed & Sun 11am–5pm; last admission 4.15pm • £9 • ☎ 01892 870347, ⓦ chiddingstonecastle.org.uk

Chiddingstone Castle is in fact a large country house, built in the sixteenth century and castellated in the early 1800s. It's an unusual place, half country manor and half museum, displaying the eclectic collection of the eccentric banker-cum-antiquarian **Denys Eyre Bower**, who bought it in 1955. The grounds include patches of woodland, a lake and a rose garden, and there's a pretty **tearoom** with a sunny cobbled courtyard.

The best of the collection is in the **Japanese Room**, though Bower, who claimed to be the reincarnation of Bonnie Prince Charlie, also collected an excellent hoard of **Stuart and Jacobite** artefacts; note the snuff box with a hidden portrait of James III, the "Old Pretender", inside the lid, and the letter from James's son, the Bonnie Prince himself. Don't miss **Bower's study**, where an overwrought letter from a fiancée, chastising him for dreadful cruelty, sits beside news clippings about his conviction in 1957 for the attempted murder of a girlfriend. Bower always professed his innocence, and was released from prison after four years when his conviction was proved to be a miscarriage of justice.

Hever Castle

Hever, near Edenbridge, 9 miles southwest of Sevenoaks, TN8 7NG • **Castle** April–Oct daily noon–6pm; Nov & Dec Wed–Sun noon–4.30pm; last entry 1hr 30min before closing • **Grounds** April–Oct daily 10.30am–6pm; Nov & Dec Wed–Sun 10.30am–4.30pm • Castle & grounds £16.50, gardens only £13.90; cheaper if booked online • ☎ 01732 865224, ⓦ hevercastle.co.uk • Hever train station is a mile west (no taxis)

A fortified manor house surrounded by a rectangular moat, **Hever Castle,** built in the thirteenth century, was the childhood home of Anne Boleyn, second wife of Henry VIII, and where Anne of Cleves, Henry's fourth wife, lived after their divorce. In 1903, having fallen into disrepair, it was bought by William Waldorf Astor, American millionaire-owner of *The Observer*, who had it assiduously restored, panelling the rooms with elaborate reproductions of Tudor woodcarvings. Surprisingly small, Hever has an intimate feel, and perhaps tells you more about the tastes and lifestyle of American plutocrats than Tudor nobles. Some original artworks and features are on display, however, along with pieces belonging to other owners, including a precious collection of Tudor portraits and a rare Jacobite sword, carved with verse claiming loyalty to Bonnie Prince Charlie.

Anne Boleyn's room is the most affecting, small and bare other than a huge wooden chest carved with the words "Anne Bullen" and a hulking piece of dark wood from her childhood bed. Next door you can see the book of prayers she carried with her to the executioner's block, inscribed in her own writing and with references to the Pope crossed out. Perhaps even more interesting than the house are the magnificent **grounds**, which cover 125 acres. Star of the show is Waldorf Astor's exquisite formal **Italian Garden** – decorated with statues, some of which are more than two thousand years old – but there's also a traditional yew maze, an adventure playground and a splashy water maze, along with ponds and weeping-willow-shaded lakes with rowing boats for rent; you can even try your hand at archery.

ARRIVAL AND INFORMATION · SEVENOAKS AND AROUND

By train Sevenoaks train station is off London Rd, about a 20min walk to the main Knole entrance.
Destinations Ashford (every 30min; 45min); Eynsford (every 30min; 15min); Hastings (every 30min; 1hr–1hr 15min); London Charing Cross (every 30min; 45min); London Victoria (every 10–20min; 45min–1hr); Ramsgate (hourly; 1hr 30min); Shoreham (every 30min; 10min); Tunbridge Wells (every 30min–2hr; 25min).

By bus Buses to Sevenoaks stop on Buckhurst Lane, in the town centre, off the High St.
Destinations Eynsford (4 daily; 30min); Tunbridge Wells (every 30min–2hr; 45min); Westerham (every 1–2hr; 20min).
Website ⓦ visitsevenoaksdistrict.co.uk.

4

ACCOMMODATION

The Bakery Westmore Green, Tatsfield, TN16 2AG ⓣ01959 577605, ⓦthebakeryrestaurant.com. Contemporary guestrooms above a lively Modern European restaurant/bar – and in a ground-floor extension, with little decks – in a quiet village near Westerham. Friendly, comfortable and good value. **£105**

Becketts B&B Pylegate Farm, Hartfield Rd, Cowden, near Edenbridge, TN8 7HE ⓣ01342 850514, ⓦbecketts-bandb.co.uk. Characterful B&B in a beautifully appointed eighteenth-century barn three miles south of Hever, near the Sussex border. There are three en-suite bedrooms – one with an antique four-poster, another with its own small garden area, and another under the eaves – with a cosy drawing room, and a flower-filled garden where you can eat breakfast in summer. Country walks head off practically from the doorstep. Minimum two-night stay in summer. **£95**

Charcott Farmhouse Leigh, TN11 8LG ⓣ01892 870024, ⓦcharcottfarmhouse.com. This gorgeous red-tile-hung sixteenth-century farmhouse, around four miles east of Chiddingstone, is a relaxing B&B with a wild garden, a terrace and rolling fields outside the front door, a few friendly cats and a laidback dog. The three twin rooms are simple, and the home-made food, from the welcome cake to the communal breakfasts, is delicious. **£80**

Hever Castle B&B Hever, TN8 7NG ⓣ01732 865224, ⓦhevercastle.co.uk. If you want to live like a queen, or perhaps more accurately like an American hotel magnate, this opulent B&B, in two Tudor-style wings that Astor added in 1903 next to the castle (see opposite), should fit the bill. The 28 luxurious en-suite rooms are each different, but all decorated in a classically tasteful style – some have four-posters. There's a swanky lounge with billiards table for guests' use and, best of all, staying here means you can wander the gardens at leisure after hours. **£165**

Ightham B&B Hope Farm, Sandy Lane, Ightham, TN15 9BA ⓣ07870 628760, ⓦwww.ighthambedandbreakfast .co.uk. Tucked away in perfect tranquility – in the garden of your hosts' house but surrounded by greenery, flowers and trees – this contemporary barn conversion offers a splendid combination of B&B and self-catering. There's one twin and one double, with a shared bathroom, plus a huge guest lounge/kitchen and secluded terrace; the whole set-up is very family friendly, with toys and a play area. The tasty breakfast – of your choosing – is brought over to you to enjoy at your leisure. No credit cards. **£125**

EATING AND DRINKING

Food for Thought 19 The Green, Westerham, TN16 1AX ⓣ01959 569888, ⓦfoodforthought.eu. This unassuming tearoom, well placed for Chartwell on Westerham Green, is popular for its simple, home-made food. The light lunches are tasty – salads, omelettes, soups – but it's really a place to stop off for afternoon tea (£9.95

for two), or a cuppa and a slab of cake or apple pie. Mon–Fri 9am–5pm, Sat 8.30am–5.30pm, Sun 9am–5.30pm.

★**George and Dragon** 39 High St, Chipstead, TN13 2RW ☎01732 779019, ⓦgeorgeanddragonchipstead .com. This friendly little village pub, effortlessly stylish with its whimsical feature wallpaper, fresh flowers, gnarled beams and bare floorboards, serves astonishingly good, generous food packed with flavour. Local sourcing is key on a menu that runs the gamut from steak sandwiches and cheese platters to wild boar and chorizo burger or baked celeriac fondue. Daily 11am–11pm; kitchen Mon–Fri noon–3pm & 6–9.30pm, Sat noon–4pm & 6–9.30pm, Sun noon–4pm & 6–8.30pm.

King Henry VIII Hever Rd, Hever, TN8 7NH ☎01732 862457, ⓦkinghenryviiihever.co.uk. Opposite the entrance to Hever Castle, this handsome tile-hung and half-timbered inn, now a Shepherd Neame pub, is an atmospheric place for a drink, with its mullioned windows and wood-panelling, and its lovely garden with duck pond. Hearty pub grub includes pies, sausages and steaks, with mains from £11. Mon–Sat noon–11.30pm, Sun noon–10pm; kitchen Mon–Thurs noon–3pm & 6.30–9pm, Fri & Sat noon–9pm, Sun noon–7pm.

The Little Garden 1 Well Court, Bank St, Sevenoaks, TN13 1UN ☎01732 469397, ⓦlittlegardensevenoaks .com. If you're heading for this buzzy bar/grill, tucked away on a pedestrianized lane, be sure to bag a table on its lovely leafy deck, festooned with twinkling lights and shaded by a spreading maple tree. The food, a mishmash of contemporary global dishes from chicken wings to Bombay lamb, duck a l'orange to chargrilled steaks, lives up to the location. Mains from £11. Mon–Fri noon–3pm & 5–10pm, Sat noon–10pm, Sun noon–9pm.

Maidstone and around

With a couple of Kent's most popular day-trip attractions within easy reach, plus good North Downs walking and a handful of lovely villages – **Aylesford** among them, which has an excellent **farmers' market** (third Sun of every month 9.30am–1.30pm; ⓦaylesfordfarmersmarket.co.uk) – there is little need to linger in the county town of **MAIDSTONE**. That said, its old centre, boasting attractive buildings dating from its seventeenth- and eighteenth-century heyday, repays a stroll. Along with the rather good **Maidstone Museum and Bentlif Art Gallery** on St Faith's Street (April–Oct Tues–Sat 10am–5pm, Sun noon–4pm; Nov–March Tues–Sat 10am–5pm; free; ⓦmuseum .maidstone.gov.uk) with its impressive Anglo-Saxon hoard, ghoulish Egyptian mummy and important Japanese prints and decorative arts, there are attractive **riverside walks** along the Medway, which runs along the western edge of town – on summer weekends you can take a boat from here to the **Kent Life** family attraction.

Kent Life

Lock Lane, Sandling, 3 miles north of Maidstone, ME14 3AU • Daily 10am–5pm; last admission 4pm • £9.50, under-16s £7.50 • ☎01622 763936, ⓦkentlife.org.uk • Accessible by boat on the *Kentish Lady* from the Archbishop's Palace in Maidstone (Easter–Oct Sat & Sun; 30min each way; £7 return; ☎01622 753740, ⓦkentishlady.co.uk)

Though it offers more than a nod to Kent's agricultural history – leaning farm buildings, a working oast house, authentic hoppers' huts – the 28-acre **Kent Life**, which occupies an old farm estate on the banks of the Medway, is actually more of a giant outdoor playground than a museum of rural life, and very popular with small kids. Along with seasonal events from sheep racing to cider festivals, star attractions include the (indoor and outdoor) play areas, farmyard pens where you can cuddle a guinea pig or stroke a cockerel, bone-rattling tractor rides, and donkey rides for the very little ones.

Leeds Castle

Near Leeds, 7 miles east of Maidstone, ME17 1PL • **Castle** Daily: April–Sept 10.30am–6pm (last entry 4.30pm); Oct–March 10.30am–5pm (last entry 3pm) • **Grounds & gardens** Daily: April–Sept 10am–6pm; Oct–March 10am–5pm • **Playgrounds, maze & grotto** Daily: April–Sept 10am–5pm; Oct–March 10am–4pm • £24.50, under-16s £16.50; tickets valid for a year • ☎01622 765400, ⓦleeds-castle.com • Shuttle bus (£5; ⓦspottravel.co.uk) from Bearsted train station, 3 miles northwest of the castle

Its reflection shimmering in a placid lake, the enormous **Leeds Castle** – it's named after the local village – resembles a fairy-tale palace. Beginning life around 1119, it has had a chequered history, and is now run as a commercial concern, hosting conferences, concerts and special events, with a branch of the zip-lining treetop adventure park **Go Ape** on site (☜goape.co.uk). The castle's interior, though interesting, fails to match the stunning exterior and the grounds, and twentieth-century renovations have tended to quash its historical charm; if you're happy to forego the paying attractions, you could simply cross the grounds for free on one of the **public footpaths**, while if you **stay the night** (see below), admission to the castle and attractions (though not Go Ape) is included.

The castle

Having started its days as a Saxon manor house, Leeds Castle was converted into a royal palace by Henry VIII. It is unusual in having been owned by six medieval queens, starting with Eleanor of Castile (wife of Edward I) and ending with Henry V's widow, Catherine de Valois; it was also home to Queen Joan of Navarre (c.1370–1437), wife of Henry IV, who was accused of being a witch. In 1926 it caught the eye of Anglo-American heiress Lady Baillie, who lived here for fifty years, entertaining guests from Charlie Chaplin to Noël Coward. Baillie upgraded many of the rooms in the 1920s and 30s, which makes it difficult to tell the originals from the reproductions – panels clarify what it is you are actually looking at. In the Gloriette, the keep, which housed the royal apartments, the **Queen's Room**, originally Eleanor's, is set up to look as it might have in 1422, while in the **Queen's Gallery** you can see a fireplace installed during Henry VIII's day, and a set of sixteenth-century busts portraying a morose Henry with his three children.

The remaining rooms look as they did in Baillie's day. Of most interest are her **dressing room and bathroom**, which were the last word in Deco chic, and the glorious **library**, flooded with golden light.

The grounds

With five hundred acres of beautifully landscaped grounds, crisscrossed with paths and streams, and with peacocks and black swans adding their elegant presence, Leeds Castle is a joy to walk around (note, though, that dogs are not allowed). There are plenty of diversions, from the **Dark Sky** audiovisual exhibit, telling the story of the Battle of Agincourt – when the sky grew dark with its volley of arrows – to the excellent **falconry** displays near the **bird of prey centre**. A tricky **yew hedge maze** sits above a kitschy **grotto** – which, full of eerie, howling sound effects and glowing-eyed sea monsters, is a little baffling. There's even a **dog-collar museum** – should you yearn to see the collar worn by Sooty's squeaky sidekick Sweep, or a jagged medieval brass collar used for bear-baiting.

ARRIVAL AND INFORMATION

MAIDSTONE AND AROUND

By train Maidstone has two mainline stations, both of them central; Maidstone East, on the east side of the river, is a 15min walk from Maidstone West, which lies across the river to the southwest.

Destinations Ashford (every 30min–1hr; 30min); Aylesford (every 30min–1hr; 7min); Hollingbourne (every 30min–1hr; 9min); London Victoria (every 30min; 1hr);

Tonbridge (hourly; 30min).

Tourist office In the Maidstone Museum & Bentlif Art Gallery (see opposite), on St Faith's St near Maidstone East station (April–Oct Mon–Sat 10am–5pm, Sun noon–4pm; Nov–March Mon–Sat 10am–5pm; ☎01622 602169, ☜visitmaidstone.com).

ACCOMMODATION

Black Horse Inn Pilgrims' Way, Thurnham, ME14 3LE ☎01622 737185, ☜blackhorsekent.co.uk. B&B accommodation in garden chalets behind an eighteenth-century country pub/restaurant, four miles from Maidstone, on the southern slopes of the North Downs (dogs are

welcome). The olde-worlde pub, where you can eat bistro food (duck breast, pork belly, gnocchi; mains from £10), is cosy. **£95**

Leeds Castle Leeds Castle, Maidstone, ME17 1PL ☎01622 767823, ☜leeds-castle.com/accommodation. The Leeds Castle estate offers various accommodation options: comfortable B&B at the *Stable Courtyard* and the sixteenth-century *Maiden's Tower*; five self-catering properties, ranging from a two-person hideaway to the gamekeeper's house, which sleeps ten; and glamping in jaunty medieval-style pavilion tents for up to four people. Stable Courtyard **£110**, glamping **£140**, self-catering **£145**, Maiden's Tower **£280**

★ **Welsummer** Lenham Rd, Harrietsham, 8 miles southeast of Maidstone, ME17 1NQ ☎ 01622 843051, ⓦ welsummercamping.com. Well-run, almost-wild camping on the slopes of the North Downs, with walking trails all around. A tent-only site, with plenty of space for the kids to romp around, it offers pitches across two car-free meadows and a small woodland area, with six bell tents (sleeping six), a well-equipped little hut (two adults plus one child) and a B&B room in the owners' cottage. A small shop sells home-grown and local produce, there are fire pits, and dogs are permitted on leads. Two-night minimum. Curfew 10.30pm. Closed Oct–March. Camping **£20**, bell tents **£70**, hut **£70**, B&B **£75**

EATING AND DRINKING

The Dirty Habit Upper St, Hollingbourne, ME17 1UW ☎ 01622 880880, ⓦ elitepubs.com/the_dirtyhabit. Dating from the eleventh century, this village pub at the foot of the North Downs – a couple of miles north of Leeds Castle – is both cosy and rather smart with its rich oak panelling, gleaming flagstones and plump leather chairs. The menu lists dishes like crab and mango *rillette*, Sicilian aubergine stew or Moroccan quinoa salad alongside gastropub staples (mains from £13). There's good walking hereabouts. Daily 11.30am–11pm; kitchen Mon–Thurs noon–3pm & 5.30–9pm, Fri & Sat noon–9.30pm, Sun noon–8.30pm.

Fortify Café 32 High St, Maidstone, ME14 1JF ☎ 01622 670533, ⓦ fortifycafe.co.uk. If gastropubs get your goat, head to this excellent vegan restaurant near the river in Maidstone, which serves everything from houmous with flatbread to seitan kebabs or lasagne, plus simple breakfasts (till noon, all day Sun). Everything is fresh and tasty, and with dishes from £5, the prices are great. Takeaway available. Mon–Wed 8am–5pm, Thurs & Fri 8am–5pm & 6–10pm, Sat 9am–5pm & 6–10pm, Sun 11am–5pm.

Mulberry Tree Hermitage Lane, Boughton Monchelsea, ME17 4DA ☎ 01622 749082, ⓦ themulberrytreekent.co.uk. Six miles southwest of Leeds Castle, this restaurant scores high for its daily-changing menu of locally sourced food, served in a smart dining room or sunny back garden. Mains, from £17, might include Kentish Middle White pork or Surrey beef rump, with starters (from £8) such as asparagus and wild garlic soup or salt-baked heritage beetroot and blue cheese mousse. The two- and three-course menus (Tues–Fri all day & Sat lunch £18.50/£21.50) are good value; on Sunday they're £21.95/£24.95. Tues–Thurs noon–2pm & 6.30–9pm, Fri & Sat noon–2pm & 6.30–9.30pm, Sun noon–2.15pm.

★ **Pepperbox Inn** Windmill Hill, Harrietsham, ME17 1LP ☎ 01622 842558, ⓦ thepepperboxinn.co.uk. You get gorgeous country views from the garden of this lovely old Shepherd Neame pub – run by the same family since 1958 – on the edge of a tiny hamlet three miles south of Leeds Castle. If your appetite isn't up to the hearty a la carte dishes – pork tenderloin wrapped in Proscuitto and stuffed with apple, apricot and ginger, say (mains from £13) – go for a fish special (crabcakes, mussels) or a sandwich (from £6), and wash it all down with a pint of real ale. Mon–Sat 11am–3pm & 6–11pm, Sun noon–4.30pm; kitchen Mon–Sat noon–2.15pm & 6.45–9.45pm, Sun noon–3pm.

Ashford and around

The ever-expanding market town of **ASHFORD** is of most interest as a public transport hub and a jumping-off point for the Eurostar. Despite the tangle of historic narrow alleyways at its core, its handsome Norman church and scores of malls and designer outlets, there is little to keep you here – head out instead to the scatter of nearby villages in the North Downs and Low Weald, **Pluckley** and **Wye** among them, which make good bases for walking.

Pluckley

Owned from the seventeenth century until 1928 by the wealthy Dering family, who left their legacy in the village's many double-arched "Dering" windows, sleepy old **PLUCKLEY**, five miles west of Ashford, distinguishes itself from other local villages by being where the phenomenally successful 1990s TV series **The Darling Buds of May**, based on the novels by H.E. Bates, was filmed. Though the tourist buzz has shifted in recent years away from the rumbustious Larkins and towards spooky ghost tours (it is said to be "the most haunted village in England"), Pluckley still trades on the fame brought it by David Jason, Catherine Zeta-Jones et al; the Larkins' **Home Farm** itself, on Pluckley Road about 1.5 miles south of the railway station, has been transformed into Darling Buds Farm, offering self-catering accommodation (ⓦdarlingbudsfarm.co.uk).

Wye

WYE, some five miles northeast of Ashford, is a quiet village that makes a great base for hikes on the long-distance North Downs Way. The **Wye National Nature Reserve**, an area of chalky grassland, woods and hills a mile or so southeast of town, is a lovely spot for a short (occasionally steep) walk, with a 2.5-mile trail offering superb views out to Romney Marsh and the Weald; the **Devil's Kneading Trough**, one of a network of narrow, high-sided dry valleys cut into the Downs, is particularly dramatic. Look out, too, for the **white chalk crown** set into the grassy slopes to the east of Wye, created in 1902 to commemorate the coronation of Edward VII. The village hosts a good **farmers' market** (first and third Sat of the month; 9am–noon; ⓦwyefarmersmarket.co.uk).

ARRIVAL AND INFORMATION   ASHFORD AND AROUND

By train Eurostar services to Paris and Brussels leave from Ashford International train station, while the domestic station, linked to it by a foot tunnel, sees regular services from London, the North Weald, East Sussex and the coast. Both are around a 10min drive from junction 10 of the M20. Destinations Brighton (hourly; 1hr 50min); Canterbury (every 10–30min; 15–20min); Folkestone (every 15–45min; 15–20min); Hastings (hourly; 40–50min);

London Charing Cross (every 30min; 1hr 20min); London St Pancras (every 30min; 40min); Maidstone (every 20–40min; 30min); Margate (hourly; 50min–1hr); Pluckley (every 30min; 6min); Sevenoaks (every 30min; 45min); Tonbridge (every 30min; 35min); Wye (every 30min; 6min).

Tourist office Ashford Gateway Plus, Church Rd, Ashford (Mon–Sat 10.15am–3pm; ☎01233 330316, ⓦvisitashfordandtenterden.co.uk).

ACCOMMODATION AND EATING

Dering Arms The Grove, Pluckley, TN27 0RR ☎01233 840371, ⓦderingarms.com. Fish is the speciality – fillet of black bream with marsh samphire, say – at this handsome creeper-covered hunting lodge by Pluckley station, but they also serve elegant meat dishes (starters from £6, mains from £13) along with a less formal bistro menu (from £10). There are three cosy and welcoming B&B rooms, two of them en suite. Kitchen Tues–Fri noon–2.30pm & 6.30–9pm, Sat noon–3pm & 6.30–9pm, Sun noon–3pm. **£85**

Elvey Farm Elvey Lane, Pluckley, TN27 0SU ☎01233 840442, ⓦelveyfarm.co.uk. Set in 75 acres surrounded by undulating fields, this farmhouse hotel offers boutique rooms – in an oast house, a barn, a granary or stables – which are rustic without being twee, with stripped beams, exposed walls and modern bathrooms. Most are suites – the light-flooded Canterbury Suite comes with its own outdoor hot tub, and there's a thrilling round room in the oast house, but there are standard doubles, too. The Italian restaurant features mains from £14. **£105**

★**Five Bells** The Street, East Brabourne, TN25 5LP ☎01303 813334, ⓦfivebellsinnbrabourne.com. All

log fires, dried hops and vintage paperbacks, this welcoming and stylish sixteenth-century inn, five miles southwest of Wye on the Pilgrims' Way, serves real ales, good wines and Modern British/European mains (from £11), plus wood-fired pizza, and snacks (from £6) including home-made Scotch eggs. Upstairs are four fabulous, colourful B&B rooms – none has TV or tea-/coffee-making facilities (though they will bring drinks to your room), but two have real log fires and all are deliciously eccentric, filled with retro and arty details. Mon–Sat 8am–11pm, Sun 8am–10.30pm; kitchen Mon–Thurs noon–9.30pm, Fri & Sat noon–10pm, Sun noon–9pm. **£130**

★**King's Head** Church St, Wye, TN25 5BN ☎01233 812418, ⓦkingsheadwye.com. It's difficult to go wrong at this good-looking, friendly food pub on Wye's main road, where seasonal, local, farm-fresh ingredients are deployed in simple but accomplished dishes such as crab croquettes, cheese fondue or ox cheek and smoked bacon pie. Snacks from £4, mains from £11. The comfy B&B rooms are attractive and comfortable, decorated with vintage and reclaimed furniture. Mon, Tues & Sun 8am–10pm, Wed–Sat 8am–11pm. **£100**

4

The Sussex High Weald

ASHDOWN FOREST

5

The Sussex High Weald

Sandwiched between the lofty chalk escarpments of the North and South Downs, the Sussex High Weald is an unspoilt landscape of rolling sandstone hills, ancient woodland and wonky, hedgerow-lined fields, dotted with farmsteads and medieval villages. Most of this chapter – bar the towns of Rye and Hastings on the coast – lies within or on the fringes of the central High Weald AONB (Area of Outstanding Natural Beauty), which also stretches into Kent. There are no large towns to speak of in this tranquil pocket of Sussex countryside, and the landscape seems almost suspended in time. Steam trains puff through bluebell woods, crumbling castles guard against long-forgotten enemies, and venerable country estates gaze serenely over the glorious gardens that are one of the Sussex High Weald's defining features.

Best-known of the great gardens are Wakehurst Place, Sheffield Park, Nymans and **Great Dixter**, the last of these just a short hop from a romantic castle at **Bodiam** and Rudyard Kipling's country retreat at Bateman's. Kipling was one of many writers and artists who made their home in the area: you can also visit Henry James's townhouse at Rye, and Farleys House and Gallery, where Surrealist painter Roland Penrose and photographer Lee Miller entertained Picasso, Miró and Man Ray. A.A. Milne, creator of much-loved fictional bear Winnie-the-Pooh, had his weekend home at Hartfield in the heart of **Ashdown Forest**, at the northern edge of the **High Weald**. The landscape changes dramatically here, with hedgerow-fringed fields giving way to beautiful gorse-speckled heathland crisscrossed with trails – a great place to strike off and get lost.

Down on the coast, the High Weald meets the sea around Hastings. This is 1066 country: the most famous battle in British history was fought in nearby **Battle**, marking the end of Anglo-Saxon England. **Hastings** itself is a buzzy and vibrant (if rough-around-the-edges) seaside town with a picturesque old core and an atmospheric fishing quarter, while further east along the coast the perfectly preserved medieval town of **Rye** is one of the highlights of Sussex, even without the added draw of dune-backed Camber Sands beach on its doorstep. Both towns are crammed with stylish boutique hotels, and excellent restaurants making the most of fantastic local ingredients – fish from the Hastings fleet, scallops and shrimps from Rye, lamb from Romney Marsh and sparkling wine from local vineyards.

GREAT DIXTER

Highlights

❶ Rye A medieval gem, with cobbled streets and ancient inns, and dune-backed Camber Sands beach nearby. **See p.166**

❷ Hastings With a pretty Old Town, a still-working fishermen's quarter and miles of glorious coastline on its doorstep, Hastings makes the perfect seaside getaway. **See p.173**

❸ De La Warr Pavilion Bexhill-on-Sea's seaside pavilion is an unmissable Modernist masterpiece and a vibrant centre for contemporary arts. **See p.184**

❹ Battle Abbey Soak up the atmosphere at the site of the battle that changed the course of British history. **See p.186**

❺ Great Dixter One of the country's greatest gardens, with innovative, imaginative planting that can't fail to inspire. **See p.188**

❻ Bodiam Castle A classic picture-book castle, complete with moat and battlements, that's best reached by river boat or steam train. **See p.189**

❼ Farleys House and Gallery Don't miss the fascinating former home of Surrealist painter Roland Penrose and his wife, the model-turned-photographer Lee Miller. **See p.191**

❽ Ashdown Forest Hunt for heffalumps in the footsteps of Winnie-the-Pooh, the world's best-loved bear. **See p.194**

HIGHLIGHTS ARE MARKED ON THE MAP ON PP.166–167

5

Rye and around

It's no mystery why **RYE** is one of the most popular destinations in Sussex: this ancient, pocket-sized, hilltop town – half-timbered, skew-roofed and quintessentially English – claims to have retained more of its original buildings than any other town in Britain, and has a street plan virtually unchanged since medieval times.

Rye lies perched on a hill overlooking the Romney Marsh, at the confluence of three rivers – the Rother, the Brede and the Tillingham, the first of which flows south to Rye Harbour and then out to sea. Though the town sees more than its fair share of tourists, especially in the summer months, it has managed – just – to avoid being too chocolate-boxy. There are plenty of good independent shops, a heartening absence of high-street chains, and you're positively spoilt for choice when it comes to great restaurants and places to stay. The main appeal of the town is simply to wander round and soak up the atmosphere: the jostling boats and screeching gulls down at **Strand Quay** (Rye's harbour in Tudor times); ancient **Landgate** – the town's only surviving medieval gate; and sloping, cobbled **Mermaid Street**, the town's main thoroughfare in the sixteenth century and today its most picturesque street.

Rye also makes a great base for the surrounding area. Within a couple of miles there's one of the finest beaches in Sussex, dune-backed **Camber Sands**, and in the other direction the once-mighty hilltop town of **Winchelsea**. Rye's acclaimed **arts festival** (ⓦ ryefestival.co.uk) takes place over two weeks in September and features a wide range

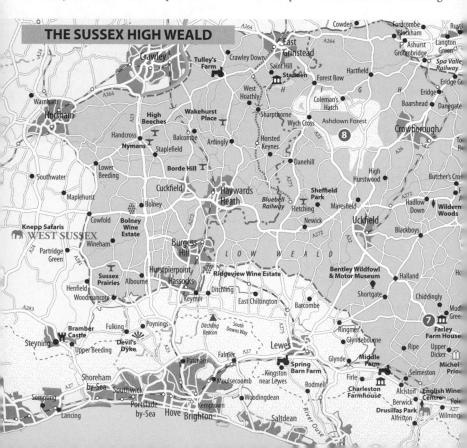

of musical and visual arts events, plus talks and walks. The other big annual event is **Rye Bay Scallop Week** (ⓦscallop.org.uk), held at the end of February.

Brief history

Rye was added as a "limb" to the original Cinque Ports (see box, p.107) in the thirteenth century, and under this royal protection it grew to become an important **port**. Over time, the retreat of the sea and the silting-up of the River Rother marooned Rye two miles inland, and the loss of its port inevitably led to its decline; **smuggling** as a source of income became widespread (see box, p.216), with the brutal Hawkhurst Gang making the town one of their haunts in the eighteenth century.

St Mary's Church

Church Square, TN31 7HH · April–Oct 9.15am–5.30pm; Nov–March 9.15am–4.30pm · Church free; bell tower £3.50 · ☎ 01797 224935, ⓦryeparishchurch.org.uk

The top end of town is crowned by the turret of the twelfth-century **St Mary's Church**, one of the oldest buildings in Rye, which dominates Church Square, a peaceful, shady oasis bordered by old tile-hung buildings. Inside the church, you can't fail to notice the massive 17ft-long pendulum beating time in front of you; St Mary's **clock** is the oldest working church-tower clock in the country, installed in 1561 – though the pendulum,

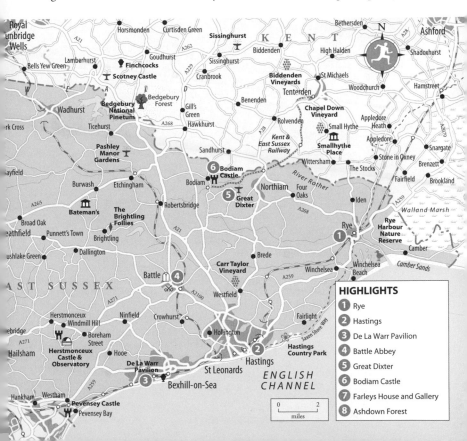

HIGHLIGHTS

1 Rye
2 Hastings
3 De La Warr Pavilion
4 Battle Abbey
5 Great Dixter
6 Bodiam Castle
7 Farleys House and Gallery
8 Ashdown Forest

5

the clock face and the quarterboys (so named because they strike the quarter hours) are all later additions. The ascent of the **bell tower** is a must, involving a fun squeeze through a 16in-wide passage and then a scramble up steep, narrow steps past the huge eighteenth-century bells to the rooftop, where there are fabulous views over the clay-tiled roofs and grid of narrow lanes below.

Rye Castle Museum

Ypres Tower Church Square, TN31 7HH • Daily: April–Oct 10.30am–5pm; Nov–March 10.30am–3.30pm • £3, joint ticket with East Street Museum £4 • **East Street Museum** 3 East St, TN31 7JY • Normally April–Oct Sat, Sun & bank hols 10.30am–5pm, but call ahead to check • £1.50, joint ticket with Ypres Tower £4 • ☎ 01797 227798, Ⓦ ryemuseum.co.uk

Rye Castle Museum is spread over two sites: the main museum is in the **Ypres Tower** (Rye's "castle") in the far corner of Church Square, and there's also a small, volunteer-run museum at 3 East Street, which contains an eclectic selection of relics from Rye's past. The Ypres (pronounced "Wipers") Tower was built, probably in the thirteenth century, to keep watch for cross-Channel invaders, though it didn't do a very good job of repelling the French raiding parties that struck in 1339 and 1377; the second attack virtually razed the town to the ground. The raids persuaded Edward III to open his

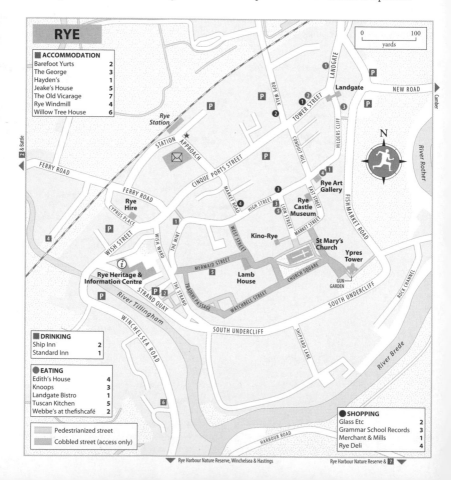

RYE

■ ACCOMMODATION	
Barefoot Yurts	2
The George	3
Hayden's	1
Jeake's House	5
The Old Vicarage	7
Rye Windmill	4
Willow Tree House	6

■ DRINKING	
Ship Inn	2
Standard Inn	1

● EATING	
Edith's House	4
Knoops	3
Landgate Bistro	1
Tuscan Kitchen	5
Webbe's at thefishcafé	2

● SHOPPING	
Glass Etc	2
Grammar School Records	3
Merchant & Mills	1
Rye Deli	4

Pedestrianized street

Cobbled street (access only)

0 — 100 yards

Rye Harbour Nature Reserve, Winchelsea & Hastings   Rye Harbour Nature Reserve & 7

5

purse and fund the construction of the town's walls and gates. In 1494 the tower became a prison, with the guardrooms in the turrets converted into cells, and it remained so for almost four hundred years, before setting up shop as a mortuary and finally becoming the town museum.

Inside the tower the modest range of exhibits includes a mocked-up cell, an interactive model showing Rye's changing coastline, medieval pottery, helmets and chainmail for kids to try on, and up the narrow stone staircase – with its "trick" steps, some deep and some shallow, to send intruders off-balance – a small exhibition on Rye's smuggling history. Another cell has been recreated in the neighbouring **Women's Tower**, which was built in 1837 to house female prisoners; thanks to reformers like Elizabeth Fry, the women's living conditions were a marked improvement on those of the unfortunate male prisoners next door. Out front, the **Gun Garden** (open access) looks out over Romney Marsh; it's hard to believe that everything you see in front of you would once have been sea.

Lamb House

West St, TN31 7ES • Mid-March to Oct Tues, Fri & Sat 11am–5pm • £5.60; NT • ☎ 01580 762334, ⓦ nationaltrust.org.uk/lamb-house

A stone's throw from Church Square, the elegant, redbrick Georgian **Lamb House** was the one-time home of author **Henry James** (1843–1916), who moved to Rye in 1897 after 22 years in London and fell in love with both the town and the house: "I have been to the South, the far end of Florida", he wrote in 1905, "but prefer the far end of Sussex! In the heart of golden orange groves I yearned for the shade of the old Lamb House mulberry tree." James wrote three of his best-known novels at Lamb House – *The Wings of the Dove*, *The Ambassadors* and *The Golden Bowl* – and entertained a wide circle of literary friends, including fellow Sussex writers H.G. Wells, Rudyard Kipling and Hilaire Belloc. You can still see some of his manuscripts, letters and photos in the house, and stroll in the beautiful walled garden.

A few years after James's death, the writer **E.F. Benson** moved in, giving the house a starring role in his comic *Mapp and Lucia* novels (see p.324), in which Rye was thinly disguised as "Tilling", while Lamb House became "Mallards". **Tours** of Mapp and Lucia's Rye run on alternate Saturdays from late May to early September (1hr 45min; £6.95; ☎01797 223114, ⓦefbensonsociety.org).

Rye Art Gallery

107 High St, TN31 7JE • Mon–Sat 10.30am–5pm, Sun & bank hols noon–4pm • Free • ☎ 01797 222433, ⓦ ryeartgallery.co.uk

The bulk of the excellent **Rye Art Gallery** is given over to exhibitions of contemporary art, mainly pottery, prints and painting, while the top floor shows changing exhibitions drawn from the gallery's permanent collection of over 450 paintings, prints and photographs. The collection includes works by artists associated with Rye, including Edward Burra, Paul Nash and John Piper, who all lived in the town.

Rye Heritage and Information Centre

Strand Quay, TN31 7AY • Daily 10am–5pm; check website for winter hours; 20min sound-and-light show every 30min • Free; sound-and-light show £3.50; audio guides £4; ghost walks £13 • ☎ 01797 226696, ⓦ ryeheritage.co.uk

Down by Strand Quay, it's well worth popping into the privately run **Rye Heritage and Information Centre** for its excellent **sound-and-light show**, which gives you a potted history of Rye using a model of the town as it would have looked in the early nineteenth century; it's fascinating to see how little its appearance has changed since then. The centre also hires out **walking tour** audio guides and offers occasional **ghost walks** in winter. Upstairs there's a room of wonderfully clunky **penny arcade** machines, some dating back to the 1930s.

5

Rye Harbour Nature Reserve

Rye Harbour Rd, Rye Harbour, TN31 7TU • Nature Reserve open access; Information centre open most days 10am–4/5pm • ☎ 01797 227784, ⓦ sussexwildlifetrust.org.uk • Free car park at Rye Harbour; bus #313 (roughly hourly) runs from Rye station to Rye Harbour

Until the late sixteenth century, most of the land that now makes up the **Rye Harbour Nature Reserve** – a triangle of land between Rye and the sea, bordered to the east by the River Rother and to the west by the River Brede – was a shallow harbour, but its slow silting up over the centuries has transformed it into a rare shingle habitat. By turns both bleak and beautiful, the reserve is at its most colourful in late spring, when the beach is speckled with spears of purple viper's bugloss, carpets of pink sea pea, and clumps of sea kale and yellow horned poppy. Miles of footpaths meander around the shingle ridges and saltmarsh, with five **birdwatching hides** set up overlooking lagoons and reed beds; you can download circular walks from the website, which also has details of **special events**, or pick up a map from the **information centre** situated down the path opposite the car park.

Camber Castle

Tours normally Aug–Oct first Sat of month, 2pm (check ⓦ sussexwildlifetrust.org.uk); meet at castle entrance • £3

The reserve runs occasional guided tours of **Camber Castle**, which was built by Henry VIII as part of a chain of coastal fortifications that also included nearby Deal and Walmer (see p.111). The castle was completed in 1544, costing a princely £23,000, only to be abandoned less than a hundred years later after the build-up of shingle rendered its defensive position useless. Its crumbling walls now lie more than a mile inland, looking out over nothing more dangerous than munching sheep.

ARRIVAL AND GETTING AROUND

RYE AND AROUND

By train Rye's train station is at the bottom of Station Approach, off Cinque Ports St; it's a 5min walk up to High St. There are services from here to Ashford (hourly; 20min), Hastings (hourly; 20min) and London St Pancras (hourly; 1hr 25min).

By bus Bus #100 runs into the centre of town from

Hastings (Mon–Sat every 30min, Sun hourly; 40min).

By car The car park at the station costs £2.70/day (£3 on Sun).

By bike You can rent bicycles from Rye Hire, 1 Cyprus Place (Mon–Fri 8am–5pm, Sat 8am–noon, Sat afternoon & Sun by appointment only; £13/half-day, £18/day; ☎ 01797 223033, ⓦ ryehire.co.uk).

INFORMATION

Rye Heritage and Information Centre Strand Quay (daily 10am–5pm; check website for winter hours; ☎ 01797 226696, ⓦ ryeheritage.co.uk). This privately-run

information centre (see p.169) sells town maps (30p) and rents out audio guides (£4).

ACCOMMODATION

RYE

The George 98 High St, TN31 7JT ☎ 01797 222144, ⓦ thegeorgeinrye.com. Rye's oldest coaching inn has almost everything you could want under one roof: 34 tasteful, individually styled bedrooms – from a Miami-themed suite with circular bed, to a cosy room lined with vintage Penguin paperbacks – plus a wood-beamed bar and a decent restaurant. It even has a shop next door selling bed linen, throws and other furnishings used in the hotel, so you can take a piece of hotel luxury home with you. **£145**

★**Hayden's** 108 High St, TN31 7JE ☎ 01797 224501, ⓦ haydensinrye.co.uk. Friendly, family-run and green-thinking, this popular B&B has seven impeccably elegant, contemporary rooms set above a restaurant in the heart of town. Rooms come with smart bathrooms, bathrobes and iPod docks, and those at the back have lovely views out

over Romney Marsh. **£120**

Jeake's House Mermaid St, TN31 7ET ☎ 01797 222828, ⓦ jeakeshouse.com. This ivy-clad seventeenth-century guesthouse has a great location on Rye's most picturesque street, and inside oozes character, with sagging beams and creaky, sloping floors. Breakfast is served in an extraordinary high-ceilinged Baptist chapel, with such treats as devilled kidneys on the menu. The eleven rooms – most en suite – are traditional in style. **£95**

Rye Windmill Off Ferry Rd, TN31 7DW ☎ 01797 224027, ⓦ ryewindmill.co.uk. Rye's 300-year-old white smock windmill is today a good-value B&B. There are eight smart en-suite rooms, plus two suites in the windmill itself: if you're splashing out, the one to go for is the Windmill Suite (£170), set over the top two floors of the mill, with a balcony giving fabulous views over the river and rooftops. Minimum two-night stay at weekends. **£90**

Willow Tree House 113 Winchelsea Road, TN31 7EL ☎ 01797 227820, ⓦ willow-tree-house.com. Immaculate, friendly B&B on the outskirts of Rye (a 5–10min stroll from the High St), with six luxurious rooms, great breakfasts and (rare for Rye) free parking. It's very popular, so book well ahead. Minimum two-night stay at weekends Easter–Oct. **£95**

RYE HARBOUR

★ **The Old Vicarage** Harbour Road, Rye Harbour, TN31 7TT ☎ 01797 222088, ⓦ oldvicarageryeharbour.co.uk. One of the nicest places to stay in Rye isn't actually in Rye at all, but down the road in Rye Harbour. This super-friendly B&B has just three peaceful rooms and a fabulous location opposite the nature reserve; bikes are available to borrow if you want to explore. Rye Harbour village has a couple of

good pubs and an excellent tearoom so you don't need to venture into Rye for every meal. **£90**

AROUND RYE

★ **Barefoot Yurts** Stubb Lane, Brede, TN31 6BN ☎ 01424 883057, ⓦ barefoot-yurts.co.uk. This magical spot, a 10min drive from Rye, comprises two beautiful yurts (hired together) nestled in their own tranquil clearing. One yurt is the bedroom, the other a sitting room (complete with sofa bed), and there's a separate hut containing a kitchen and shower room, with a covered veranda for sitting and watching the world go by. With wood-burning stoves in both yurts you could even brave a (cheaper) stay in winter. Two night minimum stay April–Sept. **£140**

EATING

There's no shortage of excellent places to eat in Rye; in addition to the places listed below, the restaurants at *The George* (see opposite) and *Hayden's* (see opposite) are recommended, as are the *Ship Inn* (see below) and the *Standard Inn* (see below) pubs. Rye Farmers' Market takes place every Wednesday on Strand Quay (10am–noon).

Edith's House 105a High St, TN31 7JE ☎ 01797 690124, ⓦ facebook.com/ediths.house.7. This sweet little tearoom – named after one of the owner's nans – is decked out as an old-fashioned living room, with armchairs, fringed lamps and family photos on the walls. A simple menu of sandwiches, salads and the like is served on dainty china; special mention must be made of the dedicated scone menu, which features five different types of freshly baked scone (from cinnamon to coconut), each with a suggested jam pairing. Cash only. Daily 10am–5pm.

★ **Knoops** Tower Forge, Hilders Cliff ☎ 01797 225838, ⓦ facebook.com/KnoopsChocolateBar. This little place only really offers one thing – hot chocolate – but it does it with style. Choose your chocolate (from 28 percent to 99 percent cocoa solids; £3), add your extras (various spices, peppers, fruits, herbs – all 50p, or a shot of something stronger for £1) and wait to be presented with your own bowl of made-to-order chocolatey loveliness. Mon & Fri–Sun 10am–6pm, plus Tues & Wed same hours in school hols.

★ **Landgate Bistro** 5–6 Landgate, TN31 7LH ☎ 01797

222829, ⓦ landgatebistro.co.uk. Perhaps the best restaurant in Rye, this small, intimate place – housed in two interconnected Georgian cottages – is known for its traditionally British food: there's plenty of fish from the local fishing fleet, Romney Marsh lamb and game in season. The three-course set menu is excellent value: £19.90 at lunch (Sat & Sun), £22.90 at dinner (Wed & Thurs). Wed–Fri 7–11pm, Sat noon–3.30pm & 7–11pm, Sun noon–3.30pm.

Tuscan Kitchen 8 Lion St, TN31 7LB ☎ 01797 223269, ⓦ tuscankitchenrye.co.uk. Book ahead at this popular restaurant, which serves up fantastic, authentic Tuscan food – the likes of potato and thyme tortellini, or roast rabbit with rosemary – in unassuming rustic surrounds. Pasta dishes cost £8/9, meat and fish mains £10–19. Usually Thurs–Sat 6–11pm, Sun noon–4pm, but check website.

Webbe's at thefishcafé 17 Tower St, TN31 7AT ☎ 01797 222226, ⓦ webbesrestaurants.co.uk. Excellent fish restaurant (mains £12.50–17.50), with an on-site cookery school offering regular day courses (£105) throughout the year. Daily noon–2.30pm & 6–9.30pm.

DRINKING

Ship Inn The Strand, TN31 7DB ☎ 01797 222233, ⓦ theshipinnrye.co.uk. This laidback quayside pub is the perfect spot for a pint by the fire after a blowy winter walk. The decor is eclectic and cheerful, and there are plenty of board games – including a Rye-themed Monopoly – for rainy days. Good seasonal food (from burgers to freshly caught fish) costs around £12–15. Daily 11am–11pm; kitchen Mon–Fri noon–3pm & 6.30–10pm, Sat & Sun noon–4pm & 6.30–10.30pm.

★ **Standard Inn** The Strand, TN31 7EN ☎ 01797 225231, ⓦ thestandardinnrye.co.uk. There's been an inn on this spot since 1420, and the current incarnation – beautifully restored, with bare brick walls and beams – is a gem. There's a good selection of craft beer and local ale, including the pub's own *Standard Inn Farmer's Ale*, plus highly rated food (mains £10–16), which runs from pie of the day to Rye Bay fish. Mon–Thurs & Sun 11am–11pm, Fri & Sat 11am–midnight; kitchen Mon–Fri noon–3pm & 6–9pm, Sat & Sun noon–3pm & 6–9.30pm.

5

ENTERTAINMENT

Kino Rye Lion St, TN31 7LB ☏ 01797 226293, ⓦ kinodigital.co.uk. Fantastic independent cinema, converted from an 1850s building that used to be the town's library, with a stylish café-bar and two screens showing blockbusters, foreign-language films and live streamings of performances from the National Theatre, Royal Opera House and others.

SHOPPING

There are **antiques shops** dotted all around Rye. A good place to start browsing is the huddle of half a dozen shops just off Strand Quay (most open daily 10am–5pm), which sell everything from upcycled furniture to vintage kitchen equipment and crockery.

Glass Etc 18–22 Rope Walk, TN31 7NA ☏ 01797 226600, ⓦ decanterman.com. A treasure-trove of antique and twentieth-century glass, run by Andy McConnell, one of the country's leading authorities on glassware. Mon–Sat 10.30am–5pm, Sun 11am–5pm.

Grammar School Records The Old Grammar School, High St, TN31 7JFT ☏ 01797 222752, ⓦ grammar schoolrecords.com. Housed in an old grammar school, this great independent record store is crammed with new and used vinyl, CDs and DVDs. Mon–Sat 10am–5.30pm, Sun 11am–5.30pm.

Merchant & Mills 14a Tower St, TN31 7AT ☏ 01797 227789, ⓦ merchantandmills.com. If this beautifully styled shop doesn't inspire you to get out your sewing machine, then nothing will: bolts of gorgeous fabrics sit alongside "sewing notions" (scissors, pins and the like) in utilitarian packaging, and Merchant & Mills' own patterns. There's also a small ready-to-wear section. Mon–Fri 9.30am–5.30pm, Sat 10am–5.30pm.

Rye Deli 8–10 Market Rd, TN31 7JA ☏ 01797 226521, ⓦ ryedeli.co.uk. Pick up your picnic provisions or foodie souvenirs from this excellent deli. Goodies include home-made pies, smoked fish, a great selection of cheeses and ales from the Romney Marsh Brewery. Mon–Fri 9am–5.30pm, Sat 9am–6pm, Sun 10.30am–4.30pm.

Winchelsea

Perched on top of Iham Hill two miles southwest of Rye, sleepy **WINCHELSEA** receives a fraction of the visitors of its neighbour, and is probably heartily thankful for it. The tiny town – a neat grid of quiet streets of white weatherboard and tile-hung buildings – is no bigger than a village really but, like Rye, it was once one of the most important ports in the country. Winchelsea was founded in the late thirteenth century by Edward I, after its predecessor, Old Winchelsea – an important member of the Cinque Ports confederation (see box, p.107) – was washed away by a series of violent storms. New Winchelsea was built on higher ground, and for a brief period it flourished until, ironically, the sea which had provided its wealth once again delivered its ruin, gradually retreating, silting up the harbour and leaving the town high and dry.

Church of St Thomas à Becket

High St, TN36 4EB • Daily 9am–6pm, closes 4pm in winter.

Perhaps the most obvious reminder of Winchelsea's illustrious past is the **Church of St Thomas à Becket**, the cathedral-like proportions of which seem strikingly out of place in pocket-sized Winchelsea. The magnificent Gothic church was erected by Edward I in 1288, with no expense spared, and would originally have covered most of the square in which it now sits – what you see today is only the chancel and side chapels, and remnants of the ruined transepts. Inside, the first things that strike you are the glorious, glowing **stained-glass windows**, the work of Douglas Strachan in the early 1930s. To your left, in the north aisle, are three beautiful **effigies** carved from West Sussex black marble that were brought from Old Winchelsea church before the sea submerged it.

Winchelsea Museum

High St, TN36 4EN • May–Sept Tues–Sat 10.30am–4.30pm, Sun & bank hols 1.30–4.30pm • £1.50 • ☏ 01342 714559

Winchelsea Museum is housed in the old courthouse, one of the oldest buildings in town, and contains maps, models, local pottery and other local memorabilia, as well

WATERSPORTS AT CAMBER

Anyone who's ever struggled to put up a windbreak at Camber won't be surprised to learn that it's a renowned centre of wind-based **watersports**: you'll often see windsurfers or kitesurfers scudding along the waves. If you fancy having a go yourself you could try one of the two local outfits, or nearby Action Watersports (see box, p.133).

The Kitesurf Centre Broomhill Sands car park ☎07563 763046, ⓦ thekitesurfcentre.com. Lessons and courses in kitesurfing (£99/day), powerkiting (£49/2hr) and kitebuggying (£59/2hr 30min, £89/4hr) on Camber Sands, plus stand-up paddleboarding lessons and trips on the rivers around Rye (£49/2hr).

Rye Watersports Northpoint Water, New Lydd Rd ☎01797 225238, ⓦ ryewatersports.co.uk. Offers windsurfing (£89/day), paddleboarding (£48/2hr) and sailing (£99/day) lessons on its own coastal lake by Camber Sands.

as a display on past residents of Winchelsea, which have included the actor Ellen Terry, artist John Everett Millais and comedy legend Spike Milligan, who is buried in the churchyard opposite under a gravestone inscribed (in Gaelic) with the immortal words "I told you I was ill".

Camber Sands

Three miles east of Rye, on the other side of the River Rother estuary, **CAMBER SANDS** is a two-mile stretch of sandy beach that's the stuff of childhood nostalgia: soft, fine sand backed by tufty dunes, with gently shelving shallows stretching for half a mile when the sea retreats at low tide. Along with West Wittering (see p.278), Camber is one of only two sandy beaches in Sussex, and the secret's been out for some time: Camber Village is awash with holiday camps and caravan parks – and the odd chic beach house – and in summer you can find yourself bumper-to-bumper in traffic on the approach road from Rye. The quieter end of the beach is to the west: park at the Western Car Park (the first one you'll come to if arriving from Rye), and scramble up one of the footpaths weaving through the scrubby dunes for your first magnificent view of the beach.

ARRIVAL AND DEPARTURE

CAMBER SANDS

By bus Bus #101 (Mon–Sat hourly, Sun every 2hr; 15min) runs from Rye station.
By car There are three car parks: Western, Central and Old Lydd Rd, which are pay-on-entry in summer,

pay-and-display in winter. On sunny weekends in summer the car parks can be full by mid-morning, so get there early.
By bike A three-mile cycle path connects Rye and Camber; bike rental is available in Rye (see p.170).

ACCOMMODATION AND EATING

The Gallivant Hotel New Lydd Road, TN31 7RB ☎01797 225057, ⓦ thegallivanthotel.com. For the perfect grown-up getaway head to this "restaurant with rooms", set just back from the beach. The twenty serene rooms are decorated "with an eye to the Hamptons", there's a complimentary tea-and-cake happy hour at 4pm each

day, and the breakfast buffet includes unlimited Bloody Marys. Even if you're not staying, the restaurant is worth a visit: it sources 95 percent of its fresh ingredients from within a ten-mile radius (mains £14–21). Minimum two-night stay at weekends. Daily noon–2.30pm & 6–9.30pm. **£155**

Hastings and around

Move over Brighton – if you're planning a Sussex weekend away by the sea, you might want to consider heading to **HASTINGS** instead. It has all the ingredients for a perfect break: some fantastic places to stay; a picturesque Old Town crammed with great pubs, cafés and independent shops; a still-working fishing quarter down on the beach where

5

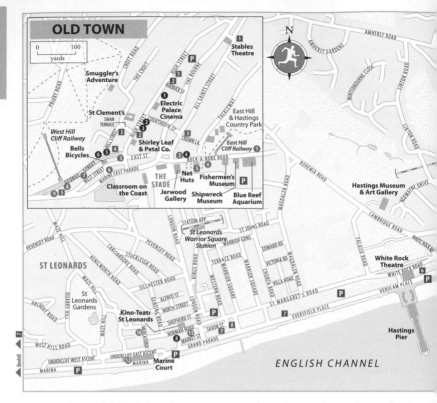

you can tuck into fish hauled in that morning; a seafront that combines plenty of tacky seaside amusements with a sleek modern art gallery and a splendid new pier; a packed festivals calendar; and miles of gorgeous countryside – the rugged Hastings Country Park – literally on your doorstep.

Sprawling along the seafront for over two miles, the town has several distinct neighbourhoods. At its eastern end, sandwiched between East and West Hills, lies the lovely **Old Town**, an enclave of handsome mossy-roofed houses, meandering twittens (passageways), antiques shops and upmarket boutiques and cafés, with the fishing quarter down on the beach. On the other side of West Hill is the **town centre**, very much the poor relation, where you'll find the station and the scruffy main shopping precinct, while further west still is fast-gentrifying, shabby-chic **St Leonards-on-Sea**, once a separate town but now more or less absorbed into Hastings.

Out of town, five miles west along the coast, the small seaside town of Bexhill-on-Sea is home to the **De La Warr Pavilion**, a peerless piece of Modernist architecture, and further along the coast you can visit **Pevensey Castle**, where William's troops encamped before marching on to Battle. Inland there's star-gazing and hands-on science at **Herstmonceux Castle and Observatory**, and wine tasting at **Carr Taylor Vineyard**.

Brief history

Hastings is perhaps best known for the eponymous **battle** of 1066 which in fact took place six miles away at Battle (see p.186); the victorious William I designated Hastings as one of the six Rapes (districts) of Sussex, and ordered that a castle be built to defend

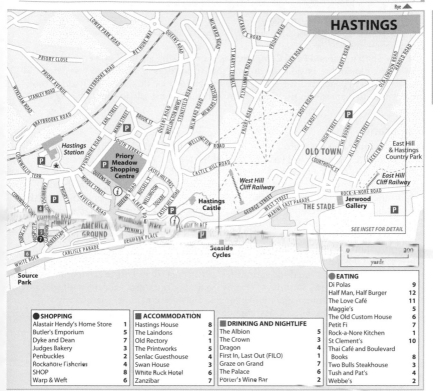

SHOPPING

Alastair Hendy's Home Store	1
Butler's Emporium	5
Dyke and Dean	7
Judges Bakery	3
Penbuckles	2
Rockanore Fisheries	4
SHOP	8
Warp & Weft	6

ACCOMMODATION

Hastings House	8
The Laindons	2
Old Rectory	1
The Printworks	5
Senlac Guesthouse	4
Swan House	3
White Rock Hotel	6
Zanzibar	7

DRINKING AND NIGHTLIFE

The Albion	5
The Crown	3
Dragon	4
First In, Last Out (FILO)	1
Graze on Grand	7
The Palace	6
Porter's Wine Bar	2

EATING

Di Polas	9
Half Man, Half Burger	12
The Love Café	11
Maggie's	5
The Old Custom House	6
Petit Fi	7
Rock-a-Nore Kitchen	1
St Clement's	10
Thai Café and Boulevard Books	8
Two Bulls Steakhouse	3
Tush and Pat's	4
Webbe's	2

his newly conquered land. In the years that followed, the town became an important **Cinque Port** (see box, p.107), but French raids and destructive storms in the thirteenth century saw the start of its decline as a port, though fishing remained the main industry. After a lucrative dalliance with **smuggling** in the eighteenth century, the town got a second lease of life as the fashion for **sea bathing** took off: in 1800 Hastings' population stood at around 3000, but by 1900 it was over 65,000, thanks in large part to the arrival of the railway. By the 1960s and '70s, seaside resorts had began to go out of fashion, and Hastings was no exception; however, recent years have seen it bounce back, and it is becoming an increasingly popular destination for a weekend by the sea.

Old Town

By far the nicest part of Hastings is the pretty **Old Town**. **All Saints Street** is the most evocative thoroughfare, punctuated with the odd rickety, timber-framed dwelling from the fifteenth century. Running parallel to All Saints Street, and separated from it by The Bourne – the town's busy main through-road – is the narrow **High Street**, lined with junk shops, galleries, hip retro shops, pubs and restaurants. Pedestrianized **George Street** – also chock-a-block with shops and restaurants – strikes off to the west; midway along, the West Hill Cliff Railway (see box, p.176) ascends West Hill.

Down at the southern end of the High Street, the view of the beach is obscured by gaudy fairground rides and arcades – the easternmost end of a long line of traditional seaside amusements that stretches west as far as Pelham Crescent, underneath West Hill.

5

Shirley Leaf and Petal Company

58a High St • **Museum** Mon–Fri 10am–4pm, Sat 10.30am–4pm • £1 • **Shop** Mon–Fri 9.30am–5pm, Sat 10.30am–5pm • ⓦ martin-enterprises.eu/shirley.html

The tiny **Shirley Leaf and Petal Company** has been making artificial flowers and leaves for theatre, film and television sets around the world for over a hundred years; descend the stairs into the cluttered workshop-cum-museum to see the original Victorian tools and moulds that are still in use today. Cloth flowers are for sale in the shop above.

The Stade

At the eastern end of the seafront, tucked below East Hill, the area known as **The Stade** ("landing place") is home to Hastings' fishing fleet – the largest beach-launched fleet in Europe – and is characterized by its unique **net huts**, tall, black weatherboard sheds built in the mid-nineteenth century to store nets, and still in use today. The beach behind the net huts is a jumble of nets, winches and other fishing paraphernalia, with boats pulled up onto the shingle. Some of the day's catch doesn't travel far: seafront **Rock-a-Nore Road** is home to a clutch of fantastic fish **restaurants** (see p.180) as well as plenty of **fish shops** (see p.182) and stalls selling fresh-off-the-boat fish, pints of prawns and piping-hot, crispy fish rolls.

Just west of the net huts, on the far side of the Jerwood Gallery, the wide expanse of the **Stade Open Space** is used for various festivals, concerts and other events throughout the year, including **Stade Saturdays** (ⓦwww.hastings.gov.uk/arts_culture/stadesat), a free programme of summertime performances. On the west side of the space is a purpose-built cookery school, **Classroom on the Coast**, where you can learn how to cook the fish that's on sale just yards away; check with the tourist office (see p.179) for details of classes.

Fishermen's Museum

Rock-a-Nore Rd, TN34 3DW • Daily: April–Oct 10am–5pm; Nov–March 11am–4pm • Free • ☎ 01424 461446

Just past the net huts on Rock-a-Nore Road, a converted seaman's chapel is now the **Fishermen's Museum**. The centrepiece is *The Enterprise*, one of Hastings' last clinker-built luggers (1912) – exceptionally stout trawlers able to withstand being winched up and down the shingle beach. Surrounding it is a wealth of photos, models, fishing nets, stuffed seabirds and other nautical paraphernalia.

Shipwreck Museum

Rock-a-Nore Rd, TN34 3DW • **Museum** April–Oct daily 10am–5pm; Nov–March Sat & Sun 11am–4pm • Free • **Tours** Check website for details of times • £6; 1hr 45min • ☎ 01424 437452, ⓦ shipwreckmuseum.co.uk

The **Shipwreck Museum** details the dramas of unfortunate mariners, focusing on two wrecks: the Restoration seventy-gun warship *Anne*, which ran ashore in 1690 when it was damaged by the French in the Battle of Beachy Head; and the Dutch East Indiaman *Amsterdam*, beached in 1749. The latter was carrying textiles, wine and 27 chests of silver bullion when she ran aground, worth several million pounds in today's money; some of it was swiftly liberated by local smugglers before the rest was removed by the

---

HASTINGS' CLIFF RAILWAYS

You shouldn't leave Hastings without taking a ride on one of its stately Victorian **funiculars** (both April–Sept daily 10am–5.30pm; Oct–March Sat & Sun 11am–4pm; return ticket £2.60). The **West Hill Railway**, with its entrance tucked away in George Street, climbs up West Hill, depositing you a short walk from Hastings Castle, while the **East Hill Cliff Railway** – the steepest cliff railway in the country – trundles up the cliff face from Rock-a-Nore Road to Hastings Country Park (see p.184). The views from the upper stations of both funiculars are sensational.

5

THE COASTAL CULTURE TRAIL

The **Coastal Culture Trail** (ⓦcoastalculturetrail.com) was set up to draw attention to the 25-mile-long coastal path that links the Jerwood Gallery in Hastings (see below), the De La Warr Pavilion in Bexhill (see p.184) and the Towner Gallery in Eastbourne (see p.207). The Coastal Culture Trail website and accompanying map and guide (downloadable from the website, or available to buy from the art galleries themselves, tourist offices and cycle outlets) have lots of useful information about walking or **cycling** the route. The stretch of cycle path between Hastings and Bexhill is especially recommended as it's off-road all the way – perfect for families. There are bike hire shops in all three towns, and bikes are allowed on the Hastings–Bexhill–Eastbourne train, making it easy to cycle one way and return by train.

authorities. The wreck is now embedded in the sand three miles west of town, with low tide revealing the tops of its ribs; the museum runs occasional **tours** to the wreck site.

Blue Reef Aquarium

Rock-a-Nore Rd, TN34 3DW • Daily: March–Sept 10am–5pm; Oct–Feb 10am–4pm • £9, under-13s £6.95; joint ticket with Smugglers Adventure & Hastings Castle £18.50/£13.65 • ☎01424 718776, ⓦbluereefaquarium.co.uk

The **Blue Reef Aquarium** is a well-presented if pricey family attraction, with both tropical and native sea life on display, from giant crabs to rays and seahorses. A small walk-through underwater tunnel brings you face-to-fin with tropical fish, and hourly talks and feeding sessions take place throughout the day.

Jerwood Gallery

Rock-a-Nore Rd, TN34 3DW • Feb–Dec Tues–Sun & bank hols 11am–5pm; first Tues of month open until 8pm • £9, free first Tues of month 4–8pm • ☎01424 425809, ⓦjerwoodgallery.org

Adjacent to the fishing quarter, the sleek **Jerwood Gallery**, covered in shimmering dark-glazed tiles – a nod to the vernacular architecture of the fishing huts – is home to the Jerwood Foundation's Modern British art collection, which includes works by Barbara Hepworth, Christopher Wood and L.S. Lowry. The paintings in the collection are re-hung regularly, and shown alongside a temporary exhibition programme. Up on the first floor there's an airy café with floor-to-ceiling windows and a small terrace looking out over the fishing boats on the beach below.

West Hill

West Hill, which separates the Old Town from the less interesting modern town centre, can be ascended by the wonderful old West Hill Cliff Railway from George Street (see box, opposite), or on foot by climbing up through the steep twittens from the junction of Croft Road and Swan Terrace, by St Clement's Church. From the top you'll be rewarded with brilliant views back over the Old Town.

Hastings Castle

West Hill • Daily: Feb–April 10am–4.30pm; May–Oct 10am–5pm; last entry 1hr before closing • £4.75, under-13s £3.95; joint ticket with Smugglers Adventure & Blue Reef Aquarium £18.50/£13.65 • ☎01424 422964, ⓦsmugglersadventure.co.uk/hastings-castle-experience

William the Conqueror erected his first castle on West Hill in 1066, a prefabricated wooden structure brought over from Normandy in sections and then built on the site of an existing fort, probably of Saxon origins. It was soon replaced by a more permanent stone structure, but in the thirteenth century storms caused the cliffs to subside, tipping most of the castle into the sea. Today **Hastings Castle** is little more than a shell, but the ruins that do survive offer a great view over the town. An **audiovisual show** inside a mocked-up siege tent describes the events of the last successful invasion of the British mainland, though for the real deal you're better off visiting Battle Abbey (see p.186).

5

Smugglers Adventure

West Hill, TN34 3HY • Daily: Feb–April 10am–4.30pm; May–Oct 10am–5.30pm; last entry 30min before closing • £8, under-13s £6; joint ticket with Hastings Castle & Blue Reef Aquarium £18.50/£13.65 • ☎ 01424 422964, ⓦ smugglersadventure.co.uk

Re-creating the eighteenth-century heyday of smuggling (see box, p.216), **Smugglers Adventure** is set in the winding subterranean passageways and caverns of St Clement's Caves, which burrow their way into West Hill. The interactive displays, eerie sound effects and narration by "Hairy Jack the Smuggler" offer a fun introduction to the town's long history of duty-dodging. As well as being used by smugglers to store their contraband, the caves have also served variously as a military hospital, a Victorian tourist attraction and a World War II air-raid shelter.

Town centre

For the most part, Hastings' down-at-heel **town centre** lacks the charm of the Old Town or the buzz of St Leonards to the west, and is eminently missable. Down by the seafront, however, the area's got a bit of a spring in its step thanks to the triumphantly rejuvenated pier and the newly opened **Source Park** (Mon–Fri 2–10pm, Sat, Sun & school hols 10am–10pm; ☎ 01424 460943, ⓦ sourcebmx.com), a huge underground skatepark converted from the long-abandoned White Rock Baths. Just inland from here, the triangle of land known as the **America Ground** is an up-and-coming enclave with a fascinating history (see box below).

Hastings Pier

Summer Mon–Fri 10am–9pm, Sat & Sun 9am–10pm; winter hours vary – check website • Free • ⓦ hastingspier.org.uk

When **Hastings Pier** was burnt down in an arson attack in 2010, after decades of neglect, it looked like the end of the road for the much-loved landmark. Fortunately, the local community thought otherwise: having purchased the pier for £1, the Hastings Pier Charity – with the help of lottery funding, donations and a community share scheme – set about its restoration, and the pier eventually reopened in 2016. The "People's Pier" of today is very different to its Victorian predecessor: there's not much on it for starters, allowing the wide expanses of deck to be used for everything from markets to concerts to open-air film screenings – check the website to see what's on. The centrepiece is The Deck, a beautifully designed visitor centre clad in recycled planks from the old pier; topped by a glass-walled café terrace and viewing deck, it also houses a small exhibition about the pier and a function room used for workshops and events.

THE AMERICA GROUND

There is a small corner of Hastings that shall remain forever star-spangled, in name at least. The **America Ground**, the area of town bordered by Robertson, Claremont and Trinity streets, gained its name almost two hundred years ago. When huge storms in the thirteenth century altered the coastline, over a long period of time creating land where once there was sea, canny locals saw an opportunity to claim the newly created no-man's-land for themselves and escape tax and rent. A ramshackle but thriving settlement gradually developed, of warehouses, farm holdings, lodging houses, even a school, and by the 1820s around a thousand people lived there. When the Corporation of Hastings attempted to seize control of the area, the inhabitants rioted, and raised the American flag, declaring themselves the 24th state of America, and independent from Hastings. Unsurprisingly the powers-that-be weren't having any of it, and in 1828 the site was claimed for the Crown; it was cleared seven years later, and stood empty until Patrick Robinson started the construction of the Crown Estate in 1850, the buildings of which still stand today.

A huge mural on Robertson Passage, on the corner of Trinity and Robinson streets, commemorates the original America Ground, while the annual **America Ground Independence Day** in early July celebrates the area's attempted American citizenship with live music and market stalls.

ST LEONARDS ARCHITECTURE

St Leonards was planned and built by the late-Georgian developer **James Burton** (1761–1837) and son, **Decimus Burton** (1800–81), and was the first ever planned Regency seaside town. The resort was centred on a private park, now St Leonards Gardens, and the streets around it today contain some of the best examples of the Burtons' elegant architecture. A booklet (£2.50) available at the tourist office describes a **walking tour** around some of the highlights.

Hastings Museum and Art Gallery

John's Place, Bohemia Rd, TN34 1ET • April–Oct Tues–Sat 10am–5pm, Sun noon–5pm; Nov–March Tues–Sat 10am–4pm, Sun noon–4pm • Free • ☎ 01424 451052, ⓦ www.hmag.org.uk

As well as hosting temporary exhibitions, the eclectic **Hastings Museum and Art Gallery** contains permanent displays on the local area and further afield, with exhibits on everything from Hastings smugglers and Native Americans to iguanodons and **John Logie Baird**, whose experiments in the town led him to transmit the first television image in 1925. Don't miss the ornately carved **Durbar Hall**, created for the Colonial and Indian Exhibition held in South Kensington in 1886.

St Leonards-on-Sea

Shabby, arty, quirky and a bit rough around the edges, **St Leonards** presents a very different side to Hastings. A few years back the national press famously dubbed the area "Portobello Road-on-Sea", and while the accolade is a bit far-fetched, St Leonards is definitely a part of Hastings that's on the up. It's well worth spending a morning or afternoon here admiring the impressive Regency architecture (see box above) or checking out some of the cool art galleries, shops (see p.182), cafés and restaurants (see p.180) along **Norman Road** and **Kings Road**.

ARRIVAL AND DEPARTURE

By train Hastings station is a 10min walk from the seafront along Havelock Rd. There's another station, St Leonards Warrior Square, at the north end of Kings Rd. Southern services along the coast and Southeastern services to London call at both Hastings and St Leonards. Destinations Ashford (hourly; 40min); Battle (every 30min; 15min); Brighton (every 30min; 1hr 5min); Eastbourne (every 20min; 25min); Lewes (every 20min; 55min); London Victoria (hourly; 2hr–2hr 15min); Rye (hourly; 20min); Tunbridge Wells (every 30min; 35–50min).

HASTINGS AND AROUND

By bus Bus services operate from outside the train station. Destinations Battle (Mon–Sat hourly; 15min); Dover (Mon–Sat every 30min, Sun hourly; 2hr 50min); Eastbourne (Mon–Sat every 20–30min, Sun hourly; 1hr 15min); London Victoria (1 daily; 2hr 35min); Rye (Mon–Sat every 30min, Sun hourly; 40min).
By car The most convenient place to park for the Old Town is the 450-space Rock-a-Nore car park, accessed via Rock-a-Nore Rd.

GETTING AROUND AND INFORMATION

By bike A 7km traffic-free route stretches along the seafront from Hastings Old Town to Bexhill, making bikes a great way to get around. Bike hire is available at Bells Bicycles, 4 George St (Tues–Sun; ☎ 01424 716541, ⓦ bellsbicycles.co.uk; £20/day), and Seaside Cycles, on the beach side of the adventure golf complex (closed weekdays in winter; ☎ 07580 426200, ⓦ www.hastings.gov.uk/cycle; £14/day).
By rickshaw Seashore Rickshaw offer guided tours along the seafront (March–Oct Sat, Sun & school hols

10am–6pm; £19–30; ☎ 01424 421231, ⓦ seashorerickshaw.com); you can book online, by phone or at their kiosk on the pier.
Tourist office On the seafront at Aquila House, Breeds Place, TN34 3UY (April–Oct Mon, Tues, Thurs & Fri 9am–5pm, Wed 10am–5pm, Sat 9.30am–5pm, Sun 10.30am–4pm; Nov–March Mon, Tues, Thurs & Fri 9am–5pm, Wed 10am–5pm, Sat 9.30am–4.30pm, Sun 11am–3pm; ☎ 01424 451111, ⓦ visit1066country.com).

ACCOMMODATION

OLD TOWN
★**The Laindons** 23 High St, TN34 3EY ☎ 01424

437710, ⓦ thelaindons.com. There's lots to love about this friendly boutique B&B, set in a Georgian townhouse

5

with bags of character. The five rooms have a crisp Scandi vibe and are flooded with light; Bedroom 1 (£140) is the pick of them, with a great view over the rooftops to East Hill. Breakfast includes coffee from *The Laindons'* own coffee bar and roastery, *No. 23*, below the B&B. **£120**

Old Rectory Harold Rd, TN35 5ND ☎01424 422410, ⓦtheoldrectoryhastings.co.uk. Elegant, double-fronted Georgian pad next to All Saints Church, with eight luxurious, quirkily styled rooms; those at the front are grander, while the smaller rooms at the back look out over the tranquil walled garden. The wide-ranging breakfast menu is a real treat, featuring devilled kidneys, own-smoked bacon and kippers from the Hastings fleet. Minimum two-night stay at weekends during busy periods. **£110**

Swan House 1 Hill St, TN34 3HU ☎01424 430014, ⓦswanhousehastings.co.uk. This boutique B&B was one of Hastings' first, and still ticks all the boxes. It couldn't have a more perfect setting, in a lovely half-timbered fifteenth-century building on a quiet Old Town street. Rooms are luxurious and tasteful, with muted paintwork and wooden floors, and there's a pretty decked patio garden for sunny breakfasts. Minimum two-night stay at weekends. **£120**

TOWN CENTRE

The Printworks 14 Claremont, America Ground, TN34 1HA ☎01424 425532, ⓦ14claremont.com. This hip B&B in the old *Observer* building offers loft-style living in the America Ground, with vaulted ceilings, wooden floors and bare plaster-and-brick walls, jazzed up with eclectic vintage furnishings. The two bedrooms have plenty of

character, with original features from the building's days as a newspaper office. **£110**

Senlac Guesthouse 46–47 Cambridge Gardens, TN34 1EN ☎01424 435767, ⓦsenlacguesthouse.co.uk. Stylish yet affordable, this friendly B&B near the station is fantastic value for money – rooms are bright and contemporary, and bathrooms gleaming. The cheapest rooms share bathrooms. Breakfast is an additional £8.50. Next door the similarly priced *Number 46 Rooms & Apartments* is equally good. **£55**

White Rock Hotel White Rock, TN34 1JU ☎01424 422240, ⓦthewhiterockhotel.com. Clean, comfortable rooms and a fab location on the seafront overlooking Hastings Pier. The cheapest rooms are at the back of the hotel; sea views will cost you £20 more. **£69**

ST LEONARDS-ON-SEA

Hastings House 9 Warrior Square, TN37 6BA ☎01424 422709, ⓦhastingshouse.co.uk. Friendly boutique B&B in a Victorian house overlooking a garden square, close to the beach. Each of the modern, luxurious rooms sports a different look; those at the front boast lovely views over Warrior Square gardens to the sea. **£99**

Zanzibar 9 Everfield Place, TN37 6BY ☎01424 460109, ⓦzanzibarhotel.co.uk. Boutique hotel with rooms themed around the owner's travels, set in a beautifully styled townhouse overlooking St Leonards' seafront – the rooms with the real wow factor face the sea. On the ground floor, the *Pier Nine* restaurant serves up excellent (though not cheap) food. **£170**

EATING

Hastings has some fantastic places to eat, especially when it comes to fish: some of the best seafood places are along **Rock-a-Nore Road**, where the day's catch appears on menus and in fish shops a pebble's throw from where it was landed that morning. As well as the places mentioned below, check out the pop-up restaurant in *Alistair Hendy's Home Store* (see p.182), open on occasional weekends, and the *Kitchen* restaurant in the cool Kino-Teatr (see p.182).

OLD TOWN

Di Polas 14 Marine Parade, TN34 3AH ☎01424 203666. The best gelato in Hastings, made on site by the Italian owner. Daily in summer 11am–6pm; winter hours vary.

The Old Custom House 19 East Parade, TN34 3AL ☎01424 447724, ⓦtheoldcustomhousehastings .co.uk. Run by the same team as *St Clement's* (see opposite), this stylish seafood and oyster bar offers "small plates" (£3.50–6.50), "large plates" (£14.50 and up) and, of course, plenty of oysters alongside a great cocktail list that changes twice a week. Drop by during Happy Hour (Wed–Fri 4–7pm) for £1 oysters and £6 cocktails. Wed–Sat & bank hols 10am–11pm, Sun 10am–10.30pm; kitchen Wed–Sun & bank hols 10am–9pm.

Petit Fi 16 ½ George St, TN34 3EG ☎01424 272030, ⓦfacebook.com/petitfihastings. This lovely little café, with big windows looking out onto pedestrianized George

St and a few tables outside, is a great spot for lunch, with a menu that ranges from sandwiches to Sussex Smokies and salted cod fritters, plus cream teas and cakes. Daily 9–5.30pm.

Thai Café and Boulevard Books 32 George St, TN34 3EA ☎01424 436521, ⓦthaicafeandbookshop.com. The town's most unique eating experience, this tiny secondhand bookshop serves up fantastic home-cooked Thai food in the evenings, with half a dozen tables nestled among the bookshelves. Two courses £13; BYO (corkage £2/ person). Bookings essential. Wed–Sun 6–10pm, Mon/Tues by arrangement.

Two Bulls Steakhouse 61c High St, TN34 3EJ ☎01424 436443, ⓦtwobulls.co.uk. Tuck into a 45-day-aged steak, grilled over charcoal and served with home-cut chips and a choice of sauces and butters, at this relaxed, informal steakhouse. Set lunches are great value, starting at £9. Thurs & Fri noon–2pm & 6.30–11pm, Sat & Sun 12.30–3pm & 6.30–11pm.

THE STADE

Maggie's Rock-a-Nore Rd, TN34 3DW ☎01424 430205. For great fish and chips look no further than this unpretentious first-floor café, right on the beach overlooking the fishing boats. Tues–Sun noon–2.45pm.

Rock-a-Nore Kitchen 23a Rock-a-Nore Rd, TN34 3DW ☎01424 433764, ⓦfacebook.com/Rockanorekitchen. Excellent, no-nonsense restaurant serving fish and other dishes in an old tannery unit in the fishing quarter. Mains such as steak and oyster pudding or roasted plaice cost £11–15, and on sunny days in summer the kitchen hatch is opened up to serve scoops of freshly cooked calamari to passers-by. There are a dozen or so tables and just one sitting a night, so book ahead. Thurs, Fri & Sat 12.30–3.30pm & 7–9pm, Sun 12.30–3.30pm; July & Aug daily 12.30–3.30pm.

★**Tush and Pat's** Opposite East Hill Lift. Husband-and-wife team Tush and Pat's fisherman's rolls are a Hastings institution – whatever the boats have brought in that day is fried in front of you and served in a roll (£2.80). Perfection. Summer Sat & Sun 11am–4pm, weather permitting.

Webbe's 1 Rock-a-Nore Rd, TN34 3DW ☎01424 721650, ⓦwebbesrestaurants.co.uk. Top-notch seafood restaurant opposite the Jerwood Gallery. Mains such as steamed panache of fish cost around £15, or you can pick and choose from tasting dishes at £3.75 each. There's plenty of outside seating in summer. Seafood cookery

school mornings with lunch included take place throughout the year – check the website. Mon–Fri noon–2pm & 6–9pm, Sat & Sun noon–9pm.

ST LEONARDS-ON-SEA

Half Man, Half Burger 7 Marine Court, TN38 0DX ☎01424 552332, ⓦhalfmanhalfburger.com. Great burgers (£6.50–9), "trashy desserts" and craft beers at this funky, cheerful place on the seafront. Burgers range from the Gonzo (with Memphis Screamin' Whiskey BBQ sauce) to the Halloumi Be Thy Name. Tues–Sat noon–10pm, Sun noon–8pm.

The Love Café 28 Norman Rd, TN37 6AE ☎01424 717815, ⓦthelovecafe.me. Quirky, laidback café on St Leonards' main drag, instantly recognizable by its striking twenty-foot-high mural of Prince Charles's pixelated face, the work of street artist Ben Eine. Inside, pull up a chair under the papier-mâché trapeze artist swinging from the ceiling (with saucy nipple on show) and tuck into crêpes (savoury £8, sweet from £3.75), sandwiches, cakes or one of the daily specials. Veggie and vegan dishes always available. Mon & Thurs–Sat 10am–6pm, Sun 10am–5pm.

St Clement's 3 Mercatoria, TN38 0EB ☎01424 200355, ⓦstclementsrestaurant.co.uk. Fish is the thing at this small, intimate restaurant: ninety percent of it comes from the Hastings fleet's daily catch, and dishes on the constantly changing menu might include fillet of seabass with a lobster cream sauce, or Sardinian fish stew (mains £14–20). A range of good-value set lunch and evening meal menus are also available. Tues–Sat noon 3pm & 6.30–9pm, Sun noon–3pm.

DRINKING AND NIGHTLIFE

OLD TOWN

The Albion 33 George St TN34 3EA ☎01424 439156, ⓦalbionhastings.com. Managed by the team behind the Hastings Fat Tuesday (see box, p.182), this Old Town pub has a great live music programme, covering everything from jazz to country. Mon–Thurs & Sun 11am–11pm, Fri & Sat noon–midnight.

★**The Crown** 64–66 All Saints St, TN34 3BN ☎01424 465100, ⓦthecrownhastings.co.uk. Great pub with a lovely ambience and a trendy crowd. There's plenty of local produce on the menu (Hastings fish, Bodiam ice cream, Rye Bay coffee, and so on) and behind the bar (Sussex ales, gins and ciders), and the classy dark-painted interior features changing exhibitions of local artists' work. Mon–Sat 11am–11pm, Sun 11am–10.30pm.

Dragon 71 George St, TN34 3EE ☎01424 423688, ⓦdragon-bar.uk. Part bar, part restaurant, this hip, buzzy little hangout has good music, scuffed wooden floors and dark-painted walls hung with art. Interesting beers and a good wine list, plus top-notch food, with a menu that changes almost daily. Mon–Sat noon–11pm, Sun noon–10.30pm.

First In, Last Out (FILO) 15 High St, TN34 3EY ☎01424 425079, ⓦthefilo.co.uk. Tiny, ever-popular traditional pub with snug booths, no jukeboxes or fruit machines, a huge roaring fire in winter, and its own microbrewery. Excellent (and good-value) food is an added bonus, and there's regular live music, too – check the website for details. Mon–Sat 11am–midnight, Sun noon–midnight; kitchen Mon 6–8.30/9pm, Tues–Sat noon–2.30pm & 6–8.30/9pm.

Porter's Wine Bar 56 High St, TN34 3EN ☎01424 427000, ⓦporterswinebar.com. Wine bar with jazz and acoustic music on Wed and Thurs nights and Sun afternoons, including a regular spot by acclaimed jazz pianist and local resident Liane Carroll. Good, home-cooked, bistro-style food is on offer too. Mon, Tues & Sun noon–11pm, Wed–Sat noon–midnight.

TOWN CENTRE

The Palace 71 George St, TN34 3EE ☎01424 423688, ⓦpalacehastings.com. Friendly, lively beer hall opposite Source Park skatepark, with a huge range of craft beers

5

(eighteen on draft), good food and a busy programme of events ranging from live music and DJs to film nights. Mon–Thurs noon–11pm, Fri & Sat noon–2am, Sun noon–11pm.

ST LEONARDS-ON-SEA
Graze on Grand 16 Grand Parade, TN37 6DN ☎ 01424 439736, ⓦ grazeongrand.com. Wine bar, café-restaurant and gallery rolled into one, this light-flooded place on the seafront has a great choice of wine (over seventy bottles – also available to take away) and a menu of "small plates" and platters. The art on the wall is all for sale, and there's regular live music, too. Wed–Fri 10am–10pm, Sat 10am–11pm, Sun 11am–6pm.

ENTERTAINMENT

The Electric Palace 39 High St, TN34 3ER ☎ 01424 720393, ⓦ electricpalacecinema.com. Tiny independent cinema showing arthouse and world cinema, with a licensed bar. Screenings Thurs–Sun; £7.
★**Kino-Teatr St Leonards** 43–49 Norman Rd, St Leonards, TN34 3EA ☎ 01424 237373, restaurant ☎ 01424 457830, ⓦ kino-teatr.co.uk. Arthouse films and new releases, plus regular live music (including afternoon jazz) at this cool little cinema-theatre with a bar at the back of the auditorium and armchairs at the front. It's attached to the Baker-Mamonova Gallery, which shows changing

exhibitions alongside its permanent collection of twentieth-century Russian art, and there's a lovely café-restaurant, *Kitchen*, perfect if you want to eat before or after a performance.
Stables Theatre and Arts Centre The Bourne, TN34 3BD ☎ 01424 423221, ⓦ stablestheatre.co.uk. Small theatre hosting amateur and touring productions.
White Rock Theatre White Rock, TN34 1JX ☎ 01424 462280, ⓦ whiterocktheatre.org.uk. The town's main venue, putting on comedy, bands, theatre, ballet, shows and the annual panto.

SHOPPING

Hastings has a great array of independent shops. We've picked out some favourites below, but great new shops pop up all the time. In the Old Town the main shopping streets are **High Street** and **George Street**, lined with antiques shops, galleries, upmarket florists and quirky homeware stores; in St Leonards the main drag is **Norman Road**, with a smattering of galleries and hip vintage shops.

OLD TOWN
★**Alastair Hendy's Home Store** 36 High St, TN34 3ER ☎ 01424 447171, ⓦ homestore-hastings.co.uk. Artfully styled utilitarian essentials – including brooms, vintage linen, woollen bedsocks, enamelware, hand-forged scissors and reclaimed furniture – arranged over three floors of a

stunning Georgian building that's been pared back to its original framework, all bare plaster and stripped wood. Out the back a small seafood kitchen opens up on occasional weekends. Tues–Sun & bank hols 11am–5.30pm.
Butler's Emporium 70 George St, TN34 3EE ☎ 01424 430678, ⓦ butlersemporium.com. A cornucopia of

---

PARADES, PIRATES AND CRAZY GOLF: HASTINGS FESTIVALS

Hastings has some brilliant (and sometimes quite bonkers) festivals. Biggest and best of the lot is the **Jack-in-the-Green Festival** (ⓦ hastingsjack.co.uk) held over May Day weekend, which culminates in a riotous parade of leaf-bedecked dancers and drummers through the streets of the Old Town up to Hastings' hilltop castle, where "the Jack" – a garlanded leaf-covered figure whose origins date back to the eighteenth century – is ritually slain and the spirit of summer released.

At the end of July, thousands of buccaneers descend on the town for **Hastings Pirate Day** (ⓦ hastingspirateday.org.uk), a phenomenally popular day of swashbuckling fun, including shanties, sword-fighting and an attempt on the world record for the Largest Gathering of Pirates – a title occasionally snatched by the scurvy pirates in Penzance.

The UK's largest Mardi Gras festival, **Fat Tuesday** (ⓦ hastingsfattuesday.co.uk), is held over four days in February, and sees hundreds of gigs, many free, taking place around town. On Fat Tuesday itself, bands move from venue to venue in the Old Town, playing a set in each, so you can put your feet up and let the music come to you.

Other events include a **comedy festival** in June; three separate **foodie festivals** celebrating Hastings' unique fishing industry; **Hastings Week** in October; and, last but not least, the nail-biting **World Crazy Golf Championship** in June. For full details of all festivals see p.32.

FROM TOP BATTLE ABBEY (P.186); CAMBER SANDS (P.173) >

5

gorgeous odds and ends – from cashmere scarfs and candles to Moroccan slippers and bolts of Merchant & Mills linen – displayed in a fabulous old hardware store complete with original shop fittings. Mon–Fri 10am–5pm, Sat & Sun 11am–5pm.

Judges Bakery 51 High St, TN34 3EN ☎01424 722588, ⓦfacebook.com/judgesbakery. Pick up organic artisan breads, tarts, quiches, cookies and meringues the size of melons at this bakery that's been making its own bread since 1826. Mon–Fri 7.45am–5.30pm, Sat 7.45am–6pm, Sun & bank hols 8.45am–5pm.

Penbuckles 50 High St, TN34 3EN ☎01424 465050, ⓦpenbuckles.co.uk. Great deli with goodies including artisan cheeses, charcuterie, Portuguese custard tarts, wines and Monmouth coffee. Tasting events held throughout the year. Mon–Sat 10am–6pm, Sun 11am–5pm.

THE STADE

Rockanore Fisheries 3 & 4 Rock-a-Nore Rd, TN34 3DW ☎01424 445425, ⓦrockanore.co.uk. One of several great fish shops along Rock-a-Nore Rd, this long-established family business is particularly well known for its smoked-on-the-premises salmon, but is also a great place to pick up wet fish. Tues–Sat 9am–5pm, Sun 10am–2pm.

Warp & Weft 68a George St, TN34 4EE ☎01424 437180, ⓦwarpandweftstyling.com. Beautiful handmade clothes and shoes in muted tones and natural fabrics, mixed with one-off vintage pieces, plus jewellery and other accessories from local craftspeople. A made-to-measure service is also available. Mon–Fri 11am–5pm, Sat & Sun 10.30am–5.30pm; sometimes closed Tues & Wed so call in advance.

TOWN CENTRE

Dyke & Dean The Printworks, 14 Claremont, TN34 1HA ☎01424 429202, ⓦdykeanddean.com. Hip interiors and homewares store in the America Ground, selling everything from lighting and utilitarian kitchenware to Welsh throws and soap from Oregon. Thurs & Fri 11am–5pm, Sat 11am–5.30pm.

ST LEONARDS-ON-SEA

SHOP 32–34 Norman Rd, TN38 0EJ ☎07763 579908. Fab little shop crammed with kitchenware, cards, furniture, home furnishings, fashion and accessories, with a small café at the back. Wed–Sat 10am–5pm, Sun 11am–4pm.

Hastings Country Park

Visitor centre Coastguard Lane, off Fairlight Rd, TN35 4AD • Thurs–Sun 10am–3pm, though hours can vary as the centre is volunteer-run • ☎01424 812140, ⓦhastingscountrypark.org.uk • To reach the East Hill end of the park, take the funicular (see box, p.176) or climb up the steep steps from Tackleway, parallel to All Saints St; for access to the eastern end of the park, take bus #101 from the Old Town to the visitor centre; there are also car parks at various locations throughout the park

Hastings Country Park extends three miles east from East Hill to Fairlight, a gorgeous and uniquely diverse stretch of coastline with more than 650 acres of gorse-speckled heathland, dramatic sandstone cliffs, rolling grassland and ancient woodland ravines cut by gushing streams and waterfalls. Most of the park is designated a Special Area of Conservation and a Site of Special Scientific Interest: its ancient gill woodlands – **Fairlight Glen**, **Ecclesbourne Glen** and **Warren Glen** – are home to rare liverworts and mosses, and are especially beautiful in the spring, when they're carpeted with bluebells and wood anemone. The **visitor centre** and main car park is at the eastern end of the park in the Firehills heathland.

The De La Warr Pavilion

Marina, Bexhill-on-Sea, TN40 1DP • Daily: April–Oct 10am–6pm; Nov–March 10am–5pm • Free • ☎01424 229111, ⓦdlwp.com • Bus #98 from Hastings (Mon–Sat every 30min, Sun hourly; 40min); train from Hastings (every 20min; 10min); or seafront cycle path from Hastings to Bexhill (see box, p.177)

Five miles west of Hastings is the seaside town of Bexhill-on-Sea, home to the iconic **De La Warr Pavilion**, a sleek Modernist masterpiece overlooking the sea. It was built in 1935 by architects Erich Mendelsohn and Serge Chermayeff – the first Modernist public building in the country, and the first to use a welded steel frame – and was the brainchild of the progressive ninth Earl de la Warr, local landowner and socialist, who had a vision of a free-to-all seaside pavilion for the education, entertainment and health of the masses. In its brief heyday the Pavilion flourished, but it slid gradually into disrepair in the years following World War II. After decades of hosting everything from bingo to wrestling while the building crumbled and corroded, today the Pavilion has been lovingly restored to its original glory – all crisp white lines and gleaming glass – and hosts changing **exhibitions** of contemporary art, and an eclectic mix of **live performances**, from big-name bands to comedy and film nights. Up on the first floor a **café** and restaurant offer glorious views from the floor-to-ceiling windows and balcony.

Pevensey Castle

Castle Rd, Pevensey, 12 miles west of Hastings, BN24 5LE • End March to Sept daily 10am–6pm; Oct daily 10am–5pm; Nov–March Sat & Sun 10am–4pm • £5.80 (includes audio tour); EH • ☎ 01323 762604, ⓦ www.english-heritage.org.uk/visit/places/pevensey-castle

If truth be told, there isn't an awful lot left of **Pevensey Castle**, and you'll need to use your imagination – or take advantage of the excellent audio tour – to really bring the rich history of the place to life. When William the Conqueror landed here in 1066, he set up camp within the crumbling walls of an old Roman fort – one of the largest of the Saxon shore forts built on the south coast in the third century. After his victory at Battle (see box, p.187), he gave the Rape of Pevensey to his half-brother, **Robert Count of Mortain**, who built a wooden castle within the southeast corner of the Roman fort, and repaired its walls for use as an outer bailey; two-thirds of the **Roman walls** still remain today. Mortain's wooden castle was replaced by a sturdier stone castle in the twelfth and thirteenth centuries.

The castle survived several dramatic sieges through the centuries, but was eventually overcome – not by invading troops but by the changing coastline, which left it without access to the sea and so without a strategic purpose. By 1500 the castle was no longer in use, though it was pressed back into action again at various times when foreign invasion threatened – the Spanish Armada in 1580, Napoleon in 1805 and Hitler in 1940. The **gun emplacements** added in World War II can still be seen today.

Entry into the Roman walls is free; you only pay to cross the moat and enter the Norman castle walls. Inside, much of what you see lies in ruins, but you can clamber down into the dungeons, and up a wooden staircase to the North Tower.

Herstmonceux Castle and Observatory Science Centre

Wartling Rd, Herstmonceux, BN27 1RN • **Castle gardens & grounds** Daily: April–Sept 10am–6pm; Oct 10am–5pm; last entry 1hr before closing • £6, joint ticket with Observatory £12.70 (£8.30 for children aged 4–16) • **Castle tours** Most days between noon & 2pm but call ahead to check • £2.50 • ☎ 01323 833816, ⓦ herstmonceux-castle.com • **Observatory** Feb, March, Oct & Nov daily 10am–5pm; April–Sept daily 10am–6pm; Jan & Dec open occasional weekends only; last admission 2hr before closing • £8, joint ticket with gardens £12.70; children aged 4–16 £6.15/£8.30 • ☎ 01323 832731, ⓦ the-observatory.org

Moated **Herstmonceux Castle**, thirteen miles from Hastings, was built in the fifteenth century, one of the first buildings in the south to be constructed from brick – at the time a new and fashionable building material. In 1946 the castle was sold to the Admiralty, who moved the **Royal Greenwich Observatory** to the castle grounds, away from London's lights and pollution. When the Observatory's prized Isaac Newton telescope was moved to the clearer skies of La Palma in the Canaries in 1979 it signalled the beginning of the end for the Observatory, and it was closed down in 1990.

The castle was subsequently bought by the **Queen's University of Canada** and is now closed to the public except on **guided tours**. You can still stroll round the lovely Elizabethan **walled garden** and surrounding **parklands**, but undoubtedly the best time to visit is during the **Medieval Festival** (see p.33) – the largest in the country – when the castle grounds are taken over by knights-at-arms, jesters and minstrels for three brilliant days of battle re-enactments, jousting, archery displays, workshops, theatre, music and story-telling.

Next door to the castle, the old observatory buildings now house the **Observatory Science Centre**, which is really two attractions in one: a fantastically well-run science centre, with over a hundred interactive exhibits, all enticingly hands-on for kids; and an observatory that's home to historic telescopes, now fully restored to working

5

order – telescope tours (free; 45min) run daily in school holidays and at weekends. **Star-gazing open evenings** offer you the chance to use the telescopes on selected dates in winter, spring and autumn.

Carr Taylor Vineyard

Wheel Lane, outside Westfield village, 4 miles north of Hastings, TN35 4SG · Daily 10am–5pm · Self-guided tours £1.50 · ☎ 01424 752501, ⓦ carr-taylor.co.uk

Family-run **Carr Taylor Vineyard** was not only one of the very first commercial vineyards in the country, but it was also the first to produce traditional-method sparkling wine (Champagne in all but name), the real success story of English wine. This remains one of its mainstays today, together with still white wine and fruit wines. You can visit the beautiful 37-acre vineyard on a **self-guided tour**, which takes you through the vineyards, winery and bottling room and finishes at the shop.

Battle

The town of **BATTLE**, six miles inland of Hastings, occupies the site of the most famous land battle in British history. Here, on October 14, 1066, the invading Normans swarmed up the hillside from Senlac Moor and overcame the Anglo-Saxon army of King Harold, in what would be the last ever successful invasion of Britain (see box opposite). Battle Abbey, built by the victorious William the Conqueror in penance for the blood spilled, still dominates the town today, its impressive gatehouse looming over the southern end of the narrow, appealingly venerable **High Street**, lined with a mix of medieval timber-framed, tile-hung and Victorian buildings.

Battle Abbey

At the south end of High St, TN33 0AD · Feb half term daily 10am–4pm; mid-Feb to March Wed–Sun 10am–4pm; April–Sept daily 10am–6pm; Oct daily 10am–5pm; Nov to mid-Feb Sat & Sun 10am–4pm; manor house tours (included in entry fee) run daily in Aug at 11am & 2pm; 30min · £10.10; EH · ☎ 01424 775705, ⓦ www.english-heritage.org.uk/visit/places/1066-battle-of-hastings-abbey-and-battlefield

The magnificent structure of **Battle Abbey**, founded by William in the aftermath of his victory, was ostensibly built to atone for the thousands of lives lost in the battle, but it was also a powerful symbol of Norman victory – not for nothing did William decree that the high altar in the abbey church should be built on the exact spot where Harold met his death. The completed abbey was occupied by a fraternity of Benedictines, and over the next four hundred years grew to become one of the richest monasteries in the country, being rebuilt and extended along the way. When the Dissolution came, the land was given to King Henry VIII's friend, Sir Anthony Browne, who promptly knocked down the church and converted the abbot's lodging into a fine manor house.

The **manor house** still stands today, though it's out of bounds to visitors for most of the year, having been occupied by Battle Abbey School since 1912; tours run in the August school holidays. All that remains of the Norman **abbey church** is its outline – with the site of the high altar marked by a memorial stone – but some buildings survive from the thirteenth century, including the monks' rib-vaulted **dormitory range**. The impressive 1330s **gatehouse** holds an exhibition on the history of the site, and allows you to clamber up to a rooftop viewing platform, but the best place to start your visit is in the modern **visitor centre**, where a short film takes you through the background to the events of the day itself.

Audio guides (40min) take you round the site of the **battlefield**, vividly re-creating the battle and its aftermath, which local chroniclers recorded as a hellish scene – "covered in corpses, and all around the only colour to meet the gaze was blood-red". The best time to visit the abbey is during the annual **re-enactment** of the battle, held

5

THE BATTLE OF HASTINGS

The most famous date in English history – October 14, 1066 – and the most famous battle ever fought on English soil, the **Battle of Hastings** saw the defeat of King Harold and the end of Anglo-Saxon England.

LEAD-UP TO THE BATTLE

The roots of the battle lay in the death of Edward the Confessor in January 1066. With no children of his own, the succession was far from clear: Edward's cousin, **William, Duke of Normandy**, had reportedly been promised the Crown by Edward during a previous visit to England, fifteen years before, but it was **Harold**, Edward the Confessor's brother-in-law, whom Edward named as his successor on his deathbed. William was enraged, his sense of injustice not helped by the fact that Harold had previously sworn an oath, on holy relics no less, that he would support William's claim to the Crown.

William quickly gathered together an army and sailed for England, landing at Pevensey on September 28. Harold heard the news in Yorkshire, where he'd just been celebrating victory over another claimant to the throne – **Harald Hardrada**, King of Norway – at the Battle of Stamford Bridge on September 22. He quickly raced his troops south to meet William, but instead of giving his footsore and battle-worn army time to recuperate, he rushed to engage William in battle.

THE BATTLE

The forces met at **Senlac Hill**. Harold's army of 5000–7000 troops occupied the superior position on the brow of the hill, his soldiers forming a protective shield wall. William's Norman army – a similar size – congregated below. Statistically, the odds were in Harold's favour, but the Saxon troops made an error: when Norman soldiers made an unsuccessful charge and retreated down the hill, some of Harold's troops, instead of staying put in their unassailable hilltop position, pursued them. Separated from the rest of their army, they were surrounded by Norman soldiers and killed. William pressed his advantage, his men feigning several more retreats, each time drawing the Saxon army down the hill, only for them to be surrounded and hacked to death. It wasn't enough to defeat the English entirely, but William had two other advantages: his mounted knights, who had greater mobility in the battlefield than the Saxon foot soldiers, and his archers, who were able to breach the English line. The advantage steadily moved in William's favour, and by nightfall the battle was his, and Harold lay dead on the battlefield. The total casualties lay at around 7000, which, at a time when the population of a large town was around 2500, would have been a shockingly large number.

THE BAYEUX TAPESTRY AND THE DEATH OF HAROLD

That we know so much about the battle and its lead-up is in part due to the existence of the **Bayeux Tapestry** – a 70m-long piece of embroidery created within twenty years of the battle. The most famous scene in the tapestry – the **death of Harold** – is, however, famously ambiguous. Harold's death by means of an arrow through the eye was first reported in 1080 (although it was not noted in any of the accounts written immediately after the battle), and by the following century had become an accepted fact. The scene in the tapestry seems to bear out the arrow story, but over the years scholars have variously argued that the figure with an arrow through his eye and "Harold" written above his head was not actually the king; that Harold was felled by an arrow through the eye and then hacked to death; and that the "arrow" through Harold's eye is just a spear he is holding, and that the fletching on it was added later in over-zealous restoration. The truth of the matter will probably never be known.

on the weekend nearest to October 14, and performed by a cast of over a thousand chain-mailed soldiers, entering into their Norman and Saxon roles with gusto.

Battle Museum of Local History

The Almonry, High St, TN33 0EA • April–Oct Mon–Sat 10am–4.30pm • Free • ☎01424 775955

At the top end of the High Street in the medieval Almonry, the small, volunteer-run **Battle Museum of Local History** contains what is claimed to be the only battle-axe

5

discovered at Battle, as well as a rare hand-coloured print of the Bayeux Tapestry, made in 1819 after a watercolour painting by Charles Stothard. The museum is also home to the oldest **Guy Fawkes** in the country, with a pearwood head dating back to the eighteenth century. Every year, on the Saturday nearest to November 5, the effigy is paraded along High Street at the head of a torch-lit procession culminating at a huge bonfire on the Abbey Green, in front of the gatehouse.

ARRIVAL AND DEPARTURE   BATTLE

By train The train station is a well-signposted 10min walk from the High St.
Destinations Hastings (every 30min; 15min); London Charing Cross (every 30min; 1hr 30min); Tunbridge Wells (every 30min; 40min).

By bus Buses #304 and #305 run from Hastings to Battle High St (Mon–Sat hourly; 15min) and then on to Tunbridge Wells.
By car The car park next to Battle Abbey is the best value for stays of more than 2hr (£4.50/day; discount for EH members).

EATING

Battle Deli 57 High St, TN33 0EN ☎01424 777810. Lovely little deli crammed with delicious stuff for a picnic or an eat-in lunch. Mon–Sat 8.30am–5pm, Sun & bank hols 10am–4pm.
★**Bluebells Café Tearoom** 87 High St, TN33 0AQ ⓦbluebellstearoom.co.uk. Just across the road from Battle Abbey, this fab tearoom is very popular for its delicious home-made cakes, breakfasts, sandwiches and light lunches. The

(very generous) afternoon teas are especially recommended. Tues–Sat 9am–5pm, Sun 9.30am–4.30pm.
Cut and Grill 17 High St, TN33 0AE ☎01424 774422, ⓦcutandgrill.co.uk. All the produce at this exemplary burger and steak place is sourced from within a 20-mile radius of the restaurant – meat, fish, cheeses, ice cream and more. Burgers start at £8, grills at £9 and steaks at £13. There's a great kids' menu, too. Tues–Sat noon–9pm.

SHOPPING

British design British made 64 High St, TN33 0AG ☎01424 777711, ⓦbritishdesignbritishmade.com. Stylish mini department store stocking everything from Harris tweed bags and Stoke-on-Trent pottery to Kentish soaps and local chutney, all made in the British Isles and, where possible, with sustainable or recycled materials.

Mon–Sat 10am–5pm, plus limited opening on Sun in Aug & Dec.
Saffron Gallery 59–60 High St ☎01424 772130, ⓦsaffrongallery.co.uk. Excellent gallery with exhibitions featuring internationally renowned artists. Mon–Sat 10am–5pm.

The eastern High Weald

A feeling of remoteness characterizes the **EASTERN HIGH WEALD**, which spills over the border into neighbouring Kent (see chapter 4). There are no really big towns – the small market town of Heathfield is the only place of any size – and most of the landscape is given over to rolling farmland and wooded hills, peppered with quiet, sleepy villages. The two big sights in the area are **Great Dixter** – one of the country's most famous gardens – and picture-perfect **Bodiam Castle**. Less known is the fascinating **Farleys House and Gallery**, the former home of the Surrealist artist Roland Penrose and photographer Lee Miller, which became a vibrant meeting place for leading figures in twentieth-century art. Other attractions include Rudyard Kipling's sleepy countryside retreat at **Bateman's**, gorgeous **Pashley Manor Gardens**, the moated Augustinian **Michelham Priory** and the child-friendly **Bentley Wildfowl and Motor Museum**.

Great Dixter

Half a mile north of Northiam, signposted from the village, TN31 6PH • End March–Oct Tues–Sun & bank hols: gardens 11am–5pm; house 2–5pm • House & gardens £10.50, gardens only £8.50 • ☎01797 252878, ⓦgreatdixter.co.uk • Stagecoach bus #2 passes through Northiam on its way from Hastings to Tenterden (Mon–Sat hourly; 45min from Hastings)

One of the best-loved gardens in the country, **Great Dixter** has come to be known above all else for bringing innovative and experimental planting to the English country

5

"MAD JACK" FULLER AND THE BRIGHTLING FOLLIES

John Fuller of Brightling (1757–1834), or **"Mad Jack" Fuller** as he's affectionately known, was a true eccentric, one of the great characters of Sussex. A wealthy landowner, Fuller was a corpulent 22 stone, wore his hair in a pigtail (despite the style falling out of fashion long before), had a bellowing voice, and drove around the countryside in a heavily armed barouche. His turbulent parliamentary career ended with him hurling abuse at his fellow MPs and being expelled from the House. And yet Fuller was also a man of remarkable philanthropy, and his name crops up again and again all over Sussex: it was he who provided Eastbourne with its first lifeboat (see p.207), bought Bodiam Castle (see p.189) in 1828 to save it from demolition, and built the Belle Tout lighthouse (see box, p.213), saving countless lives. He was also a champion of science, founding a reference library and two professorships at the Royal Institute.

His fame endures today in the main because of the **follies** he erected around his country estate at **Brightling**, a small village five miles northeast of Battle. In true Fuller fashion each one has an outlandish tale attached to it: the **Rotunda Temple** in Brightling Park was supposedly used for gambling sessions and carousing with ladies of the night; the 35ft-high circular **Tower**, just off the Brightling–Darwell road, was perhaps erected so that Fuller could keep an eye on the restoration work going on at nearby Bodiam Castle; and the **Sugar Loaf** (visible from the Battle–Heathfield road), was built after Fuller made a wager he could see the spire of nearby Dallington church from his estate – when it turned out he couldn't he had the tower, a replica of Dallington's church spire, built overnight so that he could win his bet. All three follies are accessible by footpath, but the easiest of Fuller's follies to visit is the incongruous blackened stone **pyramid** in the churchyard of squat-towered **Brightling church**: this is Fuller's burial place, though the story that he was interred bolt upright, dressed for dinner and with a bottle of claret on the table in front of him, has sadly been proved apocryphal.

---

garden. Exuberant and informal, it spreads around a medieval half-timbered house, which was home to the gardener and writer **Christopher Lloyd** until his death in 2005. Lloyd's parents bought the house in 1912 and, with the help of a dazzling young architect, **Edwin Lutyens**, stripped it back to its medieval splendour, ripping out partitions and restoring the magnificent Great Hall – the largest surviving timber-framed hall in the country – to its original double-height. A new wing (to the left of the lopsided porch) was built, and another medieval house was moved piece-by-painstaking-piece from nearby Benenden and tacked on to the back of the building.

Lutyens also helped design the **garden**, planting the hedges and topiary, incorporating old farm buildings where possible and laying the paving (recycled London pavement). As you wander round it today, through a series of intimate garden "rooms", the first thing you're struck by is its informality; all around are sweeps of wildflower-speckled meadow, and flowers spilling out of crammed, luxuriant borders. Christopher Lloyd loved change and colour, and with his head gardener **Fergus Garrett** (who continues to manage the garden today) he experimented with unusual juxtapositions and imaginative plantings, most famously ripping out his parents' rose garden to plant dahlias, bananas and other exotics. Look out, too, for occasional reminders that this was a personal garden; Lloyd's beloved dachshunds, which had a tendency to nip unwelcome visitors, are remembered in a pebble mosaic by the entrance.

Bodiam Castle

Bodiam, 9 miles north of Hastings, TN32 5UA • Daily 10.30am–5pm (or dusk if sooner) • £8.20; NT • ☎ 01580 830196, ⓦ nationaltrust .org.uk/bodiam-castle • Parking £3 non-members; bus #349 from Hastings (Mon–Fri every 2hr; 40min); steam train from Tenterden (see p.151); or boat from Newenden (April–Oct 3 daily Wed, Sat & Sun & bank hols; 3 boats daily in school hols; 45min one way; £11 return; ☎ 01797 253838, ⓦ bodiamboatingstation.co.uk)

Ask a child to draw a castle and the outline of the fairytale **Bodiam Castle** would be the result: a classically stout, square block with rounded corner turrets, battlements and a wide moat. When it was built in 1385 to guard what were the lower reaches of the

5

River Rother against the French, Bodiam was state-of-the-art military architecture, but during the Civil War, a company of Roundheads breached the fortress and removed its roof to reduce its effectiveness as a possible stronghold for the king. Over the next 250 years Bodiam fell into neglect until restoration in 1826 by "Mad Jack" Fuller (see box, p.189) and later Lord Curzon.

Inside the castle walls it's a roofless ruin, but a wonderfully atmospheric one nonetheless, with plenty of nooks and crannies to explore and steep spiral staircases leading up to the crenellated battlements. It also boasts its original portcullis – claimed to be the oldest in the country – and murder holes in the ceiling of the gatehouse, through which defenders would fire arrows or drop rocks, boiling oil, tar or scalding water on to their enemies.

The nicest way to arrive at Bodiam is on a **steam train** from Tenterden, operated by the Kent & East Sussex Railway (see p.151), or on a **boat trip** from Newenden, four miles down the River Rother.

Bateman's

Bateman's Lane, Burwash, off the A265, TN19 7DS • Garden daily 10am–5pm (or dusk if sooner); house April–Oct daily 11am–5pm, Nov–March daily 11.30am–3.30pm • £10; NT • ☎ 01435 882302, ⓦ nationaltrust.org.uk/batemans

Bateman's, the idyllic home of the writer and journalist **Rudyard Kipling** from 1902 until his death in 1936, lies half a mile south of **Burwich**, a pretty Sussex village of

---

RUDYARD KIPLING

God gave all men all earth to love,
But, since our hearts are small
Ordained for each one spot should prove
Beloved over all…
Each to his choice, and I rejoice
The lot has fallen to me
In a fair ground – In a fair ground
Yea, Sussex by the Sea!

Sussex, by Rudyard Kipling (1902)

The reputation of **Rudyard Kipling** (1865–1936), author of *Kim*, *The Jungle Book* and the *Just So Stories*, has taken a bit of a battering over the years. In 1907, when he won the Nobel Prize for Literature, he was at the peak of his popularity, but just 35 years later George Orwell was famously writing of him: "Kipling is a jingo imperialist, he is morally insensitive and aesthetically disgusting."

Kipling was very much an author of his time. He was born in India in 1865, and after a childhood spent in England he returned aged 16 to take up a position on a small local newspaper in Lahore, where he started publishing his poems and short stories, and soaking up the sights, smells and experiences that would inform so much of his later writing. Kipling left India in 1889, travelling, writing, marrying and finally settling in Vermont, and by the time he returned to England in 1896, he had published *The Jungle Book* and its follow-up, and was famous.

In the successful years that followed he captured the mood of the nation with his poem *The White Man's Burden* (1899), a celebration of noble-spirited British empire-building that was regarded by just a small minority as imperialist propaganda. *Kim* (1901) and the *Just So Stories* (1902) followed, and Kipling's fame grew so great that he decamped to **Bateman's**, in the heart of the Sussex countryside, to escape his fans. Behind the scenes, however, all was not rosy. Kipling's beloved daughter, Josephine, died of pneumonia in 1898, and his son, John, was killed in 1915 at the Battle of Loos, having been encouraged to enlist by Kipling himself. Bateman's was indeed a haven, but it was also the place Kipling retreated to lick his wounds, and – if Orwell is to be believed – to "sulk" at the collapse of British colonialism, and perhaps his tarnished reputation too.

Despite it all, though, even Orwell admitted that Kipling could write a good line, a sentiment seemingly echoed by modern readers, who in recent years have crowned Kipling's *If* the nation's favourite poem.

redbrick and weatherboard cottages with a Norman church tower. For Kipling, the seventeenth-century manor house was a haven from the outside world. By the turn of the century he was one of the most popular writers in the country, and he had grown heartily sick of the fame that came with his success. Bateman's gave him the seclusion that his previous home in Rottingdean (see p.245) had not.

In his book-lined **study** – which is today laid out much as he left it, with letters, early editions of his work and mementoes from his travels on display – he wrote *Pook's Hill* and *Rewards and Fairies*, the latter containing his most famous poem, *If*. Outside in the garage you can see Kipling's beloved 1928 Rolls Royce Phantom I, which despite his childlike enthusiasm for motor cars he never drove himself, preferring to be chauffeured around the countryside. At the far end of the garden, across the stream, is a still-working **watermill** which was converted by Kipling to generate electricity. Special **events** run throughout the year, including occasional talks on the author and *Jungle Book* days and *Just So* story days for kids.

Pashley Manor Gardens

Off the B2099 south of Ticehurst, TN5 7IIE · April–Sept Tues–Sat & bank hols 11am–5pm; Oct Mon–Fri 11am–4pm (shop & café closed) · £10 · ☎ 01580 200888, ✆ pashleymanorgardens.co.uk

Romantic and quintessentially English, **Pashley Manor Gardens** are a gorgeous confection of lakes, follies and fountains, ancient oak trees, walled gardens and luxuriant borders, all set against the backdrop of Pashley Manor itself (closed to the public); the manor house dates from Tudor times, though the handsome Georgian facade added to the back of the house gives it an entirely different character. **Sculpture** (changing every year) is displayed dotted around the lawns and lakes, and special **events** include the late spring Tulip Festival, when over thirty thousand bulbs erupt into bloom.

Farleys House and Gallery

Muddles Green, Chiddingly, BN8 6HW · **Garden** April–Oct Sun 10am–3.30pm · £2 · **House tours** April–Oct Sun 10.30am, 11.30am, 12.30pm, 1.30pm, 2.30pm & 3.30pm; 50min · £12 (includes garden access) · **Private tours** Several times a year, with Antony Penrose; 3hr · £40 · ☎ 01825 872691, ✆ farleyfarmhouse.co.uk

Though nowhere near as well known as nearby Charleston Farmhouse (see p.220), **Farleys House and Gallery** is just as fascinating. After World War II this redbrick house became the home of painter and biographer **Roland Penrose**, American photographer **Lee Miller** and their son, Antony (who still lives at the farmhouse today), and over the years that followed it became a meeting place for some of the leading lights of the modern art world – Picasso, Man Ray and Max Ernst among them. Penrose was a key figure in the English Surrealist movement, curating the first International Surrealist Exhibition in 1936, and writing biographies of Picasso, Miró, Man Ray and Tàpies. Miller, too, was known for her Surrealist images, though she also found fame as a portraitist and a World War II photographer; she was one of the few female war reporters to witness battle first-hand.

Informative **tours** of the house take you through the ground-floor rooms, in the main left as they were in Penrose and Miller's day, decorated with Penrose's Surrealist paintings, sketches by artist friends and an eclectic array of *objet trouvé* and tribal art. The homely **kitchen** was the heart of the house: Miller was a gourmet cook, and dinner parties would feature copious amounts of whisky alongside eclectic creations ranging from blue spaghetti to pink cauliflower breasts. A couple of Picasso lithographs (one produced at the farmhouse during a visit) hang on the far wall, facing a well-worn tile by the artist above the Aga – the Surrealists believed art was there to be lived with and for all to enjoy. The **dining room** showcases Penrose's paintings and his journey to Surrealism, while the photographs and objects in Lee Miller's **office** tell the story of this

5

THE CUCKOO TRAIL

One of the most popular traffic-free cycle rides in Sussex is the **Cuckoo Trail**, which runs for fourteen miles – almost entirely off-road – past broadleaf woods and farmland along the path of a disused railway from Heathfield down to Hampden Park in Eastbourne. The Cuckoo Trail **leaflet** can be downloaded from ⓦeastsussex.gov.uk. There's **parking** at Heathfield, Horam, Hellingly, Hailsham, Polegate and Hampden Park, and **train** stations at Polegate and Hampden Park. The trail slopes very gently downhill as it runs south, so there's much to be said for starting at the southern end to make your return trip slightly easier.

---

most extraordinary women, whose life included spells as a supermodel in New York, as student, lover and muse to Man Ray in Paris, and as a war photographer who witnessed the liberation of Paris and of Dachau concentration camp.

Check the website for dates of the engrossing **extended tours** led by Antony Penrose, who grew up at the farmhouse and was a favourite with the visiting Picasso.

Michelham Priory

Upper Dicker, BN27 3QS, signposted from the A27 and A22 • Daily: mid-Feb to end Feb & Nov to mid-Dec 11am–4pm; March–Oct 10.30am–5pm • £8.90 • ☎ 01323 844224, ⓦ sussexpast.co.uk

Venerable **Michelham Priory** has a lovely setting amid immaculate gardens and encircled by the longest water-filled moat in the country. The Augustinian priory was founded in 1229, with the medieval gatehouse and moat added at the end of the fourteenth century, but in 1537 it was dissolved and partly demolished under Henry VIII, and transformed into a private country house. Only the refectory, the undercroft (now the main entrance) and the prior's room above it remain from the original structure; the Tudor wing of the house was added in the late sixteenth century.

Inside, you'll find Tudor rooms and furnishings, including a re-created kitchen complete with working spit, and a goggin – an early baby-walker. It's the **grounds**, though, that are the real treat, with a beautiful little kitchen garden, a medieval orchard, a working watermill (with wholemeal flour available to buy) and a moat walk giving lovely views back towards the house. Most weekends there's have-a-go **archery** on the sweeping South Lawn.

Bentley Wildfowl and Motor Museum

Halland, 7 miles northeast of Lewes, signposted from the A26, A22 & B2192, BN8 5AF • **Grounds and museum** Mid-March to Oct daily 10am–5pm; Nov to mid-March Sat & Sun & school hols 10am–4pm • Grounds & museum £8, children £6 • **Miniature railway** Generally runs weekends & school hols (Sun only in winter), but check website • £1 • ☎ 01825 840573, ⓦ bentley.org.uk

The **Bentley Wildfowl and Motor Museum** is tucked away along a winding country lane, and is a lovely, peaceful spot to while away a summer's day. The 23-acre parkland crams a lot in: there's a huge wildfowl enclosure of over a thousand geese, swans, ducks and flamingos; a bluebell wood that shelters a handful of reconstructed ancient buildings; a small adventure playground; and a volunteer-run miniature railway that connects the three. Near the entrance and café is a museum of roped-off Edwardian and other vintage motorcars and motorbikes. Every September, the popular three-day **Bentley Woodfair** features woodland crafts, demonstrations, axe racing teams, tree climbing and more.

Branching Out Adventures

At Bentley, 7 miles northeast of Lewes • Feb–Nov Thurs–Sun & school hols 10am–5pm, but check website • Adults/under-16s: high ropes £16/14; low ropes £14/12; giant swing, zip wires & climbing wall £6/5 each • ☎ 01825 280250, ⓦ branchingoutadventures.co.uk • Follow signs to the Bentley Wildfowl and Motor Museum, and then signs to Branching Out

Zip through the trees, wobble your way round a high ropes course or brave the adrenaline-pumping Giant Swing at **Branching Out Adventures**, nestled in woodland on the Bentley Estate. If you're bringing kids, note that they need to be age 6 (and

1.2m) for the low ropes course and climbing wall, and age 8 (and 1.3m) for the high ropes, giant swing and zip wires; there's a woodland play area for littler ones.

5

ACCOMMODATION

The Bell High St, Ticehurst, TN5 7AS ☏ 01580 200234, ⓦ thebellinticehurst.com. The seven rooms at *The Bell* are as quirky as the rest of this eccentric pub (see below); for starters, each comes with its own silver birch tree growing up out of the floor. Outside are three similarly funky, eclectically styled lodges (sleep 2–4 people) – one featuring a turntable and selection of vinyl – and a "Love Nest" with roof terrace and fire pit. Doubles **£115**, lodges (2 people) **£245**

Dernwood Farm Little Dernwood Farm, Dern Lane, Waldron, near Heathfield, TN21 0PN ☏ 01435 812726, ⓦ dernwoodfarm.co.uk. Car-free campsite in a lovely location, in a large meadow in the middle of coppiced woodland. The farm sells its own field-to-fork bacon, sausages, beef and lamb for cooking on the fire pit. More expensive bell tents, a safari tent and a cabin are also available. April–Sept. Per person **£10**

George Inn High St, Robertsbridge, TN32 5AW ☏ 01580 880315, ⓦ thegeorgerobertsbridge.co.uk. The four comfortable, well-priced rooms in this eighteenth-century former coaching inn make a great base for the area. There's excellent food, too, sourced where possible from within a thirty-mile radius of the pub. Tues–Sat noon–11pm, Sun noon–8pm. **£110**

Glottenham Bishops Lane, Robertsbridge, TN32 5EB

THE EASTERN HIGH WEALD

☏ 07865 078477, ⓦ glottenham.co.uk. Eco-glamping at its most luxurious, with four gorgeously appointed "tents" (sleeping 2–5 people), ranging from the romantic pre-Raphaelite Rossetti yurt, with an antique bed and oriental carpets, to the secluded de Etchyngham geodome, decked out with stylish Ercol and G-plan furniture. Four more yurts are available (Aug only) in the Family Fields. On-site therapy treatments and courses in everything from wild cooking to crafts can be arranged, and there's even a pop-up off-grid cinema. April–Sept. Three nights' minimum stay. From **£120**

Original Hut Company Quarry Farm, Bodiam, TN32 5RA ☏ 01580 830932, ⓦ original-huts.co.uk. Four quirky "shepherd's huts", with wood-burners and their own fire pit, plus bell tents and camping pitches, all dotted about the tranquil woodland of a working farm. It's a great location – just a fifteen-minute stroll to Bodiam Castle, the battlements of which you can see peeking up over the trees. Loads of activities can be arranged, from paddleboarding to bread-making; bike hire is available, and there's also an on-site spa and shop selling local food and crafts. There's an additional per-person charge of £3.30 for camping and yurts. Three nights' minimum stay peak season weekends. Huts **£105**, camping **£22**, bell tents **£77**

EATING AND DRINKING

★ **The Bell** High St, Ticehurst, TN5 7AS ☏ 01580 200234, ⓦ thebellinticehurst.com. There's a bit of an Alice in Wonderland feel to this great village local: on the surface It's all old beams, wooden floors and battered sofas, but look a little closer and you'll see bowler hat light fittings dangling from the ceiling, coat hooks fashioned from old cutlery and, in the gent's, a row of upturned tubas for urinals. Food (mains £11–17.50) is excellent, seasonal and local, and there are plenty of Sussex ales on tap. Mon–Sat noon–11.30pm, Sun noon–10.30pm; kitchen Mon–Sat noon–3pm & 6.30–9.30pm, Sun noon–4pm & 6.30–9pm.

Blackboys Inn Lewes Rd, Blackboys, TN22 5LG

☏ 01825 890283, ⓦ theblackboys.co.uk. This lovely old 1300s coaching inn comes into its own on a summer's day, when drinkers spill out onto the terrace and front lawn under the chestnut trees. Decent food (mains £13 and up) includes burgers, pies and steaks, and they have Harveys and guest beers on tap. Daily noon–11pm; kitchen Mon–Fri noon–2.30pm & 6–9pm, Sat noon–3pm & 6–9.30pm, Sun noon–8pm.

The Curlew Junction Rd, Bodiam, TN32 5UY ☏ 01580 861394, ⓦ thecurlewrestaurant.co.uk. Just up the road from Bodiam, this weatherboard former coaching inn produces some of the best food in the Southeast but isn't at

---

ROCK-CLIMBING NEAR ERIDGE GREEN

Some of the best **climbing** to be had in the Southeast is around Eridge Green, straddling the Sussex–Kent border. Two of the sites – Eridge Rocks (owned by the Sussex Wildlife Trust; ⓦ sussexwildlifetrust.org.uk) and Harrison's Rocks (owned by the British Mountaineering Council; ⓦ thebmc.co.uk) – are open access, while a third, Bowles Rocks, is owned by the Bowles Outdoor Centre (ⓦ bowles.ac; £5/adult; climbing courses and lessons also available). The sites are all open to experienced climbers with their own equipment, while novices can get roped up with **Nuts 4 Climbing** (☏ 01892 860670, ⓦ nuts4climbing.com), who offer taster sessions (£40), and one-day (£99) and two-day (£185) beginner's courses, at Harrison's Rocks – a perfect introduction to the sport.

5

all stuffy. The short seasonal menu features dishes such as double-baked Sussex cheese soufflé with kirsch cream (£8.50) and lamb belly with goat's curd, anchovy and sea beet (£23), and there's a good-value set menu Tues–Fri lunch and Tues–Thurs dinner (two/three courses £22.50/27.50. Tues–Sat noon–2.30pm & 6.30–9.30pm, Sun noon–2.30pm & 6.30–9pm.

Six Bells The Street, Chiddingly, BN8 6HE ☎01825 872227. A proper pub, old-fashioned and unpretentious, with plenty of cosy nooks and crannies, log fires, Harveys on tap, excellent-value pub grub and a great atmosphere. Try to catch one of the regular folk and blues nights if you can (alternate Tues nights; ⓦ6bellsfolk.co.uk). Mon–Thurs noon–3pm & 6–11pm, Fri & Sat noon–midnight, Sun noon–10.30pm; kitchen Mon–Thurs noon–2pm & 6–9pm, Fri–Sun noon–9pm.

Ashdown Forest

The first thing that surprises visitors to **ASHDOWN FOREST** is how little of it is actually forest. Almost two thirds of the Forest's ten square miles is made up of high, open **heathland** – particularly lovely in late summer, when the gorse and heather flower and the heath becomes a riot of purple and yellow. It's a peculiarly un-Sussex scene, a complete departure from the rolling green hills and patchwork fields that surround it, and all the more beautiful for it.

Walking in the Forest couldn't be easier, with footpaths and bridleways striking off in every direction. Orientation can be difficult, so it's well worth picking up the excellent map (£2.50) from the Ashdown Forest Centre Information Barn (see opposite), which marks all the trails. The Barn also has plenty of free leaflets (also downloadable from

---

A BEAR OF VERY LITTLE BRAIN

Probably the most famous bear in the world, Pooh Bear, also known as **Winnie-the-Pooh**, is the much-loved creation of **A.A. Milne**, who wrote the classic children's books – *Winnie the Pooh* (1926) and *House at Pooh Corner* (1928) – from his weekend home at Cotchford Farmhouse near the small village of **Hartfield**, on Ashdown Forest's northeastern edge. The stories were inspired by Milne's only son, Christopher Robin, who appears in the books along with his real-life stuffed toys: Edward Bear, Piglet, Kanga, Roo, Eeyore and Tigger (Owl and Rabbit were invented for the books).

The places described in the stories were modelled closely on Ashdown Forest: the fictional **100 Aker Wood**, where the animals live with Christopher Robin, is named after the real-life Five Hundred Acre Wood; **Galleon's Leap** was inspired by the hilltop of Gills Lap; while a clump of pine trees near Gills Lap became the **Enchanted Place**, where Christopher Robin never managed to work out whether there were 63 trees or 64. The original illustrations by **E.H. Shepherd** took direct inspiration from the Forest, and perfectly capture the heathland landscape, with its distinctive hilltop clusters of pine trees.

POOH WALKS

The *Pooh Walks from Gills Lap* **leaflet**, available from the Ashdown Forest Centre Information Barn (see opposite), details two short walks that take you past some of the spots featured in the book, including the Enchanted Place, the Heffalump Trap, the Sandy Pit where Roo played, and the North Pole, but by far the most popular Pooh destination is **Pooh Bridge**, where the bear-of-very-little-brain invented the game of **Poohsticks** one lazy sunny afternoon with his good friend Piglet. The bridge is an easy one-mile walk from the Pooh Bridge car park, at the Forest's northern edge, just off the B2026.

POOH CORNER

The shop where real-life Christopher Robin went with his nanny to buy bulls' eyes is now **Pooh Corner**, High St, Hartfield, TN7 4AE (Mon–Fri 10am–5pm, Sat 9am–5pm, Sun 10.30am–5pm; ☎01892 770456, ⓦpooh-country.co.uk), a small **shop** – with attached tearoom (see opposite) – selling a mind-boggling array of Pooh memorabilia, from soft toys, books and cross-stitch kits to tea towels, T-shirts and Sussex honey, as well as maps and guidebooks of the Forest, and a rule-book for playing Poohsticks.

Ⓦashdownforest.org) describing individual walks. With one notable exception – Pooh Bridge (see box opposite) – the Forest never really gets too busy, and you'll generally find yourself able to enjoy the expansive views in solitude, with only the odd free-wandering sheep for company. Ashdown Forest Riding Centre (Ⓣ07818 093880, Ⓦashdownforestriding.co.uk) offers one- to three-hour **horseriding** sessions (£25–65), while the Llama Park at Wych Cross (Ⓣ01825 712040, Ⓦllamapark.co.uk) leads daily **llama walks** (1hr 30min; £35). Note that off-road **cycling** in the Forest isn't allowed.

ARRIVAL AND INFORMATION
ASHDOWN FOREST

By bus Wealdlink operates the summer-only, hop-on, hop-off #262 bus (Sat 4 daily; Ⓦwealdenbus.org.uk), which runs in a circuit from Uckfield station via various attractions in the Forest including the Pooh Bridge car park, Hartfield (for Pooh Corner), the *Hatch Inn* and the visitor centre. Alternatively, Metrobus #291 runs between East Grinstead and Tunbridge Wells, stopping at Coleman's Hatch and Hartfield (Mon–Sat hourly, Sun every 2hr), and #270 runs from Brighton to East Grinstead via Wych Cross

(Mon–Sat hourly).

Tourist information Ashdown Forest Centre Information Barn, Wych Cross (March–Oct Mon–Fri 2–5pm, Sat & Sun 11am–5pm; Nov–March Sat & Sun 11am–5pm; Ⓣ01342 823583, Ⓦashdownforest.org).

By car There are dozens of free parking sites dotting the main roads through the forest; the Information Barn sells a map (£2.50) with parking spots marked.

ACCOMMODATION AND EATING

Hatch Inn Colemans Hatch, TN7 4EJ Ⓣ01342 822363, Ⓦhatchinn.co.uk. The nicest pub in the Forest itself is this ancient weatherboard inn, dating from 1430, which ticks all the boxes for a perfect pub lunch: a cosy, beamed interior, a gorgeous garden for the summer, well-kept Harveys on tap, and good, home-cooked food. At lunchtimes you can opt for a sandwich or ploughman's (£7.50–11.50), or more expensive mains such as haddock kedgeree or belly of pork (£11–16.50). Mon–Fri 11.30am–3pm & 5.30–11pm, Sat 11am–11pm, Sun noon–11pm; kitchen Mon–Fri noon–2.15pm & 7–9.15pm, Sat noon–2.30pm & 7–9.30pm, Sun noon–3.30pm.

★**Piglet's Tearoom** High St, Hartfield, TN7 4AE Ⓣ01892 770456, Ⓦpooh-country.co.uk. If it's time for a

little something, make a beeline for the excellent tearoom in the Pooh Corner shop, with plenty of seating outside. The menu runs from "Strengthening Medicines" (drinks) to "Smackerels" (snacks), and includes quiches (£4.50), sandwiches, cakes and cream teas (from £3.95) – all tasty, generously portioned and fantastic value. Mon–Fri 10am–4.30pm, Sat 9am–4.30pm, Sun 10.30am–4.30pm.

St Ives Farm Butcherfield Lane, Hartfield, TN7 4JX Ⓣ01892 770213, Ⓦstivesfarm.co.uk. This lovely low-key campsite has three shady camping fields set around a fishing lake, three miles from the nearest main road. Evening brings the crackle of campfires; barbecue supplies can be bought from Perryhill Orchards farm shop, a 20min walk away. April–Oct. Per person **£10**

The western High Weald

The **WESTERN HIGH WEALD** feels surprisingly sleepy and remote, given that it's sandwiched between sprawling Crawley and East Grinstead to the north, Horsham to the west, and Haywards Heath and Burgess Hill to the south, with the busy A23 roaring through the centre. Scattered villages and stately manor houses pepper the landscape: when the railway arrived in the mid-nineteenth century, making the area easily accessible from London, this was a popular spot for wealthy Londoners to buy or build a mansion and a slice of rural living.

The main draw of the area is its **gardens**: the big hitters are **Sheffield Park**, **Nymans** and **Wakehurst Place**, but **Borde Hill** and **High Beeches** come a close second, and the modern **Sussex Prairies** garden provides a wonderful modern counterpoint. There's another beautiful garden surrounding the Arts and Crafts house of **Standen**, though it's the house itself which is the real star, crammed full of decorative treasures by William Morris and his contemporaries. To the south lies the **Bluebell Railway**, a vintage steam railway that puffs its way north from Sheffield Park through the bluebell-speckled woodlands that gave it its name.

5

Sheffield Park and Garden

On the A275 East Grinstead–Lewes main road, about 2.5 miles north of the junction with the A272, TN22 3QX • Garden daily 10am–5pm (or dusk if sooner); parkland dawn–dusk • £10.50; NT • ☎ 01825 790231, ⓦ nationaltrust.org.uk/sheffield-park-and -garden • Free parking; bus #121 from Lewes (Sat every 2hr; 30min); Bluebell Railway (see p.196) Sheffield Park station is a 10min walk away through the parkland

The beautiful landscaped garden at **Sheffield Park and Garden**, first laid out by Capability Brown in the eighteenth century, is at its very best in autumn, when it puts on the most spectacularly colourful show in the Southeast. Pick a cloudless sunny day and you'll have peerless views of the brilliantly hued foliage reflected in the mirror-like waters of the garden's five deep lakes, linked by cascades and waterfalls – though if you want to enjoy the views in relative solitude you're best off avoiding weekends and the busier, middle part of the day, when it can seem as though the whole of Sussex has turned up to see the spectacle. The 120-acre garden is equally lovely – and much quieter – in the springtime, when daffodils and bluebells start to emerge, and in May and June when the azaleas and rhododendrons are out.

On the other side of the access road lies the estate's 265-acre **parkland**, dotted by grazing sheep. A ten-minute walk from the car park brings you to a small copse where you'll find a natural play trail and a "sky glade" for cloud watching.

The Bluebell Railway

Sheffield Park station, on the A275 East Grinstead–Lewes main road, about 2 miles north of the junction with the A272, TN22 3QL • April–Oct daily; Nov–March Sat, Sun & school hols • Day-ticket with unlimited travel £17 • ☎ 01825 720800, ⓦ bluebell-railway .co.uk • The railway is connected to the mainline station at East Grinstead; bus #121 from Lewes (Sat every 2hr; 30min) runs to Sheffield Park station

Probably the best-known vintage steam railway in the country, the **Bluebell Railway** was started by a small group of enthusiasts in 1959, just four years after the old London–Lewes line was closed, and today has blossomed into a huge operation, with more than thirty steam locos, over one hundred pieces of rolling stock and more than eight hundred volunteers keeping the wheels rolling. The locos take around forty minutes to puff the nine miles north from Sheffield Park station – the southern terminus of the railway – via Kingscote and Horsted Keynes stations to East Grinstead, where they chug into a platform alongside the mainline station.

The three original stations have all been beautifully restored to different periods: **Horsted Keynes** in 1920s splendour, with old posters and newspaper headlines on the walls and luggage on the platforms; **Kingscote** with 1950s trimmings; and **Sheffield Park** in the style of the 1880s, decorated with wonderful reclaimed enamel signs proclaiming the benefits of Gold Flake cigarettes and Virol ("anaemic girls need it"). Sheffield Park is also home to the **railway sheds**, where you can wander

---

CYCLING THE FOREST WAY

Running for just over nine miles from East Grinstead in the west to Groombridge in the east, the **Forest Way** follows the path of a disused railway line that skirts the northern fringes of Ashdown Forest. The route is flat and peaceful, shadowing the River Medway as it wriggles its way east past patchwork fields, farms, small villages and wooded hills. With dragonflies darting over the water and swallows flitting above you, it's an idyllic ride – perfect for families – and gives you a real taste of the beautiful High Weald. There are picnic benches along the track, or you can detour off to pubs along the way or the excellent tearoom at Hartfield (see p.195). A map of the route can be downloaded from ⓦ eastsussex.gov.uk.

There's **bike rental** at Forest Row Cycle Hire in Forest Row (☎ 07539 927467, ⓦ forestrowcyclehire.org; £12/half-day, £20/day), towards the western end of the route.

amongst some splendid old locomotives, and a small **museum** which charts the development of railways from horse-drawn to electric, and also tells the story of the Bluebell Railway.

Special services run throughout the year, everything from afternoon tea services to Santa specials. Especially popular is the **Golden Arrow** Pullman dining train, re-creating the luxurious *Golden Arrow* which once linked London and Paris (£27 for the Pullman ticket, plus £48 for dinner).

Sussex Prairies Garden

Morlands Farm, Wheatsheaf Rd, near Henfield on the B2166, BN5 9AT • June to mid-Oct Mon & Wed–Sun 1–5pm • £7 • ☏ 01273 495902, Ⓦ sussexprairies.co.uk

In comparison to the grand old gardens of the Sussex Weald the **Sussex Prairies Garden** is a mere whippersnapper – it was only established in 2009 – but it's already made a bit of a name for itself. The naturalistic planting of the eight-acre site features extraordinary, vibrant drifts of summer-flowering perennials and tall grasses – some thirty thousand plants in total – with pathways snaking between them. It's quite an experience weaving your way between the borders in late summer when you're dwarfed by grasses 8ft high. In winter the garden is burned to the ground, ready for it to spring into life again the following year. Every year the work of a different group of sculptors is featured, and there's also a lovely tearoom, with tables outside overlooking the riot of colour.

Bolney Wine Estate

Bookers Vineyard, Foxhole Lane, Bolney, RH17 5NB • **Vineyard trail** June to mid-Sept Tues–Sat 10am–3pm • Trail map £3 • **Tours** Feb–Nov; must all be pre-booked except for the drop-on tour (45min), which runs July–Sept Tues, Wed & Thurs noon • Drop-on tour £10, taster tour £16, afternoon tea tour £34.50, lunch tour £42.50 • **Shop** Mon–Fri 9am–5pm, Sun 10am–3pm • **Café** Tues–Fri 9am–5pm, Sun 10am–3pm • ☏ 01444 881894, Ⓦ bolneywineestate.co.uk

Grapes have been grown on the land that is now the **Bolney Wine Estate** since the Middle Ages, but the tradition was only reinstated in 1972, when Rodney and Janet Pratt planted their first three acres of vines. The vineyard is perhaps best known for its red wines – unusual in the UK – but it's also won awards for its sparkling wines. A variety of pre-bookable **tours** are available, some including lunch or afternoon tea in the on-site café, and there's also a **vineyard trail** (open summer only) and a handy summer-only **drop-on tour**, which lasts 45 minutes, includes a couple of tastings and allows kids to tag along.

Borde Hill Garden

Borde Hill Lane, near Haywards Heath, RH16 1XP • April–June & Sept Mon–Fri 10am–5pm, Sat & Sun 10am–6pm (or dusk if sooner); July & Aug daily 10am–6pm • £8.20 • ☏ 01444 450326, Ⓦ bordehill.co.uk

Beautiful **Borde Hill Garden** ranges around a handsome honey-coloured Elizabethan manor house (not open to the public) on a narrow ridge of the Sussex Weald, with fantastic sweeping views all around. The gardens were planted by **Colonel Stephenson R. Clarke**, an enthusiastic naturalist, in the 1890s, from exotic trees and shrubs collected by famous plant-hunters (see box, p.198).

The **formal gardens** closest to the house form a series of "garden rooms", ranging from a formal English rose garden and terraced Italian garden (originally the house's tennis court), to a fabulous secret, subtropical sunken dell. Further afield the estate's **woodland** is blanketed by drifts of bluebells and anemones in spring, and later ablaze with rhododendrons – a favourite of the Colonel's. By the entrance there's a small adventure playground, as well as a café and the excellent *Jeremy's Restaurant* (see p.201).

5

Nymans

Handcross, just off the A23, RH17 6EB · Garden daily: March–Oct 10am–5pm; Nov–Feb 10am–4pm; house March–Oct daily 11–4pm · £11.50; NT · ☎ 01444 405250, ⓦ nationaltrust.org.uk/nymans · Free parking; Metrobus #273 (Mon–Sat hourly; 1hr) from Brighton to Crawley stops nearby

The thirty-acre gardens at **Nymans** were the work of the Messel family, who took on the estate in 1890 and set about creating one of Sussex's great gardens. The main draw of the garden is its plant collection – the Messels sponsored many plant-hunting expeditions that brought back rare, exotic trees and shrubs from the remotest corners of the world. It's also a garden that prides itself on its year-round interest: daffodils, bluebells, rhododendrons and rare Himalayan magnolias in spring; stunning borders and the rose garden in full bloom in summer; autumn colour at the back of the garden; and witch hazel, winter-flowering bulbs and camellias in winter.

The gardens are arranged around the ruins of a mock-Gothic **manor house**, which burnt down one winter shortly after World War II: the night of the fire was so cold that although fire engines arrived in plenty of time, the water was frozen solid and they were forced to stand by and watch the house burn. Only a change of wind direction spared the portion of the house that remains open to the public today: the last of the Messels, Anne, lived in these few, modest rooms until her death in 1992, and they are preserved as they were when she died, decorated with flowers from the garden.

High Beeches

High Beeches Lane, near Handcross on the B2110, just off the A23, RH17 6HQ · April–Oct Mon, Tues & Thurs–Sun 1–5pm · £7.50 · ☎ 01444 400589, ⓦ highbeeches.com

The landscaped woodland garden of **High Beeches** has a wilder feel to it than the other great Sussex gardens, with steep, meandering paths cut through long grass, tumbling streams, woodland glades, and a gorgeous wildflower meadow speckled with golden buttercups and ox-eye daisies in early summer. The 27-acre garden has beautiful displays of autumn colour, but it really comes into its own in spring, when the woodland is cloaked in bluebells, magnolias are in bloom, and early rhododendrons, followed by azaleas, set the garden aflame with splashes of red and pink.

The estate's grand house was destroyed when a stray Canadian bomber crashed into it in World War II, but the garden – much of which was created by **Colonel**

PLANT HUNTERS AND GATHERERS: GREAT GARDENS OF THE WEALD

Some of the greatest gardens in the Southeast – **Wakehurst Place**, **Nymans**, **Borde Hill** and **High Beeches** – can be found in a pocket of sleepy Sussex countryside, all within a few miles of each other. Their proximity is no coincidence: they were established at roughly the same time, in the 1890s and the decade that followed, by men who knew and influenced each other, and who would often visit one another's gardens and exchange ideas, advice and plants.

In contrast to the prevailing Victorian fashion for orderly formal planting, the Sussex gardens share a love of **naturalism**, partly due to the influence, encouragement and advice of the great gardener **William Robinson**, whose own garden at *Gravetye Manor* – now a hotel (see p.200) – was only a stone's throw away. The other defining feature of the Sussex gardens is their **exotic planting**, which often includes rare and important trees and shrubs. The fertile acid soil and high rainfall of the Weald provided perfect conditions for experimentation with non-native species, and Messel, Stephenson R. Clarke and the Loders all helped finance the perilous **plant-hunting expeditions** around the globe, which brought back some of the rare and exotic rhododendrons, azaleas, magnolias and camellias which are today such a central feature of the gardens.

SPOOKS AND SCARES: SHOCKTOBER FEST

The month of October sees zombies, ghouls and other blood-splattered creatures of the undead take over **Tulley's Farm** near Crawley for one of the largest Halloween events in the country (⊕ halloweenattractions.co.uk). There's family-friendly spooky fun in the daytime at the **Pumpkin and Spook Fest**, followed by properly terrifying immersive scare experiences for grown-ups in the evenings at the **Shocktober Fest**, including a horror hayride through the woods and several different interactive haunted houses, plus street theatre and live music.

Both events run on selected dates in October, including all of Halloween week. **Tickets** for the Shocktober Fest cost £28–38 (depending on the date); for the Pumpkin and Spook Fest they are £8–10, or £10–12 for children aged 5–13.

Giles Loder, who ran the estate for sixty years until his death in 1966 – survived the neglect of the war. On the Colonel's death the garden was bought by another noted plant-loving family, the Boscawens, who had heard it described as the most beautiful in Sussex.

Wakehurst Place

On the B2028 between Ardingly and Turners Hill, RH17 6TN • Daily: March–Oct 10am–6pm; Nov Feb 10am–4.30pm; Millennium Seedbank closes 1hr earlier • £12.50 including parking; NT members and other groups with reciprocal arrangements get free entry but are required to pay for parking (£2/1hr, £5/2hr, £10/day) • ☎ 01444 894066, ⊕ kew.org/visit-wakehurst • Metrobus #272 from Haywards Heath (Mon–Sat every 2hr; 15min)

The country cousin of Kew's Royal Botanic Gardens, **Wakehurst Place** sprawls over 465 acres and you'll need a whole day if you want to explore it properly. The main appeal of Wakehurst is its diversity, from the formal gardens surrounding the Elizabethan mansion (of which a few rooms are open) near the entrance, to the wilder meadows, wetlands, steep-sided valleys and ancient woodland further afield. At the far end of the site is the **Loder Valley Nature Reserve**, a mix of meadow, woodland and wetland, with several bird hides, which allows access to a maximum of fifty people a day (no booking).

The garden was originally planted by **Sir Gerald Loder**, a member of the illustrious local family also responsible for High Beeches. Many of the exotic and rare trees Loder planted in the early twentieth century were torn down in the great storm of 1987, but Kew – which has managed the site since 1965, when it took on a long-term lease from the National Trust – responded with its trademark emphasis on conservation, by replanting Wakehurst with different types of woodland from around the world, re-creating endangered habitats.

The Millennium Seedbank

Wakehurst is also home to the **Millennium Seedbank**, which opened in 2010 with the aim of conserving the most endangered and important seeds from around the world. It has already collected and stored around ten percent of the world's plant species (around thirty thousand in total), including almost all of the UK's native species; the next target is 25 percent by the year 2020. The vast storage vaults are hidden underground beneath the laboratories, which you can look into from the **exhibition room**.

Standen

West Hoathly Rd, 2 miles south of East Grinstead, RH19 4NE • Jan garden daily 10am–4pm; house Sat & Sun 11am–3.30pm; Feb–Oct garden daily 10am–5pm, house daily 11am–4.30pm; Nov & Dec garden daily 10am–4pm, house daily 11am–3.30pm • £10.75; NT; ☎ 01342 323029, ⊕ nationaltrust.org.uk/standen-house-and-garden; parking free

Set in lovely countryside at the end of a long winding lane, **Standen** is a beautiful Arts and Crafts house, creaking at the seams with treasures from many of the key figures in the **Arts and Crafts movement** (see box, p.200).

5

THE ARTS AND CRAFTS MOVEMENT

The **Arts and Crafts movement** started out in Britain in the nineteenth century as a reaction against the evils of mass production. There was a strong vein of socialism underpinning it – the movement believed that mechanization threatened to dehumanize the lives of the ordinary working classes – and both John Ruskin and Alexander Pugin (see p.100) were influences.

The central ideas were a rejection of shoddy, mass-produced goods in favour of handcrafted objects; an emphasis on simple, honest design – in contrast to the over-elaborate showiness and artificiality of much Victorian design; and the use of nature as a source of inspiration.

The father of the Arts and Crafts movement was **William Morris**, one of the most influential designers of the nineteenth century, who in 1861 set up Morris, Marshall, Faulkner & Co (later Morris & Co), with other figures including Edward Burne-Jones, Dante Gabriel Rossetti and Philip Webb, to make and sell beautiful handcrafted objects for the home. "Have nothing in your home that you do not know to be useful or believe to be beautiful" was Morris's motto. Many of the designs that came out of Morris & Co were inspired by nature, and Morris named many of his own hand block-printed wallpapers after trees and flowers.

The Arts and Crafts movement flourished in the 1880s and 1890s but by the early twentieth century it became clear that its grand ideals were flawed; only the very wealthy could afford to buy Morris & Co's handcrafted designs, which were much more expensive to manufacture than the mass-produced items they were intended to replace.

The building was the creation of the architect **Philip Webb**, friend of William Morris, and a central player in the foundation of the Arts and Crafts movement. Webb was at pains to make the house functional as well as beautiful, and it was at the cutting edge of modern technology for its time, with both electricity and central heating fitted. The beautiful original light fittings – by **W.A.S. Benson**, one of Morris's protégés – can still be seen today. Webb was famed for his attention to detail, and this is evident all over the house, from the intricate fingerplates on the doors to the meticulously designed fireplaces.

The highlight, however, is Morris's exuberant **wallpapers and textiles**, deliberately offset by plain, wood-panelled walls. Look out for Morris's trellis wallpaper, his first marketed wallpaper design, in the conservatory corridor – the birds were drawn by Webb because Morris wasn't happy with his own efforts. Other gems include red lustreware and Islamic-inspired ceramic tiles by **William De Morgan** in the billiard room, and paintings and drawings by Edward Burne-Jones, Dante Gabriel Rossetti and Ford Madox Brown.

Surrounding the house are twelve acres of terraced hillside **gardens**, encompassing formal gardens and wilder areas, as well as a traditional Victorian kitchen garden.

ACCOMMODATION   THE WESTERN HIGH WEALD

Gravetye Manor Vowels Lane, West Hoathly, RH19 4LJ ☎ 01342 810567, ⓦ gravetyemanor.co.uk. Unashamedly old-fashioned, in a thoroughly good way, this sixteenth-century manor house hotel nestles amid beautiful gardens planted a hundred years ago by former owner William Robinson, the pioneer of the natural-style English garden. The seventeen bedrooms – named, fittingly, after trees found on the estate – are elegantly luxurious, there's a Michelin-starred restaurant, and afternoon tea can be taken in the flower-filled garden. **£340**

★**Ockenden Manor** Cuckfield, RH17 5LD ☎ 01444 416111, ⓦ hshotels.co.uk. This stately Elizabethan manor house has not one but two trump cards up its sleeve: a Michelin-starred restaurant, and a sleek spa housed in a separate modern building. The rooms vary from traditionally styled doubles to glamorous open-plan spa suites. Look out for dinner, bed and breakfast packages, which are often excellent value. **£199**

★**WOWO Wapsbourne Farm** Sheffield Park, TN22 3QS ☎ 01825 723414, ⓦ wowo.co.uk. This lovely streamside campsite is a local favourite. Campfires are encouraged, there's bags of open space for kids (with rope swings aplenty), plus regular bushcraft workshops, and the "village" area offers live acoustic music (musicians stay free in return for an hour's performance). Yurts, shepherd's huts and bell tents (sleeping 3–7 people) are also available. Camping available March–Oct, yurts and shepherd's huts available all year; two-night minimum stay at weekends. Camping/person **£10**, yurts & huts from **£80**

EATING AND DRINKING

The Ginger Fox Muddleswood Rd, on the A281 at the junction with the B2117, near Albourne, BN6 9EA ☏ 01273 857888, ⓦ thegingerfox.com. This relaxed foodie pub is the country outpost of the Brighton-based "Ginger" empire, and it's equally popular, with a lovely big garden, great food (mains £14–22) and a play area for kids. Daily 11.30am–midnight; kitchen Mon noon–2pm & 6–9pm, Tues–Fri noon–2pm, Sat noon–3pm & 6.30–10pm, Sun noon–4pm & 6–9pm.

★**The Griffin Inn** Fletching, TN22 3SS ☏ 01825 722890, ⓦ thegriffininn.co.uk. On a summer's day look no further than this fabulous country pub, which boasts what is surely the most perfect beer garden in Sussex, with views across the Weald from the huge sloping lawn. Weekend lunchtimes in summer see the barbecue lit, with lobster, tuna, steak and local bangers all sizzling on the coals. Year-round there's local ale on the pump, twenty wines by the glass and excellent food (mains £13–22). Daily 11am–late; kitchen Mon–Fri noon–2.30pm & 7–9.30pm, Sat noon–3pm & 7–9.30pm, Sun noon–3pm & 7–9pm.

Jeremy's Restaurant Borde Hill Garden, Balcombe Rd, near Haywards Heath, RH16 1XP ☏ 01444 441102, ⓦ jeremysrestaurant.com. This award-winning restaurant in Borde Hill Garden (see p.197) is especially lovely on a summer's day, when tables are set up on the terrace overlooking a Victorian walled garden. The a la carte menu (mains £15–24) might feature suckling pig or South Coast John Dory, or there's a cheaper set menu (two/three courses £20/25; available Tues–Sat lunch & Tues–Thurs dinner). Tues–Sat 12.30–2.30pm & 7–10pm, Sun 12.30–2.30pm.

The Royal Oak Wineham Lane, Wineham, BN5 9AY ☏ 01444 881252. Everything a traditional English country pub should be, this ancient, unspoilt boozer sits on a quiet country lane, with plenty of tables on the lawn out front. Inside the thirteenth-century building it's all low beamed ceilings and uneven brick floors. Don't be thrown by the lack of hand pumps at the bar – the beer (Harveys, Dark Star and guests) is served straight from the cask. There's good, seasonal food on offer, too, including chunky ploughman's boards (starting at £8.95). Mon–Fri 11am–3.30pm & 5.30–11pm, Sat 11am–4pm & 6–11pm, Sun noon–4.30pm & 7–10.30pm; kitchen Mon–Sat noon–2.30pm & 7–9pm, Sun noon–3pm.

East Sussex Downs

THE SEVEN SISTERS

East Sussex Downs

The South Downs, a range of gently undulating chalk hills protected within the South Downs National Park, stretch across much of Sussex, but nowhere are they more beautiful – or more dramatic – than in the pristine pocket of countryside just west of Eastbourne. Here, the Downs meet the sea at the Seven Sisters, a series of spectacular chalk cliffs culminating in the dizzying 530ft-high Beachy Head, the tallest chalk sea cliff in the country. The gorgeous countryside continues as the South Downs sweep westwards towards Ditchling Beacon – the highest point in Sussex – with splendid views all around, over sleepy villages and spired churches, rolling grassland dotted with munching sheep, poppy fields, vineyards and patchwork fields that change colour with the seasons. Little wonder that this bucolic corner of Sussex is so popular.

The nicest way to soak up the views is on foot: the long-distance **South Downs Way** footpath follows the ridge of the Downs, crisscrossed by any number of other footpaths – the South Downs have one of the densest networks of public rights of way in the country. But the area's charms aren't all scenic: there's also a renowned opera house at **Glyndebourne**, an ever-growing number of vineyards producing award-winning sparkling wine, plenty of fine country pubs, and dozens of pretty little villages, the pick of the bunch being the old smugglers' haunt of **Alfriston**. One of the biggest draws of the area is its associations with the **Bloomsbury Group**: Virginia Woolf settled at Monk's House near Lewes, while her sister Vanessa Bell and other members of the set made Charleston their bohemian home. More of Sussex's art trail can be explored in the village of **Ditchling**, where the beautifully designed Ditchling Museum of Art + Craft displays the work of a group of artists and craftspeople – Eric Gill among them – who set up a community here in the early years of the twentieth century.

All of the sights in this chapter are an easy drive from buzzy Brighton (see chapter 7), but two other towns make great (and quieter) alternative bases. The seaside town of **Eastbourne** has an elegant promenade, a fine modern art museum and the chalk cliff of **Beachy Head** on its doorstep. Or just northeast of Brighton, straddling the River Ouse, there's the county town of **Lewes**; with a handsome centre, a Norman castle, its own brewery and a lively, arty vibe, it's full of character and charm.

CHARLESTON FARMHOUSE

Highlights

❶ Beachy Head and the Seven Sisters The unmissable scenic highlight of the South Downs National Park: soaring white cliffs backed by wildflower-rich chalk grassland. **See p.211**

❷ Alfriston A contender for the title of prettiest village in Sussex, with a picturesque main street, an idyllic village green and a clutch of historic smuggling inns. **See p.216**

❸ Charleston Farmhouse The Bloomsbury Group's uniquely decorated country home gives a fascinating glimpse into the lives of Sussex's most famous bohemians. **See p.220**

❹ Paragliding on the Downs You can be flying solo in a day, in one of the country's finest paragliding destinations. **See p.224**

❺ Lewes One of Sussex's loveliest towns, with a medieval castle, a brewery, the Downs on its doorstep, and even its own currency. **See p.224**

❻ Sussex Bonfire Night Bonfire Night as it should be: spectacular costumed processions, flaming torches and plenty of proud tradition. See p.228

❼ Ditchling Museum of Art + Craft Admire the work of Eric Gill and his contemporaries in the beautiful village where it was made. See p.231

❽ Devil's Dyke Any view described by painter John Constable as "the grandest in the world" has got to be worth seeing for yourself. See p.232

HIGHLIGHTS ARE MARKED ON THE MAP ON P.206

Eastbourne

The archetypal English seaside resort, elegant **EASTBOURNE** has a certain timeless appeal. A stroll along the three-mile-long prom will take you past old-fashioned ice-cream parlours, brass bands playing in the bandstand, floral displays and grand hotels offering afternoon tea. Over the years it's gained a reputation as a retirement town by the sea, derided as "God's waiting room", and "a graveyard above the ground". But Eastbourne is slowly changing, with families and creative types, priced out of Brighton, moving into the area; it even has that hallmark of seaside-town regeneration – a state-of-the-art contemporary art gallery, the Towner. Eastbourne may still lack the hipness of neighbouring Brighton, but some would say it's all the better for it.

The seafront

Eastbourne's well-conserved seafront is an elegant ribbon of Victorian terraces and villas, entirely unblemished by shops – thanks to an edict of **William Cavendish**, one of the two landowners who developed the upmarket seaside resort ("planned by gentlemen for gentlemen") in the nineteenth century. With its palm trees and fairy lights there's a distinct holiday vibe to it on balmy summer evenings. The seafront strip stretches for three miles from one of Europe's largest marinas, **Sovereign Harbour** (ⓦeastbourneharbour.com), in the east to the cliffs of **Holywell** in the west. From Holywell, paths zigzag back up to the main seafront road and the start of the footpath up to Beachy Head (see p.212). The beach is resolutely pebbly, but stretches of sand emerge at low tide. In August huge crowds on the beach and the roar of jet engines overhead announce the arrival of the **Airbourne** International Air Show (see p.33).

Eastbourne Pier and Bandstand

Grand Parade, BN21 3EL • Open access • Free • ⓦeastbournepier.com

The focal point of the seafront is the elegant **pier**, designed by master pier-builder Eugenius Birch and opened in 1872. The pier made the headlines in 2014 when a

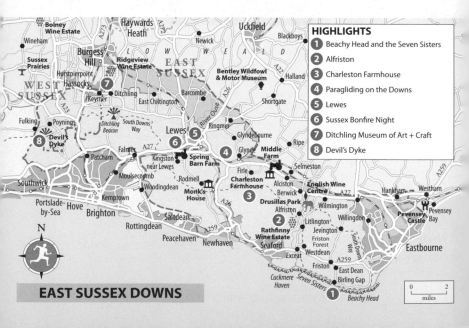

HIGHLIGHTS

1. Beachy Head and the Seven Sisters
2. Alfriston
3. Charleston Farmhouse
4. Paragliding on the Downs
5. Lewes
6. Sussex Bonfire Night
7. Ditchling Museum of Art + Craft
8. Devil's Dyke

EAST SUSSEX DOWNS

devastating fire ripped through its shore end, destroying the old ballroom pavilion; it quickly reopened, but at the time of writing a bare expanse of decking still stands in the pavilion's place while the pier's new owner plans its future.

The seafront's other pride and joy is the much-loved **bandstand** (ⓦeastbournebandstand .co.uk), just west of the pier, with its jaunty azure-blue domed roof. In summer, traditional brass bands take to the stage on Sundays (May–Sept Sun 3pm; 1hr 30min; £3.50), and big bands and tribute shows play on occasional evenings; check online for details.

Eastbourne Lifeboat Museum

King Edward's Parade, BN21 4BY • Jan & Feb Sat & Sun 10am–3pm; March, Nov & Dec daily 10am–4pm; April–Oct daily 10am–5pm • Free • ⓦeastbournernli.org/museum

A five-minute walk west of the pier, the tiny **Eastbourne Lifeboat Museum** recounts some of the more daring rescues the town's lifeboatmen have made since 1822, when local eccentric John "Mad Jack" Fuller (see box, p.189) donated Eastbourne's first lifeboat. Cork lifejackets weren't introduced until 1854, making the bravery of those first volunteers, who generally couldn't swim, all the more astonishing. The museum is overlooked by a grassy mound topped by the **Wish Tower**, one of a series of Martello towers (see box, p.125) built along the south coast at the end of the eighteenth century.

Redoubt Fortress

Royal Parade, BN22 7AQ • Daily: mid-March to Sept 10am–5pm; Oct to mid-Nov 11am–4pm • £4.50 • ☎ 01323 410300, ⓦeastbournemuseums.co.uk

The splendid **Redoubt Fortress**, at the eastern end of the seafront, was one of three fortresses built at the same time as the Martello towers to counter the threat of Napoleonic invasion, and was garrisoned on and off until World War II. The 24 casemates (rooms) around the central circular parade ground feature recreated rooms and reproduction objects from the fortress's past, while a new purpose-built museum adjacent to the Redoubt is planned to open in 2019, housing a permanent exhibition on the history of Eastbourne and the surrounding area.

The Cultural Quarter

Eastbourne's "**Cultural Quarter**" is centred on **Devonshire Park**, best-known for its world-class **lawn tennis courts** which play host to big-name players during the Aegon International Eastbourne in June. Two elegant Victorian **theatres** – the Devonshire Park Theatre and the Winter Garden – lie on the park's southern edge, alongside the modern Congress Theatre, but the Cultural Quarter only really gained its moniker when the **Towner Gallery** relocated in 2009. A £40-million regeneration of the area, due for completion in 2019, will see the park and theatres spruced up and a new plaza created, with the aim of establishing Devonshire Park as a "tennis and cultural destination".

Towner Art Gallery

Devonshire Park, BN21 4JJ • Tues–Sun & bank hols 10am–5pm • Free • **Tours** Times vary; 1hr • £6 • ☎ 01323 434670, ⓦtownereastbourne.org.uk

First opened in 1923 in a former manor house in Manor Gardens, the venerable **Towner Art Gallery** was relocated to a glamorous new home in Devonshire Park in 2009 – a sleek modern edifice of glass and smooth white curves. The award-winning gallery is the largest in the Southeast, and shows four or five major exhibitions of contemporary art a year, alongside rotating displays from its own permanent collection; it's especially well-known for its modern British art, in particular the work of **Eric Ravilious** (see box, p.208). Fascinating **tours** of the collection store (showing some of the four thousand-odd works not on display at any one time) run a couple of times a month, and there's a busy programme of events for children and families. Up on the second floor *Urban*

6

ERIC RAVILIOUS

Of all Sussex artists, **Eric Ravilious** (1903–42) – painter, wood engraver and designer – is perhaps the one who captured the local landscape the best. Ravilious was a local lad: he grew up in Eastbourne, the son of a shopkeeper, and in 1919 won a scholarship to the Eastbourne College of Art. In 1922 he started at the Royal College of Art in London, where he studied under Paul Nash, became close friends with Edward Bawden and spent much of his time chatting up women. He accepted a part-time teaching job at his old Eastbourne college in 1925, during which time he took his students sketching in Alfriston, Jevington and Wilmington, but it was only in the mid-1930s that Ravilious really rediscovered Sussex, travelling back to stay at **Furlongs**, a shepherd's cottage near Beddingham belonging to his friend and fellow artist Peggy Angus – a radical with a fondness for folk songs, home-made elderflower champagne and wild Midsummer's Eve parties. It was during these visits that Ravilious painted some of his best-known watercolours – quintessentially English evocations of prewar Sussex, where people are almost completely absent and the landscape takes centre stage.

By this point Ravilious was one of the best-known artists of the time, not only for his watercolours but also for his ceramic designs for Wedgwood and his wood engravings – one of which, of two top-hatted cricketers, graced the front cover of *Wisden Cricketer's Almanack* from 1938 to 2002. When war broke out, Ravilious served in the Observer Corps before becoming an **Official War Artist**. In 1942 he was out on a search-and-rescue mission in Iceland when his plane came down, and his life was cut tragically short, aged just 39.

Ground (see p.211) has a **café** with a small terrace looking over the Eastbourne rooftops to the Downs beyond. The Towner is one of three contemporary art galleries along the **Coastal Culture Trail** (see box, p.177), a joint initiative between the Towner, the Jerwood Gallery in Hastings and the De La Warr Pavilion in Bexhill.

Eastbourne Heritage Centre

2 Carlisle Rd, BN21 4BT • Mid-March to Oct Mon, Tues & Thurs 2–5pm, Fri 10am–1pm, Sat 10am–4pm; Nov to mid-March Sat 10am–4pm • £3 • ☎ 01323 411189, ⓦ eastbourneheritagecentre.co.uk

The compact **Eastbourne Heritage Centre** houses a modest collection of exhibits about the town, including old maps showing its growth from a few small villages into

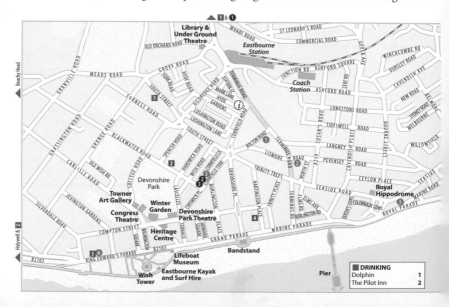

a grand Victorian resort. Changing exhibitions run a couple of times a year, and a small cinema in the basement shows films about the town, including a couple of fun promotional films from the 1960s and 1970s which enthusiastically extol the delights of the "suntrap of the South". The small shop is a good place for Eastbourne-themed souvenirs.

ARRIVAL AND DEPARTURE

EASTBOURNE

By train Eastbourne's splendid Italianate station is a 10min walk from the seafront up Terminus Road.
Destinations Brighton (every 20min; 35min); Hastings (every 20min; 30min); Lewes (every 20min; 30min); London Victoria (Mon–Sat 4 hourly, Sun 2 hourly; 1hr 20min–1hr 50min).
By bus The National Express coach station is on Junction Rd, right by the train station. Most local bus services are run by Stagecoach.
Destinations Brighton (every 10–15min; 1hr 15min); Hastings (Mon–Sat every 20min, Sun hourly; 1hr 10min); London Victoria (2 daily; 3hr 15min); Tunbridge Wells (Mon–Sat hourly; 50min).
By car There's pay-and-display parking all along the seafront.

GETTING AROUND AND INFORMATION

Dotto Train This land train (ⓦ stagecoachbus.com) runs along the seafront in summer, from Sovereign Harbour in the east to Holywell in the west, stopping en route at the Redoubt Fortress, the pier and the Wish Tower. June Sat & Sun, July & Aug daily 10am–5pm; hourly; £2, day-ticket unlimited travel £5.
Eastbourne Sightseeing bus Hop-on, hop-off buses (ⓦ eastbournesightseeing.com) run along the seafront and in a loop to Beachy Head, Birling Gap and East Dean.
Mid-March to Oct daily 10am–5pm; every 30min; 1hr for circuit; £10, valid 24hr.
Taxis Eastbourne and Country Taxis ☏ 01323 720720.
Tourist office 3 Cornfield Rd, just off Terminus Rd (March–May & Oct Mon–Fri 9am–5.30pm, Sat 9am–4pm; June–Sept Mon–Fri 9am–5.30pm, Sat 9am–5pm, Sun 10am–1pm; Nov–Feb Mon–Fri 9am–4.30pm, Sat 9am–1pm; ☏ 01323 415415, ⓦ visiteastbourne.com).

ACCOMMODATION

The Grand Hotel King Edwards Parade, BN21 4EQ ☏ 01323 412345, ⓦ grandeastbourne.com. The best address in town is the "White Palace", a grand Victorian edifice at the western end of the seafront, which over the years has welcomed Winston Churchill, Charlie Chaplin and – most famously – Charles Debussy, who worked on *La Mer* during a stay in 1905. Standard rooms are traditional in style, and there are two excellent restaurants (see p.210)

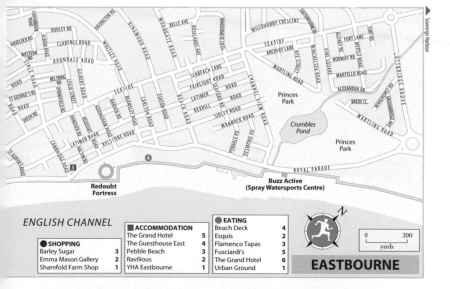

6

WATERSPORTS IN EASTBOURNE

If you thought tea dances were as animated as things got in Eastbourne, think again. Several outfits offer you the chance to get out and active on the water, whether exploring underwater wrecks, zipping along on RIBs or paddling more sedately in a sea kayak.

Buzz Active Spray Watersports Centre, Royal Parade, BN22 7LD ☎01323 417023, ⓦbuzzactive .org.uk. Taster windsurfing, sailing, kayaking and stand-up paddleboarding lessons (from £20, depending on size of group), plus longer courses. The last two activities are also available at Cuckmere (see box, p.214). Jan–April & Dec Mon–Fri; May–Nov daily.

Diving charters The Sussex coast has some of the best wreck dives in the country, and a handful of charter companies offer trips from Sovereign Harbour – check

out ⓦchanneldiving.com, ⓦsussexshipwrecks.co.uk and ⓦdive125.co.uk.

Eastbourne Kayak and Surf Hire By the Wish Tower ☎07917 863791. Sea-kayak and paddleboard hire on the beach (May Sat & Sun; June–Sept daily; £10/1hr, £15/2hr, £60/day).

Sussex Voyages Lower Quay Side, The Waterfront, Sovereign Harbour Marina, BN23 5UZ ☎01293 888780, ⓦsussexvoyages.co.uk. Popular trips in a rigid inflatable boat along the coast to Beachy Head (£25/1hr), and other RIB excursions.

and an in-house spa. **£240**

The Guesthouse East 13 Hartington Place, BN21 3BS ☎01323 722774, ⓦtheguesthouseeast.co.uk. Six of the seven en-suite rooms in this award-winning guesthouse come with their own small, well-equipped kitchenettes – perfect for families. If you're feeling too lazy to cook your own eggs in the morning you can pay extra for a delicious breakfast delivered to your door, or eat at the communal table. **£100**

Pebble Beach 53 Royal Parade, BN22 7AQ ☎01323 431240, ⓦpebblebeacheastbourne.com. Popular B&B with six stylish, good-value rooms set across three floors of a Victorian seafront townhouse, at the eastern end of town by the Redoubt. The nicest room (£110) is up on the first floor, with floor-to-ceiling windows and a private balcony

looking out to sea. Two-night minimum stay year-round. **£85**

Ravilious 16 Blackwater Rd, BN21 4AJ ☎01323 733142, ⓦravilioushotel.com. Stunning rooms – wooden floors, high ceilings and contemporary furniture – and a great location by Devonshire Park make this townhouse B&B a winner. The attic room (up three flights of stairs) is a bargain, but even the standard rooms (£105) are good value for the quality. Licensed bar. **£80**

YHA Eastbourne 1 East Dean Rd, BN20 8ES ☎0845 371 9316, ⓦyha.org.uk/eastbourne. Modern hostel in a quiet, leafy location on the western outskirts of town, just a mile from the centre. It's 400m from the start of the South Downs Way footpath (see p.212), so a good location for walkers. Dorms **£19**, doubles **£39**

EATING

★**Beach Deck** Royal Parade, BN22 7AE ☎01323 720320, ⓦthebeachdeck.co.uk. There's no better place in town for an alfresco meal than this lovely spot, with a big suntrap deck overlooking the beach and great food (including gluten-free options), ranging from crowd-pleasing burgers to fish caught fresh that morning. Summer Mon–Wed & Sun 8.30am–6pm, Thurs–Sat 8.30am–late; winter daily 9.30am–4pm.

Esquis 1 Pevensey Rd, BN21 3HJ ☎01323 430885. What this unprepossessing French bistro lacks in kerb appeal it more than makes up for with its fabulous food – and it's brilliant value, too. Two courses of traditional home-made food (Toulouse sausages, confit duck leg, tartiflette and the like) cost £12.95, three courses £13.95 (both £1 more at weekends). A little gem. Tues–Thurs & Sat 6–11pm, Fri noon–2pm & 6–11pm.

Flamenco Tapas 8 Cornfield Terrace, BN21 4NN ☎01323 641444, ⓦflamenco-tapas.co.uk. A little corner of Spain in Eastbourne, this traditional restaurant

– with cheery red paintwork and big windows opening onto the street in summer – has over 45 different tapas dishes (most around the £5 mark), 26 Spanish wines, and live flamenco and guitar performances throughout the year. Mon–Fri 5.30–9pm, Sat noon–2pm & 5.30–9pm.

★**Fusciardi's** 30 Marine Parade, BN22 7AY ☎01323 722128, ⓦfusciardiicecreams.co.uk. Established in 1967, this fabulous ice-cream parlour is an Eastbourne institution, with queues out the door on summer weekends. Over 18 flavours of home-made ice cream are on offer, as well as light meals and piled-high sundaes that are a work of art. Daily 9am–7pm; June–Aug generally open until 10/10.30pm.

The Grand Hotel King Edwards Parade, BN21 4EQ ☎01323 412345, ⓦgrandeastbourne.com. Of the two restaurants at *The Grand Hotel*, the award-winning *Mirabelle* is the one to go for if you want to treat yourself, with a dining room that's all timeless elegance and crisp white linen. Three courses at dinner cost £44 (£26 at lunch), or there's a tasting menu for £64. Elsewhere in the hotel, afternoon teas are served in the grand surrounds of the Great Hall (daily 2.45–6.30pm; £26). Tues–Sat 12.30–2pm & 7–10pm.

★**Urban Ground** 2A Bolton Rd, BN21 3JX

☎01323 410751, ⓦurbanground.co.uk. Fab little independent coffee shop – with a second branch in the Towner Gallery – serving up Union coffee alongside sandwiches, soups, Lebanese flatbreads and cakes. Mon–Sat 7.30am–6pm, Sun 9am–5pm.

DRINKING

Dolphin 14 South St, BN21 4XF ☎01323 746622, ⓦthedolphineastbourne.co.uk. Victorian pub in the centre of town, with a beautifully restored interior featuring open fires and comfy leather chesterfields. There's Brakspear and local ales on tap, and good home-cooked food including burgers (from £10.50) and local fish. Mon–Thurs 11am–11pm, Fri & Sat 11am–midnight, Sun noon–10.30pm; kitchen Mon–Thurs noon–2.30pm &

6–9.30pm, Fri & Sat noon–9.30pm, Sun noon–8pm.

The Pilot Inn 89 Meads St, BN20 7RW ☎01323 723440, ⓦpilot-inn.co.uk. Lovely, laidback pub in leafy Meads that's handy for lunch or a drink after a walk up Beachy Head (see p.212). It's dog- and walker-friendly, and (a big plus) the excellent seasonal pub food is available throughout the day (most mains £10–12). Mon–Sat 11am–11pm, Sun noon–10pm; kitchen Mon–Sat noon–9pm, Sun noon–6pm.

6

ENTERTAINMENT

Eastbourne is well-known for its plethora of **theatres**, three of which are clustered side-by-side in Eastbourne's "Cultural Quarter", backing onto Devonshire Park. At the time of writing, this area was undergoing a massive **redevelopment**, which will see the interior of the Grade II-listed Congress Theatre returned to its 1960s heyday, the Victorian facade of the Winter Garden restored and a new Welcome Centre built. The Congress Theatre will be closed during the works, reopening in mid-2018.

Congress Theatre Carlisle Rd, BN21 4BP ☎01323 412000, ⓦeastbournetheatres.co.uk. Modern, large theatre with an eclectic programme of live bands, comedy, musicals, theatre, ballet, classical music and more.

Devonshire Park Theatre Compton St, BN21 4BP ☎01323 412000, ⓦeastbournetheatres.co.uk. Drama, musicals and children's theatre are the mainstays of this Victorian theatre, as well as the annual panto.

Royal Hippodrome 108–112 Seaside Rd, BN21 3PF ☎01323 802020, ⓦroyalhippodrome.com. For many years the home of music hall in Eastbourne, the Hippodrome shows a year-round programme of comedies,

musicals and variety shows.

Under Ground Theatre Below Central Library, Grove Rd, BN21 4TL ☎0843 289 1980, ⓦundergroundtheatre.co.uk. Small, independently run performance space, hosting everything from jazz and folk bands to drama and film. Tickets available on the door, from the tourist information office or from the box office (☎0845 680 1926).

Winter Garden Compton St, BN21 4BP ☎01323 412000, ⓦeastbournetheatres.co.uk. Once a skating rink, the Winter Garden now hosts comedy, children's theatre, music, tea dances and big bands.

SHOPPING

★**Barley Sugar** 1 Cornfield Terrace, BN21 4NN ☎01323 734442, ⓦbarley-sugar.co.uk. This "artisan deli and lifestyle store" has a great deli counter, plus a small selection of homeware, toiletries, furniture and other goodies. There's also a lovely little café attached, which whips up tasty breakfasts and lunches using products from the deli. Mon–Sat 9am–5pm.

★**Emma Mason Gallery** 3 Cornfield Terrace, BN21 4NN ☎01323 727545, ⓦemmamason.co.uk. This fab little gallery sells original prints by British printmakers,

from the postwar period to the modern day, as well as books and cards. Regular exhibitions held throughout the year. Thurs–Sat 10am–5pm.

Sharnfold Farm Shop Stone Cross, BN24 5BU ☎01323 768490, ⓦsharnfoldfarm.co.uk. A 10min drive from Eastbourne, this excellent farm shop sells the farm's produce, home-made bread, cheeses and chutneys; it's also one of the best pick-your-own spots in this corner of Sussex. Tues–Sun 9.30–5pm.

Beachy Head and the Seven Sisters

The glorious stretch of coast between Eastbourne and Seaford is one of the longest expanses of undeveloped coastline on the south coast, a stunning, nine-mile-long pocket of pristine shoreline, dizzying white cliffs and sweeping chalk grassland, with beautiful views at every stride. It's one of the undoubted highlights of the South Downs National

6

THE SOUTH DOWNS WAY

The glorious, long-distance **South Downs Way** rises and dips for over a hundred miles along the chalk uplands between the city of Winchester and the spectacular cliffs at Beachy Head. If undertaken in its entirety, the bridle path is best walked from west to east, taking advantage of the prevailing wind, Eastbourne's better transport and accommodation, and the psychological appeal of ending at the sea: the heart-pumping hike along the Seven Sisters and Beachy Head makes a spectacular conclusion to the trail. Steyning, the halfway point, marks a transition from predominantly wooded sections to more exposed chalk uplands.

The OS *Explorer* **maps** OL11 and OL25 cover the eastern end of the route; you'll need OL10, OL8, OL3 and OL32 as well to cover the lot. A **guidebook** is advised, and several are available, including the official *South Downs Way National Trail Guide* (east–west; 1:25,000 OS mapping; Aurum Press); *The South Downs Way* (either direction; 1:50,000 OS mapping; Cicerone Press); and the *South Downs Way Trailblazer Guide* (west–east; hand-drawn maps; Trailblazer). Cicerone also publish *Mountain Biking on the South Downs*, which includes the South Downs Way. For more **information**, including details on **accommodation**, see ⓦ nationaltrail.co.uk/south-downs-way.

Park (see box above), and far from a secret – there's always a steady stream of walkers tramping along the blowy clifftops, enjoying what is arguably the finest coastal walk in the Southeast.

Beachy Head is the tallest of the cliffs and the closest to Eastbourne; to the west of it is the tiny hamlet and pebbly beach of **Birling Gap**, and then come the gently undulating cliffs of the **Seven Sisters**, which end at beautiful **Cuckmere Haven**. Inland lie the pretty villages of **East Dean** and **West Dean**, the latter nestled among the beech trees of **Friston Forest**.

ARRIVAL AND GETTING AROUND   BEACHY HEAD AND THE SEVEN SISTERS

By bus Bus #12 runs daily every 15min between Eastbourne and Brighton, via East Dean and Exceat. Bus #13X takes a detour along the clifftops and runs between Eastbourne and Brighton via Beachy Head, Birling Gap, East Dean and Exceat (late April to mid-June Sat & Sun hourly; mid-June to mid-Sept Mon–Fri 3 daily, Sat & Sun hourly). The Cuckmere Valley Ramblerbus runs between Berwick Station, Alfriston, Seaford, Exceat, Friston Forest (West Dean) and Wilmington (April–Oct Sat, Sun & bank hols;

hourly; ☎ 01323 870920, ⓦ cuckmerebuses.org.uk).
By sightseeing bus Hop-on, hop-off Eastbourne Sightseeing buses run from Eastbourne (see p.209).
By car Pay-and-display car parks at Beachy Head, Birling Gap (NT), Crowlink (NT), Exceat and Friston Forest (on the western side of the forest on the Litlington road; and on the eastern side at Butchershole on the Jevington road). There's also a free car park at East Dean.

INFORMATION

Seven Sisters Country Park Visitor Centre Exceat, on the A259 between Seaford and Eastbourne (March & Nov Sat & Sun 11am–4pm; April–Sept daily 10.30am–4.30pm; Oct daily 11am–4pm; volunteer run, so opening times can vary, especially in winter; ☎ 0345 608 0194, ⓦ sevensisters.org.uk). Information on walks and activities in the park, plus displays and exhibitions on its history, geology and wildlife.
Beachy Head Visitor Centre Beachy Head Rd (Easter–Oct Mon 1–4pm, Tues–Sun 10am–4pm; Nov Sat & Sun 11am–3pm; volunteer run, so opening times can vary,

especially in winter; ☎ 01323 737273, ⓦ beachyhead.org). Mainly a souvenir shop (which also sells maps and walking guides), but also has a small exhibition on the area's plant and animal life.
Birling Gap National Trust Visitor Centre Birling Gap (daily 10am–5pm, or 4pm in winter; ☎ 01323 423197, ⓦ nationaltrust.org.uk/birling-gap-and-the-seven-sisters). Lots of information on walks and the local area, with displays on wildlife, fossils and the changing coastline, including a dramatic video of a recent cliff fall. Free tracker packs for kids are available.

Beachy Head

At 530ft, majestic **Beachy Head** is the tallest chalk sea-cliff in the country, and probably the most famous, too, having been the backdrop for music videos, television dramas and films from *Quadrophenia* to *Atonement*. Every year the cliff recedes a little further, eroded by the battering waves below – up to 1.5ft a year, though in 1999 a record 20ft were lost in one spectacular early morning cliff fall, a warning to anyone tempted to stray too close to the edge. The views from the top on a clear day stretch as far as Dungeness in one direction and the Isle of Wight in the other, while down below at the foot of the cliffs is **Beachy Head lighthouse**, with its cheery red and white stripes, looking exactly as a lighthouse should. The construction of the lighthouse, completed in 1902 to replace the Belle Tout lighthouse further west (see box below), was no mean feat; 3600 tonnes of granite had to be winched down from the top of the cliff.

6

Beachy Head can be accessed by car or bus, but the nicest way is of course on foot. A steep two-mile-long path climbs up from the western end of Eastbourne to the blowy clifftop, where you'll find the Beachy Head Visitor Centre (see opposite) on Beachy Head Road.

★**Belle Tout** Beachy Head ☎01323 423185, ⓦbelletout.co.uk. For a real treat book into this old lighthouse (see box below), perched high up on the dramatic cliffs just west of Beachy Head. The cosy rooms boast stupendous views, there's a snug residents' lounge and – best of all – there's unrestricted access to the lamproom at the top of the lighthouse, where you can sit and watch the sun go down. **£195**

Birling Gap

Heading 2.5 miles west along the windswept clifftops from Beachy Head will bring you to **Birling Gap** – as its name implies, a natural dip in the cliffs. The cliff here is just 40ft high, and the pebbly **beach** below can be accessed via a metal staircase. It's a magical spot – totally unspoilt and never really overrun, with endless rockpools and even a stretch of sand at low tide, and all with the stunning backdrop of the Seven Sisters.

Up on the clifftop, the tiny hamlet of Birling Gap consists of little more than a few cottages and a National Trust-owned **visitor centre** (see opposite) and café, and is set to shrink even further; the cliff is retreating by over 2ft a year – with a whopping 9ft collapsing during winter storms in 2014 – and the National Trust is implementing a policy of "managed retreat", which in essence means abandoning the hamlet to its inevitable fate. Of the row of eight **coastguard's cottages** built in 1878, only four remain, and in a century the whole hamlet will have vanished and Birling Gap will have reverted to grassland. The National Trust runs special **events** throughout the year, everything from rockpool rambles to guided archeology walks – see ⓦnationaltrust.org.uk/birling-gap-and-the-seven-sisters for details.

East Dean

A mile inland from Birling Gap, **EAST DEAN** village is a popular starting point – or lunch stop – for walks along the Seven Sisters and Beachy Head. The old part of the village lies on and around the idyllic green, encircled by flint-walled cottages and a scattering of places to eat and drink.

BACK FROM THE BRINK: THE BELLE TOUT LIGHTHOUSE

Perched in glorious isolation on the clifftop between Beachy Head and Birling Gap, just 70ft from the crumbling edge, dumpy **Belle Tout lighthouse** was erected in 1832 and remained operational until 1902, when a more effective replacement was built at the foot of nearby Beachy Head. It hit the headlines in 1999 when its then owners, faced with the prospect of their home tumbling into the sea, had the 850-tonne building lifted up onto runners and slid back onto safer ground – an astonishing feat of engineering by any stretch of the imagination. The lighthouse has since been converted into a smart and stylish B&B (see above).

6

ACTIVITIES AT CUCKMERE HAVEN AND THE SEVEN SISTERS

While most visitors to Cuckmere Haven do little more than stroll the three-mile round-trip down to the sea and back, there's plenty to entertain more energetic types. **Walking trails** strike off in every direction and it's easy to lose the crowds; a couple of classic walks from Exceat are suggested below (both routes marked on OS *Explorer* map OL25). For cyclists there are excellent **mountain-bike trails** through Friston Forest, with climbs, drops and singletrack; at the time of writing the cycle hire shop at Exceat was closed – check with the Seven Sisters Country Park Visitor Centre (see p.212) to see if it has reopened. There's even the opportunity to get out on a **canoe** on the River Cuckmere's famous meanders.

WALKING

Exceat – Seven Sisters – East Dean – Friston Forest – Exceat 8 miles. This full-day walk takes in many of the area's scenic highlights, heading down along the beautiful Cuckmere Valley before climbing up and along the Seven Sisters, turning inland just before Birling Gap. The village of East Dean makes a perfect lunch stop, before you continue north to Friston Forest, where shady trails lead back to Exceat.

Exceat – Chyngton Farm – South Hill – Hope Gap – Cuckmere River – Exceat 4.5 miles. This walk takes you up onto the other side of the Cuckmere estuary, for superlative views of the Seven Sisters. From Exceat Bridge, you follow the west bank of the Cuckmere River for 200m before heading up a gentle incline to Chyngton Farm, and then south up to South Hill. From here a trail leads down to Hope Gap – where there's beach access at low tide for rockpooling – and then along the clifftop to the classic viewpoint of the Seven Sisters with the coastguard's cottages in the foreground. Once down at the beach, you can follow the west bank of the river upstream back to Exceat.

CANOEING AND STAND-UP PADDLEBOARDING

Buzz Cuckmere ☎ 01323 491289, 🌐 buzzactive .org.uk. Taster kayaking and stand-up paddleboarding lessons (from £20/person, depending on size of group), plus longer courses. Book in advance.

ACCOMMODATION AND EATING   **EAST DEAN**

Beehive on the Green The Green, BN20 0BY ☎ 01323 423631, 🌐 thebeehiveonthegreen.co.uk. This great little deli-café can provide everything you need for a picnic, from freshly baked pastries and artisan bread to local chutneys, cured hams, cheeses, local beer and home-made cakes. There are a few tables available. Tues–Sat 9.30am–4pm; Easter–Sept & Dec also open Sun 10am–4pm.

Tiger Inn The Green, BN20 0DA ☎ 01323 423209, 🌐 beachyhead.org.uk. With an idyllic location on the green in East Dean, this quintessentially English pub is the perfect spot for a summertime drink; ales include the award-winning Legless Rambler from the village's own Beachy Head Brewery. Five understated yet luxurious rooms make a good base for the area. Mon–Thurs 11am–10.30pm, Fri & Sat 11am–11.30pm, Sun 11am–10pm; kitchen daily noon–3pm & 6–9pm. **£130**

The Seven Sisters

From Birling Gap, the majestic, undulating curves of the **Seven Sisters** cliffs swoop off to the west, ending at Cuckmere Haven, where the River Cuckmere meets the sea. The three-mile walk along the springy turf of the clifftops, counting off the cliff summits (the Sisters) as you go, is exhilarating, though out-of-puff walkers beware – the "Seven" Sisters are actually eight, the result of the coastline retreating since they were named. The peaceful **Crowlink Valley** runs inland between two of the Sisters, Flagstaff and Brass Point, leading to a handy car park; the four-mile circular walk from Crowlink along the Seven Sisters to Birling Gap, then north to East Dean village and back to Crowlink (marked on OS *Explorer* map OL25), gives a perfect taster of the scenery.

At the western end of the Seven Sisters, Haven Brow rewards you with a wonderful view over Cuckmere Haven, before the trail heads down to the grassy valley floor. On the far side of the estuary you can see Seaford Head and the old **coastguard's cottages** that feature in the iconic view of the Seven Sisters you'll see on all the postcards; you can't cross the river mouth here, so to climb Seaford Head and see the view for yourself you'll need to head inland for 1.5 miles and then back to the coast along the river's western bank.

Cuckmere Haven

Beautiful **Cuckmere Haven**, the only undeveloped estuary in Sussex, is a famed beauty spot, and always busy with walkers, families and tourists ambling along the 1.5-mile-long main path that runs between the beach and the Exceat car park and visitor centre (see p.212) on the A259. Despite the steady flow of visitors it's still a gorgeous spot, with chalk downland, saltmarsh and shingle habitats all encountered in a half-hour stroll. The river's much-photographed **meanders** are actually nothing more than picturesque relics – the river itself flows through an artificial arrow-straight channel to the west, and has done since the channel was built in the 1840s.

6

As you follow the paved path you'll notice several **pillboxes** – squat concrete forts – set into the hillsides, and the remains of a tank trap between the beach and the saltmarsh – reminders of the role the valley played in **World War II**, when defences were put into place against a possible invasion. At night the valley was lit up to look like a town, in the hope that German planes would mistake the lights for Newhaven and so set their coordinates wrongly and miss their targets further north.

Friston Forest

The hilly slopes of tranquil **Friston Forest** (Ⓦforestry.gov.uk/fristonforest), which covers two thousand acres north of the A259 coast road, are popular with **walkers** and **mountain-bikers** alike; a free leaflet on the main trails is available from the car park. Buried away among the trees at the forest's western edge is the tiny village of **West Dean**, with a duck pond and squat-towered Norman church, while to the east, just outside the forest boundaries, is the old flint-walled smuggler's village of **Jevington**.

EATING AND DRINKING   FRISTON FOREST

Eight Bells Jevington, BN26 5QB ☎01323 484442, Ⓦ8bellsonline.co.uk. A proper country pub with loads of character and plenty of history too: the colourful Jevington Jig, leader of the Jevington smugglers' gang (see box, p.216), was once innkeeper here. Good home-cooked food features the likes of steak and ale pie (£10.50) and sausage and mash (£10), and there's a lovely garden. Mon–Sat 11am–11pm, Sun noon–10.30pm; kitchen Mon–Sat noon–3pm & 6–9pm, Sun noon–9pm.

LIE OF THE LAND

Chalk downland is one of Britain's richest **wildlife habitats**, thanks in large part to the sheep which have been grazing the Sussex downland since the Middle Ages, keeping the turf cropped short and allowing a unique – and rare – ecosystem of slow-growing plants to develop. Over forty different types of plants can grow in a single square yard, supporting an equally rich diversity of insects and small animals, including skylarks, six species of grasshopper, and the rare Adonis blue butterfly.

Chalk downland is in fact made up of a few different habitats, of which **grassland** – with its short, springy turf – is just one. Others include **scrub**, characterized by low-growing shrubs or bushes such as yellow-flowered gorse, hawthorn and blackthorn, which you'll see bent double by the wind up on Beachy Head; and **dew ponds**, man-made, clay-lined ponds built to retain rainwater for watering livestock.

Along the length of the Downs you'll see plenty of evidence, if you look closely enough, of **ancient settlements** and people, including flint mines dug by Neolithic man at Cissbury Ring; and Iron Age hillforts at Cissbury, Devil's Dyke, Chanctonbury Ring and Mount Caburn above Lewes, to name but a few. Even the footpaths that cut across the hills tell a story: many are old **drovers' routes** that have been worn away through centuries of use.

6

SMUGGLING ON THE SOUTH COAST

In the heyday of **smuggling**, in the late eighteenth to the early nineteenth centuries, there was scarcely a community along the Sussex and Kent coast that remained untouched by it, from Chichester in the west right up to Deal in the east. The counties were perfectly situated for the smuggling trade, just a short hop across the Channel from France – source of much of the contraband – and within easy distance of the rich consumers of London. Smuggling actually started with illegal exporting, when "owlers" smuggled wool to the continent to avoid paying wool tax. Later tobacco, brandy, tea and other luxuries were brought in from France in huge quantities; illegally imported gin was supposedly so plentiful in Kent at one point that villagers used it for cleaning their windows.

Smuggling was very much a community-wide affair, with whole villages involved in the trade, from wealthy landowners providing the capital and members of the clergy receiving the illegal goods to farm workers carrying and hiding the contraband. In Rottingdean near Brighton, the local vicar himself reportedly acted as a lookout.

Despite the air of romance, smuggling was often a brutal and unpleasant business, carried out by well-organized **gangs** with a reputation for violence. The gang leaders were often hardened criminals, and the locals who helped them generally did so due to a combination of fear and extreme poverty: a farm labourer could earn a week's salary in one night as a "tubman", carrying cargo from the beach to its hiding place.

Almost every village in the Alfriston area has its own infamous smuggler. At East Dean it was **James Dippery**, who managed to retain his enormous fortune by informing on his fellow smugglers. In Jevington, colourful petty criminal and innkeeper James Petit, known as **Jevington Jig**, ran a local gang that reputedly stored its ill-gotten booty in the tombs of the churchyard and the cellars of the local rectory. The Alfriston gang was led by the notorious **Stanton Collins**, and had its headquarters at *Ye Olde Smugglers Inn* – a perfect smugglers' hideaway, with 21 rooms, 6 staircases, 48 doors (some of them false) and secret tunnels thought to lead as far away as Wilmington.

The smuggling trade met little resistance from the authorities. The power of the Customs men was limited, and they could often be bribed to turn a blind eye. Although the arrival of the **coastguards** and blockade men had some success in curtailing the smugglers' activities, it wasn't until **free trade** – and reduced import duties – was introduced in the 1840s that smuggling finally came to an end.

Alfriston

As the River Cuckmere draws close to the sea, the final part of its journey takes it through the lower reaches of the beautiful Cuckmere Valley, where it loops lazily through the water meadows around **ALFRISTON**, one of the prettiest villages in Sussex. Its main street is a handsome huddle of wonky-roofed flint cottages, narrow pavements and low-slung timber-framed and tile-hung cottages, punctuated with not one but three creaky old hostelries, each awash with history and tales of smuggling derring-do. The weathered stump of the medieval **Market Cross** marks the High Street's northern end, while a hundred metres south a twitten cuts down to the idyllic village green, **The Tye**, and a view that's remained virtually unchanged for centuries, with the spire of fourteenth-century St Andrew's Church rising above a ring of trees.

Clergy House

The Tye, BN26 5TL • Mon–Wed, Sat & Sun: mid-March to Oct 10.30am–5pm; Nov & Dec 11am–4pm • £5.15; NT • ☎ 01323 871961, ⓦ nationaltrust.org.uk/alfriston-clergy-house

The small but perfectly formed **Clergy House**, a fourteenth-century Wealden hall house, was the very first building to be saved by the newly formed National Trust, who bought it in 1896 for the princely sum of £10 and rescued it from demolition. The thatched, timber-framed dwelling has been faithfully restored, with a large central hall and a floor made in the Sussex tradition from pounded chalk sealed with sour milk. The brick chimney was a later addition – fires would originally have been lit in the open hall in the middle of the house, with smoke rising up to escape from the eaves.

Rathfinny Wine Estate

Estate Alfriston, BN26 5TU • Tours generally April–Oct Fri & Sat: wine-makers' tour with lunch £55; afternoon tea tour £35 • ☎ 01323 871 031 • **Gun Room** The Tye, Alfriston, BN26 5TL • Daily 10am–4pm • ☎ 01323 870022 • ⊚ rathfinnyestate.com

The **Rathfinny Wine Estate**, on the southern outskirts of Alfriston, was founded in 2010 with the aim of producing some of the world's best sparkling wine, and is on track to become one of the largest single vineyards in Europe. Its first sparkling vintage will be bottled in 2018; until then you'll have to make do with its still wines, which can be sampled on a vineyard **tour** or at the winery's shop-cum-cellar door, the **Gun Room**, on Alfriston's village green. The Gun Room also has a small exhibition area upstairs, with displays about Alfriston and the Cuckmere Valley. You can pick up maps here for the **Rathfinny Trail**, a 1.5mile-long walking trail which winds through a small section of the beautifully sited vineyard.

ARRIVAL AND DEPARTURE

ALFRISTON

By train and bus The nearest train station, in Berwick, has hourly connections to Brighton, Lewes and Eastbourne. The Cuckmere Valley Ramblerbus operates an hourly circular service (50min) from Berwick Station via Alfriston, Seaford, the Seven Sisters Country Park and Wilmington (April–Oct Sat, Sun & bank hols; ☎ 01323 870920, ⊚ cuckmerebuses.org.uk).

By car The village's two car parks – one pay-and-display, the other free (max 3hr) – are on either side of the road at the northern edge of the village.

ACCOMMODATION AND EATING

★**Badgers Tea House** North St, BN26 5UG ☎ 01323 871336, ⊚ badgersteahouse.com. Once the village bakery, this sixteenth-century cottage is now a classy tearoom with a courtyard garden and a cosy, flagstone interior. Tea is served the way it should be – in silver teapots and with bone china crockery – and cakes are freshly baked on the premises. Especially recommended are the cheese and pecan scones, and the signature cake – a gloriously artery-clogging fresh cream, gooseberry and elderflower sponge. Breakfasts, sandwiches, soups and salads are also available. Mon–Fri 9.30am–4pm, Sat & Sun 10am–4.30pm.

GUARDIAN OF THE DOWNS: THE LONG MAN OF WILMINGTON

Ancient fertility symbol or eighteenth-century folly? No one really has a clue what the **Long Man of Wilmington** is, how long he's been there or why he was carved into a Sussex hillside in the first place. This huge figure – 231ft tall, and designed to look in proportion when seen from below – is sited on the steep flank of Windover Hill, two miles northeast of Alfriston by the tiny village of Wilmington. He's one of only two human hill figures in the country (the other is the Cerne Abbas Giant in Dorset).

Various **theories** have been put forward for his origin: some believe that the figure is Roman or Anglo-Saxon; others that it is the work of a medieval monk from the nearby Wilmington priory; while recent studies have suggested that the figure may well date from the sixteenth century, perhaps the work of a landowner "marking" his land.

The Long Man was originally an indentation in the grass rather than a solid line – the pin-sharp outline you can see today was only created in 1874 when the lines were marked out in yellow bricks, replaced by concrete in 1969 (and briefly painted green during World War II, to prevent enemy planes using the landmark for navigation). The earliest known drawing of the figure, made in 1710, suggests that it once had facial features, and a helmet-shaped head. Sadly, local folklore claiming that the Long Man once sported a penis, later removed by prudish Victorians, is probably apocryphal.

A **car park** lies at the southern end of Wilmington village, from where footpaths lead up to the figure.

6

Flint Barns Rathfinny Estate, BN26 5TU ☎01323 874030, ⓦrathfinnyestate.com. Set amidst the vines at Rathfinny Estate, this beautifully converted barn has a mix of doubles and family rooms (ten in all) – all equally tasteful, with oak floors, crisp white duvets and woollen throws – plus a cosy lounge equipped with books, board games and a wood burner. Dinner is available if there's enough demand (order in advance – two courses £20). Closed for harvest (generally mid-Sept to mid-Oct) and pruning (six weeks in Jan/Feb). Doubles <u>£95</u>, family rooms <u>£200</u>

George Inn High St, BN26 5SY ☎01323 870319, ⓦthegeorge-alfriston.com. Venerable timber-framed inn with sloping floors, low beams and a huge inglenook

fireplace, plus a peaceful walled garden out the back. The food is very good, and ranges from platters and sandwiches (£7.50) through to mains (£12–18) such as rack of South Downs lamb or monkfish wrapped in Parma ham. Daily 11am–11pm; kitchen noon–9pm.

★**Wingrove House** High St, BN26 5TD ☎01323 870276, ⓦwingrovehousealfriston.com. A stay at this stylish, colonial-style "restaurant and rooms" is a treat from start to finish. There are just seven rooms, and it's popular, so book ahead. The excellent restaurant (mains £14–20) uses local, free-range, seasonal ingredients, and lists its suppliers on the menu. Mon–Sat noon–2pm & 6–9.30pm, Sun noon–2pm & 6–8pm. <u>£120</u>

SHOPPING

Alfriston Village Store By the Market Cross, BN26 5UE ☎01323 870201. This great little village store, with a well-preserved 1891 interior, has all you could possibly need for a picnic on the riverbank, including freshly baked bread and a well-stocked deli. Mon–Sat 8am–7pm, Sun 10am–5pm.

★**Much Ado Books** 8 West St, BN26 5UX ☎01323

871222, ⓦmuchadobooks.com. Award-winning bookshop with a great selection of both new and secondhand books (including lots on the Bloomsbury Group and the local area). Craft workshops and other events are held in the neighbouring barn. Mon–Fri 10am–5pm, Sat 10am–5.30pm, Sun 11am–5pm.

From Alfriston to Lewes

A mile north of Alfriston, the Alfriston Road meets the A27, which zips west towards Lewes, shadowing the hulking South Downs ridge. Detours off the busy main road include **Charleston**, the fascinating country home of the Bloomsbury Group, as well as some lovely village pubs at **Berwick**, **Firle** and **Glynde** – each of them perfectly sited for post-pub rambles into the hills. Foodies should make a point of stopping off at **Middle Farm**'s excellent farm shop and at the English Wine Centre, where you can pick up a few bottles of Sussex's world-class bubbly – essential if you're planning on an interval picnic on the lawns of the famous Glyndebourne opera house.

| GETTING AROUND | FROM ALFRISTON TO LEWES |

By train Hourly trains run from Lewes to Eastbourne via Glynde and Berwick stations.

By bus Bus #125 runs from Lewes along the A27 via Glynde, Firle, Berwick and Alfriston to Eastbourne (Mon–Sat 4 daily).

On foot A 14-mile section of the South Downs Way long-distance footpath runs between Alfriston and Lewes, along the top of the Downs escarpment. A low-level alternative, the Old Coach Road, threads along the foot of the Downs between Alfriston and Firle.

Berwick

The village of **Berwick** is split in two by the A27: the village proper – where you'll find a beautiful **church** decorated by the Bloomsbury Group – lies just south of the road, while Berwick train station sits two miles north. The big-hitter tourist attraction in the parish is **Drusillas Park**, a few hundred metres east of the village, which calls itself (with some justification) the best small zoo in the country.

Berwick Church

Berwick village, off the A27, BN26 5QS • Daily 10am–dusk • Free • ⓦ berwickchurch.org.uk

From the outside, the little flint-walled **Berwick Church** looks distinctly ordinary, but step inside and you'll see why there's a steady trickle of tourists to this quiet spot. During World War II, **Duncan Grant** and his lover **Vanessa Bell** – residents of nearby Charleston Farmhouse (see p.220) – were commissioned by Bishop George Bell of Chichester to decorate the church with murals, a rather enlightened move given that the couple were unmarried, not practising Christians and pacifists to boot. Bell was keen to promote the relationship between Art and the Church, and also to continue the tradition of mural painting in Sussex churches, which had come to an end after the Reformation. What resulted was a series of murals painted by the couple and Vanessa's son, **Quentin Bell**, depicting biblical events set against a backdrop of rural wartime Sussex. Sir Charles Reilly, who had recommended Grant to Bishop Bell, commented that entering the church was "like stepping out of a foggy England into Italy".

The artists used themselves, locals and friends as models. In **The Nativity** (north side of the nave), Vanessa's daughter, Angelica, was the model for Mary, with farm workers posing as the shepherds, and the spruced-up children of Vanessa's housekeeper and gardener forming the onlookers – all set against the local Sussex landscape. The largest painting in the church, on top of the chancel arch, is **Christ in Majesty**; here Christ is flanked on the right by the then Rector of Berwick and Bishop Bell, and on the left by three local men representing the three armed forces; the soldier, Douglas Hemming, son of the stationmaster, was later killed in action. Perhaps the most beautiful of the murals, however, are also the simplest: four roundels on the rood screen depicting the **Four Seasons**, scenes of ordinary rural life, interspersed with two panels depicting the pond at Charleston at dawn and dusk.

Drusillas Park

Alfriston Rd, just off the A27, BN26 5QS • Daily: March–Oct 10am–6pm; Nov–Feb 10am–5pm • £14–18.50 depending on season; cheaper tickets available if booked online • ☎ 01323 874100, ⓦ drusillas.co.uk

Multi-award-winning **Drusillas Park** is a massive hit with kids, though it does get full to bursting in the summer holidays. There's been a zoo here since the 1930s and today it houses more than a hundred different small species, everything from penguins to porcupines. There are plenty of other attractions alongside the animals, including a brilliant adventure playground and a water play area.

English Wine Centre

Alfriston Rd, by the A27, BN26 5QS • **Shop** Tues–Sun 10am–5pm • Free • **Wine-tasting lunches** Monthly, first Sat • £42.50 • ☎ 01323 870164, ⓦ englishwinecentre.co.uk

If you've not yet caught on to the success story of English wine (see box, p.28) you're in for a big surprise at the **English Wine Centre**, where a whopping 150 varieties are on sale. The shop generally has a few wines out for tasting, and also runs monthly **wine-tasting lunches** – a taster of eight English wines followed by a slap-up lunch of Sussex bangers and cheeses.

ACCOMMODATION AND EATING   **BERWICK**

★**Cricketers' Arms** Berwick village, just off the A27 (south side), BN26 6SP ☎01323 870469, ⓦ cricketersberwick.co.uk. Get here early in summer to bag one of the picnic tables in the flower-filled cottage garden of this pretty flint village pub – one of the nicest spots in the area for an alfresco pint. Food ranges from seafood platters (£13) to ham, egg and chips (£12), and there's well-kept Harvey's on tap. Mon–Thurs 11am–10.30pm, Fri & Sat 11am–11pm, Sun noon–10.30pm; kitchen daily noon–8/9pm.
The English Wine Centre Alfriston Rd, by the A27

roundabout, BN26 5QS ☎01323 870164, ⓦ englishwinecentre.co.uk. The excellent *Flint Barn Restaurant* at the English Wine Centre is a good place to crack open a bottle or two of England's finest and tuck into some Sussex-sourced food, perhaps rump of Sussex lamb or sea bass with samphire (mains £15–22, cheaper at lunch). Five super-comfortable bedrooms in the adjoining *Green Oak Lodge* are just a short waddle away if you want to over-indulge. Restaurant Wed, Thurs & Sun noon–3pm, Fri & Sat noon–3pm & 6.30–9pm. **£135**

Charleston Farmhouse

Six miles east of Lewes, signposted off the A27, BN8 9LL • Late March–June & Oct Wed–Sat 1–6pm, Sun & bank hols 1–5.30pm; July–Sept Wed–Sat noon–6pm, Sun & bank hols 1–5.30pm; note that Wed–Sat entry is by guided tour only (1hr), while on Sun & bank hols rooms are stewarded and you can move about freely; garden open same hours as house (not part of tour); last entry 1hr before closing • House and garden £12, garden only £4.50 • ☎ 01323 811626, ⓦ charleston.org.uk

Hidden away at the end of a meandering lane under the hulking Downs, **Charleston Farmhouse** was the country home of the **Bloomsbury Group**, an informal circle of writers, artists and intellectuals who came together in the early decades of the twentieth century (see box below). The farmhouse was rented by **Vanessa Bell** and the love of her life **Duncan Grant**, who moved here in 1916, in order that Grant and his lover **David Garnett** – pacifists and conscientious objectors – could work on local farms (farm labourers were exempt from military service). It was a rather unconventional household to say the least, housing not only the amicable love triangle of Vanessa, Grant and Garnett, but also Vanessa's two young sons from her marriage-in-name-only to **Clive Bell**, who himself was an intermittent visitor, until he settled permanently there in 1939. The farmhouse became a gathering point for other members of the Bloomsbury Group, including the biographer and historian **Lytton Strachey**, the novelist **E.M. Forster**, economist **John Maynard Keynes** and Vanessa's sister **Virginia Woolf**.

Vanessa's children enjoyed a childhood of almost complete liberty, and perhaps not surprisingly all grew up embracing the artistic life, her eldest son Julian becoming a poet, second son Quentin an art historian and potter, and Angelica, her daughter with Duncan Grant, a painter. Vanessa died in 1961, and Duncan Grant in 1978. The dilapidated house was bought by the Charleston Trust, restored and opened to the public, retaining the warm, lived-in feeling of a family home.

THE BLOOMSBURY GROUP

The group of artists, writers and thinkers that came to be known as the **Bloomsbury Group** had its beginnings in Cambridge, where the brother of **Virginia Woolf** and **Vanessa Bell**, Thoby, studied alongside Leonard Woolf (Virginia's future husband), Clive Bell (Vanessa's future husband), E.M. Forster, John Maynard Keynes, Roger Fry and Lytton Strachey (whose cousin, **Duncan Grant**, would later set up home with Vanessa at Charleston Farmhouse). The men graduated in 1904, the same year that Virginia and Vanessa's father died. Vanessa promptly rented a property in Gordon Square in **Bloomsbury**, painted the door a defiant red, and set up home with her siblings. Thoby's Cambridge friends began to meet at the house, sharing ideas and discussing their work with each other and the sisters, and in time, the "Bloomsbury Group" was born.

Artistically, the art critic **Roger Fry** was a huge influence on the group. It was he who brought over the first post-Impressionist exhibitions from France in 1910 and 1912, which were greeted with horror by the general public whose idea of proper art was the photorealist representation of the Victorian age. In the wake of the exhibitions, Fry, Grant and Vanessa set up the **Omega workshops** in 1913, to bring post-Impressionism to the decorative arts – furniture, ceramics, textiles and more. The idea that art did not have to be confined to a picture frame was a guiding principle behind the exuberant decorations at **Charleston Farmhouse**, where Vanessa and Grant moved in 1916.

The **values** of the Bloomsbury Group were, primarily, a loathing and rejection of Victorian conventions – its worthiness, hypocrisy, prudishness, militarism, sexism and homophobia. Instead there was a focus on individual pleasure, friendship, pacifism and truth to oneself and one's sexuality – the last of these resulting in a bewildering amount of bed-hopping and all sorts of complicated **love triangles**: Keynes was a lover of both Strachey and Grant before he settled down with a Russian ballerina; while Vanessa, though married to Clive Bell, lived with Grant and had a child with him, **Angelica** (who was recognized by Bell to avoid scandal). Grant slept with any number of men during his years with Vanessa, among them Keynes, Strachey and writer **David Garnett**, who eventually ended up – in a move that horrified Vanessa and Grant – marrying the young Angelica.

The house

Bell and Grant saw the house as a blank canvas: almost every surface is **decorated** – fireplaces, door panels, bookcases, lamp bases, screens. Many of the fabrics, lampshades and other artefacts bear the unmistakeable mark of the **Omega workshops** (see box opposite), the Bloomsbury equivalent of William Morris's artistic movement. In the **dining room**, the dark distempered walls with a stencilled pattern might seem commonplace to modern eyes but at the time would have been daringly modern; so too the painted circular table, signifying equality between the sexes, where women were not required to leave the table after dinner and could enter into discussions with men on an equal footing.

Around the house, the walls are hung with **paintings** by Picasso, Renoir and Augustus John, alongside the work of the residents. Portraits of friends and family abound, nowhere more so than in **Vanessa's bedroom**; above her bed is a large portrait of her beloved son Julian, who was killed in 1937 while working as an ambulance driver in the Spanish Civil War. Vanessa never really recovered, and a further blow came in 1941, when her sister committed suicide.

The garden, gallery and other buildings

Charleston's **walled garden** was created by Vanessa and Duncan Grant, working to the designs of their friend, the art critic Roger Fry. The garden was very much a painters' garden, crammed with plants chosen for their colours and shapes, and dotted with idiosyncratic sculptures by Duncan Grant and Quentin Bell; Quentin wrote that it was "as though the exuberant decoration of the interior had spilled through the doors". The garden was neglected after Vanessa's death, but over the last thirty years it has been beautifully brought back to life.

Elsewhere on the Charleston site, work has begun on the brand-new, purpose-built **Wolfson Gallery** which will host changing exhibitions exploring the Bloomsbury Group's artistic and literary heritage. Other buildings such as the listed Barns (being restored in 2017) are used for the Trust's programme of creative **workshops, talks and events**, including the **Charleston Festival** at the end of May and the **Small Wonder** short-story festival in September.

Middle Farm

Firle, 4 miles east of Lewes on the A27, BN8 6LJ • **Farm shop, restaurant & cider centre** Daily 9.30am–5.30pm • Free • **Open farm** Generally daily 9.30am–5pm • £5 • ☎ 01323 811411, ⓦ middlefarm.com

Opened in the 1960s, **Middle Farm** is one of the oldest farm shops in the country, and is a great place to stock up on local produce. The main draw for many, however, is the **National Collection of Cider and Perry**, a small barn crammed floor-to-ceiling with barrels housing over a hundred varieties of draught cider and perry, alongside meads, country wines, ales and more; tasting glasses are provided so you can compare ciders before filling a bottle with the tipple of your choice. Elsewhere on the site there's an open farm for children and a café-restaurant.

Firle

Four miles from Lewes, tiny **West Firle** – known generally as **Firle** – is a perfect Sussex village, with brick- and flint-walled cottages lining the main street, a handsome old pub, the *Ram Inn*, and an idyllically sited cricket ground fringed by swaying oaks – home to **Firle Cricket Club** (ⓦ firlecc.com), one of the oldest in the world, formed in 1758.

Several members of the Bloomsbury set, Vanessa Bell among them, are buried in the churchyard of **St Peter's**, at the far end of The Street. Inside the church, there's a beautiful piece of modern stained glass in the organ vestry – a depiction of Blake's *Tree of Life*, designed in 1985 by English artist John Piper; look out for the local Southdown sheep at the bottom of the window.

6

Firle Place

The Street, Firle, BN8 6NS • Generally June–Sept Mon–Thurs & Sun 2–4.30pm; see website for more details • £9 • ☎ 01273 858567, ⓦ firle.com

Beyond St Peter's church lies handsome **Firle Place**, originally Tudor but remodelled in the eighteenth century with Caen stone, probably taken from the Priory ruins in nearby Lewes (see p.226). Firle Place has been the home of the Gage family for over five hundred years – Sir John, who built the manor house, served as Lord Chamberlain under Henry VIII, while his son, Edward, has a rather more ignominious place in history, having supervised the arrest and burning of the Lewes martyrs (see box, p.228). The family still lives in the house today, giving it an appealingly homely air, with family knick-knacks sitting alongside Gainsborough family portraits, Chippendale cabinets and Sèvres porcelain. It's best to visit on a weekday if you can, when visits are by informative guided **tour**.

ACCOMMODATION AND EATING   FIRLE

Beanstalk Tea Garden Old Coach Road, Firle Estate, BN8 6PA ☎ 01273 858906, ⓦ facebook.com/ BeanstalkTeaGarden. Idyllic summer-only tea garden – complete with resident peacock – hidden away at the foot of the Downs, a 20min walk (or bumpy drive) from Firle along the Old Coach Road. Cakes, afternoon teas and light lunches are served all day. Generally April to early Sept Wed–Sun & bank hols 11am–5.30pm.

Firle Camp Heighton St, Firle Estate, BN8 6NZ ☎ 07733 103309, ⓦ firlecamp.co.uk. Lovely back-to-basics campsite in a gorgeous meadow location, overlooked by the Downs, and with the Middle Farm shop (see p.221) and a handful of good pubs within walking distance. Fires allowed. Per adult **£11.50**

Ram Inn Firle village, BN8 6NS ☎ 01273 858222, ⓦ raminn.co.uk. This sprawling pub is a corker, with a lovely walled garden and, inside, wooden floors, slate-grey walls and roaring fires in winter. Food is good, and local – bread is baked in nearby Glynde, and game comes from the Firle Estate – though not cheap (mains £12–22). There are five gorgeous rooms above the pub. Daily 9am–11pm; kitchen Mon–Sat 9–11am, noon–3pm & 6.30–9.30pm, Sun 9–11am, noon–4pm & 6.30–9.30pm. **£110**

Glynde

Three miles east of Lewes, just north of the A27, the tiny estate village of **Glynde** is best known for its world-famous opera house, **Glyndebourne**, which lies just up the road. The village itself is a bit of a backwater, mainly visited by people heading to Glyndebourne and walkers stopping off at the excellent *Trevor Arms* pub.

The village was built and is still owned by the Glynde Estate; the estate's manor house, **Glynde Place** (☎ 01273 858224, ⓦ glynde.co.uk), a handsome Elizabethan affair built in Sussex flint with wonderful views across the Weald, lies at the northern fringe of the village. It's currently closed for restoration, but is due to reopen in 2017 – check the website for information.

Glyndebourne

1 mile north of Glynde, BN8 5UU • ☎ 01273 812321, ⓦ glyndebourne.com

Founded in 1934, **Glyndebourne** is one of the world's best opera houses, and Britain's only unsubsidized one. It's best known for the **Glyndebourne Festival** (mid-May to Aug), an indispensable part of the high-society calendar, when opera-goers in evening dress throng to the country house with hampers, blankets and candlesticks to picnic on the lawns; the operas themselves are performed in an award-winning theatre, seating 1200. **Tickets** for the season's six productions sell out quickly, and are eye-wateringly expensive, but there are some standing-room-only ones available at reduced prices (from £10), as well as discounts for under-30s (register beforehand to be eligible).

6

UP, UP AND AWAY: PARAGLIDING IN SUSSEX

On balmy summer's days, you can't fail to notice the colourful canopies of **paragliders** floating in the thermals above the Downs near Lewes. Two local companies offer lessons; you can be up in the air flying solo in just one day.

Airworks Paragliding Centre Old Station, Glynde ☎ 01273 434002, ⊛ www.airworks.co.uk. Small-group tuition in paragliding and paramotoring (powered paragliding). One-day introductory paragliding or paramotoring courses £130 (£150 weekends); five-day Elementary Pilot course £590; 20min tandem rides £99.

FlySussex Paragliding On the A27, 2 miles east of Lewes, between Glynde and Firle ☎ 01273 858170, ⊛ flysussex.com. The largest flying centre in the UK, with their own private flying sites and year-round lessons. One-day introductory paragliding courses £130 (£150 weekends), five-day Elementary Pilot course £590; 30min tandem rides £130.

EATING AND DRINKING   **GLYNDE**

Trevor Arms The Street, BN8 6SS ☎ 01273 858208, ⊛ trevorarms.com. Great village pub with a big garden, and good home-cooked food at non-gastro prices; mains such as pies and fish and chips are around the £10 mark. Best of all, you can come here for lunch or a pint after the lovely three-mile walk over Mount Caburn from Lewes, then take the train back. Daily noon–11pm; kitchen Mon noon–3pm, Tues–Fri noon–3pm & 6–9pm, Sat & Sun noon–9pm.

Lewes and around

East Sussex's county town, **LEWES**, couldn't be in a lovelier spot, straddling the River Ouse and with some of England's most appealing chalk downlands right on its doorstep. With a remarkably good-looking centre, a lively cultural and artistic scene, plenty of history, and a proud sense of its own identity (it even has its own currency), Lewes is one of Sussex's finest towns.

Lewes Castle

169 High St • Mon & Sun 11am–5.30pm (dusk in winter), Tues–Sat 10am–5.30pm (dusk in winter); closed Mon in Jan • £7.40, joint ticket with Anne of Cleves House £11.80 • ☎ 01273 486290, ⊛ sussexpast.co.uk

The town's splendid Norman fortress, **Lewes Castle**, was the work of William de Warenne, who was given the land by William I after the Conquest. Originally a simple motte-and-bailey construction, the castle was enlarged in 1100 and a second motte (or mound) was added, together with a gateway and curtain walls. Castles built on two mottes were very unusual: Lewes is one of only two examples in England (Lincoln is the other). Just a single wall remains of the Norman gateway today; the majestic arrow-slitted gateway you see in front of it – the **Barbican** – was built in the early fourteenth century for added fortification. The last of the De Warennes died without heir in 1347 and the castle began its slow slide into decay, until the romantic ruins were reinvented as a tourist attraction in the eighteenth century.

Inside the complex, narrow stone steps climb up inside the Barbican to the roof, with its excellent views over the town. The best views, however, can be had from the eleventh-century **Shell Keep**, which tops one of the castle's two mottes. From here you can see the other motte, **Brack Mount**, now just a grassy hillock and closed to the public, as well as the hills to the north of town where the **Battle of Lewes** took place in 1264. The battle was the bloody culmination of a clash between Henry III and a rebel army of barons under Simon de Montfort; the king was defeated and the resulting treaty, the **Mise of Lewes**, restricted his authority and forced him to assemble a governing council – often described as the first House of Commons.

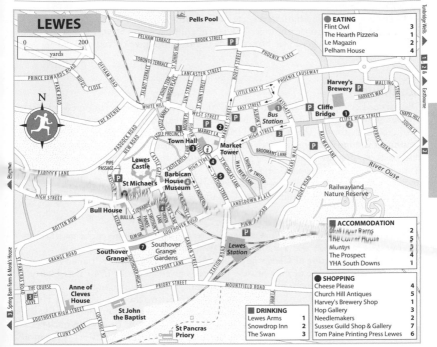

Barbican House Museum

The castle ticket office is also the entrance to the **Barbican House Museum**, which has exhibits on Sussex life from the Stone Age through to medieval times. A twelve-minute film tells the history of Lewes with the help of a model of the town as it would have looked in the 1880s. You can also see a tapestry created in 2014, using thirteenth-century embroidery techniques, to mark the 750th anniversary of the Battle of Lewes.

The High Street

Georgian and crooked older dwellings line Lewes's handsome **High Street**. A few minutes' walk west from the castle you'll pass **St Michael's Church**, one of the oldest in Lewes, with unusual twin towers, one wooden shingle and the other flint. On the opposite side of the road is the fifteenth-century **Bull House**, where revolutionary and pamphleteer **Thomas Paine** lived from 1768 to 1774 before emigrating to America, where he wrote *Common Sense*, the pamphlet that made his name and earned him the title "Father of the American Revolution".

THE LEWES POUND

Created to encourage the local economy, the **Lewes pound** was launched to much fanfare and national press attention in 2008. The currency's still in circulation – though it's rare to be handed one in your change – and is available in £1, £5, £10 and £21 denominations, with the same value as sterling. It's accepted by over a hundred businesses around town, including stallholders at the farmers' markets, and is issued at various locations, among them the Town Hall, Cheese Please (see p.229) and the Harvey's Brewery Shop (see p.229). The current issue of Lewes pounds is valid until 2020. Visit Ⓦ thelewespound.org to find out more.

On either side of the High Street, enticing narrow lanes – "twittens" – strike off into the backstreets; most photogenic is steep, cobbled **Keere Street**, down which the reckless Prince Regent (see box, p.240) is alleged to have driven his carriage for a bet.

Southover

The part of Lewes known as **Southover**, to the south of the High Street, grew up around St Pancras Priory (see below) and was separated from Lewes by the Winterbourne stream. The stream still trickles, sporadically, through beautiful **Southover Grange Gardens** (daily dawn–dusk), a favourite picnic spot with locals. A hole-in-the-wall kiosk (Easter–Oct) sells ice creams, sandwiches and snacks. The gardens surround **Southover Grange**, built in 1572 from St Pancras Priory's remains, and once the childhood home of the diarist John Evelyn. A section of the Grange is given over to the Sussex Guild Shop & Gallery (see p.229).

Anne of Cleves House

52 Southover High St, BN7 1JA • Feb to mid-Dec Mon & Sun 11am–5pm, Tues–Sat 10am–5pm; sometimes closed for private functions – call to check • £5.60, joint ticket with Lewes Castle £11.80 • ☎ 01273 474610, ⓦ sussexpast.co.uk

Despite the name, Anne of Cleves never actually lived in the timber-framed **Anne of Cleves House**: it was one of nine Sussex properties given to her in 1540 after Henry ignominiously cast her aside after less than a year of marriage, making her one of the richest women in the country – not a bad deal considering the fate of some of Henry's other wives. The building, a Wealden hall house, was constructed in the late fifteenth century by a wealthy yeoman farmer and would originally have been open to the rafters like the Clergy House in Alfriston (see p.216). The house today is for the most part presented as it would have been in Tudor times – the highlight being a magnificent oak-beamed bedroom complete with a 400-year-old Flemish four-poster – but two rooms are given over to exhibits on the Sussex Wealden **iron industry** and the **history of Lewes**.

St Pancras Priory

Access via Cockshut Lane or Mountfield Rd • Always open • Free • ⓦ lewespriory.org.uk

South of Southover High Street sprawl the evocative ruins of **St Pancras Priory**, founded around 1078 by William de Warenne, who also built Lewes Castle. Little remains of the priory today, but interpretive boards do an excellent job of conjuring up what the crumbling stones would have looked like in its heyday, when it was one of the largest and most powerful monasteries in England, with a church the size of Westminster Abbey and land holdings as far north as Yorkshire. Most of the priory was destroyed during the Reformation, and the site became a quarry for building materials – stones from here ended up being used all over Lewes.

Cliffe

At the east end of the High Street, School Hill descends towards **Cliffe Bridge** – the entrance to **Cliffe**, commercial centre of the medieval settlement. On the far side of the bridge you can't miss the Victorian Gothic tower of **Harvey's Brewery**, while semi-pedestrianized **Cliffe High Street** strikes off ahead, with antiques shops and cafés spilling out onto the pavements. At the end of the street, steep, narrow **Chapel Hill** leads straight up on to the Downs – the start of a lovely three-mile walk to the village of Glynde (see p.222) – while South Street runs south to the *Snowdrop Inn* (see p.229), named after the deadliest avalanche in British history when, in 1836, a ledge of snow fell from the cliff onto the houses below, killing eight people.

Harvey's Brewery

The Bridge Wharf Brewery, BN7 2AH • ☎ 01273 480209, ⓦ harveys.org.uk

Affectionately known locally as Lewes Cathedral, **Harvey's Brewery** is the oldest brewery in Sussex. Sussex Best bitter – one of a handful of cask ales – is the most popular brew, but the brewery also produces a dozen or so seasonal ales, including Bonfire Boy (available every Nov) and an 8.1-percent Christmas ale which the brewery advises should be "treated with respect". The brewery **shop** (see p.229) on Cliffe High Street is a great place to stock up on the award-winning cask ales and bottled beers.

6

Pells Pool

Pells St, BN7 2PW • Mid-May to mid-Sept Mon & Wed–Fri 7–9am & 10am–7pm (from noon in May), Tues noon–7pm, Sat & Sun 10am–7pm (from noon in May), sometimes later in fine weather • £4 • ☎ 01273 472334, ⓦ pellspool.org.uk

A five-minute walk from the High Street brings you to the Pells area, where you'll find **Pells Pool**; built in 1861, it proudly holds the claim of being the oldest freshwater open-air swimming pool in the country. Fed by an icy freshwater stream, a dip here is certainly not for the fainthearted, but that doesn't seem to put off the locals, who throng here at summer weekends to sprawl on the tree-lined lawn surrounding the pool. There's also a paddling pool, and a kiosk selling ice creams and home-baked goodies.

ARRIVAL AND INFORMATION

LEWES

By train The station lies south of High St down Station Rd; there are good connections with London and along the coast.

Destinations Brighton (every 10–20min; 15min); Eastbourne (every 20min; 30min); London Victoria (Mon–Sat every 30min, Sun hourly; 1hr 10min).

By bus The bus station is on Eastgate St, near the foot of School Hill.

Destinations Brighton (Mon–Sat every 15min, Sun every 30min; 30min); Tunbridge Wells (Mon–Sat every 30min,

Sun hourly; 1hr 10min).

By car There's no free parking in the centre of Lewes, and wardens are vigilant. There are plenty of car parks around town.

Tourist office At the junction of High St and Fisher St (April–Sept Mon–Fri 9.30am–4.30pm, Sat 9.30am–4pm, Sun 10am–2pm; Oct–March Mon–Fri 9.30am–4.30pm, Sat 10am–2pm; ☎ 01273 483448, ⓦ www.lewes.gov.uk). They hold copies of the excellent free monthly magazine *Viva Lewes* (ⓦ vivalewes.com).

ACCOMMODATION

The website ⓦ lewesbandb.co.uk is a good directory of B&B **accommodation** in Lewes and the surrounding area. If you're hoping to get a room on Bonfire Night, book as far in advance as possible.

Blue Door Barns Beddingham, just outside Lewes, BN8 6JY ☎ 01273 858893, ⓦ bluedoorbarns.com. Stylish B&B and holiday lets in four luxurious barns, complete with on-site treatment room. Horseriding packages are available, as well as a picnic porter service for opera-goers at Glyndebourne. Two-night minimum stay at weekends. **£130**

The Corner House 14 Cleve Terrace, BN7 1JJ ☎ 01273 567138, ⓦ lewescornerhouse.co.uk. There's a real home-from-home feeling about this friendly B&B, set back from Southover High Street on a quiet Edwardian terrace. The two rooms have cheery patchwork quilts on the beds, wooden floors, plenty of books and small, immaculate bathrooms. **£95**

Montys Broughton House, 16 High St, BN7 2LN ☎ 01273 476750, ⓦ montysaccommodation.co.uk. Boutique B&B in a nineteenth-century townhouse, with two rooms in the basement and a third stunning loft-style room (£160 – cheaper outside summer season) occupying

the entire top floor. All three rooms come with kitchenettes, and a breakfast of warm croissants and home-made granola is delivered to your door. **£75**

The Prospect St Martin's Lane, BN7 1UD ☎ 01273 472883, ⓦ theprospectbandb.co.uk. This lovely B&B is in a great spot, on a quiet twitten running down from High St. It's a modern, upside-down house, with two peaceful, light bedrooms (one en suite) on the ground floor. Breakfast is served upstairs in the light-flooded breakfast room, crammed with plants, books and art, and with huge windows giving views over the Downs. **£90**

YHA South Downs Itford Farm, Beddingham, 5 miles south of Lewes ☎ 0870 371 9574, ⓦ yha.org.uk/hostel/south-downs. The nearest hostel to Lewes is a gem, newly renovated from a characterful old farm, and in a great location right on the South Downs Way footpath, with good transport connections (Southease station – with

6

LEST WE FORGET: LEWES BONFIRE NIGHT

Each November 5, while the rest of the country lights small domestic bonfires or attends municipal fireworks displays to commemorate the 1605 foiled Catholic plot to blow up the Houses of Parliament, Lewes puts on a more dramatic show – not for nothing has it been called the "**Bonfire Capital of the World**". The town closes to traffic, shops are boarded up and, come nightfall, the narrow streets are thronged by dozens of processions of elaborately costumed locals wielding flaming torches, burning crosses and flares, accompanied by marching bands and drummers. Each of Lewes's six tightknit **bonfire societies** – Borough, Cliffe, Commercial Square, Southover, South Street and Waterloo – has their own colours and themed costumes (Mongol warriors, monks, Vikings and more), and every year each produces a massive (often controversial) tableaux of a contemporary public figure, which is paraded through town and later burnt; the 2016 event saw no fewer than four tableaux of Donald Trump wheeled through the streets. After the main procession of the night (normally around 7.30pm), each society heads off to its own bonfire site and fireworks display on the outskirts of town.

The origins of Lewes's celebrations lie in the deaths of the town's seventeen Protestant martyrs during the Marian Persecutions of 1555–57, when Mary Tudor sentenced 288 Protestants around the country to be burned alive for their heretical views. By the end of the eighteenth century, Lewes' **Bonfire Boys** had become notorious for the boisterousness of their anti-Catholic demonstrations, in which they set off fireworks indiscriminately and dragged flaming tar barrels through the streets. Lewes's first bonfire societies were established in the 1850s to try to introduce a little more discipline into the proceedings, and in the early part of the last century they were persuaded to move their street fires to the town's perimeters.

The Lewes Bonfire experience is undeniably brilliant, but it does get packed, especially on years when November 5 falls on a weekend, and the official line is that it's an event for the people of Lewes only. If you decide to come, be aware that roads close early, parking is restricted and there can be horrendously long queues for trains at the end of the night; it's best to stay over if you can (book early). With loud bangs, flying sparks and lots of open flames, the event is definitely not suitable for small children. If the 5th falls on a Sunday, the celebrations take place on the 4th. For more, see ⓦlewesbonfirecouncil.org.uk.

OTHER SUSSEX BONFIRE CELEBRATIONS

Although Lewes is the best known of Sussex's bonfire celebrations, dozens of other villages and towns have their own societies which celebrate with torchlit processions and fireworks between September and the end of November, attending each other's processions, as well as the big one in Lewes. Though on a smaller scale, these events are a great way to experience the unique Sussex bonfire tradition; you can check dates on the societies' websites below. In Lewes itself, a seventh bonfire society, **Nevill Juvenile** (ⓦwww.njbs.co.uk), is specifically for children and holds its celebrations in October.

September Burgess Hill (ⓦburgesshillbonfiresociety .co.uk), Crowborough (ⓦcrowboroughbonfireandcarnival .com), Mayfield (ⓦmayfieldbonfire.co.uk), Uckfield (ⓦuckfieldcarnival.co.uk).

October Eastbourne (ⓦeastbournebonfiresociety .co.uk), Ewhurst & Staplecross (ⓦesbs.org.uk), Firle (ⓦfirlebonfire.com), Fletching, Hailsham (ⓦhailsham bonfire.org.uk), Hastings (ⓦhbbs.info), Littlehampton (ⓦlittlehamptonbonfiresociety.co.uk), Newick (ⓦnewick

bonfire.com), Ninfield (ⓦninfieldbonfire.co.uk), Northiam (ⓦnorthiambonfiresociety.co.uk), Rotherfield (ⓦrmcbs.co.uk), Seaford (ⓦseafordbonfire.co.uk).

November Barcombe (ⓦbarcombebonfire.co.uk), Battle (ⓦbattlebonfire.co.uk), Chailey (ⓦchaileybonfire.co.uk), Hawkhurst (ⓦhawkhurst-gang-bonfire-society.org.uk), Lindfield (ⓦlindfieldbonfiresociety.co.uk), Robertsbridge (ⓦrobertsbridgebonfiresociety.com), Rye (ⓦryebonfire .co.uk), South Heighton (ⓦsouthheighton.org/bonfire).

---

regular connections to Lewes – is just 200m away). Camping pods (sleeping 3) and bell tents (sleeping 5) are

available, and there's a café and licensed bar too. Camping pods **£49**, bell tents **£89**, dorms **£25**, doubles **£55**

EATING

Lewes's weekly **food market** (ⓦlewesfoodmarket.co.uk) takes place in the Market Tower on Market Street every Friday (9.30am–1.30pm). There's a larger **farmers' market** in the shopping precinct at the bottom of the High Street on the first and third Saturday of the month (9am–1pm).

6

★**Flint Owl** 209 High St, BN7 2DL ☎01273 472769, ⓦflintowlbakery.com. The café of the Glynde-based Flint Owl Bakery – which supplies its pastries and artisan bread (made using stoneground organic flour and little or no yeast) around Sussex – is a stylish space with a small courtyard garden out the back, and counters piled high with freshly baked pastries, savouries and cakes. Sandwiches, quiches and salads are also served, and there's a great selection of bread for sale, too, if you just want to pop in to buy a loaf. Mon–Sat 9am–5pm.

★**The Hearth Pizzeria** Eastgate, BN7 2LP ☎01273 470755, ⓦthehearth.co. Whether you opt for the Holy Grail (a margarita with Italian DOP buffalo mozzarella) or the Dalai Lama ("one with everything") you're in for a treat at this fab, down-to-earth pizzeria above the rough-and-ready Lewes bus station – their wood-fired sourdough pizzas (made with their own locally grown heirloom wheat) were voted among the best in the UK by the BBC's *Good Food* magazine. Downstairs *The Bakehouse* hatch-in-the-wall offers takeaway breads, home-made cakes and Sicilian-style *sfincione* pizza slices. The Hearth Mon & Tues 5–10pm, Wed–Fri noon–2pm & 5–10pm, Sat noon–10pm; The Bakehouse Mon–Sat 8.30am–5pm.

Le Magazin 50a Cliffe High St, BN7 2AN ☎01273 474720, ⓦle-magasin.co.uk. Stylish, laidback little bistro-café with a few tables outside on semi-pedestrianized Cliffe High St. It's popular all day, from breakfast through to dinner (Thurs–Sat eves only); mains such as *moules* or pan-fried sea bream cost £11–13, or opt for the two-course set menu (£34.95 for two people, with demi-carafe of wine). Mon–Wed 8am–5pm, Thurs–Sat 8am–10pm, Sun 9am–4pm.

Pelham House St Andrew's Lane, BN7 1UW ☎01273 488600, ⓦpelhamhouse.com. Set in a beautiful sixteenth-century townhouse, this hotel restaurant has a stylish little bar for pre-dinner cocktails, a wood-panelled dining room (two courses £20, three courses £25) and outdoor terrace seating with lovely views across to the Downs. Mon–Sat noon–2.30pm & 6–9pm, Sun noon–3pm & 6–9pm.

DRINKING

★**Lewes Arms** Mount Place, BN7 1YH ☎01273 473252, ⓦlewesarms.co.uk. One of Lewes's best-loved locals, this friendly pub has bags of character, with several cosy bare-boarded rooms and a tiny bar serving a good selection of real ales, including Harvey's. Annual events range from spaniel-racing and dwyle-flunking (tossing a beer-soaked dishcloth) to the World Pea Throwing Championships (the record currently stands at over 44m). The home-cooked pub food is great value, too. Mon–Thurs 11am–11pm, Fri & Sat 11am–midnight, Sun noon–11pm; kitchen Mon–Fri & Sun noon–8.30pm, Sat noon–9pm.

Snowdrop Inn 119 South St, BN7 2BU ☎01273 471018. This cheerful, family-friendly, dog-friendly pub offers live music a couple of nights a week, has a great range of beer (including Harvey's, Burning Sky and guests), and a good-value, daily-changing menu of locally sourced food, generally with a couple of vegetarian options (most mains around £12). Mon–Sat noon–midnight, Sun noon–11pm; kitchen Mon–Sat noon–9pm, Sun noon–8pm.

The Swan 30 Southover High St, BN7 1HU ☎01273 480211, ⓦfacebook.com/theswanlewes. Friendly, always-busy pub at the end of Southover High St, a 5–10min walk from the station, with four or five different Harvey's on tap, a vinyl-only music policy and a small, sunny beer garden out the back. Great home-cooked food, too, including enormous and very tasty roasts. Daily noon–late; kitchen Mon–Sat noon–9pm, Sun noon–5pm.

SHOPPING

Cheese Please 46 High St, BN7 2DD ☎01273 481048, ⓦcheesepleaseonline.co.uk. Award-winning shop stocking over one hundred different cheeses, mainly British, as well as locally baked bread and chutneys. Tues–Thurs 8am–4pm, Fri & Sat 8am–5pm.

Church Hill Antiques 6 Station St, BN7 2DA ☎01273 474842, ⓦfacebook.com/ChurchHillAntiques. This antiques centre houses more than sixty dealers selling furniture, interiors, jewellery and more. It's one of more than a dozen antiques shops in Lewes; also worth checking out are those along Cliffe High St, and the Lewes Flea Market on Market St. Mon–Sat 9.30am–5pm.

Harvey's Brewery Shop 7 Cliffe High St, BN7 2AH ☎01273 480217, ⓦharveys.org.uk. The brewery shop is crammed floor-to-ceiling with award-winning cask ales and seasonal bottled beers. Mon–Sat 9.30am–5.30pm.

Hop Gallery Castle Ditch Lane, off Fisher St, BN7 1YJ ☎01273 487744, ⓦhopgallery.com. Well-regarded art gallery within the eighteenth-century Star Brewery building, with regularly changing exhibitions of contemporary art for sale. Check the website for exhibition times.

Needlemakers West Street, BN7 2NZ. A collection of independent shops set over two floors of an old candle factory, selling everything from jewellery, homeware and ceramics to vintage gear and fairtrade goods. Most shops Mon–Sat 10am–5pm.

Sussex Guild Shop & Gallery Southover Grange, Southover Rd, BN7 1TP ☎01273 479565, ⓦthesussexguild.co.uk. A wonderful selection of textiles, prints, ceramics and jewellery produced by Sussex craftspeople. Daily 10am–5pm.

6

Tom Paine Printing Press Lewes 151 High St, BN7 1XU ⓦ tompaineprintingpress.com. This tiny shop-cum-gallery is home to a working eighteenth-century-style printing press, of the type that would have been used to produce Thomas Paine's pamplets (see p.225). Prints and cards printed on the press are on sale, alongside the work of contemporary printmakers. Tues–Sat 10am–5pm.

Spring Barn Farm

Kingston Rd, BN7 3ND • **Farm park** Daily 10am–5pm • £7.50–8.95, depending on season • **Farm shop & restaurant** Daily 9am–5pm • ☎ 01273 488450, ⓦ springbarnfarm.com

Spring Barn Farm, a working farm a mile south of Lewes, is idyllically situated at the foot of the Downs, with bucolic views in every direction. Its well-run **farm park** has plenty of stuff to keep children entertained, from animal handling sessions to tractor and trailer rides and a large indoor play barn; in spring kids can help bottle-feed the lambs. There's a good restaurant on site, serving local Sussex produce, as well as a **farm shop** selling local fruit and veg, Sussex game and the farm's own beef and lamb.

ACCOMMODATION   SPRING BARN FARM

Spring Barn Farm Kingston Road, 1 mile south of Lewes, BN7 3ND ☎ 01273 488450, ⓦ springbarnfarm .com. You can unzip your tent in the morning and look straight out onto the South Downs at this simple, car-free site. Campers can take advantage of reduced entry to the adjacent farm park, making the site a great option for families, and other bonuses include fire pits and an adjacent farm shop and café. Per person **£12**

Monk's House

Rodmell, BN7 3HF • Easter–Oct Wed–Sun & bank hols: house 1–5pm; garden 12.30–5.30pm • £5.50; NT • Free parking • ☎ 01273 474760, ⓦ nationaltrust.org.uk/monks-house

Three miles south of Lewes on the Lewes–Newhaven road, the pretty, weatherboard **Monk's House** was the home of novelist **Virginia Woolf** and her husband, Leonard, first as a summer and weekend retreat, until their London house was bombed in 1940 and it became their permanent residence. Like Charleston Farmhouse, where Virginia's much-loved sister Vanessa Bell lived, Monk's House hosted gatherings of the Bloomsbury Group (see box, p.220), and over the years E.M. Forster, Maynard Keynes, Vita Sackville-West, Lytton Strachey and Roger Fry all visited; informal snapshots of these guests, accompanied by Virginia's occasionally acerbic comments, are on show in the writing room in the orchard.

The **house** – of which you can see just four rooms – is presented as though the Woolfs had just popped out, and is unmistakeably "Bloomsbury" in style, with painted furniture, decorated ceramics and paintings by Vanessa and her partner Duncan Grant in every room, though on a much smaller, calmer scale than at Charleston. The real highlight of the property is the **garden**, with its beautiful views over the Ouse Valley, and paths weaving between overflowing borders.

When World War II broke out Virginia sank into one of the deep depressions that had afflicted her throughout her life. On March 28, 1941, she wrote a letter to Leonard

---

BOATING AT BARCOMBE

At **Barcombe**, four miles upstream of Lewes, you can take to the water for a gentle paddle along the **River Ouse**, one of the South's most beautiful and unspoilt waterways. The eighteenth-century *Anchor Inn* (☎ 01273 400414, ⓦ anchorinnandboating.co.uk) – actually half a mile northeast of Barcombe, but signposted from the village – hires out two-, four- and six-seater **canoes** (1hr £6/person) for the two-mile trip upstream past grassy banks and meadows to Fish Ladder Falls. The only building visible en route is the spire of Isfield Church, and if you're lucky you'll spot kingfisher, heron and cormorant – though on summer weekends your most likely sightings will be boatloads of other paddlers.

– "We can't go through another of those terrible times" – and walked to the River Ouse, where she filled the pockets of her coat with stones and drowned herself.

ACCOMMODATION

MONK'S HOUSE

Monk's House Garden Studio Rodmell, BN7 3HF • ☎0344 800 2070, ⓦnationaltrust.org.uk/monks -house. Wander in the footsteps of Virginia Woolf with a stay in the cosy garden studio at National Trust-run Monk's House (see opposite). The simple studio looks out onto the beautiful garden, which you can have all to yourself once the visitors have gone home. The rate drops sharply out of high season. Three-night minimum stay. **£170**

6

Ditchling and around

The pretty, affluent village of **DITCHLING** lies eight miles west of Lewes at the foot of the Downs, overlooked by famed beauty spot **Ditchling Beacon** – one of the highest spots on the escarpment. Handsome half-timbered and tile-hung buildings cluster around the traffic-clogged crossroads at the centre of the village, with two great lunch spots, *The Bull* and *The Green Welly*, facing each other across the street. A few steps away, the village green is overlooked by the striking **Ditchling Museum of Art + Craft** and the chunky flint **church of St Margaret's**, where many of the artists featured in the museum are buried, amongst them Edward Johnston and Hilary Pepler.

Ditchling Museum of Art + Craft

Lodge Hill Lane, BN6 8SP • Tues–Sat 10.30am–5pm, Sun & bank hols 11am–5pm • £6.50 • ☎01273 844744, ⓦditchlingmuseumartcraft.org.uk

The small but beautiful **Ditchling Museum of Art + Craft** houses a fascinating assortment of prints, paintings, weavings, sculptures and other artefacts created by the artists and craftspeople who lived in Ditchling in the last century, amongst them typographer and sculptor **Eric Gill**. Gill moved to Ditchling in 1907, and was later followed by like-minded artists and craftspeople, amongst them **Edward Johnston** (who designed the iconic London Underground font and roundel while living in the village), printer and writer Hilary Pepler, poet and painter David Jones, weaver Ethel Mairet and artist Frank Brangwyn. In 1920 Gill, Pepler and two others co-founded the **Guild of St Joseph and St Dominic**, an experimental Catholic community of artists and makers inspired by the Arts and Crafts movement – "a religious fraternity for those who make things with their hands" – with its own workshops, chapel and printing press on Ditchling Common just outside the village. Gill left Ditchling for Wales in 1924, but the Guild continued to flourish, only disbanding in 1989.

The museum's **permanent collection** includes small carvings and pencil drawings by Gill, paintings by David Jones – including a beautiful *Madonna and Child* set against a lowering Sussex landscape – and weavings by Ethel Mairet, her apprentice Valentine KilBride, and Hilary Bourne and Barbara Allen (who designed the textiles for the Royal Albert Hall in 1951). One room centres on Hilary Pepler's printing press which, as well as being a creative outlet, also functioned as the village's press, printing everything from beer labels to posters advertising productions by the Ditchling Dramatic Circle. Temporary **exhibitions**, changing every six months, feature contemporary commissions alongside objects loaned from other collections, plus there's a busy programme of **talks, events** and **workshops**.

Ridgeview Wine Estate

Fragbarrow Lane, Ditchling Common, off the B2112, BN6 8TP • **Cellar door** Daily 11am–4pm • **Tours** June–Sept tours run on occasional Fri, Sat & Sun (check dates on website; pre-booking essential); 1hr 30min–2hr • £15 • ☎01444 241441, ⓦridgeview.co.uk

Just north of Ditchling, the **Ridgeview Wine Estate** has picked up a staggering array of trophies over the last ten years, including best sparkling wine in the world. Its sparkling

6

ERIC GILL IN DITCHLING

One of the country's great twentieth-century artists, **Eric Gill** (1882–1940) is probably best known for his sans-serif **Gill Sans typeface**, which was famously used on the covers of the early Penguin books with their two coloured stripes. He was also a lauded sculptor, who revived the technique of direct carving in Britain and was a major influence on British sculptors such as Moore and Hepworth. His commissions included the *Stations of the Cross* at Westminster Cathedral, and *Prospero and Ariel* on the front of the BBC's Broadcasting House.

Gill was a complicated character. He was deeply **religious**, and had a horror of the twentieth century's mechanistic culture, despising everything that went with it, including typewriters, contraception, Bird's custard powder, and the fashion for tight trousers that constricted "man's most precious ornament". Having moved with his wife to Ditchling in 1907 he relocated in 1913 to a run-down cottage outside the village, where he and his family lived in ascetic squalor, eschewing all modern conveniences and to all outward appearances living a life of pious simplicity.

Beneath the surface, however, Gill's family set-up was anything but wholesome. When his **biography** was published in 1989, he was revealed to be an incestuous polygamist, who regularly had sex not only with two of his sisters, but also with two of his daughters, not to mention the family dog. For Gill, sex was inseparable from his deeply held religious beliefs – he believed that "sexual intercourse is the very symbol of Christ's love for his church" – but whatever bizarre morality underpinned his actions his reputation has never completely recovered.

---

whites and rosés – produced using traditional Champagne grape varieties and methods – are available nationwide, but it's much more fun to pitch up at the cellar door and taste before you buy. The vineyard also runs **tours** most weekends in summer.

Ditchling Beacon

Towering above Ditchling village, 820ft-high **Ditchling Beacon** is one of the highest points in the South Downs, and from its breezy summit there are glorious views out over the patchwork of fields, copses and tiny villages of the Weald, to the hazy outline of the North Downs beyond. The summit gained its name from its warning beacon, one of a chain of bonfire sites across the Downs lit to warn of the Spanish Armada and other invasions.

A 1.5-mile lung-busting path leads up the hill from Ditchling village, or there's a car park at the summit, from where **trails** strike off in all directions; an easy 1.5-mile stroll westwards along the South Downs Way footpath brings you to the two **Clayton Windmills**, also known as Jack and Jill; the latter, a white wooden post mill built in 1821, is open to the public most Sunday afternoons in summer (normally May–Sept Sun 2–5pm, but check website; ⓦjillwindmill.org.uk). Continue along the South Downs Way for another 3.5 miles – past Saddlescombe Farm (see opposite) – to reach Devil's Dyke, just over the county border in West Sussex.

Devil's Dyke

One of the most-visited beauty spots in the South Downs, **Devil's Dyke** has been luring tourists for over a hundred years. In its Victorian heyday it was a positive playground of new-fangled delights, featuring swingboats, a funicular, a single-track railway running from Hove, and most thrillingly of all, a cable car – the country's first – that took tourists across the 275m-wide Devil's Dyke valley. Thankfully, only the concrete footings of the cable car's pylons remain today.

The **views** from the grassy slopes of the summit, described by John Constable in 1824 as "the grandest view in the world", are really something special: the hill drops off steeply in front of you giving a stupendous panorama over the Weald and westwards along the grand sweep of the Downs.

The **Dyke** itself, a steep chasm on the north side of the escarpment, is often overlooked; it lies around the other side of the *Devil's Dyke* pub and a hundred yards back along the access road. The longest, widest and deepest chalk valley in the country, it was formed by melting water in the last Ice Age – or, if you're to believe local legend, dug by the Devil to allow the sea to flood in and drown the infuriatingly pious parishioners of the Weald. The Devil was only thwarted when an old lady, hearing a noise, lit a candle to investigate and the Devil fled, fearing the light was the rising sun.

ARRIVAL AND INFORMATION

By train The nearest station Is Hassocks (on the Brighton–London line), two miles away.

By bus Compass Travel bus #167 runs from Lewes to Ditchling (Mon– Fri 4 daily; 30min). From Brighton, Breeze up to the Downs buses run on spring/summer weekends: bus #77 to Ditchling Beacon and bus #79 to Devil's Dyke (both approx hourly; end April to Sept Sat, Sun and bank hols only; every 45min– 1hr; 25min).

On foot or by bike Both Ditchling Beacon and Devil's

DITCHLING AND AROUND

Dyke are on the South Downs Way footpath, eight miles apart; if you're staying in Brighton you can use the Breeze up to the Downs buses (see box, p.247) to walk or cycle between the two. From Lewes it's a beautiful six-mile walk or cycle to Ditchling Beacon across the Downs.

By car There's free parking (2hr max stay) in Ditchling's village hall car park, and there are National Trust car parks at the summits of Ditchling Beacon and Devil's Dyke.

Website ⓦ ditchling.com.

6

ACCOMMODATION AND EATING

DITCHLING

The Bull 2 High St, BN6 8TA ☎ 01273 843147, ⓦ thebullditchling.com. Splendid sixteenth-century village inn, with beamed ceilings, huge fireplaces and the smell of wood smoke in the air. The menu changes daily, but mains (around £13–16) might include ale-battered cod or pork belly. Upstairs are four stylish rooms with compact but sleek en-suite bathrooms; four additional, larger rooms are planned. Mon–Sat 11am–11pm, Sun 11am–10.30pm; kitchen Mon–Fri noon–2.30pm & 6–9.30pm, Sat & Sun noon–9/9.30pm. **£120**

★**Green Welly** 1 High St, BN6 8SY ☎ 01273 841010, ⓦ thegreenwellycafe.co.uk. Lovely little café with lashings of charm. All the food – soup, quiche, cakes, sandwiches and the like – is made on site in the open kitchen, and there's a pretty walled garden out the back. It's walker- and dog-friendly, too. Tues–Sun & bank hols 9am–5pm.

AROUND DITCHLING

★**Blackberry Wood** Streat Lane, near Ditchling, BN6 8RS ☎ 01273 890035, ⓦ blackberrywood.com. Book

early if you want to get your hands on one of the twenty tent pitches at this fab campsite, each in its own secluded woodland glade, complete with fire pit. Elsewhere on the site, there's an eclectic range of accommodation including a gypsy caravan, a double-decker bus, a 1960s search-and-rescue helicopter and a wonky fairytale treehouse (all sleeping two). Camping/person **£17**, caravan **£60**, bus or helicopter **£99**, treehouse **£245**

Saddlescombe Farm Saddlescombe Rd, near Poynings, BN45 7DE ☎ 01273 857712 (camping), ☎ 01273 857062 (B&B), ⓦ nationaltrust.org.uk /saddlescombe-farm-and-newtimber-hill. Right on the South Downs Way, National Trust-owned Saddlescombe Farm offers camping (backpackers only) April–Sept. Alternatively, the tenant farmers run a comfy B&B in the farmhouse, and stays can be combined with lambing open days and shepherd-for-the-day events. There's also a simple café on site. While you're at the farm check out the seventeenth-century donkey wheel – one of only four left in the Southeast. Camping/person **£5**, B&B doubles **£70**

Brighton

BRIGHTON PAVILION

Brighton

Sandwiched between the sea and the South Downs, Brighton (or Brighton & Hove, to give it its official name) is the jewel of the south coast – colourful and creative, quirky and cool. On a summer's day, with the tang of the sea in the air, the screech of seagulls overhead and the crowds of day-trippers streaming down to the beach, there's a real holiday feel to the city. Vibrant, friendly and tolerant, this is a city that knows how to have fun. The essence of Brighton's appeal is its bohemian vitality – a buzz that comes from its artists, writers, musicians and other creatives, its thriving gay community, and an energetic local student population from the art college and two universities. Despite the middle-class gentrification that's transformed the city over the last decade or so, it still retains the appealingly seedy edge that led Keith Waterhouse to famously describe it as a town that always looks as if it's helping police with their enquiries.

A visit to Brighton inevitably begins with a visit to its most famous landmarks – the exuberant **Royal Pavilion** and the wonderfully tacky **Brighton Pier**, a few minutes away – followed by a stroll along the pebbly beach, lined with beachfront bars and shops, to the futuristic **i360**, the city's newly opened observation tower. Just as fun, though, is an unhurried meander around some of Brighton's distinct neighbourhoods: the car-free **Lanes**, a maze of narrow alleys marking the old town, crammed with restaurants, jewellery shops and boutiques; the more bohemian **North Laine**, where you'll find the city's greatest concentration of independent shops, and some fabulous cafés and coffee shops; **Kemp Town** village, the heart of Brighton's gay community, with antiques shops and some cool little cafés; and **Hove**, with its elegant beachfront.

Brighton's other great joy is its fantastically vibrant and eclectic **cultural life**. On any given night of the week there'll be live music, comedy, plays, concerts, talks and films, so whether you want to catch a big-name band in an intimate venue, a free acoustic gig in a pub, a string quartet in a concert hall, a subversive theatre production or a family-friendly mainstream show, you'll find something to entertain you. The city's packed **festival calendar** partly accounts for this, with festivals devoted to film, literature, music and comedy taking place throughout the year, as well as the Brighton Festival – the country's largest arts festival after Edinburgh – which runs for three weeks in May.

Brief history

Recorded as the tiny village of Brithelmeston in the Domesday Book, Brighton remained an undistinguished fishing town until the mid-eighteenth century, when the new trend for **sea bathing** established it as a resort. The fad received royal approval in the 1780s, after the decadent **Prince Regent** (the future George IV) began patronizing the town in the company of his mistress, thus setting a precedent for the "dirty

BRITISH AIRWAYS i360

Highlights

❶ Royal Pavilion This extraordinary Oriental-style palace is the city's must-see sight, with jaw-dropping, no-expense-spared opulence. See p.238

❷ North Laine Brighton at its bohemian, buzzy best, heaving with hip coffee shops and quirky independent shops. **See p.241**

❸ British Airways i360 Get a bird's-eye view of the city from the futuristic viewing pod of the world's tallest moving observation tower. See p.243

❹ Brighton Festival and Fringe The biggest arts festival in England is an all-singing, all-dancing three-week culture-fest of art, dance,

music, comedy and theatre**. See p.248**

❺ Beach sports The beach may be pebbly but you can still feel the sand between your toes at the beach volleyball courts. **See p.249**

❻ Eating out From *Jack and Linda's* takeaway mackerel rolls on the beach, to cutting-edge cooking at *64 Degrees*, Brighton's eating scene covers all budgets and tastes. **See p.251**

❼ Komedia You're spoilt for choice when it comes to nights out in the city, but make sure at least one of them is spent here, at this great arts venue that puts on comedy, cabaret, film, live music and club nights. **See p.259**

HIGHLIGHTS ARE MARKED ON THE MAP ON PP.238–239

weekend", Brighton's major contribution to the English collective consciousness. By the end of the 1700s the town was the most fashionable resort in the country, visited by the great and good of high society – though the arrival of the train in 1841 soon put paid to that, kickstarting mass tourism and a level of popularity with day-trippers from the capital that's continued unabated to this day.

Royal Pavilion and around

4/5 Pavilion Buildings • Daily: April–Sept 9.30am–5.45pm; Oct–March 10am–5.15pm; last entry 45min before closing • £12.30, audio guides £2; 2-day pass with Brighton Museum & Preston Manor (April–Sept only) £15 • ☎ 0300 029 0900, ⊛ brightonmuseums.org.uk /royalpavilion

In any survey to find Britain's most loved building, there's always a bucketful of votes for Brighton's exotic extravaganza, the **Royal Pavilion**, which flaunts itself in the middle of the Old Steine, the main thoroughfare along which most of the seafront-bound road traffic gets funnelled. Commissioned by the fun-loving **Prince Regent** (see box, p.240) in 1815, the Pavilion was the design of **John Nash**, architect of London's Regent Street.

HIGHLIGHTS

1. Royal Pavilion
2. North Laine
3. British Airways i360
4. Brighton Festival and Fringe
5. Beach sports
6. Eating out
7. Komedia

BRIGHTON

ENGLISH CHANNEL

SEE 'THE LANES AND NORTH LAINE' MAP FOR DETAIL

▮ NIGHTLIFE	
Bleach	1
Concorde 2	19
Patterns	13
Proud Cabaret Brighton	18
Volks	17

▮ LGBT	
The Bulldog	9
Camelford Arms	11
Legends	15
Velvet Jack's	3

▮ DRINKING	
Bee's Mouth	5
Black Dove	12
Brighton Beer Dispensary	7
Brighton Music Hall	10
Craft Beer Co.	6
The Greys	2
Hand in Hand	16
Lion and Lobster	8
Setting Sun	4
The Sidewinder	14

What Nash came up with was an extraordinary confection of slender minarets, twirling domes, pagodas, balconies and miscellaneous motifs imported from India and China, all supported on an innovative cast-iron frame, creating an exterior profile that defines a genre of its own – Oriental-Gothic.

Inside, one highlight – approached via the restrained Long Gallery – is the **Banqueting Room**, which erupts with ornate splendour and is dominated by a one-tonne chandelier hung from the jaws of a massive dragon cowering in a plantain tree. Next door, the huge, high-ceilinged **kitchen**, fitted with the most modern appliances of its time, has iron columns disguised as palm trees. The stunning **Music Room**, the first sight of which reduced George to tears of joy, has a huge dome lined with more than twenty-six thousand individually gilded scales and hung with exquisite umbrella-like glass lamps. After climbing the famous cast-iron staircase with its bamboo-look banisters, you can go into Victoria's sober and seldom-used bedroom and the **North-West Gallery** where the king's portrait hangs, along with a selection of satirical cartoons. More notable, though, is the **South Gallery**, decorated in sky-blue with trompe l'oeil bamboo trellises and a carpet that appears to be strewn with flowers.

7

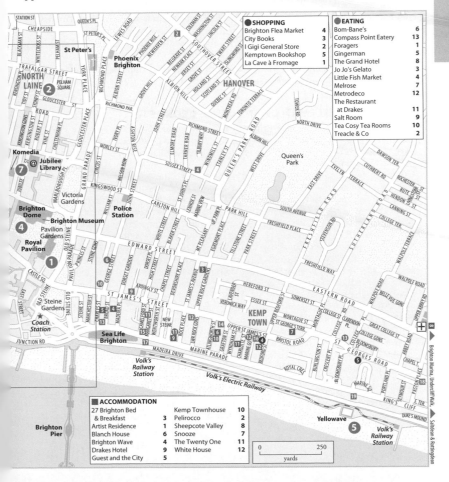

● SHOPPING	
Brighton Flea Market	4
City Books	3
I Gigi General Store	2
Kemptown Bookshop	5
La Cave à Fromage	1

● EATING	
Bom-Bane's	6
Compass Point Eatery	13
Foragers	1
Gingerman	5
The Grand Hotel	8
Jo Jo's Gelato	3
Little Fish Market	4
Melrose	7
Metrodeco	12
The Restaurant at Drakes	11
Salt Room	9
Tea Cosy Tea Rooms	10
Treacle & Co	2

■ ACCOMMODATION			
27 Brighton Bed & Breakfast	3	Kemp Townhouse	10
Artist Residence	1	Pelirocco	2
Blanch House	6	Sheepcote Valley	8
Brighton Wave	4	Snooze	7
Drakes Hotel	9	The Twenty One	11
Guest and the City	5	White House	12

Brighton Museum

Royal Pavilion Gardens, BN1 1EE • Tues–Sun & bank hols 10am–5pm • £5.20, free to Brighton & Hove residents; 2-day pass with Royal Pavilion & Preston Manor (April–Sept only) £15 • ☎ 0300 029 0900, ⓦ brightonmuseums.org.uk/brighton

Across the gardens from the Pavilion stands the wonderful **Brighton Museum**, which houses an eclectic mix of modern fashion and design, archeology, art and local history in a grand building that used to form part of the royal stable block.

Downstairs, the central hall houses the museum's collection of **twentieth-century art and design**, a procession of classic Art Deco, Art Nouveau and modern furniture that includes Dalí's famous sofa (1938) based on Mae West's lips. Across the hall the **Ancient Egypt** galleries contain some mummified animals and wonderful painted coffins from 945–715 BC, courtesy of famous Egyptologist – and Brightonian – Francis Llewellyn Griffith. Two other rooms on the ground floor take you through the **history of Brighton**, covering everything from the rise of the dirty weekend to the famous 1964 clash of the Mods and Rockers on Brighton seafront that inspired the film *Quadrophenia*.

Upstairs are three **Fine Art** galleries, as well as a room themed around "Performance", which has some fantastic **puppets** from the museum's world art collection, alongside a willow-and-paper model from Brighton's very own Burning the Clocks celebrations (see box, p.248). The **Costume gallery** includes garments belonging to George IV, whose love of fashion (and his own appearance) led his wife to comment rather sniffily "I ought to have been the man and he the woman to wear petticoats."

Adjacent to the museum, and part of the same complex of buildings, is the town's main concert hall, **Brighton Dome** (see p.259).

THE FIRST GENTLEMAN OF ENGLAND: GEORGE IV

Born on August 12, 1762, **George, Prince of Wales**, was the eldest son of George III and Queen Charlotte, and a constant source of disappointment to his straight-laced father. He was vain, indolent and profligate, with a life devoted almost entirely to pleasure – gambling, heavy drinking, dining, mistresses, racing and fine clothes.

George's love affair with Brighton started in 1783, when on the advice of his physicians he visited the small seaside town – by that stage already a popular health resort. He liked it so much that he rented a farmhouse, which he later transformed into a lavishly furnished villa. His presence over the next forty or so years was instrumental in the town's meteoric transformation into a fashionable and slightly racy "London by the sea". George had the time of his life there, building up unspeakably large debts (running to tens of millions of pounds in today's money), and spending his days in the pursuit of pleasure – promenading, horseriding, partying, and frolicking with his mistress, **Mrs Maria Fitzherbert**, whom he secretly – and illegally – married in 1785, and installed in a house on the west side of the Old Steine. A twice-widowed commoner, and Roman Catholic to boot, Fitzherbert couldn't have been a more unsuitable partner.

In 1795 George's disapproving father forced a marriage with **Princess Caroline of Brunswick**. It was not a success. Caroline had as much contempt for her portly husband as his father did, and George continued his dissolute lifestyle unrepentant, with the couple separating soon after the birth of their only child the following year.

In 1811, George became **Prince Regent** after his father was declared insane, and within a few years he hired John Nash to transform his villa into the extravagant palace that stands today. When his father died in 1820 he was crowned **King George IV** – by this time morbidly obese, suffering from gout and digestive problems, and frequently caricatured in the national press as being completely out of touch with a nation reeling from famine and unemployment in the aftermath of the Napoleonic Wars. When George died in 1830, aged 68, his passing was neatly summed up by *The Times*: "There never was an individual less regretted by his fellow-creatures than this deceased king."

BRIGHTON GALLERIES

There are several excellent art galleries in the city. As well as the places listed below, check out the Brighton Museum (see opposite), its sister museum in Hove (see p.246) and the seafront Artists Quarter. A great time to see – and buy – art is during the biannual Artists Open Houses events (May & Dec; ⓦaoh.org.uk), when artists around the city open up their homes to the public.

Fabrica 40 Duke St, BN1 1AG ☎01273 778646, ⓦfabrica.org.uk. Three main shows a year (free), often featuring installations, in an old church on the edge of the Lanes. Wed–Sun.

Phoenix Brighton 10–14 Waterloo Place, BN2 9NB ☎01273 603700, ⓦphoenixarts.org. Half-a-dozen shows a year (free), opposite St Peter's Church. Wed–Sun.

University of Brighton Gallery 58–67 Grand Parade, BN2 0JY ☎01273 643010, ⓦarts.brighton .ac.uk/whats-on. Exhibitions of students' work, plus retrospectives of well-known artists.

North Laine

7

If you're looking for the Brighton that's bohemian, hip and slightly alternative, you'll find it in **North Laine**, which sprawls west and north of the Royal Pavilion as far as Trafalgar Street, bordered by Queens Road to the west and the A23 to the east. What used to be the city's slum area is now its most vibrant neighbourhood, packed with coffee shops and pavement cafés, cool boutiques and quirky independent shops selling everything from vintage homeware and vinyl to mod clothing and bonsai trees. Several streets are pedestrianized, while others become temporarily car-free at the weekend, when the crowds descend en masse and café tables and stalls spill out onto the streets. The city's striking, state-of-the-art central **library** is also down this way, on Jubilee Square. The North Laine **website** (ⓦnorthlaine.co.uk) features a downloadable map, as well as reasonably comprehensive listings for the many shops and eating places.

The Lanes

Tucked between the Pavilion and the seafront is a warren of narrow, pedestrianized alleyways known as **the Lanes** – the core of the old fishing village from which Brighton evolved. It's a great place to wander, with some excellent cafés and restaurants, and plenty of interesting independent shops and boutiques, including the long-established jeweller's shops for which the area's known.

The seafront

Every visitor to Brighton will find their way down to Brighton's **seafront** at some point, and in summer it certainly feels that way, with crowds of holidaymakers and Brightonians soaking up the sun in the beachfront cafés, or crunching their way over the pebbly beach to find an unoccupied spot.

The section of seafront between the two piers is where most of the action takes place. Here, down beneath the street-level prom with its distinctive turquoise-blue railings, the **Lower Esplanade** runs west from Brighton Pier along to the new **i360** tower, lined for much of the way by bars, clubs, cafés, galleries and gift shops, many snuggled into the old redbrick **fishermen's arches**, and with stalls or tables out by the pebbles. The beach is quieter farther west, around Brighton's beautiful Victorian **bandstand** – the only one to survive of eight that once graced the seafront; during summer it puts on free Sunday afternoon concerts. Keep heading west and you'll soon reach **Hove Lawns** (see p.246).

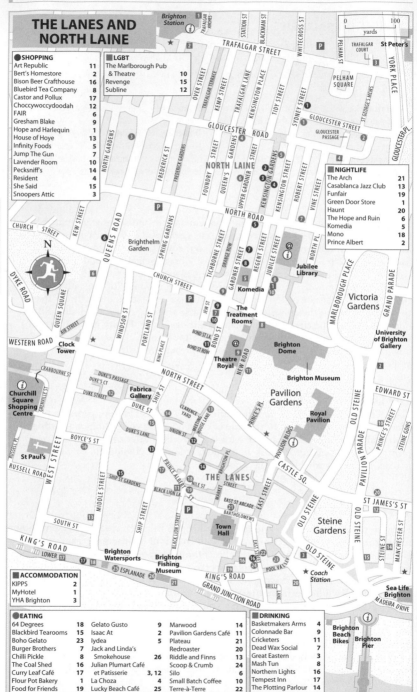

THE LANES AND NORTH LAINE

● SHOPPING

Art Republic	11
Bert's Homestore	2
Bison Beer Crafthouse	16
Bluebird Tea Company	8
Castor and Pollux	17
Choccywoccydoodah	12
FAIR	6
Gresham Blake	9
Hope and Harlequin	1
House of Hove	13
Infinity Foods	5
Jump The Gun	7
Lavender Room	10
Pecksniff's	14
Resident	4
She Said	15
Snoopers Attic	3

■ LGBT

The Marlborough Pub & Theatre	10
Revenge	15
Subline	12

■ NIGHTLIFE

The Arch	21
Casablanca Jazz Club	13
Funfair	19
Green Door Store	1
Haunt	20
The Hope and Ruin	6
Komedia	5
Mono	18
Prince Albert	2

■ ACCOMMODATION

KIPPS	2
MyHotel	1
YHA Brighton	3

● EATING

64 Degrees	18
Blackbird Tearooms	15
Boho Gelato	23
Burger Brothers	7
Chilli Pickle	8
The Coal Shed	16
Curry Leaf Café	17
Flour Pot Bakery	1
Food for Friends	19
Gelato Gusto	9
Isaac At	2
Iydea	5
Jack and Linda's Smokehouse	26
Julian Plumart Café et Patisserie	3, 12
La Choza	4
Lucky Beach Café	25
Marwood	14
Pavilion Gardens Café	11
Plateau	21
Redroaster	20
Riddle and Finns	13
Scoop & Crumb	24
Silo	6
Small Batch Coffee	10
Terre-à-Terre	22

■ DRINKING

Basketmakers Arms	4
Colonnade Bar	9
Cricketers	11
Dead Wax Social	7
Great Eastern	3
Mash Tun	8
Northern Lights	16
Tempest Inn	17
The Plotting Parlour	14

7

East of Brighton Pier the beach is much quieter. The venerable Volk's Railway trundles along for a mile to the **naturist beach** – the first public naturist beach in the country, and usually the preserve of just a few thick-skinned souls – and then on to Brighton Marina. Running parallel is Madeira Drive, end point for some of the city's biggest events, including the London to Brighton Bike Ride, the Veteran Car Run, the Brighton Marathon and the Burning the Clocks parade. Plans are afoot to spruce up the slightly neglected seafront here; projects in consultation stage at the time of writing include a 300m-long **zip wire** running along the seafront, and a 50m open-air **saltwater swimming pool**.

Brighton Pier

Madeira Drive, BN2 1TW • Daily: April–Oct 10am–10pm; Nov–March 11am–5pm; opening hours can vary depending on weather • Free; various fees apply to rides • ☎ 01273 609361, ⓦ brightonpier.co.uk

Every inch of kitsch, brash **Brighton Pier**, opened in 1899, is devoted to fun, from the side stalls and cacophonous amusement arcades to the kiosks selling bubblegum-pink candyfloss and striped Brighton Rock. The **fairground rides** at the end of the pier range from the traditional (helter-skelter, carousel and dodgems) to the downright terrifying (the Booster, which lifts you 40ft in the air, leaving you dangling over the sea).

Brighton Fishing Museum

201 King's Rd Arches, Lower Esplanade (at beach level), BN1 1NB • Normally daily 9am–5pm • Free • ⓦ brightonfishingmuseum.org.uk

The golden days of Brighton's local fishing industry are revisited at the **Brighton Fishing Museum**, which displays old photos, video footage and memorabilia, and houses a large Sussex clinker, a boat once common on Brighton beach. Before Brighton's rise as a fashionable resort it was the most important fishing town in Sussex, with four out of every five men working as fishermen; the rise of tourism led to the decline of the fishing fleet, leading some resourceful fishermen to turn to tourism instead, offering pleasure cruises or becoming dippers or bathers for Brighton's bathing machines.

The surrounding area is known as the **Fishing Quarter**; head to *Jack and Linda's Smokehouse* (see p.252) for delicious hot mackerel rolls and fish soups.

British Airways i360

Lower King's Road, BN1 2LN • Hours vary but generally Mon–Thurs & Sun 10/11am–7/8pm, Fri & Sat 10am–9/10pm; check website for the latest • £15 • ☎ 0333 772 0360, ⓦ britishairwaysi360.com

There's no missing Brighton's newest attraction, the **British Airways i360**: at 162m high, it's the world's tallest moving observation tower, and it dominates the skyline from its seafront site by the ruined West Pier (much to the disapproval of some locals). Designed by the architects of the London Eye, the i360 is essentially a pod on a pole: visitors board the gleaming, saucer-shaped pod – complete with champagne bar serving local fizz – and are whisked up for 360-degree views over the city and beyond. On a clear day the views, extending up to 26 miles, are great: inland to the South Downs, west as far as Chichester and east to the Seven Sisters cliffs and beyond. The whole experience is a bit pricey, given you're only aloft for fifteen minutes or so, but it's a fun one-off; just be sure to plan your visit around the weather.

At the bottom of the tower there's a good restaurant, the *Belle Vue*, and a tearoom housed in one of the restored nineteenth-century tollbooths that previously marked the entrance to the West Pier.

7

> **BEST OF BRIGHTON FOR KIDS**
>
> **Brighton Pier** Arcade games, stalls, scary rollercoasters and gentler rides – a surefire hit with most ages. See p.243
>
> **Yellowave** This beach sports venue is a great spot for kids, and you can take an old electric train along the seafront to get to it. See p.249
>
> **Biking along the prom** Rent bikes at the seafront and you can cycle for miles along the promenade; the quieter end around Hove Lawns is best for smaller cyclists. See p.249
>
> **Gelaterias** Ice cream is bound to feature in your stay – just make sure it's from one of the city's top-notch *gelaterias*. See box, p.254
>
> **Komedia** This brilliant, family-friendly venue has a regular programme of shows for kids. See p.259

West Pier

All that remains of the once-grand **West Pier** is a blackened skeleton, no longer connected to the mainland. Built in 1866 by Eugenius Birch, the pier was one of the finest in the country – and the first to be Grade I-listed – but after decades of neglect it was all but destroyed by storms and two separate fires in 2002 and 2003. Today the rusting carcass has become an iconic sight, especially in winter, when the skies above the pier are filled at dusk with swirling clouds of **starlings**.

Sea Life Brighton

Marine Parade, BN2 1TB • Daily: May–Aug 10am–6pm; Sept–April 10am–5pm; last entry 1hr before; times can change so check website • £10.50–17.50 depending on ticket type; cheapest online • ☎ 01273 604234, ⓦ visitsealife.com/Brighton

Sea Life Brighton is the world's oldest operating aquarium, opened in 1872. The atmospheric main aquarium hall still looks largely as it would have done in Victorian times, lined with tanks and with a wonderful vaulted ceiling, and is the real star of the show. Elsewhere there's a short tunnel leading you through a tank populated by sharks and stately giant turtles, and a small, dark room of jellyfish floating mesmerically in glowing, colour-changing tubes.

Volk's Electric Railway

Trains are planned to run Easter–Sept daily, plus special events in winter, but check website for the latest information • ⓦ volkselectricrailway.co.uk

Just east of Brighton Pier, the antiquated locomotives of **Volk's Electric Railway** – the first electric train in the country, dating back to 1883 – trundle eastward for just over a mile to Black Rock, by the Marina, stopping off halfway near the excellent Yellowave beach sports venue (see p.249). The railway was built by **Magnus Volk**, a nineteenth-century inventor and engineer, who was also responsible for setting up the first telephone line in the city and installing its first electric lighting. A new visitor centre and museum is planned for 2017, which will affect the 2017 operating season – see the website for the latest information on operating hours and prices.

Brighton Marina

One mile east of Brighton Pier, BN2 5UF • ⓦ brightonmarina.co.uk • Bus #7; free parking

The antithesis of boho central Brighton, **Brighton Marina** – the largest in Europe – is a somewhat soulless sprawl of factory outlet shops and chain restaurants, with a cinema, bowling alley, casino and superstore. On a summer's day, however, it's pleasant enough to wander around, trying out the free ping pong and chess tables in Marina Square and finishing off with an alfresco lunch overlooking the bobbing, clanking boats. Various boat trip operators and **watersports** outfits operate out of the Marina (see p.250).

Kemp Town

East of the city centre, **Kemp Town** is the heart of the city's LGBT community and one of Brighton's liveliest, most colourful neighbourhoods. From the city centre, head along busy, bustling **St James's Street** (Brighton's "Gay Village"), which strikes off east from the Old Steine. Partway along, at New Steine Gardens, look out for the country's only dedicated Aids Memorial.

St James's Street runs east to its quieter continuation, **St George's Road**, where you'll find a clutch of antique and vintage shops, delis, cosy pubs and laidback coffee shops. Here, you can't miss the elaborate copper dome of *Proud Cabaret Brighton* (see p.258), originally built as a **mausoleum** by Sir Albert Sassoon in 1892, in the same Oriental-Gothic style as the Pavilion. One can't help but wonder what the old baronet would make of the exotic burlesque supper clubs held under the dome today.

7

THE UNDERCLIFF WALK

Built between 1928 and 1935 to provide sea defences for the crumbling cliffs, the **Undercliff Walk** stretches 3.5 miles from Brighton Marina east to Saltdean. It's one of Brighton's lesser-known treasures, and makes a wonderful day-trip from the city if combined with a wander around the pretty village of Rottingdean or a swim in Saltdean's Art Deco lido. The walk is lovely on a summer's day at low tide, when you can drop down to the beach to poke around the rockpools, but it's definitely best – and most exhilarating – in stormy weather, when at high tide the wind carries the spray right over the sea wall onto the promenade.

If you're walking the route in one direction, you can catch **buses** #12, #14, #27 or #47 back to Brighton (every 10–15min) from bus stops on the coast road at Rottingdean or Saltdean.

ROTTINGDEAN

Two and a half miles along the Undercliff Walk you'll come to the Gap – a natural break in the cliffs, which allows access to the little village of **Rottingdean**. Cross over the busy coast road and head up the High Street to reach The Green, the picturesque, leafy hub of the village. It was here that Pre-Raphaelite painter **Edward Burne-Jones** and his nephew **Rudyard Kipling** both moved in the late nineteenth century: the Burne-Jones' former holiday house, North End House, sits on the western side, just a stone's throw from Kipling's house, The Elms, on the village green itself. Neither building is open to the public today, but you can wander through the peaceful flint-walled **Kipling's Gardens** (daily until dusk; free) beside his old home.

Kipling wrote many of his best-known works while in Rottingdean, including some of his *Just So* stories, but eventually he lost patience with tourists coming to gawp at him and removed himself to a more secluded haven at Bateman's near Burwash (see p.190). Burne-Jones remained in Rottingdean until his death in 1898 and is buried at the flint-walled thirteenth-century **church of St Margaret's** on the northeastern corner of The Green, which contains some wonderful **stained-glass windows** created by him in collaboration with William Morris. Just south past the duck pond the **Grange Museum and Art Gallery** (Mon, Tues & Thurs–Sat 10.30am–4.30pm, Sun 1.30–4.30pm; ☎01273 301004, ⓦrottingdeanpreservationsociety.org.uk), originally the vicarage, has plenty of material dedicated to its two famous residents.

SALTDEAN LIDO

A mile further on from Rottingdean, you'll come to **Saltdean** with its wonderful **Art Deco lido**, designed by architect Richard Jones and opened in 1938; with its two curved wings swooping away from a main block topped by sun terraces – a design intended to emulate the bridge of an ocean liner – it's a real gem, and the only Grade-II* listed lido in the country. After the lido was saved from the threat of residential development by local residents, the iconic building and pool have been restored and are due to reopen in 2017; see ⓦsaltdeanlido.co.uk for details of hours and prices.

Farther east is **Sussex Square**, part of the grand **Kemp Town Estate** erected by the neighbourhood's namesake, Thomas Kemp, in the early nineteenth century. The author **Lewis Carroll** was a regular visitor to no.11, and it's said that the tunnel that runs down to the beach from the Estate's private gardens was the inspiration for the rabbit hole in *Alice in Wonderland*. If you're heading down to the beach yourself you can take the restored Victorian **Madeira Lift**, which will whisk you down from Marine Parade to *Concorde II*, close to the Yellowave beach sports venue.

Hove

Although it forms a continuous conurbation with Brighton – and to most visitors' eyes is just another neighbourhood – **Hove** was, until quite recently, a completely separate town. It grew up as the resort of Brunswick Town in the 1820s, separated from Brighton by open fields, and it was only in 1997 that it was merged with its flashier neighbour to form the borough of Brighton and Hove, which achieved city status three years later.

Hove has always been rather protective of its separate identity: its tongue-in-cheek slogan, "Hove, actually", originates in the sniffy response of local residents to outsiders asking if they live in Brighton. It definitely has a calmer, less raffish air to it, with handsome Regency architecture around **Brunswick Square** and an elegant lawn-backed **seafront** – where the division between Brighton and Hove is marked by the **Peace Statue**. The wide grassy expanses of **Hove Lawns** start just beyond here, backed at their western end by a row of brightly coloured beach huts. Further west still is **Hove Lagoon**, one of the best places in the city to try out a new watersport (see p.250).

Hove Museum

19 New Church Rd, BN3 4AB • Mon, Tues & Thurs–Sat 10am–5pm, Sun & bank hols 2–5pm • Free • ☎ 0300 029 0900, ⓦ brightonmuseums.org.uk/hove • Buses #1, #1A, #6, #49 or #49A from North St or Churchill Square

Like its sister museum in Brighton, **Hove Museum** is a bit of an eclectic treasure-trove. Its single most prized possession is the 3500-year-old **Hove amber cup** – discovered nearby in 1856 and considered to be one of Britain's most important Bronze Age finds – but it's equally known for its wonderful **contemporary crafts collection**, one of the finest in the country, comprising over two hundred pieces of ceramics, textiles, metalwork and other crafts by local and international makers. You also shouldn't miss the **Film Galleries**, which record Hove's important role in the early silent film industry, and show some of the wonderful films made in a tiny six-seat cinema.

Elsewhere there's an interesting display on the **history and architecture** of Hove, with some great pictures of the earliest stages of development, with a ribbon of grand seafront crescents and squares backed by open fields. For kids, the **Wizard's Attic**, an imaginatively interactive room stuffed full of antique toys, is a sure-fire hit, while the museum **café** is surely the most cultured place for a cuppa in town, with tables surrounded by cabinets of exquisite pottery from Wedgwood and other big names.

Out of the centre

Most of Brighton's sights are very central, but there are a few a little further afield that are well worth seeking out. Remember also that Brighton sits on the edge of some stunning countryside, and in a surprisingly short time you can be out of the city and soaking up glorious views at some of the loveliest spots in the South Downs National Park (see opposite).

Booth Museum of Natural History

194 Dyke Rd, BN1 5AA, 1 mile from the centre of town • Mon–Wed, Fri & Sat 10am–noon & 1.15–5pm, Sun 2–5pm • Free • ☎ 0300 029 0900, ⓦ brightonmuseums.org.uk/booth • Buses #14, #27, #27A or #27B

A half-hour walk from the city centre, the **Booth Museum of Natural History** is a wonderfully fusty old Victorian museum with beetles, birds, butterflies and animal skeletons galore. The museum was purpose-built by nineteenth-century natural historian and eccentric Edward Thomas Booth to house his prodigious collection of stuffed birds – one of the largest in the country. Rumour had it that Booth kept a locomotive under steam at Brighton station so that he could be ready to set off in pursuit of a rare species at a moment's notice. Booth's technique of mounting birds in a diorama of their natural habitat, rather than on a simple wooden perch, was completely new, and copied around the world.

Preston Manor

Preston Drove, just off the A23, BN1 6SD • April–Sept Tues–Sat 10am–5pm, Sun 2–5pm • £6.60; 2-day pass with Royal Pavilion & Brighton Museum £15 • ☎ 0300 029 0900, ⓦ brightonmuseums.org.uk/prestonmanor • A 5min walk from Preston Park train station, or buses #5, #5A, #17, #40, #40X or #273

Two miles north of Brighton, pretty **Preston Manor** dates from 1738, though it was extensively remodelled in 1905 by the Stanford family, who lived there for 138 years before gifting it to the city of Brighton in 1932. Its series of period interiors engagingly evokes the life of the Edwardian gentry, from the servants' quarters downstairs to the luxury nursery upstairs; the Stanfords were ferocious entertainers, counting Queen Victoria's daughters and Rudyard Kipling among their regular visitors.

Chattri memorial

ⓦ chattri.org • Bus #5A runs to Old London Rd in Patcham (where there is also free parking), from where it's a 1-mile walk

On the outskirts of the city, up on the Downs and only accessible by footpath, the **Chattri memorial** commemorates the Indian soldiers who died during World War I. Around 12,000 wounded Indian soldiers were brought to Brighton for treatment – some ending up at the Royal Pavilion Hospital – and the 53 Hindus and Sikhs who died were cremated at this peaceful site. The simple marble memorial was erected in 1921.

Stanmer Park

Two miles from Brighton, off the A270 • Bus #78 (Sat, Sun & bank hols only) or buses #23 or #25

Covering around twenty square miles of woods and downland, sweeping **Stanmer Park** lies just within the South Downs National Park, and is a lovely place to escape the city, especially in spring when bluebells speckle the woods. One of the nicest walks – with buses back to Brighton at each end (see box, p.248) – is the three-mile stroll across to Ditchling Beacon (see p.232).

BREEZE UP TO THE DOWNS

The year-round **Breeze up the Downs** bus service (ⓦ brighton-hove.gov.uk/breezebuses) connects the city to three nearby beauty spots in the South Downs National Park: Devil's Dyke (see p.232), Ditchling Beacon (see p.232) and Stanmer Park (see above) – all just a twenty-minute ride away from the centre of Brighton. Buses run at weekends and bank holidays throughout the year, with daily departures to Devil's Dyke in high summer. The Breeze Return ticket (£4.50) allows you to travel to one destination and return from another; the six-mile walk from Devil's Dyke to Ditchling Beacon is a splendid way to soak up some of the national park's finest scenery.

BRIGHTON'S BEST FESTIVALS AND EVENTS

Scarcely a week passes in Brighton without a festival or event taking place. We've picked out some of the best below, but there are many more; check out ⓦvisitbrighton.com.

Brighton Festival ⓦbrightonfestival.org. The largest multi-arts festival in England, taking place over three weeks in May, with a different Guest Artistic Director each year.

Brighton and Hove Fringe Festival ⓦbrightonfringe.org. Running at the same time as the Brighton Festival, this is one of the largest fringe festivals in the world, with over seven hundred acts, from cabaret to club nights to comedy.

Artists Open Houses ⓦaoh.org.uk. Hundreds of artists around the city open up their houses and studios to the public in this biannual event (May & Dec).

Great Escape ⓦgreatescapefestival.com. Three-day music festival in May, showcasing the best new and up-and-coming local, national and international bands.

Paddle Round the Pier ⓦpaddleroundthepier.com. Weekend beach festival held in July, featuring watersports, live music and a pier-to-pier race.

London to Brighton Veteran Car Run ⓦveterancarrun.com. Taking place in early Nov on a Sun, this long-established event (which first took place in 1896) sees hundreds of vintage vehicles – all built before 1905 – attempt the 60-mile run from the capital.

Burning the Clocks ⓦsamesky.co.uk/events/burning-the-clocks. To mark the winter solstice on Dec 21, hundreds of beautiful paper and willow lanterns are carried through the streets before being burnt on the beach.

ARRIVAL AND DEPARTURE   BRIGHTON

BY TRAIN

Brighton station At the top of Queen's Rd, which descends to the Clocktower and then becomes West St, eventually leading to the seafront, a 10min walk away.

Destinations Arundel (hourly; 1hr 10min); Bognor (every 30min; 45min); Chichester (every 30min; 45–55min); Eastbourne (every 20min; 35min); Hastings (every 30min; 1hr 5min); Lewes (every 10–20min; 15min); Littlehampton (every 30min; 45min); London Bridge (Mon–Sat 2 hourly; 1hr); London Victoria (1–2 hourly; 55min); Shoreham-by-Sea (every 30min; 15min); Worthing (every 30min; 25min).

Hove station Much smaller and quieter than Brighton, it is at the top of Goldstone Villas; it's a 10min walk south along Goldstone Villas and then George St to reach Church Rd, the main drag.

Destinations Chichester (1–3 hourly; 45min); Littlehampton (every 15min; 35–45min); London Victoria (1–2 hourly; 1hr 10min); Shoreham-by-Sea (every 15min; 10min); Worthing (every 10min; 15–20min).

BY BUS

The bus station is just in from the seafront on the south side of the Old Steine.

Destinations Arundel via Littlehampton (Mon–Sat every 30min, Sun hourly; 2hr); Chichester via Bognor, Littlehampton, Worthing & Shoreham-by-Sea (every

20–30min; 1hr 45min); Eastbourne (every 10–15min; 1hr 15min); Lewes (Mon–Sat every 15min, Sun every 30min; 30min); London Victoria (hourly; 2hr 20min); Tunbridge Wells (Mon–Sat every 15min, Sun hourly; 1hr 50min).

BY CAR

The main A23 road into Brighton often suffers from traffic jams at weekends in summer, and once you're in the centre free on-street parking is non-existent, so it's best to avoid driving if you're just coming for the day. If you're staying overnight, most accommodation options can supply you with parking vouchers.

Park-and-ride Free at Withdean Sports Complex, north of the city centre (Tongdean Lane, BN1 5JD, signposted from the A23); bus #27 runs into town every 15min Mon–Sat, every 20min Sun. A City Saver bus ticket costs £5 (see below).

Parking Pay-and-display parking in central Brighton costs £3.60/hr, £6.20/2hr and £10.40/4hr (max stay). Seafront parking charges drop outside the central zone (east of Yellowave, and west of Brunswick Square), and allow longer stays (£7.20/11hr). The cheapest long-stay multistorey car parks are Regency Square and Trafalgar St (both £18/24hr). Brighton and Hove Council's website ⓦbrighton-hove.gov.uk/content/parking-and-travel/journeyon has a useful car parking map.

GETTING AROUND

BY BUS

The website ⓦbrighton-hove.gov.uk/content/parking-and-travel/journeyon is a great resource, with a journey planner. Most of the city is walkable, but buses can be

useful for west Hove and some further-flung sights.

Tickets The City Saver gives you one day's unlimited travel in the city for £5. Short-hop journeys cost £2.

BY TAXI

The main taxi ranks are at Brighton and Hove stations, East St, Queens Square near the Clock Tower, outside St Peter's church and outside Hove Town Hall.
Brighton and Hove Streamline Taxis ☎01273 202020.
Brighton and Hove Radio cabs ☎01273 204060.

BY BIKE

There's a downloadable cycling map of the city at ⓦ brighton-hove.gov.uk/content/cycle-facilities-map; a cycle path runs the length of Brighton seafront, meeting up just east of the Marina with the Undercliff Walk (see box, p.245) – note that cyclists must give way to pedestrians here. Bike tours are also available (see box below). The two most central bike hire outlets are:
Brighton Cycle Hire Unit 8, under the station, off Trafalgar St (Mon–Fri 9am–6pm, Sat 9.30am–5pm, Sun & bank hols 10am–4pm; ☎01273 571555, ⓦ brightoncyclehire.com). Bikes cost £7/3hr, £10 /24hr.
Brighton Beach Bikes 250 King's Rd Arches, west side of Brighton Pier (Mon–Fri 11am–5pm, Sat & Sun 10am–6pm; ☎07917 753794, ⓦ brightonbeachbikes.co.uk). Californian beach-cruiser-type bikes cost £12/3hr, £16/4hr or longer.

INFORMATION

Tourist office There are fifteen staffed visitor information points throughout the city (☎01273 290337, ⓦ visitbrighton.com), including at the train station, the Royal Pavilion Shop, Brighton Pier, Jubilee Library, Churchill Square and the Old Market in Hove. Opening times vary; see the website for a full list.
Apps, magazines and websites VisitBrighton produces a free app for smartphones – search for "Brighton official visitor city guide". The best listings magazine is *Source Magazine* (ⓦ brightonsource.co.uk), but *XYZ* (ⓦ xyzmagazine.co.uk) and *BN1* (ⓦ bn1magazine.co.uk) are also worth a look. Viva Brighton (ⓦ vivabrighton.com/viva-brighton) is a monthly magazine of articles and reviews, with covers designed by local artists, distributed free around the city and also available online.

ACTIVITIES

BEACH SPORTS

★**Yellowave** 299 Madeira Drive, BN2 1EN ☎01273 672222, ⓦ yellowave.co.uk. The country's only year-round beach sports venue is a brilliant spot, with six sand courts offering volleyball (courts and ball £22/hr; beginners' classes £5.50) and other beach sports. Even if you don't want to play it's a great place to hang out, with a sandpit to keep youngsters happy, and a great café with plenty of tables outside. Summer Mon–Fri 10am–10pm, Sat & Sun 10am–8pm; winter Tues–Thurs 10am–9pm, Fri–Sun 10am–5pm.

CITY TOURS

In addition to the recommended tours below, you can take advantage of the **Brighton Greeters** scheme, which pairs up visitors with a volunteer Brighton resident tour guide for a free two-hour tour; see ⓦ visitbrighton.com/greeters for more information.

The Grand Brighton Bike Tour ☎07914 786843, ⓦ brightonbiketour.com. A fun 2hr 30min tour of the city by bike (£19.50); morning and afternoon tours available.
Brighton City Walks ☎07941 256148, ⓦ brightoncitywalks.com. This 1hr 30min traditional tour of the city runs most days; the price depends on the number of people on the tour.
Brighton Sewer Tours ☎01903 272606, ⓦ sewertours.southernwater.co.uk. Brighton's famous, award-winning tours of its Victorian sewers are much more fun than they sound, taking you through narrow corridors and up and down metal ladders to see the still-working legacy of the Victorians, and filling you in on lots of interesting stuff about the city along the way (May–Sept; 1hr; £12).
Ghost Walk of the Lanes ☎01273 328297, ⓦ ghostwalkbrighton.co.uk. Fun (and family-friendly) ghost walks around Brighton's atmospheric Lanes, visiting eight apparently haunted sites (Wed–Sat; 1hr 10min; £8).
Only in Brighton ☎07954 482112, ⓦ onlyinbrighton .co.uk. Equally popular with locals and visitors, this quirky tour (April–Oct Fri & Sat; 1hr 30min; £8) answers all the important questions about Brighton life: how did a song performed at the Brighton Dome help trigger the Portuguese Revolution? Why did the Prince Regent need a stiff brandy when he met his future wife? And just what connects Mount Everest and the Hove branch of Tesco? The same guide runs "Piers and Queers" tours, exploring the city's LGBT history (check website for dates; prices vary).
Sightseeing bus Hop-on, hop-off buses run around the city's main sights (April & May daily 10am–6pm, every 1hr; June–Sept daily 10am–6/7pm, every 30min; Oct Sat & Sun 10am–5pm, every 1hr; 50min for whole circuit; £15, valid 24hr; ⓦ city-sightseeing.com).

7

Lower Esplanade beach volleyball ☎ 01273 292716. There's a council-run beach volleyball court on the Lower Esplanade between the piers. April–Sept £24.50/hr (£16.50 before noon Mon–Fri), rest of year free. April–Sept daily 10am–6pm; Oct–March daily open access.

WATERSPORTS

Brighton Watersports 185 King's Rd Arches, on the Lower Esplanade, BN1 1NB ☎ 01273 323160, ⓦ thebrightonwatersports.co.uk. Right down by the pebbles, this well-established outfit offers stand-up paddleboarding (board rental £10/hr; 2hr 30min introductory lesson £40), wakeboarding (30min; £40), ringo rides (15min; £20), kayak rental (£10/person/hr) and scuba dive equipment rental. They can also arrange a fun 3hr kayaking taster session (£40) with BK Kayaking (ⓦ bkkayaking.co.uk) and scuba diving with Brighton Diving (ⓦ brighton-diving.co.uk).

Lagoon Watersports Hove Lagoon, BN3 4LX ☎ 01273 424842, ⓦ lagoon.co.uk/hove-lagoon. This sheltered beachfront lagoon offers windsurfing (3hr taster £69); stand-up paddleboarding (2hr taster £50); and cable wakeboarding (1hr taster £58). Their sailing school based at Brighton Marina offers longer dinghy sailing courses, an introductory half-day session (3hr; £99) and high-speed powerboat rides (30min; £35).

BOAT TRIPS

Ross Boat Trips Pontoon 5, West Jetty, Brighton Marina, BN2 5WA ☎ 07958 246414 & ☎ 07836 262717, ⓦ watertours.co.uk. Mackerel fishing trips (March–Nov; 1hr 30min; £22), powerboat rides (25min; £17.50) and sea cruises (45min; £8.50).

SIGHTSEEING FLIGHTS

Brighton Scenic Shoreham Airport, Shoreham-by-Sea, BN43 5FF ☎ 07918 902721, ⓦ brightonscenic .co.uk Scenic flights in a four-seater aircraft. Lots of options, from a short city flight (20min; £61), to a longer tour that takes you over the Downs and along the coast (1hr 15min; £133).

WINE-TASTING

Great British Wine Tours ☎ 01273 278474, ⓦ greatbritishwinetours.co.uk. Minibus tours (£79) of two or three Sussex vineyards, leaving from Brighton, including tutored wine-tastings, lunch and a vineyard tour.

SPA TREATMENTS

The Treatment Rooms 21 New Road, BN1 1UF ☎ 01273 818444, ⓦ thetreatmentrooms.co.uk. Aromatherapy, facials, wraps and other treatments, for both men and women.

ACCOMMODATION

There're no two ways about it: accommodation is pricey in Brighton. The prices we give are weekend, high-season rates, but if you're visiting out of summer – especially during the week – these rates can fall dramatically, so it pays to check out a few options online. Year-round, you'll be required to stay a minimum of two nights at the weekend. Some of the nicest, most characterful B&Bs are in **Kemp Town**, on the eastern side of the city; with some excellent cafés, restaurants and antique shops up at the "village" end of Kemp Town, this can be a great place to base yourself.

CENTRAL BRIGHTON

★**Artist Residence** 33 Regency Square, BN1 2GG ☎ 01273 324302, ⓦ artistresidencebrighton.co.uk; map pp.238–239. Characterful, cool and quirky, this uber-stylish 23-room townhouse hotel sits at the top end of a seafront square overlooking the i360. Rooms are individually decorated – some of them by local and international artists – plus there's a cocktail bar and two very good restaurants. **£170**

KIPPS 76 Grand Parade, BN2 9JA ☎ 01273 604182, ⓦ kipps-brighton.com; map p.242. This hostel – an antidote to the party hostels of Brighton – feels more like a small hotel, and has an unbeatable location opposite the Royal Pavilion. Rooms and dorms are plain but comfy, there's a licensed bar and excellent-value breakfasts (£2.50 for dorms, included for rooms). Dorms **£32.50**, doubles **£45**

MyHotel 17 Jubilee St, BN1 1GE ☎ 01273 900300, ⓦ myhotels.com/my-hotel-brighton; map p.242. This hip, fun contemporary hotel has a great location, right in the heart of North Laine, and incorporates not only one of the city's best restaurants, *Chilli Pickle* (see p.253), but also one of its best coffee shops, *The Small Batch Coffee Co* (see p.253). The rooms have been designed along feng shui lines, so you'll find curved walls inset with crystals, vibrant colour and spiritual artwork. Rates vary according to demand, and can drop as low as £75 out of peak times, so check online for bargains. **£120**

★**Pelirocco** 10 Regency Square, BN1 2FG ☎ 01273 327055, ⓦ hotelpelirocco.co.uk; map pp.238–239. "England's most rock'n'roll hotel" is a real one-off, featuring extravagantly themed rooms inspired by pop culture and pin-ups. There's a Pop Art "Modrophenia" room featuring bedside tables made from scooters, a cosy "Do Knit Disturb" room created by a Brighton knitwear/crochet artist, and the decadent "Kraken's Lair" that comes with a circular bed with a mirrored canopy and a pole-dancing pole in the corner of the room. **£145**

★**YHA Brighton** Old Steine, BN1 1NH ☎ 01273 738674, ⓦ yha.org.uk/hostel/brighton; map p.242. The cheapest sea views in Brighton can be found at the stylish YHA hostel, less than a minute's walk from the pier. All of the 51 rooms (including twenty doubles – the smartest of them with roll-top baths) are en suite, and there's a lovely café-bar. Prices drop dramatically mid-week and out of season; book well ahead for weekend stays. Breakfast £5.75. Dorm **£33**, double **£80**

KEMP TOWN

★**27 Brighton Bed & Breakfast** 27 Upper Rock Gardens, BN2 1QE 📞01273 694951, 🖰 brighton-bed-and-breakfast.co.uk; map pp.238–239. The five rooms at this Georgian townhouse B&B – each of them named after someone or something associated with the Prince Regent – are beautifully elegant, featuring old-fashioned brass beds, antiques and Chinese-inspired furnishings, and the hosts couldn't be more welcoming, too. Decanters of sherry in the rooms are one of many lovely touches. **£120**
Blanch House 17 Atlingworth St, BN2 1PL 📞01273 603504, 🖰 blanchhouse.co.uk; map pp.238–239. Brighton's original boutique hotel is still going strong, with a mix of styles and prices across its twelve chic rooms. The main draw though is the wonderful high-ceilinged champagne and cocktail bar down on the ground floor – the perfect start to a night on the town. **£149**
Brighton Wave 10 Madeira Place, BN2 1TN 📞01273 676794, 🖰 brightonwave.com; map pp.238–239. This friendly B&B has a lovely relaxed feel, with a bright and cheery breakfast room that features art for sale on the walls and fairy lights in the fireplaces. Rooms are smart and contemporary, with en-suite showers, and welcome extra touches include a large DVD library and breakfast served late at weekends. **£125**
Drakes Hotel 33–34 Marine Parade, BN2 1PE 📞01273 696934, 🖰 drakesofbrighton.com; map pp.238–239. The seafront location is the big draw at this chic, minimalist boutique hotel, which boasts the best sea views in town: the most expensive rooms come with freestanding baths by floor-to-ceiling windows looking out over the twinkling lights of the pier. The excellent in-house restaurant (see p.252) is one of Brighton's best. **£160**
★**Guest and the City** 2 Broad St, BN2 1TJ 📞01273 698289, 🖰 guestandthecity.co.uk; map pp.238–239. A

great central location, super-friendly hosts and stylish rooms. It's worth spending a tiny bit more to bag one of the two nicest rooms (£140), which feature stained-glass windows of classic Brighton scenes and a covered balconette. **£90**
Kemp Townhouse 21 Atlingworth St, BN2 1PL 📞01273 681400, 🖰 kemptownhouse.com; map pp.238–239. Sophisticated, stylish and very friendly, this Regency townhouse – the city's only five-star B&B – has nine lovely rooms decorated in muted tones, with black-and-white prints of Brighton or the sea up on the walls, subway-tiled wet rooms and carafes of complimentary port. **£155**
Sheepcote Valley Wilson Ave, BN2 5TS 📞01273 626546, 🖰 caravanclub.co.uk; map pp.238–239. Brighton's leafy campsite lies a mile or so inland from Brighton Marina (take bus #1 or #1A from the centre to Wilson Ave), on the far side of Kemp Town, a 10min walk from the city centre. The site is mainly for caravans, but there are eighty tent pitches, and camping pods (sleep 2 people). Camping **£42.90**, pods **£50**
★**Snooze** 25 St George's Terrace, BN2 1JJ 📞01273 605797, 🖰 snoozebrighton.com; map pp.238–239. This cool B&B in the heart of Kemp Town is crammed with fun touches, including a graffiti-style re-creation of the Sistine Chapel in the breakfast room. The six en-suite rooms are styled with a hotchpotch of vintage furnishings, plus there are two uber-cool 1970s-style suites. **£140**
★**The Twenty One** 21 Charlotte St, BN2 1AG 📞01273 686450, 🖰 thetwentyone.co.uk; map pp.238–239. This Regency townhouse is a super-friendly home from home, with stylish rooms – chandeliers, fluffy cushions and cream linens – immaculate bathrooms, a DVD library, iPads, bathrobes and a well-stocked hospitality tray. The lovely owners and their attention to detail make it very popular. **£135**
White House 6 Bedford St, BN2 1AN 📞01273 626266, 🖰 whitehousebrighton.com; map pp.238–239. Set back from the road slightly, and facing south, this lovely townhouse B&B seems flooded with light. The eight serene rooms are impeccably tasteful, and those at the front even boast that elusive thing in Brighton – a proper sea view. **£130**

EATING

As you'd expect from cool, cosmopolitan "London-by-the-sea", there's a thriving café culture in Brighton, with hip little cafés and **coffee shops** sprouting up all over the city, but especially concentrated around the lively North Laine area; sitting over a coffee and watching Brighton life go by is an essential box to tick on any trip to the city. Brighton also boasts the greatest concentration of **restaurants** in the Southeast after London, among them some highly rated fine-dining options, the country's first zero-waste restaurant, and some long-established gems including, appropriately enough for a town that embraced lentils and tofu long before they became mainstream, two of the country's best vegetarian restaurants. If you're visiting on a Friday, be sure to check out **Street Diner** (🖰 streetdiner.co.uk), a weekly open-air foodie market held in Brighthelm Garden, a couple of minutes' walk from the station (11am–3pm).

7

THE SEAFRONT
CAFÉS, SNACKS AND AFTERNOON TEA

The Grand Hotel 97–99 King's Rd, BN1 2FW ☎01273 224300, ⓦgrandbrighton.co.uk; map pp.238–239. With its elegant lounge and peerless sea views, you really can't beat afternoon tea (£29.95) at *The Grand*, Brighton's iconic seafront hotel. Three sittings daily at 12.30pm, 2.30pm & 4.30pm.

★**Jack and Linda's Smokehouse** 197 King's Rd Arches; map p.242. This tiny beachfront takeaway is run by a lovely couple who've been traditionally smoking fish here for over a decade – the diminutive black-painted smokehouse is on the pebbles just across from Jack and Linda's arch. Grab a fresh crab sandwich or hot mackerel roll (£4.40) to eat on the beach for a perfect summer lunch. April–Sept daily 10am–5pm; Oct Sat & Sun 10am–5pm; March & Nov weather dependent.

Lucky Beach Café 171 King's Rd Arches, BN1 1NB ☎01273 728280, ⓦluckybeach.co.uk; map p.242. Popular beach café, with lots of outdoor seating and a great menu of burgers made from organic beef (£8–9), sandwiches and local beers. Mon–Fri from 8.30am, Sat & Sun from 8am; closing times vary depending on season and weather.

RESTAURANTS

Melrose 132 King's Rd, BN1 2HH ☎01273 326520, ⓦmelroserestaurant.co.uk; map pp.238–239. Along with the *Regency* next door, this traditional seafront establishment is a bit of a Brighton institution – it's been dishing up tasty, excellent-value fish and chips (£7.25), seafood platters (£7.75), roasts and custard-covered puddings for over forty years. Daily 11.30am–10.30pm.

The Restaurant at Drakes 33–34 Marine Parade, BN2 1PE ☎01273 696934, ⓦdrakesofbrighton.com /restaurant; map pp.238–239. The stylish restaurant in the basement of one of the city's best hotels is an absolute winner (two courses £34). Arrive early if you can, for a pre-dinner drink in the cocktail bar with its lovely sea views. Daily 12.30–1.45pm & 7–9.45pm.

Salt Room 106 King's Rd, BN1 2FU ☎01273 929488, ⓦsaltroom-restaurant.co.uk; map pp.238–239. One of the city's best fish and seafood restaurants, with a stylish exposed-brick interior, peerless sea views and fantastic charcoal-grilled fish and seafood (mains £20 and up). Make

sure you leave room for the "Taste of the Pier" dessert, a fun confection of candyfloss, ice-cream cones, doughnuts and chocolate pebbles. Mon–Thurs & sun noon–4pm & 6–10pm, Fri & Sat noon–4pm & 6–10.30pm.

CITY CENTRE

Gingerman 21a Norfolk Square, BN1 2PD ☎01273 326688, ⓦgingermanrestaurant.com; map pp.238–239. You can't spend long in Brighton without stumbling on one of the foodie outposts of the Ginger empire – there's a *Ginger Pig* in Hove, a *Ginger Dog* in Kemp Town, and a *Ginger Fox* (see p.201) in nearby Albourne – but this one-room restaurant was where it all started. Recently given a chic minimalist makeover, it still serves up some of the best food in Brighton: a three-course dinner will set you back £37, just over half that at lunchtime. Tues–Sun 12.30–2pm & 7–10pm.

THE LANES
CAFÉS AND COFFEESHOPS

Blackbird Tearooms 30 Ship St, BN1 1AD ☎01273 249454, ⓦblackbirdtearooms.com; map p.242. Smart, traditional tearoom, with dainty crockery, white tablecloths, shelves lined with vintage tins and old black-and-white photos of Brighton on the walls. Superb cakes and afternoon teas (£16), plus Welsh rarebit, sandwiches and all-day breakfasts. Daily 8.30am–5.30pm.

Marwood 52 Ship St, BN1 1AF ☎01273 382063, ⓦthemarwood.com; map p.242. A real one-off, this relaxed coffee shop's eclectic, cluttered decor includes Action Men abseiling from the ceiling and a stuffed cat mounted on the wall. The coffee is "kick arse", plus there are great cakes and a simple menu of snacks. Mon–Wed 8am–8pm, Thurs & Fri 8am–11pm, Sat 9am–11pm, Sun 10am–8pm.

RESTAURANTS

★**64 Degrees** 53 Meeting House Lane, BN1 1HB ☎01273 770115, ⓦ64degrees.co.uk; map p.242. This pocket-sized restaurant in the Lanes is one of the best places to eat in the city. The seats to go for are up at the counter of the open kitchen: choose several small plates of food (£6–12) to share from the short menu, which features four options each of fish, veg and meat dishes (example dish: "pig head, corn, mustard"). The food's inventive and

---

BEST PLACES FOR...

Afternoon tea *Blackbird Tearooms* (see above), *The Grand Hotel* (see above), *Metrodeco* (see p.254), *Terre-à-Terre* (see opposite).
Quirky Brighton *Bom-Bane's* (see p.255), *Marwood* (see above), *Tea Cosy Tea Rooms* (see p.255).
Treating yourself *64 Degrees* (see above), *Gingerman* (see above), *Isaac at* (see opposite), *Little Fish Market* (see p.254), *The Restaurant at Drakes* (see above), *Salt Room* (see above).
Veggies *Food for Friends* (see opposite), *Iydea* (see p.254), *Terre-à-Terre* (see opposite).

delicious, and the whole experience is brilliant fun. Daily noon–3pm & 6–9.45pm.

The Coal Shed 8 Boyces St, BN1 1AN ☎01273 322998, ⓦcoalshed-restaurant.co.uk; map p.242. Seriously good steak, aged for 35 days and cooked on a charcoal grill, is the main draw here, though the fish is equally good (mains £12–27). Worth a special mention are the Sunday sharing roasts (£35 for 2 people): a 500g sirloin presented on a platter with all the trimmings. Mon–Thurs & Sun noon–4pm & 6–10pm, Fri & Sat noon–4pm & 6–10.30pm.

Curry Leaf Café 60 Ship St, BN1 1AE ☎01273 207070, ⓦcurryleafcafe.com; map p.242. Delicious South Indian street food in the heart of the Lanes; tuck into masala dosas, thalis and street food platters at lunch, or more formal mains (£12/13) in the evening. Craft beers and delicious cocktails are added bonuses. A takeaway branch is planned for Kemp Town. Daily noon–3pm & 6–10pm, Fri & Sat until 10.30pm.

Food for Friends 18 Prince Albert St, BN1 1HF ☎01273 202310, ⓦfoodforfriends.com; map p.242. Brighton's original veggie restaurant has been going strong for over 35 years, and its sophisticated cooking is imaginative enough to please die-hard meat-eaters too. Mains £12–14. Mon–Thurs & Sun noon–10pm, Fri & Sat noon–10.30pm.

Plateau 1 Bartholomews, BN1 1HG ☎01273 733085, ⓦplateaubrighton.co.uk; map p.242. "Wine, beats and bites" is the tagline of this buzzy little restaurant-cum-wine bar. Sharing platters and small bites (£5–8) run alongside a good range of cocktails, organic beers and organic and biodynamic wines (some from Sussex producers). Daily noon–late; kitchen noon–3.30pm & 6–10pm.

Riddle and Finns 12b Meeting House Lane, BN1 1HB ☎01273 328008; ⓦriddleandfinns.co.uk; map p.242. This bustling champagne and oyster bar is justifiably popular. There's a huge range of fish and shellfish on offer, served on communal marble-topped tables in a white-tiled candlelit dining room. No bookings. Daily noon–late.

★**Terre-à-Terre** 71 East St, BN1 1HQ ☎01273 729051, ⓦterreaterre.co.uk; map p.242. One of the country's best veggie restaurants, this multi-award-winning place is famed for its inventive cuisine (mains around £15/16). The taster tapas plate for two (£30) is a good way to sample some of the weird and wonderful creations on offer, everything from Sneaky Peeking Steamers to Better Batter and Lemony Yemeni Relish. Mon–Fri noon–10.30pm, Sat 11am–11pm, Sun 11am–10pm.

NORTH LAINE
CAFÉS AND COFFEESHOPS

Flour Pot Bakery 40 Sydney St, BN1 4EP ☎01273 621942, ⓦflour-pot.co.uk; map p.242. Tuck into crumbly pastries, cakes and sandwiches made with artisan bread at this hip bakery/café, with bench seating in the bare-brick interior and more tables outside. Mon–Sat 8am–7pm, Sun 9am–6pm.

Julian Plumart Café et Patisserie 48 Queens Rd, BN1 3XB ☎01273 777412, ⓦjulienplumart.com; map p.242. This little French patisserie showcases the glorious patisserie creations of chef Julien Plumart – trained by Raymond Blanc. Choose from exquisite tarts, classic pastries or jewel-like macarons, which come in over a dozen flavours (£1.65 each). There's a separate shop and *salon de thé* on Duke St. Mon–Fri 7.30am–7pm, Sat & Sun 8.30am–7pm.

Pavilion Gardens Café Royal Pavilion Gardens, BN1 1UG ☎01273 730712, ⓦpaviliongardenscafe.co.uk; map p.242. Run by the Sewell family ever since it opened back in 1941, this no-frills café serves up sandwiches, jacket potatoes and legendary rock cakes from its idyllic location in Pavilion Gardens. All seating is outside. Hours weather dependent; closed in winter.

Small Batch Coffee 17 Jubilee St, BN1 1GE ☎01273 697597, ⓦsmallbatchcoffee.co.uk; map p.242. This Brighton-based coffee chain, with its own roastery in Hove, has seven branches around the city but the sleek flagship shop is here, in the ground floor of *MyHotel*. Coffee lovers can choose from espresso, cold-brew (brewed for five hours to create a delicate flavour), pour-over (filter), or a brewed coffee at the syphon bar. Beans change seasonally. Mon–Sat 7am–7pm, Sun 8am–6pm.

RESTAURANTS

Burger Brothers 97 North Rd, BN1 1YE ☎01273 706980, ⓦfacebook.com/burgerbrothersbrighton; map p.242. "Strictly burgers, no chips!" reads the sign at this independent burger joint, whose offerings – from the Simple Jack (£5) to the Benetton burger with stilton, wasabi mayo, Portobello mushrooms and a choice of charcuterie (£8.50) – have recently been voted the best burgers in the UK. There are a few seats but it's mainly takeaway. Tues–Sat noon–10pm.

★**Chilli Pickle** 17 Jubilee St, BN1 1GE ☎01273 900383, ⓦthechillipickle.com; map p.242. You really can't go wrong with a meal at this fantastic, award-winning restaurant. From thalis (£13) to tandoori platters (£16.50) to street food (£6–8), everything on the menu is innovative and delicious. Daily noon–3pm & 6–10.30pm.

Isaac At 2 Gloucester St, BN1 4EW ☎07765 934740, ⓦisaac-at.com; map p.242. A unique fine dining experience: choose the six-course (£47) or the four-course (£32) menu, with optional alcohol or Sussex juice pairings (£29/22 respectively). The food – inspired by Sussex and all sourced locally – is prepared in front of you in the open kitchen, and served to guests by the chefs. Tues–Fri 6–10.30pm, Sat 12.30–2.30pm & 6–10.30pm.

7

★**Iydea** 17 Kensington Gardens, BN1 4AL ☎01273 667992, ⓦiydea.co.uk; map p.242. Good value, wholesome and delicious veggie food served up cafeteria-style. What's on offer changes every day, but there tends to be a quiche, a lasagne, a curry and enchiladas, alongside half a dozen other dishes; pick one main, add two vegetable dishes or salads and two toppings, and you're away (£4.70–7.70). Daily 9.30am–5.30pm; lunch served Mon–Thurs & Sun 11.30am–4.30pm, Fri & Sat 11.30am–5pm.

La Choza 36 Gloucester Rd, BN1 4AQ ☎01273 945926, ⓦlachoza.co.uk; map p.242. Fun and flamboyant Mexican street-food restaurant, with great-value food: snacks such as deep-fried jalapeños or calamari with chipotle mayo cost £5–6; more filling burritos, quesadillas and tostadas are £7.50–9. Mon 11.30am–4pm, Tues–Sun 11.30am–10pm.

★**Silo** 39 Upper Gardner St, BN1 4AN ☎01273 674259, ⓦsilobrighton.com; map p.242. The country's first zero-waste restaurant aims to deliver a "pre-industrial food system": food comes from local suppliers; all waste is composted on-site and the compost sent back to farmers; the restaurant mills its own wheat, churns its own butter and even brews its own fermented drinks using "foraged and intercepted" plants; the furniture is upcycled, jam-jars are used as glasses, and plates were originally plastic bags. And the food – the likes of Shiitake mushrooms, Worksop Blue and dumplings (£14), or Mallard breast, crab apple and rye (£18) – is delicious. Mon 11am–4pm, Tues–Sat 11am–4pm & 6–11pm, Sat 10am–4pm & 6–11pm, Sun 10am–5pm.

HOVE

Foragers 3 Stirling Place, BN3 3YU ☎01273 733134, ⓦtheforagerspub.co.uk; map pp.238–239. Relaxed and unpretentious, this gastropub serves up seasonal, sustainable food, with greens and herbs foraged locally, and meat and fish sourced from Sussex and Kent suppliers. Mains are around £12–15. Mon–Thurs & Sun noon–11pm, Fri & Sat noon–midnight; kitchen Mon–Fri noon–3pm & 6–10pm, Sat noon–4pm & 6–10pm, Sun noon–4pm.

★**Little Fish Market** 10 Upper Market St, BN3 1AS ☎01273 722213, ⓦthelittlefishmarket.co.uk; map pp.238–239. This exceptionally good fish restaurant isn't cheap (all that's on offer is a set five-course menu for £50) but it gets rave reviews and is well worth it for a special occasion. It only serves twenty diners a night, so book ahead, especially at weekends. Tues–Fri 7–10.30pm, Sat noon–2pm & 7–10.30pm.

Treacle & Co 164 Church Rd, BN3 2DL ☎01273 933695, ⓦtreacleandco.co.uk; map pp.238–239. Lovely little café with a simple menu (Welsh rarebit, pies, sandwiches and the like, in the £5–7 range) and stupendously good cakes and tarts, all baked here – everything from gargantuan meringues to gooey salted caramel tarts and (equally good) gluten-free loaf cakes. Mon–Fri 8.30am–5.30pm, Sat 9am–5.30pm, Sun 10am–5pm.

KEMP TOWN

CAFÉS AND COFFEESHOPS

Compass Point Eatery 19 St Georges Rd, BN2 1EB ☎01273 672672, ⓦcpeatery.com; map pp.238–239. Welcoming, laidback café decked out with American memorabilia and with an American-inspired menu featuring hoagies, NY subs and po' boys (£5–6), plus great breakfasts served till noon. Tues–Sat 9.30am–5pm.

Metrodeco 38 Upper St James's St, BN2 1JN ⓦmetro-deco.com; map pp.238–239. Choose from over twenty blends of tea at this 1930s Parisian-style tearoom, which also has a good selection of boutique gins and tea cocktails – served in teapots, of course. The afternoon teas (£20), served on vintage crockery, are a real treat. Mon–Thurs & Sun 10.30am–7pm, Fri & Sat 10.30am–10pm.

Redroaster 1d St James's St, BN2 1RE ☎01273 686668, ⓦredroaster.co.uk; map p.242. One of Brighton's first independent coffee houses, *Redroaster* has its own coffee roastery and serves over twenty different cups of coffee, from

---

GLORIOUS GELATO

Happily for ice-cream lovers, a handful of top-class *gelaterias* have opened in Brighton in the last few years.

Boho Gelato 6 Pool Valley, BN1 1NJ ☎01273 727205, ⓦbohogelato.co.uk; map p.242. Weird and wonderful flavours abound (Gorgonzola and rosemary, anyone?) at this tiny hole-in-the-wall place. Summer daily 11am–7pm; winter daily 11am–6pm.

Gelato Gusto 2 Gardner St, BN1 1UP ☎01273 673402, ⓦgelatogusto.com; map p.242. *Sorbettos* and ice creams to eat in or take away, plus fabulous sundaes. Mon–Fri 11.30am–6pm, Sat & Sun 11am–6pm.

Jo Jo's Gelato 123–124 Western Rd, ☎01273 771532, ⓦjojosgelato.co.uk; map pp.238–239. Big, bright and beautiful, with a massive selection of gelato (over fifty flavours), and long opening hours. Daily 8am–11pm.

Scoop & Crumb 5–6 East St, BN1 1HP ☎01273 202563, ⓦscoopandcrumb.com; map p.242. Sundaes (more than fifty of them) are the big draw here, but you can also tuck into waffles, hot dogs and sandwiches. Mon–Fri 11am–6pm, Sat 10am–7pm, Sun 11am–7pm.

the usual lattes and espressos to *bombóns* (espresso layered over condensed milk). The properly thick hot chocolate is legendary. Mon–Sat 7am–7pm, Sun 8am–6.30pm.

Tea Cosy Tea Rooms 3 George St, BN2 1RH ⓦtheteacosy.co.uk; map pp.238–239. Taking quirky to a whole new level, this kitsch tearoom is decked out from head to foot in royal memorabilia, and serves afternoon teas named after royal residences and members of the royal family. A strict code of etiquette forbids the dunking of biscuits on pain of removal from the premises. Wed–Fri & Sun noon–5pm, Sat noon–5.30pm.

RESTAURANTS

★**Bom-Bane's** 24 George St, BN2 1RH ☎01273 606400, ⓦbom-banes.com; map pp.238–239. Fabulous café-restaurant run by musician Jane Bom-Bane (famous for her mechanical hats), where each of the tables – from the TurnTable to the Twenty Seven Chimes Table – has a surprise in store. Once a month there's a performance by Jane accompanied by a set two-course meal (£15). Food runs from salads and sandwiches to *stoemp* (Belgian mash) and sausage (£10.95). Wed 12.30–11pm, Thurs 5–11pm, Fri 5–11.30pm, Sat 12.30–11.30pm.

DRINKING

Brighton has an illustrious history of catering to drinkers and partygoers: in 1860 the town boasted 479 **pubs** and **beer shops** – more than the combined number of all the other local shops. Though drinking establishments no longer make up the majority of the town's businesses, the perfect venue and tipple can still be found for all comers, from traditional boozers to indie hangouts, and sleek and chic **cocktail bars**.

7

THE SEAFRONT

Brighton Music Hall 127 King's Rd Arches, BN1 2FN ☎01273 747287, ⓦbrightonmusichall.co.uk; map pp.238–239. The main draw of this bar is the fantastic location, right on the beach with a huge open-air heated terrace, and free live music when the sun shines. Hours vary but generally summer daily 9/10am–late; winter most days from noon – call ahead to check.

Tempest Inn 159–161 King's Rd Arches, BN1 1NB ☎01273 770505, ⓦtempest.pub; map p.242. Head inside this quirky beachfront pub to find a warren of lantern-lit subterranean caves, forming over a dozen cosy snugs. There's a good selection of real ales, craft beer, cocktails and gin (including Brighton Gin, distilled in the city), good locally sourced food, and live music, plus a large front patio. Mon–Wed & Sun noon–1am, Thurs–Sat noon–3am.

CITY CENTRE

Brighton Beer Dispensary 38 Dean St, BN1 3EG ☎01273 710624, ⓦfacebook.com/BRTNDispensary; map pp.238–239. This appealingly down-to-earth pub has a regularly changing selection of nine keg beers, six cask beers and four ciders, including offerings from the city's own Brighton Bier. Interesting (and great value) bar food ranges from oxtail nuggets with mushroom ketchup to battered mackerel hot dogs. Daily noon–late.

★**Craft Beer Co.** 22–23 Upper North St, BN1 3FG ⓦthecraftbeerco.com; map pp.238–239. A must for beer aficionados, this pub boasts an incredible range of nine cask ales changing daily, eighteen keg taps dispensing beer from around the world, and two hundred bottled varieties on offer at any one time. Staff are super friendly and keen to talk about the beers, and they offer free tasters. Mon–Thurs noon–12.30am, Fri & Sat noon–1.30am, Sun noon–11pm.

★**Lion and Lobster** 24 Sillwood St, BN1 2PS ☎01273 327299, ⓦthelionandlobster.co.uk; map pp.238–239.

One of the best pubs in Brighton, the *Lion and Lobster* has a traditional feel – patterned carpet, velvet seats and framed prints and pictures – but a young and fun atmosphere. Though usually busy, various booths offer privacy. Pub quiz on Mon nights, and live jazz on Sun. Good food is served until late. Mon–Thurs 11am–1am, Fri & Sat 11am–2am, Sun noon–midnight.

★ **The Plotting Parlour** 6 Steine St, BN2 1TE ☎01273 621238, ⓦtheplottingparlour-brighton.co.uk; see map p.242. This dimly lit, snug cocktail bar is a real treat, with exquisite cocktails (£8 and up), table service and stylish decor that includes flip-up cinema seats and copper-clad walls. Mon–Thurs & Sun 3pm–midnight, Fri & Sat 3pm–1am.

THE LANES

Colonnade Bar 10 New Rd, BN1 1UF ☎01273 328728, ⓦthecolonnadebrighton.co.uk; map p.242. Right next to the Theatre Royal, the *Colonnade Bar* has an appropriately traditional feel, with plenty of tasselled velvet, and black-and-white headshots of actors who have graced the boards next door. Mon–Thurs noon–11pm, Fri & Sat noon–midnight, Sun noon–10.30pm.

Cricketers 15 Black Lion St, BN1 1ND ☎01273 329472, ⓦcricketersbrighton.co.uk; map p.242. Brighton's oldest pub – all red velvet and gilt – was immortalized in Graham Greene's *Brighton Rock*, and remains an old favourite. Mon–Thurs 11am–midnight, Fri & Sat 11am–1am, Sun 11am–11pm.

Mash Tun 1 Church St, BN1 1UE ☎01273 684951, ⓦmashtun.pub; map p.242. This very popular studenty pub is often heaving, particularly at the weekend. The inside is fairly basic, but cool tunes, trendy bar staff and a "celebrity wall of death" sweepstake contribute to the young and lively atmosphere. Mon–Thurs & Sun noon–2am, Fri & Sat noon–3am.

7

Northern Lights 6 Little East St, BN1 1HT ☎01273 747096, ⓦnorthernlightsbrighton.co.uk; map p.242. This cosy, laidback bar is a real Brighton institution. The Scandinavian theme is very apparent in the drinks and food: there are over two dozen flavoured vodkas (including an amazing tar flavour), plus aquavit and a selection of Swedish flavoured ciders, plus a menu featuring reindeer and herring. Mon–Thurs 5pm–midnight, Fri 3pm–2am, Sat noon–2am, Sun noon–midnight.

NORTH LAINE

★**Basketmakers Arms** 12 Gloucester Rd, BN1 4AD ☎01273 689006, ⓦbasket-makers-brighton.co.uk; map p.242. A cosy, traditional boozer, serving a wide selection of real ales. The only downside is that the pub is more popular than it is spacious; at the weekend it can be difficult to find a seat. Mon–Thurs 11am–11pm, Fri & Sat 11am–midnight, Sun noon–11pm.

Dead Wax Social 18a Bond St, BN1 1RD ☎01273 683844, ⓦdeadwaxsocial.pub; map p.242. Vinyl, craft beer and crispy sourdough pizzas are the USPs of this cavernous bar. Every evening DJs play some of the bar's five thousand-strong vinyl collection – or you can bring your own along. Mon–Wed & Sun noon–2am, Thurs–Sat noon–3am.

Great Eastern 103 Trafalgar St, BN1 4ER ☎01273 685681; map p.242. This cosy, candlelit pub at the bottom of Trafalgar St eschews TV screens and fruit machines in favour of bookshelves stocked with well-thumbed books and board games. The craft ales and impressive array of whiskies on offer make it a local fave. Mon–Thurs & Sun noon–midnight, Fri & Sat noon–1am.

HOVE

Bee's Mouth 10 Western Rd, BN3 1AE ☎01273 770083, ⓦfacebook.com/beesmouth123; map pp.238–239. Stepping into this dimly lit, surreal pub is a little like falling down the rabbit hole. The pub descends three floors and the subterranean levels host life-drawing classes and a diverse schedule of live music (particularly jazz) and DJs. A

fantastic range of bottled beers, too. Mon–Thurs & Sat 4.30pm–12.30am, Fri 4.30pm–1.30am, Sat 3.30pm–1.30am.

KEMP TOWN AND HANOVER

Black Dove 74 St James's St, BN2 1PA ☎01273 671119, ⓦblackdovebrighton.com; map pp.238–239. This trendy, justifiably popular bar at the top of St James's St has a cool, speakeasy vibe, with lots of dark wood and antiques, plus a decent cocktail list and a wide selection of bottled beers and ciders. Live acoustic music throughout the week. Daily 4pm–late.

The Greys 105 Southover St, BN2 9US ☎01273 680734, ⓦfacebook.com/TheGreysPub; map pp.238–239. There seems to be a pub on every street in this part of Hanover, but *The Greys* is particularly nice, with a chilled-out atmosphere, cosy decor and a good selection of beer and bottled cider, plus regular live music. Mon–Thurs & Sun noon–midnight, Sat & Sun noon–1am.

Hand in Hand 33 Upper St James's St, BN2 1JN ☎01273 699595, ⓦhandbrewpub.com; map pp.238–239. This tiny, eccentric brewpub is the downstairs room of a yellow-and-red building which also houses the Hand Brew Co brewery (established in 1989). The ale made upstairs is sold downstairs, along with a wide selection of other interesting beers. Mon–Sat noon–midnight, Sun noon–11pm.

Setting Sun 1 Windmill St, BN2 0GN ☎01273 626192; map pp.238–239. The name of this hilltop pub sums up what makes it such a popular destination, in spite of the hike required to reach it. It has fantastic views over Brighton – particularly impressive at sunset – which can be enjoyed from the decking in warm weather or from the conservatory in winter. There's also good-value food. Daily noon–late.

The Sidewinder 65 St James's St, BN2 1JN ☎01273 679927, ⓦsidewinder.pub; map pp.238–239. This large, comfortable pub has a lot going for it, not least the two enormous beer gardens. During the day the atmosphere is relaxed, while at weekends the pub hosts DJs. Mon–Thurs & Sun noon–1am, Fri & Sat noon–2am.

NIGHTLIFE

Brighton is renowned for its vibrant nightlife, which, reflecting the city's personality, comes in various flavours. From the kiss-me-quick, stag and hen, messy hedonism of West St, right through to a flourishing alternative and live music scene, the party never stops. Although there's plenty of dependable, mainstream clubbing to be had, some of the more interesting nights are in smaller, quirkier venues. Note that, while the following listings have been split into "Clubs" and "Live music", there's a lot of crossover between the two.

CLUBS

The Arch 187–193 King's Rd Arches, BN1 1NB ☎01273 208133, ⓦthearch.club; map p.242. The first-rate sound and lighting system at this mid-sized seafront club no doubt helps its pulling power, frequently attracting big-name DJs,

particularly at weekends. The programming is balanced between emerging talent and big-name DJs and live performers. Drinks prices are moderate. Entry £7–15, gigs vary.

Casablanca Jazz Club 3 Middle St, BN1 1AL ☎01273 321817, ⓦcasablancajazzclub.com; map p.242.

CLOCKWISE FROM TOP LEFT CAFÉ CULTURE(P.251); FOOD STALLS IN NORTH LAINE (P.241); PAVILION GARDENS (P.240) / *GIGI* (P.260) >

7

Established in 1980, this Brighton stalwart has ensured its longevity with a dependable mix of jazz, funk, Latin and disco, washed down with cheap drinks. Head downstairs for live bands and to salsa 'til you sweat. Entry £3–7.

Funfair 12–15 King's Rd, BN1 1NE ☎ 01273 757447; map p.242. This kitsch, vintage funfair-themed club has a lot of fun quirks, including a ball pit, distortion mirrors and themed booths available for private hire. Exotic performers such as snake charmers and sword swallowers entertain punters, and the music is a fun, accessible mix of Motown, rock 'n' roll, soul, pop, disco and 90s. Entry £5–7.

★ **Green Door Store** Trafalgar Arches, Lower Goods Yard, BN1 4FQ ⊛ thegreendoorstore.co.uk; map p.242. Hip young things dance the night away in this uber-cool club and live music venue in the arches under the train station. Bare brickwork and an alternative array of music that covers anything from psych, blues, punk and rock 'n' roll to powerdisco make it eye-wateringly trendy but still good fun. Best of all, the bar is always free entry. Gig entry varies.

Haunt 10 Pool Valley, BN1 1NJ ⊛ thehauntbrighton .co.uk; map p.242. Set in a converted cinema, this club and music venue is a great space, with a dancefloor and raised stage overlooked by a balcony. Club nights are on-trend electro and indie, and retro 80s and 90s. Also regularly hosts up-and-coming live acts. Club entry £3–6, gigs vary.

★ **Komedia** 44–47 Gardner St, BN1 1UN ☎ 0845 293 8480, ⊛ komedia.co.uk/brighton; map p.242. This top-notch arts venue (see opposite) also hosts live music and fun, unpretentious and frequently retro-themed club nights, playing rock 'n' roll, 60s and alternative 80s. Devoted punters of all ages turn up in era-appropriate attire. Club entry £4–6.

Mono 169–170 King's Rd Arches, BN1 1NB ⊛ monobrighton.com; map p.242. Newcomer *Mono* has a clear and focused remit: a simple decor of black walls and exposed brick, a top-class sound system and a commitment to serious electronic music concentrating on house and techno. Door costs are kept low with long DJ sets (3–7hr) priced at £5. Wed–Sat, opening times vary.

Patterns 10 Marine Parade, BN2 1TL ☎ 01273 894777, ⊛ patternsbrighton.com; map pp.238–239. Trendy seafront venue set on two floors. Watch the sunset from the laidback terrace and soak up the LA vibes, then move downstairs to the basement club. The range of club nights is broad but specializes in electronic music and attracts internationally renowned DJs, including a residency from Horsemeat Disco. Club entry £6–8.

★ **Proud Cabaret Brighton** 83 St Georges Rd, BN2

1EF ☎ 01273 605789, ⊛ proudcabaretbrighton.com; map pp.238–239. Evenings at this decadent burlesque and cabaret venue kick off with dinner and a show, before the tables are cleared away for dancing. Dinner, show and club from £29 (Thurs), £39 (Fri) or £54 (Sat); show only £10.

Volks 3 The Colonnade, Madeira Drive, BN2 1PS ☎ 01273 682828, ⊛ volksclub.co.uk; map pp.238–239. This small, long-running club peddles all things bass, with a schedule chock-full of dubstep, drum 'n' bass, reggae, jungle and breaks. The venue is appropriately dark and sweaty, and has some of the latest opening hours of any Brighton club, often keeping the party going until 7am. Entry £3–8.

LIVE MUSIC

Bleach 75 London Rd, BN1 4JF ⊛ bleachbrighton.com; map pp.238–239. Tucked away above the popular *Hare and Hounds* pub, this intimate 150-capacity venue hosts local bands as well as touring international talent. The programming is proudly and defiantly indie, carving out a distinctive niche for this spirited newcomer to the Brighton live music scene.

Concorde 2 Madeira Shelter Hall, Madeira Drive, BN2 1EN ☎ 01273 673311, ⊛ concorde2.co.uk; map pp.238–239. It's worth the walk along the seafront to get to this slightly out-of-the-way live venue and club. Housed in a high-ceilinged Victorian building, it feels intimate but not cramped, and has a much better atmosphere than the city's larger live venues. The line-up ranges from big-name acts (The White Stripes, Kaiser Chiefs and Florence + the Machine have all played here) to up-and-coming musicians and varied club nights.

The Hope and Ruin 11 Queens Rd, BN1 3WA ☎ 01273 325793, ⊛ facebook.com/hopebrighton; map p.242. This cool indie music pub is modelled on Budapest's famous ruin bars, making it the only pub in Brighton with a caravan and a (purposefully) broken piano inside. Upstairs, the 100-capacity venue showcases mainly rock and indie bands, with weekend club nights. There's a great range of craft beers.

Prince Albert 48 Trafalgar St, BN1 4ED ☎ 01273 730499, ⊛ facebook.com/ThePrinceAlbert; map p.242. A Brighton institution, this pub-cum-music venue is immediately recognizable from the Banksy kissing policemen and graffiti portrait commemorating John Peel emblazoned on the building's side wall. The ground floor is a spacious pub, while upstairs a small venue hosts alternative live acts of various stripes.

ENTERTAINMENT

CINEMA

★ **Duke of York's Picturehouse** Preston Circus, BN1 4NA ☎ 0871 704 2056, ⊛ picturehouses.com/cinema /Duke_Of_Yorks. Grade II-listed cinema – one of the oldest still-functioning cinemas in the country, opened in

1910 – with buckets of character, velvet seats and a licensed bar. The programme is a great mix of arthouse, independent and classic films, alongside live-streamed opera and ballet, all-nighters and themed evenings. If you don't want to trek out to Preston Circus, there's always Dukes at Komedia, its sister cinema in North Laine (see below).

THEATRE, COMEDY AND CABERET
88 London Road 88 London Rd, BN1 4JF ☎07580 716575, ⓦ88londonroad.com. Housed in a former Methodist church, this professional theatre also shows film, dance, poetry and spoken word, and has a great café.

B·O·A·T Dyke Road Park, Hove BN3 6EH ⓦbrightonopenairtheatre.co.uk. The Brighton Open Air Theatre operates from May to Sept and hosts national touring productions, local theatre, and some music, comedy, screenings and spoken-word events.

Brighton Dome 29 New Rd, BN1 1UG ☎01273 709709, ⓦbrightondome.org. The Royal Pavilion's former stables is home to three venues – Pavilion Theatre, Concert Hall and Corn Exchange – offering theatre, concerts, dance and performance.

The Dance Space Circus St ☎01273 696844, ⓦsoutheastdance.org.uk. Part of the Circus Street regeneration project, just off Grand Parade, The Dance Space is due to open in 2018 and will provide a permanent home for South East Dance. The building will incorporate performance space, too – check the South East Dance

website for the latest.

★ **Komedia** 44–47 Gardner St, BN1 1UN ☎0845 293 8480, ⓦkomedia.co.uk/brighton. A Brighton institution set across three floors, this fantastic arts venue hosts comedy and cabaret, as well as live music and club nights (see opposite). The Duke of York's cinema (see opposite) has three screens upstairs.

The Marlborough Pub & Theatre 4 Princes St, BN2 1RD ☎01273 273870, ⓦmarlboroughtheatre.org.uk. This sixty-seat venue specializes in provocative and unusual theatre, music, comedy and spoken word events. Also home to local LGBT production company Pink Fringe.

The Old Market (TOM) 11a Upper Market St, BN3 1AS ☎01273 201801, ⓦtheoldmarket.com. Theatre, comedy and live music all feature on the programme of this stylish performing arts venue on the border of Hove.

Rialto Theatre 11 Dyke Road, BN1 3FE ☎01273 725230, ⓦrialtotheatre.co.uk. Theatre, comedy and cabaret in a Grade II listed building; the main space is upstairs, plus there's a less formal studio bar downstairs.

Theatre Royal New Rd, BN1 1SD ☎01273 764400, ⓦatgtickets.com/venues/theatre-royal-brighton. One of the oldest working theatres in the country, offering predominantly mainstream plays, opera and musicals.

SHOPPING

Brighton's a great shopping destination, with plenty of interesting independent shops. The places to head for are the **Lanes** and (especially) **North Laine** (ⓦnorthlaine.co.uk), though for antiques shops you'll need to head out to **Kemp Town**, where a wander along the main street – which changes name from Upper St James's St to Bristol Rd to St Georges Rd – will uncover lots of gems. For work by some of Brighton's thriving population of artists and makers, there are galleries scattered throughout town but the best– and most fun – time to buy is during the biannual **Artists Open Houses** events (May & Dec; ⓦaoh.org.uk), when you can visit the artists in their homes. Brighton's high-street chains are around **Churchill Square**, with higher-end chains concentrated on **East St** at the bottom end of the Lanes.

THE SEAFRONT
Castor and Pollux 165 King's Rd Arches, Lower Promenade, BN1 1NB ☎01273 773776, ⓦstore .castorandpollux.co.uk; map p.242. This great beachfront gallery sells limited edition prints (by Rob Ryan, Mark Hearld and others), alongside posters, art and design books, jewellery, pottery, stationery and more. Daily 10am–5pm.

THE LANES AND AROUND
Bison Beer Crafthouse 7 East St, BN1 1HP ☎01273 809027, ⓦbisonbeer.co.uk; map p.242. Independent bottle shop stocking over 350 craft beers from around the world, including draught growlers – 1.9-litre amber glass bottles that you fill with one of the shop's four draught beers (£10). Mon–Sat 11am–8pm, Sun 11am–6pm.

Choccywoccydoodah 3 Meeting House Lane, BN1 1HP ☎01273 329462, ⓦchoccywoccydoodah.com; map p.242. Check out the seasonally changing window display of this renowned chocolaterie, whose fantastical creations – cakes shaped like fairytale castles, mermaids or giant

stags – are all made from solid chocolate. Inside you can buy smaller-scale chocolatey treats, or head upstairs to the small café to gorge yourself on proper hot chocolate, chocolate dipping pots and other gooey delights. Mon–Sat 10am–6pm, Sun 11am–5pm.

House of Hoye 22a Ship St, BN1 1AD ☎0845 094 3175, ⓦjeremy-hoye.com; map p.242. A favourite of the fashion press, contemporary jeweller Jeremy Hoye's creations include silver charms featuring Brighton landmarks (from £50). Mon–Sat 10am–5.30pm.

Pecksniff's 45–46 Meeting House Lane, BN1 1HB ☎01273 723292, ⓦpecksniffs.com; map p.242. Independent British fragrance house, which has been creating its own perfumes and bespoke blends for over 25 years. Its perfumes and body products make great gifts. Mon–Sat 10am–5pm, Sun 10.30am–4pm.

She Said 12 Ship St Gardens, BN1 1AJ ☎01273 777811, ⓦshesaidboutique.com; map p.242. As you'd expect from the home of the dirty weekend, Brighton has its fair share of erotic emporiums, but this one is a touch above the rest: it's even been featured in *Vogue*. The ground floor is largely devoted to undies and corsets, with the saucier stuff kept downstairs. Mon 11am–5pm, Tues–Sat 11am–6pm, Sun noon–5pm.

NORTH LAINE AND AROUND

Art Republic 13 Bond St, BN1 1RD ☎01273 724829, ⓦartrepublic.com; map p.242. Limited edition prints from both local and big-name artists, plus open-edition museum prints and poster art. Mon–Fri 9.30am–6pm, Sat 9am–6pm, Sun 11am–5pm.

Bert's Homestore 10 Kensington Gardens, BN1 4AL ☎01273 675536, ⓦbertshomestore.co.uk; map p.242. Fabulous kitchenware and homeware, featuring polka dots, floral prints and bright primary colours. Mon–Sat 9.30am–6.30pm, Sun 10am–6pm.

Bluebird Tea Company 41 Gardner St, BN1 1UN ☎01273 325523, ⓦbluebirdteaco.com; map p.242. The UK's only tea mixologist, selling a huge variety of fine leaf teas from Gingerbread Chai and Rooibos Earl Grey to Enchanted Narnia (with Turkish Delight) and Pandalicious Liquorice. Mon–Fri 10.30am–6pm, Sat 10am–6.30pm, Sun 10.30am–5.30pm.

FAIR 21 Queen's Rd, BN1 3XA ☎01273 723215, ⓦthefairshop.co.uk; map p.242. A pioneer in ethical fashion, this boutique stocks the big-name ethical fashion brands, plus fairtrade homeware, jewellery and more. Wed–Fri noon–7pm, Sat 10am–6.30pm, Sun noon–5pm.

Gresham Blake 20 Bond St, BN1 1RD ☎01273 609587, ⓦgreshamblake.com; map p.242. Bespoke tailoring, made-to-measure and ready-to-wear suits, plus a range of eye-catching ties and bright shirts, at this hip contemporary designer-tailor. Mon–Thurs 10am–5.30pm, Fri 10.30am–5.30pm, Sat 10am–6pm, Sun 11am–5pm.

Hope and Harlequin 31 Sydney St, BN1 4EP ☎01273 675222, ⓦhopeandharlequin.com; map p.242. Beautifully presented vintage shop stocking clothing and modern collectables from the late 1800s to the 1970s, though it's especially strong on the 1930s and 1940s. Mon & Wed–Sat 10.30am–6pm, Sun 11am–5pm; call ahead to check Tues opening.

Infinity Foods 25 North Rd, BN1 1YA ☎01273 603563, ⓦinfinityfoodsretail.coop; map p.242. This organic vegetarian and vegan store – run as a workers' cooperative – has been going for over forty years, and sells seasonal fruit and veg, fresh bread, natural bodycare products and more. Mon–Sat 9.30am–6pm, Sun 11am–5pm.

Jump The Gun 36 Gardner St, BN1 1UN ☎01273 626333, ⓦjumpthegun.co.uk; map p.242. This much-loved gentlemen's outfitters – often with a moped parked outside – has been selling mod clothing (parkas, shirts, suits, T-shirts and button badges) from this shop for over twenty years. Mon–Sat 10am–6pm, Sun 11am–5pm.

Lavender Room 16 Bond St, BN1 1RD ☎01273 220380, ⓦlavender-room.co.uk; map p.242. There's a bit of a boudoir vibe at this pretty boutique; inside you'll find fragrances, bath oils, lingerie, silk robes, jewellery and vintage-inspired home accessories. Mon–Sat 10am–6pm, Sun 11am–5pm.

Resident 28 Kensington Gardens, BN1 4AL ☎01273 606312, ⓦresident-music.com; map p.242. This award-winning independent record shop often has limited editions and indie exclusives, and also sells tickets for local venues. Mon–Sat 9am–6.30pm, Sun 10am–6pm.

★**Snoopers Attic** 1st floor of Snooper's Paradise, 7–8 Kensington Gardens, BN1 4AL ☎01273 945898, ⓦsnoopersattic.co.uk; map p.242. Run by a cooperative of over twenty designers, makers and vintage collectors, this attic space is crammed full of vintage and handmade treasures – clothes, jewellery, hats, homewares and textiles. Mon–Sat 10am–6pm, Sun 11am–4pm.

HOVE

★**City Books** 23 Western Rd, BN3 1AF ☎01273 725306, ⓦcity-books.co.uk; map pp.238–239. Brighton's largest independent bookshop is a thriving and much-loved fixture in the city, organizing big-name literary talks and readings. Mon–Sat 9.30am–6pm, Sun 11am–4.30pm.

I Gigi General Store 31a Western Rd, BN3 1AF ☎01273 775257, ⓦigigigeneralstore.com; map pp.238–239. Beautifully styled little shop stocking homeware and gifts: pottery, hand-blown glassware, antique linen tablecloths, scented candles, bangles and more. Upstairs there's an equally chic café, while the stylish I Gigi Women's Boutique is a few doors along at no. 37. Mon–Sat 10am–6pm, Sun 11am–4.30pm.

La Cave à Fromage 34–35 Western Rd, BN3 1AF ☎01273 725500, ⓦla-cave.co.uk; map pp.238–239. There are over two hundred cheeses – plus thirty types of cured meats and fifty wines – at this cheese emporium, which also has a tasting café and runs regular events. Mon–Wed 10am–7pm, Thurs–Sat 10am–10pm, Sun 11am–6pm.

KEMP TOWN

Brighton Flea Market 31a Upper St James's St, BN2 1JN ☎01273 624006, ⓦflea-markets.co.uk; map pp.238–239. The unmissable pink facade of this long-established flea market houses over a hundred stalls and cabinets on two levels, selling furniture, bric-a-brac, jewellery and more. Mon–Sat 10am–5.30pm, Sun 10.30am–5pm.

Kemptown Bookshop 91 St Georges Rd, BN2 1EE ☎01273 682110, ⓦkemptownbookshop.co.uk; map pp.238–239. Award-winning independent bookshop, with a good selection of cards, prints and book-related gifts. Mon–Sat 9am–5.30pm.

LGBT BRIGHTON

As you would expect from a city as synonymous with gay life as Brighton, the nightlife here doesn't disappoint. Radiating outwards from St James's St in **Kemp Town**, the scene is surprisingly compact but varied. **Brighton Pride** (date varies each summer; ⓦ brighton-pride.org) is an LGBT parade and ticketed party in Preston Park. In recent years Pride has diversified to include a range of cultural events including film, theatre and performance art alongside the alcohol-fuelled celebrations.

INFORMATION AND TOURS

Brighton and Hove LGBT Switchboard ⓣ 01273 204050, ⓦ switchboard.org.uk. Running since 1975, the switchboard provides information about the Brighton scene, support and advice and a counselling service.

GScene Magazine ⓦ gscene.com. LGBT lifestyle, listings and community magazine for the local area.

Piers and Queers tour ⓣ 01/934 482112, ⓦ onlyinbrighton.co.uk. Fun, illuminating walking tour looking at the city's LGBT history, personalities and stories.

BARS AND CLUBS

The Bulldog 31 St James's St, BN2 1RF ⓦ bulldogbrighton.com; map pp.238–239. Brighton's longest-running gay bar pulls off the difficult trick of being both cruisy and welcoming. With the best-value drinks prices on the scene, it's packed at weekends, and is popular both as a post-club spot and for the karaoke and cabaret upstairs. Entry fee applies on weekends and membership is required for entry after midnight Fri & Sat. Mon–Wed 11am–2am, Thurs 11am–3am, Fri 11am–7am, Sat 11am–8am, Sun 11am–2am.

Camelford Arms 30–31 Camelford St, BN2 1TQ ⓦ camelfordarmsbrighton.co.uk; map pp.238–239. This cosy community pub, with a welcoming atmosphere and excellent food, is a popular first stop at the weekend for a crowd that includes plenty of bears, otters and their admirers. The Sunday roasts are legendary. Mon–Wed & Sun noon–11.30pm, Thurs noon–midnight, Fri & Sat noon–1am; kitchen Mon–Sat noon–9pm, Sun noon–5pm.

Legends 31–34 Marine Parade, BN2 1TR ⓦ legendsbrighton.com; map pp.238–239. Comprised of the ground-floor *Legends Bar* with terrace overlooking the sea, and the free-entry *Basement Club*, this venue has a friendly, mixed crowd. Downstairs the music runs from chart pop to dance; upstairs the bar hosts cabaret nights with local drag stars. Opening times vary; check website.

The Marlborough Pub & Theatre 4 Princes St, BN2 1RD ⓦ marlboroughtheatre.org.uk; map p.242.

Attracting a truly diverse crowd and welcoming to all, *The Marlborough* is unarguably Brighton's queerest pub; it's particularly popular with Brighton's lesbian and trans communities. There are DJs every weekend, regular open-mic nights and a weekly quiz, and upstairs in the sixty-seat theatre, local LGBT company Pink Fringe programme provocative and entertaining queer theatre and performance art. Mon–Thurs 1pm–midnight, Fri 1pm–2am, Sat noon–2am, Sun noon–11.30pm.

Revenge 32–34 Old Steine, BN1 1EL ⓣ 01273 606064, ⓦ revenge.co.uk; map p.242. A leading presence on the city's gay scene and a key player in Brighton Pride, with a young studenty crowd regularly packing out the two floors and roof terrace. Nights include foam parties and themed events around bank hols, plus regular packed-out, raucous appearances by the international stars of RuPaul's Drag Race. Entry free to £10. Opening times vary; check website.

Subline 129 St James's St, BN2 1TH ⓦ sublinebrighton .co.uk; map p.242. *Subline* is Brighton's only men-only cruise bar. Dark and subterranean, with industrial decor, the bar runs theme nights including leather, underwear-only and foam parties. Members only; join via the website for £10 prior to visiting. Wed & Thurs 9pm–1.30am, Fri & Sat 9pm–4am, Sun 8pm–2am.

Traumfrau Various venues, check website for details ⓦ traumfrau.co.uk. Monthly queer club night that moves location every month, with a varied roster of DJs playing everything from electro, disco and pop to punk and rockabilly. With provocative live performances and a DIY aesthetic that encourages the crowd to get truly involved, *Traumfrau* is lively, joyous, unpredictable and always truly inclusive.

Velvet Jack's 50 Norfolk Square, BN1 2PA ⓣ 01273 661290; map pp.238–239. Cosy and friendly lesbian café-bar – a great spot for coffee during the day, and in the evening the bar has a welcoming community feel. Tues & Wed 4–11pm, Thurs 4pm–midnight, Fri & Sat noon–midnight, Sun noon–11pm.

7

West Sussex

WEST WITTERING BEACH

West Sussex

One of the surprising but wonderful things about West Sussex is that over half of it is protected countryside. A large swathe of the county lies within the South Downs National Park, which sweeps west to east across the whole of the region, encompassing not only the steep scarp slopes of the South Downs themselves but also, to the north, the beautiful woodland and heathland of the Western Weald around Midhurst. Down on the coast, the estuarine landscapes of Chichester Harbour are protected as one of the county's two Areas of Outstanding Natural Beauty (AONBs); the other lies northeast in the High Weald (and is covered in Chapter 5, The Sussex High Weald). The only city in West Sussex is Chichester, and the only other settlements of any size are concentrated in the east around the busy A23 or along the built-up coastal strip, leaving the rest of the county in splendid rural tranquillity.

The county town of West Sussex is **Chichester**, a pocket-sized, culture-rich city with an unbeatable location sandwiched between the South Downs National Park to the north and the sea, sand and sails of Chichester Harbour and the **Manhood Peninsula** to the south; with the city as your base it's perfectly possible to be tramping the Downs in the morning and basking on the beach by the afternoon. Chichester Harbour aside, the jewel in the crown of the Manhood Peninsula is pristine, dune-backed **West Wittering Beach** – one of only two sandy beaches in Sussex, and consequently besieged by windbreak-toting holidaymakers in summer. There are plenty of opportunities on the peninsula for watersports, walks and cycling, or you can simply relax and take in the shifting tidal landscapes of Chichester Harbour on a leisurely boat trip.

The South Downs National Park begins just a few miles north of Chichester and, unsurprisingly, there's plenty of wonderful walking to be had, including along the South Downs ridge at Harting Down, and at Kingley Vale, one of the county's oldest yew forests. The cluster of sights up this way includes the Weald & Downland Open Air Museum, where you can get a fascinating snapshot of Sussex rural life in days gone by, the Cass Sculpture Foundation with its outdoor displays of modern British sculpture nestled amongst the trees, and the Goodwood Estate, host to three of the county's biggest events (see box, p.275) which book up hotels in the area months in advance. Further north is the attractive market town of **Midhurst**, home to the national park visitor centre, and nearby **Petworth**, a handsome town crammed with independent shops that has grown up around magnificent Petworth House. Nearby, you can get one of the best views in the national park at **Black Down**.

CHICHESTER CATHEDRAL

Highlights

❶ Chichester Cathedral Chichester's great medieval cathedral is as well known for its modern devotional art as for its more ancient treasures. **See p.267**

❷ Pallant House Gallery This modern art gallery is Chichester's pride and joy: a roll call of the great and the good in twentieth-century British art. **See p.269**

❸ Fishbourne Roman Palace One of the country's most important collections of Roman remains, and the biggest Roman dwelling ever discovered north of the Alps. **See p.272**

❹ Chichester Harbour The stunning watery landscapes of Chichester Harbour are best enjoyed on a boat trip. **See p.277**

❺ West Wittering Beach Even the summertime crowds that flock to this undeveloped sandy beach can't quite dispel its magic. **See p.278**

❻ Black Down Climb to the highest point of the South Downs National Park to see the sweeping view that inspired Tennyson. **See p.286**

❼ Petworth House One of the finest stately homes in the Southeast, with a magnificent haul of art, and a deer park immortalized by Turner. **See p.287**

❽ Arundel Castle This splendid castle, with a Norman keep and richly furnished state rooms, dominates the skyline of sleepy Arundel. **See p.289**

HIGHLIGHTS ARE MARKED ON THE MAP ON P.266

Moving east, the picturesque town of **Arundel** makes a lovely alternative base for a visit, with a splendid castle, some great places to eat, and a clutch of sights nearby that includes the industrial heritage museum at Amberley, Elizabethan Parham House and Bignor Roman Villa – a fascinating counterpart to the larger **Fishbourne Roman Palace** near Chichester. Further east again is **Steyning**, with two ancient hillforts nearby and a ruined Norman castle. From Arundel, the River Arun meanders gracefully downstream through water meadows to the coast at **Littlehampton**, one of a handful of low-key seaside towns along the **West Sussex coast**.

Chichester and around

The handsome market town of **CHICHESTER** has plenty to recommend it: a splendid twelfth-century cathedral, a thriving cultural scene centred on its highly regarded Festival Theatre (see p.277), and one of the finest collections of modern British art anywhere in the country at the Pallant House Gallery. There are some excellent attractions within just a few miles of the city, too: the Roman ruins at **Fishbourne**; ancient woodland in **Kingley Vale** nature reserve; beautiful **West Dean Gardens**; the **Weald & Downland Open Air Museum**, which contains more than fifty reconstructed historic buildings; the **Cass Sculpture Foundation**, home of contemporary British sculpture; and finally, the dashing **Goodwood Estate**, host to three big annual events. Only very slightly further afield are the Witterings and Chichester Harbour (see p.277), and the scenic splendour of the South Downs National Park.

8

Market Cross and around

The centre of Chichester is marked by its splendid Gothic **Market Cross**, an octagonal rotunda topped by ornate finials and a crown lantern spire, built in 1501 to provide shelter for the market traders. The buzz of commerce still dominates the surrounding area today, with the four main thoroughfares leading off from the Cross – North, East, South and West streets – each lined with shops, and a **farmers' market** setting up its stalls on the first and third Friday of the month (9am–2pm; ⓦ chichester.gov.uk/farmersmarket). There are several fine buildings up North Street, including the dinky little **Market House** (also known as the Butter Market), built by Nash in 1807 and fronted by a Doric colonnade; a tiny flint **Saxon church** with a diminutive wooden shingled spire; and the redbrick **Council House**, built in 1731, with Ionic columns on its facade.

The city walls

The centre's cruciform street plan, and the **city walls** that encircle it, are a legacy of Chichester's Roman beginnings. The city started life as the settlement of Noviomagus Reginorum, connected to London by the arrow-straight Stane Street. The **Roman city walls** were built in the third century, and large sections (much restored over the years) still stand today, though the ancient gateways are long gone. Pavement markers, signposts and interpretive boards guide you round the 1.5-mile circuit; for much of the route there's a footpath on top of the walls, and it's a fun way to see the city, hopping on and off at various points to visit Chichester's other sights.

Chichester Cathedral

West St, PO19 1RP • Mon–Sat 7.15am–6.30pm, Sun 7.15am–5pm; tours (45min) Mon–Sat 11.15am & 2.30pm • Free • Café Mon–Sat 9am–5pm, Sun 10am–4pm • ☎ 01243 782595, ⓦ chichestercathedral.org.uk

Chichester's splendid **cathedral** has stood at the heart of the city for over nine hundred years. Building began in 1076, after the Norman conquerors moved the bishopric from Selsey, ten miles away. The cathedral was consecrated by Bishop Luffa in 1108, and since about 1300 has only been minimally modified, with the exception of the unique freestanding fifteenth-century bell tower and the slender spire; the latter had to be rebuilt after it came spectacularly crashing down in 1861 when the choir screen was dismantled.

The interior is renowned for its prestigious **modern devotional art**, which includes a font of smooth Bodmin stone and beaten copper by **John Skelton** just inside the entrance; an enormous altar-screen tapestry by **John Piper**; and a stained-glass window – an exuberant blaze of ruby-red – by **Marc Chagall** nearby. Perhaps the cathedral's greatest artistic treasures, however, are its oldest: in the south aisle, close to the tapestry, you'll see a pair of exquisite Romanesque carvings – the **Chichester Reliefs** – created around 1125, and showing the raising of Lazarus. Notable for the wonderfully expressive faces of the figures, the reliefs would once have been brightly painted, with semiprecious stones set in the eyes.

Elsewhere you can see a couple of enormous **Renaissance wooden panel paintings** by Lambert Barnard – depicting the past bishops of Chichester (north transept), and Henry VIII confirming the Chichester bishopric (south transept) – as well as the fourteenth-century **Fitzalan tomb** of Richard Fitzalan, thirteenth earl of Arundel. The earl's stone effigy, lying sweetly hand-in-hand with his countess, inspired Philip Larkin's poem *An Arundel Tomb*, which famously concludes "What will survive of us is love."

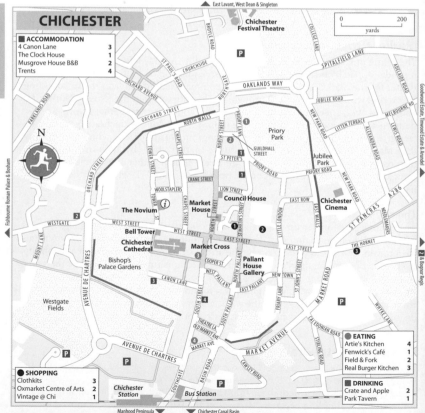

Behind the cathedral, Canon Lane leads to the fourteenth-century gateway to the Bishop's Palace; the Palace itself is not open to the public, but the beautiful **Bishop's Palace Gardens** (daily 8am–dusk; free) are one of the city's hidden gems and a perfect picnic spot, with expansive lawns, great views of the cathedral, a Tudor walled garden and sections of Roman wall.

Pallant House Gallery

9 North Pallant, PO19 1TJ • Tues, Wed, Fri & Sat 10am–5pm, Thurs 10am–8pm, Sun & bank hols 11am–5pm • £10, Tues £5.50, Thurs 5–8pm permanent collection free (£5.50 for temporary exhibitions) • Tours Sat & Sun 2pm; 30min • Free • ☎ 01243 774557, ⓦ pallant.org.uk

Hidden away off South Street, in the well-preserved Georgian quadrant of the city known as the Pallants, is the wonderful **Pallant House Gallery**, Chichester's answer to the Tate Modern. The gallery contains one of the most important collections of modern British art in the country, with works by almost every notable British artist of the last hundred years, including Moore, Freud, Sickert, Hepworth, Blake, Piper, Hodgkin, Sutherland and Caulfield. The collection started with the bequest of **Walter Hussey**, the dean of Chichester Cathedral – who commissioned much of the modern art in the cathedral, including the Piper tapestry and the Chagall window – and has grown with subsequent bequests to become an eclectic "collection of collections", encompassing paintings, ceramics, furniture, sculpture and more.

The rotating **permanent collection** is housed in a creaky-floored Queen Anne townhouse, with **installations** often taking over its sweeping stairwell. The gallery also holds several excellent **temporary exhibitions** each year in its award-winning contemporary extension, where there's also a designated room for **prints and drawings**. A free **tour** of the collection's highlights runs at weekends.

The Novium

Tower St, PO19 1QH • April–Oct Mon–Sat 10am–5pm & Sun 10am–4pm; Nov–March Mon–Sat 10am–5pm • Free • ☎ 01243 775888, ⓦ thenovium.org

The city's museum of local history – the **Novium** – is housed in a state-of-the-art building a stone's throw from the cathedral. The first sight that greets you as you walk in is the recently excavated **Roman bath house**, which stood on this site nearly two thousand years ago; after its discovery in the 1970s it was buried under a car park for safekeeping until the Novium build allowed it to see the light of day once again. If you've seen the remains at Bignor (see p.295) and Fishbourne (see p.272) you might be a bit underwhelmed, but a film projected onto the wall behind does a good job of bringing the excavation to life. Also here are the incomplete but beautiful fourth-century **Chilgrove mosaic**, discovered in the Chilgrove valley nearby, and the second-century **Jupiter Stone** statue base, unearthed during excavations in West Street.

The other two floors display artefacts from the museum's huge, eclectic collection – over 500,000 items in all. The first floor is arranged chronologically, telling the story of Chichester using artefacts that range from prehistoric stone tools to Roman hipposandals (protective horse-shoes), Saxon grave goods and the old toll board and

8

CHICHESTER'S FALCONS

If you're visiting the cathedral in spring (April/May), you'll get a chance to spot the cathedral's pair of **peregrine falcons**, which have been returning here to nest every year since 2000. There's a webcam of the nest in the café garden, and telescopes in front of the cathedral – the southwest lawn is a good place to catch them in flight, especially in the early evening.

weighing scales once used at the Butter Market. The second floor concentrates on thematic displays; from the foyer up here there are great views of the cathedral. The whole museum is very child-friendly, with dressing-up, games and child-height drawers labelled "open me".

Chichester Ship Canal

Canal Basin, Canal Wharf, PO19 8DT • **Boat trips** Mid-March to early Nov daily 10.15am, noon, 1.45pm & 3.30pm; 1hr 20min return • £8 • **Rowing boats** £7 for first 30min, £5/30min thereafter • ☎ 01243 771363, ⓦ chichestercanal.org.uk

Just outside the southern city walls, Chichester Canal Basin is the start of the **Chichester Ship Canal**, which skirts the fringes of the city before flowing lazily through flat countryside to Chichester Marina at Birdham, four miles away. The canal opened in 1822 to carry cargo between the sea and the city, but it was never a commercial success and was abandoned in 1928. Today the Chichester Canal Trust hires out **rowing boats** and runs **boat trips** as far as the Crosbie Bridge at Donnington two miles away; the more energetic might fancy a go at **stand-up paddleboarding** (see below) – the non-tidal water makes it a perfect place to learn. A **towpath**, part of the long-distance Lipchis Way (see box, p.280), runs the length of the canal down to the marina. Whether on foot or on the river the canal makes a lovely, peaceful outing from the city, with wildflowers speckling the riverbanks in summer, dragonflies flashing above the water, and swans and mallards gliding along; from Hunston Bridge you also get a great view back across the meadows to the cathedral, a vista immortalized by J.M.W. Turner in 1829.

ARRIVAL AND DEPARTURE

By train The station, on Stockbridge Rd, is a 10min walk south of the Market Cross.
Destinations Arundel (Mon–Sat 2 hourly, Sun hourly; 30–50min); Brighton (2 hourly; 45–55min); London Victoria (Mon–Sat 2 hourly, Sun hourly; 1hr 35min).
By bus The bus station lies across the road from the train station on Southgate.

Destinations Brighton via Bognor, Littlehampton, Worthing & Shoreham-by-Sea (every 20–30min; 1hr 45min); Midhurst (Mon–Sat every 30min, Sun hourly; 40min).
By car Chichester has plenty of long-stay (3hr-plus) car parks – at Cattle Market, Westgate, Northgate, Basin Rd and Ave de Chartres – all signposted from the city's approach roads.

GETTING AROUND

By bike There's bike rental at Barreg Cycles, two miles from the centre in Fishbourne (£18/day; ☎ 01243 786104,

ⓦ barreg.co.uk).
By taxi Chichester Taxis (☎ 01243 330015).

INFORMATION AND ACTIVITIES

Tourist office At the Novium, Tower St (April–Oct Mon–Sat 10am–5pm & Sun 10am–4pm; Nov–March Mon–Sat 10am–5pm; ☎ 01243 775888, ⓦ visitchichester.org).
City walks Guided city walks run throughout the year, bookable through the tourist office (April–Sept Tues & Wed 11am, Sat 2pm, Sun 11.30am; Oct–March Tues

11am, Sat 2pm; 1hr 30min; £5).
Stand-up paddleboarding TJ Board Hire (☎ 07548 619578, ⓦ tjboardhire.co.uk) offers fun SUP lessons on the flat waters of Chichester Ship Canal – perfect for beginners and families (£40; 2hr).

ACCOMMODATION

There's generally no problem finding a place to stay in or around Chichester other than during **Goodwood**'s three big annual events (see box, p.275), when the most popular accommodation can fill up more than a year in advance. Note that the prices below exclude the Goodwood periods, when rates rise across the board.

IN TOWN
4 Canon Lane 4 Canon Lane, PO19 1PX ☎ 01243 813586, ⓦ chichestercathedral.org.uk. What makes a stay here special is the location: this eight-bedroom

Victorian house, once home to the Archdeacon of Chichester, is owned by the cathedral and located in the grounds, just by the Bishop's Palace gateway. The rooms are big, comfortable and tranquil, if a little bland; two come with baths, the others showers. An added bonus is the top-notch art on the walls, lent by the Pallant House Gallery. Breakfast costs extra (£8.95). **£99**

The Clock House St Martin's Square, PO19 1NT ⓦ clockhousechichester.com. This bijou converted coach house is a stylish self-catering option for two people, with a cosy lounge complete with wood-burner (logs included), a small kitchen out the back and a courtyard garden. Lovely extra touches include Molton Brown toiletries and fluffy robes; hampers and meals are available on request. It's in a fab location, too, set on a quiet back road between North St and Priory Park. Minimum two-night stay. **£180**

★**Musgrove House B&B** 63 Oving Rd, PO19 7EN ⓣ 01243 790179, ⓦ musgrovehouse.co.uk. This friendly, stylish boutique B&B, just a short walk from the centre, is a real bargain. The three lovely rooms are all impeccably tasteful, decked out in cocooning shades of grey, with shutters on the windows, super-comfy beds with silk duvets, and fun high-tech touches like bathroom mirrors you can light up with a wave of your hand. **£80**

Trents 50 South St, PO19 1DS ⓣ 01243 773714, ⓦ trentschichester.co.uk. As long as you don't want an early night, the five rooms above this bar-restaurant are a good bet – you're right in the thick of things, and the rooms are modern and well appointed. **£110**

OUT OF TOWN

As well as the options listed below, check out the *Goodwood Hotel* (see p.275) and the *Tinwood Estate Lodges* (see p.276). **Richmond Arms** Mill Rd, West Ashling, 5 miles from Chichester, PO18 8EA ⓣ 01243 572046, ⓦ therichmondarms.co.uk. There are just two B&B rooms above this excellent village pub (see p.272), a 10min drive from Chichester. Rooms are smart and luxurious, with bathrooms featuring polished wooden floors, roll-top baths and walk-in showers; the larger room (£125) comes with a sofa bed, so is a good option for families. The real selling point, however, is the great food on offer downstairs, though bear in mind the restaurant's not open every day. **£115**

Royal Oak Pook Lane, East Lavant, 3 miles from Chichester, PO18 0AX ⓣ 01243 527434, ⓦ royaloakeastlavant.co.uk. This lovely dining pub (see p.272), set on a quiet lane just north of Chichester, offers a range of gorgeous, stylish rooms – five rooms and three cottages (sleep 3), all kitted out with DVD players, plump down duvets and local aromatherapy toiletries. **£165**, cottages **£225**

EATING

IN TOWN

Artie's Kitchen 33 Southgate, PO19 1DP ⓣ 01243 790365, ⓦ facebook.com/Artieskitchen. Tuck into authentic, beautifully cooked tapas (£7–9 each) at this stylish bare-brick and beams tapas bar. Tues–Thurs 11am–11pm, Fri & Sat 9am–11pm, Sun 9am–4pm.

Fenwick's Café Priory Park, PO19 1NL ⓣ 01243 839762, ⓦ fenwickscafe.com. In a lovely spot in tranquil Priory Park, this friendly café is a top pick for a simple summer lunch – sandwiches, salads, platters and a small selection of hot food. Summer Mon–Wed & Sun 9.30am–5pm, Thurs–Sat 9.30am–9pm; winter daily 10am–7pm.

Field & Fork 4 Guildhall St, PO19 1NJ ⓣ 01243 789915, ⓦ fieldandfork.co.uk. One of the best places to eat in the city, serving up imaginative, locally sourced food in a tranquil restaurant with a sun-flooded conservatory at the back. Mains such as wild sea trout with local broad beans and maple-glazed short rib of beef will set you back £12–19. Tues–Sat 11.30am–3pm & 5pm–late.

Real Burger Kitchen 5-6 South St, PO19 1EH ⓣ 01243 788398, ⓦ burgerkitchen.co.uk. Cheerful, independently-run burger place, with red leatherette booths and a great range of burgers (£7–12) made from locally sourced meat, plus tasty veggie/vegan alternatives. Tasty extras include sweet potato fries, supershakes, freakshakes and "hard shakes" (featuring hot fudge and Bourbon, or Terry's chocolate orange and Baileys) and a good range of craft ales and lagers. Takeaway also available. Mon–Fri 11.30am–9pm, Sat 9am–9.30pm, Sun 9am–7pm.

OUT OF TOWN

Some of the best food in the Chichester area is found in the country pubs around the city.

Earl of March Lavant Rd, 3 miles from Chichester, PO18 0BQ ⓣ 01243 533993, ⓦ theearlofmarch.com. Renowned foodie pub a few miles north of the city, with a lovely terrace garden which backs right onto the surrounding fields and has fabulous views across the Downs. Mains cost £17–22, though lighter lunches (including sandwiches and salads; from £8) are also available, and there's a good-value set menu (2/3 courses £21.50/24.50). Daily 11am–11pm; kitchen Mon–Sat noon–2.30pm & 5.30–9.30pm, Sun noon–3pm & 6–9pm.

Fox Goes Free Charlton, 6 miles from Chichester, PO18 0HU ⓣ 01243 811461, ⓦ thefoxgoesfree.com. This seventeenth-century flint country pub oozes character – think well-worn brick floors, sagging beams and inglenook fireplaces – and history: back in the 1600s William III used to drop in to refresh his hunting party here. The large garden is the crowning glory, with picnic tables under the apple trees and beautiful views of the Downs. Food is traditional and home-made, and runs from sandwiches to the Fox fish pie (£7–16). Mon–Sat 11am–11pm, Sun noon–10.30pm; kitchen Mon–Fri noon–2.30pm & 6.15–10pm, Sat noon–10.30pm, Sun noon–5pm & 6.15–9.30pm.

8

★ **Richmond Arms** Mill Rd, West Ashling, 5 miles from Chichester, PO18 8EA ☎ 01243 572046, ⓦ therichmondarms.co.uk. West Ashling's village pub is a real find, with heaps of style and great food: a meal here might start with hot and runny chorizo Scotch egg with pickled fennel and saffron aioli, followed by hot molten Selsey crab Kiev, and finish with a hot, sugared chocolate and banana spring roll served with lavender ice cream. Most mains £15–18. On Fri and Sat evenings a converted wagon serves up artisan-style pizzas. Wed–Sat noon–2pm & 6–9pm, Sun noon–3pm.

Royal Oak Pook Lane, East Lavant, 3 miles from Chichester, PO18 0AX ☎ 01243 427434, ⓦ royaloakeastlavant.co.uk. Two-hundred-year-old, vine-covered coaching inn in a pretty village just outside Chichester, with bags of character and tables out the front overlooking the quiet village lane. The food is great, sourced from local suppliers where possible: mains (£15–22) might include wild local sea bass or the Royal Oak pie of the day. Daily 8am–11pm; kitchen Mon–Fri noon–2pm & 6–9pm, Sat noon–2.30pm & 6–9.30pm, Sun noon–3pm & 6.30–9pm.

DRINKING

Crate and Apple 14 Westgate, PO19 3EU ☎ 01243 539336, ⓦ crateandapple.co.uk. This smart, family-friendly pub is justifiably popular. Craft ales, local gins and cocktails sit alongside really good locally sourced food (mains £12–17), and there's a small beer garden out the back. Mon–Sat 10am–11pm, Sun 10am–4pm; kitchen Mon–Thurs & Sun 10am–3pm & 6–9pm, Fri & Sat 10am–3pm & 6–9.30pm.
Park Tavern 11 Priory Rd, PO19 1NS ☎ 01243 785057,

ⓦ parktavernchichester.co.uk. A proper pub with a great atmosphere, overlooking Priory Park. Great-value food such as sandwiches and ploughman's (£7.50–8), plus mains around the £10 mark and superior bar snacks (£4–5) including whitebait and pork pie with home-made piccalilli. Fuller's ales on tap, plus a seasonal guest beer. Live music on Sun afternoons. Mon–Sat 11am–11pm, Sun noon–10.30pm; kitchen Mon noon–3pm, Tues–Fri noon–3pm & 6–9pm, Sat 11am–9pm, Sun noon–4pm.

ENTERTAINMENT

Chichester Cinema New Park Rd, PO19 7XY ☎ 01243 786650, ⓦ chichestercinema.org. Chichester's excellent arthouse cinema screens up to four films a day.
Chichester Festival Theatre Oaklands Park, PO19 6AP ☎ 01243 781312, ⓦ cft.org.uk. One of the best regional theatres in the country, the newly refurbished

Chichester Festival Theatre opened in 1962 when it was the very first thrust-stage theatre, with Laurence Olivier as artistic director. Today, many productions from the theatre's annual season (roughly Easter–Oct) move on to the West End and abroad; in winter it hosts touring shows.

SHOPPING

★ **Clothkits** 16 The Hornet, PO19 7JG ☎ 01243 533180, ⓦ clothkits.co.uk. Chichester-based Kay Mawer has breathed fresh life into the much-loved Clothkits brand of ready-to-sew mail-order clothes, which dressed a generation of 1970s children. The shop here in Chichester sells clothing kits for women and children (featuring unique prints by contemporary artists and textile designers) alongside a vast array of fabrics and haberdashery, and there's a busy programme of workshops running upstairs. Kay also runs Draper's Yard next door, an alley of pop-up market stalls and studios selling everything

from jewellery to prints to furniture. Mon–Sat 9.30am–5.30pm.
Oxmarket Centre of Arts St Andrews Court, off East St, PO19 1YH ☎ 01243 779103, ⓦ oxmarket.com. Housed in a twelfth-century church, this gallery houses the work of local artists, with exhibitions changing monthly. Tues–Sun 10am–4.30pm.
Vintage @ Chi 2 Jays Walk, St Martin's St, PO19 1NP ☎ 01243 773644, ⓦ vintage-chi.com. For good-quality vintage clothing look no further than this tiny shop, crammed with great pieces. Tues–Sat 10am–4.30pm.

Fishbourne Roman Palace

Salthill Rd, Fishbourne, PO19 3QR • Daily: Feb & Nov to mid-Dec 10am–4pm; March–Oct 10am–5pm • £8.90 • ☎ 01243 789829, ⓦ sussexpast.co.uk • Train from Chichester to Fishbourne (hourly; 3min)

Fishbourne Roman Palace, two miles west of Chichester, is the largest and best-preserved Roman dwelling in the country, and the largest north of the Alps. Roman relics have long been turning up in Fishbourne, and in 1960 a workman unearthed their source – the site of a depot constructed by the invading Romans in 43 AD, which is thought later to have become the vast palace of the Romanized king of a local tribe, Cogidubnus. The palace was built around 75–80 AD, on a huge scale, with around a hundred rooms, 160 columns, 43,000 roof tiles and up to two miles of masonry walls. The one surviving wing – the **north wing** – represents just a quarter of the site; a large part of the complex lies buried beneath Fishbourne village.

Fishbourne has the largest collection of in-situ **mosaics** in the country, and some of the earliest too. When the palace was built, craftsmen laid the black-and-white geometric mosaics that were popular in Rome at the time, but as tastes changed from the early second century onwards, these were supplanted by polychrome mosaics, which featured a central panel surrounded by a large border – the dolphin-riding cupid being Fishbourne's most famous example. Nearby Bignor Roman Villa (see p.295) also has some stunning polychrome mosaics, and makes a fascinating follow-on visit.

An **audiovisual programme** gives a fuller picture of the palace as it would have been in Roman times, and the extensive **gardens** attempt to re-create the palace grounds – which might well have been the earliest formal gardens in the country – with new planting in the original bedding trenches. There is at least one **guided tour** a day (free), as well as occasional handling sessions, and special events take place throughout the year.

Kingley Vale National Nature Reserve

5km northwest of Chichester, near West Stoke village • Download Natural England's leaflet (including a map of the reserve) at ⓦ publications .naturalengland.org.uk/publication/32044 • Car park near West Stoke village (signposted); the reserve is a 15min walk from here

The magical **Kingley Vale National Nature Reserve**, a few miles northwest of Chichester in the South Downs National Park, is perhaps best known for its ancient **yew trees**, which are thought to be amongst the oldest living things in Britain. The massive, twisting trees here are at least 500 years old and probably much, much older – one story goes that they were planted back in 859 to commemorate a victory against Viking invaders. The 3.5-mile circular Nature Trail (accessed from the West Stoke car park) climbs up through the dark, atmospheric yew forest to rolling chalk grassland with wonderful panoramic views over Chichester Harbour; look out for the Devil's Humps nearby, Bronze Age burial mounds.

8

West Dean Gardens

West Dean, PO18 0RX • March–Oct Mon–Fri 10.30am–5pm, Sat, Sun & bank hols 9am–5pm; Nov–Feb Mon–Fri 10.30am–4pm, Sat, Sun & bank hols 9am–4pm • March–Oct £8.50, Nov–Feb £5.50 • ☎ 01243 818210, ⓦ westdean.org.uk/gardens • Stagecoach Coastline bus #60 from Chichester or Midhurst (Mon–Sat 2 hourly, Sun hourly)

With wildflower meadows, sweeping lawns, flower gardens and fruit orchards, all set against a backdrop of the South Downs, **West Dean Gardens**, five miles north of Chichester, are among the loveliest in Sussex. You could happily spend half a day or more exploring: highlights include the walled **Kitchen Garden** – one of the most perfect examples you'll see anywhere, with neat, white-painted Victorian glasshouses, fruit trees trained into sculptural shapes, and supernaturally neat rows of flawless vegetables – and the pretty **Spring Garden**, where you'll find dinky flint bridges spanning the crystal-clear River Lavant, and two Surrealist fibreglass **tree sculptures**. The sculptures were created by poet and writer **Edward James**, who once owned the West Dean Estate and is best known for his early support and patronage of Surrealist art; Salvador Dalí's iconic *Mae West Lips Sofa* and *Lobster Telephone* were both created in collaboration with James. James is buried up in the fifty-acre **arboretum**, half a mile or so uphill across sloping parkland dotted with grazing sheep; it's at its most beautiful in spring, when rhododendrons and azaleas daub the pathways with splashes of red and pink.

Edward James's mansion, at the centre of the gardens, operates as **West Dean College**, an internationally renowned residential college dedicated to creative arts and conservation. To get a taster, you can enrol on one of the twenty-plus **day courses**, which span everything from stained-glass making and woodcarving to blacksmithing and botanical painting.

Weald & Downland Open Air Museum

Singleton, PO18 0EU • March & Nov daily 10.30am–4pm; April–Oct daily 10.30am–6pm; Dec limited opening – see website; Downland Gridshell tour daily 1.30pm • £11.50 • ☎ 01243 811363, ⓦ wealddown.co.uk • Stagecoach Coastline bus #60 from Chichester or Midhurst (Mon–Sat 2 hourly, Sun hourly)

Five miles north of Chichester, the **Weald & Downland Open Air Museum** is a brilliantly engaging rural museum. More than fifty buildings from the last seven hundred years – everything from a medieval farmstead to a Tudor market hall and a pair of Victorian labourers' cottages – have been dismantled from sites around the Southeast and reconstructed on this fifty-acre site. None would have survived without the museum's intervention: some were virtually tumbledown, while others were due to be demolished to make way for development.

Many of the buildings have been decked out as they would have been originally, using replica furniture and artefacts. In the working Tudor kitchen in sixteenth-century **Winkhurst Farm** you can even taste some of the food of the period – handmade butter and cheese, griddle bread and pottage. Stewards inside the buildings are on hand to talk about what life would have been like for those who lived there, and there are regular **demonstrations** – different every day – of rural crafts and trades. Spend some time at the brand-new **visitor centre** and information galleries at the entrance to get the most out of your visit; the daily **tour** of the modern, innovative **Downland Gridshell** building, the museum's vast workshop and store, is also recommended. Numerous events and activities run throughout the year.

Cass Sculpture Foundation

Goodwood, 5 miles north of Chichester, PO18 0QP • Easter–Oct daily 10.30am–4.30pm • £12.50 • ☎ 01243 538449, ⓦ sculpture.org.uk

The magical **Cass Sculpture Foundation** is an absolute must for anyone interested in contemporary art, with more than fifty large-scale works nestled among the trees in a beautiful 26-acre woodland setting. Uniquely, all of the sculptures are for sale – ranging in price from a few thousand pounds to well over a million – meaning that the pieces on display change from year to year as they are sold. The dynamo behind the operation is retired businessman **Wilfred Cass**, whose own Modernist house lies hidden among the trees. Plenty of big names have been on show over the years – Tony Cragg, Antony Gormley, Thomas Heatherwick, Eduardo Paolozzi, Andy Goldsworthy, Rachel Whiteread and more – but the Foundation also commissions sculpture from lesser-known British talent, meeting the cost of the materials and then taking a share of the profits when the piece is sold, before ploughing the money back into the Foundation.

The Goodwood Estate

Goodwood, 4 miles north of Chichester, PO18 0PX • **Motor Circuit** Track Days £175 (summer) or £140 (winter) per half-day • **Aerodrome** A range of flights are available, from a 20min sightseeing flight (£135) to the 2–3hr "Top Gun Combat Mission" (£499) • **Golf** Day membership £99 • ☎ 01243 755055, ⓦ goodwood.com

Goodwood's name is synonymous with glamorous sporting pursuits, and its three big annual events – **Glorious Goodwood**, the **Festival of Speed** and the **Goodwood Revival** (see box opposite) – draw spectators from around the world. At the centre of the estate is the magnificent **Goodwood House**. Surrounding it are a famous **racecourse** high up on the Downs, which has hosted horse racing since 1802; a celebrated **motor-racing circuit**; an **aerodrome**; two **golf courses** (one ranked in the top 100 in the country); a hotel (see opposite); and a members-only **sporting club**, The Kennels, built in 1787 to house the third Duke of Richmond's hounds and huntsman – the prized dogs apparently had central heating in their quarters a hundred years before it was installed in the main house.

If you've got deep pockets, all of the above is yours to enjoy. You can drive your car round the historic Goodwood Motor Circuit on a **Track Day**, take the controls of an aircraft on a short flight from the aerodrome, or play a round of golf on the prestigious

GLORIOUS, GLORIOUS GOODWOOD

Goodwood's three big **events** are all incredibly popular. Book your accommodation as far in advance as you can – many hotels and B&Bs are booked up more than a year in advance – and be prepared for **accommodation** prices to soar. For exact dates, prices and further details, see ⓦ www.goodwood.com.

Festival of Speed 4 days in late June/early July. This long weekend of vintage and special cars – featuring everything from Formula One racers and supercars to motorbikes, rally cars and classics – bills itself as "the largest motoring garden party in the world", and is held in the grounds of Goodwood House, attracting around 150,000 petrolheads. The 1.16-mile hill climb is the main event of the weekend (Sat & Sun), but there's plenty of other stuff going on, and the public can wander around the paddocks and get up close to the cars and the stars. Tickets cost £32–65, depending on the day.

Glorious Goodwood 5 days in late July/Aug. One of *the* events of the social and racing year, as much about celeb-spotting, champagne and fashion as it is about horse racing – Edward VII famously described it as "a garden party with racing tacked on". Ticket prices depend on which enclosure you're in: cheapest is the Lennox Enclosure (£18); then comes the Gordon Enclosure (£41); the Richmond Enclosure is members-only.

Goodwood Revival 3 days in mid-Sept. This nostalgic motor-race meeting relives the glory days of the Goodwood Motor Circuit, welcoming the cars and motorbikes that would have competed during the 1940s, 1950s and 1960s. Many cars are driven by famous names from the past and present, and the entire event is staged in an authentic period setting, with staff – and most of the 100,000 spectators – dressing up in period garb. Tickets cost £51–73, depending on the day.

Downs Course. A day at the horse races is a positive bargain by comparison, with the cheapest tickets under £10; see ⓦ goodwood.com for fixtures.

Goodwood House

March–July & Sept–Oct most Mon & Sun 1–5pm; most of Aug Mon–Thurs & Sun 1–5pm; check website for exact dates • Entry by obligatory guided tours (every 30min; 1hr 15min), except in Aug when rooms are stewarded • £9.50 • ☎ 01243 755055, ⓦ goodwood.com

Seat of the Dukes of Richmond, Lennox, Gordon and Aubigny, **Goodwood House** is every bit as splendid as the rest of the estate. When the first Duke of Richmond – the illegitimate son of Charles II and his French mistress – bought the house in 1697 it was little more than a hunting lodge, but over the years successive generations improved and enlarged it into what you see today. The Earl and Countess of March live in the house, so only the **staterooms** are open to the public, and those only on certain days of the week for parts of the year. The rooms are furnished in opulent Regency style, a fitting home for the family's stellar art collection which includes Sèvres porcelain and paintings by Stubbs, Reynolds, Van Dyck and Canaletto. Each year, an **exhibition** in August (included in entry price) highlights a different aspect of the house's history.

ACCOMMODATION	THE GOODWOOD ESTATE

Goodwood Hotel Goodwood Estate, 4 miles from Chichester, PO18 0QB ☎ 01243 775537, ⓦ goodwood .com. The Goodwood Estate's country-house hotel isn't cheap, but you're not just paying for the rooms – which are suitably deluxe – but for the whole Goodwood experience. A night here gives you access to the health club and spa, two golf courses, and a couple of excellent restaurants supplied in part from the estate's own farm. Rates vary according to demand. **£170**

Tinwood Estate

Tinwood Lane, Halnaker, PO18 0NE • Daily 9am–6pm • Free; wine-tasting £5 • **Tours** Thurs, Fri & Sat 3pm (book ahead); 1hr 30min • £15 • ☎ 01243 537372, ⓦ tinwoodestate.com

The **Tinwood Estate** planted its first vines in 2007, and today the smart 65-acre estate produces three sparkling wines, all made from classic Champagne-variety grapes. You can pitch up to taste the wines in the stylish, modern tasting room, or buy a bottle and enjoy it on one of the picnic benches outside, looking out over the vines; book in advance to join one of the **tours**, which take you around the vineyard and include tastings of the three different fizzes. Tinwood also runs special events throughout the year, including a pop-up restaurant and live music.

ACCOMMODATION	TINWOOD ESTATE
Tinwood Estate Lodges Tinwood Lane, PO18 0NE ☎ 01243 537372, ⓦ tinwoodestate.com. Three ultra-smart wooden lodges, named after the vines grown on the estate – Chardonnay, Pinot Noir and Pinot Meunier. Each lodge has big windows looking out onto the vines, an enormous bathroom	with two-person jacuzzi and walk-in shower, a fridge well-stocked with wine and a lovely decked terrace on which to drink it. The lodges share a wine barrel-shaped sauna, and free mountain bikes are available for exploring the area. It's not cheap, but it's all done impeccably. **£250**

Tangmere Military Aviation Museum

Tangmere, PO20 2ES • Daily: Feb & Nov 10am–4.30pm; March–Oct 10am–5pm • £9 • ☎ 01243 790090, ⓦ tangmere-museum.org.uk

An operational airfield from 1916 through to 1970, RAF Tangmere, just east of Chichester, is perhaps most famous for the pivotal role it played during the Battle of Britain in World War II, when it defended an area of the south coast from Portland Bill to Brighton, including the crucially important Portsmouth dockyard. Today a corner of the historic airfield houses the **Tangmere Military Aviation Museum**, an Aladdin's cave of aviation memorabilia covering both World Wars and the Cold War, with a couple of flight simulators and a clutch of historic aircraft thrown in for good measure, amongst them the red Hawker Hunter in which Neville Duke set the world airspeed record in 1953, and the poignant remains of a Hurricane shot down during the Battle of Britain. Displays range from stories of individual heroism by RAF pilots to a recreated ops room; particularly fascinating is an exhibit about Tangmere's role in delivering SOEs (special operations executives) into Europe under cover of darkness, armed with maps concealed in the false interiors of thermos flasks, and fountain pens loaded with capsules of deadly gas.

The Manhood Peninsula

Just south of Chichester lies the flat **MANHOOD PENSINULA**, with Selsey Bill – the southernmost point of Sussex – at its tip, Bognor Regis (see p.298) to the east, and the beautiful creeks of **Chichester Harbour** on its far western edge. Its rather wonderful name probably comes from the Old English *maene-wudu*, meaning "men's wood" or common land, though there's no remaining woodland to speak of today, with the peninsula mainly given over to agriculture. Inland the landscape is flat and featureless, but the main appeal of the area is around the coast, where you'll find some of the last remaining stretches of undeveloped coastline in Sussex.

The best way to enjoy the peninsula, known locally as "God's pocket" for its benevolent microclimate, is to make the most of the great outdoors, whether by taking a boat trip, enrolling in a watersports taster course or simply striking off on a coastal footpath.

ARRIVAL AND GETTING AROUND	THE MANHOOD PENINSULA
By bike Bike routes crisscross the peninsula (see box, p.280), most of which is no more than 6m above sea level, making it easy cycling territory. **By bus** Stagecoach bus #52 runs from Chichester to West Wittering, East Wittering and Bracklesham (Mon–Sat every 15–30min, Sun every 30min–1hr), and #56 to Old Bosham (Mon–Sat every 1hr 30min). Compass Travel bus #150 runs	between Itchenor, East Wittering, Bracklesham, Sidlesham and Selsey (Mon–Fri 4 daily). **By car** Be aware there can be daily traffic jams on the road to and from West Wittering beach on summer weekends; get there early, or consider hiring a bike (see p.270). There's plentiful pay-and-display parking around the peninsula.

8

Chichester Harbour

Chichester Harbour is the Southeast's smallest Area of Outstanding Natural Beauty, a glorious estuarine landscape of inlets and tidal mudflats, pretty creekside villages and hamlets, big skies, and sparkling water dotted with sails. One of Sussex's few remaining tracts of undeveloped coastline, the harbour shelters a rich diversity of habitats (shingle banks, saltmarsh, mudflats, sand dunes and ancient woodland) and wildlife – over 50,000 birds use the harbour every year, making it a top site for birdwatching, especially in winter. Exploring is easy: boat trips (see box, p.278) run all year, and 28 miles of footpaths wiggle around the coastline. **Chichester Harbour Conservancy** (Ⓦconservancy.co.uk), which manages and conserves the harbour, also runs an excellent programme of **activities**, everything from nature walks, foraging and stream-dipping to kids' activities, birdwatching and art events.

Bosham

One of the prettiest villages on the harbour, and certainly the most popular, is historic, creekside **Bosham** (pronounced "Bozzum") The village's appearance changes dramatically throughout the day as the tidal creek fills and empties: at low tide it's surrounded by green- and dun-coloured mudflats and marooned boats, while at high tide the water comes slapping right up against the back walls of the buildings along waterfront Shore Road. Despite warning signs, and tell-tale seaweed on the road, you still get the odd hapless parked car caught out by the tide; pop into the village pub, the *Anchor Bleu* (see below), and you'll see photos up on the walls of cars in various sorry states of submersion.

Fittingly, Bosham is one of the places put forward as the possible location of **King Cnut**'s (994–1035) failed attempt to turn back the tide – a deliberate display to show the limits of his power to his fawning courtiers. Cnut's young daughter is said to be buried in pretty, shingle-spired **Bosham Church**, parts of which date back to Saxon times. Look out for the reproduction of a scene from the **Bayeux Tapestry** in the north aisle, which depicts Harold, the Earl of Wessex and soon-to-be last Saxon King of England, praying in the church in 1064 before sailing off to Normandy to settle the matter of the English throne's succession with his rival, William of Normandy.

Beyond the church, over the millpond stream, lies National Trust-managed **Quay Meadow**, with **Bosham Quay** at its southern end; in summer it's a popular picnic spot, with good crabbing from the quay wall at high tide.

8

EATING AND DRINKING   BOSHAM

Anchor Bleu Bosham High St, PO18 8LS Ⓣ01243 573956, Ⓦanchorbleu.co.uk. The back terrace of this whitewashed eighteenth-century inn is the perfect spot to sit and watch the tide turn; at high water the sea laps right up against the terrace wall. Inside there are low, beamed ceilings and flagstone floors; the food is classic, well-done pub grub – baguettes and ploughman's (£5–9), fish and chips (£12), fresh dressed crab (£9) and the like at lunch, plus proper, satisfying puds like spotted dick and treacle sponge. Mon & Tues 11am–10pm, Wed & Thurs 11am–11pm, Fri 11.30am–11.30pm, Sat 11am–11.30pm, Sun noon–10pm; kitchen opening hours vary – check website.

Itchenor

The long, winding country lane leading to the quiet sailing village of **Itchenor** ends at the slipway, with lovely views across to Bosham Hoe on the far side of the creek across a sea of masts and sails. There's a viewing platform next to the slipway, a lovely place to sit and watch the bobbing, clinking boats, but most people come to Itchenor to get out on the water themselves (see box, p.278): **boat trips** run throughout the year, and from spring to autumn a small **passenger ferry** shuttles across the creek to Bosham Hoe, a thirty-minute walk from picturesque Bosham. Just by the slipway, the office of the **Chichester Harbour Conservancy** (Mon–Fri 9am–5pm, plus Easter–Sept Sat 9am–1pm; Ⓣ01243 513275, Ⓦconservancy.co.uk) has plenty of information on the harbour, boat trips, walks and other activities.

Ship Inn The Street, PO20 7AH ☎01243 512284, ⓦtheshipinnitchenor.co.uk. Just up the lane from Itchenor's slipway, this redbrick pub is always busy in summer with boaties and tourists, and the picnic tables out front are a fine spot to settle down with a pint. Food is decent pub grub (sausages, burgers, fresh fish, steaks), with most mains in the £10.50–12.50 range, and there are Sussex-brewed beers and guest ales on tap. Daily 10am–11pm; kitchen daily noon–2.30pm & 6.30–9pm (no food Sun eve in winter).

West Wittering Beach and around

Beach daily: mid-March to mid-Oct 6.30am–8.30pm; mid-Oct to mid-March 7am–6pm • Parking £1–8 depending on season, day & time • ☎01243 514143 (Estate Office), ⓦ westwitteringbeach.co.uk

The wonderful thing about unspoilt **West Wittering Beach** is what *isn't* there: no amusement arcades, caravan parks or lines of shops selling garish seaside tat. Instead you'll find acres of soft white sand dimpled by shallow pools at low tide, a line of candy-coloured beach huts, grassy dunes, a modest **shop** and **café** (mid-March to mid-Oct daily 9am–6pm; mid-Oct to mid-March Fri, Sat & Sun 10am–4pm) – and that's about it. It could all have been so different, had a band of foresighted locals not scraped together £20,546 in the 1950s to buy the land and prevent it being turned into a Butlin's holiday camp; the West Wittering Estate is now managed as a conservation company, with parking fees paying for the maintenance of the beach and surrounding area.

The big grass field behind the beach serves as the car park; at its eastern end by the entrance you'll find a small cabin housing 2XS, which offers **watersports** tuition and equipment hire (see box, p.280), and at its western end is National Trust-owned East Head (see opposite). **West Wittering village** – which counts among its residents Rolling Stones guitarist Keith Richards – lies less than a mile inland.

The beach gets incredibly busy on summer weekends, when as many as 15,000 holidaymakers can descend in a day. Queues on the access road can snake back for miles; if you're staying in Chichester and don't want to spend an hour or two in traffic,

---

CHICHESTER HARBOUR BOAT TRIPS

The best way to appreciate gloriously scenic Chichester Harbour is on the water. The harbour is one of the most popular boating waters in the country, with over 12,500 craft using it annually, and there are several ways you can join in.

HARBOUR TOURS

Chichester Harbour Conservancy ☎01243 513275, ⓦconservancy.co.uk. The Conservancy runs boat trips on the *Solar Heritage*, a solar-powered catamaran with virtually silent engines that allow it to glide peacefully along the inlets and creeks, getting up close to wildlife; various cruises are available, including the standard "harbour discovery" tour, evening cruises, nature tours and winter-only birdwatching cruises. Departures are from Itchenor (1hr 30min; £8.50; advance booking only) throughout the year, apart from mid-July to early Sept, when the catamaran departs from Emsworth (1hr; £8.50; book in advance or pay in cash on the day), just over the border in Hampshire.

Chichester Harbour Water Tours ☎01243 670504, ⓦchichesterharbourwatertours.co.uk. Boat trips around the harbour leave from Itchenor up to four times a day during high summer, daily during spring and autumn, and weekends only during April and Oct (1hr 30min; £9).

BOAT HIRE

Itchenor Boat Hire ☎01243 513345, ⓦitchenorboathire.co.uk. Offers self-drive, small-boat hire to those with prior experience, by the day or half-day (April–Oct only). A four-person dory costs £65–70/half-day, £105–115/day.

ITCHENOR–BOSHAM FERRY

Itchenor Ferry ⓦitchenorferry.co.uk. Runs from the end of the jetty at Itchenor across the channel to Smugglers Lane at Bosham Hoe (mid-May to Sept daily 9am–6pm; April to mid-May & Oct Sat & Sun 9am–6pm; £2.50, bikes 50p).

your best bet is to hire a bike and cruise past the jams on the Salterns Way cycle route (see box, p.280).

East Head

Coast Guard Lane, Chichester, PO20 8AJ • Open access • Park at West Wittering beach car park (see opposite) • ☎ 01243 814730, Ⓦ nationaltrust.org.uk/east-head

At the mouth of Chichester Harbour, National Trust-managed **East Head** is a pristine salt-and-shingle spit that's prized for its rare sand dune and saltmarsh habitats. It's connected to the western end of West Wittering Beach by a narrow strip of land known as "The Hinge", and covers around ten hectares – you can walk its length in just fifteen minutes, but despite its proximity to West Wittering's hordes it never really gets too busy. Boardwalks snake across the spit, protecting the fragile dune system. On the western (seaward) side there's a **beach** of fine sand backed by constantly shifting dunes knitted together with clumps of shaggy marram grass; on the eastern side there's a large area of saltmarsh which fills and empties with each tide – a popular **birdwatching** site, especially in winter. At the far northern end of the spit you'll often see boats anchored in the summer, and, in winter, the occasional seal basking on the beach.

From The Hinge, a **footpath** runs north for a quarter of a mile to a specially constructed **crabbing pool**, and on to the village of Itchenor, a further 3.5 miles away. The path skirts the shoreline all the way, with flat farmland on one side and beautiful views across the water on the other.

ACCOMMODATION AND EATING   WEST WITTERING

Beach House B&B Rookwood Rd, PO20 8LT ☎ 01243 514800, Ⓦ beachhse.co.uk. The best option if you want to stay close to West Wittering Beach is this friendly, family-run B&B with attached restaurant; it's just a 15min walk from the beach, in the heart of West Wittering village. Food is available throughout the day, from breakfast onwards: the lunch menu features burgers, ciabattas and sharing plates, with mains (£11–19) such as Southdown leg of lamb at dinner. Summer daily 8am–2.30pm & 6–8.30pm; rest of year opening times vary – call ahead. **£120**

The Lamb Inn Chichester Rd, PO20 8QA ☎ 01243 511105, Ⓦ thelambwittering.co.uk. Midway between West Wittering and Itchenor, this great pub has a lovely ambience and food to match – not surprising, given it's run

by the same team as the acclaimed *Samphire* (see p.280). The locally sourced food (seafood linguine, rabbit pie, fish of the day, and the likes) is in the £13–16 range. There's a nice garden out the back for summertime eating or drinking. Mon–Sat 11.30am–11pm, Sun 11.30am–10pm; kitchen Mon–Sat noon–2pm & 6–9pm, Sat noon–3pm & 6–9pm, Sun noon 3.30pm & 5.30–8pm.

The Landing Pound House, Pound Rd, PO20 8AJ ☎ 01243 513757, Ⓦ facebook.com/thelandingcoffeeshop. This tiny coffee shop brings a dash of style to West Wittering, with its bare boards, Eames chairs and art on the walls. On the menu you'll find great coffee, cakes, fresh crab sandwiches and artisan ice cream. Daily: summer 8am–6pm; winter Mon–Fri 9am–4pm.

East Wittering and Bracklesham Bay

Along the southwest coast of the Manhood Peninsula, the seaside villages of **East Wittering** and **Bracklesham Bay** merge together in an unremarkable modern sprawl of bungalows and shops. The beach along this stretch lacks the wow-factor of famous West Wittering; it's pebbly for a start (though there's plenty of sand at low tide), and is backed by modern residential blocks in place of West Wittering's grass-flecked dunes. It does, however, have some of the best places to eat on the peninsula, and is also one of the best stretches of coast for **fossil-hunting**, in particular around Bracklesham Bay, where every day at low tide hundreds of fossils including bivalve shells, shark's teeth and corals are washed up on the sand – the easiest fossil-hunting going, and perfect for families. The best hunting ground is around Bracklesham Bay car park and the few hundred yards east towards Selsey; see Ⓦ westsussexgeology.co.uk for details of organized fossil hunts.

East Wittering is a popular location for **surfing**; you can hire boards and wetsuits from the Wittering Surf Shop (see box, p.280).

ACCOMMODATION AND EATING

EAST WITTERING AND BRACKLESHAM BAY

Billy's on the Beach Bracklesham Lane, Bracklesham Bay, PO20 8JH ☎ 01243 670373, ⓦ billysonthebeach .co.uk. Blue-and-white-striped Billy's has a great location right on the beach, cheerful beach-themed decor and a menu of pancakes, toasties (from £5.25), fish and chips, *fritto misto* (£7.95), ice cream sundaes and more. June to early Sept Mon–Sat 9am–9pm, Sun 9am–5pm; mid-Sept to May Mon–Wed & Sun 9am–5pm, Thurs–Sat 9am–9pm.

Drift-In Surf Café 11–13 Shore Rd, East Wittering, PO20 8DY ☎ 01243 672292, ⓦ driftinsurfcafe.co.uk. As you might expect from a café that's connected to a surf shop, this place has a cool, laidback vibe, and a menu full of perfect energy fodder after a morning catching waves – smoothies, shakes, hot chocolate, wraps and an enormous selection of pancakes. Mon–Sat 9am–5pm, Sun 10am–4pm.

Drifters Kitchen & Bar 61 Shore Rd, East Wittering, PO20 8DY ☎ 01243 673584, ⓦ drifters-ew.co.uk. On a sunny day make a beeline for the big outside deck at this relaxed restaurant – run by the same folks as *Drift-In* up the road (see above). The crowd-pleasing menu runs from burgers (from £10.50) and baguettes through to chilli, meze and tapas-style "small plates" (£6.50–8), and there's a good kids' menu too. Craft beers, cocktails and wine are all available. Mon & Wed–Sat 9am–3pm & 5pm–late, Sun 9am–3pm.

★**Samphire English Kitchen** 57 Shore Rd, East Wittering, PO20 8DY ☎ 01243 672754, ⓦ samphireeast wittering.co.uk. The Witterings' culinary star is this cosy, intimate restaurant with a focus on fresh produce: its menu changes regularly to make the most of the best local ingredients, including fish from the beach 100m away. A typical meal might start with a Selsey crab Waldorf salad (£8), followed by fish stew (£18.50); there's also a good-value set lunch menu (2/3 courses £13/16). Mon–Sat noon–2pm & 6–9pm.

Stubcroft Farm Stubcroft Lane, East Wittering, PO20 8PJ ☎ 01243 671469, ⓦ stubcroft.com. This no-frills,

---

WALKS, WATERSPORTS AND TWO WHEELS ON THE MANHOOD PENINSULA

The great outdoors is what the Manhood Peninsula does best. The area is very well set up for walkers and cyclists, with miles of footpaths and cycle paths crisscrossing the peninsula – bikes can be rented in Fishbourne near Chichester (see p.270). If you want to get out on the water, sample the huge variety of watersports on offer around the coast.

WATERSPORTS

2XS West Wittering Beach (daily 9am–5.30pm; ☎ 01243 513077, ⓦ 2xs.co.uk). This well-established outfit is the only one on the sands of West Wittering. Taster sessions run for most watersports, with longer sessions/courses available: windsurfing (2hr/£48); surfing (2hr/£37); stand-up paddle surfing (2hr/£42); powerkiting (2hr/£37); kitesurfing (2 days/£225).

Equipment rental (wetsuits, body- and surfboards, kayaks etc) is also available.

Wittering Surf Shop 11–13 Shore Rd, East Wittering (Mon–Sat 9am–5pm, Sun 10am–4pm; ☎ 01243 672292, ⓦ witteringsurfshop.co.uk). Surfboard hire costs £12/half-day, £16/full day; wetsuits are £10/15.

CYCLING

Maps for the cycle routes below are available at ⓦ conservancy.co.uk/page/cycling/346.

Bill Way Signposted route from Chichester Canal Basin to Pagham Harbour nature reserve along a canalside path and minor roads.

Chichester–Itchenor–Bosham circular This summer-only route follows the Salterns Way as far as Chichester Marina, then continues to Itchenor, where you can pick up the ferry (April–Oct only) across to

Bosham Hoe. You then cycle back up through Bosham and Fishbourne before returning to Chichester. This route is easily accessible if you're hiring bikes from Barreg Cycles in Fishbourne (see p.270).

Salterns Way This signposted route runs for 11.5 miles from the Market Cross in Chichester to the dunes of East Head, partly on cycle paths, partly on country lanes and roads.

WALKING

Chichester Harbour Walks There are lots of downloadable walks on the Chichester Harbour Conservancy website, including a lovely four-mile low-tide circular walk around West Wittering and East Head – see ⓦ conservancy.co.uk/assets/assets/walks_easthead.pdf.

Lipchis Way This long-distance north-to-south

footpath (ⓦ newlipchisway.co.uk) runs from Liphook in Hampshire to West Wittering. The latter part of the walk runs from Chichester along Chichester Ship Canal, past Itchenor and along the coast to West Wittering (10 miles), where you can pick up bus #52 back to Chichester (Mon–Sat every 15–30min, Sun every 30min–1hr).

eco- and wildlife-friendly campsite is the nicest place to camp on the Manhood Peninsula, and very popular, so book ahead in summer. The slightly cramped pitches are spread over three paddocks on a working sheep farm; BBQs are allowed, there's a small shop, and as an added bonus you can help bottle-feed the lambs in springtime. The nearest beaches (East Wittering and Bracklesham Bay) are a 20min walk away. £18

Pagham Harbour RSPB nature reserve

Nature reserve Near Sidlesham, PO20 7NE • Open access • Free • **Visitor centre** Selsey Rd, 1 mile south of Sidlesham, PO20 7NE • Daily 10am–4pm • ☎ 01243 641508, ⓦ rspb.org.uk/paghamharbour • Car parks at visitor centre (donation suggested) & Church Norton; bus #51 from Chichester (20min); cycle route #88 (Bill Way) from Chichester Canal Basin

On the east side of the Manhood Peninsula, **Pagham Harbour nature reserve** feels blissfully remote – you wouldn't think that brash Bognor lies just five miles away along the coast. The bay at the heart of the reserve is intertidal, and the landscape transforms dramatically throughout the day: at high water it's filled by the sea, while low tide sees the water ebb away to reveal expanses of mudflats and saltmarsh, picked over by wading birds. Surrounding the bay is a patchwork of meadows, farmland, copses, lagoons, reed beds and, on either side of the harbour mouth, two long shingle spits that are speckled with sea kale and yellow horned poppies in early summer.

The reserve is an important wetland site for wildlife, with the tidal mudflats attracting scores of **bird** species throughout the year, including thousands of Brent geese in winter; there's a hide at Church Norton and a second near the **visitor centre** just south of Sidlesham. The visitor centre is also the starting point for the circular 1.75-mile **Discovery Trail**, which takes you along the edge of Pagham Harbour as far as Sidlesham, home to the excellent *Crab and Lobster* pub. The RSPB, which manages the reserve, runs **guided walks** and activities.

8

ACCOMMODATION AND EATING	PAGHAM HARBOUR

Crab & Lobster Mill Lane, Sidlesham, PO20 7NB • ☎ 01243 641233, ⓦ crab-lobster.co.uk. If you want to treat yourself, this classy sixteenth-century inn on the edge of Pagham Harbour is the place: the rooms are effortlessly stylish, and the restaurant has an upmarket menu (mains £17–25) focused on local produce. At the back of the pub there's a peaceful terrace and beer garden with lovely views over the countryside. Mon–Fri noon–2.30pm & 6–9.30pm, Sat noon–10pm, Sun noon–9pm. £165

Medmerry RSPB nature reserve

PO20 7NE • Open access • Free • ⓦ rspb.org.uk/medmerry • Car parks at Earnley & Pagham Harbour visitor centre (see above)

A few miles southwest of Pagham Harbour, a new intertidal nature reserve has been created at **Medmerry**. The scheme, completed in 2013 and designed to reduce flood risk, involved constructing over four miles of new clay banks inland and then breaching the shingle beach, allowing the sea to flood in; the new wildlife habitats created will take several years to fully develop, but already you can see plenty of birdlife. Access to the reserve's footpaths, cycle paths and viewing mounds is from either Earnley, on the western side of the reserve, or the Pagham Harbour visitor centre (see above).

Midhurst and around

Lying smack-bang in the middle of the South Downs National Park, and home to the park's headquarters, the small market town of **MIDHURST** proudly trumpets itself as "the heart of the national park". The sleepy town has plenty of charm and a lovely location, bordered to the north and east by the wiggling, willow-fringed River Rother, but the main draw is the surrounding countryside – a gorgeous patchwork of ancient woodland, heathland and sweeping, humpbacked hills. A few miles to the north lies wild and beautiful **Black Down**, the highest point in the national park, while just south is the South Downs Way, which threads east along the rolling chalk downlands to **Harting Down** nature reserve. Just south of here is the fascinating **Uppark House**, destroyed by fire in 1989 and since painstakingly restored by the National Trust.

Market Square and around

Midhurst grew up around the medieval market in **Market Square**, still the most picturesque corner of town. In the centre of the square, the **Church of St Mary Magdalene and St Denys** (ⓦmidhurstparishchurch.net) has Norman foundations but has been much rebuilt over the years. By the church stands the **Old Town Hall**, now *Garton's Coffee House*, which was built in 1551 as the town's market house, originally open-sided for traders to display their goods. In 1760 the building became the town hall, with law courts on the first floor and cells below (which you can still see in the coffee shop today). The town **stocks**, last used in 1859, sit in an alcove underneath the steps at the side of the building.

Behind the Old Town Hall on **Edinburgh Square** you'll see a row of redbrick houses with distinctive saffron-yellow paintwork, a sign they belong to the local **Cowdray Estate**, which covers 16,500 acres northeast of Midhurst; the colour, now known as

---

8

THE SOUTH DOWNS NATIONAL PARK

The **South Downs National Park** came into being in April 2010. Covering over six hundred square miles, it stretches for seventy miles from eastern Hampshire through to the chalk cliffs of East Sussex, encompassing rolling hills, heathland, woodland and coastline – and plenty of towns and villages, too. More than 112,000 people live and work in the national park – more than in any other – and it is crisscrossed by a dense network of over 1800 miles of footpaths and bridleways.

The South Downs themselves, a range of gently undulating chalk hills famously described by Rudyard Kipling as the "blunt, bow-headed, whale-backed downs", form the backbone of the park; the southern slopes slant gently down to the sea, while the steep escarpment on the northern side drops abruptly to give spectacular views over the low-lying Weald. West of Arundel, the South Downs become more wooded on their journey into Hampshire, and the boundaries of the national park extend northward to cover the Western Weald, an area of woodland and heathland that, after much debate, was included in the park in recognition of its outstanding natural beauty.

In 2016, the South Downs National Park was designated an **International Dark Sky Reserve** (IDSR), only the second IDSR in the country and one of only twelve in the world. Check out ⓦsouthdowns.gov.uk/enjoy/explore/dark-night-skies for more information about the International Dark Sky Association, as well as tips on stargazing, details of events and a map of the darkest skies in the national park.

PARK PRACTICALITIES

Information The park's headquarters and visitor centre, the South Downs Centre (see p.284), is in Midhurst. ⓦsouthdowns.gov.uk has comprehensive information on public transport, walks, cycling, horse-riding and other activities, plus an events calendar.

Getting around If travelling by public transport, the Discovery Ticket (£8.50, family ticket £16) is a good option, allowing a day's unlimited bus travel across the National Park; see ⓦsouthdowns.gov.uk/enjoy/plan-a-visit/getting-around/discovery-ticket for details.

Walking and cycling ⓦsouthdowns.gov.uk has over a dozen downloadable walks and cycle rides that start and finish at a bus stop or train station, and the National Trust – which manages some of the finest tracts of land within the Park – also has a series of downloadable walks on its website (ⓦnationaltrust.org.uk/visit/activities/walking). There's a list of bike hire outlets at ⓦsouthdowns.gov.uk/enjoy/explore/cycling.

Food and drink The ⓦsouthdownsfood.org portal has lots of information on local produce, everything from Southdown lamb to award-winning Sussex fizz. The site's interactive food-finder map lists over two hundred businesses that champion locally produced food and drink – from farmers' markets and farm shops to vineyards, microbreweries, pubs and restaurants. You can also find downloadable food trails at ⓦsouthdowns.gov.uk.

"**Cowdray Yellow**", was chosen by the second Viscount Cowdray in the 1920s as a statement of his Liberal politics and has remained ever since.

North Street

Midhurst's main thoroughfare is **North Street**, which cuts through town to the west of Market Square. At the north end of the street, up by the causeway to the Cowdray Ruins, you'll see turreted **Capron House**, headquarters of the South Downs National Park Authority and home to its visitor centre (see p.284). A plaque on the wall recalls the building's past life as Midhurst Grammar School, which was attended in the 1880s by novelist **H.G. Wells** while his mother worked as housekeeper at nearby Uppark House (see p.285).

Further south, the Georgian-fronted *Angel Hotel* is the first of Midhurst's two splendid **coaching inns**, and was the favoured drinking hole of a certain Guy Fawkes, who masterminded his infamous plot while butler at Cowdray House. Its rival, the gloriously higgledy-piggledy *Spread Eagle* (see p.284), opposite Market Square, dates back in part to 1430.

Cowdray Ruins

Access via The Causeway from the North St car park; GU29 9AL • May–Aug Sat, Sun & bank hols 11am–4pm • £6.50 • ☎ 01730 810781, ⓦ cowdray.org.uk

The ruins of **Cowdray** have a fabulous approach, across a 300m-long causeway bordered by water meadows. From afar the castle-like gatehouse and crenellated walls appear relatively intact, but as you draw closer jagged walls draw into view, glimpses of sky can be seen through the window frames, and the gutted, roofless shell of a once-grand Tudor house is finally revealed.

When Cowdray was built in the sixteenth century – principally by **Sir William Fitzwilliam**, favoured courtier of Henry VIII – it was one of the grandest homes in the country, but in 1793 a disastrous fire broke out which destroyed almost all of it. It was left to rot, and by the nineteenth century had become a romantic ruin, painted by Turner and Constable. Some fragments of the house's former splendour still remain, notably the 1530s **porch**, with its intricately carved fan-vault ceiling, and the **Tudor kitchen**, which escaped unscathed thanks to its extra-thick walls, designed – ironically – to prevent any fire that might break out in the kitchen from spreading to the rest of the house. Many of the interiors were recorded in the 1780s by a Swiss artist, Samuel Grimm, and some of his pictures are reproduced on interpretive boards around the site, giving a poignant before-and-after snapshot of some of the magnificence the fire destroyed.

In the vaulted **wine cellar** a fascinating fifteen-minute film tells the story of the house and its owners, who managed, despite their Catholic allegiances, to keep on the right side of the Protestant royals throughout the turbulent sixteenth century, right up until a certain **Guy Fawkes** – butler at Cowdray under the second Viscount Montague – hatched his plot in 1605. The Viscount was unaccountably absent from parliament on the planned day of the explosion, and was sentenced to forty weeks in prison for his suspected involvement in the plot.

Woolbeding Gardens

Poundcommon, Woolbeding, 2 miles north of Midhurst, GU29 9RR • Early April to Sept Thurs & Fri 10.30am–4.30pm; pre-booking required • £8.40; NT • ☎ 0844 249 1895, ⓦ nationaltrust.org.uk/woolbeding-gardens • No parking at site; a minibus shuttle service operates from Midhurst

You'll need to pre-book to visit hidden-away **Woolbeding Gardens**, which are only open to the public for two days a week in the summer. The magical gardens, which occupy a lovely spot by the River Rother just north of Midhurst, were created over a period of forty years by the late Sir Simon Sainsbury and his partner, Stewart Grimshaw, and vary hugely in style, from formal "garden rooms" divided by neat clipped hedges to a wilder water garden, complete with grotto, ruined chapel and Chinese bridge.

ARRIVAL AND INFORMATION

By train and bus The closest stations are at Haslemere (connected by bus #70 to Midhurst: Mon–Sat hourly; 25min); Petersfield (bus #92: Mon–Sat hourly; 25min); and Chichester (bus #60: Mon–Sat every 30min, Sun hourly; 40min).

By car There are car parks at North St and Grange Rd.

South Downs Centre Capron House, North St

MIDHURST AND AROUND

(Mon–Thurs 9am–5pm, Fri 9am–4.30pm; May–Sept also Sat 10.30am–4.30pm; ☎01730 814810, ⍵southdowns .gov.uk). The visitor centre of the South Downs National Park contains a small exhibition about the national park, plus has plenty of leaflets and information on walks and public transport. There's also information on Midhurst (⍵visitmidhurst.com), including town maps and trails.

ACCOMMODATION

The Church House Church Hill, GU29 9NX ☎01730 812990, ⍵churchhousemidhurst.com. A great location by Market Square, five gorgeous rooms and home-made cake on arrival are just some of the things to love about this B&B. Splash out on one of the suites (£170) if you can. **£140**

Park House Bepton, near Midhurst, GU29 0JB ☎01730 819000, ⍵parkhousehotel.com. Small, luxurious country-house hotel with glorious views, elegant rooms (from standard rooms to suites, plus cottages in the grounds), a croquet lawn, grass tennis courts and a spa – a real retreat. Rates vary according to demand. **£160**

Spread Eagle Hotel South St, GU29 9NH ☎01730 816911, ⍵hshotels.co.uk. This wisteria-covered former coaching inn, dating back in part to the fifteenth century, oozes antiquity, from the creaking corridors and stained-glass windows to the wonky-walled lounge. Standard rooms are comfortable, and rates include use of the hotel spa. **£130**

Two Rose Cottages 2 Rose Cottages, Chichester Rd, GU29 9PF ☎01730 813804, ⍵tworosebandb.com. Friendly B&B in a Victorian cottage, with just two tasteful rooms, both en suite. A cosy sitting room, private front door, great breakfasts and plenty of local maps and books all round off a tip-top B&B experience. **£90**

EATING

MIDHURST

Cowdray Café Easebourne, 1 mile north of Midhurst, GU29 0AJ ☎01730 815152, ⍵cowdrayfarmshop.co.uk. Attached to the Cowdray Farm Shop, this café is a popular spot for breakfast and lunch, with lots of local produce on

the menu, from rarebit made with Sussex Charmer cheese to rib-eye from the Cowdray Estate's organically reared beef (£8.50–15). Daily 9am–5pm.

Garton's Coffee House Market Square, GH29 9NJ ☎01730 817166, ⍵gartonscoffeehouse.co.uk. Bright and

---

THE SPORT OF KINGS: POLO AT COWDRAY PARK

Polo has been played on the lawns of **Cowdray Park**, just north of Midhurst, since 1910. It was introduced to the country much earlier – in 1834, by the 10th Hussars at Aldershot – but it's Cowdray that's credited as its spiritual home. During World War II polo had all but died out; that it didn't is due entirely to the late **third Viscount Cowdray**, whose passion for the sport turned Cowdray into one of the most famous polo clubs in the world and kick-started a polo renaissance around the country. In 1956, the **Cowdray Park Gold Cup** – now also known as the Jaeger-LeCoultre Gold Cup – was inaugurated, and it remains the highlight of the Cowdray polo season today; the final is one of the most glamorous events in the sporting calendar, with world-class players in action on the field and celebrities looking on.

The **game** is fast and furious, played on horseback on a grass field 300yd long by 160yd wide, with two teams of four riders attempting to score goals against their opponents. Matches are divided into seven-minute periods of play called **chukkas**, and a match will generally be four to six chukkas long, with players changing ends after each goal. At half-time spectators take to the field for "treading in" – stomping back the loose divots on the field.

The season at Cowdray Park runs from the end of April to mid-September, with **matches** held every Saturday and Sunday and most weekdays at one of its two grounds – the Lawns and River grounds near Midhurst, and the Ambersham pitches between Midhurst and Petworth. To watch, all you need do is turn up on the day; **tickets** can be bought at the entrance gate (£5, more for the Gold Cup quarter-finals, semi-finals and final). See ⍵cowdraypolo.co.uk for details of fixtures, and to buy Gold Cup tickets in advance.

airy coffee house situated in the Old Town Hall, with tables outside on the cobbles in the summer – the nicest place in Midhurst for an alfresco cuppa. Good soups, sandwiches and salads range from £4 to £8. At the back you can still see the wooden-doored cells once used to house the town's criminals. Mon–Sat 8.30am–5pm, Sun 9.30am–5pm.

The Olive & Vine North Street, GU29 9DJ ☎ 01730 859532, ⓦ theoliveandvine.co.uk. Very popular, contemporary restaurant-bar that covers all bases, from morning coffee through to evening meals and late-night cocktails. The dinner menu features burgers, salads, *moules frites*, platters and tasty, tapas-style "small plates" (£3-6). Daily 9am–late; kitchen noon–9pm.

AROUND MIDHURST

Some of the best food in the area can be found in the pubs in nearby villages, many of which have the added bonus of splendid views; booking ahead is recommended.

Duke of Cumberland Fernhurst, 5 miles north of Midhurst, just off the A286, GU27 3HQ ☎ 01428 652280, ⓦ dukeofcumberland.com. Fifteenth-century pub with bags of character and spectacular views. To see it in its full glory visit in summer and grab a table on the lovely deck or in the enormous sloping garden. Food is delicious but pricey: mains cost £17 and upwards at dinner, and simpler lunch dishes are £11–18. Daily noon–11pm; kitchen Mon & Sun noon–2pm, Tues–Sat noon–2pm & 7–9pm.

Lickfold Inn Highstead Lane, Lickfold, 6 miles northeast of Midhurst, GU28 9EY ☎ 01789 532535, ⓦ thelickfoldinn.co.uk. This foodie pub is a real gem. Downstairs, the bar offers log fires, local ales, comfy sofas and a long list of lip-smacking bar snacks (£3–5), while upstairs is a beautiful dining room where you can tuck into dishes such as hake with treacle bacon and salsify (£16–29). Wed–Sat 11am–11pm, Sun 11am–8.30pm; kitchen Wed–Sat noon–2.30pm & 6–9pm, Sun 12.30–5.30pm.

Noah's Ark Inn The Green, Lurgashall, 7 miles northeast of Midhurst, GU28 9ET ☎ 01428 707346, ⓦ noahsarkinn.co.uk. Traditional village pub in a perfect setting looking out onto the pretty village green. Great food, from pasta and burgers to Sussex rib-eye (£13–22), plus lunchtime bar snacks and kids' meals. Mon–Sat 11am–11.30pm, Sun noon–8pm (10pm in summer); kitchen Mon–Sat noon–2.30pm & 7–9.30pm, Sun noon–3.15pm.

SHOPPING

8

Cowdray Farm Shop Easebourne, 1 mile north of Midhurst, GU29 0AJ ☎ 01730 815152, ⓦ cowdrayfarmshop.co.uk. Excellent farm shop selling Cowdray and other local produce, including meat and eggs from the estate. Mon–Sat 9am–6pm, Sun 9am–5pm.

The Exceptional English Wine Company Easebourne, 1 mile north of Midhurst, GU29 0AJ ☎ 01730 814671, ⓦ theexceptionalenglishwineco.com. Finish off a visit to the Cowdray Farm Shop by popping into this little shop across the courtyard, where you can sample and buy a great range of English wine, much of it locally produced. Tues–Sat 10am–6pm & Sun 10am–4pm.

Harting Down Nature Reserve

Near South Harting • Open access • NT; parking £2 for non-members • ⓦ nationaltrust.org.uk/harting-down

Wonderful views, wildflowers, butterflies and skylarks abound at the National Trust-run **Harting Down Nature Reserve**, where there are plenty of options for walks including an easy four-mile circular route (see box, p.286) – walkers thin out the further you get from the hilltop car park. The highest point is steep-sided **Beacon Hill** (794ft), site of an Iron Age hillfort and home to the remains of a Napoleonic War telegraph station.

Uppark House

South Harting, Petersfield, GU31 5QR • **House** March–Oct daily 12.30–4pm; Servants' Quarters and dolls' house mid-Feb–Oct daily 11am–4pm, Nov to mid-Feb daily 11am–3pm • £10 (includes garden); NT • **Garden** Mid-Feb to Oct daily 10am–5pm; Nov to mid-Feb daily 10am–4pm; tours March–Oct Thurs 2pm • £6; NT • ☎ 01730 825857, ⓦ nationaltrust.org.uk/uppark

Handsome **Uppark House** sits, as it has done for centuries, perched high up on the Downs, with no hint that things might have been very different. For in 1989, a fire caused by a workman's blowtorch started a blaze that virtually reduced it to ruin. The house was open at the time, and National Trust staff, volunteers and members of the family managed to carry most of the art and furniture collection to safety. The decision was made to restore the house as it would have been on the day before the fire broke out, and this kicked into action a £20-million restoration, involving hundreds of craftsmen, many of whom had to relearn skills that had been lost for decades. The house finally opened once more in 1995, and it's fascinating today to play detective

WALKS AROUND MIDHURST

There are some fabulous walks to be had in the countryside around Midhurst. The **South Downs Way** (see box, p.212) can be joined two miles south of town, accessed from the village of Cocking at the foot of the scarp (bus #60 from Midhurst; Mon–Sat every 30min, Sun hourly; 10min). From Cocking you can head east along the Way towards Upwaltham or west towards Harting Down (see p.285). The walks below are marked on OS *Explorer* **maps** OL33 and OL8.

Midhurst River Walk This easy three-mile circular route (waymarked Rother Walk) runs northwest from Midhurst's North Bridge Weir along the River Rother to Woolbeding, before returning via sweeping parkland to town.

Harting Down circular This four-mile route takes you east along the ridgetop South Downs Way, with panoramic views across the Weald, before cutting south around the lower slopes of Beacon Hill, and then heading back to your starting point through a cool, dark yew wood and up onto Harting Hill.

Serpent Trail Pick up the Serpent Trail, a 64-mile-long route which wends its way in a serpentine S-shape through beautiful heathland from Haslemere in Surrey past Black Down (see below), Petworth and Midhurst to Petersfield in Hampshire; the section from Midhurst to Petersfield is around 10 miles, and there's a handy bus for the return leg (bus #92: Mon–Sat hourly). You can download a trail map from ⓦ westsussex.gov.uk/media/2206/serpent_trail.pdf, or buy the newer version for £3 from Midhurst's South Downs Centre (see p.284).

and spot the (often seamless) joins between original and restored woodwork, curtains, carpets and wallpaper (with commendable foresight, strips were ripped from the walls as the fire blazed, so that colours and pattern could be matched later).

Even before the fire, the house had seen its fair share of excitement. It was built in 1690, and bought some fifty years later by **Sir Matthew Fetherstonhaugh**, who lavished some of his huge fortune on furnishing the house with treasures acquired on the Continent. When he died, his playboy son **Sir Harry** took up the reins with some relish, installing the teenage Emma Hart (the future Lady Hamilton, Nelson's mistress) as his live-in lover in the house, where she would reportedly dance naked on the dining-room table. Harry certainly knew how to enjoy himself: at the ripe old age of 70 he scandalized Sussex society by marrying his 21-year-old dairymaid, Mary Ann Bullock.

The elegant Georgian **interior** is crammed with treasures from Sir Matthew's Grand Tour; highlights include the sumptuous gold and white Saloon, and an eighteenth-century doll's house with miniature oil paintings and tiny hallmarked silverware. The **servants' quarters** are presented as they would have been in the late nineteenth century when the mother of **H.G. Wells** was housekeeper here.

Uppark's beautiful **gardens** have lovely views over the Downs, and contain the elegant Georgian dairy where Mary Anne Bullock's singing first caught the roving Sir Harry's attention.

Black Down

Tennyson's Lane, GU27 3BJ • Open access • NT; parking free • ⓦ nationaltrust.org.uk/black-down

Black Down (917ft), up near the Surrey border, is the highest point in the national park – a wild and rich landscape of heathland, ancient woodland, bogs and wildflower meadows, crisscrossed by trails. **Tennyson** lived here for almost a quarter of a century before his death, and immortalized the beautiful view from his study in a poem: "You came, and looked and loved the view/Long-known and loved by me/Green Sussex fading into blue/With one gray glimpse of sea." To capture the view for yourself, park at the free car park on Tennyson Lane (southeast of the town of Haslemere) and follow the footpath for a mile to the **Temple of the Winds**, one of the finest viewpoints in Sussex, where the ground falls away before you and miles of patchwork fields and copses stretch into the distance, backed by the blue-green smudge of the South Downs; on a clear day you can indeed glimpse the sea, forty miles away. Black Down is also one of the best **star-gazing**

destinations in the country: see ⓦnationaltrust.org.uk/black-down/trails/summer-star
-gazing-walk-at-black-down for a downloadable star-gazing walk.

Petworth

The honey-coloured, high stone walls of Petworth House loom over the handsome little
town of **PETWORTH**, seven miles east of Midhurst. The town owes its existence to the great
house and its estate: for centuries the Leconfield Estate employed virtually everyone in the
town, and reminders of its importance can be seen in the brown-painted doors of the
hundreds of estate cottages built in the mid-nineteenth century (and numbered according
to when they first appeared in the rent records). Even today, it's **Petworth House** that
brings in the tourists, and most visitors, justifiably, make a beeline straight for it; the rest of
town, though, is a bit of a gem, with an extraordinary number of vibrant independent
shops for its size, centred around a thriving **antiques trade** (see p.288). East of the town,
attractions include family-friendly **Fishers Farm Park** and the peaceful **Wey and Arun Canal**.

Market Square and around

The centre of town is **Market Square**, site of the town's marketplace since at least 1541.
In the centre of the square is **Leconfield Hall**, built in 1794 as a courthouse; the old fire
bells, which once served as the town's fire alarm, can be seen up on the pediment above
the clock. The hall is one of the venues for July's **Petworth Festival** (ⓦpetworthfestival
.org.uk), a two-week-long arts festival.

From Market Square, cobbled **Lombard Street** – once the town's busiest thoroughfare
and still its prettiest – climbs north to Church Street and the **Church of St Mary's**; to the
left of the church is the entrance to Petworth House, while to the right you'll see a
fantastically elaborate iron **streetlamp**, designed by Charles Barry (of Houses of
Parliament fame) and erected by the townspeople in 1851 as a token of thanks to Lord
Leconfield for installing gas lighting in the town.

Petworth House

Petworth, GU28 9LR • **House** Mid-March to early Nov daily 11am–5pm; rest of year opening hours vary – check website • **Pleasure
Ground** Daily: mid-March to Oct 10am–5pm; Nov–Jan 10am–3.30pm; Feb 10am–4pm; early March 10am–4.30pm • House and Pleasure
Ground mid-March to early Nov £13.50, rest of year £7.20; NT • Parking £4 • ☎01798 342207, ⓦnationaltrust.org.uk/petworth
Petworth House, built in the late seventeenth century, is one of the Southeast's most
impressive stately homes. The grounds alone are worth the visit: seven hundred acres of
stunning parkland, ponds and woodland, roamed by the largest herd of fallow deer in
the country and dotted with ancient oaks. The park – containing the thirty-acre
woodland garden known as the **Pleasure Ground** – was landscaped by Capability
Brown and is considered one of his finest achievements, but it was **Turner** who made
the sweeping vistas famous, immortalizing the park in several of his paintings. Turner
was a frequent visitor here, given virtual free rein of the house by the art-loving third
Earl of Egremont; Mike Leigh's 2014 film *Mr Turner* was partly shot on location here.

Twenty of Turner's paintings are on view in the house, and form just part of
Petworth's outstanding **art collection**, with works by Van Dyck, Titian, Gainsborough,
Bosch, Reynolds and Blake. Other treasures include the **Molyneux globe**, dating from
1592 and believed to be the earliest terrestrial globe in existence, and the **Leconfield
Chaucer** manuscript, one of the earliest surviving editions of the *Canterbury Tales*.

The opulent **decor** is equally jaw-dropping. Highlights are Louis Laguerre's murals
around the **Grand Staircase**, which trace the myth of Prometheus and Pandora, and the
dazzling **Carved Room**, where flowers, fruit, vines, musical instruments and birds have
been carved in joyfully extravagant detail by master woodcarver Grinling Gibbons.

The **servants' quarters**, connected by a tunnel to the main house, contain an impressive series of kitchens bearing the latest in 1870s kitchen technology, and a copper *batterie de cuisine* of more than a thousand pieces – all polished by a team of strong-elbowed volunteers every winter.

Petworth Cottage Museum

346 High St, GU28 0AU • April–Oct Tues–Sat & bank hols 2–4.30pm • £4 • ☎ 01798 342100, ⊛ petworthcottagemuseum.co.uk

For an alternative and intriguing view of the life of one of the great house's former employees, **Petworth Cottage Museum** is well worth a visit. Seamstress Mary Cummings lived in this gas-lit abode, which has been restored using her own possessions to show how it would have looked in 1910, with family photos on the wall, the washing-up by the sink and the kettle on the range.

ARRIVAL AND INFORMATION   PETWORTH

By train and bus The closest stations are Haslemere (no bus connection) and Pulborough (bus #1: Mon–Sat hourly, Sun every 2hr; 15min). Bus #1 also connects Petworth with Midhurst (15min).

By car There's a large car park in the centre of town and another at Petworth House.

Website ⊛ visitpetworth.com.

ACCOMMODATION AND EATING

★ **Horse Guards Inn** Upperton Rd, Tillington, GU28 9AF ☎ 01798 342332, ⊛ thehorseguardsinn.co.uk. Lovely little gastropub two miles west of Petworth, decked out with informal, shabby-chic panache; in summer you can grab a deckchair (or hay-bale) in the idyllic garden. Harveys and guest ales on tap, plus excellent seasonal food; mains (around £15) might include Selsey crab with sea vegetable salad in summer, or pheasant with hawthorn jelly in winter. The pub also has three serene, pretty B&B rooms. Daily noon–midnight; kitchen Mon–Thurs noon–2.30pm & 6.30–9pm, Fri noon–2.30pm & 6–9.30pm, Sat noon–3pm & 6–9.30pm, Sun noon–3.30pm & 6.30–9pm. **£100**

Hungry Guest Café Lombard St, GU28 0AG ☎ 01798 344564, ⊛ thehungryguest.com. This smart, modern café on cobbled Lombard Street serves up top-quality food, as you'd expect from the sister café of the excellent *Hungry Guest Food Shop* (see below). The breakfast menu offers freshly baked croissants from the bakery near Chichester, while the lunch menu features sourdough pizza (£10), open sandwiches, sliders and burgers. Mon–Sat 9am–6pm, Sun 9am–4pm.

The Leconfield New Street, GU28 0AS ☎ 01798 345111 ⊛ theleconfield.co.uk. One for a treat, this high-end restaurant delivers superb food in a characterful

seventeenth-century building with courtyard garden. It's not cheap (mains are £20 and up), but there's a cheaper Market Menu available midweek. Tues 6–10.30pm, Wed–Sat noon–3pm & 6–10.30pm, Sun noon–4pm.

★ **Old Railway Station** 2 miles south of Petworth on the A285, GU28 0JF ☎ 01798 342346, ⊛ old-station .co.uk. Petworth's former railway station (1892) has been converted into a smart, colonial-style B&B, with breakfast and afternoon tea served in the high-ceilinged old waiting room; in summer there are tables out on the platform. The largest rooms are upstairs in the station house, but for sheer character they can't compete with the rooms in the stylishly converted Pullman carriages on the platform. **£160**

Petworth Penthouse Park Rd, GU28 0EA ☎ 01798 215007, ⊛ penthousepetworth.com. If you're travelling in a small group, consider a stay at this luxurious three-bedroom self-catering penthouse, with a light-flooded, double-height open-plan living area and views over the rooftops to Petworth House. The space was once the studio of Victorian portrait photographer Walter Keevis (his dark room is now the kitchen) and, in a nice touch, some of his old photographs adorn the walls. No children under 8. Two-night minimum stay. Two people **£160**, six people **£390**

SHOPPING

Petworth has over thirty **antiques and decorative arts** dealers within a mile of the centre – one of the greatest concentrations of any town in the Southeast. Check out ⊛ discoverpetworth.org/petworth-antiques for a comprehensive list, or pick up the free town guide (with map) – most shops will have copies.

Hungry Guest Food Shop Middle St, GU29 0BE ☎ 01798 342803, ⊛ thehungryguest. This award-winning produce store sells its own bread, pastries and brownies (baked at its own wholesale

artisan bakery), and sells local Wobblegate apple juice, a good selection of charcuterie, and cheese from a dedicated cheese room – all you need for a picnic at Petworth Park. Mon–Sat 9am–6pm, Sun 10am–5pm.

Kevis House Gallery Lombard St, GU28 0AG ☎ 01798 215007, ⓦ kevishouse.com. Changing exhibitions of works on paper – prints, drawings and photography, including an annual wood-engraving exhibition. Mon–Sat 10.30am–4.30pm.

Wey and Arun Canal

Loxwood, RH14 0RH • April–Oct Sat, Sun & bank hols 3 cruises each afternoon (30min–3hr 15min); also open for occasional special mid-week events • £4 for 30min cruise, £5 for 45min, £7 for 1hr 30min, £12 for 3hr 15min • ☎ 01403 752404, ⓦ weyandarun.co.uk

"London's lost route to the sea", the 23-mile **Wey and Arun Canal** was built between 1813 and 1816 to provide an inland barge route between the capital and the south coast, carrying agricultural produce, coal and imported goods. The coming of the railways spelled an end to its brief period of usefulness, however, and in 1871 it was formally abandoned. The Wey and Arun Canal Trust, which began its quest to restore the canal in the 1970s and has today cleared more than half of it, runs **narrowboat trips** on the canal which take you through some of the restored locks.

Fishers Farm Park

Newpound Lane, Wisborough Green, RH14 0EG • Daily 10am–5pm • £9.75 low-, £12.75 mid- & £15.75 peak-season; under-2s free • ☎ 01403 700063, ⓦ fishersfarmpark.co.uk

If you've got younger kids you really can't go wrong with the award-winning **Fishers Farm Park** – the farm park to end all farm parks. There are all the usual animals on show, ready for petting, bottle-feeding and riding, plus a ten-acre adventure play area featuring everything from swingboats, slides and sandpits to pedal karts, jumping pillows and climbing walls, with a few scare-free "rides" thrown in for good measure. It's not cheap, but it's friendly and well run, jam-packed with things to do, and once you're through the doors everything's included.

Arundel and around

Your first view of **ARUNDEL** if you're driving in from the east is a corker, with the turrets of its fairytale castle rising up out of the trees, and the huge bulk of the Gothic cathedral towering over the rooftops. The compact town's well-preserved appearance and picturesque setting by the banks of the River Arun draw the crowds on summer weekends, but at any other time a visit reveals one of West Sussex's least spoilt old towns. The main attractions are the **castle**, seat of the dukes of Norfolk, and the **WWT Arundel Wetland Centre** on the outskirts of town, but the rest of Arundel is pleasant to wander round, with some good independent shops, cafés and restaurants on the High Street and Tarrant Street. At the end of August, **Arundel Festival** (ⓦ arundelfestival .co.uk) features everything from open-air theatre to salsa bands.

Out of town, there are some lovely walks through the water meadows, as well as a handful of sights further afield, including **Bignor Roman Villa**, the **Amberley Museum** of industrial heritage and the graceful Elizabethan **Parham House**.

Arundel Castle

Mill Rd, BN18 9AB • April–Oct Tues–Sun & bank hols: keep 10am–4.30pm; Fitzalan Chapel & grounds 10am–5pm; castle rooms noon–5pm • Castle rooms, keep, grounds & chapel £18; keep, grounds & chapel £13; grounds & chapel £11 • ☎ 01903 882173, ⓦ arundelcastle.org

Arundel's standout attraction is **Arundel Castle**, which, though pricey, has enough to keep you occupied for a whole day. Despite its romantic medieval appearance, most of what you see is little more than a century old: the original Norman castle was badly damaged in the Civil War in the seventeenth century, and was reconstructed from 1718 onwards, most extensively by the fifteenth duke at the end of the nineteenth

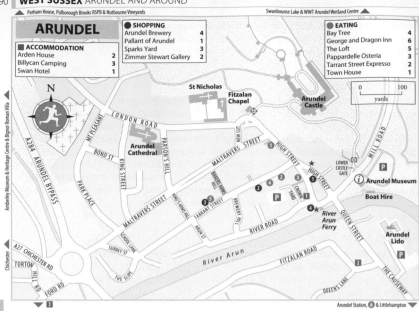

century. Parts of the original structure still remain, notably the 100ft-high **motte** on which it stands, constructed in 1068 by **Roger de Montgomery**. The **keep**, built in 1190, is a steep climb up 131 stairs, but rewards with wonderful views over the town and out to sea. **Events** take place throughout the year, including re-created sieges and medieval tournaments – see the website for details.

Over in the main, remodelled part of the castle, the opulent **castle rooms** provide a dramatic contrast to the medieval keep, with cold stone walls replaced by extravagantly carved woodwork, fine tapestries, ornate sixteenth-century furniture and masterpieces by Gainsborough, Holbein, Van Dyck and Canaletto. Treasures peep out from every corner, easy to miss amid the general splendour: in the **dining room**, hidden away in a small cabinet, is the gold and enamel rosary carried by Mary, Queen of Scots at her execution. Other highlights include the palatial **Barons' Hall**, the Victorian **private chapel** and the stunning Regency **library**, carved out of Honduran mahogany.

In the castle grounds, the **Collector Earl's Garden** is a playfully theatrical take on a Jacobean garden, with exotic palms and ferns, and pavilions, obelisks and urns made from green oak rather than stone. Adjacent is the beautiful fourteenth-century **Fitzalan Chapel**, burial place of the dukes of Norfolk, who have owned the castle for over 850 years in a more-or-less unbroken line. Like the castle, the chapel was badly damaged in the Civil War, when encamped Roundheads stabled their horses among the tombs, but it was restored in the late nineteenth century. Carved stone tombs are dotted around the chapel, among them the rather gruesome twin effigies of the seventh duke – one as he looked when he died and, underneath, one of his emaciated corpse.

Arundel Cathedral

Corner of Parson's Hill & London Rd, BN18 9AY • Daily 9am–6pm or dusk • Free • ☎ 01903 882297, ⓦ www.arundelcathedral.org

The flamboyant **Arundel Cathedral** was constructed in the 1870s over the town's former Catholic church by the fifteenth duke of Norfolk; its spire was designed by John Hansom, inventor of the hansom cab. Inside are the enshrined remains of **St Philip Howard**, the canonized thirteenth earl, who was brought up Protestant but chose to return to the Catholic faith of his birth, thereby turning his back on a life of great favour at Elizabeth I's royal court; he was sentenced to death in 1585, aged 27, when he was caught fleeing overseas, and died of dysentery in the Tower of London ten years later, refusing till the very last to renounce his faith.

St Nicholas' church

London Rd, BN18 9AT • Daily 9am–5pm • Free • ☎ 01903 882262, ⓦ stnicholas-arundel.co.uk

What you see when you walk into the fourteenth-century **church of St Nicholas** is really only half a church: behind an iron grille and glass wall lies the Fitzalan Chapel (see opposite), once the church's chancel but now part of Arundel Castle, and accessible only through the castle grounds. This unique state of affairs – which has resulted in a Church of England parish church and a Catholic chapel under one roof – came about in 1544 with the Dissolution, when Henry VIII sold off the chancel to the twelfth earl, and it became the private chapel and burial place of the earl's family. The screen has only been opened eight times in the last 35 years, most recently in 1995 for the funeral of Lavinia, Duchess of Norfolk. Elsewhere in the church, look out for the red consecration crosses on the walls, which date from the church's construction in 1380, and the beautiful carved stone **pulpit**, one of only six pre-Reformation pulpits in the country, believed to be the work of Henry Yevele, who also designed the nave in Canterbury Cathedral.

Arundel Lido

Queen St, BN18 9JG • May to mid-Sept daily noon–7pm, opens 10am Sat, Sun, bank hols & school hols • £7 • ☎ 01903 882404, ⓦ arundel-lido.com

Just south of the river lies **Arundel Lido**, which celebrated its fiftieth anniversary in 2010. It's a great spot for a dip on a hot day, with grassy lawns surrounding the heated pool, a separate paddling pool for kids and, best of all, a view of the castle as you swim along.

Mill Road

From the castle entrance, **Mill Road** curves north through an avenue of trees up to **Swanbourne Lake**, an old millpond encircled by trees, with **rowing boats** for hire (March–Oct Sat, Sun & school hols from 9/10am; £3.50/person for 30min) and a tearoom. Swanbourne Lake is the entrance to the thousand-acre **Arundel Park**, which is crisscrossed with footpaths that meet up with the South Downs Way three miles away near Houghton.

Arundel Museum

Mill Rd, BN18 9PA • Daily 10am–4pm • £3.50 • ☎ 01903 885866, ⓦ arundelmuseum.org

At the southern end of Mill Road by the river, the small and immaculately presented **Arundel Museum** tells the story of the town and the surrounding area through exhibits that range from 500,000-year-old Palaeolithic hand-axes to a model of Arundel Castle during the Civil War. There's also an informative display on the castle's owners over its almost 1000-year history, from the first Norman earls to the current dukes of Norfolk – well worth a read if you're planning to visit the castle.

WWT Arundel Wetland Centre

Mill Rd, BN18 9PB • Daily: April to mid-Oct 9.30am–5.30pm; mid-Oct to March 9.30am–4.30pm • £11.95, under-17s £6 • **Pond-dipping** April–Oct Sat, Sun & school hols • **Boat trips** Daily: spring–autumn 11am–4.30pm; winter 11am–3.30pm • ☎ 01903 883355, ⓦ wwt.org.uk/visit/arundel

The excellent **WWT Arundel Wetland Centre**, a mile out of town along Mill Road, is a great place to spend half a day, especially if you've got children in tow. The centre is home to endangered waterfowl from around the world, but a wander around the scenic 65-acre site, divided into different habitats, can also turn up sightings of native wildlife including water voles, kingfishers, sand martins, dragonflies and peregrines. Don't miss the tranquil, rustling **reedbed boardwalks** – where artist Chris Drury has created a camera obscura sculpture – or the free **boat trips**, probably your best chance of spotting water voles. There are a couple of imaginative play areas for kids, as well as popular **pond-dipping** sessions.

ARRIVAL AND INFORMATION

By train Arundel's station is half a mile south of the town centre over the river on the A27.
Destinations Brighton (hourly; 1hr 10min); Chichester (Mon–Sat 2 hourly, Sun hourly; 30–50min); London Victoria (every 30min; 1hr 20min).
By bus Buses arrive either on the High St or River Rd, and run to Brighton via Littlehampton (Mon–Sat every 30min,

Sun hourly; 2hr).
By car There's free parking all along Mill Rd, though spaces fill up quickly on summer weekends; failing that try the large pay-and-display car park on Mill Rd.
Tourist information There's a visitor information point in Arundel Museum, open the same hours as the museum, (ⓦ sussexbythesea.com).

ACCOMMODATION

Arden House 4 Queens Lane, BN18 9JN ☎ 01903 884184, ⓦ ardenguesthouse.net. Smart and very friendly B&B, in a great location just south of the river. The cheapest rooms share bathrooms (fluffy robes are provided to protect your modesty); en-suite rooms are just £10 more. There's bike storage, and muddy walking boots are welcomed. **£89**
★ **Billycan Camping** Manor Farm, Tortington, near Arundel, BN18 0BG ☎ 07766 742533, ⓦ billycancamping.co.uk. You know you're onto a winner as soon as you arrive at this lovely campsite, a fifteen-minute walk from Arundel. The snug, vintage-style tents and yurts (available in various sizes) come decked out with bunting, pathways are lit by tealights at night, and campers

are welcomed with a communal stew around the campfire on a Friday night. The two-night minimum stay includes a breakfast hamper stuffed with local goodies. Open May–Aug. Four-person scout tents **£122.50**, five-person bell tents **£122.50**, four-person yurt **£175**
Swan Hotel 27–29 High St, BN18 9AG ☎ 01903 882314, ⓦ swanarundel.co.uk. The fifteen rooms above this pub have a bit of a seaside-chic vibe, with coir carpet or wooden boards underfoot, white tongue-and-groove panelling, shutters and seaside-themed photos and paintings. The cheapest rooms are on the small side, so consider paying extra for a superior double. Family rooms are also available. Prices fluctuate according to demand. **£99**

EATING

Bay Tree 21 Tarrant St, BN18 9DG ☎ 01903 883679, ⓦ thebaytreearundel.co.uk. Cosy and relaxed little restaurant squeezed into three low-beamed rooms, with windows opening out onto the street in summer and a small terrace out the back. It's very popular, and justifiably so; bistro-style mains such as pheasant breast wrapped in bacon cost £16–18 at dinner; lunch features simpler dishes, including salads and paninis. Mon–Fri 11.30am–2.45pm & 6.30–9.30pm, Sat & Sun 10.30am–4.30pm & 6.30–9.30pm.
George and Dragon Inn Burpham, BN18 9RR ☎ 01903 883131, ⓦ georgeatburpham.co.uk. Seventeenth-century pub in the gorgeous village of Burpham, three miles upstream of Arundel. There's a beamed, flagstone interior, picnic tables out front and plenty of Sussex ales behind the bar, as well as local champagne and spirits and a good-value house lager. The daily-changing seasonal, local menu runs from filled ciabattas (£6.50) to burgers (£12.50), fish, salads and steaks. Mon–Fri 10.30am–3pm & 6–11pm, Sat 10.30am–11pm, Sun 10.30am–10pm; kitchen Mon–Fri noon–2.30pm & 6–9pm, Sat noon–

3pm & 6–9.30pm, Sun noon–4pm & 6–8.30pm.
The Loft Sparks Yard, Tarrant St, BN18 9DJ ☎ 01903 885588, ⓦ sparksyard.com. Up on the top floor of the Sparks Yard shop (see p.294), this relaxed California-inspired restaurant is a great spot for both brunch (with everything from fluffy American-style pancakes to corn hotcakes to avocado toast on the menu) and lunch; delicious burgers (£13–17) and cream-laden sundaes share the menu with healthy salads. It also opens Thurs–Sat evenings for dinner and cocktails, and puts on occasional live music. Mon–Wed 9.30am–5.30pm, Thurs–Sat 9.30am–11pm, Sun 10am–5pm.
★ **Pappardelle Osteria** 41 High St, BN18 9AG ☎ 01903 882024, ⓦ pappardelle.co.uk. This friendly café-cum-wine-bar, with its long copper communal tables, has a sociable buzz about it, with people chatting over coffee or reading papers in the daytime. In the evening there are cocktails, over twenty different grappas, and more than thirty wines by the glass – the "flites" (£8.95) allow you to sample three 100ml measures, perfect if you can't choose. Food is served all day, from breakfast through to antipasto

ARUNDEL CASTLE (P.289) >

WALKS AND BOAT TRIPS FROM ARUNDEL

Footpaths line both banks of the River Arun, and wandering even a short way up the river's reedy banks will reward you with wonderful views of Arundel Castle, rising majestically from the water meadows. Follow the **west bank** for two miles to reach the *Black Rabbit*, an idyllically sited pub that's a lovely spot for a drink, though there are better lunch options elsewhere; or head three miles up the **east bank** to reach the village of Burpham (pronounced "Burfham") and the *George and Dragon* (see p.292). Both routes are marked on OS *Explorer* **map** OL10.

 River-boat cruises set off from the town quay on the River Arun Ferry (several daily in summer; 1hr; £9; ☎07473 255889), but it's more fun to have your own hand on the tiller – four-seater self-drive **motorboats** cost £35 for an hour from the *Waterside Tea Garden and Bistro*, by the river behind Arundel Museum (☎01903 882609, ⓦ thewatersidearundel.co.uk), which will get you a fair way up the river and back. Look out for kingfishers and herons en route.

plates (£8.25), bruschetta, salads, *cicchetti* (Italian-style canapés – 5 dishes £10.95) and pizza platters served with chopped preserves and fresh chillis (£19.95). Mon–Sat 9am–11.30pm, Sun 10am–10.30pm.

Tarrant Street Expresso 17 Tarrant St, BN18 9DG ☎01903 885350. The best place to grab a coffee in town is this stylish, pocket-sized coffee shop, with just a couple of tables inside and a few stools outside on the pavement in good weather. Coffee comes from Square Mile Coffee Roasters, milk from the nearby Goodwood Estate, and bread and pastries from the Hungry Guest Bakery (see p.288) in

Petworth. Tues–Sat 8.30am–4pm, Sun 9am–2pm.

Town House 65 High St, BN18 9AJ ☎01903 883847, ⓦ thetownhouse.co.uk. This Regency townhouse overlooking the castle walls is the grandest place to dine in town, with starched linen tablecloths, a stunning ceiling – hand-carved and gilded in Florence in the late sixteenth century – and a menu that might feature foie gras and lobster alongside local lamb or game (£25.50 for 2 courses and £29.50 for 3, less at lunch). It's not at all stuffy, despite the grandeur, and is very popular, so book ahead. Tues–Sat noon–2.30pm & 7–9.30pm.

SHOPPING

Arundel Brewery River Rd, BN18 9DF ☎01903 883577, ⓦ arundelbrewery.co.uk. Pick up some bottles of Arundel Brewery's own ales (also available from the cask) at the brewery shop on the quay. The shop also has a good wine selection, and offers tastings of local Sussex wines. Normally Tues–Fri noon–5pm, Sat noon–6pm, Sun noon–4pm.

Pallant of Arundel 17 High St, BN18 9AD ☎01903 882288, ⓦ pallantofarundel.co.uk. Great little food shop, deli and wine merchant, with crusty bread from several local bakeries, a well-stocked cheese counter, and plenty of tasty-looking home-made pork pies, Scotch eggs and the like, plus takeaway coffee. Mon–Sat 9am–6pm

(5pm in Jan), Sun & bank hols 10am–5pm.

Sparks Yard Tarrant St, BN18 9DJ ☎01903 885588, ⓦ www.sparksyard.com. Homeware store spread over three floors of a handsome redbrick building, stocking stylish cookware, toiletries, stationery, toys and more. Mon–Sat 9.30am–5.30pm, Sun 10am–5pm.

Zimmer Stewart Gallery 29 Tarrant St, BN18 9DG ☎01903 885867, ⓦ zimmerstewart.co.uk. This excellent small gallery features contemporary painting, prints and photos, as well as ceramics and sculpture. Exhibitions change every month or two. Tues–Sat 10am–5pm.

Amberley Museum and Heritage Centre

Amberley, on the B2139 between Arundel and Storrington, BN18 9LT • March–Oct Wed–Sun & bank hols 10am–5pm (last entry 3.30pm); school hols also open Mon & Tues (same hours) • £10.35 • ☎01798 831370, ⓦ amberleymuseum.co.uk • Amberley station is adjacent to the museum (regular trains from Littlehampton and the south coast)

Dedicated to the industrial heritage of the Southeast, the excellent **Amberley Museum and Heritage Centre** is an open-air museum spread around the 36-acre site of an old lime works and chalk pit. The museum contains dozens of workshops, re-created shops and listed buildings (many rescued from elsewhere in Sussex), housing everything from a brickyard drying shed to a re-created 1920s bus garage. Craftspeople are on hand to demonstrate traditional skills – woodturning, pottery, stained-glass making, letterpress printing, even broom making – and hop-on, hop-off vintage green-and-yellow Southdown buses trundle regularly round the site, with a narrow-gauge train running round the perimeter. There are a few larger exhibition halls, including a Railway Hall stuffed full of old engines and wagons, and a fun Telecommunications Exhibition, with a display of telephones from 1878 onwards – an exercise in nostalgia for anyone old enough to remember the old dial telephones and the first, brick-like mobiles.

ACCOMMODATION   AMBERLEY

Amberley Castle 4 miles north of Arundel, BN18 9LT • ☎ 01798 831992, ⓦ amberleycastle.co.uk. For a real splurge, crunch up the sweeping gravel drive of this 800-year-old castle, complete with portcullis and sixty-foot curtain walls, and ensconce yourself in one of the nineteen luxurious bedrooms. Many rooms come with four-posters, and a couple even have doorways leading directly to the battlements. Outside are acres of landscaped grounds, roamed by peacocks, and a grass-covered moat that serves as a croquet lawn. **£310**

Bignor Roman Villa

Bignor, RH20 1PH • March–Oct daily 10am–5pm; last entry 4pm • £6 • ☎ 01798 869259, ⓦ bignorromanvilla.co.uk

Six miles north of Arundel, in a beautiful spot at the bottom of the Downs scarp, the excavated third-century ruins of the **Bignor Roman Villa** aren't on the same scale as nearby first-century Fishbourne (see p.272), but they do contain some of the best Roman mosaics in the country. Bignor started life as a farmstead and was gradually expanded over the centuries, ending up by the fourth century as a seventy-room villa set in a square around a central courtyard. The western end of the north wing, and the bathhouse in the southeast corner, are all that remain today. The villa's location, for all that it seems like a sleepy backwater, was carefully chosen: **Stane Street**, one of the first paved roads in the country, passed just a few hundred yards away. Local materials were used to make the stunning **mosaics** (chalk for white, sandstone for yellow and orange, and Purbeck marble for blue and black), which increased in complexity and sophistication as the villa grew in size and wealth. Perhaps the finest mosaic is in the **winter dining room**, where the head of Venus stares out above a series of wonderful winged gladiators; adjacent to it you can see the original Roman hypocaust (underfloor heating system).

Pulborough Brooks RSPB nature reserve

Pulborough, RH20 2EL • Daily 9.30am–5pm • Visitor centre free, nature trails £5 • ☎ 01798 875851, ⓦ rspb.org.uk/pulboroughbrooks • Pulborough train station (services from Littlehampton and south coast), 2 miles away, then taxi; alternatively, Compass bus #100 from Steyning (Mon–Sat hourly; 25min) stops outside the reserve

Spread over the water meadows of the River Arun, the **Pulborough Brooks RSPB nature reserve** is one of the southeast's most important wetland habitats, supporting ducks, geese and swans in winter, wading birds and nightingales in the spring, and butterflies, dragonflies and nightjars in the summer, as well as a population of deer and shaggy Highland cattle year-round. Two short circular **nature trails** from the visitor centre – the 1.5-mile wooded heathland trail and the 2-mile wetland trail – meander through the different habitats of the site, the latter taking in four bird hides, where volunteers are often on hand to help identify species. Guided walks and hands-on family activities are held throughout the year, normally for an extra fee.

Parham House and Gardens

Storrington, near Pulborough, RH20 4HS • **House** 2–5pm: mid-April to Sept Wed–Fri, Sun & bank hols; Oct Sun • £10.50 (includes gardens) • **Gardens** Noon–5pm: mid-April to Sept Wed–Fri, Sun & bank hols; Oct Sun • £8.50 • ☎ 01903 742021, ⓦ parhaminsussex .co.uk • Pulborough train station (services from Littlehampton and south coast), 4 miles away, then taxi; alternatively, Compass Bus #100 from Pulborough or Steyning (Mon–Sat hourly; 10–15min) stops outside the main gate

Built in 1577, **Parham House** has only ever been owned by three families: the Palmers, the Bisshopps and, most recently, the Pearsons, who took over in 1922 and rescued the beautiful but dilapidated Elizabethan house from decay – the Pearson family still lives there today. Inside, the highlights are the **Great Hall**, a magnificent Elizabethan room with tall leaded windows overlooking the grand sweep of the Downs (look out for the enormous narwhal horn hidden away in a corner), and the 160-foot **Long Gallery**, which runs the length of the house, with a flamboyant ceiling featuring vines, birds and butterflies designed by the famous theatre-set designer Oliver Messel in the 1960s.

Outside, the eighteenth-century **gardens** feature a four-acre walled garden containing an ornamental vegetable garden, herb garden and orchard, as well as exuberant mixed borders that supply the fresh flowers seen in every room in the house; a lavish two-storey Wendy House is built into the brickwork in the northwest corner, a gift from Clive Pearson to his three daughters in 1928. Beyond lie the pleasure grounds and deer park, where a three hundred-strong herd of dark fallow deer wander beneath ancient oaks.

Nutbourne Vineyards

Gay St, near Pulborough, RH20 2HH • May–Oct Tues–Fri 2–5pm, Sat & bank hols 11–5pm; at other times by appointment• Free • **Tours** Two days a month in summer – see website for details • £15 • ☎ 01798 815196, ⓦ nutbournevineyards.com

The vines at family-run **Nutbourne Vineyards** were first planted way back in 1980, making this vineyard one of the pioneers of the now-thriving English wine industry. The vineyard is in an idyllic spot, with beautiful views across to the South Downs – you're free to wander around the vines before visiting the tasting room, uniquely sited in an old windmill tower. Scheduled **tours** of the vineyard, which include tutored tastings, also run in summer.

8

Steyning and around

The pretty little town of **Steyning**, fifteen miles east of Arundel, has plenty of appealingly rickety half-timbered buildings, a bustling main street and a ruined Norman castle in neighbouring **Bramber**, a one-street village that Steyning has all but swallowed up. Nearby are a couple of ancient hillforts at **Chanctonbury Ring** and **Cissbury Ring**; to the east is the popular beauty spot Devil's Dyke, (see Chapter 6).

Steyning's oldest buildings can be found along **Church Street**, with Wealden and jettied timber-framed buildings rubbing shoulders with flint-walled cottages as the road slopes down to bulky **St Andrew's Church**, with its lofty double-height Norman nave and comparatively squat sixteenth-century tower. There are plenty of independent shops along the **High Street**, including the quirky **Cobblestone Walk** arcade at no. 74 (ⓦcobblestonewalk.co.uk); the town's excellent **farmers' market** takes place on the first Saturday of the month in the car park on the High Street.

Bramber Castle

Signposted from the A283, BN44 3XA • Open daylight hours • Free • ⓦ www.english-heritage.org.uk/visit/places/bramber-castle

Don't go to **Bramber Castle** expecting to clamber up the battlements: all that remains of this Norman stronghold is a section of fourteenth-century curtain wall and one tall finger of stone that once formed part of the eleventh-century gatehouse. Bramber was one of the six Rapes (districts) of Sussex established by William after the Conquest, and the castle was built here by **William de Braose** on a grassy knoll to defend the Adur gap through the South Downs. The tree-covered motte (mound) at the castle's centre, and the defensive ditch around the outer bailey, have both survived much better than the castle itself, which by 1558 was already being described as "the late castle of Bramber".

Sheltering on the hillside just below the ruins, the **Church of St Nicholas** was built at the same time as the castle and served as its chapel, making it one of the oldest Norman churches in Sussex, though in fact only the nave dates from this time.

ARRIVAL AND INFORMATION

By bus Buses #2A and #20X run from Brighton via Shoreham (daily hourly; 1hr 15min); Compass bus #100 runs from Pulborough (Mon–Sat hourly; 30min).

By car The central High St car park (2hr max stay) uses

STEYNING AND AROUND

parking discs, which are available free of charge from local shops.

Website ⓦ steyningsouthdowns.co.uk.

EATING

★**Steyning Tea Rooms** 32 High St, BN44 3YE ☎ 01903 810103, ⓦ facebook.com/steyningtea rooms. This cosy, diminutive tearoom is a real treat, with cheery floral wallpaper, scrubbed wooden tables, bunting and mismatched furniture. Great cakes, and a pear-and-stilton rarebit that's to die for, though you might have trouble squeezing out of your seat afterwards. No credit cards. Spring–autumn daily 10am–6pm; winter Mon–Thurs 10am–5pm, Fri–Sun 10am–6pm.

Sussex Produce Company 88 High St, BN44 3RD ☎ 01903 815045, ⓦ thesussexproducecompany.co.uk. This award-winning café-cum-produce-store features heaping piles of fruit and veg, freshly baked bread, a deli counter groaning with Sussex cheeses and Harveys on tap – while at the back of the shop there's a small, laidback café serving great breakfasts, lunches (mains from £13) and dinners (Fri & Sat only). Mon–Thurs 8am–5pm, Fri & Sat 8am–5pm & 6pm–late (shop closes 8.30pm), Sun 9am–4pm.

Chanctonbury Ring

Three-mile walk from Steyning to Chanctonbury, or there's a car park nearer the Ring just off the A283

The site of an Iron Age hillfort, and later two Roman-British temples, hilltop **Chanctonbury Ring** (783ft) gained its fame from the clump of beech trees planted in a circle in 1760 by **Charles Goring**, heir to the nearby Winton Estate. The hurricane of 1987 decimated the Ring, and although the trees have been replanted it will take many years before the grove is fully regrown. Nothing, however, can detract from the magnificent views from the lofty hilltop lookout, stretching north across the patchwork of fields of the Weald and south towards Cissbury and the sea beyond.

Legend has it that if you run seven times anticlockwise around Chanctonbury Ring you'll conjure up the Devil, who'll offer you a bowl of soup that, if accepted, will cost you your soul. The Devil's the least of your worries if local **folklore** is to be believed: Sussex author Esther Meynell wrote in 1947 that the Ring was best avoided at midnight as "curious things are apt to happen", and over the years Chanctonbury's been the site of numerous alleged **UFO sightings**, mysterious lights and unexplained paranormal happenings, not to mention the odd black-magic ritual.

8

A SUSSEX SAFARI

Kent's Port Lympne Reserve may promise sightings of exotic giraffes and zebras on its African-style safari (see p.129), but Sussex's **Knepp Safaris**, based eight miles north of Steyning (☎ 01403 713230, ⓦ kneppsafaris.co.uk), offers a very different – and altogether more local – experience. Here the animals you'll see are all native: herds of English longhorn cattle, red and fallow deer, Tamworth pigs, Exmoor ponies, turtle doves, bats, butterflies and beetles. The project is set on the Knepp Castle estate, where 3500 acres of Sussex countryside has been given over to one of the largest "**rewilding**" projects of its kind in lowland Europe; in the decade or so that the project's been running it has seen the re-emergence of previously scarce species such as purple emperor butterflies, cuckoos and nightingales (two percent of the UK's population of nightingale are now found here).

Knepp Safaris run various safaris at different times of year from Easter through to October, all led by experts; these include dawn **walking safaris** (£25), half-day **vehicle safaris** (£35) and a raft of **specialist safaris** focusing on everything from bees to deer rutting to "reading trees". For the full experience, **stay overnight**: shepherd's huts and luxurious bell tents and yurts are all available (2 nights midweek in July/Aug from £160, 3 nights at the weekend from £235), as are regular tent pitches (£15/person).

Cissbury Ring

Just above the village of Findon, 4 miles west of Steyning • There's a free car park a 20min walk from the Ring, signposted off the A24; on foot, the Ring lies 2 miles off the South Downs Way, but is connected to it by footpaths

One of the biggest Iron Age hillforts in the south, **Cissbury Ring** would have been a magnificent site when it was built, with a 3ft-deep ditch backed by a raised bank topped with a 15ft-high timber palisade, stretching for over a mile around the hilltop. It's estimated it would have taken two hundred men over two years to complete, involving the excavation of a staggering 60,000 tonnes of chalk. Both ditch and bank can still clearly be seen today, and the half-hour stroll around the top of the earth ramparts will give you a good sense of the scale of this most massive of earthworks. At the westernmost end of the Ring, look out for bumps and hollows in the grass – the remains of **flint mines** dug by Neolithic man thousands of years before the hillfort was built. There are over two hundred mineshafts beneath the soil, some as deep as 40ft – quite a mind-boggling feat when you consider that the miners had only antlers for tools.

The coast: Bognor to Shoreham-by-Sea

With the exception of the Manhood Peninsula (see p.276), the West Sussex coast is in the main one long ribbon of development, with only the odd pocket of undeveloped coastline here and there holding out against the sprawl. Heading west to east, you'll pass a trio of **seaside towns**, part of a wave of genteel resorts which grew up along the south coast in the eighteenth century, hoping to emulate the success of royally favoured Brighton. First stop is brash buckets-and-Butlins resort **Bognor**, followed eight miles on by spruced-up **Littlehampton** – by far the nicest of the bunch, with a great setting on the River Arun and two good beaches – followed by sedate, humdrum **Worthing**. The final worthwhile stop along this stretch of coast is the low-key port and town of **Shoreham-by-Sea** on the banks of the River Adur, just a few miles from Brighton. The **beaches** along this stretch are all pebbly, with sand at low tide; none get too crowded, and at their best – at the **nature reserves** at Shoreham-by-Sea, Littlehampton's West Beach and nearby Climping – they possess a wild, windswept beauty, with rare vegetated shingle that bursts into flower in summer.

GETTING AROUND AND INFORMATION   BOGNOR TO SHOREHAM-BY-SEA

By train Southern run trains along the coast from Chichester to Brighton via Worthing and Shoreham-by-Sea (every 30min); you'll need to change for Bognor and Littlehampton.

By bus Stagecoach Coastliner bus #700 (every 20–30min) runs along the coast from Chichester to Brighton via Bognor, Littlehampton, Worthing and Shoreham-by-Sea.

THE INTERNATIONAL BOGNOR BIRDMAN

Brilliantly bonkers and quintessentially British, the **International Bognor Birdman competition** (ⓦ www.birdman.org.uk) sees hundreds of daredevils strap themselves into human-powered flying machines and fling themselves off the end of Bognor pier in an attempt to fly 100m and gain the prized Birdman Trophy.

The event started back in 1971 in nearby Selsey, but moved to Bognor in 1978 and over the next decade started to gather interest internationally, with TV crews and competitors arriving from around the world. There's a (semi-) serious contingent who take part – the Condor Class is for standard hang-gliders, while the Leonardo da Vinci Class is for self-designed and -built flying machines – but what the competition's best known for is the fancy dress **"fun flyers"** taking the plunge for charity. Over the years flying doughnuts, vampires, pantomime horses, a Dr Who tardis and a chicken-and-mushroom pie have all tipped themselves over the edge. The date for the event varies year by year; check the website for the details.

Websites For information about Bognor and Littlehampton visit ⓦsussexbythesea.com; Worthing and Shoreham are both covered by ⓦvisitworthing .co.uk.

Bognor Regis

"Oh, bugger Bognor!", George V famously exclaimed of the little seaside town, and the words have stuck – perhaps a little unfairly. Despite its royal associations ("Regis" was added to its name after the king's visit in 1929), **Bognor Regis** is best known today for a slightly lower-brow connection – Billy Butlin of holiday-camp fame – and for its traditional, unpretentious seaside entertainments. Behind the Blue Flag pebble-and-sand beach you'll find tacky amusements aplenty, crazy golf, a miniature railway, a boating lake and fish-and-chip shops at every turn.

Butlin's

Upper Bognor Rd, PO21 1JJ • Funfair and indoor water park mid-Feb to Oct school hols & selected days: funfair 10am–8pm; water park noon–8pm • Day-tickets from £17, under-15s £10 • ☎ 0845 070 4754, ⓦ butlins.com

The flagship **Butlin's camp**, which opened here in 1960 and now boasts a couple of funky hotels alongside the more basic chalets, sits at the eastern end of the seafront; you can visit its funfair and indoor water park on a day ticket – a good option for kids on a rainy day.

Littlehampton

The low-key seaside town of **LITTLEHAMPTON** ticks all the boxes for the perfect summer day-trip, with a lovely setting by the River Arun, good beaches, a stylish beach café and, as you'd expect of any self-respecting seaside town, plenty of fish and chips, crazy golf and traditional entertainment on tap. With Arundel just a few miles away up the river, Littlehampton is also worth considering as a good-value base for a longer stay.

The seafront

The seafront is an attractive affair, with lawns backing onto the promenade, and a shingle **beach** that at low tide reveals large swathes of sand. Along the prom runs **Britain's longest bench**, a funky ribbon of candy-coloured reclaimed slats that twists and loops its way for over 300m along the seafront, bending around bins and lampposts. The bench ends near the rippling, rusted steel shell that houses the **East Beach Café** (see p.300); the multi-award-winning design of the café was the work of design supremo Thomas Heatherwick, and when it opened back in 2006 it was to a fanfare of media attention – *Vogue* magazine even dubbed the town, rather overenthusiastically it has to be said, the "coolest British seaside resort".

Adjacent are Norfolk Gardens, from where the **Littlehampton Miniature Railway** (ⓦlittlehamptonrailway.co.uk) trundles along in summertime to nearby **Mewsbrook Park**, where there's a large boating lake with pedalos and kayaks for rent. At the other, western, end of the seafront is **Harbour Park** (ⓦharbourpark.com), a small-scale, run-of-the-mill amusement park that's been pulling in holidaymakers ever since Billy Butlin started operating the first rides here in 1932.

Littlehampton prom comes to an abrupt halt at its western end as it meets the **River Arun** – one of the fastest-flowing rivers in the country – which rushes out to sea in a dead-straight channel. A riverside walkway leads up the east bank of the river, past fish-and-chip shops, bobbing boats and kids waiting patiently with crabbing lines, to the smart, pedestrianized **East Bank Riverside Development**.

Look and Sea Visitor Centre

63–65 Surrey St, BN17 5AW • Daily 9am–5pm • £2.50 • ☎ 01903 718984, ⓦ lookandsea.co.uk

Along the East Bank you can't miss the **Look and Sea Visitor Centre**, with a viewing tower up on the third floor giving fabulous 360-degree views over the town and inland to Arundel Castle and Chanctonbury Ring; lower floors cover the town's history, taking you through its trading and shipbuilding past, and its subsequent rise (and fall) as a holiday resort, with plenty of interactive elements to keep kids entertained.

West Beach

Cross the pedestrian bridge a quarter of a mile upstream of the Look and Sea Visitor Centre, then follow Rope Walk down the western bank of the river, around a 20min walk; or take the Littlehampton Ferry south of the Visitor Centre by the Harbour Board office (Easter–Sept weekends & school hols 10am–5pm; £1; ⓦ littlehamptonferry.co.uk); there's also a car park at West Beach, but it's a long detour inland to get to it

Over on the west bank of the River Arun, Littlehampton's wild and windswept **West Beach**, backed by sand dunes flecked with marram grass, feels a world away from the mini-golf and boating lakes of the town. Follow the beach westwards for 1.5 miles to reach **Climping Beach**, which together with West Beach is protected as a Site of Special Scientific Interest for its dunes, rare vegetated shingle and sand flats.

ARRIVAL AND INFORMATION   LITTLEHAMPTON

By train Trains running along the coast from Chichester or Brighton (every 30min) arrive at Littlehampton station, a 5min walk north of the Look and Sea Visitor Centre; from here it's a 10min walk down the east bank of the River Arun to the main beach.

By car There's plenty of pay-and-display parking along the seafront.

Tourist information In the Look and Sea Visitor Centre, 63–65 Surrey St (daily 10am–4pm; ☎01903 721866, ⓦ sussexbythesea.com).

ACCOMMODATION AND EATING

Bailiffscourt Hotel Climping St, Climping, BN17 5RW ☎01903 723511, ⓦhshotels.co.uk. With its flagstone floors, mullioned windows and weathered stonework, *Bailiffscourt Hotel* looks like it's been in this spot for centuries, but it was in fact only built in 1927. The 39 luxurious rooms vary hugely in size, price and decor – some are traditional, some full-blown medieval, others more contemporary. There's also an excellent spa, 30 acres of parkland roamed by peacocks and, best of all, wild and all-but-deserted Climping Beach right on your doorstep. **£259**

★ **East Beach Café** East Beach, BN17 5NZ ☎01903 731903, ⓦeastbeachcafe.co.uk. The food in this striking seafront café is every bit as good as the award-winning architecture: the menu features plenty of fish

(mains £12–15), from locally caught pan-fried sea bream to fish soup and fish and chips, and there's a small breakfast menu, too. The cave-like interior, with its rippling ceiling, has wonderful floor-to-ceiling views out to sea, and there are also plenty of tables outside. It gets busy, so book ahead. Summer Mon–Fri 10am–5pm & 6–8pm, Sat & Sun 10am–5pm & 6–9pm; winter Mon–Wed & Sun 10am–5pm, Thurs & Fri 10am–5pm & 6–8pm, Sat 10am–5pm & 6–9pm.

Regency Rooms 85 South Terrace, BN17 5LJ ☎01903 717707, ⓦregencyrooms.net. Stylish, friendly and brilliant value, this guesthouse opposite the beach is a little gem, with sleek bathrooms and rooms decked out with funky wallpaper and fabrics. No breakfast, but the *East Beach Café* is only a short walk away. **£69**

Worthing

The seaside town of **Worthing** was, like nearby Brighton, a fishing village until the fashion for sea bathing took off in the eighteenth century. When the Prince Regent's younger sister, Amelia, was sent here to recover from tuberculosis in 1798 (Brighton being deemed too racy), Worthing's smart, respectable reputation was sealed. While Brighton has blossomed over the years into a brash, beautiful London-by-the-Sea, Worthing has struggled to throw off its rather boring reputation – "duller than a weekend in Worthing" was the phrase one newspaper chose to describe tennis player Andy Murray in 2015.

That said, Worthing's low-key charms make a welcome breather from the frenetic pace of Brighton: the pebbly **beach**, backed by five miles of prom, never gets too busy, and the seafront boasts an elegant Art Deco pier and one of the oldest working **cinemas** in the country, the Dome (ⓦworthingdome.com), opened in 1911. The **Worthing**

Museum and Art Gallery, set back 500m from the seafront on Chapel Road (Tues–Sat 10am–5pm; ⓦworthingmuseum.co.uk), is also well worth a look, especially for its excellent costume and archeological collections.

East of the pier, you can kick off your shoes and have a go at beach volleyball, beach tennis or sand soccer at the **Worthing Sand Courts** (£15/hr; ⓦworthingsandcourts.co.uk), while out on the waves you can try out **kitesurfing** or stand-up paddleboarding (see below) – Worthing has been described as the kitesurf capital of the UK, and the large bay in which the town sits is one of the best places in the country to learn.

INFORMATION AND ACTIVITIES   WORTHING

Tourist information There's a Visitor Information Point at Worthing Museum and Art Gallery, Chapel Rd, BN11 1HP (Tues–Sat 10am–5pm; ☎01903 221066, ⓦvisitworthing .co.uk).

Kitesurfing and stand-up paddleboarding Plenty of companies offer kitesurfing tuition in the area, including BN1 Kitesurfing (ⓦbn1kitesurfing.co.uk), Brighton Kitesurf and SUP Academy (ⓦbrightonkitesurfandsupacademy .com), the KiteSurf & SUP Company (ⓦthekitesurfandsup .co) and Lancing Kitesurf School (ⓦlancingkitesurfschool .com). Many of these outfits also offer stand-up paddleboarding tuition.

EATING

★**Crab Shack** 2 Marine Parade, BN11 3PN ☎01903 215070, ⓦfacebook.com/CrabShackWorthing. Laidback seafood café in a top spot on the seafront, with tables outside. The regularly changing menu might feature crab sarnies, pil pil prawns or posh fish and chips (pan-fried hake with a chorizo crumb, served with minted pea puree; £15) – all exceptionally tasty. It's very popular, so book ahead.

Tues–Sat noon–4pm & 5–9pm, Sun noon–4pm.
Macaris Restaurant and Café 24–25 Marine Parade, next to the Dome, BN11 3PT ☎01903 532753, ⓦmacarisrestaurant.co.uk. A Worthing institution that's been serving up ice creams to holidaymakers since 1959. Summer daily 9am–7pm; winter Mon–Fri 9am–5pm, Sat & Sun 9am–6pm.

Shoreham-by-Sea

The little town and port of **Shoreham-by-Sea** probably won't be top of anyone's list of Sussex must-sees, but you might well pass through to take in a comedy or music gig at the excellent Ropetackle Centre (ⓦropetacklecentre.co.uk), or to visit the award-winning **Farmers' market** or **Artisans' market** (every second and fourth Sat of the month respectively 9am–1pm). Once in town it's worth poking around a little further to find a couple of gems dating back to the twelfth century: the church of **St Mary de Haura**, set in a peaceful square along Church Street; and the diminutive, chequerboard **Marlipins Museum** of local history on the High Street (May–Oct Mon–Sat 10.30am–4.30pm; £3; ☎01273 462994, ⓦsussexpast.co.uk).

It's a ten-minute wander from the centre to peaceful **Shoreham Beach**, a nature reserve with rare vegetated shingle habitat above the high tide mark and a good sweep of sand at low tide. En route, look out for the row of **houseboats** hauled up on the mudflats on the far side of the River Adur, converted into bohemian homes from an assortment of rusting ferries, gunboats, steamers and other retired vessels.

Just west of town, across the River Adur, Shoreham's fabulous Art Deco airport – the oldest licensed airfield in the country – is the base for Brighton Scenic's sightseeing **flights** (see p.250).

EATING   SHOREHAM-BY-SEA

Ginger & Dobbs 31–32 East St, BN43 5ZD ☎01273 453359, ⓦgingeranddobbs.co.uk. This lovely little organic greengrocer-cum-café, in a tranquil spot opposite St Mary de Haura church, serves up local Pharmacie coffee, home-baked bread and cakes, salads and daily specials – and stocks a selection of affordable French homeware, too. Mon–Thurs 9am–5pm, Fri & Sat 9am–11pm, Sun noon–4pm.

8

Surrey

RHS WISLEY

9

Surrey

Too often dismissed as a well-heeled swathe of suburbia, Surrey has much to recommend it, particularly for outdoors-lovers. Carpeted with woodlands, the county is bisected laterally by the chalk escarpment of the North Downs, which rise west of Guildford, peak around Box Hill near Dorking, and continue east into Kent. Within the Downs lie the Surrey Hills, an Area of Outstanding Natural Beauty, with a number of excellent year-round cycling paths and two gentle, long-distance walking paths: in the north, the North Downs Way, which starts at Farnham and follows ancient pilgrims' routes to finish in Dover; further south, the Greensand Way leads from Haslemere to Hamstreet, near Ashford. These, along with countless shorter footpaths and hedge-tangled bridleways, lead you within a hiking-boot's throw of ancient bluebell woods, gently undulating fields, butterfly-speckled chalk grasslands, and sleepy villages that have dozed here since medieval times.

Surrey's wealth dates largely from the sixteenth and seventeenth centuries, when farming and the local paper, gunpowder and iron industries were booming; later industrialization effectively passed the county by, and it remained largely rural until the coming of the railways. In the nineteenth century, before rampant road- and suburb-building changed Surrey's aspect forever, its vernacular architecture, bucolic beauty and pre-industrial ambience inspired many artists – among them architect Edwin Lutyens and his gardening partner Gertrude Jekyll, potter Mary Watts and her husband, painter G.F. Watts – to settle in these leafy surrounds. Fine examples of Arts and Crafts architecture include **Mary Watts'** astonishing **chapel** at Compton.

Other key attractions include the Surrey Hills, where grand estates, such as the Edwardian **Polesden Lacey**, and beauty spots, primarily **Box Hill** and Leith Hill, offer sweeping views over pristine countryside. These chalky slopes provide perfect conditions for viniculture, with Denbies, currently the largest vineyard in England, offering tours. The handsome market towns of **Guildford** and **Dorking** provide restaurants, hotels and train connections, but it's far nicer to stay out in the countryside, kicking back in peace and quiet just a handful of miles from the capital. In the pretty cluster of villages between Guildford and Dorking, Shere, Abinger and Peaslake offer sleepy, chocolate-box appeal and excellent local walks.

In the west, Surrey has a different flavour. Here protected areas of wild lowland heath dominate, with the eerie natural amphitheatre of the **Devil's Punch Bowl** near **Farnham** making a dramatic destination in the Greensand Hills. **North Surrey**, cut through by the roaring M25 orbital motorway, is far less rural, though beyond the collection of satellite towns and light industrial installations are a few attractions, chiefly Wisley, the Royal Horticultural Society's flagship garden.

Farnham and around

The attractive market town of **FARNHAM** lies tucked into Surrey's southwestern corner on its border with Hampshire. Notwithstanding its thousand-year history, its most striking buildings date from the eighteenth century, when hop farming boomed hereabouts. The Georgian architecture is at its best along **Castle Street**, which links the centre with the

BOX HILL

Highlights

❶ Devil's Punch Bowl Swathed in myth, this dramatic natural amphitheatre has a wild, raw beauty unseen elsewhere in the county. **See p.307**

❷ The Watts Chapel The bucolic village of Compton is home to this extraordinary Arts and Crafts chapel, part of a fascinating complex devoted to the life and works of British artists George and Mary Watts. **See p.308**

❸ Box Hill Hikers, cyclists and Sunday strollers make a beeline for this popular beauty spot – as featured in Jane Austen's *Emma* – near Dorking. **See p.311**

❹ Polesden Lacey The immaculate, extensive estate, crisscrossed with walks, and the quirky Edwardian house give Polesden Lacey the edge over many other stately homes. **See p.311**

❺ Hannah Peschar Sculpture Garden Wander through another world in this magical, artistic spot. **See p.312**

HIGHLIGHTS ARE MARKED ON THE MAP ON P.306

castle – the castle's small motte-and-shell **keep** gives good views across to the Downs (Feb–Dec Mon–Fri 9am–5pm; Sat & Sun 10am–4pm; free; EH; ⓦenglish-heritage .org.uk/visit/places/farnham-castle-keep). Meanwhile, the quirky **Museum of Farnham**, 38 West St (Tues–Sat 10am–5pm; free; ⓦfarnhammaltings.com/museum), offers a lively jog through local history, with a strong emphasis on crafts. The long-distance **North Downs Way** (150 miles) starts at Farnham, signposted from the railway station.

Devil's Punch Bowl

London Rd, Hindhead, GU26 6AB · Daily dawn–dusk · Free; NT · Parking £3 · ☎01428 681050, ⓦnationaltrust.org.uk/hindhead-commons -and-the-devils-punch-bowl · Haslemere station (on the line from Guildford) is 3 miles south

A large natural depression, created by subterranean springs eroding the clay soil from below, the **Devil's Punch Bowl**, some nine miles south of Farnham, offers a startling counterpoint to the softer countryside elsewhere in Surrey. Its wild heathland slopes carpeted with heather and gorse, surrounded by ancient woodlands, the Bowl is a daunting, occasionally eerie vision, offering long walks around the rim and down into the valley. No one quite knows how it got its name, though many folk tales describe it as the devil's handiwork – one story suggests the bowl was created when he flung clods of earth at the god Thor. The Punch Bowl segues seamlessly into neighbouring **Hindhead Commons**, particularly lovely in summer and early autumn when the heather is in flower; Sir Arthur Conan Doyle, who lived for ten years in the village of Hindhead, was inspired to write *Hound of the Baskervilles* here. Accessible on the Greensand Way, the Punch Bowl and commons are crisscrossed by bridleways and walking paths, including five NT trails that strike off from the café.

ARRIVAL AND INFORMATION

FARNHAM AND AROUND

By train Farnham station – on Station Hill, across the River Wey in the south of town – is a 10min walk from the centre. There are connections with London Waterloo (every 30min; 1hr) and Woking (every 30min; 23min).

Tourist office On South St, midway between the station and the centre (Mon–Thurs 9am–5pm, Fri 9am–4.30pm; ☎01252 712667, ⓦfarnham.gov.uk).

ACCOMMODATION AND EATING

Dovecote B&B Pickhurst Rd, Chiddingfold, GU8 4TS ☎01428 682920, ⓦbedandbreakfastchiddingfold.co.uk. In a sixteenth-century house near Chiddingfold village green, this delightful three-room B&B has a lush garden and a cosy, beamed guest lounge with a real fire. The best room, a large double, is en suite, while another double and twin share a bathroom, complete with clawfoot tub. **£110**

Farnham Maltings Bridge Square, Farnham, GU9 7QR ☎01252 745444, ⓦfarnhammaltings.com. Farnham's excellent community arts centre, which hosts live music, theatre and movies, and crafts workshops, also has a riverside café. Here you'll find books to browse, good coffee and cakes, breakfasts and simple home-made food, including sandwiches, filled croissants, soups and salad, from around £5. Mon & Tues 9.30am–5pm, Wed–Fri

9.30am–8pm, Sat 10am–5pm; kitchen Mon & Tues 10am–2.30pm, Wed–Fri 10am–7.30pm, Sat 10.30am–2.30pm.

Swan Inn Petworth Rd, Chiddingfold, GU8 4TY ☎01428 684688, ⓦtheswaninnchiddingfold.com. One of a number of good pubs with rooms in Chiddingfold. Mains (£8–20) range from venison haunch with roasted pumpkin, via pulled pork in a bun, to wild mushroom *arancini*, with sandwiches for around £5 and bar "snacks" – roasted fig, goat's cheese and walnut salad (£8.25), smashed avocado with *umami*-dressed watercress (£7.45) – served all day. The terraced garden is lovely, and they offer eleven luxurious bedrooms, sometimes on a B&B basis. Mon–Fri 7am–11pm, Sat 9am–11pm, Sun 9am–10.30pm; meals served Mon–Sat noon–9.30pm, Sun noon–9pm. **£90**

Guildford and around

GUILDFORD is an appealing county town, set on the River Wey and with lovely views across the surrounding countryside. To get a broad panorama, walk up to the medieval **Guildford Castle** (March & Oct Sat & Sun 11am–4pm; April–Sept daily 10am–5pm; £3.20;

9

 guildford.gov.uk/castle), circled by flower-filled gardens, which has a viewing platform in the tower. Otherwise, the **river** itself is a nice place for a walk, as is the lively cobbled **high street**, lined with half-timbered townhouses and with an elaborate seventeenth-century bracket clock overhanging the Guildhall. At no. 155 – sharing a building with the tourist office – the **Guildford House Gallery** (May–Sept Mon–Sat 10am–4.45pm, Sun 11am–4pm; Oct–March Mon–Sat 10am–4.45pm; free; guildford.gov.uk/guildfordhouse), stages art and crafts exhibitions and has a courtyard **café**.

Watts Gallery Artists' Village

Down Lane, Compton, GU3 1DQ • **Watts Gallery, Watts Studios & grounds** Tues–Sun 11am–5pm • £9.50; half price on Tues • **Limnerslease tours** Various days and times; check website and book in advance; 1hr • £5 • **Chapel** Mon–Fri 9am–5pm, Sat & Sun 10am–5pm • Free • **Shop** Daily 10.30am–5.15pm • Free • 01483 810235, wattsgallery.org.uk • #46 bus (hourly Mon–Sat; 15min) from Guildford town centre

Hidden away in the leafy lanes of **Compton**, a pretty village on the North Downs Way just ten minutes' drive from Guildford, the fascinating **Watts Gallery Artists' Village** offers insight into not only a unique artistic partnership but also the important role Surrey played in the cultural life of the late nineteenth and early twentieth centuries. There is a great deal to see; reckon on at least three hours for a visit.

In 1891 husband and wife **George Frederic Watts** (1817–1904) and **Mary Seton Watts** (1849–1938) – he an esteemed painter, she a sculptor/decorative artist 32 years his junior – escaped the pollution and crowds of London to this peaceful Surrey Hills spot, setting up home in a solid, half-timbered pile designed for them by Arts and Crafts architect Sir Ernest George.

Here the ageing Watts, previously best known for his portraits, shifted his attention to landscape paintings and sculpture, while Mary began a furiously creative phase, making decorative panels for their home, designing the astonishing Compton chapel, teaching pottery classes and establishing the **Compton Pottery**, whose decorative terracotta pieces, hand-carved with distinctive Art Nouveau motifs, remained in production until the 1950s.

In 1903 the couple commissioned a simple museum to display George's art. He died just a year later, after which Mary lived and worked here until her death. Today the **Watts Gallery** still focuses on his paintings, its vibrant crimson and turquoise walls displaying his portraits, light-infused metaphysical landscapes and socially conscious think pieces. Around the corner in the **Sculpture Gallery**, life-size models of Watts' monumental works include *Physical Energy* (1878), a huge, equestrian piece.

A ten-minute woodland walk away from the main complex, **Limnerslease**, the couple's home, is visitable only on **guided tours**. These are rich in personal snippets – not least that George, who modelled himself on Titian and liked to be called "signor", would keep his devoted (insomniac) wife awake with his pronouncements on the state of the world. None of the furnishings are original, but you can see Mary's lively ceiling panels, moulded in gesso (a mix of hemp, plaster and glue), packed with natural and spiritual imagery from around the world. In the east wing, the **Watts Studios** give glimpses into the pair's working methods, with George's canvases hung on easels next to paint-smeared palettes, illustrated explanations of Mary's gesso technique, and her detailed diaries, sketchbooks and beautifully decorated photograph albums

The star of the show, though, is the **Watts Chapel** (1896–97), Mary's masterpiece, a three-minute walk from the museum. Within this little red-brick and terracotta building, reminiscent of a Byzantine church, every patch of wall and vaulted ceiling is covered in a riot of imagery – lustrous jewel colours and burnished bronze gesso reliefs, natural and floral motifs, Celtic knots, Art Nouveau styling and spiritual symbols combining to create a peaceful, profoundly spiritual whole.

The **tearoom** (daily 10.30am–5pm), in Mary's old pottery, serves cakes and light lunches on crockery based on Compton pottery, and has outdoor seating for sunny days, while the museum **shop** is a winner, packed with art books, cards, artsy gifts – and, of course, ceramics.

Winkworth Arboretum

Hascombe Rd, Godalming, GU8 4AD • Daily: Feb & March 10am–5pm; April–Oct 10am–6pm; Nov–Jan 10am–4pm • £7.25; NT • Parking free • ☎ 01483 208477, ⓦ nationaltrust.org.uk/winkworth-arboretum • Godalming station is 2 miles northwest

Surrey doesn't get much leafier than at **Winkworth Arboretum**, a dazzling hillside ensemble of trees seven miles south of Guildford. It is particularly spectacular in **autumn**, when the views down the steep wooded slopes into the valley below blaze with reds and oranges; but spring, with its haze of bluebells, cherry blossom and azaleas, is also stunning. The arboretum was the creation of Dr Wilfred Fox, who in the 1930s and 1940s planted more than a thousand exotic and rare trees among the existing oak and hazel woods; exhibits in the old boathouse by the tranquil lake reveal intriguing historical snippets.

Shere and around

SHERE, its half-beamed and rough-plastered cottages clustered around the River Tillingbourne – more of a stream, really, populated with ducks and with a tree-shaded green alongside – is among Surrey's prettiest villages. The likeable **Shere Museum**, on Gomshall Lane (April–Oct Tues & Thurs 10am–3pm, Sat & Sun 1–5pm; Nov–March Sat & Sun 1–5pm; free; ⓦ sheremuseum.co.uk), has two intriguing rooms packed with local curiosities, while walks and biking trails shoot off in all directions. Other appealing villages nearby include picturesque **Abinger Hammer** – once home to author E.M. Forster and complete with stream and village cricket pitch – and the quiet hamlet of **Peaslake**, whose surrounding woodlands and hills are perfect for rambles and mountain biking. There's **bike rental** at Pedal and Spoke (☎ 01306 731639, ⓦ pedalandspoke.co.uk), and on fair weekends the village centre, with its one pub, fills up with super-keen cyclists.

ARRIVAL AND INFORMATION

GUILDFORD AND AROUND

By train Guildford station is a mile west of the centre, across the River Wey.

Destinations Godalming (every 30min; 8min); Gomshall (for Shere; hourly; 15min); Haslemere (every 10–25min; 15–25min); London Waterloo (every 30min; 35min);

Witley (every 30min–1hr; 15min).

Tourist office 155 High St (May–Sept Mon–Sat 9.30am–5pm, Sun 11am–4pm; Oct–April Mon–Sat 9.30am–5pm; ☎ 01483 444333, ⓦ guildford.gov.uk /visitguildford).

ACCOMMODATION

Angel Hotel 91 High St, Guildford, GU1 3DP ☎ 01483 564555, ⓦ angelpostinghouse.com. Ignore the chains and head for this timber-framed sixteenth-century inn in the centre of town. The standard rooms don't have the atmosphere of the public spaces – all creaking floorboards, rustic beams and maze-like corridors – and some are tired, but the history and location compensate. Breakfast costs extra, taken in *Bill's* downstairs. No parking. **£109**

★**Hurtwood Hotel** Walking Bottom, Peaslake, GU5 9RR ☎ 01306 730514, ⓦ hurtwoodhotel.co.uk. This 1920s inn at the heart of Peaslake makes a great base for cycling and walking breaks, with stylish, comfy boutique rooms and a pub/Italian restaurant (ⓦ hurtwoodinn.com)

– run by different people – downstairs. The front terrace is a sociable suntrap. **£95**

Leylands Farm Leylands Lane, Abinger Common, RH5 6JU ☎ 01306 730115, ⓦ www.leylandsfarm.co.uk. Luxurious, peaceful B&B in a self-contained, two-storey barn conversion – complete with living/dining room with a toasty woodburner – next to a rustic farmhouse in seven acres of grounds. **£90**

★**Rookery Nook** The Square, Shere, GU5 9HG ☎ 01483 209382, ⓦ rookerynook.info. In the centre of Shere, this cute half-timbered fifteenth-century cottage offers friendly B&B in two clean, quiet rooms, one with North Downs views, with shared bath. Breakfasts are excellent. **£100**

EATING AND DRINKING

GUILDFORD AND AROUND

Café Mila 1 Angel Court, Godalming, GU7 1DT ☎ 01483 808569, ⓦ cafemila.co.uk. A light, airy, colourful café, walls lined with local art and tables filled with yoga bunnies (classes are held upstairs), offering tasty, home-made food – avocado on toast, macaroni cheese, falafel in pitta – plus

fresh juices, coffee and fabulous cakes. Mains around £6. Mon–Fri 8am–5pm, Sat 8.30am–5pm, Sun 9am–4pm.

Coffee Culture 2 Angel Gate, Guildford, GU1 4AE ☎ 01483 564200, ⓦ mycoffeeculture.co.uk. It's easy to while away time in this independent coffee shop – tucked off the high street in a cobbled pedestrian lane – lingering

9

over good coffee and freshly made cakes and sandwiches. Mon–Fri 8am–5pm, Sat 8am–6pm, Sun 9am–5pm.

★**Onslow Arms** The Street, West Clandon, GU4 7TE ☎01483 222447, ⊚onslowarmsclandon.co.uk. Friendly, unstuffy country pub with a cosy beamed dining room and large patio garden, serving good food with a few surprises (Padron peppers with chilli salt, lamb kofta with harissa) alongside tasty gastropub staples (liver and bacon, fish and chips). Mains from £10. Daily 11am–11pm; kitchen Mon–Thurs & Sun noon–9.30pm, Fri & Sat noon–10pm.

SHERE AND AROUND

The Abinger Hatch Abinger Lane, Abinger Common, RH5 6HZ ☎01306 730737, ⊚theabingerhatch.com. This comfortable pub offers good, locally sourced food in a peaceful setting. Dog- and family-friendly, it's popular with walkers and cyclists, and on Sundays for its roasts, but worth visiting any time – whether you fancy bangers and mash, pheasant pie or a tasty macaroni cheese with herb salad. Mains from £11.50. Mon–Sat 11.30am–11pm, Sun noon–11pm; kitchen Mon–Thurs noon–9pm, Fri & Sat noon–10pm, Sun noon–8pm.

Kinghams Gomshall Lane, Shere, GU5 9HE ☎01483 202168, ⊚kinghams-restaurant.co.uk. In a seventeenth-century building surrounded by a gorgeous cottage garden, *Kinghams* offers upscale dining in cosy surroundings. Creative takes on classic British and French cuisine might include pan-fried guinea fowl with cream cheese mousse or roast monkfish with crayfish risotto. Mains from £16; two-course set menu £17.95 (Tues–Thurs lunch & dinner, Fri & Sat lunch). Book ahead. Tues–Sat noon–3pm & 7–10pm, Sun noon–3pm.

The William Bray Shere Lane, Shere, GU5 9HS ☎01483 202044, ⊚thewilliambray.co.uk. Large Edwardian pub where you can eat Modern British gastropub food in a smart dining room or buzzy bar, or on the terrace. The locally sourced food (mains from £13) is full of robust flavours – smoked haddock with pancetta mash, maybe, or wild garlic and goat's cheese risotto. Mon–Sat 10am–11pm, Sun 10am–10.30pm; kitchen Mon–Sat noon–3pm & 6–10pm, Sun noon–6pm.

Dorking and around

Set at the mouth of a gap carved by the River Mole through the North Downs, the historic market town of **DORKING** has quite a crop of **antique stores** – the handsome sixteenth-century **West Street** is a good place to start – and is also surrounded by some of the Surrey Hills' biggest sights. **Box Hill**, on a chalk escarpment above the Mole north of Dorking, draws streams of walkers and cyclists at the weekend; you can also stroll around the nearby **Leith Hill**, in the grounds of **Polesden Lacey**, and through the vineyards at **Denbies**, which offers tours. Further south, the idiosyncratic **Hannah Peschar Sculpture Garden** is a glorious spot, hidden in the woods towards Sussex.

Denbies Wine Estate

London Rd, RH5 6AA • **Estate** Daily: April–Oct 9.30am–5.30pm; Nov–March 9.30am–5pm • Free • **Tours** March–Oct daily hourly (except 1pm) 11am–4pm; Nov–Feb occasional tours; check online • Indoor tours £10.95, £14.95 with sparkling wines, £16.95 with food; outdoor "train" tours (March–Oct only) £6.50, £10.50 with sparkling wine • ☎01306 876616, ⊚denbies.co.uk • 15min walk north of Dorking train station

With 265 acres of vines, planted on the sunny south-facing slopes of a sheltered valley, **Denbies** is the largest privately owned vineyard in England. It's a commercial operation, centring on a busy restaurant and gift store where you can buy the wines; the estate is also home to the independent Surrey Hills Brewery (⊚surreyhills.co.uk), and a good farm shop, selling produce grown on site.

The chalky soil and the warm, dry microclimate in this area, remarkably similar to the Champagne region of France, are ideal for wine production – indeed, the Romans grew grapes just 300yd away – and nineteen varieties are now planted here. With many prestigious awards to its name, Denbies specializes in traditionally produced **sparkling wines** – champagne in all but name – including the delicious sparkling Greenfields, but they also offer superb whites (among them the Surrey Gold, a very drinkable blend of Müller-Thurgau, Ortega and Bacchus), the Noble Harvest dessert wine and the dry, light Chalk Ridge rosé.

Indoor **tours** lead you through the winery, explaining the process, with tastings at the end. Even nicer, though, especially on a sunny summer's day, is to ride the little "train" through the vineyards, which are part of a much larger estate, dipping in and out of beautiful dappled woodland and affording wonderful views over the slopes to Box Hill, Dorking and Leith Hill. You can also simply **walk** through the estate, following some seven miles of public footpaths.

Box Hill

Box Hill Rd, KT20 7LB • Daily dawn–dusk • Free; NT • Parking £3 • ☎ 01306 885502, Ⓦ nationaltrust.org.uk/box-hill • Box Hill & Westhumble train station is 850yd west; from Dorking take buses #516 (Mon–Sat) or #465 (daily)

It's a stiff cycle ride up the zigzagging path to the top of **Box Hill**, a mile from the North Downs Way, where various walks and paths lead you through woodlands of rare wild box trees, yew, oak and beech, and across chalk grasslands, designated as a Site of Special Scientific Interest, scattered with wildflowers and fluttering with butterflies. A number of NT trails include an adventurous "natural play trail" for kids, the two-mile Stepping Stones walk along the River Mole, and some longer, more strenuous options. Brilliant views abound, most famously from the **Salomons Memorial** viewpoint near the café, where on a clear day you can see across the Weald to the South Downs.

Polesden Lacey

Near Great Bookham, RH5 6BD • **House** Daily: March–Oct 11am–5pm; Nov–Feb 11am–4pm • £13.60 (includes gardens); NT • **Gardens** Daily: March–Oct 10am–5pm; Nov–Feb 10am–4pm • £8.50; NT • Parking £5 • ☎ 01372 452048, Ⓦ nationaltrust.org.uk/polesden-lacey • Box Hill & Westhumble station is 3 miles east; take bus #465from Dorking

Four miles from Dorking, and minutes from the North Downs Way, the grand Edwardian estate of **Polesden Lacey** practically begs you to while away the day with a picnic. In summer, deckchairs and rugs are provided on the velvety lawn of the South Terrace, where you can enjoy uninterrupted views of the Surrey Hills. If you're feeling more active, take a wander around the gardens – which include a fragrant lavender garden, apple orchard and a stunning walled rose garden – and the 1400-acre surrounding estate.

The **house** – remodelled in 1906 by the architects of the *Ritz* – is worth a look. It's largely set up to appear as it would have in the 1930s, when owned by wealthy socialite Margaret Greville (1863–1942). Guests here included Winston Churchill, the Queen Mother and three kings, including Edward VII and his lover Alice Keppel – Camilla Parker-Bowles' great-grandmother – and while filled with priceless artworks, it's the human details that linger. Make sure to take a quick shot in the billiards room, where nostalgic tunes on old 78s crackle in the background.

Leith Hill

Near Coldharbour, Dorking • **Leith Hill Tower** Mon–Fri 10am–3pm, Sat & Sun 9am–5pm • £2; NT • Parking £3.50 • ☎ 01306 712711, Ⓦ nationaltrust.org.uk/leith-hill • **Leith Hill Place** Leith Hill Lane, RH5 6LY • March–Oct Thurs–Sun 11am–5pm • £5; NT • Parking £3.50 • ☎ 01306 711685, Ⓦ nationaltrust.org.uk/leith-hill-place • 5 miles west of Holmwood train station

Reaching the lofty heights of 967ft, **Leith Hill** is the highest point in the southeast, topped with a neo-Gothic eighteenth-century **tower**, a folly from the top of which you can peer through a telescope to see the sprawling mass of London in the north and the Channel to the south. Four designated trails wind through open heathlands and through the woods, particularly lovely in spring, when drifts of **bluebells** shimmer across the floor, and the **rhododendrons** burst into colour. Below the tower, you can also visit **Leith Hill Place**, childhood home of British composer Ralph Vaughan Williams. With a small display dedicated to the composer and a forty-minute "soundscape tour" (an evocative musical sound installation) bringing the house to life, this is an informal, low-key visit, and the views are lovely. Tea can be taken on the lawn.

9

Hannah Peschar Sculpture Garden

Standon Lane, near Ockley, RH5 5QR • April–Oct Thurs–Sat 11am–6pm, Sun 2–5pm • £10 • ☏ 01306 627269,
ⓦ hannahpescharsculpture.com • Ockley station is 3 miles northeast

Tucked away off a hedgerow-tangled lane outside the hamlet of Ockley, a twenty-minute drive south of Dorking, the **Hannah Peschar Sculpture Garden** has a fairytale feel. Owned by an artist/landscape designer couple, the setting is a work of art in itself: a secret forest of lofty mature trees, giant ferns and towering broadleaf plants. A vision of impossibly green lushness, dappled with light, it's all amazingly peaceful, silent other than the burble of rushing streams and the rat-a-tat of distant woodpeckers. Follow winding, mossy paths and cross honeysuckle-tangled footbridges to discover modern sculptures hidden among the giant ferns, dangling from branches, or standing alone in glades. Some, made of weather-battered wood, or cool green and brown marble, look as if they have grown from the soil, while others, constructed from steel, cement and fibreglass, make a striking contrast with the organic world around them.

ARRIVAL AND INFORMATION

DORKING AND AROUND

By train Dorking's main station, with services to London, is a mile north of the centre. The town's other two stations, Dorking Deepdene and Dorking West, only run a few local services.

Destinations Hill & Westhumble (hourly; 2min); London Victoria (every 30min; 1hr); London Waterloo (every 30min; 50min); Ockley (hourly; 12min).
Website ⓦ visitdorking.com.

ACCOMMODATION

Denbies Farmhouse London Rd, Dorking, RH5 6AA ☏ 01306 876777, ⓦ denbies.co.uk. With a rather special setting on the Denbies estate, at the edge of the vineyards, this farmhouse offers seven simple en-suite B&B rooms and a peaceful front garden where you can sit and enjoy a glass of something good. Bike rental available if prebooked. **£105**
Garden Cottage Polesden Lacey, near Great Bookham, RH5 6BD ☏ 03443 351287, ⓦ nationaltrustcottages.co.uk. This handsome, ivy-strewn National Trust property – somewhat larger than a cottage – is in a gorgeous spot next to the Polesden Lacey rose garden, with two patios and a real fire in winter. Three smart bedrooms sleep six. Minimum stay two nights. **£600**
Running Horses Old London Rd, Mickleham, RH5 6DU ☏ 01372 372279, ⓦ therunninghorses.co.uk. Old coaching inn near Box Hill, with six luxurious B&B rooms,

Brakspear ales in the bar and seasonal British food, both traditional (guinea fowl; devilled crab on toast) and modern (superfood salad with kale, broccoli and quinoa) in the restaurant. Mains from £13. **£110**
★**YHA Tanners Hatch** Off Ranmore Common Rd, nr Dorking, RH5 6BE ☏ 0845 371 9542, ⓦ yha.org.uk /hostel/tanners-hatch. Deep in the woods (it's a 15min walk from the nearest car park) next to the Polesden Lacey estate, this charming seventeenth-century cottage, surrounded by an old English garden, has wonderful views. Inside is simple, snug and cosy, with low-beamed ceilings, creaky narrow stairs and a small lounge with a real fire. It's self-catering, and hostellers and campers alike can make campfires and stoke up barbecues in the woods. The 25 bunk beds are spread across three rooms, with the toilet/shower block outside. No wi-fi. Dorms **£13**, camping/person **£13**

EATING AND DRINKING

★**Duke of Wellington** Guildford Rd, East Horsley, KT24 6AA ☏ 01483 282312, ⓦ dukeofw.com. This gastropub conversion of a sixteenth-century inn, near Polesden Lacey, is family-, cyclist- and dog-friendly, with plump armchairs, an open fire and lashings of vintage cool. House-smoked meat stars, with a delicious brisket (£16.50) and ribs. Mon–Fri 11am–11pm, Sat 10am–midnight, Sun 10am–10.30pm; kitchen daily 11am till late.

Two to Four 2–4 West St, Dorking, RH4 1BL ☏ 01306 889923, ⓦ 2to4.co.uk. Dorking's best restaurant, with seasonal, locally sourced nouvelle-ish mains – sea trout with crushed potatoes and watercress purée; confit pork belly with sesame crust and chorizo – from £18, and good-value set menus (two-/three-course lunch £12/£16; Mon–Fri two-course dinner £19). Mon–Sat noon–2.15pm & 6.30–10.30pm.

North Surrey

North Surrey, straggling out beyond the Greater London borders, lacks the rural atmosphere that defines the hills and heaths to the south. However, there are a few key attractions here, including the **Epsom Downs racecourse**, home of the Derby (Ⓦepsomderby.co.uk) since 1780, and **RHS Garden Wisley**, a dream-come-true real-life catalogue for keen gardeners. The appealing village of **Ripley**, with its excellent eating options and luxury B&B, makes an obvious base.

RHS Garden Wisley

Four miles east of Woking, GU23 6QB • Mid-March to mid-Oct Mon–Fri 10am–6pm, Sat & Sun 9am–6pm (Glasshouse daily 10am–5.15pm); mid-Oct to mid-March Mon–Fri 10am–4.30pm, Sat & Sun 9am–4.30pm (Glasshouse daily 10am–3.45pm) • £14.50 • Parking free • ☎ 0845 260 9000, Ⓦ rhs.org.uk/gardens/wisley • Bus #515 (Mon–Sat) and #515a (Sun) between Kingston-upon-Thames train station and Guildford bus station stops on the A3 nearby

Established in Victorian times to cultivate "difficult" plants, **RHS Garden Wisley**, given to the Royal Horticultural Society in 1903, is still today a working and demonstration garden, experimenting with new plants and cultivation techniques. Its sheer size – 240 acres – means it remains blessedly uncrowded even in summer (though the glasshouse can fill up); it is also, with its trails, woodlands and lakes, the kind of garden that even non-gardeners can enjoy.

Things are constantly evolving, but one perpetual crowd-pleaser is the vast, 40ft-high **Glasshouse**, with three climatic zones teeming with rare and exotic plants, all set around waterfalls and pools. It's particularly lovely during the **butterfly show** early in the year, when countless species of butterfly flutter around you. Elsewhere, don't miss the **wild garden**, an abundant woodland featuring camellias, witch hazel, magnolia and bamboo. **Battleston Hill** comes into its own in late spring, when you might catch not only the bluebells but also the firework display of rhododendrons, along with exquisite wisteria, tumbling through the branches of a stand of silver birch; autumn sees the arrival of the unusual, purple-spotted toad lily. The **Mediterranean Walk** features plants from five Mediterranean climatic areas, complemented by majestic eucalyptus trees.

From the **orchard**, planted with hundreds of varieties of fruit trees, to the **pinetum**, with its mighty redwoods, Wisley's trees are as fascinating as its smaller plants. If you're here in October make for the **Seven Acres**, where the broad-leaved Wisley Bonfire and *Liquidambar* trees present a thrilling blaze of burned golds and fiery reds.

ACCOMMODATION AND EATING   NORTH SURREY

The Anchor High St, Ripley, GU23 6AE ☎01483 211866, Ⓦripleyanchor.co.uk. Run by the same team as the Michelin-starred *Drake's*, opposite, this stylishly but simply restored historic pub serves similarly intriguing food – rabbit cannelloni with pea shoots, perhaps, or roast cod with pomegranate *vierge* – at lower prices. Mains from £12; two-/three-course menu (Tues–Fri 6–9pm) £15/£19. Tues–Sat noon–11pm, Sun noon–9pm.

★ **Broadway Barn** High St, Ripley, GU23 6AQ ☎01483 223200, Ⓦbroadwaybarn.com. Luxury B&B in a historic building peacefully set back behind the high street. Each of the four rooms is different, balancing cosy comforts (home-baked biscuits; plump bedding; towelling robes), rustic cool (beams; bare brick walls) and easy-going elegance to create a gorgeous retreat. The gourmet breakfast, an array of home-baked treats, is outstanding. **£110**

Inn at West End 42 Guildford Rd, West End, GU24 9PW ☎01276 858652 (pub) or ☎01276 485842 (rooms), Ⓦthe-inn.co.uk. This light, good-looking food pub serves accomplished Modern English dishes (crispy buttermilk pheasant with sweet potato, say, or ham hock terrine with

treacle soda bread), interesting wines, real ales and gorgeous desserts. Mains from £13; set menus at lunch (Mon–Sat) £12.95/£15.95, and dinner (except Fri & Sat) £16.50/£19.50. They also offer twelve contemporary guest rooms, a couple of which welcome dogs. Daily 11am–11pm; kitchen Mon–Fri 7–10.30am, noon–2.30pm & 6–9.30pm, Sat 8.30–11am, noon–2.30pm & 6–9.30pm, Sun 8.30–11am, noon–3pm & 6–9pm. **£125**

★ **Stovell's** 125 Windsor Rd, Chobham, GU24 8QS ☎01276 858000, Ⓦstovells.com. Special occasion, on-trend food – from osmanthus and chrysanthemum broth with abalone mushroom to rabbit with fermented turnips, pistachio and nettles – dished up in a beautiful Tudor farmhouse. They distil their own gin, too. Two/three courses £18/£22.50 at lunch, £37/£45 at dinner. Tues–Fri noon–2.30pm & 6–10pm, Sat 6–10pm, Sun noon–2.30pm.

Swallow Barn Milford Green, Chobham, GU24 8AU ☎01276 856030, Ⓦswallow-barn.co.uk. Set in 4 acres of gardens, with an outdoor swimming pool, *Swallow Barn* offers three comfortable double/twin B&B rooms in a quiet spot near Wisley. **£95**

Contexts

History

As the part of the country closest to mainland Europe, the southeast corner of England has played an important part in British history. It was here that Caesar landed his troops in the Roman invasion of Britain in 55 BC, and here too, over a millennium later in 1066, that William of Normandy defeated King Harold in the last successful invasion of Britain. Over the years the coastline of Kent and Sussex has been at the frontline of potential invasion, facing off threats from Napoleon and Hitler among others, with the coast's iconic White Cliffs standing as a symbolic, and practical, bulwark against would-be invaders.

Prehistory

Southeast England has been inhabited, intermittently at least, for half a million years or more. For much of this period it was covered by snow during successive ice ages, but a land bridge to continental Europe allowed early man to come and go. The earliest hominid remains so far discovered in Britain – a shinbone and two teeth, alongside worked flint implements – were unearthed at **Boxgrove**, near Chichester in West Sussex, and date back between 524,000 and 478,000 years. "Boxgrove Man" was a nomadic hunter, over 5ft 10in tall, who roamed the shoreline, hunting large mammals using worked flint tools.

The last spell of intense cold began about 17,000 years ago, and it was the final thawing of this Ice Age around 7000 years ago that caused Britain to separate from the European mainland, with the warmer temperatures allowing natural woodland to cloak the land. The earliest farmers appeared about 4000 BC. These tribes were the first to make some impact on the environment, clearing forests, enclosing fields, constructing defensive ditches around their villages and digging mines to obtain flint used for tools and weapons. The **flint mines** in Sussex are among the oldest in England: they were begun around 4000 BC and continued until 2800 BC, with the resulting flint axes being used for barter and trade along the South Downs. At Cissbury Ring in West Sussex (see p.298) you can still see the bumps in the grass from the network of shafts, some 40ft deep.

The transition from the Neolithic to the **Bronze Age** began around 2000 BC with the importation from northern Europe of artefacts attributed to the **Beaker Culture** – named for the distinctive cups found at many burial sites. The 3500-year-old **Hove amber cup** – considered to be one of Britain's most important Bronze Age finds – is on show at Hove Museum in Brighton (see p.246). The spread of the Beaker Culture along European trade routes helped stimulate the development of a comparatively well-organized social structure with an established aristocracy. Large numbers of earthwork forts and round barrows, or burial mounds, were constructed in this period, with settlements across the Southeast, including just outside Eastbourne underneath Shinewater Park – thought to be one of the largest Bronze Age villages in Europe, though it remains unexcavated.

c.500,000 BC	4000 BC	2000 BC
Boxgrove Man roams the shore around present-day Chichester.	Farming and the mining of flint for trade begins.	The start of the Bronze Age; earthwork forts and villages are built.

THE PILTDOWN HOAX

The skull of "**Piltdown Man**" was discovered in a gravel pit in Piltdown in East Sussex in 1912 by **Charles Dawson**, a respected lawyer and amateur geologist, and sensationally hailed as the missing link between apes and humans, a paleontological find of immense significance. As the years went by, and more ancient hominid fossils were unearthed around the globe, it became increasingly clear that Piltdown Man was a bit of an anomaly that didn't quite fit with other discoveries. It took more than forty years, however, until 1953, to unearth the truth: what had been presented as a five-thousand-million-year-old skull had in fact been cleverly assembled from a medieval skull and an orang-utan jaw, and the Piltdown hoax passed into history as one of the greatest archeological hoaxes ever perpetrated.

The Iron Age and the Romans

By 500 BC, the Southeast was inhabited by a number of different Celtic tribes, each with a sophisticated farming economy and social hierarchy. Familiar with Mediterranean artefacts through their far-flung trade routes, they gradually developed better methods of metalworking, ones that favoured **iron** rather than bronze, from which they forged not just weapons but also coins and ornamental works. Their principal contribution to the landscape was a network of **hillforts** and other defensive works, among them the hillforts of Mount Caburn near Lewes, Cissbury Ring (see p.298), Chanctonbury Ring (see p.297), the Trundle near Chichester and Oldbury near Ightham.

The Roman invasion of Britain began hesitantly, with small cross-Channel incursions in 55 and 54 BC led by **Julius Caesar**, who landed near Deal in Kent. Almost one hundred years later, the death of the king of southeast England, Cunobelin (Shakespeare's Cymbeline), presented **Emperor Claudius** with a golden opportunity and in August 43 AD a substantial Roman force landed, though the jury is still out on precisely where – possibly at Richborough (see p.108) in Kent, possibly further west beyond Chichester. The Roman army quickly fanned out, conquering the southern half of Britain and subsuming it into the Roman Empire.

Roman rule lasted nearly four centuries. Commerce flourished, cities such as Canterbury and Chichester prospered, and Roman civilization left its mark all over the Southeast: in coastal forts at Richborough and Pevensey (see p.185), a clifftop lighthouse at Dover (see p.116), arrow-straight roads, city walls still standing in Chichester, which also retains the original Roman cruciform street plan (see p.267), and wealthy **Roman villas** at Lullingstone in Kent (see p.153), and Bignor (see p.295) and Fishbourne (see p.272) in Sussex – the last of these the largest and best-preserved Roman dwelling in the country.

The Anglo-Saxons

From the late third century, Roman England was subject to **raids** by **Saxons**, leading to the eventual withdrawal of the Roman armies at the beginning of the fifth century. This gave the Saxons free rein to begin settling the country, which they did throughout the sixth and seventh centuries, with the **Jutes** from Jutland establishing themselves in eastern Kent. The southeast of England was divided into the **Anglo-Saxon kingdoms of**

500 BC	55 and 54 BC	43 AD	410
The Iron Age sees a network of hillforts established across the Downs.	Julius Caesar first arrives in Britain, landing on the Kentish coast.	The Romans invade under Emperor Claudius, and rule for nearly four centuries.	The Romans withdraw from Britain, leaving the Saxons and Jutes to settle the Southeast and establish the Anglo-Saxon kingdoms of Kent, Sussex and Wessex.

Kent, Sussex and Wessex – the last of these stretching west into Somerset and Dorset – with power and territory fluctuating and passing among them over the centuries that followed. The Anglo-Saxons all but eliminated Romano-British culture, with the old economy collapsing and urban centres emptying.

The early Anglo-Saxon period saw the countrywide revival of Christianity, which was driven mainly by **St Augustine** (see box, p.50), who was despatched by Pope Gregory I and landed on the Kent coast in 597, accompanied by forty monks. Ethelbert, the king of the Kingdom of Kent and the most powerful Anglo-Saxon overlord of the time, received the missionaries and gave Augustine permission to found a monastery at **Canterbury**, where the king himself was then baptized. The ruins of Augustine's abbey, including the remains of its seventh-century St Pancras church, can still be visited today (see p.50).

By the end of the ninth century the Kingdom of Wessex had established supremacy over the Southeast, with the formidable and exceptionally talented **Alfred the Great** recognized as overlord by several southern kingdoms. His successor, **Edward the Elder**, capitalized on his efforts to become the de facto overlord of all England. The unifying realm continued under Edward's son, **Athelstan**, and **Edgar**, crowned King of England in 959.

After a brief period of Danish rule – most famously under the shrewd and gifted **Cnut**, whose failure to turn back the tide may have taken place at Bosham (see p.277) – the Saxons regained the initiative, installing **Edward the Confessor** on the throne in 1042. On Edward's death, **Harold** was confirmed as king, ignoring several rival claims including that of William, Duke of Normandy. William wasted no time: he assembled an army, set sail for England and famously routed the Saxons at the **Battle of Hastings** in 1066 (see box, p.187). On Christmas Day, **William the Conqueror** was crowned king in Westminster Abbey.

The Middle Ages

William I swiftly imposed a Norman aristocracy on his new subjects, reinforcing his rule with a series of strongholds. The strategically important kingdom of Sussex was divided into five **rapes** (administrative divisions), each with a newly built **castle** at its centre, controlled by one of William's most loyal supporters: Robert, Count of Eu, in Hastings (see p.177); Robert, Count of Mortain, in Pevensey (see p.185); William de Warrene in Lewes (see p.224); William de Braose in Bramber (see p.296); and Roger of Montgomery in Chichester and Arundel (see p.265). In Surrey castles sprang up at Guildford (see p.307) and Farnham (see p.307), and in Kent at Canterbury, Rochester, one of the best-preserved Norman fortresses in the country (see p.69), Leeds (see p.158) near Maidstone, and Dover (see p.114), although Kent itself retained some autonomy under Norman rule, possibly because of the resistance it put up against its invaders; the county motto, "Invicta", meaning undefeated, was adopted after the Conquest, and the "Man of Kent" term (see box, p.318) may also date from this time. The earliest Norman castles were motte-and-bailey earth-and-timber constructions, later replaced with more permanent stone castles.

Alongside the castles, mighty stone-built **cathedrals, abbeys and churches** were erected. William raised the great Benedictine Battle Abbey (see p.186) on the site of his

597	973	1066
St Augustine lands on the Kent coast to spread Christianity around the country; he establishes a church and a monastery in Canterbury.	Edgar becomes the first king of England.	The Battle of Hastings sees the Norman William the Conqueror defeat King Harold, marking the end of Anglo-Saxon England.

famous victory and in Lewes, William de Warrene founded **St Pancras Priory** (see p.226), which was to become one of the largest and most powerful monasteries in England. The Saxon See at Selsey was moved to Chichester, where the mighty Chichester Cathedral (see p.267) was founded, and up in northern Kent, Rochester Cathedral was built on the site of an Anglo-Saxon place of worship. In Canterbury the Norman archbishop Lanfranc rebuilt the existing cathedral in 1070 following a huge fire, and the Normans established a Benedictine abbey on the site of the Saxon St Augustine's Abbey. A hundred years later the cathedral became an important pilgrimage site – second only to Rome – when the murder of Archbishop **Thomas Becket** ended up with Becket's canonization (see box, p.43).

In 1264, the countryside around Lewes in East Sussex saw one of just two major battles to have taken place in the Southeast (the other was at Battle in 1066). The **Battle of Lewes** was the bloody culmination of a clash between Henry III and a rebel army of barons under Simon de Montfort; the king was defeated and the resulting treaty, the **Mise of Lewes**, restricted his authority and forced him to assemble a governing council – often described as the first House of Commons. De Montfort's role as de facto ruler of England was short-lived; the following year Henry III's son Edward (later Edward I) routed the barons' army at the battle of Evesham in Worcestershire, killing De Montfort in the process.

The outbreak of the **Black Death** came in 1349. The plague claimed about a third of the country's population – and the scarcity of labour that followed gave the peasantry more economic clout than they had ever had before; for the first time dwellings such as the Clergy House in Alfriston (see p.216) were erected by wealthy yeoman farmers. Predictably, the landowners attempted to restrict the accompanying rise in wages, thereby provoking the widespread rioting that culminated in the abortive **Peasants' Revolt** of 1381, led by **Wat Tyler** of Kent. Another popular uprising, this time organized by Kentish man **Jack Cade**, took place in 1450, with Cade leading an army of five thousand to London, where he listed the grievances of the common people and demanded reform from the King; the rebellion was quickly crushed and the fleeing Cade was caught and killed while hiding in a garden in Lewes.

KENTISH MEN AND MAIDS OF KENT

To call oneself a **Kentish Man (or Maid)**, or a **Maid (or Man) of Kent**, would seem at first to be simply a matter of semantics. However, these proudly held labels in fact refer to geographical areas: although the division is generally taken to be the River Medway, strictly speaking Kentish Maids and Men are born west of a line that cuts through a point just east of Gillingham, and Men and Maids of Kent in the more rural area to the east. Some believe that this east–west division may date back to the fifth century, when, following the departure of the Romans, **Saxons** moved into the west of the region, while the **Jutes**, who called themselves Kentings, or "Men of Kent", settled in the east. Others say that "Men of Kent" only became an accepted term after the **Norman invasion**, when people of East Kent resisted William the Conqueror with more force than those in the west, were granted certain privileges because of it, and were bestowed with the name as an unofficial form of honour.

1170	1264	1349	1450
Canterbury Cathedral becomes one of Christendom's greatest pilgrim shrines after Archbishop Thomas Becket is murdered within its walls.	The Battle of Lewes is fought between Henry III and Simon de Montfort's army of rebel barons.	Black Death decimates the region.	Jack Cade marches an army from Kent to London, demanding reform for the common people.

The Tudors and the Stuarts

The start of the **Tudor** period saw the country begin to assume the status of a major European power. Henry VIII – best remembered for his multiple wives, whose former homes can be found scattered all over the region, from Anne Boleyn's childhood home of Hever Castle (see p.156) to the various properties granted to Anne of Cleves in her divorce settlement – built coastal fortresses at Deal and Walmer (see p.111), designed to scare off the Spanish and the French, and around 1570 he founded the vast **Chatham Historic Dockyard** (see p.72), which quickly became the major base of the Royal Navy. This effectively spelled the end of the **Cinque Port federation** (see box, p.107), which had been established in 1278 and granted trading privileges to the south-coast ports of Dover, Hythe, Sandwich, Romney and Hastings in return for their providing maritime support in times of war – though their demise was only a matter of time anyway, with the shifting coastline leaving many of them stranded high and dry miles inland.

Henry VIII also presided over the establishment of the **Church of England** and the **Dissolution of the Monasteries**, which conveniently gave both king and nobles the chance to get their hands on valuable monastic property in the late 1530s, and reduced the monasteries at Battle, Lewes and elsewhere to ruin. In 1553 Henry's daughter Mary, a fervent Catholic, ascended the throne and returned England to the papacy. Her oppression of Protestants during the **Marian Persecutions** of 1555–57, when seventeen Protestants in the Sussex town of Lewes were condemned to be burned alive (along with 271 others around the country) is at the root of the Sussex town's riotous bonfire celebrations today (see p.230).

The country reverted to Protestantism with Elizabeth I, but tensions between Protestants and Catholics remained, and Protestants' worst fears were confirmed in 1605 when **Guy Fawkes** – butler at Cowdray House in West Sussex (see p.283) – and a group of Catholic conspirators were discovered preparing to blow up King and Parliament in the so-called **Gunpowder Plot**. During the ensuing hue and cry, many Catholics met an untimely end and Fawkes himself was hanged, drawn and quartered.

In the turbulent years of the **English Civil War** (1642–51), the Southeast, which remained almost entirely Parliamentarian, saw little serious fighting – though the castle at Arundel was reduced to rubble when it was held under siege first by Royalists and then by Parliamentarian troops. For the next eleven years England was a **Commonwealth** – at first a true republic, then, after 1653, a **Protectorate** with Cromwell as the Lord Protector and commander-in-chief. The turmoil of the Civil War unleashed a furious legal, theological and political debate, and spawned a host of leftist sects, the most notable of whom were the **Levellers**, who demanded wholesale constitutional reform and whose first manifesto was drafted at Guildford in Surrey, and the more radical Surrey-based **Diggers**, who proposed common ownership of all land. Cromwell died in 1658 to be succeeded by his son **Richard**, who ruled briefly and ineffectually, leaving the army unpaid while one of its more ambitious commanders, General Monk, conspired to restore the monarchy. Charles II, the exiled son of the previous king, entered London in triumph in May 1660. For the next 150 years the Southeast was to remain largely untroubled by conflict.

1509	1555–57	1642–51
Henry VIII comes to the throne and orders the Dissolution of the Monasteries.	The Marian Persecutions of Mary I sees hundreds of Protestants burned alive around the country, including at Lewes and Canterbury.	The Southeast escapes relatively unscathed from the English Civil War, though Arundel Castle is reduced to rubble.

The Georgian era

The next serious threat to the region's peace came in the form of the most daunting of enemies, **Napoleon**. "All my thoughts are directed towards England. I want only for a favourable wind to plant the Imperial Eagle on the Tower of London," Napoleon threatened. Henry VIII's coastal fortresses were garrisoned once again; a thirty-mile canal – the Royal Military Canal (see p.128) – was dug between Hythe and Winchelsea in Kent, with a raised northern bank forming a parapet; and more than a hundred squat Martello towers (see box, p.125) were erected along the south coast, stretching from Suffolk all the way round to Sussex. In the event, by the time the fortifications were completed – the canal in 1809, the Martello towers by 1812 – the threat of invasion was long past, with Nelson's decisive victory over **Napoleon** at **Trafalgar** in 1805 helping to put paid to his plans for invasion. Final defeat for the French emperor came ten years later at the hands of the Duke of Wellington at **Waterloo**, signalling the end of the Napoleonic Wars (1803–15).

England's triumph over Napoleon was underpinned by its financial strength, which was itself born of the **Industrial Revolution**, the switch from an agricultural to a manufacturing economy that changed the face of the country in the space of a hundred years – though it only scratched the surface of life in the rural Southeast. By the time James Watt patented his **steam engine** in 1781, Sussex and Kent's industrial era had already been and gone, with the collapse both of the **Wealden iron industry** (see box below) and of the **Wealden cloth industry** which had been centred around Cranbrook in Kent and had all but disappeared by 1700. Surrey's great **paper and gunpowder mills**, at their peak in the seventeenth century, fared a little better, clinging on until the late nineteenth and early twentieth centuries, and Kent did develop its own small but significant **coal-mining** industry, but overall the Southeast remained largely agricultural throughout the Industrial Revolution. Kent in particular relied heavily on **hop-growing**, which peaked in the late nineteenth century – and retained its rural landscape of small towns and villages.

While the landed gentry spent their money on splendid country estates, life for **agricultural labourers** was hard: low wages, high rents, soaring bread prices thanks to the

---

THE WEALDEN IRON INDUSTRY

Little evidence remains today of the great furnaces of the **Wealden iron industry** that once roared and blazed in the ancient forests of Kent, Sussex and Surrey. During the Tudor and early Stuart periods the Weald grew to become the most important iron-producing centre in Britain: wood from the forest was used not only for **shipbuilding** (Sussex oak was especially prized) but also to cheaply power the furnaces of the Weald's great **iron ore mines** – with the iron used not just to produce domestic firebacks and the like, but also the cannons and weaponry for the great Tudor and Stuart navies. By the mid-sixteenth century there were fifty **furnaces** and forges, and double that number 25 years later. **Ironmasters' houses** sprang up in the Weald, among them Gravetye Manor (see p.198) and Bateman's (see p.190).

The good times couldn't last forever; iron ore supplies started to dwindle, prices were undercut by foreign imports and production elsewhere in the country, and by 1717 the number of furnaces had dropped to fourteen. The ironworks at Hoathly near Lamberhurst in Kent lingered on until 1784, and those at Ashburnham in Sussex until 1796, but they simply couldn't compete with the great coke-fired factories of the North with its vast coalfields.

1685	1736	1783–1826
Protestant French Huguenots, fleeing religious persecution in their home country, flee to England, with significant numbers settling in Kent.	The first seawater baths open at Margate.	George IV frequents the small seaside town of Brighton, helping it become the south coast's most fashionable resort.

Corn Laws, and the introduction of labour-displacing agricultural machinery all contributed to widespread discontent, and it was in Kent that the **Swing Riots** began in 1830, with peasants rising up to destroy the much-hated threshing machines, and unrest spreading throughout the whole of southern England and into East Anglia. It was really little wonder that **smuggling** (see box, p.216) was such an attractive proposition to the rural communities along the Sussex and Kent coasts: a desperately poor farm labourer could earn a week's salary in one lucrative night as a tubman, carrying contraband cargo. Smuggling reached its peak in the late eighteenth and early nineteenth centuries, and only really died out with the introduction of free-trade policies after 1840.

A series of judicious parliamentary acts made small improvements to the lot of the rural labourer: the **Reform Act** of 1832 established the principle (if not actually the practice) of popular representation; the **Poor Law** of 1834 did something to alleviate the condition of the most destitute; and the repeal of the Corn Laws in 1846 cut the cost of bread. Significant sections of the middle classes were just as eager to see progressive reform as the working classes, as evidenced by the immense popularity of **Charles Dickens** (1812–70), whose novels – many set in and around his native town of Rochester (see box, p.70) – railed against poverty and injustice.

The general sense of inequity felt by the rural poor can't have been helped by the antics of their future monarch, **George IV** (see box, p.240), along the coast at **Brighton**, where he was living the high life with his mistress, helping turn the little fishing town into the most fashionable resort on the south coast. The town's transformation had begun in the second half of the eighteenth century when Dr Russell of Lewes began to recommend sea-bathing as an alternative to "taking the cure" at spa towns such as fashionable **Tunbridge Wells** (see p.136). Brighton was one of the earliest **seaside resorts** in the country, but it was not the first: that honour goes to Margate (see p.89) on the North Kent coast, where the first seawater baths opened in 1736. It was only in the Victorian era, however, that the phenomenon of the seaside town really took off.

The Victorian era

In 1837 **Victoria** came to the throne. Her long reign witnessed the zenith of British power: the British trading fleet was easily the mightiest in the world and it underpinned an empire upon which, in that famous phrase of the time, "the sun never set". Sussex-based author Rudyard Kipling (see box, p.190) became the poet of the English empire, coining such phrases as "the white man's burden"; wealthy landowners thought nothing of dispatching plant hunters to scour the globe searching for exotic specimens to populate their great Wealden gardens (see box, p.198); and Victorian explorers proudly displayed their hunting trophies in museums such as the Powell-Cotton Museum in Margate (see p.93). There were extraordinary intellectual achievements too – as typified by the publication of *On the Origin of Species* in 1859, written by Charles Darwin from his home in Kent (see p.155).

Perhaps the biggest change the Victorian era brought to the Southeast was the **arrival of the railway** between the 1830s and 1860s, which at one stroke opened up the region to Londoners, commuters and holidaymakers alike. The world's first scheduled steam passenger service, the **Canterbury & Whitstable Railway**, began puffing its way between cathedral town and coast in 1830, carrying day-trippers to the beach and back.

1796	1803–15	1830
The last furnace of the great Wealden iron industry closes, just as the Industrial Revolution is gathering steam elsewhere in the country.	Defences are erected along the south coast during the Napoleonic Wars, which end with the defeat of Napoleon at Waterloo.	Agricultural labourers rise up in the Swing Riots, which start in Kent and spread across the south.

Newcomers built villas and country houses in the Weald, settlements grew up along the railway routes – the start of the **commuter belt** – and the **seaside town** boomed. All along the Sussex coast the resorts expanded rapidly: the population of Hastings grew from 3175 in 1801 to 17,621 in 1851, to a staggering 65,000 by the end of the century. The fishing industry in many towns dwindled, as tourism became a major source of income, and piers and bandstands sprang up all along the coast. In Kent, Herne Bay, Margate, Broadstairs and Ramsgate all thrived, as the train replaced the slower, weather-dependent steamboats. Kent also saw another phenomenon on the rise, as thousands of **hoppers** from London's East End migrated down to the hop fields of Kent every autumn to pick up casual work during the harvest (see box, p.139).

The world wars

The outbreak of **World War I** in 1914 saw an ever-present threat of invasion hang over the southeast corner of the country. In Dover Castle you can visit a fire command post with a chart room – its broad table spread with maps, charts and tin mugs of tea – and an observation room, where binoculars and telescopes were used to keep a 24-hour watch on the harbour and the Straits.

The war dragged on for four miserable years, its key engagements fought in the trenches that zigzagged across northern France and west Belgium. Britain and her allies eventually prevailed, but the number of dead beggared belief. The Royal Sussex Regiment alone lost nearly seven thousand men. The number of men enlisting caused a severe shortage of agricultural labourers, and conscientious objectors moved to the countryside to work the land, thus exempting themselves from military service; among them were Duncan Grant and his lover David Garnett, who with Vanessa Bell set up house at Charleston, marking the beginning of Sussex's famous connection with the **Bloomsbury Group** (see box, p.220).

When **World War II** broke out in September 1939, the Southeast was once more at the frontline: the Nazis' **Operation Sea Lion** had gone so far as to identify Camber Sands, Winchelsea, Bexhill and Cuckmere Haven in Sussex as potential invasion points. Barbed wire was strung up along the coast, pillboxes and anti-tank obstacles put in place, the Martello towers, built in Napoleonic times, re-employed and the Home Guard mobilized. The Cuckmere Valley – where you can still see tank traps and crumbling pillboxes today (see p.215) – was lit up at night to look like the nearby port of Newhaven to confuse enemy planes, while the nearby Long Man of Wilmington hill figure was temporarily painted green so it could not be used for navigation. Idealized posters of the Sussex Downs ("Your Britain – Fight For It Now") were used in propaganda, and Dame Vera Lynn sang the iconic *(There'll be Bluebirds Over) The White Cliffs of Dover* (see box, p.119).

Kent in particular played a crucial role in the war. It was from here in 1940 that **Operation Dynamo** – the rescue of around three hundred thousand troops stranded at Dunkirk by a flotilla of large and little boats – was masterminded from secret underground tunnels beneath Dover Castle (see p.114). That same summer saw the **Battle of Britain** fought in the skies above Kent – a famous victory that put paid to Hitler's invasion plans and led charismatic prime minister **Winston Churchill**, who had his own home in Kent at Chartwell (see p.137), to dub it the nation's "finest hour".

1859	1830–60	1914–18	1939–45
Charles Darwin publishes *On the Origin of Species*, much of which was written from his home in Kent.	The railway reaches Kent and Sussex; seaside resorts boom along the coast.	World War I; the Bloomsbury Set arrives at Charleston Farmhouse.	World War II: the Southeast takes heavy bomb damage; Dunkirk rescue is planned from Dover Castle; Battle of Britain is fought in the Kent skies.

As the war continued, both Kent and Sussex suffered heavily from **bombing raids**. In June 1942 a Luftwaffe raid on Canterbury left whole streets and hundreds of houses destroyed, though amazingly the cathedral came through unscathed. The ports of Ramsgate, Dover and Folkestone all took a battering too – citizens of Ramsgate took refuge in a network of underground tunnels as their homes were blown to bits above them (see p.100). In the summer of 1944, 1500 doodlebug bombs fell on Kent on their way to London, bestowing the unenviable nickname of "**doodlebug alley**" on the beleaguered county.

To the modern day

A very different **landscape** emerged after World War II, particularly in Sussex, where there had been widespread ploughing up of the Downs' chalkland turf for wartime grain production – a change from the traditional mixed "sheep and corn" farming that was practised before the war. The ploughing up of grassland continued in the postwar period, leading to an enormous loss of biodiversity that has only recently started to be reversed. Some estimate that during this period the percentage of chalk grassland on the eastern Downs fell from fifty percent to just three or four percent. As early as 1929 there had been calls for the South Downs to be protected as a national park, to guard against the urban sprawl fast swallowing up the countryside, but instead after World War II the government opted to give the Sussex Downs partial protection as an AONB (Area of Outstanding Natural Beauty), with the High Weald AONB following soon after. It was only in 2010 that the South Downs finally gained full **national park** status and protection.

Elsewhere in the region, the **transport** infrastructure improved dramatically, making the Southeast even busier, and cementing its status as affluent, prime commuting territory. Motorway building took off in the 1960s and 1970s; Gatwick Airport saw its first flights to the continent in 1949 and became Britain's second largest airport in 1988; and the Channel Tunnel opened in 1994. The Local Government Act of 1972 saw Sussex divided into the separate counties of **East** and **West Sussex** in 1974, spelling an end, on paper at least, to the ancient Saxon kingdom of Sussex.

Alongside the expansion there was also decline. By the 1960s, the **hop-farming industry** was on its last legs, as machines replaced hop-pickers and cheaper hops were imported from abroad. Kent's **coal mines** – discovered near Dover in 1890 but beset by difficulties from the beginning – were closed by the National Coal Board in the 1980s; the county's miners were among the most vocal in the year-long **miners' strike** (1984–85).

Around the coast, the traditional **seaside towns** were suffering too. The rise of the package holiday (and later budget airlines) saw holidaymakers abandon the traditional train-served resorts in droves in the 1960s and 1970s. By the end of the century, seaside towns such as Margate had become sorry shadows of their former selves, with boarded-up shop fronts and derelict seafront attractions, and areas of huge social deprivation.

The new century, however, brought about a decided sea change at the seafront. In Margate the arrival of the **Turner Contemporary** gallery in 2011 brought a raft of young artists in its wake, with vintage shops, galleries and creative restaurants breathing new life into the Old Town. This artist-led gentrification process has been repeated around the coast at Folkestone, Hastings and elsewhere (see box, p.6); the Southeastern seaside, it seems, is in fashion once more.

1974	2010	2016
Sussex is divided into the separate counties of East Sussex and West Sussex.	The South Downs National Park is created.	Hastings' historic pier reopens after a devastating fire in 2010, and the i360 – the world's tallest moving observation tower – opens on Brighton seafront.

Books

Many writers have lived or worked in Kent, Sussex and Surrey, using real-life historical incidents, people and locations to inspire them. The list below is necessarily selective – we've marked our very favourites with the ★ symbol.

FICTION AND POETRY

★**Daisy Ashford** *The Young Visiters.* Written in 1890 by a 9-year-old from Lewes, this warm and witty tale of Victorian love was first published in 1919 – complete with wonderfully idiosyncratic spelling – and has never been out of print since.

★**Jane Austen** *Emma.* Austen's slyly witty novel about a misguided matchmaker was written while the author was living in Surrey; the famous picnic scene, in which Emma attempts to enjoy a fashionable alfresco foray that all goes horribly wrong, is set on Box Hill.

★**H.E. Bates** *The Pop Larkin Chronicles.* Made into a hugely popular TV series, *The Darling Buds of May*, Bates's stories of the ever-optimistic Larkin family, with their earthy, often transgressive ways, are splendid examples of storytelling, portraying Kent as a land, in many ways, unto itself – both deeply conservative and rumbustuously independent.

E.F. Benson *Mapp and Lucia.* Comic novel – one of a series – set between the wars, following snobbish rivals Emmeline Lucas and Elizabeth Mapp, each vying for social supremacy in the fictional town of Tilling (modelled very closely on Benson's home town of Rye). Fans of the books can join tours of *Mapp and Lucia*'s Tilling (see p.169).

A.S. Byatt *The Children's Book.* Set in 1895–1919, Byatt's complex, wordy novel – which gives more than a nod to the real lives of writer E. Nesbit and artist Eric Gill – tells the story of a tangled set of bohemian families tussling with their creative, and procreative, urges. While the characters can be too narcissistic to be likeable, the sense of time and place – Romney Marsh and around – is striking and original.

Nick Cave *The Death of Bunny Monroe.* Rock musician Cave's Brighton-based novel follows Bunny Munro – travelling salesman, sex addict and all-round loser – as he takes to the road with his son after the death of his wife. Funny, sad and downright filthy in equal measure, and as the title suggests, there's no happy ending.

Geoffrey Chaucer *The Canterbury Tales.* Chaucer's great work of poetry, written in the mid-fifteenth century, takes the form of a series of yarns recounted by a motley crew of pilgrims heading from Southwark to Canterbury (see box, p.47). Full of wit and deftly drawn characters, it changed English literature forever and remains an entertaining read today.

★**Charles Dickens** *David Copperfield; Great Expectations; The Mystery of Edwin Drood; Nicholas Nickleby; Pickwick Papers.* Dickens frequently used North Kent locations in his books – including the opening pages of *Great Expectations*, which rank among the most atmospheric passages in English literature.

Edwin Drood is a complex and engaging mystery largely set in Rochester, where Dickens spent much of his childhood, while *David Copperfield*'s Miss Trotwood was inspired by a real person, in Broadstairs. Of course, Dickens hopped about all over southern England, with Surrey locations included in *Nicholas Nickleby* (Devil's Punchbowl) and *Pickwick Papers* (Dorking).

★**T.S. Eliot** *Murder in the Cathedral.* Spare, visceral, overwrought and intellectual, Eliot's short play (see box, p.44) tells the story of the assassination of Thomas Becket in Canterbury Cathedral. A beautiful piece of writing, shedding light on the man whose violent death made the city one of the most important pilgrimage sites in the world.

E.M. Forster *A Room with a View.* The second part of Forster's Edwardian romance has his heroine, Lucy, return to life in Surrey after a tumultuous Grand Tour of Europe; inevitably, however, she's driven to reject the Home Counties' respectable civility for something rather more passionate.

Stella Gibbons *Cold Comfort Farm.* First published in 1932, this comic classic is a merciless parody of the rural melodramas popular at the time. The orphaned, no-nonsense Flora Poste descends on her crazy, gloomy relatives, the Starkadders, in deepest rural Sussex, and sets about tidying up their lives.

★**Graham Greene** *Brighton Rock.* Melancholic thriller with heavy Catholic overtones, set in the criminal underworld of 1930s Brighton and featuring anti-hero Pinkie Brown, teenage sociopath and gangster, who is hunted down by middle-aged avenging angel Ida, representing the force of justice.

★**Patrick Hamilton** *Hangover Square.* Hamilton's 1941 masterpiece, set in seedy 1930s London, Brighton and Maidenhead, tells the dark story of lonely, schizophrenic George Harvey Bone and his obsession with greedy, unscrupulous Netta, a failed actress, whose cruel rejection of him ultimately leads to tragedy.

★**Russell Hoban** *Riddley Walker.* Cult sci-fi fantasy set in a loosely disguised, post-apocalyptic Kent – with towns including Ram Gut, Sam's Itch and Horny Boy – thousands of years after a nuclear holocaust. Told in a futuristic pidgin English, it's a compelling and hugely affecting read.

Peter James *Dead Simple.* The first title in a series of bestselling crime thrillers featuring Brighton-based detective superintendent Roy Grace, with the city and its surrounding area looming large on the covers and in the storylines.

Rudyard Kipling *The Collected Poems.* Collection of poems by Sussex-based poet and author Kipling, which includes the wonderful *Smuggler's Song*, as well as *Sussex*, his poem in praise of his adopted county (see box, p.190).

Marina Lewycka *Two Caravans*. Lewycka's follow-up to the wildly popular *A Short History of Tractors in Ukrainian* sees a young Ukrainian woman, Irina, working as a seasonal fruit-picker in a less-than-bucolic contemporary Kent, along with a ragged band of overseas workers dreaming of a better life. The wordplay, and humour, are as sharp as in the first novel, though the issues are dark.

W. Somerset Maugham *Of Human Bondage; Cakes and Ale*. As a youth Maugham lived in Whitstable with his aunt and taciturn uncle, a vicar. He writes about it, disguised as "Blackstable", near the cathedral town of "Tercanbury", in these two novels. The first, written in 1915, portrays the Kent coast as a lonely and rather bleak place, while the second, from 1930, is a little cheerier.

★**Melanie McGrath** *Hopping*. The title is a little misleading – while the annual "hop", in which the main characters decamp from the East End to East Kent to work on the hop harvest, is key to this compelling family saga, the novel's scope reaches far beyond that, offering a detailed history of how London's East End changed through the course of the twentieth century.

★**A.A. Milne** *Winnie the Pooh; The House at Pooh Corner*. Milne's much-loved children's classics, beautifully illustrated by E.H. Shepherd, were written from his home in Ashdown Forest, with many of the Forest's real-life locations appearing in the books (see box, p.194).

George Orwell *A Clergyman's Daughter*. Orwell's short novel tells the story of a young country woman who suffers a bout of amnesia and finds herself lost in London. The chapter in which she hooks up with a group of hop-pickers and travels to Kent draws on Orwell's own hopping seasons. Unsurprisingly, he reveals a bleaker side to the whole business than is usually described, conveying in detail the poor conditions and pay suffered by the transient workers.

Julian Rathbone *The Last English King*. Fictionalized account of the 1066 invasion seen through the eyes of Walt, the last surviving of King Harold's bodyguards. A lively, gripping story which vividly brings to life that most tumultuous, momentous year in English history.

★**Vita Sackville-West** *The Edwardians*. This mischievous dig at the English upper classes, published in 1930 but set during the final years of the Edwardian era, is Sackville-West's most popular novel. On one level a coming-of-age tale about siblings Sebastian and Viola, who together create an amalgam of Vita herself, it's also an expression of the author's tortured ambivalence about her background – her passion for her childhood home (the vast Knole estate in Kent); her bitter disappointment at not being able

to inherit; her shame at enjoying privilege based upon a feudal system. Above all, however, *The Edwardians* is a paean to Knole itself, as strong a character as any in this book and described in vivid and romantic detail.

★**Graham Swift** *Last Orders*. Beautifully written, moving account of a group of ageing men on an expedition from London to Margate, where their recently deceased friend has asked them to scatter his ashes. Stop-offs include Rochester, Canterbury and a hopping farm, with the poignant climax taking place on the bleak, windy Harbour Arm at Margate.

Russell Thorndike *Doctor Syn* novels. Swashbuckling adventures of the wonderfully named vicar whose wife's betrayal turns him to revenge, piracy, murder and smuggling. The books, published between 1915 and 1945, take us from the sleepy Kentish village of Dymchurch in Romney Marsh, via the high seas and the American colonies and back again.

Sarah Waters *Tipping the Velvet*. Waters' debut, alive with the author's now-familiar storytelling genius, follows the fortunes of Nan, an oyster girl from Victorian Whitstable. After encountering a charismatic male impersonator, she sets off on a picaresque journey through the London lesbian demi-monde. The oysters' potential for erotic metaphor is, as you might expect, exploited with verve.

H.G. Wells *Kipps; The History of Mr Polly; Tono-Bungay*. Wells conveys a convincing sense of place – including Romney Marsh and Folkestone – in *Kipps*, his 1905 comic novel of an ordinary man, trapped in a stultifyingly lower-middle-class life, whose fortunes change with a huge inheritance. *Mr Polly* (1910), much of which is set around "Fishbourne" – based on Sandgate, near Folkestone – explores similar themes, but with a darker edge. The semi-autobiographical *Tono-Bungay* (1909) tells the tale of George, an apprentice chemist, whose uncle's medicine becomes a spectacular success despite having no medical benefits whatsoever. The first part of the book describes George's life as a servant's child at Bladesover House; Wells' own mother was housekeeper at Uppark House.

Virginia Woolf *Orlando; Between the Acts*. Nigel Nicolson, Vita Sackville-West's son, called *Orlando* the "longest and most charming love letter in literature". It's an astonishing gift to Sackville-West, with whom Woolf had an affair, and who in this book lives for three centuries, changes sexes, and muses on the nature of life, love, art and history. The book is populated with thinly disguised characters and real-life photos, and at the heart of it is Knole, the grand Kentish estate that Sackville-West was never able to inherit (see p.137). *Between the Acts* was Woolf's final novel, published in 1941, and follows the staging of a play at Pointz Hall, an Elizabethan manor house inspired by Firle Place and Glynde Place, near Woolf's home at Rodmell.

HISTORY, BIOGRAPHY AND TRAVELOGUE

★**H.E. Bates** *Through the Woods*. This compelling, slim volume, beautifully illustrated with exquisite engravings, sees Bates weave a year's observations of his local Kentish

woods into a musing on the particular quality and primeval allure of English woodlands as a whole. With the author's trademark deft touch, clear-eyed observations and determined lack of sentimentality, this is nature writing at its best: nostalgic, evocative, personal and profound.

Pieter and Rita Boogaart *A272: An Ode to a Road*. Now in its fourth edition, this eccentric homage to the A272, which runs from Poundford in East Sussex through West Sussex into Hampshire, has become a bit of a cult classic. Quirky, humorous and informative, it covers both the road itself and the surrounding countryside, with hundreds of photos.

Peter Brandon *Sussex*. Authoritative and encyclopedic, this illustrated book traces the history of Sussex from its earliest peoples to the modern day, taking in wildlife, artists and writers, history, folklore, geology, castles, gardens, market towns and cities along the way.

Julie Burchill and Daniel Raven *Made in Brighton*. The controversial journalist and her husband take a look at Britain through the lens of Brighton, interspersing personal stories of their lives in the city with wider observations on everything from the Labour party to former glamour model (and fellow Brightonian) Katie Price.

Sophie Collins *A Sussex Miscellany*. Quirky dip-in-and-out-of collection of Sussex trivia – one of a series of beautifully produced and illustrated books published by Sussex-based Snake River Press (⊚snakeriverpress.co.uk). Other titles in the series include books on Sussex wildlife, writers and artists, food and drink, landscape, gardens (see box, p.198) and walks.

Richard Filmer *Hops and Hop Picking*. Written in 1982, this slim volume offers a deft historical account of the hopping industry in Britain, taking it from its Roman roots to its demise in the late twentieth century, with lots of clearly written technical detail and intriguing historic photos.

David Howarth *1066: The Year of the Conquest*; **Frank McLynn** *1066: The Year of the Three Battles*; **Peter Rex** *1066: A New History of the Norman Conquest*. Three excellent books on the Norman Conquest of 1066. Howarth's book puts the invasion in the context of the year it took place; McLynn overturns some of the myths about the battle and takes a closer look at Harald Hardrada, whom Harold defeated at Stamford Bridge before his own defeat at the hands of William; and Rex not only covers the background to the Norman invasion but also continues the story to the final crushing of lingering English resistance in 1076.

★**Olivia Laing** *To the River*. This acclaimed account of the author's midsummer walk along the River Ouse from source to sea is beautifully observed, interweaving nature writing, history and folklore, with plenty on Virginia Woolf, who drowned herself in the river in 1941.

Terence Lawson and David Killingray (eds) *An Historical Atlas of Kent*. This intriguing, comprehensive history, sponsored by the Kent Archaeological Society, uses around 250 maps and short essays to illustrate everything from Anglo-Saxon churches to medieval almshouses, breweries to suburban sprawl.

Philip MacDougal *Chatham Dockyard: The Rise and Fall of a Military Industrial Complex*. A lengthy account, published in 2012, of the great royal dockyard, which, founded in the late sixteenth century, built hundreds of warships for the Royal Navy before being wound down in the 1980s. It's a good read even if you're not wild about ships, putting the docks into a broader historical context.

★**Judith Mackrell** *The Bloomsbury Ballerina*. Engrossing account of one of the fringe members of the Bloomsbury Group – Lydia Lopokova, the larger-than-life Russian ballet star who became the much-adored wife of sober economist and Bloomsburyite John Maynard Keynes (who had previously identified as homosexual) – much to the disgust of Vanessa Bell, Virginia Woolf and Lytton Strachey, who snidely dismissed her as a "half-witted canary".

Adam Nicolson *Sissinghurst: An Unfinished History*. Fascinating book by the grandson of Vita Sackville-West and Harold Nicolson about his struggles with the National Trust to revitalize the estate around Sissinghurst in Kent, with a broader, personal and lively history of both the estate and Kent itself thrown in.

Juliet Nicolson *A House Full of Daughters*. Just when you thought there couldn't be anything left to write about the Sackville-Wests, along comes this 2015 title. Nicolson, Vita's granddaughter, uses personal experience and historical record to explore seven generations of family history from the point of view of its fascinating women. Bold, emotionally honest and pulling no punches.

Richard Platt *Smuggling in the British Isles*. A good introduction to the smuggling trade that operated up and down the coastline of Britain in the eighteenth and early nineteenth centuries; Kent and Sussex's smuggling outfits – including the notorious Hawkhurst Gang – had the most fearsome reputation of the lot.

Vita Sackville-West *Pepita*. Sackville-West's biography of her grandmother, a half-Gypsy Spanish dancer, and her mother, the illegitimate, volatile Victoria, catapulted into the aristocracy to become mistress of the Knole estate, reads like a rollicking melodrama and is all the more compelling for being entirely true.

ART

Quentin Bell and Virginia Nicholson *Charleston: a Bloomsbury House and Garden*. This fascinating account of the Bloomsbury Group's country home – written by Vanessa Bell's son, Quentin, and his daughter – gives an insider's view of life in the bohemian household. With plenty of photographs of the farmhouse's inimitable

decorative style, as well as snapshots from the family album, it's the perfect souvenir after a visit.

Ruth Cribb and Joe Cribb *Eric Gill: Lust for Letter and Line*. An excellent illustrated introduction to the late, great artist, typographer, sculptor and engraver Eric Gill (see box, p.232), whose controversial personal life has received as much attention as his art. Fiona MacCarthy's authoritative, fascinating biography, *Eric Gill*, is equally recommended; her commendably non-judgmental book was the first to reveal Gill's sexual improprieties.

Desna Greenhow (ed) *The Diary of Mary Watts 1887–1904*. Watts was an accomplished potter, artist and designer who managed at once to be the perfect Victorian wife to famed painter George Frederic Watts and a major player in the Arts and Crafts movement. These diaries, kept meticulously and in great detail, chronicle the world of Surrey's turn-of-the-century artistic set, her own creative process and life with G.F. Watts – who liked to be called "Signor" – himself.

Anthony Penrose *The Home of the Surrealists: Lee Miller, Roland Penrose and Their Circle at Farley Farm House*. Written by the son of photographer Lee Miller and painter and biographer Roland Penrose, this illustrated book gives a first-hand account of life at Farley Farm House in Sussex (see p.191), which hosted some of the twentieth century's greatest artists, Picasso, Max Ernst and Miró among them.

★ **James Russell** *Ravilious in Pictures: Sussex and the Downs*. Twenty-two colour plates of Eric Ravilious's beautiful watercolours landscapes of Downs, painted in the 1930s before his death in World War II. Social historian James Russell's accompanying short essays provide the background on Ravilious's life (see box, p.208) and the quintessentially English scenes he painted.

GARDENS

Jane Brown *Sissinghurst: Portrait of a Garden*. Lavishly illustrated coffee-table book that brings the ebullience and abundance of Sackville-West's garden to life, as well as providing a good chunk of history about the estate itself.

★ **Lorraine Harrison** *20 Sussex Gardens*. A succinct, well-illustrated tour of twenty of the best Sussex gardens, taking in various different historical periods and horticultural styles, from the excellent Snake River Press. A sister title, *Inspiring Sussex Gardeners*, focuses on the designers and plant hunters behind the gardens.

★ **Derek Jarman** *Derek Jarman's Garden*. A poignant diary, illustrated with arty photos, recording the last year of Jarman's life as he created his shingle garden in Dungeness. Bittersweet, poetic and full of simple joy, much like the garden itself. The preface is by Keith Collins, Jarman's friend and current inhabitant of Prospect Cottage (see p.132).

Stephen Lacey *Gardens of the National Trust*. Lavishly photographed volume on the National Trust's expansive national collection of gardens, which includes some of the finest gardens in Sussex, Kent and Surrey.

★ **Judith Tankard** *Gertrude Jekyll and the Country House Garden*. Using a wealth of luscious photos from *Country Life* magazine, for whom Jekyll was the gardening correspondent, this stunning coffee-table book celebrates the work of the influential Surrey-based garden designer, both with collaborators – including her great friend, the architect Edwin Lutyens – and on her own.

Various *Essays on the Life of a Working Amateur 1843–1932*. A highly readable compendium of personal essays about Gertrude Jekyll, written by members of her family and various experts, covering a broad range of Jekyll's work – including interior design – beyond her garden design.

FOOD AND DRINK

★ **Mandy Bruce** *The Oyster Seekers*. Charmingly illustrated tome, produced in association with *Wheelers Oyster Bar* in Whitstable (see p.86), which works as both an excellent recipe book and a lively, nostalgic history of the oyster industry and fishing on the east coast.

Jessica Haggerty *Brighton Bakes*. Part cookbook, part travelogue, this fun, gorgeously photographed book contains a delicious collection of recipes inspired by the author's home town.

★ **Amanda Powley and Phil Taylor** *Terre à Terre: the Vegetarian Cookbook*. Innovative, exciting recipes – from Dunkin Doughnuts (parmesan and porcini-dust doughnuts served with chestnut soup) to No Cocky, Big Leeky (sausages and mash) – from Brighton's multi-award-winning vegetarian restaurant (see p.253), which is regularly voted among the best in the country.

WALKING AND CYCLING

AA *40 Short Walks in Kent; 40 Short Walks in Sussex; 40 Short Walks in Surrey*. Easy-to-follow routes spanning anything from one to four miles, with good, concise background on local history, wildlife and landscape. They also include useful details for dog-owners, include refreshment-break and public-toilet information, and suggest more detailed maps.

Deirdre Huston and Marina Bullivant *Cycling in Sussex*. Twenty bike rides, from 4km to 28km, on off-road trails or quiet roads, with routes divided into "family", "easy", "medium" and "hard". Huston's *Cycling Days Out: South East England* covers Sussex, Kent, Surrey and Hampshire, with half a dozen or so rides suggested for each county.

Pathfinder Walks Series of excellent practical walking guides with OS maps and route descriptions. Titles include *East Sussex and the South Downs; West Sussex and the South Downs; Surrey and Sussex; Kent;* and *Surrey*.

Helena Smith *The Rough Guide to Walks in London and the Southeast*. Handy, pocket-sized book covering walks for all abilities around the Southeast, all starting and finishing at train stations. Each walk suggests places to stop for lunch or a pint, and there's plenty of background information on everything from smugglers to stone circles.

Small print and index

A ROUGH GUIDE TO ROUGH GUIDES

Published in 1982, the first Rough Guide – to Greece – was a student scheme that became a publishing phenomenon. Mark Ellingham, a recent graduate in English from Bristol University, had been travelling in Greece the previous summer and couldn't find the right guidebook. With a small group of friends he wrote his own guide, combining a contemporary, journalistic style with a thoroughly practical approach to travellers' needs.

The immediate success of the book spawned a series that rapidly covered dozens of destinations. And, in addition to impecunious backpackers, Rough Guides soon acquired a much broader readership that relished the guides' wit and inquisitiveness as much as their enthusiastic, critical approach and value-for-money ethos. These days, Rough Guides include recommendations from budget to luxury and cover more than 120 destinations around the globe, from Amsterdam to Zanzibar, all regularly updated by our team of roaming writers.

Browse all our latest guides, read inspirational features and book your trip at **roughguides.com**.

ABOUT THE AUTHORS

Sam Cook is a London-born and -based writer and editor. She researched and wrote the Kent and Surrey chapters of this guide and has authored Rough Guides to London, Paris, New Orleans and Chick Flicks, among others.

Claire Saunders grew up in Brighton, which wasn't anywhere near as cool then as it is now. After almost ten years of working as an editor and then Managing Editor at Rough Guides in London, she moved back down to Sussex, where she now lives in Lewes and works as a freelance writer and editor. She researched and wrote the Sussex chapters for this book.

Acknowledgements

Sam Cook: For practical help during research I am very grateful to Lucy Ashley, Lana Crouch, Sinead Hanna, Lauren Hoskin, Sandra Killick, Rowena Moore, Natasha Najm and Diana Roberts. Thanks also to Alison Cowan and Cefn Ridout for splendid sunny (and rainy) seaside jaunts; to Becca Hallett for eagle-eyed editing; Claire Saunders for being the best co-author there could be; and above all to Greg Ward, always, for everything.

Claire Saunders: A huge thank you to everyone who helped me to produce this second edition, in particular Danny Weddup. Special thanks too to my lovely and talented co-author, Sam Cook, who was as great to work with as ever, and to Becca Hallett, who was unfailingly calm and cheerful throughout and whose keen-eyed edit made the book much better. Thanks also to

Michelle Bhatia for some beautiful pics, Ankur Guha for layout, and Ashutosh Bharti, Animesh Pathak and Richard Marchi for maps; to Jane Ellis for her very helpful Hastings tips; to Joanna Thomas for pointing me in the direction of my new favourite cocktail bar; to Amber Rose for Eastbourne help; to Margaret Murphy and Barbara Hogan in Arundel; to Katie Martin at Visit Brighton; and to Sarah Ryman from England's Medieval Festival. An enormous thank you to mum, dad, Anita, Christine and Terry for summer holiday childcare, and apologies to Tom and Mia for the long months of maternal neglect. Above all, love and thanks to Ian for putting up with it all.

Thanks are also due to **Danny Weddup** for his knowledgeable update of the nightlife and LGBT sections of the Brighton chapter.

Readers' updates

Thanks to all the readers who have taken the time to write in with comments and suggestions (and apologies if we've inadvertently omitted or misspelt anyone's name):

Kate Andreopoulos and family; John Lloyd Parry; Stefanie Lüdtke; Anna Morell.

Rough Guide credits

Editor: Rebecca Hallett
Layout: Ankur Guha
Cartography: Ashutosh Bharti, Animesh Pathak
Picture editor: Michelle Bhatia
Proofreader: Anita Sach
Managing editor: Edward Aves
Assistant editor: Divya Grace Mathew

Production: Jimmy Lao
Cover photo research: Zoe Bennett
Photographer: Chris Christoforou
Editorial assistant: Aimee White
Senior DTP coordinator: Dan May
Programme manager: Gareth Lowe
Publishing director: Georgina Dee

Publishing information

This second edition published June 2017 by
Rough Guides Ltd,
80 Strand, London WC2R 0RL
11, Community Centre, Panchsheel Park,
New Delhi 110017, India
Distributed by Penguin Random House
Penguin Books Ltd, 80 Strand, London WC2R 0RL
Penguin Group (USA), 345 Hudson Street, NY 10014, USA
Penguin Group (Australia), 250 Camberwell Road,
Camberwell, Victoria 3124, Australia
Penguin Group (NZ), 67 Apollo Drive, Mairanqi Bay,
Auckland 1310, New Zealand
Penguin Group (South Africa), Block D, Rosebank Office
Park, 181 Jan Smuts Avenue, Parktown North, Gauteng,
South Africa 2193
Rough Guides is represented in Canada by DK Canada, 320
Front Street West, Suite 1400, Toronto, Ontario M5V 3B6
Printed in Singapore
© Samantha Cook and Claire Saunders, 2017
Maps © Rough Guides
Contains Ordnance Survey data © Crown copyright and
database rights 2017

336pp includes index
A catalogue record for this book is available from the
British Library
ISBN: 978-0-24127-235-0
The publishers and authors have done their best to
ensure the accuracy and currency of all the information
in **The Rough Guide to Kent, Sussex & Surrey**, however,
they can accept no responsibility for any loss, injury, or
inconvenience sustained by any traveller as a result of
information or advice contained in the guide.
1 3 5 7 9 8 6 4 2

Help us update

We've gone to a lot of effort to ensure that the second
edition of **The Rough Guide to Kent, Sussex & Surrey** is
accurate and up-to-date. However, things change – places
get "discovered", opening hours are notoriously fickle,
restaurants and rooms raise prices or lower standards. If
you feel we've got it wrong or left something out, we'd like
to know, and if you can remember the address, the price,

the hours, the phone number, so much the better.
    Please send your comments with the subject line
"**Rough Guide Kent, Sussex & Surrey Update**" to mail
@uk.roughguides.com. We'll credit all contributions and
send a copy of the next edition (or any other Rough Guide
if you prefer) for the very best emails.

Photo credits

All photos © Rough Guides, except the following:
(Key: t-top; c-centre; b-bottom; l-left; r-right)

1 4Corners: Justin Foulkes
2 AWL Images: Jon Arnold
7 4Corners: Irek (tr). **Alamy Stock Photo:** Howard Taylor
(tl). **Getty Images:** LOOP IMAGES / Andrew Ray (b)
9 Alamy Stock Photo: Martin Bond (b). **Alamy Stock
Photo:** Peter Gates (t); PCJones (c)
11 Alamy Stock Photo: Derek Croucher (b). **Alamy Stock
Photo:** UrbanImages (c). **Visit Kent Limited** (t)
12 Alamy Stock Photo: David Baker (b)
13 arcblue.com: Peter Durant (bl). **Getty Images:** Andrew
Errington (br)
14 Visit Kent Limited (br)
16 Alamy Stock Photo: Travel Pictures (c); Tony Watson (b)
17 Alamy Stock Photo: Robert Bird (bl). **Getty Images:**
Laurie Noble (br)
18 Getty Images: Lyn Holly (t)
55 Compasses Inn (br)
64–65 Visit Kent Limited

67 Alamy Stock Photo: Andreas von Einsiedel
79 Alamy Stock Photo: Gregory Wrona (tr).
Dreamstime.com: Neillang (b)
102–103 AWL Images: Nadia Isakova
117 Alamy Stock Photo: Stewart Mckeown (t)
134–135 SuperStock: Nelly Boyd
137 Visit Kent Limited
147 SuperStock: EWA Stock (tr). **Visit Kent Limited** (b)
162–163 AWL Images: Nature in Stock
183 Alamy Stock Photo: Ian Dagnall (t)
223 Alamy Stock Photo: Scott Hortop Travel (b)
237 Alamy Stock Photo: TravelMuse
293 SuperStock: age fotostock / Philip Enticknap
302–303 Corbis: Martyn Goddard
305 Corbis: John Miller

Cover: *Fishing boat and net huts in Hastings* **Robert
Harding Picture Library:** Eurasia

Index

Maps are marked in grey

Map symbols

The symbols below are used on maps throughout the book

- County boundary
- Chapter boundary
- Road
- Motorway
- Pedestrianized/restricted access road
- Steps
- Railway & station
- Private/tourist railway & station
- Funicular railway
- Wall
- North Downs Way
- South Downs Way
- Saxon Shore Way
- Greensand Way
- Other footpath/cycling route

-)(Bridge/tunnel entrance
- One-way street
- Point of interest
- Museum
- Castle
- Stately/historic home
- Abbey
- Gardens
- Ruins/archeological site
- Viewpoint
- Zoo/wildlife park
- Nature reserve
- Vineyard/wine estate
- Arboretum/forest park
- Farm/farm park

- Observatory
- Airport
- Minor airport/airfield
- Rock formation
- Cliffs
- Bus/taxi stop
- Tourist office
- Parking
- Post office
- Internet access
- Public toilets
- Gate
- Surf beach
- Windsurfing

- Lighthouse
- Hospital
- Swimming pool
- Statue
- Golf course
- Building
- Church
- South Downs National Park
- Park/forest
- Cemetery
- Beach
- Marshland
- Tidal flats
- Shingle

Listings key

- Accommodation
- Eating
- Drinking/nightlife
- Shopping